SEPTEMBER STARLINGS

RUTH HAMILTON

The September Starlings

BANTAM PRESS

LONDON · NEW YORK · TORONTO · SYDNEY · AUCKLAND

TRANSWORLD PUBLISHERS LTD
61–63 Uxbridge Road, London W5 5SA

TRANSWORLD PUBLISHERS (AUSTRALIA) PTY LTD
15–25 Helles Avenue, Moorebank, NSW 2170

TRANSWORLD PUBLISHERS (NZ) LTD
3 William Pickering Drive, Albany, Auckland

101049064

Published 1994 by Bantam Press
a division of Transworld Publishers Ltd

Copyright © Ruth Hamilton 1994

A catalogue record for this book is available from the British Library

ISBN 0593 034619

Typeset in 10/11pt Linotype Plantin by
County Typesetters, Margate, Kent.

Printed in Great Britain by
Mackays of Chatham Plc, Chatham, Kent.

For Margaret Vincent

Many thanks to:

Michael & David

Diane & Meg

Danielle & Kevin

Irene Cunningham, who made house-moving almost bearable

also

The Reverend Geoffrey Garner, Anglican Rector of St Mary-le-Bow in London, who certainly knows more about the Catholic saints than I do.

Author's Note

There are two real people in this book – Danielle McGregor and Kevin McCann. I 'stood in' for Laura Starling and asked the questions Laura might have asked. I thank Kevin for his poetry, especially for 'The Trouble with Wings', and Danielle for allowing me to read her work on Sachsenhausen. Without the support of people like these two, writing would not be such a joy.

Part One

Chapter One

The water dances, seems lighter than the soft breath of air that fans my cheek, brighter than the lofty dome of sky. I bite my lip, force back a tide of emotion too mixed to be identified. The fear has gone, has left me cold and bare. The fear has been my closest companion for many months and I cannot imagine how I shall live without its presence. Like an old toothache, it became my familiar, a nagging, complaining escort.

The village of Barr Bridge is smaller, shabbier than the image I brought with me this morning. When I was ten, the bridge across this stream was wider, stronger, a substantial part of my existence. Now, my eyes reach high above the pitted and corroded rails, while two adult strides can almost cover the meagre span. Middle age has come to me and I have carried it to a place that was always old. Yes, I have come here to remember, to collect my thoughts.

I fell in once. We were throwing things over the sides, through the bars and into the happy brook. It still giggles and gurgles, prances hysterically over time-slicked stones, celebrates its own prettiness as it splashes and splits into prisms of pure joy. For what reason? How brief its self-laudatory pleasure will be! There is water in my eyes, a wetness whose salt pricks like onion-tears. Do I feel pity for this tiny ribbon of stream, do I mourn already for the reach it will become as it makes its merry way to town?

Anne called to me. 'You'll fall in, Laura!'

'I don't care.' And I really didn't care. In the first decade of a child's life, safety does not sit high on the agenda. 'My paper boat will get through before yours does,' was my rash response. I hung from the bridge in the manner of a trapeze clown who purposely courts disaster so that an audience might be amused. It was a long way down and I took an age to meet the water. The cold thrill of it snatched my breath away, but the spasm of terror that was almost pleasurable was wrenched from me and I felt no more. She dragged me out, heaved my waterlogged body up among the reeds. I was wakening, becoming aware, yet she screamed wonderfully at the sight of my torn and bleeding forehead.

She loved me, loves me still, continues to worry about her wayward cousin. My hand raises itself until it finds the scar, a small and crescent-shaped blemish that hides coyly beneath the hairline. Anne, too, has a scar, larger than mine, a silver blemish on her lovely face. Her mark was made by a man whose name I seek to forget, though it is hard to erase from memory the creature who shaped my young adult life.

I am here for a reason, have followed my instincts to this bridge. Did I come just to remember a summer day in 1950? Do I want to hear my mother's voice again? 'You've ruined that frock,' she snapped. There were sutures in her daughter's face, yet she worried more about ripped stitches in two yards of gingham. And yes, the socks were new and spoilt.

A flash of silver catches my eye as a small fish is swept along towards its doom. The stream bustles on, displays that familiar, manic glee as it plumes over the sloping bed to dash thoughtlessly into the future. Just as I did. This carefree babble knows nothing of its fate, is blissfully unaware of its destination. If it knew what was in store, would it defy nature and gravity, would it stop and turn back? I didn't. I just kept going, was as stubborn and stupid as Barr Brook. Down there, in the town of Bolton, the stream's beauty will die, turning first to pewter, then to a stinking foam of bleach and effluent. Won't it? Does it happen, is there a bleachworks, is cotton still spun here in 1992?

I had no more sense than this blind waterway. Although I could reason, could listen to advice, I bumbled and blundered along into my own premature decay. With this place, I have an affinity.

I turn and look at the village, just one street of cottages with an 'everything' shop at its centre and a pub at the base of the slope. Like the stream, Barr Bridge totters down the hill, each house leaning on its neighbour, the whole lot depending for support on the Black Horse. The Black Horse has not stood still, though. It has moved on, has become an eating place for Sunday families. There is tarmac at the back, a grey surface sectioned by thick white lines where cars can be stabled to recover after the climb from town. Rustic tables and benches front the pub, red and white umbrellas advertise vermouth, spread their gores above the seating area. Progress. They probably have prawn cocktails, chicken-in-a-basket, Black Forest gateau, foreign cheeses. There'll be quiz nights, folk music groups, theme parties.

I walk across the cobbles, stand on the narrow pave-ment. These flags have shrunk – I recall that they were huge and uneven. Steps punctuate the path, but they are no longer steep. I lived here through my teenage years, when I was fully grown, returned as a mother for temporary stays, yet I still see this village with the vision of a child. It is true, then, that we remember in patches, that our minds leap about and settle where they will. Although I reached my present height at the age of fourteen, I keep Barr Bridge firmly in the 'childhood' compartment of my memory.

The inner doors of the Black Horse have not been renewed. The brewery has kept the coloured glass, though one small section has been repaired, replaced by a pane of thick, plain frost. Twin brass handles do not shine, but they are comfortingly familiar. I will hold this in my mind, because the rest of the place will be altered past recog-nition.

There is a deep-piled carpet of red and gold stretching

its garish opulence right up to the bar. I smile. We used to run in here for dares, used to take pennies from evening domino players whose days were spent tilling the land and tending animals. They never told our mothers, never brought trouble on our heads. Anne and I were probably a part of their fun, something to take minds off a difficult calving or a broken fence.

The bar is the same, chunky, solid, hewn from a dark red wood that boasts a beeswax sheen. A small blackboard at one side announces PUB GRUB, and a glass case houses sandwiches, pork pies, pasties, a few ploughman's lunches. The tables are various, some square, some circular. A huge painting of a black horse occupies the upper half of a wall, the animal's stance reminiscent of an advertisement for one of the bigger banks.

The place is empty save for one very small old lady who crouches over a glass of flat amber fluid, possibly cider. The landlord emerges from a door marked PRIVATE. 'Can I help you?' he asks. He is young, agile, wears tracksuit bottoms and colourful training shoes. Once behind the bar, he is smart in the white polo-necked jersey, displays manicured nails and two gold rings. 'A tomato juice,' I answer finally. Who will come and eat all his food? The unmistakeable smell of Lancashire hotpot has followed him through from the PRIVATE rooms. 'And a cheese sandwich,' I add, worrying about his profits.

He serves me, is deft with the steel tongs as he removes my food from the case. 'One pound forty,' he states dispassionately. No need to concern myself about him, then. It's a small sandwich with a large mark-up, so he'll doubtless survive. 'Anything else?' His mouth tweaks, promises a smile, does not deliver.

'No, thank you.' I take plate, glass and change, decide on a whim to linger. Each New Year, I promise myself that there will be no more whims, yet I continue erratic, impulsive. 'I used to live here.' Why am I talking to this sullen young man? 'My father was John McNally.'

16

At last, a stiff and rather professional smile. He reaches out a hand, waits until I have deposited my lunch on the counter. The grip is firm. My sapphire and diamond cluster has twisted, cuts into an inch of the adjacent finger. I struggle against the urge to flinch and draw away. 'Charles Roe.' His tone is clipped, especially when he spits out the 'Charles'. I would wager a small fortune that few have dared to call this man Charlie. 'Your father did Barr Bridge a lot of good, Mrs . . . er . . .'

'Starling. Laura Starling.' I win back my hand, feel the blood as it stings its way back into crushed digits. 'I've just come to have a look at the old place.'

The arms fold themselves, while the dark head nods pensively. 'This village would have died off but for McNally's. Do you have anything to do with McNally's these days?'

'No. My mother is the major shareholder.'

He whistles. 'She'll be worth a bob or two, then.'

I am used to Lancashire bluntness, but this man is more calculating than the usual Bolton lad. 'I wouldn't know.'

He is staring at me, the cold marble gaze seeming to cut my soul. Barr Bridge remembers me, then, has engraved me into its folklore. I was the one who ran away, who turned her back on a comfortable life, disappointed her mother, broke her father's heart . . . 'Where are you living these days?'

'In Crosby.'

'Liverpool?'

'That's right.'

He leans closer. 'Your mam?'

'She lives in Crosby too.'

Snow-white incisors bite the lower lip for a split second. 'Does she live with—'

'No. She has a retirement apartment.' He is annoying me. I should not have begun this conversation, am beginning to lose patience with myself. 'I'll sit down now.'

My table faces the rear of the building. The geriatric car I have named Elsie is cooling off just outside the back door

– I can see her right-hand headlight fixed on me like another calculating stare. To the right of the main bar, a large extension of glass and wood crawls further down the hill. A NO SMOKING sign sits over the entrance to this pine-clad dining area. The cloths are white and crisp. Some quiet music escapes from the smokeless zone, creeps across the bar and into my ears. It is 'nothing' music, the sort that lulls its victims into a comatose state. With their senses dulled to the point of paralysis, the Black Horse customers no doubt pay inflated prices without too much thought.

Mr Henderson used to sit here, at a longer table. Five or six of his cronies would join him, each with a pint glass in one hand and some small change in the other. Brows would furrow beneath caps whose peaks were pulled low as shields for giveaway facial expressions. Poker-physogs, these old men used to have, though Anne and I called them domino-sulks. Sometimes, when the game was really vicious, my cousin Anne and I would stand unnoticed for minutes, our breath held tight in our young chests as we watched the silent fighting. A domino would tap sharply to announce a pass. Mr Henderson always cleared his throat before placing a tile on the ale-stained wood. Sometimes, the quiet was broken by an angry shout. ''Ow long 'as tha 'ad yon three, Bert Entwistle? 'As tha just picked it up? On'y yer passed afore till tha got a double. Nay, I'm not sayin' tha's cheatin'. 'Appen it were a mistake. Sit thee down, no need to jump off th' 'orse, its nobbut a game.'

I can hear them now. If I close my eyes and breathe in the smell of stale beer, I can be a child again. Halfway up the slope, Auntie Maisie will be baking bread. Boys from the little school will be chasing about, running after wooden hoops or chasing a rubber tyre. Inside the school, Miss Armitage is no doubt picking at her lunch, two fish-paste sandwiches with the crusts cut off, an apple, a piece of white, crumbly Lancashire cheese. She has a secret. Anne and I are sure that she has a secret.

Doors slam, bring me back to the here and now. The car-park is filling up and some men have entered by the back door. McNally's. That's how the landlord makes his profits, then. I have a sensitive nose and, even from this distance, I can pick up that slight liquorice scent. While Father's patent medicines were in various stages of development, the smell of liquorice often clung to coats and shirts, used to enter our house with him. Mother tried to wash it out of clothes, but it was a stubborn odour, a comforting one. This is my father's empire. He is now a pile of dust in the ground, yet he still lingers here, on the farm he bought for a pittance after the war. These men and women who stand at the bar with their Kalibers and lemonade spritzers are the children of John McNally. They are not of his loins, but they are born of his brain.

I must go outside. The landlord is leering in my direction, pointing me out with a brown, beringed finger. Old McNally's daughter has come home, perhaps she's wanting some power, a say in the running of the factory. Maybe she's regretting that hasty exit with . . . what was his name, now? Did she marry him? Will you go and talk to her, Doreen, it'll come better from a woman. I imagine the gist of their talk, flee outside before I can be accosted by a Doreen out of quality control, a Rita from the packing department.

When I stand on the pavement again, the old woman who was drinking cider is waiting for me. In my hand, I carry the remnants of a dry cheese sandwich. I break it, scatter it for the birds. She has fixed her gaze on me, is boring through me with her eyes.

'I know you.' The rusty tone is quiet, yet accusatory.

'I lived here. A long time ago.'

She coughs and extends a yellow claw in my direction. 'Laura. Is it Laura?'

'Yes.' I need to be alone, must find out why I have come here. It's hard to work out the answers when the questions are still a mystery.

'Laura.' The two syllables drift out of her mouth, then

the lips clamp themselves tightly while the ancient crone considers me. 'Laura,' she repeats at last. 'McNally.' She congratulates herself, straightens the drooping shoulders. 'Anne Turnbull was your cousin. She went on to university and became a solicitor. I was so proud of her.' A grin bares dentures that are as jaundiced as the fingernails. 'What did you do with yourself?'

'Nothing.' Who the hell is she?

The mouth is sucked inward again, works in an infantile fashion that seems to be a part of growing senile. 'You must have done something. We all do something, you know. I was your teacher and you loved my stories. I remember how your face would light up when I opened the book.'

Oh no, this woman is older than God! When I was ten, she must have been nearing thirty. She wore romantic blouses and a hopeful expression, always had a cameo pinned to the lace-trimmed neckline. Five blouses, she had – white, cream, blue, mauve and pale pink. If we were uncertain of the day, we needed only to look at Teacher's blouse, because her life had a rhythm that defied interruption. To this very day, I remember that Monday meant blue. Her skirts were either navy or grey, always long. When the 'New Look' came in, Miss Armitage was suddenly fashionable with her just-above-the-ankle clothes. Anne and I would whisper behind our sum books. 'Do you think he died in the war?' And, 'Someone will come to marry her, because she is so beautiful.'

She is no longer lovely, looks older than her years, which probably number seventy, perhaps seventy-three. 'Miss Armitage.' I reach out and touch a frail shoulder. There is no substance here, no discernible bone in the flesh. If I press hard, she will crumble like an autumn leaf – no – more like a leaf from a withered and unread tome of ancient poetry in some dead, forgotten language. 'How are you?' I manage.

'I am very old and very tired, but I hang on just to make a thorough nuisance of myself.' The beady eyes are keen, do not match the rest of the picture. 'The pension pays my rent, buys me a glass of cider on a Friday.' The eyelids droop as she rakes my body with a stare that almost makes me shiver. 'Come into the house.' She turns, stumbles on, knows that a child from her class would never presume to disobey. I am fifty-two, yet I follow as meekly as a mindless sheep.

The cottage has a sitting room and a kitchen on the ground floor. Stairs rise out of a corner of the front room, but there is a bed here, in an alcove to the left of a tiled grate. She lowers her frailty into a padded rocker. 'Can't get upstairs any longer. They come once a week, carry me to the bathroom and give me a lick and a promise. Thank goodness the landlord didn't demolish the outside lava-tory, or I would now be totally robbed of my dignity.'

There's another seat, a squarish armchair upholstered in a linen-effect cloth whose pattern consists of roses in improbable shades of pink and fuchsia. I sink into it, study the room. There are prints of flowers with plain wooden frames, some certificates, a sepia photograph of a child with its parents. On the beige mantelpiece, between two candlesticks of heavy brass, sits a young man in an RAF uniform. Above his head hangs a scroll whose mount is plainly home-made, just a sheet of glass and passe-partout. I know instantly that Miss Armitage has managed this herself, that few have been allowed to handle the item.

I check myself, curse my own rudeness, open my mouth to speak. But she is sleeping, has fallen into that deep slumber which is reserved only for the very young and for the ageing. Her jaw sags, while the ill-fitting upper denture rests on her tongue. In the hearth sits a rack containing three short-stemmed pipes, but there is no man here. And these are ladies' pipes – I saw them on sale in Devon many years ago. Miss Armitage has, it seems, discovered tobacco rather late in life. The stains on her teeth are caused by pipe-sucking, then. The pipe is her pacifier, her security blanket.

So, forty-odd years on, I have seen Miss Armitage's

secret. The mantel is like an altar with the photograph as its centrepiece. Some tired violets sit to one side of the young airman, while a pale silk rose fills another small gap. Beribboned medals lie flat among the flowers, while twin steel cufflinks squat in a saucer, their oval surfaces displaying a worn crest. A matching tiepin skulks behind them and I cannot bear her pain, her loss. Was this her brother? No. A dead brother might be kept upstairs in a drawer, but only a lover would merit long years of naked devotion.

'He's dead now.' The false teeth click as she speaks. Does she know that she has been sleeping?

'I . . . presumed that he was dead.'

She nods. 'Last year. After I lost him, I too became infirm. They talked about me, you know. After all, I brought him here in the sixties, didn't marry him. They realized eventually that I was fit to continue as a teacher in spite of my loose morals.' The irises glisten wetly. 'And they even helped, came into the house while I was in class, bathed him, took him for little walks. Bless them, bless them all.'

My memory stirs, tries to speak to me. Yes, there was talk, but I was too busy with my own problems, too caught up in trying to keep one step in front of my biggest mistake. Auntie Maisie spoke about a man, and I didn't listen. But I must say something now. 'So . . . he didn't die in the war?'

She shrugs and I hear a bone grating and creaking. The woman has wasted almost to nothing, so her skeleton must be wearing away too, leaving her bones brittle and fine. 'The war killed him. For over ten years, he stayed in a hospital for ex-servicemen. When the hospital was closed, the authorities wanted to move Richard to a psychiatric unit. His father was dead and his mother was ill, so I brought him to live with me. I could not have allowed him to go into an asylum.'

I swallow audibly. 'Was he difficult?'

'Not with me, not with the Barr Bridgers. He was at

22

home, you see. I was the only person he remembered well. When I explained to him that I would need to continue working, he accepted the kind people who replaced me during school hours. At the end of a couple of years, we even managed to throw out the sedatives.' The small head lifts itself proudly, causing the bundled hair to loosen at the base of her skull. The bun wobbles, threatens to break free, settles like the ill-placed nest of some hasty bird.

Does she want me to ask? If I do ask, she might become upset. If I change the subject, then I might be accused of coldness. 'What happened to him, Miss Armitage? If it's too painful, don't talk about it.'

She sighs heavily, blinks a few times. 'Richard was a rear gunner. His plane went down and the rest of the crew died, they were all burnt to death. Over the years, in his darker moments, he could hear them screaming. The plane was low when he jumped – or so I was told by those whose fighters survived the mission. The Germans got him and his wounds were treated after a fashion.' She halts, fingers a crocheted armrest. 'A bump on the head, you see. Some of his brain died. He was judged to be so deranged that he was not imprisoned in the normal sense. The Nazis placed him in a mental hospital in Poland. No-one spoke English and most of the patients were probably beyond communication in any language.' She leans back, closes her eyes.

'And he stayed there till the end of the war?' I ask.

'Longer than that, my dear. He seldom spoke, you see. In 1947, a Polish doctor recognized that Richard's few words were in English, so he was brought home and put into the veterans' hospital. Somehow, his story was pieced together and he was reunited with his mother. But she could not have managed him. When she told me the details, I went immediately to visit him. And he knew me, responded to me. Laura, I could not have allowed them to put him behind bars again. We were engaged to be married, but that was not to be.'

'No.'

23

The blue eyes are wide again. 'We had some happy years. Not as man and wife, you understand. It was like having a child of my own, someone who depended on me for almost everything. Then, when I retired, we were together all the time.'

'I'm so sorry, Miss Armitage.'

'Don't pity me. My life has not been wasted, Laura. I taught many children, gave them a good start. There would have been no other man for me. At least I got back what was left of him, was able to cater for his needs.'

This is all too much for me. I am so near to her – my recent experience mirrors hers too closely. After a few garbled words about being excused, I dash up the steep and narrow stairs, find myself in a bathroom whose area has been stolen from the rear bedroom. Everything is pink. Although the house is rented, she has probably renovated it herself, has chosen warm and hopeful colours. Clusters of carnations spill down the walls until they meet rose-hued tiles. The bath, the washbasin, the lavatory are all pink, but the fitted carpet is a plain burgundy to match the towels. It is all so clean. They look after her, then.

With my face still damp after a cold wash, I stand on the landing, hear the clatter of teacups. His door is open. Blue and white striped pyjamas are folded on a candlewick bedspread. Brown slippers stand on a mat beside the bed. On a pine chest, shaving instruments are laid out next to a man's handleless hairbrush. I am reminded of a piece I read years ago, something like, 'I am not dead, I am just in the next room.'

The handle to the front bedroom creaks as I push the door wide. It's all peach and cream in here. Over the space where her bed used to stand, there is another photograph of Richard, but she is with him this time. They hold their hands towards the camera, fingers intertwined so that her tiny engagement ring will show. And I am crying now, weeping for the gentle soul who bathed my scraped knee, comforted me when Mother's cruelty showed on my face. Twice I had Liza McNally's fingermarks printed crimson

24

on my cheeks. But Mother left my face alone after Miss Armitage's visit. From that day, I was seldom beaten, and when Mother did lash out, she made her mark where it would not show.

Richard. I touch his image, whisper his name. I did not know him, though I heard and ignored the gossip during my brief stays here. My own difficulties swamped me then, left little space for interest in the troubles of others. But I understand, oh God, I understand. Miss Armitage's Richard has gentle eyes and a firm chin, is justifiably proud of his wife-to-be.

She calls. 'Tea, Laura.'

I am summoned, so I descend.

She is enthroned again in her rocker, has pulled out the mismatched Doulton for me. 'You've been crying.'

'Yes.'

There are roses on the cup, bluebells on the saucer and I am shaking. Was I sent here so that I would know the question? Does she have an answer? I sip, can scarcely swallow.

'He died in the back bedroom.' The tone is down-to-earth, commonsensical. 'I was with him. Would you like some cake?'

'No. No, thank you.'

She drinks greedily, noisily. 'What do you do for a living, Laura?'

'I write.'

The grey head nods. 'I should have known that. You are comfortable?'

No need for lies here. 'I am wealthy, Miss Armitage.'

'My name is Alice. I can see from your clothes and from your jewellery that you have done well.'

'I married well.'

The miniature face is clouded by confusion as she remembers my flight from this village. 'But that boy was . . .'

'I married well the second time. He was a jeweller.'

She regains her composure, is glad that I gave her the

opportunity to resume the perfect manners. 'Was? Is he dead, dear?'

I shake my head. 'He's . . . he's in a nursing home.'

'Oh.' There is so much wisdom in her face, and it has nothing to do with age. She was always wise, always sensible. 'Richard raved so. I bought the television set for him, because it seemed to soothe him. The memories were so dreadful. I should have hated for him to die when he was hearing the pilots' screams. It was important that he should go in peace, or I might have imagined him suffering that terrible nightmare for all eternity. Are you sure about the cake, Laura?'

I nod. She is telling me something and I am impatient to hear the end of her message.

'Then I shall eat it. The old are allowed to be gluttonous.' She bites, chews, gulps, swills down the residue with a draught of tea. 'He is older than you?'

'Yes.'

Her cup clatters in its ill-fitting saucer. She probably uses a mug when she has no visitors. '*Coronation Street* tonight,' she states. 'I do enjoy that programme. Richard liked it. He died on a Monday, just before *News at Ten*. Though it hasn't been the same since Hilda left. The Street, I mean. Don't worry, this isn't quite dementia. I've always been a scatterbrain.' She sniffs, nods her head repeatedly, reminds me of Katherine Hepburn in that *Golden Pond* film.

I know all about dementia . . . 'And he was peaceful?'

'Oh, yes.' She is staring again, is pushing her knowledge into my head. Her next words come in a whisper. 'There is the Maker in all of us, a little piece of the Lord. He tells us what is best, Laura. God guides our hand when the time comes.'

The breath catches in my throat. 'Did you . . . ?'

'Did I what?'

The clock's ticking is metallic and harsh. There are no words on my tongue and I feel weak, stupid. Who or what sent me here? Which entity planned that I should meet

26

this old woman, drink tea with her, watch the dentures wobbling about as she stuffs herself with angel cake?

'I am terminally ill,' she says softly. 'At this great age, most of us are knocking on death's door. But I've a definite and specific condition. The diagnosis was made on the Friday.' She pauses, drags a dry, age-weathered hand across her mouth. 'And Richard passed away three days later. Just before the ten o'clock news.'

'Alice?'

'Yes, dear?'

'Are you suffering?'

Her smile is bright and brave. 'No, I'm just dying an inch at a time. I've no regrets, Laura, none at all. Will you wash the dishes for me?'

'Of course.' I stand, lift the tray. 'Thank you.'

The kitchen is tiny. In the parlance of today's estate agents, it might well be a 'galley type' or a 'kitchenette'. There's a porcelain sink, a gas cooker, a 1950s-style unit with glass doors in the top, two shallow drawers, a let-down centre cupboard, two further drawers, then a couple of cupboards at the base. Tomato plants flourish on the tiny sill next to a miniature brown, blue and cream teapot with DEVON announced on its belly. Home-made recipe books are propped on a shelf, their covers made from school drawing paper, yellow, purple, fading magenta. There's a rack of pans, a kettle whose whistle has been lost, an aged toaster, a colander on a hook. So clean, so poor.

Her garden is long and narrow, is not suffering. Someone has cut the grass, weeded the borders. No, she is not poor. They come and look after her, keep up her standards, love her for educating their families. This lovely lady is rich beyond measure and deservedly so.

'Many of them have gone, moved on.' She is behind me, reading my mind. 'The cottages are mostly sold, bought by first-time buyers with babies and cars. But the farms have been handed down, you know. It's the farmers who look after me. I miss your aunt.'

'So do I.' Auntie Maisie Turnbull was a wonderful woman, a giver of love. She was the only real mother I ever knew. 'Anne's living in Bromley Cross.'

'She sends me flowers and plants, ruins me.' There's a catch in her voice and she covers it with a quiet cough. 'And she takes me to her home at Christmas. She never married and that's a pity, because she would have made an excellent mother. Have you kept in touch with her?'

I smile grimly. 'Oh, yes.' Without Anne, I would have been insane years ago. Anne does not discuss me, has not shared my troubles with Miss Armitage. Like her mother, Anne is caring, trustworthy.

Alice Armitage walks back into the sitting room, shuffles as she goes. 'He might have lingered for a while longer,' she mutters quietly. 'But I was unable to calculate my own span. Perhaps it was all for the best.'

I replace the Doulton, pile it carefully into the top of the unit where a mixture of china gathers in happy confusion. Did she help him on his way? Did she?

She is tired, has placed herself in the armchair. 'Is this jeweller husband of yours going to get better?'

Ben's face leaps into my mind. 'No.' I bite back an unexpected sob. 'He suffers. Like . . . Richard did.'

She smiles sweetly. 'God is good. Be His messenger.'

Again, she is asleep. I creep from the house, tiptoe past the window, have almost reached the Black Horse before I breathe normally. Something is working in a mysterious way today. Questions, answers, an old woman who drinks flat cider and smokes a pipe.

I shall not go up to McNally's, because my father is not there. But I'll visit his grave, drive through Bolton, head for home on the M62. In Crosby, I shall rest until the morning, then the future will begin. But first, I shall wade through my past, look through the pages of my life and try to make some sense of it.

They've done things to my town. I always feel proprietorial about Bolton, wonder why I haven't been consulted by developers. How dare they tart up the old

Market Hall, get rid of the Palais de Danse, stick a fast-food place just yards from the Victoria Hall? I can't drive through the main square, as it's been pedestrianized, but I can see the clock. When my insecurity showed, Dad used to say, 'Laurie-child, I'll leave you when the Town Hall clock strikes thirteen.' It never did strike more than twelve, but my sweet father went softly into his own night.

I'm going to my other home now. And I'm going to write everything on bits of paper. Elsie grinds her gears up Derby Street's slope, seems to be in a temper since I changed my mind about the motorway. This is the old route to Liverpool – St Helen's Road, Atherton, Leigh, Lowton, East Lancs Road. When this long stretch was laid, families used to come and picnic on the verge. Watching the great road coming to life was easily as much fun as sitting in a picture house.

We take so much for granted, refuse to take the world seriously. Wars on TV, real wars with real victims. And we fail to notice because our senses have been dulled by over-indulgence in passive pleasures. I have just been cured of a disease that would have seen me off ten years ago, yet I sing no songs, fly no flags. Somewhere inside, I'm relieved to be alive, yet I feel nothing except the worry about my husband, my Ben. Perhaps I'm like the rest, then, all Barclaycard and Big Macs, no effort, no gratitude, no wonderment. Oh no, I tell myself firmly. If Ben could be cured, I'd be dancing on air to celebrate a double reprieve.

I am in Merseyside now, driving past Kirkby with its tower blocks filled with displaced persons who used to have a real life in a wonderful city. Again, we didn't scream our displeasure when Liverpool lost its soul.

Anyway, I'm all right, Jack, should be happy, relieved, shouldn't be thinking all these morbid thoughts. Was the fear my prop? Did my illness sustain me, allow me to be justifiably self-centred?

Now, I have to face it all. I have a fresh start with a mended body and a healed mind. Not many people get a second chance, an extra stab at life. A lot to think about now. There's Mother, Ben, my children, the activity I laughingly call my career. Time has been given back to me. And time is the most precious gift of all.

I must use it and use it well.

Chapter Two

I am forced to sleep alone these nights, and I miss his arms, his breath in my hair, even the snoring I once recorded for him on a thirty-minute cassette, a din that might have registered high on the Richter scale. He laughed, of course. Laughed, stroked his chin thoughtfully, chased me round the kitchen and, armed with a wooden spoon engraved with the legend A SOUVENIR OF SKEGNESS, threatened me with GBH. I love him so much. If I love him so much, then why can't I bestir myself on his behalf, why don't I keep him with me and . . . ? Yes, Dr Ashby, I heard you all right. Even now, your dulcet tones echo in my lughole. 'The treatment has taken a lot out of you, Mrs Starling. An all-clear doesn't mean you can pick up a broom and start sweeping the world's problems into a neat pile.' Bloody doctors. They carry on as if every last one of them is an emissary from God.

Benjamin Starling is here in this house, so I must not let the bubble of self-centred guilt rise up. I must go and see to his breakfast, paint on a smile, be happy. Yes, I'll do all that in a minute.

We had our honeymoon in Skegness, bundled the children into the car, deposited them at Anne's house, then went off to find a boarding house on the other side of the Pennines. It took a while to pick out the right place. People must have thought us weird, because we pressed our noses against a dozen windows before we found what we wanted. She stood in the hallway of the Shoreside Haven, wrap-around pinnie, arms folded, a turbaned scarf failing to hide the curlers. Mrs Hyatt was her name. She

31

was terrifying, of a breed that had begun to die out in Blackpool.

Ben was courteous, as always. He wanted a double room for six nights, plus full board with HP Sauce, the *Daily Mirror* and a gingham tablecloth. She didn't do papers. 'I don't do papers,' the dinosaur said.

'This isn't the Park Lane,' I advised him gently.

'Then I shall manage without my newspaper,' he said gravely.

His humour was infectious, virulent. The bed did not squeak, so he loosened a few springs, tested the tone until he achieved what he chose to identify as middle C. According to him, 'Air On A Bed Spring' should be played on everyone's wedding night. The next day, my disgraceful husband sat for two whole hours on the beach in a string vest, knee-length swimming trunks, flippers. And he wore a knotted handkerchief on his head. He was getting into the swing of it, he said, was becoming a comic figure from a postcard. Skegness was not ready for him, had become too sedate. But I was not sedate and I was ready for that lovely man.

This bed is vast, king-sized. Entombed in its barren acres, I miss the squeaks and I feel like a pea on a drum, a pimple on the moon's cold surface. Perhaps I should buy another, a single bed for a single woman. No, I'll never be single in Benaura. What a name that is! He manufactured it, of course, took one syllable from Benjamin, two from Laura. 'It's daft,' I said. He had prepared an answer. For him, it almost translated into 'bene' and 'atmosphere', implying that our house is surrounded by a halo of goodness. Has it been extinguished, then? Ben, Ben, my poor, sweet, gentle man.

As soon as the curtains are opened, I smell rain and feel the wind rushing across the creaking leaded window. Weather can be shut out now by a second sheet of plain glazing, costly interior panes supplied by some company in Speke. The rep did not understand my desire to hold on to the frail lights, but I studiously resisted his photographs

32

of patio doors in pale-brick dormer bungalows, of square pebble-dashed semis with sturdy plastic bays that were 'a dead ringer for mahogany'.

After a quick wash in the *en suite* so-called master bathroom, I make up my face. Sometimes, when he isn't here, I loll about in Jodie's old cast-offs, frayed jeans, long sweaters that almost cover my knees, then ankle boots or, if the climate is friendly, those thonged sandals called Jesus-wellies. But today, I pat my face dry, apply moisturizing foundation, blusher, lipstick, a greyish shadow that emphasizes my irises, still clear and blue after fifty-odd years. The 'odd' doesn't matter – half a century is enough, a reasonable number at which to stop counting.

I have kept my hair long, because Ben loves flowing tresses on a woman. All the fashion magazines insist that ladies of mature years should have short hair, but what do they know? The comb catches in a knot, twangs its teeth while breaking free. Perhaps those women's weeklies are on the right track after all. Tresses is definitely the wrong word. Wires might be nearer the mark, because my hair has toughened over the years and with various treatments, some performed by an effeminate and very pleasant young man called Adrian, others delivered in a hospital and against my better judgement. Still, they saved my life, I have to admit grudgingly. But my once healthy mop has faded to a salt-and-pepper blonde that performs cruel dentistry on many a comb.

I pull on my French navy suit, a good jersey wool with a scooped neck and elbow-length sleeves. A pearl choker hides the slight creping at the throat, while a quick dab of Chanel does its best to lift my spirits. She will be here shortly. She will stand on my doorstep with her back to the sea and she will make me know my guilt, my inadequacy.

It is not my fault, I tell myself firmly, noting yet another worn patch on the stair carpet. It is a beautiful staircase with three turns and two small landings partway up. We bought the big, draughty house for its stairs and for an ill-treated fireplace in one of the living rooms. We have been kind to the fireplace, have released it from its prison of paint and Formica. My cat has not been kind to the staircase, though. He has sharpened his claws on the carpet and on some finely carved rails.

It is not my fault. A chap called Alois Alzheimer messed about with brain tissue in 1907. He left his findings and his name for posterity, so my husband suffers not from senile dementia, but from Alzheimer's disease. I am twenty years younger than Ben and, until lately, I have been robust. But during my own recent illness, Ben has slipped even further away from reality. My sin is that I did not notice, was too wrapped up in my fear. Now, he is . . . he is almost gone from me. I shouldn't have been ill. Even if I'd allowed myself an illness, I should have kept an eye on him. And the dragon's on her way again. She will look at me and she will think that I am uncaring, self-indulgent, a feeble-minded and ageing bimbo who hides behind face powder and good clothes.

Ben is in his room. He may be sleeping, may be rambling. Worse by far than the confusion are those rare moments of clarity when his eyes blaze triumphantly and he knows me. 'Laura,' he says. 'I do love you.' Inside, I bleed for the man I adore, for the stranger who had five decades apart from me, before me. I arrived late in the life of Benjamin Charles Starling and we have not discussed our separate pasts. Instead of reminiscing and indulging in unsavoury anecdotes, we made a pact, threw ourselves into what was probably a near-perfect marriage, total trust, abiding love and close friendship. Dear God, help me to bear this sorrow, broaden my shoulders and dry my stupid female eyes. This is a Sunday, but You are here, not just in churches where people bend and scrape and show off a new hat.

The kettle whispers, simmers, bubbles and boils. I brew his tea thick and strong, using loose tea from the tin marked YORKSHIRE. No perforated bag for Ben, just honest-to-goodness leaves, one sugar and a splash of milk. I think he must have lived for a while in Leeds or Halifax or somewhere over the Pennines, this wonderful man whose English is too perfect. Tea mashed and stewed the Yorkshire way has been his favourite beverage.

Handel eyes me lugubriously, whiskers to attention as he waits for his dollop of catfood. Cats are supposed to be friendly when hungry, but he remains cool, offhand, paralysed by laziness. A psychologist once told me that laziness does not exist, that those who sit and wait for life to happen are suffering from lack of motivation. He never met my cat. I feed the monster, toss a bone outside for his partner in crime, a big soft dog who makes the mistake of loving and trusting all humans. The psychologist never met him, either.

The sea is wind-tossed, angry waves vying for position as the tide forces its urgent way up the Mersey's throat. The Vikings landed here, settled in Crosby, Thornton, Blundellsands. Had they arrived today, those ridiculous horned helmets might have provided some protection from elements whose anger is far from decorous, certainly unjustified. The holiday season, and the beach is as empty as Anfield when the lads are playing away. The Vikings might cheer things up a bit – even a bit of pillage would break the monotony. It could be reported in the *Crosby Herald* – 'HORNED MAN BREAKS INTO LIFEBOAT STATION, STEALS PETTY CASH'. That would make a change from the usual shoplifting. The porridge is ready, the tray is set. I place a yellow rose in a narrow glass. On my second wedding day, I carried yellow roses.

For twenty-one years, I have asked no questions. Now, as I ponder and worry my way through lonely nights, I accept that there can be no complete answers. He is a good man. His illness makes him no less a person, though I allowed myself to be considerably diminished by a disorder from which I emerged intact. So I am now less than I was. Dr Ashby echoes again in my head. 'You have not failed! Whatever you'd done, he would have deteriorated. And you've been ill, girl.' Dr Ashby has no idea. Ben saved me years ago, took my life in his hands and held it like a piece of porcelain, protected me from all harm. And when he needed me, I was not here for him.

Why didn't I ask? Now, I find myself wondering constantly, dwelling on the subject of Ben's beginnings. Where did he come from, this foreigner with an accent that is almost BBC *circa* 1950? I remember those commentators, all rounded vowels and clipped consonants, have read the famous stories of dress suits and bow ties for men, elegant dresses and straight seams in fully-fashioned stockings for 'ladies' who talked on the wireless. Yet Ben has failed, but only just, to reach Home Service standards. Each syllable of Ben's is awarded almost equal stress, so he is probably European. I have been touched to the point of tears by his need to belong in this, his chosen country. If any of our friends has noticed Ben's quaint speech, then he or she has held back query and opinion, just as I have. There was something in my husband's eyes, a look that seemed to beg, 'Don't ask.'

She rings the doorbell, and I dash like a timid schoolgirl who is late for registration. Running makes me breathless, reminds me of my weakness. Slowly, slowly, the doctors said. I press my palms flat against the door, breathe deeply through my nose, exhale through my mouth. I am recovering, convalescing after surgery, emerging from a breakdown that was ghastly. I don't know which was worse – the physical pain or the emotional collapse. But I won't panic. And I won't panic about nearly panicking just a moment ago. I'm in charge, coping.

I open the door. A dark grey raincoat is unbuttoned over a dress of royal blue whose seams have faded beneath the weight of an assiduous iron. A badge proclaims her status, announces to the world that she is a fully-fledged nursing sister. On her rigid bosom, an upside-down watch dithers in time with her asthmatic respiration. 'Cold,' she mutters.

The tang of heavy smoking hangs around her. She must take the inhalations without using her hands, because the fags have stained her moustache a darker yellow on the left side. Yes, I can imagine her labouring over a patient, filter-tip clenched between nicotined incisors. 'Not exactly summery,' I reply. 'Shame about those on holiday in Southport.'

'Never had time for holidays, myself,' she announces, her tone harsh. 'All you get from holidays is sore skin and a pile of rubbishy photos. Waste of effort and money.'

God, what I'd give for a fortnight in the Bahamas among healthy, strong people . . . Selfish again. She thinks I've been having a beano, dashing round and socializing while my husband languishes. 'I had to go away, Nurse Jenkinson. It was unavoidable – business, you see.'

She grunts, runs her muddy eyes over my thinning body. 'What you need is a good dose of vitamins and three squares a day.'

'Yes.' I am meek again, and the meekness infuriates me.

She passes me, jabs her brolly into the stand as if impaling an opponent on a skewer. 'Is he awake?'

'Yes. I've just made his breakfast. It's on the tray in the kitchen.'

She makes a great business of looking at her watch, long-sightedness forcing her to narrow the strange green eyes. 'He needs his breakfast earlier than this, Mrs Starling. When he goes back to Heaton Lodge tomorrow, he will be out of his routine and that will cause problems.'

I pretend to study my hands, because I know that this woman resents my manicured hands. Almost every week, Adrian does what he calls 'a French job', managing somehow to imply naughtiness in the term. But he simply paints the nails a natural pink, then whitens their tips. 'Ben will be here until Tuesday morning,' I reply, trying not to gloat over the small mistake. Nurse Jenkinson is always right. Nurse Jenkinson never forgets a schedule. 'It's a bank holiday.' I look straight at her. 'And you don't need to come tomorrow. I shall see to him.'

'But you can't.' She is speaking to a fool whose mantle of bravado is clearly slipping. I have not changed a nappy since my youngest child was two years old. But the

37

stubbornness persists. 'I am quite capable of looking after my own husband.'

Her tongue clicks quietly as she rejects the lie. 'I shall come tomorrow, as Mr Starling is on my list of regulars. Later, we shall decide what to do about his weekends.'

Lists. She probably makes lists for everything, probably keeps an input and output chart on her own visits to table and bathroom. 'As you wish.' I step aside as she claims more space in the hall, her bulky body seeming to grow as it claims its right of entrance. She removes what she calls her mac, hangs it at the bottom of the stairs. While she fetches Ben's breakfast tray, I make a point of transferring her outer garment to the hallstand. Sometimes, I am unbearably small-minded.

She clomps her flat-footed way up the stairs and I notice how worn her shoes are, how snagged the black stockings. She is poor, gets monkey wages for taking care of people whose families have failed them, rejected them. In future, I will try to control my thoughts about her, try to appreciate her position. She runs about in an aged Metro, cleans up food and vomit, takes pulses, temperatures and abuse, washes faces and bottoms, sticks needles in sagging flesh, talks nonsense to corpses that refuse to stop breathing. Nurses have always been undervalued, though they probably save more lives than do the so-called specialists. The masters just sit and pontificate, hide behind seventeen-letter qualifications, make no effort to disguise superiority complexes big enough to make Adolf Hitler seem submissive. They wouldn't know a bedpan from a first-class stamp. Bitterness again. They saved me and I curse them. Mind, they have ruined my hair . . .

I walk into the kitchen, make coffee, pick up the newspaper from the side porch which doubles as a utility room. His pyjamas are in a bucket of cold water and Napisan, trapped air making the blue striped cloth bubble upward like a beachball. He bought a beachball in Skegness. And a bucket and spade, some paper flags, those awful green flippers. During the daylight hours of our honeymoon, he entertained the children from the boarding house. 'My castle's better than yours,' he would say to some indignant seven-year-old. Budding architects came to light that day. By the end of the week, the competition was fierce and all the mothers were grateful to their unexpected childminder. 'I told you to bring Jodie and the boys,' he said repeatedly.

'It's our honeymoon,' I insisted.

He would then wear an expression that was tailored to infuriate. 'Is it? Oh, I must have forgotten.'

He forgets almost everything these days. Almost everything . . . I tip the pail's contents into a deep porcelain sink, turn the tap until the flow is torrential, watch the stains as they separate and gurgle down the drain. I am glad that I decided to preserve this part of the old kitchen, grateful for the aged sink. When the machine is programmed for a half-load, I peel off the Marigolds and retrieve the newspaper from a wicker washing basket.

I sit at the table in my beautiful newish kitchen, half-price one hot June with a portable telly thrown in. It took six months to persuade the firm to part with the television, a year to encourage its employees to fit the kitchen properly, preferably with the units actually fastened to the walls. The surfaces are pristine, a sort of imitation marble in cream and brown. Cupboards and drawers are white with fancy mouldings and brass handles. Nothing gets used, so nothing gets dirty. I cannot remember when I last cooked a proper meal in here, a real supper for more than two people.

Yes. Yes, I can remember. It started then, when we got the wobbly kitchen. Ruth and Les Edwards came. We had avocado and smoked salmon to start, lemon chicken for the main course, sorbets for pudding. Ruth was on one of her diets, as usual. She's short and beautiful and rather round at times. Throughout the meal, we drank a cold crisp hock, then Ben drifted out to crush some ice. Whether dieting or bingeing, Ruth always indulges her passion for *crème de menthe frappé*. I followed him, loaded the percolator, dug deep in an unhinged cupboard for some Kenya medium and a half-empty box of After Eights.

My eyes brim with salt water as I stare at the space Ben occupied that night, the spot in front of the freezer where he stood, forehead creased, hands uncertain and dangling loose by his sides. 'Where is it?' he asked in a voice unlike his own.

'The ice is usually in the top,' I replied, still blissfully ignorant of anything amiss. Ben was . . . past tense again! Ben is a mimic, often disguises his voice.

'My gun,' he said clearly. 'What the hell have you done with my gun?'

The ice was forgotten immediately, though I felt as if a glacier had been compressed and pushed down my throat by a giant hand. 'Ben?' I ventured. 'Why do you need a gun?' My tone became ordinary, I think, very low and steady. I might have been asking why he needed a new shirt or some clean socks.

'They must be shot,' he said clearly. 'And we can use their valuables to carry on the work.'

Flesh does creep. I felt as if my spine had raised itself from my body, as if it crawled like a slow, cold snake into my hair. He was a stranger. More than that, he was almost an enemy. His eyes were dull, frozen in their sockets. The kind face was twisting itself in response to some inner fury that he had suddenly accessed, something that had lain dormant over a long period. He was not Ben. He was a man with a mission, a man anxious to defend, attack, survive.

Les came in and Ben jumped on him, leapt like a panther across the room and seized this good friend by the throat. 'Pig,' growled my husband. 'Did they let you live, then? How many more, *cochon*? *Combien*?' Ben turned his head and addressed the kitchen door. 'Come, Ziggy. See what has crawled into the apartment.'

Les is a strong man, but was too shocked to act for at least half a minute. He looked at me, his eyes round and fear-filled, bulging as the hold on his throat tightened.

'Stop him!' I yelled. 'Do what you have to do, Les.'

The violence was terrible. Ben fought, struggled, cursed in several languages as Les restrained him. After a quick glance round the door, Ruth ran screaming from the house. That was strange, I think now, because Ruth is not a screamer. I phoned for an ambulance, sat still as a gravestone while my husband was handled by blue-clad men. Les and Ruth left, followed the ambulance to Fazakerley. I stayed, listened as the coffee bubbled, inhaled the smell, came to hate the wonderful aroma of coffee. Humans are resilient, but it was some time before a percolator was used again in this kitchen.

The next day, I visited my husband, brought flowers, purple grapes and a book about birds to a normal man who kissed me, discussed the weather and pied wagtails, asked about my children. The previous night had been wiped from his memory, but I knew in my bones that the initiating buzzer was still stored in some compartment of his brain. Like a file on a computer, the information simply waited for the buttons to be pressed in a certain sequence. I was also aware that Ben was not in charge of himself. The programming was random, not controllable. Up to that point, I had never been so terrified in my life. Even when Tommo was beating me, even when I ran away to save my children, I was not conscious of such intense, almost immobilizing fear.

A babyish doctor took me on one side, his upper lip still downy, as if he had not yet begun to shave. This sad child spoke about tests, asked me to be brave, outlined the cruel and merciless symptoms of Alzheimer's. Ben would be patchy, he said, would have good days and bad. My theory was wrong, he insisted. I was imagining that Ben had suffered some sudden return of memory, had perhaps recalled a traumatic experience that had lain dormant and had been followed by a bout of comforting amnesia. This was nothing to do with shock, the doctor said sadly. Ben was remembering things he had always known, but his decaying brain could no longer cope. If we were lucky, this sort of episode might not repeat itself for years. On the other hand . . .

On the other hand, my husband is upstairs being fed and cleaned by a woman whose moustache is well established, whose hands, unlike mine, are sure and steady and used to such labours. In a few minutes, I shall make some more tea. Tetley bags for her. After all, she is my husband's mother at weekends.

The newspaper is not readable – I just look at the pictures. Wars, rumours of wars, starvation and threatened drought. Little black faces, huge eyes in masks of death. I am useless, stupid, unimportant, a failure.

She comes in, surprises me. 'Don't cry, Mrs Starling.'

I have not felt the tears escaping, but her words alert me to the moisture on my cheeks. 'It's a hard life.' I wave a hand towards the newspaper, try a grin, but a disobedient sob escapes my custody. 'Sorry, nurse. I'm a bit tired.' Oh, she will hate me now. I'm just a wealthy fashion plate with a big house, a special car, painted nails and a bad attitude to duty.

She sits opposite me, uncertain because she has not liked me. Then she takes my hands in hers. The nurse's poor fingers are red, nails bitten so low that the pads above them are swollen, look sore. 'He's quiet enough just now,' she says soothingly. 'Please try not to fret yourself, love. It's just one of them things what happens.' The Liverpool accent, which usually trims just the edges of her words, spreads its gushing splendour throughout the suddenly enlivened speech. 'Me dad had this, you know. We found him down Scottie Road one night in his 'jamas, three sheets in the wind and no shoes on. No socks either. He flushed his teeth down the toilet and wouldn't go for any new ones. It killed me mam, the way me dad was. She just keeled over one day in the butcher's, spark out in sawdust, she was. They tried to fetch her back, but she'd given up. Don't you be doing that. It often happens, the partner going first. Why don't you go away for a few days, have a proper break? You like your little holidays, don't you?'

I shake my head. The only person who knows the truth about my 'breaks' is Ruth Edwards, and I trust her completely. 'I'll go again sometime, but not just at the moment.'

Nurse Jenkinson releases my hands, props her fat elbows on the stripped-pine table. 'Play one of your records, then.' She has caught me cheerful once and has not forgotten. 'You like the Beatles, don't you? He lived near me auntie, that Ringo one. Little terraced house, gone posh now, all white paint and hanging baskets. Yanks come and take photos of it.'

The Beatles Tour. I've done it with my own New Jersey relatives, 'Strawberry Fields orphanage on your left, ladies and gentlemen', then, 'Penny Lane, there's the barber's shop, sorry there's no fire engine today.' Another avenue, tree-lined, grass-verged, a hundred eyes feasting on the oriel bay where Lennon twanged his guitar until he got it right. But I'm in no mood for *Sergeant Pepper* today; the weather is too Wagnerian.

She tries again. 'You look peaky. Take a course of vitamins.'

'I will.'

'And eat your greens.'

My appetite has not yet returned. That, according to Dr Ashby, is thoroughly understandable, though he insists that I try to eat a little more each day.

Nurse Jenkinson brews her own tea, changes the subject. 'He's talking in different languages again.'

Immediately, I am alert and defensive, yet I don't understand this quick reaction of mine. 'Ben is fluent in five or six languages. He's travelled a lot.'

She sits, slurps noisily on the cup's edge, is one of those infuriating people who tackle hot drinks from a safe and sloppy distance. 'What are you going to do today?' Greedy eyes fix on the biscuit jar. I nod and she pounces on an innocent custard cream. 'There's been no inroads made

43

here,' she comments, spitting crumbs on to her uniform. 'Don't you eat biscuits?'

'Sometimes.' She's nosy, far too inquisitive for comfort. My diet is a private matter between me and myself. However, I must remember to throw out some biscuits for the birds, or this woman might make a chart for me too if the biscuit jar stays full. 'I don't eat much between meals,' I say. I haven't been eating much at all, but that's my business. Progress is being made and that's the important thing. Two squares of chocolate and a whole Cup-a-Soup yesterday. And that's not bad going for someone who was drip-fed only weeks ago, who accepted virtually no nourishment during the subsequent breakdown.

She attacks a bourbon, breaks open the sandwich, scrapes pale brown incisors across the chocolate filling. 'He likes birds, doesn't he? That garden of yours is a real sanctuary. Nice to have an interest like that. Very nice.'

It's more than an interest, was a consuming passion for Ben. He worked alongside the Royal Society, was one of the chosen few. Like Tiggywinkles hospital for hedgehogs, we have been a nursing home for gulls, sparrows, owls. And for many, many starlings. They are his favourite birds, and I'm sure that his surname was adopted deliberately. One owl refused to leave, returned each night and twitted about all over the place until his saviour woke and twitted back. Ben has walked on the shore with a starling in each hand, one perched on his foot. I am doing my best, but the feathered world misses Ben's knack of communication.

'I've no animals because the flat's too small. But I like dogs and horses. Most of all, I'd like a donkey.'

She's human after all! 'Why a donkey?' I ask, trying to keep the surprise out of my tone.

'Stubborn. They're stubborn like me. Most of my patients are bloody-minded, so I'd know how to handle a donkey. They need a rest at the end of their life, specially if they've been giving rides at Blackpool.'

Animals and people never fail to surprise me. The boys

44

once kept a fifteen-foot python in the house. He used to wind his soft, kid leather length around me and flick his tongue rudely at the television, always hissed when I stroked him. Some people are so phobic that we had to hide the poor creature in the attic and pretend we'd given him away. The terrified were often men, big men whose prime urge was to kill our snake. (Ben thought the whole thing was connected with penis envy, but I wasn't convinced.) The taller and broader the man, the bigger the terror. Two large heroes yelled, 'Kill it, get the poker, get rid of it!' Brave warriors, those men. They want to kill what they don't understand, and that is how wars begin. Kill it, occupy it, devour it, subjugate it. And thus *Homo sapiens* makes his way towards his own destruction.

Nurse Jenkinson amazes me, reminds me of that long-dead reptile. We expected him to be vicious, were pleasantly surprised by his docility. This woman's outer appearance belies her true self. She loves donkeys, probably loves her patients. But I, like the cowardly men I decried, judged her on her negative points.

'You look depressed.' She is longing for a cigarette.

'Smoke if you want to, nurse. It doesn't bother me – I used to smoke myself.'

She lights a Benson's, waves the match until it gives up its spiralling ghost of blue smoke. 'How did you stop? I've tried time after time, even got the new nicotine patches, but they made me itch and gave me nightmares. And I'd be twenty stone but for these.' She waves the glowing end in my direction and my gorge rises as ash spills and scatters on the table. 'How did you stop?' she asks again, thick eyebrows scurrying up her face in amazement. She plainly assesses me as one who is too weak to break free from the weed.

I shrug. 'I was frightened of being ill.' That excuse will have to suffice, though my real reason for quitting lay in the fact that my children needed food and shoes.

She nods sagely. 'I'm scared too, but the more I worry, the more I smoke.' She looks me up and down. 'The weight's dropped off you these last three months. I reckon that suit would cover you twice.'

'Menopause,' I reply briskly. 'Some get thin, some get fat.'

'Don't I know it. I'm like you, I never eat between meals. I wouldn't care, only I've no sweet tooth.' She remembers the biscuits, flounders. 'I need a bit of carbohydrate of a morning, but I never finish a full meal. It's no fun being fifty, is it?'

Being fifty was all right by me. At fifty, my body was healthy, firmer, and my husband was sane. We had our final good year, travelled through Normandy and Brittany, camped out in fields, watched the birds, marked our cards every time we saw a new one. At seventy, my husband was agile, quick on his feet, flat-bellied, demanding in bed. And even more urgent under two spread-out sleeping bags and a French navy star-spangled sky.

Nurse Jenkinson finishes her smoke, heaves herself up, crimson hands splayed on the table. 'I'll go now. Six o'clock, I'll see to Mr Starling again.'

I do not follow her. She is capable of making her own way out of the house and I am feeling sluggish. Chewbacca is barking in his kennel and the cat is still staring at me. He must have hollow legs, he eats more than I do. I wait, listen as her car grumbles itself to life. Like its owner, the car is shabby and asthmatic.

Ben is in his chair, a rug across his knees. He can walk, but he chooses not to, or has forgotten a skill he learned seven decades ago in a place he has not loved. The television is on, Channel 4, something meaningful and Open University-ish. Ben stares, slack-mouthed and dribbling, at a young woman in folksy clothes that she probably made herself out of wool culled from briar-edged sheep fields. She wears owlish glasses, half a dozen earrings and an intelligent expression, discusses earnestly with an invisible interviewer the merits of paganism. I flick the tuner to BBC 1 and the hymn-singing. 'Hello, Ben,' I say.

He answers in code, a mixture of what sounds like

46

Greek and Russian – something with an upside-down alphabet, anyway.

'Speak English,' I say.

'Order arrived . . . from the top. Strawberry yoghurt,' comes the disjointed reply.

I crouch, place myself in front of him and at his level. 'Do you want a strawberry yoghurt?'

'There are more.' His mouth has tightened, looks almost normal. But the eyes are vague and I notice that a white age-ring has appeared around each hazel iris.

I use my handkerchief to mop up the saliva on his chin. 'More of what, Ben?'

'No shoes. We took the cow to the market and it was too thin, Mama. Has Ruth been lately?' The face crumbles, collapses inward. 'Laura, what is happening to me? Get me to a telephone. I must speak to them, warn them that I am . . . that I am not here.' His tongue protrudes, licks the lower lip. 'Damson wine, so sweet and strong. They are drunk, you know. My mother will not be pleased. The singing is so lovely. It is all written down. Such pretty music.' His head droops, the chin resting on his chest. Like a young animal, he tires quickly, falls asleep easily. The end of life is so like the beginning . . . Is this the end? Or will he go on and on? The mild sedatives keep him quiet up to a point, yet the nightmare returns regularly, shines the cold light of misery in his eyes.

Music. He was talking just now about music. I mute the television, search the radio bands for something suitable. There's heavy metal, then a guttural contralto followed by somebody talking rubbish – something to do with compost and roses, anyway. Perhaps I should carry the music system upstairs, or have extra speakers placed in this room. He loves Mozart, Verdi, the Ying-Tong song by Milligan and Secombe. But he's too far gone. I've tried it all before, have clung to straws for months on end.

Outside in the garden, the congregation has gathered for its Sunday service. On a podium that doubles as a bird table, a lone blackbird stands, his wings not quite folded.

47

He reminds me of a dark-gowned schoolmaster whose patience is thinning, whose arms are not quite akimbo as he wills his charges to be still and quiet.

There are starlings everywhere, sleek, oily fellows with glints of purple in their plumes. This disorganized choir shuffles and struts, beaks pretending to search the ground for food. They know, though. They know I'll be out in a few minutes with their 'suitable supplements'. I learned from Ben to be careful with summer feeding. Mrs Blackbird, brown and dowdy, is a floating voter. She sits on the fence, separate from everything, one eye on her bossy mate, the other on some sparrows in the apple tree.

'Your birds are here, Ben,' I say without turning my head. 'They miss you, sweetheart. Woeful Wally comes back some nights, twitting and twooing outside our window. And we've hedgehogs, you know.'

'Don't give them bread, Laura.'

I swing round, capture the moment and hold it like a precious flower in my mind. I dare not move, speak, breathe.

'Hedgehogs do not thrive on flour and yeast. Dog food, perhaps.' He shivers. 'I am afraid of the dogs.'

He loves dogs. But since the change in him, I have kept poor Chewy away.

'They bite. We thought he would not do it, but these people cannot be trusted. Of course, it's all written down. But will they learn? Do you think that they will learn?'

'Who?' I whisper.

'Well, I think it's time to go.'

'Ben!' He is slipping through my fingers like water from the tap, trickling away to leave me alone, thirsty. 'Ben!'

'There is no need to shout, Laura, because I am not deaf. Where's that bloody woman? The trouble with these people is that they're never here when they're needed.'

'The nurse?'

'Yes. She doesn't know about the strawberry yoghurt. I haven't told anyone else about it. Could she be trusted? Do you think she's on our side?'

48

'Yes. Yes, I think so.'

He grunts, allows his eyes to travel round the room. 'So many allegiances, so many partisans. I am late for school,' he announces clearly. 'The bell went ten minutes ago, I'll need to hurry. Will you come with me?' So he sleeps, goes back to school in his dreams. Still, school is better than the other place. A shiver travels the length of my spine, pricks my scalp with its sharp and chilly fingers. There is a place in Ben's past and I can't find it. But it finds him day after day, pushes him into a nightmare whose duration increases as the days move on.

And I fear that he will be consumed by his memories, that soon he will go into that horror forever. 'No, Ben.' I am answering his latest question. 'No-one can go with you.' I cannot save him and my tears begin again.

Chapter Three

'The answer is Winston Churchill. It really is this time. Honest, Les. Cross my heart and hope to end up losing. See, it says here, "Winston Churchill". Now, do you believe me?' She waves the card beneath his bulbous nose. 'He was made an honorary citizen of the United States. And that's an end of it.'

It is not the end, because they continue their argument for several minutes, quarrelling loudly about Churchill and any other subject that might have cropped up in the game since it began an hour ago. When I intrude, when I dare to ask for my own question, they carry on fighting about bits of trivia.

It's great being the mistress of your own house. You just get ignored while the neighbours come to blows over a game that's supposed to be pleasurable. It occurs to me that a room containing Ruth and Les Edwards can seem very full, can render me all but invisible. 'Would anyone like a drink?' No response. I am now sure that I'm not really here.

There is a lull in the shouting, and they both glare at me as if it's all my fault. Something childish giggles in my breast. 'I'm not playing. And you're not playing any more either. This is my toy, so you can both go home to Mummy, see if she'll put up with the tantrums.'

Ruth and Les are mortallious when it comes to Trivial Pursuit. Ben never played the game – I bought it just before his absences began. Ruth arches the perfect brows. 'Are you sulking, Laura Starling?'

'Yes.' I fold up the board and sweep all the awkward little playing pieces into the box. 'You are both becoming

50

extremely naughty. I can't manage all this "I'm cleverer than you are." It's like being back at school in the infant department.' I wear what is meant to be an expression of sweet innocence. 'Shall we try Scrabble?'

The noes are simultaneous. We have played Scrabble for so many years that the board is almost worn away. Ben was good at Scrabble. I blink, swallow, suggest three-handed bridge.

'I'd sooner wrestle with a crocodile.' Les makes another exit towards the cloakroom. He has been talking lately about cutting out the middle man by pouring the beer directly into the toilet. 'I worry about his prostate,' laughs Ruth. Then, suddenly sober, 'When do you see the quack again?'

The 'quack' is the specialist who saved my life. 'In a week or so.'

'Worried?'

I shake my head. 'The results will be negative. I'm all clear. Oh God, Ruth, I wish I could say the same about Ben. There I was all those months, wrapped up in myself—'

'You were very ill.' Her voice is as soft as a caress. 'There were times when we thought . . . when Les and I thought we were losing you.' Her little face is grave. It wasn't the idea of my death that frightened her, because she had been convinced from the start that I would be saved. It was the aftermath that terrified her, when my mind took a holiday. So Ruth and Les watched Ben with Alzheimer's and me with a total breakdown. It must have been very unpleasant, and now I blame myself all over again. Perhaps I should have been a Catholic – my enormous sense of guilt would surely have been big enough, even for the Church of Rome.

I get up from the kitchen chair, remove the Trivial Pursuit from the table, fuss about with cheese, biscuits, coffee. Ruth is my best friend. She's an accountant, but she manages to be human in spite of this dry calling. And Les is the salt of the earth, a Liverpool lad with his own business and a sense of humour that is wicked and lively. I love them both, I owe them much. 'You've done a lot for us, you and Les. I'll never be able to thank you enough.'

She snorts. Ruth's equine snorts would frighten the real horses. 'Segal said that love means never needing to say "sorry". The same applies to "thanks". Anyway, we need you. We weren't going to let you off the hook so easily, Laura. Are you sure you're in the clear now?'

I shrug. 'I've to be tested regularly, but I've as good a chance as anyone else.' I swivel, grin at her. 'I'm a miracle.'

Les finds us laughing, then we sit for an hour or two discussing their daughter, my scattered children, the state of the building trade. He waves his arms a great deal, gets excited about recession, lack of development, the poor quality of cement. We have had many evenings like this one, and we all continue to miss Ben. When Ben was here, we played four-handed bridge and the dummy freshened drinks, filled the peanut dishes. There is no dummy these days. Except for me. I was stupid enough to crack up when I was truly needed. He drifted then, my dear Ben, got worse when I stopped visiting him. Though Ruth insists that this might have happened anyway, that I noticed the deterioration because I had not seen him for a couple of months. The analogy she used was odd, yet so right. 'When a child goes away to school, the parent notices how he has grown during term time. If the son or daughter had remained at home, such changes would have gone unnoticed.' Ben is a child, yet he is not a child. Children learn, grow, mature. Here, we have that process in reverse . . .

Ben is upstairs in the land of Nod. I realize that Les has been up to see him, has pretended to visit the bathroom. My Ben is in a world of his own. And we are all lonely without him.

We have lived here for years, on an expensive road that faces the erosion. When I first arrived, I had to roll the word around my mouth for a while, taste its oddness before allowing it to spill from my lips. Erosion. There's something medical about the term, as if it is meant to describe a weeping sore or a time-worn wound in the gynaecological department. It does not seem appropriate when applied to the wide neck of Liverpool's famous river.

When he was a pup, Chewbacca and I began our walks along the shore, one of us picking her careful way across mud-coloured and oil-streaked sand, the other cavorting in pools of grim grey water, his neck usually festooned with dirty seaweed. Even at his best, Chewy is far from beautiful. He is large and stupid, is the sole owner of a broad and vacant smile and a tail that might, in its cleaner moments, do justice to a Coldstream Guard's helmet. Covered in grease, sewage and discarded picnic debris, he is not a pretty sight. He also has a marked penchant for discovering and collecting used condoms, an activity that can be embarrassing to his innocent companion. Especially when the vicar approaches with that yappy Yorkshire terrier.

We took the dog's name from the Star Wars films, because he bears an uncanny resemblance to the matted creature who threw in his lot with the good people like Harrison Ford. Yes, he is very like a Wookie. We have loved him for five years now, but I cannot allow him anywhere near Ben. Ben used to take the dog everywhere, has been known to walk him all the way to Formby at low tide. With the demise of so many brain cells, my husband has acquired a terrible fear of canines. And no matter what the medics say, I know that Ben is stuck in some abominable time warp, that he is revisiting a place in his past, an awful place. When he was whole, he could cope with the memories, could keep them in perspective. Yes, he has Alzheimer's, but he has not lost all his yesterdays.

When our walks began, I started to understand the word 'erosion'. The river/sea is eating its way inland. In a hundred years, perhaps less, this area could well be flooded. There are stones heaped upon stones, every item rounded by a million tides. Were these boulders at the start of time, did dinosaurs clamber around them, hide behind them? Yes, there is erosion here, and it is contained, held back by concrete walls and ugly steps. For the moment, the wearing away of Blondel's villages has been postponed.

The dog and I enter the house by the rear porch, find Ruth waiting for us. She has been husband-sitting for me, has kept an ear cocked for sounds from upstairs. And she has visited him, I know that, has talked endlessly into ears that blank out most sounds. Ruth and I have occupied this kitchen for hours without speaking. Like most true friends, we enjoy comfortable silences. She occupies herself four times a year with my VAT forms, once annually with Income Tax. She is a person who does not interfere during working months, when Georgina Dawn, my *alter ego*, labours to give birth to characters and plots that will suit the True Hearts editor. Unlike so many friends, she chooses not to visit when I'm sweating over a hot computer, understands that I cannot indulge in small talk while one of my little stories is germinating.

Chewy hurls himself at Ruth, washes her face, woofs his loud way through the usual enthusiastic greeting. Handel, my large and largo cat, is unmoved, sits by the sink, mesmerized by a slowly dripping tap. A Garfield in the furry flesh, Handel is economical with his movements except when organizing some form of destruction. His superiority over the dog is never questioned; Chewy has been known to run a mile from those sharp if slothful talons.

We sit, drink coffee. The dog gets bored, claws his way outside and barks at the birds. 'Ben's quiet.' She waves a hand towards the upper storey. 'I suppose you can't just go out and leave him, can you?'

I shrug. 'Sometimes, I have to. Ben-sitters are not always available.'

Ruth stirs, clatters the spoon, sips the black and

sugarless Nescafé. 'Aren't you afraid that he might walk out one of these weekends – if he remembers how to walk, that is? I mean, what if you came back from one of your strolls and found his room empty? He could fall under a car or into the water . . .' Her voice fades, trails away. 'Sorry,' she whispers. 'I'm not meaning to pile guilt on top of everything else.'

'He's probably happier here, even on his own.' That's a lie, because Ben isn't happy anywhere, has lost all joy in life. And that was the most noticeable thing about him. He had joy, and he expressed it daily. 'At Heaton Lodge, I've watched him becoming agitated when the others scream or cry.' The fact that I've also seen him totally unresponsive does not bear talking about. Anyway, she knows, she's seen it all. I remain quiet for a moment, dare not attach speech to my thoughts. If he walked out and died, I would be grateful on his behalf, calmer about my own part in his downfall. If I hadn't been ill, if I'd worked with him . . . No, don't even think about it. 'He won't walk, Ruth, doesn't seem to have the strength to make any kind of effort,' I manage. 'He's made no strides in any direction for the past six months, either physical or mental. Even when he did walk a bit, he just paced about, four steps this way, four steps back, always counting under his breath.'

She catches the full lower lip under teeth that are white and even. 'What's going to happen to him, Laura? Are you absolutely sure that he can only get worse? Is there no hope, no chance that somebody, somewhere might find an answer?'

'I don't know. I'm seeing that specialist about Ben. Thank God I can afford to have him looked after properly. I'm going to make as much noise as I can, try to get some new treatment, anything at all that's on the market. You know, Ruth, I'll even offer him up as a guinea-pig if I get the chance. There must be a doctor, even at the other side of the globe, who would be willing to have a go.' I nod wearily, am made aware yet again of my post-operative

55

tiredness. 'I'd send him to the moon if that would make him well.'

'I know you would.'

'And I sometimes think he'd be better off . . .'

'You'll be ill again if you're not careful,' she whispers. 'You can't keep your mind fixed on Ben all the time—'

'If I don't think about him, who will?'

'I'm not tellng you to stop thinking, I'm just asking you to slow down and—'

'And accept the inevitable?'

A blush stains her cheeks. 'Not exactly. I mean, try for a cure, put some feelers out, but consider yourself as well. What about your children? Do they know the score?'

I shrug. 'They know what they need to know. Or what they want to know. They can take care of themselves.' There are still a few gems in an upstairs safe, I remember irrelevantly. I must make a real effort to find Ben's contacts, get the valuables out of the house. He would want everything to be tidy. Though locating Ben's business associates will not be easy.

She is studying her solitaire. 'He was a good cutter and polisher, Laura. He made this for our twentieth anniversary – remember? Les said it was so cheap, it was criminal. Ben should have had a shop, he would have made a fortune.'

'He has shops.' And God knows where they are. I've no chance of reaching them, no easy way of offloading the gems into hands that are friendly and fair. Because Ben never let me see inside his business . . . 'Pardon?'

'I asked about the shops. Are they in London?'

I raise shoulders and eyebrows. He never said much, but the calls and letters came from far and wide. 'There are several partners, I think. Probably in European cities. He talked about Paris, Amsterdam, Geneva – visited those places too. But he never brought his work home, always kept his home life separate.'

'Except for the cutting in the attic.'

'Quite.' What wouldn't I give now for the sound of his

tuneless whistle floating down two flights of stairs? I used to moan about the whirring noises, about his tone-deafness. I wish he were here now, humming, whirring, polishing a perfect diamond.

'Laura?'

'Yes?'

She clears her throat, shuffles towards the edge of her seat as if seeking privacy in a room filled by people. 'He must have relatives. Wherever he was born . . . Look, Les tried to talk to him once, tried to work out where Ben had come from and—'

'Why?'

She lifts a hand in a gesture that is meant to be casual, nonchalant. 'It's only natural to want to know where a good friend comes from. I mean, he's not English, is he?'

I stand, walk to the drawer where I keep the Silk Cut. Although I have not smoked for years, I always keep fresh tobacco in the house in case I crack. But I won't crack, I'm not the cracking type. Which is why that breakdown was so terrifying.

'Don't smoke,' she begs. She's a member of ASH and can be very boring about it. Most people with a mission manage to be tedious at times.

I choose my words, pick them over before speaking. 'Ruth, I'll smoke if I want to, so don't start rocking the hobby horse.' There's some Wrigley's next to the cigarettes, and I take time to unwrap a piece, chew for a few seconds while I learn the lines. 'What doesn't matter is where Ben comes from. Wherever it is, he has never expressed the desire to return or to contact anyone there. It hasn't mattered to me. And where I came from never mattered to him.' The chewing gum is ancient. I put it in the rubbish where it belongs.

'Sorry,' she mumbles.

'It's OK, don't worry. But as far as we are concerned, our lives began when we met. He pulled me out of hell, never asked what I'd done, what sin I'd committed to merit damnation. So I never asked about the pain behind

57

his eyes.' He made me face Tommo, though. Yes, he knew a lot about me, much more than I ever discovered about him.

She swallows. 'I've seen the agony in his face, too. But only recently.'

Ruth knows, then. Ruth recognizes his misery.

'It's awful, isn't it?' It's good to talk to someone who has seen his fear, who understands the dilemma. He's remembering something, living it again. 'I don't know what to say to him, Ruth, don't know how to comfort the man I love.'

She touches my hand, guides me into the chair. 'Are you feeling guilty again? Are you? Is it because of Robert?'

The smile on my face does not touch my eyes. I can feel them cold and dead as they reflect Ben's unhappiness. 'That's one thing I'm easy about. When we married, Ben instructed me to take a lover if necessary. "I'm old already," he said. "Don't leave me, but find comfort if I get worn out." He got worn out, Ruth.' The tears brim and threaten again. 'I needed Robert before I was ill. Now, he's surplus to requirements. All things change after you've expected to die. All my years from now will be a bonus. It's time for reassessment, and Robert's not a part of my future.'

'Have you told him that?'

'No. He'll catch on in a year or two. Young men are so . . . slow to learn. All those qualifications and he doesn't understand the word no.'

Ruth chews her lip for a second. 'You wonder what it's all been about, don't you? Like Ben – I mean, he's worked damned hard, made a good life for both of you – and look what happens.'

'I know.' He sits upstairs with a small fortune in this country, God knows how much abroad. He cannot write a cheque. He cannot write his name. He toiled, he saved, he prospered, he got confused.

'I'm sorry if I've been indelicate,' she says.

At last, I can smile properly. 'Ruth, you always were

about as delicate as an elephant in clog-irons. Will you stay for a bite of brunch?'

'No, I'm roasting pork. Les can't even butter a scone, you know. As a New Man, poor old Les is hopeless.'

'Trade him in.'

She shakes her head. 'Can't. I'm the sort that gets used to toothache after a while. Take care.'

After she has disappeared down the path, I hang out more of Ben's washing. The birds are still quarrelling, chattering over a few scraps. He doesn't hear them, even though his chair is near the window. I want to enter his mind, share the terror, hold his hand through dark days. There is nothing I can do and the knowledge of my uselessness is strangling me.

The stairs are like Everest, there to be conquered. But I push myself, throw open his door, place myself at his feet. 'Ben! Where are you? Look at me, please.' I hold his face in my hands, watch closely as his eyes fail to focus. 'Tell me about it. Speak to me.' Oh God, I am shaking a sick man!

'No matter,' he says. 'No matter. He will come for us.'

'Who? Ben, who will come for us?'

He sniffs, licks dry lips, blinks rapidly. 'Have you found it yet, Laura?'

'Yes, that's right, Ben. I'm Laura, your wife. Where have you been while I have needed you? I was ill and you didn't visit me. I went out of my mind after my body was mended and you still didn't come. Where are you? Where the hell are you?'

He is humming, and his deafness of tone has not improved.

'Ben. What do you think about? Tell me. Tell me about what frightened you all those years ago. Who are you? Where did you come from and why? Ben.'

The tuneless noise stops. 'I burned my arm.'

'Yes.' I lift the sleeve and look at the old purple scar. 'How did that happen?'

'It is all written down.'

'Ben—'

'I don't like frozen peas. They don't listen, you know. I said several times that I eat only fresh vegetables.'

My heart pounds. He is talking about the here and now, about the nursing home. 'Are the meals terrible? What do you have for breakfast?'

He nods sagely. 'It is all written down. Strawberry yoghurt.'

I have failed again. He sleeps, moans, snores softly. Even his snoring has lost heart. Somewhere inside this figure is my husband. And I can't find him. I can touch him, see him, hear him. But he is no longer of this world.

After lunch, Ruth's husband arrives to carry Ben downstairs, bundles him into an armchair that I have covered in plastic sheeting. The sweat drips from Les's hair, runs down his face like tears. 'He's still putting weight on. Mind, I suppose he feels heavier with being so limp.' He straightens, pushes a wet and stringy length of hair from his damp face. 'I'll come back this afternoon and carry him upstairs again.'

Ben studies us with eyes that are untypically alert. 'I can walk,' he says, the tone imperious. He stands, stumbles over the dropped car rug, rights himself slowly. The legs are uncertain, jellyish. A large paunch throws him off-balance again, and he sinks into the chair. '*Rien ne va plus*,' he mutters, the voice conveying acceptance rather than hopelessness.

'Sounds like a bloody Monte Carlo croupier,' remarks Les, his face half-hidden by a handkerchief. He emerges, less moist but still hot. 'Is he a gambler?'

'I don't know.' That is the truth. Ben came, went, came home again. Sometimes, he phoned or wrote to say when he would be home. Occasionally, an operator would talk to me, the English broken and brushed with foreign tones. I don't know. When we were together, I didn't think about where Ben had been, always understood that I should not ask. During separations, I wrote Georgina Dawn's books, shopped, improved the house, looked after children and animals. My husband is a stranger, a beloved and broken man who remains a mystery to me, though I have held him in my arms and shared the laughter and the loving.

Les touches my shoulder. 'Are you all right, girl?' He's very much a builder, is constructed like one of his thrown-together houses, straightish, tallish, but not very well appointed. Les always manages to smell of sand, cement and putty, even when he's dressed up. We took him to a wedding once, and when he knelt in the pew, a screw-driver and a couple of washers clattered from a pocket of his good suit and rolled across the aisle, cheering up the proceedings no end. Today, Les is a bundle of rags, T-shirt, jeans, a tatty maroon cardigan. 'You look a bit pale, love,' he says.

Tenderness cuts me these days, makes me brusque, puts me on my guard. 'I'm fine.'

He blinks, turns his head slightly, as if trying to hide his grief. 'We'd have been out at West Lancs now, me and him.' He jerks a gnarled thumb towards my husband. 'After our nine holes, we used to skip the rest and sit in the clubhouse. Ben always had to be near a window with his binoculars. He loved a round of golf, even if he did spend half the time looking at the sky through the bloody binoculars. Him and his birds. They called him Birdy at the club, and it was nothing to do with his score card. I sometimes wonder what we've done wrong. I mean, why did he have to finish up like that? It's no life for him, worse for you in a way.' The thick lower lip trembles. 'He's a good man.'

Ben stirs himself. 'Sarah,' he announces. 'Light brown hair, ribbons. Running in the sand . . . dog.'

I kneel, rub life into waxy hands. The weather is fair, predictably so because the forecast last night predicted storms. But there's a chill in the air, the crisp nip of autumn, and Ben gets cold so easily. I turn on the fan heater, angle it towards him. 'Sarah is Les's daughter, Ben. She used to run on the sands with you and Hector.

61

Do you remember Hector? He was a great dane – we had him before Chewbacca.'

'Thousands of them,' says Ben sleepily. 'Millions. Where did they all come from? And under the stove . . .' The eyes fix on me, yet I know that he is seeing somebody else. 'The singing is so beautiful. Why is she angry? Why should the singing have to stop?' He nods, snores, is gone again.

Les shuffles towards the door. 'Wharrabloodymess.' The exclamation tumbles from his tongue as one angry, bruised word. He slips back into the bowels of Liverpool's demolished slums when he is disturbed or worried. Twelve children, two rooms up, two down, a tin bath on a nail in the yard, accents like warm molasses. Out of such beginnings Les clawed his way until he owned his own business, until he managed to buy out several competitors. One of his favourite sayings to Ruth is, 'Well, we're all right now, don't want for nothing, queen.'

'Thanks,' I call to his disappearing back. He can't cope with the deterioration of his nearest friend, and I can't offer comfort. I hold back, because there are no words for Les.

I find a book of cheques, pay bills, write to my agent whose hand is outstretched for Georgina Dawn's next *magnum opus*. Perhaps this time he will get 10 per cent of nothing, as I am too busy to write. And I'm working towards some kind of decision, trying to clear a path to the future. The pen pauses. I am remembering the day when he realized, when my poor husband began to talk about his 'gaps'. 'I am not always with you, Laura,' he said. 'So you must take care of all domestic bills, gas and rates and so on. I'll show you how it's done . . .'

I sat here then, in my house by the sea, and I held out my arms, gathered him to me as if he were a child. There were papers for me to sign, witnesses to find. On that day, I removed from him the last of his small powers, the final shreds of his ragged dignity. He never went abroad again, seldom groomed himself, needed to be prompted to eat, to sleep, to put on the right clothes. He needed to be taught how to pretend to be alive.

The phone rings, startles me. Like a frightened rabbit, I am bolt upright, listening to the instrument's shrill cry. There's an extra edge to it, an urgency. It's my mother. Even from the bottom of the garden, or from the shore, I imagine that I can identify my mother's demanding ring.

'Laura?' Annoyed, lively. God help me. Ben just sleeps on, has reached a place where she can no longer find him.

'Hello, Mother.'

A sniff, deep and meaningful. An iciness seems to travel along the wire and into my hand. Sometimes, my imagination plays tricks with me. 'You've not been to see me,' she whines. 'It's Monday and you've not been.' She would have made a fabulous diva had she been able to sing.

I will be patient. 'I told you last week. It's a holiday, so I'm keeping Ben for a bit longer.'

'What for? What bloody good will that be to him? He's only tenpence in the bob, so it doesn't matter where he is.' The Bolton accent is stronger of late, as if she needs to be markedly different while living here among the Scousers. When I was a child, she was sometimes – not always – quite the lady. 'Oh, my husband has a chemist's shop on Blackburn Road, he's a qualified dispenser, you know.' And she deteriorated even further, became a total embarrassment when he made his fortune in McNally's Cooling Tea. 'He's a genius, my husband, on a par with Einstein for brains.' All her life, she's been trying to prove something. To me, to my poor old dad, to anyone else who stood still long enough to be judged a captive audience. She certainly never told her husband that he was clever, never praised any soul who was actually within earshot.

I try to relax. This is the woman who gave birth to me, clothed me, fed me, ruined my life, drove my father to a premature grave. 'I'll come tomorrow.'

'I've no cigarettes,' she screams.

With the receiver held at a decent interval from an

aching ear, I wait while she wades through the compulsory lecture on my selfishness, my lack of consideration for a good mother, my unfeeling attitude towards a sick old woman.

I suck a mint while lending half an ear to what looks like becoming yet another revised version of the statutory sermon. Her monologue is a well-rehearsed one, contains all the familiar words, though not necessarily in the same order as last time. At last, a gap between words. 'Smoking is bad for you, Mother,' I manage. 'You know what the doctor said to you last month—'

'Don't you tell me how to live my life!' The blast of her temper cuts through my slow, careful speech. 'All those holidays you've had lately without a thought for me. Remember, I can change my will any time, and that'll be you in rags. I want my bloody fags and you'd best go and get me some.'

It's no use. It's no use telling her that my 'holidays' were spent in hospital. That would just give her pleasure, would allow her to gloat about being in better condition than a woman who is thirty years her junior. And I need her money like a fish needs a bicycle. The writing has made me comfortable, while Ben has signed a small fortune to my name. Still, there's no point in telling her that she's completely useless. The last will and testament of Liza McNally is her only weapon, and she wields it like a sabre. Her sole pleasure in life is gleaned from the suffering of others.

'Well?' she yells. 'Lost your tongue?'

'Mother, I can't leave Ben till Les comes at six o'clock. If he'll stay for a while, I'll nip down to the Ten Till Ten.' The Ten Till Ten opens every day, makes its money from forgetful people like me who make lists and leave them in a safe place, too safe to be discovered until the next major clear-out. I spend hours in supermarkets, stare at the shelves, try to conjure up what has been written by me on the previous evening. I'm an incompetent, a total failure. Especially when my mother's on the phone. 'So you'll have to wait,' I add lamely.

'What do I do till then?'

As far as I am concerned, she can bite her toenails. And she probably could, too. She's eighty-one years old, will be eighty-two in November. She marches every day to the shops, pretends to me that she has not been out, insists, mournfully, that she is permanently confined to barracks. The woman could complete a triathlon after three big meals and sixty Embassy Regal. She is a living monument to the saying about exceptions proving the rule, has defied medical science since the 1960s, during which decade she began to die. Now, almost thirty summers and winters on, she sits in a blue fug, terrifying the life out of a succession of cleaning women, many of whom have grown old during their first few days with 'that rotten owld Woollyback'. My dear mother screams down the phone daily at me, at my cousin Anne in Bolton, at anyone who fails to pay regular court to her royal flaming highness. 'There's nothing I can do for you till six o'clock.'

She inhales, fuels her lungs for a renewed assault on me, her beloved daughter. 'You're stubborn. You always were stubborn, you. Many a time you treeped me out, wouldn't listen to sense, would never do as you were told. If you'd had half a brain, you'd have stayed away from the first queer fellow, and from the second one too. But oh no, you treeped me out even then, and I knew you'd finish up divorced from that Tommo, told you right at the start that you were going off your trolley. Madness, that's what it must be. You've married wrong twice, but you still treep me out.'

'Treeping out', a term she culled from a mixture of Lancashire idioms, means not agreeing 1,000 per cent with everything she says. 'I am not going to discuss my shortcomings on the phone,' I say mildly. With Mother, it is best to be mild.

'No, you're not. If we talked about you and your waywardness, we'd be here till Christmas on my phone bill. King size.' She means the cigarettes, not the bill. 'And I want three packets, they'll do me till weekend.'

Three packets will do her till tomorrow. At the crack of morning, while all self-respecting birds are still snoozing, she'll be toe-tapping outside Mapley's, waiting to pounce on the *Daily Mirror*, which she will hide inside *The Times*, as the latter is a better class of paper to be seen in the company of a lady. A carton of 200 Regal King Size will sit in her handbag alongside rolls of money in rubber bands, my father's death certificate and a heap of mouldering premium bonds. In the side pouch of the said handbag, there is always an apple and a small, sharp knife.

The one time she was supposed to have been mugged, Mother put the boy's eye out, impaled him on three inches of finely honed steel. The police accepted her sweet and appealing story. 'Oh, officer, what have I done? My poor stomach cannot digest the peel of an apple, so I carry my little knife when I go to Moorside Park. I was just about to take the skin off, because there's a litter bin just there, outside Mapley's. So when that misguided young man grabbed me, the knife was in my hand, and I simply lashed out.' Much wringing of hands accompanied this heart-rending 'confession'. 'What have I done?' she cried repeatedly to me and to the sad police sergeant. 'I shall never forgive myself. Never.' In fact, my mother had waited years for this opportunity, always longed for the chance to fight back. I've often wondered who was the real criminal. Did he grab for her, or did she make the first move?

These Scousers don't know what they're talking about, really, don't know what they've taken to their bosom here. 'Woollyback' is a term applied decades ago to Lancashire miners who wore sheepskins on their backs as a layer of protection between skin and heavy burden. It is used these days as a derogatory yet affectionate name for Lancastrians, is comparable with the southern term 'yokel'. But Mother has not the gentleness of those brave working men, could knock them into a cocked pit helmet plus lamp when it comes to sheer determination. And she's no yokel, no simple-minded peasant.

66

'Are you heeding me, Laura?'

'Yes.' She pored for weeks over local presses, even read about her heroism in several of the national tabloids. The boy has a glass eye and hunched shoulders now, could wear a raincoat and double for Columbo on the telly. Most people who come into contact with my mother look older than their years.

'He's dead downstairs, you know.' The salacious lip-licking is audible. 'Keeled over last night when his daughter brought him back from church.' Another loud sniff. 'She took him out twice a week, did Shirley. I said to her, "Shirley," I said, "you've nothing to reproach yourself for, because you looked after him," I told her. All of which is a great deal more than can be said for you, Laura McNally.'

'Starling, previously Thompson.' My response is automatic.

'Stupid name. And Starling's not his proper name, either. What's he been hiding all these years? Is he one of them like Burgess and Maclean? You should put him away for good, send him where that Ian Brady's kept. They've got all the lunatics there, so yon husband of yours would fit in a treat.'

I hate my mother. I hate her and I forgive myself for the crime. 'Honour thy father and thy mother'? I cannot love her, cannot even like or respect her. At best, I manage to be another of her servants, a target for her barbs. My father, on the other hand, was a gentle man and a gentleman. All my affection went to him, because he was thoroughly lovable.

'And me bowels are bad again.' Mother is passionately involved with her digestive system, has suffered through thirty years from a plethora of disorders with interesting names, anything that caught her eye in a much-thumbed tome which sits constantly by her side. The name of her volume is something I cannot remember, as the lettering on the broad spine has been eroded by regular handling. It's likely to be called *Diagnosis for Beginners*, or *Treat*

Yourself to an Illness – some crazy name, anyway, probably compulsory reading for the average hypochondriac.

Early on in my mother's apprenticeship as a sick person, a hiatus hernia was favourite, but this was forced to make way for colourful descriptions of gastric reflux caused by gallstones. She invested in enough Milk of Magnesia to warrant a substantial wad of shares in the company, then enjoyed a brief flirtation with slippery elm food. After a liverish episode – 'don't you think the whites of my eyes are on the yellow side?' – she placed her trust in an ulcerated colon, which merited many X-rays and visits to a private clinic. 'I'm all bunged up,' she announces now to me and, judging by the volume, to every other resident in the retirement apartments. 'I am suffering from chronic constipation.'

'Then take some un-bunging medicine.'

'You don't care, do you? One of these days, I'll be stretched out at that funeral home and you'll wish you'd listened to me. It'll be too late then. Oh and make sure they put me in the green suit, I'm not going in a shroud. Shirley won't be feeling it as bad as you will, because she looked after that daft man downstairs who was her father. Nothing was too much for her, nothing at all. Whereas you're not worth the paper you're written on. I shouldn't have bothered getting that birth certificate, because you're no daughter of mine. "John," I'd say, "I think they've given me the wrong one here."'

I've had enough now. But she's waiting for me to reach the point of saturation, wants to be able to tell her cronies that her daughter's a nasty piece. 'I hear you won at bingo last week, Mother.' My voice is soft. 'So nice for you to have an interest that gets you out.'

Stunned silence. Then, on top note, 'Somebody picks me up and takes me in a car, a nice big comfortable car with good springs and plush upholstery, not like that boneshaker you drive. They know I can't walk, so they help me down the steps and drive me to the Legion.'

She wants driving. With a whip, like beef on its way to

68

market. Except that I don't approve of cruelty to animals, even though I have eaten a cow or two in my time. No, a beast should never be whipped, though my mother deserves . . . I squash my wicked imagination. 'You walked for your prize, though. I was so thrilled to hear how you managed to move so quickly all the way to the stage without help. It's wonderful to hear that your health is improving. Must go now, Mother. Ben needs a drink.'

My hand trembles as I place the receiver in its cradle. She frightens me with her venom, has always scared me. I am a woman well into middle age, because few humans survive to the age of 100 and a bit. Real middle age is reached at about thirty-eight, and I passed that marker some considerable time ago. But with her on the scene, I remain a child, her child, her property. My sons have not visited her for some time, while my daughter, who is a force to be reckoned with, chose the occasion of her own twenty-first birthday as a suitable opportunity to tell Granny to eff off.

I gaze through the window. A few brave souls tramp up and down the erosion, dogs at their heels. A clutch of children flies past, all jumbled limbs and colourful training shoes. Two men are in the water, fishing lines extending from their arms. Surely there can be nothing edible in that muck? The tree in my garden looks worried, leaves beginning to curl and darken. Seasons are changing, breaking the rules. Summer arrives earlier now, spills backward into spring. Perhaps Christmas will bring a heatwave in a century or so.

I feed Ben, wait for Les, nip out for Mother's shopping, rush back and wait for the nurse. A lot of time is spent waiting these days. She comes, bustles off upstairs, returns with a decision plastered across her face. 'Mrs Starling, he needs changing more regularly than this. I suggest that you have him home for just one day from now on, because he is developing sores. If you insist on full weekends, then you will need a nurse in residence.'

Her words make me weak, take away my breath. Her anxious face swims in and out of focus as I absorb the message. I am about to lose him altogether, will not even have his shell at the weekends. 'No,' I gasp. 'Please.'

She forces me into a chair. 'Look, let's cut the bullshit, as the Americans say. No more games, Mrs Starling, no more little holidays. I've friends in the hospitals, you know. I've been told about your operations and about your breakdown.'

I narrow my eyes to achieve a clearer picture. 'What about Hippocrates?'

She shrugs, sits opposite me. 'He's a bit dead, Mrs Starling, passed on with all the other ancient Greeks. Look, there's been no law broken, love. Human nature breeds gossip and you've an unusual name. I know how ill you've been.'

'Oh.'

'Listen, here's my phone number. If you ever need me, give me a call. My name's Susan, but most friends call me Jenks. There's an answerphone, so leave a message if I'm out. You need support. I wish I could help all the folk whose relatives are in permanent residential care. The whole family is affected by Alzheimer's. You need a shoulder, girl.'

She's a good woman. Goodness weakens me, and I cry buckets. 'It's his home,' I scream. 'It's his home and he loved this house. We chose it together.' Hysteria threatens. Sometimes, I realize how alone I am, and this is one of those times.

'Mrs Starling.' I hear the scrape of a chair, feel a substantial arm coming to rest across my shoulders. She smells of iodine, talcum powder, tobacco. 'Where are your children?'

'No.' The tears dry miraculously, while alertness strengthens my spine, forcing me upright, making me rebellious. 'They are not to be told.'

'Told what?'

'That I've been ill, that I cannot manage my husband.'

With the three of them as witnesses, I would feel like a totally incompetent has-been.

'But you're their mother and he's their—'

'He is not their father.'

'Oh.'

'My children have their own problems.' I am a master of understatement. I have not been a perfect mother, partly because I did not understand the role, mostly because of difficulties over which I had little or no control. 'I have a daughter in medicine. She'll come home sooner or later. But I will not ask, Nurse Jenkinson.' No, I will not hang round their necks like my mother hangs round mine.

'Jenks. Call me Jenks, or Susan.'

I dry my cheeks on a cuff while she pulls away and sits down again. 'I'm Laura.'

She chews for a moment on a non-existent thumbnail. 'I'll visit you sometimes.'

'Thank you.'

'Who does the housework?'

'A woman called Eileen comes twice a week.' Eileen is the one who got away in time, the one I rescued from Mother's clutches before true despair could set in. 'And her husband does the garden.'

'Good.' She peers at the watch. 'I'll be off now. Have to go to a terminal case down the road. Laura.' Her voice is stern, yet I can hear kindness lurking in the background. 'You've done your best, queen. Nobody can ever do more than that. When I first . . . you know, when I met you at the start, I thought you were a bit uppity. I was wrong. You're hurt. It's all right to be knocked sideways by what's happened to that lovely man.' She nods, glances at my clock, judges me to be worth the delay. 'My heart bleeds for people like you, and I'm not supposed to let it show. "Be positive," they keep saying on these community care courses. But I'm telling you no lies. He's not likely to get better. Brain cells don't grow back again. You've had your breakdown and you've faced the worst.' A hand

71

touches my shoulder. 'Make a future, girl. Don't turn your back on him, but find a life.'

My throat is choked as I walk her to the door. She picks up her brolly, throws the coat over a thick arm. 'Be good,' she says. 'And if you can't be good, be bad in a corner where no bugger can see you. Ta-ra.'

When she has gone, I sit with Ben and wonder if he will ever spend the night in his own house again. It's so unfair. He smiles, drinks, hums a crippled tune. And talks about strawberry yoghurt.

Chapter Four

Ben has gone. The attendants came with Nurse Jenkinson – Jenks – and they carried him downstairs, placed him in the wheelchair, ferried him over to the ambulance. There's a lift at the back of the vehicle, so that Ben's chair can be lifted automatically to the right level. Jenks held my hand while the men took Ben away. 'He'll be back, love. Just for a few hours now and again. It's best, Laura. Please believe me – it's all for the best, really.'

Her head was turned away when the double doors closed, but I knew that the muddy eyes were full of unshed tears. What does she do for recreation? Does she have a life, some pleasure, a true friend? Oh, I hope she has somebody!

I stood out under my wind-bent tree till Norman arrived, didn't want to come into this empty house. He had a cup of tea in the kitchen, passed some time with me, allowed me to think about ordinary day-to-day things like peat, pruning, lawn food. He's outside now, bent double as usual, a slight hump on his back.

I scan the *Express*, do the Target. The nine-letter word is 'insinuate' today. Ben used to do those cryptic crosswords in the *Telegraph* or the *Guardian*, used to sit here with me sometimes. I jump up, pace about, cannot cope with solitude today.

Again, I watch Norman. He looks after almost everything out there, leaves to me just the patch behind the garage where Ben and I built our bird sanctuary. Norman never complains about Chewy or Handel, though both animals go through periodic bouts of destructiveness. On poor Norman's beds, they roam free; round the birds' section, we put a fence that Strangeways might be proud of.

Norman, sixty-two at the last count, is brown as a berry and green-fingered. I've known him to visit a sick plant at the crack of dawn with one of his organic cures. Like my long-dead father, Norman is a believer in home-made remedies and natural treatments. His wife, Eileen, 'does' for me a couple of times a week. She invests most of her time in the cleaning of ornaments, loves china, crystal, silver, spends little of her considerable energy on Chewy-chewed carpets and Handel-marks on lino tiles. Still, she's pleasant and they need the money.

'You should be working, Georgina,' I tell my *alter ego*. 'You're standing here talking to yourself, and you know damned well that the book's due. What will Walter say when you miss your deadline? There'll be no Christmas card from your beloved agent this year, Georgie, no pretty little lunches or suppers in those exclusive London clubs. Whatever will you do without Perrier water and olives on sticks? All that nouvelle cuisine, all those egos squashed into one small room – oh, you will miss it.'

Laura, who frequently loses patience with Georgie, has a quiet laugh. I was not meant to laugh today, so a hand covers the grin. I'm the one with the ego, because I am so flippant with Georgina, who has worked damned hard in the past and made me rich. The truth is that I hate being in a room with 'real' writers, because they are expressing themselves properly and proudly, whereas I work within certain rigid confines which pay good money while stretching nobody's mental prowess. To hell with it, I don't feel at all like working.

I slump down onto a chair, stretch out my legs, try not to frown as *A Heart Divided* flashes its neon garishness in my wilful brain. This latest composition, if I finish it, will be translated into thirteen languages and, believe me, it will lose little or nothing in the process. I bake the same literary cake three times a year; only the icing is different. We are allowed a little sex now, but the handsome hero and the hand-wringing heroine must meet, separate after some gross misunderstanding or as a result of some nasty quirk of fate, then come together in great triumph after about 55,000 words. And amen to that, I'd rather defrost the freezer.

The bell rings. Well, alleluia, I don't have to write if there's a visitor. When I open the door, I find a girl, long blond hair whipping across the throat like a silk garotte. She has been before, will not provide me with an excuse for idleness. She is selling double glazing. 'I am double-glazed, thanks,' I say in my sensible and rather don't-waste-my-time-on-my-own-doorstep type of voice.

She takes a pace back, looks at my windows. I don't know why she bothers, she's seen them before. It's like a play that we enact from time to time, rusting lines still remembered, just about. We've had plenty of rehearsals, but there's no chance of an opening night. 'Secondary glazing,' she says rather mournfully. 'I've been to you before. Sorry.'

'That's all right.'

It's another day of fierce winds. Gusts blow in more than one direction, making the girl's hair fly in long yellow streamers. I glance over her shoulder to the beach where a few brave souls struggle to remain upright on filthy sand. A hat is wrenched off, is chased by a long-limbed dog, possibly a greyhound or whippet cross, brindled and thin in the tail. He pounces, tears the hat apart. The owner mouths at him, but her voice is snatched away by twisting currents of air.

The girl's eyes have attached themselves to my weather-beaten and varnish-starved door. (Ben used to cover it twice a year, but I'm dangerous with a paintbrush, so I leave well, or not-so-well alone.) 'We do a nice one of those in UPVC,' she ventures.

'Aren't they the tripe people?' I wonder aloud. She does not smile, and I flounder through my next words. 'No, the tripe shops were UCP, weren't they?'

She thinks I'm insane, has no memory of post-war

75

years, manifold tripe doused in vinegar, parents fretting because a child would not eat her portion. 'Eat your tripe,' Mother would say. 'It's brain food.' Well, that might explain my non-academic mind, my stupidity. And Mother's too, since she never ate her tripe either.

'The UPVC doors are great,' she insists. 'They really do look real, because they're a dead—'

'Dead ringer for mahogany,' I finish for her.

The intelligent blue eyes are wary now. She is taking my measure, wondering whether to wade right in and pin me against the ropes. The wrestling match continues. There is desperation in her voice. 'Lasts a lifetime, though. You're only young, Mrs . . . er . . . You'll be replacing wooden doors for ever, because the salt eats into timber. Can I give you a leaflet?'

What difference will one more make? I already have two poorly fitting kitchen drawers filled to the brim with junk mail and 10p off something I would never dream of buying. I accept the proffered literature and am judged to be hooked.

'Would you mind if I phoned you?' So thin, that face, so vulnerable. She looks starved halfway to death, stick-like legs in black leggings, slender fingers whose joints are purpling from the cold.

'Don't phone me,' I reply. 'If I want anything, I'll contact the office.'

This does not suit. 'I'd get no money that way, because I have to order the survey. I'm saving up to do a course in pharmacology at Liverpool Uni.' The reedy lower limbs are finished off by a pair of huge Doc Martens, making the bottom half of her body into twin exclamation marks. 'This is cold canvassing in more ways than one.' She blows on her hands, looks thoroughly pathetic.

'Sorry,' I mutter. And I am sorry. It must be dreadful to be so young, so worried. In fact, I can verify the concept, can remember my own tortured late teens and early twenties. Who said that youth is wasted on the young? It's true. If some of us oldies could be young again, we'd make the most of it to a point where we might well become dangerous. I am weakening, but will not have a new door. This is Ben's door and it stays. 'If you're short of work, come back and do my ironing on Thursday night.' I hate ironing. 'And you might put a couple of coats of emulsion on a few walls at the weekend. I'll pay you three pounds fifty an hour.'

The promise of such bounty makes her smile hopefully. She lifts a foot, is preparing to walk into my life. 'Anything,' she says breathily. 'I'll do anything at all.'

'Are you cold?'

'Freezing.' The grin broadens, displays teeth that are not quite perfect, spoilt by slightly crossed incisors that are strangely childlike, endearing. 'I'd love a cuppa.'

I lead her through to the kitchen, wave her into a chair, set the kettle to boil.

'Posh house,' she comments, betraying her roots. This is no incoming student, no nomad from another town. The girl is as Scouse as the Liver birds, as Liverpool as the naked statue outside Lewis's stores.

'I can do you a quick bacon and eggs,' I say, turning from the stove to look at her. Twin spots of colour dwell expectantly on the fine cheekbones. 'When did you last eat?' I ask.

She shrugs, but the gesture is not careless. 'What day is it?'

'As bad as that?'

'Yeah. I can't afford rent, food and books, so I've paid the landlord, nicked the books and cut right back on food. It's funny, you don't miss eating after a while. You get a bit . . . a bit other-worldly.'

'That's dangerous.'

'Well, life's dangerous, isn't it? Like this double-glazing lark – there's men who made a living out of it in the good old days, the eighties. They'd wives and children to keep – what's happened to them? They'll be in bed and breakfast, houses snatched back by the building societies. My only dependants are me and my books, so I'm lucky in a way.'

But nobody's spending. It takes folk all their time to pay the mortgage, and that's killed the market stone dead. At least I've not got a wife and kids to feed. I run three catalogues and sell kitchen things door-to-door, brushes and plastic plates for microwaves. I used to do a paper round as well, but I got a bit tired, kept falling asleep during *Granada Reports*, never woke up till *Good Morning Britain*.'

I try not to smile. 'Not surprised.' I pause for a split second before cracking the eggs. 'Can't your family help?'

The pink sparkle fades quickly from her cheeks. 'Have you any sausages? I love sausages.'

I root in a cupboard, find a tin of frankfurters. They will have to do. Walls' best pork sausages haven't played a part in this house since my children departed. As the eggs bubble and set, I realize that I am actually enjoying myself. Ben has gone, will not sleep in his own house ever again. I should be mourning, grieving. Instead, I am loving the company of this educated waif.

Over a steaming plate, she smiles, the eyes brimming with unspoken gratitude. I fold my arms, pray that she won't cry. 'It smells like me ma's cooking,' she says. 'She always bought smoky bacon and free-range eggs.' A fork is crammed into her hungry mouth, leaps out again, stabs at another big portion of food. I find a cob, some Flora, a bread knife, a butter knife. She tears at the bread, devours three large and ragged lumps. 'I don't like margarine, ta,' she manages through a stuffed mouth. As with my daughter Jodie, I am reminded of the honesty of today's youth. Even if something is free, these young ones will reject it, will not respond to kindness, refuse to resort to what my mother would call 'manners'.

She finishes, lines up her cutlery, leans back and burps behind a hand. 'That's the emptiness coming back up,' she announces. 'Now, that was great, absolutely A one, full marks for presentation.' She is laughing at me. The laughter is inside, but I still hear it. 'What's for pudding?'

I like this girl, like her a lot. She is lovable, open, tough and hurt. 'Tinned rice any good? Or I think I've a fruit salad in light syrup, you could have that with some Carnation.'

The blond head shakes merrily, reminds me of a pale summer daisy, heavy on a too-slim stem. 'How did you know that Carnation is my favouritest thing? It's made in heaven, I reckon. When the nuns used to go on about manna falling from the skies, I knew it tasted just like angel cake dipped in Carnation.'

The bowl empties quickly, then she drinks a second cup of instant coffee. She adds so much sugar that a cement mixer might prove useful to stir the mixture. 'God, I'm stuffed,' she remarks. 'Good job these pants have an elasticated waist. My mother's dead.' She leaves no space, no mark of punctuation between topics. 'And my dad's in Walton.'

I hesitate. 'Hospital?'

'Prison. When me mam died, he was away with the mixer, our old man, nutty as a monkey's dinner. Missed her, you see. It was like something out of a women's magazine, their marriage. Worshipped Mam, he did, went wrong as soon as she popped her clogs. After a lot of messing with the cops, bits of receiving and stuff like drunk and disorderly, he did an aggravated burglary. I didn't listen properly, I was too aggravated myself, mad with him. I think he sort of altered the shape of a policeman's face too, so he's no favourite with the Liverpool busies. Been in and out of prison for a while now, me dad. Have you got a steam iron?'

'Yes.'

'Well, that's all right, then. I can't be doing with all that sprinkling water – it reminds me I've not been to benediction for a while. Being a Catholic's a bugger, you know. You can tell yourself you don't care, you've educated yourself past all that stupid indoctrination, but it never works.' She has not honed her vowels and the last word comes out as 'werks'. 'I stand in front of the mirror some days and tell myself that it was all fairy tales, all that mortal sin and absolution. But they've got you and you know they've got you. When I spray dry clothes or plants, it's all dominoes and biscuits, can't help it.'

A small beat of time passes. 'Dominoes and biscuits?'

'Old Latin. Services are boring now, all in English. *Dominus vobiscum*, I think it is, but Mam always said "dominoes and—"'

'And biscuits.'

'Yes. It really means "The Lord be with you."'

'And with thy spirit.'

She giggles. '*Et cum spiritu tuo*. Are you a holy Roman?'

'No. But I know a man who is.'

She taps dirty fingers on the table. 'Are you ill? You look a bit on the pale side.'

'Recovering.'

'Oh.' An unclean nail prises a bit of bacon from a gap between two teeth. 'What did you have?'

I chew this over for a moment. 'A curable problem that used to be incurable. I'm a miracle.'

'Ooh.' She likes this, is fascinated. 'They can shift most of the sods these days, can't they? There was a woman down by us with that much wrong with her – well – I think she'd had absolution so many times, they were giving her discount on the holy water, 'cos she used it by the barrel. Ninety-seven, she is now. Me mam used to say, "Look at Mrs Foley. Seventy-odd if she's a day and so many spare parts she rattles. When she does go," me mother said, "the rag man'll take her, 'cos she's at least 50 per cent scrap metal." It's like the bionic man – we have the technology. Great, isn't it?'

'Wonderful.' Why am I talking to this stranger? 'It's just that afterwards, when it's all over and you're pretty sure about being cured, everything seems different.'

'It must do. I suppose you start reorganizing your life, don't you? As if you've just come fresh into the world again, like a rebirth. Are you going to make a lot of changes?'

'I don't know. I . . . er . . . had a breakdown. The fact

that I was cured – or seemingly cured – hit me like a ton of bricks. Sometimes, good news can be as disturbing as bad. And you feel a bit guilty too, getting better while other people still suffer.'

She nods. The wisdom in her eyes belies the youthful appearance. 'So you've got to get it right this time. Sort of pay back God for saving you.'

'Yes.' Where did she get all that knowledge? I always believed that such insight arrived with age. 'It's not so much the paying back of God that matters to me, it's the relieving of others' suffering.'

'Same thing.'

'Yes, I suppose it must be.'

She cocks her head, gives me the once-over. 'Hey, you're not bad looking for a woman who's getting on a bit. Why don't you get your hair tinted, wear some decent clothes?'

We both look at our own shabby garments, then cast a quick eye over each other's, crack off laughing simultaneously and very loudly. 'Where did you find the Levis?' she asks between giggles. 'Church jumble sale? The arse is nearly out of them. And that jumper should have been on the tip years ago.'

I pull defensively at my fisherman's knit, grey, grimy, obviously made for a ten-foot giant and all his family. 'This is an heirloom, I'll have you know.'

'Oh?'

'It was my husband's. I washed it on the wrong cycle and it grew and it grew. No matter, it heats my hind quarters.'

'And what heats his?'

At the nursing home, he has an electric blanket and one of those new hot-water bottles. After a quick blast in a microwave, the bottle stays cosy right through till morning. 'He's not here,' I say quietly.

'Oh.' The hands, a paler purple by this time, fiddle with a chain of worry beads. 'Has he buggered off and left you?'

'No, he's ill.'

There's a crucifix on the beads, so this must be a rosary. Her attention is straying again. 'Do you live here all by yourself? How many rooms are there? Is there an attic?' Her gaze fondles all my kitchen cupboards. 'Good idea, having the kitchen at the front. You can see the water and the beach all the time. What's wrong with him?'

I sigh. This one's mind is plainly capable of homing in on just about anything. She is over-endowed with what I call Scouse radar, a knack of cutting through protocol, discarding the fat, pouncing on the juicy innards. 'Alzheimer's.'

'Kids?'

'Three. Mine, not his. They're not children any more and they're not here.' I still don't understand why I feel so easy with this girl, why I am talking to her so openly.

The blond head nods, drops slightly. 'This was Mam's rosary. He won't get any better, you know.'

'No.'

'A woman down by me sister's house got it. She was frying frozen veg at midnight and she started putting the cat in the sideboard next to the phone. Poor cat howled every time the phone went off in its lug'ole. Two o'clock one morning, she knocked the priest up and asked him for two hundredweight of nutty slack. It sounds funny, but it's not. They put her away at the finish and she was really happy, brewing tea all hours for the staff, she was.'

I bite my lip, try to stop the words, but they escape. 'He's not happy.'

'I'm sorry. Sometimes, they are and . . .'

'And sometimes they suffer.'

She looks at me, sends me a message of total empathy, yet I cannot grasp the fact that I am communicating with someone of such tender years. She jumps up, awards me an impish grin, dives for the door. 'I'll get my bits and pieces out of your porch and leave you in peace.' The slender figure stops, swivels, would look as graceful as Anna Pavlova except for the boots. 'Sorry about your old man. Get down the pub with a mate, have a jar and a laugh. Life's too short, you know.'

Before allowing myself time to think, I call after her, 'What's your name?'

'Diana.' The three syllables float through my house like sharp, high-toned chimes.

I shout back, 'I'm Laura.'

'See you.' The slam of my front door has a hollow quality, sounds like a death-knell. I wonder for a moment how those prisoners cope, Americans who live for years in single cells next-door-but-one to the electric chair. Now, that must be real depression. The quack says I'm not depressed any more, that I'm ready to jump back into life. But he hasn't got a husband on death row. I am so morbid, feel better when I occupy myself with dirty dishes and pawmarks on the draining board.

The maker of these marks stalks by, tail erect, ears pricked for the joyful sound of fork against tin. This cat is not normal. Most cats curl up when they stop walking, but Handel simply keels over sideways. His life is so exhausting, all that eating and sleeping and washing of whiskers.

After a Cup-a-Soup and two crackers, I venture upstairs and face my monster. It's a computer called Giles, very upmarket and attached to a laser printer whose habits are not all good. The printer often develops hiccups, flashes 'paper jam' on its LCD, goes into a sulk for hours on end. I kick the system to life, stare at the latest few pages of *A Heart Divided*. 'He held her close, so close that her spine turned to molten gold.' What a load of tripe. 'As he drowned in her eyes, he knew that he wanted no help, no lifebelt. He would go willingly to his doom, happily to his kismet.' The whole thing is a sea of adverbs, a morass of adjectives. Wait till the Pulitzer committee claps its eyes on this lot! Wait till my editor sees it . . .

I make another file, call it *Laura*. It won't sell, but I'll write my story one of these days. When I look at the time, two hours have passed and I've produced twenty pages of this *Laura* thing. It seems I've had quite an interesting life.

Perhaps I'll finish the tale one day, see if anyone else finds it riveting.

The bell rings. Is she back? Has she left her clipboard, her rosary beads? A second ring sounds impatient, angry. It won't be Mother. Mother wants me to think that she can't get about, that I've abandoned her to a life of solitude and desolation. And Ruth's out for the day.

I open the door. 'Oh, it's you.'

Robert pushes past me, turns, grabs my shoulders, kisses my hair because I've turned away to close the door. 'Where the hell have you been?'

Robert is tall, decorative, angry. I pull away and rearrange my sloppy sweater. 'Nowhere,' I say loftily.

'It's becoming a habit, isn't it? Going off without saying a word, having your little holidays. I mean, have a break by all means, but tell me. I've been worried to death.'

'Would you like something to drink?'

His eyes are angry. When he is angry, he becomes unnecessarily beautiful. 'No, I don't want a drink. I've had a hell of a day and I've come to ask a favour. Oh and to tell you that you are an impossible woman and I love you.'

'It's over, Robert. There are things I have to do—'

'Where the hell has it gone?' He stands by the hall table and begins to empty his pockets. There are small bottles and boxes, some tangled elastic bands, a chewed pencil and a comb that is almost toothless. 'Ah yes,' he breathes. 'I remember now.'

He is like a child. When I was young, little boys carried string and conkers in their pockets with marbles, ballbearings, small creatures in matchboxes. Tommo was a bigger boy and he carried a knife. I don't want to think about Tommo, but I'll have to if I'm going to write it all out of my system. That's it! I'm standing here watching this man emptying his pockets, and at last I know what I'm doing. The past has to be swept away before I can begin a future. So simple, so complicated, so bloody enormous.

An inside pocket gives up the bounty at last. It is tiny, impossibly so, jet black and squealing fit to burst. 'It's a

84

cat,' he says hopefully. 'I've christened her Snowflake. Snow because she's definitely black, Flake because she's crazy.'

For a moment, I am nonplussed. Then I rally, anxious to defend myself against all intruders. 'I've already got a cat. You should know, because you brought him here in the first place after you put Ellie down.' Ellie was magnificent, every inch the lady in spite of being ginger. 'Can that thing lap?'

For answer, he places a dropper on the table beside the rest of his hoard. 'She's only four and a half weeks old. I had to put the mother down and this is the sole survivor of the litter. She needs you, Laura. I've brought some formula because cows' milk would make her ill. Please, Laura.'

The kitten is attached to his hand like a koala on a tree, all four feet wrapped around his wrist. She is biting him and her eyes are wide, as wide and surprised as only a kitten's eyes can be. 'Take her away,' I beg.

'It's only for a few days and—'

'In a few days, I'll be in love with her. If you move her in, I'll not let her go.'

He laughs. 'If I move in, will you fall in love with me and keep me for ever?'

'No. Can't one of your gaggle of adoring old ladies take her in?'

'She'd be too much for an old lady.'

'I'm tired. I've been ill. I wasn't on holiday, I've been . . . taking a rest.' I wave a hand at the cat. 'It would mean litter trays all over again. And Handel won't like Snowflake.'

'Handel won't notice Snowflake.' He knows Handel almost as well as I do, has been the family vet for years. 'And this is a lovely cat. Special too, because her mother never saw the inside of a house. She was on a farm over towards Lydiate, got fed by the farmer's wife, wouldn't settle inside.'

'Great.' I step away, afraid to touch that wonderful

kitten-fluff. I'm a cat lover, take the whole business far too seriously. I understand the Egyptians' fascination with cats, can see why they made gods of them. They are so delightfully arrogant and I'm not having another one. 'You are asking me to take in a feral kitten? It won't behave. It'll be ripping the house to pieces once it gets its bearings.'

'Laura, you have a way with animals.'

'So do you. Take it home. I'll still take birds into the garage if anyone fetches them. Ben may not be here, but I've learned a lot and the RSPB knows we do good work here and that cat might kill a bird in a box and—'

'You always talk fast when you're unsure of yourself, Laura. Will you throw this little cat out into the cold? Will you?'

'Will you?' I ask. 'You're the one in charge. Take it home, the kids will love it.'

The eyebrows are almost knitted together now. 'Laura, I've four cats, two and a half dogs and a parrot that swears all the time and plucks its feathers out. My so-called housekeeper can manage that lot while I'm away, but a new kitten might put her off. I'm taking the kids down south for a fortnight.'

He's a lovely man. The half-dog has useless back legs, so Robert made a wheeled contraption for him. Bonzo enjoys this strange mode of travel, has worn out his wheels several times, needs to be serviced at regular intervals, gets oiled and adjusted every week. 'You're a fool, Robert. OK, pass her over.'

The huge grin lights up his face. I love two men and I cannot have either of them. I can't have Ben because he hardly exists any more, and I can't have Robert because Ben's still alive in the technical sense. Snowflake is warm, soft, skinny beneath the fur. 'Will she make it? Is she going to be healthy?'

'I think so. The diet is written down here. Intelligent creatures, cats. You'll find that she'll start lapping early, probably within a week. She's decided to live. All you

86

have to do is feed her a few drops every hour or so.'

My jaw sags. 'In the middle of the night?'

'She'll let you know, crawl up to your face when she's hungry.'

'I see. So I take her upstairs, do I?'

'You're her mother now. Do your best.'

I am an appalling mother – my sons and my daughter could testify to that. If this lovely creature is going to depend on me for positive support . . . 'You'll kill me if she's dead when you come back.'

'Probably.' He looks me up and down, latches on to a key word that he half-remembers from a minute ago. 'Ill? What kind of ill?'

'Operation. I'm OK now.'

'You didn't tell me.'

'No.'

'Why didn't you tell me?'

Flakey is eating my sleeve. See, I've already christened her properly, I'm on a loser before I start. 'It was my business, not yours. And I didn't want you languishing by my bedside during visiting hours. It would have been the talk of North Liverpool, the vet having an affair with poor old Ben Starling's wife.'

He tut-tuts, barges into the kitchen, makes a din while setting the kettle to boil. I follow with Flakey, who has fallen asleep in the crook of my arm. 'Don't sulk, Robert.'

'Don't sulk? How bloody long were you in hospital? I came round nearly every day, caught Ruth feeding the cat a few times. What happened to Chewbacca?'

'Kennels. He's a gregarious chap, likes a change of scenery.'

'But you were gone for ages.'

I'm not going to tell him about the breakdown. That frail young Diana could take it, but this big macho vet would worry and fret for days. 'Convalescence, then a month by the sea. How are the children?'

He bangs two mugs on to the table. 'Tom's learning the viola. He's sent Charlie almost completely bald. It's one

87

thing having a parrot who's a compulsive plucker, but it's awful watching insanity move in on the poor creature. The noise is dreadful.'

'And Melinda? Is she still missing her mum?' Robert's wife died four years ago, because the remedy did not come in time. I have just survived the very problem that deprived a little girl of her mother.

He stands very still, studies me. 'Ask her yourself. She likes you, needs someone like you.'

Here comes the old argument. 'I'm not moving in with you, Robert.'

'Because of how it would look? Because the neighbours wouldn't like it?'

It's hopeless. He's so infantile, so determined and stubborn. 'I don't want to take Carol's place. I couldn't. And I am not suitable material anyway. Stepmotherhood is not for me, Robert. I've done my stint and I wasn't terribly good at it.'

'Rubbish.'

My temper is grumbling like an appendix that threatens to burst. 'I've three kids. One's an inch from prison, another's breaking his heart because his boyfriend doesn't love him any more, while my daughter's wandering about England trying to find herself. They're not exactly steady.'

'It's not your fault.' His voice raises itself. 'You didn't tell Gerald to go out and mix with fraudsters, and Edward's homosexuality is nothing to do with you. As for Jodie, she'll give herself the boot up the arse that's sadly needed. Jodie will come good.'

I sit and wait while he pours water on to the Nescafé. When he is seated, I try again. 'Edward's sexuality is not a problem. It's the fact that he's insecure, can't settle. Edward doesn't trust anyone to stay with him, and that's because I didn't give him enough love and attention. Gerald's the same, uses money as a crutch. Jodie's a law unto herself. She modelled herself on me, became selfish and self-indulgent. I do not want any more children in my life. And that is an end of it.'

He isn't pleased. It began as a friendship, developed into mutual comfort and companionship after our losses, got out of hand when he fell in love with me. I'm older, wiser, don't need the kind of stability that Robert seeks. His lower lip protrudes slightly, makes him into a displeased child. 'I love you,' he insists.

'Then let me go.'

He drains the cup in one gulp, must have an asbestos palate. 'Look after the cat,' he says brusquely.

'I'm sorry.'

'No, you're not. This is a great trip for you, turning down a man who'd do just about anything for you. And don't start the age difference crap, it's boring. Ten years is nothing, nothing at all. You like me, you enjoy my work, could have a good time helping with the animals. My kids adore you . . .' His voice tails away and a hand pushes its way through the tousled mop of hair. 'I don't mind waiting. Ben won't get well, we both know that. And he told you to take a lover if he ever became ill—'

'He didn't tell me to go and start another life.'

'But you'd still be there for him. You'd still visit him and—'

Something snaps. 'I will stay in his house until he dies, Robert. He's my husband and my best friend. While Ben is in this world, I will be his and he'll be mine. And that's not romantic garbage, it's elemental, a part of who he is, who I am.' My yelling causes Handel to ruffle slightly, but the kitten slumbers on. Still, if she was born in a shed among a crowd of vicious cats, she'll be used to noise.

He is furious, hates my shouting. 'You don't bloody know who he is.'

I should never have told him that. Pillow talk is dangerous, does not look good in the light of day. 'I might have known that you would use that, Robert. Ben is one of the finest men I've ever met. You've no idea at all of what he did for me and my children. Please go home now.'

He is sorry, worried. A hand reaches across the table. 'Laura.'

'I'll talk to you when you've calmed down a bit. But I'd advise you to get out of this house. Now.'

Life is so sad. In a bedroom, Robert and I are good partners. But on a day-to-day basis, the arrangement could never work. His son is precocious, his daughter needs affection. Robert and I would be fine, but I could never accept his children. Tom is wont to rhyme off lists of meaningless facts, and Melinda needs warmth, love, a reader of fairy tales.

He shouts from the hall, 'I'll be back. I'm not giving up, Laura.'

Neither am I. When I was a child, I didn't really like children – except for my cousin Anne. As a mother of young children, I struggled against enormous odds just to keep food in the house, just to feed and clothe them. There was no time for love, no chance to escape the fear that kept me cowed and silent. Children were a part of the terror, a part of the nightmare.

And when we got away, it was too late. There were too many worries. There is no excuse for depriving children of love, because that is their birthright. But I had a reason, and the reason was that I didn't understand what a mother's love was, what it ought to be. My children are well and strong. They have good bones, good teeth, good health. But they never had a good mother, never had a pattern of security that they might copy, learn from. I've tried not to scream at my own mother for being such a burden, because I look at her and see myself in thirty years. She was my model, but who was hers? Were they really sweet, those parents of hers? Or did she, too, have to escape, has that made her bitter?

We go upstairs, Flakey and I. She lies in a shoe box, all tiny and warm, a nest of handkerchiefs beneath her. I place her liquid food on my desk, lie the dropper beside the jar.

And I carry on writing *Laura*.

Part Two

Chapter One

It's hard to remember in detail the very early days of your life. There are flashes, of course, mind-pictures of a particular garden, a porcelain sink in a kitchen, raincoats dripping, a mousetrap under the stairs. How I worried about those poor mice.

Smells are easier than pictures. Auntie Maisie used a light, powdery perfume, something on the lines of Je Reviens, but less cloying. Her house was always full of baking and sewing, rich, yeasty scents and that crisp aroma of new calico. Uncle Freddie smelled of coffee or of wet earth and potato skins, depending on what he'd been dealing with at the Co-op. My dad was liquorice and peppermint and Mother reeked of bad temper. Bad temper is something to do with cigarette smoke and a particular brand of eau-de-Cologne that seems to have disappeared from the market.

Sounds, too. Oh yes, the noises are there. The rag-and-bone man with his 'aynee owld raa-aags', the clatter of metal scoop against metal churn when the milkman filled our jugs, the gentle snort of his horse as it champed on the bit. Mill hooters, the clang of a tram on Chorley Old Road, the whirr of a trolley bus in town. *'Bowton Evernin' Newers'* sang the boy on the corner. Bolton was a noisy, smoky, comforting place.

There were other noises, not so welcome. 'Laura, have you tidied your room?' and 'I should never have had you, you are a dreadful child.' The crack of flesh on flesh when she struck me, the screams I kept inside my head because whenever I yelled, the violence got worse. My father singing to me, my poor dear father who never understood her, never understood me. He was a great man and a weak human being.

No, I must try to remember the better things, like the noises from the house next door. 'Pull up a chair, Laura. Now stand on it and give us a song.' Uncle Freddie was the most terrible tease in the whole world. That knowledge had been passed on to us by his wife, Auntie Maisie.

'What shall I sing?'

'A pretty song. A pretty girl should always sing a pretty ditty.'

I was not a good singer, but they listened while I murdered 'Alice Blue Gown'.

Then Anne would do 'The White Cliffs of Dover' or 'Run Rabbit Run'.

'Treacle toffee, that'll shut you up, Annie.' Auntie Maisie's face was round, glowing like the sun. 'Here, Laura, you get some before Freddie pinches it. Keeps swallowing bits of his teeth, greedy old bugger.'

My mother never said things like 'bugger', so I would giggle and keep the secret. Secrets from my mother were rare and as sweet as the toffee. I would sit in the warm glow of Maisie Turnbull's love, would soak up the happiness, try to keep it in my heart where it would warm me till morning. But it never did. Somewhere on the way from their door to ours, I always grew chilled and lonely.

There was bunting in the street when the war ended. Liza McNally, my supposed mother, wouldn't let me go to the party in the avenue. I often dreamed of the whole thing being a mistake, hoped that someone in authority would come along and say, 'Sorry, Mrs McNally, but Laura is not your child.' She would have been pleased, too, had I not been hers, because she was always saying that I wasn't good enough. I hoped, but the hope grew dim with the passing of time. The facts of life were a topic for the future, and I imagined that I might keep the same father and get a better mother. 'You are not going outside to mix with those people,' she announced through a cloud of

Craven A exhaust. I was not to be allowed to celebrate the end of a war.

My father spoke up for me, but she refused to be moved. John McNally believed that the rearing of infant children was a woman's job, so she often had the last word when I was very young. Father said, 'It's not worth upsetting her, Laurie-child.' He brought me sweets that night, barley sugars and Uncle Joes. He was a kind man, but he was powerless in her presence.

My mother closed our curtains on Victory Day. 'It's common,' she said, pursing her reddened lips. 'No child of mine is going to run about outside with sandwiches.'

'But Mother—'

'Don't argue with me. I've had enough of your cheek just lately.'

I sat in the dark and imagined rescue, but no-one came. Cousin Anne did not arrive to knock on our door, to urge me to step outside, because Mother had severed relations with next door some weeks earlier, had cut me off from my kith and kin. Although cowed for much of the time, I was moved to speak up on this occasion. 'You don't want me to have anybody,' I accused, my feet spread wide, arms folded to demonstrate my anger. That's a thing I recall quite clearly, the way I copied her body language.

She clouted me across my left cheek. 'You do not need Maisie and Freddie. Anne has a coarse mouth, something she's inherited from that unbearable man. Laura McNally, you will be a lady if I have to drag you up screaming all by myself.'

My face was stinging. 'I don't want to be a lady. Cyril Mort's got fireworks, saved up since before the war. His dad said they'd be lit once Hitler was in the muck where he belonged.'

She dragged me into the kitchen, waved a bar of red carbolic before my eyes. 'Must I wash your mouth out, girl? You do not use such words in my house.' Carbolic burns, sears the skin from your tongue. I knew that, because I'd received mouthwashes before for simple words

95

like 'ta-ra'. Common words, she called them. Above all, I was to become an uncommon child.

It was sickening. I'd heard my dad asking the milkman for horse-muck to put on the roses. The word she objected to must have been 'muck', as it was the only unusual one to have slipped from my tongue.

'You are not to look at me in that fashion,' she screamed before smacking my head so hard that it crashed against the sink. Immediately, she panicked. Although Mother was a vicious woman, she made it her business to ensure that the marks of cruelty seldom showed. My head was grabbed, pushed over the sink, doused in cold water. 'It's your own fault,' she mumbled, choking slightly because she had no hand free to take the cigarette from her mouth. 'The way you look at me, the way you disobey . . .' The towel was hard and rough. I kept my expression neutral as she rubbed me dry, but my dislike of her grew larger and heavier, even as I stood in that kitchen.

'We shall go into the sitting room.' Her voice shook; she had frightened herself with her actions, was terrified of being out of control, even for a second.

Liza McNally lived on her nerves and announced that fact regularly to me, to my father and to anyone else within earshot. The nerves were visible that afternoon, the day of the street party. She stood by the fireplace smoking, smoothing her perfect hair, picking at the buffed and painted nails. I can see her now if I close my eyes, pearl choker, round-necked navy frock with lace on the collar, dark shoes, nylon stockings donated by an American serviceman whose life had reputedly been saved by my father's stomach balm. Even with my eyes open, I can see the seeds of bitterness in her expression, a clear acidity of temperament that would not abate with the passing of time. After contact with the sink, my head was already sore, and she did not improve matters when she pulled at my hair till I heard some of it snapping away at the scalp. 'Selfish child,' she muttered as she dragged me out of the kitchen.

Hatred is a strong word, perhaps too strong to express the feelings of a five-year-old child. But something boiled in my chest, got brewed up in the summer of 1945, has simmered ever since. I was perplexed, lonely, excluded. She watched me, fastened me to the chair with her eagle vision, willed me not to move. It was a long day, one of the longest in my whole life. The cruellest part was the party dress. She made me wear it, pretended that we were having our own 'select' gathering in the dining-room at the back of our house. The curtains were closed, of course, to keep out the noise of the 'rabble' outside. The 'rabble' consisted of hard-working middle-class people, factory managers, shopkeepers, self-employed businessmen. Whatever, they were not good enough for my mother. The party dress was washed and pressed just in case anyone outside should catch sight of me and pity my isolation. Saving pride and face was my mother's way of life, even her *raison d'être*, but I had only just begun to learn that.

I fidgeted, of course. Sitting straight and still in a chair is difficult for an adult, impossible for a child. There was a pattern on the oilcloth at the edge of Mother's Indian carpet, brown and beige squares with diamond shapes inside the beige bits. The toes of my patent shoes tapped out a message in the diamonds. 'I am not her little girl, she is not my mother.' It was silly, but it helped. Inside, I was defying her; inside, I had a secret.

'Stop that stamping. You are so irritating. Go upstairs and stay away from the windows.'

I obeyed. Well, I obeyed by going upstairs, but I broke the second law, of course. A long table had appeared in the middle of the road as if by magic. It was made, I'm sure, from lots of ordinary dining tables swathed in sheets and coloured paper, but to my infant gaze, this was a miracle. There was dandelion and burdock, jelly, a huge cake with red, white and blue icing. I saw sandwiches and pies and jam tarts. And Anne saw me, glanced up and waved, looked sad without me.

My door burst inward. 'I saw her waving at you, Laura

McNally. Thank goodness I had the foresight to peep through a crack downstairs. You are shaming me. Why can't you do as I ask? Why?' I cowered in a corner as she raised an arm to strike again.

The shape behind her spoke. 'Because your requests are unreasonable sometimes.'

She turned on him. At least her attention had strayed from me. 'This child is a disgrace. You are never here, so don't criticize me and my methods of dealing with her. I cannot have her mixing with the people next door, not after the way they insulted me.'

'The people next door are your sister and your brother-in-law. Anne is Laura's cousin, so there should be no bad blood.' My father must have seen the anger in her face. He stepped back, one foot in my room, the other escaping to safer territory on the landing.

'Do not tell me how to behave,' she screamed. The revels outside seemed quieter, as if the whole party had slowed to listen as Mother ranted. 'I could have married Eddie Cross. He would have been glad to have me, and there would have been none of this staying at work all hours. He's got his own building business, and it puts your pathetic shop to shame. Even through the war, Eddie made money. And I'm condemned to stay here with your wayward child while you linger on Blackburn Road with your potions and lotions – what sort of a life is this for me?'

Father's voice was quiet. 'Then your father should have taken his shotgun elsewhere. He should perhaps have sent Eddie Cross up the aisle instead of me.'

She threw a glance over her shoulder, had a quick look at me, pushed him outside and slammed my door. But I could still hear it all.

'As it turned out, the shotgun was unnecessary.' John McNally had one of those voices which, though very soft, seem to carry well.

'I didn't know that. As far as I was concerned, you had had your way and the symptoms indicated—'

'No, you had had your way. And your way was the

98

fastest route out of the weaving sheds. Why do you impose all this nonsense on the child? Are you so anxious to avoid questions about your humble beginnings? I am proud of mine, grateful that my parents worked so hard to give me a chance. As for you believing that you were pregnant at the time of our marriage, I'll have to take your word for that.'

I fastened my ear to the door, tried to ignore the drumbeat that was my heart. Never before had I known Father to interrupt her and to use strong words. I feared for him, feared that she might turn on him. But after a small pause, he continued, the voice still calm and conversational in tone. 'Your word,' he said. 'I had to accept it then just as I must now take your word about Laura. She will grow, Liza. And she will grow away from you, beyond your reach. Already, she doesn't love you. The girl will have the sense to get away in ten years or so. God, I hope that she can escape your clutches.'

'How dare you!'

'I dare. But for the most part, I shall keep my opinions to myself, just as I always have. She will have some stability. She is the reason why I tolerate this silly situation. When she is grown, I hope she is a match for you.'

He did not often stand in my corner. When he had time for me, he was considerate and loving, but for the most part, John McNally was a man with a mission, a brain full of formulae and chemicals, no space for life's trivia. He loved me, but he had little room for me in his busy life. So he left me to her, trusted to luck, but my meagre store of luck kept running out.

We lived in a large semi-detached house on a spoon-shaped avenue called a cul-de-sac. Our house was right at the tip of the spoon and it was fastened to Cousin Anne's. Auntie Maisie was my mother's sister, while Cousin Anne was almost my twin, as we were born within a week of each other when the war was a few months old.

As babies, we saw a great deal of one another, because our mothers worked shifts at a paint factory down Bridgeman Place. I was not very old when I realized that my mother was 'too good' for such labour. Liza McNally was simply making her patriotic contribution towards the downfall of somebody called Hitler who had a funny moustache and a strange way of talking. As the wife of a dispensing chemist, she would not normally demean herself in such a way.

She would stand in front of the mirror dabbing a smelly liquid on her hair. 'Laura! Is it gone? Can you see any more paint in my hair? Laura, bring my manicure set. The paint is eating into my skin. Laura, get my hand lotion. Where are my slippers? You are four years old and you know that my feet are tired. Some eau-de-Cologne for my head. See if there are any Aspros in the cupboard. If not, go next door, see if Maisie has a spare tape of Aspros.'

When I went next door, things were completely different. Auntie Maisie might have paint in her hair, on a hand, on a shoe, but she would be laughing with her husband or toasting bread in front of the fire. She even laughed when she got a blob of blue on her nose, a big smudge that took days to wear off. I would look at her, try to fill my mind with the sights and sounds of her home. 'Have you any Aspros, Auntie?'

She frowned sometimes. Even when she frowned, her face was happy. 'Another headache, sweetheart? Look in my brown bag.' And I heard them whispering about me, about my parents. Things like 'No wonder he stops out late', and 'Time she started thinking about that kiddy'. There were always smiles and cuddles, bites of toast, a finger-dip of condensed milk, a spoonful of treacle. I did not mind their concern even when it bordered on pity, because they loved me. Any feeling born of love must be good – even a child can sense that.

During the war years, I stayed at Anne's when Mother was on duty. The two sisters' shifts were staggered so that children could be minded by members of their own family. Sometimes, Uncle Freddie was with us in Anne's house, and such times were filled with so much laughter that I often suffered from hiccups for several hours after returning home. Anne didn't like coming in our house, but I was safe when she was there, was free to act like a child.

The oddest and funniest of days were brought to us courtesy of Freddie Turnbull Esquire. He always called himself 'Esquire', said it gave some standing to a poor man who spent his days knee deep in spuds and spilled sugar. Uncle Freddie Turnbull, a huge man with whiskers and a limp from the Great War, was considerably older than my gentle father. He was what everybody called 'a scream', because he was forever imitating people. Not famous names, just the folk from round and about. 'They'd not make one straight man between them,' he would say about those who traded in our area. 'If they'd a pair of eyes or legs among them, they'd be stood up in the front lines with a pop-gun and a tin of corned beef.'

It was awful, even excruciating, but it brought excitement into our narrow lives. 'Sithee,' he said, the face serious and concerned. 'Just go to the door and pay yon feller. He'll be stood waiting for his money while bedtime if you don't shape. Come on, Laura, come on, our Annie.'

'I'm not doing it.' I stood my ground, felt the butterflies trembling in my chest. 'I'm not doing it unless you promise to behave.'

'I promise.' A hand lay on his heart. 'I'll upset nobody.'

Anne snatched the money, sniffed, knew what would happen. 'Don't laugh, Laura,' she said. 'Mam says we've to be polite no matter what Dad does.'

Hand in hand for companionship and security, we opened the door like a pair of Christians who expected death at the claws of some enormous feline. 'How much is it?' we asked the tradesman.

It was truly dreadful, extremely testing for two robust and high-spirited young girls. The milkman had a lisp, the coalman suffered with a stammer, while the insurance man, cross-eyed and bow-legged, always said the same thing. 'Eeh, aren't you a pretty pair, a sight fer sore eyes come rain nor shine.'

The insurance man was the worst. Uncle Freddie posed on the stairs, out of sight of any callers. Our peripheral vision was drawn to him like base metal to a magnet, because we knew that he would not be good. His whole body sagged downward, and the good leg curved itself like a letter C. We did not dare look straight at Uncle Freddie until the Prudential man had wobbled off on his bike, because Anne's dear daddy was gifted with the ability to make irises and pupils all but disappear into the sides of his nose. Then he 'did' the insurance man's voice, echoed the words perfectly.

Auntie Maisie rushed out of the kitchen. She pretended to have no time for such behaviour, though she always listened and giggled while the pantomime was in progress. The damp tea-towel was slapped across Uncle Freddie's face. 'For a crippled man, you don't half take the Michael out of other unfortunates. What are you teaching these two, eh? Our Liza will have you drawn and quartered if she catches you carrying on like this in front of our Laura.' Her cheeks glowed when she looked at him, and a smile hovered on the edges of her mouth, held back by sheer willpower and a strong sense of fun.

Uncle Freddie acted hurt and contrite. 'Ooh, Maisie, you're lovely when you're angry. Look at her, girls, isn't she beautiful? There's a dimple now, see, she nearly smiled. Anyway, Maisie Turnbull, I'll have you know that my game leg entitles me to make fun of my fellow cripples. Straighten your face and put that kettle on, Missus. Early to bed for you tonight.'

She was lovely, my Auntie Maisie. Round, plump and pretty, always smelled of yeast mixed with soap and gentle perfume, wore flowered pinnies and a string of coloured glass beads that she'd won on the fair years earlier. The fine blond hair was scraped back into a bun, but little wisps tended to escape round her ears and at the nape of her neck. Uncle Freddie used to kiss the back of her neck and whisper in her ears till she went pink.

I loved them. I suppose that they loved me too, because

they never left me out of anything – unless my mother intervened, of course. At weekends, Uncle Freddie took us to Queens Park, trained us in the art of 'handling the Americans' and forbade us to tell our mothers about our unseemly behaviour. There were two ways of 'handling the Americans'. Sometimes, it was best to look sweet, pretty and twinnish, ask for 'some gum, chum'. But that worked only when we were clean. After skirmishes with roundabouts and swings, we had to use a different ploy to attract the support of our allies.

Anne, who was endowed with great acting ability, lay on the cinder path and blubbered a lot, rubbed her big blue eyes. I ran to the soldiers, my face twisted with suppressed laughter which was usually mistaken for some other emotion. 'My sister's hurt.' We got chocolates, sweets, biscuits, lectures about being careful near strangers. And once, we were given a whole silver dollar and we polished it, took turns to have custody of the shining disc.

Anne and I must have been five when the trouble happened. The war was dwindling towards its chaotic and supposedly triumphant end. Mother and Auntie Maisie were working shifts of just four hours. Uncle Freddie was still managing the local Co-op, while my father continued to spend most of his time at the shop, probably mixing medicines and working at his bench in the upstairs rooms. Everything was normal one minute, terrible the next.

There was a row. We children did not hear it and, for a while, we had no knowledge of its subject. But in the middle of 1945, I was forbidden to go next door, was ordered never to speak to Auntie Maisie, Uncle Freddie, Cousin Anne.

Grief overcame fear several times and I tackled my mother repeatedly. She was more agitated than I had ever seen her, so I took the opportunity to dig deep into her mind. I think she must have been a lonely woman, but perhaps solitude was what she deserved. In a way, she was turning to me, using me as a sounding board, a figure at which she could direct her thoughts.

'Please, Mother. I want to play with Anne.'

Anger and frustration coloured her cheeks, made her truly radiant. My mother was a woman of exceptional beauty. She had copper-gold hair, clear blue eyes and a skin of alabaster that stained itself pink when she became excited. 'You will do as I say, young lady. Exactly as I say.'

I don't know where or how I got the knowledge, but for a few weeks after the Big Row, I felt confident that she would not hit me. She was somewhat depleted and lacklustre after the argument, kept failing to finish off sentences. I was brave enough to keep asking why. 'Why can't I play with Anne?'

'Because I am your mother.'

Sometimes, adults made no sense at all. I tried to be good, obedient and quiet, failed totally, attempted to rekindle my newborn courage. 'Auntie Maisie is my auntie. Uncle Freddie is my uncle. You told me to mind grown-ups and to be nice to them. Why is it all different now?'

She was floundering in a pit of her own digging. Because of her rigorous persistence, I was a precocious child, could read and write, add and subtract, chant a list of capital cities, sing after a fashion, blunder through two simple pieces on the piano. She enjoyed showing off her creation, wanted me capable when it suited her, like on the days when her 'friends' visited and 'took' tea and dainty cakes. I was Mother's party-piece-by-proxy, and she lapped up the shallow praise like a cream-hungry cat.

My talents were not particularly remarkable, but I drew lavish accolades from Mother's attendants. These people formed a gaggle of polite and dull women whose husbands were professional men. Auntie Maisie, even before the disagreement, was never invited to the afternoon teas, was definitely not good enough to be on show when high society descended on our home. 'We shall move away,' Mother declared hotly when I was still struggling to mend the breach between the two houses.

My temper bubbled. 'You can go if you want to. I'm staying here, I shall move next door and live with Anne.'

She wrung her delicate fingers, turned to the fireplace, groped for the umpteenth cigarette. When her lungs were filled with confidence, she looked at me again. 'We got them that house. I persuaded your father – it was my doing – mine!' The hands waved a lot, one leaving in its wake a trail of smoke like the emissions from a fighter plane's engines.

She was proud of her hands, kept a bone-and-silver manicure set in her dressing room. The dressing room was the tiniest front bedroom, linked to the larger room by a doorway made by my father after much harassment. I spent a great deal of time running to and from the dressing room, bringing her this and that, returning hairbrushes, mirrors, powder boxes.

She wandered to the sitting-room window, tugged at the lace curtain, cleared her throat of pretended emotion. 'I thought we should all be together while the war was on. Your daddy paid for that house, Laura. He used money from your grandpapa, money that might have been useful in the business. Oh!' Exasperated by my obvious lack of empathy with her grief, she tried a few tears but, finding it difficult to smoke and cry simultaneously, she opted for the former occupation and stopped snivelling.

'Anne is my favourite person,' I persisted. 'And Auntie Maisie is good and kind and she makes her own bread. And Uncle Freddie is . . . is just Uncle Freddie. I miss him, I miss them all.'

'Laura, you will heed me!' All attempts at presenting a dignified front had suddenly been abandoned, and I found myself afraid again. It wasn't the shouting, it wasn't the idea of being beaten that scared me. No, it was Mother, the woman herself. I was beginning to realize that my mother was not predictable, that even she herself was not aware of how she would act or feel. Her face was grim and set. 'I shall never speak to Maisie again as long as I live.

She has betrayed me – they both betrayed me. I am your mother, so you must be on my side.'

I squashed my misgivings, swallowed them with a gulp of air. She might beat me, scream, shout, tear at her hair – I didn't care. She was wrong. Something about her was wrong. I always knew how Auntie Maisie would be. If there was sad music on the wireless, she might allow her lips to tremble, but Auntie Maisie didn't swing from one thing to another, didn't strut about shouting at people and hitting out. My mother was silly. And I was going to stick up for myself and for what was right.

I watched her, waited for a few moments. Like most infants, I was on the side of fun and good food. As my mother provided neither of these vital factors, I could not be on her side. My mother's grey and often leaden attempts at pastry compared poorly with Auntie Maisie's rich flatcakes, succulent fruit tarts, feather-light raisin pound loaves. As for fun, Mother thought that it was common, that it had no place in a decent semi-detached with three bedrooms, a piano and an inside toilet. My fun had been fruit-picking, glorious days spent out in the hedgerows with Uncle Freddie, stolen apples in our bags, hands and faces stained purple with the juice of black-berries. All gone, no more fun from now on, no more nice cakes. I drew myself to full height, a few inches taller than the bookcase filled with Mother's romantic novels. 'Auntie Maisie told Uncle Freddie that you're no better than you ought to be.'

'What?'

I stood my ground as the shrieked word echoed round the room and rattled in my head. There might be a land-slide any minute, or one of those clips across my ear that often made me sick and dizzy. 'You're a mill girl, she said. A mill girl like she used to be. You . . . you seducinged my father. And when he was sedu . . . what I said before, you nearly got in trouble with a shotgun and you had a blue frock at church.' I stopped, studied her, marvelled at the range of colours on her face. For colour, my mother was an admirable woman at times. The middles of her cheeks had gone a sort of deep rosy mauve, then there was a red ring, a pink ring, and a very white, very wet forehead. I had never seen my mother sweating before. Though coming from her skin, this moisture was probably perspiration rather than common sweat.

'I'm no mill girl.' The tone was soft, dangerously so. The words seemed squashed, as if they were being forced from somewhere deep inside her. 'I never belonged in a weaving shed, should not have been sent there, not with my frail health. Maisie was the troublesome one, the one who gave us grief. Both my parents died of broken hearts after Maisie married that old cripple.' She approached me slowly. 'And I was married three years before you were born. Remember that, Laura McNally.'

I understood none of the implications, vaguely remembered Auntie Maisie going on about 'the phantom baby', decided to keep my mouth shut.

'If my mummy and daddy were here, if they could see and hear how I am treated, they would make sure that Freddie Turnbull got a thorough horse-whipping,' said my irate mother.

Uncle Freddie deserved no such treatment; of that, at least, I was completely sure. Tomfoolery sat on my tongue again, jumped out with hardly any warning. This wasn't courage, it was sheer lunacy. 'You're the naughty one,' I shouted. 'They would never, ever hurt anybody. And I won't eat any more of your nasty stews and puddings. I am going to starve to death.' In my mind, I held a beautiful picture of a blond girl-child, a smile frozen on its pale face, the eyes closed, hands clasped on its chest. Then the mind-picture sat up like Betty and said, 'Mama.' Betty was my largest doll. I never played with her because she was boring, and I couldn't think how she'd got tied up in my imagination with the concept of my dramatic starvation.

It seemed that I had hit yet another of her raw nerves, because she contemplated me for a second or two. Mother would not like it if I refused to eat. My plump little body was the cause of much self-congratulation on Mother's part; she was often heard to say, 'My daughter has not suffered because of this war. I always manage to keep her fed and properly clothed.' She used to remove my cardigan, hold up my arm, pinch the fleshy upper with her sharp, bright nails, demonstrate the depth and quality of my upholstery. Then all the tea-ladies would put down their cups and study the pattern and the fine sewing on my dress. Well, I would tear up all my clothes too. No, I wouldn't. Auntie Maisie had made most of them, love and warmth stitched into every seam.

'Right,' snapped Mother. 'Your father will deal with you later. Get up to your room immediately.'

My father would deal with me? Even at the age of five, I found this funny. Dad would tell me not to worry, not to upset Mother. Then he'd give me a sixpence and some sweets before reading a story and kissing me good night.

'Go upstairs,' she repeated.

'No.' Who said that? I wondered vaguely. Surely it wasn't me, surely I could not possibly be so courageous, so stupid? 'I'm not going nowhere.' Sometimes I surprised myself and sometimes I was a fool.

'Anywhere,' she said wearily, automatically. At last, she advanced on me, gripped my upper arm in a vice that did not match those pale and delicate fingers. 'Laura, you will be starting school soon, a very nice school with—'

'With Anne.' I would have to start treading more carefully. The shock of the row with next door was bound to wear off soon, and she was already pinching my flesh, making it sting and burn.

She released me then, but her mouth was twisted, and I sensed that bad news was on its way. That sinister dip of the lower lip was a sure sign of victory, and I shivered inside when I saw the cunning brightness of her lovely eyes. 'No, you will not be going to a low-class school.' She patted her hair, lit another cigarette. I should have gone to my room after all, should have obeyed and escaped from the smoke, from the awful thing that she was beginning to say. 'You will be going to a little convent, a private place for nice young ladies.'

I could not help myself, could not deny such overpowering curiosity. 'What's a convent?'

She awarded me one of her coy shrugs. 'It's a place where education is taken seriously, a place where nuns pray and slap little girls who won't do exactly as they are told. The Catholics do one thing right, it seems.'

Now, Catholics were things I knew about. My feeling that my mother was an unusual and even crazy person was strengthening by the minute. She kept changing her mind. You could never be sure of what she would do, of what she would say. Worst of all, her erratic behaviour distorted issues for those of us who were condemned to live with her. 'You don't like Catholics,' I ventured. My father used to be one of those. I had heard Uncle Freddie and Auntie Maisie talking about that, too. 'Liza wouldn't budge, wouldn't marry him at St Patrick's, said she wanted no little Catholics bred in her house.'

Boldly, I stood my ground. But my ground was at a safe-ish distance from those long arms and those scratchy nails. She was a slapper, a pincher, a puller of long ringlets. 'You don't want anything . . . papist.' I managed to drag the word from a meagre store acquired while sitting on the stairs next door. 'And nuns are papists, aren't they?'

She was not going to lose. There was triumph in her expression as she approached me. 'Your father wants you brought up as a Christian. He is very pleased that I have chosen the convent for you. And we don't want to upset your dear daddy, now.'

'I'm going to Brook Lane Mixed,' I shouted.

'No.' She was giggling and shaking her head so that the bronze curls bobbed about all round her face, as if they, too, were laughing at my stupidity.

'I want to go with Anne.'

She shook her finger at me. The talon was long, sharp,

threatening. 'To be well educated, a girl needs to be with other women and as far away as possible from boys. These nuns are quick to spot any talent you may have, so you'll no doubt be on your way to Bolton School in the fullness of time.'

I did not want to go to Bolton School, had no intention of finishing up in silly dresses and thick lisle stockings. 'Well, I'm not going there, either. Uncle Freddie says they all get humps on their backs and thick glasses and pale faces from stopping in the house instead of playing outside.' I took a breath, recharged my batteries. 'I shall run out of class every day at that silly convent. Those nuns will have to tie me to the desk. They won't make me learn, 'cos they can't make me listen.' I jerked up my chin. 'I am going to Brook Lane with Anne.'

'We'll see.' She turned away then, dismissed me with one of her shrugs. Some days, she didn't care enough even to dislike me. Being at odds with your mother is not a comfortable sensation. There were many days like this one, many occasions when she locked me in, separated me from life, 'bested' me. As a child, I had to accept the convent, the exclusion from the street party, had to bend to her will time after time.

I could not go to the Bolton Fair for fear of nits, was forbidden to enter a public lavatory for fear of disasters even deadlier than nits. The fivepenny Saturday matinee with its serials and cowboy stories was out of my reach until I grew older and wiser, until I learned to be devious and clever.

But in the early spring of my life, I had no power. And now, in my September, the woman who gave birth to me continues to shape and distort my existence.

Chapter Two

My bedroom was next to Anne's, even though we lived in separate houses. We learned quickly how to attract each other's attention by tapping on the party wall with a shoe. When I look back on some of our acrobatic displays, I think it must be by the grace of God that we are still alive, my cousin Anne and I.

'I can lean out further than you can.'

'Go on, then.'

'And if I kneel on the window-sill and grab the curtains, my top half dangles right down the wall.'

'Yes, but I've had both my legs hanging out, all the way up to the waist, too.'

'That's a lie. I saw the edge of your knickers, but only just. You were never a long way out.'

'I was.'

'You weren't.' And so on. We were daring in those days. Daring, foolish and naughty, but it was fun. The sad thing was that we could not reach one another, were unable to touch, hold hands and whisper secrets. Secrets from the grown-up world were our speciality. If we had gathered no real ones, then we made them up as we went along, each fully aware of when the other was lying. It didn't matter whether our words embraced truth or fiction – just the fact that we were communicating was enough to satisfy us.

'It's all your mother's fault, the row and everything,' she declared one cold night when the trouble was some months old. 'Your mother is the awfullest person.'

I sighed, made no attempt to defend my female parent. 'What's she done this time?' My tone was offended, resigned. I might have been my own mother speaking about me.

'She's gone cheap.'

'What?'

'I heard Mam saying that their Liza is cheap.'

I'd encountered the word before, of course, knew that people went to Bolton market on Tuesdays, Thursdays and Saturdays to buy inexpensive things. Somehow, I could not envisage my mother seated on a stall, even in the more select and covered area of the market, with a price pinned to her blouse, 'Marked down to 7/6, bargain of the week'. 'Well?'

'Well, what?' Anne was staring at the moon, had decided to be infuriating again. She sometimes went a bit coy when a tasty morsel had fallen in her path, some real gossip picked up from Auntie Maisie and Uncle Freddie's talks.

'What does it mean?' I asked, my patience slipping a little.

'It means . . .' The tip of her tongue curled over her upper lip. 'It means kissing and things like that.'

I pondered. 'Mother has never kissed anybody in her whole life.' She had certainly never kissed me or hugged me.

'She has, though.'

'How do you know?'

The thin arms waved about in the 'be quiet' signal that we had developed between us during our evening conversations. She disappeared and I heard the bedsprings twang as she leapt beneath the covers. Her window was closed by an unseen hand, then I had to wait for an endless time until she was alone again.

The window slid upward. 'It was Mam. She read me a story.'

I felt a small twinge of jealousy. Mother never read to me at bedtime, and Dad seldom had the opportunity. But I squashed the bad feeling, because I didn't want Anne to be as unhappy as I was. 'Tell me about my mother.'

Anne giggled. 'She kissed my dad. Mam said that Liza was making up to him, trying to get him to kiss her just like he kisses Mam. Dad said your mother had been drinking sherry and gin and all sorts when it happened.'

My spine went cold and I felt shocked to the core. Mother had always called Uncle Freddie 'that silly old cripple', had vowed repeatedly that she would never like him. Why would she kiss him? Why would she want him to kiss her?

Anne continued to lisp through gaps where her front teeth had recently resided. 'I heard them when they were in bed. They said your dad's had enough of Auntie Liza and that he's a nice man. He stays behind late at the shop because he's fed up to his back teeth with your mother. My dad says Auntie Liza is looking for it. Do you know what she's looking for, Laura?'

I considered the possibilities for a moment. 'She lost her purse, but she found it again in the sideboard drawer.' I did not doubt Anne, not for a single moment. If this had been make-believe, some silent signal would have passed between us. 'What else did you hear them saying?'

Anne screwed up her face, just as she often did when doing battle with difficult words. 'She's a . . . a harlot. She caught your dad through being a harlot. It sounds like a bird with coloured feathers, doesn't it? Or one of them small monkeys in my zoo book. Mam said that Uncle John should go off somewhere and have a fresh start, 'cos Auntie Liza's only interested in his money. But Dad said Uncle John is too soft and gentle to leave you.'

My world was threatening to crumble completely. How would I cope if Dad left me? I'd have to live with her, just her and her face creams and stupid tea parties and horrible meals she insisted on inventing from time to time, usually after reading a magazine. A life stretched before me into the darkening sky, a whole era with myself and Mother, cardboard pastry, chewy meat, barley and lentils still hard and nasty. And all that running, all that bring-me-fetch-me-carry-me. And even more batterings, I guessed. 'My dad loves me,' I muttered.

'Yes, he does. He's always talking about you to customers in his shop, 'cos Mam's friends have told her about it. He won't leave you, Laura, so don't worry. Mam says she'd like to see him getting away from Auntie Liza, but Dad said it won't happen. He's clever, my dad. What he says is usually right.'

I could not help worrying. The worst thing was that I did not for one moment consider my mother. My mind was firmly fixed on my own potential loss – her position was of no interest to me.

For several weeks after the clandestine talk with Anne, I watched my father like a hawk, stared at him across the breakfast table, neglected my homework in the evenings, waited for him to come in. Every minute without him was like an hour, because I feared that he would simply go missing one day.

When he was home on time, we always sat together in the dining room, Dad with his plate of reheated and totally unpalatable food, I with sum books, writing books, maps of the Empire waiting to be coloured in, pink for British, green for all other countries, blue for sea.

'What's the matter, Laurie-child?' he asked me one night. 'Why are you so down in the mouth?'

I stared blankly at my three-times tables till they seemed to melt and merge into grey squiggles. Apart from anything else, I didn't know where to begin my list of complaints. I hated the school, was different from most other pupils. Ninety per cent of them were Catholics but, because of my mother's aversion to papism, I had to sit in a corridor during religion, with a girl called Norma Wallace. Norma Wallace was a Methodist who sported bitten nails and a nasal drip, and who was judged by the nuns to be 'highly strung' and therefore a budding genius. They would say to her, 'Not so fast with the arithmetic, Norma. We don't want you to be having a brainstorm. You are highly strung and must take things slowly.' I wished that I might see her highly strung, preferably from one of the beams in the school hall.

I coloured in a bit of sea, pretended to be busy, didn't answer Dad's question immediately. Norma Wallace was expected to reach her 'full potential' at the convent of St Mary, so while we were relegated to the corridor, she read books and chewed her fingers while I swung my legs and stared at pictures of miserable saints. If a person had to be so ugly to be a saint, then most people of my acquaintance would never qualify for beatification. All the saints at our school had big noses and turned-down mouths. Norma Wallace had a miserable mouth and she snerched all the time. 'Snerching' was an Uncle Freddie word and it certainly did justice to Norma Wallace's periodic inhalations of mucus. She would probably be a saint and finish up on a corridor wall with a long frock and praying hands, her face frozen in a silent snerch.

Uncle Freddie. He was on my list of miseries too, with Auntie Maisie and Cousin Anne. I loved them, was not allowed to spend time with them. The days of blackberrying and apple-pinching were long gone, and I wanted them back. My mother had forbidden me to set foot next door. My mother's word was law, because she had appointed herself judge, jury and prison warder.

My mother. While Dad and I sat at the table, she was upstairs, trying frocks on, creaming her hands, her face, shaving all those little gingery hairs off her legs. She was cruel and silly and selfish. My mother was at the top of my catalogue of grievances.

'Laura?'

I looked up at him. 'I'm all right,' I said. If I hadn't said that, if I'd made a fuss, then he might have blamed the whole sorry mess on me and my sulks. If he was staying because of me, I would need to be good. Dads left bad children, stayed with good ones.

'I'm going to London next week.'

My heart sank like a stone. I glanced at the floor, as if I expected to see this most vital of organs slipping through the base of a shoe. He was going. He was leaving me with all that face cream and powder and Norma Wallace and her snerches. He would never come back, because I was not worthy of him, was not good enough for him. Had I been good enough, he would not have wanted to live in London. I would miss him, would be deprived of his quiet, gentle love, even if it did come in small doses and on a part-time basis. 'Don't go.' My voice was strangled with fear. 'Please don't leave me, Dad.'

'I'm not leaving you, Laurie-child. I will never leave you, not while you still need me.'

I swallowed, breathed again. 'Then why are you going?' London was one of those far-away places that no-one ever visited except on matters of great importance. It was somewhere to do with King George and a big, noisy clock and some men on the wireless. Like the moon, it was there, but too far removed in time and space to be real and touchable. 'And how long are you going for?' It would be awful without him. When he was in the house, he often sat with me, talked, asked questions, told me about his customers and their funny ways. Mother never spoke to me, except to tell me what I was doing wrong. And she used me as a plate-carrier when her cronies came, spoke nicely to me so that everyone would judge her to be a perfect mother. 'Why do you have to go, Dad?'

He laughed quietly, reached across the table and lifted my face. 'You are so beautiful,' he whispered. 'And so transparent. Laurie-child, you are an open book. You detest that school, I know all about that. But you will thank your mother one day, because those nuns are excellent teachers. As for the situation here . . .' He jerked a thumb towards Auntie Maisie's house. 'That will come right in time.'

'He didn't kiss her,' I said.

'I know that.' His brow furrowed and he said, to himself, 'The man's no fool.' That reassuring smile sat briefly on his face. 'It will come right. You and Anne will grow, then all decisions can be your own. For now, it's best not to rock the boat. Your mother . . .' He thought for a few seconds, stroked his moustache. 'She's not a happy lady, love. It's just the way she is – nothing can be done for her. We must try to make no waves.'

'Why is she unhappy, Dad?'

'I don't know.'

'Can you make her happy, make her smile more?'

He coughed, scraped his chair backward by an inch or so. 'Honesty is my policy, you know that, love. I don't believe in lying to children, even when they are too young to grasp the facts. Your mother's unhappiness is a part of her, like hands and feet. It's just how she's made.'

'But why does she make everybody else sad too?'

He sighed. 'That, too, is a part of herself. She doesn't know she's doing it, Laurie. Like breathing. We all breathe, but we don't think about it, do we?'

The nuns at school often went on about self-control, about having good thoughts, a pleasant attitude towards others. My mother had no self-control. She pretended to be in charge of herself, got upset when she lost her temper and struck me, but even when she wasn't lashing out, Mother was simmering, hiding how she felt. It came to me then in a flash. In the sixth year of my life, I learned to accept the fact that my mother was a totally unpleasant person. The words to describe her were not in my vocabulary, but I realized that the female who had brought me into the world was on no-one's side except her own. 'She says I'm naughty,' I mumbled.

'You're not naughty. You're healthy and high-spirited.' His head dropped for a moment. 'God, I hope she doesn't beat the nature out of you.' He looked up, smiled reassuringly. 'Try not to dislike your own mother, sweetheart.'

'Everybody hates her.'

'Laurie—'

'Well, they do. Me and Anne heard the postman talking about her ages ago. He told the man at number twelve that Mrs McNally is a hoity-toity bitch.'

He coughed. 'A bitch is a lady dog, child.'

'Is it?'

'Yes.'

I considered the implications. 'I like dogs. Except for that tiny long-haired thing in Greenslade Avenue. It's a Yorkshire terrier, stupid and snappy. My mother could be one of those, but not a proper lady dog. I'd better tell the postman when I see him that Mother isn't a bitch unless it's one of those nasty, yappy Yorkshire things.'

'I wouldn't bother if I were you.' His moustache was twitching. He was trying not to laugh at me. 'Laurie, you are so old-fashioned. Don't talk about your mother when you're outside, dear.'

My mind, after taking one of its mystery tours, found its way back to the main route. 'Why are you going to London? I've never known anybody who's gone to London.' Perhaps it was a frightening place where people got lost and never came home again. 'Do you have to go?'

'Yes.'

'Why?'

He chuckled. 'To see the King.'

'No!' My jaw dropped. 'Without Mother?' Mother would get annoyed about being left out. And if she went with him, then I, too, would have to go. She liked kings and jewels and stuff, so she'd be annoyed if Dad met the King and she never got the chance.

My lovely father shook with suppressed laughter. We had learned, he and I, to keep our conversations quiet, not to indulge in loud expressions of emotion. Mother seldom spoke to either of us, but we sensed that our closeness to each other would displease her. 'No, I'm going to see a man about a patent,' he said. 'I've invented a sort of medicine, a gentle drink that tastes nice and brings a fever down.'

My mother's empire was born that night, the night when I sat and joked quietly with my father about living in a pa-tent. While I coloured in the British Empire, my father painted a picture of Mother's territories. His eyes were bright as he told me about his hopes of a small factory just outside Bolton, about little muslin bags filled with dried herbs, mint, secret ingredients. 'I found a lot of it in my grandmother's recipe books,' he said. 'Your great-grandmother was a very clever woman, Laurie-child.'

'When I grow up, I'll be a chemist too,' I decided with my usual recklessness. 'Then I'll be able to work with you and make the medicines.'

'McNally's Cooling Tea,' he pronounced, his chest puffing out with exaggerated pride. 'It works, it's non-addictive, can be sold to an infant.' He relaxed, stared steadily at me. 'There'll be money in this.'

'Thousands and thousands?' I asked.

'Probably. And I shall spend it all on you. You shall have dresses and coats and shiny new shoes. Sweets, toys—'

'And a dog?'

'Of course.'

'A horse?' I was going a bit far, but it was fun. And Mother wouldn't like me to have a dog or a horse, so it was really silly, but so exciting. 'What about Mother?' I asked in a sober moment.

'What about me?' We froze, had not noticed her standing in the doorway. 'What about me?' she repeated, her tone harsh and sneering.

My father jerked himself upright, became stiff and steady, ready for her jibes and criticism. 'I was just explaining to Laurie that I am going to London for a few days.'

'Her name, in case the birth certificate has escaped your scrutiny, is Laura.' She smoothed her dress, a beautiful silky affair, its colour just about matching that incredible burnished hair. Mother's hair was brushed three hundred times each night and was washed twice weekly in a special powder that she mixed with water, something called a beauty shampoo. Liza McNally, all preened and lovely, but with nowhere to go, stepped into the room and placed herself between father and daughter. 'We've been through all this before.' She sounded unimpressed, even bored. 'It will come to nothing, you'll see. Beechams and Fennings have the market in that sort of thing. There's no room for another proprietary brand, especially one with a name like McNally. I'm afraid you will be laughed at, John. Still, London is far enough away. No-one here will know about your failure.'

I wanted to leap on her there and then, longed to pull her hair, slap her face. She should not have spoken to Dad like that. As a demonstration of my support, I shuffled nearer to him, would have held his hand except for the look on Mother's face.

He cleared his throat, took out his watch and studied it for a moment. 'We shall see about that.' The half-hunter was pushed back into a pocket of his waistcoat. 'Yes, we shall just have to await developments.'

The air almost crackled with tension as they stared coldly at each other. A shiver ran the length of my spine, because I felt as if I might reach out and touch their hatred. If I could have trapped the feeling and contained it, it would have been very hot or very cold, certainly poisonous. There was no doubt in my mind that this was my mother's fault. John McNally was not the sort of man who would hate – or love – easily.

He coughed again, was uneasy in her presence. 'Yes, we shall just wait and see. Perhaps you will be forced to eat your words, Liza. And I trust that they will not prove as indigestible as this evening's meal.' He patted my head, then strode out of the room.

I watched her. The eyes were larger than usual, seemed to be brimming with icy anger. Her head moved about in quick, jerky movements, as if a puppeteer were pulling her strings. The hands, white and softened by creams, were tipped with splashes of scarlet on the long nails. Stains from cigarettes had been removed with emery board, and the fingers were curling in temper. 'That man,' she said softly. 'If he can be called a man.'

I walked away and stood by the fire, watched as she clattered the china into an unsteady mound and whisked it away to the kitchen. Water poured, dishes rattled. 'A man?' she asked herself. 'His own bed, his own shop, his own bloody cooling tea?'

So, Mother did swear at times, then. I would tell Anne tomorrow – no. No, I would not tell Anne unless I managed to meet her after school. Because the woman in the kitchen had taken Anne away from me, had ruined my life. I blinked back the tears and listened with renewed interest.

'. . . laugh their heads off at him if they knew.' Bang, clatter, went the cupboard doors. 'Doesn't want a wife, wants a skivvy.' Cutlery jangled as it was thrown into the drawer. '. . . sleep by myself, live by myself. Then he wonders why I look around . . . blast! Laura? Run upstairs and fetch my manicure case. I've broken another nail.'

I walked slowly upstairs, stepped past my father's bed. He was lying on top of the quilt and his eyes were closed. In the dressing room, I found the leather case, turned to carry it downstairs. His eyes were still shut. 'Laurie?'

'Yes, Dad?'

'Don't let her turn you against me.'

'No. I won't.'

'And don't be cheeky to her. Remember that she can't help how she is.'

I was young, far too young to be dragged by either of them into the quagmire of their dreadful marriage. But I was on my father's side at all times, would not have reached for Mother even if he had abandoned her.

I thrust the case under her nose. She sat at the dining table and filed her broken nail. 'What was he doing?'

'Lying down.'

'Reading?'

'No.'

She held out the hand, stretched the fingers wide so that she could assess her workmanship. 'Did he speak to you?'

I paused for a moment. 'No.'

The wedding ring was being twisted round and round.

'Your father does not care about us, Laura. All he thinks about is that wretched shop and some crazy invention that will never work. There is no time for us, no time for his home. I've been asking him to distemper the bathroom walls for three years. Three years, Laura. He doesn't care what happens to us, you know.'

I didn't know what to say, wasn't sure what she expected. Was I supposed to speak? Or should I just stand and listen?

Her voice was low. 'He doesn't love you.'

I swallowed, maintained my silence.

'He pretends to, but he could not care less about his own daughter, his only child. There won't be any more, not from me, not while the sleeping arrangements—' She cut herself off, glared at me. 'I'm all you've got.'

If this was really the case, then I was totally alone. 'He loves me,' I said, unable to hold back any longer.

'He loves his pestle and mortar, his bottles of crystals and coloured water. People are nothing to him.'

I would have argued sensibly, would have reasoned with her, but the whole situation was just a jumble in my head. Some of the words I needed were hard to remember, and my chest was hot, bubbling, boiling with a mixture of fear and anger. I erupted suddenly, could not help allowing the scalding words to fall from my mouth. If I hadn't spat them out, I might have exploded. 'The postman says you are a hoity-toity bitch.'

An implement clattered to the floor, a metal thing with a tortoiseshell handle. It was a strange item, rather like a tiny spoon, something she used when digging away at the base of her nails. 'What did you say?'

My voice was quieter now. 'A hoity-toity bitch. Like a lady dog.'

Her teeth were bared as she drew a long breath. 'No. You've got that from your father, haven't you?'

I shook my head. 'The postman said it. He's always saying it.' Oh God, why couldn't I just sink through the floor? It was as if I were on automatic pilot, just floating at the behest of an invisible power that propelled me into waters that were so dangerous.

Instead of hitting me, she smiled that one-sided smile, the look that announced to the world, 'I am better than all of you.' 'The postman is a common person, unused to dealing with culture. It's a pity that we lost Mr Oakes, because he was a gentleman.' Our previous postman, the Mr Oakes whose praises she was singing, used to warrant clean blouses, cups of tea and a few kind words from Mother. He had even come into the house sometimes, had taken a glass of sherry and a slice of cake during his afternoon round.

'Mr Oakes was no fun,' I insisted stubbornly. 'The new one sings like George Formby.'

'Yes.' She nodded sagely. 'Common. An attractor of attention. And what he said about me is slander. I might see a solicitor about him, make sure he loses his job.'

She was so nasty! 'You can't help being sad, I suppose.' I was trying to remember what my father had said. 'It's part of you, like . . . like breathing, but it's not fair. You're always smacking me. I don't even know why I get smacked sometimes.'

But she had latched on to my earlier words, was ignoring my plea for clemency. 'Who says I can't help it? That's not something you made up, Laura. Who has been discussing me?' A hand pushed itself through her hair, made it untidy and quite interesting for a change. 'You will answer me.'

I was too young to plead the fifth amendment, too afraid of her to answer with a 'mind your own business'. 'I can't remember.' My brain slipped desperately into top gear. 'Oh yes, it was at school. Sister Ignatius went on about unhappy people making other people unhappy. It's selfish, she said. But sometimes they can't help it.'

Mother's dander was up. 'Have you been sitting in those stupid catechism and Latin lessons? Have you?'

'No. I sit under St Anthony next to Norma Wallace. She's under St Joan and a big bonfire. And she snerches all

123

the time, never has a hanky.' Yes, I would distract Mother. 'It's Norma who snerches, not St Joan. Her nose is red because she has to wipe it on toilet paper. She should go to the doctor's and get seen to. We could all catch her colds. I could catch one and bring it home, then we'd all be snerching all the time—'

'"Snerch" is a vulgar word. When did you get this lecture from Sister Ignatius?'

'During history. She said that greedy and unhappy people start wars. If people would be . . .' I groped for the word. 'If they'd be satisfied with what they had, there'd be no misery and no wars.'

'How nice.' She was sneering again. 'I suppose they can't keep that religion out of anything, can they? I do my best, try to stop you becoming indoctrinated, so they let it spill over into history. Don't listen to them when they start being pious.'

Pious. What did that mean? I supposed that it referred to nothing simple. 'That's the Pope's name. He's number twelve,' I remarked, my tone helpful. One way or another, I had to guide the direction of her mind, send her off course. She must not find out about Dad talking to me.

'Who is the Pope?' she asked.

'Head of the Church.' My reply was immediate and automatic.

'Head of which church?' She lit a cigarette, blew a plume right up into the air where it curled and twisted round the shaded light. 'Of which church, Laura?'

'Well.' I tried to keep my face blank, but could not help hoping that my answer might engender a change of school. What did they say in the playground? 'He's in Rome with cardinals and he's the head of the . . .' Ooh, I wished with every fibre that my mind would catch up soon. 'Of the one true faith.' Good. With any luck, that would do it.

'And who is the King, Laura?'

Oh dear. 'Dad was only joking. It's not King George he's going to see, its the patent.'

She stamped a foot. 'Stop being clever. The King is

124

head of the Church of England. Catholics were cruel, they burned people and tortured them. The King had to stop the Catholics being in charge, because they were killing everyone who didn't agree with them.'

Ah. Sister Ignatius was useful after all. 'Henry the Eighth,' I announced innocently. 'He was fat with sores on his legs and he wore knickers and he cut the queen's head off. So after that, he told the Pope that England wasn't Catholic any more. Sister Ignatius said that the Church of England was made so that Henry the Eighth could have a lot of wives.'

'Preposterous!' I had never before known Mother to throw away a half-smoked cigarette. 'You will leave that school at once. I believed that I was doing the right thing by enrolling you at a kindergarten where proper subjects are taught from the start. But what use are history and geography if the teachers are filling your head with propaganda?'

I didn't care what my head was full of as long as I could get away from St Mary's. 'They hid in cupboards,' I said, anxious to strengthen my position. 'The priests had to go behind bookshelves and stuff so that the soldiers wouldn't find them. Some of them starved away to skellingtons. Kings are wicked and popes are good.' I was breathless, overcome by my new power.

'Skeletons, Laura, skeletons.' She wrung her hands. 'This is awful.' In my mother's book, there were rich people, poor people and Catholic people. The latter category was the lowest, as Catholics usually had a lot of children. I didn't know the reason behind Mother's philosophy, because I thought that big families were wonderful, but for once, I was glad of her prejudices. 'You will transfer immediately to another private school.'

'But—'

'Enough!' She sank into a chair. 'You are not going to have your way, Laura McNally.'

I sorted through my scrambled list of priorities. I wanted to go to school with Anne, but that wasn't going to be allowed. If I had to go to a private school, then I preferred to stay where I was. Although I was only five, I clung to the devil I knew, was not happy about transferring and starting again. And it was no use trying to be clever, I told myself. She would win in the end, even if she had to knock my head against a wall to achieve her victory. Still, I must try, I must do my best . . . 'It's so funny, isn't it?' I asked mildly. 'When they're talking, those nuns, I have to be good and pretend to be on their side. But I know they're just papists like you said before. And we're up to our five-times tables now. They teach very fast, don't they? We are all in front of Anne's class – they haven't even heard of times tables.' For a child who struggled to keep up in class, I was doing a grand job, I thought. Perhaps I might turn out nearly clever after all.

She was eyeing me with mistrust, but she held her tongue.

'It would be a shame if we had to buy another set of uniform. They all have different uniforms. If I went to Brook Lane, I wouldn't need any more clothes and—'

'You are not going to Brook Lane.'

'Then I'll need all new things.'

She began to think aloud. 'And there might be no places. Yes, we could well be in trouble if you leave now. I shall ignore all this for the moment, but we shall think again at the end of the year.'

I sighed with relief. Even Norma Wallace was a part of my life. I didn't like her, but I always knew what to expect.

'You will take no notice of the sisters' opinions,' said Mother. 'Just learn your history – all the dates and battles – but never mind the rest of it.'

There was no way of besting her. I washed, went into my room, crawled beneath the covers. Anne banged on the wall, but I ignored her. This was a special kind of misery, the sort that does not improve with an airing. My parents hated one another, stayed together because of me. Dad might have been happier elsewhere, but I was making him stay, making him miserable. And Mother was getting worse, more fidgety, more fractious. But I counted my blessings, because I hadn't been beaten that day, hadn't lost any hair.

Dad went to London. During his absence, I watched my mother like a hawk. At first, I didn't know what I was looking for. But after a while, things changed, she changed, and I realized that I had expected some alterations, had been waiting for them. She took to leaving the key in the shed, wrote messages on smelly pink paper on the dining table. 'Laura, your meal is in the pantry. If the coalman comes, the money is under the tablecloth in the sideboard drawer.'

When she came in, she failed to say anything about where she had been. But she was giggly and silly, smelled of sherry, smoke, make-up. Sometimes, she would pick out a tune on the piano, sing quietly to herself, songs like 'We'll Meet Again'. I became used to caring for myself, learned to make toast by the fire, brewed coffee from the Camp bottle, even tried custard, but it came out too thin.

Then one night, I was disturbed by a lot of whispering and laughter. From my slightly open door, I watched her coming up the stairs. She stumbled, swore, righted herself, toppled over again. I thought that she had three hands, then I saw a strange man reaching out to help her, guiding the faltering steps. He was tall and bald, with a silly moustache all thin and oily at the ends.

I came out onto the landing. 'Mother?'

Her eyes were glazed. 'Is that you, Laura?'

'Yes.' Who was she expecting? 'Are you ill, Mother?'

The man guffawed. 'She's in the grip of the grape, little girl.'

She was in his grip – his large hands almost circled the tiny waist. I didn't like him. His eyes were not quite straight, as if they had been put into his head on a day when God was all fingers and thumbs. 'Why are you here?' I asked him.

'Well, she'd never have got herself home, would she?

Could have been run over by a tram. Found her in the Wheatsheaf. Landlord asked me to fetch her home.'

My mother had been in a pub. I could not believe that my mother had been in the Wheatsheaf, especially after what she'd always said about women in pubs. 'Why were you there?' I asked.

She belched, grinned. 'Wouldn't you like to know?' An unsteady finger waved itself in front of my face. 'Miss Clever-Clogs, aren't you? Tommy?'

'Aye?' The man paused, took his hands from mother's waist and heaved himself onto the landing. 'What's up, lass?' he enquired of Mother.

'Take me to my room.'

'Right-o.'

I pointed, sent him in the right direction, crept back to bed. She screamed a couple of times but I stayed where I was. After what seemed like an age, Tommy clomped downstairs and slammed the front door. The oilcloth was cold against my toes as I made for the landing. She was sobbing, moaning to herself. Through a gap in the door, I watched as she fell about the room, the lovely dress torn from her body. 'Men,' she spat over and over. 'They don't do it at all, or they attack. Attack,' she repeated. 'I have been attacked.' She vomited then, heaved her stomach's contents onto the floor.

I ran towards her, tried to help her to the bathroom. For my pains, I received a hefty swipe across the ear. 'Keep away,' she screamed. 'A lot of this is your fault. You just sit there, little daddy's girl, no time for me. I've got nothing and nobody, nothing, nobody—' Her self-pity was cut off by another bout of vomiting.

I backed away, scuttered across the landing and into my own bedroom. She didn't want me and I didn't want her.

It was to be years before I understood that my mother was raped in her bedroom that night. Nothing came of it. She had been out looking for excitement, had found the wrong kind. No policeman came and, as far as I know, my father was never told of the incident.

After this occasion, I was filled with more uncertainty and revulsion than I had ever known. There were people I had heard of, drunks, layabouts and thieves – the sort who got their names in the *Bolton Evening News*. My mother was like two different women then. She was a posh lady some of the time, a wandering streetperson at others.

Dad came back and life returned to normal. Except that some of the zest had gone out of the beatings. Perhaps a few grey cells had been uncorrupted by booze that night. Perhaps she worried that I might remember her behaviour and report on it. The cruelty continued for many years, but the earlier intensity had been diluted.

As I grew up, as I began to understand my parents, I never once felt safe or secure. I have heard it said that a bad mother is better than no mother at all. That is a gross untruth. A bad mother is an affliction, a chronic disease that distorts your thinking to the end of your life.

And I still had a long way to go.

Chapter Three

As I had to be almost good at home, school was the place where I let down my hair. I also let down my family, though Mother and Dad were not aware of that fact for quite some time.

My early stabs at rebellion were not severe enough to warrant parental intervention, but I did become naughty, almost wilful in some instances. Many of the nuns were old, severe, used to handling fractious little girls. Yet among their number were one or two young ones, newly qualified as teachers, with the bloom of Ireland still glowing on their cheeks, the bright light of vocation shining its powerful torch in their eyes.

One such was Sister Maria Goretti. She became our form teacher, replaced Sister Ignatius who was returning to the Mother House for rest and recuperation after a bout of rheumatism. Maria Goretti floated into our classroom on a cloud of lavender water, hope and charity. She told us her name, then asked us all some questions about ourselves. She called this a 'getting to know you' session.

My turn came. 'My name's Laura McNally,' I answered sweetly.

'And what is your favourite lesson, Laura?'

I looked at her, wondered what to say. History was good, especially when old Ignatius got worked up about wars and persecutions. Sums were all right, spelling was easy. 'Religion,' I said. 'That's the best subject.'

Her eyes burned with renewed intensity. 'It is so wonderful to meet a child who takes an interest in the most important of all our lessons, girls. When I was a small girl in Ireland, I knew straight away that I would take the veil, for I loved our religious classes. Do you know your catechism, Laura?'

I smiled, tried to simper. Other girls were beginning to giggle and snort behind hands and handkerchiefs, because they knew that Norma Wallace and I spent forty minutes each morning in a corridor with a lot of dead people. 'I'm not sure, Sister Maria Confetti.'

The 'Confetti' was a genuine mistake, but it added greatly to the air of tense delight that was beginning to pervade the room. 'Maria Goretti,' she corrected gently. 'I have been allowed to keep my baptismal name, you see.'

I didn't know what she was on about, but I nodded in a way I imagined to be sage.

'Maria Goretti was a little Italian girl who was a virgin martyr.'

They were hot on martyrs, were the Catholics. I had been wont to call them 'tomatoes' till one of the sisters had put me straight with a lecture and two playtime detentions.

The nun was warming to her subject. 'Maria Goretti died when she was twelve, was murdered while defending her purity. One day, she will become a saint.'

I rallied, waded in. 'Was she pretty?'

Two gentle eyes smiled down on me. 'Yes, she was pretty.'

Well, that would be a bit of a change in the corridor, then. If we got a nice-looking saint in a frame, life might improve minimally for those condemned to 'sit out' during religious lessons.

'So I was baptized Maria Goretti in memory of that wonderful child,' she continued, 'and I have been fortunate enough to keep the name within our sisterhood. So remember Goretti, child.'

'Sorry, Sister,' I said. The girl next to me, who was already six and ought to have known better, was doubled over with the pain of trying not to laugh, so I kicked her under the desk, though the smile of innocence never left my face. At last, I had found a victim, someone more vulnerable than I was. Confetti had the face of an angel, was plainly unused to the carryings-on of sophisticated English infants. Years later, whenever I pondered about poor Confetti, I came to the conclusion that bullies are the bullied who are simply passing on the pain. As my mother's victim, I chose my target and homed in on it. And even then, as I teetered on the edge of my sixth birthday, I was filled with guilt and shame. My tormenting of Sister Maria Goretti was short-lived, so perhaps I did have a heart after all.

The nun adjusted her veil, fiddled with the huge rope of beads that dangled from her waist. 'Who made you, Laura?'

Ah. I knew that one from the playground. Mary Pickavance had taught me the first two or three in exchange for a halfpenny Spanish and a back-to-front ladybird in a matchbox. Back-to-front ladybirds – the few that were black with red spots – were valuable currency at the Convent of St Mary. 'God made me,' I replied triumphantly.

'And why did God make you, Laura?'

I inhaled in preparation for this longer answer. 'God made me to know Him, love Him and serve Him in this world and to be happy with Him for ever in the next.'

Mary Pickavance could contain herself no longer. Although I kicked her again, she held up her hand and jiggled it in that annoying way that says, 'Teacher, I'm great and important.' St Mary's was packed to the rafters with great and important little egos.

'Yes, dear?' asked Confetti.

'Sister, she's not a Catholic. She doesn't come in for religious lessons.'

Confetti blinked, put her head on one side. The class groaned its displeasure, as its members had been waiting to see where it would all end. If Sister had got as far as question four, life might have become really interesting. 'My poor child,' said Confetti soberly. 'The faith is in you. And one day, you will be welcomed into the arms of God's family.'

'Yes, Sister.'

I sat down, belted Mary Pickavance with my ruler, bit my lip against the agony when she stabbed me with the very sharp point of her pencil.

The next day, I brought a bunch of flowers to our lovely form tutor. She made a fuss of me, put the blooms in a vase, sent me to the cloakroom with the pitcher. I watched as she poured in the water, marvelled that a nun, who would probably become a saint in time, was putting stolen flowers on her desk.

Norma Wallace, the class sneak and snercher, lifted her hand. There was so much righteousness behind the movement that her arm trembled under the weight of so much stiffness and indignation. 'Sister?'

'Yes, Norma?'

The girl's tongue pressed itself against a couple of remaining incisors as she performed one of her noisier inhalations. 'She pinched them. Off a few gardens on the road. There was an old man trying to chase her, but she ran too fast.'

The silence was deafening. It was broken only by the sound of a huge, collective sigh, then by the rattle of Norma Wallace's laboured breathing. Sister shook her head and her eyes were huge pools of misery. 'Did you steal the flowers, Laura?'

I scratched the side of my nose. 'I picked them.'

'Where did you pick them?'

'Out of the floor.'

'The ground, Laura.'

'Yes.'

She approached me and I backed away. Confetti might have been slow in some ways, but I'd seen enough Irish tempers running riot at St Mary's, was aware that many colleens are born with too many words, hard hands and far-seeing minds. Some nuns knew what you'd done simply by looking at you. 'Laura?' She sounded so wounded, so beautifully sad.

I swallowed, stopped moving away, wedged my back

against the edge of a desk. 'They were just growing and they were pretty. You hadn't got any flowers on your desk.'

'I don't need flowers. I need good girls.'

'Yes, Sister.'

'And what must we do now, Laura?'

I shrugged. I didn't know what Confetti must do, but I would surely separate Norma Wallace from her chronic catarrh at the first opportunity. 'Not sure,' I mumbled.

They were all enjoying it. A drama of this nature took the pressure off them, relieved five-, six- and seven-year-old minds from the torture of chattering in French when they hardly knew English, from chanting lists of battles and prime ministers and capital cities. Such distracting little performances were a regular occurrence, their theme varying from holes in paper caused by assiduous erasers to Someone Who Did Not Know The Ten Commandments. Not knowing the commandments was a bit like treason, a crime for which no excuse sufficed. However, theme and plot were unimportant – entertainment value was what counted. Twenty-odd rapt faces watched Sister and me taking centre-stage. Short of applause and encores, we could not have been nearer to stardom.

'We must take them back, Laura. I shall get Sister St Thomas to sit with the class. You and I will go directly to the old man's house and you can explain your lack of manners, Laura.' She paused, wrung her hands for a few seconds. 'It is perhaps as well that you are ignorant, child, because a Catholic girl would know that absolution can only be granted when full restitution of property has been achieved.'

This was another load of mumbo-jumbo, nearly as bad as the '*Bonjour, ma Soeur*' that was required each morning. And exercise books were suddenly *cahiers* or *livres*, and a proper book was whatever an exercise book wasn't, and we sat on *chaises* and *ouvred portes* and now she was on about restitution of what?

She must have noticed my blank expression. 'To be

forgiven in confession, a sinner must return stolen things, Laura.'

'Oh.' I thought about it. 'What if you can't? Like if the man isn't in?'

'We wait for him.'

'Right.' I glanced at the wilting blooms, wondered whether they were worth all the *angst*. 'What if he's gone till tomorrow?'

'Then we return tomorrow.'

My imagination was heating up, oiling itself for further hypothesis. 'What if he's gone on holiday? Or to London to see the King or the patent?' After a suitable pause, I added, 'What if he's dead? Old people fall over dead sometimes. My Auntie Maisie told me about their next-door neighbour in Florence Street – he died on the outside toilet and my grandad – he was Auntie Maisie's dad and my mother's dad – he had to go in and—'

'Yes.' Confetti was suddenly as colourful as the mis-nomer with which I had endowed her, several shades of pink and off-white, with glorious violet eyes that grew wider by the minute. 'If we cannot repay directly, then we contribute to the poor box.'

I thrust my hand under the gymslip skirt, heaved two pennies from my knickers pocket. 'There you are, Sister. For the poor box.'

She shook a hand, would not take the money. 'No. You must go back with these flowers, Laura. I will accompany you. There can be no forgiveness unless you visit the old man.'

'Sister?' I eyed her cautiously.

'Yes, child?'

'I don't have to do the resti . . . restichewing . . .'

'Restitution, Laura.'

'Yes, well, I'm not a Catholic, so I don't go to confession. My mother hates papists.' At last, I had found a use for Mother. 'She says confession's just so that you can go out and do the same things all over again. Like Catholics say they're sorry, only they're not. Mother says

135

if they're not drinking, they're stealing and if they're not stealing, they're . . . breeding. What's breeding?' This was a fair enough question, as I thought 'breeding' must be something to do with having a fight, because Catholics were supposed to go in for that sort of thing, fighting and shouting.

Confetti's face could have used a frame at this point. Although she wasn't ugly, she looked dead, sort of strangled. 'Laura?' she gasped eventually.

'Yes, Sister?'

'Confession is about being sorry, about asking God to give strength against sin.'

I looked straight at her. 'So my mother is telling lies?'

Oh God, the poor woman would have been happier in a den of lions at that moment. 'Not . . . er . . . not quite, Laura. Your mother is simply mistaken. Now, we shall go down the road and find the garden from which you took the flowers.'

The man was waiting for us. He had gathered around him a clan of supporters, men in flat caps, women in aprons and slippers. As we approached the group, I felt Sister's hand tighten in mine. She was scared to death, and so was I.

The offended party separated himself from the gaggle. 'Is it thee?' he asked.

'Yes,' I said. Well, no matter who I was, the answer had to be right.

'I've took prizes fer my dahlias in t' past,' he announced. 'And along comes this one, nobbut a kid, and takes t' bloody 'eads off me good blooms.'

'Nay,' said a bystander. 'They're moth-ate this year, Nat. Sithee.' He snatched the tattered bouquet from Confetti's hand. 'No colour in 'em. You'd not 'ave got far wi' these.'

Nat squared up to the main speaker. 'Listen, Ernie Grimshaw,' he spluttered through teeth that bobbed up and down a lot. 'Get thissen 'ome an' shut thy gob about other folks' gardens. Tha wouldn't know a cabbage from a rhodo-bloody-dendron.'

Ernie Grimshaw went purple. 'That lass did thee a good turn when she lopped yon dahlias. They're weak an' weedy, just like thee.'

The women giggled and shuffled off in their slippers, then the men broke ranks and wandered in various directions away from the house. Nat grabbed the stolen flowers from Ernie Grimshaw, pushed the man away, then dragged me and Confetti up the short path into his house. In the narrow hallway, we all breathed again.

'Lass,' he said to me after a second or two. 'Get thissen in t' front room and peep through t' curtains, see 'as 'e gone, nosey owld bugger.' As I went on my secret mission, he spoke to Sister. 'Cum in, love. I'll just put t' kettle on an mek a brew.'

I found them in the kitchen, he bustling about with a tea caddy and some cups, she sitting demurely at the table. 'He's gone,' I said. 'And I'm sorry about your flowers, Mr . . .'

'Evans, love. Me father were a Welsh farmer. I'm Nathaniel Jacob Evans and God alone knows what I ever did fer t' deserve a moniker like that. Dust tha like sugar, Sister?'

'Well, I do.'

He nodded. 'Thought so. Are you a country girl?'

'I am.'

He settled down across from her and began to talk to her as if she were a real person with legs, not a nun who floated about in a long black frock. 'Dust tha like England, then?'

'Well, I do and I don't. Noisy, but very nice people.' She looked at the clock. 'Good heavens—'

His loud laughter was infectious. 'That's me, Sister. Good Evans.' We all giggled at the feeble joke and Sister went bright pink. 'I never thought,' she gasped. 'But we must go.'

''Ang on a mo.' He beckoned me with a bony finger,

drew me towards a large box in the corner. 'You done me a turn, lass, 'cos me flowers was rubbish – I'd never 'ave won t' wooden spoon wi' that load o' weeds. So I'll show thee this, 'cos tha's a fine grand lass.' He drew back an old grey blanket to reveal a squirming mass of fur. 'Kittens,' he said unnecessarily. 'Their mam's gone fer a walk. Nobbut five days old, they are.'

My heart was won in that moment. I felt as if love came to me first of all through my fingers, flooded into my whole body as I touched the tiny creatures. Some part of me wanted to cry, but it was nothing to do with sadness. There was just me and the kittens, everything else disappeared. 'Kitty,' I whispered to the nearest one. 'So pretty, little kitty.'

Somebody said, 'Poetry' – probably Mr Evans. A hand touched my shoulder and drew me back into the other world. 'Come, Laura.'

'Sister . . .'

'Yes.'

'Look at these kittens, please.'

Her face went all soft as she bent over the box. 'Laura,' she whispered. 'Just look at the beauty in there and you will know God. All that fur, those lovely faces. Wouldn't it take a great architect to design such perfection?'

I knew what she meant. 'Mr Evans?' I pleaded. 'Can I come again? I'll . . .' I looked round frantically for something I might do. 'I'll clean up, do the dusting and fetch coal.'

He placed a hand on my head, and I thought how lovely it would have been if I'd known my grandparents. There's something wonderful about old people, as if they know all our sins and forgive us anyway. 'Any time, luv. The owld place misses a bit o' spit an' polish since Elsie died. She were a good 'un, my missus, but she were fierce wi' a duster. Would you 'appen like one o' these 'ere cats?'

My heart did a little dance, but the music lasted just a few bars. 'My mother doesn't like animals.'

Sister drew me towards the door. 'Ask her this evening, child. Every girl should have a pet, a bit of responsibility. Goodbye, Mr Evans. I shall call again with another sister. We might do some shopping for you when you're in need? Will that be of use to you?'

He followed us to the door. 'I'm not a Roman, luv,' he said to Sister Maria Goretti.

She beamed at him. 'Mr Evans, we do not confine friendship to those who practise our faith. It's not about them and us, you know. We're all in the one mess together, and we must take each other's arms for guidance.'

I loved the woman from that moment. I still tortured her, still came out with remarks that stained her fair cheeks to beetroot. But there was an empathy between us. On our way back to school, she straightened my hair, redid my school tie and dug in one of her many pockets for an inch of barley sugar. 'Don't steal again, Laura McNally,' she chided gently.

'I won't.'

We stood at the wrought iron gates and grinned at each other. 'No,' she said. 'But you'll torment the life out of me all the same. Ah well, such is the will of God. If you are one of my crosses, then I shall bear you gladly.'

I wanted to tell her there and then that I loved her, but I hadn't the words for how I felt. We walked into the classroom, endured Sister St Thomas's gimlet stare, carried on with arithmetic in the same old way. But Confetti looked at me sometimes and smiled a secret smile. In a way, I had found my real mother.

By the time we reached the grand age of eight, Anne and I had developed sufficient independence to meet each other on the sly. I was still forbidden to go next door, and my mother continued the silent feud. But I learned how to create happy accidents, became used to Auntie Maisie's timetable. At weekends, I would manage to be near the shops she patronized, would turn up at the butcher's, the grocer's, the tripe shop. And I always got a hug and a kind word, which was a great deal more than I received at home.

Anne and I took to loitering after leaving our separate schools. We had a favourite wall, and we would sit on it for ten or fifteen minutes to discuss matters of great importance. 'I learned a new word,' pronounced Anne one afternoon. She whispered it in my ear, her heated breath stroking my cheek. 'It's very rude,' she added as she backed away, the skin on her cheeks stained bright with excitement. 'Of course, you won't hear stuff like that at St Mary's. Everybody's too posh there to know about these interesting things.'

I shrugged, would not be outdone. 'It's to do with babies,' I said confidently. 'How they get inside their mothers. And what you said is just another word for kissing. Kissing makes babies, then the babies grow in women's stomachs.'

She kicked her heels against the wall on which we were perched. Anne's shoes were always badly scuffed. She was lucky, never got smacked for a torn dress, for ribbons lost on the way home. 'How do the babies get out?' she asked.

'Belly button.' I was more than confident, as the truth had been told during recreation by a girl called Rita Turner whose parents were of a medical persuasion. 'It's like letting the air out of a big balloon, only you get a baby instead of air. The nurse undoes the knot and a baby pops out.'

Anne thought about this for a few moments. You could always tell when Anne was thinking, because she frowned deeply and chewed her lower lip. Her mouth was often sore and chapped in winter because of all the meditation. 'So if my dad had kissed your mother when she wanted him to kiss her, then she would have had a baby.'

'Yes.' This was becoming rather intricate, but I wasn't one to let go and admit defeat, was stubborn enough to stand my ground, even when the foundation was made of quicksand. I was the one with the superior education, so I had all the answers to life's many questions. In a way, I was like my mother – never more 'right' than when I was completely wrong.

'But, Laura – why hasn't my mum had a lot of babies? 'Cos my dad's always kissing her. Sometimes, she even starts the kissing, so I should have some brothers and sisters. Well, sisters.' Anne and I disliked boys, could not entertain the concept of brothers. 'And my dad kisses me too. Why haven't I got a baby?'

I clicked my tongue and adopted a haughty stance. 'For goodness sake, Anne, you're too young. Anyway, dads don't kiss children on the lips. It has to be on the lips and with your mouth open a bit so that the baby can crawl down into your stomach. It is very small, too small to see.' After what I considered to be a visionary and very conclusive statement, I sat back and basked in the warmth of my own glory.

But the trouble with Anne was that she was persistent. 'They are always kissing,' she repeated stolidly. 'And there's no babies. I asked them about it and they said they weren't going to have any more children.'

I scratched my nose – just as I always did when flummoxed. 'Perhaps they only want you. Children are very expensive, you know.' My mother went on constantly about how much I cost to feed and clothe. 'So if they only want you, they don't do the magic spell first.'

'Eh?' Anne, a practical soul, did not go a bundle on sorcery. 'What spell?' She fixed me with a hard stare, pulled at the sleeve of my hideous navy blue uniform gaberdine. 'There's no such thing as a spell except in stories.'

My imagination ploughed another furrow from the depths of which I would be lucky to climb. I puffed out my chest and looked at her with disdain. 'Rita's dad is a doctor and her mother is a midwife, so Rita knows all about the special things that happen to grown-ups.' Thus I gave birth to another piece of McNally wisdom. It hung in the air for a few seconds before my cousin pounced on it. 'Sometimes, you are so daft, Laura.' She paused for a second or two. 'Go on, then.' The tone was challenging. 'Tell me.'

'Well . . .' I looked quickly over my shoulder into the garden behind us, wore the air of a secret agent in the midst of some world-altering intrigue. 'Listen, Anne. Never turn round three times on the spot before you kiss a boy.'

She made a loud vomiting sound. 'I don't kiss boys. They smell of dirt and Derbac soap and you never know whether they've got a spider or a worm in their lunchbox. There's always worms at our school and frogs and beetles and caterpillars.'

I liked the sound of her school. All we got in our St Mary's dining-room was an overcooked dinner with watery vegetables and grace before meals, grace after meals, lectures all through meals. We couldn't even talk at the table, let alone compare our back-to-front ladybirds. During lunch, we were supposed to be 'ladies' while the Mother of the convent read out stories about Jesus and Noah and some poor fellow whose head finished up on a plate. John the Baptist put most of us off our treacle sponge, while Jonah's brief residence in the belly of a whale was hardly designed to improve the appetite.

The nuns were always harping on about gratitude. We were to be grateful for our school, for our parents, for the smelly cabbage on our plates. We were to be grateful for our teachers, for the weather, for the fact that we weren't starving like some black babies in Africa. We all adopted one of these babies for five shillings and were allowed to choose a name. My baby was called Maureen and she sat next to my beaker all through lunch. We had to look at our babies and pray for them and hope that they all had a nice plateful of smelly cabbage and tough meat.

Each girl had what the sisters called a serviette, and though this item was provided to protect clothing, any spot of gravy or sago pudding had to be washed out immediately by the offending pupil. Before the meal, our hands were examined. After the meal, both sides of our serviettes were scrutinized. 'I wish I could come to your school,' I groaned.

She laughed. 'Your mother would go mad if she knew we were meeting on the way home.'

She would have gone madder still had she discovered that I owned one of Mr Evans's cats, a little grey one called Solomon, and that Solomon was in residence with Anne and Uncle Freddie and Auntie Maisie. Anne was very fair about my cat. She never called him hers, tried not to get close to him. Anne was and is the most equitable person I have ever known. I attempted a careless shrug. 'Bugger her. She's never in when I get home. I have to get the key from the shed and let myself in.'

Anne stopped laughing. 'She'll be out with one of her boyfriends,' she whispered. 'I heard my mam saying something about it. She said Liza's never happy unless someone's crawling all over her and calling her beautiful.'

I stared blankly across the road. My dad was terribly busy, had sunk every halfpenny of profit from the shop into his new venture. Mother was buying lots of dresses and costumes, had three pairs of high-heeled shoes. And she no longer worked, so she was spending Dad's money instead of her own. We couldn't afford any of it. 'She's always dressed up,' I grumbled. 'And I'm learning to cook things because she can't.'

Anne placed a companionable hand on my chilled fingers. With all the wisdom of the mature eight-year-old, she comforted me by saying, 'The boyfriends will be paying for the new clothes, not your dad.'

'Oh.' What else could I have said?

'With any luck,' confided Anne. 'She'll take a fancy to one of them and buggar off to the other side of town. My dad says you and Uncle John would be better off without her, 'cos she's a disgrace.'

It isn't easy knowing that your mother is a disgrace. It

143

was becoming obvious that Liza McNally had moved on after her years of wartime patriotism, had lost that bevy of admiring sycophants who haunted our house once a fortnight during the conflict. She was out for some fun and she would bring trouble on my father's head, I felt that in my bones. For my own part, I was not concerned about Mother's behaviour. It suited me to have peace after school sometimes, while I actually enjoyed the culinary efforts I made for myself and for my father.

Anne leapt down from the wall. 'You go first. She might be in today, and we'd best not be seen together in case she's in a mood.'

I ran the rest of the distance home, sped past the house as usual, made for the shed where the spare key was kept. I unlocked the door, replaced the key under its plantpot in the shed, walked into the kitchen. 'No!' The scream pierced its way past the slightly open door to the dining-room.

'It is my business.' This was my father speaking. 'And I shall employ whomever I choose.'

It was a large kitchen, because Mother had hired a builder to extend it into the rear garden. The dining-room was also spacious, but I felt as if I were standing right next to my mother, since her voice was shrill with anger. 'The Co-op has no further use for him. They've able-bodied men now with strong legs and a bit of brainpower. He was bound to get the sack sooner or later. So you are taking pity on him, is that it? How will you cope with a cripple managing your stupid factory?'

Dad's voice was quieter, so I had to creep across the kitchen to hear his words properly. 'Of course, you would know all about the able-bodied demobbed men, wouldn't you? After all, you did ask me to give the job to one of your escorts.'

Even her breathing was noisy by this time, rattling through a short pause while she considered her response. 'David Moxton is my friend's husband and I simply—'

'Friend? How can Ada Moxton be your friend when you

are intimate with her husband? Liza, you are behaving like a whore. And when you're not behaving like a woman of the street, you come over all bountiful, handing out jobs like Maundy money. This is my concern, my factory, so I shall choose my workers with care.'

She lit a cigarette. I heard the match trembling on the rough edge of the box, heard the strike when it came, listened as she grabbed a deep breath of noxious courage. 'You never take me anywhere. Every single hour, you are with your customers, your inventions, your daughter. You have no time for me, so I go and—'

'I've time for Laura. If I had the opportunity, I'd spend every day with the child.' Though he kept his tone soft, I knew that my mother was wary, because she stopped her screeching each time he spoke.

'You never wanted her,' he continued. 'I married you because you said you were expecting my child. You lied then, and you have continued dishonest for evermore. When Laura was eventually on her way, you resented that little unborn baby, became ugly in your own eyes. I've watched you with my daughter, and you are an appalling mother. And now you are cavorting about like a cheap trollop. Have you any idea of how you look? It's like having a gangster's moll in the house. This whole town is laughing at you.'

My father was not one for long and meaningless conversations. He was economical with words, so I knew that he must have felt very strongly to talk so clearly, almost elaborately.

Mother was having trouble digesting the concept of being a laughing stock. 'I have not been a subject of ridicule,' she said loftily. 'Furthermore, I have not been unfaithful.'

'That is no concern of mine,' he replied. 'All I worry about is Laura. How will she react when she grows up to understand that her mother is a tart?'

'Nonsense.' Her rope was shortening – I could tell by the voice that she was nearing the end of her patience.

145

'Nonsense,' she snapped again. 'And no-one is laughing at me, John McNally. It's you they mock, you! What would they say if I told them about our sleeping arrangements? You're not a man, never were a man. Which man insists on separate beds because of his so-called insomnia? What sort of man never touches his wife?'

'The sort who would rather reach out to Satan.' The short pause that followed was punctuated by a gasp from her. 'I am the sort of man who has too much self-esteem to meddle with the unclean.' He stopped again, coughed, raised his tone slightly. 'Laura will be here in a moment. For her sake, this will stop now. You may, if you wish, remain under my roof for the sake of continuity, for Laura. She would be ridiculed if we separated, especially while she is with Catholics. I shall employ Freddie, because he is a trustworthy man, far too sensible for your gin-soaked advances. And you, my dear wife, have my permission to return to hell's flames and enjoy your-self.'

'You . . . you have a woman!' she cried. 'You are . . . having an affair, aren't you?'

'I will not dignify that question by awarding it an answer,' he said. 'Think what you like. I am here for Laura and only for her. And you are here to make things look right for our small-minded community. Keep your activities to the centre of town, will you? And try not to be recognized – you could perhaps try a disguise – sun-glasses?' Even I was able to identify the sarcasm in his words. 'I shall go upstairs now for a rest. You would exhaust the resources of a saint.'

I didn't know why, am ignorant to this day of the reason for my exit, but I dashed from the house, tore to the end of the avenue, fled down Chorley New Road until I was almost in town. When I reached the fire station, I was moving in a slightly more decorous fashion, though my ribs still ached with panting for breath.

On a whim, I crossed the road and walked down the brew towards Bolton's finest park, passing a little shop that sold delicious pasties and ice-creams. I was starving and I had no money. For a long time, I sat on a park bench and watched other children playing, saw them running to their mothers for comfort when they tumbled, for food when their bellies screamed for sustenance. These were proper mothers. Proper mothers took their children to the park, smiled at them while they played, sat down and talked to other proper mothers about the sort of things that proper mothers do with their families. My mother had never brought me to the park, not once. Uncle Freddie used to bring me with Anne, but he wasn't allowed to do that any more. Self-pity is an unattractive emotion, and I wallowed in it for just a short time. It was something I needed to work through, a path I had to walk until I reached a sunnier place.

I sniffed, felt sorry for myself, craved Auntie Maisie's fat arms round my shoulders, longed for her to have yet another row with my mother about taking me to the fair. Auntie Maisie loved the fair, took Anne to the rides and sideshows twice a year, bought her black peas with vinegar, toffee apples, candy floss, celluloid dolls on elastic, lumps of tooth-cracking treacle toffee, bags of hot salted nuts. And a present for me. Oh yes, there was always a present for poor Cousin Laura.

I was a deprived child, I suppose. Deprived of love and adventure, starved of maternal support, paternal guidance. My dad did what he could, but he was a man of ambition with just one life to live, one chance to leave a mark. I had everything. I had enough to eat, decent clothes in spite of shortages, a room of my own, books galore, music lessons, ballet and tap classes, a large garden.

I saw the poor children sometimes, watched them clodding along in iron-soled clogs, skimpy frocks or over-long trousers that had been bought to last. And I heard them singing, shouting, caught them tumbling about in fun, in anger. Outside the pubs, they would wait for their parents, sneak in occasionally, be dragged out by an irate father, an unsteady mother. After the customary clip round the ear, the urchins would flee with the pennies they had culled from elders whose senses were numbed by alcohol. Then they would sit outside a nearby mill, huddled over a meshed vent where warm air escaped, and they would pounce on their two penn'orth of greasy chips, would taste their parents' guilt, repentance, love. I envied them.

One of the park keepers approached me. 'Are t' alreet, lass? Where's tha muther?'

'At home.'

'Oh.' He stroked his shadowy face and I could hear the sandpaper roughness of newgrown stubble. 'Dun't she fret while tha's in t' park on tha own?'

'I don't know.'

He squatted, poked his kind and rugged face towards me. 'There's funny folk about,' he said. 'Tha mun't 'ang round 'ere when t' day's growin' dim. Nobbut last week, a lass got took out of a park down Manchester way. Sithee.' He drew a large twist of barley sugar from his top pocket, handed it to me with great solemnity. 'Tha mun tek this from me, then tha mun never tek nowt from no bugger. Dust tha understand?'

I nodded. His face had gone strange, was distorted by my own unshed tears. 'You are very kind,' I said.

'Ay, and tha'rt a lady. I can tell a lady, tha knows. And there's other folk that's not so kind, lass. There's them that'll 'urt thee if they catch thee. Wilt tha mind my words?'

'I will.' And I did. I only saw that man once, yet he taught me more about self-preservation than I had learned from my parents in eight long years. He reminded me of Mr Evans, whom I visited regularly. Both were good men, old men with hearts of gold.

After that day in the park, I looked after myself, indulged less frequently in bouts of self-pity. Life was what I made of it, and I tried to make the best. We do grow up in jerks, I think. We start the process towards maturity at school, then little incidents jog us closer to adulthood. After my encounter with a generous soul who really cared about children, I became my own guardian.

Chapter Four

Norma Wallace looked as miserable as sin, or as miserable as the markedly unsinful saints who jostled for space on the walls above our heads. I messed about with my jotter, struggled to decipher a few notes about adjectives and adverbs, tried to sort out in my mind which were which. 'Norma?'

She looked up, the pale eyes red-rimmed and sore. 'What?'

'Does an adverb usually end in "-ly"?' Our teachers were keen on grammar, taught us to decline and parse at an age that now seems ludicrously young.

'Yes.'

'So it says how something was done, like quickly or slowly?'

'Yes.'

I pencilled in some crude corrections. 'Have you lost your pass?'

She sniffed loudly, blinked several times. 'Not yet. She doesn't want me any more, though. She says I'll be giving germs to the babies. I like babies. Even when they're wet and dirty, I like them. But I can't go any more. I suppose I'll have to hand my ticket in to one of the sisters.'

The ticket was a rectangle of yellow cardboard, and its value was beyond pearls in our school. If we were good – or, as in my case, if we were astute enough not to get caught being bad – we were granted a Special Permission Pass. These were so rare and so coveted, that they merited capital initials even in speech. I had a pass. My pass had been granted by Sister Maria Goretti so that I could go out of school at lunchtimes to help Mr Evans with his chores.

Special Permission Pass girls ate their meal early, were released from the dining-room by 12.15 to go out and work in the community. So as well as a degree of freedom from supervision, the chosen few also escaped formal grace and stories about Lazarus and lepers.

'I thought she liked me, the babies' mother.'

I suddenly felt sorry for the ugly little girl. We all mocked her because she looked unusual, and because of her permanent drip. A girl in the top class even brought a washer to school one morning, threw it across the playground and advised Norma to get a plumber to fit it. Now she had been dismissed by a local housewife for being a health hazard. It was an awful shame. 'Come with me to Mr Evans's,' I said, immediately regretting my impulsive behaviour. 'We're supposed to go in twos anyway. Margaret Fishwick was coming with me, but she's found an old woman with a dog that wants walking.' I have always been one of those stupid people who regret their haste, then compound the stupidity by being over-effusive. 'It's up to you,' I added lamely.

'You don't want me. Not really.'

She was right. Having Norma Wallace nearby was like sharing a meal with a noisy eater. The sound of her sniffing and snerching was so infuriating that I had to stop myself from screaming out loud. But it was still a pity. She had a permanent cold, summer and winter, was blessed with uneven features, teeth that had started to grow in crooked, and eyes that were pale enough to be almost invisible in the pasty white face. 'Norma, you can come if you want to.'

The pallid eyes were searching my face. 'I might do. I might come tomorrow. Today, I'm having extra maths.' It was a well-known fact that Norma's prowess in maths was almost of School Certificate standard. At eight years of age, she was delving into algebra, geometry, logarithms. The rest of us, the Philistines, continued to struggle with twelve-times tables and the odd bit of long division.

I scrutinized my messy English prep. 'So an adjective describes a thing, not a happening?'

'Yes.' She sounded impatient. 'Just listen to the words, Laura. A verb's a doing word, so it stands to sense that an adverb qualifies it, relates to it.' She was like something from another planet. 'Learn it,' she said quickly. 'It will help when you come to clauses. I'm doing clauses at home.'

I stared at her. Clauses? Whatever next?

She sighed, and the outflow of air rattled in her clogged throat. 'A clause is a group of words containing a verb and it makes sense but not complete sense—'

'Never mind,' I said. 'We all know you're a clever-clogs.'

The hurt look was back. 'See? I don't mean to be clever, Laura. It's more that I want to help people, want to tell them what I've been learning. It's so exciting, you see. Words, numbers – they are so . . . so great.' Her face had come to life, was colouring along the cheekbones. I caught a brief glimpse of what she meant, could feel the joy as it poured from her. And in those seconds, she looked almost pretty – no. That would be going too far. She looked normal for a while, alive and kicking. 'But I did want to help with the babies, Laura. The mother said I was unhealthy, too chesty to go near her twins. Still, never mind.' She straightened her shoulders. 'I can always read instead.'

'You really love school, don't you?'

She nodded. 'Books. I like books and solving problems and learning lists. It's like being hungry or very greedy, I just can't get full.'

She was a brilliant girl, too honest to hide her difference from the rest of us. She could have played the game, might have acted up in class, pretended to be as silly and childish as the rest of us. But she ploughed a lonely furrow, and my heart went out to her. 'Norma? Come if you want to. I mean it, honest. See, he's nice, Mr Evans. He's got a load of cats that he couldn't get rid of. Sister Maria Goretti took them to a vet so they couldn't have more kittens. Mr Evans has a terrible name – Nathaniel Jacob, I think it is. So he says if he has to have a wicked name, then his cats can suffer too. There's Bathsheba and Cleopatra – they're the girls – then Jeremiah, Ezekiel and Henry.' I could see that the Henry had confused her. 'Henry's blind. Mr Evans said he didn't want to burden Henry with a terrible name.'

'How awful.' Her forehead was creased into deep frown lines. 'That poor cat. Yes, I'll come with you tomorrow, Laura.' She glanced at her book, looked up again. 'How does the blind cat manage?'

'Oh, he's all right. Animals are better than people when it comes to things like that. He soon got used to going blind.' I loved Henry. He was the prettiest of all the cats, prettier than my little grey Solomon who lived next door with Anne. Henry was black, fat and sleek. He had the longest whiskers in the world, and he could sniff out a sardine from miles away.

After my lunch of shepherds' pie and red cabbage, I ran out with my yellow pass, waved it under Sister St Thomas's nose. She peered at me through her wire-framed glasses, gave me one of the hard looks for which she was famous. I had the feeling that she did not approve of me, that she wanted to take the ticket and tear it up, fasten me to the chair and force me to eat my way through the more popular chapters of the Old and New Testaments.

Mr Evans always left the front door on the latch for me. I went into the hallway, picked up blind Henry and carried him through to the kitchen. 'Mr Evans? I'm here.' He wasn't around, wasn't in the back yard poking about in his flower tubs, hadn't been in the front garden either.

I put Henry in the hearth, watched him settle on his old towel, dragged Ezekiel and Bathsheba out of the scullery slopstone. An enamel bucket stood under the kitchen copper, and I filled it with warmish water, topped it up at the cold tap, tipped in some soapflakes and washed all the pots. Where was he? He hadn't lit the fire – the copper's contents were no better than tepid, cooler than ever once I'd put some cold in to make sufficient for the dishes. His boots were under the mangle and the brown jacket dangled from a peg on the back door. When he went out, he usually changed into his boots and put on the coat, even in warm weather. I opened the back door, crept down to the lavatory, called, 'Are you in there, Mr Evans?' No answer came.

Back inside the house, I stood at the foot of Mr Evans's stairs. 'Mr Evans? Mr Evans, are you asleep?' Silly question, I thought. If he'd been asleep, he wouldn't have answered. And if he'd answered, he would have been awake. Blind Henry was winding round my ankles and crying for food. Two of the others were in the slopstone again. I found some cooked fish heads in the meatsafe and divided them among the troops.

The stairs were dark and narrow. When I got to the top, there were two doors, one leading to the front bedroom, the other leading to the back. The latter was empty except for an old birdcage and some piles of newspapers. The frame of a bed stood against a wall, some of the base-springs loose and dangling. I crossed the landing, knocked, walked in to Mr Evans's bedroom.

He was on the floor with his legs jack-knifed at an impossible angle. His face was crooked, as if all his features had been pushed to one side. The top teeth jutted out and covered his lower lip. He was dead. My dear old friend was dead. He was the loveliest old man, kind enough to forgive me for stealing, generous enough to let me love his cats. Being in a room with death is not easy for any of us, but it had a devastating effect on me. I was eight years old and I knew about dying, realized that none of us was here for ever. But I'd never seen it until now.

I froze for several moments, wanted to walk out of the room, couldn't move. It was like being paralysed, because my legs would not respond to messages from my brain. Mr Evans's pyjamas were made of a blue and white striped material. My dad had a pair of the same, and I wondered how I would feel if I found my father like this, folded up on the floor with his face all lopsided and his hands curled into tight, white fists.

I got out, sat on a stair, took some greedy gulps of air, picked up Henry. Henry knew. He knew what all the seeing cats had failed to notice – that their master was dead. The tears came, and Henry shared them, pushed his fluffy body against my face and acted like a handkerchief. I didn't know what to do. There were neighbours, people walking past on the pavement. All I needed to do was to go out and shout for help. But I didn't. If I stayed, then something would happen eventually, someone would come to help me.

They came. 'Laura? Are you in there? It's time for registration. Coo-ee. Mr Evans?' It was Confetti.

'Sister! Sister, I'm on the stairs.'

She ran to me, climbed until her face was level with mine. 'Laura? My dear girl, you look like a mammy who's heard the banshee. Whatever has happened here?'

'Mr Evans is dead. I had to stay with Henry. What'll happen to the cats? Is he in heaven? Is he? Do they all go, do they?' I clung to her sleeve. 'Is it just for Catholics and has he gone to limbo? Or purgatory? Sister . . . ?'

'Whisht, child.' She muttered a few more unintelligible words, removed my hand from her sleeve, climbed over me. I heard her walking in his room, waited through several seconds of silence. Sister St Thomas bustled to the bottom of the stairs. 'Sister?' she called.

Confetti was behind me. 'He must have gone last night,' she said. 'It looks like a massive stroke. Probably went as he got ready for bed.'

'He didn't lock the door,' I remarked, wondering how I could think of such a mundane thing. 'He died with the door unlocked.'

Sister St Thomas came up and tried to separate me from Henry. 'Come away back to school, Laura.' Her eyes, though made smaller by the spectacles, were rounder and gentler this time.

'I'm stopping with Henry. He's upset.'

'Look.' A heavy arm came to rest across my shoulders. 'Laura, the sisters will see to the cats.'

'Honest?'

'Honest, child.' She looked so kind, so lovable, not at all like the usual old Tommy-gun. 'Come on now, I'm not as bad as I'm painted.'

'This one's blind.' I clutched the cat to my bony bosom. 'I don't care about my mother not liking animals, Sister St Thomas. Solomon's already living next door even though he's mine. But Henry is staying with me.' My head was nodding all by itself, as if someone had wound a tight spring that just wouldn't slacken off. 'I'll run away if she won't let me keep Henry.'

'Come on, pet.'

'She's a bad bitch, you know. The postman said it on account of her being hoity-toity.' A brilliant idea flashed across my muddled brain, cut through all the dross and found expression on my wayward tongue. 'Am I too young to be a nun?'

She didn't laugh at me. 'Oh yes, dear. Seventeen's the very youngest for a postulant.'

'Oh. See, if I came in the convent, she wouldn't find me, 'cos she says she steers clear of papists. Then I could keep Henry with me. My mother will try to stop me having Henry, you know.'

She eased me to my feet, guided me down the stairs. All the way back to school, I held Henry, would not allow Tommy to take him away. She left me in a corridor, made some phone calls, explained that the police and the ambulance men and Sister Maria Goretti would look after my poor old dead friend. Then we went through the chapel, Sister St Thomas doing one of her bobs down and up again in front of the altar. 'Here, Laura. Come and visit with me. We shall have tea and biscuits and some milk for Henry.'

She had a lovely little room with cheerful saints on the walls and dark yellow curtains at the small window. Her bed was neat and hard with a woven white cover and a very

156

flat pillow. She sat in the one chair at a tiny table while I perched on the bed with Henry. A girl came in. She wore a knee-length black dress and a dark veil, but she still had all her hair and it was dry and gingery. 'Hello now,' she said brightly, placing a tea tray on the table. 'Aren't you the one with the cat? Oh, Sister, isn't he just the most beautiful thing? We had five cats at home, and me mammy could never bring herself to part with a one of them. Clever creatures, they are.'

Sister St Thomas prised Henry out of my arms and dumped him on the table with a saucer of milk. 'Here ye are, God love ye.' She spoke to the girl. 'He's blind, Katherine.'

'Oh no.' She dropped to her hunkers and pushed her face close to Henry's. 'Do you know I'm here, lad? Would you speak to Katie and tell her hello?' And the cat stopped lapping, sniffed the air, then did one of those prr. . .rr. . .aws that cats seem to use as a greeting. 'I'll keep him,' she said.

I eyed her with a degree of distrust. 'Are you a nun?'

'I'm a postulant.'

'You've got hair.'

'Indeed I have and far too much of it. When I start to be a novice, I'll have a big veil like the proper nuns, but it'll be white till I take my final vows.'

I considered her statement. 'Why?'

'I beg your pardon?'

'Why do you want to be a nun? Are you trying to get away from your mother?'

'Ah no, not at all. Me mammy's a grand woman, but I'm wanting to serve God full time, you see. So I came over the water and Sister St Thomas is looking after me. She's my special sister and she'll help me to be a good nun if it's God's will.'

She was nice. She was one of those people you can just look at and know they're nice. 'What about if you change your mind? What'll happen to Henry if you go back across the water?'

'He'll come along of me.' She had a lovely lilting voice, as if she were singing instead of talking.

'Will you be a teacher?' I did not trust teachers, not completely. Except for Confetti – and Tommy-gun was beginning to look a bit more human. Still, it was better to assess the qualities of Henry's would-be adoptive owner.

'No. I'll be like a clerk, someone who looks after the fees and the dinner moneys. And I'll probably help out in the dining hall when I'm old enough.'

I tried to smile, but my heart wasn't in it. 'Do something about the gravy, will you? And stop them reading about lepers when we're eating.'

A strange sound came from Sister St Thomas. She had a hand to her face and she seemed to be choking. 'Goretti's told me about you, Laura McNally. You would shame an angel, so you would.' She let the laughter out, then apologized. 'We shouldn't be making merry when your friend is just dead. But he's gone to a good place.'

I bucked up a bit, responded to the empathy that hung in the miniature room. 'Mr Evans didn't like people to be sad. He said tears were only good for watering dahlias with. And I don't know where he's gone, 'cos he's not a Catholic.'

'That doesn't matter. There's a place in heaven for all good people.'

This was news to me. According to what I'd heard in the playground, St Peter granted admission just to those who had been baptized in the one true faith. With only Catholics floating about playing harps, heaven might have been a bit boring, so I felt glad that Mr Evans would have a wider choice of company. 'Will you really look after Henry, Katherine? He likes cod and evaporated milk, but not together. Liver makes him . . . do things on the floor, but he loves other meat like lamb and chicken and he likes a drink of water.'

'I will care for him. Sister St Thomas will bring him to you sometimes, let you play with him.'

'And the other cats?'

Sister St Thomas stood up and touched my face. 'Goretti will place them, dear. She's a soft spot for all creatures, so she'll be out knocking on all the doors till she settles them. Laura, trust us. You can trust nuns, you see. We don't tell lies and we don't hurt animals.' Her eyes searched my face, as if she were learning things about me, accepting me as a person and not just as a terrible nuisance. 'Trust somebody, please. Don't be going around with your face in your boots, don't be thinking that the world's a bad place full of bad people. Life's hard, but we can help one another through any vale of tears.'

Katherine went out with Henry, closed the door, left me to the mercies of a woman who was universally known as a tyrant. And the tears chose that moment to begin flowing down my cheeks like small rivers. Old Tommy pulled me into her arms and sat down with me on her bed of concrete. I could feel her sobs as she held me close against her. The big rosary dug into my leg, but I clung to that dear old lady as if she were a raft in a stormy sea.

'God, look at the pair of us,' she managed after a while. 'We'll be flooding out the convent and the Reverend Mother will come on the warpath after us with the fire brigade and the Black and Tans.'

I looked up at her fat, sad face. 'Sister? Why do good people have to die?'

She rocked me in her arms. 'Ask that one of Jesus, Laura. He died and He was better than any of us.'

It made sense, yet it didn't, because I was too angry for reason. The only nice thing was that I was being held as if I mattered, as if I were a worthwhile person. If it hadn't been for the wimple, I might have been in the arms of yet another substitute mother. A lovely mother who liked cats and wept when good men died.

It was a black church, its masonry stained by the emissions of a hundred chimneys for a century of time. The clock on the steeple had only one finger, which dangled down just after the six.

Some men carried in the coffin, a light wood affair with shiny golden handles. I crept in and sat at the back, well away from all those who had a real right to grieve. The neighbours were there, many of them almost unrecognizable due to hats and best coats. Not a single curler or flat cap was in sight as they rose to sing the first hymn.

'Move over, Laura.'

I turned, and my mouth fell open. 'You're not supposed to come here, Sister.'

Confetti shunted me along the bench and perched beside me. It was a sin. They'd said in the playground that they couldn't go to a wedding, even a family wedding, if someone was 'marrying out'. Sister Maria Goretti would go to hell. She would go to hell because I'd stolen some flowers and dragged her into Mr Evans's life, then into his death. 'Go outside,' I whispered.

She blessed herself. 'And why would I be doing that, now?'

'Protestant church.'

She waited for a noisy bit in 'Abide With Me'. 'Jesus said that wherever men gathered in His name, then He would be there with them. They pray in pits and factories and on farms and the Son of God is with them. So He is surely here.'

She had what you might call a determined chin, Sister Maria Goretti. It was pointed but not sharp, and she had a habit of lifting it when she meant business. Tommy-gun hadn't come. Tommy-gun had enough sense to stay away and not risk losing her place on the right hand of God. Oh heck. Confetti would get in trouble from the priest, she would have to say about three miles of rosary, would wear the beads out.

The vicar stood in a pulpit and went on about Mr Evans. Mr Evans had been in the First War, had won a lot of medals for being brave. It made me think when the vicar said that. I had looked at people and had seen that they were old, I'd never imagined them young and healthy. But Mr Evans had been a strong man with a gun and an army uniform. At one time, he had fought for his country and had saved lives. When I met him, he was tired. I stood in that church and I knew that I would not always be young, that people would gather one day and talk about me. And children would think me ancient, a bit silly, worn out.

They sang another hymn and Sister joined in. It was a beautiful song about the Lord being a shepherd and about not being afraid of death. Then Mr Evans's box was lifted high by the men and they carried him out. As the sad procession passed us, I turned to look at the door. Father Murphy was holding one side open, and Sister St Thomas held the other handle. Katherine was there, with that tiny black veil perched on the back of her carrotty frizz, and our headmistress stood with the priest, her head bowed in prayer. Sometimes, people's goodness gets in your eyes and makes them so full that the tears come silently.

Those lovely sisters gathered round me, and Father Murphy gave me a sixpence and a big hug, said what a brave girl I was. A man arrived by my side and spoke to me. 'Are you Laura?'

I nodded, too full for words. They had come, my sisters, my priest, my friends, and they had defied a piece of church folklore by attending Mr Evans's service.

'He said you'd to have this,' said the black-clad man. He had red-rimmed eyes and a big nose. 'Thank you for looking after him, love. He was a good dad to me.' For the rest of my life, I was to keep that sovereign. Even when the dark days came, I managed to hide it, managed not to sell it for food, for clothes.

The cats found homes, settled and thrived. Henry was spoiled rotten by the sisters, sat in French classes, English lessons, was never impressed by any of our syllabus. Solomon assumed a new importance, because he was a living piece of Mr Evans's legacy. In my garden, I played with him, fussed over him, bought fish with my spending money. And Mother continued to fret because next door's feline was on her property. So my love for her, if there ever was a seed of affection, did not grow. Like Mr Evans's last dahlias, it failed to flourish. But my guilt thrived in all weathers, because disliking my mother was a grievous sin.

I didn't do it. To my dying day, I would carry the scar in my heart, because I was innocent. The worst thing was that they sent for my father. They seemed to know things about my mother, seemed to understand that she should not be summoned. So they phoned Dad at the shop and he came to school, looked smaller there than he did at home, a bit lost in Sister Agatha's office.

Sister Agatha was the headmistress. Her heart was full of love, but she never let her face know about it. Sometimes, her face was like an empty house, no movement, no expression, just blank and absent. Perhaps she was praying or meditating when she looked distant, or perhaps she had learned how to appear noncommittal and unprejudiced. 'Mr McNally,' she said gravely. 'We found these in your daughter's desk.'

'These' were a pearl rosary and a white missal with the price tags still attached. My father picked them up, weighed them in his hands, returned them to the desk. 'My daughter is not a thief,' he said.

Sister Agatha leaned back in her chair, swept her eyes over me, then over my poor father. 'Every other girl in the class has her own rosary and missal. Laura is fascinated by the faith, so she must have taken these from the repository.'

'I've never been near the repository,' I said, my temper beginning to simmer. 'And if I did go, I'd pay for what I wanted. And,' I mumbled heatedly, 'Norma Wallace hasn't got these things either, because she's not a Catholic.'

Sister Agatha rattled her beads, then clicked her tongue. 'Norma Wallace would not steal things and put them in your desk, Laura.'

I was getting really worked up by this time. 'Neither

would I, Sister. If I was going to steal something, I'd make sure I hid it well away from my desk.'

'Ah.' The cold grey eyes flickered momentarily. 'So you've it all worked out, have you?'

'No.'

Dad stepped nearer to the desk. 'Sister, I would bet my life that Laura didn't do it. If she'd done it, she'd say so. She has a rosary at home – mine. There's a missal too, in Latin and in English.'

She put her head on one side. 'So you are Catholic and your daughter isn't?' She made this sound like a charge being read out in a court of law.

He straightened his shoulders in preparation for an argument. 'My parents were Catholic, but my wife isn't.'

'You married out?'

He nodded, seemed cowed.

'She hates Catholics,' I shouted. 'It's not my dad's fault. Mother says that Catholics are only any good when it comes to educating people.'

Sister Agatha ignored me. 'Mr McNally, you must excuse my digression, as we are not gathered here to discuss your faith or your lack of it. Laura has taken these things from the repository during recess. We keep our stock on display so that the children may choose freely when they want a holy picture or a missal. Laura took the items without attempting to pay for them.'

'I did not! Why won't you listen to me? Why do you keep talking about me as if I'm not here? I did not take the bloody stupid things!'

Dad's complexion paled when the swear word fell so easily from my lips.

'She's a handful, Mr McNally. A very strong-willed girl with a good brain that she fails to use much of the time. Laura has shouted before, has been disobedient, but we never bothered you till now. Stealing is not a thing I can deal with in isolation. If we have a thief in our school, then you have the same thief in your house.'

He stepped closer to the desk, and I noticed that a

muscle in his cheek was twitching, as if the anger in his mouth wanted to jump out and spit itself all over Sister Agatha's office. 'I shall tell you just one more time that my daughter has not stolen, that she would not, under any circumstances, steal from you or from anyone else. Her language may have been a little . . . adventurous just now, but Laura did not take these.' He picked up the missal and slapped it on the blotter. 'I suggest you look elsewhere for your criminal.'

The door burst open and Confetti fell in, her cheeks red and the veil a little off-centre. 'Sister?'

'Yes?' Agatha shook her head slightly at the sight of her dishevelled colleague.

'May I speak with you in private?'

In response to Sister Agatha's nod, Dad and I stepped into the corridor. He stared at a red light that flickered at the feet of a Sacred Heart statue. 'You mustn't swear,' he said softly. 'But I know that I don't need to lecture you about stealing. A soul as generous as yours would not choose to offend itself by such lowly behaviour.'

Well, my father believed in me, or so it seemed.

The office was growing noisy. 'I tell you here and now that the child did not do it!'

'Goretti, are you questioning my wisdom?'

'In this case, yes. Yes, I am.'

A chair scraped along the floor, then a drawer seemed to slam shut. 'I am your superior in this matter, in all matters connected with your work here. Did you not learn humility on your way to the altar, Goretti Hourigan? Are you still running with the wind like you did when I tried to teach you some sense back at home?'

'You are no longer my teacher. I am not a barefoot seven-year-old now, Sister Agatha. I'm a teacher, and I work closely with that child out there. There's trouble in that house, trouble you've talked about to me. Even if she had taken those trinkets, then who would blame her when her mother—'

'Whisht.' That was a noise the Irish nuns often made

164

when they were impatient and wanted quiet. 'Leave the girl's mother out of it and don't be calling a missal and a rosary trinkets.'

There was a short pause. 'They're trinkets till they're blessed.'

Confetti's remark did not go down well. Agatha was probably mad because the girl she had taught in Ireland was bright and clever, was determined to have the last word too. 'Then we shall let the matter lie. As you say, your contact with Laura McNally is a daily occurrence. Perhaps I have been hasty. But what am I supposed to think when the goods are found in her desk?'

'That there is jealousy.'

'Oh. And why?'

'Because I . . . I try to take an interest in the child.'

My father pulled me away from the door. 'Best not listen to any more of it, Laurie. The young one's on your side, so you'll be all right.'

I stamped a foot. 'I want to leave. I want to go to a proper school with real teachers in real clothes instead of blackout curtains. I'm fed up with everything, specially the dinners and being called a thief.'

He smiled sadly. 'Life's unfair. Growing up is just learning to accept the unfairness.'

I turned on him, my frustration making me unreasonable. 'You're never there. I'm stuck in that house on my own or with her when she comes back from wherever she goes. And you don't talk to me as much as you did and I can't go next door and . . . and everything is horrible.' I breathed rapidly, puffed myself up for the big drama. 'I wish I was dead.'

A hand touched my shoulder. 'You're a bit young for those words, Laura.' It was Confetti. 'Usually a girl is twelve or thirteen when her parents hear that sort of noise. And then it's all "I should never have been born" and "It's your fault that I'm here." But then, you are advanced in some ways, Laura McNally.'

'I'm not a thief.'

'And you're no mathematician either, so don't brag about the good points.' She looked kindly at my dad. 'You shouldn't have been dragged all the way up here, Mr McNally.'

He pulled at his collar, appeared to be embarrassed by the whole episode, as if he were unused to witnessing real emotion. 'Send for me, Sister. If you've any problems at all, don't tell my er . . . don't hesitate to call on me.'

Ignored for the moment, I searched for my place at centre-stage. 'I still wish I was dead. And if I can't be dead, I want to be at Anne's school.'

'Shut up, Laurie.' He did not raise his voice. 'There's trouble enough in the world without you turning all contrary.' He shook Sister Maria Goretti's hand. 'Thank you. She's a good girl, you know. Spirited, but good.'

'I know.'

He walked away and left me standing in a dark corridor with the Sacred Heart and a nun who loved me. I knew that she loved me when she said, 'Come along of me, Miss Imp. There'll be no dying done, for the planet needs folk like you to keep the rest of us on our toes. It's me you'll be the death of, so get back and do some work. And stop copying your English homework out of other books.'

This was going too far! I heaved up my spine until I achieved a height well in excess of my usual standing. 'I don't copy,' I snapped. 'That's another lie about me.'

She chortled quietly, adjusted her veil and stuck a black-headed pin into the front. 'Just testing, Laura McNally. It'll be English for you at the university, then.'

'But you said I copied.'

Her face positively beamed. 'Well, it worked, didn't it? Now you have to stay alive to prove me wrong. One day, we'll see your name in print. And comb your hair, you look like an angry hedgehog.'

This was one of my more daring moments. 'And you look like a big penguin, Sister Maria Goretti.'

She giggled like a five-year-old. 'You still call me Confetti, don't you?'

'Sometimes.'

'And your other good friend is old Tommy-gun.'

'I didn't invent that name. She already had it when I came, so don't blame me.' We wandered down the corridor. 'Sister?'

'Yes?'

'Did you never want a little girl of your own?'

She thought for a moment or two. 'Oh yes. And I wanted a pony of my own, long hair, a big house, a handsome husband. Oh and I wanted to be a film star.'

We both stood still and stared at one another. I asked her, 'Do you have to find the most important thing and give up all the others? Is that what grown-ups do? Like you being a nun and looking after us – is that more important than all the other things you wanted?'

'Well, I wouldn't know. See, we had on our farm horses for field work and horses for breeding. The breeding stock were good Irish Arabs for the racing. The same thing happens with people, it's how we're built. It sort of comes to you when you get to a certain age. And you realize that you're just a work horse, not a brood mare. Whatever, horses for courses.'

'What will I be?'

She steered me towards the classroom. 'A terrible torment. But not a thief, Laura McNally. You are never a thief.'

Chapter Five

We never discovered who put the beads and the missal in my desk, but then we didn't hire Mother as a detective. She found out everything, always. She found out about me and Anne meeting after school. One predictable thing was that my mother would always catch you unawares, would discover where you had been, even what you were thinking. Sometimes, she would scour me with her eyes, and I would glance quickly over my shoulder, as if I expected to see a hole burnt into the wall behind my head.

Every time I have looked back on my childhood, I have seen the same thing. Mother and me standing near some furniture, always with at least one piece between us. It might have been a table, a chair, a piano, but it was always there. She never touched me except in anger. For most of us, infancy is something we seem to view through the wrong end of a telescope, little pictures that are slightly distorted, misty round the frames. And I have always had the one endless scene, small, tinged with sepia, but a definite portrait inside my head. It is as if most of my formative years were spent in this single circumstance.

Brown is the chief colour of my early life, because the furniture was usually brown, while most walls in our house were of a dull beige or mushroom. Mother strayed only once from her 'tasteful' theme, allowed a decorator to paint my room yellow. For three days, she fretted and fumed about the gaudiness, then she hauled the workman back and reduced my happy room to a miserable fawn. Miserable fawn was 'tasteful'.

In my dreams, which have often been in colour, a red light has usually surrounded my mother. Red is the colour of anger, of lipstick, of nail varnish, so I suppose that my young brown days were edged with scarlet. Mother towered over me, is the one big thing I remember. Memories of her are not all reduced by the passage of time. Even now, her essence hovers over me, makes my spirit shrink and cower. When I was a child, she plainly needed me to look up to her both physically and mentally. Respect was what she craved and never got. Because my mother is and was a bad angel.

'You've been meeting Anne on your way home from school. You were seen more than once, by a friend of mine, and you were sitting side by side on a garden wall in Chorley New Road.'

I made no reply. Replies, in my mother's massive tome of domestic etiquette, were cheeky unless she had actually solicited an answer. 'What were you doing sitting on a garden wall like a common person for all the world to see?'

I tried to think about this one before answering, but I failed to come up with something inventive or self-protective. Even as I opened my mouth to speak, I had no real concept of what I might say. So I slipped into automatic, just allowed my tongue to do the work. 'I was sitting on a wall, I suppose.' Well done, Laura, I said to my inner self. That will get you a big gold star.

Her cheeks went pink and she reached across to the mantelpiece for her Craven A. 'That is worse than dumb insolence, Laura McNally. A gifted girl? Who does that Maria Goretti think she's fooling when she writes your school report? What are they teaching you at the convent? Do you have lessons in how to make your mother ill?'

'No.'

She slapped her hand down on the chair back. 'I know that you were sitting on a wall. I do not need a picture, thank you. I have just said that you were sitting on a wall. What I require to know is why you were doing it against my express wishes.'

'I was tired, I think.' An express was a train, so I wondered vaguely whether my mother's express wishes

169

moved as fast as the 9.15 from Manchester. Or Blackpool. No, it would definitely not be Blackpool, as Blackpool was for common people with yellow bedrooms and poor taste. I shifted about, wondered where I'd ever got the courage to argue with her a few months earlier. I'd told her that she was bad, and that hadn't done any good. And I was still frightened of her . . .

'What is the matter with you, girl? Look at yourself, just look.'

In the absence of a mirror at the correct height, I could not obey this new command, not without turning myself inside out.

'You are no daughter of mine. I always imagined that I would have a pretty girl child, but you look like a tramp, all rumpled and dirty. What are you thinking of?'

'Nothing.' I tightened my lips to stop my loud thoughts escaping into the room, because Liza McNally was capable of reading a person's innermost imaginings.

She took a chestful of smoke, blew it out in a long blue stream that caressed my face with its filth. 'Dumb insolence again,' she announced. 'I should have thought that the nuns would not allow this type of behaviour.' She flicked non-existent ash in the direction of a crystal ashtray. Even the air I breathed was an unpleasant shade of nicotine in those days.

My mother was really peculiar. If you talked back, it was cheek, if you stood still and listened, it was this dumb insolence thing. The hardest part was trying to work out which was worse; it was impossible to fathom what to do. 'If I don't talk to Anne when she talks to me, then I'll be rude. Sister Maria Goretti says that we shouldn't be rude.'

She took a step closer to me, and I wondered whether this was the right time for me to stoop and cover my head with my hands. I really hated that. Cowering and protecting the skull from a larger person is so dehumanizing and humiliating. 'Don't quote that dried-up nun at me, miss. When you leave that school at four o'clock, you obey my rules. The Turnbull family is just trouble. I don't want you growing up wild like Anne – she gets far too much of her own way. As for Maisie and Freddie – they are no better than they ought to be. I have asked you to stay away from them, and I expect obedience, not criticism.'

The seeds were planted, had been sown when I was very young, but I was too inexperienced to verbalize, even inwardly, the contempt I felt for this thin, selfish, chain-smoking woman. 'I like Auntie Maisie and Uncle Freddie.' The words were out before I could check them for flaws.

She nodded, but her mouth was thin with displeasure. 'You are too young to differentiate between people, so you must simply accept what I say. In time, you will discriminate for yourself, you will realize that the family next door is not up to the mark.' She was a talking dictionary once she got heated, or even warmish. 'They are not our sort.'

Anne was my sort, would remain my sort throughout life. I stood and waited for the tirade to continue. Mother might follow up with a lecture on gratitude, a homily on good behaviour, a speech about her own martyrdom. Or perhaps I would get a mixture, a few bits from each well-worn monologue. Whatever, the delivery would take time, but at least she didn't seem to be lashing out with fists and nails on this occasion.

'No-one knows how I suffer.' She looked at herself in the mirror over the fireplace. She had opted for martyr-dom, then, was practising a pose that might gain her a halo in the fullness of time. And she could be hung in the corridor at St Mary's with a lunch menu to her left, a timetable to her right. And Joan of Arc staring across from the opposite wall. I swallowed the wry laughter. No way would my mother merit sainthood.

'I am alone so much.' A small kiss-curl above her left ear was smoothed, pasted down with a bit of spit. For a woman who worried about manners, she had some queer habits. 'Nobody cares about me, considers me, worries about me. You don't care, your father doesn't care, and I'm—'

'He's busy.' Where my father was concerned, I was inclined to snappiness, even if my own physical safety was at risk. 'My dad works very hard.'

She turned, dismissed the holier-than-thou look from her face. 'Did I ask for your opinion? Did I?'

'No.'

'Then keep it to yourself, please. A lot of men are busy, but they still find time to take their wives out for a meal, or to the cinema. He never talks to me. Never.'

She was searching for sympathy, even for love, but I had nothing to offer. 'He talks to me,' I said quietly. 'He tells me about the factory and the shop.'

'Huh.' She tossed the cigarette into the fireless grate where it fell among its predecessors, twenty or thirty orange-coloured cork tips resting in the iron basket. 'How fascinating for you. So now you know all about silly little bits of herbs and muslin bags. How utterly wonderful.'

Dad was not silly. What Dad was making was not silly, yet I held my tongue again. There had been so many days like this one, many of them culminating in a beating. Looking back on life is seldom easy; days have a habit of mixing themselves up, merging into one. When I was eight or nine, I felt as if I had already spent a lifetime rooted to the spot, listening as my mother complained about me, berated and belittled me, undermined my father.

On one such day (there were many, as Anne and I continued to meet after school) a knock at the door interrupted Mother's moanings and groanings. She crept to the window, twitched the thick lace curtain, fell back with a hand to her throat. 'You must help me,' she mumbled. 'Quick – do something.'

This was quite interesting, as I had never before seen my mother nonplussed. 'What shall I do?' I asked. The door was almost breaking away from its hinges. Whoever was outside had no intention of remaining on the path for very long.

'Say I'm not in,' she gasped. Her lips were turning an exciting shade of purple, as if her fear had triggered some chemical that reacted violently with her Sunset Flame lipstick. 'Whatever happens, you must say that I've gone out.' Her head bobbed about like a cork in water. 'I won't be back for some time. Say it!'

'Why?'

She was whispering now, though the quiet voice was harsh, reminded me of an angry snake I once saw at the pictures with Uncle Freddie. It was a cowboy film, I suddenly remembered. The man in the white hat had been tied to a tree by a crowd of men in black hats. Men in black hats were bad, and they invariably rode black horses. And they let this long, poisonous snake out of a sack and then the man in the white—

'Laura!'

I felt myself jump, knew that she had seen me jump, felt foolish about it. 'Yes, Mother?'

'Go to the door right away and get rid of that dreadful woman. She's wicked and she tells a lot of lies. Now, say to her . . . tell her that I've gone to the doctor's.'

'That's a lie,' I answered coolly.

'Of course it's a lie!'

'You said that she's the one who tells—'

'Shut up, you foolish girl.' Mother was forgetting her manners again. 'Tell her I'm ill, very gravely and seriously ill and—'

'What with?' The door was in danger of collapsing inward at any moment. A female voice screamed, 'Come out, you whore,' and the letter box was rattling furiously.

'Never mind what with, just say I'm ill. Get rid of her.' Mother's face was now a fascinating shade of red that tended towards magenta. The colour defied foundation cream and powder, shone like a beacon in the ditchwater-dull room. She seemed to be having some difficulty with her breathing, was panting as fast as a dog in hot weather. Seeing her crouching as I had crouched so often was thoroughly enthralling. She had no dignity, no standing. I stepped closer to her, so close that I could almost smell her fear.

'Laura . . .' The eyes were huge and round.

'It's a lie,' I said. 'We're not to tell lies.'

'You will do as I say.'

I hopped from foot to foot, physically expressing the fact that I was in at least two minds. Half my body pulled towards the hall, while the rest dragged me back, made an effort to stay out of the other danger zone. In this room, I was with the devil I knew, but the dark angel on the front doorstep was an incalculable threat. And my whole body and soul ached with the knowledge that whatever I did, there would be trouble.

Her eyes started to bulge from her head, were plainly ready to pop out and roll across the carpet, twin blue and white 'bobbers' that would be worth ten plain 'glassies' in the streets and playgrounds of Bolton. Shining beads of sweat collected on her brow, ran in small rivers down her cheeks, left stripes in pale powder, small canyons in patches of rouge. One hand reached out, almost touched me, the fingers shrivelling inward at the last split second to avoid contact with my shoulder. 'Please,' she moaned. 'Do this one thing for your mother. God will not mind – this is a white lie. You must, you really must . . . save me.' The hands folded themselves against her throat, reminded me of doves fluttering in a nest. But this was no dove, no gentle herald of peace.

I opened my mouth to frame a question about the various shades of lie, snapped it shut immediately, knew that this was not the time for one of my queries about the less tangible aspects of living. I was shaking like an autumn leaf. My mother's terror was filling the room, was invading me, choking me. I did not like my mother, but nor did I enjoy watching the scaffolding that supported my small existence disintegrating before my eyes. Fascination made way for discomfort, discomfort became fear. The person on the path might have come here to murder my mother.

She ran across the room, bent down low behind a chintz-covered chair. 'I'll have to stay in here,' she babbled. 'She might see me if I go into the hall.'

A few more seconds marked their own passing while I absorbed the fact that my dignified mother was a shivering coward with no pride at all. My stomach was sick, ached beneath the weight of tangled and nameless emotions. I longed for Anne, longed to clutch the hand of my 'twin' in this hour of dire and dreadful need. The eleven-times table chanted itself in my head, as if my subconscious had dredged up a piece of normality to which I might cling. I backed out of the room, my whole body trembling with apprehension. There was pain in my gut now; I needed the bathroom.

Ten elevens, eleven elevens . . . It took me a week to walk through the hall and into the small front porch. The letter flap was raised, so the intruder would have seen Mother in the hall, as the inner door was half-glazed. A pair of angry eyes glared at me. 'Get a move on,' screamed an invisible mouth.

When I turned the key, the door crashed inward, pinning me against the wall. Winded, I remained where I had been thrust, waited until the door swung away from me. Oh for a few moments of blessed invisibility! My eyes were screwed up and seven elevens were seventy-seven, it all rhymed and made sense . . .

She was a vast woman, tall, fat, with several loose chins that wobbled every time she moved her head. The body was encased in a tight-fitting coat through which all the blubbery bulges seemed to do battle for freedom. Round her shoulders and neck hung a dead fox with sad, beady eyes and unnaturally red fur. 'Did I hurt you?' Like my mother, the woman was rather breathless. 'I'm sorry, I didn't mean to crash into you like that. You're not the one I'm looking for, and you have my sympathy, you poor little thing.' The chins were on overtime, bouncing about all over the dead fox's middle portions. 'What a mother you have. Are you all right, my dear?'

I fought for some oxygen, ironed my bruised ribs with the flat of a hand. 'I'm very well, thank you,' I answered untruthfully. Was that a white lie, or would it be grey . . . ? And would several charcoal greys and a few off-whites add up until they became a black? Because that was the case with powder paint – if you mixed colours, you usually got muddy brown or black . . . The girls at school said that black sins stuck fast to the soul, ruled out any chance of heaven until wiped out by a priest. And I didn't fancy the idea of hell, did not wish to be banished to the valley of torment just because of my mother, who was forcing me to deny the truth until my soul was as black as soot. And she would go to hell. They all smoked in hell. And if she and all the other smokers went to hell . . . The woman was staring at me as if I were a very odd person.

'Come in,' I managed. She was already in, so I felt really daft by this time.

'Where's your mother?'

I paused for several seconds, couldn't achieve a second lie straight away, no matter what the colour of this new sin might have been. My eyes moved of their own accord to the sitting room. Mother would kill me, would beat the back of my head until it broke wide open. So I had to do it, had to! Breathing hurt, but I finally found the necessary presence of mind. 'She says . . . she said she was going to the doctor's because she's very ill.' There was water in my eyes, the sort of stinging moisture that usually comes with the peeling of onions. Because of my dampened vision, the fat lady seemed to be swimming about in a huge pond, a great fish with staring eyes. I coughed and blinked a few times. 'So she must be at the doctor's, I think. She'll be waiting in the waiting room.'

The ridiculously tiny mouth pouted. She had made herself even sillier by painting the Cupid's bow a dark and unbecoming pink, a strange shade that bordered on brown, and I was not a lover of the colour brown. The lips sat pursed and tight in the acres of lard that formed this unfortunate face, but the eyes above were liquid, vibrant, dangerous. 'Then I, too, must wait,' she announced ominously, her words coated with acid. 'She'll not get away from me this time, love, I'll see to that.'

She stamped into the sitting room, her broad feet threatening the house's stability. I leaned against a wall, buried my face in a coat of my father's, sought comfort in the aromas of peppermint and black Spanish. After several loud beats of time, I lifted my head until the noise of my heart was no longer crashing on nerve-tightened eardrums. Silence. The angry woman and my mother were sharing a room, yet there was no fight, no conversation. I lingered in the hall, watched the hand on the grandmother clock, dreaded the outbreak of war in our own living quarters.

I peeped round the door, was reminded of Uncle Freddie and the films again. Was it the Three Stooges? I wondered. Or perhaps Laurel and Hardy? Whatever, whoever, there had been a fat woman sitting on a chair behind which the heroes of the piece had concealed themselves. I dared not laugh, forbade myself to think about Uncle Freddie sneaking me out to the Odeon. 'Don't tell your mother, Laura,' he had said. 'Your mother doesn't approve of the cinema unless the film is what she calls a classic. Comedians are not classical, so keep your lip buttoned once you get home.'

Well, the current situation was not a celluloid story on a sticky reel, would not be punctuated by adverts at half-time. Or would it? It felt so unreal, so funny, so hazardous. Perhaps the film might stick in a minute, might even melt and leave a silly hole on the screen. And everyone would boo and jeer and sing, 'Why are we waiting?' Oh, I must take control of myself. The hilarity of the scene was making me worse, was causing my stomach to grind like a butcher's mincer. It was a farce, a hoot, I had to run!

I fled past the open door and into the kitchen, spread my hands across the coal-burning stove, gripped its enamelled edge. My mother was in the front room, was in a pickle that was terribly amusing and dangerous. Would the fat lady hit Mother about the head, would she be my revenge? No, that must not happen. Although I had little love for my female parent, I didn't want her brains bashed in by an ugly person with a dead fox round her neck. Somehow, I had to find a way of getting rid of the fat lady. A snort of hysteria squeezed its way down my nose, and I altered it into a very unprofessional sneeze. Anne was the actress – I wasn't terribly good at imitating sneezes, voices and suchlike.

'What's your name, dear?' The voice was high-pitched, probably strangled by corsetry on its journey to the outside world. 'Dear? Can you hear me?'

Several more seconds elapsed before I made full contact with my own Christian name. It was silly, being so frightened that I forgot who I was, but not silly enough to make me laugh again. 'My name's Laura,' I replied at last. I definitely needed to go to the bathroom by this time, dared not move, was too scared to pass the woman on my way to the stairs. What was happening to my thinking? I had talked my way out of many tricky situations, could surely manage one more. But this was not my tragedy, it was Mother's. Talking my own way out of a corner was one matter, but I didn't fancy my chances of pleasing my mother, no matter how hard I tried.

'Are you there, Laura?'

'Yes.' I swallowed a great mouthful of air, and it landed in my stomach like a lead pellet. 'Would you care for a cup of tea, Mrs . . . er . . . ?'

'Mrs Morris, dear. And no, I don't want anything, thank you. This is not a social call.'

'Oh. Right.' I had to get her out of that room. Should I shove some papers inside the stove, waft the smoke into the house and scream about fire? No. Mother might be fooled too, might come out of her hiding place and into the clutches of this intruder. There had to be something, some ploy that would work. On tip-toe, I moved along the hall, pushed myself to stand in the doorway, tried to act casual and normal. 'Would you like to look at our garden?' I asked. We had a very ordinary garden, just some grass, a few flowers and an apple tree, but it was worth a try. My mother was curled up like a cat, limbs drawn in, head so far down that it touched her knees. She would get cramp any minute, I thought. And for a dignified woman who set a lot of store by 'doing the right thing', she looked like a completely graceless bundle of clothing.

'I don't want to see your garden, Laura. What did you say was the matter with your mother?'

I raised my eyes to the ceiling, tried to take my attention away from this painfully ludicrous scene. 'Headaches,' I replied. 'She gets a lot of headaches.'

'Hmmph.' The dead fox had slipped when I looked down, was hauled up cruelly by huge, dimpled hands until it sat high on plump shoulders. 'She'll have more than a headache when I catch up with her. Anyway, isn't your father a chemist?'

'Yes. He's at work. He works up . . .' My mother was stirring in her den behind the chair. 'Up Blackburn Road. In a chemist shop. And . . . he's making a factory some-where on a farm.' Any minute now, I would surely explode in gales of laughter or in floods of tears. Mother's head was up and she was mouthing at me, but I couldn't concen-trate. If I'd stared behind the chair, Mrs Morris might have followed my gaze and . . . I gulped. She was such a big woman that she could have killed my mother by sitting on her for a minute or two. 'He's working,' I repeated lamely.

'Pity he can't cure a simple headache, then,' snapped Mrs Morris. 'When does he come home?'

'Er . . . about six o'clock, usually.'

Mrs Morris drew back her head until I could count three full chins, plus one more that was still in a developmental stage. She turned and looked at the mantel clock. 'Ten to six now. I'll wait for him, he'll do.' She nodded thoughtfully. 'Yes, he'll do very well, will Mr McNally.' She settled back, was just a couple of inches away from the crouching figure. All that separated them was the padding on the armchair.

Mother was mouthing again, something that looked like 'Get her out.' My need for the lavatory was suddenly urgent. After a gabbled 'Excuse me', I fled up the stairs like a real living fox with the hounds snapping their fangs at its brush.

I was never fond of the bathroom. From a very early age, the toilet terrified me with its strident gurgling, made me worry about demons and dragons and slimy opportunists that might live in dark water and bite people's extremities. Even when I was almost nine, mature enough for the voice of reason to reside more frequently in my head, I was still scared. I told myself every time that there were no evil forces in our drains, yet something elemental made me shiver each time I pulled the chain.

But on this occasion, with the rest of the house full of ill-concealed malevolence, I decided to opt for whatever lived down the pan, because the devil downstairs, which was now known to me, was far fiercer than any reptile that might poke its forked tongue out of a U-bend.

When the cistern had refilled itself, I went through the eleven-times table again and added on two Hail Marys, a Glory Be and the Catholic version of the Lord's Prayer. After the pipes had settled, I squatted on the floor and counted diamonds on the wallpaper. Each diamond had three flowers in it, and I struggled to multiply the diamonds by three. It must have been six o'clock. I stood on the toilet seat and opened the small window, strained to hear the Town Hall clock as it announced the safety zone. Dad was on his way. Dad was sane and comfortable; he would take away the dragons.

The landing was silent. I stood as still as a stone and listened to the ticking of the grandmother clock. It hiccupped, creaked, played its tune and bonged six times. He was late. If he'd decided to stay and invent something, then Mother might very well squat behind that chair till midnight. And Mrs Morris could stand up at any minute, walk round the room, find my mother hiding like a criminal in her own house.

I heard him. My father clopped when he walked, because he always bought real leather shoes with real leather soles. The gate moaned, swung open, took an age to shut. He pushed wide the front door, stepped inside, paused in the hall. Papers shuffled as he looked through the mail, and I heard the soft sound of his coat as he removed it and hung it on the stand.

'Mr McNally?' She was in the doorway of the sitting room. I crawled along the landing, held on to the rails, held on to my breath.

'Hello?' he said.

'I want a word with you.' I could picture her chins wobbling indignantly. 'Really, I wanted a word with your wife, but she seems to be out.'

'I see. What do you wish to talk about?'

'My husband,' came the swift response. 'I'm not the first to come after your wife. Doreen Shipperbottom had a do with her last year, because that woman of yours was chasing Ernest the length and breadth of the Market Hall, pretending she was after a particular brand of Turkish delight.' She cleared her throat in a way that thoroughly expressed her disgust. 'The delights she was interested in had nothing to do with Turkey, Mr McNally, nothing to do with Ernest Shipperbottom's sweet stall.'

My father's sigh was loud enough for me to hear quite clearly. He was a man with a problem, and the problem was not a new one. 'Why should this concern you?'

'Why?' she screamed. 'Why? Can't you keep her under control? It's like having a bitch on heat wandering the streets. I've heard of folk locking up their daughters, but it's coming to a pretty pass when we have to keep our husbands on a lead. She's not normal. She's one of those nymphomaniacs, can't leave the men alone for a minute.'

He took her into the kitchen – I followed their path with my ears, then I crept like a cat down the stairs as the kitchen door clicked into its jamb. In the sitting room, I beckoned, urged her to come out of her hide. One of her knees cracked, sounded like a bullet emerging from the throat of a pistol.

'Come on,' I whispered. 'Be quick, please!'

She put a finger to her lips, stared at me with so much pleading in her eyes that I almost worried about her for a few seconds. As she pushed past me and into the hall, the kitchen door flew open. 'I told you!' screamed Mrs Morris. 'I told you I could hear something.' She flew with a speed that was commendable in a woman of her weight, grabbed Mother's hair, swung her round and smashed her face into the wall. 'Bitch!' she screamed. 'Dirty, fornicating bitch!'

Instinctively, I beat my father to the scene of the crime, lifted my foot and kicked the wide rump. 'Don't you dare hit my mother. Don't you dare touch her, you ugly, fat person.' The tears streamed down my cheeks. My foot kept reaching its target until Dad dragged me away. 'Go upstairs, Laura,' he said.

'No, I won't. Mother had to hide behind a chair, so I'm going for a policeman.'

My mother turned and looked at us, an arm coming up to protect the already injured face. I knew how she felt. I knew all about it, because I had had a bloody nose more than once. Yet I hated seeing Mother suffering as she had made me suffer. 'Laura, go into the sitting room. We don't need the police,' she said.

I bit my lip, fought to stem the weeping. 'I'm stopping here.'

Mrs Morris glared at me, then focused her attention on her victim. 'And what were you doing behind a chair, Liza McNally?'

'I was . . . playing hide-and-seek with my daughter.' Mother never played games, unless they were adult and dangerous, but there was no point in disabusing the unwelcome visitor, so I held my tongue. 'Laura? Weren't we playing?' pleaded Mother.

'Yes.' Another black blotch stuck to my soul. I almost felt it rushing into me and sinking its claws deep in my belly.

The bloated woman screamed again, 'You were hiding from me. You're a liar as well as a scheming witch. Adulterous, that's what you are.'

Adulterous meant old, grown-up, I thought. My mother didn't look old, certainly nothing like as old as Mrs Morris.

'Have you finished?' Dad sounded as if he were asking a diner to pass him an empty plate.

'She's been going with my husband for ages. They are at it in his office every lunchtime. I've three children, Mr McNally. How will they feel when they find out that their father is having an affair with the chemist's wife? And how will you feel when I name her as co-respondent in a divorce suit?'

'Calm yourself, please.' My dad sounded tranquil, quite resigned and unruffled. He was, I decided, a dignified man. His wife ached to be dignified, missed by a mile. But he was a true gentleman. 'It will stop, I promise you,' he said to the fat woman. 'There will be no further trouble.'

'She'll only start on somebody else's husband. Have you any idea of the number of men in this town who have received favours from your wife?'

He gazed at me. 'Go away, Laura.'

'No.'

'Laura? This is the wrong place for you. Please go upstairs.'

I walked past them, went up six or seven steps, sat down out of sight, listened avidly.

My father spoke first. 'Mrs . . . er?'

'Morris.'

'Mrs Morris, my daughter is only nine years of age and she is in this house. If only for her sake, I beg you to leave. We may, if you wish, discuss this matter further on neutral ground.'

There followed a short pause that was punctuated only by my mother's irregular breathing. I pressed my face against the banister, prayed for the fat woman to go away and leave my father in peace.

But she started to yell again. 'Go anywhere near my husband again, and I'll kill you. There's a lot of us in Bolton wouldn't mind turning your guts into garters, so be warned. One of these days, we'll organize a posse and come after you. There'll not be one single hair left on that dyed head of yours—'

'My hair is not dyed.' Even now, in the midst of chaos, Mother defended her natural beauty. 'Which is more than can be said of yours, Florrie Morris. As for your husband – who on earth would want a man as bald as a coot and with a beer belly down to his knees? Talk sense. I've too much pride to be dallying with the failures of this world.'

'You've had him, I know you have,' snarled Mrs Morris. 'He's a rich man, just the sort you're after. Well, he'll not leave his kiddies for a trollop like you, and if you try any more of your tricks on him, I'll separate your arms from your body.'

She could probably do that too, I thought. She was about a foot taller than Mother, and a yard or so broader across the beam.

'Can't you be more like a man?' screamed the distracted Mrs Morris. 'Can't you put your foot down, keep her in her place?'

'Will you please leave my house?' he asked.

I crawled to the top of the stairs and lay flat on the landing. Something told me that my dad might be distraught if he discovered that I had overheard every syllable of the argument.

The sitting room door slammed, and I gathered that Mother had escaped from her tormentor. Heavy feet plodded after my father's tap-tapping of leather along towards the front door.

She wanted a few final words, stopped walking when she reached the porch. 'Mr McNally, I realize that your life must be difficult. No man likes to be married to a loose woman, but I beg you to do something about her. She's becoming a public nuisance – everybody's talking about her. She never left my husband alone, never gave him a minute's peace. I got it out of him this afternoon, finally went down to the works and faced him with it. He's terrified of divorce, but he couldn't get rid of her. She's had a fortune in meals and clothes, you know and—'

'Please.' His tone remained level, but I felt his grief as if it had travelled up the stairs like an invisible gas. In that moment, I knew the depths of my father's despair. 'Your husband's weaknesses are no concern of mine,' he said.

'But your wife is your business, surely?'

'I have no more to say to you, Mrs Morris.'

I heard the outer door as it opened, felt a draught of quickened air.

'I'm sorry for you,' she said, and her voice was kinder, softer.

'Save your pity for your children,' he replied. 'My own concern is for my daughter. I trust that there will be no further repercussions?'

'I've said my piece.'

She left. My dad lingered in the hallway for what seemed to be a very long time. Curious now, I climbed on to the landing railings, leaned down and looked at him. He was crying. There was no noise, but my lovely father was wiping the tears from his eyes. I swallowed my own sobs, dragged myself away, entered my bedroom.

But in one sense, the worst was yet to come. He did not speak to my mother, did not shout at her, did not allow her the chance to explain the afternoon's happenings. I heard him walking up the stairs, listened as he paused outside my door. When he seemed satisfied that I was unaffected by the day's events, he went into his bedroom and closed the door quietly. He did not crash about, pound his fist, slam doors. He simply walked away from the problem.

My father didn't care one jot about his wife's behaviour. I suppose I had already known that my parents' marriage was not a good one. I had seen Auntie Maisie and Uncle Freddie together, had witnessed the language of love in its spoken form and in gestures, touches, glances. But now, I suddenly knew that my dad was going through hell for me, for his beloved little girl. For my sake, he continued to live with Mother. It was my fault, all of it.

Chapter Six

The conversion of Liza McNally took place just a few weeks after the famous altercation with Mrs Florence Morris and all her chins. It was very dramatic, very sudden, and it gave Mother the opportunity to put to use the saintlike expression that had been practised in mirrors all over the house since the dawn of time.

She began to attend the Methodist chapel every Sunday, sometimes twice, and she took to wearing what she called 'quiet' clothes, navy suits, dark coats, white blouses with high necks and prim collars, usually with a discreet little cameo brooch perched neatly at the throat. Her walk became sedate, decorous and slow, but this new demeanour was probably another pantomime for the neighbours' benefit. It was the same whenever we got any new furniture. She had to be out in the avenue directing the delivery men, making sure that everyone knew how well she was doing. John Willie's men were well used to my mother, always wore caps pulled down to conceal knowing grins when they came to our house.

Many years later, I came to realize what a good hatchet job Mrs-Morris-of-the-chins had achieved, even though her effectiveness dwindled with the passage of time. But when the chapel saga began, no-one had visited us for some time, while few spoke to my mother when we went shopping. Inside shops, conversations would stop abruptly as soon as we entered, and discomfort crackled in the atmosphere while we made our purchases.

Mother did not choose to remain permanently in the *persona non grata* slot, so she launched herself upon religion in a very big way, a way that was meant to show her fellows the enormity of their mistakes, the error of their collective judgement. In the beginning, before the next lot of trouble arrived, she was doing a form of penance, I suppose, wearing her weeds like sackcloth and ashes, presenting the aura of a wronged woman who has seen the blue-white flame of eternal joy, the orange embers of infinite damnation.

I suffered, of course, was dragged along in weathers fair and foul, my reluctant patent-leather-clad feet dragging in the wake of Mother's urgent need to be seen doing the right things. The whole caboodle got me down, wore me out with its monotony. I was forced to wear a silly, babyish, royal blue coat with a gored skirt, velvet collar and velvet strips above the pockets. 'It's a princess line,' Mother announced when she witnessed my dismay. 'It will be all the rage in a year or two.'

I scowled. 'Let the princesses wear it in a year or two, then.' I could not imagine Princess Margaret putting up with this sort of garb. 'I hate it,' I said.

'You'll wear it. You'll wear it and be glad that you have a coat. There are many children who would be delighted to have a coat that cost three pounds.'

The coat was bad enough, but the matching hat was almost too awful to mention, though I learned to laugh in later years about my mortal agony. A nine-year-old girl does not enjoy wearing a poke bonnet of dimensions so enormous that it might have served as blinkers for a brewery shire. 'I am not wearing that. I could get killed wearing it. You couldn't see a tram coming or a car or anything.'

'It is very fashionable and it hides your sulky face.'

'Anybody would sulk in these clothes. Can I send them to Africa for my black baby?'

'No.'

'What about the mission in town, or the Salvation Army?'

'Laura, do be quiet. You look very nice.'

I went as far as stamping a foot, but this won me

nothing more than a hefty slap across the head. My ears rang with the pain while she repeated from behind gritted teeth, 'You look very classy, so stop the nonsense.'

I looked stupid and felt stupid. The one benefit of the terrible hat lay in the fact that when sitting, standing or kneeling in a pew, I could not always see my mother praying earnestly by my side. Mother's idea of earnestness was ludicrous. She screwed up her face and moved her lips, so I was minimally glad for the narrowing of peripheral vision while we were at service.

It was a solid, well-built chapel with good windows and polished pews. We lived in one of the 'better' areas that clung by the skin of its teeth to the rim of affluence. Had we been truly rich at that time, we would have entered the hallowed acres of Heaton, would have settled ourselves further along Chorley New Road. But we were still up-and-coming, would arrive elsewhere in a year or so.

The preacher was a noisy zealot with a handsome face, a dowdy wife and a terrible fixation about hell and all its horrors. His three children sat in a front seat with their mother, whose nondescript looks they had inherited. They never flinched when their dad roared, never showed the slightest response to his ravings. I wondered occasionally how they reacted at home when he asked for the salt to be passed along the table. Did he yell, promise everlasting banishment to those who did not hand the condiments to God's messenger? In actuality, he advertised Satan far more vigorously than he commended God, and this implied that several among his congregation must have known little about the alternative to Hades.

Each Sunday, my mother would emerge from the chapel with a smile of such beatitude that the minister could not fail to notice how powerful his sermonizing had become. This meant that Mother and I received a lot of attention, and I was embarrassed as much by my mother's sighs and flutterings as I was by the dreadful hat. He shook hands with everyone, made the odd comment to some people, peered down his long nose at others. Mother's glowing face always made him stammer. When we came out through the door, I bowed my head and listened to the stammering. Then Mother would show me up, go on at length about how soul-cleansing he was, how gifted in the art of translating the will of God so that it might be understood by lesser beings. I kept my head so low that all I could see was the pavement and my shoes. If the ground had opened up, I would have jumped gladly into the hereafter in spite of the heat, the horns and the cloven hooves.

I got fed up with it. Getting fed up with chapel, saying that I was sick to death with it, was the first sign of my next attempt at rebellion. I had taken Mother to task before, but previous problems paled into insignificance in the face of the ranting pastor and when compared to that hat and coat. This time, I was determined to get my own way, was not prepared to negotiate a treaty, had no intention of giving one inch of ground to anyone. Even Mother. If she wanted to kill me, then she could just get it over and done with. I would leave a note for Dad, would let him know that I must not be buried in my 'Sunday best'.

At first, in spite of firm resolve and several hours of rehearsal, I took the coward's way out, a headache, stomach pain, an ankle twisted on uneven paving along Chorley Old Road. But I ran out of lies, ran out of my father's remedies for illnesses and injuries that I'd made up in the first place. After depleting my store of excuses and imagination, after emptying my father's store of medicaments, I simply said no.

Mother was never a woman to take no for an answer. It was as if the word 'no' should not exist in my vocabulary. 'You will do as you are told this instant, Laura McNally. Put on that lovely coat immediately. It cost three pounds, and I am not leaving it to hang with the mothballs.'

'I'm not going.'

'Oh yes, you are.'

If she was dug in, then I was even further entrenched,

sinking lower by the minute into the sea of mud that was my own determination. 'I'm not wearing that stupid coat again as long as I live. And I'm not wearing that stupid hat, either.'

We were in the dining-room 'enjoying' our Sunday breakfast. My father, vague as usual until my voice was raised, put down his newspaper and stared mildly at his belligerent daughter. 'What is the matter, Laurie-child?'

'Laura,' snapped my mother. 'She's a big girl, and it's time you dropped that baby name, John.'

He ignored her. 'Laurie?'

I was suddenly inspired. 'Well, he frightens me. That Mr Openshaw has a terrible loud voice and he screams all the time and goes on about the day of judgement and burning in the flames of hell.' I glanced at my mother as she pushed the orange end of a Craven A into her mouth. 'Drinking is a sin and so is smoking. Mother will go to hell because of smoking and you will go too Dad, because you have a glass of whisky at night. It's best not to be a Methodist if you drink and smoke.' The ensuing pregnant pause aborted itself as Mother coughed against the day's first dose of nicotine. 'Anyway,' I continued, 'it's all a terrible waste of time when I could be getting on with homework and things.'

He folded the paper and placed it next to his napkin on the table. Dad and I didn't approve of napkins, so we avoided using them whenever possible. I followed suit with my own napkin, crushed it into a ball and set it in the centre of my plate where the egg had congealed. Mother's fried eggs were always burnt or still clear and runny where they should have been white. This had been one of her runnier days.

Dad cleared his throat. 'You should try to go for your mother's sake, dear. There's no need to take the man too seriously. Close your ears when he shouts about hell.'

'He's like thunder,' I insisted. 'He's the sort of thing you'd hear even with cotton wool in your ears.'

'Try,' he repeated gently.

I had expected support, was floored for the moment. Dad kept giving in to Mother, kept opting for the line of least resistance. I was annoyed with him and there was a lump in my chest, a knot that I recognized as real anger. Life was beoming a permanent lump in my chest and it wasn't fair, I was always in trouble. Mrs Morris hadn't shouted at me – she'd been quite nice till I kicked her. Mrs Morris hadn't meant for me to go to chapel twice a week in a funny hat. Although the connection was not completely clear, I felt that the fat woman was the cause of my mother's interest in Christianity. 'Well, I'm not going.' I often began rebellions with a 'well'. 'I will not go. If you make me go, I shall scream all over the place, and I'll shout louder than Mr Openshaw does. And I'll be sick. Mary Ashurst at school showed me how to be sick when I want to stay in at playtime. You just stick a finger down your throat and wiggle it about . . .' My finger was in my mouth and I managed a retching sound. 'Like that,' I concluded.

Mother rose. She never stood up, she rose like a swan preparing for flight, all long neck and smooth plumage. 'You are a terrible disappointment to me, Laura. I expected you to be refined after a few years at St Mary's. After all, those nuns are paid to teach you manners. Unfortunately, you are still a difficult child. You will go to your room and you will stay there until four o'clock.'

'Why?' Only one word, but enough to start a war. Though she wouldn't hit me, not with Dad in the room.

'Go upstairs,' she said, her tone cool but dangerous. You could always hear the threat, even when she didn't actually promise a beating. 'Go now.'

'No.'

Her eyes were narrowed, seemed to spit out little sparks of kindling as she heated up her temper. She spread one of her hands on the table, leaned forward, curled the fingers into talons that scratched the white linen. 'Sometimes, I don't know what will become of you, girl. This defiant attitude is too much. John – deal with her.' She marched out of the room and slammed all the doors between ground and first floors, started stamping about in her dressing room. Even from the back of the house, we could hear the heavy footfalls.

Dad looked at me for a long time. 'You are your own worst enemy, Laurie.'

'She'd have hit me except for you being here. She's always hitting me. Remember when she cut my face with her ring and I had to stay at home till it healed? Well—'

'Laurie, she's an impatient woman and you must try not to anger her. She's your mother. My mother and father were not always easy people, but I respected them, tried to please them. You must make an effort.'

'She's never pleased. I keep winning prizes for my stories, but she takes no notice. And when I make her a cup of tea, it's too strong or too weak or too hot. How can I please her?'

He dropped his head. 'It's not easy. Just do as she asks, go to your room and sit quietly.'

Sometimes, I couldn't seem to get through to anyone. I had the feeling that he understood, that he loved me and wanted me happy, yet communicating with him wasn't easy. I walked out of the room and up the stairs, threw myself on the bed like a ham actress in a poor melodrama. Dad loved me and was too busy; Mother didn't love me or anyone else. The person she really cared about lived in a mirror and I was terribly lonely, mistreated, underprivileged and sick to the back teeth of everything.

I heard him walking up the stairs, listened as the bedroom door clicked, crept out to the landing in the hope that I might hear something to my advantage.

'Don't push Methodism down her gullet,' he said. 'If you do, it will make her as sick as any finger down her throat. Methodism's all well and good for some, but it can be a bit grim, and grim isn't everybody's cup of tea.'

'Would you prefer Catholicism?' She said the last word

in a silly voice, as if trying to convey her continuing contempt for the Church of Rome.

'No. I don't want any religion forced on her. She's just a child, and children don't need to sit and hear about hell and damnation. It's obscene, making her stay there while the man roars about doom. Leave Laurie out of it.'

'Laura,' she said automatically. A chair scraped, then there was silence.

Back in my room, I lay on the bed and counted books on the shelf. I had twenty-seven complete books, two torn ones and about ten copies of the *Beano*. The *Beanos* were hidden under two shoeboxes in my wardrobe, as Mother did not approve of modern comics. Modern comics, she often said, corrupted young minds. Yet she bought the *News of the World* in spite of my father's misgivings. In Catholic homes, the *News of the World* was only seen second-hand, covered in grease and vinegar.

My father used to read to me sometimes, but now I was left to my own devices, was old enough to read by myself. No-one cared, no-one worried about my terrible loneliness. If Anne had lived a few streets away, I might have seen her at the weekends, but sneaking next door was difficult. Mother had a habit of turning up at the oddest times, had even been known to come out of chapel before the service ended. This was because she had discovered a new illness called migraine. Migraine meant four Aspros, a darkened room and a wet flannel over her eyes.

It was boring in the bedroom, because I had not chosen to be there. On many occasions, I spent a whole afternoon in my room, crayoning, reading, writing bits of stories. But being forcibly constrained was a different matter altogether. I heard Mother slamming out to go to service, then I walked to my window, watched Dad pottering half-heartedly about the garden. He didn't care. So I pulled on my older blazer, emptied my piggy bank, left the house. No-one would miss me.

Running away is all well and good in the heat of the

moment, but the details tend to crowd into your mind after a half-mile walk. Like not having enough money, being without company, clean knickers, food. Names of places jump into your mind, London, Blackpool, Manchester, but there is no way of working out how to reach any of those destinations. And I worried a bit about somewhere to sleep, though the day was only ten hours old.

Bolton is a big place, particularly huge for a child who has not been allowed to wander. I saw many liberated children who had been permitted to discover their own town. Some were free enough to wear clogs on a Sunday, one or two sported nit-caps under which they would be shaven, possibly still bald. They played rough games, threw each other against walls, spat on pavements, made sparks with iron-shod soles. Oh, they sounded so happy, so free. They looked down on me, saw me as a lesser being. In my blue gingham print dress, navy blazer, hair ribbons, shiny leather shoes, I must have looked like something from a different world.

I passed the fire station, turned left into Deansgate, found an alley. It had rained during the night, so getting dirty was not difficult. I smeared blazer and dress with mud, rubbed grey water on my face, on my shoes, dried my fingers on socks that had recently been snowy white. When I emerged, I peeped in a shop window just past the post office. My hair was too tidy. The ribbons went into a pocket and I left the braids to untangle themselves. Now, I might begin to belong.

'She's mad,' announced someone behind me.

I spun round, held my breath for a moment.

'What the bloody 'ell are you doin'?'

It was the group of children I had seen earlier near the entrance to Queens Park. 'Nothing,' I replied.

'Daft,' said one.

'Double daft,' giggled another.

They spread themselves out, surrounded me in a semi-circle from which there was no escape, as there was a wall to my rear. For a few seconds, a shaft of pure panic darted through my breast, but then I comforted myself with the knowledge that these were children. It had been my experience thus far that while the ones to watch had two legs and no feathers, they were usually fully grown when they became dangerous.

'Is that an 'Oly Mary blazer?' asked the nearest girl.

'Yes, it's a St Mary's blazer.'

A boy laughed, doubled himself in two with the pain of his merriment. ''Ey, listen to 'er. Dun't she talk posh, eh?'

They all agreed, including the pair of girls with nit-caps. They were twins, carbon copies of each other. 'Can me an' our Enid 'ave yer ribbons?' asked one of them.

A large and noisy boy, obviously the leader of this motley crew, guffawed crudely, displaying an array of teeth that were greenish and broken. 'What d' yer want ribbons fer, Irene? Are yer goin' t' fasten 'em round t' cat's neck? Yer've no 'air.'

The two girls went pink. Each put a hand to her head, then a finger on the lower lip. It was as if some choreographer had trained them in the art of synchronized movement, though they seemed to need no prompt, no glances from one to another to assess the state of play. Feeling sorry for them, feeling anxious to belong, I gave them the lengths of blue satin. 'They're a bit creased,' I said timidly. 'But they'll be all right ironed. And your hair will grow back again, Enid.'

'I'm Irene, she's Enid.' They each stuffed one of my best ribbons up a knicker leg. ''Ave yer got owt else?'

I lifted my chin, worked hard to dredge up a bit of courage. 'Yes, I've got some money, but if you want it, then you'll have to do something for me.'

The boss stepped forward, spoke through the chewed mush of a mouthful of liquorice root. 'I'm in charge 'ere, Miss Muffet. What dust tha want?'

My imagination shot into top gear. Running away did not seem to be a wonderful idea. I would have to go home at some stage, because people like these could scarcely care for themselves, let alone for someone who had hardly stepped out of the house on her own. But there was time for an adventure. There'd be trouble at home no matter what time I returned, so I might as well take the chance for a bit of excitement. 'Take me to a Catholic church,' I ordered. 'That stone one near Trinity Street Bridge.' My father was a Catholic, used to be a Catholic. I'd been forced to attend Mother's stupid services, so I would take a look at Dad's religion.

'Are you a bloody baby?' This tall, ungainly boy had carrotty hair and some gaps in rotted teeth, was old enough for the adult incisors to have been knocked out of him. 'What's t' matter? Can't yer find yer own road round t' corner?'

Three or four non-speaking extras drifted away, one of them finding his tongue to mutter briefly that he wasn't going near any churches as he intended to play 'footie' in the park. So now there were the four of us, Enid and Irene, the Boss and myself. I fixed narrowed eyes on him. 'Listen, you,' I said carefully. 'I can't help it if I've never been allowed out of the house.' My inventiveness was working overtime. I dropped my voice, glanced left and right. 'I'm in trouble,' I said, amazing myself with the sense of mystery I was managing to inject.

His green eyes flickered with interest, though he was fighting to suppress it. 'Oh aye? Go on, then. Tell us all about it.'

My hands folded themselves, were still not as dirty as his in spite of my encounter with the mud. My companions' dirt was very professional, had eaten into their skins, was an inherent part of their construction. They had probably been born dirty, and might well remain in that state for the rest of their natural lives. They were alive, exciting, so much more vibrant than I would ever be. So I needed to make it all up, needed to become vaguely interesting at the very least. 'I was stolen as a baby,' I announced in a whisper. 'And you mustn't tell anyone,

197

ever. My parents were Catholics, that's all I know, and they went to St Patrick's, near the station. They lock me in my room, the people who stole me. And I climbed out this morning, came down a drainpipe.'

'Must 'ave bin a bloody clean drainpipe,' remarked Ginger acidly.

'Everything is clean where I come from. They make me eat with a napkin and wash my hands seventeen times a day.'

'Bloody 'ell,' he said. 'An' there's me wi' no bath fer more than a fortnit.'

The twins, slower than Ginger, but endowed with female intuition, looked at me with suspicion. 'They must let yer out fer school. 'Ow d' yer get ter school if yer locked in all t' time? Down t' drainpipes?'

A pertinent question, I thought. 'They guard me. Somebody watches outside the school gate.'

The red-headed chairman of this bedraggled committee took up the debate. 'An' wot yer doin' at a Catholic school? Is them wot pinched yer Catholics an' all?'

'No.' I used the necessary pause to step closer to Number One, pushing my brain into a canter as I crept towards him. He smelled. Of things I had no way of identifying, but the odour was warm, though unclean. 'It was all in my grandfather's will with the money. I had to go to St Mary's, it was written down on rolled-up paper in front of a judge. The paper's in their wardrobe at home, tied up with ribbon at the bottom of a box. With the jewels and the money.'

I could see that this was getting a bit complicated for the gang of four. They were four again, because a thin boy had crept back and listened to my last statement. 'No footie,' he said sadly. 'No ball. Bloody park keeper took t' ball again. 'Im an' them rotten flowerth.'

The leader awarded the new arrival a glance of sympathy. 'We could sue 'im fer all t' balls 'e's took. I might get me dad fer t' drop in on 'im, give 'im a good 'idin'. Anyroad, we've got fer t' 'elp this 'ere 'Oly Mary.

'Er dun't know where t' look for 'er real mam an' dad.'

The second boy, whose most noticeable feature was protruding teeth, said nothing at all at this point. The twins were round-eyed with amazement. Somewhere in the deep recesses of their poverty-sharpened wits, they must have seen the holes in my story, yet they had not the vocabulary to express their doubts. 'I've got one and eightpence,' I said. 'Take me to the church so that I can look for my true mother.' I would have to be careful. Although Anne was the dramatic one, I was overacting and might spoil the fun if I went too far with this off-the-cuff drama. 'You can get ice-creams with it.' Their stomachs were probably their first concern. 'With raspberry on from Manfredi's cart.'

For a sum of 1s 8d, they would have flown me to the moon and back. But when we reached St Patrick's, my new-found protagonists would not abandon me, even after I had handed over the money. The gang leader had decided to become concerned about me, and kept expressing the intention to 'do right by 'er'. Really, he wanted to be important, the hero of the piece, the magician who would create a happy ending to my transparent tale of woe. Or perhaps he just wanted the last laugh, the chance to call my bluff.

We went in. There was a man at the back with a collection plate. His jaw dropped when the five of us trailed in, but he managed, only just, to save the dish from clattering to the floor. The big lad bobbed down and up again before entering the pew, so the rest of us imitated him. The buck-toothed boy made a disastrous stab at this, ended up prone in the aisle till one of the twins clouted him and heaved him onto the bench.

After about three or four minutes, other occupants of our section began to move, slowly and decorously, out of our line of fire. The smell of my companions was strong, yet it comforted me, and I felt a degree of indignation when members of the congregation edged away from us. They were soft. This was the aroma of life –

199

nothing to be ashamed of. To my untrained nose, the gang's odour was fascinating. I did not know that my friends teemed with life of the lowest order, that their garments and hair were sublet to tenants whose stay would be indefinite.

There was another man at the front, a priest. He stood at the top of some steps and wore a long frock with a green sleeveless cape over it. The language he spoke was not English, and I suspected that this was the Latin in the missals at school. Four boys were with him, and they wore long black frocks and white shirts with lace borders. These boys did all the answers in Latin. Everybody sounded bored with the whole thing, especially the priest.

Ginger-head dug me in the ribs. 'That's Tommo – 'e goes to my school.'

'I beg your pardon?'

Ginger sighed. 'Th' altar boy – yon lad givin' stuff ter t' priest. That's Tommo in our class. 'Appen 'e knows yer mam.'

Two people in front 'shushed' and we went through the rest of the service in silence. It was weird. They rang tinkly little bells and bobbed about a lot, but at least nobody screamed about hell. Every time one of the altar boys went past the middle of the elevated table, he knelt on one knee, bowed his head, then got up and walked the rest of the way. If he wanted to come back from where he'd just been, he had to do the same thing all over again.

The plate was passed along our row beneath the eagle stare of the collection man. I had no money, Enid and Irene had none, and Buck Teeth put a brass button in the dish. The button clanked about and sounded nothing like money. Ginger saved our bacon, flourished a threepenny bit, whispered to the man, 'That's fer all of us, me mam said', before clattering the coin in amongst the others. There followed an embarrassing episode while Buck Teeth retrieved his button, then we settled back for the rest of the mass.

Ginger had been up for some bread, had shown us the white disc melting on his tongue. He carried his Catholicism with a strange mixture of pride and contempt, bowing his head some of the time, breaking loud wind during moments that were particularly tedious. Irene or Enid looked adoringly at their leader, then whispered to me, ''E can blow off any time 'e wants. Sometimes, 'e even does a tune.'

This statement prompted me to double over with unseemly mirth. Really, I was terrified of what I was doing in the house of God, yet the fear served only to increase my hysteria. It was a truly terrible thing, but I could not control myself. The thought of Ginger and his built-in set of bagpipes provided me with some imaginings that were not appropriate in a Catholic church. In the end, they dragged me outside and propped me against the wall. Ginger looked at me with affected disdain. ''Ave yer got no self-control?'

This made me worse. His self-control was masterful – he could even get his body to make noises, could explode to order and, furthermore, he managed an air of total nonchalance every time he broke wind. 'Sorry,' I mumbled. 'It was so funny.'

Buck Teeth chose this moment to give voice to his views on the matter. 'It'th not funny, thomebody fartin'. It'th thometimeth theriouth, ith bad wind in the gut. Me granny were a martyr to wind, me mam thayth. Me granny thuffered all 'er life an' at the finish, they 'ad to thtick a tube up 'er arthe to let it out. The 'ole thtreet were nearly gathed with it. It'th not a laughing matter.'

The lad's explanation nearly killed me. I wondered if it might be possible to die laughing, because the pain in my belly was acute and my lungs were starved of oxygen to the point where one of the twins said, ''Asn't 'er gone a funny colour?' That poor, unfortunate buck-toothed boy had a lisp that tickled not just my ears, but my eyes too had been suffering from hysteria. Every time he attempted an S, his tongue poked past the terrible tombstones that pretended to be teeth, and I could scarcely bear to look at him for another second. My sides ached with cruel stitches and the tears poured down my cheeks. I had never laughed like this before. It was a wonderful way of releasing tension, yet I still pitied that ugly little boy.

'It's a shame,' said Irene or Enid (whose complete twin-ness was causing me even more uncomfortable glee). ''Er wants 'er muther. An' we was just sat there in t' church doin' nowt.'

The other twin compounded the felony. 'Ginger were doin' summat. I've smelt sweeter pongs round t' back end o' t' muck cart on a Friday.'

Ginger, wearing an expression of mild hurt on his battle-scarred face, came to stand next to me. Fortunately, he seemed to have suspended his musical interlude for the moment. 'We'll wait fer Tommo,' he announced. 'Tommo'll know what's best fer t' do. 'E's bin an altar boy three month.'

The church door opened, and members of the congregation hurried past, gave us an unnecessarily wide berth, I thought. Then after a few more minutes, a smaller back door shot open and four boys were propelled, by an unseen hand, onto the pavement. While they sorted out their tangled limbs, a disembodied voice found them. 'If I catch you lot smoking again, I'll cane your backsides.' It was the priest, I suddenly realized. His bobbing and scraping altar boys were being threatened with actual bodily harm. Mind, they looked a rough lot without their white blouses. Three of them clattered off in iron-soled clogs, while the fourth, a boy with impressive pinkish hair, sauntered towards us.

The priest poked his head into the street. 'Bernard Thompson?'

'Yes?' The pink head did not turn towards the priest, as its owner was coming towards me.

'Have you stuck this chewing gum on the Immaculate Conception?'

'No, Father.'

'Then who did?'

The boy's shoulders shrugged and he made no reply.

Within ten seconds, the man of God was upon us. 'Did you hear me, boy?'

'Yes.' After a short pause, 'Father,' was appended to the curt answer.

'Look.' The priest was white with anger, looked strange in his proper clothes, black trousers, a black top with no sleeves and hardly any back, just strings fastening the cloth to his chest. The back-to-front collar wasn't anchored down, so it hung like a hoop that had been thrown at a prize on a fair stall. 'There's boot polish all over the chair in the vestry. You are a wicked boy, Bernard. What would your father say if I told him? And there's two more bottles of unconsecrated communion wine missing from the cupboard.'

At last, Tommo rewarded the priest with his full attention, the main part of which was a winning smile that displayed perfect teeth. 'Father, there's mischief afoot. The choir was out of tune during Benediction last Sunday. Perhaps some of them had been drinking?' He talked nicely, wore decent clothes.

The priest was still fuming. 'Listen, Thompson. It took my cleaning ladies two hours to get the candle wax off the Sacred Heart the other day. Since you started serving, St Patrick's has gone to the dogs.'

Tommo shook his head slowly, sadly. 'In that case, Father, I shall remove myself from your church and I shall not darken your door again.'

A twin nudged me. ''E reads books,' she whispered. 'Proper books with 'ard backs, not like wot you buy at t' paper shop. 'E can do right big words, Tommo.'

The reverend father clouted Tommo round the ear. 'You are a menace, boy. I have always believed, or have tried to believe, that a human being is not born bad. In your case, however, I have to admit that you may be the exception which proves the rule. In time, you will no doubt go to prison.' He cast an eye over the rest of us. 'As for you, stay away from this boy. Unless you want to spend your days in trouble, of course.' He marched off, stopped when his collar dropped off, bent to retrieve it.

Tommo rubbed his ear. 'I should sue him,' he grumbled. 'He always goes for an ear. I could finish up deaf or brain damaged.' He moved his eyes over me. 'New girl?'

'Yes.' I felt shy, embarrassed.

Ginger pushed himself forward. 'This 'ere girl got stole when she were a babby.' A filthy thumb jerked itself in my direction. ''Er's bin brung up wi' folk wot keeps 'er locked up. In t' will, 'er grandad said about 'er 'avin' fer t' go an' be an 'Oly Mary. So we're lookin' fer 'er mam.'

Tommo walked round me, bored into my spine with his gaze. 'That, in my opinion, is a load of my eye and Betty Martin. This young lady is having you on.'

'Don't 'e talk luvely?' asked a twin. No-one bothered to reply.

Ginger confronted me. 'Is 'e reet? Is Tommo reet? 'Ave yer bin pullin' our legs?'

Something about Tommo made me straighten my skirt and push the hair from my face. 'Of course,' I answered sweetly. 'It was a joke.'

Several emotions did a procession across Ginger's face, then he grinned hugely. 'That were a good un,' he yelled. 'D' yer want fer t' be one o' t' gang? There's me an' Art,' he pointed to the buck-toothed boy, 'an' t' twins an' Tommo. We've a few more, but they jus' cum part time, like. Are you in wi' us?'

In? I would have donated an arm and a leg just to hover on the edge of it all! 'Yes, please.'

'What's yer name?' asked a twin.

'Laura.'

'We'll call 'er Lo,' pronounced Ginger.

'I shall call her Laura,' said Tommo. 'It suits her.' He raked his eyes over the church. 'He can't be allowed to get away with that. The bloody priests have no right to hit us and knock us about.'

204

Art grabbed Tommo's sleeve. 'What yer goin' fer t' do, Tommo? Thmash a winder?'

Tommo grinned, but his face was cold. 'No. I shall just leave my mark.' From his pocket, he took a crumb of chalk. Then he strode to the large double doors of the church and wrote, THE PRIEST HERE IS A BIG F. A hand shot out of the porch and dragged Tommo inside. There followed several moments of silent tension, the twins clinging together in mortal fear, Ginger chewing his lip, Art doing his best to hide behind a street lamp.

Tommo emerged, his face red, the lower lip bleeding. With amazing coolness, he finished off his written message, then joined us on the corner.

'Yer mouth's bleedin',' cried a twin.

Tommo leered at her. 'He's in a worse state than I am, Enid. He'll be afraid to put his face out of the presbytery for weeks.'

'Why?' Ginger's eyes were saucers. 'Whar 'ave yer dun?'

Tommo whistled under his breath. 'Remember that vicar up Chorley way – it was in the paper last year? He liked little boys, didn't he? Liked them a bit too much?'

Everyone looked as puzzled as I felt, but Tommo continued unabashed. 'Father Sullivan will have to watch his step. I told him I'd go to the police and accuse him of interfering.'

'Oh.' Art seemed satisfied with this, nodded a few times, kept saying 'Oh.' 'They alwayth interfere, grown-upth. 'Appen he'll thtop interferin' now, Tommo.'

The worldly wise boy hooted and shook his pink curls. 'Where shall we go now?' he asked.

Ginger grabbed my arm and dragged me off, beckoned to the rest of the group. 'Cum on, we've a bob an' fivepence.'

It was the first happy day of my life. No matter what happened from now on, I would have the gang. No-one would take my special new friends away from me. And the most special of them all was the boy called Tommo. He had hair of a gentler shade than Ginger's, a colour that I would learn to call strawberry blond. His real name was Bernard Thompson. Bernard Thompson was to have an effect on me that would last for ever. But on that day, he was Tommo, just another ally.

Chapter Seven

Tommy-gun left our school soon after my first encounter with Tommo and the gang. It was strange that I should lose one person and gain another with a similar name. Sister Maria Goretti could see that I was pretending not to be upset after the farewell assembly. She cornered me under St Francis of Assisi, who seemed a nice chap, because he actually smiled and was surrounded by animals. 'Laura, she's getting on in years and she needs to retire.'

'I know.'

The young nun took my hand when all the other girls had disappeared. 'Look, she's away back to Ireland in a day or so. She's very fond of you. Would you like to come into the convent and say a private goodbye?'

The emotion of it all would have been too much for me. Since meeting the gang, I was tense, excitable. Saying goodbye to Tommy-gun could well turn out to be the last straw, and I didn't want to show myself up by weeping and gnashing my teeth. 'No, Sister. I've got to finish my story.'

'Ah.' The other hand went up to touch the pin on top of her head. For a nun, Confetti was a rather harum-scarum type, with a veil that was often off-centre and a black skirt that always looked as if it needed ironing. 'You'll win.'

I shrugged. 'I won the school prize, but there's only two classes in our year. In the whole of Bolton, there'll be hundreds of kids entering.'

'But you're talented.'

No-one at home had ever said that I was talented or clever. Auntie Maisie had always loved me, Uncle Freddie had often said that I was a nice good girl, but even Anne treated me as a very ordinary soul. If I turned out extraordinary, then I would be the most surprised of all. 'I just like stories,' I said.

Confetti put her head on one side and the top pin tumbled to the floor. I retrieved it, tried not to flinch as she skewered the headgear to her skull. 'Does your mammy read your stories when you carry them home from school?'

'No.'

'And your father?'

I shrugged. 'He's busy inventing things.'

'So they don't know that a budding author resides in their midst?'

'No.' I tended to ignore Confetti's enthusiasms. She reckoned that Norma Wallace was the next Madame Curie, that Lizzie Boardman would be the greatest nurse since Nightingale, and that I might well finish up in libraries like Shakespeare and some fellow called Dickens for whom she carried the brightest of her many torches. 'I'm just Laura to them,' I said. 'Not a budding author or anything much. Well, Dad calls me Laurie-child, and that annoys my mother.'

She nodded, looked pensive for a moment or two. 'Are you . . . are you unhappy at home?'

'No.'

She coughed. 'Happy, then?'

'No. I'm just all right.'

'Do you get punished often?'

The third degree did not please me. 'Sometimes I get smacked. Not as often as I used to.' My first outing with the gang had been expensive. It had cost me 1s 8d and a battering from Mother, but it had been worth every penny, every blow. And I wasn't getting too many hidings lately, because Mother was out a lot, doing good deeds with Mr Openshaw from the chapel, taking food parcels to the poor and helping out with big families. This new behaviour of Mother's had opened my eyes slightly, had made me look at her differently. Perhaps she had found her good side, perhaps she liked some people and I wasn't one of the people she liked. 'I go out more now, Sister. I've got friends.'

'Ah. And which school do your friends attend?'

Again, I lifted a shoulder. 'Different ones. Some go to Peter and Paul's, some go to Derby Street.' I didn't tell Sister Maria Goretti that I'd met these friends while I was trying to find sufficient courage to run away from home.

'What do you do with these friends?'

Sometimes, people were very nosy. 'We write stories. We sit in Enid and Irene's parlour and do poems and things.' Enid and Irene probably had no parlour. 'And we go to church at St Patrick's.' Well, we'd been once.

She wore an expression of disbelief in her eyes. 'I suppose I'll get silly answers if I ask silly questions?'

'Yes.' At last, we understood one another.

'Laura. Be careful. You've brains and a tremendous energy that could be easily misdirected.'

I wondered if she'd heard anything. There'd been several scrapes, and one head-on encounter with police after some apples got pinched from the market. 'I'll be careful,' I said. And I would indeed take care, especially when speaking to an adult. Yet I didn't want to alienate her, needed her on my side. And I hated the idea of being without old Tommy-gun. She had what Auntie Maisie would call 'a face like a clog back', but I'd seen the other side of Sister St Thomas. She had been good to me, and now she was going away. It seemed that I kept on losing people who liked me. Auntie Maisie and Uncle Freddie lived just feet away from me, yet I had lost them. Would Confetti go next? Or Tommo? My heart missed a beat when I thought about life without Bernard Thompson.

'Go back now to class and finish your story. We have to send it in today for the judges. Good luck, Laura.'

I walked away from my friend and wrote one of my better stories. It was about Mr Evans, who had called himself 'Good Evans' and who had looked after cats and helped to win a war. And it was about the sovereign he bequeathed to me, even though I'd stolen flowers from his garden. Love, I suppose, was the theme of my scribbling. Those who read it must have recognized a lonely child who sought affection, but I simply scribbled down what came into my heart as a tribute to a wonderful old man.

My name was placed on the short-list together with many others from schools throughout the town. There was to be a function at the Victoria Hall, some singing by choirs from various schools, a few tunes from discordant youth orchestras. We received an invitation with a crinkly edge and curly writing. It popped through the letterbox a day or so before the event, and Dad stood it on the mantelpiece next to the clock. 'We'll be proud of you, Laurie-child, whether you win or not.'

On the evening of the presentations, I went back to school and climbed into a cramped charabanc with the choir, the orchestra, three nuns and a thin woman called Miss Bridges. Miss Bridges taught music, so she was a vague and wispy person with vague and wispy hair. Norma Wallace always said that Ida Bridges was a genius and that geniuses did not make good teachers. There was a lot of messing about during music lessons, whispering and giggling and throwing of bits of blotting paper dipped in watery ink. Geniuses appear not to notice much.

I slipped into a vacant seat next to some very small violins and a box of recorders. So the evening promised to be hilarious then. The St Mary's orchestra was like cats on the tiles, just a lot of wailing and screeching. Confetti leaned over me. 'Are you all right there, Laura?'

'Yes, thank you.'

She lowered her tone. 'They're going to play in public. And the choir's going to sing.'

'Oh.' I didn't know what to say.

She pulled a wad of cotton wool from her pocket. 'May God preserve us,' she muttered. 'Do you want some of this?'

'No, Sister. I'm used to the noise.'

Miss Bridges was standing in the centre aisle, her hair messier than ever. 'Where is she? We shall have no first violin if Mary doesn't come. Audrey? Look outside and see if she's there. Who has the sheet music? Has anyone seen my baton? Please give it to me, Susan. No, it is not a fencing sword, this is my conductor's baton. There's a music case somewhere, and my handbag. Ah no, I remember that I didn't bring my handbag. Mary – come along, stop dawdling. No, your mummy must take the tram or the bus to town, as we have no room on the coach. Who threw that?' Toffee papers were flying round the bus like a plague of cabbage white butterflies. 'Really, girls, I do wish you would settle down and behave like young ladies.'

They quickly became young ladies when Sister Agatha appeared, her voluminous skirts spread as wide as any crinoline. She climbed into the vehicle, stared straight ahead, simply waited for silence. Sister Agatha would have been very useful during the war, because even the Germans would have fled from an expression as sour as hers.

We trundled off to town, unloaded ourselves outside the Market Hall and marched across the road in an untidy crocodile. Sister Maria Goretti stood in the middle of the traffic waving her arms as if bringing in an aeroplane. Some loving parents accosted their daughters, straightened ties and collars, pulled up wrinkled stockings, brandished combs and brushes. No-one waited for me. Dad would no doubt be inside. I wondered whether Mother would turn up, but she'd probably gone out again to save some family from starvation and fleas.

The music was unbelievably bad. Even the Mayor of Bolton squirmed in his seat, while I wished with all my heart that I'd taken the cotton wool from Confetti. The best performers were from Peter and Paul's, a group of little girls in their best white communion frocks. They sang about a gypsy woman called Meg and made a good job of it. Everyone else's renditions were murderous, though nothing was quite as wonderfully appalling as the St Mary's Strings. The St Mary's Strings were accompanied by Miss Bridges on the piano. She played all the right notes, probably in the right order, but my colleagues were, as ever, a law unto themselves. When those tortured miniature violins were finally put out of their misery, a collective sigh of relief hovered in the air above the audience. But I looked at Sister Agatha in that moment and saw something on her face. It wasn't pride, but it was certainly love. Seeing that made me special again, because I was close to these holy women. They knew me and some of them allowed me to know them. They were full of charity, those brides of Christ, but they made sure that few of us discovered their inner gentleness.

The Chief Education Officer stood on the platform and peered through glasses that were just halves of circles. He seemed a jolly man, especially when he made jokes about his own schooldays. He talked about three classes in one big room, three teachers at the front teaching three different subjects. The pupils on the ends of benches listened to two lessons simultaneously and either learned too much or nothing at all. 'We all kept hutching up,' he said, 'pushing one another along the forms till the end one fell off. That was our entertainment.' Then he told us how lucky we were to have powder paint and books and paper and bright classrooms.

The first prizes were for art, then we went through music (St Mary's won nothing in that category) and mathematics. Norma Wallace came out top, beat every child in Bolton, even those from the private establishments that crammed for Bolton School itself. I knew now that my story about Mr Evans had been silly and ordinary. None of these posh folk would be interested in an old man who grew flowers and made a fuss of cats.

The Chief Education Officer announced that he would now give out the essay prizes. Sister Maria Goretti turned in her seat and winked at me. I learned two things in those few seconds – a composition was an essay and a nun can wink. I felt terrible about letting Confetti down. She set a lot of store by me, would be disappointed when I didn't win. My father would be sad too. He must have been at the back of the hall, because I hadn't seen him yet.

Third prize went to a boy from Castle Hill, then the second was collected by a very beautiful girl from the Bolton Preparatory. The Chief Education Officer stood centre-stage and waved a paper. 'The first prize goes to someone whose story is very real and moving. Will you come up and read your essay, Laura McNally?'

I was stuck to the chair. My legs were of no earthly use to me and cold sweat ran down my neck, tickling as it travelled along the bumps of my spine. Sister Agatha got out of her seat and came for me. 'Come along, child.' Her eyes were wet and bright. 'I am so proud of you.'

I did it. To this day, I don't know how I managed not to faint, but I got on to that platform and read my sad little piece about an unsung hero. Applause is addictive. When they clapped and stamped their feet, I wanted more and more of it. Some of them even stood up and turned to one another, and I knew that they were talking about me.

I needed just one face in that audience, needed to see Dad, wanted him to share my moment of glory. My eyes raked back and forth along the rows and did not discover him. It was like the evening in the park all over again, because I was learning anew to be there for myself, to be my own guardian.

I was given a lovely leather-bound book full of Shakespeare, another item that I would keep till my dying day. The nuns clustered round me, their skirts spreading like a dark womb in which I could stay and be myself. They were my mothers, would continue forever to be my supporters, my guides. Norma Wallace gave me a germ-ridden kiss, then snerched in my ear. We were told to sit down, to remain in our seats until the schools nearer the door had left the hall.

Confetti knew. The pain in her lovely face was horrible,

while her eyes kept darting all over the place as she searched for some member of my family who would come forward and be proud. When hopelessness filled my heart, Uncle Freddie hobbled in. I learned that he had heard my composition, had gone outside for a breath of fresh air. But whatever emotion he had taken out with him was still working on his face. 'Eeh, lass,' he said, picking me up and holding me to his chest. 'I don't know what to say to you. I went back out in case . . . well . . . Liza might have been . . . We love you, Laura. Always remember that, sweetheart.'

Confetti beamed like a lighthouse, pleased to see that someone had cared enough to come. 'This is my uncle,' I told her. 'He's called Freddie and he lives next door.'

'Yes, I know,' she answered. 'Mr Turnbull and I have met before.'

'Sister Maria Goretti sent me an invitation,' he said, placing me back on my feet. 'Maisie's got a bad cold, so I've left our Anne to see to her. I wouldn't have missed this for the world. You're a great kid, Laura. Sister here has told me how well she thinks of you. And she's not wrong.' He beamed broadly at Confetti.

The thing about nuns is that they find out everything. In that one small sense, they are not unlike my mother. Even if you pretend that life at home is all right, they ask questions, make sure that they know your business. It hurt. Realizing that Confetti and old Tommy-gun and our headmistress (whom we called Aggie) knew all about my parents was not comfortable. It was as if my skin had been made of glass, as if they could look through me and see all the details of my inner workings.

Confetti was still grinning from ear to ear, while her affection for me shone wetly in her eyes. My indignation evaporated within a moment, because Confetti was a precious soul, had picked me from the crowd and watched over me ever since the death of Mr Evans. Even Aggie was my friend. After our headmistress had made a fuss of the other winners, she came and put a hand on my head. 'That was a wonderful piece of work, Laura McNally. In time, we shall expect great things of you.'

On an impulse that was undeniable, I spread my arms wide and hugged the unhuggable, pressed my face into the celluloid wimple of an immovable woman. And she laughed at me, laughed hard and tugged at my hair. 'She'll have the heart out of you, Goretti,' she said. 'For the child is a character and no mistake.'

Oh, it was so good to be a character and no mistake, to be noticed and valued, to be appreciated, touched, applauded. I turned to Uncle Freddie. 'Where's my dad?'

He stroked his moustache. 'The thing about your dad is that he's a genius. Geniuses do not make good time-keepers.'

'Or good teachers.' I saw that Sister Agatha had turned away. Her back was shaking, so I knew that I had said something amusing. 'One of our teachers is a genius. But Dad promised that he'd come. I read my story and didn't make any mistakes and—'

'He'll have forgotten, lass. He's a busy man.'

It was hard to accept that a person who loved me could forget an occasion such as this one. If Dad loved me, then why had he not been here on my special night? 'He should have come,' I said softly. 'It was my story that won and he should have come.'

Confetti mouthed at Uncle Freddie, something about my mother, I thought.

'Out, I think,' he answered curtly. 'Charity work, which should start at home.'

'Exactly.' Confetti's mouth was suddenly so tight that it looked mean. 'Some people don't appreciate God's gifts, Mr Turnbull. And gifts need nurturing.'

'I'll speak to John,' he said. 'This just isn't good enough.'

We filed out to the charabanc. I clutched my Shakespeare and my certificate of merit, curled my fingers round a florin from Uncle Freddie. Then I saw him. He was leaning against the wall, his face turned away from

215

me, but I knew that hair. Tommo. Tommo had come, had heard my story. When he swivelled round, I smiled at him.

'I stood in the porch,' he said. 'I heard you.'

He cared. Well, life wasn't too bad after all. Confetti and Aggie liked me, Uncle Freddie loved me, so did Auntie Maisie. If she hadn't been ill, she would have come, would have brought my cousin too. And Tommo . . . Tommo must have cared. Otherwise, he would not have bestirred himself to come and hear my story.

Tommo didn't say any more, but I could feel his gaze following me into the vehicle. As we drove away, he was still standing there, still staring at me. We turned into St George's Road, and I saw a man running down the slope towards the Victoria Hall. My father had come too late for me. But Tommo had been on time.

Life with the gang was hilarious, invigorating, extremely dangerous. For a while, I convinced Mother that I was taking extra music classes after school, but she was disabused of this concept when she met my piano teacher.

'Where is the extra money I gave you for the lessons?' asked Mother.

I placed the money on the mantelpiece, had not dared to spend the pound note on myself, hadn't dared to tell the gang of its existence. I prepared myself for the showdown, expected and got the usual stuff, furniture between us, a lot of hand-wringing and smoking on her part.

But I had changed, had toughened considerably. People like Enid, whose hair and dignity had been removed by high authority, whose mother collected rags and fleas in more or less equal quantities, were beyond caring, and they had dragged me into a state of near-nonchalance. The twins beat me, I clouted them back – it was all a part of the ethos. Tommo stayed aloof and superior, while Ginger worshipped me, stole things for me, put his freedom on the line many a time. Art worshipped me too, but he was just a little brother, a sad waif with strange teeth and a lisp. He was a friend, though, was a part of the gang. I needed them all, was getting used to people taking notice of me, felt encouraged by their interest. Mother was suddenly less significant than before.

'Where have you been going?' my mother asked shrilly.

'Out.' I was alone, yet not alone. In the slums of Deane and Daubhill, my mates were behind me. They might not have been visible at this particular juncture, but they held me up, supported the grim campaign I waged against my mother.

She stubbed out another Craven A. It had taken the length of a whole cigarette for her to persuade me to open my mouth in the first place. 'I am asking you where you go, Laura. Smart answers that tell me nothing are useless.'

I shrugged. Although I had not yet reached double figures in the age stakes, I was righteous about my rebellion. The righteousness sprang from the knowledge that while I was not necessarily right all the time, Liza McNally was definitely wrong on most occasions.

'Will you say something?'

I eyed her with what probably was dumb insolence. I had learned, from Ginger and under the watchful gaze of Tommo, how and when to kick back, when to speak up, when to be silent. Art was a big help too – when he did bestir himself to speak. According to him, if you said nowt, 'they' could do nowt to you. He'd probably gleaned that from films about courtrooms and from life experience. My mother was a member of the 'they' who could do nowt. 'I've got friends,' I said eventually. My tone was dark and sinister.

'Their names?' She arched the perfect eyebrows, leaned an elbow on the mantelpiece, looked like Bette Davis in one of her many dramatic roles. 'I wish to know the names and addresses of all your friends.'

'Why? Why do you need to know?' I was finding that if I stared straight at her, if I made my face cold and hard, she glanced away. 'I don't know the names of the people you go out with,' I said, believing this to be a seed of reasonable debate.

I had struck a nerve. She blinked, seemed vague for a second, propped herself more firmly against the dark wood shelf. 'I am not a child. When I was a little girl, I told my mother everything. My parents always knew where I was.'

I sat down on a dining chair, ignored the look of surprise that had invaded her face when I dared to sit without waiting for the order. During my lectures, I was expected to remain erect and alert unless otherwise advised by present company, present company always being Mrs Liza McNally. 'How could your mother know where you were all the time? What about when she was out scrubbing the Town Hall steps?'

She swallowed, pushed a lock of hair from her cheek. 'Who told you about that?'

'Auntie Maisie.'

'I ordered you not to go—'

'Ages ago. She told me a long time ago. Before you . . . before you upset Uncle Freddie.'

I had overstepped the mark by miles. Her hand was sharp and dry as it whipped across my face, but I managed to remain upright in the chair, did not cower. The skin of my cheek glowed with pain – I could almost feel it swelling, as if it had been stung by a wasp.

Mother stared hard at me, raised a hand, saw that I did not flinch. My stomach was fluttering and threatening to heave as she spoke. 'Don't talk about my parents,' she whispered as her hand dropped. 'My parents were decent people who worked very hard. It wasn't their fault that they got no education. My father might have been a great man if he'd been given a chance. Anyway, I listened to them, obeyed them.' She swallowed again, gulped down her shame. I thought that she was ashamed of being ashamed of her beginnings, but perhaps I was being too generous. Liza McNally was never eager to talk about her poor home background.

My breathing was hurting as it rushed past a constricted throat. She might kill me. She might just do it this time.

Yet I sensed some kind of watershed, as if I had to push for a conclusion, a solution to my problem with her. 'Auntie Maisie said you were . . .' I searched for the word, dug my teeth into it, 'humiliated by where you lived and that you pretended not to live there. I don't know why you should worry about things like that. Auntie Maisie said that nothing is good enough for you. So you read a lot of books and followed my dad till you caught him.' Auntie Maisie had said none of this to me, but had been overheard by Anne, then Anne had furnished me with this delicious ammunition. Sometimes, I was not a nice child. Although rather young to organize my revolution properly, I fired some more bullets anyway. 'You didn't do as you were told all the time. You were naughty sometimes, Auntie Maisie said.'

'Auntie Maisie, Auntie Maisie,' she mimicked spitefully. 'Stop wandering away from the point. Where have you been when you ought to have been taking your music classes?'

'Out.' And thus we returned to square one. Inside, I was scared, but I laughed secretly at her discomfiture, tried to smother my frail misgivings. Yet my own discomfiture was still there, because although I never loved my mother, I was destined to remain uneasy with my feelings towards her.

She lit yet another cigarette.

'I wish you wouldn't do that.'

The hand which held the lighted match paused, froze in mid-air. 'What did you say?' She yelped as the flame matured and licked a heated tongue against her fingers, then she flung the match away. 'What did you just say to me?'

I made my eyes cold and hard again. It was easy to do – I just blinked as infrequently as I could manage. 'Every day – well, nearly every day – I come in here and you tell me how bad I am. That's all right, but I wish you wouldn't smoke, because I find it hard to breathe when you are smoking all the time.' It was as if I wanted to be slapped, as if I deliberately courted her anger just to see how far she would go.

She darted round the chair and grabbed my hair, forced my head back until I thought my spine would snap. The noise that escaped from her throat was guttural and nasty. 'Don't you dare criticize me, girl. I smoke when I am nervous, and your behaviour makes me nervous. This is all for your own good. If you are running about the streets and misbehaving yourself, then you will only bring dishonour to this family.'

It's hard to know where the strength came from, difficult to work out where I got the courage and the inspiration, but I said, very softly, 'I don't bring great fat women knocking on our door.'

She was still tugging at my hair, and her eyes had become frantic, were darting about in her head as if seeking somewhere to hide. The lids dropped for a moment, hid her panic. Mother was afraid because I appeared not to fear her. Had she heard the clamour of my heart, she would have known the terror.

I was tossed aside like a rag doll, came to rest against the door. The brass knob crashed into my temple, filled the room with flashes of colourful light. But I would not fall, would not allow myself to sag.

The silence almost defied description. There was a small fire that crackled and spat, making the smoky atmosphere even more electric and frightening. My mother seemed to petrify, the cigarette halfway to her mouth, her lips parted and slackened by something that looked like a blood brother to astonishment. When she finally moved, it was towards me, the free hand lifted to strike anew.

At times like this, I had always cowered low down to make myself small, to reduce the visibility of target areas like head and neck. Until this day, my hands had covered my face and as much of my skull as they could encompass, so Mother had been very sure of her power, even if her dominance over me had been merely physical. But on this occasion, I did not move, did not even blink.

Her progress slowed itself, and she looked silly with her hand raised above her head. 'You are . . . not natural,' she whispered. 'You are not my child. I have often said that they must have given me the wrong one.'

My knees threatened to buckle as I steadied myself, but I managed to stand fairly still. 'I'm Daddy's,' I said, the tears dangerously close.

'Are you? Did he come to your precious presentation? Oh, I heard you telling him off. Let you down, did he?' As she spoke, she lowered her arm and took a pace back.

'I am the right one,' I screamed. 'It's you who are wrong, you, you, YOU! Uncle Freddie says that Dad ought to leave you and find a proper life with somebody nice, but Dad won't leave me. He stays with me. So . . . so just be very glad that I'm here, that's all. Because if I wasn't here, he'd go off and live all by himself in the rooms above the shop.' My temper slipped into neutral, coasted along with no brake to hinder it. 'He might even find a nice lady with no cigarettes or red lipstick, somebody who can cook.'

She walked out of the room. Had she stayed, she would probably have battered me to death. The whole of my back had weakened to pulp, then my limbs became affected, started jerking and trembling like saplings in a skittish wind. Breathing was not easy. I had to open my mouth wide, found myself gulping down air that was heavy with smoke. There was no strength in me, so I could not cough. I simply heaved, waited for my legs to return to me, rested until the flashing lights had settled, then I crept out of the house and fled down towards the town.

They were waiting for me on the open-air market. Tommo, careless as ever, had struck a pose on an empty stall, his expression aloof and magnificent. He was the real boss of the gang, the brains behind all our wickedness, though Ginger provided weight, voice and muscle. Tommo rarely addressed the group, preferring to brief Ginger privately before each assembly. But it was strange how we all came together as if responding to some magnetic force. Nobody seemed to state properly where we should be, when we ought to arrive at a certain place, yet we would turn up as if driven by an unseen hand, would simply arrive, nod at each other and meld together into a single unit of mischievous humanity. Though Tommo remained detached for most of the time, seemed to be amused by half the things we did.

'Yer on a job, Lo,' announced Ginger without preamble. 'Down near t' station.'

I gulped, swallowed a mouthful of air. This was to be my proper initiation, then. I had not been 'on a job' yet, a job of my own. I had served my apprenticeship as a mere labourer by helping to carry stuff from one disused air-raid shelter to another, from Ginger's back yard to Art's coalshed. 'What are we doing?' I asked.

Tommo nodded, gave Ginger the awaited permission. 'Yer've got fer t' stand on Trinity Street,' said Ginger.

'Why?'

Enid simpered, cast a veiled glance in the direction of her hero, Ginger Nelson. ''Cos yer've lost yer busfare 'ome.' The twins fluttered quite frequently, were both in hot pursuit of Ginger's affections. But Ginger's heart was mine. Enid and Irene knew it, I knew it, while Ginger remained blissfully uncomfortable in my presence. If Tommo was aware of any of this, he kept it where he kept most things, in a place that never showed in his eyes.

'Can yer cry?' This came from Irene, the other twin. I could tell the difference now, because their shorn heads had reseeded themselves, and the vegetation was dark brown on Irene, a lighter brown on Enid.

'I can cry.' Well, I supposed that I could. And I had to look right, had to do the right thing in front of Tommo. He seemed to be a very judgemental person, very quick with a sniff and a raised eyebrow when one of us failed to meet standards that he had never bothered to lay down in the first place. 'I can pretend to cry,' I added lamely.

He sniffed now, jumped down from his throne of weather-beaten and splintered wood. 'You'll cry,' he said coldly. 'I'll guarantee it.' His English was quite good, though he seldom used it. Tommo's father had been an altar boy, had even been a candidate for the priesthood till Tommo's mother got the better of him. According to Ginger, there were books in Tommo's home. Not magazines, not romances like my mother's collection, but proper books with a lot of pages and leather covers. Also according to Ginger, Tommo was a 'jeenyus'.

Tommo made me cry. On the railway bridge, he thumped me on the chest, pinched the backs of my hands till they glowed with pain, hit me across the mouth with an oustretched palm. While he did these things, he smiled. The smile was almost gentle, almost kind. He even remarked on a handprint left by Mother, asked if I had been a naughty girl at home.. If only I had remembered the expression on Tommo's face, the serenity, the calm, then my life would have been so different . . . But I had something to prove, so I did not flinch, though my tears ensured that the evening was a success.

I worked the 45, 46 and 47 buses, the ones that stopped outside the ladies' toilet on Trinity Street before driving off up the moor to decent houses. After an hour and a half, I had collected 3s 7½d, because I was quite good at being a little girl who had lost her fare. Back on the bridge, Ginger was sulking. I felt sure that he had tackled Tommo about the beating, and I felt sorry for my staunch red-haired friend. I gave him the money, but it was grabbed quickly by Tommo.

'Divide it,' I said. I felt stubborn and strong, because I had defeated my mother, had refused to let Tommo break my spirit, had collected the day's booty. Although Tommo fascinated me, I knew that he needed fetching down a peg or two.

Tommo looked at me, swept his arrogant eyes the length of my body. He smiled again, then gave the five of us sixpence each. It was not good enough. I walked to the edge of the bridge and tossed my handful of coppers through the iron trellis. Everyone except Tommo screamed at me, berated me for throwing money onto the rails. Tommo remained as still as a statue. He knew why I had committed the foolish deed, but he simply smirked and walked away.

'I hate him,' I said softly.

Ginger heard me, blushed to the roots of his colourful hair, bent his head and stared at his boots. They were ugly things, brown and scuffed and lacking laces. Occasionally, he stepped out of them when running, had to dash back and retrieve one or both. These had been his brother's boots, and his brother was four years older, four years bigger. 'Tommo's all right,' he muttered. 'Yer've just got ter get used ter 'im, that's all.'

Enid shook my arm. 'Th' art a reet 'Oly Mary. Yer could 'ave give us t' money if yer di'n't want it.'

I was suddenly tired of the whole thing, fed up with waiting while they pinched empties from the back yards of shops, while they tied people's door knockers to lamp posts. It was boring. 'I'm going home,' I said.

Ginger grabbed me. 'Are yer finished wi' us?'

'Yes,' I replied smartly. 'The people on the station gave me money because of a lie. It's not right – they've worked for that bus fare. I'm not doing it any more.'

As I trudged off the bridge, I heard Irene saying, 'See? She is an 'Oly Mary.' It might have been Enid who said that. But I couldn't see their new batch of hair and I wasn't going to turn round. I had left them behind me and I was the loneliest girl in all the world.

Chapter Eight

Life alone was not exactly thrilling. Several times, I almost gave in to the urge, almost ran all the way from our house up to Deane, but I managed to stay away from the gang. Had I returned to Ginger and the rest, I would probably have become inured to bad ways, might even have slid into the habit of juvenile crime. It was time to put a stop to my sinful behaviour, because my father was an honourable man. Although he had let me down in my brief moment of triumph, he had done nothing to deserve a delinquent daughter.

Gang or no gang, trouble followed me wherever I went. Even when a day started out bright and normal, something unforeseen would crop up – a pile of spelling mistakes, a blotted sum book, an unlearned poem. I was a lively child, and I always seemed to meet misfortune halfway, had a habit of sticking out chest and tongue, a tendency to over-defend myself.

But I was not ready for Norma Wallace. We had got on quite well for a while, would have shared Mr Nathaniel 'Good' Evans had he lived, but Norma turned on me. And I retaliated. She cornered me one morning during our enforced absence from a lesson about Gifts of the Holy Ghost. I felt quite smug about the missed class, as I'd almost learned the list from a girl in Standard Four – something about wisdom, understanding and fear of the Lord with a few other bits in between that I was trying to discover in the recesses of my cluttered mind. One was fortitude. I liked the word, wrote it down in my rough book.

She snerched extra loudly. Norma had developed a

variety of snerches, or perhaps I had learned to interpret their hidden meanings. There were the necessary snerches – those she employed to keep her face clean – and the intentional ones. The latter usually preceded an announcement of great moment, so I looked up from my 'fortitude' and waited for her statement.

She pushed the stringy hair from her face, fixed a red-rimmed eye on me. (She hadn't been crying. Her eyelids were constantly red owing to her everlasting cold.) 'It's your mother's fault,' she snapped. 'Mr Openshaw's had to leave.'

My mouth hung open for a moment, then I snapped it shut as soon as my wits began to return. 'I beg your pardon? What are you talking about?' I sounded like a child who was pretending to be grown-up all of a sudden.

'He was a good preacher. Mummy says he's the best we've ever had.'

It was a pity that Mummy didn't supply snot-rags, I thought. Then a dim light began to break amongst the clouds of my fuddled thinking. Openshaw. She was talking about that terrible man who ranted and raved at the Methodist chapel. 'You mean the minister? The one who shouts about hell?'

She heaved another strangled breath up the clogged nostrils. 'Don't pretend you don't know him, Laura McNally. I used to see you at the morning services.'

I hadn't been able to see anyone who had sat outside the eight or so inches of vision allowed by that stupid bonnet. 'I never noticed you.' This was the truth.

'She went after him, followed him all over the place,' said Norma. 'She chased him till he had to run away to another chapel in a town near London. My mother says that your mother is very cheap. And I heard my dad saying that Liza McNally is a Jezebel.'

Norma Wallace had annoyed me – albeit off and on – for some years. I hated and pitied her for her appearance, disliked the filthy habits, the bitten nails, the way she courted the nuns and did all her work efficiently, proudly.

Had someone pleasant spoken ill of my mother, I might not have minded. But to have this prudish, judgemental and ugly girl saying anything at all about my private life – well – it made me angry beyond endurance. I belted her full in the face with my atlas, a solid weapon with a hard blue cover.

The scene became extremely colourful when a mixture of red and yellowish-green poured from her ruptured nose. Mother Hyacinth, a high-grade non-teaching nun who was visiting the school, rushed to the scene, mopped the mess from Norma's face, fetched the cane, gave me six stinging strokes on each hand. Mother Hyacinth spoke to me after the caning, seemed rather shaken by the whole thing. Perhaps she was not qualified to issue corporal punishment, as she worked in an administrative capacity at both school and convent. 'It is a shame that you lost your temper. Norma was wrong to bait you, but you really must pray for self-control.'

'Yes, Mother.' I was beyond caring. And the easiest way with nuns was to agree completely, especially when they were in the wrong. They were educated women, but their life experience was narrowed to the point where they saw little, because their vision was as narrowed by their vows as mine had been by the silly hat.

I stood outside Sister Agatha's office, listened while Confetti pleaded my case. It didn't matter. I would be leaving St Mary's eventually, would have a fresh start at another school where no-one would know about my mother. Or so I hoped. 'She's a good girl,' said Confetti. Then I heard a few splinters of conversation like 'her mother' and 'Methodist chapel' and 'didn't deserve to be caned'. And it still didn't matter, except that I wanted Norma's nose to be a proper shape when it settled down.

When I arrived home that afternoon, I entered the front room on a voluntary basis, looked at my mother with an expression that was meant to echo her own.

'What's the matter?' She was plainly uncomfortable.

'What's a Jezebel?' I asked.

227

Several emotions did a procession across her face. She knew what I meant, knew that I had heard all or some of the story. 'I'm not sure,' she answered, her voice crippled and low.

I nodded. 'Neither am I. But Norma Wallace from the Methodist chapel understands it. And so does Mr Openshaw. He's had to move to London because of a Jezebel.'

I walked upstairs, threw myself on the bed, tossed my homework into a corner. Life without my friends was boring, but at least I could relieve myself of learning.

Things started to happen after a short while, events that served to take my mind off the isolation I had imposed on myself. Men arrived from London, Birmingham, Coventry, big men in bulky black suits and bulky black cars. I looked at them and thought of funerals, then I sat back to watch.

My father had no proper office yet, so he was forced to bring home these people after showing them round his almost ready factory. Mother was coy, discreetly made-up, secretly overwhelmed. I knew about the secret overwhelming, because I'd seen her practising in front of mirrors. 'How do you do, Mr Simpson, Mr Lewis, Mr Charnock?' She always put her head on one side when she greeted them, whether she was in the mirror or face to face with flesh and blood reality. She was a Jezebel who was preparing to go up in the world; she was uncertain, afraid of letting herself down among all the business folk who were invading our home. Her unease communicated itself to me, and I began to fret slightly about developments, about major changes. Mother was worried even though she was grown up, so how would I cope with my father's promising future?

Dad wore an air of great seriousness, explained to me that some of the visitors wanted to buy him out before production had even begun. But he had registered McNally's Cooling Tea with the patents office, was determined to go it alone if no-one would back him with cash. I wore a blue dress and a winning smile, was declared 'sweet' by the funereal financiers as I passed out biscuits and tiny sandwiches. In the end, several of the bankers lent money, so Dad was able to set his empire in motion.

There were ten muslin bags to each box, and my father's mother's coat of arms was emblazoned on the packaging, a pig's head with a shield surrounding it. I studied the first real packet, yet another item that I would preserve for ever. 'Nice except for the pig,' I judged.

'Never dismiss the pig, Laurie-child,' he answered. 'My forefathers made a living out of pigs. A porker is an animal of great wisdom and intelligence, and it makes a good parent.' Mother came in, stood with a foolish smile on her face while Dad concluded, 'And don't forget the swine's sheer stubbornness.'

My dad's signature was on the side of the box under some words about the product's efficacy. The legend PATENT PENDING sat on the lid to warn others not to copy the recipe. In reality, no-one could have managed it, because the secret was guarded for years like the crown jewels. 'Very nice, John,' said Mother.

He did not look at her. She was just beginning to realize that her husband was not a fool, and was trying, against all odds, to revitalize a marriage whose soul had passed on for all eternity.

'You'll be a great success,' she added quietly.

He nodded, looked at his watch. 'Not with Fennings and Beechams so well established. Haven't you always said that?'

'Well . . . perhaps I was wrong.'

At last he awarded her a cursory glance. 'We were both wrong.' He was not talking about the kind of chemistry that comes in liquid or powder form. 'But then we all make mistakes, don't we?' He walked out, leaving her with a silly expression on her face, as if she had just been clouted with a wet dishcloth. She would never be close to my father again, would never be a wife to him.

There followed a difficult time, the duration of which I

have never managed to assess accurately. There was less coal to burn and the meals were smaller, a blessing for which I was thankful, as my mother never learned to cook properly. She became thinner, keener, watched me like a hawk, pinned me to the table and stood over me as I laboured with history, geography, sums. She was going up in the world, so I must not disgrace her on the academic front. My father stopped coming home regularly, sometimes labouring for two whole days at a stretch without a break. He was an honourable man, and honourable men do not play the fool with investors' money.

Then suddenly, it was all over and Dad came home with a baby doll in a large cardboard and cellophane box, a full quarter of Keiller's butterscotch all for me and, in a long brown envelope, a description of the house in which we were going to live. It was an old farmhouse with barns and stables, but Dad had already converted the outbuildings into factory sheds. The doll stayed in its packaging, but I made much of the sweets, as Mother's stews were becoming totally indigestible.

He spread our future on the table, some drawings of a kitchen, living room, laundry, bedrooms. His face glowed with pleasure as he outlined his plans, while he ignored Mother, who sat motionless in a chair pulled out slightly from the table. To me, her separateness was total. She was an alien being, had no part to play in my father's great step forward. But I wished that she were different, someone who could sit with us and share the excitement. 'The barn conversions are almost completed,' he said proudly. 'Electric power is going in as we speak. I shall be able to fall out of bed and straight into work each morning.' He paused, loosened his tie, as if success seemed so unbelievable that it threatened to choke him. 'Anne will be moving to the village of Barr Bridge with Maisie and Freddie. Our house is just outside Barr Bridge, a few hundred yards up the moor.'

I could feel her eyes boring into my spine. I shivered, found something to say. 'Will I still go to St Mary's?'

He shook his head. 'Too far away, I'm afraid. You'll have to make do with the village school for a year or two.'

My heart leapt at the thought of school with Anne, then sank like a lead weight at the thought of school without Confetti. I hadn't realized how much I cared for my surrogate mother until separation was threatened. And would Mother accept this? Would she allow her daughter to associate with 'common people'? I was old enough now to understand that my mother was seriously odd, if not deranged. She acted common, ran round with men, expected me not to show her up. It was hilarious and horrible.

She continued to say nothing. It had been my experience thus far that Liza McNally was at her most dangerous when keeping quiet. It was like the calm before a storm. Mother often exploded after a long, quiet sulk. But that happened with the weather too, I thought irrelevantly. There was usually a dark grey lull before thunder, but at least the hall barometer told us what to expect. Life would have been a lot easier for me and my dad if Mother could have been fitted with a barometer.

She struck a match. I froze as she scraped the box, waited until she breathed her first sigh of smoke. 'Shopping,' she said, leaving a meaningful pause behind the word, 'will be very difficult.' She extinguished the flame with a small puff of air from between pursed lips.

My father kept his tone light. 'If you feel that the country will not suit you, then you can stay in town. Freddie and I will be selling the two semis, but I could have the rooms over the shop made into a decent flat. I've taken on a young dispenser, but he's a married man with his own house, so he won't be needing the upper floor.'

She inhaled deeply. 'If I remain in Bolton, then Laura must stay with me and continue with her schooling.'

'No.' His voice was even, emotionless. 'Laurie comes with me.'

My cheeks burned in anticipation of a long argument, though none was forthcoming. As the heavy, smoke-laden seconds ticked by, I began to feel the edge of my father's power. He was a polite man, a correct one. But he had brains, the sort of inventive cleverness that breeds a non-aggressive success. She knew it. In later years, I looked back and understood a little of the young woman who was my mother. He would become rich and she needed his money, craved the kudos that went with money. I was the weapon she used to stay with him, as I was the one person in the world he really cared about. Father's capacity for human love was not immense. He liked rhyme, reason, a formula. In people, he found no strict pattern, nothing to analyse. But he allowed Liza to come along for the ride because she was the one who gave birth to his daughter.

Busy days followed this one, hours of packing and cleaning and casting out of the rubbish that accumulates in an established family. For the first time in years, I was given permission to go next door. In fact, I was asked to go. She was casual about it, so deliberately nonchalant that I knew straight away that my errand had been planned. 'Ask Maisie if she needs any more packing cases. And see if they've a pat of butter to spare.'

When my bated breath became easier, I ran to the adjoining house and almost wept when the door was opened to me. Auntie Maisie cried for both of us, hugged me tightly against her ample chest, called me a dear girl and a poppet, sat me down, made me eat three lemon curd tarts. The house was so much brighter than ours, with bordered patterns on the walls and a yellow-painted ceiling. Uncle Freddie came in from the garden where he was trying to grow potatoes. He threw some sad-looking specimens onto the table, swung me up in his arms, staggered beneath my weight. 'By Christ,' he muttered. 'Have you been eating lead piping? She's solid, Maisie, is our Laura.' And Anne just stood still with her heart in her eyes. I could feel Anne's relief and happiness, needed no words.

'The country,' I said to Uncle Freddie. 'We'll be all grass and stuff.'

232

He laughed. 'Aye, we'll be bumpkins inside a fort-night, wearing our nightshirts while we drive the cows home. We're having a cottage in Barr Bridge, a little stone place with climbing roses in the back yard. And Maisie's planning on getting a suntan.'

Auntie Maisie giggled and flicked him with the ever-present tea towel. I'd forgotten how she always wore one on her left shoulder. She mopped her face with the same cloth, found me a glass of dandelion and burdock, cut the butter in half and wrapped my portion in greaseproof paper. 'Take this to our Liza, lass. And tell her we'll be round when we're nearly packed, see then if we want any more boxes.' The rift was not mended, but a bridge had been built. Auntie Maisie's relationship with my mother would never be an easy one, and my heart went out to her. All her life, she had made room for her sister. Now, it was my turn to make room for Liza. We understood and pitied one another, though nothing was said.

Anne took me to the door. 'I'm glad things are right, Laura.'

Things would never be right. 'So am I.'

She closed the living room door. 'Hey,' she whispered. 'There's been a lad looking for you. He keeps hanging about and asking everybody have they seen you.'

'Oh?' This came out squeaky. 'I don't know any boys.'

'Well, he knows you. Another lad with red hair hangs around with him.'

The lad with red hair would be Ginger. Was little Art pining for me, standing at the end of a cul-de-sac and lisping his way nearer to my house? 'Take no notice,' I advised. 'We'll be gone in a few weeks.'

'Tommo, he's called,' she said.

'Well?' I was hot, unaccountably so. The butter would be dripping out of my hands in a minute. 'Well?' Anne was still infuriatingly slow to part with a secret.

'He says he's got his eye on you. He means he likes you, wants to know if you've got any other boyfriends.'

The sweat dripped down my spine. 'It's Ginger who

likes me,' I mumbled. 'Ginger, not Tommo.' When you are nine, underfleshed, big-boned and a coward, it's nice to know that a boy is interested in spite of your shortcomings. 'I don't like red hair much,' I said smartly.

'Not him,' she said. 'It's the other one who likes you, the one with the funny colour of hair. It's not red, more sort of pinkish, I'd say.'

'Strawberry blond,' I remarked, smart again. 'I saw it in a magazine of mother's. That's what they call that colour of hair. Strawberry blond,' I repeated, aware of Anne's fierce scrutiny.

'You like him.' The tone was accusatory. 'Didn't we say we'd never—'

'Shut up. I don't know him, not properly. I've seen him a few times and—'

'And you know the colour of his hair. Well, I'd never have believed it.' She looked and sounded just like Auntie Maisie. 'Laura with a boyfriend.'

'He's not my boyfriend.' I transferred the butter to my left hand, hoped that it would keep in spite of the heated conversation. 'I can't help it if he's following me.'

She softened, looked sorry for me. 'Well, he says he'll follow you wherever you go.'

I did not understand this at all. As a thief, I'd been useless, as a beggar, I'd been a terrified amateur. And Tommo had never even spoken to me, not properly, except when we'd walked on the station bridge that evening. Even then, he had hit me and commanded me to be a beggar. 'Are you sure it wasn't the other one, the boy with the carroty red hair?'

Anne shook her head. 'No, it was Pink-Head,' she whispered, shielding her words from any adult with acute hearing. 'I think he loves you. The one called Ginger says Tommo's smitten. When Ginger found out that I'm your cousin, he came to see me on his own. "He'll never let go now," he said. "Tommo always gets what he wants, so tell her to be careful." Is he dangerous, this Tommo boy?'

234

I tried to look dignified. 'How should I know? He's not somebody I've seen more than once.'

She stood her ground. 'He loves you and he'll not let go.'

This was getting really stupid. Grown-ups were the ones who loved and refused to let go. 'Rubbish,' I announced. I stalked off with the watery butter, stopped on our doorstep to try shaping the oozing grease into something resembling a newly-patted quarter. The smile on my face was probably idiotic, very broad and stupid. He loved me. The selfish, strong and silent Tommo was my very own boyfriend. And soon, he would have to walk a terribly long way to find me if he wanted his sweetheart. Well, if he really liked me, he would do just that.

'Laura, I am so sorry to be losing you.' She was losing her veil too, had been hasty when dressing. 'It's such a shame, because you're doing well. Your English homework got top marks again. Is there no way that you can carry on at St Mary's?'

'I'm not old enough for the bus, Sister. Dad says you've given me a good grounding, so I should be all right at the village school. It won't be for long. Once I'm eleven, I'll have to come to one of the big schools in Bolton.'

She poked a pin into her head, flinched slightly as it caught her scalp. 'I'm always attacking myself with these pins,' she said, as if talking to herself.

'You shouldn't have been a nun.' I bit my tongue, marvelled yet again at my own audacity. Perhaps I was brave because I was leaving the school.

'Why?'

'Well,' I shifted in the chair, groped for a reasonable explanation. 'You wouldn't have needed pins if you'd just been a woman.'

'I'm still a woman.'

'Yes, but you're a nun with pins. A lot of the little girls think you don't even have legs. When I came to St Mary's, I was sure you all went back to heaven every night to play your harps. A few of us were scared of you because of the black clothes. But now I know you're just like everybody else underneath.'

She grinned. 'My mammy said I'd never make a nun. I was always in trouble, you see. I mind the time we all went strawberry-picking over to Father Martin's place. He was a wealthy priest who'd given up a large house as part of a seminary for young boys who were called to the priesthood. But he still owned the garden, and he grew fruits and vegetables for the market, then he used the money for his church. Well, I was in the most awful state, Laura, for I'd eaten more than I'd collected in the punnets. And didn't we find out that I'm allergic to strawberries? So off we went to hospital, me and Mammy and Father Martin and him so grim-faced you'd have thought the world was at its end. God's punishment, he called it.'

I stared at her. 'So you've done ordinary bad things like ordinary people do?'

'Well of course. Did you think we were all born clutching a rose and with a halo like the Little Flower?'

'I never thought about it.'

'You surely did think, for you said just now that we all played our harps after sunset. Nuns are not perfect, Laura. We still go to confession and tell all the sins we've committed. Don't let the habit fool you, for we're as mortal as the rest of humanity.'

I swallowed, bit back the tears. 'I'll miss you.'

'Ah, so you'll miss old Confetti, will you? Would you write to me, Laura?'

'Yes.' I was not going to cry.

'Every week?'

I nodded. I was definitely not going to cry.

'Until one of us dies?'

I was going to cry. 'Don't die.' The world would be a dark place without people like Confetti. 'Please don't die.'

'Well, I'll do me best to carry on alive. Is that you weeping, Laura McNally?'

'I've got something in my eye.'

She hovered over me, poked around with a corner of a

handkerchief, made me blink against her clumsy attempts to remove the non-existent foreign body. Confetti had a gentle soul and a heart full of love, but she was all fingers and thumbs. 'There's nothing there at all, child. So you're crying.'

I flung my arms round her and buried my face in the rough cloth of her uniform. 'I want a mother like you,' I mumbled.

She was shaking. 'Laura, I can adopt you in my heart. It's a tiny sin, because I should have no favourite, but I feel your need for a good friend. When you write, tell me everything, even if it's bad. It will go no further.'

'Like confession?'

'Exactly like that.'

'And you'll write back?'

'Even if they send me to Africa with three priests and a brass band playing. Even if they send me to the Eskimos and make me skate five miles across frozen water to the post office. Even if I get caught by cannibals and stewed in a pot with praties and onion, so help me, Laura McNally, I shall still write to you.'

I stood back and fought for my dignity, dashed the drops of wetness from my face and forced a smile to appear on lips that were stiff with grief. It was like giving up my family. I knew now what these nuns had. They'd found sisterhood and God. While God was an important being, fellowship with other people was the first step towards Him. More than ever, I wanted to wear that veil, but with pins that wouldn't fall out. 'I'll be a nun,' I said. 'I'll come back and be a teaching nun like you.' Perhaps safety pins would suffice. Though being a nun and a pharmacist might prove difficult, and I'd already promised Dad that I would work with him one day.

'We'll see.' She sounded just like any other grown-up who pretended to believe what a child was saying. That disappointed me, because Maria Goretti had always taken me seriously. 'You don't think I'll do it,' I said.

'You'll go with God, my child. Listen to Him and hold

His hand. If He wants you to join the order, then He'll tell you. If He wants you to marry and have babies, then He'll find a way of letting you know.'

'I'll miss you, Sister. I really, really will miss you.'

She grinned and her face shone, but it was like a rainbow after a storm, because the tears made her eyes brighter. 'Call me Confetti. And when you write to me, put "Confetti" on the envelope, because the sisters think it's hilarious. Mind, it's not as funny as the other name I'm called. Is it?'

'You mean Spaghetti?'

She started to giggle. 'Very Italian, isn't it? Still, perhaps it's apt – after all, Rome is the seat of the Church. And the real Maria Goretti – God rest her gentle soul – was from Italy. She's to be a saint soon, you know.' She bent down and delivered a peck to my left cheek, then to the right. '*Au revoir*, Laura. Come and see me.'

I walked out of that school and did not turn my head. I had not left her behind. Confetti was a part of me, because she had done more for me than anyone else except old Tommy-gun, and poor Tommy had retired now on health grounds, something to do with rheumatics and poor circulation. But I carried Confetti home with me, prayed fiercely that her goodness would shape my thinking, make me generous, kind, more tolerant of my mother.

She was waiting for me. 'Laura, your room was in total chaos. Didn't I tell you that the Pearsons are coming to measure for curtains? This is not really our house any more. I've scrubbed and scrubbed at that desk of yours. And why do you leave a coat hanger on the floor almost every day? I could have broken my neck . . .'

On and on she went. There was no charity in me, because I was tempted to imagine how much better life could be if she had broken her neck. If she went and broke her neck, she'd be in a wheelchair and I would leave her in a place far away from me, in a room at the other end of the farmhouse. Then I could do as I pleased and there'd be no more speeches and—

'Are you listening to me? He knocked at the door as bold as brass and asked for you. Now, he was a well-spoken boy in decent clothes, but I do not know him. Where has he come from? Laura, why is this boy coming here and asking for you?'

'I don't know.'

She took a deep breath and prepared to pick up the threads. 'He says that you know him as Tommo, which sounds very common in my opinion. His real name is Bernard Thompson, and he wanted to know our new address. Well, I am not going to stand all day on the doorstep telling my address to every Tom, Dick and Harry—'

'Tommo, Dick and Harry.' Here came Clever-Clogs again, little Miss Brains with the untamable tongue.

Her expression was vague. 'What did you say?'

'Nothing. I coughed.' There'd be no place for me in a convent. Strawberries were one thing, lying to your mother was another matter entirely.

'So I sent him away. But he's been hovering about at the end of the avenue. He can be seen from a mile away with that odd hair. Go and send him away—'

'He's not there.'

'Oh yes, he is.'

'I've just come up from the road and he wasn't there.'

Mother stepped to the window and peered through the curtains, careful not to twitch the cloth in case the neighbours thought she was interfering again, watching their every move. 'He's there now. Go and send him away.'

Bernard. That was a Catholic name. One of the priests who visited the convent was called Father Bernard. Of course, Tommo was a Catholic – I'd seen him serving at the altar in St Patrick's church. Well, if I wasn't going to be a nun, I'd marry a Catholic boy and have Catholic children. Which would make Mother furious and might turn out to be a wonderful way of paying her back for all her cruelty. Not that she hit me much these days. I was getting too big for her to batter now, too solid to be dragged about by the hair, too strong and wilful to cower in a corner with my hands over my head and—

'Why are you standing there? Go and send him away at once. When you come back, you must peel some potatoes, since I've had no time at all to prepare a meal. The hairdresser's was crowded out and smelled awful, because some stupid woman was having a hot perm. She'll come out like a French poodle . . . And don't slam the door.'

I didn't slam it, but I closed it noisily, just to let her know that I didn't care, wasn't afraid. We lived in a quiet street where nobody shouted or banged doors, so my naughtiness was probably noticed by at least a dozen eyes and ears. But I didn't care, because I was important. Tommo had come for me, so I was very, very important.

'What do you want?'

He turned slowly and examined me, his expression calm and cold. 'Where have you been?'

'Here.' I waved a hand across the house-fronts. 'This is where I live.'

'I know that. Where have you been when you weren't here?' His eyes were warming up, as if the kindling had caught beneath a coal fire. 'We've seen nothing of you for months.'

'Well.' I thought of saying something interesting, but all my interesting statements tended to be lies. 'I've been at school and doing homework and getting ready to move. My dad's starting his own factory in Barr Bridge.'

He handed me a mint, one of those clear, glassy ones in clear, glassy paper. 'Eat it.'

'I'm saving it.'

'Please yourself.' He strutted to the edge of the pavement, looked down Chorley New Road, looked up Chorley New Road. 'When are you moving?'

'Next week.'

He stalked back to me. 'I'll be coming up to see you. Your mother doesn't like me, so you'd be best not telling her. I'll come Saturday or Sunday afternoons, depending on what I'm doing, and I'll wait in the bushes at the far side of the bridge, away from the houses.'

'Why?'

His cheeks reddened. ''Cos I want to come, that's why. Are you as daft as that mother of yours? "Where do you live, young man, who are your parents?" Anyway, there's no need to ask me why. I do as I please, always have and always will.'

There is something completely fascinating about a truly selfish person. I found myself drawn to him as a moth is attracted to a fatal flame, wanted to climb inside his head so that I might truly know him. Tommo loved himself completely, was a clever boy who was not easily satisfied, who did not tolerate fools. So he must have been an interesting person, or he would not have found himself so totally absorbing. While I processed these confused and confusing thoughts, I found my voice again. 'I meant why do we have to meet in the bushes?'

'Because your mother won't like us seeing one another. I've met her sort before. She thinks she's the bee's knees, doesn't she?'

I shrugged, didn't want to speak for or against the motion.

'Well, she'll only make a fuss. So we'll meet in the bushes – right?'

I didn't know. 'I don't know,' I said.

He fixed his gaze on a point somewhere behind my head. 'You like me, don't you?'

'Well . . . yes.'

'So you'll want to see me.'

It was nice to have a boy wanting to see me. My world thus far had been populated by females, the biggest of which would now be twitching her curtains in spite of what the neighbours might say. Dad loved me, but he had no time for anyone. It might be fun to have a friend all to myself, someone who wasn't a girl. 'Will you bring Ginger?'

The fire in his eyes roared with life, seeming to send out

sparks as he glared at me. 'Why? Do you want him for your boyfriend?'

'No, I—'

'Well, he won't be coming with me.'

I swallowed, began to worry about Mother's reaction if I didn't go back soon. 'What about Art and Enid and Irene?'

'I'll fetch nobody.'

'Oh.' My lips were dry, so I ran my tongue over them, but the dryness had gone right through me, into my mouth and right through to my soul. He frightened me, but I liked him. I liked him a lot. 'Well, they're all in the gang,' I said.

'There's no gang.' He rattled some things in his pockets, marbles or ballbearings, though Tommo seemed too mature for normal games. 'If there is to be a gang, it'll be the two of us. Just you and me, Laura. Just you and me.'

I felt weak as I stood and watched him walk away. It was as if I had just been bought and paid for, as if the boy had actually begun to own me. Yet the positive side still appealed, the idea that I might be wanted just for myself.

When my legs found strength, I walked back to the house and peeled the potatoes. Mother continued to rant and rave, carried on fretting about the packing, the cancelling of the milk, the number of people who needed notification of our new address.

I poked out the eye of a potato and smiled to myself. Tommo loved me. And no-one in the whole wide world knew about it.

Chapter Nine

Living in the country was, at first, a bit of a bore. The local children were quieter than my contemporaries in town – even the St Mary's girls had been rumbustious when compared to the simple souls who inhabited the village of Barr Bridge. At least, that was the impression I got early on in my career as a Barr Bridgeite. But country folk were deep, as my mother found out after a month or so.

'She says these are the only potatoes she has.' Three sad and greenish tubers lolled in the centre of our kitchen table. 'We are surrounded by fields and farmers, but that dreadful woman has no decent produce on sale.'

On later shopping expeditions, Mother was refused candles, semi-sweet biscuits, ready-chopped firewood and Craven A cigarettes. The cigarettes were the last straw. The war was over, the fug of Turkish tobacco had cleared, and my mother wanted her rights. 'Go to that shop,' she snapped at me. 'And get whatever the woman will sell you.' I managed, after very little effort on my part, to come home with candles, a bundle of firewood, half a pound of Marie biscuits and twenty Craven A.

This meant war of another kind. Although I was not present during the battle, I understood that my mother had taken the shopkeeper to task. The village was agog with it all. It seemed that Liza McNally had taken no pains to hide the fact that she was too good for country life. She had never before cooked at a range that was both cast iron and geriatric, had never been forced to live with stone floors, had never patronized a shop as filthy and ill-kempt as Mrs Miles's General Store. Mrs Miles had heard these vicious criticisms as they passed from one customer to another, and she chose to deal with the situation in her own way. So Mother got the treatment she deserved.

'I asked for plums. I could see the plums in a basket by the door. But she would not sell them to me. They were spoken for, she said. John? Are you listening to me?'

'Hmmph,' grunted Dad from behind the *Bolton Evening News*. Now that he was 'a success', Mother often punctuated her lectures with a request for his opinion, and he was not best pleased by the intrusions.

'So I asked her straight out, demanded to know why she treats me so badly. And the woman had the effrontery to say that she saves the better stuff for her regulars. So I told her that I might well become a regular, and she simply turned away and said something about not wanting regulars like me.'

Dad had no comment to make, and I dipped a Marie into my tea.

'Laura, don't do that. Well, I don't know how I'm going to manage, really. There's no electricity – when are you bringing it into the house, John?'

'Soon.' His head was buried in the radio listings. He stood up, switched on the wireless, fiddled with a connection. 'Didn't you get the charged one brought back?' He waved the paper at the battery, a huge square thing that was almost as big as the radio it served, twice as heavy as the dresser. 'Didn't the man deliver and collect today?' Dad loved his radio.

She threw up her hands in despair. 'For goodness sake, I've had a boy here all afternoon trying to get a goat out of the coal shed. This is no laughing matter, Laura. And those hens from down the lane came strolling up here again, five of them dripping loose feathers all over the kitchen. That goat was black when it finally ran out to the yard. And it wrapped itself up in my sheets, so I had to start again. Have you any idea how long that copper takes to heat enough water for the dolly tub? And when the electricity comes, I'll have one of those washing machines with automatic wringers. That Victorian thing is ruining my nails.'

He looked at her, raised his eyebrows. 'I've oiled the wringer,' he said.

'Oh, I know you've oiled it, because most of the oil is on my best pillow slips. Laura, stop dipping those biscuits in your tea. I can't carry on here, I really can't.'

He lowered himself into his favourite chair, an old wooden rocker that had been left behind by the previous householder. 'Well, you can always go back to town, I suppose.'

She stormed out in a huff. I watched him for a while as he reached across and fiddled with the wireless knobs, listened to his tut-tuts when he failed to get anything except the noise of half-hearted and power-starved static. Then I wandered outside and looked at my new stamping ground.

The land that used to belong to Ravenscroft Farm had been split up and sold to neighbouring farmers. We still had a large lawn at the front, a piece of rough land at the side, and a vegetable garden at the back of the house. To the right of the house, alongside the patch of weed and thistle, were a few sheds and a greenhouse with broken windows. A path led away from this side piece to the barns where Dad was making his Cooling Tea. Most of the workers came from Bolton, were brought up each morning by coach, then taken back in the evening.

Mother had made much of the workers' travelling arrangements. 'Laura could travel down on the coach in the morning when it goes back empty, then the driver could bring her home each afternoon.' But Dad refused to allow this, as I would have been early for school and late home every day. He was beginning to put his foot down, though they seldom argued. There was no fire in the marriage, so quarrelling was not necessary.

During my first few days at Ravenscroft, I wandered about and studied things, because I'd never seen so much green stuff except in the Bolton parks, and even there the green was contained behind railings and gates. Here, it seemed to go on for ever, dipping and rising eastward into the mists that formed over foothills of the Pennine Chain. 'That is the backbone of England,' my father said to me on our first day. 'In more ways than one, it's the spine. We're a fierce lot, Lancastrians and Yorkshiremen, built to last like the mountains that divide us. We fought one another for a long time, you know. There's a white rose and a red rose, and we are the reds. That war never really ended. Somebody married somebody, then everybody pretended to be satisfied. But never cross a Yorkie and never expect him to pay his way. A Yorkie's like a Scot with his pockets sewn up.'

'Are they selfish, then, the people from over the mountains?'

He smiled at me and placed a hand on my head. It always felt good, having his hand on my head, as if things were safer and surer while he touched me. 'It's a myth. Some Yorkshiremen are tight with their money and some aren't. But the fact remains that we're made of good stuff up here, so never regret your roots. There's money down south, money and not much more. The Government keeps the south safe and out of trouble, because trouble down there would be trouble in Parliament's back yard. So all the fretting and fuming goes on up here. We don't know the difference between a depression and a boom, because ordinary folk here are usually poor no matter what the state of the country. But it'll not last for ever. One day, the southerners will need us and we'll be too busy feeding ourselves to worry over them and their fancy houses.'

I felt so grown-up when he talked to me like this, when he told me about politics and money and people. 'You don't like them from London, then?'

He chuckled. 'I use them, Laurie. I use their money and their big ideas, pay them back a bit for their trouble. But on the whole, they're nowt a pound.'

This was really funny, because Dad hadn't much of an

accent and wasn't given to the use of colloquial speech. I thought it was a shame that he had no respect for the people from the cities – the funeral men, as I called them. Like many from the north, he was proud and angry, had clear memories of poverty, filth, dying children and men who marched on the capital with empty bellies and no boots on their feet. Although I was sad about his anger, it was good to know that he felt strongly about something.

He wasn't around very often, so I explored the countryside with Anne. There were all kinds of creatures, slugs and frogs and creepy-crawlies, rabbits, hares, farm animals, dogs and cats. Solomon was still living with Anne, though she always called him 'Laura's cat', so I still had no real pet of my own. Instead, I adopted everything I met, had a special affection for Monty, a billy goat from up the road. He used to live on our farm in one of the sheds, and he returned to base with a frequency that was monotonous and infuriating for my mother. She hated and feared him, but I fed him on vegetables from our garden and steered clear of his horns.

Our house was wonderful. There was a huge kitchen with flag floors and a black-leaded range. This room stretched all the way across the back of the house, and we lived in it for much of the time. Mother made a few quips about our rustic existence, but she set about the business of cleaning up, scrubbed out an aged dresser, balanced some plates on a rack above the fire, scraped the dirt off a massive table with bulbous legs and drawers at each side for cutlery.

When the kitchen was clean enough for her, she tackled the two front rooms, made one into a parlour and the other into a kind of study. Sometimes, Dad worked at a desk in the study, and Mother used the same room for her sewing, though never when Dad was working on account books. The sewing was not sensible stuff, as Mother's seams were about as straight as a dog's back leg, but she amused herself for a while with tapestry work, cross-stitched pictures of flowers and country cottages. I watched and waited, knew that the novelty would wear off eventually, wondered where she would go for some adventure.

The upstairs of our house was in the roof, which made the bedrooms odd and exciting. There were two staircases, both of them narrow and tortuous. One led to my bedroom, and the other went up to a pair of interconnecting bedrooms where my parents slept. They no longer pretended to have a marriage, so Dad slept at the back of the house while Mother used the front room.

I loved my bedroom. It had lots of odd little corners, big beams, a shiny wooden floor and two windows, one at the front and the other at the back of the farmhouse. I used to stand in the dormer and stare at the mountains, spent hours wondering about fierce Yorkshire folk with sewn-up pockets and white roses in their buttonholes.

The bathroom was a nightmare. It housed a terrible bath with brown stains all over it and a single cold tap suspended from a bent lead pipe under the window. Above the bath sat a gas heater with a bad temper and an explosive cough. The farmer had been very proud of this acquisition, had demonstrated it to my father some months earlier while the sale was being negotiated. 'He lit it,' Dad said, 'and it sent forth a long blue flame and a shower of sparks. The farmer's face was black and his eyes looked terrified. I couldn't remember whether he'd started out with eyebrows, but he had none after his adventure with the dragon. I think we'd better use a tin bath for now.'

The tin bath was where Mother drew the line. Once a week, she travelled on a rickety bus to Bolton and went to the slipper baths. I am sure that she must have gone to the public bath house in disguise, probably with a scarf on her head and dark glasses covering her eyes. When she returned, she was happier for a while, could even be heard humming under her breath. There was no doubt in my mind that Mother had found some entertainment in town, though her temper was always back to normal within twenty-four hours. 'Laura, get some coal for this fire.

Laura, go to that awful shop for your father's *Bolton Evening News*, and don't dawdle on the way. Laura, lay the table, sweep the floor, peel these carrots, find me a tablet for this dreadful headache.' She clouted me a few times, but the blows were almost half-hearted. I no longer crouched and cowered, refused to hide in the house when the marks of her blows shone bright on my face. As her power diminished, I relaxed, enjoyed my freedom.

Every weekend, I waited at the bridge, looked for Tommo, felt disappointment when he didn't arrive. Anne came with me, wondered why I lingered for so long in the same spot. I distracted her, played games, fell into the water, cut my head and got stitched up by the local doctor. And he still didn't come.

There seemed to be no poverty in the country. Everyone was robust and rosy-cheeked, no-one wore nit-caps, no-one sported heavy clogs with irons on the soles. There was no knock-a-door-and-run, no swinging from lamp posts, no fun. When I thought about it, there'd been no fun of that sort since I'd left the gang. And even snerchy Norma began to look vaguely interesting when viewed retrospectively. But gradually I grew used to the pace, slowed myself down, looked around until I found something to attract my butterfly attention. And I had Anne. Anne was the balm for any wounds I might have sustained during the lifting of roots. There were other compensations too, like a sky that was prettier, cleaner and bluer away from all the dust and smoke of a cotton town.

We had no proper pavements near the farm, just muddy dirt tracks and clinkered lanes that seemed to wander in circles that had lost any sense of direction they might once have had. The village street was cobbled, while the narrow pavements consisted of very uneven flags with steps here and there when the single thoroughfare dipped too deeply for paving stones.

There was just one shop, the place where Mother was not welcome, and it seemed to sell everything from postage stamps to lamp oil. The keeper, Mrs Miles, wore fingerless gloves all the year round and sported a long black skirt that swept the floor as she walked. The shop was so dirty that Anne and I decided that Mrs Miles's skirt served two purposes – one to cover her thin, bent frame, the other to gather the worst of the mess from her filthy floors.

This remarkable lady was a relic from bygone days, the sort of figure that was usually seen only in books about the Victorian era. Her hair was scraped back so tightly that it stretched the skin of her forehead, made it almost smooth, though the flattened wrinkles still showed and looked as if they had been drawn with a greyish pencil. She would have been tall except for the stoop, and the rounded shoulders were always covered by a fringed shawl that dangled in butter, sugar and any other commodity that required weighing and bagging. Anne and I liked her because she was weird – her individuality appealed to our romantic souls.

After a very short time, Mother refused outright to be insulted by the keeper of the village store, so she travelled to Bolton more frequently. The Bolton coach ran twice a week on market days, and my mother sat in its ramshackle front seat as it bounced to and from the metropolis on Tuesdays and Saturdays.

Auntie Maisie, a gregarious soul, was quite content to do her buying in Barr Bridge. The village took to her, and she was quickly on nodding terms with most of the inhabitants, on cup-of-sugar terms with her immediate neighbours in the row of cottages that climbed up the hill towards our house. As Auntie Maisie's cottage was fastened to Mrs Miles's shop, she never wanted for anything, even when the store was closed. So sunny was my aunt's nature, that she soon melted old Ma Miles's frost, became the aged crone's nearest and dearest within a fortnight. 'She's mortallious troubled with her back, poor soul,' said Auntie Maisie a few days after our arrival in the district. 'So I've got her some of John's liniment.' Auntie Maisie would have fitted in anywhere with the possible exception of hell, as she was a good Christian woman.

Of course, we had to go to school. Until now, education had been one of the elements in the tragedy we called life, a necessary poison that could not have been sweetened with a thousand sugar canes. I'd made friends among the holy women at St Mary's, but the endless lists of places and battles and French verbs had been too much for a mind already saturated by images found in *Heidi* and *Little Women*. Because of my grounding in a 'crammer' school, the Barr Bridge centre of education made easy going for me. I became lazy and complacent, concentrated on the social aspect of school, learned little or nothing in my short time at St Mark's.

Our school was attached to St Mark's C of E church, and St Mark's was also connected to the vicarage. The vicar was a round fat man with a round fat wife. Their plump children had married and wandered off, but photographs of the offspring sat in lines of military precision on a desk in the vestry. Apart from this small symptom of organization, our vicar was a hale-fellow-well-met sort of chap who blundered through life like a drone bee, dependent on others for some pattern to his existence.

Anne and I were summoned to the Reverend Conley's presence early on in our career at St Mark's. Reverend Conley was a favourite with all children. For a man of God, he was unusual, because he was not judgemental by nature. This lovely and loving man was a source of great comfort, because he gave tea parties to boys and girls in the vicarage and encouraged them to talk about anything at all. Troubles, however difficult to talk about, were blown away in an instant by the vicar, and no sin existed that he could not forgive and understand. He was a man of vision who recognized that children are people in the making, and he was there to listen to our opinions in a serious and sensible way.

He gave us an Uncle Joe's apiece, a stick of barely sugar between us, and some advice on how to settle to country living. 'Cows,' he said seriously, 'are the ones with milk-bags hanging underneath. Bulls don't have that particular equipment, but they can be savage, girls. The farmer across the road from you breeds cattle, Laura. Keep your gate closed and your eyes open. Don't sit in nettles, don't jump in the crop fields. Clean up after a picnic, say your prayers morning and night, and keep away from the Black Horse on Friday evenings. Labourers are paid on Fridays, and their language can get a bit dreadful after a pint or two of ale.' He was not a solemn man by nature, so he twinkled at us then. 'How are you getting along with Miss Armitage?'

One thing I knew by the age of ten was that I got on better with some grown-ups than I did with most children. They had to be fairly sensible adults, though, and I hadn't met many of those. In fact, I could count them on my fingers with a few digits to spare for any future encounters that might be lucky. So far, I had collected Uncle Freddie and Auntie Maisie, who were warm and loving, and my father, who was vague, but charming. Then there was Sister Maria Goretti with whom I corresponded on a weekly basis, and Sister St Thomas who was in Ireland with bad rheumatics. I hadn't forgotten the park keeper who had told me to look after myself, and I had recently met the vicar and our teacher, Miss Armitage. Miss Armitage promised to be secretive and of a romantic nature, so she was interesting. Nathaniel 'Good' Evans was dead, but he still counted as dead people didn't really die . . . I was running out of fingers. Perhaps I was a lucky girl after all.

I was thinking about my mother, who was not charm-ing, not sensible, not really an adult, when Anne kicked me on the shin. 'Mr Conley wants to know how we are getting along with Miss Armitage.'

I pulled myself together and gave my full attention to the round-faced vicar. 'Has she been crossed in love?' I asked sweetly. Anyone could have asked this good man anything at all.

Anne awarded me another kick and I glared at her. The

blow was so hard that it might have propelled me to the other side of the vestry had I not hung on to my chair. To thank her for this favour, I narrowed my eyes, treated her to one of my hard looks.

The vicar folded his hands across a belly that was pleasantly rounded and comfortable. 'Funny you should ask that,' he muttered, as if talking to himself. After a small cough, he raised head and voice. 'Why do you ask, Laura?'

'It's the way she dresses, Mr Conley. Frilly bits round the tops of her blouses and lipstick sometimes too. Not on her blouse, on her mouth – a nice, soft pink. She seems . . . very sad. As if she ought to give up waiting, but she still waits.' Like I did. On a rusty bridge. For a boy called Tommo with peculiar hair.

Mr Conley twinkled again. When he smiled, his whole face lit up until the brightness spilled from him into the room. 'You have an active imagination,' he said. 'Perhaps you will write stories when you grow up.' He was so sweet, a real father to the whole village. He turned his attention to Anne, 'And what will you be, dear?'

'Rich,' she said. One of the things I loved about Anne was the fact that she never pulled a punch.

His laugh was deep and booming. For some unfathomable reason, his chuckle reminded me of dark fruit cake, the sort you get at Christmas with almond paste and white icing. I had to laugh too, because I realized that Anne also had fallen under the spell of this magical man.

'How will you get rich?' he asked.

'By marriage.' She had been reading again, I guessed. Something Victorian, probably about a beautiful girl who pined for a poor young man, waited for him to return from a war or something. And when he came back, he was rich after all, so everything ended well. 'It's the only way for a girl,' she continued. 'If I'd been a boy, I might have become a solicitor.'

Mr Conley pushed himself away from his desk and leaned back in the chair. 'You can be a lawyer, Anne. Get your scholarship, go to a good school, work hard. The universities are for women too. Of course, you'll have to prove yourself once you get a job, but there's no reason why you shouldn't succeed in time.'

'Oh.' Anne's mouth remained round long after the quiet word had been breathed. She studied him closely to assess his seriousness. 'Is that really true?' she asked eventually.

'I am a man of God. Would I lie?'

'He wouldn't lie,' I said to Anne solemnly. 'Because if he did, he'd go straight to hell for all eternity in sackcloth and ashes.' For a child of supposed intelligence, I showed a marked tendency towards confusion. 'Isn't that right, Mr Conley?'

His fat fingers looked like a row of pork sausages looking for a pan, all stretched skin and pink blotches. 'You've been to a Catholic school, haven't you?'

'Yes.'

'Well, God is more forgiving than you think, my dear. But mendacity is not in my nature, so I do tend to speak the truth. You may look up "mendacity" in the dictionary later.' He looked at Anne again. 'Unfortunately, you will have to travel to school next year, when you leave St Mark's. There's a secondary school two miles away, but for a grammar education, you will need to go back to Bolton.'

Anne sucked noisily on her Uncle Joe's. 'There's no bus, no tram.'

The vicar heaved himself up from the chair, easing the arms away from his heavy body. 'If I grow any fatter, I shall need a sofa to sit on and a crane to pick me up.' He walked to the door. 'Pass your scholarships first, worry about buses when the time comes.'

We came out into the school yard just as the home bell sounded. In the cloakroom, Anne was pensive as she buckled the belt of her navy raincoat. 'Your dad is going to have to buy a car,' she said. 'Or a van or something.'

'Why?' My buttons were hanging off again. I would need to remember to sew them back on again after tea, because my mother's relationship with needle and thread was not an easy one. 'Why shall we need to have a car?'

Anne picked up her half of the barley sugar. 'To get on in life,' she said loftily. 'To get to where we are going.'

Sometimes, my cousin Anne really annoyed me. I was the one who had received the so-called education, yet she was becoming brighter, quicker by far than I was. 'You can do as you please with your cars and vans,' I snapped. 'I'm going to the secondary.'

She grinned at me. 'Well, you'd better go in a hearse. Your mother won't allow you to mix with common people.'

I smiled back. 'I'm mixing with you, aren't I?'

The other annoying thing about Anne was that she was bigger and stronger than most ten-year-olds. The satchel swiped across my head, leaving me with ringing ears and teeth that felt slightly deciduous. 'It'll all even out, Laura McNally. We'll both go to university and we'll both get good jobs.'

We wandered down to the bridge from which the little village had taken its name. As we dangled over the bars, Anne asked me, 'What's university?'

I wasn't sure, but I held my ground in more ways than one, made sure that my feet were on terra firma and that my brain was in gear before I answered. 'Just goes to show how stupid you really are, Anne Turnbull. University's like a big castle with towers and a lot of rooms and important people and books. It's where you go to get really clever.' This was, I thought, the best response I could dredge up at such short notice. Then I remembered something else. 'And you wear a daft hat, like a flat thing with a curtain tassel hanging from it.' I'd seen that on a photograph in the corridor at St Mary's, some ex-pupil with a grim smile in a gilded frame with curly bits on the corners. 'And you carry rolls of paper with ribbons tied round them.'

She stared at me for a moment. 'He was watching you last Saturday.'

'Eh?'

'What would Auntie Liza say if she heard you saying "eh"?'

'Who was watching me?' She was at it again, savouring a secret.

'That boy with pink hair. He was hiding in the bushes and you were standing on the bridge for hours.'

'I wasn't.'

'You were. Anyway, he seemed pleased that you were standing there, because he smiled before walking away.'

So. Tommo had been hiding and watching me waiting for him. I would never wait again. Why had he come all the way from Bolton without speaking to me?

'University sounds a bit daft to me,' pronounced Anne. 'And that Tommo's daft too. Come on, I'll race you home.' And she did, of course.

I was the ink monitor, while Anne was in charge of milk. Ink was all very well as long as you didn't spill it, but milk was another matter altogether. The real problem was the milk mats, woven circles of raffia with bacteria and matured cheese threaded into every frayed strand. As newcomers, we were the victims of Miss Armitage's kindness, so we got these awful jobs as perks. Miss Armitage laboured under the delusion that children like to be helpful, and she beamed on us most magnificently when we agreed, albeit reluctantly, to accept the dubious honour that was monitordom.

On Mondays and Thursdays, I arrived ten minutes early to do battle with a cardboard carton of navy-blue powder, a chipped enamel jug and water from a tap of uncertain temperament. This monstrous outlet either dripped slowly like Chinese torture, or erupted in a fashion violent enough to warrant the building of a second ark. I learned to equip myself with sou'wester, wellingtons and raincoat when mixing ink for our class.

When powder and water were united in relative harmony, I transferred the resulting potion into brown bakelite inkwells that sat in holes on each age-wearied desk. The writing in our classroom depended on the mood of the tap and the extent of my patience, a virtue I did not possess in abundance at the age of ten. Sometimes, our work was runny and covered in blots. On other days, the ink would be so glutinous that a trowel would have served better than a pen, and we would need to reduce the glue in our wells by topping them up from the ever-present enamel water jug.

Anne got fed up with the milk mats. One Thursday morning, she arrived extra early, accompanied by me, a large apron, a scrubbing brush, a wedge of carbolic and a very determined expression. 'I'm going to wash them,' she announced. I stood back and watched as she wound her mother's pinny twice round herself. 'Don't laugh,' she warned me before fixing a peg to her nose. 'Your job's easy cobpared to bilk. Dothig is as bad as bilk.' The *m*s and *n*s had been squashed out of her vocabulary by the dolly peg that pinched her nose flat. The tap splashed angrily, was in volcanic mood. Water bounced from the shallow slopstone and drenched her within half a second.

My recipe sat to one side, a newly mixed batch of reasonably malleable ink. The smell of stale milk was overpowering as she lowered mats into the metal wash-bowl. She scrubbed energetically for ten minutes or so, her face rosy from exertion and lack of oxygen. 'I could do with breathig through by dose,' she gasped. 'But I cad't stad the sbell.' Even at that age, I was given to levity when a situation became grave. As the milk mats disintegrated and floated to the surface, I indulged in a bout of giggles that bordered on hysteria. 'They're ruined,' I offered at last. 'Miss Armitage will have a pink fit, she'll probably faint and need a doctor.' We imagined that Miss Armitage was of a delicate disposition on account of all that waiting for love.

Completely unfussed, Anne tossed the soggy mess into a waste basket, then removed the peg from her nose. 'I shall be back in half an hour,' she pronounced with rather too much dignity for a girl with white marks where the clothes peg had pinched. 'Tell Miss that I have gone on important business.' On her way to the 'important business', she tripped over the hem of Auntie Maisie's voluminous apron and knocked all my new ink down the drain. 'Well,' she said. 'That'll give you something to do when you've stopped laughing.'

I think that was the day when I realized that my cousin Anne was a rather fine character. Where she acquired such presence of mind, I shall never know. But she returned halfway through long division, her father limping behind her. Uncle Freddie, rather rosy in the face from exertion and because we were all staring at him, placed a large box on the floor next to Miss Armitage's desk. 'Quarry tiles, Miss,' he said, removing the tweed cap from his dripping brow. 'They're heavy in a lump, but all right a few at a time. They'll be more hygienic as milk mats, because all the spills can be wiped away.'

'Very kind,' simpered Miss Armitage, who always simpered when a man came in, even when the vicar arrived to tell us one of his Jesus stories.

'We've done the workshop floors with them,' he explained. 'And our Anne thought they'd be just the job, these spare ones.'

Anne was rewarded with a huge smile from the teacher and a knowing nudge from me as she took her place by my side.

Miss Armitage looked fondly at her two 'town girls'. 'Very thoughtful,' she said. 'And so clever. You may arrange the flowers in the church this Friday, Anne. Laura, will you give out some more squared paper? After sums, I shall continue with our story.'

Storytime was always a real treat. Miss Armitage should have been on the stage or in films, because she made us laugh, cry and live every line of 'The Little White Horse'. But first, we had to make our solitary journeys through the maze that was long division, a skill I would never master in a month of Sundays.

I reached the back row with my bundle of squared paper, froze as my eye was caught by something across the road. It wasn't Uncle Freddie, though I could see him limping his way back towards our farmhouse. Again, I saw a flash of colour, stood still for a second until I was sure. He was there. It wasn't Saturday, wasn't Sunday, but Tommo was near the bridge.

When I sat down to do my sums, Anne nudged me. 'You've gone all red,' she whispered.

'Shut up.'

'Have you seen him?'

'Have I seen who?'

'The boy with pink hair. He's outside.'

I took a deep breath. 'Sometimes, you are very silly, Anne Turnbull.'

But I was the one with the glowing face, the one whose heart was hammering in uncertain rhythm. Why? Why was he out there when he ought to have been at school? He was old enough for senior school, old enough to know better. And why did he keep coming and staring without ever speaking, without ever coming near me?

Well, I was a girl who had been forced to make the ink twice, a girl who was useless at long division. But outside, a boy looked for me, stood for endless hours until he caught sight of me. Perhaps long division didn't matter, because I had an admirer, someone who travelled miles, probably on foot, just to catch a glimpse of his princess.

'Laura?'

'Yes, Miss Armitage?'

'Are you ill? Your face is rather flushed.'

Anne kicked me. 'She's not ill, Miss. She's just excited about having ten whole long divisions to do. Laura loves doing long division.'

Miss Armitage, who was nobody's fool, nodded wisely. 'Then perhaps you might get one or two of the sums right this time, Laura. I shall take a special interest in your efforts afterwards, when I mark the work.'

I bent my head, kicked my poor cousin again, got on

with my work. Life was waiting for me outside. As I struggled with a seven fours are twenty-eight and carry one from the other column, I wondered whether he would always be there on that bridge. Encouraged by such perfect devotion, I went on to get nine out of ten sums right. Anne took top marks, but I still felt superior. My knight in shining armour had arrived at last.

Chapter Ten

It was like an extraordinary meeting of some governing body, perhaps a ministry of defence that was about to turn itself into a war office. And I had caused it, was standing near the door in our kitchen while everybody's eyes bored into what was left of my soul. Of course, there wasn't much soul left, because I had done the unforgivable. I had deliberately and with malice aforethought failed my scholarship examination. In fact, I had failed both parts, plus the common entrance paper. I knew as I stood there that I was the only person in the world to have committed such a pernicious crime.

'Laura.' Mr Conley's face was at its gentlest, no blame, no accusation, just sympathy trimmed with deep concern. 'You are one of the cleverest girls we have ever had at St Mark's. What went wrong, dear?'

I shrugged my shoulders and wished that Tommo could have been here. He had the right attitude and the bravery to back up his opinions. Education was all right in the long run, especially for boys, but grammar school meant more years at my books, an endless stretch before getting away from home, away from the woman who was wringing her hands and crying softly and prettily into a scrap of lace-edged cotton with roses embroidered on a corner.

I counted the beats of time as they passed, watched her movements, knew exactly when she would speak, how her voice would sound. She would perform the 'good mother' act any second now, would sound so ill-treated and sad. Ah, she was beginning. 'She doesn't care. She doesn't care about me or her father, never considers our

261

feelings. We just wanted the best for our daughter, Miss Armitage.'

Miss Armitage was the one who looked truly grim, and I had never seen her so discomfited before. The battle was already lost as far as she was concerned. 'You had the ability and you were not ill when you took these examinations. There can be only one answer, Laura, and that is that you do not choose to attend a grammar school. In time, you will regret this more than you know.' She shook her head and narrowed her lips until she looked old and weary. 'Unfortunately, you are too young to understand the gravity of your mistake. By the time you do understand, it may well be too late for the matter to be put right. You need an education. You deserve an education, but you have closed the door in your own face. Before our time, ordinary people fought for the right to learn. And you have thrown away the opportunity that was gained for you.'

Auntie Maisie and Uncle Freddie, who had been summoned by my father to this summit conference, stared miserably at me. It had all been planned. Anne and I were supposed to start at the County Grammar in a few months' time. It had been expected that we would travel together, learn together, do homework together. After five years, we would gain our School Certificates, then aim for further education and successful careers. The world had widened its arms so that a few women could be embraced as doctors, lawyers, lecturers. Those women had to be special just to survive in the world of work, and everybody knew that we were special, Anne and I.

'It's that damned boy!' Mother checked herself, nodded an apology at the vicar who smiled his forgiveness. After all, wasn't the poor woman at the end of her tether? 'He comes every weekend, has been coming for as long as we've lived here.' Liza McNally dabbed at her wet cheeks, looked every inch the Hollywood queen of melodrama. 'She goes into the woods with him. My eleven-year-old daughter has been playing about like an infant, running around and looking for wild animals when she ought to have been—'

'We were trying to find an ant colony,' I interrupted. 'Ants are fascinating creatures.'

My dad sighed and glanced at the clock. He was working on a new flavour for his Cooling Tea, didn't want to be away from the laboratory for too long. 'She will go to a private school,' he said. 'We can afford it now.'

No-one cared about what I wanted, or so it seemed. My chief desire was to be with Tommo. In four years, I would be able to escape from the school system, could get a job in a shop or in an office, might start saving so that Tommo and I could find a place, get married, get away from this awful woman whose mascara was running down her face.

Uncle Freddie cleared his throat. 'The nuns will take you back, Laura. I had a word with Sister Maria Goretti, and she knows that you would pass the entrance examination. So if John and Liza can pay the fees, then everything will be fine.'

They'd all been talking behind my back, they'd been arranging my life, deciding what I would be, where I should go, how long I'd stay wherever they chose to put me. That temper of mine simmered, bubbled and popped open. 'I'm not going.'

'You see?' screamed Mother, all attempts at ladyhood finally abandoned. 'She won't listen. She writes every week to that nun, tells her all the secrets, never talks to me. I have done my best, but this wilful child is determined to ruin her own life. That terrible boy is at the back of this. Until he started coming regularly, Laura worked hard at school.'

Miss Armitage sighed. 'Laura has never worked hard. She has relied solely on her wits. If she had tried her very best, she would have left the rest of the scholarship year standing. But she never tried. Isn't that right, Laura?'

Tommo had told me never to listen. They would run my existence for me, he always said. He had very special eyes, the sort of eyes that say things. He loved me. After a few years, once we became grown-ups, Tommo would tell me in words about his love, then he would take me away to a magic place and we would have children and cats and a dog and—

'Laura!' My father did not often raise his voice. 'Look at me. The nuns at St Mary's have taken a house on Chorley New Road. It is for girls who live out of town, girls whose parents work away or abroad. You will live in that house as a weekly boarder. I shall drive you to school each Monday morning, then I shall fetch you home on Fridays.'

I could not believe my ears. He was sending me away. The man who had loved me, who had bought me sweets and dolls that I'd kept in their wrappings, who had provided me with books and a shoulder to cry on . . . that same man was sending me away to live with a lot of other unwanted girls. 'I'm not going there, either. If you don't want me, I'll go to Tommo's, see if his mother and father will let me live with them till I'm old enough for work.'

He stared at me and there was nothing in his expression, no hatred, no anger and no love. 'I will not have you wasting yourself on that boy. You are young and im-pressionable, and you might drift into an unsuitable relationship when you are older. He is a bad lot, Laura. Because of him, you have failed to get a free place at the County Grammar. But you will go to school and you will behave yourself. In years to come, you will realize that we made the best decision here today.'

I swallowed the tears, almost choked on my fury. 'That's the first time you've ever agreed with her,' I yelled, waving a hand in the direction of my mother. 'You've always been on my side, always, always. She used to hit me and you were nice to me when you came in from the shop. She hurt me, threw me about and banged my head on the wall. Even since we've lived here, she's gone for me a few times. Miss Armitage came to see her about my slapped face, didn't you, Miss? And then—'

'Laura!' Now my father was really shouting. 'There is no need for all this.' He turned to the vicar, then cast an

264

eye over Miss Armitage's unhappy face. 'Laura's imagination never deserts her.'

Yet he had deserted me. After a while, I would begin to understand my father's reason for such behaviour, his fear of being shamed before the representatives of such a small community. As the owner of the McNally works, he dared not allow his wife's misdeeds to be widely broadcast. In time, I would know him, but on that evening in 1951, I simply felt betrayed.

When Tommo came the following weekend, we ran far from the village across farm and moorland until I had put enough space between my parents and myself. 'I'm to go as a weekly boarder to the nuns,' I gasped breathlessly. 'Confetti's all right, but she teaches the juniors, so I'll never see her. It'll be all Latin and stuff and I'll be living with the awfullest nuns, the ones who don't teach. They just pray all the time and scrub floors. It'll be best if I run away and never come back.'

He lay on the grass and closed his eyes. 'Where will you go?'

'To your house.'

He laughed mirthlessly. 'Mater and Pater wouldn't allow it.' He'd been calling his parents Mater and Pater since starting at Bolton School. 'And you'll be near me if you go to the nuns. My school's a stone's throw from the girls' boarding house. I'll come and throw stones at your window.'

I dropped down beside him. 'This was all your idea, you know. You said you wouldn't pass your scholarship, but you went and passed it. Then you said you wouldn't work at school, promised you'd be a duffer and leave at fifteen so that we could run away to a circus or something. And you keep coming top of the class.'

He opened one eye. 'Brains will out. I can't help being brighter than most.'

He was so sure of himself, so wrapped up in his narcissism. But I adored him, could not see that I was being manipulated into a shape that suited him. 'You'll be at Bolton School till you're eighteen, then you'll buggar off to some university a million miles away. I did what you told me to do. I answered hardly any of the questions on the papers, and they were dead easy. But you're breaking your promise to me.'

He opened the other eye. 'Look, one of us will need a good job. That'll be me. Women stop at home and look after the house. No point in both of us working too hard at school.'

I was content. The proposal had not been formal, there had been no bending of the knee, no bunch of red roses. But Tommo had plans and I was a part of his scheme. 'Anyway, you're always missing school, always coming up to Barr Bridge and waiting for me.'

A cold expression took up residence on his features, as if he had chosen this facial aspect to disguise or hide a weakness. If he had a weakness, it was his need for me, his need for me to be exactly the girl he wanted. 'How did she take it?' he asked. There was no necessity for him to nominate the 'she'.

'All hankies and runny make-up. She says she's done her best and I've let her down.'

He sat up, tore a piece of grass out of the ground, chewed on the white root for a second or two. 'She's doing a favour for somebody at the moment, but not for you and your dad. In fact, I'd say she's in trouble.'

'Why? And how do you know?'

He raised an eyebrow. 'I've legs and eyes, haven't I? She's been knocking about with a policeman from Tonge Moor, a man young enough to be her son. They go in that sports pavilion at the back of Castle Hill School – the one near the railway embankment. I've listened to them.'

I swallowed, was afraid to ask. But I had to ask, was forced by factors elemental to find out the worst about Mother. 'What do they talk about?'

Tommo laughed, but there was no joy in the sound. 'They don't talk. What they get up to leaves no room for words.'

I understood some of what he meant, had seen enough of animals' behaviour to realize that odd things happened in the world of nature, but the details were still vague. 'Tommo?'

'Yea?'

'What do they do?' I was blushing, didn't want a reply, desperately needed an answer.

'They do it. You know what "it" is, don't you? He goes inside her and she lets him. In fact, I'd say she likes it, judging by how she carries on, all moaning and shouting. But there's more to it than that, Laura.' He smiled the smile of a man who knows all the answers. There was no embarrassment in his face as he told me the language and the mechanics of a sexual encounter. 'Anyway,' he said when the details had made my face hot. 'She's been hanging round Mary Dunbar's house.'

I didn't know who Mary Dunbar was, and I was too ashamed to ask. No way could I imagine my mother doing what Tommo had just described with frightening clarity. I wanted to run away from him, too, because he had managed to make himself a part of an unpalatable world.

'She's a midwife,' he announced.

'Oh.' What would Mother want with a woman who delivered babies?

'She brings them into the world, but she also makes sure they never arrive in the first place. It's a sideline. She doesn't always do a good job. They say she can get a bit slapdash about cleaning her instruments. Some women call Mary Dunbar's kitchen the torture chamber, but they still visit her when they're desperate. Men aren't supposed to know about it, but Art heard his mother talking one night about their next door neighbour. Their neighbour died in hospital after one of Mary Dunbar's mistakes, but nobody spoke up. They're too scared of sending Mrs Dunbar to prison, because she's the only one who knows how to do it.'

Confusion reigned in my overloaded mind. 'Do what?'

'Get rid of the baby.'

267

'What baby?'

He shook his head with impatience. 'And you think you could have passed the scholarship? The baby that gets made in pavilions behind schools, of course. Or any other baby that gets made in a bed or up against a back yard wall. That's what happens when men and women get together. They make babies, and babies aren't always wanted.'

I began to shake with a violence that affected my teeth to the point where my tongue tasted of blood. Mother having a baby? Mother trying to get rid of a little baby? What would Dad say if he knew? I voiced this last thought when the shaking slowed.

'It's not his,' said Tommo bluntly. 'They don't sleep in the same room, so they don't do it. Your mother's been doing it with other men for years, so if she had a baby, it wouldn't be your dad's.'

I nodded as understanding finally penetrated the cotton wool in my head. 'Because they never do together the thing that makes the baby. And if she had a baby, Dad would be angry because of the policeman in the pavilion.'

'Ten out of ten.' The sarcasm in his tone was heavy. 'Never mind, Laura,' he said. 'You'll learn about it all in good time.'

I heaved myself away from him and ran home almost as quickly as I had fled from it just a few minutes earlier. For most of that journey, I hated Tommo with a passion that defied reason. He was saying bad things about a bad woman, and those things were probably true. But he had hurt me, hadn't even tried to offer comfort and understanding.

There was no time, no space in my heart for diplomacy. I simply burst into the kitchen and came to a dead stop near the table. Mother was smoking and drinking tea. 'You look like a tramp,' she snapped.

'Who's Mary Dunbar?'

The cup dropped like a stone from her hand, split the saucer into two neat half-circles. Hot liquid poured into her lap, but she was plainly visiting a place where physical sensation did not register. 'What?' she mouthed silently.

I was stammering, and the words came out disordered. 'The policeman in the pavilion gave you a baby and Art's neighbour died in Bolton Royal Infirmary after seeing Mrs Dunbar. She must have got the baby in the wrong place like you did and . . . I mean Art's neighbour, not Mrs Dunbar got the wrong baby, and sometimes the instruments are dirty and you die in hospital when the baby's already dead in the torture chamber.'

Her face was as white as one of Dad's bleached work overalls. For several seconds, there was no movement in her, then she picked up her teaspoon and hurled it at my face, missed me by a mere half-inch. 'Shut up,' she hissed. Her mouth froze into a thin line, while the eyes grew huge, seemed to protrude from their sockets. 'If I had the strength, I'd give you the hiding you've deserved for weeks,' she muttered.

I backed away, afraid of her, almost afraid for her. Something was terribly wrong. Her face was paler than pale, was becoming the sort of white that I had seen emerging from a tub of Dolly Blue. All at once, she slumped forward into spilled tea and broken china, her hands dangling uselessly towards the floor.

It was difficult to know what to do. This was Saturday, and Dad always did his special work at the weekends, tended to get a bit experimental when the factory was empty. He would no doubt be in the laboratory with beakers and bunsens, would be weighing and measuring all those delicate herbs that went into his medicines. If I ran across and disturbed him just because Mother had fainted, then he might lose his place in the experiment, might be forced to start all over again. And I knew enough about human nature to understand that Dad didn't care one jot about Mother.

In the end, the decision made itself. Beneath Mother's chair there was a pool of liquid, a pale brown mess made by the spilled tea. But it continued to grow in volume and

269

began to change in colour as bright red spots dripped from the seat of her chair. She was bleeding to death. I was standing by and watching and doing nothing while my mother bled to death. Galvanized by terror, I flew down to Auntie Maisie's, then sat in a frightened heap next to Anne while all the female adults in Barr Bridge went about the business of saving Liza McNally's life.

'She'll be all right,' whispered Anne, trying to comfort me.

The worst part of all this was the fact that I didn't really care, because I'd never had much of a mother and I was able to take care of myself now. I didn't love her, didn't worry about her being in pain. But the flame of guilt raged healthily and fiercely in that part of the mind that craves to save humanity in a state of bodily integrity. I didn't want her crippled, didn't want her dead. It was an instinct that flourishes in all of us, yet it served only to confuse me. 'She's killed a baby,' I said to Anne. 'And it's not Dad's baby. That's a secret even from Uncle and Auntie. My mother's a bad woman.'

Anne pulled me close. I hadn't bothered much with her since I'd decided to be a duffer. Duffer was one of Tommo's terms, something he'd picked up from a Biggles book. 'Anne, there was blood everywhere. She's been to the midwife to get the baby killed, and Art's neighbour died in hospital after the same thing. It would be awful if she died, as if I'd wanted it to happen. And what about that poor little baby?'

Anne's face was nearly as white as Mother's had been. 'What about Uncle John? Has anyone told him?'

I sat up straight and thought about this. If anyone told Dad that Mother had been doing those things with another man, then there might be trouble. No. I remembered. I remembered the fat woman and Norma Wallace. They had known about Mother's goings-on, and Dad had been told about one or both of those situations. So now I knew exactly what my mother had been doing with the screaming preacher. When she was supposed to be giving out bits of charity, she was lying down somewhere, or standing up somewhere and . . . The pictures painted by Tommo were very clear. And Dad had known all along, had realized that his wife was performing these unspeakable acts with all sorts of men. No, this would not disturb him unduly. 'He won't care,' I answered at last. 'Because it's not the first time, not the first man. She's been doing things all over the place since you and I were little.'

'Oh, Laura. How awful for you and Uncle John.'

I stared at my cousin as if seeing her for the first time. She was older, more adult than I had pictured her, even recently. 'Do you know what men and women do?'

'Yes.'

I shook my head. 'Who told you?'

'Mam and Dad. They told me about cows first, when I went up with Dad to watch a calf coming out of its mother. But with people, all those things happen in love. Mam says it's only right for people if they're married to one another.'

'It's a huge sin for Mother, then.'

'Well . . . it's wrong. But Mam says that their Liza can't help it. She was a very pretty little girl with beautiful curls and a sweet smile. Everyone made a fuss of her and gave in to her. People like that grow up selfish, Mam says. It's as if they want all the attention all the time, as if the world owes them things. Your mother takes from men, just as she took from the grown-ups when she was little.' Anne swallowed. 'Dad and Mam were talking the other night, and I heard Dad say that the only difference between Auntie Liza and a streetwoman is that Auntie Liza doesn't get paid for each performance. She takes the men's money in clothes and meals and drinks.'

I'd always known all of this, but hearing it organized into words, having those words spoken to me, was awful. I'd heard other things too, sayings such as 'like mother, like daughter' – would I be like Liza McNally? Would I lie down and lean on walls and let men do that terrible thing?

'Don't cry, Laura.'

'Tommo knows. He followed her to the woman's house,

271

the woman who kills babies. My mother has killed . . .'
Sobs choked me, cut off the flow of words.

'She'll get well again, you'll see.'

Even Anne didn't understand completely, then. She had a good mother, a father who hadn't dedicated all his life to his work, a father who was there when it mattered. It was plain that Anne believed in loving even a bad mother. 'I don't love her,' I managed.

'She's your mother.'

'She's cruel. She used to hit me and hit me and hit me and she wouldn't stop and I put my hands over my head so that she couldn't give me a headache and you don't understand what it was like till I learned to make my eyes hard and nobody knows what she's really like because—'
A hand swiped itself across my face.

'Sorry, lass.' Mrs Miles stood over me, the musty smell of her clothes hitting me as hard as the calloused hand. 'It were fer t' best. I allers 'its somebody wi' th' 'ystericals. Yer'll be reet in a minute, luv.'

I caught my breath. 'Where is she?' I asked after a second or two.

''Ospital. Yer dad's gone down wi' 'er. They'll 'appen give 'er some new blood, top 'er up, like. 'Er's lost more nor a couple o' pints, I'd say.'

I rose, found my legs to be rubbery, leaned against Auntie Maisie's table for support until the sobs died in my throat. The room was all yellow and white, gingham curtains and tablecloth, yellow flowers on the sills, deep gold rug, white wallpaper dotted with primroses. It was a happy room. 'I'd best go home.' Back to beige and brown and bottle green, back to misery.

'That lad's lookin' fer you,' said Mrs Miles.

I sat down again. A part of me blamed him, accused him of being the architect of the day's disaster. But it wasn't his fault. All he'd done was to colour in the gaps and make me face the whole truth. Yet he knew my mother's shame, and I did not want to see him for a while. 'Tell him to go home, Mrs Miles.'

Mrs Miles ambled out, leaving the room all the sweeter for her departure.

'You should keep away from him,' said Anne quietly.

'Why?'

'Because he's distracting you, making you fail the exams.'

I shook my head. 'No, that's not true.'

But she persevered. 'You'd have passed except for him. You always wanted to pass.'

I looked at her. Was she jealous of my friendship with Tommo? Was she upset because I wasn't spending much time with her? 'Anne, I like being with Tommo. If I go back to St Mary's as a paying pupil, I'll be near him. He's a good friend, my best friend.'

She coloured slightly. 'I used to be your best friend.'

Things were going to change anyway. Anne would be going off to the County Grammar where she would find new friends, new interests. It was time to leave behind childish things. At eleven, I was old and wise, and my destiny was planned. He understood. Tommo was the only one who could grasp my need to get away from Mother, to begin as soon as possible a life of my own. 'You'll always be my special cousin,' I said.

'I'm your only cousin.'

'That's why you're special.' I stood up and walked to the door. 'I'd better be in when they get back from the hospital.'

'That boy is bad.' Her tone was soft, pleading.

'You're wrong,' I said. 'You don't know him.'

Anne leaned back on the horsehair sofa. 'Laura, I've seen his eyes. They are not the eyes of a kind person. Why does he come all this way to see you? Has he no pals down there in the town? It's as if he wants . . . to buy you, like something in the window of a shop. He doesn't like me. I can tell that he doesn't like me. He wants everybody to stay away from you so that he can have you all to himself.'

Perhaps that was what I wanted. Perhaps his need for me fulfilled a need of my own. 'He's not bad,' I said. 'He just likes me a lot. Tommo comes from a nice family – they have books and things. And he goes to Bolton School and—'

'That's where you should be.'

I stood in the doorway and looked at her. 'I don't need Bolton School, or the County Grammar. Girls just have to look after a house and babies.'

'Did he tell you that?'

My cheeks were heating up. And this didn't feel right, standing here and talking about Tommo while my mother was bleeding to death. 'Leave me alone, Anne.'

'You'll marry him.' This was an accusation. 'And you'll be sorry for evermore.'

I tried to laugh, failed completely. 'I'm only eleven. I'm not marrying anybody for years and years.'

I walked out of the house and up the street until the village was behind me. Halfway to the farm, I stopped and turned, looked back along the single street that was Barr Bridge. He was leaning on a gas lamp, ankles crossed, hands in pockets, the stance deliberately nonchalant. Tommo knew when to approach, when to keep his distance. He stayed, waited for me to continue. He did not follow me, but I knew that he would simply be there. Like the air I breathed, like the earth I walked upon, Tommo would be there for the rest of my life.

She lay in bed for almost three weeks after being discharged from the hospital. It was a strange time, because she was almost pleasant, but I realized as the days passed that she was simply healing herself. Later in life, I was to learn that people are typically calm and gentle after a brush with death, as if they are so grateful to be alive that they forget to be vicious.

'I'm sorry,' she kept saying when I took up a meal or a cup of tea. 'I'm sorry if I seemed cruel to you.'

It was like dealing with a stranger – I didn't know how to react. 'It's all right. Just eat this and drink this, then you'll soon be better.' I always escaped quickly, was reluctant to return when the next meal time arrived.

Auntie Maisie did a lot of our cooking, kept puffing her way up the hill with steak and kidney pie, Lancashire hotpot, pea and ham soup, apple dumplings with custard so thick and smooth that it was almost set. 'Get this down her,' she would say. 'Line her ribs for the winter.'

One day, when Mother had been home for a month or so, Dad took some time off work and talked to me. 'She's been very ill,' he said. 'She'll take a while to pick up. The . . . illness she had was very weakening, so she needs a nice long rest. Do you fancy a week or two in Blackpool?'

I thought about this. 'Will you be going?'

'Er . . . no. I've a lot on, because we're trying a new mint flavouring that might be more palatable. And there's that lung healer I told you about, the little pills for people with bronchitis. And . . .' He faltered, knew that he wasn't fooling me. 'Laurie, your mother might not want me there.'

I picked up a tea towel and started to dry the dishes. 'I want to stay here. When the summer's over, I'll be going to St Mary's, so I'd like to spend the holidays at home.'

'She needs someone with her.'

I dried a fork, placed it on the table. 'I don't want to go.' If I went, I wouldn't see Tommo, and Tommo was going to take me to the fair in town, had arranged a ride through a coal-bagger who delivered in the country. 'Thank you, but I'd rather stay here.'

He sank into a chair. 'She's your mother, Laurie.'

She was his wife. 'You'll have to find somebody else,' I said. 'Auntie Maisie might like to go.'

'No. Maisie and your mother don't get on.'

I polished a fruit dish. 'No-one gets on with my mother. If she goes to a boarding house, she'll be moaning about the food and complaining about the beds. You know what she's like.'

'Don't you think she's changed just lately?' There was little hope in his voice, as if, underneath it all, he recognized his own stupidity. 'She seems quieter and calmer. Things happen, you know, things that alter people's attitudes to life. She might carry on the way she is now.'

I stacked the plates in the dresser cupboard. 'Auntie Maisie says that a leopard keeps its spots no matter what. She wasn't talking about Mother – she was laughing at Uncle Freddie, saying that he'll never grow up and behave himself if he lives to be ninety.' I closed the dresser door and turned to look at my poor father, the man who had loved me until I began to fail. 'I'm sorry about the exams, but I'll go to St Mary's if that's what you want. Nobody ever does all the things that other people want. I can't go away with her.' I paused, looked for words, found none, fiddled about with the buckle on my belt. 'I don't love her, Dad. I don't love my own mother and I feel . . . I feel ashamed because I can't love her.'

'Don't worry, pet,' he said. 'Just try to keep your temper, be as good as you can be.'

I folded the tablecloth, smoothed out the green baize cover that always occupied the kitchen table, placed a bowl of rosebuds in the centre. 'I'll do my very best,' I said. 'But she'll not improve.' I must have sounded about fifty.

'I'm sorry,' he said.

'Why? Is it your fault?'

'She's my wife,' he muttered, echoing my earlier thoughts. He dropped his head. 'I've failed. I can't manage her, never could manage her. And now I'm talking to a child whose life should be carefree. Oh God, what a failure I am.'

I stood still, wondered what to do or say. 'Well, that makes two of us, Dad. Those exams – remember?'

He shrugged. 'You'll be better away from here, I suppose. I can't be at home every evening, Laurie. There are men depending on my success, folk with families to feed. I look after them when I should be taking care of you.'

I smiled at him. Dad had been in the *Evening News* several times, because he employed a lot of crippled

276

people, men who had lost limbs in the wars, women who arrived on the bus in wheelchairs and worked at benches that had been specially lowered for them. He was a good man with a breadth of vision that encompassed all mankind, yet he wore blinkers in his own house. This was his survival kit. If he had chosen to use his energies on the domestic front, then the marriage would have been over almost from its start. 'I love you, Dad,' I said softly. 'And I'm sorry about the exams and about not going to Blackpool.'

A single tear made its way down his face. 'What sort of a life have I made for you, Laurie-child?'

'You're busy.' My own water table was rising, and I bit down on my lip. 'You have the factory.'

'I have a daughter.'

'I can look after myself.'

He dried his face. 'You've always done that. You can cook and sew and keep house. But you shouldn't be doing those things. You ought to be out enjoying life while you're young enough.'

'I like housework.' This was true.

He opened his arms and I ran to him, inhaled deeply to trap my tears and to enjoy the smell of him, all those herbs and mints and aromatic lotions. 'Oh Dad, I do love you, honest. And everybody else likes you too because you're so kind. Don't worry about me.'

'Laura?' She was in the doorway. 'Aren't you a little old for that?' She was back to normal, then. Well, she was halfway back to her robust self, though the face was still pale, and the hand on the doorknob trembled slightly. 'Make me some more tea. That last cup was cold.'

I pulled away from my father, went for the kettle, filled it at the sink. The silence behind me was deafening as I placed the kettle on our new gas cooker. She scraped a match, threw it into a metal ashtray. 'Why aren't you at work?'

He cleared his throat. 'I've been talking to Laurie.'

'Perhaps you'd better return,' she said sarcastically.

'After all, the place could well fall down if you're away for more than a few minutes.'

I spooned tea from the caddy, placed three cups on the table, cast a glance in her direction. 'Sugar?' I asked with all the sweetness of tone I could muster.

She sniffed. 'You know full well that I do not take sugar in my tea. Only the uneducated take sugar in tea.'

I nodded as if considering the depth of her statement. 'Yes, but I wondered if you might need building up, Mother. I mean, you've been so ill and sugar's for energy.' When she shook her head, I turned to Dad. 'Two sugars as usual?' I asked. He was an educated man, and he loved sweet tea.

'Thank you,' he answered.

We drank our tea in silence, then Dad rose from the table. 'There is no point in trying to keep anything from Laurie,' he said to his wife. 'She already knows things that should not reach the ears of so young a child. So what I have to say can be said in front of her. Liza, you may remain here in this house until you are well, then I shall rent a place for you in Bolton. There will be no divorce. I shall make it known that your health is uncertain and that you need to live close to a hospital. If you want to fight me, then I shall be forced to go to the courts and lay you bare in public.' He placed a hand on my head. 'I'll look after you, Laurie-child. You'll be fine with me and the good sisters.'

When he had left, my mother turned on me. 'Don't you dare to criticize me to your father. This is your fault, isn't it? You're the one who has begged him to be rid of me, and I will not have you standing in judgement. What I do is my own affair. And as for him . . .' She waved a hand towards the back door. 'He is useless. I'm going nowhere, because he'll put me nowhere. No way will he go to court and tell lies about me. I shall stay put.'

I walked right up to her. 'They aren't lies. He knows what happened – I know too, because people followed you to that sports pavilion and to the midwife's house. And that's the truth.'

She raised her hand and swiped it across my cheek. Without hesitation, I grabbed her wrist and pinned it to the table. 'I'm bigger now, Mother. You can't drag me round by the hair and bang my head against the walls. You can't hurt me any more.'

But she did. She never left the farm, never went to live in a rented house in town. And at every opportunity, she made my life a misery.

Part Three

Chapter One

'I'm not going to Mary Dunbar's. I don't care what happens, but she's not getting hold of me.' There was no bulge yet, no outward sign of my sin, but my body clock had missed a beat, and there could be only one explanation for the failure of a metronome that had always been so steady.

He leaned against a dry stone wall, his hands plucking at the spiky petals of a dandelion. 'She loves me,' he said with near-sarcasm as he threw away the mutilated remains. 'And I don't mean Mary Dunbar. I can't work out why you're worrying. There's no way I'm going back to Imperial College. My interest in organic chemistry petered out months ago. I'll get a job and a day off to get married, so where's the problem?'

I didn't know why I was so worried. There would be the usual encounters, of course, a couple of showdowns with parents, my hasty exit from St Mary's, a hurried wedding in a registry. But none of those things bothered me.

He grabbed my arm, squeezed it tight. He was always doing that, hurting me a little then stroking me better. That was how I'd managed to get pregnant, when the stroking better had gone too far. Even that thirty seconds of frantic activity had been rather painful. But he loved me, was looking at me with such naked devotion that I dispelled the misgivings from my mind.

'Right,' he said. 'Tomorrow, we'll tell Mater and Pater what's going on. Take no notice of my mother – she tends to go on a bit, gets rather hysterical when threatened with change. Then we'll tackle your parents in a day or two.' His eyes gleamed, as if he were looking forward to these encounters. 'You'll soon be mine, Laura, all mine.' He grinned, but there was no amusement in his expression.

I tried hard not to mind. Belonging completely to somebody might prove a little difficult, as I had not belonged to anyone before. I was blessed with a mother who, in defiance of her husband's requests for her to leave, remained ensconced at Ravenscroft Farm. And my father was always up to his armpits in ingredients and recipes. Being owned did not promise to be easy. In fact, childhood for me had been rather pleasant, in spite of the absence of love and attention. Freedom was a privilege I had come to enjoy, and my sweet liberty was about to vanish into history.

We went first to Tommo's house in John Street. It was in a large terrace with steps up to front doors and grilles under windows where the cellars were. I hadn't been inside before, had never met Tommo's parents. It was a pleasant house with bookshelves everywhere and a nice painting of the Town Hall over the fireplace. Tommo's dad, who had painted the picture, was an avid reader. He was a balding man with coal-miner's eyes screwed up against the light. As I walked in, he put on a pair of dark glasses and placed a book on the table. 'Hello,' he said pleasantly. 'Are you the girl who's being mercilessly chased by Bernard?' Daytime brightness plainly bothered him, though he seemed able to read without spectacles.

I had to search for a sensible reply until I remembered Tommo's real name. 'Yes,' I answered feebly. 'I'm Laura McNally.'

'Sit down, please.' His hand waved towards a chair, and I noticed the blue-black marks of coal eaten into the skin. 'Phoebe should be here in a minute. She . . . er . . . might enjoy a bit of female company, because we've just the two boys, you see.' From his tone, I gathered that Mrs Thompson didn't really want any company at all.

I hadn't known that Tommo had a brother, and I shot a look of surprise in his direction. He was leaning casually against a dresser where some statues sat, the sort of statues

284

that lined the corridors of St Mary's school. This wasn't going to be easy, then. A practising Catholic family would not welcome a non-believer into its midst, would not be pleased about a hasty wedding. I sat down, waited for Tommo to say his piece.

He didn't even clear his throat. 'We're getting married,' he announced. 'And I'm not going back to college.'

Mr Thompson stared at his son, then glanced at me. 'Pregnant?' he asked.

Tommo nodded.

'Well, that's exactly what I might have expected from you, Bernard. Really, you were wasting everyone's time at university, so I expected you to leave before completing the course. But there was no need for the drama. I was already concerned about the money that was being wasted on your education.' He looked at me for a second or two. 'How old are you?'

'Seventeen.' My cheeks were burning like a foundry furnace, were warm enough to heat the whole room. 'Seventeen and a bit.'

Mr Thompson took a step towards his son. 'Go to Butterworth's and fetch your mother. She'll be gossiping in the queue.'

Tommo turned towards the door. 'Coming, Laura?' he asked.

'She is staying here,' stated Mr Thompson. 'I want to have a word with her.'

Tommo slammed the door in his wake, then Mr Thompson drew back the curtain, as if making sure that his son was out of earshot. 'Laura,' he said, coming to sit in a green-covered armchair. 'You must not make this dreadful mistake.' He removed the dark spectacles and placed them on the table.

I searched his face for clues, found nothing but concern in the coal-stained features. 'But I can't kill a baby, Mr Thompson. My m— I know somebody who did that, and she finished up in hospital. Anyway, I think it's wrong.' I didn't want the baby, didn't want to murder it, didn't want to die because of dirty instruments. 'I'll have to get married.'

He shook his head. 'No. Someone who has no children will adopt your baby. I'll talk to the priests and the nuns, because they always know how to place a child. Don't think about ending your pregnancy except by giving birth. And don't marry that boy.'

'That boy' was his son. He seemed a genuine sort of man, looked concerned for me. 'I love him, Mr Thompson. We met ages ago when he was going round with Ginger and Art and the twins. Then when I moved out to Barr Bridge, he started to come up at weekends. It was funny at first, because he just watched me, took weeks to come and talk to me.'

'Stalking his prey,' said Mr Thompson. He dropped his head, moved his lips in what looked like prayer, pleaded with me again. 'Just stay away from him, please. He isn't right for marriage.'

'Well, we're both a bit young,' I answered carefully, 'but he's the father and he wants to marry me. I know it won't be easy. I'll have to leave the convent and Tommo will need to get work and find somewhere for us to live.'

He sighed, rose from the chair, went to lean on the fireguard. 'I'll get you a rentbook if you really want one. There's a house on the other side of John Street, one of the smaller ones without cellars. If you insist on going through with the marriage, I can at least make sure that you are near me.'

I studied my hands, kept folding and unfolding them in my lap. Mr Thompson was a nice man who seemed not to like his own son. Up to now, I had believed that my mother was the only person in the world who managed to dislike her own flesh and blood. But this man was sitting on something, was withholding some of the truth. Or perhaps he was simply trying to save his family from disgrace. He looked uncomfortable, preoccupied. 'We'll be all right, Mr Thompson,' I said. 'Tommo will do his best to look after me and the baby.'

He raised his head, and I saw a flicker of hope in the gentle eyes. 'You may be right. My son has never been one to shoulder his responsibilities, you see. So he may well take to fatherhood and prove me wrong.' He sighed. 'I hope for your sake that I am completely mistaken.'

Phoebe Thompson rushed in and stopped abruptly when she saw me sitting by her fireside. It seemed that the top half of her body was still running, as if she had ground to a halt at the lower level while continuing to move above the waist. 'You're not getting your hands on my boy, you evil little minx,' she snapped.

'She spoils him, thinks he's special,' said Mr Thompson to no-one in particular. 'He's special all right, but not in the way she imagines.'

Mrs Thompson rounded on her husband. 'Shut up, Colin. Can't you see what's happening here? This girl has trapped our son in the usual good old-fashioned way. She's trying to take him away from me, from his home, from his studies—'

'He'll not study, Phoebe. You know damned well that he's doing no good in London. He'd be better off at work.'

The tiny woman turned on me again. She was like a little doll with red cheeks and black hair painted on to its head, because she had scraped back every thread into a tight bun at the nape. 'You're not having him.'

Throughout all this, Tommo had been casting his eye over the *Green Final*, a sports edition of the *Bolton Evening News* that was issued each Saturday. 'They'll not get the cup again,' he muttered. I assumed that he was referring to the local football team. 'And don't shout, Mater. I've made my mind up to marry Laura, so leave her alone.'

She dumped a basket on the table and stared hard at me. She had blackcurrant eyes that seemed to pierce my flesh so deeply that they might well have found my innermost core. 'Well, you made sure you got first prize, eh? There's many a girl would open her legs to catch a good man, but—'

'Phoebe!' roared her husband. 'There's no necessity for that sort of talk. You've ruined that lad all his life and now you're reaping the benefit. It's not a cat he's fetched home this time, not a dumb creature that can't defend itself against his wickedness. He's caught a human being now, and my pity goes to Laura, not to this so-called good man you've reared.'

They were frightening me a bit. He clearly disliked Tommo, she obviously doted on him. How would I cope if I lived in this street? There would be Tommo's parents across the cobbles, one of them cursing him and the other one praising him, damning me. The future seemed rather bleak.

Tommo tossed aside the newspaper and grabbed his mother's arm. 'This is what I want,' he said between lips that had narrowed to a thin line. The words continued to force themselves out from behind clenched teeth. 'You can have me and Laura, or you can have just our Frank. Laura and I are a team now, so if you want to keep me, you must take her on as well.'

Mr Thompson touched my arm. 'Frank is Bernard's older brother. He was born lame, so he is not considered by his mother to be a proper person. Bernard has been my wife's whole life. She can take full credit for the man he is today.'

Although Mr Thompson's voice was soft, a silence hung in the room at the end of his short speech. Tommo plucked a cherry from the table, tossed it into his mouth, tipped the stone into his hand after chewing the flesh. 'I'm nineteen,' he said. 'So I don't really need permission to marry. When the church hears about Laura's condition, a way will be found so that we can marry. Laura needs permission, but with her expecting a baby, she'll be allowed to get married just to give it a name. So it's all as good as cut and dried.' He stared hard at his own male parent. 'You've no time for me, Pa, and that works both ways. As for Mater, she'll come round in a while. Laura, let's get you home in time for tea.'

288

Phoebe Thompson was taking my measure, running those dark, beady eyes over my body as if assessing a beast on its way to market. 'Well.' She slid the tip of an extremely red tongue along her lower lip. 'Then I must welcome you to the family, I suppose.'

'I'll get them the empty house across the way,' announced Mr Thompson. 'So that we can keep an eye on them.'

The door opened and a beautiful young man hobbled into the room. Like Tommo, he had red-gold hair and grey eyes, but everything about him was softer, gentler. I glanced at the boys' father, realized that he too had hair of this rare colour, but he had lost most of it, and the little that remained was weary and running to salt-and-pepper. Frank Thompson leaned against the mirrored dresser and awarded me a shy smile. One of his boots was built up in an effort to lengthen a shrivelled limb, yet he still depended heavily on the healthy leg. 'I'm Frank.' He blushed like a teenager, jangled some coppers in his jacket pocket.

'This will be your brother-in-law,' said Tommo. 'Frank, this is Laura.'

He held out a hand and shook mine firmly. 'Pleased to meet you, Laura.'

'He's a clerk with the corporation,' sniffed Mrs Thompson. 'He had to have a sitting down job because he's a cripple.'

I wanted to hug Frank in that moment, wanted to shake him too. He needed telling that he was beautiful, because his mother was making him so small and useless. 'For hair like yours, Frank, a woman might commit murder,' I said.

Tommo stared at me. 'His hair's the same as mine.'

'It's a bit quieter,' I said. 'And his eyes are a warmer grey.'

Tommo laughed. 'Our Frank's a good chap.' He clapped a hand on his brother's shoulder, causing a degree of unsteadiness that made Frank's blush even deeper. 'I'll be trying to get a job alongside you, old boy. This university business isn't up my street at all.'

Mr Thompson walked to Frank's side. 'College would have been just the ticket for you, Frank. All you needed was confidence and you'd have walked an honours.'

Mrs Thompson sidled towards the kitchen. 'He can't walk half a mile, never mind the honours. Will you be back for tea, Bernard?'

'I don't know.' Tommo led me to the door. 'I'll see you when I see you.'

We walked down towards Deane Road, then ambled into town until we reached the bus station. 'I'll go on my own,' I said.

He stared at me. 'Oh no. I'll be with you from now on. Wherever you go, I'll be there.'

When he said that, I shivered as if cold steel had touched my spine. But I dismissed the sensation, took my lover's hand and caught the bus to Barr Bridge. It was August, and no-one shivers in the summer time.

As far as I have been able to remember, John McNally only raised his voice once or twice during the length of my time in his house. But when I told him of my pregnancy, his behaviour disturbed me beyond measure. He did not scream and shout, did not scold me for my sins. No, his reaction was far worse than anything I might have imagined. My father simply sat down on a stool in his laboratory, laid his head in his hands and wept.

I didn't know what to do, what to say. Tommo had chickened out at the last minute, had asked me to do the job by myself. 'He'll not want me there, Laura. This has got to be done by you alone.' So much for his speech about us being together for all time, I thought. Still, I was glad that Tommo wasn't standing here watching my father's tears.

I hadn't even considered talking to my mother. She would have made a feast of it, would have enjoyed telling me what a disgrace I was. Of course, I could have brought

Mary Dunbar into it, could have ranted on about police-men and sports pavilions, but I wasn't up to much. If this was pregnancy, then I wouldn't be wanting more than one child.

'Laurie. Oh my Laurie-child.' He got down from the stool, mopped his cheeks and made for the door. 'Back in a moment,' he said. I guessed that he was going to the washroom where he might clear his head sufficiently to cope with this latest shock.

I walked to a door at the opposite end of the laboratory, looked through a pane of toughened glass, saw a part of my father's kingdom. There were long benches where the workers sat during the day, some stretches made lower than others to accommodate the disabled. Overhead, small vats hung from an upper floor where the Cooling Teas were mixed, then pipes led down to the benches. Each pipe fed a measure into a circle of muslin, then the operators tied and boxed the bags for the warehouse. The place was empty now, gloomy in the parsimonious glimmer of a few dim lamps. I was seventeen, pregnant and alone, and my father was in the washroom, probably being sick.

I cast an eye over his bench, saw sheaves of notes piled high next to pipettes, beakers, boxes of herbs, bottles of essences. A gas burner sucked its nourishment from a tube of reddish-brown rubber, gave forth a long pale flame with a yellow core. He worked hard, my poor father, and I was killing him.

When he came back, I looked at him as if for the first time. He was a man of moderate height, but the feet and inches were variable in accordance with his mood. On this evening, he was shorter, as if his shoulders had been weighted by all the worries in the world. Of late, he had taken to wearing spectacles, because his startlingly blue eyes were feeling the strain of many hours spent hunched over notes and theories. He was old, older than his years.

'I'm sorry, Dad,' I whimpered. Really, I was sorry for myself too, felt like a tragic princess whose fairy tale had not yet managed to come right. But I pushed away the pity I felt for my father, because the fear of my condition was greater than any other single thing. I had to get married quickly, and my father would be required to help me achieve my goal.

He walked up to me, lifted my chin with a finger. 'I think you're wrong,' he said. 'For some time, I have believed you to be anaemic, so your symptoms will be caused by a lack of iron. You are not pregnant, Laurie.'

Hope stirred in my breast, fluttered like a small caged bird that has heard a promise of freedom. I did not want to be married. I did not want to be married to Tommo, not yet. 'How can you be so sure?' I asked. 'Don't we need a doctor?'

Dad pursed his lips, shook his head slowly. 'I think not, dear. I know that doctors are supposed to keep quiet, but Barr Bridge is such a small place and Dr Horrocks is an ageing man, too old, really. He'd be running about gossiping, telling everybody how John McNally let his daughter suffer from anaemia. Oh yes, he'd get some mileage out of that, Laurie. All you need is a few doses of ferrous sulphate. There's no point in visiting a semi-retired doctor when your dad's a chemist. I can treat you myself. It's just a matter of a tonic, two or three doses, then some bed rest.'

'But I feel pregnant.'

He swallowed, the Adam's apple bobbing in his thinning throat. 'And how does "pregnant" feel, Laurie?'

I thought for a moment. 'Just different. A bit heavy, very tired. Everything seems to be dragging downward towards my feet, as if I'm made of lead.'

'Anaemia,' he said authoritatively. 'You aren't expecting a child. Please believe me. You must stay at home for a few days, allow me to treat this weakness. In a week or so, you will be back to your normal self.'

I breathed a sigh of relief. 'What about Mother?'

'Leave her to me also. I'll tell her that you need a rest.'

I pondered again for a moment. 'Well, why don't I tell Dr Horrocks that we think I need iron? There's no need for me to say I might be pregnant, I can just go in and—'

'No.' His voice, though soft, was forceful. 'The man couldn't treat a horse with bellyache. And as I said just now, he'd make me into a laughing stock. You don't need a doctor, love. I'll sort you out. Just leave the details to your old dad.'

He sorted me out, all right. When he had finished with me, I felt as if I had been through the Victorian wringer, that aged monument which had been relegated by Mother to the back garden since the advent of her washing machine. I bled copiously, suffered severe back pain, had cramps in my belly that precluded me from standing, even from sitting up in bed.

When the pain subsided, I sat in our new bath, stared ahead at the frosted window, paddled my hands idly in steaming water. The baby was gone. My father had killed the child. The anaemia had been a figment of my father's educated imagination, had been dreamed up during his lonely sojourn in the washroom on the night of my confession.

I hadn't wanted the baby any more than I had wanted any of the dolls in my bedroom. For years, those silly faces had sat behind their cellophane wrappings, the tiny clothes fading into rags, the rosebud lips still perfect, untouched, unkissed by a loving child-mother. Perhaps I was not normal. Anne had always loved her dolls, had wheeled them in a pram, had dressed them, given them tea-parties, had talked to them and cuddled them. 'I'm not normal,' I said aloud. 'And my mother and my father are both murderers.' Living on the fringe of Catholicism had given me a strong sense of guilt where birth control was concerned. Abortion was wrong. I wouldn't go to hell, because I'd been taking a tonic for my blood, but Dad was condemned now to an eternity of heat and pain.

When I was dressed, I made my way downstairs,

depending heavily for support on the iron handrail. Mother was smoking in the kitchen, and the smoke made me sicker than ever. I walked past her, went looking for air in the garden. But she stopped me before I got outside, stood by my side, raked my face with her eyes. 'It's all right for you, then, is it? All right for you to run around like a tramp with that horrible boy? Oh, I heard you moaning and rolling about. It hurts, doesn't it?'

I didn't look at her, didn't want to see her face. She had heard me crying out in my agony and she had not come to me. 'Go away,' I said softly.

'His precious daughter. Oh, he'd risk prison for you, but not for me.'

I held on to the door jamb, cursed the weakness in my knees. 'Your baby wasn't his.'

'And yours wasn't exactly a welcome guest, was it? Your baby wasn't legitimate, Laura. At least I was old enough to know what I was doing.' She sounded smug.

'And still stupid enough to get into a mess,' I said. 'I betrayed no-one, Mother. I love Tommo and I'm going to marry him one day. There'll be no running about with other men, because I'm not cheap.'

She stepped back a pace, took in a sharp breath of air. 'You don't know what you're talking about. You've no idea what it is to live with a man who isn't right, a man who's hardly a man at all. I needed warmth, needed some love. All he wants is a science book and a silly box of medical tricks. Your father isn't made of flesh and blood.'

I turned and gave her a quick glance, then fixed my eyes on the open door. 'He's a good man. The reason why he doesn't bother with you is easy to work out. You're an unpleasant person, Mother.' The bitterness was rising in my gullet, and I was unable to hold it back this time. Something had happened to me, something that had left me unbalanced, out of control. 'You don't deserve him, and he deserves better than you. Why didn't you go when he asked you to? Are you waiting for his fortune?'

'How dare you speak to me like that?'

At last, I gave her my full attention. 'I just open my mouth and let the words come out. It's quite easy, really.'

I stumbled down the dirt track, stood still and looked at the sign over the big yard, RAVENSCROFT FARM, HOME OF McNALLY'S FEVER TEAS. An outer door stood open, and I could see him at his desk. He was alone. As if drawn by invisible factors, he lifted his head and looked at me. His face was lined with misery, and I wanted to run to him and offer comfort. But in my weakened state, I had to walk slowly. Dad didn't rise to meet me, and I knew suddenly that he feared me, dreaded what I might say to him. I gathered around me the shattered remnants of self-control, kept my pace steady, walked into his workshop. 'Dad?'

'I'm sorry. I'm sorry, love.'

'Why? Why did you do it, Dad?'

He gulped, but managed not to weep this time. 'It was your baby, Laurie. I should have asked, should have cared about what you wanted. But I couldn't sit by and watch your life ruined before it's even started.'

'It's all right,' I muttered at last.

'No. No, it isn't all right. What I did went against everything I believe in. I've lost my soul, Laurie. Whether what I did was right or wrong in earthly terms, I've broken my bond with God.'

He hated himself and it was all my fault. 'I'll take you to church,' I said. 'And you can tell a priest.'

He smiled, but there was no joy in his face. 'Lady Macbeth knew all about God's wrath, Laurie. Nothing could ever cleanse her heart, nothing in this world. It's the same for me.'

I remembered something that Confetti had written in a letter. 'The biggest sin is despair,' I reminded him. 'There is no sin that can't be forgiven.'

He dropped his pen, closed the book of notes with a sharp snap. 'Perhaps you're right.'

'I am. So's Confetti.'

He rose from his seat and walked towards me. 'You must forgive me first. Without your absolution, there's no point in seeking a priest's blessing.'

So I opened my arms and my heart, drew my father close and forgave him. Forgiving him was an act of will, as I was very young, very confused about what had taken place. There had been a baby and I had not wanted it, and I had not wanted it killed. The decision had been made outside of me, but the ultimate responsibility had been mine. I should have gone to a doctor, should have guessed my father's plan.

John McNally was received back into the church at the end of the same week. I sat in a pew and watched him going up for communion, saw the wetness in his eyes when he returned to my side. He had been lapsed for years, and that tiny unborn child had dragged John McNally back into Rome's maternal arms. The priest had mediated between layman and God, had forgiven my father's enormous sin. It was a great comfort to him and, from that day on, he kept Sundays and holy days right up to his death. So my poor little baby had had a purpose, even though it had not survived to enjoy the light in its newly devout grandfather's eyes.

He was furious, kept pulling at the railings as if he wanted to bend them over. 'How the hell did you come to lose it? Have you been messing about climbing trees?'

'No. It just happened. One minute I was pregnant, and the next minute I wasn't. It often happens like that the first time. I read about it in a magazine of my mother's.' I was emotional, still unwell, was hanging on to my temper with the skin of my teeth. Tommo could be annoying at times.

He kicked at a clump of grass, shook his head from side to side. 'Well, we can still get married, can't we?'

'No.'

The grey eyes were suddenly hot with anger. 'Why not? You've already decided not to go back to school. Aren't you going to work with your dad, do his notes and his letters?'

'Yes.'

'Then why can't we get married and have it over with?' He sounded as if he were discussing some painful surgical procedure. 'Why do we have to wait?'

'Because I'm only seventeen and you're only nineteen. We need to save up some money, buy things.'

'What things?' Now he was acting the part of a hurt child who is begging for a toy on display in some shop window. I was his favourite plaything, and he was being deprived of his pleasure. 'What bloody things?' he shouted.

I sighed. 'Chairs, tables, knives and forks. Towels, plates, cups and saucers. Rugs and—'

'Sod it.' He thrust his hands deep into trouser pockets. 'Well, we've done it once, so we can do it again. If it takes a baby, then we'll just have to make another one.'

'No.' I took a step away from him. 'I'm not going through that again. I don't want a baby, Tommo, don't want to have to get married. We'll wait a few years, till I'm twenty-one, then we can do everything properly, have a party and somewhere decent to live.'

He grabbed my arm, squeezed the flesh between his fingers. 'John Street not good enough for you? Am I not good enough? What the blazes do you want to go waiting for? Arma-bloody-geddon?'

'Let me go.'

He strengthened his hold, and I knew that there would be bruises tomorrow. 'I'll not let you go,' he said. 'I'll never let you go, because you're mine, Laura. We should be getting married. We should leave home and start up by ourselves, get away from our moaning parents. She's just got used to the idea. Mater's not an easy woman, you know. Now I've got to go and tell her it's all off, and she's already found some curtains for the house across the street.'

My face was heating up as I finally threw caution and

temper to the winds. 'Leave go of my arm,' I shouted. Several passers-by stopped and stared at us, while people in the park, on the other side of the railings, turned and looked before carrying on with their walks and games. 'You're always hurting me,' I said, quieter now. 'And telling me what to do. You treat me as if I'm stupid, and I'm not. I'll get married when I'm ready, Tommo. And when I do, I'll choose my own blinking curtains.'

He dropped his arm and stepped back, a look of amazement narrowing his eyes. 'You don't like my mother.'

'No, I don't like her at all. She's a very nasty piece of work, and I won't live near her.' I'm sure that I was wearing the look of a person who is surprised by what she's hearing, even though the words were coming from my own mouth. I had lost all self-control, was whizzing along in the jaws of a hormonal whirlwind.

He nodded. 'So if I find another place, away from her, can we fix a date?'

'No.' He was upsetting me, making me experience all kinds of negative emotions. But Dad had told me that I would be unsteady for a while, something about too many shocks to my system, too many changes. 'I want a couple of years first.'

'Why?'

'To grow up.'

He curled his hand into a fist, smashed it against the opposite palm. 'Your dad's done this, hasn't he? He's persuaded you to stop at home and be a daddy's girl. Well, please yourself. I'm not hanging about waiting for you, Laura McNally. There are other girls who'll take me on, especially now that I've got a job. I'm doing accountancy,' he said proudly. 'Starting next week. Just office duties at first, but I'll pass the exams and get higher up the payroll. Some girl will be glad of a chap with prospects.'

I swivelled on my heel and stalked off towards the bus stop. Although my eyes were overflowing, I maintained a steady pace and did not look back. I heard him calling my name, heard him threatening not to see me again, yet I did not falter. He was the love of my young life and I left him there, outside Queens Park in the middle of Bolton.

Instinct in a woman should never be ignored. I was strong that day, determined that he would not get the better of me. Had I held on to that decision, my path would have been smoother. But Tommo was tough, and he had seen what he wanted. Unfortunately, I was the subject of his wildest dreams.

'Go back.' Anne leaned on the wall outside the Black Horse, arranged the skirt decorously round her knees. 'School is the most important thing in your whole life. Go back and finish the sixth form. You've six good passes at ordinary level – why not go on and do the advanced? Then you'll have more jobs to choose from.'

Everyone in my small world was getting on my nerves. Mother wore an everlasting secret smile, was enjoying the fact that I had been brought down from my ivory tower. Dad had tied himself in knots once more, was trying to invent a type of aspirin that would not irritate the digestive system. John McNally's whole system was taking a battering, yet he did not have the sense to slow down. Bernard 'Tommo' Thompson had taken to staring at me again from a distance, Anne was being all holy about education, and Confetti's letters were frantic. 'It doesn't matter now what you did with your boyfriend, because God is good. Laura, if there were no sinners, God would be out of a job, so get right back to school this minute.' Et cetera.

'Shut up, Anne,' I said. 'You don't know what you're talking about. In this world, there are readers and doers. I'd prefer to belong in the latter category.'

She stared at me. 'Swallowed a dictionary? What's all this "latter category" stuff? Just get off the high horse for a minute, Laura. You know I'm talking sense. If you're ever alone, a widow or something, you'll need some qualifications to fall back on. Just because that dozy chap has left university . . . Christ, if you listen to that lad, you'll end up a pauper.'

'I've finished with him,' I snapped, careful to keep my voice down. The domino set was arriving at the pub, all flat caps and bow legs. 'Hello, Mr Henderson,' I called.

They smiled, tottered into the snug where the usual battle would commence after a pint or two. There were two religions in Barr Bridge – Church of England and dominoes. I wished with all my heart that my life could be so simple. Cut a bit of grass, sweep the path, pick up a pension, wage war over a cheat with a double six up his sleeve.

'You might have finished with him, but he's not started with you yet.'

My mind was still on the dominoes. 'What?'

'Tommo. He's hanging round again.'

I shrugged. 'So's the smell from the cowsheds, but you get used to it after a while.'

She shook her mane of hair. 'Don't come over all clever with me, Laura McNally. That boy is trouble. You're going to waste your life if you stick with him.'

'I told you – we're finished.'

'Ha ha.' There was a hollow sound to this pale imitation of amusement. 'No way. He'll get you back.'

I wondered briefly whether I should tell Anne the reason for my sudden maturation, but decided that she could make much of my short pregancy. If she knew about that, then Tommo's name would be blackened for ever in my cousin's book. 'Anne, you are so good at minding my business. Have you none of your own?'

She nodded. 'Yes, I'm going to do a history degree, then I'll go into law. I've mapped it all out, Laura. It's no use reaching your twenties without some idea of the future.'

I sniffed, got down from the wall, searched for a scathing answer. There was none, of course. Anne was going about her life properly, was steering in the direction of a career, a good job. And I was drifting on the tide of life like a piece of flotsam. I should have listened to her. I should have gone back to school, then college, should have broadened my horizons.

But I didn't. And Tommo simply waited until he got his own way.

Chapter Two

He finally wore me down towards the end of 1960. After several bouts of painful activity, I became pregnant again and ran away from home so that my father might be prevented from performing a second act of kindness. I was also anxious to escape from Mother, whose temper had not improved with the years. She had stopped showing me off long ago, had given up on her early plan to make me into an 'educated young lady', but she continued to criticize my every move. So I upped and offed into territory that was no more welcoming than home and a great deal less attractive than our farmhouse on the outskirts of Barr Bridge.

At first, we lived in John Street with Tommo's parents. As there were three bedrooms, I was allowed to sleep in the house as long as the usual proprieties were observed. Even though I was pregnant, Phoebe Thompson ruled that any contact between her son and me should be strictly verbal.

I hated Phoebe Thompson with an intensity that was both sinful and frightening. She constantly made remarks about my appearance – 'You really should get that hair cut, because long hair drains a pregnant woman of her strength' was one of her favourite statements. It was as if she were setting out to destroy me by picking at little bits of my anatomy – my hair, my hands, my complexion. Perhaps she hoped that I would disintegrate before her very eyes if she kept eroding my confidence.

Dad arrived, of course, visited me, tried to persuade me to return home. 'And you could continue to work for me,' he said. 'Just till you get married.' My job had been a good one, especially since my graduation from the secretarial college. I was a competent typist, could do shorthand, bookkeeping, filing and office management. Office management at McNally's had been easy enough, as there had been just one person to manage – myself. Now Dad was taking on a proper staff, was expanding the business in Bolton, Leigh, Chorley and Preston.

I sat on a dining chair and studied my hands. According to Mrs Thompson, my hands were big and ugly, didn't fit with the rest of me at all. 'I'm not coming back. Anyway, the wedding's going to be at Sts Peter and Paul, so I'm going there for instruction. Barr Bridge is too far away.'

'Are you intending to convert?'

'No.' I had been considering becoming a Catholic, had decided to wait until a time when pregnancy had ceased to guide the hand of fate. 'But I suppose any children will have to be Catholic,' I added.

Phoebe came in then with a brown teapot and some mugs, eyed my father with the distrust she reserved for me, the dustbin men and strangers. 'Will you have a flour cake with boiled ham?' she asked, sounding as if she would prefer to feed both of us to the lions.

'No, thank you.' Dad wore the look of an injured man whose final breath might well be choked off by the smallest morsel. 'I'll have to be getting back to my work.'

'Cooling Teas,' mused Mrs Thompson. She had a habit of sucking her teeth while musing, and she sucked them now as she considered my father's products. 'I've tried them and they're no good for fever.' Before anyone could cut in, she asked, 'Sugar, Mr McNally?'

'Two, please.'

She doled out the sugar, stirred vigorously, plonked the mugs in front of us. 'Fine kettle of fish when they've got to get married. Unheard of in my day, it was.'

Dad looked at her. 'I thought it was rather commonplace, actually. Many of the people in our area had weddings that were somewhat hasty. And perhaps you might like to try our latest tea, Mrs Thompson. This is the adult version of a new recipe. There's camomile in it, and most folk find it palatable and good for the lowering of temperature.' He placed a muslin bag on the table. 'I would be grateful for your opinion, Mrs Thompson. Market research, you see.'

Phoebe pushed out her non-existent chest. 'Well, I've never been one to reserve my opinions. Speak as I find, I do. As soon as one of us is poorly, I'll brew this up and see what it does for us. But I'll say my piece, whichever road it turns out.'

Dad sipped his tea. 'Yes, that's the way to be. Though I've found that many of us who speak as we find don't like others to do the same.' He replaced his mug and sat back. 'What brand was that?' he asked pleasantly.

'I think it was Horniman's,' she replied.

'Not good,' said Dad. 'Strange, because it's always been a top brand.'

She didn't enjoy listening while Dad spoke his mind. After snatching up her free sample of McNally's, she tripped out of the room and banged a few pans in the kitchen. Dad looked at me and grinned sheepishly. 'I couldn't help it,' he whispered. 'The woman's a bully. You're not going to carry on living here, are you?'

'Not likely,' I mouthed. Tommo was out looking for a house as we spoke – as we whispered – and I had ordered him to find something at least half a mile away.

He swallowed, pulled at the top button of his shirt. 'No need to get married, love. I'll not give you medicine like I did last time, but I'll stand by you, whatever you do. Don't go rushing in with this lad, Laurie. He's been no more than a weekend visitor. You don't know what he's like. Come home and wait a while.'

I sipped my tea, replaced the mug on Phoebe Thompson's best tablecloth. 'Go home, Dad,' I said quietly.

He inhaled deeply. 'I've got no home. You are my home, love.'

I looked at my father, thought about his life. He had a factory and a grand big farmhouse with modern conveniences and green wallpaper. He had several bank accounts, a motor car, two vans and a workforce that adored him. He had a daughter who was getting married to a boy who was disliked by most people, and a wife who was hated by all who met her. He had tobacco smoke, silence and the *Bolton Evening News*. 'Oh, Dad. I wish it could be different for you.' If only Mother had carried on with her waywardness; if only she'd gone off with some rich man to America or Africa, or even to Manchester.

'I'm not your responsibility,' he said. 'And I shouldn't make you feel guilty. I've had my chance, and I've mucked some of it up, but I shouldn't be holding you back.' He looked at his watch, measured it against Phoebe's mantel clock. 'If you're ever in bother, come to me.'

My dad was an old man, had been old for as long as I could remember. In 1960, he must have been about fifty-two, but as he walked out of Phoebe Thompson's house that afternoon, I saw age in his walk, on his lined face, in his eyes. My heart was heavy and sad, because although my mother had been fashioning his coffin for years, I knew that I had just knocked in a nail or two.

Tommo found us a house to rent in Horsa Street on the other side of town, two long bus rides away from his clucky mother. With a cheque from my father, I bought furniture and utensils, and we moved into our new home on the day of our wedding. Dad gave me away, and Anne was my bridesmaid. Mother stayed at home with a chill on her kidneys, but Auntie Maisie and Uncle Freddie did me proud in their newest clothes and happiest smiles.

The best man was Frank, who had ordered a new pair of boots for this special occasion. It may have been my imagination, but he seemed to walk a little taller and straighter that day, as if making an effort to be whole under the critical gaze of his mother. Even so, she chided him outside the church, pushed and bullied him as we posed for the photographs.

After the strain of the wedding, I was tired to the point of pain. Pregnancy did not suit me, and I was glad to arrive in our pretty bedroom with its cream lace curtains and yellow bedspread. Tommo had been drinking, was listing somewhat to starboard as he entered the room. He stood at the foot of the bed and grinned at me, then launched an attack that left me bruised and sore. At the end of a few minutes, my wedding dress was in ribbons and the bridegroom was snoring in a heap on top of me. I looked at his handsome face, saw a twist in his lip, wondered whether he would always be so brutal in drink.

Downstairs, I brewed tea in a virgin pot, put balm from my father's shop on the bruises, curled up on the couch and slept for a short time. When I woke with a jump, I knew with a blinding certainty that I had done the wrong thing. The realization came to me just like that, in a flash of burning light that seared my brain with its intensity. I had made a mistake. It wasn't just the injuries, the torn dress, the lack of concern for my condition. No. It was a picture in my memory, an image of a man with red-gold hair and grey eyes. The man was not Tommo. It was his brother who sat in my head. Because I recognized the expression that had sat on Frank's face when the service was partway through. It had been a look of pity.

Being married to a brute is completely demoralizing. From the very start, I felt stupid, was anxious to hide my inadequacies. My husband had little patience with me, and I was strongly convinced that everything was my own fault. I was even sure that Frank's pity was born out of his knowledge that I was a poor creature. It never occurred to me that Tommo might be in the wrong, that his behaviour sprang from some sickness within him.

The knowledge that I was subnormal and unsuited to marriage made me determined to make a good stab at it, and my first efforts began in the kitchen. I made cakes and scones, pies and casseroles, spent the change from my father's wedding gift on the best cuts of meat, the freshest vegetables.

Tommo came in from his day at the office, flung himself

into a chair, ate the main course in silence, threw my rice pudding at the wall. 'I don't like skin,' he said. I thought at the time that everybody liked skin. Whenever Auntie Maisie had sent up a pudding, Dad and I had always locked ourselves in hysterical combat about who should get the larger piece. 'I'm sorry,' I said. 'Most people like to eat the skin.'

He jumped from the chair and pinned me against the wall. 'I'm not most people,' he snarled. 'And look at you, just take a look in that mirror.' He dragged me to the chimney, thrust me towards my own image. He was my mother all over again, but I could not fight because my husband was right. I looked forty, all limp hair and dark circles round the eyes. 'I'm sorry,' I said again.

This only served to infuriate him even further. 'Years I followed you,' he shouted. 'I even gave up the chance of a degree to marry you. And what have I finished up with? A clerk's job and a woman who looks like an unmade bed.' He tossed me aside, stamped out of the room and plodded noisily up the stairs.

He was excited, would call for me shortly so that he could indulge that frantic need for physical contact with me. I was beginning to notice that Tommo always wanted sex after or during one of these one-sided arguments, that he was not interested in love-making when things were quiet between us. But I had no way of comparing him with anyone else, could remember nothing of my parents' marriage, nothing that might guide and comfort me.

I lay under him yet again, saw the anger in his eyes, marked the instant when it changed to triumph as he dominated me, watched the upper lip curling in response to the premature end of his staying power. At least it was always quick. I had some vague idea that the process should last longer, should be accompanied by expressions of love and tenderness. I often felt that something important was missing, but since the act had never given me pleasure, I was uncertain of what this absent element was.

Until Frank. Frank was a complete accident and a shock to my system that would reverberate down many years to come. He was delivering some council papers to the Tonge Moor Branch Library, decided to pop in on his way back to town. As was the custom among families in those days, he let himself in at the back door, found me crying in a heap on the couch.

'Laura?' His voice did not match the uncertainty of his stance. 'Laura?' The second time, there was urgency in the tone.

'Sorry.' That was the word I used most in those days. I had almost forgotten its meaning, as it was so often on my lips.

He sat next to me, put an arm round my shoulders. The whole thing happened so quickly that I have never been able to recount it properly. I responded to him. At the time, I could only compare the situation to ice-cream, felt foolish about finding such a poor analogy. I touched that man and I could not stop touching him. My first encounter with a vanilla cornet had been like that, a veritable orgy of self-indulgence. Nothing much was said, but there was a lot of fast breathing as we stared into each other's eyes. Very little happened for about ten minutes, but I could see that he, too, was feeling this unseen power that seemed to bear a close relationship to electricity. He moved away, I followed. I dropped my hand from his neck, he dragged it back. It was a dance, a sitting-down dance without music and without properly choreographed steps.

'What is he doing to you? Come on, Laura, spit it out.'

I gulped, dried my face with his handkerchief. 'I'm no good as a wife,' I finally managed. 'He doesn't like my cooking and he gets really mad with me.'

He took the square of cotton and dabbed at my cheeks. 'Is he hitting you?'

I shrugged. 'Not hitting exactly. He . . . sort of throws things at me and pushes me.'

Frank nodded. 'So that he has power over you. I've put

up with that all my life, you know. When he pushes me, I fall over. Then he stands over me and curls his lip—'

'Don't!' Tommo's face hung in the air above me, was insinuating itself between me and this man who was trying to understand my shortcomings. 'I can't bear it,' I said quietly. 'It's my fault, all of it. I'm pregnant and ugly and I'm no good at keeping the house clean.' I pulled away from him, tried to place myself on the outside of this unwelcome spell, but the magnetism still encircled me.

He kissed me. He kissed me for an endless time, and I thought that the baby had quickened, though I soon realized that I was the one coming alive. Like a woman in a trance, I allowed myself to be led to the rug, then I stood aside in my mind and watched while he undressed me. His hands on the bulge of my belly were cool and kind. There was no pain, although the experience was shattering, unnerving. Even though I worried about disturbing the unborn child, I had no wish to stop Frank as he made slow and gentle love.

He cried with me afterwards. 'Oh Laura,' he said. 'There've been a few women, but not like this. Nothing like this, ever.' Then he stroked my trembling body until all our tears had run dry.

'I don't know what to do,' I whispered, practical as ever now that the pleasure was over. 'I don't belong with Tommo, but he's my husband.'

'I love you.' His voice was sweet, made even gentler by the strength of his emotions. 'Loved you the first time I saw you, hated him for marrying you. No-one would have me, not with this game leg.'

'I'd have you, Frank. You are just so . . . so lovely.'

Frank was one of those people who teach others not to be fooled by appearances. He had a shrivelled leg and a mind that might have extended itself endlessly with the help of education. He had a shrivelled leg and a body that was beautifully strong. After our second coupling, the bad leg was a thing that was just fastened to him, an item that made walking difficult, a nuisance. He took off all his clothes and he was still a fine figure with one unfortunate flaw that detracted not one bit from his overall appearance. Somebody with a bit of sense would snatch him up soon, would marry him and take him away from me.

'Why are you smiling?' he asked. 'And why is the smile so sad, Mona Lisa?'

I laughed, was invigorated, no longer felt lumpy and unattractive. 'I'm a married woman and I'm frightened of losing you. I can't lose you, because I can't have you.'

'Yes, you can.'

'No. I belong to him. I must try my best to make it work.'

He sat up, dragged on his trousers, fiddled with the clumsy surgical boot. 'When did you realize your mistake?'

I frowned, thought about my wedding night. 'Soon after we were married.' Strangely, I still had a lot of loyalty, still wanted to protect Tommo.

'He's brutal,' announced Frank clearly. 'He used to do things to animals, torture them, kill them. And I was a sitting target, of course, was there just for his amusement. He was always hiding the calliper I wore when I was young. Even lately, he has burned my boots so that I couldn't go out.'

I sat up, covered myself with a cushion. 'Why?'

'Sadism.' He fastened the lace, leaned across me to reach his shirt. 'You are beautiful,' he whispered hoarsely.

'Don't start again, Frank. You'll be missed at work and Tommo will be here in an hour or so.'

He smiled, showed off those perfect white teeth. 'I'm sorry, ma'am, but even I am out of steam now.' He began to fasten the shirt buttons. 'Bernard isn't exactly a good lover, is he?'

I frowned, wondered what to say, decided on silence.

'He used the twins to practise on – that pair called Irene and Enid. They're nice girls, a bit free with their favours. They told me about him, about his problem. People talk to me, you see, because they think their confidences will go no further. I'm just about half a person, so my opinion of their morals is not important. He was having sex with both of them.'

'Oh.' This was the only syllable I could lay my tongue on. What I felt for Frank was not pity. It was empathy, because he had not been loved. I had thought I knew all about not being loved, yet I was still learning. Nor could I put a finger on my attitude to Tommo. We had been married for just a few weeks, yet I didn't mind hearing about his other dalliances. There was no anger, just numbness. Also, I glimpsed the edge of pity for the brother who was truly crippled. Tommo was the one with the disability, I thought as Frank carried on talking.

'Cruel, the twins said. Apparently, he enjoyed watching them suffer, got a kick out of giving them pain. He has to be angry to get . . . to be in a state where he can do anything. And no marathons for our Bernard, or so I'm told. That makes him even angrier. It's a vicious circle, very vicious.' He knotted his tie, picked up the jacket which had lain in a crumpled heap for the past hour. 'More of a downward spiral than a circle, I suppose. He had to be sure of a virgin bride, had to get somebody who didn't know the score. If you'd been with anybody else, you would have known the difference between Bernard and normality.'

'I wasn't a virgin.'

'But there's been just him?'

I nodded.

'And now, I've shown you what you're missing.' There was no false pride in his tone, no hint of sarcasm. He struggled to his feet, gazed down at me. 'In a way, I'm sorry about that. Perhaps if I hadn't come, you might never have known about real loving.' He grinned broadly, yet there was nothing lewd in his expression. 'I shall come again, Laura. I've been offered a post as assistant librarian at Tonge Moor, so I'll get along to see you quite often.' He paused. 'Do you want that? Do you want me?'

I wanted him. I wanted him to come back that night, to

take his brother's place. What I felt for Frank was not love, not yet, but my body screamed for more of his attention and affection. 'I'll have to think about it. If he ever found out . . .'

'He'd kill me. And what happened here today is worth dying for, Laura. It was wonderful.'

My teacher walked out of the house after giving me a last kiss. I stood at the back window, watched as he limped out of the yard. He had shown me the possibilities, had steered me right into the eye of my own sexuality. For a moment or two, I even understood my mother. For a chance of repeating the day's pleasure, I might well have laid my marriage on the line. My body glowed, was alive, aware. But I was still married to Tommo. And Tommo, as he often reminded me, was not like other people.

My head hit the edge of the open cupboard door, then I felt no more. When I came to my senses, I was naked from the waist down and the pain in my legs was intense. He must have flung himself on to my inert body, probably neglected to arrange my limbs into a natural position. I knew that one leg was broken. When I attempted to move, fire shot into my groin and I feared yet again for the innocent unborn baby who had shared the battering.

I summoned the tattered remnants of strength and yelled for him. 'Tommo! Come down, I can't walk.' The sky outside was darkening, and I did not want to sit all night with my back propped against the kitchen cupboard, with my leg broken beneath me. The house carried the sort of echo that advertises emptiness. He was out. He would be drinking in the Starkie, would be back to make another attempt to prove his flagging manhood.

I reached for the pan rack, grabbed a saucepan, banged on the wall. After ten or fifteen minutes, a woman threw open my back door. She took in my appearance, ran her eyes over my effort to cover myself. 'At it again, love?' she asked. 'I've heard him many a time. Can't he get it up proper?'

312

I blushed, wiped some beads of sweat from my brow. 'I've broken the long bone,' I said. Even talking rattled the wound, made me cringe. 'Get the ambulance, I need to go to hospital. And if you'd be so kind as to go upstairs for my dressing gown. It's hanging on the bedroom door, pink candlewick.'

She poked her head into the yard. 'Ernie? Run up yonder and do us a nine-nine-nine, ambulance. She should be getting the bloody cops to him, but we'll save that for when she's mended. He's broke her leg, Ernie.'

She dragged her upper half back into the room. 'That was Ernie,' she said unnecessarily. 'And I'm Ida Bowen. I only wish we could have met under better circs, if you get my drift. Now, I'll fetch a pair of knickers and all. If you'll point me to the scissors, I'll fathom a road of making you decent. You can't go riding in an ambulance with your ha'penny on show, can you?' She went off to sort out my wardrobe while I continued to pour with pain-induced sweat. He had done this. He had done this to me and to my passenger, who was his son or daughter. And now I knew about lovemaking, knew full well that my husband was not a normal man. Was my dad normal? I wondered, probably in an effort to take my mind off my own tragedy. He would be, I felt sure. Perhaps Mother was one of those nymphomaniac people, then.

Ida Bowen came back, knelt beside me, cursed as she hacked at my underwear and pushed my arms into the dressing gown sleeves. 'I'll safety-pin you into these knickers, love.' She puffed, panted, did her best to give me some dignity. 'You want to report him, get him stopped. We've been worried ever since you moved in, lass. Thompson, isn't it?' She ignored my nod, went on chattering. 'He wants to have a couple of years in jail, that thing you've married. They'd soon sort him out, the thieves and robbers in there. Decent folk, some of them, can't be doing with a man who hits women. They'd separate him from his jukebox, they would. Aye, he'd soon be two balls short of a bowling match, yon feller. Is that all right?'

'Yes. Thank you.'

She sat back on her haunches and wielded the scissors before my eyes. 'You want to do it yourself, wait till he's asleep and then cut off his privileges.'

Ernie dashed in. He was as thin as his wife was fat, as short as she was tall. 'All right, lass?' he asked of both of us.

'You'd never hit me, would you, Ernie?' asked Ida.

Ernie shook his head. If I hadn't been in pain, I might have laughed at the concept of this tiny man taking on his gargantuan wife. 'What's up with your hair?' he asked.

I lifted a hand, felt the blood. 'I fell against the kitchenette door. It was open.' The kitchenette was the article of furniture on which I was leaning, a green-and-cream affair with many compartments and drawers.

'Were you knocked out?' asked Mr Bowen.

'I can't remember.' Talking was exhausting, and I didn't really know what to say anyway.

Ida struggled to her feet and they stared at one another above my throbbing head. 'He's done it to her while she was unconscious,' announced the furious woman. 'That's the truth, isn't it, love?'

I wiped the blood on to my torn skirt. 'I can't remember,' I repeated in a monotone that sounded nothing like me. Not being able to remember had been useful in infancy, but it seemed to cause more trouble here.

'See?' screamed my next-door neighbour. 'He's bloody well raped her while she was spark out on the floor. He wants his membership withdrawn, he does. You'll have to deal with him, Ernie.'

Ernie looked too weak to deal with the peeling of an orange. 'Right, sweetheart,' he said.

'Sweetheart' adjusted the turban that failed to cover a headful of curlers, orange and blue with little spikes sticking out of their surfaces. 'Ernie'll see to him, just you mark my words.'

The ambulance and Tommo arrived simultaneously, the

314

former announcing its presence with clanging bells, the latter standing with his mouth open and gazing down on his prostrate wife. 'What happened?' He had the face of an angel and hair like gold, was the devil in a Saturday night suit.

Ernie squared up to Tommo, who was at least four inches taller than the little man. 'You've forced yourself on an unconscious woman,' he snapped. 'And that's bad news for any right-minded bloke. A bloody disgrace, you are, putting her through this. She must have been knocked out, else she'd have screamed blue murder when you broke her leg and we'd have heard her, me and Ida. We've heard her many a time before now. Well? Anything to say for yourself, you rotten young sod?'

'No.' Tommo shook his head, tried to look innocent. 'I didn't do that, I didn't hurt her.'

Ida Bowen wanted a few lines in the script. 'Listen, toe-rag. We've heard you. These walls are like paper, you know. What sort of a man are you? Why do you keep making her cry? Does she have to be knocked senseless to put up with you? Well, she'll have to go in hospital now. I hope you're proud of yourself, you blinking evil bully.'

Tommo raised a fist, seemed intent on hitting Mrs Bowen, but her husband intervened, made a strange sound in his throat, then smashed the outer edge of his hand into Tommo's neck. Tommo gagged, made a choking sound, then fled out to the yard just as the ambulance crew came in.

'See?' Ida looked thoroughly satisfied with everything. 'I told you that there judo stuff would come in useful.' She turned to me. 'He's what they call a master or a dan or summat. Shall we fetch your mam?'

'No.' Good heavens – Mother on top of all this?

'Right.' She stood back while the ambulance men placed me on the stretcher. The pain seared my flesh, but I still managed to mouth my thanks at the Bowens. 'Nay,' she said. 'You just knock on this wall, love. And get bloody shut of him, he's no use at all to man nor beast.'

She was right. All the way to the infirmary, I knew that she was right. But there was no way out of the situation. I was married with a baby on the way and a leg that wanted attention. Fortunately, it was a bad break, and I stayed in hospital until my pregnancy reached its end. Perhaps fatherhood would change him. Perhaps . . .

The pain was terrible. I'd just recovered from traction after my leg had healed, was reasonably sure that my lower limbs would be a matching pair, and now I was back where I had started, filled to the brain with an agony that was next to unbearable.

A blue-clad sister messed about with the blood-pressure gauge, gave me a friendly if somewhat professional smile, patted my hand. 'Very nice, dear. Coming on a treat, you are.'

Tommo had gone out, was sitting somewhere along the corridor reading *Titbits* or *Reveille* or *Woman's Weekly*. He seemed capable of getting away with everything, had clearly been put in this world to cause me as much trouble as possible. There had been no repercussions, as I had felt too shaky to send for the police. And what could they have done? Even in the 1960s, it was difficult for a woman to sue the man to whom she was married. I was his property, just another piece of furniture for his home.

Mother and Dad had been, had been coming for months to visit a daughter whose bones, though young, seemed to be on strike, refused to heal within a decent time scale. Today, I had sent them away, could not bear to have anyone near me. Even Frank, who had been arriving at my bedside several times a week, would have received no smile of welcome at this juncture. There was just me and the pain, and one of us had to win.

A doctor came in, one I hadn't seen before. He talked to me about distress, something to do with the baby's heartbeat. He intended to allow me just a few more minutes, after which I would be down in theatre for an emergency Caesarean. With that awesome possibility in mind, I went to work, co-operated with the contractions, produced a healthy boy whose lungs might have put a cathedral organ to shame.

Tommo stood by the bed, his face wreathed in a wistful smile that might have touched my heartstrings in days gone by. He ran a finger over his son's head, caught my cheek with a fingernail, flinched when he saw the cold stillness in my face. 'He's grand,' he said at last.

'Yes.'

'Can we call him Gerald?'

'Yes.' I really didn't care.

'After my grandfather. My mother's father.'

I shrugged. 'Whatever you like.'

'Gerald John?' His eyebrows were arched as he quizzed me. 'The John after your dad?'

'Gerald John sounds stupid,' I said. 'Gerald Thompson will do.'

Tommo edged away from the bed, though his eyes never left my face. 'I'll be different,' he muttered. 'Now that I'm a dad, things will get a lot easier.'

'Yes.' Even that didn't matter. It wasn't tiredness or depression that was causing my lethargy – I really and truly didn't give a damn about anything. Tommo, the baby, Frank, my father – as far as I was concerned, I wouldn't have cared if everyone and everything had just disappeared in a puff of smoke. I included myself when I didn't bother to count my blessings. We could all have faded away, then I might have enjoyed just being nothing and nobody for all time.

'Are you all right?' he asked.

'Yes.'

'Do you want me to bring anything in for you or for Gerald?'

'Ask the nurses.'

He took a tiny step towards me. 'Some more fruit? Some of Mam's cake?'

'I don't mind.'

'Laura?' There was a sharp edge to his voice, though he

was plainly fighting for self-control. 'I'm sorry. What more can I say? I didn't know you were unconscious. I didn't know that your leg was broken.' He breathed in a bit more courage. 'Even when you are awake, it's like being with a corpse. How was I to know the difference?'

I stared at him, wondered what he was talking about. Was love-making the subject of his meandering? Should I tell him about his brother, his delicious brother who knew how to pleasure a woman, how to bring her to the brink of an experience that felt like a mixture of disaster and screaming joy? Ah, I was feeling something at last, was beginning to remember, beginning to care. Should I say it? No, it wasn't worth it, wasn't worth upsetting an applecart that had no value anyway.

'Does your dad know what happened that night?' He was worried, then.

'Not unless he's talked to the Bowens. And I don't think he has.' I paused, fiddled with the baby's blanket. 'No, he doesn't know about your problem, Tommo.'

'What?'

I looked up at him. Since coming into hospital, I had learned a lot from my stays on several women's wards. Women in a group without men could be lewd, coarse and very funny. But underneath their banter ran a strong thread of disdain for men, for their inadequacies, their infantile minds, their stupidity. 'Premature ejaculation,' I said with the air of one who is learned about such matters. 'It's what's wrong with you, why you can't do things properly.'

He staggered back as if I had hit him with a brick. 'I've been coming here for bloody months visiting you,' he spat. 'I even offered to stay with you during the birth.'

'Big of you.' Yet again, I couldn't believe what I was hearing, even though the words were coming from me. It was probably hormones, I thought wearily. My mouth seemed to be developing a habit of going into freefall whenever I suffered a hormonal upset. 'I don't want to live with you any more.'

His face coloured until it matched the rim of a picture on the wall, a pale watercolour of a mother and baby that was trimmed with burgundy. 'You'll do yourself a mischief if you're not careful, Tommo,' I said. 'There's temper in your face. You'd better watch out for strokes and heart attacks in a few years.'

'You can't leave me.'

'Can't I?'

He pulled at the collar of his shirt as if it choked him. 'Where would you go?'

Away with your brother, I answered internally. 'To a place where I won't be raped. Somewhere quiet and peaceful where my bones won't get broken.'

'I've promised, haven't I?'

'Oh, yes, you've promised all right. But it makes no difference. I'm going away. You won't find me, so don't try. And I promise you that I'll name this baby after your grandfather. When he's older, I'll make sure that you see him from time to time. One of the many differences between us is that I am capable of keeping my promises.'

He darted across the room and grabbed my wrist. 'You'll not get away from me, Laura. I'll make damned sure of that.'

'Let go of my arm.' I pressed the button by my side, heard the bell screaming somewhere down the corridor. 'They'll be here in a minute. Get out.'

He ran from the room and I suddenly realized that I was shaking, that I had probably been shaking throughout the whole ten or so minutes. But Tommo had gone. I was rid of the monster.

Chapter Three

We sat on Darwen Road in Dad's parked van. I was in the passenger seat next to my father, while poor Frank squatted in the body of the vehicle with his hands on a small wicker cradle that contained my son. Dad screwed his head round and looked at the man behind him. 'What have you done to your hair?'

Frank grinned wryly. 'It's a noticeable shade if left to itself, Mr McNally. I've got the sort of crowning glory that can be relied upon to be visible in a crowded room. I bought the dye from your shop on Blackburn Road. Does it not suit me?'

Dad chose not to answer the unanswerable, turned his attention to me. 'Look, Laurie, this is taking things a bit too far. I mean, how do you expect to get away with it? Running off with the man's brother, leaving all your possessions behind, carrying a new-born child into God alone knows what.'

I closed my eyes and dropped my head, longed to be somewhere peaceful, some place where nobody asked questions. 'I love Frank.'

'It's not five minutes since you loved Tommo.'

'That was a mistake, Dad.'

Dad tapped an impatient rhythm on the van's steering wheel, nodded his head jerkily in time with the beat. 'You've forbidden me to tell your mother, and she's asking all sorts of difficult questions. You know what Liza's like with scandal – unless she's at the centre of it, of course. Come to think, you're acting rather like she used to behave, completely amorally.'

Frank touched my dad's shoulder. 'You don't know

what Laura's been through, sir. None of us knows – even I'm not sure of the details. But I can tell you what my brother is. He's a curse, a blind boil on the face of humanity. Ever seen a cat with its neck broken? That was just to prove that a cat's neck could be broken, because he'd read somewhere that a cat can jump from the highest window without severing its spinal column. Mind you, the book said nothing about hitting an animal with a brick.' He paused, swallowed, clearly had difficulty in admitting kinship to such a bestial man. 'Shall I go on? Small dogs, rabbits, birds?'

Dad shook his head, eyed me seriously. 'Were you just another of his little animals, Laurie?'

I tried to sound brave and practical, didn't want to think, needed not to remember. Forgetting was impossible, but actively remembering was not something in which I intended to involve myself. 'There's a baby now, Dad. A small animal, I suppose. Because we are just animals, aren't we? He might hurt Gerald. In drink, he's capable of anything—'

'And sober, he's positively dangerous,' Frank muttered.

My father swivelled in his seat again, fixed his eyes on my brother-in-law. 'Why have you got yourself involved in this, Frank? And what are your parents thinking of? Don't they know what he is?'

Frank shook his dyed brown hair. 'Dad knows. Dad tried to warn Laura, then started hoping that marriage would work a miracle on Bernard. As for Mam – well – she's said all along that her Bernard is playful, that he has an inquisitive mind. She can't accept my brother's sadism any more than she can embrace my bad leg. Her eyes are closed, Mr McNally. But what she says and what she thinks could well be two different things.'

The baby whimpered. Frank lifted him out of his basket and passed him to me. Under a thick white shawl, I fed my child, the child for whom I had no feeling. Because of my lack of love, I determinedly did everything right, breast instead of bottle, followed the feeding-on-demand

321

school of thought, talked endlessly to the poor little thing.

'Where have you been staying?' Dad asked me.

'In a bed and breakfast on Bromwich Street. Frank bought some things for the baby, and I emptied my account for my own clothes and food. Now, I'm destitute. And Frank's left home too.' I waved a hand towards the suitcases at the back of the van. 'It won't take Tommo long to put two and two together. He knows I get on well with Frank, so he'll be looking for both of us any minute now. Which is how Frank came to make such an awful mess of his hair. It's supposed to be black, but it's actually greenish in some lights, especially when the sun shines. A bit like Anne Shirley's in the Green Gables book.'

Neither of them smiled at my attempt to lighten this dynamite situation. Dad was still tapping, this time on the dashboard. 'You'll have lost your job at the library, of course,' he said to Frank.

'Daren't go back.' Frank looked sad, because he had loved his work. 'So I'll get no reference. But I've no address either, you see. Even if and when we do get an address, I won't be able to give it out. Bernard will be at the library as soon as it opens. As my brother, he can soon persuade them to help in the search for me.'

Dad stopped tapping, had plainly started thinking. 'Can you drive, Frank?'

'Never had the chance. But the bad side of me could use a car clutch, I'd say.'

'Then we'll get you driving and you can work for me.'

Frank's face lit up like a Christmas tree, then darkened just as quickly. 'I can't come near Barr Bridge, Mr McNally. I really do appreciate your offer, but it's out of the question. He'd find me. When he finds me, he finds Laura. I'd starve before I'd let him near her again.'

My father's face softened. 'You want to protect this daughter of mine, don't you?'

The pale cheeks showed twin spots of colour as he said, 'He'll not break her leg again, sir. I'll break his bloody back first.'

Dad smiled. 'Have you never heard of a telephone, lad? You'll be a traveller, you'll be drumming up more outlets for McNally's products. You see, there are a lot of smaller shops that still don't stock the teas and the other bits and pieces. You'll have a map and a car, and you'll travel.'

Frank glanced at me. 'She'll be on her own. I don't fancy leaving her alone, not after what she's been through.'

My father touched my cheek. 'Would you feel safe with forty-odd miles between you and Bolton?'

Tommo would be no respecter of distance. I would never feel safe anywhere on the planet as long as Tommo lived. It was going to be just a matter of time, wherever Frank and I went. 'I'll feel safe enough,' I lied. 'Just get us out of Bolton.'

We spent the following week or two at an inn near Ramsbottom, emerging from our hide only to seek fresh air for the baby. Our names remained unchanged, as Thompson was not uncommon, and we continued to call ourselves Mr and Mrs. Although both titles were technically correct, I felt as if everyone knew the truth. This was my husband's brother, and I was the most awful sinner.

The Sister House,
Chorley New Road,
Bolton.

3 September 1961

Dear Laura,

I am sending this via your father's factory, as I understand your need for secrecy at such a difficult time. My poor girl, how can you carry on being so hard on yourself? I know that what you have done is unusual, but you really could not have carried on with that terrible fellow. And him a Catholic too!

Laura, the main thing for you is to be safe and to keep Gerald safe also. Please do not worry about your lack of maternal affection. You will learn to love that little boy – I know you will. After such brutal treatment, you cannot expect life to turn instantly into a bowl of cherries. I am praying constantly for you and Frank. God is good, and He will surely understand your love for that kind man. Old Tommy-gun over in Mayo is praying like billy-o as well – I bet she has worn out a whole rosary these past weeks.

Well, I'm still getting into trouble for what the Revd Mother calls my unconventional views on topics like birth control and the ecumenical movement. I suppose I just feel that all Christians should bury hatchets – not in each other's brains, though. Sometimes, I get as confused as you are, my dear girl. Life's not simple. The commandments make it seem clear enough, but living's an art form and getting it right seems to be a matter of luck (God forgive me for such blasphemy). But factors outside of us often affect and guide our instincts, and instinct affects our interpretation of God's laws. I had better start praying for myself, too. You are not the only sinner in this world, Laura.

Please write to me soon.

God bless you,

Confetti.

I smiled at Confetti's words of encouragement, then passed the letter to Frank. 'Do you think I've got this post-natal depression thing?'

His eyes sparkled. 'No sign of that last night, old girl. I think you're just having a bit of trouble getting used to motherhood, that's all.'

My feelings for Gerald were similar to those I'd had for dolls. I didn't want to play with him, wasn't struck on showing him off in his pram, didn't enjoy dressing him up and going for walks with him. I did all these things, but they required a great deal of energy and were founded not in what I recognized as love, but in willpower. I made an act of will each morning, then every day I worked hard at being a good parent.

'He should have stayed in the cardboard box. I wouldn't have minded looking at him through cellophane. Oh, Frank, I feel so bloody awful. This poor little lad. Just look at him, will you? All that lovely blond hair turning brown, those beautiful eyes staring at me all the time. Does he know, Frank? Does he know how I feel about his dad?'

'Stop it, Laura.' He took a step towards me, folded his arms around my neck, dropped his chin and smiled at me. 'It will come. Your love for this baby is just buried under a few other things.'

Like rape and a broken leg, I thought. Like rice pudding and a broken heart. Thick pudding dripping down the wall and a man shouting for me, ordering me to lie beneath him so that he could hate me properly, fully. 'I'm not normal,' I insisted. 'I don't like myself. Someone else should be Gerald's mother, someone kind and loving.'

'Stop it, sweetheart.' His hair looked really peculiar, was starting to grow. Although he kept it short, the roots looked bright pink compared to the lifeless greeny-brown that was cropped close, too close for the fashion of the day. 'Keep your hat on,' I advised yet again.

He laughed. 'When I take it off, I tell any onlookers that I used to be an actor and that my latest bit part required a cripple with brown hair. They are all waiting for the film to come out, but they're in for a very long wait. I've called this non-existent epic *The Luck of the Devil*. I hope there isn't one coming out with that title.' He stepped away, pulled on the old-fashioned trilby, tipped it over one eye.

'I can always look sad and say that the brown-haired cripple is on a cutting-room floor.'

I didn't think of him as a cripple. He was the kindest person I had encountered for ages – with the possible exception of my pen-pal, Confetti – and I loved him with a passion I had not expected to discover in someone of my nature. I was a cool person, humorous but detached, a watcher rather than a doer. I remembered telling my cousin Anne that I wanted to be a doer, but things hadn't turned out that way for me. I was a collector, a gatherer of people. Often, I wrote people in a little book, wondered vaguely whether I would ever find the energy to write novels or short stories.

'What are you thinking about?' asked the man in my life.

'Becoming a writer.'

He didn't laugh. Frank never laughed at people's hopes and dreams. 'Yes. I can see you scribbling at a desk in some quiet attic. Try it.' He gathered up his briefcase and kissed the top of my head, tickled Gerald under the chin. 'See you later.'

I watched as he drove away in his brand-new Ford, waved until he disappeared round the corner. Gerald, whose bloom of health was even rosier this morning, was sitting propped up by cushions in his pram. He stared at me solemnly. This was a serious baby who took in everything that went on around him. He frightened me, because I guessed that he felt my lack of love. 'Smile,' I said to him. 'Come on, give Mummy a smile.'

He had lovely eyes of a soft grey-blue, and hair whose colour was either dark blond or light brown. His crowning glory was shiny and thick, had begun to thicken shortly after birth. At almost four months of age, he was solid, crammed with nourishment, deprived of real love. He continued to stare at me until I walked away.

We were living in a village just outside St Helens, a tiny place that nestled amid some of Lord Derby's rich crop fields. It was safe enough, I mused as I washed the breakfast dishes. We were surrounded by emptiness, attached to half a dozen cottages that housed labourers from tenant farms. No-one ever came here. He would not find me, I insisted while drying the cups and saucers.

The telephone screamed at me. It was an angry-looking red thing, was attached to a wall in the kitchen. I lifted the receiver, inhaled deeply to prevent my heart from forcing its noisy way up my throat. 'Hello?'

'It's only me.'

'Dad.' I felt the tension running out of me, almost heard the stiffness cracking as it melted in my shoulders. 'Are you all right?'

'Yes.' He paused. I knew that he had covered the handset, could hear muffled words as he talked to someone else. 'Laurie?'

'Yes?'

'Is Frank there?'

'No, he went to work a few minutes ago.'

Dad left me hanging on again, this time failing to cover the phone. 'Look, Freddie, just go out and buy another bloody gallon of it.' To swear, John McNally needed to be at the end of his tether. 'And tell them out there that I'll be cutting their wages if they spill any more. That stuff's four pounds a quart.'

'Dad?' By this time, my nerves were on edge again. 'Is it Tommo? Has he been up to see you?' Tommo had threatened my parents with everything from a law-suit to physical pain, was causing not a little gossip in my father's village.

He cleared his throat. 'Sorry, love. It's a bit hectic here today. I wanted to talk to Frank. Have you any idea where he is?'

I flicked through the schedule on the cork notice-board next to the phone. 'Formby, Ainsdale, Southport.'

'Right. I'll try one of the shops on his route, get him to call me back.'

'Why?' I shouted. 'Is it business or is it Tommo?'

'Both,' he answered softly. 'But there's nothing to

worry about. Really, Laurie, don't start getting yourself upset.'

'He's been round again, hasn't he?' Gerald was grizzling and I needed to go to him. As a dutiful mother, I did not leave my infant to cry on his own. Most of the time, I cried with him, was uneasy when Frank was out, couldn't cope by myself. I was not a coper. I was useless, no good—

'Laurie?'

'I'm still here.'

'Look, I'll get away tonight when it's dark. Fix up the bed in the spare room and get a nice meal together. Do you need anything?' He often did our shopping, filled up freezer and cupboards at least twice a month. 'I can get off early and pick up some things in St Helens.'

'No, Dad. You do too much already.'

'Only for you, Laurie-child. Oh and Liza's moaning again about never seeing her grandson.'

'Don't bring her,' I yelled. 'Please don't bring her.'

He laughed, though the sound contained little humour. 'That's my other ear-drum punctured,' he said. 'Your mother's done my left in, and now you've completed the set. See you later.'

I rang off, spread the tea-towel to dry, gazed through the window at the endless flatness of the fields. It was a boring place. I hadn't thought about it before, but now I missed my own undulating countryside. Perhaps movement in the land made for interesting people, because this lot round here were surely the dullest crowd I had never met. They hadn't even bothered to introduce themselves after we had moved into the house at the end of the terrace. Flat land, flat folk. I closed the window, went back to my son in the living room.

He had slipped sideways, so that his little head was resting on the side of the pram. I walked round to him, reached out to lift him into a more comfortable position. My hands froze in mid-air. Gerald's skin was a pale blue-white, and there was no movement in him. My baby was dead. My baby had died from lack of love. I backed away from the tiny embodiment of my mortal sin, crouched down in a corner of the room, screamed and yelled for help until the house threatened to burst open.

It did burst open. The woman in the doorway was short and fat, with red hands and a pale face, but her face wasn't as pale as Gerald's. Needing my neighbours was becoming a habit. I should not have called the people hereabouts flat and dull, because there was nothing placid about this rounded lady. And I shouldn't be thinking about neighbours, shouldn't be cataloguing folk for my collection when my baby had just breathed his last. The newcomer's work-scalded hands plucked my child from his pram and turned him upside down. 'Water,' she snapped at me as she pummelled the little body. 'Hot and cold, sink and bowl.'

I ran out, chanted in my head, 'hot and cold, sink and bowl', filled the sink, filled the bowl, called to the woman, 'I've done it, I've got the water.'

She rushed into the kitchen, dunked Gerald in the bowl, clouted him, immersed him in the sink. 'He's right now,' she said. 'Must have got a bit of a temperature, love. It doesn't mean he'll always have fits, but you'd best see a doctor all the same.' She unveiled my son, pulled the towel from his face. And he smiled at me. The cheeky little rascal grinned so widely that his face was almost in two halves.

'I'm Hetty Hawkesworth,' she stated defiantly. 'No jokes, please. They call me Hetty the Hawk because I miss nowt.' She thrust the wriggling bundle that was Gerald into my arms. 'Get out of me road,' she ordered, launching herself at the telephone. Within ten seconds, a taxi was on its way. 'I'll not mither the ambulance, because this is no more than an infantile convulsion. Don't look at me as if I'm daft, I've done more than enough auxiliary nursing in my time.'

'Thank you.' He was beautiful. He was beautiful and he was smiling and I had nearly lost him and I didn't love him.

Hetty the Hawk dragged some clothes from a pile in the corner. 'Give him here. Now get shaping, go and make yourself ready. Take him to the Provvy, tell the sisters that I sent you.' Although she was plump, Hetty deserved to be likened to a bird of prey, because her nose was definitely hooked.

I stood in the doorway and tried not to look at the predatory nose. 'The Provvy?'

'Providence Hospital, love. Nuns run it. If you'd rather, you can take him to Whiston – or all the way to Alder Hey Children's. The Provvy's the nearest.'

Nuns. I liked the sound of that, trusted it. I realized that day that I would always run to the sisterhood when I was troubled. There was Confetti in the post and there was a convent in St Helens. They would find me wherever I went, the sisters.

Gerald was weighed and measured, played with and cosseted, fussed over by half a dozen women in hospital white and the usual veils. The doctor was a layman, of course, and he expressed the opinion that this had been a one-off, a sudden rise in temperature, probably caused by a passing virus, and that Gerald had shaken off his fever in the age-old way, by having a short fit. 'There'll probably be no more,' said the doctor. 'A fine boy, a credit to you.'

The nuns walked me to the door, asked after Hetty, told me to keep an eye on her. 'She's had a bad bout of illness, can't work any more. Tell her we're thinking of her.'

I waved from the taxi, blinked against my filling eyes, remembered the charabanc with the awful orchestra and the puny choir, saw Sister Agatha's face when 'her girls' assassinated a perfectly innocent piece of music. Love. It was all about love.

He was clutching my finger all the way home, holding on to me, willing me to look at him and be his mother. At some traffic lights, the driver turned and stared at me, took in the sight of my tears dripping down onto my son's head. 'Eeh, that's a picture,' he said contentedly. 'There's no mistaking a mother's love, is there?'

So this was mother-love, was it? This feeling of relief that had replaced my terror? Was this it? Or had my anguish sprung from guilt, was it the same emotion I would have experienced had a dog almost died of my neglect?

'Da,' said Gerald.

I dashed a palm across my moist face. 'You're too young to talk, Gerald Thompson. People do not talk until they have teeth and a proper backbone and no holes in the middle of their skull.'

'Da,' he said.

I touched the spot where the four sections met, where Mother Nature had left room for my child's brain to grow before closing its container. He was going to be clever. That was why he stared all the time. Like me, Gerald would be a collector, an assessor of things or of people. 'Silly,' I said aloud. 'How on earth can I tell what you're going to be? As long as . . .' I paused, because the thought was frightening. 'As long as you don't turn out like your dad.'

He grinned wetly, toothlessly, the bright red gums seeming sore and swollen. 'Da.'

And I hugged him all the way home.

By the time my father was due to arrive, my toothless son had four thin wafers of bone in his mouth, two in the upper storey, two in what Frank called the balcony seats. 'Teething,' said Frank. 'It can drive them nuts, give them all kinds of peculiar symptoms.'

'Not fits.' I clutched the baby to my bosom, refused to leave him out of my sight even for a second.

'You can't keep taking him to the bathroom with you,' said Frank. 'Come on, Laura, this has got to stop.'

Dad entered by the front door, was immediately accosted by me. I told him about the fit, the neighbour, the hospital. Dad wasn't unduly impressed or worried. 'Those things happen. Get him off to bed, Laurie. He'll be exhausted after producing four incisors in one fell swoop.'

I obeyed reluctantly. As I placed him in his cot, Gerald 'Da-ed' again, chuckled loudly when I tickled his ribs. 'Listen, you little monkey,' I said. 'There'll be no more of this caper, right? If you want a bit of attention, just yell "Da".'

'Da,' he repeated.

I crouched down and looked at him through the wooden bars. 'Why didn't you say something about those nasty teeth, kid? How the hell am I supposed to read your mind? Couldn't you just have stuck your fingers in your gob? I mean, you don't even give clues, do you?'

He laughed again, obviously found me amusing. He was so alive, so pretty, that I forgot all about meals waiting downstairs, cleared my mind of threats that had been issued by the so-called natural father of my son. Gerald and I got through *The Three Bears*, *Rumpelstiltskin* and *Little Miss Muffet* before I remembered that there were other people in the house. But it was a good feeling, a positive change for the better. I had just learned how to be a reasonable, if not an excellent parent.

My meal awaited me. I sat down in the kitchen, picked up my fork, tackled the chicken casserole that Frank had served on my plate.

'Is he settling?' asked Dad.

I nodded, swallowed some food. 'He'll be OK.'

My father looked at Frank, at me, at Frank again. 'Tommo's in trouble,' he said carefully. 'He's . . . been charged with rape.'

The fork hung in mid-air for a split second, then clattered onto my plate. Some other poor woman, some other poor girl . . . 'How old was she?' It was important that his victim should be mature, capable of understanding what had happened to her, capable of anger. Though, whatever her age, any woman would be shattered by such an experience.

'No name has been issued, but the folk around Deane think they know the girl. She's eighteen. Laura, you may be called upon to answer questions.' He held up a hand to still my clear apprehension. 'It's more than likely that the questions will come from a doctor. You won't be required to give evidence in court against your husband. But the rumour is that Tommo's . . . out of control.'

'Insane.' I did not lift up the second syllable, did not need to frame questions about Tommo's state of health. I knew now. Since Frank, I knew about my husband's sickness. 'Is she . . . is the girl all right?' Damned silly thing to ask, but I was so concerned for her.

'Well, she's in hospital,' answered Dad. 'He knocked her about a bit, cracked a couple of ribs. Rumour also has it that Tommo's insisting that the girl consented, that all the injuries were accidental. It's going to be his word against hers.' He paused, sipped at his glass of water. 'That's if the girl decides to testify at all. Raped women do tend to get a raw deal sometimes. He may even get off scot-free. Unless you tell this doctor that Tommo needs some kind of treatment for his problems.'

I realized that I was shaking like a leaf. Frank came to my side, knelt on the floor, held my hands until the ague passed from me to him. Our eyes locked until he had absorbed my terror. 'Laura, you don't need to do anything unless you want to.'

'He'll find me. If I talk, he'll find me.'

Dad pretended to busy himself by cleaning his glasses on a paper napkin. Obtusely, I thought of Mother, wondered how she would react if she learned that her daughter used paper serviettes. 'Any answers or opinions given to a doctor will be kept secret,' he said. 'Tommo won't know anything about it. But the medical folk in Bolton were not fooled by your story, Laura. Didn't you insist that you had fallen down the stairs?'

I nodded mutely.

'But . . .' My father paused, dreaded the pain he would suffer if I spoke the whole truth about my leg. He placed his spectacles on the table, steadied himself, cleared his throat. 'But he hurt you.' He jumped up from his chair and paced about. 'Sometimes, people can be really stupid.

When you had the broken femur, I wondered, I worried. But I wanted so badly to believe your version . . . I believed what suited me, Laurie. Because I couldn't have coped with the truth.'

I watched him as he travelled back and forth across my kitchen. 'It's over now,' I said. 'And I would like to help that girl. But I don't want to think about him, don't want to talk about what he did to me. I'm sorry.'

Frank shook his head. 'Talking might help you, love.'

'No. I'm not ready.'

My father came back to the table. Frank went off to make coffee, kept one eye on me as I talked to Dad. 'Sorry,' I muttered. 'Perhaps I'll be able to talk about it one day. But not yet.' I swallowed, felt dry and sore in my gullet. 'I can't always remember all of it. But he's not right, Dad. I might manage to tell the doctors that he's not right, but I can't discuss what he did.'

He patted my hand. 'All right, sweetheart. Whatever you decide will be all right.'

I couldn't eat any more, couldn't even drink Frank's coffee. The enormity of it all sat on my shoulders until I felt like Atlas, as if the future welfare of the globe rested on my shoulders. If I talked to a psychiatrist, a doctor who would, no doubt, be working for the prosecution side of the case, then the whole sordid mess would be brought to the front of my consciousness. The possibility of nervous illness did not appeal to me any more than it might have appealed to any person. But if I refused to help the doctors, then Tommo might run free to rape again. A crowd of anonymous girls squatted in my head, every one of them weeping and bleeding.

'Laura?' There was concern in Frank's tone, and not a little love. 'What are you thinking about?' This wonderful man always tried to share my troubles.

'I'll have to do it,' I said. 'But nothing I say can be used in court. There are things known only to me – I haven't even told you what really happened during my marriage, Frank. If those facts are used against Tommo, he will know who has given the ammunition to the prosecution.' I swallowed. 'It's Gerald. He's too little to take care of himself. We have to mind him, you and I – you too, Dad. We can't take chances with the baby. But at the same time, if Tommo carries on doing these things, then I'll share his guilt. We have to do all we can to get him stopped.'

'Brave girl,' said Dad.

Frank said nothing, needed to say nothing, because he and I had quickly reached the stage where words were not always required.

I gulped against the rising panic, sat perfectly still with my hands on the table, angled my thoughts away from the evening's main topic. 'Dad, send some flowers to Ida Bowen – the woman who lived next door to me and . . . Tommo. She found me when I was hurt and she helped me. I'm beginning to realize how important neighbours are. I'll get something in St Helens for Hetty the Hawk.'

Two pairs of male eyebrows were raised. 'Hetty who?' asked Dad.

'Hetty lives here.' I pointed to the next house. 'She saved my baby's life. And would you make a donation to the sisters at the hospital, Dad? They were lovely.'

Dad relaxed a little. 'She's always had a soft spot for nuns,' he told Frank. 'At one point, she even considered joining their ranks.'

After Frank's hollow laughter had died, I said, 'It was only to get away from my mother. And a convent's not for runaways, it's for people who really want to be in the sisterhood. It's a job like any other, except that there's only one boss and no unions. And anyway, I'm just not good enough.'

Dad wasn't smiling. 'I tried to get Liza to leave. If I'd persuaded her to go, you'd never have needed to run away. But getting rid of a person is not easy. Perhaps I ought to have insisted, then your childhood would have been a little rosier.' He coughed, wiped his face. 'My fault, Laurie. It was all my fault.'

When I lay in my bed with Frank that night, I wondered about people and happiness, people and disappointment, people and guilt. Dad felt responsible for the actions of his wife, just as I must now admit my own part in Tommo's wickedness. Had I stayed, I might have been his only victim. Had Dad got rid of Mother, then I might not have been her only victim. But really, all my father could have achieved was the thinner spreading of Liza McNally's malevolence. As for Tommo, I simply could not have borne any more of his cruelty, especially now, with a baby in the family. So I had left him and he now chose to prey on others.

My relationship with Gerald was an odd one, because I did not yet know how to love him properly. I mused on, thought again about the dolls in their boxes, the toy pram which had been used just to contain my collection of caterpillars, beetles, stones. In the drawers of my tallboy, I had kept piles of baby-doll clothes, lemon matinée jackets, rose-printed frocks, little bootees, tiny underclothes. I remembered giving them all to Anne, recalled the unspoken questions as they sat on her face all those years ago. I was not a mother. I would never be a mother. The mere act of giving birth could not make me into a maternal woman.

But the more I lay and thought, the more determined I became to make a decent stab at life. I liked my baby now, and surely I could build on that, could use it as a foundation for the future? I loved Frank, but that was different, easy. Frank looked after me, made a fuss of me, courted my favours. Frank pleased me. The baby in the next room was a burden, I supposed, someone who would depend on me until he became old enough to make his own way. If I treated him badly, or even coldly, then he might turn out to be another lost soul.

I watched the sky as dawn began to stain it pink, heard the birds twittering outside, listened to Hetty the Hawk as she stirred the fire and made breakfast for her husband. Days in the country started early, finished early. We always kept the volume low in our house after ten o'clock in the evening, as those next door were often in bed by nine.

Life was about catering for others, then. All I could hope for was the chance to do my best, especially for Gerald. I tried hard not to blame my mother, but the fact remained that there was no pattern for me to follow, no outline that I could colour in. A bad parent breeds another, but I would break the chain now.

I stood over his cot, waited until those huge eyes opened. 'Hello, you,' I said. 'This is the first day. From now on, we shall get on a treat.'

He yawned, blinked, didn't smile. Gerald was weighing me up, was making the first collection of his life. At last, he could start compiling his list. At last, he had a mother.

Chapter Four

We led a simple life. The winters were cold and crisp, as the pancake-flat fields offered no shelter from the sea. Although we were some miles inland, the winds whipped off the Mersey, through the suburbs of Liverpool and straight into our small world. Summer days could be merciless unless we found shade under our old apple tree, so my favourite times were spring and autumn, as I was never fond of extremes of temperature.

Frank travelled, expanded my father's business, never left me overnight. I grew stronger, more cheerful, while Gerald blossomed into a sturdy youngster with limbs that were brown, eyes that were bright with intelligence. Even though there was a darkness at the back of my mind, I seldom allowed the fear to have a front seat. We painted walls, dug the garden, made silly meals from foreign recipes, enjoyed ourselves.

No-one ever came to ask me about Tommo. As the months went by, I got snippets of information from my father, items of gossip that he had gleaned from the floor of his factory. Owing to some weird technicality, Tommo was out on bail, then he was dragged in for questioning again, then he was home. For a long time, I feared that his victim was having second thoughts.

Finally, the girl and her family left Bolton and the matter was at an end. I understood that young woman, felt for her, empathized completely with a decision that might have seemed rash on the surface. She couldn't face it. She couldn't talk about what had been done to her, balked at the concept of reliving the ordeal in a courtroom full of men. When I heard about her flight, I cried. He was free now, at liberty to search for more prey. He reminded me of a cowboy with notches on his gun, or of an Indian with scalps hanging from a rawhide belt. My flesh crawled for a while, but I settled determinedly to my new way of life, found comfort in my lover, in my son who was growing at an alarming rate. I never stopped waiting for Tommo, but I did not always actively expect him. He would come one day, and I hoped that I would be strong enough, well enough protected to survive the showdown.

Mother sent letters via Dad, pulled him to pieces on paper for his refusal to tell her of my whereabouts. 'I have a grandson, but I am not allowed to see him. Life is boring here and I would like to visit you occasionally. John stays with you sometimes, I am sure of that. These pharmaceutical meetings are just a figment of an imagination I never knew he had. That Tommo has been lurking about again. I hear that he lost his job when he was arrested, but he seems well-to-do, is always extremely well dressed . . .' She had decided to be an invalid, was always asking Dad for medicines. I could not manage to worry about her, scarcely gave her a thought unless she wrote to me. I never replied, never bothered to put pen to paper. My coldness towards her still bothered me, but I was busy with my son, very busy with my neighbour.

Hetty Hawkesworth had taken over my life, had shown me how to make what she called 'bother-money'. I asked her what it meant, and she tapped the side of that little hooked nose. 'It's for getting you out of trouble, girl. Or into it. Whichever road, bother's easier when there's a bob or two in your pocket.'

Hetty and I baked three times a week, and the Chapman's Country Fayre van picked up our offerings on Mondays, Wednesdays and Fridays. We made scones, date loaves, pies, tarts, angel cakes, devil cakes and any other kind of cake that showed its face in the women's magazines. These were sold to various shops in the region, then the Chapman's Country Fayre man paid us a commission once a month. We did not invite the taxman to

339

join our party, so we made a tidy profit, even when the ingredients were expensive.

Gerald was an easy child, would sit happily for hours with a rolling pin and a bit of grey pastry, always enjoyed licking out our mixing bowls. He walked early, talked early, but reserved his speech for special occasions. When he was almost two, he made his first jam tarts and Hetty made him a junior partner. Gerald was happy. I felt his happiness even when he was serious, knew that I had passed my test as a mother.

After six months or so of baking, we were rich women. Hetty had a new three-piece suite and a perm, while I had £417 in the bank. We sat in her garden drinking tea and making plans. 'I'm going in for pots,' she declared. 'Nice pots, Doulton and the like. I've never had a set that matched. Mind, I'd have to stop chucking stuff at him.' 'Him' was her husband, and she ruled him with a rod of steel. 'I'll pick a pattern from the catalogue.' She cast an eye over me. 'And what will you do with your money?'

'Save it.' I watched Gerald as he chased a butterfly. His little brother or sister was a cluster of cells in my womb. How would I cope with two? Would the second one be easier? Oh no, there was no better-behaved boy than my little Gerald – angelic, he was. I smiled, knew that I was becoming a mother in spite of myself.

'Laura? Have you got cloth ears?'

'Sorry.'

'I asked you why you don't treat yourself.'

'Well, you never know what's going to crop up, do you?'

Hetty shrugged. 'That man of yours is on good money. You should use what you earn to buy some pleasure, a holiday or something.'

The problem was that I could never relax completely. I had a good man, a sweet little son, a pretty house that was rented by my father for me, decent clothes, television, fresh air and sunshine. Letters from Anne, who was studying in London, and weekly missives from Confetti kept me smiling, wiped out the anxiety that my mother's messages brought. Auntie Maisie and Uncle Freddie phoned once a week, passed on some of the Barr Bridge gossip. In spite of some tension, I was quite content, fairly happy with my lot. But it might all disappear. If he found us, if he came . . .

'What's up, lass? You shivered then as if somebody had stood on your grave. Is there trouble?'

I trusted Hetty, could have depended on her for my life. But I couldn't talk. Not about that, anyway, not about Tommo. 'I'm pregnant,' I said. 'So the money will do for the baby.'

She grinned, displaying a beautiful array of teeth whose architect had no doubt been commissioned by the National Health Service. The top set slipped, and she clicked the plate back into position with the tip of her tongue. 'Well, I'm glad about that, love. He could do with company, could Gerald.'

Hetty was a caution. She had a bad heart, arthritis and a thyroid condition, but she moved as fast as anyone I had ever known. She was one of those people who seem to do everything at running pace, so I asked her about this terrible need for speed. 'Why are you in such a rush, Hetty?'

She poured more tea, gave Gerald a cup of orange, swept the crumbs off the rickety-legged card table that doubled as an al fresco dining piece. 'Well, I'm fifty-five and it's catching up with me,' she said. 'See, we always have a past, even when we're only two minutes old. It kicks off like a little pebble, but it picks up all sorts and gathers weight and speed as we get older. Gerald! Come away from that cat, it scratches.'

Gerald looked at her, ignored the order, carried on tormenting her cat. 'He'll learn the hard way,' I said. 'Go on, Hetty.'

'I'm running away from my avalanche,' she said. 'That snowball has grown bigger while it's rolled down the hill. When it catches me, I'll be dead, because it'll crush me. So I just keep on the bloody move all the while.'

It was a strange philosophy, yet it was right for her. She would be running the day she died, would fight till her eyes closed. 'We all run from the past, I suppose.' Was my snowball gathering weight and speed, would it crash through my door and pin me against a wall? My snowball had strawberry blond hair and a cruel upper lip and I wasn't running, I was sitting in a back garden waiting for the landslide to happen . . .

She glanced at me sideways. 'What about your past? Why doesn't your mam come to see you? You've mentioned her in passing, so I know she's not dead.'

'She's ill,' I answered. Well, she was practising to be ill.

'Then why don't you go and see her?'

'I can't stand her.'

Hetty nodded. 'Aye, well that's as good a reason as any. My kids were glad enough to see the back of me and all. Mind, they come at Christmas and other holidays, but it's lovely when they've gone. Peaceful, like. What's she done?'

'Who?'

'Your mam.'

I ran to rescue Gerald from the claws of Hetty's furious feline. 'Leave her,' I said. 'Stop poking sticks at her.'

'Bad cat,' he muttered. Then he forgot the whole incident, went off to dig for worms. He loved worms, was always bringing them into the house, especially at meal times.

I went back to Hetty, drank my tea. 'Mother's not a nice woman,' I told her. 'She's very selfish, very demanding. And she used to play the field, liked the men.'

Hetty grinned. 'Men? I'd sooner play bingo any time. Are you sure you won't come with me one night? They have a big payout every so often, you know. Mrs Millichamp takes us down in her Mini, but I'm sure we could squeeze you in.' It was just like Hetty to change the subject in this way. Because she realized that I didn't want to talk about Mother, she skipped easily onto safer ground. 'Will you come to bingo, Laura?'

'No, thanks.' I never went out without Frank. We had started to use the car more often, sometimes driving to Liverpool or Southport, but I didn't dare to go out alone. Sometimes, I was scared at home, spent minutes at a time staring through various windows, scanning the fields as if I expected Tommo to materialize. Perhaps he would forget me. Perhaps I would be able to go home one day. No. He would never forget that I had left him, would never forgive Frank for winning me and taking me away.

'You should get out more. You worry too much.'

Sometimes, I felt that I didn't worry enough. I gathered up my son, said cheerio to my chatty neighbour, went home to cook a meal for my husband. Because he was my husband, except for a little scrap of meaningless jargon with a rubber stamp mark.

He came home early, threw down his old canvas satchel – Frank never went a bundle on briefcases – and ordered me to pack. 'We're moving,' he announced. Those spots of colour were on his face again, twin roses that sat on his cheeks whenever he was disturbed.

'Why?' My jaw hung. I felt stupid, shouldn't have asked, knew the answer. 'Tommo?'

He nodded, scooped up Gerald, held him tight. 'He's mobile and he's following me. I don't know how long he's been doing it, can't work out how much information he has, whether he knows about this place and so on. I've rung John and I'll not be working for him for a while. We're going to Manchester.'

'Manchester's near Bolton,' I said.

'It's a city. It's either Manchester or Liverpool. We're sitting ducks here if he gets the address. It seems that somebody told him about me being employed as a traveller for McNally's. So he's got himself a job with Rumworth's, the toffee people. Puts you off Rumworth's famous rum truffles, doesn't it?'

The advertisement ran across the front of my brain, the Rumworth's Rummy cartoon that was on telly almost

343

every day. 'I'll phone Rumworth's,' I decided. 'I'll tell them what he's doing.'

Frank frowned. 'He's doing nothing, love. Mr Walker in Ormskirk just mentioned that a man called Bernard Thompson had been in to sell him some sweets.'

'And Bernard Thomson enquired about his long-lost brother, I take it?'

Frank smiled grimly. 'He did better than that, Laura. He's looking for his nasty older brother who ran off with you. So folk will start to look at me sideways, I'm afraid. Even so, Bernard's doing nothing wrong. He's just telling enough of the truth to make himself look like the injured party. And there's no point in getting involved with details, because the whole truth isn't particularly believable.'

'Stranger than fiction.' I touched his face, stroked Gerald's thick brown hair. 'Where to, then? Which bit of Manchester?'

'Sale. It's Cheshire, really, but it's densely populated, a Manchester suburb. Your father knows some influential people, so we're to be allowed a new house for a while. Only one pair of semis is finished, and we'll occupy one of the two. It seems that I'll be there as a nominal night-watchman just to look after the building materials when the men are off site. Strange job, but I think your dad's had it tailor-made for us.'

'Hetty will miss me,' I said. 'She's going to be doing all the baking herself.'

Frank lowered Gerald to the floor and put an arm across my shoulders. 'You can't tell Hetty anything. If Tommo gets to her, she might give him our address.'

'I can't lie to her.'

Frank shrugged, then straightened his shoulders. 'There is an alternative, love. We can just stay put and face him. But he won't fight fair. The difference between fighting with my brother and with an ordinary human will be as big as the gap between warfare and terrorism. He'll not stand up to be shot at. He'll come carefully. I think

344

we'd best just do a bunk when Hetty's at one of her afternoon bingo sessions.'

'I know you're right, I do know.'

'So?' His eyebrows were raised. 'It's up to you, Laura. I can't carry on in the job, because he's going to blacken the name of McNally in every shop while I'm involved with the firm. But I can always find another job in St Helens or Liverpool—'

'No, we'll go to Sale.'

We moved while Hetty the Hawk was out for a few hours. One day, when I could talk, I would tell her why. And she would understand.

Edward Thompson was born in 1963. He had sandy hair, deep grey eyes and a fine set of lungs. He screamed as soon as his head was born, and he continued in the same vein for several months. Gerald did not like his little brother, thought that the new arrival was a pest. 'He's a pest,' he said daily.

Daily, I agreed with him. 'He'll grow up, Gerald. He won't always cry.' We kept the radio on all day, had the volume turned as high as we could bear. When Dad brought us a Hoover, I used it more often than was really necessary, because even the drone of the machine was preferable to Edward's screaming.

The small estate on which we were living was almost completed when I came home from hospital, so we faced another packing session when Edward was just a few weeks old. This time, my father had found accommodation for us in a Liverpool suburb called Woolton, and we were expecting to move to our new home by the end of August.

Sale had been OK, but we hadn't been able to settle. Frank became restless there, grew tired of having no proper job. So the idea of moving on appealed to us, as Frank was confident about getting work in Liverpool on the strength of my father's reference. But I had grown fond of the house, which was not much more than a

345

modern box, all open-plan and pale cream walls. There was a school at the back, and I often watched the children playing on the field. The shopkeepers in Sale were friendly without being inquisitive, which taught me that a larger community, especially a middle-class one, was probably the safest place in which to hide. Everyone was too wrapped up in his or her own ambition to take an interest in us.

We were due to move on the Friday. By Wednesday, our bags and boxes were packed and the house was being subjected to my final clean-up. I was sweeping the bare boards in an unoccupied bedroom when the phone rang. Frank answered it – I heard his soft, deep voice as he talked into the instrument.

'Laura?' There was a lift in the word, a sound that was not a stranger to panic. 'Laura?'

I stood at the top of the stairs, the broom still clutched in my hand. 'What is it?'

'Come down, love.'

I went slowly, strongly aware that I was walking towards something unpalatable. As soon as I reached the bottom of the flight, he grabbed me, held me tightly. 'Darling, your dad has had a stroke.'

This couldn't be right. I knew that the whole thing had to be a mistake, because my father was going to live for ever. 'No,' I said. My voice was even, as I was quite sure of my ground.

'Yes, Laura.'

'No, he can't do that. My father can't do that, Frank. It's not true.'

He was shaking. The dear man was trembling like a leaf in the wind, all because someone had played this terrible trick on us. It would be Tommo, of course. Tommo had got someone to phone us with this disgusting lie. I held Frank close, listened to the pounding of his heart. 'Who was on the phone, Frank?'

'Maisie,' he said.

'My Auntie Maisie? Why would she ring and tell us such a pack of lies? Are you sure it was Auntie Maisie?'

'Yes.'

I pulled away from him, held him at arm's length. 'A stroke? A brain thing?'

He nodded, his eyes bright with water. 'Laura, he's very sick. We must go to him. Maisie and Freddie will mind the boys while we get to the hospital. We have to go right away, love.'

'No, no, NO!' Someone was screaming and it wasn't Edward. There were words in the scream, horrible words full of hatred and pain. The screamer was me. When Frank's hand swept across my face, I dissolved into tears, ran away from him and crouched in a corner, my hands over my head. I was a child again and Mother was standing over me. In a moment, she would pull my hair and lift me up, then she would swing her palm against my face. No. I was with Frank. If I allowed myself to go back into my history, I would surely court insanity.

'Sorry,' he was saying.

I rose, patted his arm, told him not to worry, not to cry. When the children were bundled into the car, I sat in the front passenger seat and saw nothing. There was nothing left, nothing to see, nothing worth looking at.

I have no memory of that journey. As we entered Barr Bridge, I stirred myself to life, climbed out of the car, handed my children to my aunt and uncle. 'We've been longing to see them,' said Maisie. 'But not like this, Laura. Not for a reason like this.' She looked old. Uncle Freddie had a marked stoop, and his eyes were red with weeping. My father was not going to make it. He would leave the hospital in a box, and I had to get to him, wanted to say goodbye, thank you, I love you, wanted to say so much to him.

Dad was in a side ward. He was a mass of tubes and wires, was connected to things that buzzed and bleeped. Mother sat by his side, her make-up perfect for the outing, her nails polished and filed to smooth, rounded shapes. It was strange, because now I took in all the details, anything that would distract my eye from the figure on the bed. She had black patent shoes and a matching bag. The handkerchief bunched in her hand was dry. It was a prop, something she needed for when the audience arrived. And we were the audience.

'Laura. So you deigned to come, then.' She sniffed, dabbed her nose with the square of cotton and lace. 'He worked too hard, poor man. This was inevitable.'

I stared at her. 'He's still alive, Mother.'

She fixed her gimlet eyes on Frank. 'So you are my daughter's husband's brother.' The tone was accusatory.

'Frank is my husband,' I said. 'And you will treat him as such.'

'Pardon me, I'm sure.' She took a mint from her bag, pushed it into her mouth. Deprived of nicotine, she needed a substitute.

I walked to the window, gazed out at the grounds. 'Will you leave me alone with Dad?' I asked. 'Just for a few minutes.'

The clasp of her bag snapped. 'This is my legal husband.' She underlined the adjective, savoured it. 'I have a right to be here.'

I swivelled, kept my eyes away from my father. 'Go, please,' I said.

Frank held out his hand, guided my mother out of the chair and towards the door. Before going into the corridor, she threw a handful of words over her shoulder. 'Tommo's mother is here,' she said, and I could hear the venom beneath this statement. She would never change, would never learn love and tolerance.

It meant nothing. I didn't care who was here, who was not, who was hanging washing out to dry. At last, I looked at him. He was grey and small, with blue veins on his eyelids and snaking up his forehead. His chest moved slightly with each breath, but apart from this small sign of life, he was as still as stone. I sat by him, picked up a hand. His flesh was smooth, clammy, cold. 'Dad?'

Nothing. He was a shell, a piece of housing that had held my father's soul.

'Dad, I love you. You are such a good man, so kind. Thank you for all you've done for me and Frank. Thank you for keeping us safe.' Who would care for us now? I chided myself, repeated inwardly the words I had said to my mother. The man was still alive. 'I love you, Dad.'

He didn't move at all, didn't respond, gave no clues about his senses. Had he heard me? Did it matter?

A nurse rushed in, shouted the word 'crash', pushed me towards the door. I was met by three or four other people, all of them pushing to enter the room. Frank was in the corridor with my mother and Mrs Thompson. 'Is he dead?' asked Mother. She tried to enter my father's room, was placed gently in a chair by a youngish nurse.

'He's gone,' I told Frank. 'I've just remembered how it sounded, though I didn't seem to hear it at the time. There was a bleep, a very long bleep. My dad's dead.'

Frank's mother approached me. 'I've been wanting to catch up with you for some time,' she said. 'A woman in our street told me about Mr McNally's stroke. He was experimenting at the time, fell down at his bench. It's been a terrible strain for all of us, wondering where you were—' She silenced herself as the door opened. 'I'm sorry,' said a doctor to my mother. 'There was nothing more we could do.'

My mother did a fair imitation of grief, patted her face with the handkerchief, tried a few sobs, sank back against the wall. Frank kept his eyes on me, was waiting for my reaction. But I felt nothing. Perhaps this was a dream. I wondered if I would waken shortly to find the sun streaming through the curtains.

'Well, I can't say I'm surprised.' Mrs Thompson still had that painted-doll look, every hair scraped to the back of her small head. 'Frank, you've a lot to answer for. Running off with that poor man's daughter, making fools of all of us.'

I turned slowly and gave her my full attention. 'Shut up,' I said softly. 'No-one here is interested in your opinion. Just go home.'

She bristled, sucked in her cheeks, looked as if she might explode at any moment. 'I'll have my day with you, lady.' She awarded her son a look of fury. 'And with you, Frank. He's heartbroken, is our Bernard—'

'He can't be,' I said. 'He has no heart to break.' My father was dead, was lying a few feet away from me, and I was arguing with this nasty creature. 'Frank's a good man,' I added. 'And your other son's a monster.'

'How dare you—'

'I dare because he broke my leg. I dare because of what he did to that girl, the one who ran from Bolton to be away from him.' My voice was still quiet. 'Please go. This is not the place—'

'And where's your place?' she hissed. 'In bed with our Frank while our Bernard's grieving? Years he's searched for you, years and years.'

Frank stepped between us. 'Then I hope he never finds us. If he does, I'll kill him.' He pulled me into his arms. 'Come on, love. Let's go and say goodbye to John.'

I clung to Frank as his mother walked away. In that moment, I felt closer to him than ever, because we shared the same problem. Mothers. Frank's mother was a nightmare, and mine was another. When we stood round my father's broken body, the tears welled up and drowned me, but I felt comforted by Frank's arms. Mother simply stared at me, a new light flickering in her bright eyes. I recognized this as a glint of victory, and I feared anew for my future.

'Come outside, Laura.' Anne reached out a hand as if to guide me through the door. She was beautiful now, had matured into a stunning woman with the figure of a model and the face of an angel. But Anne was no angel. Anne was practising law, was a new force to be reckoned with when it came to litigation. 'Come on, we'll talk about divorce,' she urged.

'No, I don't want to go outside.'

She clicked her tongue, reminded me of Confetti.

'The nuns used to tut like that, Anne. Don't tut at me.'

'Sorry.' She brushed a speck of invisible dust from the white blouse. 'Just a short walk. We could take the little ones—'

'I'm not going out. And the children can't go out either.'

'Why not?'

'He might be there. Frank's gone to pick up the rest of our stuff from Sale and I want to be here when he gets back. It's bad enough knowing that we'll be staying in Barr Bridge for a while, but I refuse to tempt fate. Tommo will be out there waiting. When he finds me, he'll kill me.'

'Nonsense.'

I looked hard at her, felt the anger colouring my cheeks. I couldn't talk about it, would never be able to talk, yet I exploded now. 'Don't you dare to minimize my situation, Anne. I will not be treated like a neurotic. There is no drama in what I'm saying, no exaggeration at all. The fact is that Tommo will kill me one day if he gets a chance, or even half a chance. Don't dare to belittle what you don't bloody well understand.'

She reached out again, placed a hand on my shoulder. 'Laura, how can I understand when you won't talk? What did he do to you? Why are you and Frank running all the time? This is why I want you to get a divorce, then you'll be rid of him for ever.'

I sighed. 'Look, it took the Great Fire to rid London of the plague. I daresay we'll need another act of arson to clear him out. It's him or me. Don't ask for details, because I've no wish to dwell on the past.'

She leaned on Auntie Maisie's table. 'I've got a junior partnership in Bolton. Divorce isn't as messy as it used to be. Look, let me talk to Tommo. After all this time, and now that you've had Frank's child, he might be wanting his freedom. He's probably over you now.'

It was hopeless. She kept talking about Tommo as if he were normal, as if he might just carry on like an ordinary, everyday type of person. 'He's obsessive,' I said softly.

351

'His behaviour follows no pattern that you or I could understand. Tommo is sick in his head, and I have no intention of discussing the subject.'

Anne poured two glasses of fresh lemon. Auntie Maisie always made this in the summer, and now that the twentieth century had reached middle age, there were ice-cubes floating amid pieces of tangy lemon peel. She had a fridge, a freezer and a shop to run, because she had taken over Mrs Miles's General Store after the old lady's death.

She came in now with Edward in her arms. He never cried when Auntie Maisie held him, seemed to recognize a born mother. 'I'm opening up again, Laura. Gerald can stay with me – he enjoys playing shop. But this little fellow needs his nap. Laura? Are you all right?'

'Yes.'

The kind and gentle woman approached me. 'Stop here, lovey. Stop here with me and Uncle Freddie. We can soon have a toilet put in above the shop, then that back room will make a kitchen. It'll mean having a bed in the front room, like a bed-sitting room, but there's loads of room for two cots in that store place. You can have a bath at our house, can't you? See, with living next to the shop, we can use our Anne's old room for storage.'

Anne nodded. 'OK by me. I've a car and a flat in town, so there'll be no problem as far as I'm concerned.'

'I don't want to live round here.' I must have sounded ungrateful and churlish. 'We can't stay,' I said firmly.

Maisie looked puzzled. 'Then where will you go? I know John was finding somewhere, but . . . but he can't do it now.'

'I know, Auntie Maisie.'

'Then—'

'He may have provided for me.' The funeral was due to take place the following day, then the reading of the will was to be held at the solicitor's office in Mealhouse Lane. 'Wait until the funeral's over.'

'He'd have wanted you to be with us.' There was a

stubborn set to Auntie Maisie's jaw. 'He'd have wanted you to be with family.'

I sighed, wished that everyone would go away and let me grieve selfishly for a while. 'Mother's my family. Dad wouldn't want me anywhere near her. And he kept moving us on for a very good reason. That wasn't a game we were playing, Frank, Dad and I. The need to be at a safe distance from . . . the past has not disappeared just because my dad's dead.'

Anne looked at her mother. 'Laura's still afraid of Tommo. From what she says – or rather from what she can't make herself say – she is probably right to be careful. So we'll wait and see what Uncle John wanted for her.'

Dad's funeral service was held at the church of St Patrick where Tommo had served at the altar so long ago. I passed the very pew where Ginger had played his foul-smelling tunes, remembered little Art spread-eagled in the aisle, wondered what had happened to Enid and Irene. There were five of us in the front pew – Mother, myself, Anne, Maisie and Freddie. Frank had stayed at home to mind the babies, was suddenly aware of his lack of proper status in my life. I missed him, missed his smile, his shoulder, his support and love.

The coffin was too small to contain my father, I thought. The requiem mass, which was solemn and long, had a calming effect on me. The priest was a tender man who seemed to care genuinely for the deceased man. He spoke of my father's generosity to his workers, of his dedication to the employment and rehabilitation of the physically handicapped. I knew that this priest had loved my father, that most people who had known my dad had probably been fond of him. John McNally suddenly belonged to the whole world, not just to his selfish daughter.

Mother sniffed a lot, rubbed at her nose, played with a slight crack in a rose-tinted thumbnail. She was dressed in lavish black, had no doubt spent a fortune on the new role she was playing. The hat had a veil, a short curtain of netting that was decorated with black polka dots. I would have expected such a pattern to cause nausea, but she seemed unruffled.

Dad was carried out to the hearse, then we all followed at a sober pace until we reached Heaton Cemetery. My tears came when I cast soil and a rose onto the coffin, when I heard the clatter of earth on the box. I would never see him again, would never hear his voice. It seemed to me in that moment that life was just a series of losses, that the older we grew, the bigger the emptiness became. In our own death, we would finally have nothing, would be nothing. Until our own death, we practised for nothingness by losing everything we cared about. On the day of my father's burial, I could see no positive reason for staying alive.

Mother appeared anxious to be on her way, was edging towards the path. 'Come along,' she chided. 'Lingering here won't bring him back.' She didn't want him back. I could tell from her jaunty walk that she was looking forward to widowhood.

'She's picked up,' I heard Auntie Maisie say. 'Last week, she'd a bad stomach, a bad back, pains in her legs. Soon got over it, eh, Freddie?'

'Shush, Maisie,' he whispered.

Out of the corner of an eye, I saw a black shape, knew that my good friend Confetti had come to pay her respects to my father. There were no words in me, so I did not bother to greet her. But at the gate there stood a man I knew well, a man whose face, even when just imagined, usually sent shivers the length of my spine. Today, his presence did not signify. As I walked past him, I heard him say, 'Sorry, Laura,' but that was of no importance.

He chased after me, grabbed my arm. 'Give me another chance, Laura,' he pleaded, though the voice was hard and cold.

'No.'

He swung me round, held both my forearms. 'I've changed,' he said. 'I still love you.'

354

There was no fear in me, no feeling of any kind. 'Take your hands off me.' I waited until he released his hold. 'Tommo,' I said softly, 'Please understand me. Please, please try to listen. I don't want to see you ever again. You and I were a mistake.'

'My own brother,' he spat.

'He's a good man,' I replied. I was tired, weary, too exhausted for this.

'He's a cripple,' said Tommo.

I nodded. 'Oh yes, he has a terrible leg, but he's a wonderful person. Forget me. You must do us all a great favour by wiping me out of your thoughts.'

He took a step back. A bright blush stained his cheeks, clashed with the pinkish-blond hair. Frank's hair was golder, softer, I thought. 'I've learned . . . things,' he mumbled.

'Really? What things?'

He swallowed. 'How to treat a woman, how to go about living without losing my temper. I'm better now, honest.' He was almost grovelling, and this was not in his nature. The anger would be enormous once he realized that the ploy had not worked.

I glanced back at my father's grave where the men with shovels were waiting for us to leave. What would Dad have me say, here and now, while I stood by his open grave? Would he want me to be respectful, or would he rather have me honest? The latter, I supposed. I stared at the man who was still my husband on paper. 'You'll never change, not really,' I told him. 'Chalk could not become cheese, or vice versa. But if you have managed to find another way of living, be happy away from me.'

'No,' he hissed. 'Never, never.'

As I watched the fury working in his face, I thought about the girl who had fled, that other young woman who was now scarred, possibly for life, by the man who stood just inches away from me. He had used her, had thrown her away when she got broken – just as he'd cast me aside that night when my leg snapped beneath the weight of his anger. For Bernard Thompson, women were toys, optional accessories that could be picked up, smashed, discarded at will. Though he had no intention of consigning me to the rubbish bin . . .

He seemed to read the words in my head, appeared to sense my deep hurt and dismay. After staggering back a few more paces, he sagged against a bench at the edge of the path, lowered himself slowly into a sitting position. He shook, trembled like an old man. 'Bloody bitch,' he snarled. 'You won't even give me a hearing, will you?'

'No.' I forced myself to meet his wicked gaze. 'No, Tommo. It's over.'

He looked like a man with asthma, was gasping for oxygen. But I knew only too well that his difficulty had arisen out of temper and sheer malevolence. The look in his eyes would have scared me, but I had just lost my father, so I was untouchable just then. I climbed into the big, black car, sat next to the woman who had given me life.

'He wants you back,' she said as she breathed out a long plume of smoke.

I wafted away the fug, pressed my lips together, opened the window and stared not at Tommo, but at the diggers who were filling the hole.

'What will you do now?' asked Liza McNally.

'I don't know.'

She giggled, hid the sound behind a manufactured cough. 'Well, there's no daddy to protect you.'

'I've got Frank.'

'And that's all you'll get,' she said.

Chapter Five

The will was almost as old as I was. There was only one codicil, a small addition that had been ordered just a few months earlier. Maisie and Freddie Turnbull were to be given deeds to the house and the shop in Barr Bridge. My father had lent the purchase price of both to Uncle Freddie, but the debt died with the lender.

For me, there was nothing. This very old will of my father's had been witnessed in 1944 when Dad had owned nothing except a small business and a pair of semi-detached houses. Everything went to Mother. She sat in a tall chair at the end of a long table, the silly polka-dot veil hiding her triumph.

The solicitor asked me to stay behind after the reading. He ushered out Mother, my aunt and uncle, then he perched on the edge of the table and peered at me over the rim of his spectacles. 'I just wanted to talk to you for a moment, Mrs Thompson. You must be in no two minds about the facts, and the facts are that your father was in the process of drawing up a new will and that he was afraid that your legal husband might get his hands on the business.' He paused, placed a yellowing hand on mine. 'We were trying to work out a way of getting you divorced without . . . without unduly annoying Mr Thompson. Your father's biggest concern was for your welfare and that of your two children.'

'I know.' I pulled back my hand, extracted it from beneath the dry, papery skin of his palm. The man reminded me of sepia parchment, looked as if he had been locked away with old documents and scrolls, possibly the Dead Sea variety. 'Please don't worry about me,' I said.

357

'He was just days away from resolving his problem. In a new will, the house and a small annual income would have gone to your mother, then the bulk was to come to you. The one provision was to be your divorce. Even without a divorce, you would have received an annuity for yourself and the children.'

'My father was a fair man, but a sensible one.'

'Quite. Of course, when the will I read today was drawn up, you were a child and there was little property to dispose of. Had John died then, while you were in infancy, then your mother would have needed the money to rear you. It is a shame that he died so suddenly. It's a great pity that the new will was not ready.'

I looked into the cold green eyes. 'It's a shame that he died at all, Mr Brownlow.'

'Yes. Yes, of course.' He did not blush, though the skin on his cheeks was stained now to a colour that approached brown. 'I trust that you will manage in spite of this unfortunate occurrence. Of course, when your mother dies, you will inherit whatever she leaves.'

'Will I?'

He put his head on one side, shoved the glasses further along the bridge of his narrow nose. 'Of course. Why do you doubt that?'

I shrugged. 'My mother would give to the cats' home before she'd give to me. And she hates cats.'

He wandered away from me and thrust his hands into the open drawer of a greyish-green cabinet, brought out a slim folder that was tied with navy ribbon. 'Mrs Thompson, I have letters here, copies of correspondence between myself and your mother's solicitors. As your father was a Catholic, divorce was out of the question. But he spent many years trying to obtain a legal separation. There was a great deal of acrimony between your parents.'

'Yes, I know all about that.' And for some unfathomable reason, I didn't like this yellow man knowing about my family's problems. He was a leech, a thing that feasted on the lives of others, yet my father had trusted him, so I tried, pushed myself to have faith. 'Where is all this leading, Mr Brownlow?'

'To a contest. We can fight this will, Mrs Thompson. I have letters here from your father, letters which state clearly that he wanted rid of his wife, that he wished her to have no share in McNally's Cooling Teas. I can try to remove the business from her. That is not to say that we would win, but—'

'Whatever, she wins.'

He put down the folder. 'I beg your pardon?'

'It doesn't matter.' Whether I won or lost, my mother would be the true winner. If I took the business from her, she would enjoy playing the part of a wronged mother. If she held on to the business in spite of the contest, then she would be doubly victorious. 'I don't want to fight the will.'

He coughed, and his throat grated dryly. 'May I ask why?'

'You may ask, but I am not bound to answer.'

'Quite.'

'It's difficult, Mr Brownlow.' I began to waver, felt a bit sorry for him. He probably led a normal life in a normal family, might have difficulty in understanding my reasons for accepting the unacceptable.

'Mrs Thompson, I do have insight into your predicament. The reason why your father employed me was simple. I do not express opinion. I am here simply as a tool for my clients. I am, if you like, an encyclopedia of the law, something to which one might refer for information. This is not to say that I am without feelings. Your father was a likeable man with whom I used to share a whisky and a joke.' The whisky could have explained his colour, yet I could not stretch my imagination to a point where this man might ever commit a joke. He went on, 'My concern is for you, because you were John's chief concern. He is dead, but I am still representing him.' His eyes were no longer cold. He was pleading with me, begging me to fight for money, for security.

I decided to come clean. 'I've never liked my mother.

She was always unpleasant and she shows no sign of mellowing. But I can't fight her, Mr Brownlow. I can't stand up in court and say that my father hated her and—'

'There would be no need for that. The letters explain it all. The letters are newer than the will, so I would stand a chance of winning, of pleasing John. If we believe in an afterlife, then we must believe in those who have gone on before us. His spirit is asking you to go for a contest. Will you think about it?'

'No.' I did not hesitate, even for a second. 'I can't.'

Once again, he wore his professional face. 'Then I shall comply with your wishes. If you ever need help or guidance, contact me. Perhaps we should go ahead with your divorce.'

'No. Not just now.'

He sat down, looked at his watch. 'There would be no question of payment. It would be a service for John, who paid me well and promptly throughout our time as client and lawyer.'

I picked up my bag, pulled on the black gloves. 'It's not the money. I just have to wait a while.'

'Until your fear of the man has gone?'

He was a human being after all. How many more times must I tell myself not to judge on appearances? 'Thank you, Mr Brownlow. I shall bear in mind all you've said.'

They were waiting in the porch. Mother had pushed back her veil, was standing in the doorway with a glow on her cheeks and a cigarette in her hand. 'Well?' she asked, an eyebrow lifted slightly.

'Nothing. He knew Dad, just wanted to talk about him.'

'I see.' She puffed away to the last quarter-inch, ground paper and tobacco into the polished floor of the vestibule. 'Then perhaps he ought to have talked to me. After all, I did live with him for a year or two.'

I said nothing. She had occupied the same house as my father for ever, had driven him to an early grave. But she had never lived with him, not really. John McNally was fifty-five years and four months old when he died. And now, Liza had everything.

Auntie Maisie touched my arm. 'What'll you do now, lass? Are you stopping with us in Barr Bridge?'

The look in my mother's eyes was like a knife that had been honed to pierce her sister's heart. 'She will not be living with you, Maisie. No daughter of mine is going to spend her life above a shop. She will live with me. I am no longer well, no longer able to take care of myself.'

I stared at her. She was fifty-three years old and she looked about thirty, all bright eyes and clear skin, a picture fit enough for *Vogue*. Women who smoked were supposed to go dry-skinned and hollow-faced in middle life, but she was as fresh as a daisy. I would not live with her. If necessary, I would go to the town and beg for corporation living quarters, but I would not stay in the same house as this awful woman.

'Laura?' Uncle Freddie, still bent beneath the weight of bereavement, looked tired enough to be another corpse for burying. 'Are you coming back with us now? In the firm's van?' It went without saying that my mother would never travel in a blue van with McNALLY'S printed on its side.

I took his arm, clung to him. He needed support, needed to be helped through the next few months. After working so closely with my father, who had been his best friend, Freddie Turnbull would be lonely during every hour at the factory.

Mother peeped out, searched for the taxi. 'Time you retired, Freddie,' she said from a corner of her mouth. 'After all, you are sixty-eight now. John kept you on out of friendship, I think. I shall be recruiting someone younger.'

I felt his arm stiffen, knew that he had just been given the worst news possible. 'You can help in the shop – can't he, Auntie Maisie?' I asked. 'We'll be quite a big family, what with the two of you and the four of us. All hands on deck, eh?' In spite of Tommo, in spite of Mother (not in order to spite her, surely?) I would stay for a while in Barr

Bridge, would make sure that Uncle Freddie was settled and occupied. 'We'll be all right, you'll see,' I told him.

Liza McNally turned very slowly until she was facing the three of us. 'You will be living with me, Laura. At least, you and the children will live in my house. I cannot give room to your fancy man, I'm afraid. He must make his own arrangements. But you must move in with me.' She shook out the tiny veil, pulled it over her face, hid the workings of her wicked mouth. 'I cannot be expected to run that factory single-handed. We shall hire a nanny for the children, then you will be free to go out to work. There is money to be made in the mechanization of all the processes at McNally's. But I cannot undertake such demanding work alone. Of course, it will be in your own interests to come home, Laura. If you don't, then I shall possibly sell the works and live on the proceeds. Your children's legacy might be gone if I live a long life.'

A place as public as a lawyer's porch would not have been my choice of venue for such negotiations, but since she had thrown down the gauntlet, I did not hesitate to pick it up. 'Do as you like,' I said, my voice carefully controlled. 'I shall be staying with Frank.'

'But he's not your husband!'

I smiled, yet I knew that my eyes were cold. 'Don't try to lecture me, Mother. I'm a grown woman now with children of my own. The money is yours, so do as you please with it. Frank and I shall manage.'

Aunt Maisie gasped and pulled me backwards just as Mother raised a hand and slapped the air near my face. 'Hateful girl,' snarled the mean red mouth.

Uncle Freddie wrenched his arm from my grip, grabbed his sister-in-law's wrist, stayed its course. 'Too late for all that now, Liza,' he said gruffly. 'She's getting on the big side for a clouting, a bit too old for you to go tormenting. We listened all those years, Maisie and I. We heard you and we hoped that our Laura took no notice of you. What you put her through was nothing short of cruel and—'

'Shut up, you old fool,' yelled Mother, every inch the fishwife in spite of expensive clothes and sweet perfumes.

Uncle Freddie cocked his head to one side. 'Aye, I'll keep me gob shut,' he whispered. ''Cos I'm ashamed. We're both ashamed, me and Maisie, we should have done something about you years back, when the lass was a babby. We kept our tongues still for the sake of John and for our little niece. But she's an adult now, and he's gone where your tongue can't reach him. God love him, he should have tossed you in the ashpit when he saw the welts on his daughter's face. But we'll not talk, 'cos we failed John and Laura, so we've nowt to brag about. As for the job, I'd not work under you for a million quid a year.'

The teeth below the black netting were bared as Liza turned her venom on me once more. 'Freddie Turnbull is beneath contempt,' she sneered, 'so I'll not bother to answer him. But you, lady, will starve. Don't come to me with your hand out, Laura McNally. I shall make that factory valuable without you. The chances we gave you! When I think of how I sent you to a decent school—'

'An uncommon one, at least,' I said. 'We were never to be common,' I told my sad companions.

'And you married a failure, then ran off with his brother. Well, staggered off with a cripple. And remember, you've an illegitimate son to whom I am quite prepared to give a home—'

'I'll remind him of your generosity,' I said.

'And you throw the lot back in my face.'

I shook off Auntie Maisie and Uncle Freddie, stepped so close to my mother that I could smell her tainted breath. 'Just stop all this, stop it now. My dad has just died, and you've no respect for the man he was and no remorse about him dying so young. There's no love in you, no charity at all.'

'You're a cunning little bitch, aren't you?' she snarled. 'Acting nice as pie, carrying on as if you're perfect. If only the world knew what a nasty piece of work you are . . .'

I nodded. 'Don't worry about the world, Mother. I'm

sure you'll manage to broadcast my sins – try the Home Service or the news on TV.'

She made a noise, something that sounded like a cross between a sob and a cough. 'I told him where you were, you nasty little bugger. I told that Tommo creature how to find you, how to get hold of that cripple you ran off with. Oh yes, I put him in the picture.'

I could have killed her then, could have slaughtered her on the spot for causing so much pain to my father, to Frank, to me, my aunt, my uncle. The pressure on Dad to move us on yet again might just have been the final straw, the one that broke John McNally's heart and stopped his brain . . . She had put that pressure there, had passed on the information that had caused everybody's stress. I needed to get away. If I stayed, I would surely drown her with the venom of my words.

Uncle Freddie must have seen something in my stance, in my face, because he pushed past us, hailed a taxi and held the vehicle's door wide until my mother had stepped inside.

I stayed with Auntie Maisie until the taxi had left the scene. 'I'll kill her,' I said softly. 'One day, I'll really lose my rag and push her down the nearest flight of stairs.'

'There, there.' Auntie Maisie patted my shoulder. 'Don't be getting yourself into a fret. Feelings run high at times like these.'

'She told Tommo where I was. I can't believe that any mother would draw a map for a monster. She put a freak on the trail of her own child, her grandchildren.'

Maisie nodded pensively. 'But you never told us, Laura. We had our own ideas, our suspicions, but we didn't know for sure that Tommo was really bad. Perhaps she didn't realize what she was doing. You don't talk about him, so how could she have known that you had left him for ever?'

I leaned against the wall. 'A real mother would know, Auntie. If it had been Anne, you would have known.'

She sighed. 'Aye, I reckon I would, love.'

We walked to the van, squeezed ourselves into a narrow

seat, drove through town and out towards the rolling moors. Frank would be waiting for me. I didn't know what our future would be, where we would live, how we would cope. But he was there just for me and the children. Perhaps I could stop running now. Perhaps Tommo would not loom so large in the corridors of my mind. The shortage of money was a small thing, a minor irritation. For peace of mind, for a world without Tommo and Mother, I was prepared to deny myself indefinitely.

I was exhausted for weeks after the funeral, too weary to plan a life. So we stayed put simply because neither of us had the energy for organization. Frank was quiet, withdrawn, watchful. He was probably waiting for Tommo; he was also waiting for me to buck up sufficiently for yet another change of location. About one aspect of life I was content. Uncle Freddie had accepted the enforced retirement, was making a good stab at shopkeeping.

Few alterations were done to the property in Barr Bridge, because Frank and I had no intention of remaining in the village. The local builder made a connecting door between the two houses' upper floors, so that we could share facilities, but beyond that, we could not commit ourselves to expenditure that might be wasted. I, in particular, would eventually need to get as far away as possible from the area, from the gap left by my father. Mother had taken very well to widowhood, was shouting the odds all over the place. The factory was invaded by engineers, electricians, chemists, specialists in time and motion. When new machinery moved in, the buses became emptier, and rumour had it that many disabled people had been given their cards. Mother was on the up, so the rest of us could go down without wrinkling the surface of her gilt-edged pond.

Anne was the one who came up with an answer. She relayed her suggestion through Frank, who had taken a job at a stationer's in Bolton. He came in one evening, joined me in a room above Auntie Maisie's shop, played with Gerald, put both boys to bed. Sometimes, he was so good that I almost wept with gratitude. He spent all day on his feet, often finishing up with dreadful pain in the bad leg, then he would come home and take over the children. 'You're too good to be true,' I whispered in his ear. 'Shall I go through and run a bath for you next door?'

'No.' He kissed me, pushed the fall of heavy hair from my face. 'I saw Anne today. She thinks it's time we stopped running.'

'Oh yes? And who are we running from? Or should I say from whom are we running? God, there are bloody two of them, Frank. There's Mother sacking the infirm and replacing them with automation, then there's our darling husband stroke brother. Where the hell is he these days?'

Frank smiled at me. Whenever he smiled, it was like the sun peeping over cloud, bright and cheerful after the most dreadful of storms. He was a handsome man, quite broad and firm about the chest, solid except for the one wasted limb. His eyes always wrinkled at the corners, while the whole face seemed to reflect any merriment that happened to be taking place. 'I love you, Laura,' he whispered. 'And I'm so happy to see you livening up again. Anyway, enough of frivolity. She came in for envelopes, paper clips and stuff.'

'Who did?'

'Anne did.'

'Ah.' I began to count the freckles on his arm, used a Biro to draw a line after fifty. This was a game we often played, as Frank's freckles were profuse and impossible to number. It was the impossibility that had created the game. 'Is this two or one?' I asked as I started on the second fifty.

'Siamese twins,' he replied, rubbing at a freckle shaped like a number eight. 'Or an amoeba caught in the act of simple fission. She's found us a flat.'

I thought about amoebae in *flagrante delicto*, wondered how they might feel about being caught in the act. Then I drew a heart just below his elbow, put our initials in it, a fancy L entwined with a curly F. 'In Bolton?'

'Yes. Laura, we can't keep skipping about. I like working with old Mr Saunders. He's talking about retirement, so he might just be looking for a manager in a year or two. I'll never get a decent job with a decent wage if we carry on hopping all over the place. And we must consider the children. They're young, I know, but they need some security of tenure. They don't want to be waking up in a different house every six months.'

Frank was always sensible. 'You're always sensible,' I said. 'Without ever managing to be boring. Yes, we need our own place. I've not had my back scrubbed since we left Sale – imagine how dirty I must be.' We needed privacy, the chance to be together properly, to live our life without even kindly spectators. I sighed, nodded, agreed with him. 'It's time to move on, darling, but I am so scared of him. It's probably safe-ish here, simply because of the shop and all the comings and goings. But I don't think I should be near Mother. I anger her, I've got on her nerves since the day I was born. The factory folk might be better off once I'm out of the way. She's sacking everybody just to hurt me.'

He yanked off his tie, threw it on the floor, heaved at the left leg till it rested on a footstool. 'Remember Cunningham's furniture?'

'Bradshawgate?'

'That's the one. Well, it's closed down. The chap who's taken over is opening several lock-up businesses on the ground floor. Anne's flat is above what was the main showroom – it's a newsagent's now – and there's another flat available. The beauty of it is that although it's upstairs, the old lift is still there, the one that used to bring the furniture down to earth. You could use that when you're fetching the pram into the street.'

I bit hard on my lip, begged the panic to go away. 'But it's still Bolton, Frank.'

'Yes. If he wants to find us, he'll find us in Cornwall or

367

Australia. This flat is a town dwelling, Laura. Bolton's just about the biggest town in England, full of bustle and noise. We both felt like sitting ducks in the country, didn't we? Well, didn't we?'

'Yes.'

'So it has to be a town. Look, there'll be Anne in the next flat. Even when she's at work, she's only a spit away from Bradshawgate. I'll be working almost next door to the police station and you'll have a phone.' He massaged my shoulder, tried to squash out the tension. 'You can't live on the edge all the time, love. Sooner or later, you've simply got to relax or . . .'

'Or what?'

'Or be ill.'

I turned and looked at him solemnly. 'You mean daft-ill, don't you? You mean that I'm still letting Tommo get to me, even though I don't see him every day. He's still winning.'

'They're both losers, Laura. Bernard and your mother are miserable people who've tried to drag you down with them.'

I snorted. 'Down? Mother's never been so up!'

'Only on the outside.'

'She's crowing, Frank.'

He dropped his chin and stared up at me, the grey eyes misted with concern. 'It's all a game. She's like a child with the longest skipping-rope, the brightest colours on her spinning top. Inside, she's sad, lonely because no-one wants to play with her.'

'And Tommo?'

'The same.' He dropped the leg, stood up, smiled at me. 'Except that he is really sick. He's daft-sick, as you so aptly put it. Only there's nothing amusing about my brother's brand of insanity. Forget both of them, please. Let's go out there and find some sort of a life.'

I reached out for him, careful to account for most of my own weight as he lifted me out of the seat. He was a strong man with two weaknesses – one in his leg, the other in his heart. I thanked God that this lovely man had chosen me to occupy that gentle, caring heart. 'OK, Buster. We'll move. What about furniture?'

He grinned knowingly. 'Cunningham's left some bits and pieces, all a bit scarred and utility-ish. We'll manage. We'll always manage.'

As he led me to the bedroom, I held those words in my mind, clutched at them as if they were a life-raft. Frank was my saviour, and I lay down with him gladly. But there was no gratitude in my love-making. In that, there was only love.

Auntie Maisie had packed as if we were going off on a picnic that would last about a fortnight. We had tins of corned beef, soup, fruit and Spam. Four two-pound bags of sugar were wedged next to grease-proofed packages containing bacon, ham and cheese. She had even made curtains for our flat, and two lace-trimmed table cloths as covers for a barley-sugar-legged table that was scarred beyond repair, an item that had plainly been used when the Cunningham's sales force had been brewing tea.

'Are you sure you'll be all right?' she kept saying as we forced all the gifts into Frank's car.

'Of course,' I replied for the umpteenth time. Sometimes, Maisie was more like a mother to me than she was to her own daughter. 'You never fussed like this over Anne,' I reminded her.

'Anne hasn't got two babies to care for.'

Uncle Freddie, who had taken to wearing a brown overall coat while working in the shop, passed me a small sack of potatoes. 'We'll not get in the car,' I told him.

He pulled a wry face. 'Then stop here, lass.'

I threw my arms about the dear man's neck. 'You've always been so good to me, both of you. When I was little . . .' I swallowed a self-pitying sob, stamped on it, continued determinedly with what I wanted to say. 'You were always there for me.'

Uncle Freddie's eyes were old and sunken, with white

rings around the irises, the rims that come with advancing years. 'We love you,' he said gruffly. 'As much as we love yon lass of our own.'

Maisie agreed with him. 'We've had two good daughters, me and Freddie. But don't tell your mam we said so.'

'Of course not.' They knew her, all right. They knew that although she hadn't wanted me, she had never liked the idea of me receiving love and attention elsewhere. 'It'll be a long time before I talk to Mother.'

'Nay.' Maisie mopped her face with a large white handkerchief. 'She is your mam. Never forget that she's your mother, Laura. Happen she can't help the road she is after getting spoilt as a young one. Life's about forgiving folk and that includes ourselves. Don't put the blame on any one pair of shoulders.'

I climbed into the car, reached for Edward, took him from Auntie Maisie's gentle arms, closed the door. Judging by the crackling of paper, Gerald, in the back seat, was making inroads into Auntie's carefully wrapped parcels. But I did not check him, because my eyes were fixed on the figure approaching us along the uneven village street. 'Oh God,' I breathed from the corner of my mouth. 'Get going, Frank.'

He had not seen her. 'Why the sudden hurry?' he asked.

'Mother is upon us,' I said, trying to keep my lips as still as possible.

'Ah.' He rolled down his window, greeted my mother. 'Hello, Mrs McNally.'

My mother, resplendent in a burgundy suit, chose to ignore Frank. She stepped off the pavement, walked in front of the car and stood motionless until I opened my window. 'Yes?' I asked, sounding like a shopkeeper who waits for an order.

'That is a company car, I think,' she said.

I looked hard at her, breathed in the disparate odours of Worth and Park Drive, studied her expensive clothes. There was no doubt in my mind that the suit and blouse had been made for her, because the fit was perfect. I decided that she had visited a city dressmaker, had probably ordered a dozen exclusive outfits. The shoes were suede, as was the handbag, a large affair that was rather like a briefcase. Here was the businesswoman, then. So the play had progressed into yet another act, with one of the scenes to be played here and now with the world passing by. 'My father gave it to Frank,' I answered eventually.

'It was for company business,' she snapped.

I glanced up the street, decided that this little bit of the world was a poor audience for Mother, too small to concern me. After all, the locals knew Liza, had enjoyed her variable temper over the years. And as far as I was concerned, there was nothing to lose.

I thrust my baby into his father's arms, got out of the car, squared up to the woman on the cobbles. As far as height was concerned, I held the advantage, but because of the heels on her court shoes, we were more or less on the same level. However, my footing was steadier than hers, and I tried not to smirk when she stumbled slightly between two age-worn stones. 'Do you want the car now, Mother?' I asked, my tone trimmed with saccharine.

'Where are you going?' she demanded.

I leaned a casual elbow on the car's roof. 'Why do you need to know? And what difference will our destination make? Oh and if we keep answering questions with questions, we shall be staying exactly where we are for the foreseeable future.'

She curled that top lip in her good old-fashioned way. 'Don't be impudent.'

'I am too old to be impudent. Just one more question, though. Why do we keep having these show-downs in public? Don't you think we should use a telephone or the Royal Mail? Or pigeons?'

She gritted her teeth, almost looked her age for a moment. 'You will not take that car out of Bolton. It is mine, it is company property.'

I leaned down, spoke to Frank. 'Put the children inside the shop, love. And then you can help me to unload all the luggage. Mummy wants her motor.'

'Don't call me Mummy. I've told you before—'

'I'll call you exactly what I choose to call you. And some of the names will probably be short and rather rude. Come on, Frank, she wants her precious car back.'

Frank climbed out, gave Edward to Auntie Maisie, lifted out Gerald, who had become firmly attached to a packet of biscuits. As he was a well-brought-up child, he offered the soggy contents to my uncle and to Frank, then to a few other people who happened to be passing.

At last, there remained just Mother, Frank and myself. I walked to the boot, threw it open, scattered our cases on to the pavement. My temper was rising – I could feel the heat on my face.

Frank spoke to Mother. 'We're not leaving Bolton, Mrs McNally. And the car is so useful to us because of the children.'

She ignored him, but used the information he had imparted. 'Laura, if you are staying in town, you may continue to borrow the car.'

I glared at her, deposited a pile of nappies on a suitcase. 'I want nothing of yours.' I paused for a second, had a think. 'Frank, give me a hand. We'll keep the bloody car and pay her for it.'

When the boot was filled once more, we collected our boys and began the process all over again, Gerald in the back, Edward with me, biscuit crumbs everywhere. Mother stood on the pavement, her body turned slightly away from her sister and brother-in-law. I didn't smile, because my temper was still simmering, but I felt as if I had won a small battle. Even so, defeating my own mother did not give me any true joy. And, as Frank had so rightly predicted on many such occasions, there were tears before bedtime.

I wept not just for myself, but for the man whose arms contained me. She would not even deign to recognize him.

'I'll get the money tomorrow,' I said between sobs. 'And I hope it chokes her.'

He patted my back, comforted me as if I were a baby with colic. 'You should just keep the car and the money, darling. She doesn't need either of them, she's only trying to—'

'I want nothing of hers,' I cried. 'Nothing. I'm an orphan.'

He bathed my face, brushed my hair, tucked me into our new and rather lumpy bed. 'From this day, I shall call you Orphan Annie,' he declared soberly. 'I hope Anne won't mind me borrowing her name.'

The trouble with Frank was that he never let anybody grieve for long. He lay down beside me and started making up names for everyone we knew. When he had finished reducing the good people of Bolton to characters from *Comic Capers*, he began on the famous, rhyming names that sounded too terrible for me to resist. 'If Bette Davis had been Mavis Davis and if Doris Day had chosen May Day—'

I cut him off with a sharp elbow. 'Shut up, Frank.'

He had no remorse in him, no mercy. 'Your life could have been a lot worse if you'd been called Sally McNally. And if Clark Gable had a sister called Mabel, and if John Wayne had a sister called—'

'Jane!' I shouted. 'Honestly, there's nothing worse than a man who makes you laugh in bed.'

He turned on the bedside lamp, a hideous thing from the thirties with a naked women stretching upward towards the shade. 'What about Myrna's brother, Roy Loy? Are you giggling? Are you?'

'No.'

The light went out. 'You're no fun,' he grumbled.

'You've missed the best ones anyway,' I said.

He let out an exaggerated sigh. 'Go on, then.'

'Well, if Clara Bow hadn't been called Clara . . .'

'Right, I'm listening.'

'If she'd been called Florence and she'd shorted it to—'

373

'Flo?' he interrupted. 'Flo Bow? Not bad for a beginner.'

I felt damned by this faint praise. 'Right. Which president of the United States had a facial tic? Go on, Clever-clogs, work that one out.'

He pretended to think for a moment, was probably miles ahead of me. 'I give in,' he said.

'Blinkin' Lincoln. Now go to sleep.' Frank was the best man in the whole world, because he loved me, looked after me and made me laugh in bed. But I wasn't going to tell him what he already knew.

Chapter Six

It was a large and airy flat with tall windows, two living rooms, kitchen, bathroom and two bedrooms. I liked living there, was comforted by the comings and goings in the street below. After a while, I gained enough confidence to put the babies in their Silver Cross, Edward at the sleeping end, Gerald seated opposite, then we would saunter forth into the town. The old-fashioned lift was a bonus, as we would never have got out during weekdays while Edward was so young. As time passed, I ventured further afield, to the Town Hall Square, to the open-air market and even along Deansgate to Queens Park.

We heard nothing of Tommo, nothing of Mother, as we both maintained a careful distance from family. Frank was fond of his father, met him sometimes for a drink in the Pack Horse, but Mr Thompson chose not to mention his other son. Occasionally, they would come to the flat after a couple of pints, and Mr Thompson would peep at his sleeping grandchildren before sitting silently in front of our rented television set. I tried to draw him out. 'How are you today, Mr Thompson?'

'All right, thanks.'

'Would you like a cup of tea?'

'Not just now, thank you.'

'Are you still at the same pit?'

'Yes.'

It was hopeless. Time after time, I tried to be a friend to my lover's father, but I failed miserably on every occasion. When I asked Frank about it, he rambled on about his dad being ashamed of Tommo, about me reminding Mr Thompson of his son's misdeeds.

Then the evening came when I didn't have to try. Frank was preparing to meet his father in the pub while I bathed the boys and tucked them into bed. Our doorbell rang, so I ran to the window and stared into the street. Although I seldom voiced my fears, I still expected to see Tommo standing at the front door. 'It's your dad,' I called. 'I'll just let him in.'

Colin Thompson followed me up the brown-painted stairs, stood in our living room, the tweed cap twisting in his hands. 'Where's Frank?'

'In the bathroom having a shave. Shall I put the kettle on?'

'No, love.' Mr Thompson was not one to call a person 'love' or 'dear'. 'I'll just sit down a bit.' He dropped into the sagging sofa.

I stood near the fireplace, fiddled with a china shepherdess whose nose had gone missing during one of Gerald's games. 'Gerald broke it,' I said, feeling gauche and stupid.

'Yes, little ones do break ornaments, don't they?' He cleared his coal-damaged throat. 'Is he a good lad?'

'Well . . . yes, he is. A bit quiet, gets into cupboards and drawers. But he's a nice little boy.'

'He doesn't smash things deliberately?'

I shivered. Was this poor man looking into the adage 'like father, like son'? 'There's no harm in him, Mr Thompson. He just gets into places when I'm not looking and breaks bits and pieces by accident.'

He nodded. 'Fair enough.'

Frank came in, continued to run a comb through his hair. 'What's the matter, Dad?'

Mr Thompson fixed his eyes on me. 'He's not given up, Laura.'

'Oh.' The syllable was more of a sigh than a word.

Colin Thompson drew something from an inside pocket, placed it on the melamine coffee table, another ugly piece of furniture that had been among the pile of Cunningham's rejects.

Frank bent down and picked up the envelope, opened

it, drew out some stiff paper and riffled through five or six items. 'Bloody hell,' he said softly. 'I thought it was all over, hoped he'd come to his senses at last.'

The man on the sofa ran a hand over his balding head. 'He's got no senses. Not human ones. I thought you should both be warned.'

Without another word, I took the cards from Frank, turned them over, saw myself sitting on a bench, my hand resting on the handle of the pram, saw myself again, this time squatting on the grass near a duckpond. There were photographs of me, of me and Gerald, of me and Edward. But my younger baby's face had been mutilated by layers of ink that had poured from an angry pen. Tommo had crossed out Edward. My legs would not bear my weight, so I sank to the rust-coloured rug, allowed the photographs to scatter around me. I was everywhere and so was Tommo.

Frank dropped down beside me, placed an arm across my shoulders. 'Come on, girl.'

'He's wiped out our baby,' I said. 'And a baby's not much bigger than a pet rabbit. Remember what he did to all those poor animals. We have to move on, Frank. We've got to go somewhere, anywhere. But he's all over the place. Wherever we go, he'll find us and he'll kill Edward and—'

He shook me, guided my chin until I faced him. 'Laura, he's not chasing us again. He can't chase people who refuse to run. We are not going to keep on the move for ever, darling.' He cast a glance over the widespread photographs. 'I'd say he was drunk when he did this to Edward's picture.' He directed a question at his father. 'Hasn't he found another woman yet?'

'No. Thank God.' The man reached out and touched my arm. 'I don't mean anything by that, Laura. I know it's a mess when you seem to be his only target. But I couldn't bear it if I'd another young woman to worry about.' He screwed up his face, looked as if he were about to cry, but he held on. 'He wants locking up. I'm not just saying that, Frank. If I had my way, he'd be having his head tested. But your mam's dug her heels in, swears there's nothing wrong with him. Even when I've come home and found her battered and bruised, she's always had a fall. The only benefit of having him back home is that I can keep an eye on him.'

I stared at the visitor. 'He hits his mother?'

'Yes. And I'm no match for him. Even if I could manage him, Phoebe wouldn't let me raise a finger. It was the same when they were kiddies – nothing was good enough for her Bernard.'

Frank picked up all the snaps and tore them into tiny pieces. 'These are going in the bin. And Dad and I are going nowhere tonight, Laura. We shall all stay in and watch a bit of telly, give you a hand if the boys wake.'

As if on cue, Edward, who was making much of his sore mouth, let out one of his roars. 'Teeth,' I explained to Grandad. 'He never does anything quietly, I'm afraid.'

A chill swept over me as I walked to the bedroom. Had the badness missed Gerald, even though he was Tommo's real son? Was it going to emerge in my husband's nephew, was there a miniature Tommo waiting for me to pick him up and rub Bonjella on his reddened gums?

Edward stopped crying as soon as I reached the cot. His cheeks were scarlet and the little chest continued to heave with the rhythm of recent sobs. Mothering still didn't come easily. I loved my children, but mostly with my head. Yet how sick I had been moments earlier when I'd seen this tiny chap's face rubbed out with what looked like Indian ink. 'No-one will get you,' I told him. 'By Christ, I'll kill him first, Teddy.'

Gerald eyed me from the bed. He was almost three years old, master of all he surveyed, very quietly superior to his little brother. 'He's a pest,' he announced for the umpteenth time. 'He's getting pesterer all the time.' Gerald's acquaintance with adjectives was short, but he insisted on using 'gooder' and 'badder' with great relish, usually when describing Edward. 'He keeps me waker,' he grumbled. 'Screaming louderer.' Ah, the courtship with adverbs was beginning. Tommo's son bore all the hallmarks of cleverness, and I hoped that he would direct himself into something useful. Tommo was bright. Bright and twisted and evil. God forbid that my child should . . . I shivered again. 'Go to sleep.'

Frank came in. 'Is this little devil disturbing you, Gerald?' The amazing man never showed any favouritism, treated both boys as his own sons. 'I'll take him away for a while.'

When Gerald and I were alone, I tucked him up and sang to him, pushed the shock of hair from his eyes, watched him watching me. 'Will you sleep now?'

'Yes.'

'We'll keep Teddy till he drops off. OK?'

'I like him really,' said the sleepy child. 'He's my brovver.'

There were times when I knew I was a mother, times when one of my children wore a certain expression, occasions when Gerald's diction was quaint and heart-rendingly infantile. Whenever he said 'tewevision' or 'bweakfast', something stuck in my windpipe and threatened to cut off my breath. This was a skill that could be learned, an art my mother had failed to master. Small people were lovable once the fear of them had passed.

In the sitting room, Frank was cradling his son and rubbing balm on the fiery gums. But my eyes were fixed on the senior Mr Thompson, because his face was twisting again as he watched his favourite son playing the part of a father. As I understood him and felt his pain, I sat next to him on the sofa and held his hand. It was dry and calloused, seemed to have healed itself after a dozen pit injuries. This was a good man, another like Frank. 'Where did he come from, Mr Thompson? How did you manage to have two sons so different from each other? What happened to make Tommo act the way he does?'

'I've asked myself that for donkey's years, Laura. It was

379

Phoebe's fault, I suppose. She favoured Bernard over Frank.'

I patted his hand, felt like a nurse looking after a patient. 'Are we all our mothers' faults?'

He smiled weakly. 'I reckon so. It might start coming right once enough men decide to take more of an interest in their children. But there wasn't a lot I could do from a seam half a mile underground. She spoiled him, made him too free. He's been a wrong 'un all his life, ever since he could walk.'

'I'm scared.' I tried to swallow the fear, but it bubbled in my throat, made me cough. 'I'm frightened to death of him, Mr Thompson.'

He shook his head, looked tired, ill and old. 'So are we all, lovey. And that includes his mother, though she'll never admit it. Time and again I'd have left home, but I've needed to keep an eye on his doings. She just says he's clever and has to have his head. I reckon he'd have battered our Frank to pulp if I'd scarpered when they were still at school. And now, it's too late for me to have a fresh start. I'm old, set in my ways.'

How well I understood. 'It's too late for my dad, Mr Thompson, but not for you. Get away from him.'

'And who'll watch him? Who'll find the photos with the kiddy's face blacked out?' He grabbed my hand tightly. 'I'm sorry about your father. Don't think I'm not sorry. Frank says that your parents didn't rub along too well. And yes, it is too late for your dad. I must sound selfish, moaning on because I've never had the courage to walk out. Marriage becomes a habit, you see. It's all to do with home and a certain chair or a pattern on a rug. We get used to the worst places simply because we've not the courage to try again.'

Frank placed the sleeping infant in his day-crib, a larger version of the Moses basket. 'We'll leave him there till Gerald's settled, otherwise we might get stuck with the pair of them.' He sat in the armchair, part of which was threatening to explode at any minute, as the moquette had worn thin against too much stuffing. 'Laura, I'm sure we've got to hang on. I've got a job I can cope with, a car that you've paid for, a decent flat—'

'She sent the car money back,' I said. 'A bundle of cash in a registered envelope. It went against the grain, but I forced myself to keep it.' I shrugged. 'Perhaps there's hope for her yet.'

Frank's jaw slackened. 'She what?'

'I put it in the bank. She sent a little note about her grandsons needing the best clothes, the best food, about her grandsons being special because their grandmother is special. So we've still got four hundred pounds.'

'Bingo,' grinned Frank. 'Let's buy some grapes and have an orgy.' He blushed, remembering his father's presence.

Mr Thompson smiled fully for the first time since arriving. 'You two are made for one another,' he said. 'Can't you have an orgy without grapes?'

Frank's tongue stumbled slightly as he answered, 'No, not a Roman one. Mind, a Lancashire orgy's different.' He grinned at the expectant looks on our faces. 'For a Lancashire orgy, you need cow heels, tripe and black puds.'

His father lost the smile, adopted an expression of great seriousness. 'Oh heck, I'll go to the back of our coalshed,' he muttered.

'What's up, Mr Thompson?' I asked.

'Well, all these years, I've seen myself as a right Lothario. I thought it took just two bags of chips and a couple of cod. No wonder I've no luck with women.'

Frank nodded, continued the game. 'Depends on the kind of vinegar, Dad. You've to make sure it's brown.'

They were two of a kind, a matching pair. Mr Thompson was clearly a man of great intelligence, one of the many who had been deprived of chances. If I closed my eyes and cut out the blue lines of coal-dust in his complexion, he might have been a teacher or a doctor, because folk these days were hanging on to their roots,

381

refusing to 'talk proper' just for the sake of protocol. The sixties crashed through all kinds of barriers, brought much of the Establishment tumbling down. It was the debs who were mocked now, the social climbers, the folk with cut-glass BBC gobful-of-plums accents.

They were both staring at me. 'Sorry, I've been thinking again,' I explained for the benefit of our visitor. 'I've the sort of brain that can only deal with one thing at a time. Have you asked me a question?'

Frank looked serious, had worry-lines on his forehead. 'He's working nights at Yates's Wine Lodge.'

I held my breath. The wine lodge was just a hundred yards from our flat. 'Every night?' I asked. I didn't need any clarification about the 'he'.

'No,' answered Mr Thompson. 'Thursdays and Saturdays up to now. He's still travelling in confectionery, but he says he needs extra cash. I don't know what to think.'

'I do.' Frank's cheeks glowed with colour. 'He's trying to get near Laura.' He gave me his full attention. 'Your mother told him once where we were, so she might just have done it again. Or he could have found out from another source, simply by keeping his eyes and ears open.'

I was sick of it, sick to death of wondering when he would turn up, what I would do if he did. And there was Frank to consider. He had a good job and a bad leg, had been dragged about enough. It was never my fault alone, because we shared the burden of Tommo, were both related to him. But I couldn't make my lovely Frank carry on moving, changing jobs, searching for homes, just because I was afraid of one man. Then Edward's face, most of it blacked out, came roaring into my mind . . . I breathed in, checked my terror. 'We stay,' I said.

Frank's forehead flattened itself out instantly, looked as if it had been ironed. 'It's for the best, love,' he said. 'Because in the end, there's no hiding place from a man like my brother.'

'And my husband.'

Mr Thompson stood up, collected his cap, bent over the

basket. 'Nice-looking little thing,' he said. 'I wish . . . Well, wishes don't count, do they?' He strode to the doorway, turned and looked at us. 'But dreams do count. Follow them and find them.'

'Oh, what a smashing bloke,' I said when the door was closed.

'Of course. I mean, look at me.'

There was just one problem attached to living with a man like Frank. He wouldn't let me fret, always made me laugh at the most unlikely times. There could be only one thing worse than being with Frank. I hugged him, buried my head in his shoulder. That one thing would be to live with a man who never made me laugh at all. A man who made me cry.

Anne looked all posh and fashion-platey in her tailor-mades, but she was still the same Anne Turnbull underneath all the worsted and silk. Well, she was almost the same . . . 'They sort of stand there like this, with a hand on each side of the gown, running their thumbs over the material. There's a bit of swaying back and forth as well, up on their toes, then down on their heels. They think it makes them look imposing, you see. It's a good job they get wigs, because most of them are bald. "My learned friend", they call each other, but you could cut the air with a blunt razor. Honestly, they're giving each other such filthy looks – you wouldn't be surprised if it was pistols at dawn. Half an hour later, there's the whole shower of them in the Dog and Duck, you'd think they'd just got married to one another. It's a bloody scream. So much for Her Majesty's Crown Courts, eh?'

I sat on her off-white sofa with my feet on a thick cream rug. One of my eyes was on Gerald, who had both of his eyes fixed on a group of Spode figures just above his head. Edward gurgled, and I tried to keep my other eye on him, prayed that he wouldn't be sick in the midst of all this opulence. For a junior solicitor, Anne was very well furnished. 'How do you afford all this?' I asked.

'I don't. The chairs are on the never-never and the carpets and stuff are courtesy of my bank manager. He's fed up with his wife, so I treat him to a meal now and then.'

'Just a meal?'

She arched a perfect eyebrow. 'Of course. I've set my sights on a doctor, because that would balance things out. I could see to all the family's legal problems while he attended to their physical well-being. But I am definitely off barristers. And I don't want to marry a solicitor, because there's no room in my life for a pair of briefs. Coffee?' She lifted a fancy percolator and grimaced. 'Catalogue,' she said. 'Three bob a week.'

I sipped politely from my Susie Cooper cup, gave Gerald a stern look as he weighed up the possibilities of a stool on which he might climb and reach the porcelain figurines.

'So, you're in purdah, I take it?' She wasn't quite laughing at me, but there was something in her tone that made me feel foolish for hiding away from Tommo all over again.

'Yes.' It was no use, she would never understand.

'What the hell for? Why don't you just off-load the bad bugger, cut him out of your life? I can do it for you if you like.'

'Thanks.' I planted the cup in its delicate saucer, noticed that my hostess had mixed up her fruits, as I had a grape pattern on one piece and a lemon on the other. They were beautiful things, lovely to hold and to behold. 'I've already had the same offer from Dad's lawyer. He wanted to contest the will, said he had some flimsy evidence of Dad's change of heart.'

She sighed explosively. 'Sometimes, Laura, you get right up my nose. Why don't you do something?'

'Such as?'

'Anything. Just something. You let things happen to you, just sit there and wait for life to arrive. It's not a bus you know, not something that runs to a timetable.'

384

'I've never known a bus to be on time anyway,' I quipped. I placed the baby on my shoulder, winded him, hoped that he hadn't done one of his wet burps. 'There are two children now, you know,' I reminded her unnecessarily. Gerald had picked up a heavy crystal ashtray, was trying to balance it on his head. 'Put it down,' I said crossly.

'Babies are happenings,' she replied. 'I'm talking about you and the rest of your life. What about it?'

'I don't know.' My older son placed the ashtray on the floor and attempted to stand in it. At home, he had been as good as gold, but now, just a few yards from his own territory, he was behaving like a thorough brat. 'Get out of that,' I ordered stiffly.

'Leave him alone,' said Anne. 'Everything's insured.'

'Even the stuff that's not paid for?'

'Especially the stuff that's not paid for. Look. You're twenty-three and you've a head on your shoulders. Why don't you go to night school and pick up a few qualifications?'

She was annoying me, had plainly joined the up-and-coming brigade of women who considered motherhood and housekeeping to be a crime. 'I'm happy,' I said lamely.

She shook her head, but every hair remained fastened down, adhered strictly to the swept-back style that she had favoured of late. 'You're scared to death. Get out of that dreary flat, find an interest, forget Tommo.'

I dropped my chin, inhaled, raised my head and looked straight at her. 'Stop being so damned superior, Anne. I never wanted an education, never needed to be anything except content. Motherhood's no picnic, but it's a challenging job.'

'And not a permanent one. You'll be redundant in fifteen years. What then?'

The rein on my patience snapped. 'How the hell am I supposed to know what'll happen in fifteen years? Do you think I've a crystal ball at the bottom of the nappy bucket?

There's no way that you can be sure of anything, either. Oh, you're all talk now, ready to take on the world and all its rolled-up bits of legal documents. No-one questions you about the rightness of your decisions. But do you really want to spend the rest of your days up to the neck in mucky divorces, boundary fences and all kinds of broken promises?'

'*Touché.*' She crossed the small space between us, mopped some baby-sick from my shoulder, sat down again with all the grace of a dancer in *Swan Lake*. 'I admit that I set great store by education and achievement in the workplace. It's as if I'm watching you drift, though, and I do worry about you. So many women finish up alone these days, husbands dead or disappeared, no way of earning money in a dignified way and—'

'What dignity?' I demanded, my hackles rising. 'How can anything be dignified when one person's paying another to dance to a certain rhythm? I see no difference between the woman who scrubs steps and the woman who types letters. They both do a job, get paid, go home, spend the money.'

'Yes, but one of them has clean hands,' she replied quickly.

'So what? She might have been typing dismissal notices or threatening letters from one mogul to another. There's nothing clean about labour of any kind. You do the job and ignore the consequences if you want to stay sane.'

Anne's nails were manicured and coated with a pearly-pink varnish. She tapped them on the arm of her white leather chair, glanced at Gerald who was trying to pluck strands from the sheepskin rug, finished her coffee. 'You should join the Labour Party and go for a seat. A purist like you ought to be gracing the halls at Westminster.'

'No, thanks.'

'Then what are we going to do with you?'

I didn't like the 'we'. The nuns used to say 'we' when one of us had been naughty – 'We aren't doing our best today, are we?' – and it made me feel like a child again.

This was my cousin, a woman who was exactly the same age as I was, with the same background, the same colouring, mannerisms, build. 'You sound like a bloody public-school prig?' I reminded her, not for the first time. 'And I am not the poor relation who gets visited by you on the odd occasions when you're not changing the world. Anne, I love Frank. Just being with him is enough for me. I don't want to plan a future without him. When the boys are older, I'll get some work and contribute to the family income.' I paused, timed the final barb. 'You see, I shall work to live, whereas you live to work. There's no-one special in your life, no-one who loves you the way Frank loves me. Don't judge me by the false standards you acquired in the corridors of so-called learning.'

She plucked an invisible speck from the skirt of her suit. 'As I said earlier, you're an orator. Use your abilities and get out of that blinking flat. I just cannot understand why you shiver and shake in there just because Tommo's in the vicinity.'

No-one except Frank would ever know how deep my fear was. And I didn't want her pity, couldn't just sit there and tell her that it had always been rape, that I hadn't known the difference between rape and loving until Frank. If I'd talked about Tommo's near-impotence, about his frustration and his cruelty, she would have taken up the cudgels there and then, would have found my husband and . . . Whatever, she could have achieved little. 'You don't know the half of it, Anne.' Divorce papers? He would have set fire to them and posted them through our letter box.

'Then tell me.'

'No.'

She gazed at me as if she were trying to work out a difficult crossword puzzle. 'Does Frank know all the details?'

'Not all of it, no.'

'So.' She inhaled, sighed heavily. 'Only you and Tommo know the score.'

I shrugged. 'Only I know. Tommo . . . he doesn't think about what he does, seems not to remember everything. Blind rage, it's probably called. Anger that's both short-sighted and amnesic.' I had said enough, rose to leave, settled Edward in my arms.

'He's dangerous?'

'Well, of course.'

She followed me, placed a flat palm on my back. 'Anyway, I wish you would get it all off your chest. The police should know, the medical people—'

'What for?' I turned on my heel, faced her squarely. 'The girl knows, remember? The girl he assaulted? She got hurt by him, she recognizes how disturbed he is. I can't stand up against him, not alone. He's charming, funny, attractive – he'd make me the laughing stock of Bolton.'

Her head shook slowly. 'Not with the other case. People won't have forgotten that he was charged with rape – they all seem to believe the theory about smoke and fire. There are two of you who have suffered through that man, even if the other one has fled. The police keep records, you know. We could have a quiet talk with a detective, make sure that the force is watching out for him.'

It was as if I had to go through it all again, because I had pondered such matters for a long time. 'No use. If Tommo gets wind of anything, he'll blow again, just go up like a time bomb. And the law won't be interested in a tale that's almost three years old. After all, I ran off with his brother, had another baby. No. I just can't talk about it.'

She walked to the window and stood still, tall and willowy, so sure of herself. But the shoulders drooped slightly after a moment or two. 'I'm sorry, Laura. Just then, for a couple of seconds, I tried to put myself in your shoes. You're right. Tommo will have to offend again.' She swung round, stared at me with eyes that were big and sad. 'I just hope you're not the next item on his agenda. Funny, it's taken me all this time to realize what you were up against—'

'But I've said nothing, explained nothing and—'

'No need. I can feel your story, Laura. It's standing right here in this room, but it's not between us any more.' She sniffed, walked towards me and took Gerald's hand. 'The other stuff – all that mithering about your own career – I'm sorry if it offends you, but I meant all that, you know. The boys are lovely and Frank's great, but you are so important. You've skills and talents and they must be used. Of the two of us, you were always the cleverer.'

I grinned. 'Then talent will out. Have you ever tasted my banoffee pie?'

'Banoffee . . . ee,' shouted Gerald happily.

'I've a talent with bananas and boiled condensed milk. So I'm not completely wasted, am I?'

'Banoffee!' yelled Gerald.

She hugged me and I felt like a little girl again. We were standing next to a wall on Chorley New Road and my mother was at home waiting for me, waiting to curse me for meeting my cousin. 'Thanks, Anne.'

'What for?'

I detached myself, collected Gerald's sticky hand, worried fleetingly about all the cream and white, all the dirty fingermarks. 'For being there after school finished.'

She laughed. 'I'll always be here, kid.'

I made banoffee pie that week, despite the fact that it was a troublesome recipe. The two men in my life loved this pudding, though Gerald was wont to spread it all around a bit. The recipe involved boiling unopened tins of condensed milk, a dangerous process that required constant vigilance throughout 2½ hours. But at least I had to be there, at least I could pretend that I wasn't skulking behind my own door like a scared rabbit.

Gerald and I baked the 'blind' case, sliced the bananas, waited for the alarm clock to sound. 'When it rings,' said Gerald, 'we can have the banoffee . . . ee.'

I fed Teddy, changed him, tried yet again to make the flat look decent. The explosive chair and the sagging sofa never looked good, no matter how hard I brushed and pummelled. Gerald hung over the clock, willed it to mark the moment when the toffee would be ready. When it finally sounded, he capered about and jumped from foot to foot until the toffee was cool enough to handle.

There were not too many accidents with the whipped cream, although much of the border had been 'Geralded'. We placed our accomplishment in the centre of the table, sat down and watched *Jackanory*.

'Is Daddy coming?' asked my son.

Sometimes, I felt like a terrible fraud. One day, this little lad would find out his true identity, but until that time arrived, I went along with the charade. 'Soon.'

'Banoffee . . . ee.' he sang. 'Toffee . . . ee, banoffee . . . ee.'

I looked at the clock. Frank had said that he would be early, because he was bringing some yellow fish from the market. It was to be an altogether yellow meal, what with the haddock and the banana pie.

The doorbell rang. 'I can go,' announced Gerald.

'No. Stay here with Teddy. Watch the television and make sure that you don't dip your fingers in anything. Especially anything in a round dish in the middle of the table.'

At the bottom of the stairs, I paused, remembered that I hadn't looked through the window. 'Hello?' I called cautiously.

'Mrs Thompson?' It was a man's voice, one I didn't recognize.

'Yes?'

'Police.'

A lot of things can go through your mind in just a tiny fraction of time. My mother was dead, Anne was hurt, Uncle Freddie had keeled over, Frank had been in a car accident. I opened the door.

'May we come in?' There were two of them, and one was female.

I froze. The man had removed his helmet, and I knew

that the police became extra-polite when delivering bad news. 'Tell me,' I said at last. 'My little boy . . . he's only two, but he . . . he understands things. Tell me here, downstairs. What's happened?'

The woman touched my arm. She had a hooked nose that made her fierce, and soft brown eyes that made her gentle. 'I'm afraid it's your husband, Mrs Thompson.'

I swallowed. 'Tommo? What . . . which one?' I had two husbands and one of them was hurt or dead. I had two husbands and this policewoman's face was swimming about in water and it wasn't even raining. 'Tell me!'

They stepped into the narrow hallway, and we were all squashed together like people in a lift. 'He's dead,' said the man. He had a mole on the end of his nose. It had three bristly hairs growing out of its centre.

'Who is dead?' I heard myself ask.

'Your husband,' said the female. 'Come on, let's go up and look at your little boy.' She sounded as if she were talking to a child. And her face was still misty round the edges.

'Which husband?'

They glanced at one another. 'Have you more than one husband, Mrs Thompson?'

I nodded. 'Sort of. One's a good man and the other's not. If the bad one's dead, then everything's all right. But if it's Frank, then I don't know . . . I can't be here without Frank. He knows that, so it's not to be him. Do you hear me? It can't be Frank.'

Between them, they led me up the stairs. When we reached the flat, the policeman took Gerald into the bedroom and closed the door. There was a dreadful finality in the click of that catch, as if my life had suddenly ended.

'How?' I asked.

She placed me at the kitchen table, then busied herself with the kettle. 'It's suspicious,' she said. 'We're treating it as a suspicous death.'

'Then it must be Frank,' I announced clearly. 'And the

killer will be Tommo.' The room had gone red, and there was no light at the windows. Everything moved, floated about, lost its proper place in time and space. Day was night, the cooker drifted in the twilight, threatened to touch the ceiling, except that the ceiling and the floor seemed to be changing places. I fell gratefully into the arms of this new darkness, gave myself up willingly.

When I woke, I was in a pale green room with painted walls and glass in the door. Someone sat next to me, a woman who was leafing through a magazine. On her head there was a white cap, very stiff and fastened with a sort of paperclip at the back. She was a nurse. Where were my children? What was I doing lying here like the Queen of Sheba when Gerald was longing for his banoffee pie?

'Hello.' She had dark hair and pale skin, was probably Irish, though the 'hello' had sounded Bolton-ish. 'You've had a sedative. You were thrashing about a bit, so we had to quieten you. The doctor's had a look at you while you were asleep, and he thinks you've a touch of anaemia.'

Something menacing lurked on the border of memory. 'Where's Frank?'

'Er . . .' She glanced at her upside-down watch. 'I'll just fetch the lady constable. I'm sure she'll be able to tell you more than I can.'

The door opened to reveal my cousin Anne. She was dressed in denim jeans and an old sweater, both articles covered in spots of paint. Yes, Anne had said that she was going to paint her bedroom. Why was she here in the middle of painting? Why? 'Laura,' she said softly.

'Where are the boys?'

'In Barr Bridge with my mother and dad.' She walked right up to the bed and clasped my hand. 'Poor Frank,' she whispered. 'And my poor Laura.'

Chapter Seven

By 1965, Gerald was four and Edward was two. After Frank's death, we had moved to a small terraced house in Maybank Street, Bolton. This purchase had taken up all my savings, plus £200 Anne had 'lent' me. Her chances of retrieving the investment were poor, though she eventually found me some work.

Every day, I baked. The cooker was a temperamental piece of electrical stupidity, a bulky thing with two rings at the back and a square hotplate at the front. This rectangle was really the lid of the grill, so it worked only when the grill decided to be co-operative.

The oven was OK once I had learned where to place things. It had cold spots, hot spots and a tendency to vary in temperature from cool to hellfire hot. But I tamed it sufficiently, managed to bake my pies, cakes and scones. These were collected by a Mr Tattersall, who sold them in his shop at Tonge Moor. The children and I ate a lot of failed cakes, and the rest of my income went into maintaining our cramped home.

Those two years had been strange, because they seemed to have changed me completely. Gone was the girl who had feared marked photographs and knocks at the door. My anger was so intense, so constant, that it burned out all the terror.

In the kitchen, I kept the cuttings from local and national papers. They were in a tin box at the bottom of a drawer, stashed away from the clutches of my older child, as his reading age was well in advance of his chronological status. Alongside them and in the same tin were the cheques from Mother. She never visited us and I never cashed her conscience payments, didn't use a penny of the money.

Sometimes, when the children were asleep, I would spread the 'mystery' across the floor, placing the cuttings in order on the scarlet rug that fronted a two-bar electric fire. 'LOCAL MAN FOUND IN RIVER' said the first. Oh I remembered that day. Anne standing beside my hospital bed, her clothes shabby and paint-spattered. Two weeks I spent in there. They were talking about sending me to the psychiatric ward, but I thought of the boys and pulled out of my nosedive. Anne dragged me from the bed, forced me to dress, took me home, took time off work, fed me, dressed me.

'WAS FRANK THOMPSON MURDERED?' was another piece of journalism from the *Bolton Evening News*. Yes, he was murdered. And no, they never punished him. Him. I knew him well. Frank's car had been parked next to the river, keys still in the ignition. A parcel of haddock was on the passenger seat, so he had bought our fish and was on his way home. This was all very understandable, all very plausible. Except for one tiny detail. He had been driving in the wrong direction.

I kept diaries now, noted down the dates and times when I had seen Tommo, when I'd thought I had seen him. The house was in the middle of the terrace, and was far from soundproof. The man on one side snored and kept me awake, while the woman at the opposite side had a consumptive-sounding cough that rattled every bedspring in the street. I was safe.

On a Saturday evening towards the end of June, Anne visited me. She brought two chops, some potatoes and a cabbage. Anne was the sort of person from whom I could accept charity. She got a bit high-horseish at times, but we had shared so much throughout our lives that I felt no shame in her presence. Had our positions been reversed, then she would have accepted help from me.

She threw herself into that old sagging sofa, wiped the sweat from her brow. 'I've had to have the bloody thing towed away,' she announced. Her relationship with her car was on a par with mine with the cooker. 'Clutch went halfway up Derby Street. I've had it decoked, tuned, serviced three hundred times, but it still fizzles out on me. In fact, the mechanic suggested that the only cure was to jack up the number plate and slide a different car behind it.' She looked at the cuttings on the rug. 'Why?' she asked.

'I don't know.'

She picked up a photograph of Frank. 'This won't bring him back, love.'

There were times when I just had to look at his face, when I had to read about that terrible day. He was slipping away from me, leaving me more alone with every passing moment. I needed him. If I couldn't have him alive, then I would carry on searching my memory and using the printed word to help me feel close to him. 'I just have to do it, that's all.'

Anne's face was a picture of misery. 'Irene and Enid Corcoran,' she muttered. 'What a wonderful alibi.'

I stared into the distant past, remembered those little clones with the matching nit-caps. 'They'd do anything for him when they were children. I suppose they're afraid of him now. Playing card games? Whenever did he sit down and play whist?'

'Well, they stuck to their story all right.'

I picked up a piece from the *News of the World*, 'MAN CLEARED OF MURDERING HIS BROTHER', and waved it under Anne's nose. 'Not guilty of murder, just as he was innocent that other time, when the girl was raped. There's absolutely nothing we can do.'

'Don't cry,' she said.

'I'm not crying.'

'Ah, so your eyes are just leaking, I take it?'

I rubbed my eyelids, mumbled that I probably needed a new washer fitted to my dripping tear duct. 'One of the most awful things was when I got into trouble for harassment. Imagine those two girls taking out an injunction just because I'd asked a few questions.' I chose not to dwell on the real facts, which were that I'd followed them mercilessly, had beaten their doors to sawdust at midnight, had written repeatedly to the twins.

Anne stretched out her legs. 'At least you can talk about it at last. I'm sure that's a healthy sign. Have you heard from Frank's father at all?'

'No.' Poor Colin Thompson had disappeared after Frank's funeral. Before leaving the town, he had visited me. 'I can't stay,' he said that night. 'There's nothing here for me now. I know I've got the two grandchildren, but Frank was . . . important to me. All we can hope is that our Bernard gets his come-uppance in time.'

'Shame,' said Anne. 'He was a good bloke.'

We put away my press cuttings, switched on the television, sat through a tedious comedy and a police series. 'Are you staying?' I asked her at about ten o'clock.

'Well, I'm not walking to town and I don't fancy waiting for the bus. Lend me a nightie and a toothbrush.'

I watched Anne as she prepared for bed. She was a true citizen of the world, never turned a hair when it came to outside lavatories and no bath or shower. She often kept me company at the weekends, and we always slept together in the double bed. On this occasion, we threw off most of the covers, as the night was hot.

Perhaps the heat affected me, or perhaps I was just overwrought, but the dreams that night were terrible. I was in a different bed, a high one with a metal frame and a white quilt. Someone held me down, prevented me from running outside. Through the window, I saw a coffin being carried by some men in black. One of the men turned and looked at me, smiled, made me shiver. The hatred bubbled up, made me fight the nurses, but I could not rise from that hard, plastic-covered mattress, could not run after the funeral and tell the mourners that my Frank was being carried to the grave by his murderer. The murderer was the one with the strawberry blond hair and the curled upper lip. As in reality, I never got to the funeral.

The scene changed. There was a nun behind a counter, a pretty nun with an Irish accent. That was all right, because I had no qualms about meeting Confetti. But she changed, her features melting then setting until they were hard, masculine, were the property of a worldly wise police sergeant. 'Mrs Thompson, there is no proof. And you never reported him when he broke your leg, did you? Or on any of the other occasions when he supposedly assaulted you?'

'No. I've been scared. But he hurt that girl, the one who ran away. It's not just me! He's killed his brother now.'

'Well, I'm sorry, but there's no evidence.'

'Then I'll tackle him myself. When you find my body, you'll know who killed me, who killed Frank, who's going to kill my . . . Teddy! If I'm not here, who'll look after the babies? Auntie Maisie's old and my mother hates children.'

He was dissolving, becoming someone else. 'You're getting exactly what you deserve, Laura McNally.' My mother wore a police uniform and an air of sheer delight. 'I told him where you were. I told him so that he would kill Frank and leave you on your own. That's all my doing, all my own work.'

'I hate you,' I said.

'Really?' She was laughing. Smoke poured out of her mouth in a stream that promised to be endless. 'You'll be next. You and your children will be next.' She reached over the counter and pushed me to the floor. I was small, wore white ankle socks and strappy brown sandals. And she hit me, beat me on the skull with her fist, crashed my head into the wall. I wondered why I had not lifted up my arms, but I realized that they were fastened down, pinned to the bed by two women in blue. 'She's crazy,' said one.

'Laura?' It was Frank. 'It's all been a mistake. I'm not dead after all.'

397

'Frank, stay this time.' I'm dreaming, I told myself. I'll wake up in a minute and Frank will be gone.

'He kidnapped me,' said Frank. 'Bernard forced me to drive to the river. I told him about the fish from the market, but he didn't care. And then he hit me on the head. That's why the doctor said I hadn't drowned.' He turned, showed me the hole in his temple. Like Doubting Thomas, I reached out to touch the wound, and my lover disappeared. 'Frank! Come back! You're not dead, so come back. We can move back into the flat and you can work for Mr Saunders again.'

The only answer was a maniacal laugh. 'I won't hit you. Come here, you're quite safe. I promise to be good.'

'Go away, Tommo. You are sick in the head.'

The room was filled by grey people. This is a dream, I said firmly. Dreams are sometimes in black and white. Anne was there, but not in her official capacity. Papers were turning over and over on a desk, as if they were being worked by some mechanical contraption. The verdict came up on a screen, UNLAWFUL KILLING. This was followed by advertisements for Camay soap and Birds Eye peas. Someone spoke about a blunt object, perhaps a hammer. It had been wielded by person or persons unknown.

'I know!' I shouted.

'She knows!' chorused the court.

I woke, sweat pouring down my face. They had questioned him, held him overnight, released him. And he had talked to the press, had told them of his grief at the loss of a dear brother. No, he didn't mind the fact that his wife had run off and set up home with Frank, didn't mind at all about the second baby. He would take us back tomorrow, would rear both boys as his own.

'Laura?'

'What?'

'Is every night like this?'

'No.' I swallowed and my throat was like sandpaper. 'It's just now and then, after I've been thinking about it.'

'You were screaming for Frank.'

'Yes.'

She held my hand tightly. 'Shall I go and put the kettle on? A nice cup of tea and a bit of toast?'

'All right.'

I lay as still as a stone, concentrated on relaxing. But every time I ironed out the tension, it simply moved to a different part of my body. Anne was clattering the kettle and I found the sound comforting. I heard the hinges on the tea caddy, a cup rattling in its saucer. The luminous green hands on my clock announced a quarter to twelve. The dream had lasted for ever, yet I had been asleep for less than an hour.

The back door opened. Anne was no doubt visiting the lavatory. No. No, she wasn't. I sat up, pulled on my dressing gown, held on to the rail at the top of the steep stairs. There was a door at the bottom of the flight, and it led straight into the kitchen. I thought I could hear Anne breathing.

'Who's there?' she called. The back door squealed – it wanted oil – and I heard her bare feet slapping the flags. 'You bloody swine!' Her voice was loud, powerful, was the voice of someone whose word was law. 'How many times have you skulked round here? Did you think she was alone? Well, don't be fooled just because my car isn't outside. I often come without my car. In fact, I practically live here, so bugger off.'

'I've every right to visit my son.' It was Tommo.

'At midnight?' asked Anne. 'He's asleep, has been in bed for hours. Anyway, you'd better stay away from here. Laura won't take kindly to your visit, I can tell you that for nothing.'

'Really? Don't solicitors always charge for advice?'

'You thought she'd be by herself, didn't you? Get away – go on, leave her in peace.'

I was down those stairs before I had thought about moving. The yard brush was next to a mop bucket under the kitchen window. I grabbed it, flew to the gate, pushed

Anne to one side. He just stood there while I went for him, didn't even try to defend himself. By the time Anne reached me, there was blood on his face. The light from the kitchen streamed out into the darkness, settled on the mess around his nose. 'They can put you away for that,' he said softly. 'Crazy behaviour, this is. Ask your fancy lawyer cousin about assault, Laura.'

Rage pumped through my veins, fed adrenalin to my brain where it exploded and prepared to fuel my tongue. There was little or no fear, as it is difficult to be furious and afraid simultaneously. Anger as justifiable as mine left no space for timidity, allowed no quarter for caution. I wanted to kill him, needed to dance on his grave. Above all, I wanted to avenge Frank and keep my children safe.

'Cage bars been rattled, Laura?' he asked smoothly as the blood dripped from his nose.

'Anne knows everything,' I managed at last. 'I've told her and she's a lawyer and—'

'Laura,' said Anne. 'Come on, now.'

I was going nowhere, listening to no-one. 'Murder,' I gasped. 'You killed my Frank. You're not a man, you're something else, something that crawled from slime, cold-blooded, evil, nasty . . .'

'Stop this, Laura.' Anne took the brush away from me. 'This will get us nowhere.'

'He was a man. Your brother, the one you murdered. He was so different from you, so gentle and loving. Killer,' I shouted. 'Killer, killer, killer!'

He took a step towards us, wiping his face as he moved. 'Being gentle and kind didn't stop him taking my wife and my son, did it? He had no right to do that.'

'He didn't take me,' I screamed. 'I went. I went of my own free will, away from you and your rotten ways. No-one took me. I'd have gone to hell before going back to you.'

A few lights appeared in surrounding windows. 'Come on out, all of you,' I yelled. 'Come and look at this murdering swine. He killed his own brother.'

'Slander,' he said. The lip curled. I wanted to smash that lip, but Anne hung on to the yard brush, wouldn't let me take it. 'I didn't kill Frank,' he said.

'Oh, but you did.' My quieter tone obviously alarmed him. He could cope with the shouting, but a normal voice seemed to unnerve him. 'You did it. You sat in that car with a hammer, then you made him drive to the river. When he got out of the car, he couldn't run. You knew about his leg, didn't you? Oh yes, you plagued him all his life about that leg. When you caught Frank, you hit him on the head, bashed out his brain. You must have felt really proud about that, really powerful. I mean, it takes guts to kill, doesn't it? When he was dead, you threw him in the river. Then you ran home across the fields.'

He stared at me as if I'd just arrived from another planet. I had re-enacted the whole scenario, was as near to the truth as anyone could possibly be without having witnessed his actions. 'Clever, aren't you?' The words were not quite clear, and he stumbled slightly over the first syllable.

Anne squeezed my arm. 'Dear God,' she whispered. 'It's written all over his face.'

A sash window shot up, banged as it reached the top frame. 'Can't you lot take your bloody din in the house? I'm working tomorrow. We don't all get Sundays off, you know.'

'Sorry,' called Anne. She took a small step towards the creature who was still my husband. 'Had the divorce papers yet?'

He cleared his throat. 'I'm contesting it. She'll have to wait another two years if she wants rid of me.'

Anne shook her head pensively, as if considering a matter of great moment. 'No. I think you'll see sense, Tommo. After all, Laura won't ever live with you again. And there are witnesses here who will testify to tonight's little charade.'

'What about my nose?' he asked. 'It's probably broken.'

'What about Enid and Irene Corcoran?' Anne's voice

was smooth, like the silk caress of a venomous snake. 'They might be persuaded to change their minds about that little whist drive. I've a few pounds in the bank that could very well make them see things differently.'

His Adam's apple moved convulsively, seemed to travel up and down his neck three or four times. He swallowed audibly, wiped his bloody nose on the cuff of a sleeve. 'They'll not listen to you.'

'Won't they? Aren't they married now and both living in Crumpsall Street? I'd bet a year's wages that they'd be happy to go out and buy a bit of furniture or—'

'I'll tell the law you've bribed them.' He was breathing very quickly, and his voice rasped, as if having to fight its way out of a narrowed passage. 'The police would come down on you like a ton of bricks.'

Anne looked at me. 'Laura, would I bribe anybody?'

'No,' I said.

'See?' She reached out her hands and lifted her shoulders in a gesture that might have suited Shakespeare's Shylock – except that Shylock probably never had a yard brush attached to him. 'No-one will ever believe that I could break the law.' She placed the broom against the wall, folded her arms, put her head on one side. 'The Corcoran twins will gladly speak up now, I'm sure. They're no longer under your twisted spell. When I explain to them that their perjury will be treated lightly, that the court will accept that you had threatened them, I'm sure we'll have you convicted of murder before you can say knife. Or, as in this filthy case, before you can cough up the words "blunt instrument".'

He stood very still, like a rabbit caught in false light after sunset. The yellow glare from my kitchen illuminated his features, made the blood on his upper lip black and menacing. 'I want my kid,' he muttered through clenched teeth. 'Gerald is my son.'

'I'll have to tell him that one day,' I replied. 'And I only hope that he will be strong enough to take the good news, because I'm sure you'll be in prison before long.' I lifted a hand, pointed at him. 'There'll be an injunction served this week. My neighbours will back me up. So get yourself out of my street.'

'You'll get no bloody divorce, though.'

'Watch me,' I said. 'And watch the Corcoran girls.'

I took Anne's arm and we walked into the house. When the door was closed, I sagged against it, allowed myself to slide down to the floor. 'My legs have gone on strike,' I said. 'And thank God for that car of yours, Anne. If it hadn't broken down, you would have been long gone by this time.'

She opened the stairway door, ran her eyes over the wall at the bottom of the flight. 'It shouldn't cost much,' she remarked thoughtfully. 'And I've a couple of grateful clients in the building trade.'

'What?'

'Well, we'll have a door here, at the bottom of the stairs, then the lavatory can be moved into that lean-to. You can use the old lavatory building as a storage shed.'

'You're too good to me, Anne.' My eyes were wet again.

'It's not a question of money,' she said. 'Safety first. That man's as crazy as a monkey behind bars, and it's bars he needs.' She sat on the last stair, reached out and held my hand. 'And to think that I used to shout at you for exaggerating. I never liked him, you know.'

'I remember.'

'Yet I thought you were being a bit dramatic at first. But just now, out there, I was standing within three feet of a psychopath. He's obsessed with you. Dear God, I'm shivering like a half-set jelly.' She struggled to her feet, picked up the kettle and warmed the pot with boiling water. 'I'm going to get him.' Her jaw was set. 'Even if I can't do it legally, I'll make sure he's finished.' She brewed the tea, swished it about to thicken the mixture. 'It would only cost about twenty-five quid to get him knee-capped. And I do work in the best circles, you know.' She handed me a biscuit. 'Eat, you need the sugar.

403

He should try living life like Frank did, with a limp and a smile.'

'No,' I pleaded. 'Don't descend to his level, please don't go breaking his legs.'

'You know I won't, Laura. But imagining him in pain is so delicious and it's no crime. However, it would do no harm to have him followed now and then. I don't like this, don't want to think about what might have happened if I hadn't been here.'

I accepted the tea, swallowed several scalding sips. 'Don't worry. These walls are thin and I've a good set of lungs. And we can try for an injunction on Monday.'

'Hmm.' She folded herself into a dining chair, placed her cup on the shabby formica table. 'Pieces of paper won't mean anything to him, you know.'

I did know, how well I knew.

'He'll still be hanging about like a bad smell.'

I got up off the floor, dusted down my dressing gown, sat opposite my cousin. 'This time, it's you worrying and me being complacent. Frank's death sort of numbed me, but I'm so ill-tempered underneath. I can't manage to fear him any more. It's as if he's done his worst.'

She dipped a bourbon into her tea, looked nothing like an up-and-coming young solicitor. 'Don't believe it, kid. Don't ever believe that.'

The youngish woman stood outside my front door, a battered suitcase resting next to her feet. She wore a navy coat which hung open over a black skirt and a white blouse, yet even though the clothes were of good quality, she managed to look untidy. A bell rang faintly in the chambers of my memory, but I could not name this person. Her hair was short, brown and wavy, and the slender feet were encased in heavy brogues. 'Help', she said.

'I beg your pardon?' It was one of those moments in life when you look at someone or something, when you know that you've seen him or it before, and you can't place the pieces of the jigsaw in a sensible sequence. It was a bit like *déjà vu,* only less weird. I dried my hands on the tea towel, pushed Gerald back into the house. I tried again. 'I'm sorry, but . . .'

'But what?'

'Well, you asked for help. How can I help you?'

'A cup of tea would go down great, Laura McNally.'

'Holy cow.' The words were out of my mouth before I could check them.

'I'm neither holy nor a cow, miss. Now let me in and give some shelter to a failed nun before she keels over on your doorstep due to lack of sustenance and low blood sugar.' She never paused for breath, didn't smile. 'My life's a mess,' she added. 'And I'm out on the streets with no future and a bagful of clothes from the last century.'

'Confetti?' I leaned against the door jamb, needed its support. 'Did they finally throw you out, then?'

She frowned. 'The sisters do not throw anyone out. I walked. I did not need to be ejected. And my name is Goretti Hourigan. However, you may call me Confetti. Throughout my childhood, I was called Hooligan, but we shall draw a veil over that.'

'But not a nun's veil?' I stepped aside, allowed her into the house. She picked up Gerald, sat him on the sofa, handed him some jumbo crayons. 'Little boy, I stole these from school. Use them in good health.' She turned to me. 'Where's the other one?'

'Upstairs. He's still young enough to need an afternoon nap. I'll put the kettle on.'

While I made the tea, I listened as she educated my son. Within five minutes, he was reciting his two-times tables and had started to make inroads on the threes. 'He's bright,' she shouted. 'Like you used to be.'

I ignored the barb, picked up a tray, carried the tea into our tiny living room. 'I made the cakes myself,' I said. 'Because I am still bright enough to follow a recipe.'

'May all the saints be praised.' She crammed half a buttered scone into her mouth, passed the remainder of it to Gerald. 'Life is about sharing,' she said. 'And I shall share with you my store of learning.'

I sat down, picked up the teapot, poured.

'Milk and no sugar.' She winked at Gerald. 'I shall have to watch my figure if I'm to find a husband.'

Sitting next to an ex-nun is not a comfortable experience. When she was a nun, I understood her, knew what she was, how she thought, how she expected me to think. But here she was, doing her best to be outrageous, pushing her way into a life that was already hard to manage. Did she intend to stay? Would I have to share my bed with a woman who used to teach me, who used to pray and go to mass when she wasn't actually working?

'I'll be taking advantage of your hospitality while I think,' she announced.

My heart sank. I loved the bones of the woman, but the woman whose bones I loved was a nun, not a . . . a woman who stole crayons and looked for a husband.

'Till my dowry comes through,' she said.

It has been my experience that most disturbing remarks are made when someone within earshot has a mouthful of liquid. When I had finished coughing, I echoed the word. 'Dowry? Is your family paying some man to marry you?'

She eyed me disdainfully. 'Well, of course they are. You don't think any fellow worth his salt would take me just for myself, surely? My dowry is to be four Arab-Irish racehorses and a smallish herd of cattle. The livestock should arrive at the docks in Liverpool at any moment. In fact, as we speak, there could well be a lorry full of beef and very superior horseflesh on its way down the East Lancashire Road.'

I decided that silence would be the best tack.

'Have you a small field?' she asked.

'No, just a back yard.'

'A tape measure?'

I pointed to my sewing basket. 'You can stop this fooling around, Confetti.'

She swung to face me, her eyes bright. 'What? I'm here

just now trying to place my animals. Would you kindly tell me how many cows can stay in your yard?'

'None.'

The tape measure fell to the floor. 'Never mind, we'll just have to keep them in the street.'

'Can I have a cow?' Gerald, who usually found adults to be boring, was fascinated by the new arrival. 'I like cows.'

'Ah, I'm only kidding. But we'll take a ride out on the bus and find some cows, eh?' She glanced at me. 'The dowry comes from the convent. It's the money I brought in with me.'

'I know.'

'Then why didn't you say so, you obdurate girl? Isn't obdurate a lovely word?'

'It was a favourite of Tommy-gun's,' I answered. 'How is she?'

'Crippled with pain and refusing to die. How many bedrooms here?'

'Two.' She was going to take over. She was going to walk into my existence, into my home, and treat it like her classroom. 'Aren't you going home?'

She shrugged the thin shoulders, ran a hand through Gerald's hair. 'They'll not have me. My brother was almost a priest till he upped and married a girl called Siobhan O'Casey with a marvellous figure except for the bulge. The bulge became twins who had been conceived during one of Eugene's breaks from the seminary.'

'Ceme-tery,' said Gerald.

'Exactly. Anyway, my mother's head was bowed in disgrace throughout the whole of Lent and right past Eastertide. No-one in our village ever mentions 1959. They say, "Well now, and didn't the donkey die the year when Eugene Hourigan had to marry Siobhan O'Casey with the great belly on her?' My mother can't take such shocks. She has a delicate disposition and a temper that's mortal cruel. So I'll be staying in England.'

'Oh.'

Confetti arranged the skirt about her knees, obviously missed the long folds of her habit. 'Don't you want me to stay? I'll be company for you and I'm to be teaching soon at one of the local schools. I'll go if I'm not wanted.'

'Oh, don't be silly. I just wasn't expecting it and—'

'You were expecting it, Laura McNally. Haven't I been writing to you since the crack of creation, telling you about my unacceptable beliefs? They may well stop me teaching in a Catholic school, just because I agree with birth control. I've been on my way out since you were knee-high to an inkwell.'

She was so . . . enthusiastic. She bubbled with energy, brimmed over with excitement. And she had chosen me to be the witness to her own rebirth. I wished with every fibre of my being that I could feel flattered by her faith in me. 'You'll have to share my bed.'

'That's fine by me unless you snore. Do you snore?'

I sighed heavily. 'I don't know. I'm usually asleep when I'm asleep, so I've no way of telling.'

'Did Frank complain ever?'

'No.'

'Right. That's the interview over and you've got the job. I'll pay you seven pounds a week and I'll share the bills.'

So that was it. The good woman had come here as if demanding bed and board, was hiding her concern for me under a blanket of noise and fuss. 'It's not much of a house, a bit cramped,' I ventured.

She clicked her tongue. 'I'm used to a room with no space for a flea. We'll be as snug as bugs here.'

'Bug,' said Gerald. 'Bugger. Bugger, bugger, bugger.'

'Exactly,' agreed Confetti. 'Now there's paper in my case, so I'll get some for you and you can draw me some cows and some bugs. Then your mammy and I will cook some food and we'll have bedtime stories if you're good.'

He ran his eyes over her. 'I'm four,' he said disdainfully. 'So I'm always good. But Teddy is a pest. His real name's Edward, but we call him Teddy.'

'Is that so? What kind of a pest is this brother of yours?'

'A bloody pest.'

She nodded. 'Ah, that sort. Ah well, we'll see if I can sort him out for you.'

It was as if she had always been there. Gerald took to her immediately, made me feel redundant. Even Edward fell under her spell, stopped moaning about Gerald pinching his toys, pinching his arms, ruining his tiny life. In a sense, I was rather jealous of Confetti, because she displayed all the hallmarks of a natural mother, whereas I had needed to train myself through books and by many bouts of trial and error, had learned mostly through my thousand mistakes.

When the boys were in bed, we sat together in front of the dreadful electric fire. The evening was warm, so we used no heat, but the fake coal glowed and flickered as a wheel of metal spun over a light bulb in the base of the fire.

'Marvellous,' she declared. 'The things they've invented. We always burned peat over to home. And here you sit with a nice clean electric heater, no grate to scrub.'

'I hate it.' My tone was petulant.

'Don't hate anything or anyone, Laura.'

'That's difficult.'

She nodded. 'I know. There's your mammy and that pig of a husband. Is your divorce done? Are you free from him?'

'Not yet. Anyway, you're not supposed to believe in divorce.'

'I'm a sinner, sure enough. I've even gone so far as to put down my name as a voluntary worker with the FPA. Family planning, that is. Of course, I'll not be involved in the mechanical side of the process, but I can answer the phone and book people in for appointments.'

I stared at her. 'Why? It's one thing believing in birth control, but to go out and actually encourage it – what would the Pope say?'

She giggled. 'Five Aves and a Pater Noster, I shouldn't wonder.' The smile wiped itself off her face. 'No, this is a deep thing with me, Laura. It's about women's freedom. You see, that Pankhurst woman and all those others, they believed in us having our franchise, which was all very well and necessary in the broader scheme of things. They began the fight, but we mustn't put down our weapons yet. We're still victims, you see. Like the men are in charge all the while, and those of us who had not the benefit of being born male are just here for those who were. A woman's life can be very small, my dear.'

'I know.' My life was the size of this house, stretched no further than the Co-op on Derby Street. 'But how can you make a woman's life more fulfilling?'

'By giving her some control. By allowing her to choose motherhood or to reject it, by letting her decide when to allow her body to be hired out as an incubator. We should all be citizens with rights, equal rights and equal duties. For example, if you were to take the bread knife and stab your husband, what would you get? A life sentence?'

'Probably.'

'Yet he can interfere with you whenever he likes. He'll come in from the pub with a bag of chips and a great drunken smile and he'll expect his rights there and then. Well, once he's eaten his chips. Can you prosecute him for his deafness when you say no? You are still his property, Laura. Until the day comes when you can sue your partner for rape – and you of all people should know about that – then we have no dignity at all.'

So I was living now with a missionary. The fire in her eyes burned far brighter than the 60 watt lamp in my two-bar heater. I could not understand how the convent had managed to contain her for so many years. Within the order, Confetti must have stuck out like a boil on the face of a saint. So she had let herself out, because a vocation as strong as hers needed freedom, not confinement. This woman must have suffered beyond measure, as she was a strong believer in God. Her arguments with Rome were fundamentally unacceptable. And I knew that she was terrified by what she was doing.

'You'll be all right,' I said.

She stared into the poor imitation of fire, sighed from the depths of her soul. 'I hope so, Laura. Oh, I hope so.'

Chapter Eight

We had a wonderful Christmas in 1965. Confetti organized me, pushed me into inviting Ida and Ernie Bowen who had lived next door to me during my time with Tommo. She also persuaded me to write to Hetty Hawkesworth, my good friend from the country. I received a note from her, read with delight her slanted hand. Hetty had won a national bingo prize, was going off on a cruise without 'him'. It seemed that 'he' had been stepping out of line, but she intended to leave him a few bob before she sailed into the sunset, just enough for the odd pint and a fish supper on Fridays.

'They're all at it,' beamed my house-guest. 'Soon, we shall be recognized as true human beings.'

Confetti was completely unrecognizable, though she still looked just about human. She had taken to wearing the strangest clothes, great full-skirted dresses in Indian cotton, headbands, beads, shawls with fringes. On her feet, she usually sported clogs with leather uppers and wooden soles, and she clanked as she moved, because both wrists were a tangled mass of slender metal bangles. During these colder months, she was making few concessions to the weather, with the exception of one or two eccentric purchases. It was with great pride that she showed off her sheepskin coat, 15 shillings from a second-hand shop, and her fluffy boots, £1 from the same establishment. Her dowry had come through from the convent, but she had plans for it.

When our Christmas meal had been consumed and our guests had wobbled off beneath the weight of laden bellies, she tackled me again. 'This coming week, you will visit your mother.'

For answer, I blew into what Gerald called a 'ter-ter', a whistle attached to a tube of paper with a feather stuck on the end. My breath expanded and unrolled the tube, sounded the whistle, caused the feather to collide with Confetti's earnest face. 'Get lost,' I said politely.

'Isn't that just great?' she asked.

'Don't be rhetorical, Goretti,' I warned. 'Or I shall become hysterical. You go and see my mother. Then, when you've seen the dragon, go and visit your own parents.'

'They'll not let me in.'

'Quite. And my mother won't put out the red carpet for me.'

She dragged some multi-coloured streamers from her hair, handed them to the children. 'She sent you a card and a cheque. There's about five hundred pounds worth of cheques in that drawer. At least she remembers you.'

I nodded. 'Oh, she remembers me all right. In the same way as we all remember the war and toothache and smallpox. Anyway, stay out of my tin and mind your own business.'

I went, of course. Goretti Hourigan was, still is, a great manipulator. She works on the theory that a drip of water, however small, can wear away stone in time. She dripped. Into every conversation, she dragged the importance of family, the sadness of growing older without seeing one's children, the futility of a life without love. The anecdotes came thick and fast as the days went by. 'And of course when she got there, her mother had passed on and the wake was starting. Her mammy was all decked out in the coffin and Padraig Mulvanny was playing a sad song on his melodeon. The fiddler from the next town was so upset that he couldn't tune up for weeping. His sadness came from the fact that the wilful daughter had neglected her mammy for so long.'

'Shut up, I'm going.'

413

'She went into a decline after that, hadn't the strength to hold the rosary. Aye, she was a broken woman and all because she had left it all too late and—'

'I'm bloody going!'

I scarcely recognized McNally's. There were new buildings, low sheds prefabricated in concrete, embellished with dark wood and large windows. In the centre of all this magnificence a garden had appeared, a sweep of lawn with a fountain at its centre. A cherub in greyish marble balanced on a plinth, one foot stretched out as if ready to walk away. He carried a pitcher, and it was from this that the water poured. The base of the fountain had been inscribed, IN LOVING MEMORY OF JOHN McNALLY, FOUNDER OF THIS COMPANY. How thughtful of Mother. How difficult it must have been for her to find those few kind words for a man who had irritated her for so many years.

I was accosted at the door by a bulky man in a navy blue uniform. He tweaked the cuffs of a white shirt, made sure that they showed for an inch or so below the blazer sleeves. There were cufflinks too, spoked circles like a pair of wagon wheels. 'Can I help you?'

'No.' I often judge people fairly quickly by listening to their first words, am sometimes right, frequently wrong. That 'Can I help you?' had been patronizing, even scornful. I glanced down at my shoes, shabby after two years' wear, straightened my shoulders, looked him full in the face. 'I'm just visiting, having a walk around.'

He coughed, placed a huge hand to his mouth, curled the fingers in a gesture that was too delicate for someone of his size. 'I'm afraid that's not allowed, miss.'

'Madam.'

'Ah.' He turned round, gazed towards the nearest building. 'This is the office complex. Do you have an appointment to see somebody, an interview for work, perhaps?'

'No.'

'Then I'm afraid I shall have to ask you to leave.'

'Really?' I perched on a low wall at the side of the path

leading up to what was now the office complex. It used to be a cow-field, I thought. 'And I shall have to refuse to leave.'

'One moment, please.' He walked away, swinging his arms like a corporal who is about to face a fierce sergeant. I became bored with watching him, stood up, sauntered across to the old section, the barns that had been used by my father. There were padlocks on the doors, bars at the windows. A man swept the ground with a stiff broom, and I asked him about the old part of McNally's. These were the storage sheds now, he informed me. I stood and looked past the bars, remembered my father weeping at his bench. Mother had wiped him out completely, had built a new and clinically clean empire.

'Laura?'

I swung round. 'Mother.' She was a true fashion-plate, a two-dimensional figure from some up-market magazine. Her face was thickly but expertly made up, and the jewels on her fingers were not paste. The suit was perfectly cut, a business outfit with a feminine finish in the finely tailored lines.

'My dear, how are you?' The accent had been worked on, was just about halfway between Mayfair and Manchester Piccadilly. 'It's been ages.' She kissed the air at the side of my face, made little squeaking noises that were meant to illustrate her supposed joy. 'Come. We'll go inside and have some tea.'

So this was Mother's latest role. Confetti would have been delighted to meet such a wonderful woman, a female who could build a business with one hand and apply face cream with the other. But Mother was not sufficiently emancipated to allow herself to be seen with a shabby daughter. We entered the office building by a side door, cut through a corridor before reaching Mother's office. A plaque bore the legend, ELIZABETH McNALLY. CHIEF EXECUTIVE. I caught sight of a pale girl at a typewriter, glimpsed her worried face before Mother closed a second door. 'My personal assistant,' she said.

'An absolute treasure.' She pressed a button and a disembodied voice asked, 'Yes, Mrs McNally?'

'Tea for two, please.'

I slouched in the chair opposite Mother's, noticed the despair on her face as she assessed my poor deportment. 'So, I just came to see how you were,' I said. 'Since you never have the time to come and see how we are.'

'I'm no worse than usual.' She screwed a pink cigarette into a white holder, flicked a switch that turned on a window fan. 'Extractors,' she mouthed. 'I know you don't like tobacco smoke.'

'Your grandchildren are very well, thank you for asking.'

'Give me time.'

'And Gerald will start school soon. He already reads, writes and counts.'

'Good.' She flicked ash into a hideous ashtray of dark onyx. 'You obviously don't need money. I notice that my cheques have not been cashed.'

'Quite.' I had done my duty, had obeyed Confetti's instincts, was ready to leave at any moment. This was a farce, though Mother probably considered it to be a drama in which she played the chief role. As ever.

'And you sent back the car. You could have kept it, you know.'

I hadn't wanted it, hadn't wanted to look at the vehicle that Frank had driven to his death. Most of all, I hadn't wanted anything from this woman. 'I can't drive.'

'But you must learn.'

'Yes, I must.'

She tapped scarlet finger-nails on the huge desk. There was a lamp on its surface, one of those brass things that are often seen in American movies, a very important-looking item designed to shine its light only on the paperwork. Her eyes followed mine and she informed me, 'It's a reading lamp.'

'Yes.' We hadn't seen one another for years, and we were talking about lamps and old cars. 'Well, I'd better go.' I stood up, smoothed my coat.

416

'Can't you buy yourself something a little more sensible, Laura? A nice camel-hair coat or something in tweed?'

'No. I've children to feed.'

She opened a drawer, pulled out a tin, took a wad from it and threw it on her desk. 'Is cash preferable to cheques?'

It was plain that she didn't remember anything, that she had wiped the slate clean not only of my father, but also of me. Perhaps I was just a small and unsavoury problem that she recalled occasionally, like a troublesome molar or a bout of flu. 'You are just like Tommo,' I said. 'You do things, say things, forget things. It's all forgotten, isn't it? The cruelty, the neglect, the nastiness?'

She sighed, put her head on one side. 'You know, dear, most of that is in your own mind. I do worry so about you. Have you mentioned to your doctor that you have these strange dreams? Because that's all they are, just nasty dreams. I never hit you, seldom shouted at you, gave you a very happy childhood.' She rose, came round to my side of the desk and perched on its edge. 'I'm a wealthy woman, Laura. Because I've a head for business, I finished what your father never had sufficient courage for. Oh, he had moved into other towns, but his thinking was too . . . too small. I expanded properly, went into mass production. But although I keep going on the surface, I am not a well woman. I need someone to live with me.'

I walked to the door. 'Then get a man. Father's dead now, so it will be legal this time. You'd enough of them while he was alive, so why are you alone now?'

Her eyes narrowed. 'Because there's too much money at stake. I don't want any man to hitch his wagon to my star.'

Someone knocked at the door through which we had entered. The second door opened, and a ghostly face peeped through a small gap. 'Shall I get that, Mrs McNally?' Mother's personal assistant looked frightened to death and I empathized with her, remembered my own fears.

'No, Susan.' Susan disappeared. 'Come in.' This order was directed towards the corridor.

The burly guard stepped into the office, came to an abrupt halt when he saw me. 'Oh,' he said, his voice rather high-pitched. He cleared his throat, descended an octave or so. 'I thought . . . I saw this young woman in the grounds and—'

'No matter,' she snapped. 'Go back to your post.'

He marched out in double-quick time. I watched my mother as she took some pills from her bag, counted them into her hand before swallowing them with a sip of water. 'I really do need you to come home.'

'No.'

The tea arrived, but I did not stay. As the nylon-aproned woman placed the tray on a side table, I left the office and fled down the passage. I shouldn't have come, would never come again. The woman who had birthed me had no concept of proper human behaviour. It was plain that she thought I'd come for cash, probably hush money. The sign on her face needed no neon lighting, no help to send its message. *'I don't know this shabby young woman,'* it had read, *'But if she cleans up her act and comes to live with me as a servant, then she will be my daughter.'*

I did not run far, just as far as the farmhouse. I stood on the front lawn, a stretch of perfect emerald grass where no weed would dare to show its face. The sheet of green was striped like a football pitch, had been carefully tended by another of her lackeys. Around its edges there were shrubs, dwarf conifers, rose-bushes that had been cut back for the winter.

But it was the house that held my attention. Gone were those lovely sash windows, gone were the cornerstones that had framed the delightfully flawed panes of glass. Mother had opted in a big way for light, had torn the once-proud house to shreds. Picture windows, six of them. They sat in the warm stone walls, huge blind eyes with lids that hung tired and expressionless, wood-framed transoms extended on metal catches to let in a little air, to let out a lot of smoke. She had murderded Ravenscroft, had done a face-lift in reverse, and the old house had not survived the anaesthetic.

Houses matter to me. That isn't to say that I'm particular about where I live, but I think places have souls. There's often one house in a terraced row, just a single dwelling where the architect's original plan still shows. A good solid door with the panels intact, no sheet of hardboard covering the pattern. Window frames cared for, painted with love and a good brand of gloss. Intact, treasured, respected. This farmhouse had been extended, had lost its character. The main part of the building had been altered to tone in with the new, so the guts had been torn out and discarded like offal in an abattoir.

I walked down the hill towards Auntie Maisie's shop, my insides twisting with an anger that went beyond mere rage. My mother had snuffed out my father's life, had tried to diminish mine, was continuing to leave a trail of rubble in her wake. That poor house, that lovely, ruined place. And all those crippled, active people thrown out of work, probably because they didn't fit in with the colour scheme.

'You look a bit fetched-up,' said my aunt after her usual fussy greeting. 'A bit on the upset side. Have you been up yonder?'

I nodded.

'She's doing well, isn't she? They're saying she'll be a millionaire come 1970. See, sit yourself down and I'll make us a bite. Freddie?'

He appeared at the back window, his face wreathed in smiles as soon as he saw me. Once inside, he took off his thick gloves and warmed his hands on my face. 'I've been tending my vegetables,' he said.

'Aye, well you can tend the shop for a bit, Freddie. I want to make Laura a cuppa.'

We settled at the big square table in the room behind the shop. They had given up the house next door, were letting it to a newly married couple. 'We can manage this road while there's only two of us. Right.' She stirred the tea, banged the brown lid home, poured the liquid into a pair of china mugs. 'What's up with you? Did she come out of the wrong side of the bed again?'

'There's only one side to Mother, Auntie Maisie. You should know that after all these years.'

'Aye, happen I should. Has she offered you no help?'

'Just money.'

She poured the milk, took a tea towel off a plate of newly baked cakes. 'Would you sooner have a butty, love?'

I shook my head, sipped the tea. 'I couldn't eat a thing.'

'You should take the money. Your dad would have wanted you to be comfortable.' She paused, waited for an answer, gave up after a few seconds. 'I hear that nun's finished up at your house. What's it like living with her?'

'Crazy.' I forced a smile, didn't want my aunt worried. 'She's gone all eccentric, looks like something from a desert island, flowery prints and wooden necklaces. To top the lot, she's very big at the family planning clinic in town. She's a feather in their caps, because she left the convent when the church found out about her faith in birth control. And she's a noisy beggar. I think I'm getting the benefit of her being cooped up in a convent for so many years. She lets off steam and I get scalded.'

The warm-hearted woman reached out a work-reddened hand and placed it on top of mine. 'Never think you've got nobody, lass. There's me and our Anne and your Uncle Freddie. Then there's your kiddies and Sister Wotsername-as-was and Miss Armitage – that old teacher of yours – she's asking after you. Bit of a scandal there, something to do with a man, but I speak as I find, and she's a good soul. Plenty of us care for you, Laura.'

'Thank you.'

She patted my arm, picked up a cake, took a healthy bite and chattered on in spite of her full mouth. 'She'll be the loser at the finish, will our Liza. She's turned that many folk away from her, she'll be lonely at the end.'

I travelled home on the bus, a box of toffees and tinned

food on my lap. Auntie Maisie was right. I was a rich woman, because so many folk cared about me, needed me. Most of all, I was wealthy after being loved by Frank. The love of a good man is beyond price. I smiled to myself, sucked a Nuttall's Minto, looked forward to going home.

'So I've to go home immediately if not sooner.'

I could not take my eyes off her. She was wearing a dirndl-type skirt that looked as if it might have started life as kitchen curtains, three rows of striped glass beads, some twenty-odd bracelets of metals so base that they left her wrists green, and a very strange coat that she'd probably pounced on at the nearly new shop. 'Where did you get that coat? No, don't tell me, Confetti-Goretti, it sticks out a mile. You got it as a bargain at that blinking second-hand shop. Well, you've surpassed yourself this time. That's a loose woman's coat.'

She glanced down at herself. 'You see, I've never gone in for a tight fit, as I can't seem to wear clothes tidily, so the more room the merrier and—'

'The term "loose" is applicable to the wearer, not to the size of the garment.'

'Oh.' I could tell by her face that she was greatly disappointed. It was one of those dreadful garments with shaggy fur all round the edges, then braided fasteners that were supposed to attach themselves to fancy toggles. Except that Confetti wore the coat open, so the effect was not quite as cheap as usual. 'Well, isn't that a turn-up for the book now, Laura? Me in a streetwoman's coat.'

'You need high boots with it,' I said. 'In purple or burgundy, boots that cover your knees. Then a very short skirt that shows your knickers every time you bend over. For the skirt, you could try black leather or very open crochet.'

She tore off the coat and tossed it aside. 'Then I'll stick to the sheepskin, even though it is adrift on two seams.' She dropped into a chair, kicked off the blue clogs. 'Mammy has forgiven us all. She's had a vision and we're

421

all summoned, have to get there immediately if not sooner.'

'Really?'

She nodded mournfully. 'She's seen the light. And as she found the light very attractive, she's decided to go into it rather earlier than originally planned.'

'Light?' I asked.

'Heaven. She's arranging her death.'

'Oh.' It was difficult to choose many words at this point.

'This incandescent glow hung over the cowshed at midnight, she says. So she's forgiven me for being a failed nun, and she's even extended the hand of motherhood to Eugene, despite the fact that he had to get married after indulging in sex and unconsecrated communion wine.' The bangles rattled as she smoothed down her fast-growing hair. 'He probably drank the wine before enjoying the sex, but who's to know the real truth of it? So I'm off in the morning.'

I thought about it, decided that I wasn't pleased. 'I'll miss you.'

'I'll be back. My mammy may have seen a vision over the cowshed, but it would be more to do with cough medicine than the hereafter.'

Confetti has never thought along the same lines as an ordinary person. In those days, the route she took was always tortuous, always exciting. If she had been a driver – and we must thank the Almighty for great mercies because she never touched a car – then Confetti would have chosen to drive on the B roads. Her arrival might have been tardy, but she would have seen some interesting sights along the way. Her head was positively bursting with information, and she would spill it out in great quantities, with the result that one needed to home in on a certain wavelength in order to extract the pertinent points. I was tuned in and I was going to miss her. 'What has cough medicine got to do with lights over the shippon?'

'She's an addict. Mammy had a terrible cough for years, was thought to be consumptive. Then Fidelma O'Flaherty came across from her farm and gave my mother one of her brews. Now, it's a well-known fact that Kevin and Fidelma O'Flaherty brewed all kinds of stuff that should never have seen the light of day and that—'

'Or a light over a cowshed at midnight?'

'Exactly. In fact, there'd been some terrible explosions over at O'Flaherty's farm, and Kevin lost a pig and a finger, and that was a terrible shame and the cause of great concern all round. The finger wasn't too important, as it was on his left hand and he is a right-handed person, but the pig was a creature of notable stock. Anyway, aside from all the aforementioned, we began to notice that Mammy had improved something wonderful when she started on this cough cure. She still had the cough, but she was beautifully happy until the bottle was empty. The upshot was that she bought a job lot of the stuff, so that'll be the light over the shed.'

'I see.' She was better than radio, heaps better than television. My children would grieve for her, because she was the most motherly woman I had ever known. 'You've got to come back.'

'Oh yes. I've got to come back and put my dowry to good use.'

I gazed into the electric fire, watched the fan as it circled over imitation coals. It wasn't going to be easy without Confetti. She was one of those people who bring joy and energy into the most mundane situation, and she had lightened my mood considerably over the past weeks. Strangely, there was still no fear in me. It had died with Frank, though the sadness remained alive and kicking.

'Will he come for you?' She often bit into my thoughts like that, frequently answered questions before I asked them.

'He's had a letter from Anne,' I said. 'She warned him that any further contact would merit prison because of the injunction.' I chewed over the thought for a second. 'I've not seen the last of him.'

'Then what'll you do while I'm away?'

'Bake, look after the boys, watch the telly.'

'But what if—?'

'Don't think about it. I've survived without you before, so I can do it again.'

She gathered up her new coat, made a bundle of it. 'I'll stick it in the yard afterwards. Will I make the cocoa?'

'Please.'

It was the humming I would miss most, I thought as she banged about in the kitchen. She was always la-la-ing or whistling or tapping a rhythm with her feet. At this moment, she was ruining a bit of Bach as she slammed down the pan, upset a cup, sent the lid of the cocoa tin clattering across the stone floor. I would have bet a tidy sum that the convent was safer without her, that plates and statues lasted longer without Sister Maria Goretti. There would be peace, that was sure. And silence. An awful, boring silence.

He came about a week after Confetti had left, a crooked old man with a flat cap and a suit that had seen better days. The headgear was pulled so low that it almost met a striped scarf, leaving little of the face visible. I studied him, knew him, didn't know him, remembered that this unrecognizable person was a good man long before he removed his packaging.

'She's gone?' he asked.

'I beg your pardon?'

'The one who's been staying with you.'

I poked my head into the street, looked left and right as if I expected to find the answer written on the cobbles. 'Yes,' I answered uncertainly.

'Don't you remember me?'

I hesitated, fished about at the back of my mind. 'I'm sure I'll . . . remember in a minute,' I said lamely. 'Would you like to come in?'

He removed the cap. 'Laura?'

Immediately, I remembered the hair, or rather the lack of it. 'Oh, I'm so sorry. Come in, Mr Thompson.

Where've you been all this time? I never got to Frank's funeral, you know. Well, of course you'll know, because you would have noticed my absence.' I was wittering and babbling like a nervous child who has just arrived at a new school.

He settled into the collapsing sofa, placed his cap on the melamine coffee table. 'Are you managing for money?'

Yes, this was definitely my Frank's father. 'I bake. There's a chap who comes and picks up the stuff, then it's sold at Tattersall's. Would you like some tea or coffee? Or shall we go upstairs and have a peep at the boys?'

The lines of tension in his face eased when I mentioned his grandchildren. 'Does Phoebe visit them?'

'Never.'

He nodded slowly, as if keeping time with a platoon that marched to the beat of funereal drums. 'I'll see them before I go. Do you get support money from our Bernard? No, don't say anything, I know the answer. He's an executive now, if you please. He's gone into what they call marketing, all to do with targets and advertising campaigns and concentrating the sales force in certain areas. Big boy these days.'

'Oh.' He hadn't answered about the tea, so I was unsure of my next move.

'Sit down,' he said.

I sat. 'Where've you been?' I asked again.

'Here and there.' He pulled a notebook from his pocket, waved it in the air. 'Dates and times. He's messing about with one or other of those twin girls, the pair who gave him the alibi. They look so alike that I can't decide which one's he's favouring.'

I fixed my eyes on the book as he placed it next to his cap. The pages were dog-eared, looked as if they'd taken a hammering. 'Irene and Enid are married,' I ventured.

'That'll not stop him. There's nothing will stop him having his own way, even if he has to wait longer these days. When he was a kid, his mother gave in to him every time. He's shown Phoebe his appreciation by beggaring

425

off and leaving her in a terrible state. With me gone and no money coming in, she's had to take up cleaning. Still, a job of work might just improve her character. You'd fine mothers, both of you. Well, all three of you. Between that wife of mine and Liza McNally, the devil himself would have a job picking a deputy.' He smiled, showed two rows of very white teeth. 'But you belonged to Frank, Laura.' He shook his head slowly. 'I'm worried about you,' he said.

I didn't want him reviving my fear. Perhaps it was only slumbering. Whatever the truth of the matter, I had no intention of skulking in corners. 'I'm safe. My cousin even had an inside toilet made so that I don't have to go outside after dark. He's done his worst, Mr Thompson. He killed his own brother. After that terrible crime, he'll be afraid of me pursuing him. No, he's leaving me alone.'

'Aye, well we'll have to see about that.' He picked up the shabby book and flicked through a few pages. 'Co-op on Derby Street last Thursday? You'd Edward in his reins and Gerald pushing that little cart with cereal packets in it. Am I right?'

I nodded.

'Well, he was in the pie shop across the way, next to the newsagents where the woman's got one eye.'

My gullet quivered, threatened to rise. 'Blind Ivy,' I muttered uselessly. 'Go on.'

'I was standing outside the school, wore an old trilby and a mac. As you've probably noticed, I disguise myself. Bernard bought his pies, got into his car, then sat eating his dinner till you turned up View Street. After that, he drove away.' The book was tossed again onto the table. 'He's still following you.'

I told him again about the letters, about the injunction. 'He daren't come near me,' I insisted.

'You'd have a job proving that he's bothering you. I reckon he's making a timetable of your movements, trying to work out when you're at the shops and so on. He's followed you to playgrounds, to the parks and he's waited outside the doctor's.'

426

I felt poleaxed to the chair, fixed like a granite statue. 'What the hell am I supposed to do?' I asked. 'I can't stay in the house. We've got to get out. The boys need fresh air and exercise, then there's food to buy, ingredients for the baking, clothes . . .' I searched his face. 'Anyway, how are you managing to watch him? What about your own job in the pit?'

'I've left.'

'Oh.' I waited for some embroidery.

At last, he spoke. 'I work for that cousin of yours. I run messages and do a bit of cleaning in the office, find out anything she might need to know. Being his dad, I can work out his movements some of the time. But there's more cases than this one, you know. I go to the Town Hall for papers for property searches, talk to bailiffs, run back and forth between police station and the office, go to the bank sometimes. She's a good woman, is Miss Turnbull. I get paid well and I work my own hours.'

'So my cousin isn't paying you just to watch Tommo?'

'No.' He pulled some more thin and tattered books from a capacious pocket. 'I've a few jobs in hand, and it's good to see daylight. This is a grand change from coal-mining.' He paused, ran a nervous tongue across his upper lip. 'Laura, I know him. There is no-one better qualified than I am. And I've talked to your cousin, asked her what she thought about him shadowing you. So she sent me up here, wanted me to tell you, because I'm the one on the spot, the one who's seen him hanging around when he should have been at work. I don't want to frighten you, yet you must be made aware.'

The flesh between my shoulder blades began to crawl, then icy fingers touched the roots of my hair on the neckline. 'He wouldn't dare, Mr Thompson. Surely, he can't risk prison?'

He sighed, shifted his legs, sagged back against the sofa. 'There's no law of man or God that will hold him back. Bernard is ill, love. He has a sickness in his head, something that recurs time after time. Occasionally, he

427

loses control over himself, obeys some other voice.'

'So . . . so he's not to blame?'

'I didn't say that.' He closed his eyes, shook his head from side to side. 'That's a clever boy, you know. When he was small, everybody remarked on how early he walked, how clearly he spoke.' The eyes opened suddenly, seemed to burn with emotions that were deep but very mixed. 'He's my son. At times, it's easier to hate those who are close, too close. I've tried to stand back, tried to believe that he would change, tried to give him a chance. But I have to tell you how I feel, how I feel inside.' A closed fist crashed against his chest, then the Adam's apple rose and dropped in his throat several times. 'He can help himself. He does choose to be evil. You see, he fixes his attention on something or on someone, then homes in for the kill. I think he becomes obsessed, but he indulges himself. A doctor would have a hard time diagnosing insanity, since Bernard has a brain that covers for him, hides the craziness. In a way, this is a man who prefers to be unwell.'

My hands had folded themselves, the finger-nails biting through thick wool and into the flesh of my upper arms. I forced myself to relax. 'What do you suggest, then?'

'Don't be alone. Get that woman back, or move into a house where there are other tenants. There's a room available where I stay. Between us, we can keep ahead of him and—'

'No. I'm not running.'

'But you need someone with you—'

'For how long?' I jumped from the chair, stood with my hands spread wide. 'For a year, ten years, for the rest of my life?' I allowed my arms to drop, struggled for composure. 'Part of me knows that Tommo isn't done with me. In a way, I want him to strike, because his next crime will be his last. You know, I would love to be there when they send him down. Is that wicked?'

He dropped his chin. 'If it is, then I'm another sinner, because I need to see him punished for Frank, for you, for

428

that young girl who couldn't face the pain. No, you're just seeking an end to him, Laura. There's nothing bad about caging a poisonous beast.'

We tucked up the boys, drank tea, watched the BBC news. It was the start of a new year, so we wished one another all the best as we said goodbye. I stood at the door for a long time, watched Mr Thompson getting smaller as he trudged down the hill towards Bolton. There walked a man who had had two sons, one now dead, the other a killer. Here stood a woman who had known both, who had borne a child to each of those two men. I almost quaked in the icy cold, yet I remained at my door until Colin Thompson's figure had disappeared completely.

Inside once again, I flicked a switch to illuminate another bar of warmth, picked up *Pride and Prejudice*, a parting gift from Confetti, curled myself into a dip in the sofa. The wind howled in the chimney, sounded like a creature trapped and lonely. But I calmed myself, began to enjoy the work of a woman who had applied common sense to an era whose literature had been lurid and sensational. As the elements clashed, Austen and I kept our feet on the ground and our minds on the marrying-off of Mrs Bennett's daughters.

When the bigger draught arrived, I had no time to assess its source. Before I could rise from my seat, he had brought into my house a sickly smell and a large pad of gauze. As he covered my mouth, I tried not to breathe, but in the end I was forced to enter a world of silence and darkness where no wind howled.

Chapter Nine

The roaring brought me back, that mournful sound of turbulent air trapped in the vertical tunnel of bricks that was my chimney. During those first moments, I felt little, saw nothing, just heard the futile screams that came from the place behind my electric fire. Opening my eyes took tremendous will-power, and I remained blind even when my lids were lifted. He had covered my upper face with a cloth of some kind, had turned me into a creature without identity.

'I know you're awake.'

My limbs began to tremble, not just from fear, but because all my clothing had been removed. He was king and I was nothing, was less than a person in the presence of his greatness. As the cold registered on my flesh, so did the pain. I had been raped again. A part of me started to wonder where my anger was, but a brain reduced by chloroform does not react quickly. I opted for silence, waited for his next move.

Something clinked – a spoon against a saucer? What kind of a man was this? He could break into a house and disable its occupant, he could beat and rape an unconscious woman, after which commonplace events he was capable of drinking tea and . . . yes . . . he was eating something crunchy, perhaps a ginger biscuit. My children – were they safe? Had he found them, hurt them, killed them? In such thoughts lay the route to insanity, so I forced myself to believe that Gerald and Edward were alive and asleep. If I kept very still, they would not be disturbed, would not shout for me, and he might forget them. Edward. Edward was Frank's son.

Frank's son had been blotted out with Indian ink . . .

'Cat got your tongue, Laura?'

I moved my legs away from the fire, imagined the red mottles that must have appeared along the calves. Electric heat was dry and unforgiving, tended to concentrate on the nearer objects, failed to warm most of the room. If I did not answer, he would attack me again, but my mouth was sore, tasted salty and unclean.

'You are my wife. I've signed nothing, sent nothing back to that cousin of yours. You'll get no divorce from me. You see . . . ah, you can't see.' He ripped the blindfold from my face, scowled down on me. 'You see, I'm staying here now. The Irish witch is out of the picture, so I'll be sharing your bed in the future.'

When my pupils had adjusted to the cruel invasion of light, I raised my head, saw blood on my chest, knew that it had dripped from my mouth. A front tooth was loose, seemed to hang by a thread next to its brothers. Something was alive in my head, a loud thing that clamoured like the wind in the chimney. Exhausted by the headache, I dropped back to the rug, flinched as the loosened tooth jarred against its own nerve.

'I'll give up the job. Hanging on to you will be a full-time caper, but I've saved money, so we'll not go short.'

'You can't keep me here for ever.' Speaking was intensely painful. I wondered whether he might have broken my jaw, because everything seemed to grate as soon as I tried to talk. As the fumes cleared, I was aware of more damage, knew that I would be black and blue within hours. He had acted completely in character, had needed me unconscious so that his near-impotence would not be noticed and mocked. All his rage was on my flesh, inside me, around me. And to survive, I would need strength and wit, qualities that had been denied to me by this grinning monster. 'You can't,' I repeated.

'Just watch me, lady. Years we were together, you and I. There's nothing I wouldn't do for you, Laura. You're my whole life, have been my whole life ever since I first met you with Ginger and the others. All I ever wanted was to be with you. And you bloody well left me and ran off with my own brother. How do you think that made me feel? Everybody was laughing at me, calling me a fool.'

'You killed him.' Several loud beats of time crashed through my head after this careless statement had escaped.

But he laughed. 'Prove it. Go on, get down to the police station and prove it.'

'I know. Everybody knows, especially your father.'

'Frank wasn't a man. He was a pathetic cripple with no sense in his head. Nobody in their right mind could choose him over me. He always hated me because I was in one piece and because I could get the girls. So he tried to teach me a lesson by taking you away. He knew how I felt about you, so he stole the one thing I cared about.'

I swallowed. 'I'm not a thing.' The tooth was threatening to fall out at any moment. 'I'm a human being and I need a dentist.' It was becoming obvious that Tommo did regard other people as things, probably tools or toys to be used for his own gain or amusement. It was difficult to assess whether his depleted sexuality was the cause of his wickedness, or whether it was just another symptom of his disordered personality. Whatever, it deserved no attention at this particular juncture.

'You don't need anybody except me.' These words were growled from a corner of his mouth. I did not look at him, but I knew that his lip was twisted.

With the tip of my tongue, I wiggled the tooth. 'This will be out by tomorrow.'

'Good.' He threw himself into the sofa. 'Then no other man will want you.' There was greed on his face as he allowed the cold grey eyes to travel over my nakedness. 'You belong to me, because I've got a certificate to prove it,' he whispered.

What he needed was a different piece of paper, one signed by two doctors. My main feeling in that moment was panic. He was going to try again. I pulled at the rug, covered some of my nakedness. If he pounced now,

I would not be able to stop my own screams. While I thought about screaming, I heard a shrill noise, thought for a moment that it had emerged from my own mouth. But no, it was the telephone.

'Leave it,' he snapped.

I inhaled deeply, winced as cool air cut damaged gum, tried to settle my shoulders in a position where the knots of muscle might relax slightly. Tension was my enemy. If I lost my cool, I might well lose my life. The phone persisted, sounded its cry twenty or thirty times. It was about nine o'clock. Those who knew me would be aware that I must be in at this time of night. Like the good cowboy in a Saturday matinée, I waited for the sheriff to arrive.

'Who is it?' he asked.

'I don't know.' A piece of the tooth flew out of my mouth and landed on the rug. 'I've no way of knowing unless I answer it.'

'Will they come?'

I coughed, cleared my throat of blood. 'Eventually. Today or tomorrow, somebody will come.'

'Wrong answer, Laura. Get dressed, we're leaving. And we take just one kid. That boy of Frank's has no place near my son. Somebody'll find him before too long, put him in the orphanage where he belongs.' He kicked out at me, caught my shin with the toe of a shoe. 'Get the clothes on. Now.'

I didn't cry, didn't make a sound, the dress was torn and bloodstained, but I managed to pull it over my head. There was no obedience in my fingers, no direct line from brain to hands. I shook, faltered, groped for underwear, dragged the garments onto my aching flesh. Buttons and zips were my enemies, especially when the phone sounded again.

'Answer it. Get rid of whoever it is.'

I crawled across the floor, lifted the receiver. 'Hello?' A thickened tongue spoiled the word.

'Laura? It's Anne.'

433

'Two dozen,' I said after a short pause. 'And I'll do a batch of pasties.'

'Are you all right?'

'No, just the meat pasties. I'll make some cheese and onion next week.'

Another pause. 'He's there, isn't he?'

'Yes, Mr Tattersall. I fell, you see, fell and banged my mouth against the door handle, so that's why I sound different. No, I'll be able to cook.' He was moving towards me, probably preparing to listen to the conversation. 'Thanks. Happy New Year to you, too.' I threw the handset into its cradle. 'Mr Tattersall,' I said. 'Wanted to know about the pies and things.'

Disbelief contorted his features. 'What's he doing on the phone at this time of night? Isn't the shop shut?'

I gulped, searched for a lie. 'He's got a liquor licence. He wants extra pies to sell with the beer.' Anne would need to be quick. 'He says they drink more if they eat at the same time and he doesn't want them going to the chip shop.' There was still half a tooth in the front of my mouth and it felt reasonably firm. 'So he'll make on the beer and on the food.' If I concentrated on the tooth, if I managed not to think about the children, then I might hang on to my reason. Just about.

His fingers curled themselves into angry fists. 'If you're lying to me, I'll kill you.'

I stared at him levelly. 'You'll kill me anyway. All your life, you've killed things, starting with animals, finishing with your own brother. Or perhaps you haven't finished? Is it my turn soon?' I needed to keep him occupied, even if I had to stand on dangerous ground. By drawing his fire, I might save the boys. 'It won't work, Tommo. If you do it now, you'll definitely be caught. If you take me away from here, you'll never manage to keep me quiet until I'm six feet under. Whichever, you'll be a long time in prison.'

His shoulders drooped suddenly, making him shorter, less menacing for the time being. But then he started to cry, great shining tears that chased each other down his face before disappearing into the front of the bloodied shirt. 'I don't know how to do it right, Laura. I want to do it right.'

In that moment, I truly knew his despair. He had beaten me, raped me, threatened my children, yet I almost pitied him. 'Tommo, you need some help.' I kept my voice quiet and even. 'None of this is your fault. If you'll go for help . . .' I swallowed against the bitter taste of bile and untruth. 'Get some help and I'll stand by you.'

'Honest?'

'Honest.' I had never been more dishonest in my life. The thoughts that sat on the rim of my mind were all connected with escape. We could go to America, Australia, Canada. I forced myself to touch his hand. 'Please calm down. Don't cry.' There was a deep pain in my belly, an agony that marked what he had done to me in my state of unconsciousness. There was no cure. He deserved no pity, yet I stood on uncertain legs and nearly managed to worry for his future. 'Please try to understand me. I've been afraid of you, so afraid that I had to run away. When you're better, we can start again.'

The tears dried, evaporated in the reborn heat of his devilish eyes. 'You think I'm bloody thick, don't you? You're making the mistake of classing me with our Frank. Now, he was stupid. Yes, he was daft enough to give me a lift that day, daft enough to stop when I asked him to. No, I didn't kidnap him, Laura. I told him that I'd forgiven him, asked him to drive me out to Belmont. "Let's look at the water," I said to him. And he just stood there staring at the bloody river while I battered him.' Hysteria lurked on the hem of his words. 'He took you. He gave you a baby. There's no way he could have been allowed to live.'

A car hurtled down the hill, squealed against the sudden application of brakes. Doors slammed, then my bell rang and a man shouted, 'Mrs Thompson?'

He leapt like a panther, slammed a hand across my mouth, pulled me against his body. 'Don't move, bitch,' he muttered.

'Police, Mrs Thompson.' A fist hammered on my front door. 'Are you all right?'

'Go away,' yelled Tommo. 'I've got her kids here. There's nothing I can lose now, so I'll kill them if I have to. The answer's in your hands, just bugger off and leave us alone. We're man and wife, in case you didn't know.'

The silence outside was ominous. His hand covered my nose, too, so the oxygen was limited. I pretended to faint, went slack and heavy in his arms. He dragged me across the floor, pulled me onto the sofa, kept one hand across my mouth. Something new was troubling him, because he started to mumble, 'That bloody door. I've got to cover . . . that door . . . a sheet of wood . . . that door . . .'

A crash from the kitchen was closely followed by Anne's voice. 'Laura?'

Before I could rise from the couch, he had grabbed a tiny but solid poker from the hearth. I jumped up just as the metal rod made contact with Anne's head. She was in the kitchen doorway, and she fell like a stone after one blow. My brain was refusing to work properly. It wasn't a real poker, so it shouldn't have hurt her like that. This little ornament had never riddled ashes, had never met coal, so why had it killed my cousin?

The house was suddenly full of people. They poured in at the back door, strode over Anne's body, took the weapons from Tommo and hurled him against a wall. He went down slowly, like a ham actor from some B-movie. Bells rang, lights flashed, someone opened the front door. My cousin was carried out on a stretcher while a police-woman wrapped me in a blanket. 'Children,' I said. 'Take them to Auntie Maisie in Barr Bridge. The shop. Take them to the Turnbull shop.'

She patted my shoulder. 'You'll be all right, love. We've got him now, it's all over.'

A man with three stripes on his sleeve stood in front of me. 'Was there just him, Mrs Thompson?'

'Oh yes. He can't do it right, you see. He told me that he can't do any of it right. I had to be asleep, so he put a

436

rag on my face. It smelled so sweet. And it's not a real poker, so she can't be dead.'

There was pity in their eyes as I rambled on about Mr Tattersall and his pies, about my Frank and the river, about Gerald's dislike for peas. 'Tell them no peas, but he'll eat a bit of cabbage.' The strangest thing was that I knew that I was talking rubbish, yet I couldn't lay my tongue across anything sensible.

They handcuffed him and dragged him out of my house. They were hitting him, and that was wrong. 'They're hitting him,' I said.

The man with three stripes had tears in his eyes. 'God love her, she's in shock,' he muttered.

I stayed in that odd state for several weeks. Everyone was kind, especially the young ones with yellow bands on their caps. A bespectacled man talked to me for hours on end, pulled the whole story from my cluttered mind. When he had separated the wheat from the chaff, I was sent to another place where crocuses and daffodils grew in sweet abundance. Life was easy, because I wasn't myself. I walked in the grounds, ignored the high wall and the guarded gate, immersed myself in simple pleasures like pottering in the gardens and arranging flowers for the dining table.

Eventually, visitors came. Auntie Maisie and Uncle Freddie arrived without the children, told me that the boys were well and happy. While my aunt and uncle were there, Anne turned up with bath cubes and scented soap, hugged me and told me how well I looked. This was all very mysterious, because something had happened to Anne, and she should have been with Frank. Auntie Maisie made excuses for my mother, said that their Liza's stomach was bad. I remembered my mother. She used to hit me and take me to chapel. My father, who was with Frank, had invented some kind of medicine in a barn.

When they had left, I started to look at other residents of the nursing home. Many were old and unloved, left in this place so that the lives of others might become tidier.

437

The younger ones were examples of all levels of society, some from wealthy families, others with dowdy clothes and accents that had survived the onslaught of education. I agreed to go into group therapy, found myself listening to troubles that made me squirm. The victims of violence jogged my memory, forced me to face the man who had reduced me to a state that had stopped just short of catatonic.

At last, it all came out in sequence, was driven by my brain out into the open. This time, I needed no doctor's help, because I was received with love and compassion, was physically pulled into the arms of those who truly understood my plight. The nightmares began in earnest, and I was kept in the home until the bespectacled doctor visited and pronounced me fit to return to the real world. He explained that the bad dreams would disappear in time, gave me some tablets, advised me to take things easy. 'You know all about what's happened to you,' he explained gently. 'When I first took your notes, I had to sift out the dross. But you've made it. We're very pleased with you.' He pushed the glasses along the bridge of his nose. 'There's still time,' he said softly.

'Time for what?'

He inhaled deeply, held onto the desk with the ends of his fingers, prayed, no doubt, that I would retain my fragile sanity through the next few seconds. 'You could have the abortion. Given the circumstances, there should be few difficulties.'

I stared through him, past him, concentrated on the garden. 'No, thank you.' Somewhere inside, I had always known about this baby, had been aware right from the start, as soon as I awoke with the cloth on my eyes. 'No abortion,' I said. Three children, I would have, two of them born of rape.

'Are you sure?'

I nodded. 'It's not the baby's fault.'

'But . . . he or she will perhaps remind you of—'

'It's nothing to do with the child.' I placed a hand on my

438

belly as if to reassure its sitting tenant. 'Tommo's in prison, isn't he?'

The man nodded.

'How long?'

'Life.' He cleared his throat. 'They got him for his brother at the same time. It seems that your father-in-law had words with a young woman and the alibi was exposed as perjury.'

I thought about this. 'Did she get into trouble?'

'No. She insisted that your husband had some kind of hold over her – over both of those twins. They were put on probation, I think.'

'Good.' He had a kind face. 'Tommo's a frightening person, you see. He can make people do things and say things.'

'So I gather.'

He stood up, came round the desk and shook my hand. 'The breakdown's over now, Mrs Thompson. It has been a bitter time for you, but you must regard this as a *learning experience*. That is not to say that you need to go through life in a state of fear. The fear of breaking down can be almost as bad as the real thing. But many who collapse under pressure early in life become strong. Learn your limits. Consider it this way.' He walked to the window and pointed to a rain barrel. 'Look at that container. It's large, but when it's full, it's full. As the water reaches the brim, all those extra drops of rain overflow. We're like that. People can take so much and no more. At least you have learned your own capacity.'

I rose and walked to the door. 'Yes, I suppose I understand how much I can take, doctor. But how do I calculate for other people? How will I recognize another Tommo?'

He smiled. 'Believe me, you will. If you meet his like, you'll run like a deer until you're out of his sights. Go on, now. Go home and start your life.'

I paused, a hand on the doorknob. 'I want to get right away. There are three children – well – almost three. Two are his, one is illegitimate. My children are brothers and

439

cousins, you see. The story of their beginnings will be widespread throughout Bolton, especially now that one of their fathers is a recognized criminal. There must be a completely fresh start.'

He followed me, placed a hand in the centre of my back. 'It's all been discussed, Mrs Thompson. The welfare people have intervened, and you will move to Liverpool very soon. Your home in Bolton will be sold, but as its value is low, you will be awarded a corporation house. In return, the Bolton authorities will accept a family from Liverpool.'

'Displaced persons moving round in circles,' I commented. 'How sad.'

He patted me, made a tutting sound that was meant to be comforting. 'Get out there and live. Take each day as it comes, remember my advice no matter how trite it sounds. There may be times when a day is too long, when you may have to get through the next few minutes, or the next couple of hours. You're an attractive young woman with much to live for and—'

'With a false tooth.' I tried to make light of the situation.

'A crown. And it matches in very well. Listen, when the adrenalin flows for no obvious reason, go into that panic happily, know that you are alive. You've been very insecure, but you do have insight into your own make-up, and that's your strength. I can't take you back in time. I can't give you a loving mother and a father with a nine-to-five job. But I do hope I've managed to teach you how to believe in yourself.'

It was going to be a struggle. I had to pick up my boys, gather our belongings, go forward into a city I hardly knew, make a life for us and for a person who was not yet born. But I couldn't stay, didn't want to put my children through any pain. 'His dad's your dad's brother and you've both got the same mother', 'Your dad's in prison', 'Your dad got life for killing your brother's dad', and so on. They deserved better than that.

'You'll make it,' he said softly.

'I must. There's no real choice, is there?'

I walked out of that home, stood at the gate until Anne came, listened to the world and knew how noisy it was, how peaceful life had been until this morning. Giving up could be easy, I thought. How simple life might have been had I stayed in the care of others. Meals prepared, dishes washed, clothes laid out each morning. For many weeks, I had made no decisions, taken no responsibility for my own existence.

Anne pulled up. 'Climb in, you look lost.' She bore his mark on her forehead, a thin line that was turning to silver.

I climbed in. 'I am lost. And I'll definitely be lost in Liverpool. They talk funny, you know. If I ask for directions, I'll not understand the lingo. And my kids will grow up to be Scousers.'

She drove off, left tyre marks in her wake. 'There's nowt wrong wi' Liverpool folk,' she said mockingly. 'It's still a Lanky town, not foreign soil.'

'They'll call me a Woollyback,' I said.

'Sod them.'

'They're very quick-witted,' I moaned.

'Then give as good as you get, and give it before you get it.'

'Eh?'

She turned slightly, allowing me another glimpse of the silver scar on her forehead. 'You're thick, Laura. You deserve to be called a Woollyback.'

I had thought that places such as this had been eradicated before the 1960s, yet I stood in a filthy room with boarded windows and ancient oilcloth sticking up in patches all over a stone floor. There was a living room and a kitchen at ground level and, so far, I hadn't dared to look at the kitchen. I was trapped in a time warp, had somehow got stuck in the fourth dimension with gas mantles and a pulley line above a black iron range.

The kitchen – not much more than a scullery, really – was no better. A meatsafe hung open, its meshed door crippled due to a missing hinge. The unmistakeable perfume of boiled cabbage hung in the summer air, mingled listlessly with dust motes in shafts of light. Lead piping emerged from the outer wall, leaked where it joined a brass tap. Cold water only, it seemed. Beneath the tap sat a slopstone, just a shallow brown trough held up by two walls of pitted brick, no plug to the sink, no frills here. Oh heck. Was this to be the start of my new life, then?

Anne came in, muttered something about car springs and cobbles, froze like a statue when she saw the house. 'Bloody hell', she finally managed. 'Well, you were only a stride from the pavement in Maybank Street, but at least there was electricity. What the hell do we do?'

I rolled up my sleeves, picked up mop and bucket. 'Go and buy white paint and a small bag of coal. I'll fill this copper and get moving. Have you any change for the meter?'

'You'll get moving?' Her eyes were round as she stared at the ancient copper that perched to one side of the fireplace. 'You're not moving in here, Laura. Who the hell do they think we are?' She marched into the kitchen, trotted back straight away, an expression of anger distorting her features. 'Get back in the car. Do you realize that the only source of water is in that so-called kitchen? To make a bath, you'll be carrying buckets through here, traipsing back and forth like a chain gang with only one member. You are not staying in a house without proper plumbing. Come on.'

'No.'

'Then I'll go on my own.'

'Where?'

She dragged a hand through her hair, dislodged most of the chic French plait. 'To the housing, of course. They can't put you here, not in a place like this. You've two children and another on the way. This is no place for a young family.'

I sat on an old orange box, folded my hands around my knees. 'I never expected the Savoy, Anne. We're here under sufferance, you know. Do you think that some displaced Liverpool family will be given a brand new council house in Breightmet, three bedrooms, bathroom, south-facing rear garden? Will they hell as like! Bolton Council has a list as long as the Nile, so whichever poor woman has gone to my town will be no better off than I am. We're as good as homeless, Anne. I'm a misfit, a woman without a man, without a fixed abode and I'm a mother whose children have no father. This is the best I'll get to begin with. After a while, I can start crying, plead overcrowding and move on.'

She stamped a foot, looked petulant and childish. 'I wish you'd try, Laura. I wish you'd stir yourself and stand up for your rights, because—'

'I've no rights, not in Liverpool.'

'You've human rights, woman! You've a duty to those boys as well, a duty to find them some decent accommodation.'

'Safety will do,' I mumbled. 'Safety is a luxury.'

She turned on her heel and stamped up the stairs. After she had made her noisy inspection of the first floor, she yelled down the stairway, 'There's not even a gas jet up here, no lighting at all.'

'That's why I need white paint,' I shouted. 'So that I can read down here under one of the mantles. I'll get an oil lantern for upstairs.' My words bounced off the walls, came back to me with their syllables hollowed out and lengthened. It was a hole, but I didn't care. We could live here, the boys and I, could make our own amusements and mistakes.

Her face was covered in smudges when she reappeared. 'Cobwebs everywhere. This house hasn't been occupied for ages – the cabbage smell must come from next door. That's another thing. What sort of neighbours are you going to have?'

I shrugged in a manner that was probably over-careless.

443

'The same sort I'd have in a Bolton slum.'

But she would not be placated. 'No self-respecting woman could live in such a dump. How can you think of setting up here? And why don't you get that bloody mother of yours to part with the price of a little semi?'

'Stop it, Anne. You know I won't let her win. She owned me once, but never again.'

She came and stood next to me, one hand resting on my hair as she tried to persuade me. 'There has to be an alternative. I can't bear this, Laura.' I heard what she said, remembered that she had uttered the same words when Solomon died. She couldn't bear me to lose a pet I'd never really owned, couldn't cope with the idea of me suffering.

'Well, I can bear it, just as I bore it when Mr Evans's Solomon died. I'm stronger than you think and I'm staying here. No-one will find me in Liverpool.'

The hand on my head stilled itself. 'He's in prison. Why the hell are you afraid of a man behind bars?'

'He'll get out. There's nothing will hold a will as strong as his, nothing man-made, anyway.'

She walked to the grimy window where one small pane had managed to survive despite footballs and stones. 'It's a hell-hole,' she insisted. 'And look,' she waved a hand towards the street. 'Just yards away, new houses, flats, playgrounds. Yet they put you here.'

I didn't mind. We could be safe in this place, secure, fresh and new. All I needed was white paint. 'Go and buy gallons of white paint,' I insisted. 'Then, when my house is sold, we can get the electricity board in.'

She frowned, chewed her lip. 'You can't do that. You can't improve the place – they'll put your rent up. And how do you know whether there's a main in the street? Don't you need a big underground wire for electricity?'

I forced a grin. 'Twenty-seven and six is what they want and twenty-seven and six is what they'll get. And of course there's a main – how do you think they managed to build flats in 1966 without mains electricity? I'll just get myself tagged on at the end of their cable.' I rummaged in my purse for coins, fed the meter, tested the nearest gas-jet. It spat, coughed, exploded, then sent a blue-centred flame towards the ceiling. 'There,' I said placidly. 'All mod cons.'

'You need a mantle,' she grumbled.

'I'll get some.'

'Where?'

'At the mantle shop.' I would never make her understand, not in a month of Easter Sundays. 'Anne, get gone for the bloody paint. At this rate, we'll be here till midnight. And I want to move the boys here next week, get them settled.'

She slammed out of the house, revved the engine to bursting point, shot off in a blaze of temper and oil fumes. Anne was a go-getter, a woman of great ambition, a woman of substance. She didn't understand my attitude, could not make herself realize that my life's ambition was simple. All I needed was to be away from two people, and one of those was my mother. There were worries in my head, of course, concerns about money, about keeping three children on an income that was non-existent. But I hadn't shared my brainwave with Anne, hadn't told her about the recipe.

I stood in the scullery, left the bucket to fill beneath a tap that seemed to have three speeds – drip, trickle and flood. I opted for trickle, then took the envelope from my pocket. They thanked me for my interest, advised me to read at least thirty True Heart romances. The ingredients were listed below this advice. I was to take two beautiful people, mix them with love and misunderstanding, lace the cocktail with some competition – an anti-hero, perhaps, then deliver both parties to the altar at the end of some 80,000 words. Well, I would have a go. Story-telling had been my forte and I would revive that small slumbering talent, try to make it pay. I lit a cigarette, despising the habit I had picked up while recuperating. It was the last in the packet, would be the last in my mouth. If I smoked, the new baby would be stunted and my boys might

445

become bronchitic. Liza smoked and I thought I knew why. Nicotine alerts the brain, stops the boredom.

After tipping the water into the fireside copper, I started a fire by breaking up the orange box and using it for kindling. How many pages for 80,000 words, I wondered. And I'd need a typewriter, was glad I'd learned to type at McNally's. A pawnshop might have a portable, then there'd be carbon paper, reams of foolscap or A4, a steady table and . . . no. I would think about all that some other time. Anne would be back in a minute, then we could carry that small bag of coal from boot to house. 'No graphic sex, no swear words or blasphemy, no reference to politics or to religion. Our readers expect a well-told story with a happy ending.' Well, OK. I must plumb the very depths of my soul, find a bit of romance somewhere. My heart lurched as I thought of Frank, who had been my one romantic interlude. For him, for his son and his nephew, I would become a writer. 'I can do it, Frank,' I whispered into the dusty air.

I walked to the back door, peered outside, saw the lavatory shed at the bottom of the yard. No, I wouldn't look in there, not today. I could not take on an army of germs while planning to become a True Hearts writer. A few crumbs of slack coal were scattered about with some sticks of chopped-up furniture, so I scooped up my find on a handleless shovel, dumped the lot on the ailing fire. Anne was right, this was back-breaking labour, especially for one who expected another sort of labour in a few months.

Anne's cheeks glowed with some emotion or other when she stepped into the front room. 'Two quid a tin.' She dumped the paint next to the gas meter. 'I've seen this for one pound fifteen shillings at home. And they talk another language altogether, it's like double flaming Dutch.'

'They're Scousers, a very clever and amusing breed.'

'Oh, I'm sure. I'm sure they're very funny once you get through the language barrier. I'd have done better in downtown Calcutta.' She inhaled a few times, cursed the smell of filth, brought in the coal. 'Actually, they were quite helpful. They said something about Liverpool Council planning to pull these houses down in a few years. But for now, they're being let to down-and-outs.'

I decided to take no notice, got busy with tepid water and cloths. She opened the stairway door, sat for a while at the bottom of the flight, then picked up a sponge and started at the other side of the room. Inevitably, our paths crossed under the window. 'You're a damned fool,' she said.

I giggled, pushed the hair from my eyes. 'I know, but I'm lovable with it.'

Chapter Ten

The Hourigan Farm,
Near Celbridge,
County Kildare,
Eire.

May 12th 1966

Dear Laura,

I don't know where you are, so I'm sending this via
Anne. I am so sorry for what happened, I should
never have left you. It even got into the papers over
here, which is why I understand your need for a new
start. I have spoken to Anne on the telephone, but
she will not give out your address, even to me,
without your permission. I agree with her whole-
heartedly in this matter, though I am hoping that
you will begin writing to me very soon. Please try to
keep the hatred for Tommo out of your heart. Apart
from it being a sin, it's also very exhausting and
time-wasting.

Have you room for me wherever you are? Just keep
the bed aired, because I'll be a while. My father has
taken to drink since my mother took to her bed. He
is all the while over to an inn on the Dublin Road
and different fellows bring him home every few
days. If I'm not careful, the dowry will be used up
before I get back to England, as the farm has gone
down with neglect. It is a terrible shame for my

father, who is a good man, because he scarcely took a drop till Mammy was ill. He cannot bear the thought of life without her, so he is burying himself in whiskey, poor soul.

Eugene has four children now and he doesn't enjoy being a daddy. I think he wishes he had stuck to his cassock, because a priest's life would have been easier. They quarrel a lot, all of them, so it's very noisy when they visit.

Mammy is really ill this time, though the famous cough medicine does take the edge off her pain. There is no hope for her, but she is happy to leave this life, since all her children have been such a bitter disappointment. I've five brothers, none of them priests, then my two sisters are married and living in Birmingham. I am the worst of the failures, as I took the veil then ripped it off. She accuses me with her eyes, but voices few opinions these days. Like I said to you all those years ago, life is not about pleasing parents, so I do not feel too guilty.

Laura, please write to me sometimes. I know it must be hard for you to find the time, but I would love to hear from my dearest friend, even if you scribble just a few words on a postcard. I am praying for you every night, so make sure you pray for me.

I was with Tommy-gun when she died peacefully some weeks ago. I visited her while a nurse stayed with Mammy, and Tommy asked about you, but I did not tell her about the piece in the paper. She remembers you as a dear little girl with a terrible loneliness in your face. The funeral was well attended – Agatha came over from England and the church was filled to bursting by Irish nuns and relations of the lovely lady. Now, she was a real nun, because she simply believed and made believing an act of will. Whereas I always asked too many questions, so I finished up sitting here in a draughty kitchen with my mother upstairs waiting for the end, my father down the road drinking himself senseless.

I will be back, Laura, that's a threat. There's something I want to do over in England, but I'll need a barrel of cash to fund it. Still, if it's God's will as well as mine, then it will happen.

My fondest love to you, also to Gerald and Edward.

Your friend and sister, Confetti-Goretti.

I placed the letter on the white tablecloth in my white room, picked up my pen, wrote a reply. We had been here for three weeks now, and the boys had settled reasonably well. Yet I was lonely, felt almost as isolated as I had as a child. The shopkeepers were pleasant and helpful, but I had met few other people until today. Today, the house next door had spat out one set of tenants and taken in another family. Two of the children had spoken to me, so I allowed myself to hope for contact from an adult neighbour. I finished the letter, wrote two pages of my embryonic True Hearts romance, made use of the remaining daylight.

When dusk fell, I went into the yard and listened. It had been an interesting and very noisy day so far, and I wasn't convinced that the excitement was over. A tousle-haired child stared at me, head and neck completely visible above the dividing wall. No child of that age could possibly have legs of such length. 'What are you standing on?' I asked.

'A bucky.' The locals often left the *t* off the end of a word. And it must have been one huge bucket. I reached up on tiptoe, peered over the wall, saw that the child was on an upturned dolly-tub.

I studied the dirt-streaked face. 'Where's your mother?'

It waved a hand towards the house. 'She's lookin' fer nits. I don't like it when she looks fer nits. Can I cum in your 'ouse?'

'I don't think so.'

A small, agile woman leapt through the doorway, pounced on the child. 'Get over here, this minute if not sooner,' she said, the tone strident and determined. 'I've got to do your head.'

'I told yer,' announced the child, directing this accusatory remark at me. 'She scrapes me 'ead. I 'aven't got no nits.'

The mother bared her incisors at me. She was tiny, and her hair was bleached not quite to the roots. These were dark brown, almost black, and the lank blonde strands were as lifeless as cotton wool. 'Hello,' she said, her accent less pronounced than the child's. 'I'm Liddy. Liddy Mansell.'

'Laura Thompson.'

'I got moved here today. They put all the social problems in this street. That's what they call us, social problems. Have you seen any more of these?' She pointed to the child. 'Only I've six, so they take some keeping up with.'

'I've seen just this one. Oh, I talked to a couple earlier on, but I don't know where they are now.'

'Halfway to bloody Manchester, I shouldn't wonder.' She dragged the infant down from its perch, pulled a fine-toothed comb through the mousy mop, scrutinized the remaining teeth on the worn plastic weapon. 'That's you off the list till next week, then. Where's the rest of the kids?'

The small body held back the tears, wriggled, escaped, fled into the house. 'They've no patience with nit-combs,' she said pleasantly. 'Where are you from?'

'Bolton. And you?'

'Halewood. Some buggers down there didn't like the cut of my jib, so I've been shifted. They've moved me away from my man, that's what they've done. How can I take this lot down to Halewood, eh? Well, he'll just have to come here, that's all.'

This was beyond my comprehension. If Liddy had a loving husband, then why had she been sent to Seaforth without him? 'They don't usually split families,' I ventured.

She stared at me, seemed to be trying to assess my worth. A loud sigh escaped from the small body, seeming to leave her even tinier. 'He's their dad, but we're not married. See.' She approached me, climbed onto the tub, made it possible for me to flatten my feet, which were aching after being on tip-toe for so long. 'See, he's a lodger and I'm not.'

She was not getting through. 'Oh,' I answered hopefully.

She glanced over both shoulders, then looked straight ahead, as if she could see right through me. 'I'm a Catholic.'

'Ah.' A dim light dawned. 'He's Orange Lodge?'

'Well, he's from a lodge family. His ma hates Catholics. So we can't get wed till she's dead, because if we did get wed, it would kill her.'

I held back a flippant remark about two birds and one stone, waited for her to continue.

'Any road, we had all these kids, me and Jimmy. Now, his old girl has had the whole lot of them round to visit her every Sunday, but she'll not let me past the front gate. It's like they've all been conjured up or born through some immaculate conception thing, because they're not allowed to have a mother. Truth is, I was quite happy to carry on and wait till she was dead, just have Jimmy on a part-time basis. But' – again she looked over her shoulder – 'then I got trouble from the other side as well.'

'Really?'

She nodded, gave me a better view of the dark roots. 'The Catholics. They started sending the priest round. Now, I can't be doing with priests. They walk in your house without knocking and start a conversation about the

452

price of fish, but they always finish up wanting donations for the church fund and a list of your sins. Well, my sins were usually crawling all over the floor and swinging from the priest's clothes, so I didn't need confession. Anyway, I took no notice. Till the windows got broke. They didn't like me going with a Protestant, and they didn't like me being loose. So they broke me windows.'

Somehow, I knew just by looking at Liddy Mansell that the broken windows were not the end of the story. At 5 feet and very few inches, she was not one to back down. 'What happened then?'

'I belted three or four faces. Might have been half a dozen, I can't remember. I'm bound over to keep the peace, so they shoved me here, right at the other end of bloody Liverpool. This must be the corporation's idea of birth control.'

I liked her right from the start. Within ten minutes, she was sitting in my front room, dipping what she referred to as a suggestive biscuit into a mug of tea. 'Well?' she asked after sweeping the crumbs from her chest. 'What have you done to finish up here?' She jumped up, pinned an ear to the party wall, hammered with her fist. 'Mary? Stop that lot bloody wingeing, will you? We're trying to have a conflagration in here.' She marched back to the chair, winked at me. 'It's all right, I say the wrong words on purpose. Or on purple, as my Jimmy calls it. You haven't answered my question.'

There was no sense of throwing caution to the winds, because I had seen right away that Liddy Mansell was a salt-of-the-earth type of person, too straight for her own good, a pure moralist whose morals would never stand up in the eyes of those Christians whose sight was diminished by dogma. She was 'loose' with her favours, loyal to her man, a woman whose ascent into the heavenly firmament would be heralded by a guard of honour comprised of all God's angels. Liddy was simply good. So I told her.

The little jaw dropped during the tale, hung slack for a few seconds after I'd finished relating the condensed version. She pulled herself together, dug with a spoon for the dregs of biscuit in the base of her mug, ran the other hand through the bleach-murdered hair. 'It was even in the *Echo*,' she said. 'And the *Daily Mirror*. You could write all that down and flog it, it's better than *Peyton* bloody *Place*.' She licked the soggy crumbs out of the spoon.

I smiled at the idea. 'No, I'm sticking to the True Hearts.' I told her of my plan, of the painstaking labour I had undertaken. 'It's all in longhand.'

'Jimmy'll get you a typewriter,' she volunteered generously. 'He can get most things, working on the docks.'

'A typewriter on the docks?'

'Well, there's offices, queen. Or he might get his hands on something he could swap for a typewriter.' The little chest swelled with pride. 'He can get you an elephant if you want one.'

'No thanks. The yard's not big enough.' It was amazing how quickly she had absorbed and dismissed my lurid story. It occurred to me that Liddy Mansell was all but beyond shock, that she must have seen a great deal of life before I came along. 'Would I be receiving stolen goods?' I asked.

'Yes. Why, does it bother you?'

I thought about this for a few seconds, recalled the occasion when, as a schoolgirl, I'd been accused of stealing a missal. Things were different now, harder. I had entered an area where survival would be confined to the fittest, and I had every intention of keeping my family fit. 'I think not. You see, Liddy, I've not much money. If my children are ever threatened with starvation, I'll go shoplifting. So it's all the same, isn't it? If I make money, I'll give some of it to charity.'

She nodded enthusiastically. 'You're honest, girl, I'll say that for you. I mean, you talk a bit posh like, but you know which end's which. We just have to get through life without making a lot of folk suffer. And if we're honest about it, we're all dishonest. See, I'm honest enough to tell you that I tell lies. I've had to tell lies to cover my back and stick hold of my children. Same as you say, you pinch from them what can afford it, and you give to them what's in need. And Robin Hooding should start in your own house.'

The door flew open and I worried fleetingly about the boys being disturbed. A female child stood on my step, her face set in a smile that was almost disarming. 'They won't go to bed. 'Ello, missus.' She dashed in, picked up a digestive, crammed most of it into her mouth.

'No manners,' Liddy said. 'It's with having no full-time dad. They'll get manners once old Mrs Hurst passes on, because Jimmy doesn't like rudeness.' She grabbed the girl and pulled her down onto the chair arm. 'This is Mary,' she announced. 'She's the eldest. There's five more if only I could find them. Mary, tell Auntie Laura about your dad.'

Mary grinned again. Her adult incisors bore scars from some disaster or other, were chipped too short for her words to be completely clear. ''E's dead big, built like a sh . . . like a lavatory shed. An' 'e's got blue eyes an' black 'air an' 'e plays the melodeon. An' I luv 'im.'

Liddy beamed. 'Best man in Liverpool, is my Jimmy. We're going to have a great big wedding when his mother pops her clogs, and all the kids will be bridesmaids and pages. Mind you, if the owld girl doesn't get a move on, her grandkids'll be wed before we are. She's one of them that'll live for ever, straight through her century and into the next. I'll be grey before she shows signs of bad health. Never catches cold, never ails a day. Even the bloody germs are frightened of her.'

When they had left, I felt warmer and happier for having made their acquaintance. It occurred to me that neighbours were more important than family, because they were geographically closer, easier to reach. And party walls were no prison while a woman like Liddy sat on the other side. I stood on my front doorstep, wondered how many women had stood there over the years. The slab had

455

a dip in the middle where generations had worn away the stone. Did they stand here in their clogs and shawls while their men fought for work on the docks? Did they scurry to the shelters when the Luftwaffe vomited its cargo on this beautiful city?

The view from the house was a new one, was filled by large concrete flats that towered into the sky. Some council houses were almost finished, tarpaulins flapping over beams that waited for tiles. There was a bit of grass across the way, some swings and a slide to occupy the children. I liked it, liked the shops, the streets, the people. There was something about Liverpool, a quality I could not quite name. It was to do with friendliness, yet it was more than that. It was almost a welcome, as if this seaport still opened its arms to all newcomers. During my excursions to the shops, I had heard Irish voices, Scottish accents, a variety of Lancashire dialects. It was a meeting place, a city where a foreigner could come, lay down his head and be at home. And a part of me knew that while I might long for my own folk and for the moorlands, I would never drag myself from Liverpool, not completely.

I closed my door and I was at home.

Loving Liverpool is easy. By the time I had plucked up the courage to venture into what the locals called 'town', I had mastered the language, could cope in any crisis.

There are many bad moments in a young mother's life, and one of the worst is met when two children are dragged through a city, one on reins, the other in a pushchair. But when I asked, doors were opened, when I looked harassed, there was always someone to take Gerald's straps or Edward's pram. I was received with more kindness than I had ever encountered before, and we wandered round Lewis's, Lee's, Marks & Spencer, took our time, made our purchases. The attitude to children was almost continental, because we were accepted and helped all the way. Yes, loving Liverpool is not difficult.

We sauntered down to the Pier Head while we waited

456

for transport, watched the gulls swooping, counted pigeons as they strutted with out-thrust chests all over the pavement. Gerald was excited by the water, wanted to stay for ever. Even Edward forgot to moan, concentrated instead on the river and the birds, especially the two stone giants that overlooked the water. 'Liver birds,' I said. 'Liber birds,' repeated my younger child.

Our return journey took a different route, brought us parallel with the dock road. Through gaps in buildings, we glimpsed ships and cranes, saw a ferry loading for a trip across to Ireland. I thought briefly of Confetti, hoped that her parents were feeling better. There was an excitement in me, because I had finally found my own feet, my own place. I still longed for Frank, but if I couldn't have him, then I would rather be without him in Seaforth.

We showed our purchases to Liddy and company, took tea and Ribena at her cluttered hearth, discussed the possibility of becoming electrified. Of course, Jimmy knew somebody, but a new mains connection would need to be done by the book.

Liddy went into her scullery, came back with a large cardboard box. 'It's your typewriter,' she said happily. 'And some paper and carbon and white ink for your mistakes.'

I opened it, looked down with eyes that were misted with gratitude. 'Thank him, Liddy,' was all I managed. It was almost new, a little portable in a brown leatherette case.

'Just don't ask where it came from. We never ask where things come from, do we, kids?'

They chorused their 'no', carried on playing with Gerald's new Lego.

Six weeks later, I sent off my first True Hearts romance. It came back very quickly with a note attached. They had found it interesting but unsuitable, invited me to try again. I looked at my rejected paper offspring, felt like a mother whose child is unfairly accused of some terrible crime. Oh, I couldn't go through all that again, couldn't sit and worry about Reginald and Lucy finding passion, losing it, rediscovering it on page 204. The books were so simple to read, so difficult to write. I had often mocked the authors of such small, thin books, but now I realized how skilful they were, how attentive to detail. There was nothing else for it. I must do it all again, because I would soon have yet another mouth to feed, and my savings were dwindling fast.

My daughter was born in October 1966, came screaming into the world on a tatty hearth-rug in front of a roaring coal fire. I had scarcely felt a twinge when the waters broke, was pushing down within seconds of this first warning. Gerald, who was quite the little man of the house, ran next door for Liddy. She shoved both my children into her house, left them in Mary's dubious care, returned in time to welcome the new arrival.

'Well, I've heard of special delivery, but this is a flaming miracle,' she declared as she washed the yelling infant. 'Keep pushing,' she barked at me. 'You've got to give me a clean afterbirth, or you'll be in the hospital come midnight.'

I pushed, delivered, was cleaned and cosseted by a woman whose life skills were truly amazing. 'This calls for a celebration,' she said when the baby had quietened. 'I'll send our Mary with a jug. Do you want black or bitter?'

I lay back on my pillow, which was really an old tapestry cushion, considered various names. 'I'll call her Joan, I think. They can't do a lot with a short name, can they? Poor Gerald will get Gerry, and Edward will be reduced to Eddie. So I'll plump for Joan and a bottle of lemonade.'

She left me alone with my daughter. Gingerly, I eased my aching bones onto the sofa, picked up the scrap of new life, counted her fingers and toes before wrapping her once more in Liddy's best towel. She was the most beautiful thing I had ever seen, and she was not the child I had expected. I was blonde, the father's hair was a golden ginger, yet I had just delivered a child with violet eyes and long black tresses that looked ample enough to be plaited. She smiled at me, grinned in a way that could not possibly be connected with wind. My Joan was born old, knew straight away who she was, who I was, where she fitted in the scheme of things. When people discuss reincarnation, I always remember that knowing look, the wisdom etched deep into crumpled features.

We drank, interviewed the family doctor who had come to assess the health of mother and baby, then we watched with baited breath while Joan's reflexes were tested. 'She's fine,' he said as he put away the stethoscope.

'Course she is,' snapped my feisty neighbour. 'She bred her and I delivered her. No rubbish round here.'

He walked round my little home, wrote some notes on a card, declared his intention to have the house upgraded. 'You need light and warmth with children. These houses can get damp at this time of year.'

I eyed him warily. 'They'll only put the rent up.'

Liddy agreed. 'We'll manage as we are. Twenty-seven and six takes some finding.'

The man smiled, pulled on his overcoat. 'They've two choices here, girls. They can pull this lot down and rehouse you, or they can update the terrace and stick in a few mod cons. Don't worry.' He pulled a scarf from a pocket, wound it round his neck. 'Your rents won't go through the roof.' He left us to our own devices.

Liddy looked glum. 'I had Jimmy round the corner, two lavvies, a proper bathroom and a big kitchen. And I lost my temper and lost the lot.'

I laughed at her. 'Keep smiling, Liddy. Something tells me that you'll win through in the end.'

She swallowed half a pint of stout. 'Tell you what, queen. If I don't bloody win, them Liver birds'll topple off their perch.'

I didn't doubt that, not for a minute.

We had our second good Christmas. In spite of the three children, I had rescued Reginald and Lucy from the rubbish bin, had tidied them up to a point where the publisher had paid me £200. The cheque sat on my Utility sideboard for three days, because I didn't want to part with it. I was Georgina Dawn and I was getting paid for being schizophrenic. Existing as two people is not the easiest of things, so I was Laura during the days, Georgina in the evenings. Georgina worked hard on her proof-reading, but she did have the benefit of electric lighting. Laura struggled through the days, entertained and pacified three children, washed, shopped, cooked, cleaned, ironed.

For Christmas, I bought an electric cooker. Eleven of us, plus one baby, crowded into the scullery, all ooh-ing and ah-ing at the sight of so much luxury. 'I've had a gas one,' said Liddy. 'But never the electric sort.'

Jimmy ran a huge finger across the pristine hob. 'It's very nice, Laura.' He was the loveliest man I had ever met – except for my father and Frank, of course. There was so much of him that he almost filled the tiny scullery, leaving the rest of us to gather together in a clutch of arms, legs and squashed bodies. 'You can do a turkey in it. I'll get you a grand bird, then you can cook dinner for my kids as well.' He would be cooking for his mother, eating with his mother. Yet even though he was so much under the dragon's thumb – it was Liddy, of course, who had christened her not-quite-mother-in-law – he remained very much a man. 'I'll be down in the afternoon to see you all,' he said.

I've never forgotten that Christmas. We all had presents from Jimmy, and we had made or bought gifts for one another. There's something about a place that's too small, a very special aura that brings out unexpected qualities in people. As we fell over one another, I realized why Westminster had never been modernized. Those small crowded chambers brought together people whose views were so opposed whereas a larger space might have absorbed some of the quarrelling, thereby rendering the arguments tepid and meaningless. When crammed together, folk are forced to get on with the business in hand, and our business was enjoyment.

We all had to do a turn when Jimmy came. He presided, acted as Master of Ceremonies, sitting on the stairs between introductions. Peter and Paul and Mark did the Beatles minus one, Gerald laughed his way through 'I Know an Old Woman who Swallowed a Fly', Mary sang 'Silent Night' in a sweet, reedlike voice. But Jimmy and Liddy stole the show, got up after Edward's 'Baa Baa Black Sheep', delivered several duets. I had not expected 'Greensleeves' and 'Early One Morning', not from such life-toughened people. The harmonizing was perfect, needed no accompaniment. This pair kept together in more ways than one.

I think they expected something wonderful from me, because I was thought to be artistic. But they received 'Albert and the Lion' very well, though they must have heard it a million times before.

We had crackers and funny hats, mince pies and cream, carols under my plastic tree. Everyone looked at my cards from Anne, from Uncle Freddie and Auntie Maisie, from Goretti-Confetti and Colin Thompson. I explained the ex-nun's name, told the story of the little Italian saint who was my friend's namesake. Then Mary asked about two other cards, items that I had relegated to the dustbin. Liddy distracted her daughter, drew the fire away from me. One of those cards had been sent by my mother, and the second had arrived via McNally's. It was from Tommo, who wished me and Gerald a happy Christmas.

Joan was passed from child to child with a level of expertise that was remarkable. At just over two months of age, she was a student of the human animal, always keeping her eyes fixed on somebody, as if she were collecting data to be used at some time in the future. When I looked at her, I knew I was a mother. My feelings for the boys, too, had blossomed with the birth of my daughter, though I've always credited Liddy for my new attitude. Being near a woman like Liddy opened me up, helped me to embrace my children. She lived hand to mouth, day to day, yet she was a mother through and through, a fiercely protective female who guarded those cubs with her life. All the flippancy, all the 'I don't know where the bloody hell they've got to', hid a heart made of something far rarer than gold.

When our Christmas was almost over, Liddy took her brood next door, and I put my three to bed while Jimmy washed mountains of dishes that had been gathered together from both houses. Then he sat with me, feet on my fender, eyelids drooping with a satisfied exhaustion. 'I knew she'd be upset when it finally happened,' he said out of the blue.

'I beg your pardon, Jimmy?'

He tilted his head to one side, rested against the chair's high back. 'Mam's got cancer, so my girl's upset.'

It was so sweet, the way he called Liddy 'my girl', because Liddy was thirty-five if a day. 'I'm sorry,' I said, and I was.

He nodded. 'Well, we've waited to get married, me and Liddy. Liddy's been so good, stopping on her own all the while and putting up with all my kids. People think I'm soft for staying with my mother, but she'd nobody else. And she can't be doing with Catholics.'

I gazed into the fire. 'Why didn't you say something earlier?'

His eyes opened wide. 'What? And spoil the kids' Christmas?'

For me, that last sentence summed up Liddy and Jimmy, embraced the Liverpool I was learning to love. People here were tough, warm, sensitive, aggressive. The large man snoozed in the chair, waited for his lover to summon him to say six goodnights in the crowded bedroom where his children slept. Jimmy had struggled on Christmas Eve, had made his dogged way from Liverpool centre to Seaforth, had borne the weight of a 16 pound turkey and presents for everyone. He had laughed, played games, had sung like an angel. And all the time, he had worried about a nasty old woman whose life was drifting to a close. Occasionally, I liked a person so much that I came near to tears. But I breathed them in, smiled at my companion, stayed silent while he enjoyed the rest of a just man.

She stepped out of the car, a coat of grey wool wrapped close to her body, as if she were afraid of touching anything in this mean and dirty street. So, here came my nasty old woman, though she looked younger than I felt. At fifty-six, Liza McNally had the legs of a dancer, the body of a teenager, the face of a Madonna. It was only when she came close that the meanness showed, two lines between the eyebrows, a slight downturn of the painted mouth, some creases in an upper lip that had sucked for forty years on tubes of tobacco.

The vehicle was a Jaguar, an elongated item with a fierce-looking bonnet and large headlights. It suited Mother, because it stared at me, seemed to accuse all who stood in its path. 'Hello, Laura,' she purred. Yes, she was in the right car, because that purred too until the man at the wheel stopped the engine. 'I hear you've had a daughter.'

I hadn't expected her, was preparing to go next door for my Boxing Day meal. 'Yes,' I replied feebly. 'Do you want to see her?'

'Of course.'

She stepped into my shabby little home, and I was glad that I'd cleaned up the mess that had sat here through Christmas night, bits of cracker, crumbs, torn party hats and strands of tinsel. Then she did yet one more unforgivable thing. Although my home was small and old, I kept it clean, was forever polishing and dusting and sweeping the carpets. But Mother was not satisfied with my standard of housekeeping, because she flicked a handkerchief over a dining chair before daring to seat herself.

'The room is clean,' I said.

463

'Well, I'm sure you do your best.' Her accent was still stuck somewhere between the Queen's English and the fish market in Bolton. 'Hello, Gerald. And hello, Edward.'

They looked at her, glanced at me, questions on their shiny clean faces.

'Where is she?'

'Upstairs. I'll go and fetch her.' As I ascended the flight, I heard her speaking to my sons. 'You may visit me any time you like. Perhaps you will all come to stay with me one day. Gerald, don't pick your nose. Edward, come here and I'll wipe that little mark off your cheek.'

There were times when I couldn't remember why I disliked my mother, occasions when I really believed that I was being unreasonable where she was concerned. Yet here she was in my house, where she had spoken no more than a few dozen words, and my hands were itching, as if they wanted to attach themselves to her throat.

I came down with my daughter. 'This is Joan.'

Mother smiled, rose from her seat, scrutinized my baby's features. 'Are you sure you got the right one? She's so dark.'

I nodded. 'Oh yes. I gave birth here in front of my own fire. So I won't be telling her that there was a mix-up.'

She coloured slightly, must have heard an echo from years ago – 'There's been a mistake, John. This is not my child.'

I sat down, perched Joan on my knee while Mother hung over us. 'She's very beautiful. How can you give such a plain name to such an adorable child?'

'I like the name.'

She simpered, tickled Joan under her chin. 'May I hold her?'

I sat there and studied my mother, remembered her hands on my forearms, felt the pain when she squeezed me too tightly. Lights danced before my eyes as she beat my skull, and the roots of my hair tingled, as if she had pulled my plaits again. 'No,' I said. 'You may not hold her.'

464

Tension crackled in the small room, seemed to bounce off the walls like the winter sun, whose over-bright rays were licking the bright, white paint. 'Why do you hate me?' she asked coldly.

'I don't know.'

She sank onto the sagging sofa, placed her bag on the floor, took a handkerchief from her pocket and blew her nose. I wanted to remind her that she had used this same item as a duster just moments earlier, but instead, I turned to my sons. 'Gerald, take Edward next door, tell Auntie Liddy I won't be long.'

When the boys were gone, I addressed the woman who had asked me a question to which I would never have an answer. 'There's no love between us, Mother, so I can't understand why you've bothered to come.'

'You're my daughter.'

'When it pleases you, yes. As a child, I wouldn't have known who I was except that my father reassured me every time you turned on me.'

She twisted round and took in the size of my new life. 'You can't stay here. It is absolutely ridiculous to think that a daughter of mine is living in such conditions. You must come home. I shall buy you a house, and I won't interfere.'

I waited until her head had stopped its journey round my living room. 'I can't live in Bolton. You know who Edward's father was, and I'm sure that you don't want the disgrace of having us living near you. After all, your son-in-law is in prison, isn't he? By the way, my divorce has come through.'

'The children,' she wailed. 'They deserve better, they need—'

'I needed.' My voice was loud, too loud for the festive season. It was no use, anyway. There was no point in self-pity, no point in whipping her for the sins she refused to remember. 'Look. Two of my children are the result of rape. My middle child is illegitimate. I'm not fit company for a woman of substance, Mother.'

'But—'

'I don't want them living in Bolton, where people remember Tommo and Frank. And that's all there is to the matter.'

She inhaled deeply. 'May I smoke?'

'No. White paint soon shows the nicotine.'

She jumped up, agitated without her fix. Deprived of cigarettes, she was like a cat on hot bricks. Her face was fixed to the window when she spoke again. 'This is an awful place. Look at those terrible flats, those nasty little council houses.' She swivelled, fixed her gaze on me. 'If you insist, I'll buy you a house here, in a better part of Liverpool. Are there any decent areas in this awful city?'

I was hardly a Liverpudlian, but I was immediately on my mettle. This was my place, and I didn't like destructive criticism, especially from a woman whose every word seemed to be trimmed with sarcasm. 'You don't know the first thing about Liverpool.'

She sighed dramatically. 'Noisy people, I should imagine. They would need to be loud to produce these so-called groups. Beatles, Pacemakers – wherever do they get such names?'

'Go home,' I said quietly. 'Go home and leave me in peace. All I want from you, Mother, is silence.'

The door opened and Liddy's small face peeped in. 'Are you coming, Laura? Only I've sliced the ham and opened five tins of new spuds – good ones – they used to be Jerseys when they were alive. Hello,' she said to the stranger. 'Are you Laura's mam?'

'Yes.' The lip was curled so slightly that Liddy might not have noticed. But I saw the contempt, the false superiority that was enjoyed by the small-minded creature who had birthed me.

I rose, clutched Joan to my chest. 'This is Liddy Mansell, my next-door neighbour. She acted as midwife when Joan was born and we have become close friends.'

Liddy grinned. 'You've got to be friends living so close to one another.' She nodded her tiny head, awarded

Mother a good view of the dark roots. She was dressed for the festivities in a short blue skirt and a crocheted blouse that showed bra straps and several inches of bare stomach through the very open pattern. The shoes were white, with very tall heels that were scuffed, and Liddy's make-up was as colourful as the baubles on my tree. 'You've a look of your mam,' she said to me.

'We're late,' I told my mother.

She followed Liddy and me out of the house, signalled to the chauffeur. He got out of the car, opened the lid of the boot and lifted out some parcels. 'Christmas presents for the children,' she said to me.

I smiled at the man, recognized him. He was the fellow who had refused to allow me near my father's factory. 'Put them inside the house,' I ordered the red-faced driver.

Liddy stepped through her front door, tottering on the stilt-like shoes. I turned to follow her, flinched as a hand reached out and stayed my progress. 'Laura, you don't belong with these people.'

I faltered, raised my chin and cast a last remark over my shoulder. 'No, you are the one who doesn't belong.'

And as I sat through the meal, I tried to think of a place where my mother might fit in. Apart from hell, I came up with no ideas.

Chapter Eleven

We had five good Christmases in Seaforth. By 1971, I was no longer a full-time mother, as the education system had finally managed to absorb all three of my offspring. But Liddy, rampant as ever, had got herself pregnant for what she declared was the 'abso-bloody-lutely' last time. 'He's only got to look at me. He's only got to stand there in George Henry Lee's – we don't even need to be in the bedding department. I can't work out how it's happened this time, 'cos we don't get many chances, like. We've three in the back bedroom, two on settees in the downstairs – there's only our Mary what's left home, and she keeps turning up like a bad half-crown and—'

'Twelve and a half pence, Liddy.'

She bridled. 'Listen, they can say what they want, but I'm taking no notice. Mind you, have you seen what they're doing? Something that used to be three bob's shot up to nearly thirty of them new pences. They've just moved what Jimmy calls the decimated point.'

I worked out that she meant decimal, sat perfectly still while she continued. Music hall had not passed on in Wordsworth Street, Seaforth, not while Liddy continued to strut the boards. Or the flags, if we were downstairs.

'And she's lingering, isn't she? Not that I wish her any harm, but she was supposed to be dead at least four years ago. Hanging on with the splinters on her broomstick, she is, always has a gob on her like something out of a nightmare. I've not seen her for years, but she won't have improved. Jimmy's running two homes, you know.' Her face softened. 'He's a good lad, is Jimmy. The old girl's got to have a colostomy next, and he's worried sick. And

468

so am I. They'll not let me stop here, Laura. It was bad enough when our Mary was with us, the housing trying to put me in one of them cardboard boxes.' She waved a hand towards my front door, indicating that she was referring to Seaforth's latest housing developments. 'Open the oven door in one of them jerry-built shacks, and you'll be dipping your bread in next door's beef gravy. There's no privacy.'

'You think they'll move you when the baby arrives?'

She glared down at her bulging belly. 'What colour are my shoes? Do they match?'

'Yes.'

She fell into a chair, puffed and panted as her belly rose, round and huge in front of the tiny frame. 'I don't want to leave you. You're my best mate, like. And it's private here, what with you on one side and owld Charlie on the other. He suits me, does Charlie, deaf as a post and easygoing.' She shifted uncomfortably, tried to find her ever-changing centre of gravity. 'We'll be needing a crane to get me out of this chair.'

I handed her a cup of tea, gave her a paper napkin so that she could balance the cup on her bulge without scalding the skin. 'Drink that and stop worrying.'

She grinned. 'How's your mam?'

'Dying. That's the fifth time in about eighteen months. I think she's been reading about the liver this time. Or it might be the kidneys – my cousin Anne gets mixed up with all these different diagnoses. When Mother finally decides to fix herself on leprosy, I'll be able to get her put away.' My lovely Uncle Freddie had died during the previous year, had slipped away during sleep. At his funeral, I was accosted by my mother. 'See? He died a healthy man. It'll be my turn next, but will you come home? Oh no, you're too busy entertaining your low-life friends. If Freddie can go out like a light, then so can I. My body is a mystery to medical science. There's so much wrong that it's a miracle when I wake up in the mornings.'

Liddy was staring at me. 'Do you think he'll be getting out soon? I mean, life doesn't mean life, not really.'

For most of the time, I tried not to think about this, was driven now to answer. 'According to Anne, he hasn't behaved himself. So he'll not be coming to torment me yet.'

'But what about when he—'

'Liddy, don't. As far as we can work out, he has no idea where I am. Unless my mother has furnished him with the information, of course. But he gets no visitors except for his own mother – his father disappeared from the scene ages ago. Mr Thompson's Christmas cards have come through Anne, and the stamps were franked all over the country. And Mrs Thompson won't know where we are.'

'Unless your mam . . . Never mind. Once Jimmy comes to live with me, you'll be frightened of nothing.'

When Liddy had gone home to do battle with her youngsters, I set about preparing a meal for my own three. They were fairly good kids. I had been lucky so far, was blessed with two children who created few waves, who seldom needed admonishment. Edward was the exception, but even he was not outright naughty.

Jodie came home first. Despite my intention to furnish my daughter with a plain and sensible name, the 'Joan' had been corrupted years earlier. I had made up a silly little song, 'Joanie, rag and boney', and she had started to join in when I sang it. A head cold had reduced her *n*s to *d*s, and she had insisted on calling herself Jodie from the age of two. So here she stood, a beautiful ruffian, the jewel-like eyes sparkling after a day at her books. She was advanced, they said at school. At the grand old age of five years, she had already stated her intention to be a doctor, 'or a nurse if I can't get to uni-vest-ity'. She flung off the winter coat, prised off the boots, grabbed a biscuit from the tin. 'Mam, have you sold another book?'

'Yes, but not for a lot of money. And it'll be Christmas in a few weeks, you know.'

She nodded, crunched the biscuit in time with the

movement. 'Only we're doing parcels at school, you see, for old people with no dinner on Christmas Day.' She finished the biscuit and arranged her face in a fair imitation of an impish angel. 'I told our teacher that you are a very kind person, Mam. I said we'd give four frozen chickens and four Christmas puds.'

Jodie was always generous with my money. So far, we had adopted several donkeys, half a dozen children in Third World countries, and a granny in the next street. The last, a tired old lady called Myrtle, was besieged twice weekly by my charismatic and benevolent daughter. Jodie washed dishes, broke dishes, went for shopping, bought the wrong things. Each granny-day, I made a secret visit of my own, went round and rescued Myrtle from the results of my daughter's mistakes. Often, this activity took me back to my own childhood, prompted me to remember old Nathaniel 'Good' Evans and the stolen flowers. Jodie was, I suspected, very like me.

'All right,' I sighed. 'But don't promise anything else without asking me first.'

'I knew you wouldn't mind,' answered my tousle-headed philanthropist. 'But in future, I'll ask first.' That 'first' would have crucified my mother, as it came out as 'fairst'. All my children were Scousers, and Mother would blame me for that.

Gerald came in next. He was a quiet boy, industrious, fascinated by numbers. At ten, he had a bank account that contained almost £30, and it was he who had led me through the Hampton Court maze that was decimal currency, the recently imposed system which was tormenting Liddy beyond endurance. I passed on my learning to Liddy, but Gerald would need to spend some time with her. 'You'll have to sort Auntie Liddy out, Gerald. She's still a bit mixed up about the change-over.'

'Right.' He nodded the mousy head, shook the drops of winter rain from his coat, hung it neatly on a peg at the bottom of the stairs. This undemonstrative child needed rhythm and reason to his life, often wore a mark of panic between his eyebrows when things changed, however minimally. Occasionally, I caught him staring at me, as if he wanted to ask questions but, so far, I had been lucky. He loved me insofar as I provided the constancy and stability he needed. In fact, I suspect that his affection for me was strong during childhood, too powerful for him to express properly. 'Get a glass of milk and a biscuit, Gerald. The pie will be ready at about six o'clock.'

Edward came in howling. Immediately, Jodie ran to his side, hugged as much of his plump body as could be encompassed by such young arms. 'What's the matter, Edward?'

The first words defied comprehension, yet Jodie interpreted their meaning with very little difficulty. 'He's lost his PE shoes and he thinks somebody's pinched them.'

My younger son was a professional victim. Wherever he went, he was troubled by others who happened to occupy the same space at the same time. In fact, I had watched him during the pre-school years, had been a witness to several of the misunderstandings that seemed to plague him. A child would ask him a question and Edward, his head bent low, would mumble an answer if his mood happened to be good, or he would simply walk away without coming up with a reply. Sometimes, this anti-social behaviour was ignored, but he took some beatings from those whose tolerance was minimal. Edward clung to me, hated school, would winge and wail until I relented and left him in bed. But as soon as school had started, the minute he realized that he was safe, Edward's headache or stomach upset would improve miraculously.

I often looked at my ginger-haired eight-year-old and wondered whether he might be an interesting specimen, an example of the theory that genetics can triumph over environment. Yet my other two, who seemed to have little or none of their father in them, proved that environment can overcome nature. Although we were not wealthy, I strove to provide stimuli for my children, did my best to entertain and teach them. But Edward was not terribly responsive and I wondered whether he would turn out like Tommo.

Tommo had been a difficult boy, but his offspring were docile by comparison. Although Edward's father had been a wonderful man, I could not help thinking that some of Tommo's genes had perhaps appeared in his nephew, had been once removed by Mother Nature on one of her less sensible days. 'Stop yelling, Edward,' I said as kindly as I could. 'You've probably mislaid the things in the cloak-room or dropped them outside.'

He sniffed back the abundant tears, pushed away his sister, looked at me with those soft grey eyes that might have been attractive had they not been surrounded by so much lard. Edward was a compulsive eater with the ability to dispose of half a pound of biscuits in a single sitting.

'One biscuit,' I warned him. 'Then we're all going for a bath.'

Everyone groaned. They hated the public baths, but they were too large now for cosy spongeings and splashings in front of a fire. 'It's icy cold,' moaned Edward. 'I've been sneezing today,' offered Jodie. Gerald said nothing, but he looked glum.

'We're going.' I relieved Edward of his coat, brought all three outer garments to steam on a maiden in front of the grate. 'One day, we'll have our own bathroom.'

Edward snorted. 'There's no space for a bathroom here.'

'We won't always be here,' I informed him.

Gerald looked at me quizzically. 'Where will we go?'

'Somewhere,' I said airily. 'Not too far, so don't start bothering your head about changes. When I've done another three or four books, we might have a deposit for a better house, one we can buy instead of renting.'

Jodie beamed. 'A garden. A dog and a cat – can we have a rabbit?'

'No, you can have meat pie like everybody else.'

473

She pretended to look hurt. 'I didn't mean a rabbit to eat, Mam, I meant—'

'Kitchen, all of you,' I said. 'Hands and face washed, then, if you've homework, do it here on the table before I set it.'

Someone knocked at the door. I pushed the fringe from my eyes, answered the persistent caller. It was a tall woman with stringy hair and pale eyes. I recognized her face, but could not place her accurately. 'Are you Mrs Thompson?' she asked.

'Yes.'

She thrust an envelope under my nose. 'We live further up, in one of the new houses. I think 22 Wordsworth Street used to be up there, before they pulled the terrace down, like. Well, the woman in the greengrocer's said your name was Thompson, so I've called on the off-chance. I think they must have meant number 2. Anyway, if it's not for you, you can always shove it back in the box, put "not at this address" on the envelope.'

'Thank you.' I turned the cheap buff envelope between my fingers, not understanding why I felt so disturbed. I was definitely number 2, the first house on Wordsworth Street. And I was definitely Mrs Thompson. I looked into the colourless eyes. 'I'll open it later.' When she had walked away, I stood on the doorstep for several seconds. I didn't want to look at this letter. It wasn't a bill or a note from my newly acquired agent, wasn't from Confetti or Anne. Mr Thompson, then? If so, why so?

We went to the public baths, came home shiny and clean, ate our supper of pie and vegetables. The letter stood on the mantelpiece, propped up behind one of a pair of candlesticks from a second-hand shop in Waterloo. It was a smallish envelope, yet it seemed to grow as it sat there, seemed to swell up until it filled my mind and the small sitting room.

When they were all in bed, I took it down, placed it on the tablecloth. My name and the wrong address were printed in block capitals, rather square ones, and the pen

474

had been a cheap ballpoint, because bits of ink had made a blob here and there. I weighed it in my hand, assessed that it contained just one sheet of paper or perhaps two thin pieces.

The same instinct that had stirred on the doorstep forced me into the kitchen. I filled the kettle, set it to boil, almost hopping from foot to foot as I waited for some steam. But I missed my chance, because Liddy's voice came screaming over the back yard wall. 'Laura! Get out here, I've bloody started.' I turned everything off, thrust the letter into a drawer, fled through the house and into number 4.

Jimmy was there looking huge and useless, his hands dangling by his sides. 'What do I do?' he asked me.

'Shift,' I answered. 'Get this lot upstairs and play cards or something.' Liddy, whose dislike of hospitals was almost paranoid, had fought to have this seventh child at home. I wondered fleetingly what its name would be, as the rest, with the exception of Mary, answered to nicknames most of the time. Bonzo, really Mark, chased Short'ouse, really Paul, up the stairs while Jimmy continued riveted to the spot. The expression on his face might have framed the word 'gormless', had it not already been invented. 'Go,' I told him.

He went, feet dragging, his face turning towards the woman he loved. 'Will she be all right?' he threw over his shoulder.

'Out,' I said again.

Liddy rallied. 'Look, Jimmy, I know some of these modern folk want their men there when the baby comes. But you're not standing near me and staring at me private parts, it's not nice. And you'd only faint over.' She gritted her teeth against one of those fierce and unproductive early pains. 'He's bloody thick,' she announced to me when Jimmy had dragged himself away. 'I've done this six times without him, so he can sod off.' She sat on the sofa, then eased herself onto the floor. 'Now, I'll be all right. Just open out this here sofa-bed, then get down to Milton

475

Terrace for that midwife, her with a face like a tinned prune. Gladys, she's called. Gladys Roberts. She's Welsh, but that can't be helped.'

As I unfolded the bed, I wondered what Liddy had against Welsh people. Liddy plainly read my thoughts. 'She doesn't talk, she warbles, goes up and down all the while. It's a nice enough voice till you're in labour, but all that "Ooh, there's lovely you are" gets you down after an hour or two. You'll find the linen clean and ready in the bottom drawer.' She pointed to the dresser, a treasured heirloom that dominated the room. 'And if this one's not a girl, you can stuff it back in, 'cos I've knitted in pink, bought a job lot on Paddy's Market.'

Being present while Liddy gave birth was a great privilege and an experience that I would never forget. She told the midwife to sit in a corner and keep quiet, then my stolid little neighbour ran through every song she knew, some of them highly unsuitable for such a serious occasion. Halfway through 'The Foggy, Foggy Dew', the waters broke. 'Not so much dew as a bloody torrent,' declared Liddy. 'Is that plastic sheet saving the sofa? And put apples on my shopping list, Laura, red delicious and Granny Smiths. Then get that kettle on, me throat's like a birdcage bottom.'

Gladys stirred. 'It would be best if you didn't drink tea, Mrs Mansell. You see, if there are complications, you might need an ambulance and an anaesthetic—'

'Belt up.' Liddy was clearly approaching the highlight of her one-woman show. 'If I need you, I'll send you a sodding telegram. Laura, two sugars and a drop of brandy.'

I concurred, but went easy on the brandy. A drunken mother-to-be would not have gone down well in most operating theatres. I stood in Liddy's kitchen, tried not to laugh out loud as the good woman worked her way through an infamous version of 'Colonel Bogey'.

When I returned, the midwife had been allowed to approach the sofa. 'Push now,' she said gently.

'What the sodding hell do you think I'm doing? Writing

476

me bloody memoirs? And do something about your hands, missus, they're like ice cubes.'

I placed the mug of tea on the table, mopped Liddy's brow with a damp flannel. 'Be nice,' I mouthed.

She winked at me. 'I'm always nice.'

A pink baby girl arrived before midnight, her face screwed up against the brightness of an overhead light. She howled, coughed when the midwife tried to clear her throat, screamed all through her first bathtime. Liddy, radiant enough to deserve a halo, took the tiny creature and placed her at the breast. 'Oh no,' she muttered. 'Not again.'

'I beg your pardon?' lilted the midwife.

'Teeth,' groaned Liddy. 'That's three of them born with their bloody front teeth.' She cuddled the newborn, lifted her head. 'Jimmy?'

'What?' The voice was very near.

'Never mind standing all breathless on them bloody stairs, I'm the one what's doing all the work. It's a girl with teeth. Now get down to Openshaw's chemist and knock him up. He'll be drunk, so make sure he does the order right. You want Cow and Gate – the weak stuff – teats, bottles and one of them sterilizers. The sterilizing stuff's called Milton. And you can drop in at the offy, get me a pint of stout and some toffees for the kids.

'Mrs Mansell,' began the midwife.

'Miss,' snapped Liddy. 'I'll get that soft beggar to marry me when his mother's shuffled off. But for now, I'm miss. That's M-I-S-S.'

Gladys raised her eyes to heaven. She'd been through all this with Liddy before, so she wasn't particularly bothered by the antics. 'Miss Mansell, you shouldn't be needing anything from the off-licence. There's a lovely cup of tea here and—'

'Shut up,' said Liddy. 'I'm celebrating. If this had been a lad, he'd have turned out a right fairy-cake. I've been worried ever since I bought that pink wool.' She eyed Jimmy. 'Are you still here?'

The large man blushed, wiped his cheek with a handkerchief. 'You're a queen, you are, Liddy.'

'And a nice bottle of rum.' She glared at the bewildered Gladys. 'As a present for the midwife.'

'There's no need . . .' Gladys picked up her bowls and went into the kitchen.

'I'm calling her Daisy.' Liddy looked at my bewilderment, realized that my attention had followed the midwife. 'Not her, you pie-can. This one. I'm calling her Daisy.' She impaled Jimmy on her gimlet stare, pushed him out of the house with the sheer power of her will. 'Soft,' she said again to herself. 'That's your dad, Daisy, and he's as daft as they come.'

I examined the child, found her very fair-haired and pretty. 'That's a lovely name. Shall I fetch the kids down?'

Liddy shook her head. 'No, you'd best get back to your own. And thanks, love.'

I smiled at my exhausted friend. 'Thanks to you too, Liddy. There was no midwife for Jodie, was there?'

The small face pulled itself into a comical shape. 'We don't need them, Laura. Good night.'

I was so tired that I fell asleep as soon as my head touched the pillow. At some ungodly hour of the morning, I was wakened by the persistent cry of a healthy newborn. As I lay listening to the latest arrival, I thought about the letter. But it was cold and dark, and I'd been allowing my imagination to run away with me. It would be a circular, a piece of nonsense. I lifted my head, saw the dim outline of the other bed, heard Jodie's gentle breathing, decided that all was well with the world. There was no need to be frightened, no need at all.

It was from Tommo. A sickness rose in my gorge, threatened to hinder my breathing. He knew where we were. There might have been a digit added to the house number, but he was on our trail. I shuddered, made sure that the envelope was intact, tried to praise myself for managing to steam it open.

478

Well, I had got through the night without reading the thing, had even lasted for most of today, but I had finally allowed curiosity to be my master. It was from him. Part of me had felt it, had sensed the venom sealed inside the folds.

I read it again. A social worker called Mrs Melia had tracked us down, had made sure that prisoner 458917 made contact with his son. With good behaviour, he would be out in a couple of years. Meanwhile, a friend of Tommo's would be visiting, would be keeping an eye on us. A friend. A criminal, an ex-prisoner, no doubt.

With fingers that refused to obey, I tried and failed to refold the page into its original shape. Where could we go? Where could we hide and from whom were we hiding? Life was going to be unbearable. Every strange man in the street would be a suspect, every knock at the door would drive me nearer to insanity. I didn't want insanity. That was something I'd encountered before, and I didn't need to pay a second visit. What? Where? When? Every hair on my body seemed to stand on end as the pores opened in reaction to my terror. Yet again, I was a hunted animal.

At last, I had the letter sealed, though I had to put a little fresh glue on the flap. When my hands were calmer, I took a pen and printed NOT AT THIS ADDRESS, RETURN TO SENDER. If the Post Office had any sense, the sorters would realize that a communication from a prisoner was not acceptable. Dead-end letters were opened in the sorting office and returned to source. I stared at the envelope for a long time, knew that Tommo was far too clever to be distracted by my feeble ploy. We would have to move again. I was tired of chopping my existence into separate sections, sick of being on the run all the time.

I sat in Liddy's house for a while, watched fondly while she tended the new baby. She was going to have Jimmy doctored, she said. It was only a small operation, just a couple of quick cuts with the bacon scissors. 'What's happened?' asked my too-astute neighbour.

479

'Nothing.'

'Have you had one of them ejections again?'

'No, they've accepted the book. I'm lucky, I've only been rejected once.'

'Then why the gob?'

I shrugged, tried to make light of the situation. 'A letter, that's all. Just a few words from someone I never wanted to hear from again.'

She whistled. 'Where is he now?'

'Walton.'

'Oh God.' She shifted the child, placed the little body against a shoulder and patted the tiny back. 'He's only round the bloody corner.'

'I know.'

Liddy's face screwed itself up as she went into one of her 'thinks'. 'Jimmy'll know somebody. There's always half a dozen dockers inside waiting to be proved innocent. Jimmy can get him sorted.'

That wasn't an option. 'No. I've returned the letter, sealed it up again. There are no Thompsons on Wordsworth Street. Except . . . the electoral register. My name will be on that. A social worker found us for him.'

She snorted in disgust. 'We were a lot better off before they invented them rotten social workers. They do nothing but damage. There's kids out there being beaten to death, but where's the cavalry? In Walton giving out names and addresses. We had a social worker, though, and she was nice. Stuck up for me in court, she did, said I was a good mother. But most of them are rubbish, bits of girls with bits of qualifications, or middle-aged women with lives that are so bad, they have to go and poke their noses in other folks' muck. Takes their minds off their own mess, like. What are you going to do? When's he coming out?'

'I don't know the answers to those two questions, Liddy.' Though I did know that I'd be leaving Seaforth, leaving Liddy and Jimmy and all those rumbustious kids with silly names and bright, hopeful smiles.

'Jesus, Mary and Joseph.' This phrase didn't sound like blasphemy, was not uttered in Liddy's usually strident tones. The girl was actually praying, had closed her eyes and woven her fingers together behind Daisy's little head. 'He's sick,' she said softly. 'Clever-sick, the sort of ill what never gets diagnosed. With people like him, you don't know what'll happen.'

I knew what was going to happen, all right. I was about to perform one of my famous disappearing acts, would melt away like boiling water on snow, leaving nothing but a muddy pool. This little woman's tears would make that puddle. 'I'm scared, Liddy. He's . . . he's fixed on me, has had me in his sights since we were both children. I'm like a deer caught in somebody's headlights, turned to stone because I don't know which way to run. He's having us watched, I think. Someone who's just been released is going to keep an eye on us. How the hell will we recognize him?'

She looked hard at me. 'You'll be buggering off, then.'

'Possibly.'

The small nose wriggled then sniffed. 'I'll not sleep. I'll not be able to sleep without the noise of that bloody typewriter. And where will you go?'

It wasn't that I didn't trust Liddy. Liddy was one of those people who could be trusted completely, yet my destination would need to remain a secret. If she talked to Jimmy, if the children overheard, if some man in the street offered them sweets and money for Auntie Laura's address . . . 'I'm sorry, Liddy.'

'So am I.' She lay down, placed the baby on her chest, wiped a tear from the corner of an eye. 'We've been good mates, Laura.'

'We have, Liddy. We have indeed.'

When Daisy was three days old, her grandmother died. Jimmy went into overdrive, kept turning up at Liddy's with a sad face, feet so itchy that he couldn't sit still for five minutes at a time, and carrying items of sombre clothing for his children. They were to attend the funeral of a woman who had refused to recognize their mother. Liddy announced that she would not go. 'She'd not want me, Jimmy. She never wanted me in life, so she'd not look kindly on me if I followed her coffin. It'd be like I was gloating.'

'You're coming,' he insisted. 'Laura can hang on to our Daisy.'

I kept out of the argument, continued to glance at the clock to see if the time to pick up my children had arrived. They had always brought themselves home from school, were not pleased about my clucky behaviour. Earlier in the day, my five-year-old had faced me across the table, arms akimbo, an expression of anger ageing her features. 'It's only across the park. You'll be showing me up. Nobody except a baby gets brung home. They'll be calling me names if you come.'

'I don't care. There are some funny people about, Jodie. It's better to be safe than sorry.'

My daughter was far from pleased. Gerald, who had long since risen above matters mundane, had no opinion in the matter. But Edward felt moved to cast his vote. 'I can look after Jodie.' He failed to acknowledge the fact that Jodie was the one who took care of him. 'I'm eight,' he said importantly. 'And I'll make sure nobody talks to us.'

My temper was fraying. So far, I'd seen three new males in our street. One had turned out to be a health inspector who was chasing rats, and two others were selling something or other, but I couldn't settle, didn't dare to call Tommo's bluff. Perhaps it hadn't been bluff. For all I knew, he might have made several friends inside, and one or even half a dozen could be watching me and my children.

'Laura?'

I jumped, looked from Jimmy to Liddy, returned to the present with a jerk that almost sent me reeling. 'Yes?'

'Look at her,' said Liddy. 'Like a cat on hot bricks. There's nobody out there, queen. And Jimmy'll be moving in after the funeral, so he'll make sure no harm comes to you.'

Jimmy touched my arm. 'You can't go on like this, love.'

'I know.'

Jimmy explained what was going to happen, told me that he, Liddy and the children would be going to the church in Halewood, then to the cemetery. I was to take care of the baby until they returned.

The next day, I wheeled Daisy to the school, watched my children as they leapt away from me in an effort to be absorbed as quickly as possible into the playground throng. Gerald was the last to disappear. He stood with his back to the building, watched me warily until I pushed the pram towards the park. My heart lurched as I registered the knowledge that he might be the target. I could imagine Tommo arranging the kidnap, pleading with some old lag, imploring a felon to come and reclaim his son. In such moments, I realized that I did love my children. I was not the best of mothers, but my instincts were in the right place.

The day passed uneventfully. I fed Daisy, dangled her on my knee, enjoyed that warm, powdery smell that always accompanies a clean baby. When my own three were safely delivered from whatever demons awaited them, I sat in my white room, put Daisy in her pram, wrote a few pages of my latest True Hearts romance.

It was about nine o'clock when Liddy rushed in. She was drained white beneath the make-up, was trying to speak in a voice that seemed to be strangled at birth. I thought she was drunk, got up from the table and guided her into the room. 'Liddy? What on earth have you been up to?'

'They're . . . coming,' she managed.

'What? Who's coming?'

She pointed towards the door. 'Jimmy's took the kids somewhere safe. It's the gangs, the ones we used to have trouble with. There's . . . oh, God . . .' Her breathing quickened. 'Fighting. They say I killed her. Me being a Catholic killed her. Then the Catholics say I'm . . . With not being married, with him being a Proddy. All drunk, Laura. Followed me here. Mind that baby.'

She ran out of the house, yelled at the top of her voice. 'Come on, you bastards. Here I am. Come on, catch me if you can.'

My brain engaged a higher gear, crashed into motion, sent me up the stairs. I woke the boys, grabbed Jodie from her bed. 'Coats,' I said. 'Get out into the back yard and stay quiet.'

Jodie rubbed her eyes. 'Why did—'

'No questions,' I snapped. 'Outside. Now.'

We huddled together in the lavatory shed, the baby plastered against my chest, the other youngsters clinging to each other, teeth chattering with cold, their breathing fast and shallow. We heard glass breaking, listened to the whoops of revellers on the warpath. So many battles had been fought in the name of Christianity, I thought. Was there any real good? Was there any perfection on earth, beyond earth?

'Why?' whispered my daughter.

'Drunk,' I answered. 'Drunk and very silly.' Little Liddy had drawn their fire to save her baby. And I was shut out of my house because the invaders had no doubt marked the spot where Liddy had reappeared. I prayed, hoped that Confetti was praying too. If there was good somewhere, we needed to access it quickly.

Eventually, we went back inside, made cups of cocoa, piled coal on the fire. The children were subdued, seemed to understand that questions would be useless, unanswerable. I tucked them into their beds, came down, nursed the whimpering Daisy.

At ten past three in the morning, Jimmy and Liddy returned. He wore a bandage over one eye, had needed treatment at the hospital. Liddy's banter had taken a holiday. Dishevelled and mournful, she took Daisy from me, wept silent tears into the downy hair.

'Are the kids all right?' I asked Jimmy.

He nodded. 'I got them to a mate, then ran down here to find Liddy. We've been across Liverpool that many times, I could write a blinking guide book. Anyway, there's a load of them banged away in the bridewell, and we're all up in court tomorrow. Disturbing the peace if we're lucky, causing an affray if we're not.'

I stared at Liddy. 'What was it all about?'

She lifted her head. 'It's about Jesus when you boil it down. Yes, that's it. We were fighting about a good man and it makes no bloody sense at all.'

Chapter Twelve

Jimmy moved in next door and I tried to feel safe, but the man's working day was long and, the more I thought about it, the more I realized that I could not become yet another of Jimmy Hurst's many responsibilities. And it was plain that the Mansell/Hurst clan would be relocated soon, as the housing people had visited several times in order to assess the level of overcrowding. With two children sleeping downstairs, three in the back bedroom and a baby with the parents, they were definitely bursting out of the small terrace. Liddy and I spent a few days looking at what was available, always coming back in time for me to pick up my three from school. I was developing eyes in the back of my head, had grown invisible antennae that could pick up the scent of a stranger from a distance of a hundred paces.

She didn't like any of the houses. 'Them walls is cardboard, never mind hardboard,' she kept saying. 'And there's too many kids messing about in the streets. I've a job keeping them in as it is, so I don't want them flying round a bloody ghetto. We'll stop here till they fetch the army.'

I stirred my tea, glanced at the pile of proofs that had arrived from the publisher. Oh God, I would have to read through my own stuff yet again. Reading my work was boring and repetitive. Bits that had started out quite well began to look trite after several perusals. Perhaps I should go back to baking, get some scones going, try to sell them to the local shops . . .

'What are you thinking about this time, Laura?' asked Liddy.

'You can't stay here,' I replied. 'They won't allow it. Some of those newer houses have four bedrooms and downstairs toilets too. Just imagine having a bathroom. They're going to close the public baths, you know, because they're making no money. Last time we went, we were the only ones there.'

'There's nothing wrong with an all-over wash.' She snapped a ginger biscuit, dunked it in the cup.

'The kids will grow, they'll get too big for that. They won't want to be stripping off in their teens, will they?'

Liddy sighed, gave me a look that conveyed agreement. 'What about you?'

'I don't know.' I didn't know. The task of moving on with the children was not easy to imagine or to arrange. It would involve new schools, new friends, changes that might impede development. The road in front of my three was already bumpy, as they would need to be told about Tommo. Gerald had been pensive for some time, was working up to something. Any minute now, the questioning must start and the answers must be given. At some stage, I would need to explain a few things, as I believed firmly that children's rights should be respected. There could be no lies, yet I was grateful for having come this far without making explanations. For as long as possible, I wanted to pave the path with security, hoped to give them a stable start so that the inevitable shocks might be minimized, cushioned by the strength gained from me. Did I have enough of that strength? 'I suppose we'll have to go. I'm frightened to death every time there's a knock at the door.'

She nodded, took another biscuit. 'Get the welfare to help you. It's their fault, anyway. It was one of their lot what told your owld feller where to find you. Tell them you want shifting.'

I considered the suggestion. 'It could happen again. I want a different area, somewhere away from here. If we let one social worker have the address, it could easily be found by the Walton Witch.' That poor woman had been given many titles, and this last one had stuck. 'I've got to get up and go, Liddy.'

She stared into my fire. 'Are you going before Christmas?'

'Probably.' Another happy Christmas with the Mansells would have crippled me. I needed to make the decision and act on it quickly before I faltered. Leaving Seaforth was going to be difficult enough without seasoning the occasion with Yuletide tears.

Liddy yawned, glanced inside the pram where Daisy slept. 'It's either her or him keeping me awake at night. A part-time bloke's all right, 'cos you get to be yourself some days. But with him living here all the while, it's like being a film star, always at my best.'

I looked at her best. The hair was still rendered lifeless by regular applications of peroxide, and her teeth were in need of attention. She always wore thick make-up, the sort of panstick that might survive in a dance hall, though it looked garish and out of place in daylight. But Liddy's charm had nothing to do with the packaging. There was life in her face, energy, movement, naughtiness. 'He won't mind how he sees you, Liddy. You could wear a potato sack and he'd still love you.'

She grinned. 'Love me? If he loves me any more, I'll be having bloody quads. How do I put him off?'

'You don't. Just get yourself equipped and hope for the best.'

'Equipped?' The over-plucked and blackened eyebrows disappeared beneath a fringe of blond candy floss. 'Listen, I've had one born clutching the flaming coil, and two that got past a Dutch cap and plenty of that suicidal jelly.' She held up her hand. 'I know it's not suicidal, but I can't think at the minute. I don't want no more, Laura. I'm thirty-eight, I should be settling down and doing the knitting. See, I used to think I was immunized, like. We had our Mary, then no more for donkey's years. But they suddenly started popping out regular, falling on the floor every time I stood up. So I've told him to get one of them operations. He says he's going to India for it, 'cos they get a free radio thrown in. Cheer up. Your gob would stop a wedding, honest.'

'I'll be all right. We'll miss you, all of you.'

'Ditto.' The eyes shone too brightly. 'I know, queen, I do understand.' Her voice was suddenly soft and gentle, not her own at all. 'But don't tell nobody where you're going, love. It's too serious and dangerous for that. See, he might even be having us watched, me and Jimmy and the kids. He's found you before and he's not lost his nastiness, not where he is. There's no way you can risk them kids. If he comes for Gerald, you'll never forgive yourself.' She stood up, angled the pram so that it might get past the furniture. 'I'll think about you. Every day, I'll say a prayer.'

When she had left, it was as if I had already lost her. Just as I'd lost other friends like Ernie and Ida Bowen from Horsa Street, Hetty Hawkesworth from that hamlet near St Helens, Frank . . . Oh, Frank. More than a friend, so much more. He would have loved Liddy, would probably have likened her to a small bird, perhaps a canary or a yellow budgie. And we would have laughed, not unkindly, might have invented a new language for her, something like Liddy-speak or Liddy-propisms. Sometimes, I ached for Frank, felt like an empty vessel, a small thing that was being tossed about on the tide of life. He had been my stability, my anchor. And Tommo had taken him away, had removed him and all my friends except for Anne and Auntie Maisie.

I brought the children home, went through the usual routine, cook, feed, clear up, wash the dishes. We practised the three-times table for Jodie, drew a map of Britain for Edward, left poor Gerald to his own devices. He sat on the sofa, head in a book, his brain geared towards solving mathematical problems that were a mystery to me. They had told me at the school that he was talented, that his teacher was having to set special work for him. My Gerald was going to be a high-flier, something in the city, no doubt. My Gerald was going to ask questions. Now. Tonight. In one sense, there's a lot to be said for single parenthood, because the lone mother or father is tuned in all the time, doesn't get the chance to off-load difficult tasks. It was down to me, and I had to cope.

When the younger two were in bed, he dawdled at my elbow, watched as I dragged a ruler down my proofs. 'Why are you doing that?'

'I'm looking for mistakes.'

'Do you make mistakes?' he asked.

'Yes. So do typesetters and copy-editors and professional proof-readers. Everyone makes mistakes.'

'I don't.' This wasn't pride – he merely stated a fact. 'But numbers are kind of absolute, I suppose. Easier, you know.' Absolute. He knew words like absolute, could connect with all kinds of concepts, was capable of analysing language and number, of understanding even the subtler aspects of a word.

'Yes. For you, but not for me.' For me, few things were absolute. But I knew that this boy was going to question me tonight, had felt his nervousness for days. Yes, it would happen now. Absolutely.

He showed no inclination to go upstairs, so I sat back. This older boy of mine did not indulge in conversations that were unnecessary. I waited, watched his deliberately calm face, knew that it masked a thousand questions, a million emotions. 'What is it, son?'

'What happened to Frank?'

My heart missed a beat. I hadn't thought that Frank would be remembered. Clearly, Gerald was aware that Frank was not his father.

'He . . . he died,' I mumbled. 'He bumped his head and fell into a river.'

Gerald nodded. 'And he wasn't my dad.'

'No.'

He sat down opposite me, looked me full in the face. 'Have I got a dad?'

'Everyone has.'

'Alive?'

Here came the crunch, then. Was he old enough – was I old enough to manage this terrible business? I took a deep breath, longed for a glass of whisky, brandy, anything that might fuel my brain and take away the anxiety. 'He's alive. He's . . . er . . .' I moved my eyes, could not bear to meet that penetrating gaze. This was an exceptional boy, one who could not be fooled, not easily, anyway. 'He's in prison.'

My son nodded gravely. 'I've been in that box under your bed, Mam. It was a week ago. I'm sorry. I was looking for things, just looking . . .'

He had been searching for himself, had been wondering who he was, where he had come from. 'It's all right, Gerald.'

'Photos,' he said. 'Of you and Frank, of me when I was a baby. Some with Edward too.' He paused. 'Is Frank Edward's dad? Because Frank lived with us then, when Edward came.'

'Yes.' My voice was squeaky, so I cleared my throat. 'Frank was Edward's dad.'

'Jodie?' he asked seriously.

'She and you are Bernard Thompson's children.'

He was ten years old, and his face was suddenly lined like that of an old man. Gerald was a boy with great dignity and self-control, yet his forehead showed the depth of his misery as he homed in on the final chapter. 'My father killed Edward's father. It's in that newspaper with the photos. And that's why he's in prison. And he hit Auntie Anne too.'

I longed to reach out and hold him, but this was not a child who wanted to be pitied. Soon, he would work out that he and Edward were cousins as well as brothers, at which point he could well suffer a crisis of identity. Or would he? Sometimes, I wished I'd had an education, but nothing in the world of academia seemed to offer the training I needed. To be a mother, a person required no certificate to prove competence. The hardest and most important job in the world was being done by amateurs who groped in the dark . . .

He clasped his hands on the table, looked like a priest at prayer. 'That was a mistake, Mam. Marrying Bernard Thompson, I mean.'

I smiled reassuringly. 'Oh no, Gerald. If there'd been no Tommo, there'd be no you and no Jodie.'

His knuckles were white. 'So you don't mind me being here, then?'

My hands grasped his, felt the tension that ran through the body of this little boy. 'I love you,' I said. 'I love all three of you. But you're very special, because you're the first. There was a time when I had just you, and that was a lot of fun. You didn't speak much, but you watched me all the time, wanted to learn things. Gerald, never apologize for being born. I don't hit children, but I'd probably lose my temper good and proper if you thought I didn't love you. We'd be like Liddy and Short'ouse, you running and me chasing you with the yard brush.'

A corner of his mouth twitched. 'I still don't talk much, do I?'

'No. But that doesn't mean you don't feel things. Often, those who say the least think the most. I've done my best some of the time, son. But there's only me between the three of you, so you may not get the attention you need.'

His eyes seemed to darken to a smokier grey. 'You're a good mother,' he said brusquely. 'I wouldn't swap.'

I laughed softly. 'Gerald, I should go to the top of the class and give out the pencils.'

'Why?'

I got up, pulled the child into my arms. He was brave and brainy, too clever for anything less than the truth. I decided there and then that I would always tell them the truth, even when it was difficult, even when a lie might be an easy option. But for now, I insisted on congratulating myself. 'Gerald,' I said, 'I think I've just passed my exams.'

*   *   *

492

Finding somewhere was hard. I got Liddy to pick up the children, made her promise that they would not have to risk the short journey from school without some adult vigilance. The *Liverpool Echo* travelled with me, rolled up under my arm, circles drawn round sections of the 'To Let' section. I wanted private sector, needed to get my name out of the council lists.

Because of the existence of seven Georgina Dawn novelettes, I had managed to save a few hundred pounds, so there was no problem when it came to what the locals called key money. I would manage the deposit and the advance rent, but I was desperate in my quest for something that would please my kids. After all, they would be leaving so much, would be experiencing so many changes and losses that I needed to compensate them.

There were houses with gardens, bathrooms and no school within walking distance. I found a good flat near enough to schools, but this accommodation allowed no children or pets. Each time, there was something missing, a reason why I decided to reject the place. After three consecutive days of searching, I came back to Seaforth through chill November rain, sat dejectedly in my little house, feet in a bowl of hot water, hands wrapped round a glass of cheap brandy.

'No luck?' asked Gerald.

'Not yet. We'll find somewhere, don't worry.'

He was worried. There was change coming, and my oldest child hated change. 'A bathroom would be nice,' he conceded. 'But make sure there's a good school nearby. I'll be moving into the seniors soon.'

'Gerald, we'll all be together. Where we live doesn't really matter, as long as we stick by one another. As for school – you'll do well just about anywhere. Talent will out, remember that.'

He apportioned me a tight smile, followed his brother and sister to bed. Gerald was a good kid. Jodie, too, was coming on a treat. If only Edward would shape a bit, if only he would stop wingeing and whining. Life was strange. I had two children from a monster, one from a wonderful man. Tommo's were turning out great, while Frank's had a chip on his shoulder the size of a canal barge. But it was no use sitting here indulging my ideas about Mother Nature and genes that were once-removed.

I slopped about the room, feet dripping as I searched for a magazine. There was an article somewhere, a piece about middle children. The theory that middle children miss out on things had been expounded by an agony aunt, a kindly female with four chins and strong opinions. I might even find an answer, or some guidance about how to cope with a boy like Edward. After years of stomach aches, I had run out of patience, was sending him to school whatever his complaint. Because of my determination, he had been brought home with measles and chicken pox, but fortunately, the teachers understood my mistrust of Edward's illnesses. The poor lad was looking for something, possibly love, attention, affection . . .

Someone knocked at the door. Maybe I thought it was one of Liddy's brood, or perhaps I was rather engrossed in looking for the magazine. Whatever, I was too tired to be careful, too busy to be alert. 'Come in, it's not locked,' I called.

The door swung open with menacing slowness, causing the hairs on the back of my neck to rise. I was reminded of those old black and white horror films, all creaky doors and dark nights, tall servants with white hair and white gloves, a flash of thunder illuminating the hand that holds the knife.

I stood, transfixed and wide-eyed, my feet bare, my hands clammy with cold sweat. A tall figure was framed in the doorway. It was a man. He was broad and strong, with grey clothes and a white scarf at the neck. Frost in the air marked his breathing, made it hang about his head in wreaths of mist. The rain had stopped, then, I thought irrelevantly. My tongue found itself at last. 'Are you looking for someone?'

'Mrs Thompson?' The words were clipped, precise. 'Are you Mrs Thompson?'

To say no would have been foolish. 'Who wants to know?'

He stepped into the room, his height dominating the small area as soon as he closed the door. This action was performed softly, as if he needed to be quiet. Why? Who had sent him? 'Who sent you?' I asked, the words almost sticking in my throat.

'No-one sent me. I am here at my own behest.'

Behest. What an old-fashioned word. I backed away, rested my hands on the table's edge. 'I don't know you.' This statement sounded feeble, childish. 'I'm . . . I'm expecting a friend to call shortly.'

He looked me over. 'Your feet will be cold. Dry them and put on your slippers.' He waved an arm towards the fender where my mules were warming. 'Don't be afraid of me. I have not come here to do any harm.'

I blundered about, managed to get the slippers to stay on feet that were rigid with tension. For a criminal, for a messenger from Tommo, this was a very gentlemanly person. But crime was not the property of one section of society. In fact, most criminals probably came from the upper strata, from levels where detection was almost impossible. As I turned to face him once more, I wondered how many of the big fish actually got caught. After all, money could silence many a complaint. 'What do you want?'

'May I sit down?'

I nodded, watched as he pulled out a dining chair and lowered himself into it. He was about fifty-ish, I guessed, a handsome man whose thinning hair had once been brown, almost black. Streaks of iron-grey sat among the darker strands, allowing him an air of dependability. His eyes were hazel, I thought, quite crinkly at the edges. They were the eyes of a man who smiled a lot. He was smiling now. 'My name is Starling, Ben Starling.'

He seemed to expect an answer. 'Laura Thompson.'

495

'Yes.' He steepled his fingers, rested his chin on the apex. 'I know your husband.'

The clock ticked so loudly that I thought it might jump off the mantelpiece at any explosive second. And I could feel my heart beating right through my body, causing my fingertips to thud, my limbs to tremble. 'I am no longer married, Mr Starling.'

'Ah. But Bernard Thompson does not recognize divorce. As far as he is concerned, you are still his property.'

In spite of the grim situation, my temper bubbled, moved me to debate the issue. 'Nobody belongs to anyone. No person can own another. The man is crazed, has always been mad.'

'Quite. There is a boy named Gerald?'

I stumbled over the rug, arrived at the table rather clumsily. My head seemed to bend of its own accord, was forcing the rest of me to face up to this unwelcome visitor. 'My children are in my custody, my sole custody. Their care and control is my business and nobody else's. He can't have Gerald, can't ever see him. If I have to kill the man, I'll keep him away from my children.'

Ben Starling took hold of my hand. 'My dear lady, I am here to protect you.'

I pulled away from him. 'Protect me? Like Al Capone protected his victims? Look, I want nothing to do with you. In fact, if you don't leave my house at once, I'll scream. Liddy next door will get the police. And that'll be you back where you belong, mister.'

He sighed. 'Mrs Thompson, I am a law-abiding citizen of this country. Here is my card.' He took a beautiful leather wallet from a pocket of what looked like £100-worth of suit. The overcoat was a Crombie, I thought. When the card was on the table, I picked it up gingerly, holding it along its edges, as if I might become contaminated by it.

'You see?' he asked pleasantly.

'There's a lot of crime committed in your sphere, Mr Starling.'

'I agree.' He did not pick up the card when I laid it on the tablecloth. 'But I am a mere prison visitor, Mrs Thompson. I spend time with those whose families do not come to the prison. Your ex-husband is a lonely man.'

'Do you know what he did?' My tone was rising in pitch, climbing the slope to hysteria.

'I never ask. I never ask because I don't wish to know. Many of us have pasts that are best left alone. I have come here simply to warn you.'

'I've already had my written warning, thanks.'

He nodded gravely. 'So you are aware that he is determined to frighten you?'

'He will try to terrorize me for the rest of my life, I think. But what has that to do with you? If you're a dealer in gemstones and precious metals' – I referred to the wording on the card as I spoke – 'then why spend time in a prison?'

He shrugged. 'Because like the men in Walton, I have a past, a past I never discuss. When I go to the jail, I see caged birds. They have offended, I understand only too well that they are criminals. But to be locked up is a terrible thing. So I do what I can for them, try to make life a little happier for those who cannot see fields and trees. Most of all, those men's minds are trapped. They lose all faith and all hope—'

'And they lost all charity before they went in there, didn't they? How can you pity thieves and murderers? Why don't you spend what's left of your charity on people who deserve it?'

He studied me for a few seconds. 'Did you never steal?'

My eyes moved of their own accord towards the typewriter that sat, idle for now, on a small table next to the stairway door. 'Not directly, no.' My cheeks were alight with shame. 'But I've fought my corner, protected my kids, made sure I had the equipment necessary to make a living. But I don't hurt people. And . . . and I've made a donation to the NSPCC.' There were times when I felt really lame and foolish. This was one of those times.

'For the typewriter.' This was not a question.

'Yes.'

He loosened the scarf, made it sit outside the heavy greatcoat. 'Most of the time, I try not to judge, attempt to draw no lines between offenders. Who am I to say that a man is good or bad? Many in prison are victims, some are held after mistakes that started off small and foolish. But there is one category that cannot be ignored.'

'And Tommo is a member of that group.'

He nodded slowly, thoughtfully. 'Tommo, yes. That's the name he gets in Walton, too.' He thought for a moment, fixed his gaze on me. 'He's a dangerous man, Mrs Thompson. He should be in a hospital for the criminally insane, I think. There's a power in him, a terrible anger that nourishes him and turns him into some sort of hero among the socially defective. He possesses a magnetic force, the sort that took Hitler from house-painter to Führer. Tommo hates, nurtures the hatred, enjoys getting what he calls his own back. I listen in there, Mrs Thompson, and I have worried for you.'

'Oh.' It was impossible to find something to say.

'You must leave here. He has been courting the attention of prisoners who are due to be released. And he has chosen carefully, concentrating on Liverpudlians with a track record of violence. As he cannot deal with you himself, he is trying to appoint deputies. So you will need to move on immediately.'

I should have been grateful, but all I could feel was an unreasoning anger born of exhaustion and disappoint-ment. Searching for a new home was not my idea of fun, and this fellow was putting poison-laced icing on a day that had already been far from perfect. 'It's all right for you, isn't it?' I yelled, knowing that I was being rude and unfriendly. Despite my guilt, I was swept along like an unwilling passenger on a roller-coaster ride. 'There are three kids up there, three little children who've never done anything to deserve this. They didn't ask to be born, did they? I know what you're saying. For weeks, I've been aware of the threats. But I can't find anywhere. It's almost Christmas and we've nowhere to go.'

His face wore no expression as I ranted and raved. He simply sat and waited until I had finished. 'Three children?' he asked. 'From what your ex-husband said, I thought there was just the one.' His English was perfect, yet it was not quite right, was slightly out of rhythm.

I closed my mouth with a snap.

'However,' he went on smoothly, 'there is no need for any explanation.'

'Thank you.' The sarcasm was plain.

'You don't understand me, Mrs Thompson. My belief is that every day is a new start for each one of us. The past does not make a person what he or she is. Intentions, goals, desires and needs – these are the prime constituents of the human soul. You must begin anew, my dear lady. At this moment in time, you need help. Because of the season, many prisoners are being considered for release, prisoners whose sentences are almost completed. There is compassion in the judicial system, and men with children may well be let out before the due date. Some of those men are under your husband's influence. So you will come now. Well, tomorrow.'

I stared at him, my eyes wide and my jaw dangling on its hinge like a worn gate. 'I don't know you. Come where?'

'To my house.'

My veins were throbbing again. 'You expect me to lift three children from their beds tomorrow morning, then lead them into the home of a stranger? I wasn't born yesterday, Mr Starling. I've learned the hard way that trust is a mug's game. They're babies, they're in need of support and guidance. I can't just whip them off without explaining why.'

He laid his hands on the table. The fingers were tanned, the nails well shaped and clean. 'Their bodily safety is the immediate aim. Stay here and someone will suffer. Bernard Thompson is an organizer. He can cope with everything from drug-smuggling to full-scale riot. Frightening you is

499

not my intention, yet I feel that you must accept a fact. That fact is that you will be safer in the house of a stranger than in your own home. So you will come.'

I found that I was held by him, riveted by the intelligence in his eyes, in his words. He was an unusual man, one who was not quite . . . not quite real. The falseness lay in his accent, in that too-perfect English which rolled from his tongue with something that fell just fractionally short of ease. Yet he was not dehumanized by this frailty, because his face was lived-in, pleasant, kind. 'Is it so urgent, then, Mr Starling?'

'Oh yes. One of the men, a good soul who was lost for a while, is a person I visit from time to time. Tommo failed to recruit him, and the man found out what was afoot, told me last week.'

I swallowed. 'What is afoot? Come on, I can take it.' Could I? Of course I could, I'd taken rape, beatings, verbal abuse . . .

'The general opinion is that Tommo wants you dead. He has money, a stash hidden somewhere on the outside. This money has come from drugs and extra tobacco. How he gets things in and out is a mystery, but it seems that most things are within his power. If he wants, he gets, if he shouts, a dozen people jump. He may put out a contract on you.'

It was like being in a film, one of those gangster movies that never ring true. Was this my Eliot Ness? Moments earlier, I had compared him to Capone. 'Do those things really happen?' I asked.

'Yes, they do.'

I was a mother. As a mother, my chief function was to protect my children. There were things I didn't know, things I couldn't understand. Like who was this man, where did he live, why did he want to help me? But there were facts, too, truths that should not be ignored. Tommo was a fact, so was his evil. If we stayed here in this house, we would become victims within days or weeks. If we moved into the unknown for a while, if we stayed with

Mr Starling until another place became available, we would have a chance of survival. 'Where do you live?' I asked.

'Waterloo.'

'Not far, then.'

'Far enough. Nothing will happen while you are in my care. I liaise with police and prison officers. You will be safe.'

I was not sure, could not work out my future. 'Perhaps we should leave Liverpool.'

'Perhaps. But you need time to work out the answers to such questions. This period will be spent with me. I have a large house, so you will have the privacy you need. And you may tell the children that you are coming as my housekeeper. This will preclude the need to give them the truth.'

I bowed my head, remembered Gerald's conversation. 'I have vowed that I will always tell them the truth, even when it's not easy.'

'Sometimes, the truth can be cruel. And there is a time for that, a better time for these explanations. The little ones will be warm and fed, they will be safe with me.'

This Mr Starling had spoken earlier of Hitler's hypnotic power, of Tommo's ability to influence others. Yet Mr Starling himself was a persuader, a man with an invisible halo about his person. Was it his voice, his appearance, his kindness? I didn't know.

Not knowing, I took the children and left my house at the end of November, carried few belongings with me. When we reached the end of Wordsworth Street, Gerald noticed something in my face. 'We're not coming back, are we, Mam?'

'No.'

Jodie tugged at my arm. 'What about our things?'

I sighed, heard my breath quivering on a sob. 'A big van will come tomorrow, Jodie.' Everything had to look normal, Mr Starling had said. I was to tell nobody of my destination, was to leave the house as if we were going to school. 'I've got a new job,' I said with forced brightness. 'We're going to look after a man called Mr Starling.'

'That's a bird,' grumbled Edward. 'And you've got a job, you write books.'

I dragged them along, wanted to get out of the area before anyone from Liddy's house appeared. 'Bird or no bird, Edward, we are going to stay with him. He has a garden and two sheds where he looks after injured seagulls and other birds.'

'That's why he's called Starling,' giggled Jodie. 'He's a bird man.'

The Bird Man of Alcatraz. I thought about Burt Lancaster, wondered whether this Starling chap had been a prisoner who looked after feathered patients. After all, he seemed to have an affinity with criminals and an affection for birds. 'In cages', he had said when talking about men serving time. He was a man of mystery. And I was taking Gerald, Edward and Jodie into the home of a person I didn't know.

I allowed myself a last look down our street, was glad that it had been ours for a while. These people had minded us so well, so lovingly. There was the greengrocer who gave me tick – 'Pay next Friday, queen', the chemist who treated Jodie's chicken pox, actually coming to the house with calamine and cotton wool. 'I've seen less spots on a leopard,' he said that day. We were moving further away from Liverpool, along the coast towards Southport and gentility. I would miss my sorties to Williamson Square where the pigeons collected to steal my sandwiches, where 'Old Jack' cavorted in his army greatcoat to entertain the pram-bound infants. The markets, the stations, the flower sellers in the streets, the streetwise lads who sold tea towels from a suitcase, 'Hurry up, missus, the cops are coming'.

He had driven me away again. How big was England? How much further would we need to run? Perhaps I would finish up in Ireland with Confetti and her family, would learn to milk a cow and churn butter.

I hadn't told anybody, couldn't risk anybody. Auntie Maisie, my cousin Anne – even Liddy and Confetti were in the dark this time. We were moving on again, going into the unknown.

Part Four

Chapter One

I saw three ships come sailing by, but not on Christmas Day in the morning; also, there were more than three. It was a couple of weeks ago, and all because Mrs Columbus of Genoa had a baby boy in 1451. If Christopher had been a girl, then Haiti might never have been discovered, might have failed to develop its strange religious mixture of Catholicism and voodoo. Christina Columbus would have sat at home, all demure, ironing her wimple, would surely have broken her dear mother's heart if she'd given up the harpsichord and gone off with a gang of roughnecked sailors. Anyway, the problem never arose.

So, during August, in this year of our Lord 1992, sail from Italy, Spain, America, Portugal and Britain swayed gently into the Mersey's docks to celebrate the fact that no-one really knows who discovered the US of A. The Portuguese claim that they were the first invaders, while poor old Columbus, whose statue was removed from Liverpool a few years ago, thought he had found Japan. The man was a fair-to-middling coastal pilot but, as a navigator, he should have stuck to ironing wimples.

The beautiful vessels stayed awhile, then drifted out to sea again. On the day of the ships' mass departure, I parked myself on the beach, the bird-watching binoculars hanging from my neck. There were thousands of people on the sands, an army of invaders who ignored traffic cones and parked just about anywhere. Those cones must have gone forth and multiplied during the previous night, there were acres of them. Offending vehicles would be clamped, but I didn't want to spoil anybody's fun by issuing a verbal warning. Ben, wrapped in his Sunday rug, sat in the wheelchair behind the railings, eyes and mind focused elsewhere, hands clasped in his lap as if prayers were being said.

It's amazing what it does to you, the sight of an almost silent exodus as it pulls away towards the horizon. Grand, Armada-ish ships hoisted sail and flags while fussy little dock boats scurried behind, like ducklings in the wake of a mother. The Liver birds, tall and too bold to need maternal guidance, would have claimed the best view, were no doubt staring down with arrogance upon the labouring sailors. Prop planes did a fly-past, their clever stunts vying for attention with the sea-bound vessels. Helicopters hovered, reminded me of busy insects, dragonflies, perhaps, searching for stagnant water. They were mere babies, these flying machines, could not hold centre-stage for too long. In every British breast there is an affection for the sea, a love that has been handed down in our blood. We noticed the fliers, but we watched the ships.

The sea-going traffic moved on just as life moves on, no pause, no backward glance at a middle-aged woman and a feeble old man. That's the way it should be, *perpetua mobile*, go forth and find the future. The creamed wakes of foam settled, flattened, became one with the sea. How speedily they pass, these moments of pure and painful joy. Soon, a flotilla of smaller vessels scuttled out, prows aimed towards the edge of the world. Too quickly, they would be gone. Some drunken youths staggered along the shore, began to render a maudlin version of 'The Leaving of Liverpool', toneless and disparate voices punctuated by heavy belches. They giggled like girls, took another swig of lager, drew breath, tortured the song anew.

Ben looked chilled, so I wheeled him back to the house, switched on the TV. On screen, eminent people sat on the Albert Dock making comments about steamships and the death of sail. Bearded men in green sweaters were singing sea-shanties on the remodelled and just-too-perfect dock. Silly teenagers jumped about, trying to wave to

Mam and Dad. I had been wrong, because not all the ships were gone. A lone Russian remained, crippled, no money to mend her damage. The people of Liverpool would care for her and the crew, would have a collection, see them right. And one or two of the naughty girls would probably address the problem, give themselves to Russia with love. At a knock-down price, of course.

'Did you like the ships?' I asked my husband.

'No room. Too many of us,' he replied. 'The child in the corner is dead. Don't cry.'

'Ben, where are you?' I knelt at his feet while the television carried on singing, commentating. 'Where is this place in your head? Ben, where do you go?'

He looked at me, through me, his lips moving quickly. 'We'll never get home. I don't want to go back, because there's no-one there for me. Did you tell them about the fresh vegetables?' He was not speaking about this home, was referring to some other time, some other location.

I nodded. 'Yes. The matron knows that you prefer fresh. What do you think about, darling? When you shout about dogs and stoves, where is that place?'

Ben smiled, almost fooled me yet again into believing that he might get better. 'Laura. My mother will like you. She's down there mending nets. Did you see her? We drank her wine and she wasn't pleased. When we've taken everything from them, they join the other queue. In the strawberry yoghurt.'

My husband is crackers. He comes home rarely these days, is allowed out for just a few hours. I am lonely. I sit here now, gaze at the empty water, remember the day of the tall ships, think about the effort I made to communicate with him. Hopeless. Well, today I go to see the expert. My own health has a clean bill at last. I am dismissed by the surgeon, sacked by the psychiatrist. Now, I can fight for my Ben.

Despite the fact that the hair is beating a fast retreat, Gordon Watson-Jones is a very attractive man. He has dark brown eyes that wrinkle in the corners whenever he deigns to award me his full attention, a strong, muscular body and enough self-confidence not to use aftershave. I believe that smell is important, that most of us are attracted to the opposite sex by something subliminal, and that our nostrils play no small part in the pairing-off ritual. Men who smell of perfume have never appealed to me. The truly clean male needs no olfactory signal beyond the one that escapes from his own washed skin. Plain soap allows a man's honest, yeasty scent to come through, the delicious aroma of uncomplicated masculinity.

I am not in the market for a partner, but I enjoy window-shopping. This senior doctor is like an expensive hat in a Bond Street window, look but don't touch. Anyway, he is a mere tool, something I need to use for Ben's sake.

He taps the ends of his fingers together, stares down at some notes, blinks just once, clears his throat. 'How is he behaving these days?' After a split second, he rediscovers the surname, staples 'Mrs Starling' to the end of his question.

'He's completely haywire. I'm here to ask you to use him as a guinea-pig. There must be some research, some untested drug—'

'He's getting worse?'

I nod. 'He jumps about in time, recognizes me, then scarcely knows me, complains about the food in the nursing home, asks to see his mother. Ben never talked about his past. Nor did I, not often, anyway. For the pair of us, the marriage was a fresh start. So I know nothing about him.'

'And you need to know now?'

'Yes. There's one particular situation that haunts him. He is spending more and more time locked into some dreadful scenario. I want him out of that.'

He looks up. A woman could drown in those eyes. Another woman, that is. 'There's no way of arresting Alzheimer's,' he says.

'Vitamins?' I ask hopefully, yet without hope. 'Vitamins, minerals, electrolytes?'

He smiles broadly, pulls at his collar. 'You've been reading again. Look, everything logical has been tried, everything that's readily available has been fed to or dripped into patients. We don't know the answer. It's important that you accept our limitations.'

I allow my gaze to wander round the consulting room. If I slow down, I might be able to persuade him to phone America, Canada, anywhere that has control groups being assessed. This is a predictably brown and green room, leather couch, tall antique bookcases, square-paned windows that overlook Rodney Street, the Pool's pool of medical excellence. My chair is of beige leather and he occupies its twin. Three of the walls are heavy with diplomas and seascapes. 'He's had his chips, hasn't he?' There's no need to be formal. Manners won't help, etiquette won't buy a reprieve. Anyway, this is just another bloke, the one who is qualified to blow the final whistle, no extra time for injury.

He takes a deep breath. 'A few improve. Some stay at the same level for many years, others deteriorate quickly.'

I will not weep. This consultation is costing £40, so I'd best not waste time with tears. 'I want you to send us abroad. There's no worry about money. There must be somebody somewhere who knows something and—'

'Mrs Starling, your husband is in no fit state to travel. You are just out of hospital too, aren't you?'

I eye him steadily. 'The doctors have sacked me. As a patient, I am currently unemployed.'

Our eyes lock and I no longer find him attractive. There is something cold-blooded about a hanging judge. He won't even try to save the condemned man, isn't even making the effort to research the bloody disease. He tunes in to my thinking, opens a drawer, pulls out charts, lists, graphs, photocopies of articles. 'I do keep abreast of my speciality. I'm sorry. I find myself apologizing every day when I face people like you, men and women whose relatives have no quality of life. All I can tell you is that we're searching. The whole world is looking for this particular answer. Why does it hit some old people and not others? Why do some fairly young patients develop these symptoms while others continue to a century with their mental capacities intact?'

I feel my eyes pricking, blink to contain the flood. 'He's such a wonderful man, you see. He took me in, took my children in and became a father to them. After doing so much good, why does he have to get this bloody awful thing?'

He puts a hand to his mouth, drops it after a split second. This small gesture tells me something, makes me know that he is sharing my pain. Perhaps he is, after all, a human being. 'Mrs Starling, I would give a lot to be able to help you, to help the next person who will occupy that chair. Apart from anything else, I'd be a very wealthy man if I could cure your husband.'

'He would be better off in some ways if . . . I wish . . .'

'No.' He shakes his head. 'There's no cause for that sort of thinking, please don't—'

'He is suffering. The torture is in his head, in his mind. Look, I've had a couple of breakdowns, but they were pieces of pat-a-cake compared to this. He's haunted, tormented. I don't even know what it is that crucifies him. I can't keep him at home, can't look after him, so he's with strangers. What sort of an existence is that, when he sits in his own soil till someone cleans him, babies him? You don't know him, nobody knows him. Ben is a dignified man. No way would he want to be nursed like an overgrown infant. He can't decide, deduce, remember anything decent. It's our duty to decide for him, and I know that he wouldn't want any of this. He's getting stuck somewhere in the fourth dimension, talking to real people who aren't there any more. And you tell me he can last for years like this.'

He allows a short pause after my outburst. 'Yes, he may live for a while yet. He's a strong man with a strong heart.'

'And you would condemn him to a half-life, when his particular portion is full of dread?'

'Do you understand the alternative, Mrs Starling? Have you really grasped the concept? Have you?'

I haven't. I look at Watson-Jones and I realize that I haven't even skirted the edges of the idea. 'I'm sorry.'

'Don't be.'

'It's just that we don't let our animals . . . well, we don't. Ben is one of the most magnificent people I have ever known. So solid, he was, so kind and dependable without being a bore. We were happy.'

'Yes.'

I feel a sudden urge to confess, to purge myself and get rid of the guilt that always hovers over me. Like a Catholic in confession, I blurt it all out, not to a priest, but to a man who is paid to listen to me. 'I took a lover. Ben always said that I should if he became senile. There was no-one there to comfort me, you see. My children are grown, have been in and out of the nest for years, are now gone for ninety per cent of the time. I was hurt, you see. I had pain and I needed to be held.' I beg myself to stop indulging this unbecoming self-pity, yet I continue regardless. 'Ben is still my husband and I love him. I became ill myself, was put into hospital, had surgery. It's awful, because my lover's wife died of the very disease I survived.' I think about Carol, think about poor Robert.

He coughs quietly. 'Do you feel remorse because you survived?'

'I don't know. In a sense, the breakdown was born of relief, because I couldn't believe that I was better, wondered whether I deserved to recover so completely.' I remember that I said none of this to the psychiatrist. 'You're the first person I've talked to except for Ruth. She's my friend. The illness was like a punishment, as if some great being looked down on me and said, "She's not looking after that sick man, she's enjoying herself." So now, I'm even more acutely aware of Ben's situation.

Every time I see him, I try to get through to him, try to find out what he needs.'

He blinks two or three times. 'Sackcloth and ashes, Mrs Starling.' The man leans forward, places elbows on the table. 'So many people come in here and say exactly what you have just said. "Oh, Mr Watson-Jones, I went out and had a good time, I went to a wedding without her or without him." This wretched disease spreads like wildfire through the whole family. Comparisons are not terribly useful, but I understand from colleagues that parents of handicapped children often react in the same way. Because one member of the family is infirm, everyone seems to feel guilty unless the suffering is shared. There are homes in this city where families don't move, don't go out for a drink or a bit of relaxation. They all sit there sharing the same space as the sufferer, as if it's wrong to leave the house. Mrs Starling, there is nothing wrong or sinful about seeking respite.'

I want to believe him, must believe if I'm going to carry on living. And I am going to carry on living.

'They are locked in houses,' he repeats softly. 'Locked in, watching sick people. They think it's the right thing to do. But it isn't, it's very wrong. Workers don't operate seven days a week, twenty-odd hours a day. It's a full-time job, but holidays and weekends are allowed.'

'Are you telling me to find a life?'

He nods. 'Don't push him out, don't let him take over. If he were physically ill, would he keep you by his side?'

'No.'

He looks at his watch, shuffles some papers, signals that my time is almost up. 'Go and walk round a gallery, look at a painting or two. Or just go shopping.' He smiles. 'Shopping is a hobby with many women.'

I stand, pick up my bag. 'Goodbye.' I look at him properly, give him the kind of once-over that I might award to a piece of decorative furniture. 'If you find any new treatments—'

'I'll let you know.'

Perhaps I am, after all, my mother's daughter. I look at men, weigh them up, play about in my mind with imagined possibilities. Ah well, men have done that to women for centuries, and now that we are equals, females can enjoy similar standpoints. And no, I am not Liza McNally's daughter, not in my heart.

I stand on his doorstep, study the brass plaque that announces his position in medical society. It shines like the sun, though there's a bit of greenish-grey Brasso stuck round one of the twenty-odd letters that squat behind his name. Beneath him, there is a list of others who make their fortune from the mortal illness we call life.

This isn't really a doorway, it's almost a portal, an ornate affair that might have sat well in the shadow of the Parthenon, scrolls on top of pillars, a small stone cherub carved into the inverted V over the top section. The solid wooden door is painted blue, while creamy white paint flakes away from surrounding masonry.

The Harley Street of the north is pleasant enough during the hours of daylight. It sits, polite and clean, coyly skirting the edge of the red light district, becomes slightly seedier after nightfall. All along the block, windows are dressed with boxes of flowers – lobelia, alyssum, a burst of cheery marigolds here and there. Steps are worn down, sagging in the middle, eroding sedately beneath the weight of the many sicknesses that have staggered up and down the once solid slabs. The blooms in tubs and window-boxes are past their best. Most who enter here are beyond their prime.

My car is parked on double yellows, sports in its windscreen Ben's orange disability sticker. Any warden worth his salt might see the disparity here, an ancient Alpine in British racing green, a car that's difficult to cope with even when its occupants are in the best of health. I drive round aimlessly, heading for home, doubling back along side streets, journeying away from whatever, then towards confusion and traffic signals. There is something I want to see, a place I need to visit. I don't know why and

I don't know where, so I continue my circular tour through Liverpool, towards Crosby, back to Liverpool. This is a mystery outing at its best, one where the driver doesn't know the destination.

I am arguing with myself, speaking out loud. 'You knew there'd be no new discoveries, Laura. What were you expecting? A miracle?' I change gear, slow down behind a bus. 'There's no harm in asking,' I reply to myself. 'He'd be better as a guinea-pig, he'd be better off . . . better off if he were . . .'

A Liverpool cabbie misses my rear by centimetres, gives me the two-finger sign as he swerves into the centre lane. 'Get yerself a bloody guide dog, luv,' he yells.

The weather is warm, yet I am freezing. I am chilled to the bone because I am praying for my husband to be released from prison. I had another husband in prison once, and I prayed then that he would never be allowed his freedom. The prayers worked in a way, as Bernard Thompson suffered a massive heart attack in his cell, is prevented by poor health from tormenting me and my children ever again. And now, I pray for release . . . I am asking God to kill my Ben, am begging for the death of a good man.

I drive down Bankfield Street, stop on the docks. It's a ghost road again today, no sound, no movement, just brick upon brick, stone upon stone. This is where my dad's Irish father first set foot on British soil, where thousands came to start a new life in a place that was up-and-coming.

There is a terrible stillness about the place. A crisp packet scutters along, driven by a wind that has lost all will to survive, a mere breeze compared to recent weather. A gull cries, his mournful wail seeming like a dirge as it falls along Liverpool's deserted miles. Here, men waited to be called for work, propped themselves up, disguised weaknesses, hid their infirmities in order to gain a shilling for a meal. Limbs were broken, backs were bent, lives were snuffed out by falling loads.

On the road that skirts the world's biggest docks, there is a woman and a crisp packet. Why am I here? The bird swoops again, shouts at me, is joined by a couple of pals. We used to stand here, Ben and I. My children too would come to this place, used to carry biscuits, bread, bits of meat for the gulls. I reach into the glove box, bring out some stale cake, wind down the window, scatter the bounty. Screaming and quarrelling, they pounce on the food. Oh Ben, how you loved the gulls.

Men perished here, formed unions on this stretch, fought bosses, police, each other. It seems right that I should pray in this pitted, damaged place with its deep scars of iron where trains ran, with its pockmarked cobbles on top of which a few thin bandages of tarmac linger in sad, grey patches.

Ben, oh Ben. I smile, remember the quickness of it all. I kept house for a week, was courted for a month, was married so quickly that my mother screamed about delicacy and good taste. We had the sort of marriage that Georgina Dawn writes about, one of those happy-ever-after things that drift along all smug and safe until . . . until a dinner party and some ice that never got crushed.

In the coronary artery of a city's slowed heart, a woman comes to terms with dementia, with Alois Alzheimer, with her husband's frailty. It happened here, too, that slowing down. Will you pick up, Liverpool? Will your ship come in? Will Ben's?

I am weeping now and it doesn't matter. No-one will come. And if someone does happen along, I shall be ignored. Women have wept on this road for years, I'm only a few decades out of step. I went into a pub once, an old-fashioned ale-house near Miller's Bridge. An aged dear wailed in a corner and nobody bothered her. Her younger companions told me, 'Oh, that's Biddy, she cries a lot.' They allow you your space, the Liverpool folk. It was a dockers' haunt, so it was empty of men. Women sat with babies, nappy bags leaning against table legs, feeding bottles stacked among glasses of stout and lager. To get to the counter, I had to fight a dozen prams. The Liverpool lasses phoned the RAC, found me a sandwich, got the landlord to dig out a dusty bottle of white wine. They were good to me. Until this moment, I had forgotten them, how they took me in, nourished me, put a ten-year-old to guard my wounded car.

I suppose they stood together when the tall ships came and went. The children would be older, wilder, possibly uncontainable. What did they think about, those girls whose grandfathers had run the greatest docks on earth? How did they feel when that last strip of canvas fell off their horizon? I bet they didn't say, 'Well, never mind, we've got all these enterprise things starting, tourists and boutiques and training schemes.' Perhaps I'm getting depressed again. I'm no deep thinker, no poet, shouldn't be standing here like cheese at fourpence. That was one of Auntie Maisie's sayings, 'Don't stand there like cheese at fourpence.'

Why Ben? Why Liverpool, why England? Are we all so unworthy? Who will look after Ben's winter birds? I did it last year and the year before, haven't his magic touch.

He was always sad about house-martins. We once sat for a whole day in a Sussex field, Ben, myself and a couple of hundred insect eaters. Ben watched the babies, worried for them. 'No nest to go back to when the weather's cold,' he said. I remember wondering what happened to their nests, should have asked at the time. 'If they fly high, that means good weather. Low means rain. Many don't get to Africa, many don't return. But look how happy they are.' Birds. He was always fascinated by them, was often emotional about his feathered children.

I've decided to go and see Confetti. She's just round the corner, is usually surrounded by dozens of people. Her dowry has been put to good use in a large house for distressed girls. She calls them her distressed girls, even to their faces, makes a joke of it. I have never met a less distressed crowd in my life. They come to Confetti when there's nowhere else, when it's too late for a lecture on birth control, too late for abortion. Confetti is vigorously opposed to what she calls 'assisted miscarriage', spends time and energy placing the newborn infants with foster parents, or finding homes for those young women who want to keep their children.

I drive on to Waterloo, past the private hospital where Confetti goes for spiritual guidance from the Augustine sisters. In a side street off South Road, I park Elsie, walk into bedlam. She's standing at the foot of the stairs, a baby in one arm, a feeding bottle in the other. 'Laura, thank goodness you're here. Get up those stairs now and tell that lot to turn down the music.' We don't need to listen, as the heavy metal is welding itself to our eardrums.

'Why me?' I ask.

'Because you're here. Did you never hear why Everest was climbed? Because it was there. Now get that racket stopped, I've babies scared halfway to death with it.'

The girls sense their mentor's anger, because the cacophony grinds to an abrupt halt. I am waved towards the kitchen. 'Kettle,' she says. 'Tea bags in the jar marked flour, sugar in the biscuit tin, milk wherever they've left it.' She must be in her seventies, yet she displays a level of energy that should put to shame many of her distressed guests.

'Anything else?' I ask sarcastically.

'Well, a cheque might help, something with six noughts to it.'

'Aren't you being funded at all?'

She shrugs, waves the feeding bottle. 'Cut-backs. Good job I'm a registered charity.'

In the stark kitchen, I find two expectant mothers at the table and a third standing near the outer doors, the arm of an expectant father round her shoulders. All of them seem to be no more than sixteen years of age. They eye me warily, as I am one of the 'them' who have caused all the trouble. At sixteen, they know everything and the parents who turn them out know nothing. With my age against me, I brew tea, place six mugs on the table, pour, hand a drink to each one of them, pick up mine and Confetti's, walk to the door.

'Ta,' says the lad. They're OK folk, just a bit wary and self-defensive.

'You're welcome.'

In the front room, my old friend is humming to herself while feeding the baby. She is sitting in an armchair that pretends to be a golden-yellow, but the moquette is badly stained and torn. 'Thanks for the tea,' she says. 'How's your mother?'

'Simmering. How's your dad?'

She lifts the infant to a shoulder, rubs the tiny back. 'He's ninety-five and still on the go. My sisters in Birmingham are fighting over him, because neither wants him in the house. He was found last week walking up the slow lane of the M6, said he was going home.'

'Oh.' I know she's worried, know she won't show it. 'Dementia?'

The grey head nods. 'Alcohol. The good man never touched a drop till Mammy took ill and died. We'd a grand farm, everything up to date, good land, valuable animals. I think he flushed the last racehorse down the toilet just before we brought him over. Sold the lot just to numb his pain with drink. Anyway, I can't have him, not with this lot.'

'Perhaps he would have been better at home.'

She sniffs. 'That's all well and good, but there was nobody for him. Eugene's showing no signs of coming back from Canada, and the rest of us are in England. I couldn't have done my birth-control classes over there, not without a lot of church opposition.' She looks me up and down. 'Have you money to spare?'

'Yes, I suppose so.' Confetti is one of my tax blessings, as I pay to the mother and baby home on a monthly basis. 'What did you do with the last cheque?'

She tut-tuts. 'I used it on cocaine, of course, ruined my nostrils. It's just gone, Laura. There are fifteen young adults living here, and four babies just now. They need food, washing powder, electricity, gas—'

'Shut up.' I am already writing the cheque. 'And get yourself some decent clothes, for goodness sake. If I see you in those old trousers again, I'll bring a gun.'

She peers over the coffee table, scans the cheque. 'That's a lot of money, Laura Thompson. Still, my need is greater than yours.' The grin is impish but short-lived. 'Ben?'

I shake my head. 'No chance. There's nothing new, no miracle on the horizon. When they do discover something, I don't think it will help him, because he's lost too much, gone too far. The best that can happen is the finding of a drug that might slow the process. There's no replacing dead brain cells.'

'Ah, God love the both of you, Laura. I pray every night for some sign of recovery, but it seems not to be the Lord's will.'

I sip the tea, pull faces at the baby. When the cup is empty, I take the child, give Confetti the chance to enjoy a break. She gulps down a mouthful, settles back in the disgraceful chair. 'They've called that one Garth. It's a great pity that these little creatures are saddled from the start with odd names. That's enough to make him different right from the word go. What's wrong with Peter and John, for goodness sake? Mind, I've done well this year, three Michaels and a Goretti.'

I laugh at her. 'That's the funniest name of all.'

'A matter of opinion.' She peers down at the navy trousers, seems to be attempting to identify the several stains mapped all over them like the pages of an atlas. 'I'll go to town and get a couple of skirts,' she mutters. 'And a blouse or three. Mind, I'll be needing some new cot blankets and a couple of baby baths. Does Mothercare ever have a sale? Laura, remember that God is good.' There is no signal to herald the change of subject. 'Ben won't go on for ever like that.'

'He's suffering,' I tell her yet again. 'It's so cruel.'

'There'll be an end.'

'And get yourself some support tights.' I am becoming as bad as she is, peppering my conversation with snippets of irrelevance.

She looks straight into my face. 'We're all tempted. I was tempted when the cough mixture stopped working for Mammy. They prescribed morphine, and the giving of a drop too much would have been the easiest thing.'

'I know.'

She stands, takes the snoozing infant. 'I'll put him in the cot. You're right, I need some support for these varicose veins. Laura, get that business out of your mind.' Sometimes, I can't quite love her, because she reads me too easily.

Chapter Two

There's a nip in the air today, a promise of October, though this month is barely middle-aged. I sit on the concrete steps and watch Chewbacca as he cavorts mindlessly, senselessly, hurling himself about all over the sands. He finds something, loses it, forgets to retrieve it as soon as he spots another piece of flotsam. Our flotsam is deserved, because much of it is just our own rubbish coming back, Coke cans, beer cans, condoms and fag packets.

The Welsh hills have remained coy all morning, have secreted themselves behind a veil of light mist, but the New Brighton dome is clearly visible. I see no ships, though I am reliably informed that Liverpool is receiving more cargo than ever before. When they do come, the vessels are huge and ugly, low in the water, many of them as grey as the scum on which they float. Who unloads them? I wonder. There must be some dockers, just a few, enough men to direct the lifting of massive containers.

I am thinking about my children. Jodie was here a few weeks ago, but I've seen little of my sons for the past eight or nine months, can remember that they came at Christmas. Gerald gave me some more shares for what he refers to as my portfolio, then a talking-to about surviving the so-called recession. He's a southerner now, all rounded vowels, clipped consonants, car phone, designer shirts and suits, designer stubble. I always knew he'd turn out to be something in the city. Sometimes, he messes about with my offshore bank accounts, frightens the life out of Ruth, my best friend and accountant. She tells me that Gerald is sailing close to the wind, suspects that he might be dealing with the aid of inside information. He's thirty-one, a big boy, but I hope he doesn't get caught, hope he stops in time.

My son Edward is gay. For Christmas, he brought me a pair of satin pyjamas and his latest boyfriend. Edward refused to accompany Gerald when the statutory visit to Tommo was paid. 'He's not my father anyway,' he said. 'And he hates what I am.' All his life, Edward was different, separate from the common herd. He has told me how he felt, how he suffered through being 'soft' and 'queer'. From a very early age, he was uncomfortable, troubled. When people go on about gays being perverts, I lose my rag a bit, stand up for my middle child's principles. Edward was always a loner. If I'd had half a brain as a young woman, I would have realized long ago that my Edward had been predisposed from birth to be extraordinary. He's a fine man with a good heart, he's a man who was programmed from the start to love people of his own sex. With the aid of money from me and Ben, Edward owns and runs a health club in Manchester. He still tends to overweight, continues to indulge in bouts of comfort-eating, so he fights the flab constantly, uses his own exercise machines to sweat away the fat. I love him, find him gentle yet cuttingly witty.

Chewy runs to me, the nine-inch tongue lolling and dripping onto my coat. 'Woof,' he says companionably. He wants me to run with him. 'Woof off,' I reply. He gives me a paw, soggy, dripping with sand and oily water.

'What about Jodie?' I ask him. 'Will she ever settle down, or is she going to carry on for ever like another bloody Confetti?'

'Woof.' He spots a distant dog, bounds away jerkily, his legs splaying like the limbs of a marionette whose master has not yet served his apprenticeship.

Jodie is a newly qualified doctor who travels about, refuses to settle to a life of medicine until she's winkled out what everybody, with the exception of her good self, calls the madness. The madness consists of Oxfam frocks, open sandals, dirty hair and a small motor home. She looks just like Confetti used to look, a nightmare from the late sixties, plaited hair-bands, tangled locks, large pendant earrings, a weather-beaten skin, eyebrows almost knitted together by all that unnecessary thinking.

I keep telling my errant and lovable daughter that the world will find its own way to hell, but she will insist on being concerned. Being concerned to a certain level is fine, even commendable. But jumping in with both feet, a BAN THE WHATEVER sign and a bad attitude is taking altruism that little bit too far, I'd say. She's been arrested on Greenham Common in her youth, more recently in Trafalgar Square (I never asked what she was doing on that occasion, could not bear to hear what she'd perpetrated in the metropolis) and, last month, outside some remand centre where she campaigned, none too quietly, for the release of one of her numerous unsuitable boyfriends.

Chewy is starting a war. A small black terrier has not accepted the attentions of the exploded sofa that masquerades as my pet, is barking furiously as Chewy leaps about in circles. I run, arrive at the scene of the crime, pacify owner and canine with words of apology. They both escape to the car park. I hold Chewy's collar, listen until the Mini's angry engine is started. Strange how some ill-tempered little people have noisy little cars and nasty little dogs. And how some tall, unkempt women called Laura have long-legged unmade beds as companions. He is a mess. I adore him.

I am not a snob. At least, I think I'm not a snob. But Jodie will pick up people with problems, folk with disorders ranging from simple dyslexia to apparent paranoid schizophrenia. And skin problems. When she does deign to arrive home, it is usually in the company of some youth whose face owns more craters than are visible on the moon when viewed through a high-powered telescope. And she isn't even remotely interested in dermatology. She came three weeks ago, breezed in, ate, had a quick bath, drifted away again. This time, she was alone and on her way to pick up some newly released and downtrodden convict with 'morals'. God help him, he'll be wishing he'd stayed inside.

For Christmas, Jodie bought me a book about somebody with Alzheimer's. 'It can be coped with, Mother. A sufferer isn't always miserable, you know.' She brought nothing for her father, did not visit him. 'I've seen him twice,' she protested. 'And there was no discernible improvement on the second occasion.' When she doesn't like somebody, she makes no bones.

Chewy and I amble home, fight in the rear porch with a bucket and a towel. He doesn't enjoy having his feet washed any more than I enjoy seeing my towels ripped to bits. When we are both breathless, we collapse in the kitchen, a cup of coffee for me, a handful of biscuits for the miscreant. Flakey drinks some formula, is lapping well. The dog stares at Handel, considers having a go at the immobile cat, thinks better of it, snores at my feet.

The gate creaks. My dog opens an eye, looks at me. 'No more barking, please,' I beg. 'It's not a burglar.' He would probably find a burglar exciting, would welcome him with a big smile and a quivering tongue.

I rise, look through the window, believe for a moment that I have conjured up Jodie just by thinking about her. But no. This is a different kettle of frankfurters altogether. I remember that she likes sausages and Carnation, not necessarily on the same plate, that her name is Diana and that it's not Thursday. She was supposed to iron my things on Thursday.

I open the door, stare at the vision before me. My uninvited guest is dressed very much *à la* Jodie, that is to say she looks extremely odd. There's a blue flat cap which has lost much of its flatness because of the blond hair bundled into it. Then there's a filthy anorak type of jacket with just a hint of green showing between dozens of badges and slogans. The leggings are purple today, but there remains some consistency in the feet, which are clad again in those huge and hideous Doc Martens. During my lifespan, I have been privileged to know three such fashion-plates – this one, my daughter, my dear friend Confetti.

After looking her up and down, I wait for her to speak, but nothing happens. 'Well?' I say, watching as she sweeps a smutty mark from the end of her nose. 'What do you want this time? I'm not having a new door.'

She placed her worldly goods at my feet, and I am reminded now of Handel, who sometimes bestirs himself to contribute to the larder by bringing home a dead bird or two. Today's offering is just as unsavoury, two aged Woolworth's bags and a filthy canvas backpack that looks as if it might have served in both world wars, perhaps the Crimea too. 'Can I come in?' She has a way of making her eyes round, looks like a neglected and wilful infant begging for sweets.

'You may come in tomorrow night, do the ironing. Then, if you like, you might magnolia the dining-room walls on Saturday afternoon.'

'I hate that colour. It's not a colour, it's a bad mood.'

'Then stay away.' I do not care, I am telling myself sternly. She is not my child, not my responsibility.

She glances over her shoulder, waves a hand towards the steely grey water. 'Where do I go till tomorrow, Laura?'

'Double-glazing, I presume.' She is a lost soul, but so am I, so are we all. Yet I am weakening, will give in any minute now. 'What happened?' I feel my shoulders sagging. If I let her in, will she stay for ever, become one of those tenants who sit there for all eternity? And will she wear me down to the point where I might buy a front door which looks like plastic, is a dead ringer for extruded UPVC?

'Why are you smiling?' she asks.

'Didn't know I was.' Gerald has made me smile – the thought of him, anyway. It would be wonderful fun to watch him pitted against Diana, she squatting in his mother's house, he waving his arms a lot, consulting his Filofax for numbers of 'contacts who know about this sort of thing'. 'This isn't a boarding house,' I announce sternly. 'Anyway, you said you'd paid your rent.'

'He wanted more.'

'More rent?'

She chews her lip. 'He wanted sex.'

'Oh.' She needs food, a warm bed, a friendly ear. I'm not feeling friendly just now. 'Do you enjoy watching *Neighbours*?' I enquire, can't think why.

'Hate that too,' she answers. 'Magnolia and *Neighbours*, both insipid, lifeless. Especially *Neighbours*.'

'Then we shall suffer it together.' I drag her into the house, force her to sit in silence through the whole episode. She hugs herself, sways gently in her seat like a baby in a cradle. We each glue our eyes to the screen, watch the cavortings. It is weird. Some people run into a house and say some things, then they dash off to another house and say the same things. After a couple of minutes, everybody gets together in a garden, and they repeat the earlier lines, but in a slightly altered order. A trio of vile teenagers giggles a bit, and a young woman with a pregnancy cushion stuffed up her skirt has difficulty rising out of a chair. This is probably because the size of the bulge would be appropriate for someone in the twentieth month of incubation.

There is no interval in *Neighbours*, as it is BBC, so we don't even get a Fairy Liquid advert or chimps with tea-cups. An older woman worries about Jim, is reminiscent of *Mrs Dale's Diary*-as-was, and a sensible yellow dog wanders about, delivers a performance that deserves an Oscar when compared to the scriptwriters' garbage. As the credits roll, we agree earnestly that the dog is a clever ad libber.

Diana fixes me with a stare that does not match her cap's rakish angle. 'Do you watch that every day?' There's a near-hysterical edge to her words, but I suspect that this young woman is a good actress.

'Twice a day. I plan my life around it, can't go shopping

or for a walk when it's on. I know I could video the show, but it's not the same, is it? I want to see it when it's actually happening. Then *Home and Away, A Country Practice, Flying Doctors*, and there's *Families*, of course, but that's British and—'

'What's it about?'

'I beg your pardon?'

'*Families*. What's it about?'

She's clever. I flounder, surface after a few seconds. 'It's about groups of people, adults and children in nuclear groups, though one family has extended all the way to Australia, Sydney, I think, so—'

'How many children?'

'Some. A few.'

'Names?' One of her eyebrows has floated up the forehead, causing shallow, youthful lines on one side. 'Go on, then. Tell me some names.'

I sigh. 'I've forgotten.' Inspired suddenly, I managed to remember some of it. 'A woman with red hair ran off with her half-brother. She didn't know who he was, so they're living in sin.'

'The old incest chestnut?' is the next piece of rhetoric. 'You don't watch that crap. I can tell just by looking at you that you've no time for rubbish.'

I smile, think of Georgina Dawn's rejected outpourings. 'I am very familiar with all kinds of rubbish.'

She nods quickly. 'And you certainly don't see any of it while it's actually happening, because we're ages behind with all the Antipodean junk. It's recorded, was recorded about a year ago. All soaps are recorded. Even *Coronation Street* runs five or six weeks behind itself.'

I rally. 'I watch *Coronation Street*.'

'That is acceptable,' comes the swift response. 'So is *PCBH*.'

I am flummoxed, cannot create a reply, am not going to beg for an explanation.

She can see my flummoxedness. '*PCBH. Prisoner Cell Block H*. Compulsory viewing in most select homes, even those with dishwashers and Axminster carpets. It is brilliantly bad.'

This girl is so likeable. 'Oh. My education is incomplete, then.'

'You can't fool me, Mrs . . . er . . . Laura.'

'Starling.'

She removes the cap and the hair tumbles down in oily, shampoo-starved rats' tails. 'Funny name, that. It's like being called Sparrow or Cuckoo or Owl – Wol, if you're an AA Milne fan. I liked Eeyore best. Bits kept dropping off him. It was all middle-class mush anyway.'

I pin my eyes to a hole in the leggings, wonder how many other such goodies she has brought in her tattered luggage. 'A rose by any other name,' I mumble. 'I'm rather fond of my surname, as is my husband.'

Her fingers are digging into the chair arm. She is tense, though none of the nervousness shows in the lift of her head, in the clean clarity of her voice. 'I need a room for a few weeks. You have plenty of rooms and I have none. We should share.'

I shift in the seat, pretend some anger. 'Are you a bloody communist?'

'I'm pinkish,' she replies smartly. 'You?'

'A professional floating voter. But nothing about fair shares is written into the constitution of this democracy. You are . . . invading my space? Isn't that the with-it term these days for pushy people who move in and refuse to leave?'

'Chill out,' she begs. She's heard that one on *Neighbours*, I reckon. 'I've nowhere to go. Are you going to throw me out into the street? There are funny buggers in Blundellsands, just as many here as anywhere else. I could get mugged or raped or knifed or anything.'

She is wearing a lot of clothes. There are at least three sweaters under that anorak – she probably ran out of plastic bags for her packing. 'Get a shower.' My tone is fairly . . . well, nearly fairly strong. 'And put yourself in the attic. There's a sleeping bag in the landing cupboard, some towels in the chest outside the bathroom. I want you gone by the end of the month.'

Her gaze is steady. 'How many bathrooms have you got here?'

'Three.' I meet her eyes, will not apologize for my living conditions, refuse to be ashamed of my comparative wealth. Inverted snobbery is as unacceptable as the usual sort. 'Does that matter?'

She lifts a shoulder. 'Not really. It's just I'm a bit messy, want somewhere to drip my underclothes.' The grin widens. 'I'd like my own bathroom.'

Yes, she is dangerously likeable. Here I stand – well, sit – with one husband broken down by Alzheimer's, the other suffering from angina, clogged lungs and narrowed arteries, and I'm taking on yet another problem. My kids are God knows where doing God knows what, but I still seem to collect people. Other women gather diamonds, designer clothes, perfumes. I attract lame ducks, not just ducks, either. There are still a couple of Jonathan Livingstones in the shed at the back of the garage, seagulls whose wings are healing in spite of my ministrations. 'You should go on the stage, Diana. It's a while since an actress of your calibre graced our theatres.'

'I'll pay,' she says generously. 'Seven pounds a week and I'll find my own food.'

I look her over. 'You won't. You've not found much food so far, anyway. Are you suffering from anorexia? Will you linger palely in my attic, then drift off to heaven all ethereal and beautiful?'

She sniffs. 'Don't talk soft, I'm just starving. It happens, you know, even in 1992. I've a good BSc, can't get a job, might as well go back to college and aim for a doctorate. So the rest of you will have to shelter my burgeoning genius.'

'We owe you that?'

'Somebody does.'

She's right. Even five or ten years ago, it was easier for young people to find a goal, work hard to reach it, enjoy the benefits of a career after all the studying. My own three went to colleges, universities, medical school; the two who wanted work got jobs. Jodie will do it soon, I tell myself. She'll settle down, get a post in a hospital, save some lives, have the occasional wash, invest in some ozone-friendly deodorant . . .

'What do you think about all the time, Laura?' The words are spoken softly, gently. 'You seem to be preoccupied.'

'I . . . I miss my husband.' That's the truth, the whole truth. Well, nearly. I miss Ben, support Tommo against my better judgement, worry about Gerald's ethics, Edward's sensitivity, Jodie's foolishness.

'I'm sorry.' The eyes burn and I know that she really is sad for me.

'Get yourself cleaned up, Diana. I'll find something for you in the freezer.' The idea of mundane tasks is suddenly attractive. 'I'll get you a quick meal.'

She leaps up, makes a dive for me, places the thin hands on my shoulders. 'You're all right, queen,' she whispers, laughter lurking in her throat. The tone lifts itself, finds a more audible level. 'And can I walk that big soft dog and is the cat allowed upstairs and have you got a spare toothbrush? And I'm good with kittens.' She points to Flakey, who is curled up in a shoe box next to the bread bin. 'It was my dad, not the landlord. My dad's a good bloke, but he cracked up when Mam died, took to drink. I've run away from him for a bit of a rest. I will go back to him, you know. But I need a break, that's the truth.'

I think of Confetti's problem. 'I've another friend in the same position. The drink affects her father's brain. He started after his wife died, was almost teetotal before.'

She sighs, looks pensive. 'When we were kids, he was really good to us. But he drank to forget about Mam, then he started going a bit violent and unpredictable.' She displays a slender, bruised wrist. 'He doesn't mean it. He's just desperate, trying to keep hold of me. And I like kippers.'

She grabs her possessions, runs out of the room, leaves me cold, empty, leaves me lonely. She is singing in the shower, a Beatles song, 'Whatever Gets You Through the Night'. I cannot afford to attach myself to anyone. Somewhere out there, three products of mine are doing damage, one insider dealing, another moaning, putting on weight, seeking a permanent lover. And the third runs round with criminals and hippies.

I find a pair of frozen kippers, linger near the microwave as I wait for the singing to stop. Tommo tonight. Ruth comes with me, though I need no protection from the feeble man. He sits, watches TV, waits for my visits. The eyes are still powerful, but the strength is diminished.

Tommo was Ben's only mistake. 'Go to him,' he insisted for years. 'Three heart attacks and chronic angina have diminished him. For your own sake, you must see this man and realize that he is just a broken creature. Then and only then will you be free in spirit.' After Ben's constant nagging/encouragement, I went and laid the ghost. But, fool that I am, I supplement Tommo's state income, look after his welfare. After all, he is a human being. I think.

And last but never least, there's my Ben. I won't cry. I won't stand here crying next to a pair of frozen, headless kippers.

'Laura?' God, they'll hear that scream in Birkenhead.

'Yes?'

'Can I have a bath as well as a shower?'

'Yes.' I bet she's dripped all over the landing, all over the bathroom too. Life will be fuller than ever if I let this one linger for too long. Three Confettis. I shudder. There's the real one, then Jodie, now this apprentice off-beat upstairs.

The phone again. 'Robert, it's over.'

'I'm coming home,' he says. 'I've had enough of this bloody holiday.'

'Stay where you are,' I order.

'I want to see you.'

'Don't blame me for shortening the children's pleasure. Look, I'll see you soon.' I'm not a good liar face to face, but I'm quite feasible on the phone. 'I promise that we'll talk if you'll give those kids another few days.' Really, I can't take him on as well! This place is going to be like Wembley Stadium if I'm not careful.

'Do you still love me?' Oh the urgency of youth. Though forty is not exactly infantile.

How many people can one woman love? How many kinds of love are there, how many kinds of truth?

'Laura?'

'Yes, of course I do.' Well, that's one kind of truth, I suppose.

Ruth makes the tea, carries it through to the tiny sitting room. My first husband is staring at me, his eyes seeming to bore into my soul. 'There you are,' my friend says to the invalid. 'And I've put the sugar in for you.'

He does not look at her. 'Thanks.'

I sit back, attempt to relax, wish with all my heart that he would stop watching me. 'Are you any better?' I ask.

'No.'

Ruth picks up the *Echo*, reads, or pretends to read.

'Do you need anything more?' I force some shallow brightness into my voice. 'Some books, a particular kind of food? Is the home help still visiting?' I ask, wishing that I could settle down and be comfortable in this little cottage. I've been coming here for about ten years, ever since Tommo's third coronary. 'Face him,' Ben said to me over and over again. 'Look at the nightmare, then it will become an everyday thing, it will go away.' For a long time, Ben came with me, waited in the car. He was a sensitive man, still is, I suppose. Degeneration of the brain cannot possibly make the soul poorer. But Ben can't come any more, and Ruth insists on being a witness. 'You never know,' she often says. 'He might get strong and turn on you again.'

'The home help comes,' he mutters. 'More of a hindrance than a help. But I'm all right.' His eyes flicker for a moment, move towards Ruth. He wants her out, has always wanted me to come alone. But I told him right at the start that I would be accompanied at all times. Tommo disapproves of Ruth, was happier when I arrived with a husband who stayed outside. 'Is he still away?' There is emphasis on the 'he'.

'Ben's in the nursing home, yes.' You were my nightmare, I want to say. Ben made you unimportant, released me from the evil dream. But he finds no solace now from his own torment.

He grins, displaying sickly yellow teeth that do little to enhance his sickly yellow face. 'You backed two losers, didn't you?'

Sometimes, I amaze myself. I come here and sit with a man who beat me, raped me, murdered a man I loved, and I still find a sort of pity for this creature who altered the course of my existence. But he's not a lot worse than my mother, I suppose. And I still visit her. I have hated this man, have hated my mother, continue to harbour negative feelings for both these people who have harmed me. But hatred is not strong enough to make me turn away completely. I'm no saint, no martyr, yet I do these 'good' deeds, keep turning up to be stared at by Tommo in his Bootle cottage, continue verbally abused in a certain person's retirement apartment.

'The kids haven't been,' he grumbles.

'I know.' They can't stand him, even for a few minutes. Neither can I, I decide suddenly. This will be the last time. If he needs money, he can have it. By post.

'Why won't they come?'

'Busy,' I reply briskly. 'Lives to lead, things to do.'

'And the fairy-boy? How's he getting on? Has he found a boyfriend yet?' The eyes narrow as he contains the glee. His brother, the man he murdered, fathered a creature who is less than a man. 'And don't start telling me he's not queer. I spotted it a mile off that time when he came with my son.'

'Edward is fine.'

535

'Your mother?' he enquires sarcastically, as if able to access my thoughts. 'Still smoking herself to death and refusing to lie down?'

'Something like that.' I place an envelope on the table, make the movement as discreet as possible. We never discuss the contents, never refer to the few pounds I leave here each time I come. This awful man is the father of Gerald and Jodie. He is diminished in body and spirit, has fought his last fight. It is impossible for me to allow him to starve. But I receive no thanks, expect none.

Ruth makes much of looking at her watch. 'Shall we go, Laura? After all, you're supposed to get your rest.'

He picks up the clear plastic mask, holds it over his mouth and nose while he inhales pure oxygen. I am supposed to worry now, am supposed to stay with him in case he has another attack. That would be taking my charity too far. I am performing a duty, no more than that, am obeying my real husband's instincts. And Tommo's a sick animal, just another patient on my rota.

We make our goodbyes, go out to the car. 'I don't know how you do this,' says Ruth. 'After all, he's never grateful, hardly even civil. I wonder about you, I really do. Are you trying to win a medal? The way he looks at you makes me shiver.'

'Shut up.' I stick out my tongue, climb into my uncomfortable driver's seat, wait till Ruth is strapped in. 'He's harmless.'

'Only because he's ill. He'd kill you if he could.'

'Nonsense.'

'All right. But don't come running to me when he breaks both your legs.' She giggles, presses my hand. 'Laura, you're incurable.'

She's wrong, I'm cured. I'm getting better every day, have come to terms with the reprieve I have been granted. Ben, Tommo, Flakey, Diana, the seagulls, my mother – these characters are not dictating my life. There are choices, so I do as I will. On an impulse, I jump out of Elsie, lean down, speak to Ruth. 'Stay here.'

'But—'

'Stay.' I return to the house, find Tommo counting my fivers.

'What do you want?' he asks, the pale face stained by anger. He isn't happy, is displeased because I've caught him in the act of accepting my charity. 'I want an answer,' I say softly.

'Fire away.'

I lean against the closed outer door. Words. I have to find the words. 'You wrote to me, said you'd be sending friends to see me. Criminals, I should think.'

He frowns. 'And?'

I clear my throat, wish I could cough the clutter out of my head. 'How did Ben manage to keep me safe? How could he be so sure that you wouldn't interfere? After all, you might still have sent someone.' I pause, remember the early days of my second marriage. I can hear Ben now, can hear him telling me that it was all over, that Tommo could never hurt me again. 'How?' I plead. 'Tell me.'

He lowers his gaze, stuffs the money down the side of his chair. 'Are you sure he won't get better?'

'Yes, the doctor tells me to expect no improvement.'

Tommo nods. 'He warned me never to tell you any of this. And he's not alone. He might not come after me, but one of his mates could do it.'

A ripple of fear rises up my spine, digs its cold fingers into my neck. 'What is it? Who are these friends of his?'

The yellowed mask of death shows its teeth, but there is no warmth, no humour in the smile. 'Look, I don't know the details, but that Ben Starling of yours gave the impression that our crimes were fairy-tale stuff. He was a prison visitor for a reason. We never found out who he was looking for, but there were rumours. He threatened me, others too, dropped a few names, London people with big money and clean slates. Your so-called husband talked like a crook, acted like a gentleman. I don't scare easily, but he put me off.' He pauses, sighs. 'I stayed away because he threatened me and because he seemed to be part of something big. He put the frighteners on a few of us, even the old lags were winded by him. Anyway, that's all I know, so make what you like of it.'

I stand very still, am conscious of my breathing. There is nothing more to be said. Tommo is making all this up, is reaching deep into the recesses of imagination. Ben is a good man, was always a law-abiding citizen. Even if Ben did say those things, they would have been manufactured just to keep me out of Tommo's reach.

Tommo leans forward, thrusts the poker into the grate, stirs the fire to life. 'The answer's in London. And, from the little I learned, in other cities, European cities. Like I said, you married two bad devils. But he's worse than me, I'm telling you. The notches on his gun—'

I move towards him. 'He never killed.'

He shrugs, replaces the poker. 'You may be right. Perhaps it was all rumour.'

His skin has paled again, and I feel sick, revolted, because this man is telling a kind of truth. And Ben travelled a lot, went to Europe on a fairly regular basis. But I decide to keep my counsel.

The drive home is silent. Ruth senses my need for quiet, does not intrude on my thoughts. Truth. How many more kinds are there?

Diana reminds me of Jodie, therefore of myself in younger days. Physically, the two girls are not unalike, both very slim, both fairly pretty. Diana is blond, as I was, but Jodie, my nomadic daughter, has dark brown hair with reddish highlights, though the lustre doesn't show until she deigns to take a bath or a shower. She used to be clean, was always getting scrubbed up as part of her job. So her 'industrial action' has taken the form of greasy hair and grubby clothes, while my own small rebellions against society – against my mother, really – were feeble battles of words followed by a near-silence that lasted for ages.

I've done the crossword, am sitting here fiddling with my nails, sawing half-heartedly with an emery board. It's time for Adrian to be let loose with his box of tricks, pink for the body of the nail, white for the tip. Diana is in the dining-room with stepladder, brushes and paint. She is pretending that the latter is luminescent green, as she can't bear magnolia. Flakey has gone missing again, is no doubt up to mischief.

'Woof.' Chewbacca eyes me lugubriously, wants a walk. Handel, whose fur has remained remarkably unruffled by the kitten's arrival, ambles by, jumps into the sink, supervises the dripping tap. He paws the drops, investigates their source, gets a wet nose. Intelligent? He does the same thing every day, finishes up mesmerized by the drip-dripping, falls asleep in the bowl.

Diana peeps round the door. 'Was this kitten magnolia when you got it?'

'Black,' I answer, unperturbed. I'm getting used to her.

'Right.' She pauses for a second or two. 'Is your sideboard worth anything?'

'Yes, why?' The sideboard is of solid English oak, darkened by age, ponderous, ugly enough to be beautiful. I bought it out of pity – I used to do that sort of thing.

'Give us a J-cloth, then, 'cos I've splashed a bit.' She is wearing a lot of Crown vinyl silk, most of it on her face. 'It's time for a brew,' she reminds me.

The kitten staggers in, a few drops of paint decorating her fluff. Flakey is one of those happy cats, the sort of animal that just accepts life's roses and thorns, treats both the same. She's feeding herself, is a real little gem. 'Have you painted before?' I ask, scraping together a faint interest.

'Course I have. I did a picture of my mam and one of our house. Oh, and I was good at cows, but they always had too many legs. We only ever had purple sugar paper in our class. You don't get a good breed of cattle out of purple sugar paper.'

'You haven't painted since junior school? You've never painted a wall?'

She shrugs. 'Walls, cows – they're all the same. Anyway, you needed new cushions in the first place.'

I will not be taken in by her, will not pick up the tossed glove. There's something about Diana that allows you to know her right away, a basic honesty that leaves her transparent and trustworthy. 'Tea or coffee, Diana?'

'Call me Di. A lager would be great, but alcoholism could be in the genes and I might finish up like my dad. He's got three gears, my dad. There's drive, reverse and park, and he's usually parked in a horizontal position after reversing into something or other. I don't really want to go following in my father's backward footsteps, so I'll settle for tea.'

I fill the kettle. 'Your dad's an automatic vehicle, then?'

'Oh yes. If he had to think about moving, he'd never engage his clutch. You can tell by his eyes that he doesn't actually think, just lets his legs dictate speed and direction. Really, we should fit him with indicators so that the folk behind him won't pile up when he changes course.'

I brew the tea while she dashes out with a cloth. When she returns, she places newspaper on a chair before sitting down. 'Well, that's spread the paint round a bit. The fireplace looks good with freckles.'

'Great,' I say as I hand her the mug.

'Aren't you bothered?'

I bang my own mug on the table. 'Biscuits in the jar. No, I'm not bothered. If you had ruined my furniture, you would be mortified, not mischievous.'

'Oh.' She nibbles at a chocolate digestive. 'He was best on escalators.'

'Your father?'

She nods. 'He'd do one of his halts, and a backlog used to form behind him, loads of people going down the up or up the down. He's a pest. Everybody knows he's a pest. I think he's banned from railway stations and big shops.'

'Sisters, brothers?'

'All wed and fled. There's only me to take the brunt.'

540

I sip my tea, manage two plain biscuits, am recovering at a rate of knots, it seems. 'He'll be looking for you.'

'You're my refuge for the moment.' The eyes cloud, darken a shade. 'Thanks for having me. It's when I go and work at the hospital that the trouble will start. Whether I'm in haematology or pain relief, he'll find me. At uni, he used to wander about the departments bellowing like a bull till security or police threw him out.'

'He sounds like a man in pain.'

'He sounds like a foghorn, more like. Don't get me wrong, I love the old bugger. But since Mam went, he's been away with the mixer, like a schizophrenic. The booze changes him, makes him horrible.' She looks and sounds so young, so confused. 'I don't know what I can do with or for him.'

Laura, I say to myself. You cannot carry any more passengers. 'Can I help?' asks my disobedient mouth.

The fair head shakes till the scarf falls off. 'No, I don't think so.'

'Why don't you do your PhD somewhere else?'

'Good question.' She leans back, stuffs her hands into jeans pockets. 'I suppose I've got to be here in case he needs me. I'm just having a holiday for a while, you see. There was only me ever visited him in hospital when he had alcohol poisoning. There was only me ever went to see the specialist about Dad's liver. He's lovely in hospital, all sad and soulful round the eyes. When he's in hospital, I can see why Mam loved him so much. Then as soon as he's out, it's beer and bloody mayhem all over again.'

'You do love him, Diana.'

She hesitates for a split second. 'He gets on my nerves. Hatred and love – aren't they the two sides of a single coin?'

I think about that. 'I've hated two people, I think. But I've never hated enough, never hated strongly. Love's a lot more powerful for women like you and me. We are likely to act out of love, not likely to act out of hatred.'

She smiles slightly. 'I come from a family where all our

feelings were strong and always on show. It was a noisy house in a noisy street. School was the same, you had to make a din to be noticed. We were always either in or out of friendship. In meant doing battle on behalf of, out meant doing battle with. We're of Irish decent.'

'My father was Irish,' I tell her.

She looks me up and down as if assessing my value before the auctioneer quotes a reserve price. 'It doesn't show. Somebody's knocked it out of you. Have you no temper?'

'I sit on it.'

'Oh.' Another loud slurp of Typhoo is followed by, 'Don't you ever have a really good belly laugh? That's part of being Irish too, having a good laugh.'

Loud glee had no place in my mother's house. If I exploded with snorts and giggles, my mother would turn off the wireless, forbid me to listen to *ITMA*. *ITMA* was not ladylike, I would be better employed practising the piano. Yes, it had all been knocked out of me. I didn't like the piano, was forced to sit on another emotion, was put to sit on the stool, too, was bullied till I pretended to learn my scales. 'Mother wanted me to be a lady,' I say now.

Diana places her empty mug on the table. 'Mother?'

I nod. 'I never called her "Mam" or "Mum". That would have been too working-class for her, too familiar.'

'Bloody hell.' The eyes take a journey round my cold and pristine kitchen. 'Was she posh, well-born?'

'No. Her parents were ordinary working folk, I think. Her father was a tackler in the mill – a weaver, really. And her mother did cleaning jobs.'

She shakes her head sadly. 'They're the worst. Not your grandma and grandpa – people like your mother who go all etiquette and magazines with shiny pages. Did you like her?'

'No.'

'Is she dead?'

'No.'

She whistles on a long exhalation. 'Where is she?'

'In sheltered housing five minutes away.' Mother followed me in the end, arranged to enact her decorous retirement on my doorstep. McNally's is in the hands of a management team whose profits soared once Liza's interference stopped. Even in recession, the firm is doing well.

The girl folds her arms, seems to be preparing to continue the third degree. But she's slowing down a bit. 'You're like me, then,' she says. 'With a difficult parent. If you told her to bugger off, it would do loads for your self-confidence, wouldn't it?'

'No, it would just make me guilty.' I don't lack self-confidence. Self-confidence is an outer garment, something we wear like a hat or, more aptly, like a very concealing coat. I don't lack a cloak. What's missing in me is an undergarment, an essential sense of identity. I was my mother's burden, my father's child, Anne's cousin, Maisie's niece, Tommo's terrified wife. I became a mother to three, then Ben's wife. Even my working life has been carried out under another name. Georgina Dawn writes the stories, and I hide behind the pretty words, the simple sentiments.

'And I'd be guilty too if I got rid of my burden,' muses Diana. 'Parents are just there, like the wonders of the world, we either appreciate them or ignore them. Mind you, the hanging gardens of Babylon don't show us up, do they? Laura? You're thinking again.'

'Yes, I do think from time to time.'

Another digestive does a quick disappearing act. I was wrong about the anorexia. 'What's the computer for in that little room at the top of the stairs?' she asks.

'Work.'

'What sort of work?' She's at it again, the third degree.

'I write small books for women who refuse to give in and take sleeping pills.'

'Mills and Boon?'

'No, but a similar type of thing. It's a difficult genre to tackle, but I'm improving with age.'

Her round eyes are riveted to my face. 'You're different,' she pronounces. 'You tell the truth.'

Well, I'm saying nothing. There are so many kinds of truth . . .

'My mother was like you, Laura. She shamed the devil all her life.'

I'm nodding as if I'm listening properly, but really I'm thinking about truth and self-confidence and identity. When Alzheimer's removed Ben, part of me stopped existing. Without a picture of myself reflected in someone else's vision, I have been nothing, could be nothing. So have I been just an idea, my mother's, Tommo's, my children's, Ben's concept of daughter, wife, mother? Is there no straight-on Laura, must I be inverted by the eye's lens, translated, righted, validated by another's brain? Did I take a lover after Ben just so that I might be visible. 'No,' I say aloud.

'Eh?'

I look at her, notice her, see the fresh young skin, the tumbled scarf, the spattered overall. 'I'm talking to myself,' I admit. 'I do that, it's a sign of age.' Actually, it's a sign of growing up. I'm fifty-plus and still developing. I am myself. I shall say that like a mantra every night, I am myself and I do as I please.

'Write a proper book,' she suggests. Ruth's always saying the same thing.

'Why?'

She heaves up the thin shoulders. 'To leave a mark, I suppose. That's why they all did it, Trollope and Austen and the rest of that shower. They didn't do it for money. They did it for eternal life. See, they're never dead. People keep reading their words and their thoughts. Musicians and writers don't really die.'

I sigh, drain my mug. 'You're just a romantic at heart, Diana. Incidentally, what's your second name?' I may be harbouring a criminal, a runaway, a drug addict.

After a slight pause, she says, 'Hulme. I'm Diana Hulme.'

'Are you sure?'

She jumps up, ties the scarf. 'Is any one of us sure?' In the doorway, she turns quickly, moves like a dancer. 'What if I spill the paint and make a mess?'

Seconds pass before I reply. 'No use crying over spilt magnolia.' The words are for both of us.

Chapter Three

I haven't thought about it for at least two days. The concept of Ben as a criminal cannot be a true one, so I've pushed it to the back of my mind, where it skirts the rest of my thoughts like a silent skater circling the rim of an ice-rink. But it's there, I must look at it.

I am in the master bathroom, looking at myself. The figure in the mirror has lived closely with Ben Starling for many years, would surely have sensed any badness in him. I remember that first meeting, hear him saying, 'I am a law-abiding citizen of this country, Mrs Thompson.' But it would take a lot to frighten Tommo. Tommo was a killer, an abuser. Nothing much short of a Chicago-style gangster could put so much fear in him.

A woman of any age has to be brave to stand like this in front of a rather theatrical makeup shelf with seventeen naked lamps glinting on flesh that is also naked, never perfect. After the big five-O, it takes courage or bloody-mindedness, and I would guess that the second of these two qualities is what forces me to judge meat and bone that is over half a century old. Anyway, I won't find any answers here, won't discover whether or when Ben did this or that. The nakedness is symbolic, then. I've stripped off my body, am preparing to denude my mind.

The human frame seems to desiccate after a while, starts to dry out no matter how many moisturizers are applied, no matter how many killer exercises are performed in the company of morning television. Ben has dried out too. Ben has lost hair, muscle, the power of co-ordinated physical movement. The poor love's brain has wrinkled too, has given up its moisture, its alacrity. At least my wrinkles are all tangible, all of the visible flesh.

He went abroad a lot. He and a number of partners dealt in gems, owned several businesses, some wholesale, some retail. Ben never took me with him, even when my children had grown old enough to be left. Our holiday trips abroad were separate from the business. I never asked; he seldom spoke of our pasts, except to help me face mine positively. He tackled the problem of Tommo head-on, asked no questions, just encouraged me to face my monster, to accept that there would be no more threats. How did he know that? Did he really threaten Tommo and other inmates, did he have some power, some force that frightened them into submission?

I perch on the cushioned seat of a wicker chair. My face is blurred round the edges, made less definite by little nests of cellulite. The cheek-skin is no longer taut, is beginning to fold inward just a fraction on each side of my nose. The lips are narrower, have probably shrunk because of being drawn in so often. Worry shows in the face first.

I have survived. This fairly well-preserved woman in the looking-glass has come back from the dead, has cut through the red tape of an illness that claimed many women for hundreds of years. Free and strong, I am promised longevity, life without Ben. Although I broke down again, cracked up beneath the weight of my pain and Ben's hopelessness, I am here at the other side, have dismissed another bad dream. How well you coached me, Ben. How I have loved you, how I still love you.

No. I won't cry. This image in the glass needs no further wrinkles, even those created briefly by watery eyes. I dress myself, wonder how I will discover yet another truth, wonder whether such truth is worth pursuing. Ben. Who are you, who were you? And will you die before I find out?

For about ten minutes, I stand in the bathroom remembering, digging right down to the catacombs of our history together. Things he said to me, things he said on the phone, bits of paper, a passport, a receipt. Millions of pounds have passed through Ben's accounts over the years. Was this good money or bad? Was he an actor of such high calibre that he managed to fool even a bed partner? No. I cannot have been sleeping with another madman.

I go downstairs. Diana, who cheers me beyond all measure, is plainly up to mischief again. The kitten is on the table, is worrying a piece of sticky tape, is worrying about the same sticky tape, as its relationship with Flakey's paw promises to be on-going. I rescue the near-crazed baby cat, peer over my human lodger's shoulder. She is taping a candle and a fifty pence coin to a postcard. 'I had to cut the candle,' she says mournfully. 'It was too long to stick on the card properly.'

There are some odd days in life, some strange people, too. I won't ask, not just yet. A spoonful of pulverized Whiskas disappears down Flakey's throat. She's a good kitty, a quick student. I make coffee, throw some bread into the toaster. I'm supposed to ask Diana what she's doing. 'What are you doing?' I ask, the tone nonchalant. For all I know, she might be following in the footsteps of Guy Fawkes. Like Jodie, she's mercurial, unpredictable.

'Charity work,' comes the tardy and deliberately vague reply.

I scrape some honey onto my toast, sit opposite her, wait for clarification.

'Have you got an address for *Neighbours*, Laura?' she asks eventually.

'No.'

'Pity. I shall never perform my good deed for today unless I find that address.' Naughtiness exudes from her, hovers in the air above her head like summer lightning with the sting removed. 'What a shame,' she moans.

I nibble at my toast, enjoy the honey, sip strong coffee. The words have to be spoken, because I cannot tolerate her giddy anticipation. 'What are you doing with a candle and fifty pence? And why have you used so much tape?'

'I don't want the candle to drop off in the post. They've run out of money, I think. The lighting's terrible – yesterday's episode of *Neighbours* was a mystery to me. So I'm sending a donation for the lecky meter and a candle to help throw some light on the subject. I'll address it to *Neighbours*, Australia.'

She's what the Scousers call 'a case', what I call daft as a brush. 'You don't watch *Neighbours*,' I inform her.

'I watched it yesterday. Well, I tried. Is there something wrong with your telly?'

'No.'

'It was all shadows and ghostly happenings. Prison's the same – you can only tell who's talking when somebody lights a cigarette or sets fire to a mattress.'

I lean back, finish my toast, count the seconds while she prints AIR MAIL in giant-size blue capitals. Eating in such pleasant company is so much easier than eating alone. Revived by caffeine and carbohydrates, I tackle her. 'Diana, don't you think you should put that lot in an envelope?'

'They'd think it was a bomb. Manchester Airport would grind to a halt while my candle got defused.' She winks at me. 'I know what I'm doing.'

'Glad to hear it. I'm sure a psychiatrist could help. Would you like to see mine? He's redundant now, could do with cheering up.'

She glares at me. 'I've pinched enough of your cast-offs, thanks. And there's a hole in the green jumper you gave me.'

'Ah, but my head-doctor's in one piece.'

She laughs. 'I doubt it, especially if you've had a go at him.'

'*Touché*,' I say politely.

She sniffs knowingly. Most Liverpudlians are knowing, are born knowing. 'You take all the excitement out of life, Laura.'

I swallow my vitamins.

'Why are you taking those?'

'I've just had surgery and a breakdown – I'm hedging my bets.'

The blond head shakes slowly. 'Go the whole hog – you're loaded, aren't you? Get to one of those health farms, I'll look after the menagerie.'

The menagerie. There's Handel the vandal sitting in the sink, Chewbacca asleep with all four legs in the air, Flakey trying to have a wash, falling over due to underdeveloped co-ordination. In the shed at the back of the garage, there are two quarrelsome gulls whose broken wings are flapping again. This is the difficult stage, as they are strong enough to be angry, too weak to fly. Members of my extended family include a difficult mother, two husbands who are strangers to me, a nun in frayed trousers, a demanding lover, a cousin who phones, seldom visits, three offspring who are widespread, two very supportive friends and a girl who sticks candles and money to postcards. A holiday would be nice.

'Go on, book yourself in.'

'Oh, I've done all that, thanks. They slap what they call natural oils all over you, call it aromatherapy. I finished up with so many allergies that I needed a doctor. The food's natural, too. We were all sneaking out to McDonalds and the pub. There were women of all shapes and sizes leaning on the bar with pyjamas rolled up under their coats.'

'No men?' she asks.

'No, the men do as they're told.' Talking, making a stab at entertaining this young woman, is keeping my mind off Ben. I need to stay away from thoughts of Ben. 'Men have no trouble with health farms. But we were a mess. One woman's winceyette dropped down in the middle of a double martini, very dry, one cherry. The locals never turned a hair, they were used to it. Anyway, the short story is that you need a rest after a week on a health farm.'

She throws down her pen. 'So you're going nowhere. You won't leave him, will you? He's why you're staying.'

'Yes.' Diana is a student of the human animal, and I am

now one of the victims of her scrutiny. She would perhaps do very well as a social worker or a window cleaner, because she's very intrusive, nosy about other folks' lives. This young madam probably picked me out three interviews ago, when she first started mithering about plastic window frames. Her assessment was correct, no doubt. She needs shelter, so she foists herself on one who seems to lack company.

I rise, grab bag and keys. 'I'm going shopping. Don't answer the telephone, the recording's on for messages. And don't paint any cows on the dining-room walls.'

She sticks out a healthy, pink tongue. 'You're no fun.'

'Thanks.'

'Buy something stupid,' she yells after me.

Elsie sits outside. She's an ancient Alpine with a British racing green complexion and a temperament to match. She has a tendency to get confused about her gears, and she's showing distinct signs of oil-dependency, is a motorized version of a human alcoholic. When I turn the key, she makes a loud vomiting sound, reminds me of my mother and her acid indigestion.

I sigh heavily, engage first gear, speed up until I manage to jump to third. Elsie no longer responds to a plea for second, seems to have dispensed with anything that's not strictly necessary. 'You'll have to go in for surgery soon, old thing,' I tell her. She grumbles, threatens to stall, is plainly disturbed by my threat.

Well, I'll have to visit Liza soon, mustn't keep putting off the next fateful day. Meanwhile, I'll seek nectarines for Ben, pick up three tubes of Smarties in Sainsbury's. My child/husband has developed a craving for coloured sweets. And yes, I may very well buy something stupid, indulge myself for a change.

I pay my 25p for the privilege of parking on a plot of land that was bequeathed to the village, wonder anew about the old dears who enjoy a stroll around the shops. A potter for some of them lasts more than an hour, and they are now forced to pay for pleasures that were once free.

They'll all stay at home and die quietly, I suppose, die for lack of company and exercise.

'Coo-ee!'

I freeze, one hand on Elsie's door. This is not Ruth's call, yet I recognize it instantly, cannot quite attach a name to the shrill sound.

'Mrs Starling. Laura!' It is Susan Jenkinson, my erstwhile husband's erstwhile district nurse. She is panting heavily, is garbed in civvies, an ancient brown coat over a Crimplene-type suit whose vintage is *circa* 1975. 'It's lovely to see you,' she gasps. 'Are you coping all right?'

There's something in the homely face that lets me know she really wants an answer. She has little money, next to no life of her own, yet she still manages to be generous, concerned. 'I'm OK. You?'

'Not bad, ta. Busy – you know how it is.' She glances round the car park. 'I'd like a word, if you've time.'

'Well, I'm just going to do a bit of shopping, but—'

'It'll not take a minute.' She places a bag on the ground, balances its uneven weight between thick legs and feet that look flat and tired. 'See, I visit Heaton Lodge, work there about three times a week, check up on residents and report to doctors. We're community nurses now, so our brief's a bit wider than it used to be. It's poor Mr Starling. He's getting on the difficult side.'

I swallow, feel the dryness of my throat. 'Yes, he can be hard work at times.'

She peers closely at me, narrows the muddy green eyes. 'What is it he keeps going on about? Everybody's asking the same questions, wondering what's making him so aggressive. We don't like over-sedating old folk, you see. It's not fair to dose them up just to make them containable. But he's screaming and shouting, using foreign words—'

'I know.'

She moves away slightly, rights the lumpy plastic bag on the ground. 'He's fretting, going over and over the same things all the time. On Tuesday, it was "close the door" and "they've got to die". Then the next day, he kept saying he'd had enough of it. "For Laura's sake", he kept saying.'

I haven't heard that one. 'He's confused,' I say lamely.

She shakes her head, causes the newly frizzed hair to stand to attention. 'The psychiatrist says that Mr Starling's accessing the past, having real memories of troubled times. We need this clarifying. Can you tell us what he's thinking about?'

'No.'

'No idea at all?'

I look towards Sainsbury's, wish I could get inside. Inside, I won't think of Ben. I shall fold him up carefully like a road map that might be needed again, will place him in a rear compartment of my head, will study vegetables and fruit and Smarties. To stay sane, I have to put my love on a back burner, keep the gas low.

She is staring at me, continues to hope for clarification. I can't help her, can't help myself. 'Ben was in his fifties when I met him,' I tell the nurse. 'I got the impression that he had been away, or that he originated from another country. There is something in his past, something he never wanted to discuss. It's too late for me to find out now.' The phone has not rung for years. After the very early days of Ben's illness, the calls stopped. Somehow, those widespread people have learned about Ben's condition. All links with the past, with the business partners too, have obviously been severed or put on hold. So the jewels in the safe will stay where they are.

'I just wish we could ease him,' she says.

'I know. Thanks for caring.'

She awards me a huge smile that lights up the whole face, making her warm, almost attractive. 'Well, I do care. It's not just a job to me, it's a way of life. Like I've been thinking about you a lot, hoping you're better. And you're not even on my list. Lists don't mean much, do they?'

In the past, I have categorized this woman wrongly. She's OK, a good sort, a woman who doesn't depend on rotas. 'No, but I wish I could find my shopping lists.'

We separate and I enter Sainsbury's, where the plot to confound me continues apace. They have reorganized, have moved everything except the building. It takes me a while to find animal food and toothpaste, but I finally stuff the lot in Elsie's boot, march onward to obey Diana by buying something silly. Nobody in Crown Records raises an eyebrow when I buy £60 worth of memorabilia. I shall sit tonight with Little Richard, Bill Haley, Elvis Presley for company. I was not a rock and roller, but I was alive then, I suppose. The music of my teens has grown on me, is attractive when compared to the current morass of metal. Will the young folk of today play Guns 'n' Roses in defiance of something even less melodic?

The jeweller has a sale. I buy a Westminster chime mantel clock and a pair of crystal hedgehogs, a mother and a baby. But after a moment or two, I relent and buy the father, too, as I have no wish to create yet another single-parent family. The proprietor congratulates me on my choice of timepiece. She is a beautiful woman with good clothes and a sincere smile. 'How's Ben?' she asks.

'No improvement, Marie.'

She knows him as well as anyone does, asked him for an opinion sometimes. 'That's a shame.' She means it, they all mean it. There are many people who would help if they could, if help were possible. But I'm on my own. He's my husband and I can't do anything for him. And I've unfolded that map, the one I was trying to store in a box at the back of my brain. He brought me joy, freedom, wealth, and I can't bear to think of him. Something must be done. Soon. I shall probably ask for my darling husband to be sedated to a point where he might become comatose. Do people in coma dream? I wonder.

Across the road, Barclays has a new branch, has cleared out of a lovely sandstone building to continue the steel, glass and plastic dream that is a nightmare for many of us. On the corner of Moor Lane and Liverpool Road, the once-proud bank hides its vacant eyes behind a FOR

SALE notice. Thatched cottages and a working mill have fallen victim to the onslaught of progress. Everything changes, diminishes, including Ben. Wherever I look, I am reminded of him.

I drive past the comprehensive where my Jodie was educated, wait at the crossing while diesels for Southport and Liverpool rattle past. Shall we ever see real trains again? Or a clean snowdrop? Ben won't celebrate any more when the blackbirds achieve their spring hatching. Our kitchen robin still comes, struts on the window-sill, one eye on Handel, the other on me. Ben was so much better with the birds, so much easier than I am. Who will love the birds as much as he did? Who?

I am sitting near the coastguard station, my vision blurred by two kinds of water, both saline. The sea throws off a pewter-coloured sheen, my eyes sting as I continue to come to terms with the end of my husband's life. I cry for him and for the birds. I cry for myself.

My heart is still breaking. Sometimes, I don't feel much, just come in, look at him, talk to a member of staff or to a resident who continues to manage a decent conversation. But today, my Ben is back with me for a few minutes. He smiles, allows me a glimpse of how he was, who he was, before the illness. His hand comes out. 'Laura, how lovely to see you. I'll come out with you today. We might walk along the shore and look at the gulls.'

I gulp, force back the sobs, plaster a false smile across my stiffened face. 'How are you, darling?' I manage, clinging fiercely to that small portion of my mind that prompts me to function automatically.

'I am good.'

He is good, so good. There's stubble on his face, a bit of dried soap on a cheek, a new puffiness round the eyes. He is the finest man I have ever known, the bravest and the best. With Ben, I was right, I made a sensible decision. We were lucky, because we had love and friendship. Without love, there's no marriage, without friendship, there's no communication. We were so fortunate. Till it all got taken away. 'Did you have breakfast?' I ask.

'Oh yes, I had cornflakes and milk. Of course, they watch me. But I'm used to being watched, just as I'm used to watching. Our eyes were the most important part of the job.'

I pat his hand. 'Which job is that, Ben?'

He is staring at one of the nurses. 'She shouldn't have gone in there, you know.'

I look at the door, still swinging after the nurse's passage through it. 'Why?'

'They never come out.'

'Ben, look at me.' I turn his face towards me, push the hair from his eyes. He won't let anyone near him with scissors. My Ben is terrified of scissors and dogs. 'What job, Ben?'

The eyes are bright, brimming with moisture. 'Why do you leave me here? Why can't I come home? Remember the rubies and that square emerald in the top safe. I must have promised them to someone. My memory is so poor. They watch me all the time.' He glances round the room again, shakes a finger at an empty space. 'Over there,' he mutters. 'Go away from me now.' Ben's brief flirtation with near-normality is almost over.

'Where are you, my love?' I whisper. 'The stove, the cow going to market, the hut you keep mentioning. Where did it all happen? Why are you so afraid? And what did you say to Tommo?'

He fixes his attention on me, though he seems not to recognize me completely. I am, perhaps, someone he knows vaguely, a face that is not quite familiar. '*Dove?*' he says. The second syllable is extended, sounds like 'vay'. Italian, then, the Italian for 'where'. He rattles off some fluent French, slips into German, confuses the two. From a stream of unrecognizable words, I pick out '*nein, nein*' and '*bitte*', watch his face as it twists into a shape that must surely echo his inner torment. I can't sit here and do this, can't bear his pain, can't bear my own fruitless agony.

He stops shouting, places a hand on mine. 'We shall make no more noise.'

I mouth quietly, 'Are you German, Swiss? Ben—'

'I am Greek,' he answers clearly, flooring me completely. 'My mother was Jewish. I am now a Christian, just as my father and grandfather were.' He blinks slowly, listens, his head on one side. 'They are gone and we are safe for now.'

In his sleep, Ben used to punctuate his terrible snoring with words in a language I could never place. Is he telling me the truth, is he Greek? Or is the Greek just another symptom of a brilliant mind going to seed? He's certainly a linguist, speaks better Paris French than any Englishman would trouble to learn. I knew he wasn't English, thought he might be French or German.

'Strawberry yoghurt,' he announces loudly, back to his old routine now. He's had a fixation with strawberry yoghurt for some time, though he never used to be terribly keen on dairy produce. 'And cornflakes.' Well, that's a change.

'Do you want more cornflakes, Ben?'

He is no longer with me. I lean back, watch his lips moving in time with thoughts that are seldom voiced. Ben is in another location, another time. I cannot reach him. I cannot find my husband.

'Hello.' A hand settles on my shoulder. 'Don't worry, he's been calmer this morning. Did you get your shopping done yesterday?'

'Hello, Susan.' I sniff, try to swallow the rising tide. Bereavement is never easy, is particularly difficult when there hasn't been a funeral at all.

Nurse Jenkinson dries my tears on a tissue, stuffs it back into a side pocket of the blue dress. 'No use you getting upset, love. They do hear things, you know. He might just remember your sadness after you've gone away.'

We shared everything, Ben and I. The grief, the joy, the tears, the laughter. 'I feel so guilty,' I say. 'He should be at home with me, should be where he belongs.'

'No.'

'But I'm his wife, I ought to look after him.'

She drops to her hunkers, takes each of my hands in a grip that is firm but friendly. 'You've been ill. Getting ill is nothing to feel guilty about. Why don't you have some rest, rent a cottage somewhere, have a break and some fresh air?'

'I can't.'

She tugs at me, forces me to look at her. 'Why not? He's going nowhere. He gets all he needs here, food and warmth and a doctor just a phone call away. There's nothing you can do to bring him back as he was. Making yourself worse won't be any good to either of you.'

The 'worse' comes out as 'werse', reminds me of Ma Boswell in *Bread*. 'He wasn't so bad when I went away for the first lots of tests. Then when I . . . had the breakdown, I couldn't even look after myself, so I had to leave him in here with the other lost souls. I drove him to this. I should have got a resident nurse, then Ben could have stayed in his own environment.'

She shakes her head, releases my hands, rises carefully because her weight is distributed unevenly over the wide frame. 'Alzheimer's goes its own way, Laura. It's just that you noticed the deterioration because you'd been away from him. Your husband would have been just as ill, but you'd have come to terms with it gradually. Mr Starling stopped responding to most exterior stimuli years ago. None of this is your doing.' They keep telling me the same things over and over, and I keep not listening.

She pats my shoulder, moves on to another group, two children, their parents and a frail man who smiles all the time. The vacant grin is not improved by threads of saliva that run down to a towelling bib under his chin. His son or son-in-law reaches out, catches a few of the dribbles on a tissue. Dear God, this is a kind of hell, a capsule trapped in some dark zone of another dimension. We sit with the living dead, then we go home and cry all over again. I won't look. I won't look at Ben, at the other stricken family. Determinedly, I gaze round a room that is becoming almost as familiar as my own house.

It's a nice enough place, lots of cheerful chintz, an open fireplace with a painted screen hiding the unused grate, coffee tables covered in *Country Life*, *Lancashire Life*, some daily papers, the odd *Merseymart*. Tea-trolleys sit sedately along walls, the pottery deliberately non-clinical – one of the Johnson's, I think, possibly Eternal Beau, flowers and ribbons painted on earthenware. No china here, no crystal, no sharp-edged knives. The carpet is moss green, one of those American Shadow types, probably scrubbable. There's a grandfather clock, a noticeboard, some hardback books on a shelf with jigsaws and a compendium of games.

Nurse Susan Jenkinson is combing an old woman's hair. This old lady sits here every day, never gets a visitor. Our nurse straddles the now slim divide between National Health and private, seems to treat all her clients equally well. She is part of the system that dictates to once-private homes, comes in here, works the district, covers both sides of the fence. She'll get no OBE, no mention in the honours, yet she represents the true heroes among real people.

I walk to a table, flick through *Vogue*. These poor folk are probably Nurse Jenkinson's only family. I picture her huddled over a gas fire in the evenings, beans on toast or Pot Noodles for supper, the TV doing its best to persuade her that she is not truly alone. There will be a photograph of her mother in a cheap frame. I could offer something, a pretty rug, some prints for her walls. But it doesn't work that way. Giving is easy, receiving is hard.

I walk out along a corridor whose red and black Axminster shows some signs of wear. Shalom sits near a door, cleans his whiskers. The home cat is a huge beast, bigger than my Handel. I cannot imagine who gave him such a peaceful name, because he is not tranquil by nature. He takes my measure, rises up, stretches, announces his desire to be released. I let him out, keep an eye on him while he bounces nimbly towards a tree. Should any stray feline come this way, Shalom will separate the intruder from at least six of its nine lives.

Ben's room is like the others, small, clean, with neat hospital corners folded into the pale green bed cover. My image sits on top of a small television set. The three children are suspended from a picture rail, their faces frozen in yesteryear's laughter. I sit in the cushioned wicker chair, listen to the soft ticking of Ben's travel clock. Where have you been? I ask this timepiece. When you came out of his suitcase, when your face was uncovered at the end of a journey, what did you see?

The room does not smell of Ben. I know that, because I bent down once and buried my nose in his pillow. Nothing. No trace of him, just clean linen, a whiff of Daz, a hint of pine disinfectant. He would be better . . . yes, he would be better dead, because he's not really alive. There's a sickening pain in my chest, because I cannot bear to think of him dead, even though most of his brain has pre-deceased him. My husband has lost much of his mind, is tormented by the few grey cells that still sign on for work every morning. He has mislaid much of the present and most of the recent past. The clearest memories are bad ones. There is no comfort for him unless we have him sedated.

What shall I do? For five minutes, I have sat here, have found no solution. Can I leave him here? Can I leave him with well-intentioned and capable nurses, a twinkle-eyed matron, a killer cat called Shalom? If I bring him home, will I manage, will someone with medical training move in and sustain me until . . . until the end?

I look out on a garden that is neatly trimmed, square, sufficiently unimaginative to be easy. 'I don't know what to do,' I mouth to an inquisitive thrush. 'He's looked after your lot for years, so when are you going to help him?' Am I going loopy? No, I think not. Strange, because I've been crazy before, and I wasn't under pressure like this. Ben has been my strength, my suit of armour. Now, I must be his.

There's a mist over the window, so I must be crying again. He doesn't need me, doesn't really know me. I am useless, stupid, incapable of patching up this one broken man. But no, he told me many times that I am not stupid. Tommo was the one who put me down, who finished off the job started by my mother. You did so much, Ben. Please tell me how I can help you.

'Come into the light,' Ben said to me many years ago. 'Do not hide in the shadows, my lovely girl. You are clever and kind and your husband was a fool to let you go.'

My blouse is damp with salt water. I need him now. Ben, where are you? Self-pity, disgusting self-indulgent tears. I powder my face, go back to say goodbye.

He looks at me, his eyes narrowed, searching, groping for a clue. Then the face clears. 'Laura?'

I sniff, smile, wait.

'It's in the bottom safe,' he says softly.

'What is?'

'Paper. Writing. The housemartin's nest.'

I drop to my knees, rub his hands, will him to be warm and alive. 'Ben. You are the only one who has the combination to the bottom safe. Can you remember it?'

He grins, grips my fingers. 'Strawberry yoghurt,' he whispers.

With this final piece of information, I am forced to be content.

Three times now I have driven past my mother's place. Today, my resentment for her is active. I must therefore stay away from her. In her eighties, the woman displays more intactness of faculty and spirit than I do. But I won't kick her, not even with words. She's old, and temper seldom improves with time.

My car is parked outside the newsagent's, has begun to grumble about its circular, boring route. With all this starting and stopping, Elsie will decide to have another coronary soon, will go down with a clogged carburettor and dirty points. I enter the shop, pick up a handful of papers, pay a small fortune at the till.

The neo-Nazis in Germany have attacked a Berlin cemetery for Jews. We pulled down the wall, so it begins again. The Hitler Youth is alive, well, throwing petrol bombs. So I'll do the crossword. Diana will be enjoying the run of the place, must be glad when her middle-aged landlady gives her some space. She'll be in my living room eating my chocolates and watching *EastEnders*.

'Laura.' He pokes his head into my car. 'How are you?'

'Fine.' I stab at the general knowledge quiz, make a hole with my angry ballpoint. 'Go away.'

He opens the door, climbs into Elsie's passenger seat, squashes my *Observer*. 'I've missed you.'

'Good holiday?' The whole of Crosby is walking down Coronation Road, is watching me with the best-loved vet in these parts. They love him for his kindness to animals; I have loved him for the same quality, also for his goodness to me. No, that's not strictly true. I've loved him because I'm selfish and he took away some of my pain by making love to me. Sex was not just an expression of love, not in my life. It became an essential like food and drink, it was necessary. It still is, but I'm staying on a diet. 'How are the children?' I ask.

'OK.' He pulls the newspaper from beneath his buttocks, smooths the creases, plays jig-saw with torn corners. 'Is it over, Laura?'

'Yes.' Five down is beyond me. I need to go back into the shop for some Tippex, whiten my mistakes. Though I can't blot out Robert with a little brush, can I? 'We should never have started it.'

'It was good,' he whispers. His arm creeps across my shoulder. A current spills from his fingers, travels the length of my spine in a long, continuous and persuasive beat. It is a gentle, familiar pulse that attempts to waken my lazy, resting body. I sit forward. They all know him. There's a gaggle of young parents, a tangle of prams outside the shop. They are standing in a queue, all waiting for Daddy to come out with the Sunday ice-cream, the weekend toffees. 'Sweets are delicious,' I am inspired to say. 'But they're no good for you. Gratification of a base hunger doesn't exactly strengthen the soul.' God, I sound like Confetti used to before she got a bit of sense.

'I won't rot your teeth,' he replies.

He is annoying me. I am annoying me. I want to jump out into the road, scream about my privacy being invaded by this handsome intruder, but I am trapped in a vice created by my own sins. Also, I don't want to show myself up unduly. 'Robert, I don't want to see you again. Ever.'

'OK.' The door swings open and he gathers up his long legs, the muscle straining against black tracksuit bottoms. I am a lustful woman, have often studied men in the same way as I look at pieces of art. He looks right in crazy clothes, would look good in a flour sack. Most men don't do justice to casuals, trainers, polo shirts, as they make the mistake of confusing 'casual' with 'scruffy'. Robert is not merely handsome, he is beautiful, like something created by Michelangelo or another of those Italian oddballs. He has a superb body and I will not look at him.

I turn the key, grit my teeth while Elsie strains herself to come to life. But she can't move, because I dare not shift her. A man sits on the bonnet, squats in a position that is almost lotus. He is a lunatic. I've been aware of that, have watched him swimming in icy November water, smelly water, too. He has climbed up trees, across trees, inside trees. He has talked to the trees, has swung in Tarzan fashion from branch to branch, his only anchor a piece of frayed washing line left behind by the scouts. Robert has nothing to lose but his reputation, and he cares not one fig-leaf for that. In fact, I ought to be grateful for the fact that he has remained fully clothed.

Well, to hell with it all. While this lot of pram-pushers is talking about me, some other poor beggar will be left alone. I climb out, straighten my coat, lock both doors. A child stares, his mouth oozing melted orange lolly-ice. Two older women have stopped mid-sentence, Sunday shopping forgotten in all the excitement. There's a button hanging off my coat. It has been my experience that when dignity is required, elastic breaks or a button comes loose. With my head held high, I stalk towards the group of witnesses, stumble over a drop in the pavement, manage to remain upright. That's another thing that spoils dramas, a tendency to lift the nose so high that nothing is truly visible.

'Laura, what about your car?'

I stop, listen to the silence. There must be fifteen or twenty people standing between us, but not one of them is breathing. 'Keep it,' I shout, throwing my voice ahead, not bothering to turn and look at him. He can have the bloody car. My feet slow long before the message from my brain has reached them. My feet remember that I've promised the car to Edward. When I get too old to drive, Edward will adopt my baby. Elsie is valuable, a collector's item. Robert catches up with me. He seems unflustered, is fit enough to endure any barb I might throw at him. 'Why do you want me?' I ask. 'I'm old, far too old. Your children need a younger stepmother, someone who can tolerate the noise, even add to it.'

'I didn't ask you to marry me.' He is so attractive, 6 feet 2 inches tall, brown wavy hair, bright blue eyes. He should be on the telly in that Nescafé advert, ought to be borrowing coffee from a female executive who pretends disinterest in his body.

I look him up and down. A dozen pairs of eyes are fixed on us. Some people have gone away, their constitutions too delicate to witness raw emotion. 'Bugger off, Robert,' I say.

'Would you?' He is serious. I know he's serious because his eyes aren't crinkling at the corners. 'If you were free? And if I asked you?'

My tongue clicks, making me feel and sound like one of those old nuns who tried to educate me many moons ago. 'How quaint. These days, the women do the asking and the telling. No, I wouldn't ask you and no, I wouldn't

564

marry you. I'm going to be a recycled virgin.' A young mother giggles, understands how I feel, pushes her pram away.

Robert is plainly intending to persist. He is leaning against the shoe shop window, has assumed the age-old attitude of the young buck on the prowl, seriously casual. He opens his mouth, 'Now, look—'

'I'm leaving Crosby.' Well, that is news to me, but what a splendid pearl of wisdom. I wonder how I'm managing to be so resourceful. There again. Perhaps I do intend to leave. That could have been the plan all along, so secret that I haven't even told me about it yet.

He falters, blinks a few times, then crosses the pavement and steels his spine against a lamppost. It's like being fifteen again, keep off the streets or the boys will get you. 'Where are you going?' The tone is low, disappointed.

'Never mind.'

'I can visit. Have stethoscope, will travel.'

'No. To go where I'm going, you'd need a visa.' I am learning so much about my intentions today.

'Rubbish. Even if you're going to Russia, the cold war's over. As for the rest of the world, a visa never was a problem.'

Again, I am inspired. 'I'm taking Ben home. He's a foreigner, wants to be with his own people.'

'But—'

'No.' I walk away, push past a few lingering witnesses, leap into Elsie and drive off at a speed that is extravagant. He is still leaning on that lamppost. Perhaps a little lady will pass by – it worked for George Formby. Sainsbury's is open, has defied the Lord's day, but it's peaceful and the parking is free on Sundays. Robert was just a plaything, I tell myself firmly. He was a toyboy, he'll find some other strong woman to amuse him.

The pigeons swoop, pick at a McDonalds carton. From the corner of an eye, I watch as a single starling awaits his turn, just as we all await ours. Time to go home.

Chapter Four

She has finished the painting, has done a good job. I saunter about, pick up the odd piece of valuable tat, a figurine, two crystal paperweights, an old Venetian vase. What will I do with these tangible memories? Ben was with me when I bought some of them, he even chose one or two while on his business trips. What was he doing, where was he doing it? No, I won't think.

I have to leave here. Some part of me realized that long before my subconscious leapt into my mouth when Robert was performing for the crowd. I'm going. This is Ben's home, our home, this is Benaura. He won't get better. He won't kick me out of bed on Saturdays, won't ever be here to persuade me to make the tea. 'Every day, I do it,' he used to say. 'Go on, woman, earn your keep.' Then he used to chase me round the bedroom and beat me with a pillow. I never made the morning tea, not once.

Benaura is my property, was signed over to me by a weary man with a weary brain. 'Take it, Laura. It is brick and mortar, no more than that. And the money in my British accounts too. What time is it?' That was an early symptom, asking the time, the day, his address. 'Are we in a hotel, Laura?' I won't cry.

Where am I going, then? Will I abandon Ben in Heaton Lodge, just turn my back on him, leave him to sit alone like the old lady who never gets visitors? Don't worry now, I tell myself. Take it easy, you've been ill, you've had a rough time, old girl.

I sit on an arm of the sofa, fix my gaze on the window. They are here, the September starlings, fighting, shouting at each other in the pear tree. Ben loved them so, envied

566

their anger, their survival skills. Among some species, when a bird fails to keep up with its peers, its life is ended by other members of the same group. Do Starlings kill Starlings? Is that the kindest thing, is it? Laura, does that idea sit with the others that have surprised you lately? You're so sure about leaving here, so positive about new starts, clean sheets. Don't think. Look at the birds, but don't think.

This is Monday. On Mondays, I force myself to face my mother. My failure to arrive at her door and at her beck and call would just cause a lot of bother on the phone. I glance at the instrument, accuse it silently. In about half an hour, her special ring will be reborn, that piercing, endless freep-freep that belongs only to Liza McNally of the School Hill Retirement Apartments, Crosby, Merseyside. Even Telecom succumbs to her special power, seems more alert when prompted by a bony, nicotined finger with pearlized varnish on the talon. Perhaps they know that she holds shares in their grasping empire.

Diana is out, has gone to bend a different ear. When I think of her, I smile. She has brought life to this house, has made me laugh, made me function. Diana is a pharmacologist, a student of drugs and their various applications. Perhaps she will find a cure for Ben after he is dead. Jodie will pen the prescription, will use Diana's medicine to cure a sufferer, a victim of Alzheimer's. I wish it had come sooner. How many of us are thinking this? How many have relatives with this terrible illness?

The phone. It's too early, won't be Mother. Mother is like an alarm clock, is tuned in to the rhythm of her joyless life. At half past ten, she will torment me. At four o'clock, it will be the turn of one of the wardens who look after the apartments.

I lift the receiver, suddenly sense bad news. 'Hello?'

Diana's voice is squeaky. 'Me father. It's me dad.' She must be in a tight spot, because the accent is thickening by the second. 'They've just found him.'

My mental picture of Diana's male parent is a sparse one, just a bundle of rags with a meths bottle peeping from a pocket. 'Where?' I ask.

She chokes, breathes heavily. 'In the river.'

It is difficult, almost impossible to think of something sensible to say. I am sweaty but cold, and my slick fingers tighten on the receiver. Gooseflesh creeps up my arms, makes me shiver. 'Diana?'

'What?'

'Is he . . . is he dead?'

A small pause is fractured by a sound that is half sob, half cough. 'What do you think? Even the bloody fish are dead in this muck. I can't . . . will you come for me?'

'Of course I will.'

She blubbers. I can imagine the poor little thing wiping her nose on the sleeve of that dreadful anorak. After a huge sniff, she tells me the address. 47, Cannonfield Street. I feel sick, an empty sick that is probably made worse by not eating. After grabbing an apple, I dive out, jump into Elsie. She's in one of her moods, needs talking to before she'll start.

From the top of Diana's street, I can see the Mersey. It killed Diana's dad. My hands are shaking. I did not know this man, but his daughter has loved him. Even as she cursed his waywardness, she loved him.

There's a policewoman at the door, a smallish person with no hat and a well-cut uniform. The hat is on the sideboard, and the cluttered sideboard is just two short paces away from the pavement. 'Mrs Starling?' The short arm of the law seeks mine. 'She's heartbroken. Can you take her back with you, let her stay in your house?'

'Yes.'

Diana is in a corner, on a chair that is already occupied by a pile of newspapers. This makes her taller, almost as tall as if she were standing. The house reeks of take-away food, rotted cabbage, stale sweat. A low mantelshelf is covered in papers, brown envelopes with windows, junk mail. Another armchair seems to have exploded, its guts pouring onto a rug that tries hard to be a shade of maroon, fails due to many spills and black-edged burn holes. An ashtray on the floor spills its dead. Hanging over the squalor is a black crucifix, Christ's agonized figure shaped from a silvery metal and affixed to dry, polish-starved timber. There's a pulley line above the fire, several pairs of greyish underpants draped over its slats.

'Laura.' She reaches out for me as the policewoman releases my arm, but there is no time for condolences. An army of people arrives, pushes past me. The newcomers talk very quickly in a language I mastered years ago. There's our Jack, our Audrey, our Peter, our Mark. Sundry spouses line up in front of the sideboard, a small platoon not at ease, but hardly ready for inspection. Our Jack has matters well in hand. 'We'll see to it, Di,' he blusters. 'He can go in with me mother, I'll soon get it sorted.'

Diana is white. She leans back in her chair, closes her eyes. 'Shut up, all of you.'

The room is instantly quiet. Everyone waits for the little waif to speak. Someone coughs, a match is struck.

'You'll see to it?' asks Diana. 'It? That "it" was my dad. And not one of you turned up when he was in the 'ozzy with the DTs. Even you never came, Sal, couldn't be bothered to see your own brother in bloody prison.' This remark is addressed to an older woman who loiters near the door, plainly anxious to be on her way. 'So you can just bugger off, the lot of you. Nobody wanted him when he was alive, so it's up to me what I do with him. Go on, get gone.'

They won't go. I've seen all this before, have witnessed these scenes a long time ago. They will fight, grieve, fight again. It's like a ritual, a pattern that must be observed. Because they are bereaved, emotions are strong, tempers frayed to lacework.

Our Audrey steps forward. She may be Diana's sister, or she may be an in-law. Whatever, she will be family, will have been absorbed into the unit as soon as the ink on the certificate was dry. Baptismal or marriage, any certificate means full membership. Our Audrey has bleached hair, an ankle chain and no bra. Her eyes have been outlined with thick, black stripes, making her into a cut-price Jean Shrimpton. When she talks, her breasts jiggle about like two animals fighting in a sack. 'Don't you be coming all the 'oity-toy with us just 'cos you've 'ad wot you might call an education, like. Me mam bought this 'ouse with that bit of a win wot she 'ad with Littlewood's in the seventies. So it's between all of us an' no messin'.'

I can't believe it. Their father is on a slab at the morgue, and they're carrying on like vultures hovering over carrion before it's begun to rot. So this is what happens, is it? The deceased is at the funeral parlour having a last hair-do, and the kids start fighting over bankbooks and other items of interest.

Diana's eyelids lift slowly. 'Take the bloody house,' she says wearily. 'I'm off back to Blundellsands.'

Our Audrey is not best pleased. 'You can't just go and—'

'Can't I? Just watch me. I saw to him when he was alive, didn't I? Well, I'm having him cremated and then—'

'Put him near a gas oven and you'll blow both cathedrals to kingdom come. There's that much bloody booze in him—'

Diana jumps on our Mark, smacks him across an acne-scarred cheek. 'Shut up, you. He was a drunk. I know he was a drunk, so there's no need for you to go disc-jockeying it all over Radio flaming City. In case you haven't noticed, he was your father. It doesn't matter what they were, what they did wrong or right. At the end, you just say, "These were my parents." We owe everything to them.'

Mark shuffles, backs away. 'I don't know about that. It was the other way round, 'cos he died owing me a fiver.'

Diana pokes a hand into her pocket, throws a jangle of coins on to the rug. 'There you are, Judas. Sorry I can't manage the rest of the thirty pieces, but that's all I've got

570

on me at the moment. You can have the rest when I've sold me Rolls Royce.'

The money stays where it is. 'Sorry, girl,' mumbles Mark. 'I was only messin'.'

Mark shuffles again, his large feet bursting out of some size 11-ish Adidas trainers whose laces trail on the floor. He lights a badly squashed Superking, tosses the empty packet in the general direction of the fireplace. 'I've left me van,' he grumbles, quieter now. Our Audrey agrees, mutters a few words about kids abandoned to the questionable mercies of ''er next door'. A woman with dyed black hair takes two steps to her left, peeps into the kitchen, freezes, pulls her head back into the room and displays an expression of complete bewilderment, looks as if she might have caught a glimpse of hell's doorway. 'Yer'll not sell this 'eap of crap. Bloody cockroaches are 'avin' a disco in the back kitchen. There's enough grease on them walls to start a chippy.'

Diana is finally tired out, routed. I step to her side, place a hand on her shoulder. Facing them isn't easy. I know people like these, have lived among them. They are honest yet cute in the proper sense, wary, talented, furious without quite knowing why. The one with the blackened hair displays all the charm of a cement mixer, yet her eyes are hurt. Liverpudlians, poor Liverpudlians, people with a history of hard work that is now so historical that it seems like folklore. Building trade, dock work, plumbing? Oh yes, they've read about jobs like those. Oh God, I've been here, I've been stuck in a grimy cottage with three underfed children, a few pennies for the gas, enough bread and jam for breakfast. An image jumps unbidden into my head. Gerald and Edward are lying in their beds. I bend to kiss them, listen as my long hair sizzles in the candle's feeble flame. Automatically, I wet my fingers, pull them the length of the burning tress, extinguish the fire. Yes, I remember when electricity was a bonus, a luxury.

They don't know that. Diana's family doesn't appreciate my true empathy, my gut-wrenching understanding of their plight. Georgina Dawn saved me, I'm a lucky one. I was frightened then, before I started to write, and I am still afraid, still angry. Which geriatric judge put the black on his head, which lord of the realm ordered the death of Liverpool? I resent this slow murder of my city – yes, it is mine. I can no longer cover my ears to blank out the pitiful cries of its adult children as they moulder on another mountain of surplus. Butter, milk, people – they're all *de trop, mon cheri*. And thus we advance into Europe.

I look at Diana's family, see mouths that are thin from waiting, eyes that are hungry for activity, for employment. How many days have they stood in that ever-swelling dole queue? I smile inwardly. It isn't just the north, isn't just us, I say to myself. The cancer has spread, begins to be noticed. The difference is that we stopped blubbering years ago. 'I'll look after Diana,' I say eventually.

Our Audrey fixes her black-ringed eyes on me. They are blue, hard as flint. 'Are you 'er from Blundellsands?'

'I am.'

She heaves back her shoulders, thrusts out the trembling chest. 'Debtors' retreat, that.'

'Yes.' I meet the unfriendly and challenging stare. And somehow, she sees me as I really am, knows from words I have not spoken that I have been here before, have been where she is. She can tell that I have endured cold and fear. Perhaps the saying is true, 'It takes one to know one'. Her lips twitch, but she kills the smile. 'I will take care of your little sister, Audrey,' I tell her.

The thickly painted lower lip quivers. 'He was all right, really, me dad. It was the drink got him. He could read stories really good, like, used to put meaning in, he done all the different voices. Mind you, he was a terrible Red Riding Hood, sounded as if he'd been doctored.' She has picked up her aitches for me.

Mark puffs on his fag, doesn't bother to wipe a tear from his cheek. ''E was good to me ma. 'E never got drunk when me ma was 'ere.'

The policewoman steps outside, leaves the family to

grieve. My hand tightens on Diana's shoulder – I can feel the sobs building up pressure inside that slender body. Like a volcano that has lain dormant for too long, she will be forced to erupt soon. 'Shall I make some tea?' I ask. Tea is always made at times like this.

Mascara trails down Audrey's face. 'There's no cups, love. He didn't live here, he just got poured through the letterbox every night, fell on the floor and slept where he dropped. If we gave him something, like pots or pans, he sold them or swapped them. There is pans and that, but they're filthy in the back kitchen. He got fed by her three doors down – she used to do him meat and veg a couple of days a week. We paid her for it.'

Like members of the one body, they close ranks and pull me into their midst. I am here, therefore I am seconded without a vote, am drawn in as an honorary sister. They weep and curse and touch one another, each living through a past that has been colourful and noisy. Neighbours slip into the house, grey shapes that move silently round the edges of the scene. Yes, they are indeed scene-shifters, fetchers and carriers of props, because the scent of their offerings cuts through the tears. I don't even know why I'm crying. I don't know why I sob anew when I see the sarnies, the teacups, knives, spoons, paper napkins.

We eat. There are scones and biscuits and little pies, sausage rolls, tarts, triangular sandwiches with the crusts cut off. Audrey puts some food in her shopping bag, 'For the young ones,' she explains to no-one in particular. They have aged in this short time, have begun to bear the guilt that attaches to a parent's death. I can read their thoughts. They wish they'd been kinder, more obedient, wish they'd listened while their mother and father were still alive to make the rules.

'These are Mrs Cooper's cups,' observes Diana, a sob still fracturing the words. 'I'll take them back in a minute.' She fingers a saucer. 'Mrs Cooper collected this set with Green Shield stamps donkeys' years ago, before I was

573

born, I think. Mam told me. Mrs Cooper only gets these pots out for special occasions.'

Audrey drains her cup, pats a non-existent crumb from the ample bosom, grins when she realizes that she has my full attention. 'I could have been a page three,' she announces proudly. 'Only I got pregnant and got married. Still, I might give it another go, eh? I've kept meself firm.'

I nod, grant my approval. Where the money comes from doesn't matter, I remember that. You just get that typewriter or whatever where you can, cut out the questions and carry on with the business of keeping your dependants alive. 'Shall we go, Diana?' I ask.

Diana inclines her head. 'In a minute. Anyway, our kid's right. How the heck are we going to get shot of this place?'

Though I should not become involved in anything else just yet, I cannot help myself. 'I'll see to it.' It is yet another of those times when I say something, feel that I haven't really said it, look round and seek the guilty party. It's me, of course. I said it.

Everyone's attention is on me. 'Yer wot?' Jack is so incredulous that his voice is near falsetto in pitch. 'D'you know the Pope, missus? 'Cos it'll take a fuc— a flaming miracle to turn this into an 'ouse again. There's no floorboards upstairs. 'E burnt 'em before we got the gas fire put in. An' that kitchen is a f— it's an 'ell 'ole.'

'Even a hell hole can be fixed.' This is me talking again, Big Mouth, the last of the big talkers. 'I've furniture, paint, we can get some wallpaper. There's a chap in Crosby who'll do the work.'

Mark bridles. 'We're not charity cases.'

I look steadily at him. 'Well, I used to be a charity case and I've not forgotten. People round here kept me and my children alive when they scarcely had enough for their own families.' Actually, it wasn't that bad, not after I'd started writing, but I've been near enough to the breadline to be glad of my Warburton's sliced. 'I've been on the receiving end,' I tell him.

'Oh, right.' He sweeps the long-lashed gaze over me, takes in the silk scarf that hides my creping throat, the Italian shoes, breathes in my Estée Lauder scent. 'Sound,' he says contentedly. 'Thanks, missus. That's sound.'

'Sound' must mean good, I think. They are truly amazing, a separate and robust breed, strong, resilient, humorous to their last breath. A few minutes ago, they were keening like sick animals. Now, the eye make-up is being repaired, cigarettes are being cadged, plates have been returned to their rightful owners. I have enjoyed their company so much that I feel bereft when they leave, am pleased to accept a kiss from Audrey, a pat on the back from the black-dyed one.

We are alone now, just Laura Starling and Diana Hulme in a room that stinks of all kinds of rot, wet, dry, human. 'We'll have to get it fumigated,' she says.

'We might put in some windows, Diana. Some of that UPVC that's a dead ringer for ma—'

'Shut up.' She fiddles with a string of hair. 'Our Mark's gone to identify him officially. Me dad'll have to go in a shroud, 'cos he's got no best suit.'

'I'm so sorry.' I am, oh I am.

She gulps. 'I'll miss him. There'll be nobody waiting for me outside college, nobody chasing me along a corridor. "Give us the cash for a pint, girl," he used to shout. He was a docker, ages ago when there were loads of jobs. A lot of them are used-to-bes, most round here are jobless.'

Again, I am slightly afraid. She depends on me, needs me. I should not have taken her on, should not be here. While I'm here, Ben is alone. I pull myself together. 'Have you seen *Bread* on TV?' I ask.

'Yes.'

'Ma Boswell has a nice house.'

'Yes.' She sounds so down, so defeated.

'We can make this place nice, then you can live in it.'

She blinks, considers. 'What about the rest of them? They'll all want their cut. There's only our Mark with a job, and that van's on its last radials. He sells fish, always

575

stinks of it, specially Tuesdays and Fridays.' She pauses, seeks her point, plucks it out. 'I can't pay them.'

'But I can.'

The jaw drops a fraction. 'Why?'

She needs the truth, deserves it. 'Because I can afford it. I want to help you, Diana. But I can't keep you with me indefinitely.' I wait for a second, allow the things that have been wedged in my subconscious to come forth and leap from my tongue. 'I'm bringing Ben home. You will need somewhere to live while you get through the course at the hospital. Ben is going to be hard work.'

The pale yellow head nods. 'I can help you with him.'

'No. There'll be nurses most of the time.'

'Oh.' She scratches her nose. 'Well, it's very good of you to offer, but I thought you were a floating voter.'

'So?'

'It's a bit communist, sharing out your wealth. What will your husband say?'

I think about that. 'He'll probably say something about strawberry yoghurt.' My hand raises itself. 'No, don't ask. Just accept my help gracefully.' She needs occupying, I decide. 'In return, you can come with me now. Diana, you are going to deal with my mother.'

She stands, walks a few paces, gazes up the stairs. 'Hang on a bit,' she says. 'I'll just go upstairs and get my crash helmet. Pity we sold the suit of armour.' One eye winks. 'These stately homes isn't wot they was, is they?'

We close the warped door, drive off to Crosby.

Mother is in a high dudgeon. Mother's dudgeons are loftier than anyone else's, I'm sure of that. Enthroned on her armchair, she dominates the room, looks like a queen who is quarrelsome about meeting lesser beings. Diana is with me. Diana is not behaving in a way that will suit, because she has already shaken Mother's hand, has introduced herself to the dragon.

'What does your father do?' My mother fixes rheumy but agile eyes on her latest victim.

576

'Nothing. He's dead.'

My heart misses a beat, but I've nothing to fear. Diana is rising to the bait, will not be trounced by this wearying crone. Even today, with her father just deceased, Diana has resources that are asking to be plumbed.

'What did he do, then?' The 'Lanky' has gone missing from the voice, is replaced by one of her awful attempts at 'poshdom'.

'He drank.' Diana sits, though there has been no invitation. I scurry into the kitchen, set the kettle to boil. Diana Hulme and Liza McNally promise to be an explosive combination. Perhaps I should make a gallon to quench the flames. No, there's an extinguisher on the wall.

'He drank for a living?'

I cough, rattle the cups.

'I suppose so. He drank for a living and it killed him.' Her voice is desolate, but old Liza will choose not to hear the sadness.

I can almost hear my mother bristling. 'Was he a wine-taster, then?'

No, Laura, you must not laugh. Diana's dad died last night, this is not the time for hilarity.

'I reckon he's tasted most things in his time,' says Diana. 'With the possible exception of Harpic.'

The tap drowns my nervous giggling. I wriggle the end of the Addis dishwashing brush in the drain, force breakfast time tea-leaves round the bend. Like Ben, my mother refuses to use tea bags. And that is the only common ground between them, though my husband was always courteous and kind to the nasty creature in the next room. I recall the occasion when Jodie gave Granny an earful some years ago – I was privileged to be present at the time. Mother had palpitations, a severe migraine and two fingers of the best cognac after dinner that day. Will Diana have the same disastrous effect? Tentatively, I turn off the tap.

Diana's tap is in full flood. '. . . all round the world.

577

You see there's all these islands that haven't been discovered properly. He used to go and visit, buy their alcohol, but he could never get the recipes out of these uncivilized people. He used to sniff at it and taste it, but he could never work out how the pygmies made such powerful stuff. It was his life's work, Mrs McNally. And it killed him in the end.'

'How sad,' says my mother.

'Anyway, we've just been sorting things out. My brother's in fish, so he's gone to Dover to collect the body. He knows all about temperatures and things, so he'll keep Dad in good condition in the back of the van.' She is so strong, yet so pathetic. While she aches for her father, she still hangs on to the reins, remains in control. I know that the humour is for me, to keep me cheerful.

'And the yacht is lost?' How interested the old woman sounds!

'Completely. Went down just as they were coming into port. The coastguards tried their best, but they couldn't save the crew.'

I am out of the apartment in a flash, am hanging, red-faced and hysterical, over the railing on the balcony. She has lost a father, has gained and lost an ocean-going vessel, has gained the interest of a woman who never listens to anyone. Diana is tough, even tougher than I thought.

We drink our tea. Diana, who has come up in the world, makes much of crooking her little finger. Between ladylike sips, she dabs at her face with a handkerchief, one of mine. Mr Hulme's boat has acquired a name, the *Esmerelda*. Her crew consisted of honest Liverpool folk who were culled from the DHSS queue. They had just returned from some remote island when the *Esmerelda* floundered as she neared Dover.

Mother is moved to speak. 'The last thing the dear man saw would be that cliff face. It's so pretty, snow white and very English. Vera Lynn sang about it during the war, you know, kept all our spirits up.'

I cannot look at Diana. She knows that the last thing her father saw was the bottom of the Mersey, and that his spirits must have been far from up when he made that final journey. If I look at her, she might become as hysterical as I was on the balcony a few minutes ago. After all, she is grieving and the wounds are still raw. 'Would anyone like a biscuit?' I ask.

Diana shakes her head, moves closer to Mother. 'Your daughter has sort of adopted me.' The tone is confidential enough to almost exclude me. 'She's a very good woman, a good mother. I can see now why she is a good mother. She learned it from you.'

I cannot stay here. Any minute now, I shall laugh or cry or both.

My young friend jumps up. 'It was so lovely to meet you. I must go now, as there is a funeral to arrange.'

Mother's eyes are dim. 'His work killed him, Diana. Oh, I know how that is. It was the same for my husband, you know. He gave his all to the work, died trying to find comfort for sick people.'

I dive for the door, prepare to escape from my father's real murderer. 'I'll keep in touch, Mother,' I say, my voice strangled by very mixed emotions. I'm sorry for Diana, delighted that she's coping so well, amazed that my mother has behaved so appropriately.

Mother waves us out. Her finishing barb catches me from behind, but I manage to close the door on her words. 'Pity your daughter hasn't the same manners as Diana, Laura,' I hear as we stand on the landing.

'Bloody hell,' breathes my companion. 'If that's your mother, you deserve the Croix de Guerre. Will you take me to the erosion? I want to look at the river.'

'Yes. I'll take you.'

We can see the hills of Wales today, rising and dipping in shades of purple, grey and green. A ship is coming in, a lead-coloured merchant that glides silently over a glassy sea. The beach is deserted, the ice-cream man's van has

579

left its post. Summer is over, the visitors have gone with the tall ships. We shall be peaceful now, except for the screams of the gulls. Even they might desert us as the weather gets colder. In the frost, they often fly inland to look for warmer air. I have watched them hovering over houses, bouncing like balsa-wood gliders over thermals provided by the heat of humankind. They are chattering now, are no doubt excited by the ship's movement, will be discussing the pros and cons of following the vessel into port.

Diana is quiet, thoughtful, stares for at least ten minutes at the gun-metal depths that claimed her father. 'You're all right,' she says at last. 'I knew you'd be all right. You don't even know who I am, but you took me in.'

I decide to leave her to it. After what she's been through this morning, she needs the stage to herself.

'The best part of it is that you like me. I can tell you like me, Laura. Don't say anything, but I've been telling you lies.'

I unravel a tube of Polos, take one, offer one, put the rest away as she raises a hand in refusal.

'Laura, my name isn't Hulme. It's nearly Hulme, though. I kept the first two letters the same, so it was only three-fifths of a lie. And I changed my Christian name yonks ago. Diana's a good name, because Diana hunted for what she wanted and got what she wanted. Even that name's only two-fifths of a lie. I turned the I and the A round, put them in reverse order.' She takes a deep breath. 'Don't say anything till I've finished. Let me get the lot off my chest while we're not looking at each other. This isn't the first time you've saved my life. You were there when I was born and you were there the night the Catholics clashed with the Orangemen.'

I think I've stopped breathing. Everything's stopped breathing. Even the ship is standing still, is listening to my companion. Forbidden to speak, I concentrate on taking in oxygen and pushing out CO_2.

'I was called Daisy,' she says. 'And my mam was Liddy Mansell.'

Things remain on hold. The air in the car continues too still to breathe, so I wind down my window, take a gulp of ozone. I hover on the brink of panic, on the edge of joy, blink stupidly while my slowed brain sorts out her words, analyses, computes. For one frozen moment, I am back in that cold, bare cottage and Liddy is at the door. She rushes in, places the baby in my arms. A window breaks, is smashed by drunks who do not approve of Liddy's ways. The other children are missing, are probably with their father. He lives with his mother at the other end of town, waits for the old woman to die, bathes her, feeds her, works on the docks.

'They got married after Grandma died,' she tells me. 'I was too young to be a bridesmaid.' She sounds so far away.

'Daisy,' I murmur stupidly.

'A cow's name,' she says. 'I used to paint cows on—'

'On purple sugar paper.' Oh, Jimmy. Jimmy, why didn't you tell me about Liddy? Why didn't you find me when life became too sad for you to bear alone? I clear the emotion from my throat. 'We used to meet in town, Liddy and I. We had coffee in a place just off Williamson Square the last time we met. She told me that she was going away, that she'd write when you were all settled.' I gulp, hang on to the steering wheel as if it might guide me out of this new sorrow. 'She didn't write, because she didn't go away. Did she?'

'Only to heaven.' Her tone is soft, careful. She knows that I am hurt, doubly hurt by these twin blows.

'Now Jimmy . . .'

'Yes.' She takes my hand, has trouble separating my fingers from the steering wheel. 'Not long before she died, she gave me your address. "If you're ever in a mess, go to Auntie Laura," she said. I was in a mess, Laura. I had a rotten landlord, a good degree, no future and a dad who'd gone so far off the rails that he couldn't find a station.' She grits her teeth, won't let the sobs see daylight. 'My dad was a really good man, you know.'

'Oh, I do know, Diana. And your mother was . . . your mother was Liddy. I've never met anyone since who was as close a friend to me. Even Ruth . . . we're close, but it's not the same. Liddy and I were mothers together, single parents of young children. When I left . . .' I pause, remember that my saviour is in a nursing home five minutes away. 'I went with Ben, the man I'm married to. There were circumstances . . . I had to keep Liddy safe, had to make sure none of you would be hurt because of knowing where I was living. After a few years, we met up again. I missed her, Di. How I missed Liddy.'

She nods. 'He really ruined your life, didn't he? That first husband of yours, I mean. It's as if he wanted to take everything away from you. How did you make him stop?'

I didn't. Ben stopped him. Ben. 'He just stopped,' I say lamely. 'Everything stops if you wait long enough.' Perhaps Audrey really did recognize me, then. 'Is Audrey your sister?'

She grimaces, then grins. 'Yes, but don't broadcast it. She's got a bit of a reputation, has our Audrey, never settled down till she got married. And even now, her husband needs eyes in the back of his head. She's a tart, a tart with a heart.'

'They all had nicknames,' I remember aloud.

'Except our Mary,' she says. 'She's in America, we'll have to phone her. I suppose you wouldn't know my family by their proper handles.' She stops, turns my hand over, looks at the lines. 'Broken lifeline,' she remarks. 'That was your big illness. See, it picks up again here. You've a lot of years in front of you.'

I am guilty again. Many years ahead for me, none for Jimmy and Liddy. 'He was such a hard worker, Di. He looked after his mother, wouldn't make trouble by marrying Liddy before Mrs Hurst was out of it. And he still managed to hand over enough money to feed all of you. Theirs was a real love story.'

'Yes.'

The tightness of my grip matches hers. I can feel the

little bones of her hand, as tiny and fragile as those in the wings that have been mended by Ben over the years. 'I'll do what I can for you, Di. I'm not a mother, wasn't really cut out for parenthood, but I've done my best.' I carried this child against my chest, gathered my own brood about my skirts, hid in the lavatory shed. Gerald was silent, Edward fought his moans, Jodie stroked this baby's cheeks. We listened while Liddy made a dash for it, heard her feet slapping on uneven cobbles in the back street. The yelling stopped and the good Christians went away, some in pursuit of my friend and neighbour, others back to their homes to celebrate their hollow victory over the whore.

'Thank you,' says this woman-child. 'Thank you for taking me in that night when the fight was happening.'

Jimmy Hurst was tall and strong, had heart enough to look after all his dependants. I want to cry for him, want to get out of the car and scream with the gulls. He could have come to me, but his baby came instead.

'They might have killed me, Laura. You saved me.'

I sigh, wonder why I haven't done more for Liddy's family, for Liddy herself.

'What's it all about, Laura? The religion crap, everybody bowing and scraping, then fighting like cats and dogs?'

'Don't ask me, Diana. That's one of life's great mysteries.'

She chews a thumb-nail, studies the view for a moment. 'Can we go home now?' she asks. 'I'm starving.'

Chapter Five

We have arranged the funeral by phone. It's amazing what you can do by proxy these days. As Jimmy is to be cremated, his ornaments will be of imitation brass, a gilded plastic crucifix and a nameplate that will melt away into the ozone layer. It's more than sad. He used to be a man of honour and great dignity, and he will be dispersed like so much rubbish in a day or two. With the exception of Ben and, perhaps, Robert, I have met few men as gentle and entertaining as Jimmy was. For Liddy, Jimmy even became a Catholic, must have lost so many family friends from the old Lodge days. Diana manages to joke about her dad's plastic trimmings, says it was the UPVC windows all over again. Like many of us, she makes light of life's tighter corners. Her levity moves me more than tears would.

She is in the bath. I sit here trying to make sense of VAT. Whoever invented this system must be closely related to Lewis Carroll or Edward Lear, because it makes the most excellent nonsense. People pass money on to me, then I pass it on to Customs and Excise. The Customs and Excise give some of it back to the people who sent it in the first place, and we all get dizzy on the roundabout. And my pen is leaking all over the return, I'll probably get thrown in prison. It seems that the VAT man can get rid of the key and ask questions later.

The phone rings. My agent wants to know when to expect *A Heart Divided*. He is not pleased when I mention the turn of the century. Fortunately, someone calls on his other line, and I am cut off to make way for a transatlantic message. I forget the VAT, watch my animals. Handel has taken to Flakey, is teaching her how to catch the drips from the tap. It's my fault, I lifted the kitten onto the kitchen surface. Even Chewy is in love with our latest resident, has set up home on the mat in front of the sink. The gulls will leave soon. I shall be richer, am running out of sardines and mackerel. Both birds are flapping, revving up, agitating to be off. Tomorrow, I keep saying. Tomorrow, or the next day, they will be strong enough to try their wings.

The door flies open and Robert stalks in, stops abruptly, cocks his head to one side. He's a good-looking man, but he is always preceded by a smell that is a bit medical, usually wears a quantity of loose hair that was recently attached to some poor, sick beast. I am not ready for Robert. 'Go away,' I tell him.

'How are you?' He is doing his best to look non-chalant.

'The same as I was a few days ago. You can't stay, because I have a guest.'

He leans against the yawning door, stumbles as it groans and almost closes itself. 'I've seen her,' he replies. 'All legs and long hair. Snowflake looks well.' He watches as the eyes of two felines follow the emissions of a slow-dripping tap. 'You need a new washer,' he says.

'It would deprive my cats of their entertainment. The drip stays.'

Robert is fiddling in the pockets of his waxed jacket. He reminds me of my children when they were young, because he is a collector of 'interesting' things. I catch a glimpse of a shell, some pebbles, a fisherman's float. 'It's here somewhere,' he grumbles. Rubber bands and coins are transferred from one pocket to another, then his attention is taken by a length of tangled string. I tap my toe, wish he would go away. I don't want to have to explain him to Diana, shouldn't need to.

About five minutes too late, the dog realizes that we have a visitor. After a woof of welcome, he launches himself upon his victim. Chewy adores Robert, even when

585

the needle is entering tense shoulder muscle. He's a brave animal, never wails while being protected from distemper, hardpad, Parvo. Robert's face is getting a thorough wash, though the man isn't bothered. He has this empathy with animals, is so close to them that no behaviour troubles him. If a scared dog has an accident while in the surgery, Robert wipes up the mess, scatters a bit of disinfectant about, accepts that the animal was disturbed enough to disgrace himself. He's lovely, is Robert. I wish he'd go away.

'Found it.' He rubs at a piece of metal, presents it to me with a flourish. 'Your earring, madam.'

'Thanks.' He probably found this in his Land Rover. His Land Rover is where we last made love, on some very rough sacks in the back. I remember the scent in that vehicle, leathery, doggy with a hint of anaesthetic.

I remember too how sensitive he is, how caring. When he put our python to sleep, he sat with him for many hours until the slow metabolism finally succumbed to the over-dose. Yes, he's sensitive, a big softy who's looking for love, for permanence.

'Come for a walk,' I say, grabbing the lead. When Chewy is attached to his unwelcome tether, he drags me out to the path. Robert wipes his dog-slicked cheeks, follows us across the road and down the concrete steps. It's better here, because Diana will not hear us. Freed from his leather shackle, Chewbacca bounds away to worry a mound of blue-ish seaweed.

I cannot look at Robert, will have difficulty in meeting his eyes until the whole thing is over. The plan isn't something I've manufactured – it's just arrived by itself. And I can't talk about it to anyone, dare not court even the most tacit of accomplices. The bare facts must suffice. 'He's not happy, Robert. I'm bringing him home, to Benaura. I was lying when I said I was taking him out of the country. He's got no home except for this one. I can't see you while Ben's with me.'

He understands. 'That's OK, Laura. We don't need to

586

be lovers, you know. There's more than that to life, isn't there? As long as I can visit sometimes.'

My peripheral vision marks his stillness. If I could bear to turn and look at him, I would see a sculpture of great merit, something Rodin might have been proud to create. He's wounded and worried, is rendered immobile by the depth of his pain. He loved Carol, kept her with him until the suffering was too much for his children. When she was away, he visited her daily right to the end. Now, he wants me to replace her. There could be no better man for me, no finer companion. I used to feel old, too old for him, but I was wrong. It's me he needs, and that has nothing to do with anyone's age. We're right together, we love the same things. If . . . when Ben is gone, I might settle for stepmotherhood and this animal doctor. If I keep my freedom, that is, if I can live with my freedom afterwards.

I walk on, think back a few weeks to the time when Robert searched for days until he found a suitable kitten for a grieving pensioner. His face lit up that night when he brought me the mewling tabby and white tom. 'He's gentle,' he said. 'See how he keeps the claws sheathed even when he plays. Mrs Blythe will take to him, I know she will.' He looks after his human patients too, knows that while he caters for the animals' bodily wholeness, he also seeks balm for the human souls who depend on him. I love this man. It's complicated, *de trop*, messy, but I do hope he'll wait until . . .

'Laura?'

I turn, smile at him. Will he wait until I've killed my husband?

'What are you thinking about?' he asks.

'That's an easy one, Robert. I'm thinking about my second chance at life. It's as if everything has to be reassessed when you win a battle with death. Since I've been ill, I've been different, I notice things I took for granted before. Sounds silly, I suppose, but a cup used to be a cup. Now, it's a pretty thing made by somebody's hands. And more than ever, I'm thinking about Ben and what's best for him.' Robert has never been jealous, hasn't wanted me to stop talking about Ben. 'He's trapped in a time before me, stuck somewhere in a place in his head. It's as if his brain's short-circuited and blacked out everything else. Sometimes, I can bring him out of it, sometimes I can't. When he's in Heaton Lodge, there isn't always a member of staff available to distract him. So that's why I'm having him home.'

He nods. 'Yes, I can understand that.'

I look at Chewy, shake my head at his antics. He has found a punctured beach ball, is torturing the thing beyond death. 'It isn't that I don't have any feelings for you,' I say carefully. 'But he has to come first.'

'Absolutely.' He stands on the greasy sand, points to my dog. 'Did you know there are animal psychiatrists?' he asks. 'Do you want me to get him analysed?'

I laugh, take Robert's hand. 'Compared to humanity, that dog is as sane as God.'

He whips me round, drags me into his arms. 'Where did you get the idea that God is sane? Would a supreme being have made this confusion deliberately? Surely the creator's faculties must be impaired.'

I pull away, separate dog and ball. A gull hovers above my head, reminds me that the creatures I am fostering will need feeding again. As we make for home, a picture flashes across my brain. It's something I've seen day in and day out for weeks now. It hasn't meant anything, might be meaningless even now. But it haunts me, is suddenly printed across my mind like one of those paper transfer pictures we bought as children, little cartoons that sat on the backs of our hands like tattoos. Well, mine didn't sit for long, because Mother thought they were common, made me scrub up before tea. But this one won't wash off, this one is permanent. Strawberry yoghurt. 'Oh heck,' I say aloud. 'The answer's been there all along. I am so stupid.'

Robert drags the unwilling dog towards me. 'Did you say something?'

'No.' At the gate, he lets Chewy go, climbs into his wrecked vehicle. 'Keep in touch,' he says.

'I will.' Strawberry yoghurt. Under the birds, under the shelf where the makeshift cages stand, there are several supermarket cartons. Ben keeps things in them, tools, rags, tins of paint and turps. One of the boxes is a Kellogg's, once held packets of cornflakes. He has mentioned cornflakes, though yoghurt has been his constant fixation. Inside that huge cereal box, there is a smaller one with Ski printed on its side. Unless I am sadly mistaken, that container also bears the legend Strawberry Flavour. The craziest thing Ben has been saying is possibly sensible after all. There is something in the boxes under the birds.

I stand in the kitchen, listen as Chewy slurps his water all over the floor. Two cats are asleep in the sink, one a huge bundle of fur, the other a tiny fluff-ball curled into the paws of her adopted uncle. Not now. I won't go now. Nothing will change in the next few hours. When Diana has left to go to Mark's or Audrey's house, I shall look in the boxes. She will be staying overnight with a brother or a sister, so there will be no witness when I find whatever it is.

Ben. Shall I find you in the yoghurt carton? Oh God, I do hope so. You have been missing for too long a time, my darling.

This day is so long. It seems an age since I walked on the beach with Robert. I could not make a commitment to him, could not promise to be here for him when it's all over. Because I could well be in prison for the rest of my days. Yes, I'm leaving this house, but I may have to go via the Crown Court.

The phone freeps quietly, it can't be Mother. But it is. 'May I speak to Diana, please?'

I am flabbergasted. The ring was different, the voice is softer. 'She's just packing a few things to take to her brother's house,' I answer.

'I'll wait.' I hear the click of a Zippo as she lights up.

There is very little for me to say. I am standing here breathing at my mother's expense. 'Would you like me to hurry her up?'

'No. I spoke to her earlier. It's just a question of tying up a detail or two.'

I am mystified. What on earth could Liza McNally want with a girl like Diana? 'May I ask what this is about, Mother?'

She sighs. 'Well of course you may ask. It's about McNally's. It's time for me to let go, Laura. There are some adequate people working for the company, but I want somebody young and fresh to go in and assess the whole business. Diana has a degree in pharmacology, and I think she'll make a good manager in time. So I'm handing over to you. I urge you to employ this girl, because she's as sharp as a razor. She is willing to take an intensive course in business studies, so she should be useful to you with all that education. It's time for me to take a back seat.'

My ears seem to be glowing as the words are translated via ear-drum to nerve, via nerve to a brain that isn't ready to accept an 'improved' Liza McNally. There must be a catch. I glance over my shoulder. A red-faced Diana is staring at me. 'It's for you,' I say tersely. What has this young madam been up to now? More to the point, what's Mother's angle? I sit down, fondle Chewy's ears, listen to half a conversation.

When the connection is severed, Diana joins me at the table. 'I'm not going behind your back or anything, Laura. I never thought she was serious, I mean, she doesn't even know me. So I thought I'd just forget what she said. She phoned me this morning while you were out with the dog. It seems she's taken a fancy to me.'

'Really?' I pull my eyebrows back into their proper place. 'You are highly honoured, then. She's never been known to take to anyone before.'

Diana sniffs, her colour still vivid. 'She asked me loads

of questions about my qualifications. I think she's offering me a job in research to start with.'

'And the doctorate?'

She lifts a shoulder. 'That was instead of a job. I can't just do nothing, can I? A job's what I need really. And she wants you to take over the firm. She talked about floating it on the market, but she says that's up to you.'

I have never trusted my mother, have never even liked her. 'What's the catch? Come on, there has to be one.'

Diana squirms in the chair. 'We all go to Bolton and live among the Woollybacks. You don't have to move in with her, she knows that wouldn't work. She's hiring a full-time housekeeper for the farm – Ravenscroft, I think she called it, and she wants me living close by, in the village. She says I'm interesting. Bolton hasn't even got a football team, has it?'

For the moment, I'm saying nothing. There's no point in digging up Bolton's history. Bolton and Blackpool were on the football map while Liverpool and Everton were still playing hopscotch, but what's the use? And we'll be back, I say to myself. Just get some eyes in the back of your heads, lads, the Bolton Wanderers are finding a sense of direction again. I tap my fingers on the table. 'Beware, Diana. She has never been guilty of a charitable act in her life. Anyway, I thought she liked the retirement apart-ments.'

The girl's face almost splits in two as she smiles. 'Laura, she can't stand living where everybody's old. She calls it a false situation. It seems that everything depends on you, though. If you don't go and take an interest in McNally's, she won't sign the business over to you.'

I mull this over for a few seconds. 'There's a lot to con-sider, Di. Firstly and most importantly, there's my husband. I'm going to bring him here, see what can be done for him. This is a difficult time for me. I'm recovering from an ill-ness, so it's not a good idea to make too many decisions just now. Yes, I'll have to think about it.' I need McNally's at this point in time like I need a hole in the head.

'It's all right,' she says. 'If you don't want to take over, she'll understand.'

I laugh, though the sound is grim. 'She's never understood before, so that would be a change.'

Di clears her throat, seems embarrassed. 'Laura, she knows she wasn't a good mother. She hasn't said as much, but I get the feeling that she's reaching out to you now.'

It's a bit late in the day, I say inwardly. Oh, she reached out, lashed out, terrified the child I used to be. 'So she needs a mediatrix, does she? Can't she tell me herself that she wants to give me something at last, that she trusts me with the business?'

Diana's head drops. 'No. She can't do that. You know how old people are with mistakes – they can never own up to them. Folk get worse as they get older. But I think she's sorry. "We never got on, Laura and I," she said to me this morning. A clash of personalities, she calls it. Anyway, I've been put in this difficult position, but I've no opinion about it. The job would be great, but it's up to you.'

More responsibility. If I'm good, if I'm nice, I can make sure that Liddy's baby has a chance in life. If I'm good, if I'm nice, I won't help Ben on his way. If I'm half human, considerably less than good, I will put him out of his misery. First, I have to live with that misery, decide whether or when he needs to die. 'I want some peace and some time to think,' I tell her.

'Right. Whatever, it was nice to be given a chance of a job.'

When she leaves, I sit for an age at the table, everything running about in my head. It's amazing that I'm not crazy again. Perhaps I am. Perhaps I have to be insane to consider what's euphemistically called euthanasia. No-one has the right to take the life of another. I've always believed that, even when considering the unborn. I know women who've had abortions, have seen the emptiness in their eyes. To kill a man I know, a man I love . . . But I can't leave him to linger in that insane place he seems to visit with monotonous frequency. That place is in a box under the birds. I don't just know it, I sense it, feel it deep in my marrow. Oh God, I can't face that awful dream of Ben's just now. Not yet. Give me a few more hours, please . . .

On an impulse, I grab the keys, shut the animals in the kitchen, jump into Elsie. There are things I should be looking at, strawberry yoghurt things, but I can't cope with any more at the moment. Ruth opens the door, drags me into the sitting room. 'You look like death on a low light,' she mutters. 'Sorry.' A hand goes to her mouth. 'I'd forgotten about your friends.' She has heard the tale of Liddy and Jimmy – I phoned her last night. 'When's the funeral?'

'Soon. Diana's sorting it out.'

She pushes me into an armchair, sits on the rug at my feet. 'What's up?'

'Nothing.'

'Come on, spit it out, Laura.'

I look into the earnest little face. I trust this woman and she trusts me. 'It's Ben.'

She puts her head on one side. 'It's been Ben for some time now. What's different? Pangs of conscience about Robert again?'

'No.' It isn't as simple as that. I wish it were. 'He's worse. You see, he remembers some things very vividly. I've told you before about the shouting, and you've seen him at his worst.'

She nods, kneels, takes my hands in hers. 'It's a silly old saying, but what can't be cured really has to be endured. Nothing can be done. You have to accept that. He's in the right place with qualified people—'

'I'm not worried about his physical maintenance, Ruth. It's the mental suffering.' I swallow, feel the rough dryness of my throat. 'Something really terrible happened to Ben before I knew him. It's been hidden all these years. We had a pact when we met, a fresh start was what we agreed on. I was glad to wipe out my past. Ben even forced me to face Tommo, made the whole thing as ordinary as

593

possible. Though I wouldn't have gone had Tommo not become less dangerous. Ben's past is elsewhere, too far away to be contacted.'

'Yes.' She tries to rub some life into my icy fingers. 'But where? When I mentioned his origins, you didn't want to discuss the subject.'

'Because I had no information. But he told me the other day that he is Greek. And I think I know where the answers are.'

She falls back onto her heels, thinks for a moment or two. 'Will the answers help?'

They won't help. Ben cannot be reached, cannot be comforted. But I have to know what he's going through. 'I can't let him suffer on his own. This time, I have to share his past.'

'And . . . you think you've found the answers?'

I jump up, pace about the floor. 'I'm scared. I don't know what I'll find and I'm scared. Half of me hopes that this is some kind of wild-goose chase, and the other half wants to get at this truth of Ben's. Have you noticed how everybody's truth is different and that there are degrees of truth, kinds of truth?'

She sighs, stands up. 'Laura, don't go all poetic on me. What do you want me to do? Shall I come and be with you when you unearth whatever this is?'

I shake my head. 'He wouldn't want that.'

'How can you be sure?'

'I just am.' I shouldn't have come. Like a child, I have run away from whatever's new and difficult, am trying to hide behind Ruth's skirts. The man in the park suddenly appears before my mind's eye, that stranger who gave me sweets and told me to be my own keeper. I have to stop hiding, I must cope alone. 'If . . . if I get upset later on tonight, I'll phone you.' There has to be someone there, someone who will help me through the aftermath. Even the park man would understand that, I'm sure. 'Anyway, I could be wrong, I may not find anything.' I will. It's there, in those boxes. And I have to be alone.

I still haven't gone home. Soon, I'll be needed as a disher-out of catfood, dogfood, kitten slops. And another tin of pilchards must bite the dust before I sleep, or the imprisoned gulls will be mortallious. I am sitting in Elsie outside the George. The George is one of those schizophrenic pubs, civilized at lunchtimes, bulging with teenagers every night. They are spilling into Moor Lane, shouting and laughing, advertising their youthful silliness. A policeman approaches, so I move on, anxious not to be caught in a no-parking zone. I wish I could work out why I'm here.

Elsie knows her way around, so I give her her head, finish up outside Confetti's refuge. A girl with a swollen belly leans against a lamppost, cigarette smoke making her eyes narrow as it floats upward from her mouth. Smoking is not allowed inside Confetti's place. Through a lighted window, I see my old friend. And she is old, seventy if a day. She is folding towels, is having an animated conversation with someone who is out of sight. Her hair is grey and thinning, and she is still wearing those awful clothes. She would tell me not to think of helping Ben to leave the world and all its horrors. She would tell me that life is valuable, no matter what its quality. She would sentence Ben to live right to the bitterest of ends.

I pass Robert's house, park across the road, see one of his dogs shambling about the front garden. Robert is in his daughter's room. He bends over, is probably kissing her good night. He's been a good parent, an excellent mother-cum-dad to those kids. What would you say, Robert? How many sick animals do you release from pain each week? My Ben has rights, too. He cannot be allowed to continue incontinent, tormented, afraid.

Outside Heaton Lodge, I turn off the engine, climb out of Elsie's uncomfortable body, stroll round the garden and look at the faded bedding plants. It's over, Ben. Summer is over. The marigolds are crunched up, wrinkled, aged.

Susan Jenkinson accosts me in the lobby. 'Hello, love. I never expected to see you at this time.'

'Is he asleep?'

She shakes her head slowly, draws me through the entrance and into Matron's office. 'Sit down,' she says. 'We can have a good chinwag here, no interruptions.'

I sit, wait.

'He's had a rough day, Laura.' She puts the matron's desk between us, settles her bulk, rests gnarled elbows on the blotter pad. 'He's needing more sedation. We can't let him carry on like this, because he's a danger to himself, you know. He's been throwing cups at doors, falling out of chairs, trying to run after somebody who isn't there.'

I place my keys on the desk, look into her eyes. 'I want him home, Susan. And before you start, I'm intending to have round-the-clock nursing, three nurses, eight hours each.'

She draws in her lips, takes a hissing breath, puts me in mind of a plumber who has just been asked when the lavatory will be fixed. 'That'll cost you a bomb. And it might take more than one to manage him when he's at his worst.'

'I'll be there.'

'But—'

'I'll be there, Susan. And if we need more than one nurse, or a strong man as well as a nurse, then we'll employ as many as are needed. He can't stay here. I put him here because I was ill. I'm no longer sick, so he can come back where he belongs.'

She studies me for a few moments, then rises from the chair. 'Come with me, Laura. Come and look at him.'

She leads the way to Ben's room, bustles along as if she means business. I have no doubt that she is intending to put me off, but I shall bring him out of here no matter what. He is mine, my husband, my beloved burden.

At his door, she stops and draws breath. It seems an age before we enter the room, she first, me bringing up the rear with a huge grin on my face. Ben has routed her. As if he expected to be caught in bad order, he is sitting in his chair with the television flickering on his face. Some aged singer is assassinating 'Always', and Ben has joined in. 'Hello, Laura,' he beams. 'Come in and listen to the singing. It is so beautiful.'

Susan shakes her head, gives me a nudge of warning as if telling me not to be taken in by my husband's improved mood. 'I'll be off, then. Don't keep him up late. It's as if he's ready for me.' She pats Ben's hand. 'Be good.'

He gives her a withering look. 'Go away,' he says imperiously. 'I wish to talk to my wife.'

After she has left, he seems to forget me, is wrapped up in the songs of yesteryear. But 'My Way' proves too much for him. He looks at me, a temporary intelligence in the fading eyes. 'How is Chewbacca?' he asks.

Ben doesn't like dogs any more. 'Fine. We have another cat, too.'

He nods. 'There were dogs, but no cats. We had rats, you know. Even the wild ones are trainable, very clever. And we didn't see many birds. I've been back, and there are still few birds.'

I wait until he seems to have finished. My spine is tingling, crawling with cold. I am beginning to know where he has been. 'Was this during the war, Ben?'

'It's over.' He frowns at the television. 'For most, it is over. For some, it continues. They cut my toenails today, I think. Yes, it was today. I don't like scissors. Are the children at school? Did you find Gerald's geometry set? He will be a mathematician, you know. Keep the door closed.'

He is leaving me. I drop to my knees, take his hands, am reminded of how Ruth held on to me just half an hour ago. 'Is it under the birds, Ben? Is it in the Kellogg's box?'

He nods jerkily, like a child who has barely mastered the art of tacit agreement. 'Strawberry yoghurt.' There is pride on his face. 'I knew I would never forget that. The key.'

'To the bottom safe?'

He is vague again. 'They went a bit crisp under the stove, but we got them out. The jewels too. Well, they paid for their own destruction, so we merely used what was left as a deposit on retribution. Diamonds, rubies and sapphires, she wanted. I made it for her, but she died.' A grim smile hovers on his lips. 'So gaudy, it was, so we broke it later in Paris. Valuable. Watch the gendarme in the Rue Albertine. What?' He is questioning an invisible companion. '*Non, c'est fini. Je vais maintenant en Angleterre.* Laura.'

'Yes?'

But he is speaking of me, not to me. He repeats that he is going to England, that he is going to Laura, that everything is finished.

'Ben? Would you like to come home?'

He focuses, recognizes, jerks the balding head. 'I am better here,' he says. 'Soon, I shall get my wings.'

'What do you want?'

I step inside, catch sight of a Fry's Chocolate Cream bar that betrays her by peeping out from its hiding place. I glance at the cushion, then at her. No sweet stuff, the doctor said. But why should I remind her? 'What's all this about McNally's?' I ask without further preamble.

'I'm tired.'

She looks about as tired as a three-week-old foal. 'Mother, you can't go picking up people like Diana. How do you know she'll be suitable?'

'I know. I know people.'

I sit on the chair that faces her throne. The throne is high, made taller for old bones. It has wings and braided joints, lacks only a royal crest and a bit of gold thread. 'I can't leave Ben.'

She fumbles with a Regal packet, picks out a fag, lights it. 'We shall take him home. He can live with me at the farm and I shall hire help – nurses and so on.'

What is the matter with her? She's never cared before, has never catered for anyone but herself. 'Why?' I ask.

She shrugs, the lifting of the shoulders emphasizing twin cavernous salt-cellars at the base of her throat. 'I'm not sure.' She has always been certain, and this ambivalence sits uncomfortably on her features. 'I've . . .' A long drag of nicotine disappears into her gullet. 'I've not been much of a mother, have I?'

There is nowhere for me to look. I am staring ahead into nothingness, would not be surprised if Jesus Christ Himself materialized in the face of so tremendous a miracle. 'No,' I reply at last. 'You were not much of a mother.'

She is plucking at her skirt, is smoking so fast that the cigarette behaves like a joint, burns hot, red, quick. 'It was not in my nature,' she offers after a few seconds. 'And I had no help, no support from your father. That is not to say that he was a bad man. We were . . . different, poles apart. And you were in the middle of it. I suppose you were our equator.'

Is this an apology, an explanation? I am counting the roses on her border. They are large and pink, extend dado-fashion around the comfortable room. There are seventeen in the alcove at one side of the chimney, seventeen and a half at the other side. The fractured flower turns a corner, marries up to another broken bloom. They are slightly off-set, rather untrue. Truth. Is she telling her truth now? 'Why did you hit me, Mother?'

She coughs, clears the phlegm from her chest. She has been a good cougher, has perhaps found a way of clearing the muck of years from her lungs. 'I don't know that, either.'

My eyes stray to her face. 'You never loved me.'

'No.' She brushes non-existent ash from her blouse, stares downward at the floor. 'But you are my daughter. I don't have long, Laura, and I can't put anything right. It was all done a long time ago. I have learned . . .' She swallows as if in pain. 'I've come to respect you.'

There's a dreadful clock on the mantelpiece, one of those domed things with gold-coloured globes that swirl back and forth, back and forth. It's a timepiece that mocks time, makes it boring and uneventful. The silly thing wheezes, spits out a tune to illustrate the hour. Nine o'clock. It's nine o'clock on a September evening in 1992, and my mother has just spoken to me for the first time ever. The clock that marks this occasion is bland, unimpressive, a quartz thing with no character, no guts. 'I used to hate you,' I say tonelessly.

'Yes.' The cigarette end is being murdered in an onyx ashtray. Mother likes onyx and silver, is surrounded by ornaments culled from such cold substances. In fact, I am beginning to warm towards the clock, because it isn't as dead as the rest of Mother's collection. 'Do you still dislike me so intensely?' she asks in a whisper.

I shake my head. 'I've not the energy for it.'

'Nor have I.' She straightens, pushes her head against the chair's high back. 'You are all I have in this world, Laura. You are a living creature, the only one that comes directly from me. I want a new start before it's too late. McNally's is yours. Sell it or work it, whatever you wish. If you work it, take on that thin girl. She looks frail, but she's as tough as shoe-leather.'

I still don't know where to rest my eyes. 'But if I don't go to Bolton, if I stay here—'

'No. I said those things to the girl, to Diana, but it's of no importance, really. I'm going home before Christmas. I came here all those years ago, followed you to Liverpool and sat here until I plucked up the courage to talk to you. You are a grown woman with responsibilities. Do whatever you need to do, but I'd be grateful if you carried on the McNally tradition.' She sniffs. 'He was a fool in many ways, but he knew his onions – well – his medicines.'

This is as near as I am going to get. She is sorry, but she can't say it, was wrong, can't admit her error. My mother is a human being after all. And that is almost enough for me. 'Thank you,' I tell her. 'This wasn't easy for you, Mother. You are right, it's no longer a question of right and wrong. We have to negotiate the terms of a treaty, and you've taken a very brave step. I admire you for that.'

She stares at me. The eyes are wet, as wet as they used to be when she missed her aim with the little mascara brush. 'You've turned out quite well after all,' she mouths. 'Close the door on your way out.'

So I secure one door and march onward to open another. I am still in shock, still reeling from this strange encounter with a woman who has breathed fire over my whole life. Now, I go towards the key to another mystery. Having found a sort of mother, I shall seek my husband in an upstairs safe.

Chapter Six

THE TROUBLE WITH WINGS by *Kevin McCann*

At first
They were just nodules
Protruding from behind
His shoulder blades
And after that
The rapid growth of membrane and quill
Was not an altogether
Unpleasant sensation.

But having wings
Can create
All kinds
Of problems:
His wife refused
To sleep with him,
He was made suddenly redundant,
Children followed him
Silently in the street.

He flew
Fishtailing and chandelle
After the wild geese
That drew him
With their cadences
As sirens drew sailors
Towards a promise
They could never keep.
Only to return,

Hedgehopping
To avoid the guns
Of frightened farmers
And the cautions
Of police.

Finally,
Tired and hounded,
He went to a surgeon,
Had his wings removed
And burned.

Now
He's got a new job
With prospects of promotion,
He makes love to his wife
Three times a week
And children
No longer regard him
With awe.

But sometimes
He will look
Towards the sky
And the flesh
Between his shoulder blades
Will tug and ache.

I am standing on the doorstep of the man who wrote this poem. His name is Kevin McCann and I can hear him walking towards me. Life has made me all kinds of fool thus far, and I am now the fool who has rushed up ten flights of stairs with a collection of verses in my hand. Kevin McCann took some finding. I searched the whole of this city's education system, found that the writer had escaped the classroom. Many do these days. They get out of teaching, discover that living is pleasant, wonder why they never tried it earlier.

A girl opens the door. She has shiny brown hair that cloaks her shoulders, a small silver ring on a slender finger, blue jeans, boots, a pale green shirt. 'Yes?'

I smile, assure her that I'm not selling anything. 'Is Kevin McCann here?' I ask. She cannot be Kevin McCann, surely?

I am led along a hall and into a cosy living room where candles flicker and cast shadows on a poet. He is approachable, almost handsome, clad in ordinary clothes. Did I expect a serious writer to wear something different, then? A smoking jacket, a toga, a suit of armour? His work has enlivened and disturbed me, because I found it good, found it among my husband's papers in the bottom safe. Kevin's hair is long, not curly, not straight, just bent a bit. He has a smile that means hello.

'I found this.' I thrust the slim green book beneath his nose. 'He's marked off this 'Trouble with Wings' one. Can you tell me why?'

His eyes seem blue, but I'm not sure. 'Can you tell me who?' he asks.

'My husband.' I sit in a comfortable chair, find myself in the company of a pretty blond rat in a cage.

'That's Basil,' says the girl. 'I'm Danielle, so the other one must be Kevin.' She sits on some cushions, draws in the long legs, rests her chin on her knees. Basil chews at a bit of apple, keeps an eye on me.

'I'm Laura. Laura Starling.'

Kevin knows my name, knew it before I opened my mouth. 'Ben,' he says. 'The bird man, the one who works hand in glove with the RSPB. Gardening gloves, he told me. He said a seagull's bite can be a lot worse than its scream. How is Ben?'

Well, I've had the surprises, the shocks. Ben's association with this young man is good news, the happiest piece of information I've gleaned so far. I tell him how Ben is, tell him all of it, not just the bearable oddments. Kevin has the kind of face that deserves the best truth you can achieve, so he gets the ranting, the dribbling, the incontinence. 'I found your poem with the other papers. The story of his life's in that safe, I think, but I've not tackled it yet.'

Danielle offers me wine. 'It's peach,' she informs me. It is sweet and fruity, slakes a thirst I hadn't noticed till the first sip.

With the minimum of Dutch courage, I ask these two how much they know. 'Enough,' says Kevin. 'Ben read Danielle's thesis about the concentration camp, showed an interest that was more than academic. A few years ago, your husband asked me about the poem. So I can only tell you what I said to him.'

I notice something hanging from an overhead lantern, cannot stop myself from interrupting, 'So it was from you, the Indian dream-catch.' Metallic threadwork converges into a central hole, making the ornament into a rounded-off spider's web. Ben told me the theory. Nightmares are supposed to be held back by the wider net, while pleasant dreams can find a way through the gap in the middle, are able to float down and access the sleeper. 'I think it works in a way,' I say. 'He's quieter now while asleep, but the living nightmare continues. I took the circle to the nursing home and hung it above his bed. I suppose the sleeping tablets help, too.'

They know when to be quiet, these two. There's a peace about this place, a tranquillity that does not argue with the field of energy that surrounds the flat's inhabitants. They have taken me in, given me wine, allowed me to pour my heavy burden onto their heads. I could stay here until the energy wakes. Perhaps the room becomes noisier then, when the words fly. He writes the words, but she is in them. Even the little rat belongs, is in its proper home. The rodent is round and content, is a squirrel with bad PR and no bushy tail. Since the plague, these intelligent creatures have been avoided and feared by the masses.

Kevin sits and focuses on Danielle, as if she is his pulse. I can feel the love between them, know that it is big enough to include me, my Ben and a million other people.

'Can you help me?' I ask at last. That Indian catch has another significance for me, because it sums up all I have learned in the past twenty-four hours. Danielle knows the camps, Kevin is the father of the poem, they both know Ben. I have come full circle within a circle of beliefs that stem from native America. This is a moment of magic.

'It was a joke at first,' he says. 'When I was a kid, I wanted wings. Then, later on, I read how the American Indians treat birds like messengers from God. In their faith, a bird wears the wings of a holy being, something like an angel.'

He is smiling slightly. 'So I kept wavering between the concepts. How would a man with wings cope in a supermarket? I imagined Heinz beans tins swept off the shelves, women scooping up children to save them from the heavy feathers. An albatross has a massive span – think how wide a human's would be.'

Danielle picks up the thread. 'But we all want to fly, even if we can only do it metaphorically. It isn't difficult to imagine how great it would be to sit up there and watch the world. An eagle is supposed to be capable of focusing on the tiniest object. At the same time, he's got this wide view of life. It's taken us thousands of years to get something that birds had all the time, but we needed machinery to achieve it.'

She leans forward, touches my knee. 'No two people have taken that poem the same way. It means so many things. Poetry's only good if it does that. What Kevin meant when he wrote it isn't the important part. It reaches people. But for Ben, it meant so much, it covered a lot of ground for him.'

I haven't been able to read the rest of the stuff yet. I've dipped into it, hurried out of it. 'There's that other pile of papers,' I remind them. 'I was all right with the poem, but his life story's going to be hard. He was in a concentration camp, I do know that much. And that burn mark on his arm was no accident.' I take a gulp of peach wine. 'He heated a poker and burned off his number.'

'He can't wash it off his soul, though,' says Kevin. 'He can't cleanse his memory, not completely. I think he's gone through a period of denial, a better beginning, he called it. To live with you, he got new wings.'

I lean back, beg support from the chair. 'And he's living the worst part of his life all over again.' Would I have treated him differently had I known his history, his youth? Would my pity and sorrow have shown? He wanted no pity, my Ben. He wanted a start that was fresh enough to squeak like a new shoe. Yet he wrote it down. 'He wrote it down,' I say. 'And he wants more wings.'

'Understandable,' offers Danielle. 'He's worn out a few pairs in his time.'

How much do they know, then? I am surprised that the answer jumps so quickly into my head. It doesn't matter. If Ben told Danielle and Kevin any of it, then at least he has managed to share the weight with strangers. A stranger can often be so much closer than a friend, as the picture arrives in black and white, no colours lent by preknowledge and prejudgement. 'Was he confused when he first came to you?'

Kevin thinks for a moment, nods. 'Yes, he thought he had started with Alzheimer's disease, though he was still together enough to know that he was missing a lot of stuff. That was the sad part, the fact that he realized what was happening to him. He came in a taxi with the address of the flat on a piece of paper.'

'Where did he find your work?' I ask.

'The book of poems was among some stuff he picked up at the university,' Kevin tells me. 'I was lecturing there, taking a couple of writers' groups. I was a bit worried about him, because he kept jumping from one subject to another when he visited us here that day. Anyway, the taxi waited, and I went down in the lift to make sure that Ben would get home OK. The driver knew where to take him, so I guessed that your husband had provided for what he was calling his gaps. We've never forgotten him. There was something about him that stayed with us.'

'We had a new kitchen.' I am remembering again, but audibly this time. 'Ben attacked a very close friend. I was getting some After Eights out of a cupboard that wouldn't shut properly. Until then, I hadn't noticed anything unusual about Ben's behaviour. Sometimes, I've hated that cupboard, even though the firm came and made it close. It was as if I'd let something out with the After Eights and the Kenya coffee. Perhaps if I'd managed to close the door . . .' I flounder, stop in my tracks. 'Silly, isn't it?'

Neither speaks, neither finds me silly.

'I've got to read the rest of it, haven't I?'

'Ben asked for my work on Sachsenhausen,' says Danielle. 'He sat there, in your chair, read every word and pored over the photographs. When he passed it back to me, he thanked me for being a new witness. He made me cry, Laura.'

Oh God, what am I going to do? The new wings he needs are to be made by me. I have to plan, stitch and sew, make sure that the ailerons will take my man upwards, 'fishtailing and chandelle' as Kevin says in the poem. 'Having wings just means being unusual, doesn't it?' I've got past trying to sound intelligent.

Kevin agrees, up to a point. 'We've all got wings if we want them,' he tells me. 'But most of us don't like them to show. Don't forget that this poem can be hopeful, too. At the end, he feels the feathers threatening to erupt again.'

I haven't read it that way. 'But I thought the tugging between his shoulder blades was regret. Like a man who has a leg amputated – he still feels when the missing knee aches or when the absent foot itches.'

'You were low when you read it,' says Kevin. 'You weren't flying when you found the words.'

We can all fly. He is telling me that and I am believing it. The girl on the cushions has known for years that she can take to the air. It's something to do with integrity, then. 'Why did Ben need more than one pair of wings?' I wonder aloud.

608

'To fit his many circumstances.' Kevin has probably travelled deeper into my husband's thoughts than any other living creature.

I decide to go further. 'Which wings does he need now?'

He shakes his head. 'Only you know that, Laura. He told me his past and a little of his present, but the present he discussed has become history now.'

Danielle has a brainwave. 'It might not help, but if it does . . .' She is excited, has risen onto her knees. 'Take the papers in, and the poem. Read them to him, let him know you're sharing it. That might bring him forward a bit, tip him out of the worst part of his past.'

I don't think so. I cannot believe that a story read aloud can darn the holes created by Alzheimer's. But I'll try anything, anything at all. I'll even make those wretched wings if necessary. The young people go into the kitchen for coffee and food. I am left with a rat called Basil and a poem that is breaking my heart.

Van Gogh sits all around the walls, his gorgeous insanity translated, printed and framed. A native American stares down at me, arms folded under his woven dress. Beneath him sits another stark truth.

ONLY AFTER THE LAST TREE HAS BEEN
CUT DOWN
ONLY AFTER THE LAST RIVER HAS BEEN
POISONED
ONLY AFTER THE LAST FISH HAS BEEN
CAUGHT
ONLY THEN WILL YOU FIND THAT MONEY
CANNOT BE EATEN

Laurel and Hardy linger in a corner, their closest companion a tiger, a big fellow, possibly from Bengal. Books teeter on top of books, Stanley Kubrick's *Clockwork Orange* is announced on another poster. Above it all, the dream catch turns on the end of its thread. Nothing is expected of me. I can stay or go, I can be myself.

She reminds me a little of Diana and Jodie, this calm-faced girl whose hair is free, whose mind has found its own liberty. She is educated, I think, but she is not hidebound by her achievements. And Kevin is a man whose ideals have made a bypass round all middle-class mores. This is what my daughter meant then, when she announced that she would find herself before settling down to practise what has been preached at her across a hollow lecture hall. The young are cautious these days. They have stopped jumping onto the roundabouts we created for them, have learned to step slowly and carefully across into adulthood.

I eat with them, read more of Kevin's brilliant work, ask if I might return. 'Any time,' he says. 'And we'll visit you, too.' I have told them about Chewbacca, about Handel and the fluff-ball kitten. Kevin and Danielle came late into my life, but they arrived at the right time. They know Ben and they care. I come away relaxed, ready to face the rest of the story.

Chapter Seven

My Darling Laura,

You may not have noticed just yet, but I am
beginning to lose my memory. At first, just the small
details of everyday life were fading, things that were
too unimportant to cause concern. If we went out, I
could not always recall where we had been, with
whom, for how long. These problems I dismissed as
trivial, until I started to struggle with addresses,
names, pieces of business. My dear wife, it is
possible that I have been launched on the slope that
leads to dementia. It is a slippery road and I can find
no purchase beneath my feet. We are both powerless
to stop what is probably coming. As I descend, I
shall no doubt gain momentum. While I can still
reach for words, I shall use my lucid periods to write
to you.

Our marriage was not blessed by a priest, but the
church knows of our difficult and unusual circumstances and accepts your divorce. Although we
married in a registry, we shall still meet again in
heaven, because all my sins are now forgiven. I
thank you from the bottom of my heart for all the
happy years we have had. My love for you is
undiminished – I wish I could say the same about my
brain power, which seems to be lessening daily.
Laura, I am forgetting our yesterdays. How many
gulls did we have then, did the thrush die, have I
eaten breakfast? I am not ready to discuss this with

you, yet I am guilty about the grief you may soon feel. I fear my steady diminution, as it is difficult to assess and understand. Dementia is a state about which little is known – as a potential sufferer, I do not possess the ability to think clearly about a situation that already clouds my judgement. I am living in a vicious circle, though I do hang on to the hope that I am mistaken. If that is the case, then I shall improve and this letter will not be needed. However, should I deteriorate, you will find this in the bottom safe. The key and the combination will be in a place I shall remember. It is so important that I know it will not be forgotten, no matter how sieve-like my mind might become.

I do have some vivid memories. They are so strong that they are threatening to take me over, so I must explain to you some details. My life has been difficult and I find myself talking aloud sometimes, as if I am re-entering the times that were most terrifying. Your terror must be precluded. I shall go gently with you, but it is vital that you understand the place and the time into which I seem to be disappearing. Do not fret if I begin to rant, because I am speaking to ghosts or to people whose powers have been taken away. Do not pity me, do not weep.

Perhaps these revelations are a form of self-indulgence, a cleansing of conscience. As you are aware, I am now a Catholic, but my past was so cluttered and confused that I had to apply to Rome for absolution. Because of the unique situation, I was granted time with the Holy Father, who prayed for me and intervened on my behalf. I am now forgiven, though I still tremble at the thought of Judgement Day. I am tired now, so I shall continue tomorrow when I hope to have a clearer picture.

We walked on the beach this morning, my love. That silly dog wagged his tail so hard that it seemed ready to drop off. I am good today. I remember that we had Alpen for breakfast and chicken with green salad for lunch. How I wish that every day could be like this! You wore that old blue coat and the green wellies, got a speck of sand in your eye.

Where to begin? I shall give no names, or perhaps I may decide to append false names to some of the characters in what is intended to be an accurate account. This is an attempt to help you make sense of who and what I am. I was born on the island of Corfu in 1918. My family fished, kept a few animals, helped in the olive groves occasionally. I had several uncles and aunts on the island, some Jewish, some Greek Orthodox, as my mother was Jewish and my father was a Christian.

My father had one brother in Athens, so I moved to the mainland and was apprenticed to my uncle at the age of fourteen. It was he who taught me the arts of gem-cutting and polishing, jewellery design and manufacture. I remained in Athens until 1938, in which year I gained my qualifications as a fully fledged jeweller. As my father had become ill, I went home to Mother, because my brothers, who were fishermen, could not spare sufficient time to tend my parents. Fishermen are at the mercy of the tides; I was elected chief nurse and goat-farmer. My father died on Christmas Day in 1938.

The day of Papa's death is so clear to me, clearer than the view from Benaura's window. My three brothers were drinking Mother's wine and singing Christmas songs. The gentle woman was hurt because her sons were drunk as they celebrated the birth of Christ. She did not object to our Christianity, but there should have been no singing while her husband lay dying. I sat with my father. He was so happy to hear the lovely music that he died with a smile on his face. His joy and her sorrow have remained with me down the years. She berated them for carousing, yet the boys could not possibly have known that their father had chosen that moment to slip away. He had been ill for so long that we never knew how many more weeks or months he might linger. He died happily, because my brother's voices were so beautiful. We were a melodic family, though I was the exception, since I have always been tone deaf.

This cat of yours is chasing my pen. I have never met a lazier animal, yet he taunts me when I need to concentrate and be quiet. Chewbacca is growing, is almost as big as the guard dogs. The guard dogs were German shepherds, but their intelligence had been directed along the evil path chosen by their masters. I digress, Laura. I must try to keep things in order, or you might become as confused as I am sometimes. The river is beautiful today, because the sky is clean.

I did not return to Athens. Our bit of land had been neglected during Papa's decline. I did what I could, but the livestock were feeble and sick. When all but the cow had died, I built her up and sold her, then opened a little stall on the market. I sold jewellery made from shells, polished pebbles, cheap stones. Children became my labourers, their small fingers proving eminently suitable for assembling little brooches and necklaces for the young girls on the island. I achieved hardly any profit, but my brothers fished and made merry, brought home enough money and food for us to survive. My mother became old very quickly, always wore sombre clothes, seldom smiled. Do not let this happen to you, my Laura. Father was but a man, just as I am but a man. Be strong, be calm and face the storm, find a lover who will keep you sheltered from the worst of the wind and rain.

The war began in 1939 and we were not much affected. Our island seemed too small and unimportant to play any part in a conflict that promised to swamp the whole of Europe. Corfu changed little, because it had not yet been targeted by masses of tourists. We ate, we slept, did our work and talked to sweethearts on the beach. Nothing could have prepared us for the horrors to come.

Preparing you is difficult. You have already heard of these things, must have read about them in history books. I sit here at my desk in a house on the edge of the Mersey, cannot imagine war. The river is flat, almost glassy, a tanker is strolling along the horizon like a snail in the heat. No rush, no hunger, no need. Liverpool suffered. It is hard to envisage the blackness, the fires, the roar of sirens along this battered coast. But wars do happen, I was there, I survived. I don't need to use my powers of imagination, because I have the memory burned into my mind. And into my flesh. The burn mark on my arm was self-inflicted. As a half-Jew, I carried a number, but again I am going too fast, am beginning to wander off course.

The tanker was days ago, I think. Days, hours, minutes – these are all being swallowed up and I can no longer gauge the time, am unable to estimate how long I have been sitting here this morning. You have gone to the shops, I believe, have driven off in that little green car. I remember your dress – it is yellow. Have you noticed how I stare at you, how I hang on to your every word so that my responses might be appropriate?

At about six o'clock one morning in June 1942, the Nazis landed on Corfu. We had noticed for some time a slight antipathy towards Jews, as if some Christians did not want to support Jewish traders. Even before the evil had landed, its doctrine had begun to contaminate our shores. It was as if propaganda infiltrated via some osmotic process that infected the whole world. Some believed that the Jews had started the war simply by existing. Had the Jews not existed, then Adolf Hitler might have kept a rein on his insane temper. But in June 1942, the Christians came out to watch 1,500 Jews being marched off to a collection of decrepit vessels. The Nazis had actually promised to pay the Greek government for 'selling' Jews, had vowed to send Athens a share of looted possessions. Some of our islanders smiled as their neighbours were marched away.

We were overlooked that first time, even though we were half-Jewish, but we were taken a week later. My mother, who was very weak, was the first in our family to be hurled onto the boat. My brother and I stepped forward to protect her, but we were clubbed by the guards. I think my brother was bludgeoned to death and disposed of before we sailed. When I woke the first time, I was on a huge raft that was towed by a small German boat. There were only three guards on the raft, as the Nazis had worked out that terror and confusion are the most efficient gaolers. My eyes were full of blood that dripped from a gash in my head. I was unconscious for a long time, for days, became aware from time to time that I was no longer on the water, that I was travelling in an upright position wedged among a suffocating mass of people. I never saw my brothers or my mother after that journey of death. Many of us who stood in the cars were the dead who remained upright because of the congestion.

Laura, I hope that you will never have to read this. Today, I have been quite well, but I am wondering now where you are. When you came back from the shops that other time, your dress was not yellow. I remembered it being the colour of buttercups, but I think you were really in a grey or beige suit. How many days am I losing, how many hours? How long is it since this amnesia began and why does it not apply also to the time I write about?

I have told you about the journey, I think, about my family having disappeared. Now, I shall stick at this, because my behaviour is becoming noticeably odd. Did I go into hospital? Did I strike our friend Les? You are watching me, listening in the night. I must finish, I must win this race.

I was thin and I was in Poland. The camp was called Treblinka. Some things I shall never forget! We all had beards. Well, there were not very many of us left, but those who walked out of the train had several inches of growth on their faces. I can hear it now, hear it, smell it, almost touch it. It never goes, Laura, even in my confusion I can hear the cries of children, the screams of women. They were taken away, the young and the female. We were left to stand, dried out, hollow-eyed, dying of a thirst that had become a part of us.

There seemed to be hope for me and another Greek Jew. An aged interpreter spoke for us, conveyed to the guards that I was a qualified jeweller and that my companion was a graphic artist. We were separated from the rest. After the numbers were tattooed on our arms, we were pushed into a small hut where we could not sit down. In fact, the space was so cramped that we almost took turns to breathe. Later on, we learned that this was a punishment cell where men were often abandoned to die slowly of thirst. After some hours, the door opened and we were given a scoop of brackish water. Nothing before or since has tasted as good as that drop of filthy water.

I keep reading this through, going back to the start so that I might remember what I have already written. It is so difficult. Memories from 50 years ago are bright and terrible, but I cannot recall what I wrote yesterday. Was it yesterday? I suppose it does not matter. You are worried, my darling. Are you concerned about me, are you ill? I must concentrate, must hurry. Time is not on our side, Laura.

I will call my companion Paul, as that was not his name. I have written Paul on my wrist so that I might see it when I glance down, might have a chance of remembering. There are people who are still alive – they might suffer if these papers are found. I must be careful to protect the cabal we became when the war was over.

Paul and I had the best of it. While others were tortured, murdered, disposed of, we slept in an office-cum-workshop with a good mattress and ample food. We were the elite. Paul and I received wedding rings, gemstone jewellery, all kinds of adornments. We were also given the terrible task of melting down gold fillings from the teeth of those who burned in the crematoria. Our workshop was near to the big furnaces as we, too, needed heat for our crucibles. We became deaf, Paul and I. We made fine ornaments to decorate the Reich. Paul designed to order, I broke jewellery, reconstructed it to order. And we ceased to hear the shouts of the guards, the explosion of a flying bullet, the screams of the damned.

Laura, I did not suffer unduly, so do not upset yourself. My ambition was to stay alive until the end. I worked, I smiled, I bowed and scraped. We enjoyed a degree of freedom, were allotted clothes that were warm and decent, items that had been dragged from the backs of new prisoners. Feverishly, we strove to please our masters, taught them to look through the glass, educated them about the form, the cut, the colour of a diamond. Our anger was deep and cold, but we made no attempt to warm it. We wanted to survive. We vowed to live so that we could tell the world what had happened in Treblinka. Laura, the Jews paid for their own disposal, paid with jewels, furs, little mementoes from home. They paid for the privilege of being put to death.

Sometimes, there were no trains and our work slowed. The days without trains were the worst, as the Germans would use the lull to pick out and dispose of the weakest among us. Even so, we were safer than the rest. We stood at the small window of our workshop and watched the old interpreter being supported by stronger prisoners on his way to the gas chamber. Paul ran from my side. I heard him as he retched over the bucket that was our latrine, found him weeping next to our little furnace.

Because of the designs, Paul and I had an almost limitless supply of graph paper. We were both blessed with photographic memories, but his skill at portraiture was far superior to mine. Under the stove in our quarters, we hid a metal box that contained detailed drawings of many Nazis, the men whose atrocities we had observed from our window. It was this collection that kept us going, because we were saving evidence that might prove useful after the war. I intended to avenge my mother, as I was certain that she had not survived the long journey from home. Paul needed to avenge the whole Jewish nation. His was the kind of fury that is lasting and dangerous, yet it is also justifiable.

There is rain today. The garden needs it, so do the birds. This morning, when I woke, you were standing over me. There is so much anguish in your face. Has someone told you about my problem, do I scream in the night? I have returned to my desk, am trying to pick up the threads of my story. I think I make the effort to come into the office every day, but I may be forgetting sometimes. Reading through takes a long time. I often need to go to the beginning more than once, as I am not absorbing what I read.

Rich Jews came, probably from Macedonia or Bulgaria. They were covered in furs and jewels, carried boxes of valuables. Paul and I, helpless and ashamed, received the gems and precious metals that would keep us alive. For Eva Braun, I made a swastika in gold and platinum studded with sapphires, diamonds, rubies. My hatred was melted into every carat.

There are good German people. There were good ones then, during the war. A young guard who had escaped active service because of a shrivelled arm became our friend, often bringing us cocoa and sugar, even bits of butter and chocolate. The lad was truly terrified of what was happening. From him we learned our German. We also learned how much he hated the camp. There were tears in his eyes on the days when mass genocide was accomplished via the 'showers'. 'Why is it happening?' we asked him.

'Why do your friends do these things to the prisoners?' 'Fear,' he replied. 'If we don't do the job, we join the Jews in the ovens.' How prophetic he was. When we had known him for quite some time, he was savaged to death by dogs belonging to a particularly crazy guard. We watched this happening, saw our young friend's bloodied corpse when his nightmare finally ended. The Nazis must have seen his fear, no doubt felt threatened and weakened by his sanity. So he was ripped apart like a rag doll, tossed into an incinerator and burned like another piece of waste. Sometimes, I fear dogs. The cabal dealt with that guard, gave him a similar end, but I am wandering ahead again.

The doctor came, Laura. Today, I'm sure it was today. I remember you saying that I was due for my MOT. He prodded me and listened to my chest, took my blood pressure. Did we have breakfast before he came? Did you and he whisper apart from me, has he told you that I am slipping away? It is becoming so vivid, my darling. These are not hallucinations. I am actually seeing people from years ago, can hear them talking, am sometimes able to join in the conversations. This is craziness, yet I am so clear about the war years.

I have not told you about my other Greek friend. Have I? Well, I shall assume that you and he have not yet been introduced, as I can no longer go back to the start of this document. After reading the last line or so, I simply continue and hope for the best. He was a violinist and he entertained the officers. He was also in charge of our food after the other man was torn to pieces. He told us things that were hard to believe, yet he was not lying. Jews were helping to kill Jews, were forced to empty bodies out of gas chambers, were made to burn the bodies. Healthy

621

people came in on the trains, were being stripped of clothes and possessions. Meekly, they filed to the showers, were lifted out as corpses and carried to the incinerators. It was a machine of superb efficiency, with prisoners aiding guards. If a man refused to assist, then he simply joined the queues for showers. More often, he would be shot. The real efficiency lay in the fact that most victims remained blissfully unaware of their fate until it was too late.

Laura, I am explaining all this so that you might understand my anger. I know that this account may be a little confused, too detailed in some parts, too sparse in others. I am running a race and I must get to the winning post before – before whatever. But you need to know what happened in order to forgive me for other deeds.

Paul and I had been spared since 1942. The commander, I'll call him Spangl, needed us. We were a part of a well-oiled team of specialists who used by-products of the holocaust to the Nazis' advantage. Under Spangl's all-seeing gaze (he haunts me now) human hair was gathered, presumably for wigs, clothes were kept, spectacles, shoes, dentures. Even human skin was used for lampshades. Paul and I were at the upper-class end of this macabre feast, as we handled the true valuables of the soon-to-be-victorious Reich.

The Czechs came, gathered in hundreds beneath fierce white floodlights. They were pushed into undressing rooms, forced out again into the cold night, arms wrapped about their nakedness. Some fought and were beaten to death on the spot. The violence was extraordinary. The blood looked black under the harsh lights. Naked children clung to naked mothers. This was real, my love. I was there. I am not a history book, I am a witness. It was the Czechs who made me determined to join Paul after the war. Those at the back of the ranks began to sing their anthem. We cried, Paul and I. While those brave Czechs were marched off to their end, the singing grew louder and my heart hardened. This would not be forgotten. I would be there when the massacre ended, I would be healthy, strong enough to bear witness, determined enough to accuse and condemn.

A Pole joined us late in 1943, I think. Because of language barriers, we learned about the Warsaw ghetto by looking at the pictures he drew. Our new friend was a goldsmith of great talent. While he worked alongside us, we taught him some German, then he regaled us with tales of even more atrocities. Hitler's aim was clear, he told us. Even if the war should be lost, the Reich would have achieved its main aim. Not one Jew would be left in Europe. His eyes were hard when he said to us, 'If you licked my heart, you would die of poison.'

Even in the camp, we could see that the war was ending and that our gaolers were on the losing side. They became careless, started to shoot people when the ovens overflowed. Bodies were buried after a fashion, but many were piled up in surrounding fields. The Nazis' carelessness extended to our department and our paperwork diminished. Instead of having to account for every item, we now began to feel free enough to stash some valuables with the portraits.

Allied planes flew over sometimes. (Have I already told you that? There are black semi-circles beneath your eyes. You are ill, my darling and I cannot help. Words come out of my mouth in the wrong order.

Only here, as I reheat an old fury, can I be clear enough to be understood. Soon, I shall be too far gone for this, too.) The end of the war was coming. The killing became haphazard, sporadic. The three of us hid in our store cupboard, listened while our work was smashed and stolen. But they did not touch the stove.

We walked out of our office one morning and into the arms of weeping Russian soldiers. Some English people arrived later. They jumped from aeroplanes, brought medicines and food. Grown men do cry. We watched as young Englishmen tried to feed those who were beyond food, tried to revive those whose need for oxygen had snuffed itself out in the night. The nurses, doctors and soldiers of your country were beyond words, Laura. There was a silence that was broken only by the thud of their boots as they walked through hell. The stench of burned flesh still lingered in the air, clung to everything it touched with its invisible talons. A sergeant sat by the gate, his legs useless, vomit and tears pouring through fingers that had fastened themselves to his face to shut out the sight. We helped him, brought him inside and cleaned him. I see that man all the time these days, in our kitchen, in our garden. I trust that he is well.

Have you heard people say that the birds don't sing there? It is true. I have been back to the emptiness. There is a poet somewhere in Liverpool – I've forgotten his name – whose friend went to the site of another camp. There were no birds in that vale of death, either.

We saved jewels, hid them, went into hospitals and became strong again. Laura, we had to do something. Nuremberg could not trap and try all of them.

There were little men, people of no importance who had gained stature and backbone from a uniform. Paul and I, together with witnesses from other camps, made it our business to find those torturers who had invented alibis and new identities.

It seemed right that we should use as a down-payment the property of those Jews who had perished. Eva Braun never got her swastika, because I broke it, opened our first establishment with the proceeds. For many, many years, I helped to capture the murderers. Some had already been tried and acquitted in spite of evidence, but we dealt with them anyway.

But I became sickened by what we were doing. We were killing old men. I began to wonder whether people remained the same, because we seemed to be murdering men who were so different from the young guards we remembered. When I met you, I walked away from it, though my business has continued to support the cabal.

Another thing I did not tell you was that I kept in touch with a man called Colin. You used to be married to his son. Colin lives not far from here. He watched over you for years. We met at the prison. I think I visited several men, but that time is not as clear as the war years. I probably became involved because I remembered what it was to be interned.

Did they pull down that wall, my love? Will it come again, the Reich? My fingers are stiff, so I guess that I must have done a lot of writing lately. I think you are going into hospital. I think you are sending me away so that I may be cared for during your absence. Do not worry for me, no matter how bad this becomes. A young man walked with you on the beach. I hope he is caring for you.

Oh, my darling, I know I am going mad. Why do I find myself in strange situations, how do I manage to do so many odd things when sometimes half of me knows that I shouldn't be going for walks in the dark or standing naked at the back door? You may have to help me if I sink too far. A poem. Somewhere, there's a poem. Yes, it's in the bottom safe. Give me my wings, sweetheart. Let me fly away and leave you in peace.

The Final Solution. We survived it. The American Indians knew the concept behind those words. They fought to avoid it too. Those three dreadful words were put together by a powerful American called Ulysses Grant. Learn not to blame one nation, learn not to sink to the level of the worst in mankind. Making sense is difficult, almost impossible. You have packed a small case. I think you have told me that you are going into hospital.

I love you, Laura. Find your wings. If I can't find mine, help me.

With all my love,

Ben.

Chapter Eight

It's Wednesday, the last day of September. I have been acutely aware of the minutes as they passed, was up before seven so that I might experience to the full these important hours. I even read my stars this morning, was advised not to feel inadequate. 'You really want to disappear behind your protective cover and let the world get on without you. But you will have to see where you can make your life easier without cutting yourself off completely.' Utter nonsense, of course.

Chewbacca is in the water, is splashing and staggering about like an old man on a day out during Wakes Week. With a knotted hanky on his head, this huge animal would really look the part. He runs from a scum-crested wave, turns, barks at the moon's handiwork. The Mersey's tides never fail to catch Chewy out. As a pup, he used to try solving the problem by drinking the river, but even this thick-headed clown learned not to imbibe such filth. I read recently that a group of amateur divers is planning to march through Liverpool to draw attention to the famous waterway's plight. They won't win. There's no beating the ebb and flow, no money to clean the water, no chance of making blue the sea that receives mess created by a whole city.

The funeral was this morning. I felt as if I were somewhere else, could not make complete contact with what was going on around me. Diana was very supportive and controlled, coped superbly. The girl is a brick. I cannot imagine life without her noise, her energy. We are managing, Diana and I.

At my feet rests a mesh cage that contains a pair of

627

mended gulls. In a few minutes, when I have composed my thoughts for Ben, I shall give the birds their wings. There's no-one on the beach today. No dog-walker will hear me if I talk to myself, no children will run helter-skelter up to the road, away from the madwoman.

I sit on the concrete steps, watch the gulls watching me. 'You'd better bloody fly, you two,' I advise them. 'Because your saviour's up there already. He's waiting for you, so be sharp.' Be sharp. Auntie Maisie used to say that. 'Come on and be sharp, Anne, you'll miss next Preston Guild at this rate.' Maisie, I did love you and Freddie.

So much has happened in recent days that my head is still spinning like a whipped top on a windy day. There is a chance that I shall become as muddle-headed as Ben was. Ben was. He isn't any more. Where Ben has gone, all is calm and peaceful. I won't cry. I'm sure I won't cry.

After reading that terrible document, I was in a zombie-like state for several days. When I surfaced, I phoned the poet, read parts to him. 'Yes,' he said softly. 'We know, Danielle and I, but we were sworn to secrecy.'

'Why didn't you tell me when I came with the poem?' I felt angry, betrayed, though I still remembered the gladness I experienced when I first realized that Ben had talked to Kevin. 'You knew how ill he was,' I said, recognizing my own petulance, disliking my tone of voice even as I spoke. 'Why didn't you shield me from the shock of this letter?'

Kevin waited for me to stop ranting. I'll never forget his answer. 'The sickness made him no less human, Laura. He was a man who asked for my promise. I keep promises.' The young are so good at putting me in my proper place lately.

For several evenings, I terrorized my cousin Anne. 'Did she do it?' I asked a hundred times. 'Did Miss Armitage help Richard on his way?' I don't know why I needed to ask. My plans for Ben should not have depended on anyone else's courage. 'Did she kill him?' I insisted.

'Why do you need to know?'

I screamed at her, must have made her head ache. 'Stop answering my question with the same bloody question. Never mind why.'

'Then stop asking,' she shouted back.

I wore her down in the end, convinced her that my need for an honest response lay in a programme of research for what I called 'a different type of book'.

'Yes, all right,' she snapped eventually. 'With a certain doctor's help and blessing, she laced that final cocoa with something or other. The doctor is long dead and Miss Armitage is failing, so there's your bloody research done. How's Ben?'

'The same,' I replied.

After a slight pause, she cleared her throat. 'You won't, will you?'

'Won't what?'

'Don't answer questions with questions, Laura. It's not legal.'

'Really?' My mind was already elsewhere. I would bring him home, talk to him, read the stuff from the safe, read it aloud, try to reach him. If there was no improvement, I would help him to move on. 'What did you say?'

'Euthanasia's not legal.'

'Right.'

'Is that girl still with you? Will she be there when you bring Ben home? Laura, are you listening to me?'

'Yes. She'll be here, I think.' I put down the phone, didn't need any lectures from my lawyer.

The dog has become excited. He tears towards me, skids to a halt, woofs quietly and raises his crazy eyebrows. He is asking about the seagulls. A hundred times he and I have stood here, or in the woods, while Ben released one or more of his patients. And at last I understand my husband's preoccupation with house-martins. Many perish because they can't find a home, a nest in which to shelter. Ben lost home, family, identity.

I have comforted myself by insisting that my husband

never performed an actual murder. He travelled, dealt in jewels, made money for the cause and researched on behalf of the cabal, but I am sure that he could never kill. The wind whistles round me, makes me shiver. I stare at the mist-shrouded Welsh hills, force myself to admit that I shall never know that particular truth, will never be able to pick it up and hold it to the light as if it were a polished diamond. Like the hills, it is clouded over. Only the cabal knows the real story, and I shall not meet its members.

I finally faced my own past three days ago, went alone to see Tommo, the torturer from my youth. I had vowed never to come again, but for once, I needed this man. He is old, grey-faced beneath a clammy slick of sweat. He breathes with determination, as if he has to think about it. When I told him of Ben's death, the cold eyes flickered with . . . was it triumph, hope, amusement? 'How did he keep you away?' I asked insistently, still dissatisfied with the previous answer. 'You weren't always so weak, and you swore many times that you'd catch up with me.'

'Bother boys.' He took a draught of oxygen, fought a cough for a moment or two. 'He threatened me exactly as I'd threatened you. An eye for an eye, he called it. Ben Starling had some powerful connections, according to rumour. Not strictly big-time, but not kosher, either.' He was sticking to the tale, then.

'He . . . dealt with Nazis,' I said softly. 'He cleaned up after the war, brought Hitler's small fry to justice.' He didn't kill, I kept saying to myself. Even if Ben did kill, I wouldn't tell this man anything. 'You would have been small fry, Tommo. Don't get any ideas – he still has friends.'

'Was he a Jew?'

I shrugged. 'Partly. But not kosher.'

He dismissed the feeble play on words. 'For a long time, I got visitors, big blokes who asked me whether I was being good.'

'If you were being good, that must have been a new

experience for you. Even the worst of criminals wouldn't commit fratricide.'

Pale hands gripped the arms of his chair. 'Well, it started in bloody Genesis, Cain and Abel. And my so-called brother took you away from me.'

My hands itched to strike him. With an effort of will, I backed away from the sick man. 'No. Your cruelty sent me away, Tommo. Frank was a good man, so was Ben.'

Since childhood, I have been capable of feeling something akin to hatred. My mother has not been a favourite, and I have loathed Bernard Thompson for many years. Yet I have never turned on either of them, not fully, not intentionally. For an endless time, I accepted abuse, tried not to care, simply shut out my mother, my first husband. Yet there I was, spending days planning to kill Ben if he didn't begin to come out of his nightmares.

Oh Ben. I stood in the street, breathed fresher air into my lungs. I knew why. At last, I knew why my Ben had made me face the monster. He must have endured so much, especially during sleep, must have dreamt of Treblinka. He forced me to go to Tommo so that my nights would be peaceful. Ben made just that one mistake, forced me to sit with a lunatic, and even that one mistake was no error. Now, at last, I fear nothing, nobody.

As I drove away from Tommo's house, I realized that love was the only emotion I had ever felt strongly. I loved Ben enough to kill him, had never hated sufficiently to strike out. Ben encouraged me to support Tommo, taught me to face the worst. Lately, I have learned so much about myself and about the wonderful stranger who became my second husband. (No, I haven't forgotten you, Frank. You were the second, but you weren't any more legal than euthanasia.)

While I prepare to release these birds, I find myself thinking about Mother, that unapproachable woman whose presence in my life has been less than comfortable. She is baffling just now, almost pleasant on occasion. Do people change as they grow older? Ben wrote that he and his friends were seeking out men who had altered beyond recognition. My husband's vigilantes were wreaking vengeance on people who no longer existed, folk who bore no resemblance to the guards who strutted, barked orders, played a part in the attempt to annihilate a whole ethnic group. Even the Nazis had metamorphosed once the climate had changed. Is Liza McNally softening? She is in my house now, is chain smoking via the gap beneath her black net veil. We are to go home, she says. Diana will become a trainee director, I shall play a leading role in my father's dream.

Diana. Liddy. All Liddy and Jimmy's children. If Diana leaves Liverpool, then the other members of her family will inherit a decent house, the place that's being gutted at this very moment. Diana's brothers and sisters will be able to sell the property, use the divided loot as a deposit on a future. How it all dovetails, how tidily it comes together, this latest chapter of my life.

Robert's there, too, his grief about Carol revitalized by Ben's passing. He has delegated his veterinary duties, is almost suave in a dark grey suit, black tie, very few dog hairs beyond those bequeathed to him this morning by Chewbacca. Mother was talking to him earlier, has probably elected him as my next husband. 'You could be a vet in Bolton,' I overheard her saying. All organized, all designed for me.

A jogger sprints by, the world shut out by a Walkman. Perhaps he and I share the same birth sign, though he has not read his stars this morning, is bent on being alone. Chewy chases him, throws up wads of grey sand, stops in his clumsy tracks when he gets no attention.

My children have come to Ben's funeral. Jodie looks fairly smart in a blue suit, though the hem dips slightly at the back. She won't sew. I've known her to use staples and sellotape to secure a drooping hem. She is working at last, has settled down to a job at Great Ormond Street. 'Children,' she announced this morning, 'are the important ones.' At least her priorities are an improvement on her needlework. I wonder how she copes with sewing up a wound? There's a man with her, no spots, good shoes, a qualification in psychology. I'm even smiling. It'll take him a lifetime to analyse my mercurial daughter.

Gerald teeters on the brink of marriage, seems to be atoning for his sins by putting most dealing, inside or not, outside of his sphere. He is in the company of an elegant woman whose mother used to be somebody, a Lady-in-Waiting, I think Gerald said. They are forming a partnership to deal in antiquities and bric-a-brac from a posh *bijou* shop near Mayfair, a shoebox with a pretty frontage. They showed me the photos, enthused about the project. She's forty if a day, talks around a gobful of marbles, is pseudo-aristocratic. I wonder about her previous liaisons. She has boys at Winchester, drives a 1939 MG, knows all there is to know about European porcelain.

Everything is working out smoothly, too evenly for me to believe. Even Edward has forgotten to sulk, though he wept when Ben was lowered into the ground. Ben understood, was one of the few older heterosexuals who truly accepted my younger son's dilemma. Edward is alone, but he looks calm, so I guess that he has found a partner. Oh, I hope so. He needs monogamy, stability.

I made the decision to bring Ben home, was intent on following through the plan to talk to him, to read aloud the contents of the safe, to help him out of the maze one way or another. Heaton Lodge was not pleased by my mulish stubbornness. Susan Jenkinson, known in the trade as Jenks, visited me after my letter had been received by Matron. 'You can't cope with this, Laura,' said Jenks, determination in the set of her jaw. 'He's started walking a bit, keeps trying to wander off. The poor man is very hard work. After the surgery and the breakdown, you're not up to it.'

Diana was there, was ironing two of my T-shirts that she'd begged from me. 'It's her husband,' she said rather peevishly. 'She can do as she likes.'

I silenced my house guest with one of my hard looks. 'He wants to be at home,' I told Jenks. My collection of sleeping pills and tranquillizers was just behind the nurse's head, in one of my famous kitchen cupboards which have never quite fitted. 'He needs me,' I told her firmly.

'He needs professional care—'

'He'll get it. He'll get whatever makes him feel better.' Above all, he might achieve that final release from a life that was fast becoming a tragedy. 'I'm well enough,' I insisted. 'And Diana will help me, I'm sure.'

'Course I will.' She stood like the Rock of Gibraltar, rigid and rather menacing, her hair plastered back into a thick rope that also looked carved from granite.

Jenks wheedled. 'Just another month, then. Give yourself till mid-October, get some rest and build yourself up.'

'No.'

When the nurse had left, I turned to my young friend. 'I want you to go back to your father's house for a few days when Ben comes home. Give me a chance to settle him while you bully the workmen.'

'OK.' She walked out, threw a parting shot over a slender shoulder. 'Me mam told me you could be a stubborn owld bugger.'

I could have shouted 'Ditto', but I didn't bother. Liddy often told me that her little Daisy was as determined as a constipated donkey. Sometimes, I really miss Liddy.

I stare at the horizon and miss a lot of people, my Ben most of all. He never did come home. In an hour of lucidity, my husband found his legs, walked to Matron's office, prised off the lid of a locked medicine trolley and stole fifty-seven tablets. They were sure of the number, as all drugs were accounted for daily. I was told that the lid showed few signs of damage, and I was not surprised. Ben must have been clever to survive a camp, to plan with others a form of world-wide retribution that was never noticed. How stealthy they must have been, those avengers.

It was decided that Ben stole the tablets in the night, as nothing was discovered until the morning shift arrived. By 7 a.m., my lovely husband was cold in his bed. 'If you hadn't managed, I'd have done it for you, my darling,' I say. He saved me from that, too, saved me from so much . . .

I look at the leaden sky, feel chilled beneath its cheerlessness. 'Goodbye, my love,' I say. 'I don't blame you for any of it.' He's better off, I keep telling myself. The world was not good enough for him, did not deserve a man of such magnificence.

Suddenly, I am not alone. A crowd of people descends on me, the approaching footfalls cushioned by wet sand. Diana and Jodie stand together, the spot-free young man behind them with Edward, Gerald and his probably Honourable fiancée. She looks better outside, younger, ordinary. Her hand is in my son's and they are each with the right person. Ruth, who is short enough to hold Chewy's collar without bending her knees, has taken charge of my wayward canine. Les supports my mother, has cupped a shovel-sized hand beneath the old woman's elbow. And she is old, thin, wasting, weak. Confetti smiles, her still-pretty face wrinkling with age and too much soap.

Robert moves to my side, though there is nothing proprietorial about his stance. And bringing up the rear is my Frank, aged, bald, slightly bent. But Frank is dead and this is the man who sent Ben to me. Colin Thompson, whom I have not seen for many years, must have read about Ben's death in the newspapers. My husband made quite a stir when he exited, though I shall not sue the nursing home for negligence. To Tommo's dad, I mouth a soft 'Hello' that falls into a silence of two decades. My cousin Anne has joined Robert, is standing between me and him.

I bend, touch the catch on the cage. A movement nudges the corner of my vision, and I look up at the rails above the concrete steps. Although they don't often

635

approach the beach, two starlings sit and stare at me. I won't cry. Did you send them, Ben? Did you? How dowdy they look as winter approaches, how dull the beaks that were recently lighter, brighter.

From behind the gathering of people, a voice reaches me. 'Give him his wings, Laura,' says Kevin McCann. He stands with Danielle, watches as I open the cage.

They bolt from their prison in a flurry of feathers, beating the air wildly as they test mended quill and tendon. We seem to hold our collective breath while they keep together, soaring upward into a sky whose curtain has opened for them. A single ray of light touches the birds, making them ethereal, angelic.

Mother sniffs meaningfully. 'Walking on sand is no good for a person of my age,' she says. A narrow, gloved hand reaches up, pulls the veil over emotions I didn't know she had. 'Well,' she says impatiently, 'he was another fool of a man, but a good enough fool.' Having framed the epitaph, she allows Les to steer her homeward.

I swivel, look at the rail, find it empty. The September Starlings have gone home.

†HE LADY OF †HE SORROWS

THE BITTERBYNDE TRILOGY:
BOOK 1: The Ill-Made Mute
BOOK 2: The Lady of the Sorrows
BOOK 3: The Battle of Evernight

Visit Cecilia's web site: http://www.dartthornton.com

CECILIA
DART-THORNTON

THE
LADY OF THE
SORROWS

MACMILLAN

First published 2002 in Tor by Pan Macmillan Australia Pty Limited

First published in Great Britain 2002 by Macmillan
an imprint of Pan Macmillan Ltd
Pan Macmillan, 20 New Wharf Road, London N1 9RR
Basingstoke and Oxford
Associated companies throughout the world
www.panmacmillan.com

ISBN 0 333 90755 8

A CIP catalogue record for this book is available from
the British Library.

Printed and bound in Great Britain by
Mackays of Chatham plc, Chatham, Kent

For my friend and muse, Tanith Lee

**Cecilia
Dart-Thornton**

CONTENTS

THE STORY SO FAR

This is the second book in THE BITTERBYNDE trilogy.

Book 1, *The Ill-Made Mute*, told of a mute, scarred amnesiac who led a life of drudgery in Isse Tower, a House of the Storm-riders. Stormriders, otherwise known as Relayers, are messengers of high status. They 'ride sky' on winged steeds called eotaurs, and their many towers are strewn across the empire of Erith, in the world called Aia.

Sildron, the most valuable of metals in this empire, has the property of repelling the ground, thus providing any object with lift. This material is used to make the shoes of the Skyhorses and in the building of Windships to sail the skies. Only andalum, another metal, can nullify the effect of sildron.

Erith is randomly visited by a strange phenomenon known as 'the shang', or 'the unstorm'; a shadowy, charged wind that brings a dim ringing of bells and a sudden springing of tiny points of coloured light. When this anomaly sweeps over the land, humans have to cover their heads with their taltries—hoods lined with a mesh of a third metal, talium. Talium prevents human passions from spilling out through the skull. At times of the unstorm, this is important, because the shang has the ability to catch and replay human dramas. Its presence engenders 'tableaux', which are ghostly impressions of past moments of intense passion, played over repeatedly until, over centuries, they fade.

The world outside Isse Tower is populated not only by mortals but also by immortal creatures called eldritch wights—incarnations wielding the power of gramarye. Some are seelie, benevolent towards mankind, while others are unseelie and dangerous.

The drudge escaped from the Tower and set out to seek a name, a past and a cure for the facial deformities. Befriended by an Ertish adventurer named Sianadh, who named her 'Imrhien', she learned that her yellow hair indicated she came of the blood of the Talith people, a once-great race that had dwindled to the brink of extinction. Together, the pair sought and found a treasure trove in a cave under a remote place called 'Waterstair'. Taking some of the money and valuables with them, they journeyed to the city of Gilvaris Tarv. There they were sheltered by Sianadh's sister, the carlin Ethlinn, who had three children; Diarmid, Liam and Muirne. A city wizard, Korguth, tried unsuccessfully to heal Imrhien's deformities. To Sianadh's rage, the wizard's incompetent meddling left her worse off than before. Later, in the marketplace, Imrhien bought freedom for a seelie waterhorse. Her golden hair was accidentally revealed for an instant, attracting a disturbing glance from a suspicious-looking passer-by.

After Sianadh departed from the city, bent on retrieving more riches from Waterstair, Imrhien and Muirne were taken prisoner by a band of villains led by a man named Scalzo. Upon their rescue they learned of the deaths of Liam and Sianadh. Scalzo and his henchmen were to blame.

Imrhien promised Ethlinn she would reveal the location of Waterstair's treasure only to the King-Emperor. With this intention, she joined Muirne and Diarmid, and travelled to distant Caermelor, the royal city. Along their way through a wilderness of peril and beauty, Imrhien and Diarmid accidentally became separated from their fellow travellers, and also Muirne. Fortunately they met Thorn, a handsome ranger of the Dainnan knighthood whose courage and skill were matchless, and Imrhien fell victim to love.

After many adventures, followed by a sojourn in Rosedale with Silken Janet and her father, these three wanderers rediscovered Muirne, safe and well. Muirne departed with her brother Diarmid to join the King-Emperor's armed forces. Recruits were in demand, because rebel barbarians and unseelie wights were mustering in the northern land of Namarre, and it seemed war was brewing in Erith.

Imrhien's goal was to visit the one-eyed carlin, Maeve, to seek a cure, before continuing on to Caermelor. At her final parting from Thorn she was distraught. To her amazement, he kissed her at the last moment.

At last, in the village of White Down Rory, Imrhien's facial disfigurements were healed. With the cure, she regained the power of speech.

Two of her goals had been achieved. She now had a name and a face, but still, no memory of her past.

THE LADY
OF THE
SORROWS

The Known Countries of Erith

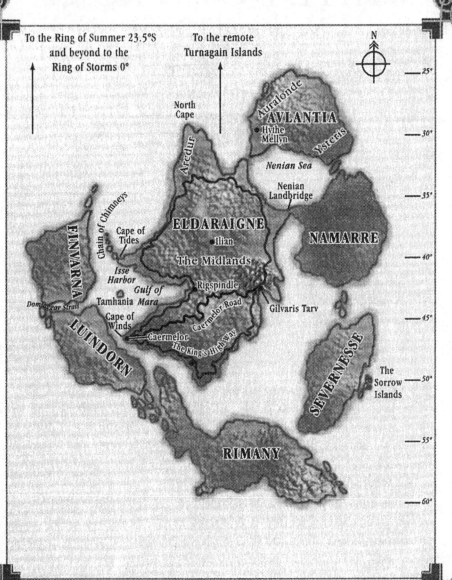

To the Ring of Summer 23.5°S
and beyond to the
Ring of Storms 0°

To the remote
Turnagain Islands

N

North
Cape

Auralonde

AVLANTIA

Hythe
Mellyn

Ysteris

Nenian Sea

Nenian
Landbridge

Arcdur

ELDARAIGNE

Ilian

NAMARRE

Chain of Chimneys

Cape of
Tides

The Midlands

FINVARNA

Isse
Harbor

Rigspindle

Domber Far Strait

Gulf of
Tamhania Mara

Gilvaris Tarv

Caermelor Road

Cape of
Winds

LUINDORN

Caermelor

The King's High Way

SEVERNESSE

The
Sorrow
Islands

RIMANY

25°

30°

35°

40°

45°

50°

55°

60°

1
WHITE DOWN RORY
Mask and Mirror

Cold day, misty gray, when cloud enshrouds the hill.
Black trees, icy freeze, deep water, dark and still,
Cold sun. Ancient One of middle Wintertide,
Old wight, erudite, season personified.
Sunset silhouette; antlers branching wide—
Shy deer eschew fear while walking at her side.
Windblown, blue-faced crone, the wild ones never flee.
Strange eyes, eldritch, wise—the Coillach Gairm is she.

SONG OF THE WINTER HAG

I t was Nethilmis, the Cloudmonth.
Shang storms came and went close on each other's
heels, and then the wild winds of Winter began to close in.
They buffeted the landscape with fitful gusts, rattling drearily
among boughs almost bare, snatching the last leaves and hunting
them with whimsical savagery.

The girl who sheltered with the carlin at White Down Rory felt
reborn. All seemed so new and so strange now, she had to keep
reminding herself over and over that the miraculous healing of her
face and voice had indeed happened; to keep staring into the
looking-glass, touching those pristine features whose skin was still
tender, and saying over and over, until her throat rasped:

'Speech is mine. Speech is mine.'

But she would discover her hands moving as she spoke.

Surrounding the unfamiliar face, the hair fell thick and heavy, the colour of gold. Lamplight struck red highlights in the silken tresses. As to whether all this was beauty or not, she was unsure; it was all too much to take in at once. For certain, she was no longer ugly—and that, it seemed for the moment, was all that mattered. Yet there was no rejoicing, for she lived in fear, every minute, that it would all be taken away, or that it was some illusion of Maeve's looking-glass—but the same image repeated itself in placid water and polished bronze, and it was possible, if not to accept the new visage, at least to think of it as a presentable mask that covered the old, ugly one—her true countenance.

'I kenned you were mute as soon as you fell through my door,' said the carlin, Maeve One-Eye. 'Don't underestimate me, colleen. Your hands were struggling to shape some signs—without effect. And it was obvious what you were after, so I lost no time—no point in dilly-dallying when there's a job to be done. But *'tis* curious that the spell on your voice was lifted off with the sloughed tissue of your face. If I am not mistaken you were made voiceless by something eldritch, while the paradox poisoning is from a *lorraly* plant. Very odd. I must look into it. Meanwhile, do not let sunlight strike your face for a few days. That new tissue will have to harden up a bit first, 'tis still soft and easily damaged.

'Tom Coppins looks after me, don't you, Tom?'

The quick, cinnamon-haired boy, who was often in and out of the cottage, nodded.

'And he will look after you as well, my colleen. Now, start using your voice bit by bit, not too much, and when 'tis strong you can tell me everything; past, present, and future. No, the glass is not eldritch. Come away from it—there is too much sunlight bleeding in through the windowpanes. And there's shang on the way—the Coillach knows what *that* would do to your skin!'

Not a day, not an hour, not a moment passed without thoughts of Thorn. Passion tormented the transformee. She whispered his name over and over at night as sleep crept upon her, hoping to dream of him, but hoping in vain. It seemed to her that he was fused with her blood, within her very marrow. Ever and anon her thought was distracted by images of his countenance, and conjecture as to his whereabouts and well-being. Longing gnawed relentlessly, like a rat within, but as time passed and she became accustomed to the pain, its acuteness subsided to a constant dull anguish.

Late in the evening of the third day, the howling airs of Nethilmis stilled. Maeve dozed in her rocking-chair by the fire with a large plated lizard sleeping on her lap. Imrhien was gazing at her own reflection by candlelight, twin flames flickering in her eyes. Tom Coppins was curled up in a small heap on his mattress in a corner. All was still, when came a sound of rushing wind and a whirring of great wings overhead, and a sad, lonely call.

Quickly, Maeve roused and looked up. She muttered something.

Not long afterward, a soft sound could be heard outside the cottage, like a rustling of plumage. Maeve lifted the lizard down to the hearthrug and went to open the door. A girl slipped in silently and remained in the shadows with the carlin. Her face was pale, her gown and the long fall of hair were jet black. She wore a cloak of inky feathers, white-scalloped down the front. A long red jewel shone, bright as fresh blood, on her brow. Maeve spoke with her, in low tones that could not be overheard, then began to busy herself with preparations, laying out bandages and pots on the table.

The carlin's activities were hidden in the gloom beyond the firelight, but a sudden, whistling, inhuman cry of pain escaped the newcomer, waking Tom Coppins. Maeve had set straight a broken limb and was now binding it with splints. When all was finished, the swanmaiden lay quivering in the farthest corner from the fire, hidden beneath the folds of her feather-cloak.

'Pallets everywhere,' muttered Maeve, leaving the dirty pots on the table. 'I shall have to take a bigger cottage next year.'

'You heal creatures of eldritch, madam?' Imrhien's voice was still soft, like the hissing of the wind through heather.

'Hush. Do not speak thus, when such a one is nigh. I heal who I can where and when I am able. It is a duty of my calling—but by no means the beginning and end of it.' Maeve fingered the brooch at her shoulder; silver, wrought in the shape of an antlered stag. 'Carlins are not merely physicians to humankind. The Coillach Gairm is the protectress of all wild things, in particular the wild deer. We who receive our knowledge from her, share her intention. Our principal purpose is the welfare of wild creatures. To protect and heal them is our mandate—care of humans is a secondary issue. Go to bed.'

'I have another affliction. You are powerful—mayhap you can help me. Beyond a year or two ago, I have no memory of my past.'

'Yes, yes, I suspected as much. Do you think I haven't been scratching my head about that? But it's a doom laid on you by something far stronger than I, and beyond my power to mend. For the Coillach's sake, come away from the mirror and go to bed. You're wearing out my glass. Don't go near her, that feathered one—she is afraid of most people, as they all are, with good reason.'

The saurian jumped back onto the carlin's lap. She scratched its upstanding dorsal plates as it circled a couple of times before settling.

'I would have liked something less armoured and more furry,' she murmured, looking down at it, 'but bird-things would not come near, if I had a cat. Besides, Fig gave me no choice. He chose *me*.'

It was difficult to sit still inside the house of the carlin, within walls, and to know that Thorn walked in Caermelor, in the Court of the King-Emperor. Now the renewed damsel was impatient to be off to the gates of the Royal City. At the least, she might join the ranks of Thorn's admirers, bringing a little self-respect with her. She might exist near him, simultaneously discharging the mission she had taken upon herself at Gilvaris Tarv: to reveal to the King-Emperor the existence of the great treasure and—it was to be hoped—to set into motion a chain of events that would lead to the downfall of those who had slain Sianadh, Liam, and the other brave men of their expedition.

Maeve, however, was not to be swayed.

'You shall not leave here until the healing is complete. Think you that I want to see good work ruined? Settle down—you're like a young horse champing at the bit. Even Fig's getting ruffled.' The lizard, dozing fatly by the fire, adeptly hid its agitation. In the shadows the swanmaiden stirred and sighed.

Three days stretched to five, then six. The weather raged again, battering at the walls of the cottage.

At nights a nimble bruney would pop out from somewhere when it thought the entire household asleep, and do all the house-work in the two-roomed cot with amazing speed, quietness, and efficiency. Under Maeve's instructions the girl feigned sleep if she happened to waken and spy it. Its clothes were tattered and its little boots worn and scuffed. When it had finished, it drank the milk set out for it, ate the bit of oatcake, and disappeared again, leaving everything in a state of supernatural perfection.

Tom Coppins, the quiet lad with great dark eyes, was both messenger and student to the carlin, performing errands that took him from the house, aiding her in preparing concoctions or help-ing her treat the ailments and vexations of the folk who beat a path to her door; everything from gangrene and whooping cough to butterchurns in which the butter wouldn't 'come', or a dry cow, or warts. Someone asked for a love potion and went away empty-handed but with a stinging earful of sharp advice. From time to time Maeve would go outside to where her staff was planted in the ground and come back carrying leaves or fruit plucked from it—potent cures. Or she would tramp out into the woods and not return for hours.

More and more, the carlin allowed Imrhien to wield her voice; it was exhilarating to converse freely; such a joy, as if the bird of speech had been liberated from an iron cage. Little by little she told her story, omitting—from a sense of privacy if not shame for having been so readily smitten—her passion for Thorn.

When the tale had been recounted, the old woman sat back in her chair, rocking and knitting. ('I like to be busy with my hands,' she had said. 'And it sets folk at ease to see an old woman harm-lessly knitting. Mind you, *my* needles are anything but harmless!')

'An interesting tale, even if you have left out part of it,' Maeve commented. Her patient felt herself blush. Maeve's perceptiveness was disconcerting. 'So now you still have three wishes, eh? Isn't that right? That's how it usually goes—yan, tan, tethera. No, there is no need to reply. You wish for a history, a family, and something more—I see it in your eyes. Mark you—remember the old saw, *Be careful what you wish for, lest—*'

'Lest what?'

'*Lest it comes true.*'

The carlin completed a row of knitting and swapped the needles from hand to hand.

'Now listen,' she continued. 'I do not know who you are or how to get your memories back, but I do ken that this house, since five days ago, is being watched.'

'Watched? What can you mean?'

'I mean, spied upon by spies who do not know they have been spied. And since they began their enterprise not long after you arrived, I deduce that it is you they are after. Nobody gets past my door without my allowing it—the world knows that. Therefore, these observers must be waiting for you to come out. What think you of that, eh? Are they friends of yours, wanting to protect you, or are they enemies?'

It was like a sudden dousing in icy water. All that had happened to Imrhien since her arrival at the carlin's house had driven out thoughts of pursuers. Now the recent past caught up with a jarring swiftness. These spies might be henchmen of the wizard, the slandered charlatan Korguth the Jackal—but more likely they were Scalzo's men who had somehow tracked her down. She had been traced right to the carlin's door! If they had come this far, across Eldaraigne in search of her, or if they had sent word of her approach by Relayer to accomplices in Caermelor or even at the Crown and Lyon Inn, then it was obvious they were determined to catch her before she went to the King-Emperor explaining her detailed knowledge of Waterstair's location. Danger threatened. Desperate men might resort to desperate methods to prevent her from reaching the Royal City.

The carlin's eye was fixed intently upon her guest.

'How do you estimate these watchers? Take care with your reply. A false decision might bring disaster. What comes next depends on what you say now. Your tongue is new to you. Use it wisely.'

'I think they are evil men,' the girl replied slowly. 'Men who wish me ill; brigands led by one called Scalzo, from Gilvaris Tarv, who slew my friends. They will try to stop me from reaching the Court.'

'That may be the case. I am not in a position to judge. If 'tis true, then it is perilous for you to depart from here unprotected. With this in mind I have already asked my patient Whithiue to lend you her feather-cloak so that you might fly out in the guise of a swan and send the cloak back later. She would not hear of it of course, but it was worth a try—she and her clan owe me many favours. Yet I have another plan. If those who watch are your enemies, then they will know you chiefly by your hair and by your name. My advice is this—when you set out for the Royal City, go not as Imrhien Goldenhair. Go as another.'

The needles clattered. A ball of yarn unrolled. The lizard watched it with the look of a beast born to hunt but restrained by overpowering ennui.

'Change my name?'

'Well, 'tis not your name, is it? 'Tis only a kenning given you. One kenning is as good as another. I'll think of something suitable to replace it, given time. But you *cannot* go to Court with that *hair* and not be noticed. By the Coillach, colleen, know you how rarely the Talith are seen? Only one of that kindred resides at Court— Maiwenna, a cousin of the long-defunct Royal Family of Avlantia. In all the lands, there are so few human beings of your colouring that they are always remarked upon. Feohrkind nobles can rinse their tresses in the concoctions of carlins and wizards and dye-mixers as often as they like, but they can never copy Talith gold. Their bleached heads are like clumps of dead grass. No, if you want to mingle unmarked, you must change the colour of your hair as well as your kenning. And for good measure, go as a recently bereaved widow and keep that face covered.'

'You know best,' said Imrhien slowly in her whispering tones, 'for I know nothing of the ways of the King-Emperor's Court. But who would recognise the face I wear now?'

'Folk from your past, haply.'

'Then that would be wonderful! I should meet my own folk, discover all!'

'Not necessarily. Who left you to die in the rain in a patch of *Hedera paradoxis?* Not folk who were looking after your interests. Safer to remain unknown, at least until you have delivered your messages to the King-Emperor. And if you cannot tell His Majesty himself, why then you would be equally well-off to confide in Tamlain Conmor, the Dainnan Chieftain, or True Thomas Learmont, the Royal Bard. They are his most trusted advisors, and worthy of that trust, more so than any other men of Erith.

'If you manage to leave my cottage unmarked and reach the Court, you will likely be richly rewarded, you understand. Gold coins can buy security, or at least a measure of it. When all is done and your work discharged, then you shall have leisure to decide whether to doff the widow's veil and show yourself, and risk all that goes with being Imrhien of the Golden Hair.'

'There is good sense in what you say,' the girl admitted to the carlin.

'Of course there is. And if you had your wits about you, you'd have thought of it yourself, but I expect you've lost them in that glass. By the way, are you aware that you speak with a foreign accent?'

'Do I? I suppose it is Talith.'

'No. It is like no dialect I have ever heard.'

'Am I of the Faêran? It is said that they lived forever . . .'

The carlin cackled, true to type. 'No, you certainly are not one of the Gentry. Not that I have ever set eyes on any of them, but there is naught of the power of gramarye in you. If there were, you would know it. You are as mortal as any bird or beast or *lorraly* folk. None of the Fair Folk would get themselves into such scrapes as you manage. And yet, your manner of speech is not of any of the kingdoms of Erith. Your accent's unfamiliar.'

'The Ringstorm that encircles the world's rim—does anything lie beyond it?'

'Let me tell you a little of the world. Some say that it is not a half-sphere but an entire orb with the Ringstorm around its waist dividing Erith from the northern half. That is why the world has two names; "Erith" for the Known Lands, and "Aia" for the three realms in one, which comprise the Known Lands, the unknown regions on the other side of the Ringstorm, and the Fair Realm. Of those three realms only Erith is open to us. Many folk have forgotten the Fair Realm. Some say it never existed at all. People believe what they can see. Furthermore, it is commonly held that nothing lies beyond the Ringstorm, that it marks the margins of the world, and if we were to pass further than that brink, we would fall into an abyss.'

'Mayhap there is some path through the Ringstorm.'

'Mayhap. Many have tried to find one. The shang winds and the world's storms are too much for any sea-craft. The Ringstorm's borders are decorated with broken Seaships.'

'Mayhap there is a way through to Erith from the other side, from a land on the other side where they speak differently . . .'

'Too many "mayhaps". Let us to the business in hand.'

'Yes! Madam Maeve, I am concerned for your safety. Should I depart hence under an assumed persona, the watchers will believe Imrhien Goldhair bides yet here, and they may keep watching for a time until they tire of it and assail your house.'

'A good point.' Maeve thoughtfully tapped her ear with a knitting needle. 'Ah, but if they *think* they see Imrhien Goldenhair leaving and they follow her, then find out it was a ruse and rush back here and see no sign of her, they will think she escaped during their absence. In sooth, she will have. An excellent plan—nay, ask no questions, it will all be clear to you soon. Meanwhile, I had better rouse Tom—he has errands to run for me in Caermelor. We shall need money to carry out this scheme. How much have you?'

'Madam, please accept my apologies. Your words remind me that I owe you payment for your healing of me, and my board and lodging. What is your fee?'

'My fee,' said the carlin, shooting a piercing glance from her bright eye, 'is whatever those who receive my services are prepared to give.'

'What you have given me is valuable beyond measure—worth more than all the treasure in the world.'

'Have I given it, or was it already yours by right? Do not be thankful until you have lived with your changed appearance for a moon-cycle or two. See how you like it then.'

'I cannot be otherwise than happy!'

'Ha! The measure of happiness is merely the difference between expectations and outcomes. It is not concerned with what one possesses—it is concerned with how content one is with what one possesses.'

Imrhien had taken out her leather pouch. The pearls she had left in Silken Janet's linen-chest, the ruby she had given to Diarmid and Muirne, but there remained two more jewels and the few gold coins she had saved when she ran from the caravan. In glittering array she spread the stones and metal before the carlin.

'This is all I have. Please, take it.'

Maeve One-Eye threw her head back and laughed.

'My dear,' she said, 'you will never survive out in the wide wicked world if you do this sort of thing. Have you not heard of bargaining? Such an innocent. And how would you fare with no money to spend on your way to the City? This I shall take.' She leaned forward and picked up the sapphire. 'The mud from Mount Baelfire is costly to obtain. And blue is one of the colours of my fellowship, the Winter shade of high glaciers and cold water under the sky. Leave the emerald out of your purse—it is of greater worth and will fetch a high price. It is necessary to sell it to pay for the purchases Tom shall make in Caermelor on your behalf. But put away the sovereigns and doubloons and the bit of silver. You may need them someday. And be more careful to whom you display your wealth—fortunately, I can be trusted, but not all folk are as honest as Maeve One-Eye!'

Her thicket of albino hair bristled untidily, like a rook's nest in a frost—her guest suspected that it was in fact inhabited by some pet animal—and she leaned back in her chair, chuckling. The needles resumed their *click-clack*.

'True to Talith type, you possess the darker eyebrows and eyelashes—those I will not need to alter. What colour of hair want you? Black? Brown?'

'Red.'

'A canny choice. Nobody would ever believe that any clear-headed person would *choose* the Ertish shade, thus they will think that you soothly *are* of Finvarnan blood. I take it you will not mind being despised as a barbarian in Court circles?'

'I have had my fill of contempt! I have been despised enough for twenty lifetimes. Not red, then. What is the fashion for hair at Court?'

'Black, or straw yellow—save for the salt-haired Icemen that dwell among them; their locks do not take kindly to dyes, nor do they wish to alter them, being a proud race.'

'It seems I must choose black. But I will not stay long at Court—only long enough to deliver my news, and then I will be away.'

And long enough to find someone.

'Be not so certain. You may not obtain an audience with the King-Emperor straight away. He is busy, especially at this time of strange unrest in the north. As an unknown, you will be seen as inconsequential enough to be kept waiting—if necessary, for weeks, despite the fact that I am going to transform you into a lady of means for the mission. If you successfully reach Caermelor and then obtain permission to pass within the palace gates, you may have to wait for a long time. And if you are eventually granted an audience, the next step must be verification of your news. They may ask you to lead them to this treasure.'

The carlin paused in her handiwork, holding it high for a bet-ter view. 'Cast off, one plain, one purl,' she muttered obliquely. With a thoughtful air, she lowered the needlework to her lap. 'So. A name you will need.' She hummed a little tune. 'I've got it! "Rohain". A tad Severnessish-sounding, but it suits you. And you must say that you come from some remote and little-known place, so that there is small chance of meeting any person who hails from there and might betray you. The Sorrow Islands off Severnesse are such a place—melancholy, avoided whenever pos-sible. Tarrenys is an old family name from those parts. Yes—that's it. Ha! *Rohain Tarrenys* you shall be—say farewell to Imrhien Goldenhair, Lady Rohain of the Sorrows.'

'Am I to be a lady? I know nothing of the ways of gentlefolk. I shall be discovered.'

'Methinks you underestimate your own shrewdness. Hearken.

Should a peasant wife arrive at the palace with a story of discovering great wealth, that woman risks her life. There are those at Court who are not as scrupulous as the Dukes of Ercildoune and Roxburgh; those who would wish to take the credit to themselves for such a discovery, and to silence the real messenger. It is possible a commonwife would not be given the opportunity to speak with the Dukes before she was bundled off with a few pennies, maybe to be followed, waylaid, and murdered. Howbeit, a *gentlewoman* must be treated with greater scrupulosity.'

'Who, at Court, could be so perfidious?'

'It will become clear to you,' said Maeve briskly. She changed the subject. 'Have you a potent tilhal for protection along the way?'

'I have a self-bored stone, given me by Ethlinn.'

'A worthy talisman,' said the carlin, examining the stone with a lopsided squint. 'You might well have need of it. Many malign things wander abroad these days. Doubtless you have heard—it is said that one of the brigand chieftains of Namarre has grown strong enough to muster wicked wights in his support. There is no denying that some kind of summons, inaudible to mortal ears, is issuing from that northern region. Unseelie wights are moving across the lands, responding to the Call. With an army of lawless barbarians, aided by unseelie hordes, a wizard powerful enough to summon wights would be an opponent to be reckoned with. They say such a force might stand a goodly chance of overthrowing the Empire and seizing power in Erith. If that should come to pass, all the lands would be plunged into chaos. It would mean the end of the long years of peace we have known.'

A chill tremor tore through the listener.

'These are uneasy times,' continued the carlin with a shake of her head. 'Even creatures which have not revealed themselves for many lifetimes of men have lately re-emerged. It is not long since I heard a rumour that Yallery Brown has been seen again.'

She returned the stone to its owner.

'What is that?' asked the girl, tucking the tilhal beneath her garments.

'Yallery Brown? One of the wickedest wights that ever was or is—so wicked that it is dangerous even to befriend him. Have you not heard the old tale of cursed Harry Millbeck, the brother of the great-grandfather of the mayor of Rigspindle?'

'I have heard many tales, but not that. Pray tell it!'

'He was a farm labourer, was Harry,' said Maeve. 'On a Summer's evening long ago, he was walking home from work across fields and meadows all scattered with dandelions and daisies, when he heard an anguished wailing like the cry of a for-saken child. He cast about for the source and at last discovered that it issued from underneath a large, flat stone, half-submerged under turf and matted weeds. This rock had a name in the district. For as long as anyone could remember, it had been called "The Strangers' Stone", and folk used to avoid it.

'A terrible fear came over Harry. The wails, however, had dwindled to a pitiful whimpering, and being a kind-hearted man he could not steel himself to walk on without rendering aid to what might have been a child in distress. With great trouble, he managed to raise up the Strangers' Stone, and there beneath it was a small creature, no bigger than a young child. Yet it was no child—rather it looked to be something old, far older than was natural, for it was all wizened, and its hair and beard were so long that it was all enmeshed in its own locks. Dandelion-yellow were the hair and whiskers, and soft as thistle-floss. The face, puckered as lava, was umber-brown, and from the midst of the creases a pair of clever eyes stared out like two black raisins. After its initial amazement at its release, the creature seemed greatly delighted.

'"Harry, ye're a good lad," it chirped.

'*It knows my name! For certain this thing is a bogle,* Harry thought to himself, and he touched his cap civilly, struggling to hide his terror.

'"Nay," said the little thing instantly, "I'm no bogle, but ye'd best not ask me what I be. Anyway, ye've done me a better ser-vice than ye know, and I be well-disposed toward ye."

'Harry shuddered, and his knees knocked when he found the eldritch thing could read his unspoken thoughts, but he mustered his courage.

'"And I now will give ye a gift," said the creature. "What would ye like—a strong and bonny wife or a crock full of gold coins?"

'"I have little interest in either, your honour," said Harry as politely as he could, "but my back and shoulders are always aching. My labour on the farm is too heavy for me and I'd thank you for help with it."

'"Now hearken ye, never thank me," said the little fellow with an ugly sneer. "I'll do the work for ye and welcome, but if ye give me a word of thanks ye'll never get a hand's turn more from me. If ye want me, just call *'Yallery Brown, from out of the mools come to help me,'* and I'll be there." And with that it picked the stalk of a dandelion puff, blew the fluffy seeds into Harry's eyes and disappeared.

'In the morning Harry could no longer believe what he had seen and suspected he'd been dreaming. He walked to the farm as usual, but when he arrived, he found that his work had already been completed, and he had no need to lift so much as a finger. The same happened day after day; no matter how many tasks were set for Harry, Yallery Brown finished them in the blink of an eye.

'At first the lad augured his life would be as leisurely as a nobleman's, but after a time he saw that matters might not go so well for him, for although his tasks were done, all the other men's tasks were being undone and destroyed. After a while, some of his fellow labourers happened to spy Yallery Brown darting about the place at night and they accused Harry of summoning the wight. They made his life miserable with their blaming and their complaints to the master.

'"I'll put this to rights," said Harry to himself. "I'll do the work myself, and not be indebted to Yallery Brown."

'But no matter how early he came to work, his tasks were always accomplished before he got there. Furthermore, no tool or implement would remain in his hand; the spade slipped from his grasp, the plough careered out of his reach and the hoe eluded him. The other men would find Harry trying to do their work for them, but no matter how hard he tried he could not do it, for it would go awry, and they accused him of botching it deliberately.

'Finally, the men indicted him so often that the master dismissed him, and Harry plodded away in a high rage, fuming about how Yallery Brown had treated him. Word went around the district that Harry Millbeck was a troublemaker, and no farmer would hire him. Without a means of earning a living, Harry was in sore straits.

"'I'll get rid of this wicked wight," he growled to himself, "else I shall become a beggar on the streets." So he went out into the fields and meadows and he called out, "Yallery Brown, from out of the mools, come to me!"

'The words were scarcely out of his mouth when something pinched his leg from behind, and there stood the little thing with its tormentil-yellow hair, its pleated brown face and its cunning raisin eyes. Pointing a finger at it, Harry cried, "It's an ill turn you've done to me and no benefit. I'll thank you to go away and allow me to work for myself!"

'At these words, Yallery Brown shrilled with laughter and piped up: "Ye've thanked me, ye mortal fool! Ye've thanked me and I warned you not!"

'Angrily, Harry burst out, "I'll have no more to do with you! Fine sort of help you give. I'll have no more of it from this day on!"

"'And ye'll get none," said Yallery Brown, "but if I can't help I'll hinder." It flung itself into a whirling, reeling dance around Harry, singing—

"'Work as thou wilt, thou'lt never do well.

Work as thou mayst, thou'lt never gain grist;

For harm and mischance and Yallery Brown

Thou'st let out thyself from under the stone."

'As it sang, it pirouetted. Its buttercup tresses and beard spun out all around until it resembled the spherical head of a giant dandelion that has gone to seed. This thistledown orb blew away, disappearing into the air, and Harry never again set eyes on Yallery Brown.

'But he was aware of the wight's malevolent presence for the rest of his life; he sensed it opposing him in everything to which he turned his hand. Forever after that, naught went aright for poor Harry Millbeck. No matter how hard he worked he could not profit by it, and ill-fortune was on whatever he touched. Until the day of his death Yallery Brown never stopped troubling him, and in his skull the wight's song went ceaselessly round and round, "... for harm and mischance and Yallery Brown thou'st let out thyself from under the stone ..."'

'That's a terrible injustice!' cried the listening girl.

'Aye,' said Maeve. 'That's the way of unseelie wights and that one is among the wickedest.'

The carlin gave detailed instructions to Tom Coppins, who went off to Caermelor on a pony and returned three days later laden with parcels.

'What took you so long?' Maeve said impatiently.

'I was bargaining.'

'Hmph. I hope you got the better of those rapscallion merchants. How much got you for the emerald?'

'Twelve guineas, eight shillings, and eightpence.'

'And what purchased you with that?'

'Shoes, raiment, and trinkets such as you asked, and a hired carriage to be waiting at the appointed place at the appointed time.'

'Good. Keep half a crown and give the rest to my lady, Rohain of the Sorrows.'

Tom Coppins was accustomed to unquestioningly accepting curious events. That a yellow-haired monster should have entered the cottage and been transformed was no more strange than many things he had seen while in the service of Maeve. He loved the old carlin with unswerving loyalty—whatever she needed, he would fetch; whatever she asked, he would do, and without question. He was an astute lad and warmhearted. In the time he had been in Maeve's service, he had seen beyond the aspect of a simple old woman, the aspect the world saw. He had been witness to the carlin's true dignity and power made manifest.

That night, Tom washed Imrhien-Rohain's hair with an iron-willow mordant. He rubbed in a thick mud of pounded and soaked iris-roots, then rinsed the hair again with the mordant, as Janet had done to Diarmid's locks in the valley of roses. The black-haired girl shook out her sable tresses in front of the fire.

The swanmaiden's eyes gleamed from the shadows. Maeve brought food for the wight-in-woman-form, speaking to her in a low, foreign voice.

The next morning, at *uhta*, the eldritch maiden departed. Before she left, Imrhien-Rohain saw her standing framed in the doorway, her fair face and slender arms gleaming white against the nightshade of her cloak and hair. The lovely wight offered a single black feather to Maeve. Then she slipped behind the doorpost and vanished. A moment later, with a rush and a whirr, dark wings lifted over the house-roof. There came a plaintive, mournful cry that was answered from far off.

Maeve stood on the doorstep, her face raised to the sky.

'She rejoins her flock at a remote mountain lake,' she said at last. 'She could not bear to be enclosed any longer within walls. The limb is not yet properly healed but it might be she will return for my ministrations, now and then, until it is whole. They always know where to find me, in my wanderings. And soon I must wander again—I have stayed here long enough and Imbroltide draws nigh.'

Consideringly she looked at the long black feather, before swathing it in a swatch of linen.

'Now it is but sixteen days until the turn of the year, the most significant time of all—Littlesun Day. There is much to be done.'

She set a fiery eye on her other visitor. 'Take this swan's plume with you. The swans of eldritch sometimes give a feather in token of payment. When the feather's holder is in need, the swan is bound to help, but once only. Her calling-name, potent only for the duration of the bitterbynde, is *Whithiue*. This is a gift of high value.'

A bitterbynde. Imrhien-Rohain recalled hearing that term when she dwelled in the House of the Stormriders. The betrothal of a daughter of that House, Persefonae, had been pledged on the day she was born. A vow, or geas, laid upon a subject willing or not; a decree that imposed bitter sanctions upon its breaking, and demanded stringent, almost impossible conditions for its removal—that was a bitterbynde. In the swan-girl's case, she was bitterbound to come to the aid of whomsoever grasped the feather and summoned her.

'Now,' said Maeve earnestly, folding the linen package firmly
into the hand of Imrhien-Rohain, 'it is your turn to go forth.'

So it was that on the fifteenth of Nethilmis, before the early gathering of morning, a cloaked and taltried figure, mounted sidesaddle,
rode swiftly from Maeve's door. White stars arrayed a fretwork of
black boughs, and the green star of the south was a shining leaf
among them. Thin chains of mist fettered the trees. Every leaf and
twig seemed carved from stone. The rider, awkward and uncertain,
continually glanced from right to left. The long skirts kept tangling
with the stirrups, but, as if in haste, the rider urged the pony on. Not
far from the house of the carlin, dark figures sprang from among the
trees as the steed cantered past. The rider cast a glance backward,
then, with surprising alacrity, threw one leg over the pony's back
and, giving a shrill cry, surged forward. As the pony's hooves clattered away, other figures ran from the trees bringing up horses with
muffled hooves. Soon they were galloping in vigorous pursuit.

The pony, although swifter than an ordinary mount of its kind,
could not outmatch the long strides of the horses. Yet for a time it
seemed the pursuers did not want to catch up, but merely to follow from a distance and mark their quarry, as though biding their
time. Suddenly they rounded a bend and were forced to rein in
their horses so sharply the steeds reared on their hind legs and
screamed their indignation. Right in their path, the pony had
halted. It wheeled, then, and faced them. The rider flung back the
hood, revealing the face of a dark-eyed lad. His hand dipped
beneath his cloak and he flung out a powder that exploded in the
faces of the pursuers with a dazzling flash, followed by billowing
smoke. When they finally fought free of the thick fog, he was gone.

Back, then, they rode like a storm. When they returned to the
house of the carlin, the windows and doors stood open, sightless.
No smoke wisped from the chimney. The place was empty and all
trails were cold.

A quarter-moon danced overhead. The Greayte Southern Star
hung like an emerald set in onyx, and falling stars peppered the
night sky.

Imrhien-Rohain ran along a narrow woodland path leading northwest, clutching her purse of coins to prevent them from clashing together. She had the advantage of a secret start, and carried a potent tilhal of Maeve's as protection against things of the night that dwelt around White Down Rory. A Stray Sod had been let fall behind her at the beginning of the path to mislead any mortal who stepped thereon, and a sudden, temporary thicket of brambles camouflaged the path's entrance. Despite these precautions, terror spurred her pulse as she fled through the black trees. The glimmering footpath seemed enchanted—no root reached across to trip her up, no wight crossed it or started up alongside. Without pause, she hastened on, casting many a backward glance, as if the mysterious riders who had watched the house might spring out of the darkness. At last, lacking breath, she slowed to a swift walk.

The money from the emerald had been well-spent. Rohain of the Sorrows, an elegant lady, would become a widow as soon as she unfolded the silk mask across her face to hide her grief, in the fashion of bereaved women. By her ornaments and garments, she would appear a noble widow of considerable means. The silk domino, blue as night, was worked with scarlet. Jet beads sparkled in her long dark hair. Matching needlework, dark red and azure on midnight blue, drenched the full bell-sleeves of her gown, slashed to show contrasting lining, and dripped down the voluminous skirts from below whose picoted hems several petticoats peeped demurely. Her waist was cinched by a crimson leather girdle, housed within silver filigree. A long, fitted, fur-lined travelling cloak, frogged down the front, covered the yards of fancy fabric. A fur-lined velvet taltry topped the outfit.

She went forward. Hours passed. A soft noise like the wind in an Autumn wood came rustling. She thought it strange, for there was no wind, and all around, stark boughs plowed black furrows into the fitful moonlight, unmoving. A tall, pale figure glided past; some wight in almost mortal form. It groaned and soon passed out of sight. The susurration of falling leaves went on and on. Suddenly the moon shone out radiantly and the sounds changed to faint murmurs of laughter and ridicule that continued for a while, then faded.

Down among the tree roots, tiny lights were moving.

The path climbed a final slope and came out on the Caermelor Road as the sky began to pale. Farther down the Road, to the left, squatted a white milestone. It was there that the coach waited, its coach-lamps glowing like two amber flowers. The horses' breath steamed, a silver mist combed to shreds by the sharp and bitter cold.

The coachman had received an enticing down payment on the understanding that his services were to be performed with confidentiality—*not* that the noble lady passenger had held a clandestine tryst in the woods with a bucolic lover, *of course*. Simply, she desired privacy and no questions. Given his utmost discretion, the pecuniary reward at the end of the journey would exceed even the down payment.

He saw a slender, cloaked figure materialize out of the darkness, silent as a moth.

Bowing, he murmured, 'Your ladyship.' Her name was unknown to him.

She nodded. He could not see her face behind the decorative blind. Handing her into the carriage, the coachman stepped up into his box-seat and shook the reins. His bellowed 'Giddap!' harshly interrupted the night.

With a sudden thrust forward, the equipage bowled rapidly along the Road to Caermelor.

Light wooden caskets were waiting in the coach. With a sense of excitement, the passenger opened them. One was filled with sweetmeats and refreshments for the journey, one contained a most risible headdress, another an absurd pair of shoes, and a fourth accommodated an ermine muff and a pair of gloves. With difficulty inside the cramped and jolting compartment, the 'widow' added these items to her person.

The wide headdress was fashioned from a thick roll of stiffened fabric trimmed with sweeping carmine plumes, beaded, latticed with silver. It possessed a crown rising to a point draped with yards of azure gauze. Altogether, the dainty, fragile shoes, the voluminous sleeves, the stiff, embroidery-crusted fabric of the gowns, the heavy girdle that made it difficult to bend forward and the wide headdress that made it impossible to approach any wall—seemed most onerous and impractical, not only for travel but for everyday living. These garments and accoutrements would impede the simplest of tasks. Could it be that such strange raiment was truly the fashion at Court? Had her benefactress and the lad been mistaken, out of touch? Quickly she dismissed the thought. Nothing escaped the carlin's notice—the costume would be correct.

Her heel kicked against a heavy object sitting on the floor—a foot-warmer. Tom Coppins had thought of everything. Housed in its elaborately carved wooden case, the brass container with its pierced lid gave off a welcome warmth from the glowing charcoal in its belly. The passenger propped her feet thereon and sat back against the padded leather upholstery.

Yet the new Rohain could not enjoy the comforts of this unaccustomed mode of travel. She fervently hoped that all she had heard about the Court had been exaggerated—the tales of the refined manners, the complicated rules of etiquette, the forms of speech. Between the fear that the carriage would be overtaken by her enemies, the dread of what was to come, and constant battles with the unwieldy headdress that threatened to slide off, she made the journey in great discomfort and alarm.

Throughout the Winter's day, the carriage rolled on.

Days were short. At its zenith, the sun had risen only marginally above the horizon, where it glowered from behind a dreary blanket of cloud.

Emerging from the woods, the Road ran through farming lands patched with fields, hedge-bordered. Here and there, a house topped with smoking chimneys nestled among its outbuildings. After passing through a couple of outlying villages, the Road began to climb toward the city walls.

The buildings of Caermelor clustered on the slopes of a wall-encircled hill that rose four hundred feet out of the sea at the end of its own peninsula. To the south, the sea had taken a deep bite out of the land to form a wide and pleasant bay fringed with white sands. The far side of this bay was cradled in the arm of a mountainous ridge reaching out into the ocean to form a second, more rugged peninsula, its steep sides clothed in forest.

Eastward, an expansive, flat-bottomed valley opened out. Through the middle of it ran the river that drained the encircling hills, flowing until it reached the sea to the north of the city-hill. There, salt tide danced to and fro with fresh current. In the estuary, waters ran deep enough for the draught of the great-keeled Seaships. Wharves, piers, docks, and jetties jutted from the northern flank of the city-hill, stalking into the water on thick, encrusted legs.

Atop the highest point, the palace overlooked all—the vast sweep of ocean to the west, the curve of the bay with its long lines of lace-edged waves, the blue-folded shoulders of the ridge dropping sharply to the water; north, the ocean stretching to distant mountains; northeast, the river-port teeming with business, forested with tall masts. Eastward, the city spread out over the plain, dwindling to scattered farms and the backdrop of Doundelding's hills on the horizon.

But blind ocean was not all that could be seen to the west, for a tall island rose up, perhaps a quarter of a mile offshore, directly opposite the city-hill. At low tide, the waters drained from a causeway that connected it to the mainland. At all other times it was completely cut off by water. Here stood the Old Castle, much like a crag itself, jagged, gray, and gaunt. Of yore it had been the fortress to which citizens had retreated in times of war. Now it stood, stern sentinel, silent guardian, facing the palace on the hill.

Late in the afternoon the coach halted at last before the city gates. There was a knock on the front wall of the compartment. Imrhien-Rohain slid back the little window that opened onto the coachman's box. His eyes appeared, goggling like a fish's.

'Where to now, m'lady?'

'To the palace.' Her new voice had crisped to a clear, ringing tone.

'Very well, m'lady.'

She slid the window shut, like a guillotine chopping off the outside world.

Guards lounging under the portals had a word with her coach-man. Through the windows they eyed the passenger with curiosity as the vehicle went by. Imrhien-Rohain drew the curtains against their intrusion. Beyond, voices rose and fell, wheels rattled, sea-gulls mewed, children yelled. In booming tones a town crier shouted, 'Hear ye! Hear ye!'

She had come at last to Caermelor.

2
CAERMELOR, PART I
Vogue and Vanity

Euphonic fountains splash, by arbor walls where climbing roses, red and yellow, cling.
Proud peacocks strut on sweeping, verdant lawns and nightingales in gilded cages sing.
Glass carriages with plumed and matching teams roll on amid this royal plenitude,
By ornamental lakes where sleek swans glide, reflecting on their mirrored pulchritude.

The silk and satin ladies with their fans incline upon the marble balustrade.
The night will see them dance like butterflies, when they attend the Royal Masquerade.
Fair jewels gleam on ev'ry courtly peer: bright rubies, sapphires, diamonds, and pearls.
The costliest of velvets, plumes, and furs adorn dukes, viscounts, marquesses, and earls.

Prosperity and luxury abound; sweet music plays as nobles feast and sport.
The rarest beauty and the greatest wealth are found within the Empire's Royal Court.

FASHIONABLE SONG AT THE COURT OF CAERMELOR

Caermelor Palace had been originally constructed as a castle stronghold and still retained its fortified outer structure. Machicolated watchtowers, siege engine towers, stair turrets, a mill tower, round mural towers, square mural towers, and numerous other outjuttings thickened the twelve-foot-deep walls at varying intervals.

The road into the park-like palace grounds crossed the moat by means of a drawbridge. Beyond the drawbridge bulked the garrisoned gatehouse and the barbican. The main outer gate was constructed of solid oak, studded with iron. It could be barred, if necessary, by an iron portcullis that remained raised in times of peace and was lowered only for the purpose of oiling the chains and maintaining the winches.

When this outer gate was shut, persons on foot might enter by a smaller postern set into it, whereupon they would find themselves in a long chamber set within thick walls, with a gate at either end—the gatehouse, a solid edifice specifically dedicated to the purpose of providing a space between the inner and outer portals. Peepholes in the walls allowed guards in side passages to inspect purportedly innocent visitors. Those approved visitors might pass through a second gate. It opened onto the outer bailey, which in recent years had been filled with walled gardens and leafy courtyards. A third gate led to the inner bailey with its stables, barracks, parade grounds, kennels, pigeon-lofts, coach-mews, and falconry-mews. It was bordered by the King's Tower winged with fluttering standards, the arsenal tower, the Great Hall with its pentise, two tall Mooring Masts, the solar, and the keep. The windows of the internal buildings had been enlarged from cross-slitted arrow-loops and narrow arches to gracious fenestrations of latticed glass, and greater opulence reigned within them than in former days. The transformation from fortress castle to residential palace had also involved the creation of ornamental gardens around the keep.

Somewhere within the vitals of that keep, Tamlain Conmor, the Most Noble the Duke of Roxburgh, Marquess of Carterhaugh, Earl of Miles Cross, Baron Oakington-Hawbridge, and Lord High Field-Marshal of the Dainnan—to name only his principal titles—strode into the richly furnished suite he always occupied when at Court, calling for his junior valet and his squire.

'Ho, John! Where is my lady wife?'

'The Duchess Alys-Jannetta is at her bower with her ladies, Your Grace,' piped the valet.

'So. Have you laid out some clean clouts for the evening?'

'The scarlet hose or the puce, Your Grace?'

'I care not, just as long as they are serviceable enough that they don't split along the crotch seam and let my backside hang out. Wilfred, is Conquest well-polished?'

'Conquest is oiled and polished, sir,' replied that young man.

'Give him here.' The Dainnan Chieftain stroked the broad-sword lovingly; held it up to the light.

'Good.' He handed the weapon back to his squire. 'See that the new scabbard is maintained as bravely. Who's that at my door? Enter.'

A footman opened the sitting-room door. A messenger ran in, went down on one knee before the warrior and bowed, offering a silver salver on which a leaf of parchment flapped. Roxburgh read the note, scratching his bluff chin.

'Very well.' He sighed. 'Conduct this lady to the Chamber of Ancient Armour. She may await me there. My wife is at her bower, you say?' Crumpling the parchment into a ball, he threw it at John, who ducked too late. The messenger bobbed his head in answer and ran out.

As the sun dipped, the clouds in the west parted, allowing a gleam of bronze to lance the lofty windows of the Chamber of Ancient Armour. The room overlooked a walled courtyard of fountains and statues. Across the tapestries on its walls, scenes from history and legend spread themselves, all with a bellicose theme. Here, two cavalry brigades charged at one another, pennants streaming, helmet plumes, manes, and tails flying, to clash in a tangled mass of armoured brawn and rearing, screaming war-horses. There, Dainnan archers in disciplined rows fired a deadly rain of darts, the back line standing with legs astride, braced to shoot, while the front, having spent its arrows, reloaded. On another wall, Warships locked each other in combat among a ferment of storm clouds above a city. Farther on, the infantry of the Royal Legion raged about a trampled field. Their enemies lay thick on the ground and the colours of Eldaraigne fluttered high above.

Antique armours stood against the walls. Dark wooden shelves housed outmoded hauberks-of-mail, habergeons, camails, coudieres, padded and quilted armour of fabric and boiled leather, mail coifs, brigandines, conical helms extruding long nasals, prick spurs, knee-cops and aillettes of leather, rerebraces, vambraces, gauntlets, baldrics, helms winged and fanged and halberds from times long past, dull and sheenless, mostly dented, torn or cloven. The high gabled lids of arming chests hinted at more.

Afternoon light spilled like brandy across an acorn-patterned carpet at the daintily shod feet of the visitor who sat waiting in a chair heaped with brocade cushions. A page boy in the livery of Roxburgh, gold and gray, stood stiffly at her shoulder.

Filigree brass lamps hung on chains from the ceiling and jutted in curled brackets from the walls. A servant scurried about, kindling them to amber glows. Disappointed, the last of the sunrays withdrew. As they did so, a white-wigged footman entered, wearing black pumps and an iron-gray tail-coat with gold trimmings. He bowed.

'Your Ladyship, His Grace will see you now.'

He held the door open. The dark-haired, masked widow passed through and was guided deferentially to a larger chamber; the Duke of Roxburgh's audience-room. In a loud voice the footman announced, 'Lady Rohain Tarrenys of the Sorrow Islands.'

The visitor was ushered in.

A hearthful of flames flung warmth into this room, cheerily bouncing their glow off polished walnut furniture and silver-gilt. A pair of cast bronze andirons with eagle motifs supported a burning giant of the forest. They matched the decorated fender, the pokers, the tongs. Crossed swords, broad-bladed hunting knives with deer's foot handles and other trophies of arms enlivened the walls alongside a mounted boar's head with formidable tusks and the masks of other game.

The fire's light was supplemented by three hanging lusters and, atop a table, a bronze urisk holding a massive bouquet of bell-flowers whose cupped petals were candle-sockets. Two more goat-legged wights in marble supported the mantelpiece, which in turn bore a set of equestrian statuettes in malachite and agate. On a bearskin rug before the hearth lay a pair of lean hounds.

Conmor, Duke of Roxburgh, stood by the window. He was still in the field-dress he had worn that day: loose-sleeved shirt, leather doublet slit to the hips, belted loosely at the waist, embossed baldric slung across the shoulder, suede leggings, and knee-boots. Firelight burnished his shoulder-length, unbound locks to dark mahogany.

At her first sight of the Dainnan Commander, a muffled gasp escaped from beneath the visitor's veil.

Thorn!

But no. Of course not—it was just that she had not been expecting to see a tall figure wearing the subdued Dainnan uniform here in the palace suites, where braided liveries stalked alongside jeweled splendors. This man with brown hair tumbling to his shoulders was not Thorn, although he came close to him in height, and if she had not first seen Thorn, she would have thought the Commander exceedingly comely. He was older, thicker in girth, more solidly built, his arms scarred, his thighs knotted with sinew. At the temples his hair was threaded with silver. Proud of demeanor he was, and stern of brow, but dashing in the extreme.

The warrior leader's hazel eyes, which had widened slightly at the sight of the visitor, now narrowed. Somewhere in remote regions of the palace, something loose banged peevishly in the rising wind.

'Go and see to that shutter, will you, lad?'

The momentary distraction allowed Rohain-Imrhien to recover her poise. She curtsied and awaited tacit permission to speak.

'Rohain of the Sorrows,' repeated Roxburgh, 'pray be seated and remove your widow's veil. Here in the palace we are joyed to look upon the countenance of those with whom we hold converse.'

His guest inclined her head.

'As Your Grace's servants have many times assured me, sir. But I am uncomfortable without it. I have made a vow—'

'I insist,' he broke in; a man used to having his demands met and impatient with those who would not cooperate. There seemed to be no choice.

She unhooked the mask and drew it aside.

Her eyes never left his face. She read all that passed across it—the look of surprise, the turning away, then the avoidance of her eyes. What could it mean? This was the first test in the outside world of this new face she wore. Was it then so strange?

'Wear the veil if you must,' the Dainnan Commander said briskly, throwing his shoulders back as though regaining control of himself after a lapse. 'Wilfred, have refreshments brought for Her Ladyship and myself.'

Murmuring compliance, Wilfred withdrew.

'For you must be weary, m'lady,' continued Roxburgh, 'after your journey. The message I received from the Doorkeeper indicated that you have travelled to Caermelor on an errand of importance, with news that you will entrust only to the King-Emperor.'

Rohain-Imrhien fastened the mask back in place.

'That is so, Your Grace.'

She perched on the edge of a velvet-covered chair. Roxburgh remained standing, occasionally striding up and down in front of the hearth.

'Have you any idea,' he said, 'how many folk come knocking upon the King-Emperor's doors with the same message as you? Petitioners, beggars, would-be courtiers, social climbers—most of them do not get as far as an audience with me. You have been fortunate, so far, due to your apparent station. I have many calls upon my time. His Imperial Majesty the King-Emperor will not hold audience with you. It is a busy time for all—meaning no discourtesy, my lady, but His Majesty has no spare time these days. Our sovereign's waking hours are devoted to the urgent business at hand. As one of His Majesty's ministers I am empowered to speak for him and take messages on his behalf. Now, what are your tidings of import?'

A page in gray-and-gold livery came in bearing a laden tray. He set it down on a table with legs carved like sword irises and inlaid with mother-of-pearl, then bowed to his lord and to the lady.

'Thank you—'

Her host glanced at Rohain sharply. Obviously she had made a mistake by thanking the lad. It appeared that those born to be served by others did not consider it necessary to show gratitude to the servants here in the palace. She must avoid such errors. To survive here among the denizens of the Royal Court, one must do what all newcomers must do in a strange country—copy the behaviour of the inhabitants. If she observed them closely, if she followed their customs and manners, then she might pass undiscovered.

'My tidings are for the ears of the King-Emperor,' she repeated. The Dainnan Chieftain frowned. He seated himself opposite her, leaning back in his chair.

'Well, My Lady of the Sorrows, it seems we can discover no common ground. Pray, partake of wine and cakes before you depart. I am sorry there can be no commerce between us.'

Ethlinn and Maeve had said that Roxburgh could be trusted, but it would be better to see the King-Emperor himself. She must try for it.

'I *must* speak with the King-Emperor.'

'And I have told you that it is impossible.'

He handed her a goblet, silver-gilt, enameled in mulberry.

'To your health.'

'And to Your Grace's.'

She raised the vessel, lifted the veil, and drank. The liquor was the essence of peaches, on fire.

''Tis a pity to travel so far only to leave with your mission unrequited,' remarked the Duke conversationally, lifting one mightily thewed shank akimbo and resting a boot on his knee.

'Yes, a pity.'

'How do they speak of us, in the far Isles of Sorrow?'

'Highly, sir. But no words I have heard spoken do justice to the wonder and wealth of the Royal City. The name of Conmor, Duke of Roxburgh, is also famous in far-flung places, of course.'

'And no doubt many a story is attached to it.'

'All are gestes of valor.'

'And honour?'

'Most assuredly!'

'If Conmor of Roxburgh is spoken of, perhaps you are aware that he has little time for secret messages, being more concerned with the safety of the Empire. It is no secret that war is gathering on the borders. Our spies reported large movements of armed barbarians in northern Namarre last month near the Nenian Landbridge. Yesterday the Royal Legions began deploying five hundred troops to the north as part of the King-Emperor's moves to guard against possible military action by Namarre. I am needed there. I sally forth on the morrow.'

'I know nothing of such matters, sir, but perhaps a show of strength may be all that is required to make these rebels think again.'

'Precisely. Otherwise, they shall know the fury of the King-Emperor's Legions.'

'It is said that they are allied with immortals—unseelie wights of eldritch who are moving northward in answer to some kind of Call; formidable foes.'

'In sooth, but so-called immortals only live forever unless they choose to die or are slain.'

'I have heard that if they are wounded so sorely that their bodies become incapable of sustaining existence, they are able to transmute and thus live on in another shape?'

'Some possess that power, yea, but they must take a weaker form, threatless.'

Conversation petered out.

The Dainnan Commander quaffed the remaining contents of his goblet. Rohain-Imrhien sipped her own, replaced it on the inlaid table, and stood up. Roxburgh also rose to his feet.

'You are leaving so soon?'

'I will not squander more of your time, sir—Your Grace is a busy man, I know. Thank you for sparing me a moment.'

'But your tidings . . .'

'Will Your Grace take me to the King-Emperor?'

'Before you stands his sworn representative. Is that not enough?'

'No, sir.'

She curtsied. Beyond the palace walls, out in the gulf of night, the wind raged, hammering at the windows.

'Good speed,' said Roxburgh, smiling slightly.

Rohain-Imrhien guessed he would not truly let her leave without divining her purpose.

She paused by the door, where two footmen of matching height stood poised to escort her. Then she turned and looked over her shoulder. The war-leader stood with his feet apart, arms folded. He nodded curtly. She walked back into the chamber.

Her bluff had not worked.

His had.

'I will tell you, sir,' she said, since there was no option.

The wind sucked along corridors. It sang weird harmonies, flinging doors open and shut with sudden violence and setting every hound in the Royal Kennels to howling.

A sleepy young footman went around the Duke of Roxburgh's audience-chamber, lowering the gleaming lamps on their chains and trimming the wicks, lighting a score of candles slender and white like young damsels, now yellow-haired. In the tall hearth, the flames had simmered down to a wary glow, enlivened now and then by a sudden gust down the chimney. The hounds by the fire twitched, dreaming perhaps of past hunts.

Rohain fell silent, her story told. Long before this night, before she had become Rohain, she had held an inner debate on what she would say, should she ever reach Court. To reveal the existence and whereabouts of the hidden treasure was her purpose, and to uncover the corrupt Scalzo and his adherents so as to be avenged. But to disclose her own identity—insofar as she knew it—was not her intention. In truth, she was nothing but a homeless waif who had forgotten a past that possibly was best left forgotten. She was a foundling, an ex–floor-scrubber, a serf, a stowaway, a misfit, and an outcast. Now a chance to begin afresh had fallen like a ripe plum into her lap. The lowly part of her life could be swept away and hidden. With a new face and a new name, she who had first been nameless and then been Imrhien might indeed become Rohain of high degree.

To begin living a lie did not sit comfortably with her, but so many reasons made it the choicest path. A noblewoman could wield so much more influence than a servant. That power might be used to help her friends. With influence, she had also some chance of finding Thorn again, of at least seeing him, from a distance, one more time. Thirdly, having once tasted dignity and luxury, it would be hard to relinquish them.

And so she had told her story to Roxburgh not as it was, but as she wished it to be heard. He had listened closely throughout, and when she had finished had asked several pertinent questions. He was no fool; she guessed that he perceived some flaws in the web she had woven, but, perhaps out of tact, he chose to overlook them.

The story went that she had left the Sorrow Islands and begun a journey across Eldaraigne in a small, private Windship. A storm had wrecked the craft over the Lofty Mountains. She and a crew member had been the only survivors of the disaster. Wandering destitute and in danger through the wight-ridden forests, they had come accidentally upon a treasure hoard of unsurpassed magnificence, at a place they named Waterstair.

'A treasure hoard? You say that it contains much sildron?'

'Vast quantities, sir.'

'Did you bring any with you?'

This might be a trick question.

'Knowing that all newly discovered sildron is the property of the King-Emperor, I did not take any from this trove—nor did my companion. But those who discover such wealth are entitled to a share of it in reward, or so I am told. We took jewels and coin, to help us, should we find our way out of the wilderness and regain the lands of men, for we were destitute, as I have recounted.'

'May I see these valuables?'

'All is spent.' She added hastily, 'We took so very little—we could not carry much.'

'Spent? Where?'

'In Gilvaris Tarv, when we reached it. Of course, my first thought was to send a message by Stormriders to the King-Emperor, to inform him of this find. However, I held back at the last moment. I was reluctant to let such precious knowledge pass out of my hands—not that I do not trust our most worthy Stormriders, but accidents may happen. I decided, then, to journey to Caermelor, in person, with the news. As I was preparing for the journey, disaster struck. My unwonted spending, and that of the aeronaut who had helped me survive in the forests, had not gone unnoticed. He was abducted, with a number of his friends, by a gang of perfidious knaves. They forced him to lead them to the trove, and there he was betrayed, slaughtered before the very doors of the vault. One of his companions escaped to tell the tale, but later perished. I barely escaped with my own life. Through adventure and misadventure I made my way across Eldaraigne until I came here, to Court. Even as we speak, those black-hearted murderers, Scalzo's men, may be raiding the King-Emperor's treasure at Waterstair—not for the first time—while the bones of brave fellows lie rotting in the grass.'

'The name of this aeronaut?'

'Oh—the Bear, he was called,' she stammered, fearing she might somehow betray Sianadh by revealing his true name.

'The Bear, indeed?'

'Yes.'

'And the haunts of these brigands?'

'Gilvaris Tarv, near the river. On the east side. I know no more.'

The Dainnan Chieftain called for more wine. He leaned forward, resting his elbows on his knees.

'But if all is as you say, my lady, then this is a very serious matter. We are talking of treason.'

She made no reply.

'Treason, perpetrated by those who have concealed and appropriated the property of the Crown. The punishment for that is severe.'

'As I imagined.'

'You will understand, my lady, that you must remain, as it were, under royal protection until your story can be verified. This is for your own safety as well as for reasons of security.'

'Of course.'

This had been half-expected. Besides, where else would she go? It had been in her mind to ask her coachman—by now no doubt comfortably ensconced in some downstairs pantry with a tankard in his hand, waiting for her—to take her to the nearest reputable inn for the night. Beyond that, she had formed no plan.

'You must bide here, at the palace, until transportation to the Lofties can be arranged. Since you know the way, you must lead us there. Your reward shall be substantial—more than a few jewels and coins easily spent.'

Untruthfully, she said, 'Sir, knowing that I serve my sovereign is reward enough. Nevertheless I accept your offer with gratitude. I hope for every success in tracking down the treasoners.'

He laughed humorlessly. 'So, 'tis retribution you are after!'

Truthfully, she said, 'Yes, but that was not my primary goal. I came here to fulfil a promise to a friend, and that I have done.'

He shrugged. 'I will have that wag Wilfred call your servants to bring your accoutrements. Your horses and carriage shall be accommodated in my own stables, your coachman in the grooms' and equerries' quarters behind the Royal Coach-Mews, and your maidservant in a chamber off the suite to be prepared for you.'

'I have no handmaiden. The coachman and equipage are hired.'

'What? No maid?'

The Dainnan scowled. He left his seat and again paced restlessly before the fireplace.

'My lady Rohain, you are a most singular noblewoman. You come here, unannounced; nobody has ever heard of you. You come masked and maidless, bearing a most extraordinary tale. You speak with disarming plainness, unlike a courtier or any member of the peerage. Are you in fact a spy?' On the last word, he spun on his heel and glared at her accusingly.

Outraged, Rohain jumped up. Her overblown skirts knocked the table. A goblet fell to the carpet, scattering its contents like spilled blood. Angry words sprang to her lips in the heat of the moment.

'Now you accuse *me* of treason! Indeed, sir, it seems you have been in the King-Emperor's service for too long—you have become suspicious of all strangers who set foot in the palace. I have come here in good faith, to carry out my duty, only to be called an infiltrator. My mask disturbs you? Well then!' She tore off the domino and threw it on the fire. Was it a sigh of the wind she heard, or the sudden intake of her host's breath? The hounds lifted their heads, snarling.

'If I speak too plainly for your Court manners,' she cried, 'teach me otherwise! And as for your treasure, I will prove that it exists. What more would you have me do?'

Her knees trembled. Abruptly, she sat down. The blood drained from her face. How had she possessed the temerity to dare such an outburst? What would happen now—would she be hanged for insolence? She fixed her eyes on the fire. The fragile mask had already been consumed. She was exposed, vulnerable.

Out across the city, a bell tolled. Unquiet fingers of air slid under the door and plucked at the curtains.

'Your pardon, lady,' said Roxburgh at length. 'I stand chastised.' He bowed. His visage softened. 'Pray do not think me unkind. It is my way, to test others at first meeting. Surely I have this night learned not to taunt the ladies of the Sorrows, should I ever meet another! Prithee, rest by the fire awhile.' He paused for another moment, as though savoring some anomaly or bizarreness, then summoned his pages. 'Lads! See to Her Ladyship's belongings and pay off the driver. Have lodgings made ready. Find a lady's maid.'

Two or three young boys hastened to do his bidding.

This Dainnan lord speaks forthrightly to say the least, thought Rohain-Imrhien. *He is a man to place faith in.*

'You are His Majesty's guest now,' Roxburgh informed her.

And prisoner? What if my ruse were to be discovered?

'Gramercie. I am weary.'

'Wilfred—play.'

The multiskilled squire took up a lyre, checked the tuning, and began expertly to coax a melody from the strings.

The wine, the warmth, and the music were sweet. Rohain may have dozed; it seemed no time had passed before a knock was heard at the door. There entered a damsel of her own age, perhaps seventeen or eighteen years, her hair corn yellow, half-encased in a crespine of gold wire. She curtsied, peeping at Rohain out of the corners of her eyes, blinking.

'Mistress Viviana Wellesley of Wytham at your service, Your Grace.'

'You are to be servant to the Lady Rohain Tarrenys,' said Roxburgh.

'Even so, Your Grace.'

'Lady Rohain,' he said, 'I beg you to dine in the Royal Dining Hall tonight.'

'Sir, I am honoured.'

Roxburgh again addressed the lady's maid. 'Miss, is the suite of chambers ready?'

'Yes, Your Grace.'

'Then pray conduct Her Ladyship to them with due consideration!'

Accompanied by a footman four paces behind to the right and the new personal maid four paces behind to the left, Rohain-Imrhien was verbally guided through a gridwork of resplendent corridors to her lodgings. The footman waited outside the door, holding it open for them to enter. She caught him staring at her and he blushed to the roots of his powdered wig.

A small, neat woman awaited them in the rooms, a bunch of jangling keys attached to her belt. She curtsied. Her mouth hung open, until she snapped it shut like a frog catching flies. After an awkward pause, Rohain concluded that servants were not permitted to speak first.

'Speak,' she offered lamely.

The Chatelaine of the King's Household introduced herself and indicated an anteroom where a bath awaited. Rohain dismissed her without thanks. The little woman bustled out with a rattle and a clash of stock, ward, and barrel. The footman closed the door and the sound of his steps echoed away.

Sixty candles lit the scene, rising from their brackets like tall yellow flag-lilies. Rohain stood staring. The opulence of the palace suite forced Isse Tower's decor into insignificance. These rooms burgeoned with decor in shades of emerald and gold, from the patterned carpet like a soft expanse of lawn studded with buttercups, to the gilded walls covered with plaster frescoes and the velvet hangings in apple green and lemon, their lush tassels dangling in bunches like ripening fruits. The bed's four posts were carved in the likeness of flowering wattle-trees whose boughs soared to a canopy of green brocade fringed with round gold beads above a matching coverlet and cushions. The windows were draped, swagged, and pelmeted in green and gold; daffodil tiles framed a niche wherein a fire blazed bravely, gleaming on a burnished grate and fire-irons. Rohain's fur-lined cloak, which had been urbanely subtracted by a butler as soon as its wearer had entered the palace, had been placed on a gilt chair next to her few pathetic belongings—the boxes from the carriage and, absurdly, the foot-warmer.

A soft clearing of the throat from the new personal maid drew Rohain's attention.

'Ah—what was your name again?'

'Viviana, m'lady. Vivianessa, in sooth, but I am called Viviana.'

'Well, Viviana, would you—ah—put away my traveling cloak?'

This was all that came to mind, on the spur of the moment. What in Aia was she to do with this girl? Were the Court ladies expected to be incapable of dressing and undressing themselves? What a nuisance, to have someone constantly bothering and fussing around!

The young servant folded the cloak carefully into a camphor-wood chest carved with woodland scenes. Rohain went into the small room indicated by the Chatelaine. Therein stood a copper tub on lion's feet, lined with white cambric that draped over the sides like falls of snow. The tub was filled with steaming water tinct with sweet oils and strewn with unseasonable primrose petals like flakes of the sun.

A marble washstand held a matching toiletry set. There was a pair of highly decorated enameled porcelain globes on high foot-rims, pierced all over to allow moisture to drain and evaporate. One contained scented soaps, the other a sponge. These were accompanied by somewhat superfluous porcelain soap stands, soap dishes and soap trays, ewers, jars, pots, candle-branches, and a vase overflowing with hothouse-forced snowdrop blossoms. Incongruously, a shoehorn lay on the floor. Made of pewter, it was mounted in ivory with carved and inlaid handles in the shape of herons.

The lady's maid spoke. 'Wishest donna mine that sas pettibob shouldst lollo betrial?'

'I beg your pardon?'

The girl repeated her strange sentence, twisting a fold of her skirt in her fingers, gazing hopefully at her new mistress.

'I don't know what you are talking about. Please speak the common tongue.'

The girl's face fell. 'Forgive me, m'lady. Methought Your Ladyship might like to practice slingua for this night. I asked only whether Your Ladyship would like me to test the bathwater.'

'Slingua?'

'Yes, m'lady—courtingle, some name it, or courtspeak. Lower ranks call it jingle-jangle. Does Your Ladyship not have it?'

'No, I do not have such palaver.'

It had sounded like childish babble, yet the girl seemed to hold great store by it. Could that curious string of quasi-words be part of the social fabric of Court?

'I will bathe now.'

By this phrase, Rohain had meant to indicate that this Viviana should leave her alone. Instead, the girl stepped forward.

'Let me unfasten Your Ladyship's girdle—'

'No! I can do it myself. Leave me!'

With a look of despair, the lady's maid rushed from the room. Rohain's conscience was stricken. The girl had only been trying to do her duty as she saw it—but how annoying and confusing it all was! Rohain almost wished herself back in the woods with Sianadh and the wights. Existence had seemed simpler then: it was life or death—none of these perplexing customs and slangish vernacular.

A sound of stifled sobs emanated from the outer room.

What a featherbrain of a girl! Fancy having nothing better to cry about than a sharp word from her mistress! To one who had faced the Direath and the Beithir, it all seemed so superficial.

Rohain removed her girdle of leather and filigree, and struggled with the gown's difficult fastenings. Presently she peered around the door.

'Viviana, will you help me unlace?'

The lady's maid came willingly, red-eyed. Together they battled the endless buttons, the petticoats, the pinching, mincing little shoes.

Timidly: 'Does my lady wish that I should soap her back!'

'No. I bathe alone.' *Providence forbid that the girl should see the whiplash-scars.*

Nervously: 'Then shall I lay out Her Ladyship's raiment for the evening?'

'I have no other clothes—only what you see.'

The girl's face crumpled as though she were about to cry again.

Rohain gathered her wits and said quickly, 'Naturally, I shall require a more extensive wardrobe. You must soon expedite some purchases on my behalf.' *It is fortunate that so much money remains to me from the sale of the emerald.*

The servant picked up her skirts and effected a dismal bob of acknowledgment.

Beyond the walls, the wind wailed.

Bathed and dressed, Rohain sat before a many-mirrored dressing-table in which she could scarcely recognise herself, while Viviana brushed out her coal-black locks. The courtier was subdued, doleful. Recalling only too well her own servitude, Rohain's heart went out to her. Anthills could appear to be mountains if one were an ant oneself, condemned to live among them daily. Softly, she said, 'I come from a faraway place where Court customs and ways are not known. This seems to trouble you. Why so?'

'Indeed, my lady!' Viviana blurted out. 'It troubles me, more than all the wights in Aia, because it will trouble you, my mistress!'

'Why should my tribulations be yours?'

'As your servant, your standing reflects on me. I shall suffer for it.'

'You speak with honesty, if not tact. How shall my plain manners trouble me?'

Viviana spoke earnestly. 'My lady, there is a way of going on that is not commissioned by those holding office, yet it has grown up in our midst. Here at Court, there is a self-styled elite Set or Circle. The Royal Family and the dukes and duchesses are not part of this courtiers' game, but many nobles below the degree of duke are counted Within the Set or Out of it, with the exception of the very old and the very young. If one is regarded as being Within the Set, one must fight to retain one's hold, for if one is Cut, which means cast Out, there is little chance of regaining one's place.'

'Is it so terrible, to be Out of this Set?'

'Indeed, I would say that life is scarcely worth living! Until she witnesses with her own eyes, my lady will not know of what I speak. But by then it may be too late. If my lady is not included in the Set, she will want to leave Court and then I shall be sent back to be maidservant to the unmitigable Dowager Marchioness of Netherby-on-the-Fens! I'd as lief die, in honesty. 'Tis unspeakable, the manner in which the Marchioness treats us. She is continually finding fault and slapping us with her broad and pitiless hand.'

Rohain assimilated this information, staring unseeing into the mirror.

'Tell me more.'

'My lady, as the daughter of an earl, you shall be seated amid the cream of the Set at table tonight—the very paragons of Court etiquette.'

'What makes you think I am the daughter of an earl?'

'Oh, simply that your finger displays no wedding band, ma'am—despite that I caught a rumour you were a widow—and to be called by the title of "Lady", you must be the daughter of at least an earl, a marquess, or a duke. Yet since the name Tarrenys is not familiar at Court, methought it must be an earl, begging your pardon, Your Ladyship.'

This was encouraging. Viviana possessed a certain acuity of mind, then, despite her frail emotional state. It seemed that during her stay at Court, no matter how brief, Rohain would need an ally. She studied the lady's maid in the mirror, seeing a rounded, dimpled face, a turned-up nose, a spot of colour on each cheek, hazel eyes with brown lashes that did not match the bleached hair. A pretty lass, Viviana was clad in a houppelande of sky-blue velvet, with a girdle of stiffened wigan. In addition to the girdle, her waist was encircled by one of the popular accoutrements known as a chatelaine, from which depended fine chains attached to a vast assortment of compact and useful articles such as scissors, needle-cases, and buttonhooks.

'And I reckoned that my lady came from a faraway place,' the girl chattered on, wielding the hairbrush, 'because of the way m'lady thanked the Duke for his dinner invitation.'

Rohain swiveled in alarm.

'Said I something incorrect?'

'Yea, verily, m'lady. A dinner invitation from a duke is a command. One must reply, "I thank Your Grace for the kind invitation and have the honour to obey Your Grace's command." I don't know what he thought, forsooth, but likely the lack of form did not irk him, for those of the Royal Attriod are above such matters.'

'But you say that I will be scorned and reviled by others if I am ignorant of these complicated forms of etiquette?'

'In no small measure, m'lady! The cream of the Set can hang, draw, and quarter the ignorant, in a manner of speaking. Those they have scathed never prosper in Society. But 'tis not merely the forms of address and the slingua—'tis the table manners and all. Entire libraries could be devoted to them. Coming from a high-born family, Your Ladyship will have all the table manners, I'll warrant.'

'Not necessarily.'

Unbidden, images formed in Rohain's mind; the table at Ethlinn's house—everyone seated around, plucking food from a communal dish with their hands and wiping their greasy fingers on the tablecloth; Sianadh clutching a joint of meat in his fist and tearing at it with his teeth; thick bread trenchers used as plates, to soak up the gravies and juices and to be eaten last.

Rohain chewed her lip. To be catapulted from shame to glory and back to shame would be more than she could bear. And what if Thorn should attend this dinner, to witness her humiliation?

'Do the Dainnan attend the Royal Dining Hall?'

'Sometimes, m'lady, when they do not dine in their own hall.'

'Are you acquainted with any of the Dainnan?'

'Not I, m'lady.'

'Viviana, why do the noble courtiers insist upon this? These dialects, these intricate manners you hint at—why are they necessary?'

'Marry, I vouch it is to show how clever they are, how much they deserve their station because they are privy to secrets of which the commoners know naught. Yet again, those of the highest degree do not concern themselves with slingua and such codes—they do not have to prove themselves worthy.'

'Viviana, you are wise. I believe I have misjudged you. Teach me, that I may not be made an outcast this night.'

'My lady, there is no time!' From somewhere down the

labyrinths of corridors, a hum mounted to a reverberating crescendo—the sounding of a gong. 'It is the dinner gong! In a few moments, a footman shall come to escort Your Ladyship to dinner. And then we are both ruined!'

'Calm yourself. Listen, you must help me. When I go to the table, stay beside me at all times. I will do as others do. Prompt me if I err.'

'But my lady's hair is not yet coiffed appropriately!'

'Shall I wear the headdress to conceal it?'

'No, no—that design is not suitable for evening wear.'

'Then attend to my hair.'

'It will take long—'

'Nonsense! Do the best you can. We have moments, do we not?'

'Verily, m'lady.'

Determinedly, Viviana swapped the hairbrush for a polished jarrahwood styling-brush inlaid with coloured enamels, its porcelain handle knopped with crystals. She twisted the heavy tresses, looping some of them high on her mistress's head. Securing them with one hand, she fumbled at the legion of assorted knickknack boxes, bottles, and jars set out on the dressing-table, fashioned from silver, ivory, wood, and porcelain. Rohain lifted a few lids, unscrewed several caps, to reveal pink and white powders, black paste, pastilles, gloves, buttons, buttonhooks, ribbons, decorative combs of bone, horn, or brass inlaid with tortoiseshell, silver pique barrettes, enameled butterfly clasps, scented essences, aromatic substances.

'What seek you?' Rohain winced in pain as Viviana in her haste tweaked a strand of hair.

'I seek pins for the coiffure.'

A carved ivory box fell open, spewing jeweled pins. Viviana snatched them up and began thrusting them ruthlessly into Rohain's cloud of curls.

'Ouch!'

'Forgive me . . .'

'What is the purpose of these paints?'

'They are for the beautification of the face. Kohl for the eyes, creams and coloured powders for the skin; rouge made from saf-flowers . . .'

Suddenly panicking, Rohain clapped her hands to her cheeks. In the looking-glass, her new visage had seemed unobjectionable to her, but how could she be certain that this was not merely wishful thinking? Her heart began hammering.

'Should I be using them?'

'Many courtiers do, but you need not, m'lady.'

'Why not, if 'tis what others do? My face—is it acceptable? Tell me truly!'

'My lady already has the look that others wish to achieve—she needs no paint.'

'What do you mean?'

Viviana halted her furious burst of hairdressing activity and planted her hands on her hips.

'Does my lady jest?'

'No. I do not jest. I wish you to tell me if my features are acceptable. Tell me now, and if they are not, I will not venture into that Hall this night, command or no command.' Butterflies roiled in Rohain's stomach.

A loud rapping at the door startled them both. A voice called out imperatively.

'Yes, m'lady, yes they are!' Viviana squeaked hastily. 'Quickly—to be late for dinner is an unpardonable lapse. M'lady would be Out before the first forkful.'

'Then let us go.'

The decoratively painted plaster walls of the great Royal Dining Hall, here and there covered with tapestries, soared to elaborately carved cornices and a domed, frescoed ceiling. Six fireplaces, three on either side, threw out enough warmth to fill its vaulted immensity. In a high gallery a trumpeter stood like a stalagmite dripped from the plaster ceiling plaques and chandeliers. He was one of the Royal Waits, wearing scarlet livery and the ceremonial chain of silver roses and pomegranates.

Along the walls, edifices of polished wooden shelves lit by mirror-backed girandoles displayed ornamental silverware, tempting platters heaped with fruits and cakes, covered cheese dishes disguised as little milk churns or cottages, silver chafing dishes with ivory handles, and glowing braziers of pierced brass ready to warm food. Liveried butlers and under-butlers stood at attention beside every board. Broad trestles ran down the length of the Hall, draped with pure white damask cloths, lozenge-patterned. The High Table, set up at right angles to this, stood upon a dais at one end. Its snowy wastes were bare of tableware, save for a quartet of surtouts, the seasons personified; grand sculptures in silver-gilt. Spring, her hair garlanded with blossom, caught butterflies. Summer, laurel-wreathed, held out her dainty hand for a perching lark. Autumn, twined with grapevines, dreamed by a corn-sheaf, and Winter, crowned with holly, danced. Candlelight glittered softly from their frozen glory.

The long tables, loaded with dinner service, made the High seem by comparison austere. A myriad white beeswax candles in branched candelabra reflected in fanciful epergnes of crystal or silvered basketwork, golden salvers lifted on pedestals and filled with sweetmeats or condiments, sets of silver spice-casters elaborately gadrooned, their fretted lids decorated with intricately pierced patterns, crystal cruets of herbal vinegars and oils, porcelain mustard pots with a blue underglaze motif of starfish, oval dish-supports with heating-lamps underneath, mirrored plateaux and low clusters of realistic flowers and leaves made from silk.

On both sides a sanap—a long strip of white cloth—lay along the table edges. Individual place settings had been laid along the sanaps at regular intervals, hedged in by an array of gleaming weaponry—knives, forks, spoons, suckett forks, soup spoons, cake forks, dessert spoons, cheese knives, miniature tongs, fish forks; a veritable arsenal, all engraved with the royal insignia, all with matching handles ending in silver scallop shells. Milk-white serviettes in front of each setting had been cleverly folded into sailing ships. Beyond these cutlery fences, gardens of tall crystal goblets sprang up from long, slim stems, like tulips. Several silver table-top Seaships on wheels served as salt-cellars to be rolled along so that diners could help themselves.

Quiet music wafted from an overhead gallery where a trio of

minstrels fifed and strummed, ignored by the dour-faced Wait. A stream of noble courtiers flooded through the doors at the lower end of the Hall. At first glance they seemed not to be human, so fantastic was their raiment.

Not one of these ladies seemed to be clad in fewer than three garments at once: a shorter surcoat, a longer half-sleeved kirtle worn beneath, and a full-length tight-sleeved undershift, the three contrasting hems and pairs of sleeves all tailored to be cleverly revealed. Their outer sleeves either fitted at the shoulder and hung in loose folds to be gathered into a tight band at the wrist, or they were tight, with a roll or gathered puff at the shoulder, or bell-shaped, sometimes turned back to the elbow, showing the fur lining, sometimes gathered into a bunch at the shoulder and left to fall in deep folds under the arm. So ridiculously long and full were many of the sleeves that the lower sections had been tied in great knots to prevent them dragging along the floor. Rich embroideries covered every yard of fabric. From the ladies' girdles and chatelaines, harnessed with silver and gilt, hung keys and purses and little knives in pretty sheaths, to match the armbands, brooches and jewelled pins of these human peacocks. Their head-dresses were exaggerated affairs, horned, steepled, gabled, flowerpot or resembling wide, fretted boxes.

Taltries being unnecessary within dominite walls, the lords burdened their heads instead with large beaver hats or generously draped millineries of velvet and cloth, or cockscombs of stiffened, scalloped fabrics. Liripipes of impractical length twined around their owners' heads and shoulders like strangler vines. There were hats with tippets dangling and flapping about, hats with coronets, hats with bulbous crowns, hats with long and voluptuous plumes and painted hoods. Dagged, jagged gorgets fell in a profusion of ornamented folds over the shoulders of the lords. Wide and embroidered tippets trailed to the ground.

The persons of the lords were gorgeously encased in laced doublets, velvet jackets, embroidered surcoats, cotehardies with bunched shoulders, parti-coloured paltocks, court-pies and striped hose. So small-waisted were the fops among them, they must have been corseted.

With painted faces floating above brilliant damasks, velvets, figured satins, samite, keyrse, tisshew, cloth-of-gold, shot silks, saffian, cambric, gauze, partridge, and baudekyn, this magnificent crowd milled around the trestles and chairs of carven oak. They stood by their accustomed places with their squires and pages and other personal attendants keeping guard at their backs. Some courtiers carried their pet cats on their arms: highly bred miniature lynxes, caracals, and ocelots, trained to sit demurely at plateside and daintily share the feast.

'An it please my lady, wait behind the doors until the assembly be seated,' the escorting footman had said. 'The Steward of the Royal Dining Hall will proclaim my lady's name as she enters, in order that she may become known to all.'

A trumpet sounded.

'Bide,' whispered Viviana, attending close at Rohain's elbow. She added unreassuringly, 'Ah, would that there had been time to enamel m'lady's fingernails—they look so *overgoren* bare.'

Between fanfares, the voice of a steward or herald announced the arrival of various aristocrats of the upper echelons who took particular precedence. When these were seated, the rest took their places with a scraping of chairs and a murmur of conversation.

'Lady Rohain Tarrenys of the Sorrow Isles!'

Rohain entered the Dining Hall.

Like a lens concentrating light beams, the appearance of a newcomer drew immediate and intense attention. Aware of the covert glances, the open stares and whispers, Rohain felt the blood rush to her face. The Hall seemed overheated and stifling.

'This way, m'lady.' An obsequious under-steward indicated an empty place and helped the new arrival arrange herself and her wayward petticoats into it. Rohain courageously lifted her eyes and nodded politely to those seated in her vicinity. Not one of them met her gaze for more than an instant, although she knew they scrutinized her intensely when she looked away. Her eyes scanned the faces of the rest of the company. Thorn was not among them. The under-steward introduced her to the young men seated on her left and right but she scarcely heard, so awed was she by the dazzling landscapes of the tables.

Another trumpet blast seemed to be a signal. At its sound, ewerers approached the tables bearing fish-shaped aquamaniles with spouted mouths, and proceeded to pour perfumed water over the diners' hands. The water fell into small porcelain bowls with perforated lids, and was thus hidden from view, being now polluted. Serviettes for drying were proffered, then whisked away along with bowls and ewers. Following the handwashing, a formidable procession of servants carried in massive covered platters that were set down in the few available spaces.

The High Table, with its canopy over the tall chair in the centre, was so far removed that it would have been difficult to make out the faces of any seated there. However, it remained empty of diners and food. The small silver tools chained to Viviana's chatelaine jingled softly as she leaned to her mistress's ear.

'They will now begin the Credence and the Assaying. Your Ladyship need only wait.'

'Why is the High Table empty?' murmured Rohain.

'The Royal Family and the Attriod, and others of the highest degree, frequently dine privately, in the Royal Dining Chamber or one of the parlors. The Lord Chamberlain, the Master of the Horse, and the Lord Steward have joined them this night; also the King-Emperor's Private Secretary, the Crown Equerry, and the Keeper of the Privy Purse. Many lords who were staying at Court have returned to their own estates, what with the threat from the north and all.'

When the courtier referred to the northern menace, her tone became grim. Her flow of information abruptly ceased. Rohain sensed the undercurrent of apprehension behind the words, and her queasiness doubled. Namarre—that strange, wild land seemed so far away, and yet its very name loured like an airborne pestilence over the Royal City.

'And the Dainnan?' Rohain's gaze roved among the knights in white satin tabards seated along trestles at the far side of the Hall.

'Their tables are poorly attended. Only one *thriesniun* dines with us this night.'

One of the courtiers seated nearby shot Viviana a censorious glance. She drew back and stood respectfully to attention as before.

At the top end of the long tables were arranged the earls and countesses, the viscounts and viscountesses, and one marquess. There, among side tables, moved the Tasters, who were commissioned with the job of dying if the food should be poisoned. They swallowed morsels with grace, deliberation, and an air of the utmost insouciance. Assayers touched the food with serpents' tongues, crystals, agates, serpentine, and jewels from toads' heads, all of which would change colour or bleed should poison be present.

'With all these boats at table, one imagines that the Cook has arranged something diverting in the way of marine vittles for the second course,' drawled the drooping-eyed courtier seated to the left of Rohain. Detached sleeves were tied at his shoulders with the laces they called 'points'. Beneath them, the sleeve of his doublet was slit up to the shoulder to reveal a third set of sleeves, those of his silken shirt.

Noting the nautical salt cellars, the sailing-ship serviettes, and the scallop-ended cutlery, Rohain forced a smile. 'One would imagine so.'

'Does my lady intend to stay long with us at Court?' casually inquired the long-jawed fellow to the right. He wore a short gown with bagpipe sleeves and a harness with bells attached, slung across his shoulder.

'I am uncertain, at this time . . .'

Butlers serenely poured wine; rose, white, and gold. Crystal goblets enhanced the brightness and colour of the liquids. The rituals of Credence and Assaying seemed to be taking a long time. Making small talk was like mincing on a tightrope. Rohain felt that at any instant she might speak a false word and plunge into an abyss of condemnation. Catching her eye, Viviana nodded encouragingly.

'Ah, the 1081 vintage Eridorre,' said Droop-Eyes, admiring the wine. 'A good year. And at last, the Tasters cease. One might expire of thirst.'

Yet another brazen fanfare clove the air.

The elderly marquess at the head of the table levered himself to his feet with difficulty, being stout and dreadfully gouty. Three long thin cords hung ornamentally from the yoke of his gown. Weighted with beads, they became entangled at the back, causing his page utmost concern. Heedlessly, the plum-cheeked aristocrat raised his goblet.

'Let the cups be charged for the Royal Toast!' he bellowed. The courtiers rose and looked around, holding high their goblets and drinking horns.

'To the health of the King-Emperor—may His Majesty live forever!'

With one voice, the company loudly echoed the marquess's sentiment. Crystal rang against crystal. At a nudge from Viviana, Rohain noted that all the other ladies were holding their goblets by the stems rather than by the bowls. Quickly she changed her grip, but not before someone snickered daintily. All then lifted their drinking vessels, tasted, looked around once more, and sat down.

'Let Dinner be served!' boomed the Master of the Dining Hall. 'The Soup! Green turtle, lobster bisque and cream of watercress!'

The elderly marquess at the head of the tables leaned back slightly. His squire draped a large and luxurious napkin over his left shoulder, it being a breach of etiquette to demolish the starched linen ships. At this signal, the other bodyservants followed suit. Silver domes were whipped off tureens of steaming liquids. The first course commenced.

'Much good do it you,' the courtiers wished each other as they fell to, imbibing without a single slurp, with the exception of those at the head of the table where rank obviated the need for manners. By scrupulously imitating the other diners, Rohain won through the soup course. When the soup bowls had been removed, the top layer of the sanap was taken away, revealing a clean, unspotted layer beneath.

The seafood course was duly announced and launched with applause. It comprised a magnificent sturgeon that was carried around to be viewed before serving, to the accompaniment of a flute and violins played by musicians dressed as chefs. Two kitchen-hands wearing knives carried the horizontal nine-foot ladder upon which the whole baked sturgeon was laid out on leaves and flowers; beside them walked four footmen bearing flaming torches. The procession was led by the Head Porter, marching with ax in hand. After being paraded once around the table, the dish was borne out of the Hall for carving. During the entremet, the diners were entertained by acrobats and a couple of over-dressed mortal dwarves riding wolfhounds.

At the actual serving of the marine fare, the diners picked up their silver fish forks in their right hands. With the edge of the implement, they cut off a small piece, then impaled it with the tines, raised the morsel to their mouths, and delicately closed their lips around it. The fork was put down while each piece was chewed, and taken up again to prepare the next bite.

Rohain had been accustomed only to eating with hands and knife. She had glimpsed forks once, in the Dining Hall of the Tower—more common had been the sight of the larger versions used to pitch hay up to stacks. Now she picked up the fork and held it as others did, with her index finger pointing toward the root of the tines. So intent was she on managing this with grace that she did not notice, until alerted by tittering, and an agonized whisper from Viviana, that all others held their forks with the curved tines pointing downward. The newcomer had been in fact partly spearing and partly scooping, using the fork like a spoon. It would seem wantonly perverse to deny the fork its useful ladle-like qualities, yet that was exactly what was expected. Hastening to turn it over, she dropped the offending instrument. It clattered boorishly against her plate. Another gaffe. She found it impossible to eat flesh anyway, and only picked at the garnishes.

Across the table from Rohain and a little to the right sat a strik-ingly handsome lady, surrounded by many admirers. The ornate roll on her head, eighteen inches high and a yard in circumfer-ence, was bent around into a heart shape, the front worn low on the forehead, the sides raised to reveal gold-fretted nets covering her ears. Her fur-edged, cutaway surcoat revealed a contrasting, skintight kirtle. Huge quantities of fur had been lavished in the wide cuffs of sleeves that reached to the floor. Having ignored the newcomer up to the middle of the seafood course, she now tossed a flashing smile in her direction, saying,

'Dear Heart, how well you look, considering the travails of your long journey. Don't you think she looks well, Lady Calprisia?

Isn't she just the prettiest thing? Lord Percival Richmond thinks so, don't you, Percival, you've scarcely taken your eyes from her all evening! Don't be alarmed, Dear Heart, Percival shall not bite, at least I don't think he shall!' She followed this with a chiming laugh. Others joined in.

'That is Lady Dianella,' whispered Viviana. 'Beware.'

'Speak up now—don't be shy,' continued the Lady Dianella. 'How do you like our maritime theme for this evening?' The lady's smile was as brilliant as the jewels flashing at her throat, waist, and fingers.

'I—ah, it is wonderful,' offered Rohain weakly, bedazzled.

The laugh carilloned.

'Wonderful, is it? Wonderful, she says, did you hear it? Marry, but she *does* have a word to say for herself after all. Such charming wit—can you believe it, Lord Jasper? I suppose you know far more about Seaships than we poor land-lovers, you coming from the Sorrow Isles. I am given to understand that those unfortunate lands are so named due to the number of shipwrecks which have occurred on their rocky shores, am I not correct? Is it true that the shipwrecked mariners are welcomed into the arms of the ladies of the Sorrows?'

As if this beauty had said something infinitely scintillating, her section of the table burst into loud guffaws, the antithesis of the restraint practiced in the Tower. Tear-eyed with mirth, Dianella added, 'Do you like sailing, Lady Rohain?' which provoked a further outburst of merriment.

Rohain burned. 'I know nothing of sailing,' she said.

'La! Of course not, Dear Heart, your time would be devoted to much feater accomplishments, naturally! Do you sing?'

'No.'

'Perhaps the Lady Rohain plays a musical instrument,' put in a lady with fake seashells and ropes of pearls bedizening her horned headdress, her hair having been drawn through the hollow horns and falling in waves from the extreme ends.

'No, I do not play.'

'Do you then dance? One would suppose that you dance blissingly! We should like to see it,' said the one referred to as

Calprisia, taking her cue. Her dainty face was framed by a steeple headdress delicately painted with black lacework, from which trailed a starry veil.

'I am sorry to disappoint you—'

'Oh come! Do not be so modest! Hide not your talents—we only wish to encourage, in good sooth,' said False Scallops.

'I can only applaud the talents of others.'

'La! What must they do with their spare time in the Isles!' Dianella exclaimed. 'One can scarcely begin to imagine!'

'And do they all wear their hair like yours?' asked Calprisia. ''Tis a most intriguing style, so simple yet so . . . ah—'

'Simple!' said Dianella innocently, and to the amusement of her friends.

Rohain sensed credibility slipping like sand from her grasp. How should she respond—should she meet affront with austere civility? Exhibit disdain or try to match them at their game?

'Of course you likely find us complete scoundrels, here at Court,' added Dianella, 'No doubt you think us utter reprobates! What brings a polished lady like Rohain Tarrenys to our midst?'

'My business is with the Duke of Roxburgh.'

That set her tormentress back, but the respite was only temporary.

Turning to the lord beside her, Dianella said, 'Athal selevader chooseth sarva taraiz blurose.'

'Fie! Aura donna believeth sa mid-uncouthants es,' he replied, laughing.

'You must know I do not understand your slingua,' said Rohain, flustered. 'Why then do you speak it in front of me?'

She knew at once that she had erred again. Dianella's smile dropped from her face like a mask. She arched her eyebrows in a look of exaggerated surprise.

'Marry, because we are not *speaking* to you, that is why! La! Is the lady endeavouring to eavesdrop on our conversations? How churlish! Selevader taketh baelificence, Lord Percival.'

'Dianella, really . . .' The droop-eyed lord protested halfheartedly.

'Pash com grape-melt es—sildrillion et gloriana. May aftermath sault-thou, et storfen-thou!' responded the other tartly. The rest went off into hoots of laughter. Lord Percival sulked throughout the remainder of the meal. Rohain sat drowning in misery.

'The Roast Beef!' roared the Master of the Dining Hall. The third course arrived. The Carver, a comely man with his knives in hand, walked into the Hall followed by the Taster, the Assayers, the Cup-Bearer, the Head Butler, and the Head Panter, all flanked by torchbearers. For the diversion of the company, he carved the meat in front of them, performing with the dexterity and flair of a juggler. He divided the beast into sections and speared entire joints on the carving fork, before lifting them into the air and shaving pieces off with a keen knife. Thin slices of meat fell to the trenchers in organised patterns, slightly overlapping. Swiftly, he used the knifepoint to place final touches to the arrangement. Salt was sprinkled over the dish before it was presented to the potential consumers. The courtiers served themselves from chased oval chafing-dishes of vegetables, side dishes and pates up and down the tables, and boats of thick sauces and gravies. Some allowed themselves a sprinkle from the personal nutmeg-graters they carried at their belts; small silver boxes with a steel rasping-surface and a hinged lid at the top and bottom.

Through the croon and purr of shallow conversation pricked by the tinkle of crystal and artificial laughter, a far-off, eldritch howling sent sudden shivers through the assembly. Then a deeper note rumbled, so deep that it was felt, not heard. The bass vibration rumbled up through their feet and set the wine to rippling in the goblets. The small table-dogs about the floor began to yap. The pet cats bristled. As exclamations of astonishment flew like angry wasps around the tables, the tall windows snapped alight with a white blaze. Cries of alarm pierced the air, followed by laughter.

''Tis only the beginnings of a natural storm,' the courtiers reassured one another. 'I heard the cry of the Howlaa.'

But what a storm.

It was as though some great pent-up anger had been unleashed, which threatened to pound the city to rubble and shake the palace to its very roots. The wind sang in a multitude of voices, like the keening of women lamenting lost lovers and the deep groaning of old men in pain, like the yowling of wolves baying at the moon and shrill pipes whistling in the chimneys, or the boom of some monstrous creature of the deep oceans. The banners and standards atop the palace had to be hastily lowered, for fear that they would be ripped to tatters. Slates tumbled from the roofs, smashing in the courtyards below. The trees in the gardens bent low, moaning. Their boughs whipped and cracked. Sudden whirls of leaves gusted by.

In the Royal Dining Hall, servants covered the light-stabbed windowpanes with heavy draperies, but no fabric seemed thick enough to banish those incandescent flashes. Bolts came hurtling out of the sky, one after another. The trio of musicians increased its volume, trying to be heard over the rain, the wind, and the thunder.

A fire-eater and a stilt-walker endeavoured to attract attention. A juggler performed amazing feats with plates and balls and sticks and flaming brands to while away the next entremet. He was largely ignored, except when he dropped something on his foot and hopped about clutching it, squawking. The Court thought it the best part of the act and applauded.

The fourth course, a pair of swans, was brought into the Hall on a silver dish by two comely young serving-girls in plumed costumes. The birds had been flayed carefully so as to leave their feathered skins intact, then stuffed and roasted before their feathers were sewn back on, their heads replaced complete with jeweled collars, and their feet gilded.

Visualizing the swan-girl at the cottage of Maeve One-Eye, Rohain recoiled in horror, then tried to disguise her reaction, dabbing at her mouth with a tiny kerchief presented by her lady's maid. *But wights cannot be slain,* she recalled with a rush of relief.

The counterfeit swanmaidens presented their dish to the elderly marquess and it was then expertly divided up into modest morsels by the Carver.

During the dispatching of the swans, Dianella and her friends conversed with each other almost exclusively in slingua. Their eyes frequently flicked over the stranger among them. Sometimes they giggled behind their hands. Rohain toyed with her food, pretending to eat, sick to her stomach. She could think of nothing to say and only wished to leave the Hall and retire to the solitude of her suite.

Out beyond the dominite walls, thunder rolled its iron ball along the metal tunnel of the sky. Wind laid both hands on the palace roof and tried to wrench it off.

In readiness for dessert, the last layer of the sanap was removed to reveal the chaste tablecloth. Now the ladies of the heart of the Set, bored with each other, flung an occasional retort at the shrinking violet in the midst of their convivial bouquet—sweet words, sharp-edged and biting, liqueur laced with poison, swords beneath silk. Airily, they tossed her dignity from one barb to another, until it hung in shreds.

Lucent jellies, glossy syrups, smooth creams and blancmanges, cinnamon curds, glazed pastries, and fruit tartlets followed the last entremet. Rohain pictured the oleaginous scenes necessarily taking place in the sinks of the palace sculleries.

'When are we permitted to depart?' she murmured to her handmaiden. She felt nauseous, but not due to fancy's images.

'Not until my lord the Marquess of Early has left the table.'

'I hope he lives up to his name.'

'Won't you tell us what you are whispering about with your maid?' entreated False Scallops, the Lady Elmaretta.

'Yea, prithee, tell us!' chorused others, eagerly, eyes shining as they scented a further delicious opportunity to savor somebody's discomfiture and win one another's approval.

'Naught of importance.'

'Oh, how provoking!' they cried in tones of astonishment.

'Fie!' Elmaretta wagged a gilt-nailed, admonitory finger. 'You must out with it. No whispering at table!'

'And besides, Dear Heart, everything you say is of importance to your friends!' added Dianella sweetly.

'Well,' said Rohain boldly, 'I was merely telling Viviana what the fox said to the ravening hounds.'

'Oh? And what was that, pray?'

'When you have devoured me, let the weakest among you look over his shoulder.'

The ladies exchanged glances.

'Is that intended for a joke?' queried Calprisia. 'Marry, 'tis not very amusing.'

'No, it is not amusing,' her friends agreed. 'What a very odd thing to say!'

'Are you sure you've not partaken of too much wine, Dear Heart?' said Dianella. 'Or maybe not enough! Look, she's scarcely touched a drop. Butler! Fill up my lady Rohain!'

Several people laughed bawdily.

Rohain held her temper in check. To lose it would be the final humiliation. Having scored, Dianella appeared to lose interest and turned away.

After distending his bloated belly a little farther by way of the inclusion of frumenty, the gouty old Marquess of Early was helped to his feet and made his exit with ceremony. Dinner, mercifully, was over.

Outside, the storm raged on.

The wattle-gold rooms were a haven.

'The lords had not such viperish tongues as the ladies,' muttered Rohain wearily. 'Not one of them said a word to degrade me.'

'The lords have their own reasons for courtesy, my lady.'

Rohain climbed the steps of the bed and sank into the feather-stuffed mattress.

In a small voice, Viviana said, 'Your Ladyship ate very little. To be of modest appetite is considered chic.'

'You are kind,' returned Rohain, 'and supported me as best you could against overwhelming odds. But I know how it is. I have failed. I shall never be included now. I am Out before ever I set foot Within.'

It seemed a terrible disgrace, as though the world's weight had been set on her shoulders.

Having helped her mistress to bed, Viviana went to dine on the leavings, with the other maids of the lower ranks.

A pair of inhuman eyes, red coals piercing the gloom of a drain.

A stench of rotting matter and feces, stifling. A skittering and a chittering and a squeaking in the shadows, which were alive, running, slithering clumps and humps, black shapes climbing over one another and surging forward in a terrible, living tide. They were everywhere, in increasing numbers—under the bed, in the folds of the curtains and the canopy, falling with soft, heavy plops from the damask pelmet and the frilled valance like malignant raindrops, jammed, wriggling in corners, swarming up the elegant brass legs of the firescreen, smothering the matching firedogs, crawling up the gold-inlaid piers of the lacquered table, upsetting the bowl of oranges upheld on its silver pedestal by four winged babies.

They were rats, and they squeaked.

Their stealthy, filthy claws scratched and scratched. As they drew near, she saw that they wore the spiteful faces of courtiers. Soon they would come running up, in long black streams, up the steps of the bed and across the embroidered eiderdown, along her arms to her face. Then they would cover her with their warm, stinking bodies and begin, with those needle fangs, to gouge, to gnaw, burrowing through the newly emptied eye sockets into the brain, until her flesh was devoured and blood gouted all over the silken pillows and ran down to pool on the meadowy carpets and all that remained was a sightless, staring skull.

Screaming, Rohain woke up.

Pale, pearly light suffused the windows. The pillars of the wattle-tree bed grew protectively all around. Her eyes roved the chamber. The fruits in the dish were not oranges but pears, onyx pomegranates, pastel-dyed marzipan plums, enameled porcelain apples, amethyst grapes.

Of rodents, there was no sign. Her hand brushed her forehead. Her breath came and went in shallow gasps, her skin felt damp with perspiration.

Viviana ran in, full of concern.

'My lady, what is it?'

''Tis naught. Only a dream.'

The windows rattled. Viviana went to them and pulled back

the lace curtains. Bright sunlight streamed in. The storm had cleared.

Outside on a green hill near the garden wall, albino peacocks swaggered, unaware of their status in the eyes of the Royal Carver. Nannies monitored overdressed children freed from the Palace Nursery, frolicking with their wooden hobby-horses, their whipping-tops, their pet dwarfhorses the size of small dogs. Citizens of Caermelor peered in through the bars of the iron fence, past the shoulders of the Royal Guards, hoping to catch a glimpse of royalty. The sequestered children stared back, equally fascinated. A diminutive son of an earl drove past the window in a child-sized carriage drawn by sheep. Savagely he wielded the whip.

'What do you fear?' Rohain asked suddenly.

'I do not understand my lady's meaning,' the court-servant parried uncertainly.

'I have a fear of rats,' explained Rohain. 'A fear most intense and unreasonable. After all, they are only small animals, relatively harmless, easily slain by foxes and lynxes. Why I should hate them so is beyond guessing.'

'My cousin Rupert is in dread of the sound of tearing cloth,' said Viviana.

'How strange!'

'Methinks it is not strange, m'lady. When he was but an infant, Rupert had a crooked hip. They used to bind it tightly so that it would grow straight. The binding was most painful for him—he used to wail when they did it. They would rip long pieces of linen to use as bandages, and this was the signal for his terror. So his fright remained, despite that he has now grown to manhood. My mother used to say everyone harbours at least one unreasonable dread, for it is human to do so. Mine is fear of spiders.'

'Spiders? But they are lovely creatures, so clever, so delicate . . .'

Viviana shuddered. 'Even to speak of them, ma'am, sets me atremble.'

'Why must we have these fears?'

'I know not, m'lady, but it is said they begin early in childhood.'

'Then,' whispered Rohain to herself, 'my childhood was troubled by rats.'

Viviana glanced again toward the window. 'Was that not the most fearful storm last night, my lady?' she asked. 'It has weakened now, but the wind's still with us, although it is past noon.'

'Past noon? I have slumbered too long. I would have been better off without those last moments.'

'It is well that Your Ladyship woke now,' Viviana said, with the air of one who has hitherto suppressed exciting news for the purpose of surprising her listener. 'The Duke of Roxburgh's footman came here earlier, with a message, but I would not waken you. The Duke has already boarded a Windship bound for the north, but he left a message bidding my lady be ready to depart from Caermelor at sunset.'

'So they are casting me out already?'

'Nay—my lady is to be taken aboard a Dainnan patrol ship, a swift craft of the air, for a voyage to the Lofty Mountains under the protection of Thomas Rhymer, Duke of Ercildoune. I have been instructed to attend Your Ladyship on this voyage.' Her voice rose with exhilaration. 'My lady, I have never travelled on a Windship before. This is the blissiest thing that's ever happened to me!'

'I am glad of it.'

'Your Ladyship, I am utterly delirious to be accompanying you from this palace. I will be well away from the clutches of the Dowager Marchioness, at least for a time.' The servant-courtier bobbed a small but exuberant curtsy.

'For longer than that, perhaps,' smiled Rohain. 'I will not give you up easily! Let us prepare.'

'My lady, you shall require several changes of attire, as befits your rank,' Viviana informed her. 'I have taken the liberty of notifying the Court tailors, who even as we speak are altering several ready-made garments in accordance with my estimation of m'lady's measurements. It will be necessary, nonetheless, for you to summon them to a fitting-session at the earliest opportunity.'

'Well done, Mistress Wellesley!' said Rohain in admiration. 'Have they told you the price?'

'Of course, m'lady! And 'twas not over-high, either. I haggled somewhat,' she added modestly.

'I shall straightway give you the money to pay these tailors.'

Despite the frenzy of preparations that day, visions of the rats did not crumble away for hours. Rohain knew it had not been a dream, but a snippet of memory.

The Dainnan frigate clove the air at speed, with a following wind strong from the west, at around twenty knots. Her timbers creaked. The decks rose and fell, lifted by rising currents on the windward slopes of the foothills and tossed by turbulent down-currents on the lee slopes. The sweet fragrance of wet leaves rose from below, and the twitterings of a multitude of roosting birds. Behind the vessel, across the sea, penduline clouds blackened the long, infernal forge-fires of the guttering Winter sun. The sails' shell-scoops glowed fuchsia for an evanescent moment before graying to somberness, scoured out by the raw and grudging westerly. Soon the stars would appear.

Clutching the lee rails in one hand and her taltry-strings in the other, Rohain of the Sorrows stood on the open deck. She was looking back through the lower rigging at the dwindling lights of Caermelor on the hill: the buttressed dominite palaces, dark and massive on the heights, their crenellated shapes squatting among their battlement-crowned turrets and spangled with many eyes; the fragile, latticed columns of Mooring Masts like a forest of webby trees; the spires; the sudden skyscraping upthrust of Caermelor Tower, the fortress of the First House of the Stormriders.

In the darkening courtyards and gardens of Caermelor, fountains would be tinkling unheard. Indoors, out of the cold, lords and ladies would be drinking mulled wine by their fires, serenaded by bards with harps and lutes. The watcher's heart ached with an abstruse longing—but not for *them*.

The ship having just entered an airflow of a greater velocity, the wind—traveling faster than the ship it drove—swept the dark tresses from Rohain's face. Long strands fluttered out on the airstream. Aloft in the rigging where shadowy sky-blue canvas cracked taut, Dainnan aeronauts called out to one another. The sails were constantly being trimmed. The men working them from the decks were standing in a snakepit of hemp and manila. The aeronaut on watch at the bows stood by the bell ready to sound warning of any ships sighted to port or starboard, ahead, above, or below. Crewmen coiled rope on the decks, checked gear and rigging for chafing, and often, in the course of their duties, strode past the two passengers at the taffrail; the only women aboard. Others of the Brotherhood voyaged aboard the Windship; a *thries-niun*, a detachment of seven-and-twenty Dainnan under their freely elected leader, Captain Heath. Thorn was not among them, and Rohain feared to inquire after him lest she besmirch his name by association, or appear to be brazen. And what would she do, should she be brought into his presence? Confess her passion? He had protected her and Diarmid on their journey across Eldaraigne, as was his duty. As a Dainnan he must safeguard the lives of citizens. The journey was over, the task done. The entwined cords of their lives had split and unraveled. But each time a tall olive-green-clad warrior strode by, her heart lurched like a ship windhooked. From sheer habit, the Lady of the Sorrows pulled her sumptuous taltry closer around her face.

The ship heeled. Viviana staggered at her mistress's elbow. She looked pale.

'Come into the chartroom, m'lady. If the air or the ground should become bumpier, there is a goodly chance of being tossed overboard.'

The courtier sidled like a crab across the deck, fell against a wall, and tiptoed back with involuntarily quick, light steps. Rohain watched in surprise. Personally, she found it little effort to compensate for the ship's movement.

The chartroom was lit by oil-lamps on hooks, sunflowers of light that swayed in a rhythmic dance with the shadows. Thomas Learmont, called the Rhymer, the Most Noble Duke of Ercildoune, Marquess of Ceolnnachta, Earl of Huntley Bank, Baron Achduart, and Royal Bard of Erith (to name only his principal titles) scratched his red goatee. He was poring over a map, alongside Aelfred, the ship's navigator. Lamplight glanced off the Bard's shoulder-length silken hanks of hair, turning them wine red against the robin's-egg blue velvet of his raiment. Around his neck coiled a torque of gold with sapphire eyes; the bardic snake-sigil.

At their first meeting, Rohain had almost mistaken him for

Sianadh, not having expected to see red hair at Court, after all she had heard of the place. This man with the neatly trimmed *pique-devant* beard and dapper mustaches was not Sianadh, although he matched her lost friend in height and girth. The features of his freckled face were strong and pronounced, the eyes deepset and hooded beneath bushy eyebrows. Winged keys were stitched in gold all over his costume. A demi-cloak swung from his left shoulder, fastened by a zither-shaped brooch. True Thomas, as he was commonly called, had not questioned Rohain concerning the story she had told to Roxburgh. He was no fool, either; shrewdness dwelt behind those twinkling eyes. But for whatever reason, he took her at her word, for now.

The Bard's pale eyes now turned toward the visitor. He bowed and kissed the back of her hand.

'My lady.'

She curtsied. 'Your Grace.'

'Thirty-four hours should see us at the Lofties, given that this fair westerly keeps up. We sail by night and day.' He turned to his apprentice, a downy-chinned youth in the Bard's blue-and-gold livery. 'Toby, is the rosewood lute restrung?'

'Yes, Your Grace,' said Toby, handing it over.

The Royal Bard appreciatively stroked the shiny rosewood and plucked a few strings, which gave out soft, bell-like notes.

'Good.' He handed the instrument back to the apprentice. 'See that it is kept tuned. As I do not have to remind you, new strings stretch, particularly in the changeable airs at these altitudes. Gerald, bring supper and wine. Roll up your maps, Master Aelfred—the lady and I shall dine here anon, with the captains. But first we shall stroll together on deck, if that is to m'lady's liking.'

'My servant tells me I am likely to be tipped overboard.'

'There is little chance of that for the duration of the next watch, m'lady,' said Aelfred with a bow. 'The ship will be passing over smooth and level territory. Turbulence is improbable.'

'Then I accept Your Grace's kind invitation,' said Rohain, exulting yet again in her newfound powers of speech.

Quarreling over the best perches, the birds settling in the tree-tops beneath the hull made noise enough for a dawn chorus. The

celestial dome arching high overhead glowed softly with that luminous, aching blueness that is only seen at twilight, and then rarely.
The rigging stood out in ruled black lines against it. The moon,
just over the half, floated, bloated like a drowned fish.

'What a strange time of night—or day,' mused Rohain politely
as they stepped along the gently canting deck. 'Is it day or night,
I wonder? The moon and the sun are in the sky both at once. Birds
carol as though they greet the morning. It is a *between* time—neither one nor the other; a border-hour.'

Her companion offered her his arm and she reached past the
wide perimeter of her petticoats to rest her hand lightly on his
lace-cuffed wrist. The Duke of Ercildoune, Royal Bard and Rhymer
to the King-Emperor, was a man of courtesy and learning. She had
warmed to him at their first meeting.

'Speaking of borders,' said the Bard, 'puts me in mind of a very
old tale. May I tell it you? There are few pleasures greater, it seems
to me, than indulging in storytelling on such an evening, at such
an altitude.'

'I would be honoured, sir, to be told any tale by the Bard of
the King-Emperor.'

He inclined his head in a gesture of dignity and courtesy.

'There was once a fellow,' he began, 'named Carthy
McKeightley—a braggart who took to boasting that he could best
any wight in a contest of wit. These brash words eventually came
to the ears of Huon himself . . .'

Panic seized Rohain. She struggled to conceal it.

'And,' Ercildoune continued, gazing out over the starboard
side without noting her distress, 'being of a sporting nature, the
Antlered One challenged McKeightley to play at cards with him, a
challenge which McKeightley, to uphold his words, must accept.
To make it interesting, the life of the loser would be at stake.

'"Be certain!" said Huon the Hunter, lowering his great antlers
threateningly, "If I outwit you, your life shall be forfeit, whether
you be within your house of rowan and iron or without it. If you
run I shall come after you with my hounds, the Coonanuin, and I
swear that I shall take you."

'To this, McKeightley blithely agreed.'

The storyteller paused. Having recovered her composure, Rohain smiled and nodded.

'Wily as McKeightley was,' said Ercildoune, 'Huon was craftier. The game lasted for three days and three nights, and at the end of it the unseelie wight was the winner.

"'Now I shall devour you," he said.

'But McKeightley jumped up and fled to his house, locking the rowan-wood doors and windows with iron bolts. It was no ordinary house, built as it was of stone, with walls four feet thick. Every kind of charm was built into it.

'The Antlered One came to the door like a dark thundercloud, with eyes of lightning, and said, "McKeightley, your iron bars will not stay me. You have pledged me your life, both outside your house and within it. I will devour you."

'With that, he struck a mighty blow on the door. Every hinge and lock in the place shivered to pieces and the door burst apart. But when the mighty Huon strode in, McKeightley was nowhere to be seen.

"'You cannot hide," laughed the unseelie lord. "My servants will sniff you out."

"'Oh, I am not hiding," said a voice from somewhere near the chimney. "After such a long game I am hungry. I am merely sitting down to dinner."

"'Not before I eat," said the Antlered One.

"'I fear I cannot invite you to join me," said the voice. "There is not enough room for a big fellow like you here in the walls where I now dwell, *neither within my house nor without it.*"

'Huon gave a howl of rage and disappeared with a thunderclap!'

'But how clever!' said Rohain with a smile. 'Did McKeightley spend the rest of his days living in his walls?'

'No, for he had in fact outwitted the Antlered One and so had won the contest. He had a sort of immunity from the creature from then on, and his boastfulness became legendary. He infuriated a good many more folk of many kinds, but surprisingly, lived to a ripe old age; overripe, really, almost rotten.

'The wrath of Huon was, however, formidable, and upon other mortals he wrought vengeance for this trick. I always air this geste when Roxburgh wishes to dispute my tenet that the brain is mightier than the thew. Do you not agree the tale indicates, my lady, that wit wins where muscle fails?'

'Why yes. The walls—how astute!'

'Yea, verily,' said the Bard, nodding his head. 'Walls and borders and marches are strange situations—neither of one place nor the other.'

Rohain looked up at the sky, now colourless. To the west, cumulus clouds converged, boiling in some disturbance of the upper atmosphere. She half-expected to see dark shapes sweep across them, howling for blood.

'Pray, tell me of the Unseelie Attriod,' she said in a low voice. 'Where I come from, they will not even speak of it, believing that the mere mention brings ill fortune.'

'They may be right,' replied Thomas of Ercildoune, 'under some circumstances; for things of eldritch mislike being spoken of and have ways of listening in. But I'll vouch we are safe enough here, mark you! In times past the Unseelie Attriod was the anathema of the Royal Attriod, of which I am currently a member, as you must be aware. An Attriod, of course, consists of seven members, one of whom leads and two of whom are the leader's second-in-command.'

He slid a jeweled dagger from a sheath at his belt and with the point scratched a pattern on the upright panels of the poop deck.

'This is how an Attriod is shaped. If the leader is placed at the top and the others in a triangle, with four along the base, a very strong structure will be created—a self-supporting, self-contained framework with the leader at the pinnacle, at the fulcrum, from which he can see afar. It may be seen as an arrowhead, if you like. Each member must contribute particular talents to the whole, such that when locked into position, the structure lacks nothing. As Roxburgh and I now stand at the left and right shoulders of the King-Emperor, so, in macabre travesty, Huon the Hunter and the Each Uisge, the most malign of all waterhorses, once long ago flanked their leader.'

'Who were the others?'

'They were four terrible princes of unseelie: Gull, the Spriggan

Chieftain; the Cearb who is called the Killing One—a monster who can shake the ground to its roots; Cuachag of the fuathan; and the Athach, the dark and monstrous shape-shifter. That is—or rather, *was* the Unseelie Attriod, whom some called the Nightmare Princes.'

'What of their leader?'

'The Waelghast was struck down. They are leaderless now, and scattered. Many centuries ago, the Waelghast made an enemy of the High King of the Faêran, but eventually it was a mortal who struck the deciding blow, putting an end to the power of that Lord of Unseelie.'

For a few moments a thoughtful silence hung between them.

'Yet these Hunters are not the only scourges of the skies, sir,' said Rohain at last. 'Mortal men can be as deadly. Do pirates frequent these regions?'

'None have been seen. If we encounter them 'twill be they who have the worst of it, for this frigate is heavily armed and those who sail in her are not unskilled in warriorship.'

'There is a place . . .' Rohain hesitated.

'Aye?' prompted the Bard.

'There is a place in the mountains, a deep and narrow cleft. The sun rises over a peak shaped like three standing men. To the west stands a pile of great, flat stones atop a crag. As the sun's light hits the topmost stone, it turns around three times. Pirate ships shelter in that place.'

Ercildoune revealed no reaction to this astonishing news, not by the merest facial twitch.

'A ravine, you say, between the Old Men of Torr and one of those un*lorraly* formations in stone they call a cheesewring,' he replied, 'of which there are said to be several in the Lofties. This knowledge may prove to be of great use. How you came by it is your own affair, my dear. Be assured, it will be acted upon. But let us speak no more of wickedness. Let us to the cabin—the night grows cold.'

Just before they bent their heads to pass through the low door, Rohain saw the Bard glance over his shoulder, to the northern horizon. It was a gesture that was becoming familiar to her since her arrival at Court. The awareness of strange and hostile forces gathering in Namarre was never far away. It was always felt, even if not voiced.

Besides Captain Heath of the *thriesniun*, another Dainnan captain sailed aboard the frigate *Peregrine*. He was the ship's captain, a skyfarer with the Dainnan kenning of 'Tide'. These two took supper with Ercildoune and their lady guide, dining in the Ertish manner, with total disregard for forks.

Conversation in the captain's mess was dominated by the kindly Bard, who was never at a loss for words. As she grew to know him better, Rohain noted some indefinable similarity between him and the Duke of Roxburgh.

'How describe they us, in the Sorrow Isles?' he asked her.

'With words of praise, sir. The name of Thomas, Duke of Ercildoune, is well-known and highly regarded.'

'And no doubt many an anecdote is told thereof.'

'All are tales of chivalry.'

'And musicianship?'

'Most assuredly!'

'Since Thomas of Ercildoune is spoken of, perhaps you are aware of the geas he carries with him,' subjoined Sir Heath.

'Is it true, then?' asked Rohain, recalling one of Brinkworth's histories concerning the Royal Bard. 'I feared that to ask about it would appear discourteous.'

'Yes, 'tis true,' answered the Bard. 'I never utter a lie. This virtuous practice, if virtuous it can be called, is a bitterbynde I have sworn to, and shall never break.'

'Such a quality,' said Rohain, 'must be as a two-edged sword, for while His Grace's word is trusted by all, he likely finds himself in an unenviable position when obliged to comment upon the charms of a noblewoman whose aspect has not been graced by nature.'

The Dainnan captains grinned.

How glibly the words came to Rohain's lips! By rights, she thought, her tongue ought to have rusted from disuse. Wordsmithing came very easily, considering that she had been for so long mute. With the birth of a new persona, she could become whomsoever she pleased. But what manner of woman was she, this Rohain of the Sorrows? Given the power of speech, she had already used it to lie and flatter, to vent anger. Could this be the character that memory had suppressed?

'Zounds, you are sympathetic!' The Bard smiled broadly at his demure guest. 'Indeed, when it comes to flattery, I am not in the contest. As for hawking my own wares, exaggerated boasting is impossible—only in song and poesy have I license to give rein to fancy. Over the years, I have learned to avoid awkward dilemmas. Never was I a liar or a braggart, but I have come to be of the opinion, since I was gifted with this bitterbynde, that a little white lying, like a little white wine, can be good for one's constitution. Unfortunately, I am incapable of it.' He reached for the rosewood lute, and as an afterthought added, 'Of course, there is a curb on truth as there is on every facility of man. That is, one can only speak the truth *as one believes it oneself.* If you were to tell me a lie and I were to believe it, I should repeat it to another as a veracity.' He plucked a string of the instrument. 'I am for some song—what say you? I have one that I think shall please you.'

'I should like to hear it!' exclaimed Rohain.

Experimentally, the Bard strummed a few chords, then began to sing:

'One holds to one's ritual customs, one's intricate, adamant code;
One's strictly correct with one's manners, in line with the mode.
Real ladies are frugal when dining; to bulge at the waist would
     be vile!
Their forms must be slender as willows; of course, it's the style.

One's speech is quite blissingly novel—'tis far from colloquial
     brogue!
And common folk don't understand it; they're not in the vogue.
One's raiment's expensively lavish and drives ev'ry suitor quite
     mad.
One's tailors are paid to keep up with each glorious fad.

One's hairstyles defy all description; each strand is coiffed
  right to the end.
One needs to put up with the anguish to be in the trend.
We carefully choose whom to cherish with fine and fastidious
  passion;
'Tis seemly for one to be seen with the doyens of fashion!'

Between each verse he led a facetious chorus of *fal-lal-lals* in
which, after the first time around, everyone joined, masters and
servants alike. The song concluded amid general merriment.

Later, talk among the Dainnan captains turned to weightier
matters, such as the strength and numbers of the rebels in the
unquiet north. Rohain could only listen in growing consternation,
untutored as she was in the ways of warfare.

'And how do their tactics serve the barbarians of Namarre?'
asked Sir Heath.

Ercildoune replied, 'Reports say they are but loosely organised
under their several chieftains. They shun pitched battles. Instead
they use their speed and horsemanship to ride swiftly from location to location, assailing isolated detachments, intercepting
convoys and plaguing columns on the march. Until they feel confident of winning, they try to avoid fullblown conflict.'

'I have heard additionally,' said Sir Tide, 'that their light horsemen also use the classic tactics of feigned flight, luring our troops
into ambushes or doubling back at a prearranged position and
charging the pursuers.'

The Bard nodded and went on to describe other maneuvers
performed by the rebels in their constant harassment of northern
Eldaraigne by land and sea. Of the unseelie wights being drawn
to Namarre by a Summons undetectable to mortalkind, little was
discussed. By this omission, Rohain guessed the true depth of the
men's unease. The ways of eldritch wights were alien, often
incomprehensible. Who could guess what horrors might come of
such an unprecedented mustering?

Thus in conversation the evening passed, until it was time for
the passengers to retire to their cabins.

The role of bard was one of the most important and highly regarded functions in society. Historian, record-keeper, song-maker, entertainer; a bard was an exalted figure and a good bard a treasured auxiliary to any person of high birth. 'Second only to jesters in consequence,' Thomas of Ercildoune himself had drily proclaimed.

He being probably the most learned man in the five kingdoms, later in the voyage Rohain tapped him for information about the Talith: how many were known to dwell in Erith, where they were located, whether any Talith maidens had been reported lost or taken by wights during the past year or so. He gave her many details about the yellow-haired people, yet although he spoke at length, nothing he revealed gave any clue as to her origins.

But he was merry company, and the Dainnan captains, if sterner and more watchful, were also quick to smile and exchange banter. In song, story, and discussion of the foibles and quirks of courtiers, the voyage passed swiftly.

An unstorm came, casting its crepuscular veil and lighting the dusky forests with jewels of multihued fires. By night, the *Peregrine* wandered through a cloudscape of long white ridges and blue-gray valleys, smooth snowfields like bleached velvet, frosted mountains, blue abysses and hoary cliffs occupied only by silent towers of ivory and flocks of teased-wool sheep. The rising sun crayoned bright gold edges on them all.

Before dawn on the eighteenth of Nethilmis, the Windship reached the snow-tipped Lofties and was onhebbed to a lower, more perilous altitude so that Rohain could view the dark land-scape. The sky, pure violet in the zenith, shaded to pale gray in the south. Northeastward, the low red rim of the sun burned, ray-less. The snowy peaks glistened brilliantly in appliqué against the dull sky.

When at last they drifted over the shadowy pine forest wherein she and Sianadh had been lured by the malignant water-horse, Rohain was able to get her bearings. Rugged Bellsteeple reared its glistening head in the north. Below it, the line of the dis-tant escarpment was dimly visible across the terrain. Westward, wild, wide *cuinocco* grasslands stretched as far as the eye could see. There was the gleaming slash of the river-gorge, gouged by the Cuinocco Road on its route to the Rysingspill in the south.

On board the Windship, all attention was directed toward Rohain.

'This is the waterway we called "Cuinocco's Way", which springs from Bellsteeple. Where the land begins to rise,' she stretched out an arm and pointed, 'that is the Waterstair.'

Now the vessel flew up the river, directly above it, the hull's sildron repelling the shallow riverbed but unable to affect the water. In such narrow confines, Captain Tide ordered all sail to be furled. The *Peregrine* ran only on her quiet, well-oiled sildron engines. Progress was slow but inexorable. Below, jacarandas reached crooked fingers skyward, their cyanic glory now vanished. The firmament unrolled overhead like a sheet of beaten pewter.

Every memory of Sianadh threatened to overwhelm Rohain. She saw the river redgum trees lining the western shores where the walls of the gorge subsided; at this season the river, deprived of its lifeblood by ice's iron grip in the higher altitudes, ran at a low mark. Farther along, the tree-bridge still lay across the channel. There she and Sianadh had fled to safety and she had brought him water in a boot. Her mood grew melancholy.

In silence and despondence the refugee from Isse Tower came, for the second time, to Waterstair.

'Before daylight grows,' said Sir Tide, 'we shall onheb down to fifty feet and bring her in behind the trees. If any keep watch on this Waterstair, this ship shall not be seen by them.'

The wind dropped. Light as ash keys, the winged, wind-dispersed fruits of ash trees, the *Peregrine* settled down amid tall firs. The port and starboard anchors were tossed out noiselessly in the brittle air. Landing-pods were rolled down on ropes and Sir Heath led his *thriesniun* forth. Like shadows they melted into the greenwood.

The sun stepped a little higher, but no rays bristled forth to pierce the greenery of a thousand shades in the cold, leafy galleries where the *Peregrine* bobbed, camouflaged by her mottled hull.

A Dainnan knight materialized silently below, the sage green of his raiment scarcely visible against the vegetation. Climbing a rope ladder as easily as another man might run up a stair, he came before the Bard and, addressing him by his honorary Dainnan kenning, delivered a message.

'My Lord Ash, the place is found. Prisoners have been taken. Lookouts have been posted through the forest. The way is clear.'

Now the other passengers descended and made their way alongside the river.

The water's loquacious tongues muttered softly. Bushes and grasses beside Cuinocco's Way lay trampled and crushed. Vines lay shriveled at the cliff's foot. Rohain searched there for any signs of Sianadh—a fragment of clothing, perhaps; a belt buckle or an earring. She found nothing. Scavengers would have dragged away any carcass left aboveground to rot. His bones would lie scattered somewhere. She had heard it said that hair was an enduring thing, that in graves opened centuries after their occupation and sealing, even the bones had crumbled to dust but the hair yet remained undecayed. Would ruby filaments hang upon twigs here and there, blowing in the wind, all that remained—besides memories—of a true and steadfast friend?

She learned from Captain Heath all that had taken place on the ground while she and the Bard had been waiting in the Windship. Perhaps a dozen of Scalzo's men had been left to guard the doors of Waterstair. Their lookouts had not perceived the approach of the Dainnan, who moved as quietly as wild creatures. Some of the eastside men had been stationed around the skirts of the rocky pool into which the cascade poured—Sianadh's 'porridge pot'. There they had lolled unwarily. The Dainnan warriors had crept up unnoticed under the cover of the waterfall's noise and taken them without trouble.

However, beneath the water curtain it was a different story. Several of the guards had managed to seal themselves inside the cavern, having slipped through the doors when the surprise attack was launched. They had pulled the doors shut behind them.

The massive, decorative portals would not budge. The Dainnan, having discovered the stone game pieces atop the cliff, had as yet embarked upon no course of action. Twelve of their knights stood ringed around the wet stone platform in the cavern facing those impossibly tall doors, which glimmered green-gold under the gaze of the carved eagle. The ever-descending torrent at their backs cast its illusions on the eyes of those who watched them. As they stood braced, the knights seemed to be moving upward.

An indication of his calm faith in Dainnan prowess was given by Captain Heath, who allowed the lady passenger to accompany the Bard beneath the falls. Now Thomas of Ercildoune stood before the doors of Waterstair. His eyes, squinting with intense concentration from beneath his embroidered taltry, moved across the motifs of twining leaves to the runes. Abruptly, the solemnity of his mien was broken by a flashing smile. He nodded at Sir Heath, who signaled his men. The Bard's chest expanded. He shouted out a single word, which rose above the cataract's thunder. Smoothly, as they had been designed to do, the doors swung open.

Instantly the Dainnan were inside. The tussle was brief; Scalzo's mercenaries had no chance of matching the King's warriors. The Dainnan took the armed guards without drawing their own weapons, in a spontaneous display of speed, strength, and force. In a short time, all were disarmed and restrained.

The treasure at last lay revealed.

So mighty was the mass of the hoard that although it had been despoiled, it seemed to Rohain there was no change in its magnitude. There lay the jeweled caskets, the candelabra, the weapons and armour, the cups and chalices, the gold plate, the coffers and chests overflowing with coins, the spidersilk garments. Over everything burned the cold, crystal flame of the swan-ship. Certainly no change had been wrought in the beauty and wholesomeness of any of the artifacts. So much beauty—and so much blood had been spilled for it.

Laying eyes on the preternatural ship, Captain Tide said, 'Now I have seen the fairest ship in Aia.' He wandered long on her decks and vowed that one day he would take her into the sky.

'All this is of Faêran make,' said Ercildoune in amazement. 'I trow it's lain here for many lives of kings—since the Fair Ones went under the hills. The door runes have kept their secret for a long time.'

'How did you open the doors?' asked Heath.

'The password was plain to discover, for those who have studied the Faêran tongue, as I have. Written on these walls is a riddle. Loosely translated, it reads:

"In my silent raiment I tread the ground, but if my dwelling is
    disturbed,
At whiles I rise up over the houses of heroes; my trappings lift
    me high,
And then far and wide on the strength of the skies my
    ornaments carry me over kingdoms,
Resounding loudly and singing melodiously; bright song.
Wayfaring spirit, when I am not resting on water or ground."

'The answer? A swan—*eunalainn*, as the Faêran would say. That word is the key.'

Now that her work had been completed by guiding the King-Emperor's men to the hidden cache, Rohain was able to withdraw to the sidelines. In the bitter chill of the morning, the captured eastsiders were brought in chains to the hold of the Windship. Sir Heath and his Dainnan took over with energetic efficiency, thoroughly exploring Waterstair's cavities and cliffs, leaving nothing undisturbed, loading objects onto the Windship under the direction of the Bard, with the use of sildron hoisters and floating transport platforms.

'Behold,' Ercildoune pointed out to Rohain, 'no war-harness exists here. All these most wondrous armours are intended for ceremonial purposes only. The Faêran had no need of bodily protection in battle. They loved it for decoration but their fighting skills precluded the need for body-shields. Also, while the Faêran could be diminished, they could never be destroyed.'

Among the booty was a set of thronelike chairs, each adorned with carvings of flowers; marigolds of topaz and crocodilite, roses of pink quartz, hyacinths of lapis lazuli, their leaves cut from chrysoprase, olivine, jade. With a spasm of pain, Rohain watched the poppy and lily chairs being loaded aboard. Visions from memory sprang to mind.

Settling himself back in the poppy throne, Sianadh took up a brimming cup, sampled it with a satisfied air, and watched the girl over the rim of it. She repeated every sign, almost to perfection.

'Ye left the fat out of the pig part.'

Having corrected this he went to check on the helm of fruit juice, which, optimistically, he was trying to coax to ferment into something stronger. The girl idly flipped gold coins in the sunlight; they winked light and dark as they spun.

'This brow ought never to be plowed with sorrow,' quoted Ercildoune as he drew Rohain aside, leaving Viviana alone to admire each new piece being hoisted on deck. They stood beneath the lichened arches of a melancholy willow that wept green tears at the water's edge.

'I grieve for departed friends,' said Rohain, to explain her frown.

'Who does not? Yet such grief is merely selfishness. Hearken, Lady of the Sorrows, and be no longer of them. What we have uncovered here is as you promised, and more. This is a wealth of vast import. It might have been whittled away at the edges, pilfered by petty thieves over time, but you have rescued the greater part of it for its rightful owner. You have done the King-Emperor a great service and therefore you shall be appropriately rewarded. An it please the King-Emperor, you shall receive honours. I myself shall nominate you for a peerage in your own right. Lands and more shall be bestowed upon you, I'll warrant.'

'I have only done my duty.'

'Do not underestimate your deed. By nightfall, this lusty little bird of a frigate shall be loaded to her ailerons and ready to lumber through the sky like an overfed duck. Then we shall to Caermelor go in haste, leaving a goodly company of Dainnan behind to protect the King's interests. We shall arrive in triumph and in good time to make ready for the New Year's celebrations! Now, if that does not make your smile blossom, then you are not the sweet-tempered wench I took you for!'

His jollity being infectious, she smiled.

'Ha!' The Bard laughed, flinging his cap in the air. 'All is well! I feel a song coming on!'

3
CAERMELOR, PART II
Story and Sentence

As warmer seasons wear away and nights begin to lengthen,
The power of the eldritch ones shall waken, wax, and strengthen.
Blithe heat and honest, artless light from all the lands shall wane,
Shadows shall veil what once was clear. Unpleasant things shall reign,
And mortal folk should all beware, who brave the longest night,
Of wickedness and trickedness—of fell, unseelie wight.

FOLK-CHANT

The Dainnan patrol frigate returned to Caermelor with its cargo on the evening of the twenty-first Nethilmis, having waited twenty-four hours in the mountains for a favourable wind and then been blown off course by its fickleness. News from the north greeted them at the Royal City. Roxburgh had returned already. Tension at the Namarran border had recently eased somewhat. It seemed that for the time being, at least, activity in Namarre had ground to a standstill. Insurrectionary lightning-raids had ceased and no spies had been seen for some time. An impasse had been reached; a breathing space in which the seditionists halted their mustering and proceeded to work only on fortifying their groundworks. As for the Imperial Legions, with most of the heavy equipment already in place, troops were kept busy performing military exercises.

This mortal state of affairs, however, did not apply to unseelie entities, which continued to be drawn, by degrees, into the north. What mortal or entity possessed the power to summon them could only be guessed, but it boded ill for the peace and stability of the Empire. A mood of suppressed fear insinuated itself throughout Caermelor, but the citizens endeavoured to go about their daily lives as usual.

New Year's Eve drew nigh. This being the Midwinter festival, Imbrol, and the most important annual feast-time in Erith, the populace spared no effort to realise every traditional custom for the decoration of their surroundings and the entertainment, gratification, and nourishment of themselves. Here was a good reason to set aside their apprehension for a time and immerse themselves in jollity. All over Erith, in hovels and bothies, in cottages and crofts, in cottages, marketplaces, smithies, and workshops, in barracks, taverns, malt-houses, and inns, in manor houses, stately homes, and Towers, in halls and keeps, castles and palaces, they set holly garlands on rooftrees, ivy festoons around inglenooks, sprays of mistletoe above the doors and strobiled wreaths of pine and fir and spruce on every available projection. They chopped dried fruits, mixed them with suet, honey, and flour, wrapped this stodge in calico and boiled it for hours, then hung the lumpy puddings like traitors' heads, high in their butteries and spences. These and numerous other things the folk of Erith did in preparation for the Winter Solstice and the birth of the New Year, 1091.

This was the season when young lasses, whose hearts were stirred by something beyond the walls of the mortal world, dwelled upon the frightening and attractive possibility of going out into the wilderness during the long, enigmatic nights of Dorchamis in case the Coillach Gairm, the blue crone as ancient as Winter, as terrible and as miraculous, should choose to come silently, unannounced, and offer to them a coveted staff of power in exchange for whatever mortal asset she might wish to take for herself.

But that way was not for Lady Rohain of the Sorrows. She had no desire to wield eldritch powers through the Wand and would rather retain any human powers of which she found herself in possession. Having lived without several, she now valued them all too highly to risk forfeiture. That was for others to choose. Those who would be carlins generally carried that ambition from childhood.

Although Rohain knew where her future did not lie, she was uncertain as to where it did. In the city, festive splendor was the order of the day. Amid the bustle and business of the preliminaries to Imbrol, Rohain learned that Ercildoune's nomination for her recognition by a peerage had indeed been sanctioned by the King-Emperor. Creation of a new peerage was a long-drawn and tedious affair; first the Letters Patent must be prepared, after which the new title would be posted and proclaimed. The appointment would be complete when she received the accolade personally from His Majesty. The scribes of the Lord High Chancellor were also arranging the handing over of titles to a modest but choice Crown Estate in Arcune, with a return of two hundred and seventy guineas per year, which was to be bestowed at her investiture. Meanwhile she, as treasure-revealer, had already been gifted with eighty golden guineas (most of which lay locked in the Royal Treasury for safekeeping, but some of which already weighed down the purses of city tradesfolk), and a casket of personal jewellery from Waterstair: rings, bracelets, fillets, torques, gorgets, pins, girdles, the value of which could only be guessed. The amnesiac lackey from the House of the Stormriders had become wealthy beyond all expectation, exalted beyond all hope.

The days leading up to Imbrol took on an insubstantial quality. It was all too much to absorb at once. Later, Rohain could not have explained what her feelings were at that time. She was conscious of performing all actions automatically, of being swept along by a tide of events she herself had set in motion, with visits to the tailor's, the milliner's, the shoemaker's, with Viviana fussing and exclaiming, dramatising and exaggerating everything in her joy at knowing that at last she was free of the threat of being relegated to the service of the dreaded Dowager Marchioness of Netherby-on-the-Fens, and as if paying for this sense of relief by means of exerting her imagination, sculpting her mistress's hair into ever more fantastic designs and decorating it in ever more novel ways. She was well-intentioned and good-natured, this lady's maid; a lass who had lived a sheltered life, whose most feared hardship was a scolding, whose thoughts skimmed like swallows over the shallows, yet every so often dived deep and shrewdly; whose hands and chattering tongue were always fretting to be busy.

Testing the new powers springing from wealth and recognition, as a youth suddenly waking to manhood would experimentally flex expanded sinews, the prospective Baroness Rohain Tarrenys inquired discreetly after her friends. Messengers were dispatched, returning with the news that both Muirne and Diarmid had been accepted for military service and were training at Isenhammer. Farther afield, of the itinerant Maeve One-Eye there was no sign, which was not surprising, given the current season: Winter was the tenancy of the Coillach Gairm. Inquiries at Gilvaris Tarv resulted in a message via Stormriders that the carlin Ethlinn Kavanagh-Bruadair also had ventured abroad in response to the subliminal call of the Winter Hag, or possibly only from habit. Her whereabouts were unknown. Roisin Tuillimh still dwelt at Tarv, hale and hearty. To Roisin, Muirne, and Diarmid, Rohain anonymously sent gifts. She wished to share her good fortune without revealing a past identity that, certainly at Court, would transform her into the subject of scandal and possibly revulsion.

Of Thorn, she dared not inquire, even discreetly, for she guessed that the Dainnan knights had ways of knowing what was whispered about any of their number. She existed in a paradoxical state between fear of meeting him again and hope of it. While her face had been masked by ugliness and there had been no question of her feelings being reciprocated, to adore him in secret had been the only possibility. She had been able to say to herself, 'He cannot look upon me with favour; I am not worthy, but if I could be otherwise, he might look again.' Now that a fairer face was revealed, she was vulnerable. If he should look upon her and dismiss her, it would be a rejection of the best she could be, rather than the worst, and thus the ultimate rebuff.

There was no doubt that Thorn had been kind to her, but kindness was of his nature. Besides, that benevolence had also been extended to Diarmid. Of the meaning of the parting kiss, she could not be certain. Had he bestowed it out of pity or—against logic—out of liking? On impulse, but with enough forethought to do it where no other eyes could bear witness? If the latter, then he would have regretted it afterward, in which case he would not wish to be reminded of his folly by a stranger who had infiltrated Court by means of deception. No: her past association with the dark-haired Dainnan warrior was like a jewel of the most rare and precious kind, but so fragile that should the rigorous light of day fall upon it, it might crack asunder, crumble away. It must be locked away in the darkness of her mind's vault, to be cherished and kept entire, even though its loveliness could never in actuality be enjoyed again.

Without meeting him, the potential existed for happiness. There could be no risk. Yet she looked for his presence everywhere, as a lost wanderer would scan for any sign of water in a desert wasteland. The first glimpse of long black hair flowing over broad shoulders never failed to make her heart turn over. All sweetness, all joy, all light existed by his side, wherever he might be, and to be without his voice, the sight of him, the proximity of him, was to secretly live in wretchedness.

Sad longing dwelt on an inner level. Only a heart of stone could remain cold amid the festive revelry that day by day ascended toward its height. What was more, Rohain found herself surrounded by convivial company. Chief among these were Viviana, the irrepressible Thomas of Ercildoune, the Duchess Alys-Jannetta, Roxburgh's wife, with whom she had formed a friendship, and, in a surprising turn of events—or perhaps not so surprising—her erstwhile foe Dianella and that lady's faddish coterie. Now that she was to become a peer in her own right, was fêted for her role in adding to the Royal Treasuries, and moreover appeared to be glaringly in favour with the King-Emperor and the greatest aristocrats at Court, Rohain had been accepted Into the Set.

Whether due to this fact or some other, a goodly number of dashing sons of peers both In and Out of the Set seemed to find her companionship to their taste. They were constantly begging her to wear their favours upon her sleeve when they fought their rivals with rapiers, at dawn, in secluded places. Like fighting cocks they tiresomely challenged each other to illicit duels over trivial hurts to their pride—contests that seldom eventuated. Some excuse was usually discovered at the eleventh hour, some pretext that allowed both parties to retire with dignity and intact flesh. Rohain scarcely had more than a moment to spare for each of these heroes. Invitations from Dianella, Calprisia, Elmaretta, Percival, Jasper, and the rest of the trend-setting circle continually bombarded her. Would she come gathering ivy and spruce in the King's Greenwood? It would be such an amusing jaunt, with just enough danger to spice it, although only seelie wights were said to dwell there and the excursion would be guarded by outriders and carriage dogs accompanying the barouches! Would she come glissanding there, or hunting? Did she like to ride to the hounds? Would she come and view the new dress Dianella's tailor was sewing for her to wear on New Year's Eve? Would she come fishing upon the sea, or ice-skating on the frozen mountain lake where they were going in the Windship of the Lord High Wizard Sargoth? And so on.

Not to appear unsociable, Rohain accepted their entreaties for her company, and they drew her into their sophisticated, butterfly crowd with joyousness, teaching her a smattering of slingua so that she could become truly as they. Their activities, in fact, turned out to be novel and diverting; their chatter boring. Rohain was glad enough of Ercildoune's frequent presence as an excuse to desert them. Taking advantage of a break in the inclement weather, she strolled away with him in the Winter Garden, their attendants keeping at a discreet distance among the trees. Caermelor Palace boasted a garden for every season of the year, each walled off from the others so that its individual theme could be enjoyed.

'You shall, of course, remain at Court until well after Imbrol,' said the Bard. 'Much time may elapse until your new title, Baroness of Arcune, is invested. Nothing can be done to advance the proclamation of your title and the securing of your estate until after the festive season.'

'I understood, sir, that one is normally presented to the King-

Emperor *before* residing at his Court. I have not yet been granted the honour of an audience with His Majesty.'

'You speak knowledgeably, my dear, but these are troubled times. With the situation as it is in the north, with all this to-ing and fro-ing, councils and moots and so forth, normal procedures fall by the wayside. The King-Emperor is busy now as Imbrol approaches, and who knows but that at any time there may be a sudden escalation of belligerence in Namarre, leading to further need of his attention at the borders. Howbeit, it is not necessary for these military matters to hinder the bestowal of honours upon you. The title can be officially recognised merely by issue of Letters Patent granting full privileges of the honour and the posting and proclamation. Still, in good sooth, 'twould be a pity not to receive the peerage from the hands of our Sovereign himself, with all due pomp.'

There were no fountains in the Winter Garden. The walks were lined instead with marble pedestals whose bases, dados, and entablements were richly carved. Atop these pedestals, great bowls of stone cupped living fires whose flames leaped like the petals of giant stained-glass magnolias.

Evergreens spread resinous boughs or stood virgate, as if upholding the sky, or else modestly wept. Barberry and cotoneaster hedges popped with ripe scarlet spheres. Here, too, grew laurels with dark purple fruits, and firethorns with their startling orange.

'I suppose I shall remain,' said Rohain after some thought. Like a shimmerfly cloyed with honey, she felt herself to be trapped by a kind of inertia, mired in the sweetness of the luxurious Court environment. Indecision played a major part in her proposal to linger.

'Marry,' said the Bard poetically and somewhat whimsically, 'had you other plans? To return to the Sorrow Isles and tell your people of your fortune?'

'No.'

'I confess, I am glad of that,' he said suddenly. 'A confirmed bachelor have I always been, and vowed to remain, for I love the fair sex too much to restrict myself to the company of only one of their number. Despite this I find myself half inclined to pay you court.'

His companion turned to him in astonishment.

'Look not askance, my lady! Am I not but one more in a long line of suitors?'

'Indeed, no!' she said emphatically.

'Then, what say you? Or is your heart already given, as I suspect?'

'Well, since you ask it—yes, my heart is already given.'

'Alas.'

His chest heaved with a gentle sigh. Subdued, they walked a little farther along the lakeside path where sharp-eyed robins bounced like plump berries, past a stone gazebo whose pillars repeated their symmetries and patterns in the water. Rohain could scarcely believe what she had heard—that she should have received homage from one of the highest in the land.

'Then,' said the Bard, 'I will not speak of courting again. However, if you should chance to receive your heart again, will you think of me?'

'Most certainly, sir.'

'And meanwhile, shall we remain friends?'

'Indeed! And sir, you honour me too much. I am not worthy.'

'Alas,' sighed the Bard once more, 'I was ever a slave to a fair face.'

Rohain stopped in her tracks, confused.

'A fair face?' she repeated.

'As fair as any I have seen,' he said. 'And when animated, so that hectic roses bloom in the cheeks and a sparkle sets fire to the eyes, why, 'tis above all others most comely. 'Pon my troth, you are exquisite in every measure!' He laughed. 'Like all women, my lady of the Sorrows loves praise, and it comes sweeter from True Thomas, verily, for 'tis not flattery but truth.'

The girl leaned out over the still surface of the lake. Like quicksilver, it gleamed.

'Mind!' he warned. 'Do not fall! 'Tis not the season for swimming!'

She did not hear him. Her taltry-enclosed face looked up at her from the water, framed by branches of evergreens, backed by the metallic sky.

'I cannot see it myself,' she said with a frown.

'What? Brazen modesty?'

She straightened and turned to him.

'Nay!' he said, and it was his turn to be surprised as he read the honesty in her expression. 'Not false humility. You see no special virtue in your own features. Odd! But charming. Let me assure you, my dear, that you are alone in your opinion. Ah, Rohain, I understated just now, thinking that you would know I jested, but I am too accustomed to the complex cerebrations of courtiers. Let me now do you justice—hearken—for yours is a beauty more radiant than a flame, more perfect than a snowflake, more enchanting than music, more astonishing than truth, and more poignant than the parting of lovers who know not whether they will ever meet again.'

'You mock me, sir!'

Soberly he shook his head. 'Not at all. When I look at you, my eyes are filled with a beauty to ache for, to make tyrants and slaves of men, a beauty to beware of. Be aware of it; others are.'

'Gramercie,' she stammered, nonplussed.

It was a revelation.

Once, between engagements, Rohain borrowed Ercildoune's coach-and-four. His coachman drove her to Isenhammer. From high on the hill overlooking the town, the drill, parades, and training exercises of the recruits for the Royal Legion Reserves were clearly visible below. Having descended, she moved among the young cavalrymen, foot soldiers, and archers, escorted by her lady's maid and two footmen.

The feeling of tension among the recruits was almost palpable. It was like the pulled-back string of a bow, on the point of letting the arrow fly. They executed their drill with extreme dedication and concentration. Sometimes, involuntarily, their eyes slid toward a certain horizon, their heads turning, in the gesture Rohain knew so well. The north: what dire events were brewing there, so far away?

Diarmid and Muirne, in cadet uniform of the Legion, appeared hale and content. They did not know her, nor did she wish that they should. She had no desire to receive thanks for the costly gifts she had sent them, nor did she want to behold the aloofness or perhaps distrust that would appear in their eyes should she reveal her identity.

It was not that she shunned her friends, but that she did not see how she might fit in with their chosen life-paths. It was her intention to ask them to share her new estate when the procedures were finalized. For now, she wanted to ensure that they dwelled in comfort, lacking nothing. She returned to Caermelor without having spoken to them.

Imbrol drew nigh. Meanwhile, Viviana Wellesley seemed to be enjoying her latest role.

'It is quite a feather in m'lady's cap, to have been invited to meet the Lady Maiwenna,' she raved enthusiastically. 'She does not mingle with many people at Court, for her manner is quite reserved. When I saw the two of you together, I thought you looked almost like sisters in some respect.'

Rohain's spirits had been lifted by eager suspense when Ercildoune introduced her to the Talith gentlewoman who was said to be the last of the Royal Family of Avlantia. Yet her hopes were shattered. No recognition had registered in the green eyes of that golden damsel.

Her own hair was showing the slightest trace of a golden glimmer against the scalp, but this had not yet become apparent to anyone but herself. The elaborate, close-fitting headdresses fashionable at Court concealed her hairline. Her maidservant, busy chattering and clattering about with jeweled combs during the tedious coiffing sessions, had remained oblivious of the colour contrast. By the way she habitually held her hand-work at arm's length, squinting, Rohain suspected her of long-sightedness or poor vision.

'Howbeit, no one can compare with my lady, of course,' Viviana prattled on. 'Upon my word, if I may take the liberty of saying so, my lady's face and figure are the envy of the Court. Such elegant limbs—no wider than my wrist, I'd swear—and a waist the size of my neck!'

Rohain ignored these compliments. Her new servant chattered more than necessary, yet she continued to prove herself a cornucopia of information about Court matters.

'When I told Dianella she would look well in green,' said Rohain, 'why did she exclaim, "Odd's fish, how revolutionary!"?'

'My lady, the green is not to be worn. Not as a main colour, anyway—only in bits for decoration, and then not the proper leaf green.'

'Why not? Is it forbidden?'

Viviana was taken aback. 'Wear they green in the Sorrow Isles then, m'lady?'

'No, no, but tell me.'

'It is not forbidden, exactly, but it is not done to wear the green.'

'The Dainnan wear it—a kind of green, at least.'

'Begging your pardon, m'lady, it is not exactly green that Roxburgh's knights wear, but the colour *dusken*. 'Tis as if a dyer mixed together brown paint, a little grayish, with mayhap a pinch of saffron—'

'And a good helping of grass green.'

'—and perhaps a hint of green. *Dusken* is not truly leaf green or grass green, m'lady, 'tis in the shades of dusty bracken-fern.'

'I see. What of green furnishings?'

'They are allowable.'

'And what of emeralds?'

'Green jewels ought to be worn with discretion. Royal purple is forbidden, of course,' added the lady's maid warily, anxious not to offend her mistress by implying she was ignorant of such matters.

'Of course,' replied her mistress. 'But royal purple is reserved for royalty. Why should green be held in reserve?'

'Oh well, it was the colour most favoured by Themselves, and old customs die hard, m'lady. It was unlucky for mortals to wear it. Green was only for the Faêran.'

The subject of the Faêran interested Rohain. For further information she went to Alys-Jannetta of Roxburgh, the wife of the Dainnan Chieftain. The Duchess, a level-headed gentlewoman of assertive spirit, liked to ride and hunt and shoot with a bow. On her chief estate she had a rose garden that she often tended with her own hands, not being afraid to dirty them. Rohain found her bold bluntness refreshing.

'I will give you one view,' said the Duchess, 'and others will give you another. For my part, I hold no good opinion of Themselves—as a race, that is—and I think it well that the Fair Realm was sundered from us so long ago. The old tales tell all. It was one law for mortals and another for the Faêran. A haughty folk they were, proud and arrogant, who thought nothing of stealing mortals who took their fancy. But if you would hear tales, why, there is only one man who knows them all and tells them so well, and that is our Royal Bard, Thomas. Come, we shall attend him.'

It was Ercildoune who opened up the subject of the Faêran for Rohain as never before; he who possessed an inexhaustible supply of stories concerning them, he who awakened her interest in their lore and history and taught her of their beautiful, dangerous, vanished world; the lost kingdom, the Fair and Perilous Realm of the Faêran.

The Bard's palace suite was decorated to a musical theme. Across the tapestries on the walls of the Tambour Room, scenes from history and legend spread themselves. Here, seven maidens harped beneath flowering horse-chestnuts. There, a youth played a gittern to charm an evil lord into sleep, that the musician might recover his stolen wife. On another wall, a virgin beneath a green oak tree sang a unicorn to her side. Farther along, a row of trumpeters sounded a fanfare of triumph to a flower-strewn parade.

The room was crowded with crested arks and dark cabinets thickly carved with leaves, rosettes and lions. A clear, red fire burned in the grate, beneath a chimney-piece whose side-panels were a carved marble relief depicting the beautiful water-wights, the Asrai, lyres held in their slender fingers. Inscrutable footmen in the pale-blue-and-gold livery of Ercildoune stood to attention at the doors.

The Duke of Ercildoune welcomed his guests and settled them near the hearth. His apprentice Toby strummed softly. A small lynx purred on a ragged appliqué cushion that it had previously shredded with its claws. Five tiny moths flitted along the ornately carved friezes and architrave moldings then fluttered down to the thickets of candles to dance with death. Viviana arranged her mistress's skirts. The Duchess of Roxburgh toyed with a tasseled fan, occasionally glancing at the velvet-draped windows that looked out over the Winter Garden, across the city to the ocean. A chill mist was rising from the river. The first star of evening had already punctured a sky both clear and dark. In the still and crystalline air, frost threatened.

To the Bard, Rohain said, 'Your Grace, in these days I have passed at Court I have heard somewhat of the Fair Realm, and it has whetted my appetite, for I have little knowledge of the place or its denizens. Will you tell me more?'

Ercildoune's demeanor altered subtly at her words. From being the jovial host, he seemed to metamorphose, to become a stranger, remote, staring now into the fire.

'The stars,' he said suddenly. His visage sharpened to a wistful look.

Rohain waited.

After a pause, he continued: 'The stars. So beautiful, so mysterious, so alluring are they—so unreachable, pure, strange, and glorious that they could only be of Faêrie. Go into the wilderness on a clear night and look up. Look long. Then you will have seen something of Faêrie.' His voice roughened to an uncharacteristic huskiness. 'Or behold, at dusk in Springtime, drifts of white pear blossom glimmering palely through the gloom, for the turn of the seasons is evanescent as the beauty of the Fair Realm, which slipped through mortal fingers like handfuls of seed-pearls. The power of the Fair Realm cannot be comprehended.'

He gazed into the fire's red world. Eventually he added, 'The Realm is a place with no frontiers.'

'You speak with longing and love, Your Grace,' said Rohain wonderingly.

'Anyone would long and love, who had heard even a tenth of what I have heard.'

'Yet is it a place? Did it exist?'

'Fie! Never say that it did not—I will not brook it!'

'Forgive me! I did not seek to denigrate that which stirs your passion.'

'Nay,' the Bard replied hastily, 'you must forgive *me*, Rohain—I spoke too harshly just now.'

'Well then,' she answered lightly, bantering in the manner she had learned at Court, 'if I am to forgive you, you must give me a tale about the Faêran, so that I can come to know them better.'

'Gladly, for this is a subject dear to my heart.'

He drew his chair closer to the hearth.

'The Faêran,' he began, pronouncing the word as if he spoke some ancient, arcane spell, 'had many names; the Gentry, the Strangers, the Secret Ones, the Lords of Gramarye, and other kennings. Their Realm had many names also. Some called it the Land of the Long Leaves. Before that, it was called Tirnan Alainn.

'Most of the Fair Folk were well-disposed towards mortals, but there were those who harboured ill-feeling, for, dare I say, the deeds of mortals are not always courteous. Of all the faults of Men condemned by the Faêran, they despised spying and stealing most of all.

'Long ago, before the ways between the Fair Realm and Aia were closed forever, there were places in Erith which the Faêran favoured above others. Willowvale, in northern Eldaraigne, was one of these. At night, the Faêran would ride out through a right-of-way that used to lie under the green hill called the Culver, and go down to Willowvale. There they would bathe in the river and sing in harmony with the water as it flowed over its rocky bed, glinting beneath the moon's glow.

'One blossom-scented twilight in Spring, a little girl who was gathering primroses by the waterside heard the sound of laughter and music coming from the Culver, so she walked up the hill to investigate. The right-of-way lay open and she dared to peep inside. There she saw a sight to gladden her spirits: the Faêran folk, in their beauty and their gorgeous raiment. Some were banqueting, others were whirling about in graceful, lithesome dances. The child hastened home to inform her father, but the good farmer could not share her delight, because he knew that the Faêran would come for her. They guarded their privacy jealously. Any mortal who spied on them would either be sorely punished or else taken away to dwell forever with them, and he did not doubt that they would choose to take a little girl so fair and mild.

'Because he cherished his daughter and could not bear to upset her, the farmer did not tell her what would happen to her for spying on the Faêran. He went straight to a carlin who knew something of the laws of the Gentry.

'"They will come for your daughter at midnight tonight," she told him, "yet they will be powerless to take her if utter silence is maintained throughout your farmstead. When they come, you must ensure that there is no noise, apart from any made by the Faêran themselves. Even the faintest sigh, the softest tap of a fingernail, will shatter the charm."

'Away to his house went the farmer. That night, he waited until his daughter had fallen asleep in her bed. Then he herded all the geese and hens into their coops, removed the bells from the necks of the milch-cows before shutting them into the byres, and locked the horses into the stables. He gave the dogs such a large dinner of bones and scraps that they lay down to sleep at once, their stomachs distended. He tied down anything that could sway and squeak in the slightest breeze. Then he came indoors, and laid the rocking-chair on its side, that it would not rock, and doused the hearth-fire so that there should be no spitting or snapping of sparks, and he sat down in the dark, cold, silent cottage to await the Faêran.

'At midnight they came.

'The latch on the garden gate went *click* and the hinges creaked as it swung open, then the farmer heard the clopping crunch of horses' hooves coming up the path. When they discovered the place so soundless and frozen, the riders hesitated. The farmer sat motionless and held his breath, lest they should hear even the slight whisper of the exhalation. The silence deepened, the minutes lengthened. The blood pounding at his temples sounded to him as loud as a blacksmith's hammer. Then there came the clatter of hooves turning around—the Faêran were leaving. He let go of his breath with no noise at all, but alas, he had overlooked one thing. At the sound of the Faêran horses beneath the window, the little spaniel that slept at the foot of his daughter's bed jumped up and barked. The charm was shattered. Instantly the farmer hastened up the stairs, his heart bolting, only to discover his worst fears realised. The bed was empty. His daughter was gone.

'Devastated by his bereavement, he resolved to try everything in his power to regain her. So wild was he with this anguish that straight away, without waiting for the dawn, without eating or drinking, he went again to consult the carlin.

'"Even in this extremity I can give you advice," said she. "Nonetheless, the challenge will be fraught with difficulty. You must take a sprig of rowan for protection and go to the Culver every night and lie down on top of it. Should they Themselves come to inquire your purpose, you must ask them to give back your daughter, but I warn you, what they may ask in return may not be easily guessed."

'The farmer did as she had advised and on the third night the Faêran appeared before him and asked him why he should be so bold as to lie down on top of the Culver.

'"I am come to ask for my daughter who you took from me," he said.

'"Well then, you shall have her back," they said, "if, before Whiteflower's Day you bring to us three gifts—a cherry without a stone, a living bird that has no bone, and, from the oldest creature on your farm, a part of its body given without the shedding of any blood. If you come back with those three things, we will give you your daughter."

'Hope sprang afresh in the farmer's heart as he departed. But then he asked himself, "How can there be a cherry without a stone, save that I should cut the stone out of it? But I am certain that is not what they mean. As for the bird, I could kill a hen and take its bones out, but how shall I find a living bird with no bone? And what of the last part of the riddle—could it mean milk from my old cow, Buttercup? Yet milk is not really part of an animal's body. What if I cut off the tips of her horns? But wait—is not Dobbin the cart-horse older than Buttercup?" He tormented himself looking for the answers but could find none, and the carlin could not help him further. Unable to rest, he took to roaming through the countryside, asking himself those questions over and over, and querying whomsoever he met, but with no success at all, and Whiteflower's Day was coming closer.'

The Bard leaned to caress the soft fur of the lynx. Taking advantage of the interlude, the Duchess of Roxburgh said, 'Whenever I hear this tale I wonder at the thickheadedness of that farmer. How could anyone not guess the answers to such simple riddles?'

The Bard smiled, saying, 'Not all folk are as clever as Alys of Roxburgh.'

'Hmph!' she returned, feinting a slap at him with her folded fan. 'Go on with the tale!'

'Barely three weeks remained before Whiteflower's Day,' resumed Ercildoune, 'when, as he trudged along the road, the farmer met a beggar.

'"Prithee, sir," said the ragged fellow, "can you spare a crust? I am famished!"

'"A crust and more," said the farmer feelingly. Opening his leather wallet, he generously handed out bread, cheese, and apples. "I know what suffering is," he said sadly, "and I would alleviate the distress of others if I am able."

'"You have succored me," said the beggar as he took the food, "and in turn I will give you aid. The answer to your first question is: a cherry when it is a blossom, clasps no stone."

'In amazement the farmer stared at the beggar, but the old fellow just walked away, smiling. Although he seemed to walk slowly he was along up the road in a trice and quickly disappeared around the corner. The farmer ran to catch up with him but when he rounded the bend all that he saw was the long, empty road stretching away to the distance, and no traveller upon it.

'Marveling, the farmer walked on. He was passing a spinney of chestnuts when he saw a thrush trying to escape from a kestrel, which stooped to kill it. Momentarily setting aside his woes, he seized a pebble from the roadside and hurled it at the hunting hawk. The kestrel fled, but the thrush returned. It fluttered down to perch on the bough of a thorn bush, regarding its rescuer with a bright and knowing eye.

'Seeing such a look, the farmer was hardly surprised when the bird opened its beak and spoke to him in melodious tones.

'"You acted in kindness. Now I will reward you with the answer to your second question. If a broody hen sits on an egg for fifteen days, that egg will hold a chicken without a bone yet formed in its body." The man gaped at the little brown bird, but it trilled three musical notes and flew away.

'The farmer was vastly encouraged. "Two answers!" he said triumphantly to himself. "Two answers have I!" Then he thought, "But what good are they if I cannot find the answer to the last question?" And he almost despaired.

'As he tramped on his way, frowning and cogitating about the third riddle, there came to his ears a pathetic wailing. In the hedges bordering the road, a rabbit was trapped in a wire snare. Its crying moved the man to pity. Crouching beside the creature, he gently set it free, expecting it to run away forthwith.

'Like the thrush, it focused its gaze upon him. This time, he was not astonished, yet a sense of wonder welled in him.

'"Sir," piped the rabbit, "you have done me a favour, therefore here is the final answer you require. If you cut off a lock of hair, it will come away from the body without shedding one drop of blood. As for the oldest creature on your farm, why the looking-glass will answer that."

'When the farmer blinked the rabbit was gone, but he threw his cap into the air and ran jubilantly home. Hurrying to the chicken coop, he placed an egg under a broody hen. When fifteen days were past he took the shears and chopped off a lock of his own hair. Then he went out into the orchard and gathered a great bough of pink-and-white cherry blossom. Throwing his cap in the air, he whooped for joy.

'He could hardly wait for night to fall. At sunset, he stuck a sprig of rowan in his cap and went down Willowvale and up to the top of the Culver. There he sat down and bided his time, and the stars came out over his head, and the night was warm and still, and yet he kept vigil. After a time he heard music and laughter, which seemed to be coming from beneath the hill, and soon the Faêran came. They were annoyed to see him there, but they could not touch him because of the sprig of rowan, and they could not abduct him because he had failed to transgress their code. When he showed them the blossom, the egg, and the lock of hair, they had to give him back his daughter. At first she gazed at her father in bewilderment, as one who has woken from a dream, but then she gave a cry of happiness and threw her arms around him. They returned home together, and never again did she try to spy on the Faêran.'

With a discordant twang, a string broke on Toby's lyre. At the sound, the listeners started.

'The Faêran had their own laws,' continued Ercildoune after a sidelong glance at his apprentice, 'as this tale shows. And when those laws were broken, they meted out their own forms of punishment. Yet they were not unmerciful. First, they gave the farmer opportunity to reclaim his kin. Secondly, they tested him to see if he was worthy of reward. Because he showed kindness, they themselves gave him the answers to the riddles. Kindness in mortals was a virtue which they esteemed highly.'

'Also great courage,' Alys contributed.

'Aye, and neatness and cleanliness, and true love, and the keeping of promises,' added the Bard.

With a practiced air, Toby removed the broken string from his lyre and unrolled a new one.

'I have learned,' said Rohain, 'that they delighted also in feasting, dancing, and riddles—a merry race, it seems they were, but also dangerous.'

Ercildoune, leaning on his elbow, called for a page.

'Bring piment!' he said. 'Does m'lady like piment?' he added, turning to Rohain.

'I know not what it is.'

'A brew of red wine, honey, and spices.'

'I am certain it would please me.'

The Bard snapped his fingers and the lad hurried away. Toby plucked a rising scale of liquid notes to tune the string as he tightened it.

'Did they live under the hills?' pursued Rohain. 'Was their Realm underground, in caves?'

Ercildoune laughed. 'Not underground, not under water, not under or over anything. Faêrie lay elsewhere. It was Away. The traverses that linked Aia and the Fair Realm—some called it the Perilous Realm—used to lie in such places as eldritch wights now see fit to haunt. There was an access under the Culver, as under certain other hills. These green mounds were known by many names, such as *raths, knowes, brughs, lisses,* and *sitheans* or *shians,* but passage existed also under lakes, in coppices, in wells, in high places and low. So you understand, Rohain, the little girl gathering primroses did not look into an underground cavern— she looked through a traverse into the Realm itself.'

'Well,' said Rohain, 'abduction seems severe retribution for an unwary glance.'

'It seems so to us,' agreed Ercildoune. 'Howbeit, bearing in mind that the Fair Realm could be a place of delight, the Faêran may have seen it merely as a way of preventing the child from telling others all that she had seen and thus pre-empting an influx of human gawkers. Generally, they considered mortal spying to be an outrageous crime and they were swift to avenge, as I shall relate. But first allow me to provide you with a further example of traverses and mortal transgression.'

A hallmarked lore-master, ever enthused by his trade, the Bard launched into another story.

'There was once a Faêran right-of-way at Lake Coumluch in the mountains of Finvarna. Coumluch is a solitary lake with a mist of white vapors ever on it and lofty cliffs rising all around. For most of the year the lake waters were unbroken by any reef, rock, or isle, but every Whiteflower's Day there would be an island in the lake's centre, and at the same time a Door would appear in the face of the cliffs. The Door stood open, and if anyone should dare to enter they would follow a winding stair descending to a long, level passageway. This traverse beneath the lake was a right-of-way into the Fair Realm. At the top of a second stairway, a Door led out onto the island. Fair and stately was this domain, with its long, verdant lawns, its great drifts of perfumed flowers like clouds of coloured silks and confetti, its arbors dappled with freckles of golden light and lacy shade.

'The Faêran made their bedazzled guests welcome, bedecking them with garlands of flowers. They plied them with dainty viands and refreshing draughts, which were not of the Fair Realm but had been brought—stolen, perhaps—from Erith; for the Fair Folk did not wish to capture their guests, only to entertain them, before letting them go. Neither would they allow the Longing for Faêrie to come over them. Eldritch wights struck up tunes on their fiddles—Faêran musicians rarely played for the amusement of mortals—and the guests were invited to join the dancing. In mirth and revelry the day fled by, and as evening drew in the mortals must take their leave.

'The Faêran imposed only one condition on their visitors: that none should take anything from the island. Not so much as a blade of grass or a pebble must be removed. The gifts of flowers must all be put aside before the guests went down the stair to the passage beneath the lake.

'For centuries, this condition was met. Eventually, however, one man's curiosity overcame him. Just to see what would happen, he plucked a rosebud from his garland before he put it aside, and slipped the bud into the pocket of his coat.

'Down the stone stairs beneath the lake he went with the rest of the departing crowd. Halfway along the passage he felt in his pocket, but the rosebud was no longer there. At this, terrible fear gripped him, for he guessed that the Faêran had ways of knowing about transgressions like his. He hastened to the Door in the cliff face, and passed through it, and all the jovial crowd with him. As the last guest passed out of the right-of-way, a voice cried, "Woe to ye, that ye should repay our hospitality with theft." Then the Door slammed shut and, as usual, not a crack remained to show where it had been.

'But from that day forth, the island never reappeared on Whiteflower's Day, nor was there ever again any sign of the Door in the cliff face. The Faêran of the Isle never forgave mortals for that theft. They withdrew their annual invitation and closed that Gateway forever. One of the traverses to the Fair Realm was closed, never to be reopened, but it was only the first. Later, at the time of the Closing, all the rights-of-way were barred forever.'

'Why?' asked Rohain.

'Mortals have done worse than steal flowers from the Fair Realm. Some of the Faêran were greatly angered by the deeds of our kind. They wished to have no more commerce with us.'

'And you say that these traverses were barred forever? Can they not be reopened?'

'No.'

'Perhaps it is for the best,' suggested Rohain. Alys nodded.

'Never say so!' cried the Bard, now heated. 'Aia has lost its link with a world of wonder such as mortals can only dream of. The Fair Realm was and remains a perilous land, aye, and in it were snares for the unwatchful and prison towers for the foolhardy, but it was far-reaching and unfathomed and lofty and filled with many things: all kinds of birds and beasts, shoreless oceans and stars beyond measure, beauty that is spellbinding and dangerous, gramarye both rich and strange, joyousness and sorrow as piercing as any Dainnan blade. In that Realm a man may have considered himself lucky to have roamed.'

A lonely thread of music arose from outside in the night. Somewhere, someone was playing a reed flute. The thin piping in the key of E-flat minor jarred with Toby's recommenced strumming in some major key. Eventually the swooping notes and trills trailed off into silence.

The Bard said loudly, 'Where's that piment?'

Two pages came hurrying in, one with a tray of goblets, the other with a steaming jug and a towel. The fragrant brew was poured. They drank a toast to the King-Emperor, then Ercildoune commenced his next tale.

'If you wish to understand more about the Faêran,' he said, 'you must hear the tale of Eilian.'

Rohain inclined her head.

'Back in those olden times, an old couple came to Caermelor from the village of White Down Rory, to get a maidservant at the Winter Hiring Fair. They saw a comely lass with yellow hair standing a little apart from all the others and they spoke to her.'

'A Talith maiden?' murmured Rohain.

'Aye, a Talith maiden, brought low by circumstance. She told them her name was Eilian, and she hired herself to them and came to their dwelling. In the villages thereabouts it was customary for the womenfolk to while away the long Winter nights by spinning after supper. The new maidservant used to take herself out to the meadow to spin by moonlight, and some passersby said they saw the Faêran gathering around her, singing and dancing. Springtime came. As the days grew longer and the hedgerows budded and the cuckoo came back to the greenwood, Eilian ran away with the Faêran and was not seen again. To this day, the meadow where she was last seen is known as Eilian's Meadow, although folk have long forgotten the reason why.

'The old woman who had been Eilian's mistress was a midwife, and her reputation was such that she was in great demand all over the countryside, but she did not get any wealthier because those she tended were as poor as herself. About a year after Eilian's flight, on a cold, misty night with a drizzle of rain and a full moon, someone knocked at the old couple's door. The old woman opened it, to see a tall gentleman, wrapped in a cloak, holding by the bridle a gray horse.

'"I am come to fetch you to my wife," said he.

'Suspicious of the gentleman's exceptionally comely countenance and not altogether pleased by his haughty tone, the midwife was about to refuse, but a strange compulsion came over her. Despite herself, she gathered her gear and, getting up behind the stranger on his horse, rode with him until they came to Roscourt Moor. If you have ever been to Roscourt Moor you will have seen the rath they call Bryn Ithibion, the great green hill rising in the centre of the moor. Bryn Ithibion resembles a ruined fort or stronghold, crowned with standing stones, with a large rocky cairn on the north slope. When the midwife and the stranger reached it, they dismounted and he led her through the side of the rath into a large cave. Behind a screen of donkey's skins at the farther end, on a rude bed of rushes and withered bracken, lay the wife. A smoky wood fire smoldered in a small brazier, hardly taking the dismal chill off the place.

'When the old woman had helped the wife to give birth, she sat on a rough wooden stool by the fire to dress the baby. The wife asked her to stay in the cave a fortnight, to which she agreed; her old heart pitied the wife, you see, for the birthgiving had grievously worn and pained her, and her surroundings were shoddy. Every day the tall stranger, the husband, brought them food and other requirements, and every day the child and the mother grew more healthy and robust.

'One day, the husband came to the old woman with a curiously carved little box of green-hued ointment, telling her to put some on the baby's eyelids but forbidding her to touch her own eyes with it. She did as he bade, but after she had put the box away, the old woman's left eye began to itch and she rubbed it with the same finger she had used on the baby's eyes.

'Instantly she saw a wonderful sight. The cave had disappeared, and in its place was a marvelous paneled chamber, decorated in green and gold, fit for royalty. Instead of being seated on a wooden stool before a guttering fire in a brazier, she found herself in a high-backed, carved chair near an open hearth, from which a glorious warmth was blazing. Deep-piled rugs covered the polished floor, gorgeous tapestries adorned every wall, and a gold-framed mirror spanned the mantelpiece. Stifling her gasps of amazement, she crept across to where the lady lay asleep, no longer upon rushes, but on a featherbed endowed with sheets of ivory silk, the most luxurious pillows, and the richest of embroidered counterpanes. None other than the lovely yellow-haired Eilian lay sleeping there! The baby, too, who had before seemed a very ordinary little chap, was the comeliest child the midwife had ever nursed.

'Even more extraordinary was the fact that the old woman could only see all these marvels with her left eye. When she closed that eye and looked with her right, she saw everything as it had first appeared: the rough stone walls, the humble couch of rushes, the crude, unplaned furniture, and the floor of beaten dirt.

'Prudently, she did not mention her acquired faculty of vision, but while she dwelled in the cave she kept her left eye open during her waking hours, although it was sometimes confusing, and she must repeatedly wink with the right—and in this fashion she came to acquire much information about the Faêran.

'At last it was time for the midwife to go home. The tall stranger took her on horseback to her door, and once there he pushed into her hands a purse bulging with coins. Before she could thank him he was up on his horse and galloping away. Hurrying indoors she poured the money out on the kitchen table. A hill of gold gleamed before her eyes, and in great excitement she counted it. Soon she realised she had enough gold to keep herself and her husband in ease for the rest of their lives.

'What with her wealth and her power of seeing through Faêran glamour, the old woman considered herself fortunate indeed. Wise enough to know that having the Sight and the gold would put her neighbours in awe of her and cultivate jealousy among them, she said nothing about it to anyone. Besides, it was well-known that the Faêran would be vexed if any kindness of theirs was revealed to all and sundry. She even concealed her faculty and her fortune from her husband, in case he should inadvertently betray the secrets.

'Sometimes in Spring she would see the Faêran lords and ladies in the orchards, walking among the apple-blossom, or in Summer dancing within grassy rings under the night sky, and once she beheld a procession of lords and ladies on a Rade.'

'A Rade?' interjected Rohain.

'That is the term for a cavalcade of the Faêran, on their way to some entertainment, or else taking horse merely for the pleasure of the jaunt. The old woman would see them riding through the fields at dusk, with a gleam of light dancing over them more beautiful than sidereal radiance. Their long hair seemed threaded with the glint of stars and their steeds were the finest ever seen, with long sweeping tails and manes hung about with bells that the wind played on. A high hedge of hawthorn would have kept them from going through the cornfield, but they leaped over it like birds and galloped into a green hill beyond. In the morning she would go to look at the treaded corn, but never a hoofmark was imprinted, nor a blade broken.

'One day she happened to go earlier than usual to market, and as she went about her business amongst the booths and stalls she rounded a corner and came face-to-face with the tall stranger who had knocked at her door on that misty evening. Trying to cover her surprise, she put on a bold front and said, "Good morrow, sir. How fare Eilian and the bonny young boy?"

'The stranger politely replied, with favourable tidings of his wife and child. Then he asked conversationally, "But with which eye do you see me?"

'"With this one," said the old woman, pointing to the left.

'At that he laughed. Producing a bulrush, he put out her eye and was gone at once. She never saw any of the Faêran again.'

'Fie!' exclaimed Rohain, sitting bolt upright. 'Another severe and brutal punishment for a small fault. After all, the woman meant no harm—she merely rubbed her own eye, and that without fore-thought or malice! Why should she be blinded so painfully?'

'Terrible was the revenge of the Faêran angered,' said Ercildoune, taking a draught from his goblet.

'The tale only serves to illustrate my point,' said the Duchess of Roxburgh.

Ercildoune laughed. 'Alys views the Faêran race as through a black crystal,' he said. 'To each his own thought. Mine is the opposite view.'

'Ercildoune would discover benevolence in the Each Uisge himself,' rejoined the Duchess drily.

'The girl Eilian must have thought well of the Faêran,' said Rohain.

'That is likely,' replied the Duchess. 'In the end, though, she was exiled from the Fair Realm for some minor transgression, and pined away to a miserable end.'

'A harsh fate,' said Rohain presently.

'But you must not judge without knowing all,' said the Bard. 'That pining was not put on Eilian by the husband, or indeed by any of the Faêran—it was the inevitable effect of the Fair Realm on all mortals who entered it. No mortal could dwell for more than a short period within the Fair Realm and return to Aia without lan-guishing thereafter, yearning ceaselessly to return, being filled with unutterable longing. The longer the stay, the fiercer the crav-ing. This affliction was called the Langothe. Wilfred, bring more piment. Another story will illustrate.'

The lynx on the cushion stood up, yawned, disemboweled its bed, and settled again. Its master began another tale.

'Perdret Olvath was a very pretty girl who lived in Luindorn. Being from a poor family, she made her living in service. It is said that she was a girl who liked to indulge in flights of fancy, or romance, as some would call it. Conscious of her own comeliness,

she was also rather vain. Pretty women have a right to vanity, in
this gentleman's humble opinion, but others would not agree.
Perdret would take great care to dress herself as well as possible,
in colourful, flattering clothes; she twined wildflowers in her hair
and attracted the attention of all the young men, to the envy of the
other lasses. She was also highly susceptible to flattery, and, being
unsophisticated and without education, was unable to conceal this
fact. If anyone praised her looks, her eyes would light up with
pleasure.

'Perdret having been without a situation for some time, her
mother was anxious to see her employed. No positions were available in the local area, so she told her daughter that she must look
further afield. The girl did not want to leave her village, but there
was no choice. She packed her few meager possessions and set off.

'She walked a long way, and everything seemed to be going
well until she came to the crossroads on the downs, when she discovered that she knew not which road to take. She looked first
one way and then another, until she felt mightily bewildered;
should she choose some path at random or return home or stay
where she was? Unable to decide, she sat down on a granite boulder and began in dreaming idleness to break off the fronds of
ferns which grew in profusion all around. She had not sat long on
this stone when, hearing a voice near her, she turned around and
saw a handsome young man wearing a green silken coat covered
with ornaments of gold.

'"Good morrow, young maiden," said he. "And what are you
doing here?"

'"I am looking for work," said she.

'"And what kind of work seek you, my pretty damsel?" said he
with a charming smile.

'"Any kind of work," said she, quite dazzled. "I can turn my
hand to many things."

'"Do you think you could look after a widower with one little
boy?" asked the young man.

'"I dote on children," said Perdret. "And I am used to taking
care of them."

'"I will hire you," he said, "for a year and a day. But first,

Perdret Olvath"—Perdret gaped in wonderment when she discovered the stranger knew her name, but he laughed. "Oh, I see, you thought I didn't know you, but do you think a young widower could pass through your village and not notice such a pretty lass? Besides," he said, "I watched you one day combing your hair and gazing at your reflection in one of my ponds. You stole some of my perfumed violets to put in your lovely hair."

'Seduced by his winning ways, the girl was more than half inclined to accept his offer, but her mother had trained her to be careful. "Where do you live?" she asked.

"'Not far from here," said the young stranger. "Will you accept the place and come with me?"

"'First, I would ask about wages."

'He told her that she could ask her own wages, whereupon visions of wealth and luxury rose before Perdret's eyes.

"'But only if you come with me at once, without returning home," he added. "I will send word to your mother."

"'But my clothes . . . " said Perdret.

"'The clothes you have are all that will be necessary, and I'll put you in much finer raiment soon."

"'Well then," Perdret said, "we are agreed!"

"'Not yet," said the stranger. "I have a way of my own, and you must swear my oath."

'A look of alarm spread across Perdret's face.

"'You need not be afraid," said the stranger very kindly. "I only ask that you kiss that fernleaf which you have in your hand and say, 'For a year and a day I promise to stay.'"

"'Is that all?" said Perdret, and she did so.

'Without another word he turned and began to walk along the road leading eastward. Perdret followed him, but she thought it strange that her new master went in silence all the way. They walked on for a long time until Perdret grew weary and her feet began to ache. It seemed that she had been walking forever, and not a word spoken. The poor girl felt so exhausted and so dispirited that at last she began to cry. At the sound of her sobs, her new master turned around.

"'Are you tired, Perdret? Sit down," he said. Taking her by the hand, he led her to a mossy bank. Overwhelmed by this display of kindness, she burst out weeping. He allowed her to cry for a few minutes before he said, "Now I shall dry your eyes."

'Taking a sprig of leaves from the bank, he passed it swiftly across one of her eyes, then the other. Instantly her tears and all weariness vanished. Perdret realised she was walking again, but could not remember having left the bank.

'Now, the way began to slope downwards. Green banks rose up on either side and the road passed swiftly underground. The girl was not a little apprehensive, but she had struck a bargain and was more frightened of going back than forward. After a time, her new master halted.

'"We are almost there, Perdret," he said. "But I see a tear glittering on your eyelid. No mortal tears can enter here."

'As before, he brushed her eyes with the leaves. They stepped forward and the tunnel opened out.

'Before them spread a country such as Perdret had never before seen. Flowers of every hue covered the hills and valleys; the region appeared like a rich tapestry sewn with gems which glittered in a light as clear as that of the Summer sun, yet as mellow as moonlight. Rivers flowed, more lucid than any water she had ever seen on the granite hills. Waterfalls bounded down the hillsides, fountains danced in rainbows of brilliant droplets. Tall trees in belts and thickets bore both fruit and blossom at once. Ladies and gentlemen dressed in green and gold walked or sported, or reposed on banks of flowers, singing songs or telling stories. Indeed, it was a world more beautiful and exciting than words could describe.

'Perdret's master took her to a stately mansion in which all the furniture was of pearl or ivory, inlaid with gold and silver and studded with emeralds. After passing through many rooms they came to one which was hung all over with snow-white lace, as fine as the finest cobweb, most beautifully worked with flowers. In the middle of this room stood a little cot made out of some beautiful seashell, which reflected so many colours that Perdret could scarcely bear to look at it. Sleeping in the cot was the sweetest little boy she had ever seen.

"'This is your charge," said the father. "You have nothing to do but wash him when he wakes, dress him and take him to walk in the garden, then put him to bed when he is tired. I am a lord in this land and I have my own reasons for wishing my boy to know something of human nature."

'Perdret began her duties and did them well and diligently. She loved the little boy and he appeared to love her, and the time passed away with astonishing swiftness. Strangely, she never thought of her mother—she never thought of her home at all. Dwelling in luxury and happiness, she never reckoned the passing of time.

'But the period for which she had bound herself finally ended, and one day she woke up in her own bed in her mother's cottage. Everything seemed unfamiliar to her and she appeared unusually abstracted or foreign to all who saw her. She could evince no interest in meat or drink. At nights, instead of sleeping, she would go out under the stars and gaze up at them. Sometimes she would wander all night, barefoot, only to be found exhausted on her bed in the morning, unable to rise. She grew pale and thin and was hardly ever seen to smile. Numerous wise persons were called in to try to cure Perdret's ailment, and to all she told the same tale, about the Faêran lord, and the beautiful country and the baby. She being known for her fanciful turn of mind, some people said the girl was "gone clean daft" but at last an old carlin came to the cottage where Perdret lay on her bed.

"'Now crook your arm, Perdret," said the carlin.

'Perdret sat up and bent her arm, resting her hand on her hip.

"'Now say, 'I hope my arm may never come uncrooked if I have told ye a word of a lie.'"

"'I hope my arm may never come uncrooked if I have told ye a word of a lie," repeated Perdret.

"'Uncrook your arm," said the carlin.

'Perdret stretched out her arm.

"'It is the truth the girl is telling," said the carlin. "She has been carried away by the Faêran to their country."

"'Will my daughter ever come right in her mind?" asked the mother.

"'I can do nothing,' said the old woman, shaking her head. "Perhaps she will, in time."

The Bard having finished his soliloquy, the Duchess added, 'Anyway, it is told that Perdret did not get on very well in the world. She married, and never wanted for anything, but she was always discontented and unhappy, and she died young.'

'Verily,' said the Bard, 'some said she always pined after the Faêran widower. Others said she pined after the Fair Realm itself. No matter the reason, it was the Langothe that plagued her.'

'And was that the same Faêran lord who had been husband to Eilian?' Rohain inquired.

'I think not. The first tale happened subsequent to the second. I have told them out of order. Over the course of time, more than one fair mortal maiden has been taken away to the Realm.'

'Did the Faêran steal mortal men as well as maids and wives?' asked Rohain.

'Most certainly,' came the Duchess's quick reply.

'Well,' declared Rohain, 'it seems to me that the Strangers were a dangerous race, selfish and arrogant, cruel in many ways, excessively wanton and proud in their immortality.'

'Yet theirs was a conditional immortality,' observed the Bard sharply.

'What do you mean?'

'Age and disease could not slay them, but they could be defeated by violence.'

'Even then,' amended the Duchess, 'they could only be diminished, not destroyed.'

'Yet what mortal violence could defeat the gramarye wielded by the Lords of the Fair Realm?' argued Rohain. After a silence, she added, 'Is it possible that any folk of their blood remained in Erith—perhaps children of mixed races, both Faêran and mortal, like the child of Eilian?'

'Historically,' said the Bard, 'very few Half-Faêran have been born—perhaps a score, that is all. None have walked our world since the Ways were closed. They chose to stay on the other side.'

'What of their progeny? The children of the Half-Faêran?'

'There is no such issue. The Half-Faêran were all barren.'

'Is it possible that one of the Faêran could be stolen by a mortal?' Rohain asked.

'Indeed!' responded the Duchess. 'There were ways, if one knew how. Many a mortal man has been drawn into desperate love after setting eyes on a Faêran damsel. To see the Faêran was to be attracted to them. In truth, some Faêran damsels who desired mortals—I will not say "loved", for I believe they were all incapable of love as we know it—allowed themselves to be caught as brides.' She paused, then added, 'And it was possible for Faêran brides to be taken by men.'

'But surely, never against their will!' exclaimed Rohain.

'Only once,' said Thomas, 'has an abduction like that occurred, and only because, as in the tale of the swanmaiden, foolish chattering wights gave away the secret of how to do it. They revealed the rules to a man of our race who, smitten with the sickness of love, was able to capture a Faêran bride.' A troubled shadow fleeted in the depths of his eyes. 'That particular tale is another example of our race stealing from the Faêran—perhaps the most significant example of all. The theft of a Faêran bride by a lowly mortal greatly roused the ire of some of the Fair Realm's greatest lords. Thereafter, one Faêran prince in particular began to take pleasure in the company of unseelie wights whose delight was to plague and torment mortals.'

'But how could a mortal man steal a Faêran damsel?', wondered Rohain.

'They could not be stolen in the same way as wightish brides,' explained Thomas, 'as, for example, power is gained over merrows by taking their combs, over swanmaidens by stealing their feather-cloaks, over silkies by purloining their skins. But there were certain words and deeds which could force the Faêran to remain in our world, at least for a time.'

'But not for long,' interjected the Duchess, nodding for emphasis, 'and after she left him he pined away to, if you'll excuse the cliché, an early grave. As ever, all love between immortals and mortals was doomed. In the end, all unions between Faêran and humankind ended in tragedy.'

Groups of peasants stamping in the cold went about Caermelor singing traditional songs on street corners and before the doors of townsfolk, to be rewarded with coins or wrapped cakes and common flagons of mulled ale. Carts rumbled along the streets bearing great logs cut from the forest to supply the Imbroltide fires. Marketplace trade rose to fever pitch. Lanterns burned all night in workshops as tradesmen hurried to meet deadlines on orders for the nobility, the exchange of gifts being one of the most eagerly looked-for customs of Imbrol.

Coloured lamps had been strung along the streets, vying with glowing garnets of charcoal in the braziers of the hot-chestnut vendors. Under the Greayte Southern Star, Caermelor bustled late into the freezing nights and scarcely slept, despite rowdy winds that knocked the lamps about and blew out the charcoal fires, despite the lightning that danced like green skeletons all across the western skies.

This was angry weather, uncharacteristic of Imbrol. Some people were blaming it on the gathering of unseelie swarms in Namarre. ''Tis *their* doing,' they muttered darkly. ''Tis but a premonition of the first assault. Wicked wights allied with barbarians! How are such enemies ever to be defeated?' Beneath the outward merriment, horror flowed through the thoroughfares of the city.

New Year's Eve.

When the bells tolled the last stroke of midnight, Misrule would reign until dawn on Littlesun Day. The tradition of Misrule entailed the annual turning of the tables that saw lord trade places with footman and lady step into the shoes of chambermaid, so that, for a few hours, the world would be topsy-turvy and Foolery would be the order of the night until cock-crow.

But hours before all that, there was the Feast.

Grander and far more expansive than the Royal Dining Hall, the Royal Banqueting Hall boasted eight fireplaces, in each of which burned a massive tree trunk, the traditional Imbrol Log. Coincidentally, eight Waits stood vigil in their splendor to fanfare the courses. The High Table on its dais was so far removed from the opposite end of the Hall that those who graced it could scarcely be expected to discern the countenances of those seated at the lower trestles, or even the central ones—a state of affairs that, despite the blaze of countless girandoles, lusters, and candelabra, was exacerbated by the soft haze of steam and incense filling the air. Below the high dais lay a second platform, innocent of furniture. Here, some of the entremets would be played out between courses.

All plate was of gold or the harder, more brilliant silver-gilt. White light dazzled over its myriad surfaces. Not a gleam of silver, copper, brass, or bronze winked forth.

For ornament there were golden surtouts in the shape of fruiting and blossoming trees. Cakes had been fashioned and frosted to resemble white castles, cities of dough and Sugar, glittering coaches-and-six, peacocks in full display, sprays of lily-of-the-valley, bouquets of roses, the traditional spinning-wheels of Imbrol, snowy ducks and geese. The sideboards struggled to support pyramids of ripe and luscious fruits from the Royal Conservatory, forced to grow out of season, all surrounded by garlands of evergreens and berries. For the occasion, the salt cellars took the shape of ceremonial snow-sleighs, hung about with tiny gold bells and emblazoned with the King-Emperor's insignia. The linen serviettes were folded in enchanting forms of snowflakes. Superfluous napkin rings, garlands of holly and other Winter leaves individually crafted in gold, lay empty next to every place setting.

More accustomed now to the dangers of mistaking blade, prong, and scoop, Rohain silently revised the different uses for each piece included in her place setting: the oyster fork nestling in the soup spoon; the marrow scoop; the pairs of knives and forks each dedicated to the fish, the meat, and the poultry; the dessert spoon and fork; the fruit knife; the tiny bonbon tongs. Beyond the boundaries of her place lay the cutlery to be shared: the suckett forks, condiment spoons, Sugar shells, mote spoons, pickle forks, butter picks, nut picks, cheese scoops, horseradish spoons, and various others, not to be confused with the soup ladles, fish slicers, jelly servers, snuff spoons, and wick scissors to be wielded by the servants.

Most of the courtiers were already drunk when they entered the Royal Banqueting Hall—Rohain among them. They had been junketing all day, insisting that she match them deed for deed, and, loathe to relinquish her new status, she had acceded. Unaccustomed to imbibing liquor, she had succumbed to it more swiftly than they. The Hall swam before her eyes.

Everyone was standing beside their chairs. The High Table filled last of all—the lords of the Royal Attriod and the chief advisors of the King-Emperor's Household entered with their wives, preceding by several minutes the young Prince Edward. When the King-Emperor appeared, an awed hush settled on the assembly, yet in good form, none regarded their sovereign directly. His Majesty took his seat in the tall chair overshadowed by its richly decorated canopy, after which everyone else followed suit.

Now Rohain noted that one of the long tables was occupied entirely by Dainnan warriors in dress uniform: thigh-length doublets overlaid by tabards emblazoned with the Royal Heraldry. She strained to view them. Some were positioned with their backs to her. Of those she could descry, none were Thorn, but her gaze fastened on that table and it was difficult to look away.

Pages and ewerers came to pour scented water for the handwashing. Rohain looked up. The face of the boy holding the ewer for her seemed familiar.

'You!' blurted Rohain suddenly, and not particularly distinctly.

'I beg your pardon, m'lady?'

'You! Where have I seen you before?'

'I am sure I do not know,' stammered the lad, embarrassed.

'I have seen you. Oh yes, I know now—'

She checked herself. Realisation had dawned. This was the cabin boy from the merchant ship *City of Gilvaris Tarv*. He would not recognise her. Joy welled in her heart—he, then, had been saved. What of his shipmates?

'You were once in the employ of a merchant line, the Cresny-Beaulais, were you not?'

'Aye, m'lady, but—'

'Your ship was scuttled by pirates. What happened to the crew?'

Nonplussed, the boy stammered, 'Some were slain, m'lady.

Others escaped. The captain, he was ransomed. Others were sold as slaves, methinks.'

His eyes showed his obvious desperation to ask how she knew so much about him, but he was too well-drilled to question a high-born lady.

'And you escaped?'

'Aye, m'lady.'

Rohain peeled a ruby-encrusted bracelet from her wrist. It matched her outfit—tonight she was clad all in crimson and gold, with a hint of jade. Viviana had braided silk rosebuds into her crimped locks. A vermilion plume within the circlet of a band of cornelians nodded over them. Tiny red roses had been appliquéd in lace all over the watered silk of her houppelande. Her bodice was scalloped, edged with appliquéd rose leaves, her waist was clasped by a scarlet-purple girdle harnessed with gold beads and lattice. The sleeves fell in lacy folds to the floor.

'Take this,' she said, proffering the bracelet. 'It pleases me to give it you. Sell it, if you wish. If ever you need help, ask for me. If ever you require a position, ask at the Estate of Arth— Argh— that is, Arcune. I am to be Baroness of it, y'know.' Unaccountably, her tongue seemed to have thickened. It appeared to be reluctant to shape words.

'By the Powers, my lady! I thank you.'

''Tis nought. You deserve it.'

A lad as acute as the erstwhile cabin boy might have been expected to complete his task in haste, in case his benefactress should sober and reverse her benevolence. Instead he performed the rest of his duties slowly and wonderingly, then bowed and withdrew.

Servitors ported trays laden with hunches of fluffy white bread up and down the tables, beginning at the top. Each diner was served, with a flourish and a pair of tongs, accompanied by a loud declaration of his title and honour, whereupon he stood up and afterward sat down again. Simultaneously, the Credence and the Assaying took place. Wines were dispensed by footman-bees, filling with nectar the goblet-flowers. Snow floated in the wine jugs.

''Tis going to be ever such a capital occasion tonight!' cried a lady in a turquoise surcoat of figured satin and a lavender kirtle with an upstanding collar of stiffened wigan. 'I adore play-acting at Misrule, don't you? I intend to be an ever so slovenly scullery maid, and make my footman a prince!'

'Don't take it too far, my dear,' rejoined another in an embroidered gable headdress and an apricot-coloured gown of shot silk. 'One never knows what a prince may ask of a scullery maid!'

'Faugh! Jenkin would never overstep the mark with me!'

'Unless you beg him,' Dianella said sweetly. Her friends shrieked, to High Collar's thinly disguised discomfiture. Dianella turned to Rohain. 'Zounds, Dear Heart, quot wroughtst-thou un sa manfant pove? Mi sugen esprait quill overgrand pash-thou es.' *What have you done to that poor lad? I should say he is mightily in love with you.*

'Ta ferle-fil?' *That page boy?* replied Rohain offhandedly. 'Quot sugen cheyen-mi al ins?' *What should I care for him?*

She had learned to answer Dianella's audacity with stoicism.

That comely doyenne of innuendo, her beautiful head encased in a pointed turban topped with clusters of golden baubles, turned to those seated near her and began to converse in rapid slingua. Shadowy tresses fell loose across her smooth white shoulders to the damask bodice, the heavy diamond necklace.

The Waits trumpeted fiercely. Far across the room, at the High Table, someone rose up from behind the table-decorations to propose the Toast. Rohain could make out a tall, distinguished figure across the tables. When he spoke, his reverberant voice revealed him to be Thomas of Ercildoune. The Royal Toast and the Loving Cup were attended to in due order, after which Rohain seemed to see many more accoutrements upon the table in front of her than had been there previously. She knew she had taken too much to drink, but to refuse the traditional pre-dinner draughts would have been uncouth. This insobriety hampered her efforts to discover Thorn among the Dainnan and her ability to converse in a sprightly manner.

With utmost pageantry, the Soup was revealed and consumed. There followed the first entremet of this Imbrol Feast—a score of dancers in sildron harness, costumed as the cicada-like species of creatures called the Five-Eyed. They had encased their faces in masks with convexities of glass for the large eyes and a triad of jewels for the small. Helmets clasped their heads, bronze cuirasses covered their chests and backs. Wings of gauze and silk like rippled glass, spangled with sequins, expanded from their shoulders in sapphire blue, gold, and emerald green. At their hips they wore factitious tymbals, and their heels were spurred.

To the rattle of nakers and other percussive paraphernalia, these exotics performed a gliss-dance of prodigious gymnastic skill, floating above the heads of the diners, grasping each other by the arms to change direction or pulling on streamers and crosiers; spinning and gliding, pushing off the walls, somersaulting, flying. At the conclusion the diners applauded enthusiastically and the next course was served: golden carp suspended in coloured gelatins and whole baked dolphins on beds of oysters, complete with pearls. The butlers built pyramids of balancing goblets and poured wine into the topmost ones. The torrent splashed lavishly down from layer to layer in a spectacular cascade of pale gold.

A display of swordsmanship next entertained the Court. A hefty purse having been promised to the winner, the combatants treated it as no light matter. Three dueling pairs, all accomplished professionals, fought with foils, sabers and épées. In a fine exhibition, they footed it up and down the lower dais in front of the High Table. Through the milky airs, beyond the candle-flames that shifted and jumped, beyond the gleams that glanced off dinner- ware and played ocular tricks, Rohain dimly descried figures leaning on their elbows, watching. At the far-off tables that stood nearest the High Table, the only identifiable faces belonged to the comely Lady Rosamonde, eldest daughter of the Duke of Roxburgh, the balding Dowager Marchioness of Netherby-on-the-Fens in her incongruous and outrageously expensive wig of real Talith hair, and the young Talith noblewoman Maiwenna, her good looks framed by naturally acquired gold.

Nearer at hand, a group from Rimany, born of the Ice-Race called the Arysk, sat like a row of lilies or plumy white birds, wearing the feathers of albino peacocks and ibis. Ivory of skin were they, their locks of pure white silk framing grave faces and eyes of palest blue. Like the trows, they favoured silver for adornment, and as for apparel, they chose only white silk and gauze and cloth-of-silver, ice blue or sea gray. Sudden blood-red, like a stab wound, was the only bright hue of their decoration, deepest carmine velvet edged with sable. They kept to themselves—Rohain had only been introduced to one of their number, the Lady Solveig of Ixtacutl. The candlelight had described in her eyes ice-pinnacles tinged by a flame of sunset.

Blood having been shed, the swordfighting event closed in time for the ensuing dish, which appeared to consist of a bloated ox. In roasted state, surrounded by glazed worts, parsley, nasturtiums, and sausages, the beast was wheeled in on a golden cart drawn by skittish reindeer, to be presented at the High Table. As the cart halted before the dais, Roxburgh stood up. His voice roared out across the Hall. A horrified silence fell abruptly over the assembly.

'What's this? An ox for dinner at Imbrol? And look at it! Is this fit to be presented to His Majesty? Has it not even been gutted and stuffed? Are we to chew entrails? Bring the Master Cook. We'll see him hanged for this incompetence!'

The Royal Cook was dragged sniveling and groveling from the kitchens. On his knees before the High Table he begged for mercy, rolling his eyes hideously.

'Your Majesty! Your Highness, Your Graces, have pity! I did my best, but there was no time—'

'Silence!' roared Roxburgh. 'I'll see *you* gutted instead!'

'But sir,' said the Cook, 'I'd rather show you the beast's innards than mine.'

With that he drew a long knife from his side and in one easy movement slashed open the ox's stomach. A cheer went up from the diners as an entire roasted cow rolled out. A slash along the cow's abdomen revealed a baked doe. Inside the venison was a nicely cooked sheep, stuffed with a pig, crammed with a turkey that contained a pigeon packed with forcemeat. By now the audience was applauding madly. The Royal Cook capered. Roxburgh threw back his head and made the Hall ring with his laughter—of course, it had all been a jest, and planned from start to finish. The Dainnan Commander threw a purse to the Cook. A tribe of footmen rolled away the Seven-In-One to be operated on by a bevy of Carvers.

The next course was roasted peacocks, brought forth with wads of burning camphor and wool stuck in their beaks, spitting flames, to be paraded in their jewelled plumage and then devoured. After that, files of liveried servitors triumphantly brought forth pies which, when their pastry lids were cut, released live birds to fly around the hall.

Barring dessert, there could not have been a more complete repast. Many a noble waistline bulged. Pages, footmen, butlers, cup-bearers, all were kept busy scurrying back and forth at the whims of their masters and mistresses. As the last sanap was removed in preparation for the final collation, all entremets disappeared and an orchestra played soft music from the gallery. The musicians gleamed with their own perspiration. Like a field of burning goldenrod flowers, feverish candles blazed, stuck in wrought brackets attached to the sheet-music stands.

The courtiers murmured expectantly.

The Royal Bard rose from his chair. Beckoning to a group of half a dozen boys who had been waiting in the wings, he strode down from the dais to a golden harp that stood there, its frame formed like a giant fish with waves streaming from its scales. All fell silent once more.

'I sing "The Holly,"' he announced, seating himself at the harp.

Backed by the harmonies of the youthful choir, the Bard sang a traditional song of Imbrol. All those assembled raised their voices in the last verse, and a grand swelling of sound it was—it seemed to rock the walls and lift the very ceiling.

Thomas of Ercildoune waved the choir away and once more touched the strings of his Carp Harp. In a voice both rich and mellow, which carried clearly to all those seated in the Hall, he began a serenade:

> 'My love, though I should never wish that we
> Should even by a hair's breadth parted be,
> There shall be times when we must dwell apart—
> Then would I keep some emblem to my heart;
> A token of thee, lady whom I cherish,
> That of the lack of thee I may not perish—

A part of thee which no one else could make,
And yet, that would not harm thee for to take;
A pledge of thy return, a treasured thing
More tender than a portrait or a ring;
A part of thee which of thee shall remain.
Thus, sundered we shall never be again;
So if beside thee, love, I cannot be—
I pray thee, spare a lock of hair to me.'

Tears brimmed in Rohain's eyes. She forbade them to fall. Had Thorn kept the twist of hair he had stolen from her, or had he tossed it away? The Bard bowed to the High Table and was commended on his performance.

'My apprentice, Toby,' said Ercildoune, 'has been practicing some epic these last days, methinks. Let us hear it now, Toby.'

'If it please Your Majesty, I shall play "Candlebutter",' said Toby, bowing low. The courtiers stirred appreciatively. It was one of those old, well-known songs that, although the words bore no relevance to the occasion, was always thought of as indispensable to Imbrol.

'For those who are not aware of the manner of speech used in some regions, candlebutter is an archaic or rustic name for gold,' said Toby in a clear voice. 'The ballad is made upon the true story of the Dark Daughter, as happened, they say, in days of yore. 'Tis an ancient song and many a minstrel has passed it down through the years. Now it is my turn. I shall try to do it justice.' Taking up a lyre for accompaniment, Toby half sang, half chanted a long, strange ballad. As the last liquid notes of the lyre trickled away, the singer bowed. His audience remained, for a time, under the spell of the curious old song.

Hardly had they begun to applaud when a loud explosion and a wizardly cloud of purple smoke from the lower doors heralded the arrival of the Puddings. Upon matching gray steeds, in rode twelve masked equestrians outfitted to represent the twelve months of the Year. Wearing sildron bracelets to bear up the weight, they held aloft flaming spheres of compacted suet, peel, Sugar, brandy, and fruits, whose purpose was to resemble the burning sun in a half-serious attempt to lure the real one back from its Winter retreat in the north. All who viewed these triumphal orbs did so with the anticipation of being fortunate enough to find within their portion one of the lucky silver tokens hidden there. These apparitions jogged once around the Hall, pausing to genuflect to the High Table, the horses having been trained to do the same. They deposited their guttering burdens on the sideboards for subsequent butchery and departed in another burst of smoke and noise.

'La! Uncle never did things by halves!' commented Dianella, covering her ears.

The uncle mentioned, being the Lord High Wizard, Sargoth the Cowled, commenced his customary Imbrol Spectacle directly after dessert. The fame of this man had reached to all the corners of Erith, even to the Tower at Isse, where he had been spoken of with awe and excitement. Rohain soon saw that his reputation had not been overpraised. He demonstrated each of the Nine Arts with utmost skill and aplomb, revealing himself as a true Master of Wizardry. Compared with Sargoth, Zimmuth of Isse Tower seemed but an apprentice.

Servants went around snuffing out candles. The darkened Hall became the scene of wizardly lightning, flame, sparks, and smoke. Between thunders the orchestra played. On the dais below the High Table Sargoth transformed maidens into wolves, wolves into tyraxes, and tyraxes to watch-worms. He sawed men in half; the halves walked around by themselves and were rejoined later. He chopped men into little pieces and restored them to life. He made them disappear, only to reappear where least expected. Inanimate objects came to life. In his ungloved hand, water turned to fire and fire to water. He levitated without a sildron harness. He seemed aflame, he walked through fire unscathed. He performed feats of gramarye that left his audience gawping. In short, he was astounding.

A bell tolled eleven. On the eleventh stroke, the wizard vanished for the last time, leaving a rain of gold, silver, and scarlet sparks to descend slowly into the foggy Hall. A cheer went up—it was time to prepare for Misrule. Footmen scurried to relight the candles. Their light, leaking through the haze, showed that the

High Table had already been half-deserted. In order of importance, the courtiers now absented themselves from the Banqueting Hall, repairing to their suites to dress for the Midnight Ball.

With a rustle of silk, Dianella, attired in the costliest of fabrics cut in peasant style, entered Rohain's boudoir. She was followed by her lady's maid.

'Are you almost ready, Dear Heart?' she said with a sweet smile. 'The night wears on! Allow me to help you with your coiffure. Servants do not know how to prosecute such affairs successfully. Besides, I have been told your maid's sight is impaired.'

Biting her lip, Viviana stepped back. Rohain allowed Dianella to rearrange her curls.

'Like this, see?' said Dianella, teasing out loose strands. 'A little messy, like a maid who's forgotten to tidy herself—'twould be true to type, I ween. What a capital costume—it does show your figure to advantage! I see your skivvy-girl here is wearing the one of your gowns I most admire, oh, I could almost be jealous! Yet breeding will tell—the most gracious of raiment cannot enhance a low-born face. What's this?' She peered closely at Rohain's hair. 'What have you done to the roots? Why, I declare! Griffin, get out of here. You too.' She rounded on the two lady's maids, who hastily removed themselves.

Rohain drooped, wine-befuddled, before the looking-glass. 'What is the matter with my hair, Dianella?'

'Only that the roots are beginning to grow out gold. How entirely fascinating! Come, come, what are you hiding from us?'

'I hide nothing! If I am Talith, what of it?'

'Of course. What of it indeed! Nobody of any consequence wears their hair yellow these days—only old quizzes like the Dowager Marchioness of Netherby, and cold fish like Maiwenna. Verily, it is out of style. You had better have it seen to quickly— Griffin shall dye it for you on the morrow; she is *taraiz* adept. There's not a moment to lose. Contrasting roots are *so* out of favour!'

She held up a strand of Rohain's hair between finger and thumb.

'La! What emulsion have you used, Heart? Your hair positively glows. Most of the usual black dyestuffs coarsen the tresses something *storfenlent.*'

'I do not know what it was called. My hair was dyed for me by a carlin in White Down Rory.'

'I must know her name, this adept witch of the hairdressing!'

Only half attending, Rohain said, 'She is called Maeve One-Eye. Shall the ladies of the Court dance with the Dainnan tonight?'

Dianella laughed her silvery tinkle.

'The ladies of the Court may do many things on *this* night of the Year. All of Roxburgh's stalwarts are *sofine* and unco' gallant—dare I surmise that your eye has rested upon one in particular, *es raith-na?*'

A gong sounded the call to the Ballroom. Dianella glided to the window and peered out. In the darkness below, torches flared.

Rohain rose unsteadily from her seat by the dressing-table.

'Do you know of a Dainnan by the name of Thorn?'

'Thorn?' Dianella paused, without turning around. 'Nay, I think not. Nay, I am certain I have not heard that name. Have you asked anyone else?'

'No.'

'Well it would be best not to, Dear Heart. It does not look so well, you understand, a lady in your position asking after one of the King-Emperor's hired men, dashing though they be. I am sure you will see this man again, by and by.' She lifted from her chatelaine an ivory mirror-case depicting a tournament. Knights jousted while nobles watched from a high gallery. Ivory heralds sounded long trumpets. After a quick glance at her reflection, she snapped it shut. 'Is he very much in love with you?'

'I hardly know him.'

'But of course! You would be saving yourself for a viscount, at the very least! I am sure your Dainnan loves you from afar, in truest chivalry, with most ardent and *untainted* passion. *Cai dreambliss!* Have you your dance-cards and fan? Come now, take my hand—let us away to the Ball. We must be there before midnight. That is when the best fun begins!'

A great stillness fell, near and far.

In the gardens and courtyards of the palace, bonfires flared, inviting the Winter sun's return. A band of well-wrapped musicians sustained the circles of dancers around each conflagration. Some maidens ran, screaming 'Bogles in the hedges!' Someone, it was reported, had seen them—but it turned out to be a mere folly.

The city bells rang a carillon for midnight.

A mighty cheer went up to the starry skies, and a blowing of horns and a rampage of bells and drums. In the Royal Ballroom, the oboe, the clarinet, the viol, the shawm and hautboy, the serpent, the trumpet, the horn and timpani, the triangle, the gittern, and the double bass struck up.

The Royal Ballroom stood wide and high, its painted, paneled, festooned walls lined with mirrors and chairs, the latter occupied by ladies with fans and gentlemen with snuff-boxes, many of these observers being in various stages of coquetry and flirtation. Dancers packed the floor. It would seem to an onlooker that servant and master, both simple and gentle, mingled without regard to propriety: cup-bearer and countess, minion and marquess, drudge and Dainnan, valet and viscount, laundry-maid and lord, nursery-maid and noble, equerry and earl, squire and seigneur, henchman and high-born lady. With blue glass gleaming at her throat like sapphires, a ragged scullion whirled in the arms of an under-butler with gold-buckled shoes, whose jacket had been turned inside out. A queenly dame in cloth-of-gold partnered an elderly, bewhiskered steward; a kitchen-maid in a stained apron trod the boards with a velveted duke while a baroness danced with a pastry-cook. The Yeoman to the Royal Wine Cellar footed it with the Countess of Sheffield, and the Master of Robes trifled with a gardener's daughter in damson silk and a golden chatelaine. It was all bewildering in the extreme, which indeed was the intention, for the period between midnight and sunrise on Littlesun Day was a dangerous time when anything might happen.

On this the longest night, dark-loving eldritch things roamed abroad—in particular, unseelie entities out to do harm to mortals—and if they should be led astray by appearances, if they should not be able to identify those upon whom they spied, then there was a chance that they would have less power to wreak mischief upon them during the coming year. With reversal in mind, acrobats walked about on their hands, their feet waving in the air, wearing gauntlets over their shoes. Jesters, dressed as birds and butterflies with stars on their heads, toddled here and there; others, wrapped in swaddling to represent the worms of the soil, glissanded near the ceiling.

The lowliest drudge, a young, uncomely maid whose distasteful daily duties included the emptying of chamber-pots, presided over the Ball. Smiling in genuine glee, this Queen of Misrule sat on one of the King-Emperor's very thrones, with a paste-and-paint crown stuck askew upon her curls and glass baubles winking on every joint. Ercildoune, who loved such occasions, made great show of falling upon his knees before her, offering tray after tray of sweetmeats and wine. In his joskin's garb, he looked quite the yokel, although rather rakish. His performance, however, was soon eclipsed by Goblet-As-Footman. His powdered wig on sideways, his long-toed shoes tripping him up at the slightest provocation, the Royal Jester fell on many people—judiciously selected. He fell into the lap of the Queen of Misrule and was mortified and begged forgiveness, but, unforgiven, tried to hang himself with a noose whose frayed end he held high in his own hand. When suicide failed, he implored pardon again; she kissed him, and he was so elated that he cut a caper, tripped on his shoes, and landed in her lap once again. In disgust, his fellow jesters heaved him up by the hands and feet and threw him into the multitude, whereupon he was passed from hand to hand over their heads around the room. None scorned to join this activity, least of all those of the Set. In all seasons Goblet was deemed fashionable by the Set, even though he was, by choice, not part of it. His scathing tongue could strip face and facade from those he chose to mock; as jester, he was licensed to lampoon; none bar a very few would not give way before him, and most would not wish to do so. He was popular despite his acerbic wit and because of it; Goblet could say and do almost anything and get away with it. Furthermore, it was deemed lucky to touch a jester on New Year's Eve.

When next seen, Goblet was wearing an elaborate farthingale, with two slightly lopsided puddings squeezed into the bodice and two more in the bustle. In this finery he skipped through the crowd, having perfected the knack of appearing at people's elbows, then kicking up his heels and disappearing with an arch wink before they had time to collect their wits. A trail of children endeavoured to follow him.

In the adjacent room, the White Drawing Room, a take-as-you-please supper had been laid out. Gold glittered everywhere; encrusted on the walls and the heavy frames of the paintings that adorned them, on the embroidered chairs, the ornate ceiling, the solid gold firescreens. About the walls, cabinets inlaid with semi-precious stones housed objets d'art. Tall doors gave on to the torchlit gardens. Before these portals posed graceful marble statues and tall ivory vases overflowing with white lilies. Overhead hovered a breathtaking tiered crystal chandelier. The floor was thick with priceless purple and gold carpets that flowed out beyond the White Drawing Room into the length of the red-and-gold East Gallery.

The Yeoman of the Silver Pantry, who compensated for his lack of height with excessive girth, was helping himself generously, piling his plate high with lobster mousse and goose pâté. Nearby, a tipsy butler with a long and equine countenance was performing the most extraordinary antics before an admiring audience of pages and porters, balancing empty plates in aspen stacks upon his head and hands. Not unexpectedly, these ceramic towers ultimately descended with a startling crash, causing the unfortunate Yeoman of the Silver Pantry to jump and inadvertently bestow his victuals on the undeserving purple-and-gold carpets.

Thus deprived, he bristled like an indignant boar.

'You there, Fawcett!' he shouted. 'Hold yer noise.'

'Shout till yer hoarse, I'll never heed *your* noise,' came the flippant reply.

The Yeoman of the Silver Pantry hitched up his belt and rolled his sleeves to his podgy elbows. His cheeks purpled like two generous aubergines.

''Tis not I who's horse but you, horse-face—and yet the face of you compares best with the hinder parts of the noble beast.'

Sniffing an entertaining discourse, servants gathered around. The Yeoman of the Silver Pantry had struck on an issue sensitive with the butler.

'If horse I be then I can draw the likes of you after me—aye, draw you whithersoever I would choose to go,' sneered Fawcett. 'Put wheels on and you are a wain—you've the build of it!'

'"Tis a pity he does *not* wane,' interjected the butler's friend waggishly. 'He waxes more than he wanes methinks—more so than a thousand candles!'

'Nay, no *drawer* you, but an artist,' shot back the Yeoman of the Silver Pantry, ignoring this interruption. 'An artist in horse manure.' Quickly reconsidering, he added, 'Had I but a pair of drawers such as you, you would be the crotch!'

The audience, who had been applauding each sally, cheered this barb of wit. Nonetheless, the butler was not to be deterred. After a brief deliberation as to whether to interpret the word 'crotch' as 'fork' and thus allude to his opponent's disgusting eating habits, he decided on a more threatening approach. Both participants were incisively aware of the retribution that would shortly be exacted from them by the Master of the King's Household in his wrath, as payment for the damage they had occasioned to the carpets and dishes of the White Drawing Room. Thus they decided that it was as well to be hanged for a buck as a fawn.

'A crutch you would fain lean upon once I have bested you!'

'Aye, *leaner* will they call me an you keep me from my dinner,' hotly said the Yeoman of the Silver Pantry, who was in fact proud of his bulk. 'But I'll dine anon, horse-face, while you shall couch upon the cold ground. Then you'll be the leaner, understand me?'

'Rather do I *over*stand you, base churl.' The butler loomed over the short figure of the pantryman, his long chin thrust forward.

'Why then, I'll undermine you!'

While the butler was thinking of a reply, the Yeoman of the Silver Pantry tackled him around the knees and bowled him over.

Fists flew. Rohain and many others prudently withdrew to the comparative safety of the Ballroom. Among the crowd that jostled there she briefly noted a tall man with a scarred face, high cheekbones, and startlingly blue eyes—one of the footmen. Wearing a

gorgeous jacket of sapphire velvet lined with white Rimanian bear
fur, he was bowing low before a curly-haired chambermaid, the
sixth granddaughter of the Marquess of Early. The girl took his
hand and they began to dance. Their eyes never left each other.

'Love knows no boundaries of rank,' murmured Rohain to
herself.

Unfolding the pleated leaves of a carved wooden fan, the
chicken-skin parchment of which was ostentatiously painted with
a scene from the Legend of the Sleeping Warriors, Viviana edged
closer to her mistress's elbow.

'I dream—am I truly wearing my lady's cloth-of-silver gown
and topaz girdle?'

'Go on with you!' said Rohain, smiling. 'You are a lady tonight.
You need not attend me.'

'Georgiana Griffin attends Dianella—'

'Nonetheless, I insist!'

'A thousand thanks, my lady! I cannot wait to join the dance.
This will surely be the best night of my life!'

With a quick curtsy, Viviana made haste to join the ladies waiting for partners.

Rohain's eyes roved the assembly. She fluttered a lacquered fan
of brilliant luster, edged with gilt. At her girdle hung a small, slender case containing ivory dance-cards. Made of mother-of-pearl, it
was overlaid with gold filigree work and had a matching pencil.
Several gentlemen had inscribed its ivory leaves with their names.
Having been plagued with offers to dance, each ardent aspirant
producing a white lace handkerchief and flourishing it under his
nose with a bow, Rohain had accepted a few and refused many.
She was an inept dancer, having learned the few steps she knew
during impromptu lessons from Viviana—a fact that none of the
gallants who whirled her in their arms had seemed to care a whit
about. But not one of her partners could match Thorn. She did not
wish to dance any more, not with anyone but him. Tired of refusing offers, she had masked her face with a feathered domino
borrowed from the Duchess of Roxburgh, dressed herself like a
chambermaid, stuck a large pair of artificial moth's wings on her
back, and teased out her black hair in a fright.

Dainnan knights were among the crowd in the ballroom, costumed as both aristocrats and servants, but she could not obtain a clear view from where she stood. It occurred to her that from the elevation of the musicians' gallery, one could be sure of commanding the scene. Eluding a dashing young earl who may have penetrated her disguise and was advancing in her direction, Rohain slipped through a service door and found a narrow stair.

As she ascended the stair a chill swept over her. She looked up and flinched. Something barred her way. It was a tall, white object, like a column of pale marble. The flicker of a torch in a sconce showed a long dark shadow stretching from the pillar's feet and up the wall. She pushed back her mask to obtain a better view.

'Oh! My lord Sargoth!'

He said nothing. He simply loomed there, looking down from the added height lent him by the staircase. Torchlight carved shadows out of his unblemished pallor, his luminous marble hair. The long face and beard matched the utter colourlessness of his wizard's robes. Here was one member of the Imperial Court not dressed for Misrule. It was all Rohain could do to prevent herself from backing away, turning and fleeing down the stair. She told herself she would not be intimidated by this man. He was a servant of the King-Emperor, after all—surely in the Court hierarchy she was his superior?

'Sir, let me pass.'

'My lady—*Rohain*, is it? Is that what you are called?'

'Yes.'

'My lady *Rohain*,' he deliberately emphasized the name. 'Far be it from me to impede your upward progress.'

He did not move. His eyes glittered oddly. What did he mean? What could he know?

Her mind groped for some anchor, and found the past. *Sianadh said never to show fear, never to run. To do so gives fearsome things power over you.*

'Well then, let me pass,' she said, evincing a boldness she did not feel.

'Assuredly.'

He moved, but she thought that instead of stepping aside he

stooped toward her. She recoiled. A voice boomed up the stair-well from below: 'Ho, my fair lady, are you there?'

Ercildoune bounded into sight. With relief, she smiled at him. When she looked again, Sargoth was gone.

'Oh! Where is he?'

'Who? Have I been so churlish as to interrupt a lovers' tryst upon the stair? Now, Rohain, you must allow me to know the name of my rival. And what an enchanting push-broom you make, I declare. Winged to boot!'

'No rival, Your Grace. No rival was here, only Sargoth the Wizard.'

'Gadzooks, you tremble like a twanged harpstring, my dear. What, has the old charlatan frightened you? I'll have his gizzards!'

'He has not.'

'That is well for him! Never trust a wizard, that's what I say. All that trickery and smoke—bah! There's no more gramarye in the Nine Arts than in a sieve. Come now, were you not directing your steps to the musicians' gallery? I would fain accompany you there. It is a place in which I feel right at ease, if they are playing well.'

They ascended together.

Yet, although she leaned long on the parapet looking down, Rohain could not spy the one for whom her eyes ached. And when the red eye of the Winter sun first opened its lid on the late, slate dawn, it seared his absence on a frost-blighted world.

Two days passed.

From the turmoil of festival, the palace was thrown into the upheaval of war. Aggression had flared again at the Nenian Landbridge. This time, the King-Emperor himself was to travel north, with many soldiers and Dainnan, leaving Thomas of Ercildoune in charge at Court. All had been in readiness for this eventuality. In two days more, they were gone. The palace fell silent. The passages echoed with their own emptiness.

A dreariness settled.

Dianella came to Rohain privately, sending the lady's maids away.

'I have tidings.'

'What tidings?'

'News for which you have waited long.'

'Well, what is it? Prithee, speak!'

'Dear Heart, you seem a trifle peeved these days. Selestorfen thou al Sorrow Isles?'

'No, I am not homesick.'

'Now, I insist that you treat me kindly, Heart,' scolded Dianella with a smile. 'I have done some hunting on your behalf. See how I put myself out to please you?' She pouted. 'You know you are dearer than a sister to me.'

'If I appeared brusque I ask your pardon, Dianella.'

'I forgive easily.' Lowering her voice, the courtier went on confidingly, 'I have heard somewhat of your Dainnan, Sir Thorn.'

Rohain started.

'What? What have you heard?' she said, unable to conceal her eagerness.

'Only that he has gone to the gythe.'

'Gone where?'

'To the gythe. He has gone to *war*, Heart, with the last detachment of Dainnan who left here with the King-Emperor. What shall you do now—dress as a soldier-boy and follow him into battle? Oh, but I only tease.'

'Then he was here! Are you sure? How can you know? Have you seen him?'

'Patience, patience! You know, Rohain, that I have certain connections here at Court. My uncle is an influential man. He has discreet methods of discovery. You can be assured that no one shall be apprised of your inquiry and that I shall keep you informed of any further word received. No gratitude, please! I have done all this out of friendship.'

'But I am grateful, Dianella. You are a worthy friend indeed. I should ask the Duke of Ercildoune to make a heroic song about you.'

'Pshaw! How singularly inventive you are. I must take leave of you for now, Heart—duty calls.'

'Don't leave—'

'I must.'

As Dianella passed through the door, her voice floated back over her shoulder;

'Until tomorrow, my—'

The last words were muffled, uttered with a laugh. She must have said '*imaginative* friend'. She could not possibly have said '*imaginary*'.

The Letters Patent would soon be finalized, but with the King-Emperor absent for an indefinite period, no date could be set for the official bestowal of Rohain's title. Ercildoune was continually occupied with matters of business, 'holding the fort' as he called it, while His Imperial Majesty was absent. The Bard had never a spare moment between receiving and sending dispatches and attending meetings.

Conflicting rumours whirled like maddened insects up and down the streets of Caermelor. The Empire was doomed; it would be smashed apart by a sweeping assault from Namarre. Some barbaric wizard-warlord would then seize governance, and the lands of Erith would be plunged into decades of suffering and strife. Unseelie wights would overrun the cities. All mortal creatures would be destroyed.

Folk cringed, darting uneasy glances northward, as if they expected to see at any moment a tidal wave of unseelie incarnations rolling down to crush them. Like fog, an atmosphere of impending ruin brooded over the city. Many members of the Set dispersed to their country estates. Those who remained became bored and discontented. They quarreled often.

There seemed nothing better for Rohain to do but to repair to her new estate, Arcune. Somberly—in harmony with the weather—she set out with Viviana in the Duchess of Roxburgh's Windship *Kirtle Green*, a topsail schooner, accompanied by that gentlewoman, who, now that her husband had departed once more for the battle zone, was eager to escape the dreary and suspenseful Court climate for the freedom of the countryside. Also on board were the Duchess's eldest child, Rosamonde, her six other children, and her large retinue of servants and nursemaids.

Viviana spent most of the journey below, lying in her cabin.

Her normally rosy face had taken on a greenish tinge, like a plum *un*ripening.

'I fear that Windship travel does not truly agree with me, m'lady,' she had said woefully. 'I never can master the art of walking on aerial decks, and the movement sets my head aspin. Waterships, on the other hand, present no problem.'

'That is well. Many folk tremble to board a Watership, fearing the possibility of drowning.'

'I have no fear of water voyages at all. I was born with a caul.'

'I have heard of such things. A caul is a membrane, is it not? A membrane, sometimes wrapped about the heads of infants newly born. Such articles are supposed to protect against drowning.'

'Even so,' said Viviana, passing her hand across her perspiring brow, 'I carry a piece of my caul everywhere with me, inside this locket-brooch.'

'A pretty ornament. I noticed you wear it regularly.'

'Oh, ma'am, prithee excuse me. The ship rocks so . . . I must lie down . . .'

Arcune, set in the rolling hinterlands, exceeded its new mistress's expectations. As the schooner docked at the Mooring Mast adjacent to the main house, Rohain leaned over the taffrail, gazing at her lands spread out below. In their Winter raiment they looked fair: fallow fields and green meadows, an orchard, woodlands, a chase abounding in game verts, a cluster of farm buildings, a river, and—most imposing of all—Arcune Hall.

This gracious *chastel*, part castle, part manor house, stood three or four stories high. Solid as a monolith yet of graceful, aerial architecture, it plumbed the ornamental lake with an exact replica of its columned self. A formal garden skirted the lake: neat flowerbeds, hedged squares of parterre laid out in gravel and sand of different colours in scrolls and arabesques, crossed and bordered by precise lines of trees. Fanning out from the garden walls lay a spacious park, with quiet tracts of velvet lawns, shady copses and spinneys, water like broken panes fallen from the sky's window.

'A fine estate,' said Alys-Jannetta of Roxburgh approvingly, 'and I shall teach you to be mistress of it.'

She did so with a will, hiring more servants, giving orders that the house—which had been unoccupied for several years—should be turned out, aired, polished, dusted, scrubbed, and refurbished. She held consultations with the Steward, the Housekeeper, and the Gamekeeper, she examined the accounts. For a week, she and Rohain indulged in no recreation, but when all was concluded to her satisfaction, they went riding in the chase.

In this open woodland, stands of leafless birch stood like stiff brooms. Horse-chestnut and elm spread black boughs over a deep, rich leaf-mold on which the horses' hooves dully thudded. A line of ravens in arrowhead formation slid over the gray glass sky. Mist rose in soft streamers, like vaporous shang images of the trees' roots themselves, as if the woodlands could ever grieve or love.

Each breath of the riders hung as a silver cloud. The day was dark. Another storm threatened. From upwind, the dire ululation of a howler rang out, to prove it.

'You have a trustworthy Steward and an honest Housekeeper,' said Alys. 'I cannot say the same for the Gamekeeper—he'll have to be watched. Howbeit, I would say that this estate, like all good properties, will run smoothly whether you live here or not, although a few unannounced visits by the landlady during the year tends to improve efficiency. On one such visit I shall return to Roxburgh shortly. How I hate these sidesaddles, don't you?'

Rohain, who could not recall ever having sat on a horse before but who felt at ease in the saddle, agreed.

'I do dislike them, yes,' replied Rohain. 'Next time you visit me here we shall dress like gentlemen and ride like them, like the wind, jumping hedges and ditches wheresoever they fall across our path. But look now, the storm clouds come rolling over. The sky is angry. We must make haste and return before the rain sets in.'

The echoing howl of the storm-harbinger again curdled the air.

'Such a Winter it is for tempests!' tutted the Duchess, turning her horse for home. 'Such disruption to Windship and Stormrider schedules.'

Arcune Hall's most ancient inhabitant was a household bruney known to all as 'Wag at the Wa'. When no kettle occupied the pot-hook hanging in the kitchen, he would sit there swinging himself to and fro, chuckling. He loved merriment and in particular the company of children, of which, until now, he had lately been deprived. He looked like a grizzled old man with short, crooked legs and a long tail that helped him to keep his seat on the hook. Sometimes he wore a gray cloak, with an old tattered night-cap on his head drawn down over one side of his face, which was always harrowed with toothache, but usually he wore a red coat and blue breeches. He would not approve of any drink stronger than home-brewed ale and used to cough furiously if strong spirits were imbibed in the kitchen. In all other ways he was a benevolent wight despite the toothache, although very fussy about the cleanliness of the house, and the bane of slipshod kitchen-maids. Like most household bruneys he had no fear of cold iron. Swinging the empty pot-hook would bring him; this the Duchess's children often did. What with the wight, the children, and the servants, the cavernous old kitchen was the heart of conviviality at Arcune. When beyond the house's thick walls the wind came in sudden gusts like heavy blows, and sharp, prickling rain fell and thunder punished the skies with flails of lightning, all was cosy by the kitchen fire. It was often there that Rohain, Alys, and the children would spend the evenings, in the company of the old Housekeeper.

Every day a Relayer of the Noblesse Squadron rode in with dispatches from Caermelor—communications about the fighting in the north and, often, snippets of Court doings in a note from Ercildoune.

'I need to stay informed,' said Alys. She looked daily for tidings of her husband. With equal impatience, Rohain awaited the incoming reports.

The messenger would be seen coming out of the southeast like some strange bird, his cloak flying, to alight on top of the spindly Mooring Mast whose structure of pointed arches was etched against the sky. Soon after, the sildron-powered lift would begin to descend, carrying both the Relayer and the eotaur with its hoof-crescents unclipped and flying-girth neutralised by andalum. The ostler of Arcune would then hasten to take the steed's bridle and lead it to the stables, while the Stormrider, pulling off his riding gloves and winged helmet, strode into the house, a butler or footman hastening before him to open doors and bow profusely.

True Thomas of Ercildoune corresponded regularly, reporting on humorous Court incidents as well as graver matters from the strife-torn north, including descriptions of battle tactics, which Alys read over and over. The Bard wrote:

> The mounted archers of Namarre are exceeding swift, and they use this to great advantage. Their preferred tactic is encirclement. Even when we outnumber them, they are often speedy enough to surround our troops or outflank us. Aware of this, our commanders try where possible to elect narrow-fronted battlegrounds, protected by natural features of the landscape such as rivers and rocky hills. As additional protection, they keep ready a reserve force in case of cavalry attacks from the rear.
>
> Some days since, the first pitched battle was fought in north-western Eldaraigne, not far from the Nenian Landbridge. The Luindorn Battalions were marching west in two parallel columns, about four miles apart, when as the first column entered the open fields it was assailed by vast numbers of rebels. In order to provide a secure base from which battle could be waged, the commander ordered his men to set up camp. However, the sorties and continual harassment of the barbarians hampered their efforts, so he sent out the cavalry to stave off the enemy, enabling the infantry to begin establishing an encampment.
>
> However the Luindorn Drusilliers were unable to engage the rebels in battle and were repeatedly forced to withdraw to avoid being cut off. The barbarian rebels successfully encircled the Imperial troops. Furthermore, our infantry were unable to hold off their lightning strikes and sallies without the Drusilliers beside them, so the Drusilliers gradually fell back until all our troops of the first column were close-packed in a dense and milling confusion, sur-rounded on all fronts by fast-galloping archers on horseback. Their position was grim. Defeat seemed inevitable, until at last, with a great blowing of horns and clashing of swords on shields, the second column appeared over the horizon behind the rebel forces.

It was not long before a Luindorn cavalry charge shattered the Namarrans, scattering them to the four winds.

'The Namarran scouts must have been careless,' commented the Duchess, folding the letter and handing it to a footman. 'On this occasion, luck was with the first column. It seems these rebels are not to be swiftly defeated.'

'I remain puzzled as to their purpose,' said Rohain.

'They are rebelling against the Empire,' explained the Duchess. 'The Namarran population comprises generations of cut-throats and thieves who have been banished to the north as punishment for their crimes. They hate the judicial system that cast them out, and wish to take revenge upon the whole Empire. Theirs is an unstable society in which violence rules. Habitually they quarrel and make war on one another, until the cruellest and most merciless butcher among them claws his way to chieftaincy. But such victories are short-lived. As soon as any flaw appears in the dictator's defences he is attacked, and the conflict begins all over again.

'Plagued by so much strife, the Namarrans cannot prosper. They have come to believe that the answer to their poverty lies in expropriating the wealth of the Empire.

'In the past they have never stopped squabbling for long enough to mount a concerted assault against us. For some unknown reason, they have finally joined forces, it seems.'

'And still there is no mention of the role of unseelie wights in this conflict,' said Rohain in troubled tones. 'It seems as if the barbarian commander is keeping them aside, waiting for some significant moment to strike with full force. But why? And what hold could any mortal man, even a great wizard, have over immortal beings so antipathetic to the human race?'

The Duchess shook her head. 'Weighty questions,' she replied, 'and ones that we all ask ourselves often. As yet, no answers have been found.'

Some three weeks after they had begun their sojourn at Arcune, there came, in the usual letter from Thomas Rhymer, a paragraph that the Duchess's daughter Rosamonde read aloud.

Unto The Most Noble the Duchess of Roxburgh, Marchioness of Carterhaugh, Countess of Miles Cross, Baroness Oakington-Hawbridge, also to the Lady Rohain of the Sorrows, Mistress of Arcune, I, Your Most Humble Servant Thomas, Duke of Ercildoune, send thee Greetings.

Madam and My Lady,

I send greeting and earnest desires that this missive should find you both hale. Be it known that following the discovery of the wealth amassed at a secret location in the Lofty Mountains and the apprehension of the culprits responsible for its treasonable looting, further questioning has revealed that members of a rival conclave were still at large. One of these, an Ertishman, 'Sianadh Kavanagh of County Lochair', also known as 'the Bear', was arrested yesterday in Caermelor. The felon has been consigned to the palace dungeons to await His Majesty's pleasure, which may well be execution for treason . . .'

'What?' shouted Rohain. 'No! It cannot be!'

She rushed to snatch the parchment from Rosamonde's hand but could make nothing of the runes and threw up her hands in despair.

'Alys, I must leave at this instant. Via, pack my chattels, have my horse saddled—nay, the sky would be faster. Is the Relayer still here, he who brought this message? Does he yet take refreshment in the front parlor? I shall ride up behind him.'

The Duchess asked no questions.

'You shall have the use of *Kirtle Green*. Dobben, run and tell the captain to make ready to sail in haste.'

'I thank you, but it will take some time to get her under way— I shall ride behind the Relayer!' cried Rohain again, in agitation.

'Their rules forbid it. Only Stormriders or the chosen of the King-Emperor may ride the skies. No need to wring your hands— the Windship shall be ready as soon as you are.'

The palace dungeons were no worse than the cellars at Isse Tower. In many ways, they were better, not so damp and slimy. The passageways had been hewn of clean stone. They were well-lit and well-ventilated. Still, they were dungeons, and cheerless. Down here, all was stone and iron, fire and shadow, with little change. The slow decay of time was signposted by the various laments of prisoners who came and went. With keys clanking, the Head Jailer led the way, lurching, down the stairs and along a corridor.

'Hurry, hurry!' urged Rohain.

'Rats,' whispered Viviana despairingly at her back. 'I heard them.'

Rohain halted, aghast. 'Rats? By the Powers, I detest them more than all the unseelie wights in Erith!' She stared desperately after the jailer's retreating back. 'The guards will chase them off,' she blurted. They ran on and caught up with the jailer. 'Hasten, man!'

'Beg pardon, m'lady, I've a crook knee. I'm goin' as hasty as I can.'

Fume and fret she might, but no more speed could be got out of him. The clatter of his bunches of keys preceded them, while the boot-crunches of the two escorting guards brought up the rear, ricocheting off cold stone.

'*Obban tesh!*' said a voice farther down the passageway. 'Can a bloke not get some sleep in here without being woken by yer racket, ye *doch* fly-blown *daruhshie* of a turnkey? Come in here and I'll give ye a right knee to match yer left, ye *sgorrama samrin.*'

'Sianadh!'

Rohain rushed forward, shoving the jailer aside. With both hands, she grasped the iron bars of the cell, gazing inside. There stood a man, bootless, in a ragged tunic of bergamot belted at the waist. His hose were riddled with holes and his cloak of coarse woollen kersey was threadbare. On his head was a taltry, worn beneath a filthy chaperon that ended in an outrageously long liripipe wound under his chin and over the top. From beneath this headgear bristled a red hedge in need of pruning, for it had overgrown to cover the jaw. Scorpions, crudely drawn and almost obliterated by dirt, crawled across the hairy feet.

It was indeed he.

Rohain's tears mingled with laughter. Sianadh stared, his blue eyes bursting from their sockets. For once, he was dumbfounded.

'My lady,' said Viviana, 'I shall fetch some salts—'

'No.' Weakly, Rohain leaned on her maid's shoulder.

'A handkerchief, please. That is all.' She wiped her face. The tears disappeared, the smile remained.

'What have ye brought me, jailer?' Sianadh had found his tongue at last, but it rattled hoarsely against his palate. 'One of the baobhansith? A siren to tempt and strangle me? Has hanging gone out of fashion?'

'Go,' said Rohain, turning to the jailer and the two guards. 'I shall be safe here. Wait in the guardroom. I would hold converse with this prisoner.'

Baffled, the yeomen warders bowed and obeyed.

'You also, Viviana. Wait around the corner. I have words for his ears alone.'

As Viviana departed, Sianadh took a step forward. His eyes squinted, as though he tried to look at something so bright it was too painful to be directly observed.

'What d'ye want of me?'

'Ah, Sianadh! That is the second time I have ever spoken your name and yet it feels not unfamiliar on my lips—I've thought of you so often. I've mourned you. How came you here? I thought you slain—I thought you dead at the foot of Waterstair by the hands of Scalzo. You live! Yes, it is true! If you were some incarnation and not a real man they would have found it out by now.'

'Who be you?' His voice was rough with wonder and suspicion.

'I am—Imrhien.'

Sianadh's jaw dropped. Then he turned on his heel.

'Trickery,' he growled, walking to the far wall of his austere cell.

Her words tumbled out.

'Not trickery. Ask me anything! What happened to the worm-skin belt that you won at Crowns-and-Anchors in Luindorn? You unbuckled it so that you could fall out of the sky after we jumped off the pirate brig—now it floats somewhere above Erith. How did we escape the Direath? You fought it until cock-crow. What did you call yourself in Fincastle's Mill? "My Own Self". What colour were the gowns you ordered for me in Gilvaris Tarv?'

'Enough! Enough! My pate addles. If 'tis in fact Imrhien before

me, then by the smoking bones of the Chieftains, her face is somewhat altered and her tongue is making up for lost time.'
Approaching, he peered through the bars.

'She was kind o' spindly, like ye be. She looked as if she'd
snap in twain, with naught but a pin to hold her two halves
together. But she was a straw-head.'

'I have dyed my hair, *mo scothy gaidair*.'

'Why?'

'It is a long story . . .'

The Ertishman stood with folded arms, shaking his head.

'Nay. It cannot be. I cannot believe what ye say, ye a fine lady
and all. Don't be taunting a condemned man.'

Rohain seized the bars again and shook them with all her force.

'Listen to me, you stupid, pigheaded Ertishman. Question me
about anything!'

He eyed her doubtfully.

'What is the name of my niece?'

'Muirne.'

'Ach, ye could have found that out. I have it! What did I, in
the Ancient City when the unstorm came?'

'You doffed your taltry. You stood by some stone dragons with
your hands upraised and said, "*I be My Own Self, and I be here, so
look ye, I have* gilfed *this town with my mark*."'

Bright-eyed and flushed with expectation, she looked at him.
He returned her gaze with a strange one of his own, as if seeing
her for the first time. His facial muscles worked in spasms. Very
softly, he said,

'Your face?'

'Healed by the one-eyed carlin.'

'Your voice?'

'That also.'

She held her breath.

Beginning deep in his chest, a roar erupted. Sianadh collided
with the cell bars at a run. Hurrying up the passageway, Viviana
beheld her mistress embracing the prisoner through the grating,
the latter still bellowing wordlessly. At the disturbance, other prisoners began to shout.

'*Chehrna, chehrna, chehrna!*' bellowed Sianadh.

Tearing himself away, he danced around the cell. Guards appeared.

'Silence! You there!'

'Leave him alone,' commanded Rohain. Unmoved by the presence of his captors, the Ertishman continued to sing, dance, and leap into the air, which caused his liripipe to unwind and tangle around his legs.

'Let this man out. Unlock this door.'

'M'lady, we are forbidden to do that without a release signed by His Imperial Majesty. This man is a treasoner. He is to be hanged.'

Sianadh stood quietly now.

'"Tis greeting and farewell, ain't it, *chehrna*,' he said.

'Not necessarily,' she replied. 'My dear friend, you are as innocent as I. I am going to try to have you pardoned. I must go now but I shall soon return.'

'Wait! Muirne and Diarmid—do they live?'

'Yes. They thrive at Isenhammer.'

'Ceileinh's arms! Take them a message for me, will ye?'

'And have them know you live, condemned? And let them lose you twice?'

'Ach, nay. 'Twill be time enough for to clap eyes on 'em when I be out of this *doch* cage. No use getting 'em worrit. Get me out quicklike, *chehrna*—my throat craves a drenching with a good tavern draught. I'd rather not save 'em the cost of a hangin' by dyin' of thirst.'

'I shall get you out, I swear it. Meanwhile, remember—there are two days you ought never to worry about.'

They left him grinning. As she moved off, Rohain said to the jailer, 'Treat him well. If you do, you shall be rewarded. If you do not, you shall answer to the Duke of Ercildoune and the Duchess of Roxburgh!'

'He must be pardoned. He must not hang.'

Rohain stood before the Royal Bard, in a courtyard of Caermelor Palace.

'And why? And why not?' demanded Ercildoune.

'He is a good man, a friend—he saved my honour, my life.'

'He is a treasoner.'

'As much a treasoner as I!'

'Never say that, Rohain. I forbid it.'

"'Tis true. At Waterstair—'

'You took booty to aid you on your return—you confessed it from the first. It has been recognised as no crime. Say no more on't!'

'With what crime is he charged?'

'The thieves we apprehended upon your advice, the men you call Scalzo's—although we did not find one by that name amongst them—they indicted him. It seems that unlike yourself, he returned to Waterstair to pilfer from it. This advice was confirmed by the man's own drunken boasting, overheard in a tavern. 'Tis not the first time a man has hanged himself with a tankard of ale.'

'His boasts are empty. The thieves lied.'

'You are determined to remain his ally. Yet I have seen this man. I cannot fancy him to be your sweetheart.'

'He is not. He is—brother or uncle. Family.'

'Since you and no other ask it, I will grant stay of execution. But only His Majesty can grant pardon for such as this.'

'Then I must have audience with His Majesty.'

'Impossible. He is at the fields of war, as you know.'

'And why should I not journey north?'

'My flower, my very bird—you upon the battle-plain? Await His Majesty's return. Until then, your friend, my fellow Ert, may live.'

By the grace of the Duke of Ercildoune, Sianadh was allowed, chained and under guard, to ascend daily to one of the parlors. Rohain would converse with him there for hours, regaling him with food and drink to his heart's content.

She told him news of his family, then, having sworn him to secrecy, revealed all of her remembered past that her muteness had kept hidden from him. She had revealed this history to nobody, ever, not even Maeve. She told him of the cruel ivy, *Hedera paradoxis,* and the callous denizens of Isse Tower, and her life as a servant. It was as if a weight had been lifted from her heart, to share such a burden of knowledge.

For his part, Sianadh was tickled to find himself enjoying the hospitality of the King-Emperor's palace, if only conditionally.

''Tis the life,' he said cheerily, sprawled on a wolfskin rug before the fire. 'If I could get these *doch* manacles off I'd be the happiest man. Fortune's smiled on ye, *chehrna*. But ye haven't your past returned to ye, yet.'

'No.'

'Ye ought to try. It be important to know history. Kings come and go and some remain. To survive, a bloke must know what comes before and after. Things be not what they seem at a given moment. They be the sum of their past and the hope of their future. The smiling stranger may offer ye wine but has he just come from the house of sickness?'

'How am I to find my history?'

'When ye lose summat, ye must retrace your steps to find it.'

'Do you say that I should return to Isse Tower?'

'That be what I say. Far as I can tell, 'tis your only hope. I cannot call ye Rohain, or Lady Muck or anything. Find out your real name, eh?'

'I could not go away, leaving you here.'

He shrugged.

'I've been worse off. The fare down there in the dungeons be plain but plenty. I be gettin' plenty o' rest and flay me for boots if I've had much of that these past years. From what I ken, the King-Emperor will not be rushing back to pardon me for trying unsuccessfully to steal some of his treasure until after we win this war. Take a Windship to Isse. Ye're wealthy—ye can afford it. Ye will not be gone for long and ye might find out summat.'

'No,' she repeated, 'I could not leave you.'

But the dormant questions had reawakened.

'Begging your pardon, m'lady, but I am surprised that you have not been Cut,' said Viviana with concern. 'There is all this talk of you having family connections with that hairy felon. M'lady, he's Ertish and an outlaw! Dianella and all of them must think it such a quiz and yet they have not Cut you.'

'Dianella is saying she thinks it an amusing novelty and she wants a condemned man of her own to keep on a chain.'

'Beg pardon, m'lady, but I would not trust her, truly I wouldn't. For all her peacock's plumage, she is nothing but a gray-malkin that tears apart birds and helpless creatures merely for sport. M'lady, until you came here she was generally thought to be the fairest in the land and now she's jilted from her high horse. She does not like it, and that's a fact. But she has not let them Cut you and she worms her way into your affections for her own purposes. She's a cold-hearted one and that's for certain. Her own uncle is unwell, having returned from an excursion black with bruises from a spriggan attack, yet she troubles herself not at all on his behalf.'

'You speak truly. Howbeit, I cannot trouble myself with Dianella's meretriciousness.'

The meetings with Sianadh brought mixed pleasure and sadness, for the Ertishman could not bring himself to meet Rohain's eyes very often, and when he did he would hastily avert his gaze. There was none of the easy comradeship of old times. That was all gone, and in its place stood an uncomfortable awareness, as if she were a porcelain figurine on a shelf and he too afraid to touch it lest it break or be sullied by his rough hands. And once or twice she caught him looking at her from the corners of his eyes with an expression of awe, as if he witnessed a vision in which he could not fully have faith.

She desired no reverence, only the banter of good fellowship. Was this distance between them, and the covert duels in the gardens, and the spurious friendship of Dianella part of the real price to be paid for the unwearing of her mask of ugliness? Maeve had said, *Do not be thankful until you have lived with your changed appearance for a moon-cycle or two. See how you like it then.*

Despite the awkwardness, she looked forward to the company of her friend and used their hours together to discover his recent history.

'The Gailledu saved me,' said Sianadh, 'as I lay below Waterstair wounded to the bone and almost breathing my last. A life for a life, he repaid me—gathered me up in his arms as if I were no more than a lad. Great strength has he, belied by his looks. It was because of that flower, ye ken, the blue one that Ethlinn preserved in an egg of resin and gave to me. It meant summat.

'He took me to some place in the forest and healed me. When I was well, I returned to Tarv and sheltered with Ethlinn and Roisin. They told me you had set out for Caermelor but that the roads were bad. By then all roads to the west had been declared impassable, wight-struck. My thought was how to swiftly get word to the King-Emperor at Caermelor to inform him of the treasure, so that it could be quickly wrested from Scalzo's cowardly *uraguhnes*, and ye and me could be heroes and Liam, *tambalai* lad, would be avenged. For I had little hope then that ye would get through, the reports being so bad and so many caravans being lost. So I scraped together all the money I could beg or borrow and went to the Stormriders.

'I get sent to a scribe of theirs and I tell him a message to write down, to send to the King-Emperor. Not wanting the world to know about it, like, I don't say exactly what 'tis about, but I give hints. Only one who knew aught could have pieced it together. Anyway, this scribe looks at me kind of strange, and he reminds me of another I saw somewhere, blast his eyes, but I couldn't recall where. I took exception to him from the start. And with good reason, as it turns out later. For when I returned to Tarv Tower with Eochaid at my side, to ask whether the message had been successfully sent for all me trouble and money, we were set upon by ruffians outside the Tower, and hunted through the streets. And in the process, I got separated from Eochaid but the heat was still on me.

'Now, I always had a plan for if something like this should happen—'tis wise to keep a couple of escape plans handy for emergencies, mark you, Imrhien. I have a friend with a boat at Tarv docks. Down there I run, for the lick of me life, but when I get there, the boat is gone. Must've gone out fishing. At this point I remember where I have seen the pox-faced Scribe before—he be one of Scalzo's accomplices. Tarv be full of them—or it was. Anyway, these sons of dogs being hot on me heels, I jump into the nearest boat and head off. This shakes them off me tail because there's a storm brewing which only a silkie or a mad Ertishman would take to the seas in. Being possessed of wondrous seamanship, I sail all the way to Caermelor, and many's the un*lorraly* tale I could tell about events along the way. But when I finally get here, strike me lucky if the entire population doesn't already know that there's a treasure at Waterstair because some ladyship's found out about it and squawked. It's sleeveless me sayin' aught about what the world already knows and expectin' a reward for it, so there's nothing left for it but to join the army.

'Now, if a lad's going to join the army he wants to make the most of the last of his freedom first. So I makes meself known at the nearest malt-house, where I meet a couple of blokes I used to knock around with in the old days, good mates. We've had a few sessions. Priz—that be his kenning and I wist no other—he was in the lock-up once. He be a fellow always dressed so clean and neat, careful with his clobber, like. Dogga, he don't fuss so much about what's on his back—'tis who's on the end of his fist that counts with him.

'So me and Priz and Dogga be sitting down to dine and Priz tells the story about how in that same malt-house last year there was a fight and the floor was rotten and eight big blokes crashed through the planking into the cellar below, which hadn't been used for fifteen years and was full of slime up to their middles and Priz nearly laughed his well-tailored breeches off at the sight. Then I be telling the story about when old Cauliflower died at the table playing cards, and his hand still on the table, and his mates looked under his hand and there were three aces so they shoved the money in his pockets before they carried him out, 'cos he'd won.

'As I be telling this, in comes Lusco Barrowclough, as loud-mouthed a bullying drunkard and want-wit as ever cheated in a hurling match or got thrown out of a Severnesse tavern. I had not had the misfortune to set eyes on the whoreson villain for a year or two—not long enough. Barrowclough's already well-oiled, and it's not long before he starts miscalling the malter and his nice little tarty servant-wenches. I up and tells this gentleman that if I want a disturbance while I be eating, I only have to go and eat at me grandmother's place. He looks down his Feohrkind nose at me, and me wearin' a Finvarnan kilt—and he says with a sneer, "Nice legs." "Would ye like one of 'em up yer backside?" I offers. He starts mouthing off a bit, then Priz says, "Pipe down while we're trying to eat," and then Dogga looks up and puts in, "I've had a gutful of ye."

'So then Barrowclough, the *uraguhne*, says, "Well, I've had a gutful of *ye*," and adds, "I'll break yer bleedin' neck." Dogga politely responds, "Ye couldn't break wind let alone break any-one's neck," and in less time than it takes to fling a curse across a tavern, the fisticuffs is on. I flatten Barrowclough with much joy and return to my seat. He runs out the door and I politely say "pass the salt" and salubriously resume eating with my two mates. Before we have quite finished dining, we look up to see our *shera sethge* gentleman walk *back* in the door. Behind him, another the same. Behind him, another. They keep walking in, until in addi-tion to Barrowclough, there be nine. None of them are comely, I can tell ye—all bull-girthed, solid, bald, scarred, toothless, ugly *skeerdas* to a man, and ropeable as wounded steers. The malter and the servants went pale, and so did all the other diners.

'Not to be taken by surprise, I punched out one of Barrowclough's cronies with no preamble. As foreseen, a fight began. There were stools being broken across blokes' backs, tables being overturned, crockery smashing, blokes flying through the air, round and round the malt-house for a goodly while. A bloke could have had another square meal and a tankard in the time it took for that fight.

'While this is going on, another two malt-house customers who have been watching with interest see that although 'tis three against ten, the three appear to be winning, so they join in on the winning side. That makes it five against ten, and pretty soon Barrowclough and his nine are being helped out the door by the malter and his brothers. We three now being five, we returned to our tables and sopped up the last bits of gravy, which had been preserved from ruin more by our own effort than by some stroke of good fortune.

'As we are eating I take time to look at the condition of my mates. Priz, always so immaculate, be missing a boot. The remaining boot be split. One of his sleeves be ripped off at the shoulder, his shirt and every other article on him be torn. Dogga and I be in a similar condition. Heedless of small inconveniences, we are partaking of the last part of our meal when a couple of fellows put their heads around the door and survey the scene. They turn out to be a sheriff and a constable.

'"Has there been a fight here?" says they.

'We look around in surprise. The malt-house looks a mite untidy.

'"Fight? I ain't seen no fight," says we. The malter says the same as we—so do the serving-wenches.

'The sheriff and the constable look us over once more, while we're licking the gravy off our trenchers and complimenting the malter's cook on the meal. They warn us against disturbing the peace, we assure them that we shudder to think of the idea ever entering our heads, then they slouch out and leave us be.

'Well, news spread around and the malt-house began to fill up until we found ourselves with a jovial company of drinkers around us. Everyone likes a winner. The night went on and someone brought in a yard of ale, which was a bit of sport, and then more ale all round, and I got to talking about Finvarna and friends I left behind, and then about other friends and relations lost to me—for I thought ye'd been devoured on the Caermelor Road—and then on to what might have been, and the riches I nearly had. I may have said things I wotted not what of. Somehow, the truth got all twisted and next thing the sheriff and his constable be back, with about fifty others, putting the strong-arm on me and dragging me outside and me throwing punches while the drink robs me of my strength and then the revels are over. That be how I ended up here.'

Not seven days after Rohain's return to Court, Dianella again sought a private audience with her. Dressed in a cotehardie of red velvet edged with fur, a kirtle of rich baudekyn, a cloak of blue-green velvet worked with a design in gold and lined with ermine, a reticulated headdress ornamented with goldsmith's work and jewels, and a hip-belt of square brooches and jewels from which depended an aulmoniere with a baselard thrust through it, alongside a hand-mirror and a pair of pincers, Dianella looked fair in the most splendid degree, although, by the frown on her brow, she was clearly unsettled.

In her glorious plumage, she paced up and down for a while, pursing her lips and continuing to frown until Rohain said, 'Unburden yourself, pray.'

'Alas! It is not that simple, Dear Heart. What I have to say distresses me deeply.'

'Thorn—he has not fallen in battle?'

'I know not. But it is not of your Dainnan that I would speak. It is of yourself. You are discovered.'

'What is your meaning?' A seed of apprehension sprouted in Rohain's mind.

'Ah, what is *yours*, Dear Heart, whoever you may be? For you are not Rohain of the Sorrows, that has become evident.'

A chill sensation ran through Rohain to her fingertips. Her blood seemed to have frozen in her veins. Dianella smiled with only her mouth, not her eyes.

'I perceive my words have an effect upon you. Good. You see, you have been found to be an impostor. Inquiries have been made, in Severnesse, in the Sorrow Isles. The family Tarrenys is an old one, granted, yet it has all but died out. Only a few members are left, all accounted for. Of them you are not one. Do you deny it?'

After a while, Rohain said, 'I do not.'

'Well, then!'

Triumph lit Dianella's mien. Rohain itched to slap her face. If it had not been for the courtier's knowledge of Thorn, Rohain would have thrust her from the room. Beneath the anger and the fear, a deep sense of shame spread out, taking root in her very bones. Through clenched teeth she said, 'What now?'

'What now? Dear Heart, there is only one course open to you. You will not, of course, claim the peerage of Arcune—instead you must leave at once.'

It was Rohain's turn to pace now.

'Leave, I say,' continued Dianella. 'This is not the place for you. You are above your station. For now, the knowledge of your deception rests with only myself and my uncle, and I swear to you as a true friend that neither of us shall expose you if you depart now. But should the word spread despite our best efforts to keep it secret, there is no knowing what steps might be taken to punish you for your wanton guile. For your own safety, go this day, this very hour.'

'You say you will not betray me?'

'La! I am cut to the quick!'

'What do you want in return?'

'More and more ungracious! Really! Do you suggest that I want payment? Friends do not buy and sell, but gifts are often passed from one to the other.'

'Take my entire wardrobe. Take everything I own in the Treasury.'

'Pshaw! How should it look, if I were to be seen dressed in your hand-me-downs?'

'Dianella, I need, more than ever now, to retain the influence of my position, if only until the King-Emperor returns. I shall leave Court at first light on the morrow, only to come back one last time for an audience with His Majesty. After that you shall see me nevermore.'

'A wise decision on your part, Dearest Heart.'

Omitting the courtesies of leave-taking, Dianella sallied from the room with a swish of baudekyn and a clash of implements. Typically, she tossed a parting shot over her shoulder: 'Have your maid bring me the costumes now. And the keys to your caskets.'

Rohain rang for Viviana.

'I intend to make an excursion from Court,' she told the courtier, carefully keeping her tone level. 'Have a letter dispatched to Isse Tower. Inform them, at the Seventh House of the Stormriders, to make ready—the Lady Rohain of Arcune sends greetings. She is coming from Caermelor Palace to sojourn for a time.'

Her heart felt wrung out like a blood-soaked mop. Now that Dianella had exiled her from Court, she had indeed lost Thorn forever.

Night drew in around Caermelor Palace. Rohain sat gazing drearily into a gold-backed looking-glass framed with ivory and mother-of-pearl. She wondered whether strange visions would trouble her this night, and whether she would wake in fear. Once, back in the cottage of Maeve, she had dreamed of three gentle, loving faces: those of a woman, a man, and a boy-child. Later there had been the Dream of the Rats. Both of these fragments had borne the hallmark of truth—she could not doubt that they were memories in disguise. It was only since Maeve had laid hands upon Rohain that her repose had begun to be been disturbed by such images. She suspected something else must have happened at that time, when her face and speech had been restored. The restoration, perhaps, had acted as a catalyst for the beginning of a gradual arousing of memory. In Gilvaris Tarv, Ethlinn had once explained, <<*Sometimes in such cases, all it takes is for the sufferer to come upon something familiar, and then the memories slowly begin to filter back into the mind.*>>

Rohain whispered to her reflection, 'My own once-familiar face . . . when I looked upon you, in the mirror of the one-eyed carlin, the sight sparked off an opening of closed doors.'

That night, through a chink in one of those doors, there issued a third dream—that of the White Horse.

It was under her, running, the horse—the apotheosis of swiftness and freedom. All was speed, all exhilaration. The wind roared in her ears, the ground passed swiftly by below—were the hooves even touching it? She laughed aloud, but a shape fell out of the sky beating its wings, dark against the sun. It dashed in close—too close—and the laughter turned to screams, but the horse itself was screaming and it was a night mare, because the horizon spun through weightlessness that gathered in the pit of her stomach and rose to her gorge, then the hillside came up with a smack and became a spear of white-hot iron that burned through the bone of her leg and she was screaming . . .

Dreams, memories—perhaps she had been better off without them.

4
THE TOWER
Hunt and Heart's Desire

The twelve mighty Houses from Belfry to Fairlaise,
From Worthing to Outreme, where thunderstorms breed,
Command the four winds on the highest of highways.
The wings of the thoroughbred glory in speed.

VERSE FROM 'SONG OF THE STORMRIDERS'

U hta: the hour before dawn.
Tidings arrived by carrier pigeon as the Wind-clipper *Harper's Carp* was being rigged for takeoff. A Dainnan Windship had captured a black pirate brig lurking in the Lofty Mountains, and seized much booty. Desperate and bloody had been the struggle. Few of the reivers had been taken alive. Those who fell had been abandoned, to be devoured by the strange mouths of the forest.

Winches rattled. Screws rotated. The wooden fish figurehead seemed to leap. As the crew vigorously onhebbed the andalum hull-plates, the Royal Bard's personal clipper began to rise, leaning her silhouette elegantly into the wind. For those on board there was no feeling of motion forward or upward—rather the impression that the Mooring Mast was leaving the ship and the launch-crew was sinking away below.

Caermelor Palace dwindled. Spreading her canvas wings, the *Harper's Carp* lifted like a long-billed crane through the clouds until she reached cruising altitude. After the first ascent there was no sense of height. The carpet of mist below appeared close and solid, beckoning the passengers to tread upon it. The Windship's shadow skipped along down there, a trick of light-interference painting a coloured halo around the keel.

Like a thimbleful of bubbles in the sky, the *Harper's Carp* sailed north along the coastline. By Windship, this journey was almost nine hundred miles. By Seaship across the mouth of the Gulf of Mara the distance would have been considerably shorter. Ercildoune, however, had insisted that Rohain take his private aircraft instead of buying passage on a merchant Seaship, claiming it would provide greater security from eldritch assailants. For the Bard, who was busy with political matters and frequently closeted for hours in discussion with members of the royal council, she had contrived an excuse for visiting Isse Tower: 'Court is become so dull of late, and I should like to behold with my own eyes one of the famous outposts of the Stormriders.'

The captain had no qualms about sailing at night, and so they reached their destination in only four days. Late on the fourth day a jagged stalk began to grow from the horizon, enlarging until it became Isse Tower, fantastically tall, crowned with prongs, its dark shape cutting the sky in half.

A brass trumpet blared—the watchman's signal. Two or three Skyhorses circled like flies against the raw wound of the western sky. When the sea-breeze had settled, the winches began their keening. The Windship was onhebbed down to the docking stair on the west side, one hundred and twelve feet above ground level. The crew flung out lines. Slowly she was hauled in to her mooring against the Tower's shelf.

Once, a grotesque servant had fled from here—nameless, mute, destitute, despised. Now she had returned, Imrhien-Rohain, to the only home she could remember.

As she descended the gangplank on the captain's arm, a young man in Stormrider uniform greeted her. Hard-faced was he, with the predatory look of a vulture. His hair was severely plastered against his skull and bound at the nape of his neck, his taltry was brazenly thrown back. Here stood Lord Ustorix, Son of the House, the Chieftain's heir, who had once been one of her tormentors.

Ustorix met the arrivals with a deep bow and a calm formality at odds with his demeanor, for his gestures evinced intense excitement and the tension in his face betrayed a desperate covetousness. At his shoulder crowded numerous other Tower gentlefolk in black and silver, led by Ustorix's sister Heligea, herself wide-eyed at the sight of this urbane newcomer.

To the Tower-dwellers, Rohain appeared the paradigm of courtiers. Prudently, she had kept aside half a dozen costumes when she handed over her wardrobe to Dianella. She was dressed in a fur-lined houppelande tightly fitting to the waist, patterned all over with a stitched motif of artichokes and vine-leaves on a ground of dark blue velvet. Dagged sleeves sweeping the ground were folded back to flaunt undersleeves of gold tisshew on deep red velvet, tight to the wrist. Three aerial feathers sprouted from her fur taltry-turban. Her cloak of ciclatoune was fastened at the shoulder by a gold filigree agraffe. From her jeweled girdle depended a sharp-bladed anlace in a decorated sheath, a gold tilhal in the shape of a rooster, whose eyes were pink rubies, and a fringed aulmoniere containing a certain swan's feather.

Two rows of bowing Tower footmen in mustard-and-silver livery lined the way from the gatehall of disembarkation. Servants swarmed deferentially. The honoured visitor from Caermelor and her retinue were guided into a wrought-iron lift-cage. Ustorix stood near enough to his guest that nausea overswept her, caused by the familiar odour of his sweat and its past associations. Fighting her illness, she smiled at him, taking note of the way he trembled and flushed. She thought it an interesting effect, as though she brandished a weapon.

'Of course, my father, Lord Voltasus, is in the north, fighting at the King-Emperor's side,' he was saying, waving a gloved hand. 'I am master here during his absence. My lady mother is on a visit to my sister at the Fifth House, in Finvarna. Yet fear not, all has been made ready for Your Ladyship's arrival, although word of your visit came but two days since. The messenger who delivered it neglected to declare that the visitor would be the fairest flower of the Court. He shall suffer for the omission,' he added, with a swaggering bow from which his visitor happened to glance away.

'No doubt,' he continued, 'Your Ladyship has long desired to admire at first hand the strength of the Seventh House, the magnificence of Isse Tower, forever acclaimed in the accolades of bards.'

'No doubt.'

Parochial, supercilious man! she thought. *Do you believe the world has nothing better to do than drone endlessly in praise of Stormriders?*

'Be assured, Your Ladyship shall not be disappointed.'

'I am certain of that.'

High expectations are a necessary prerequisite of disappointment.

The lift-keeper stopped the cage at Floor Thirty-seven, where Ustorix solicitously offered to hand his guest from the cage. Her hands, however, were occupied with lifting the hem of the velvet houppelande. She stepped scrupulously through the door.

'My lady might wish to rest . . . shall be conducted to your quarters . . . obliged if you should sit by my right hand at dinner . . .' The words tumbled out of Ustorix's mouth like fried onion rings—well-oiled, pungent, and hollow. It appeared the Son of the Seventh House waged an inner battle that pitched his innate arrogance against a desire to present himself in what he considered a flatteringly humble manner. He bestowed a second lavish bow. His sister Heligea curtsied. With a brusque nod—she could not bring herself to make polite obeisance to this kindred—Rohain, accompanied by Viviana and a bevy of upper level servants, left them and entered her designated chambers.

It seemed that the more she scorned Ustorix the more he adored her. Deference would have encouraged his contempt, but ill-usage attracted respect. He, like most bullies, must exist either as a boot-heel to crush, or a doormat to be trodden upon.

At dinner Rohain shone like a peacock among crows—and the

crows hung on her every word, copied her every gesture. They presumed that everything she did was the epitome of the latest mode. Of course, they said among themselves, she must be conversant with the latest trends—she had been dwelling at Court. What endeared her to them further was that there was no indecorous laughter from this fashionable courtier, no overt show of emotion to offend their stoicism. A complete model of detachment, she displayed admirable aloofness. Furthermore, she was wealthy, titled, and beautiful into the bargain.

The Greayte Banqueting Hall on Floor Thirty-one seemed small and austere after the glitter of Court. Rohain scrutinized every dish, insisting on learning the name of the cook who was responsible for each. The dishes were numerous, designed to impress. Most she waved aside, barely glancing at them. Beckoning her maid to lean closer, she whispered, 'I advise you to partake of nothing prepared by the hands of the cook named Rennet Thighbone. I know he never checks the vegetables for snails. He also cleans his filthy fingernails by kneading pastry, and spits into the sauces—and those are not the worst of his habits.'

'Gramercie, m'lady. With gladness I take this advice.'

'The masters of this place are unaware of it,' added Rohain.

Ustorix fawned, pouring out blandishments. He began intentionally addressing Rohain with the archaic forms 'thee' and 'thou', whose meaning had evolved from olden times to convey the close association of brotherhood, as between high-ranking Stormriders—or an intimacy of affection, such as between lovers.

'May I tempt thee with a slice of pigeon pie, my lady? The pastry looks interesting—spiced, I fancy, by the spotted look of it. Or perhaps thou wouldst prefer to taste of this dish of cabbage with, I think, rather charming raisins—or baked leveret glazed with quinces and a little of this excellent foaming sauce?'

Rohain said softly to Viviana, 'Tell Lord Ustorix's page to instantly inform his master that it is hardly appropriate to address me with such familiarity.'

The message having reached its destination, the heir of the House upset his wine in startled mortification, thus adding to his distress. Both he and the page blushed to their ears. Ustorix kicked the lad, sending him sprawling, and bawled a petulant criticism at a passing steward.

The sauce foamed in its pewter boat. Avoiding it, Rohain sipped the fern-green wine, whose flavour had probably been beneficially influenced by the presence of moss-frogs in the cellar.

'My Lord,' Rohain remarked conversationally, turning the twin weapons of her glance on Ustorix, 'the fact that Stormriders possess nerves of steel is well-known.'

'Of course, my lady. As Riders we are born to it. Courage flows in the bloodline of the Twelve Houses. Howbeit,' he added hastily, 'an infusion of new blood may sometimes be of benefit, should it be particularly pure.'

'As I was saying, the Stormriders' unrivaled reputation for performing death-defying acts has achieved its pinnacle, methinks, with this latest rumour from Isse Tower which has at last reached the Court.'

'The tale of my brave ride to Ilian during the storms of Imbrol?' The vulture puffed out its chest. 'True, many attempting such a hazardous undertaking would have perished, but I—'

'No. The tale of the Stormriders who stood balanced on sildron, four hundred feet above the ground, wearing no flying-harness or safety ropes.'

Ustorix afforded no reply.

'Zounds, what a feat,' expounded Rohain, warming to her topic. 'We all asked ourselves, *what manner of men are these?* There is naught so charming as a man of heroism and bravery, one who can perform acts of great daring and remain icy cool. Do you not agree, my lady Heligea?'

'Certainly,' replied that lady, who until now had exhibited only bored sullenness.

'One must indeed respect such a man,' persisted Rohain. 'One must adore him. Pray, leave me not in suspense—who were the perpetrators of this rumoured exploit?'

'A couple of the servants,' drawled Heligea insouciantly, before her brother could reply. 'Grod Sheepshorn and Tren Spatchwort.'

The knuckles of Ustorix whitened, like a range of snowy peaks. Gimlet-eyed, he shot a glance of pure hatred at Heligea.

'Servants!' Rohain smiled. 'Well, if the servants are so remark-able, the masters by rights must be doubly so. I suppose 'tis quite a common feat among Stormriders. No doubt you practice it every day. Dearly would I love to witness such a valorous act!'

Am I becoming another Dianella? Oh, but the vulture deserves this, and more.

'May I watch *you* at this trick, my lord?' Rohain asked sweetly. 'It would be something to tell them, at Court.'

Ustorix's face had grayed. He cleared his throat, attempting a thin smile. The object of his adoration gazed at him expectantly.

'Assuredly . . .'

'Delightful,' she said, raising her wineglass in salute. 'I look forward to it. By the by, where are these dauntless servants to be found, this Tron Cocksfoot and Garth Sheepsgate?'

'One of them enlisted. The other—well, I am told he joined the crew of a Windship,' advised Heligea, who seemed to keep herself informed about all events both Below the dock and Above.

'Was there not talk of some other servant,' Rohain continued airily, inwardly remarking on her new persona's ability to dissim-ulate. 'A deformed lad with yellow hair?'

'It is surprising how much talk of Isse Tower's servants reaches the Court,' purred Heligea. 'One wonders how, since Relayers would hardly bother. Yes, there was once one such as Your Ladyship describes. I know not whence he came, nor where he went. Nobody knows.'

'Unfortunately, there may be no time for the sildron demon-stration,' grittily interjected Ustorix. 'I had planned to throw the Tower and demesnes open for a tour of inspection tomorrow, should my lady so condescend.'

'Such an undertaking must prove diverting, but do not deny me, my lord, I pray you! I am certain there will be enough time for other diversions. It is not necessary for me to leave here until I receive word of the King-Emperor's return to Caermelor.'

And so it was arranged. Before her visit came to an end, the Lady Rohain would be granted the entertainment she desired.

Keeping company with Isse Tower's masters soon palled. After dinner, Rohain pleaded travel fatigue and retired to her rooms. There she instructed Viviana to go discreetly among the Tower servants.

'Find an old drudge-woman called Grethet. She works on Floor Five, around the furnaces. There must be no fuss—concoct some story that I've heard she's skilled at healing and wish to ask her advice, or some such explanation. And discover all you can about another servant who once worked here—a lad, yellow-haired, misshapen.'

Shang harbingers prickled Rohain's scalp as she stood in the doorway watching Viviana, gray-cloaked, flit like a thought to the lift-well. There, the lady's maid rang the bell and waited. From the deeps, the cage could be heard clunking upward on its rails. The wrought-iron gates slid apart and Dolvach Trenchwhistle burst forth beefily, followed by a quartet of chambermaids bearing laden trays. On beholding Rohain, the Head Housekeeper came to a sudden halt.

'Oh, er, my lady,' she stammered with a curtsy, 'I was just comin' ter see if there'd be anything Your Ladyship might be wantin'.'

'No. Only peace.'

'Yes, m'lady. Very good, m'lady.'

Dolvach Trenchwhistle turned back toward the lift.

'Trenchwhistle!'

'Yes, m'lady?'

'Carry that tray for that little chambermaid. It is too heavy for her. I am surprised at you. At Court, we hear everything. I had been told that the Head Housekeeper treated her underlings as she would nurture the finest roses. Do not disappoint me.'

'Yes, m'lady. Forgive me, m'lady.'

Flustered, the Head Housekeeper blundered into a tray, knocking it against the wall. Half the contents spilled. She muttered imprecations. As the lift-gates closed, she crooned aggressively to Viviana, 'And what might you be wantin' downstairs my dear?'

Rohain's skin tautened. The air smacked of lightning. Her dark-dyed hair, relieved of the fur turban, lifted of its own accord. She was alone in her chambers in the Tower.

Her door opened onto a wide passage, at one end of which
stood a pair of high and narrow portals. She walked to them,
pushed them apart. They gave onto a balcony with a dominite
balustrade. Spoutings sprouted winged gargoyles, their tongues
protruding. The cool night wind shouldered its way past, bringing
a whiff of the sea that knocked at memory's gates. Down below
at the dock, the *Harper's Carp* bobbed, waiting to return to
Caermelor with the morning breeze, since it could not be spared
from duty. The Greayte Southern Star winked like an emerald beacon gemming the horizon. It being the middle of the month, the
moon was full. A silver note sounded from somewhere in the
crenellations overhead. An impossible silhouette flew across the
moon's face—a Stormrider coming in from a Run.

The unstorm travelled close in his wake. Rohain watched it
cover the forest, far below, with tiny firefly glows, here and there
shining brighter where a tableau pulsed. Isse Harbour was transformed into a carpet of gaudy fish-scales, green and gold. A real
Seaship lay at anchor there. A ghostly galleon foundered off the
headland, like the Seaship in a song Sianadh had once sung about
a vessel caught in the Ringstorm:

'If ye go forth into the north ye'll see her evermore—
The ship and crew so brave and true, do perish o'er and o'er.
Outlin'd in gold from top to hold, each clew and spar and
     cleat—
She founders ever and again in terrible repeat.'

'From whence come I?' Rohain said softly. 'From beyond the
Ringstorm? Could it be that I sailed from unknown lands beyond
the girdle of outrageous winds, and survived?'

The unstorm's terrible splendor rolled by. She walked back
toward her chambers but had not yet reached the tall doors when
a disquieting occurrence took place, a jarring note in the paean of
her triumphant return to Isse Tower.

Almost soundlessly, out of the moonshadows, something
limped rapidly across the passageway.

'Stop!' she reprimanded.

It checked, for the space of a heartbeat, then backed away.

'Pod—it is Pod, isn't it?'

A hoarse sob broke from a throat.

'You! You back again! I told you to leave me alone,' Pod gasped. 'Go away. Go from here. You might bring doom on this place.'

'You know me?' She was incredulous. 'But how—'

'Yes, I know you. You used to live here. Now you have come back. Come back to bring ruin on us all.'

'No, I have not—' but she knew herself to be at his mercy. Pod alone knew her, instantly, when in her altered persona she had scarcely known herself. It lent him a certain power.

'Grethet,' she said. 'Tell her to come to me. Prithee.'

'Cannot do that.'

'Why not? I shall pay you.'

'I do not want *your* tainted gold. Anyway, the crone's dead— Grethet's cold in her grave.'

With that, Pod limped to some hitherto unnoticed slot in a wall and sidled into it. Rohain called into the darkness after him but he did not reappear. Perhaps he was lying . . .

Clouds ate up the moon and a rapid wind slammed the doors shut.

'A rum and gloomy lot they are, m'lady,' announced Viviana, 'the servants here. All save three of them—the old codger they call the Storyteller, he's all right, and there is a rather strapping strapper among them, by the name of Pennyrigg. He knows how to laugh, at least, not like the rest. And one little girl—she seems ever so nice—name of Caitri Lendoon.'

'The daughter of the Keeper of the Keys.'

'How clever is my lady, to know all the names of the servants!'

'The yellow-haired lad—what did they say about him?'

'Where he came from and where he has gone are mysteries.'

'What did you find out about Grethet?'

'Why, she died, they told me. That's all they said.'

Rohain fell silent. Eventually, she sighed. She must not reveal her grief. Inwardly she was crying, aching for the sake of the old woman who had roughly nurtured her, and who had been the last possible link to her old life.

''Tis late, my lady,' said Viviana gently. 'Oughtn't you to be abed?'

'I suppose so. You were long away, Via, what else did you hear?'

'Well, the Storyteller, he told a couple of wondrous interesting tales. I could not help listening. He has a way with him; he reels his listeners in like fishes, so to speak.'

'Yes. Maybe that old Grethet had a story too. It will never be told now.'

The tidings of Grethet's demise caused Rohain to despair about her future. What course should she choose now? She might not return to Caermelor or Arcune. In the absence of any other plans she resolved to remain at Isse Tower until inspiration or opportunity should present itself.

They walked in the demesnes: Rohain, Ustorix, Viviana, the captain and first mate of the *Harper's Carp*, numerous hangers-on and attendants, and the disconsolate Heligea dressed in black with silver buttons. The solemn shadow of the Tower unrolled itself across the Road and fell into the Harbour. Gulls scourged a cloud-ridden sky.

At Rohain's side, Ustorix raved grandiosely. 'These are the hattocking-circuits, m'lady of the Sorrows,' he proclaimed, giving an expansive wave. 'Smithy and stables are over that way. All that you can see is under my sway. Isse is the keystone of the entire Relay network, and without the network the Kingdom grinds to a halt, the Empire stalls.

'Yeoman Riders, operating at an altitude of three hundred feet, are the younger Sons of the House. They ride for us on miscellaneous errands, or Relay for simple folk with urgent personal messages and enough coin scraped together to pay the fee. The largest squadron, the Regimental, makes its runs at four hundred feet. These are the mercantile wings. They Relay for wealthy merchants, who lavish upon them the appropriate deference and reimbursement, being dependent on our goodwill.' He turned eagerly to Rohain. 'Knowledge is power,' he proclaimed, as though he had invented the phrase. 'The merchant who learns of enterprises early might send his own ships ahead to catch his rivals' trade. He who is blessed with first tidings of a shortage might buy up that commodity before prices rise!'

Absently, Rohain acknowledged his words.

'The Noblesse Squadron, of course,' he ranted, 'rides sky for the peers of the realm—their assigned altitude of five hundred feet is second only to the fastest and highest ranked, the Royals, also known as the King's Emissaries, who are entrusted with state business.' Rohain stifled a yawn.

'Would my lady like to see the ornamental gardens?' suggested Heligea halfheartedly, diverting attention from her brother. The visitor's eyes had meanwhile alighted elsewhere.

'For what purpose are those long buildings roofed with slate tiles?'

'They are the workshops of our wizard,' smoothly replied Heligea, 'Zimmuth, who was introduced to my lady at dinner. Most dull and cluttered are his sheds. Now, the gardens—'

'Let us visit the workshops.'

The interior of Zimmuth's main lair was grossly cluttered. Springs, alembics, coils of copper tubing, buckled sheets of metal, gear systems both rack-and-pinion and epicyclic, pendulums, levers, cams, cranks, differentials, bearings, pulleys, assorted tools, and stone jars containing alkahest and corrosive substances crowded every horizontal surface. The well-thumbed pages of a couple of ephemerides flapped weakly, held down by embossed leather bookmarks. Magnetic compasses, theodolites, telescopes, and pocket sundials had been shoved arbitrarily into worn wooden cases with specially shaped satin-lined compartments. Constructions resembling metal innards ticked and whirred. An impossibly configured planetarium dangled from the roof-beams, hitting the heads of all who passed under it. In one corner a clock struck fifteen and fell over with a *sproing*.

Men in skullcaps, with stained taltries and disfigured faces, hammered and filed and sawed. Zimmuth waxed enthusiastic, buzzing like an obsessed bee.

'The sildron hoister project is over here,' he spouted, 'a new and more efficient lift system. And here is a modern skimmer being built. We had another but it blew asunder in the end. You understand, sildron and andalum will not bind to any other metal—these types of rotors tend to fly apart eventually, like the propellers of Windships. There is inherent instability. And yet I predict that every Tower shall have one someday. And over there, we are developing an improved andalum girth for eotaurs, to make the onhebbing easier.'

'Wizard.'

Zimmuth broke off his monologue. 'Er, yes—um?' Already he had forgotten the visitor's name.

Rohain idly flicked a scrap of iron off a bench. It rang dully on the raddled flagstones.

'Fashion a sildron-powered butterchurn,' she suggested.

'What?' Uncouthly, the wizard gaped.

'And try your hand at designing a powered spinning-wheel, or better still, a loom.'

He scratched his matted beard. An earwig dropped out. 'But what's the point of it? I mean, that is women-servants' work.'

'Precisely. Facilitating it would give the women more time.'

'To do what?'

'Other things.'

'Well, yes, I suppose so. But they do not know how to do other things.'

'Such as building precondemned vehicles out of incompatible materials? Doubtless they could work it out if they had time to try, and the inclination.'

The wizard had already transferred his attention away from her words. He sucked on his teeth, then jabbed a finger in the air.

'A butterchurn. Yes! It can be done.' Like a blinkered horse he trotted away, summoning his henchmen.

'My lady sows interesting ideas,' commented Heligea as the party of gentlefolk moved out of the workshops and toward the gardens. Musingly she twisted her beaded taltry-strings.

'I have heard tell of another, here at Isse, who dabbles in the Arts,' said Rohain. 'Who is that?'

'A false rumour,' interjected Ustorix. 'No one here is acquainted with wizardry save Zimmuth.'

'That will be Mortier,' said Heligea deliberately. 'He used to be Master at Swords.'

'No longer?'

'No. You see, m'lady, he used to try to transact with wights, outside the demesnes. He thought they would give him power over the unstorm.'

'Heligea!' Ustorix rapped.

'One day he was out in the forest with some servants who were a-gathering,' his sister went on blandly, 'and—'

'We are now come to the gardens,' pompously interrupted her brother. A footman ran to open the gate and, bowing, stood aside to let them enter.

'And the unstorm came,' persevered Heligea.

'Be silent, chit, or you will answer to me!'

'My lord Ustorix, pray allow dear Heligea to continue,' reproved Rohain. In the Stormrider's neck, the tendons popped.

'Well,' said Heligea, breaking off a woody stem of poplar and using it to idly thrash its mother tree, 'our good Master Mortier took fright at being caught by the unstorm in the open. He ran away.'

The party strolled down a gravel path between uninspiringly leafless hedges. Heligea prodded moodily with her whip-stalk at the groin of a skeletal rosebush, avoiding the furious gaze of her brother.

'We sent out searchers, of course,' she went on, 'and we finally found him. But it was vile.'

'What had happened?'

'We saw his boots first, dangling some way off the ground, swinging slightly. His feet were in them. He was hanging high on a Barren Holly, strung up cruelly on its branches. We cut him down—a wind sprang up as we did so—how the Holly thrashed and hissed!'

'Nay!' exclaimed Rohain in horror and disbelief.

'He was still alive when we cut him down,' blithely said young Heligea. 'He survived, but he could not speak. His throat was ruined, from hanging there. In truth, his mind was deranged too. He could not teach swordsmanship anymore, but when he recovered partially he took to hammering late at nights at some invention he was working on in his chambers. One night as he was working away with only his servant nigh, his rushlight suddenly blew out and the hammer was knocked from his hand. When the servant managed to kindle a light he found Master Mortier pinned to his bench by his own hands. His fingers had to be forced apart to prise him off. After that he lost the use of his hands entirely. Now he has to be fed through a straw. He sits and does nothing. His hair drops out from his scalp until he is smooth and moist. He is no better than a great slug.'

The skycaptain and the first mate laughed boorishly. 'A sluggard, no less!' they joked.

'Cry pity!' gasped Viviana, grimacing. Her mistress shuddered. She felt the hairs rise on her scalp and recalled with misgivings a curse she had once mouthed at the Master at Swords.

A strung-out note pierced the sky from high above. Prim Heligea craned her neck to catch a glimpse of the incoming Stormrider.

'I must be informed at once if that Relayer brings word from the Royal City,' said Rohain.

But from Caermelor there came no tidings.

Rohain felt uneasy. Like a sticky cobweb, a restless melancholy settled over her. It seemed that all plans, all hopes, had come to a standstill. Sianadh sat alone in a cell, the shadow of a rope falling across his neck. She, Rohain so-called, stood un-alone in a tower, the thorn of hopeless passion piercing her heart, the burden of a friend's life weighing heavily on her shoulders, while the picture she had so foolishly allowed herself to paint, of life as a baroness at Arcune, was being washed away in the bleak rains of Fuarmis, the Coldmonth.

Far away in Namarre Thorn was fighting. Perhaps his life was even now in danger. Worse, perhaps he had been slain . . . That possibility did not bear contemplation and she thrust it from her mind. What weird and malignant enemies might he be facing? And what would happen if the strength of the Empire's legions should fail and be vanquished? Stormriders would come hurtling back with messages: *Escape, flee for your lives. The Empire is overthrown, all is lost* . . .

Rohain envisioned the network of Relayer runs reaching from point to point across the kingdom like a mightier cobweb, their tension increasing so that they must thrum like overstretched wires. Dianella crouched like a spider in a corner, waiting. Beside that lady lurked a darkness that was not her shadow but another like herself, only more heinous: the wizard Sargoth. At the ganglion of the cobweb loomed the Tower. At a pitch too high for human hearing, the word *impasse* screamed through Rohain's head.

What would this waiting bring?

'I hope the King-Emperor shall return soon to Caermelor,' said Rohain, in a private moment with her maid. 'Think you that he will spare Sianadh's life, Viviana? What *kind* of man is he, the King-Emperor? A merciful man?'

Viviana waxed circumspect.

'Wise is how I should describe him, my lady—merciful when mercy is justified, ruthless to warmongers and other evildoers. A shame it is, that he should dwell in widowerhood.'

'Ah, yes. Queen-Empress Katharine met her death in terrible circumstances, that much I know. What exactly happened to her? Nobody will enlighten me. Indeed, it seems forbidden to mention the topic, except in the most cursory way.'

The girl replied in low tones, 'It is not spoken of at Court anymore. But we all know. Leastways, we know the main events, but some tell the tale one way, some tell it another. I can tell it the way I heard it but I know not if 'tis correct in every detail.'

'Prithee, say on.'

'It happened by the sea. Their two Imperial Majesties were out riding, late, along the strand, when a mist came down and they were separated from their retinue. For a time they rode on, calling to their guards and courtiers, but they could find none. All of a sudden the Queen's horse took fright and bolted. His Majesty spurred his horse and rode after her, hearing her screams through the mist, but when he caught up, he saw her horse in its death throes, mangled, and the Queen being dragged into the sea. He sprang off his steed and ran into the water. Something unspeakably unseelie seized him. It was none other than Nuckelavee, the flayed centaur—no doubt my lady has heard of this terrible monster. His Majesty slashed at it with his sword but it would have dragged him under too, only that with the last of his strength he put his hunting horn to his mouth and blew a long call. At the sound, his attacker loosened its grip and drew back. When his men found him, King James was half-perished, but still trying to drag himself into the waves. They had to pull him out of the water—he would have plunged in after his lady. She was never seen again, and she not yet five-and-twenty.

'That happened some ten years ago, when the Prince was but a lad. Prince Edward seems older than his years, methinks, but has grown up fine and handsome.' Viviana clasped her hands, staring into some unguessed distance. 'His Majesty never took another bride. At that time, all the royal princesses of Erith's lands were either too young or already wed. Besides, it is said he loved Katharine so much that he could never love another.'

'A tragic tale.'

'Verily. The grief of it changed His Majesty in some ways. He is at once sadder and merrier than before, so they say, although I never knew him aforetimes. I was but a child. They say, too, that sorrow sobered him, for since that time he has thrown all his fervour into ruling well and wisely. The lands of Erith, before this Namarran uprising, have never been so peaceful and prosperous. But then, the House of D'Armancourt has ever been the most powerful dynasty. The historians tell us there has been some special quality, something beyond the ordinary, in all who are born to that line. They say that royal blood is puissant. It sets them apart.'

Twice the Winter sun opened its shrunken eye. Both days were soused with rain. The next morning dawned clear.

Enclosed within the Tower, daily confronted by its horribly

familiar smells and sights, and their painful associations, Rohain grew restless and irritable. She longed to be free of these environs, but had no notion of where she might go.

One evening, after dinner, a wild mood seized her. Leaning toward the sulky Heligea, she asked quietly, 'Do you ride?'

'It is my most favoured pursuit.'

'Do you ride sky?'

'To shoot the blue,' said the Daughter of the House, 'is of all things what I desire most.'

'You are of the Blood.'

'It is forbidden. And will ever be.'

'Why?'

'It is simply not done.'

'Not a good enough reason. Ride sky with me on the very morrow.'

Heligea turned disbelieving eyes on Rohain. 'Hoy-day! You would never dare!'

'I would. You would too. Wait until your brother is otherwise occupied. The equerries, the grooms, the ostlers—they will not gainsay the daughter of Lord Voltasus.'

''Sblood! 'Tis impossible!' Heligea seemed lit up from within, as if a lamp burned behind the porcelain skin of her face.

Unfolding their mighty wings the next morning, two eotaurs sallied forth from Gate East Three Hundred on the Yeoman Flight level. They circled the demesnes and galloped out across the forest. Beneath flying-helmets, the Riders were masked. They rode astride, demonstrating consummate skill, like Relayers of many years' experience; yet instead of following a Run they branched off, toured the local terrain, and were back in the Tower before noon.

Ustorix's rage was uncontainable.

At first he directed it at his sister, threatening her with death for breaking one of the most ancient and honoured tenets of the Twelve Houses. He scandalized the Tower's occupants with the vulgar raising of his voice, his fiery displays of temper.

When he had finished haranguing his sister, Ustorix rushed

unexpectedly through the door of Rohain's suite. His colour
burned high, his nostrils flared. His hair had escaped its bonds and
now draggled in sweaty tendrils.

'What is the meaning of your bursting so rudely in upon me,
Lord Ustorix?' demanded Rohain, rising from the chair by the fireplace where she had been seated.

'You know it!' He strode forward, careless in his wrath. 'Riding
sky is *not* the prerogative of women. Women have not the strength
for it. Only noblemen possess the finesse and acuity required to
learn the skills of governing eotaurs and the fickle currents of the
atmosphere. How will Isse Tower be regarded when word of your
folly is spread abroad? It will be said that we of the Seventh House
cannot keep our women in their place. It will be said that we are
weak, and our women are frolicsome and willful. You have
destroyed the reputation of the Seventh House. You have brought
ruin upon us all.'

'I hardly think so. Take control of yourself, sir. These emotive
scenes are scarcely seemly. We ladies can ride sky as featly as any
gentleman. No harm has been done. It is a lesson—'

'Hear me!' He gripped her by the arm. 'I'll be hanged if you
don't need lessoning, and hanged if I'll not teach you.'

'Unhand me!'

The young Stormrider glanced down. In his guest's hand, the
point of the anlace, still chained to her girdle, jabbed the hard
flesh of his stomach. He released his grip on her arm.

'How dare you!' Rohain enunciated carefully. Every ounce of
hatred and scorn for him that she had ever stored flung its weight
behind those words. Suddenly Ustorix dropped to one knee.

'Forgive me. Forgive me,' he gasped over and over. 'I was not
myself. I did not mean—'

'Depart!'

'Rohain, I am in . . .' He squirmed in anguish, groping for
words of apology and excuse.

'Avaunt! Get out!' At the sight of his groveling, Rohain felt only
revulsion.

He went.

She wished that she had never thought of riding an eotaur,

joyful as the experience had been. She scrubbed her arm raw where he had touched it.

At dinner, Ustorix was all scrupulous politeness. He said, 'Tonight I will demonstrate the balancing feat.'

'It is not necessary,' said Rohain.

'It will be done,' he stated tightly.

Gate South Five Hundred gaped, the cusps of its portcullis pointing like daggers. Far below the overhanging threshold, miniature outbuildings were pricked by tiny lights shining from their windows. A light tracery of vapor sculled past, upon a thermal layer, about a hundred feet below. All was black and silver: the forest, as dark as Dianella's hair; the ocean, as silver as a trow's desire; the sky, as colourless as cellar slugs.

Heligea was present, with Ustorix and Rohain and a young Relayer displaying three stars on his epaulettes.

'Lord Ustorix,' said Rohain formally, sincerely regretting her taunting, 'I beg you not to attempt this.'

Now this pompous ass was going to lose his life because she had craved vengeance. It had seemed a good idea at the dinner table, considering her past sufferings, but now that the time had come she wished she had held back her words. She would not relish witnessing anyone's life being snuffed out. Revenge was supposed to be sweet. This tasted sour.

Her anxiety only served to fuel Ustorix's intent.

'Stand aside,' he commanded heroically.

A refractory wind, which had been pummeling the Tower, tapered off. The Stormrider carefully placed the sildron ingots. They hovered. He ran and jumped. Agile and strong from riding sky, he found his footing and, as the momentum transferred to the metal bars, caught his balance. Like an acrobat he stood poised, slowing.

'Well done, sir!' breathed the three-starred Relayer.

'The deed is done,' Ustorix called back over his shoulder. His helper tossed him a rope to haul him in. He glided back like a tremulous skater, until, without warning, the quiescent wind reawoke. With a gust forceful enough to shake the Tower walls, it pushed him sideways.

He fell.

Heligea screamed. Rohain squeezed her eyes shut.

'My lord!' The three-starred Relayer peered over the edge. 'Are you hale?' he shouted, rather redundantly. The rope hung slack in his hand. The sildron ingots had shot away into the night and were nowhere to be seen.

Ustorix's hand appeared in midair. He had been floating, unharmed.

'The rope.' His voice was cracked and strained.

The aide reeled him in. As he clambered onto the salient door-sill, Ustorix pulled off his jacket and began unfastening the buckles of the sildron harness he had worn beneath to provide him with complete safety.

Heligea's laugh was cut short by her brother's virulent scowl.

'I shall do it again,' he grated.

'No, Ustor, you are safe now. It does not matter that you cheated,' cried Heligea.

Ustorix flung down the harness. 'Give me the spare ingots, Callidus.'

'Ustorix, you must not!' beseeched Heligea. Gallant Callidus dragged her away.

For the second time that night, the heir of the House threw sildron into the outer airs. He took a deep breath and walked toward the edge. The whole of Eldaraigne yawned below, an expanse so vast and distant that it seemed to suck the very marrow out of his bones.

He collapsed on the floor in a faint.

When a pair of footmen had carried away the young lord, Rohain remained, for a time, alone in the gatehall. The wind was rising. From the core of this thirty-second story, the sound of horses came to her ears. They moved in their stalls, scuffling their hooves. She walked past the alcoves and vestibules leading off to either side, and continued down the wide straw-strewn corridors that circumnavigated the fortress's walls. Eotaurs leaned over their demi-doors to blow their warm breath on her hands, allowing her to scratch their ears and stroke their forelocks.

From the corner of her eye she viewed a small shape edging furtively past.

'Pod.'

It shrieked.

'Pod, do not go away. I will depart from here if you tell me something.'

'What?'

'Where did Grethet find me? How came I here?'

The lad mumbled.

'I do not understand what you are saying. Prithee, Pod, I returned here to find this out—for that reason only.'

'Carters brought you in. Road-caravan.'

'Did the carters say anything about me?'

'Said they found you.'

'Where?'

'At the old mines—near the accursed place.'

'What accursed place?'

'Carter-captain had on a fine cloak, he did. A very fine cloak.'

'What accursed place?' she repeated insistently.

'Got to go now.'

'Pod! You are my one chance. If there is any kindness left in you, have pity!'

'You had no pity. You made me go on the ship.'

Rohain seized Pod's wrist. 'Is force the only thing you heed?'

He wriggled. She released him and he scrambled away.

'I shall tell them you hide in the goat-caves,' she called.

'No!' wailed the lad, already out of sight. His voice floated back: 'Don't tell them where I hide. Huntingtowers. It was at Huntingtowers they found you.'

Huntingtowers. Rarely had that place been mentioned by the servants when the yellow-haired lad had lived among them. Like the Fair Realm, like the Unseelie Attriod, it was considered to be a subject that, if discussed openly, attracted ill-fortune in the guise of the wrath of some unspecified agency; yet, like children with an itchy scab, the lowly denizens of the Tower could not leave it quite alone, and sometimes they hinted at it in whispers. It was the name of the haunted crater-lake lying northwest of Isse Tower.

Huntingtowers had another name, but what it was, none of the servants knew. It lay some two days' ride away, toward the Cape of Tides, and it was said to be most evilly infested with unseelie wights—a hub of all things eldritch that irrevocably hated mortal men. A hill rose from the land there, but it had no tall and rounded peak. Instead, its centre was sunken and hollow, resembling a giant cauldron. Within this crucible of soil and stone lay a black lake whose level almost reached to the barren rim. Many cone-shaped islands were scattered across this forbidding water, some large, many small. On the central islet, the largest, a strange building had existed for as long as anyone could remember. It was a grim tower surrounded by eight others in a circle, each joined to its two neighbours and the central edifice by the stone arches of several flying bridges. From this fortress, the place had received its kenning, for it was said that an eldritch Hunt dwelt therein, the most terrible Hunt of all, so cruel and merciless that for miles around this black cauldron no mortal folk dared to dwell and even *lorraly* birds and beasts shunned the region. Folk who dwelled on the fringes would speak of their horror as, huddled in their cottages at night, they listened to sounds from high above: the baying of unnatural hounds, the weird and hideous screams of the Hunter, the rush of wind as eldritch steeds careened through the skies.

On nights of a full moon the Wild Hunt would debouch from its stronghold. Indeed, it had sometimes been seen through the spyglasses of the watchmen on the parapets of Isse Tower. So far the unseelie hunters had ignored the heavily fortified House of the Stormriders, but whosoever witnessed the Wild Hunt trembled at the certainty that come morning some road-caravan, or remote-dwelling charcoal-burner or cotter, or someone straying late abroad, would be gone, never to be seen again; or else would be found, far from home, lying torn to pieces in a pool of blood.

Viviana found out from the servants that lately the region of Huntingtowers had fallen into an unusual quietude. The Wild Hunt had not been sighted for many months and it was thought that the dwellers in the black caldera had removed to the north, responding to the mysterious Call; but of that there was no certainty, for no one dared venture there to see.

The moon was just past the full. If from Huntingtowers she had come, reasoned Rohain, then to Huntingtowers she must return. There existed no other clue to her past. From the high windows of the strange edifice in the centre of the crater-lake, any aerial approach would doubtless be spied. The only chance for her to reconnoiter undetected in its environs lay in getting there by the deserted and therefore less scrutinized land-routes.

'Viviana.'

The lady's maid looked up at her mistress. She had been sewing by candlelight, cocking her head and holding the work at arm's length, peering with utmost concentration as she stitched loose beadwork more securely onto the fringed aulmoniere. Her softly rounded face looked younger in the candle's dandelion glow. Her large and limpid eyes reflected the flame. She held the needle poised for the next stitch.

'Yes, m'lady?'

Rohain seated herself beside the girl.

'I wish to tell you something in the strictest confidence. Viviana, you have been a good servant to me, and a kind friend.'

The hand holding the sliver of silver abruptly dropped to its owner's lap.

'Some events have taken place,' said Rohain, 'which make it impossible for me to keep you on.'

'Oh no, my lady, prithee do not say that!' Viviana stuck the needle through the purse and put it aside. 'I do not want to leave your service.'

'I have with me enough items of value to pay the wages you are owed, and a little extra for a gift, in thanks,' said Rohain. 'After that I shall not be able to afford a maid.'

'But you are a lady! Your estate, your jewels—'

'Are no longer mine. And I am not a gentlewoman—not by birth, I think. I am just like you.'

'I cannot believe it!'

'It is true. Furthermore, I am about to embark upon a perilous journey to a perilous place. You cannot come on this path with me, Viviana, and so I am going to send for a Windship to take you back to Caermelor.'

'My lady, you could not say anything that would make me more miserable,' Viviana said quickly and tremulously. 'Send me back? Never. I shall not go.'

'There is no choice. You belong at Court, not here.'

'I shall be sent back to the Marchioness! Ugh! I'd rather be a scullery maid. No—I shall stay with you.'

'But I cannot pay your wages, after this day, and how should you make a living?'

'In the same way as you, I expect,' said Viviana, spreading her hands palms upward. 'Whatever that may be.'

'As for that, I suppose I shall go into service again if I return alive.'

Viviana pondered. 'Go you into some kind of adventure?'

'Yes—no. It may be a tedious mission or it may be tremendously dangerous and life-threatening.'

'Well then, that's not much different from life at Court, m'lady.'

Rohain laughed. 'It is not necessary to hail me by a courtesy title now.'

'I cannot help it, m'lady. Prithee, let me accompany you.'

'After what I have told you, do you still wish to come?'

'Yes.'

'Why?'

'I'd rather be here than there, if you take my meaning.'

'Would you?' It was Rohain who pondered now. 'I like you,' she said at last, 'which is why I'd rather not put you at risk.'

'Seeing as how you're not paying my wages anymore, you have no say in the matter,' said Viviana primly, picking up the aulmoniere and resuming her sewing. 'And now you had better tell me the whole story, m'lady.'

So Rohain launched into the tale of her service at Isse Tower, her escape and the finding of the treasure that had allowed her to purchase a cure for her deformity, some fine clothing, and a new identity. She told also of her quest for the past, but, suffering from an ache that throbbed in her heart, she could not bear to mention

Thorn—not yet. To her words, Viviana listened with equanimity. At the conclusion she said, 'I declare, m'lady, you have been through more adventures than the Dowager Marchioness's crook-tailed tomcat. Yet I have no doubt you are of noble birth, judging by your bearing, and this history you tell has not changed my opinion of you in the slightest. To me, you remain the Lady Rohain.'

Rohain shook her head with a nonplussed smile, taken aback at her friend's stubbornness and heartily grateful for it.

No breath of wind ruffled the day. In Isse Harbour, the sea lay satin-smooth, barely moving. Hanging in seaweed valleys far below, countless jellyfish pulsed like glacial moons, blue-white, see-through, finely fimbriated. The Seaship that Rohain had spied from the gargoyled balcony lay becalmed. Its departure had been delayed. This was not the stillness of tranquillity; rather the deadly motionlessness of a predator poised to attack.

Rohain had spun a fabrication to her hosts, made of half-truths, improvisations, and prevarications. She told them that all she had heard about Huntingtowers had piqued her curiosity; that the vogue among the jaded courtiers of Caermelor was to journey in search of novelty and exciting adventure; that the moon was just past the full and therefore this was the best time to explore, or at least to view from the caldera's rim the infamous abode of the Hunt, thus obtaining a delicious thrill of horror. It was a fabrication as full of holes as lace, but it was the best she could concoct on short notice. So bedazzled were they by this living jewel in their midst that her hosts accepted it.

How easily the lies roll out, she thought again, ashamed. *I am no better than Dianella.*

As a groom helped her mount a landhorse Rohain fought a stifling sense of dread. Once in the saddle, she looked around at the other riders. Ustorix in light armour, Viviana, the wizard Zimmuth and one of his scarred henchmen, Dain Pennyrigg, Keat Featherstone from the stables, and Lord Callidus had all wanted to accompany her. Sensing doom, she wished them out of her retinue. If catastrophe struck, their blood would be on her hands.

'Now is your final chance to turn back,' she said, 'one and all. If I choose to ride into danger, merely for the purpose of satisfying my curiosity concerning this ill-famed place, it is not your responsibility. You have the right to withdraw.'

The wizard's henchman made as if to dismount and was stayed by a gesture from Ustorix. Nobody spoke. Like the ship in the harbour, the party's departure had also been delayed. They had set out earlier that morning, but after they had ridden a few miles the wizard's horse had cast a shoe and he had insisted upon them returning to have it reshod. Most of the morning had worn away by the time they set out again.

Ustorix raised his visor. 'We shall have to set a good pace now,' he said, 'if we are to reach the Hill of Rowans by nightfall.'

Heligea stood plucking at her brother's cloak.

'Please, Ustor. Take me with you.'

'No.' He pushed her away with his boot. 'Forward,' he added over his shoulder.

The twelve landhorses, four of them carrying only packs, moved off. Heligea stood watching them leave, her hands planted defiantly on her hips.

'I hate you, Ustorix!' she shouted, kicking one of the grooms in the shins.

The party passed through the heavily fortified front gate of the demesnes, turned right, and disappeared from view. The Tower stared out to sea. Behind it, in the servants' graveyard, no wind ruffled the wreath of leaves and berries placed by Rohain beneath the wooden stick marking Grethet's last resting place.

The riders hastened along the beaten dirt of the road. Trees burned black by wintry gales locked fingers overhead, forming a dark tunnel. Every portable precaution against wights accompanied the travellers: bells on bridles, salt, bread, ash keys, the ground-ivy *athair luss*, sprays of dried hypericum tied with red ribbons to rowan staves, tilhals and other charms, self-bored stones, and amber. Every fabric garment was worn inside out, save for the taltries tied closely around their heads. Lords Ustorix and Callidus, flanking Rohain on strong war-horses, had encased themselves in armour of plate and chain. Thus iron-clad, they must surely be invulnerable. The wizard carried a tall, whirring contraption that resembled a windmill, which he said was a modern wight-deterrent and which he cast aside after a couple of miles because it was too heavy for him or his henchman to carry for long.

Their plan was to halt for the night at a hill crowned with rowans, where the serving-men would set up pavilions. Zimmuth was to weave a tight wall of spells about the encampment to keep it safe during the long hours of darkness, the most dangerous time.

After noon the sky darkened with unusual rapidity. The sun became obscured behind a wall of somber gray clouds; its location could only be guessed. Judging by the deepening dusk, it must have been starting to slide toward the horizon when the road began to twist back on itself, climbing steeply.

'We have reached Longbarrow Ridge,' announced Callidus, pushing back his talium-lined visor. 'On a clear day, the Hill of Rowans can be seen from the summit. Once we have crossed the ridge, we shall be less than an hour's ride from the hill. I'll warrant we'll be there by nightfall.'

As he spoke, a heartbeat awoke out of the southeast.

It was an urgent, syncopated throbbing, deep and dire, the supple-wristed thudding of polished wood against goat-hide stretched over a resounding concavity. The voice of Isse Tower was broadcasting a warning.

'The drums!' exclaimed Ustorix echoingly from within his helm. 'The drums of alarum!'

The riders urged forward their horses, hearkening to the compelling rhythm, their pulses rousing to its thrill. The trees thinned and gave way to stunted vegetation. Emerging at the top of a bald ridge, the riders were able to command an unobstructed view. Under clear skies, they might have been able to see the landscape for miles around.

There they reined in, by mutual agreement. Not a word had been spoken, but the presentiment was almost palpable. Why were the drums being sounded? What had the distant Tower watchmen seen? Fear had begun to overtake them all, and they looked to the north from whence, unaccountably, the fear emanated.

Something unseelie was coming.

Swiftly, it was coming.

The evening darkened. Low thunderclouds completely covered the sky like a blanket, from horizon to horizon, and a thick gray mist roiled up from the hollows of the land. Even the sea, so close at hand, was hidden. By now, it seemed to the riders that they stood on an island in an ocean of fog, with a heavy ceiling pressing down on their heads and threatening to crush them. They all faced north, straining their eyes to pierce the thickening murk. From that direction came a certainty of sheer horror that enveloped them like some oppressive mantle. Their limbs weighed so heavily they could scarcely move a muscle. It was onerous, in that ghastly miasma, even to think of lifting a hand to guide the horses toward shelter. An unnatural lethargy pinned the riders to the ridgetop.

Their terror increased as sounds approached along the roof of the sky—a baying and yammering, a deep thunder, the crazed hallooing, the berserk screaming of carnivorous horses like the screech of metal ripped asunder. A denser cloud ballooned out of the rest and raced straight toward the watchers. Bursting from its depths loomed the shapes of fire-eyed hounds and dark riders on mounts that snorted flame. Ahead of them plunged their leader— a thing shaped like a man.

Yet it was no true man.

It was a darkness with two sunken sumps for eyes; and, not worn as a helm would be worn, but growing from the head, magnificent when gracing a stag, yet obscene on this human parody—the appalling tines, a pair of wide skull-claws, the antlers.

At the instant these apparitions appeared, Ustorix screamed and launched himself sideways off his horse. In panic, Callidus's steed reared and threw its rider. Zimmuth's mount bolted downhill, followed by the four packhorses. His henchman spurred after him. The Hunt galloped right over the heads of the remaining four riders and receded in the direction of Isse Tower, invisible somewhere in the mist, twenty miles away.

The two men of the stables cursed softly, calming their horses. Rohain's mount shivered beneath her, slippery with the sweat of terror. Leaning over its neck, she murmured into its ear. Keat Featherstone spoke rapidly to his three companions.

'Isse Tower is in dire peril. My lady, forgive us. We are obliged to leave you and return to the aid of our comrades in the Tower. Our lords remain hereabouts—they will guard you.'

'I give you leave, Featherstone and Pennyrigg. Wind be with you.'

'And with you, lady. We must ride hard. Let those follow who will!'

Without further ado, the two stablemen leapt away down the hill at a great pace.

Clanking, the armour-plated lords lurched on foot after their chargers, whistling and calling. They disappeared down the north side of the ridge, leaving the two damsels alone.

'Well, Viviana,' said Rohain. She was dazed and reeling from shock after witnessing such appalling visitations, and was alarmed by their unexpected abandonment. 'Well, Viviana, it seems our guardians are otherwise occupied.' She mustered her thoughts. 'Meanwhile, mayhap we can help our hosts. I vote we follow those who ride to the Tower's aid.'

Viviana seemed to shrink. 'Those things . . .' she said in a low voice. 'Those things that hunt through the sky . . .'

'We are pinched between a sword and a spear, as the saying goes,' said Rohain. 'The Tower is beleaguered, for sure, but it is well-manned and fortified. Would you rather we camped on this hill waiting for the Wild Hunt to fly over our heads on its return journey? Or that we continue on to the haunted caldera, two ladies unguarded and alone?'

'Marry,' said Viviana in weary disgust, 'this is a sorry state of affairs. That Ustorix is a craven bumbler and no mistake. First he falls from his horse in his terror, then he runs away, leaving us vulnerable. So much for his vaunted boldness and chivalry.'

'Will you return with me to the House of the Stormriders?'

'I am loathe to do so, m'lady, but we have little choice.'

They cast one glance over their shoulders in the direction of

the horizon where Huntingtowers brooded unseen, unconquered.
Then, pointing the heads of their steeds back toward the stronghold of the Seventh House, they set off at a gallop.

Below the hill, the road dived back under its roof of trees. The
dank wall of mist and the obscuring vegetation afforded no view
of the Tower to Rohain and Viviana as they rode. The sonorous
pattern of the drums continued on for a while, then ceased
abruptly, leaving a calm broken only by the hammering of iron-
shod hooves on wet clay and leaf-mold.

The pale vapors drew back among the trees and frayed to
invisibility. A wind brooming through the upper atmosphere
swept most of the dirty clouds away to the west. Only the last rays
of the sun lingered by the time the travellers cantered their weary
horses along the last stretch of road leading to the demesne-gates
of Isse, and a translucent moon was already rising, swimming up
into the unfathomable sky like some pale jellyfish. Now rowans
crowded in thickly toward the road. To the left, the stone walls of
the demesnes rose high, topped with metal spikes and shards.

Through the black lacework of boughs the Tower loured in the
half-light, tapering from its wide base to become a slim needle in
the sky. So high it soared that its turreted head was hidden in a
shredded remnant of cloud. Much winged activity was taking place
around the upper stories. Darkly etched on the clouds, dozens of
eotaurs whirled in descending spirals, onhebbing toward the
ground. Their riders' cloaks billowed up like broken bubbles.
Shouts issued from behind the demesne walls, accompanied by
the crunch of hooves on gravel. From high above speared shrill,
inhuman yells, deep roars, the clash of metal and stone. A howling
bundle plummeted from a balcony, its limbs writhing.

Just before a bend in the road that concealed the gate from
view, the travellers crossed a stone bridge over a little rill and cantered beneath a long arch of overhanging willows.

'Stop, my lady, I beg you!' They reined in. Rohain glanced
quizzically at her companion. 'My lady, the Tower is overrun by
wights. There is nothing we can do—we must turn back! We must
ride for our lives!'

Two more victims hurtled, screaming, from above.

'In good faith—we cannot leave! We must help them fight.'

'There is nothing we can do. We are not warriors. To bide here means certain death.'

Rohain hesitated. 'You have the right of it,' she admitted reluctantly, 'and yet . . .'

As she faltered, something like a fish-hook raked across her chest. It caught in the fine gold chain of her tilhal, ramming it tight into the flesh of her throat and crushing her windpipe until she could not breathe. Mercifully, the chain snapped. The rooster with pink rubies for eyes shot away into the grasses at the roadside. A scrawny arm whipped like a leather belt across Rohain's eyes, blinding her.

A scrawl of hobyahs had swung down from the willow-boughs overhanging the road. Their grotesque limbs were thin and strong as whipcords. Wrapping them around the heads of the riders, they wrenched off the talium-lined riding hats. Others of their kind dangled by their skinny legs and gripped the damsels by their hair, whereupon their terrified horses ran from underneath them. Both mortals were let fall to the ground.

The hobyahs rushed at their victims. No more than two feet tall, they leered through bright needles of eyes that slanted upward at the outer corners, narrowing to mere slits. Their noses were large and uptilted. Pointed ears stuck up on either side of their conical caps and their mouths grinned maliciously. Avoiding contact with turned-out garments or bridle-bells, they hung off the saddles and surcingles, then jumped in twos and threes on the horses' backs and rode them away. Possessed of the hideous strength of eldritch, they hooked their clawlike fingers into their victims' hair and easily dragged them off the road. The struggles of the girls were futile. There could be no escape.

Yet in the next instant, the hobyahs' yodels of victory turned to screeches. Red-and-gold lightning flashed among them, and suddenly there were horsemen brandishing swords. A skirmish broke out. The cold iron blades of the superior force broke the wights' resistance, scattering them, routing them. Staggering to their feet, Rohain and Viviana clung to each other. Blood trickled in runnels from their scalps. Their garments were torn. Hair tumbled over their faces.

'Let us to the safety of the demesnes!' gasped Rohain. But even as they started for the gates, equestrians emerged from both banks of the road ahead, blocking their way. In dismay, the girls whirled about, only to be faced with a second blockade closing in behind.

"Tis some eldritch trickery!' cried Viviana. 'These men wear the Royal Livery—this cannot be!'

In scarlet jackets and gold braid the riders sat tall and straight. The final thin shafts of sunlight, sword-bright, pierced through disintegrating clouds and struck golden gleams from their face-guards and plumed helms. They appeared like a vision from the Fair Realm.

Five of them rode slowly forward. The damsels exchanged frightened glances.

'We wield iron!' cried Rohain in desperation. 'Approach at your peril!'

Calmly, the horsemen reined in a short distance away.

'You mistake us,' their leader, a lieutenant, shouted. His tone was grave. 'We are cavalry of the Royal Legions.'

Wights were incapable of lying.

'Out here it is perilous for mortals,' he said. 'The lower stories of the Tower are now secured against the enemy. Come. We shall bear you to safety there.'

He gestured to two of the cavalrymen. Dismounting, they helped Rohain and Viviana up behind the other two. A black smoke spewed from a southern gate in the Tower, just below the cloud ceiling. Dimly within it, the Wild Hunt soared in outward flight. They seemed this time to be fewer in number. Unseelie hounds and horses swooped around the Tower and struck out northward over the lifting moon, pursued by a company of eotaur-riders who, although great in number, could not match the speed of their eldritch quarry and were sure to be outdistanced.

'Welladay! Huon is driven forth!' exclaimed the lieutenant. His men cheered; several yelled triumphantly and punched the air above their heads.

In perfect formation, six men of the platoon rode up and

closed ranks around the officers with the pillion riders. Together, they made toward the gate.

Red-jacketed men-at-arms patrolled throughout the shadowy demesnes. Guards at the Tower doors saluted and allowed the lieutenant to pass through with his wards. He consigned them to the care of some doughty stewards of Isse and returned to his business of scouring the area immediately outside the demesnes.

Within the Tower, all was in uproar. Rohain and Viviana were escorted to a kitchen in one of the lower stories. There they found crowds of house-carls and nobles mingling, making a tremendous hubbub, some chattering, others sobbing.

'Wickedness! Oh, wickedness!'

''Tis an evil hour that brought these fell fiends upon the House.'

'Lend me your kerchief, for I bleed.'

'All fate be praised for bringing us our rescuer in time of need!'

'I cannot yet grasp that *he* is among us!'

'And more striking than the stories ever told!'

'Cursed be this day that saw such evil fall on Isse. Yet bless'd it be also . . .'

Some were uncharacteristically shrieking and wringing their hands, and several, in a sorry state, lay prone on the tables while their wounds were tended. Pet capuchins loped about, jabbering and hindering.

Rohain stared at the scene, sickened and appalled. Questions and offers of help surged at her and her companion as soon as they entered. Dolvach Trenchwhistle cleared a path for them with her elbows.

'Make way for the fine ladies from Caermelor! Can't you see that they are hurt, you dolts? Get out of the way.'

She seated the fine ladies by the hearth and proffered glasses of brandy. Heligea shouldered her way through the press and stood before them.

'My brother and Callidus! Are they with you?'

'No,' said Rohain, sipping brandy to give her strength. 'I do not know how they fare.'

'Ill tidings, then.'

'Yet I would vouch for their safety, encased as they are in all that iron.'

''Sbane! You are wounded, my friend. Blood runs from your hair. You, servant, bring oil.' A young girl hastened away.

'What has happened here?' asked Rohain.

'The Tower was attacked at nightfall,' said Heligea. 'Terrible ravagers they were. Powerful. They landed in at the top stories and went down through the Tower at speed, like rats down a drainpipe. We had no time to escape. Methinks they were hunting for something, or somebody. When they couldn't find their target, they turned on us like boars at bay, and took our people and began to torment them. Then he came.'

'Who?'

'Why, none other than the King-Emperor himself!'

'His Imperial Majesty here?' cried Viviana. 'I can scarce credit it!'

Heligea's eyes blazed as though with pride, or triumph, or battle-lust. 'He came from the south, riding to our rescue, leading the Duke of Roxburgh and others of the Royal Attriod, and regiments of the Royal Legions and *thriesniuns* of the Dainnan, all mounted on Skyhorses. They'd got word that the Scourge was on its way here, and they came. Ah!' Dreamily, she clasped her hands at her throat. 'The King-Emperor himself, here at Isse! I never thought to see this hour. Dainnan and men-at-arms swarm all over the Tower. I'll be honest, at first it seemed impossible that even such great fighting men could drive off the Wild Hunt, but victory has been won!'

'Won?' echoed Rohain. 'So the wights are all gone and the Tower is safe?'

Heligea waved her hand dismissively. 'Yes, yes. Almost safe. A few of the lesser wights that rode with the Hunter remain scattered throughout the upper stories and must be flushed out. We are to remain locked up down here until all things unseelie have been ousted and the Tower thoroughly scoured. As yet I have not set eyes upon His Majesty, but as I am, for the moment, the Mistress of the House, I am sure to be summoned soon by his gentlemen. I confess to a little nervousness, but in good sooth, how I look forward to the moment I am presented!' Lowering her voice, she leaned forward confidentially. 'You have seen him at Court. I never have. Is he as fine as they say? Do the images stamped on the coins of the realm do him justice?'

Rohain felt reluctant to admit she had never been in the King-Emperor's presence. She could not know whether the portraits hanging in gilt frames all over the palace were good representations, or the worn and blurred profiles in relief stamped into the coins. Besides, she had only ever seen older coins, depicting the D'Armancourt ancestors. Of the portraits, she recalled only cascades of velvet and brocade. She could barely remember them, not having paid much heed. In any event, she supposed he had aged greatly since those images had been created.

'Via,' she said, 'tell Heligea what he looks like.'

'Well, ma'am, no artist has ever been able to featly capture his likeness,' said Viviana. 'Just barely do the portraits represent His Majesty. I look forward to seeing him again with all my heart, if only from a distance, for upon my word he is a gentleman any maid or wife would sigh to look upon—a gentleman after every lady's heart. All the ladies at Court are in love with him, I doubt not—every one; and I'd warrant that every woman throughout Erith who has ever set eyes on him would share that passion.' Her eyes sparkled. 'So handsome is he and so kingly. Just to think of him causes the strangest thrill, as if the shang were passing over.' She balked, blushing suddenly. '*Sain* me—I hope you'll not think me impertinent for speaking thus of His Imperial Majesty.'

'You *are* impertinent,' interrupted Heligea impatiently, 'and should be thrashed for presuming to such familiarity, insolent girl. Ah, here comes a servant with the oil.'

A girl approached, carrying a stoneware jar. She was young, almost a child, thin and pale-cheeked but vigorous-looking, with large, deep-lidded eyes and a neat, bow-shaped mouth. Rohain recognised that triangular face, surrounded by its abundant cloud of wavy brown locks. The daughter of the Keeper of the Keys, the girl's name was Caitri Lendoon, and she had shown kindness to the deformed, yellow-haired lad.

Before Rohain could acknowledge her former friend, the smell of the oil assaulted her, closing in on her like a dark jail. Her throat and back were on fire. She gagged.

'What is in that jar?' she said hoarsely, holding the folds of her skirts to her nose. 'Whatever it is, I beg you to take it away from me. I wonder you don't all expire from the stench.'

''Tis only siedo-pod oil,' said Heligea in astonishment. 'A pungent scent, aye, but tolerable enough.'

'I will not have it near me!'

'It will soothe your hurts, my lady,' said the little girl, backing away.

'Mayhap. But I cannot stand the stink of it. I would rather endure the pain of my hurts and take another drop of brandy. You may anoint Viviana, if she is willing, and I will move from her side. Heligea, I must be brought into the King-Emperor's presence as soon as possible.'

'None but His Imperial Majesty's gentlemen may attend him now. That is how I am informed.'

'Yes, but as soon as the Tower has been secured—'

'Of course. Come, my lady, let these servants bathe you with lavender water if you will not have the oil. And take another sip of the spirit.'

There was to be no sleep that night. The moans of the wounded filled the lower halls. Those who had escaped harm spoke of nothing but the disastrous attack, and the unprecedented presence of royalty at the Tower. Occasional noises of belligerence echoed down the stairwells and the lift-shafts as malevolent presences were flushed out of oblique crannies. These became more infrequent, and eventually ceased altogether. Alone in a quiet room of the servants' quarters, Rohain sat by a window embrasure. It was forbidden to open the shutters until the danger had passed, but a cold night breeze crept in through the cracks and this she inhaled with relish.

Viviana approached.

'My lady—'

'Come no closer, Via. I cannot endure the stench of the oil in your hair.'

'It is strong, I'll concede, but not truly offensive, surely? Some might consider it pleasant.'

'I have ill recollections of the stuff,' said Rohain. Her face closed in on itself.

Sensing some inner perturbation, Viviana nodded silently. She curtsied and withdrew.

Rohain remembered: *Here in Isse Tower they use siedo-pod oil for many purposes, including the assuaging of every hurt from cuts and scratches to bellyaches and warts. Grethet used the stuff for the cuts on my back—yet I detested it well before then. I fought against her but I was too weak. She smeared it on, and as soon as I could I rubbed it off, rolling on rough bags, which opened the wounds afresh; but the stench—the stench clings for ages.*

Restlessly, she stood up and walked to the next window. Along the hairline crack between the shutters, a glimpse of starry sky ran like a black thread stitched with seed pearls. The brandy had warmed her, had taken the edge off the pain of her tortured scalp, but she ached with the longing to go straight away to the King-Emperor and plead for Sianadh's life. And she blazed with a desire to see which of the Dainnan had accompanied him to the Tower.

All of that lay outside the barred doors.

Around midnight, a hammering on those doors announced the end of the waiting period—the Tower had been cleared of eldritch incarnations.

Chaos resumed. As the Stormriders and their ladies returned to the upper floors, all able-bodied servants were ordered into action preparing billets and provender for the King-Emperor and his attendants and men-at-arms. Heligea disappeared precipitously, in a clanging lift-cage.

Rohain, eluding Viviana to escape the siedo-pod fumes, took another lift-cage up to Floor Thirty-seven. Lords and ladies moved to and fro shouting orders. Overworked servants hurried to obey.

'Where is the King-Emperor?' Rohain asked.

'His Majesty is at the topmost floor, my lady,' was the reply. 'He may be in conference or at meat. Is there anything you require? A repast is being set out on the tables in the dining halls.'

'Thank you—no.'

A passing Dainnan knight started at the sight of her face. Simultaneously she jumped, taken by surprise at the sight of his uniform. Recovering his composure, he bowed.

'May I be of assistance, lady? I am Sir Flint.'

His unbound hair fountained in bronze filaments to the small of his back.

'The King-Emperor's quarters on the top floor—do you know where they are?'

'His Majesty holds conference there with the Royal Attriod. The while, the Stormriders of the Tower are gathering in the dining halls to take refreshment. May I conduct you there instead? Allow me to call your servants.'

Seeing herself suddenly as he must see her, it struck Rohain that she could not kneel at the feet of the King-Emperor dressed in a torn and inside-out riding habit, with her hair tousled. To beg for a man's life, she must appear sleek and well-groomed, as etiquette demanded. She sighed.

'You are kind, Sir Flint. I wish only to retire.'

'Your name, my lady?'

Already she was walking away, not wishing to delay.

He bowed again and watched her go.

When she was out of his sight, she ran to her suite. On reaching it, she checked abruptly with her hand on the door-jamb and stared in.

The rooms had been ransacked.

Furniture lay splintered. Chests had been forced open and turned out, then apparently picked up and thrown across the chamber by some agency far stronger than any man, to crash and sprawl open, lids twisted awry, spilling out the remains of their contents. Garments had been strewn, torn to shreds. The looking-glasses lay in splinters on the floor—even their backings had been punched through. Only the frames of their obliterated faces remained. The bed had been reduced to no more than a welter of kindling and rags, scattered with dead leaves and a couple of live loam-worms, dusk pink and jointed. Rohain's jewellery was unrecognisable—misshapen as though melted in a hot fire. Every

item she owned had been broken or corrupted. An odour of compost hung over the whole scene.

Softly, she left the scene of the shambles. There was no sign
of a door—save for buckled hinges half torn off the door-frame—
or she would have closed it.

The hour had grown very late. Made aimless with shock she
wandered, dazed. The torchlit halls were empty now that the nobles
had gone to their supper. Dry leaves eddied along the floors, whispering, blown by a bitterly cold breeze from the gargoyle-wreathed
balcony overlooking Isse Harbour. It was there she had stood on the
night of the unstorms, watching a ghostly galleon being wrecked off
the heads, and wrecked again, over and over.

One of the balcony doors stood open. Beyond, stars dripped
thick radiance down the sky and the sight drew her. Thomas's
words came back: *'Go into the wilderness on a clear night and
look up. Look long. Then you will have seen something of Faêrie.'*

Heedless of the slap and sting of the cold, she stepped out. A
wide vista opened across gray water. The moon and the Greayte
Southern Star had wheeled out of sight on their inevitable courses
and only the fantastic splendor of the other starry realms
remained, to draw heart and mind out through the eyes and send
them spinning into the void.

Someone else was already on the balcony. A Dainnan leaned
on the parapet. Ribbons of black hair rained across his wide
shoulders and down his tapered back, reaching to his belt. A sea-
draft driving up the walls of the Tower lifted fibers of darkness
across the winking stars—the weft from which night itself was
woven.

He straightened, turning. He was looking down at Rohain.

Instantly, all her thought was swept away by intense emotion.
Speech and movement became impossible under that piercing
gaze. Every wish, every hope, had come true in front of her eyes.
The sight of him, so often imagined, was hard to invest with
reality. For so long had his image existed only in intangible form
that she had become accustomed to knowing him as a dream, and
could not at first believe what she saw.

As from a distance, a dark, strong voice said,

'So, you came at last to Court, Gold-Hair.'

A response was required. Rohain's numbed mind could prepare none. Mechanically, she murmured, 'Yes.' Her eyes remained wide, fastened on him steadily, drinking him in. The action of speech released her paralyzed thoughts.

'Is it really you . . . ?' She faltered.

'It is I.'

She must say something else, something to keep him here, for the longer he remained the more substantial he became.

'I am glad to see you.'

The statement seemed so feeble an offering, compared with the intensity of feeling it represented—as if she'd held oceans in readiness to offer him and instead, through lack of expertise, had handed over only a spoonful of water.

'And I you.'

Like Pod, he had known her immediately, despite the complete transformation, and yet he uttered no comment about her hair, her face, her voice.

'How brightly the stars shine tonight,' said he, turning again to look out at the spectacle. She, moving to his side, was now blind to the radiant glory of the glittering haze spread across the sky. Only, she was aware of a heat on her left where he stood, like the heat of a beacon-fire, pulsing warmth all down one side of her body while the other was chilled. And so they stood together looking outward, and the rising thermals caught their hair, making it flow out behind them, the dark locks mingling.

An hour passed, or it might have been half an hour, or a minute. It was not forever, although Rohain craved that it should be. Although they kept vigil in silence, it seemed to Rohain that a million words were traced upon the air. They hung there in runes of fire, slowly fading. It was unspeakable to be there beside Thorn at those moments. It was to fall into stars, to ride sky in a thunderstorm, to dance in a riot of jewels at a masquerade ball on the uttermost peak of an ice-mountain, to be swept up on the winds of shang.

'I have searched long for you,' Thorn said quietly at last. 'Will you come with me to Court?'

'I will.' Terror and delight swarmed, fizzing like sweet and savage acid.

'I want you to belong to me, and to no other.'

Just like that, with no preamble. She was too stunned to ask questions.

'That I do already. I will be yours for my life.' *Did he truly speak those words? Am I sane?*

'Do you swear it?'

'Upon the Star, upon my life, upon anything you wish to name, I swear it.'

He held out his hand. She grasped a levin-bolt whose convulsion sizzled from fingers to feet.

'Now we are troth-plighted,' he said, as though he had noticed nothing about the effect of his touch. Indeed, she would swear he had felt nothing.

The sound of boots approached, crunching along the corridor. A group of Royal Legionaries came to the open doors. At the sight of the two on the balcony they dropped to their knees, heads bowed.

'Speak,' said Thorn.

'Your Imperial Majesty,' said the colonel, 'the one we seek is here in the Tower—the Lady Rohain.'

'You are too tardy to avail me,' laughed Thorn, 'for I have found her myself.'

Have I heard aright? The aftermath of the past day's fear and exertion, which until now Rohain had subjugated, arose again and challenged her consciousness. It mingled with her exhilaration and terror, her pain and confusion. If she allowed it to overwhelm her, she would faint like some overcorseted courtier; it would sunder her from him and when she awoke he would be gone, because this could only be a cruel dream.

She hid her face in her hands. Tears trickled in a pewter rain between her fingers.

Someone caught her up in a hammock of thunder-webs and carried her along. The voice of Thorn, deep and musical, spoke. She could not properly understand the words, but soon a cup was placed in her hands, and she drank, and felt the effects of a sleeping-draft coursing through the pathways of her body. The walls fell in, one by one, and she tumbled in a circle.

Which closed over her head.

He *was* gone, after all.

Music sounded, heartbreakingly sweet and haunting; a piping that described an existence beyond mortal grasp, beyond knowledge, a prize to stretch out and yearn for, unreachable, and she, not knowing what it was, awoke crying because she could not follow.

The sleep-memory troubled her waking mind, and a clear young voice sang:

'I'll sing you nine-O. Heark, how the winds do blow!
What are your nine-O?
Nine for the Arts of Gramarye and eight for the notes of singing.
Seven for the riders in the sky and six for the gamblers' flinging.
Five for the rings on my love's hand and four for the seasons
    winging.
Three, three, the Chances,
Two, two the lovers' hearts joinèd close together,
One is one and all alone and shall be so forever.'

It was a well-remembered voice, a linnet of a voice that softly sang that old song. It belonged to Caitri, the daughter of the Keeper of the Keys, a daydreamer given to composing ditties that she often hummed to herself. The child seemed oblivious of the world beyond her small horizon, but in fact was the opposite. She sat nearby, playing cat's cradle as she sang. She was dressed in servants' subfusc and smelled of orange blossom.

'Did I dream again?' Bemused, Rohain raised herself on one elbow. She found herself reclining on a sumptuous couch within a richly decorated, spacious room. In a wide hearth, a fire flamed like evanescent castles of light. The windows were obscured by lengthy velvet draperies emblazoned all over with the Stormrider device, but the curve of the outer wall betrayed the room's status as a Tower chamber.

Young Caitri smiled, still half musing on her song.

'What is dream and what is reality?' she asked, philosophically, rhetorically, and somewhat pedantically for one so young. Such a childish face could not have weathered more than thirteen Winters.

'Where are we?'

'Your Ladyship is at the fortieth story, the most exalted level of the Tower, barring the somewhat cramped turret rooms. The apartments here shall henceforth bear the title "Royal Suites", and all future guests shall wish to occupy them. I was called upon to attend Your Ladyship and right glad I am to escape, for a time, the sorrow of the misfortune that has descended upon the Seventh House.'

'Your mother,' said Rohain suddenly, 'is she hale?'

'Why yes, my lady,' returned the child, frowning her puzzlement. 'My mother escaped the scourge . . .' She put aside her string game.

'That is well. Now I must make myself presentable at once.'

'Take refreshment, an it please you, lady—here are both victuals and drink. A bath awaits and raiment is laid out. My lady Heligea has gifted part of her own wardrobe, since Your Ladyship's was destroyed by the Antlered One and his unseelie wights. Seamstresses have lengthened the hems in haste, while you slept. Methinks the colours of the Seventh House shall become you. Your Ladyship is to be received by His Majesty this very morning.'

'Has the night passed already and is morning come? Where is the King-Emperor?'

'I know not, m'lady. I have not yet beheld His Majesty. Since I was called I have been in a constant state of excitement in case I should happen to glimpse him.'

'And Viviana?'

'She was, in sooth, the one called to attend Your Ladyship but she asked me to take her place, since she cannot rid herself of siedo's faithful stench.'

'Caitri, I am glad it is you who came.'

'Do you know me?'

'Yes. I wist that you are worthy.'

'I thank you, m'lady.'

'I wist you show kindness to unfortunates, to outcasts.'

'I suppose you mean Pod—that I treat him fairly.'

'Oh, Pod—yes. A curious lad.'

'Your Ladyship has seen him, then? Some say he has the Sight, you know.'

'Indeed! That would explain much.'

'And somewhat of a gift of prophecy. Yet it is sad, for part of his wit is lacking. Possessing such wondrous gifts, he is unable to use them profitably and is betimes erratic in his augury. Dine now, prithee, or I shall be taken to account for failing to sustain you. I can assure you, our chief cook had no part in the preparation. Confidentially, Rennet Thighbone is a slovenly one.'

'What is the Sight, exactly?' asked Rohain, taking up a cup of milk and honey. The girl's talk distracted her from the one thought that churned around and around in her head, threatening to drive her to the brink of madness. She welcomed the distraction.

'Well, I suppose it is the gift of seeing what is real. It is a rare talent—only a very few folk are born possessing it, although the Sight disregards all barriers of social distinction. The rest of us must try to find four-leafed clover, for when its leaves are carried, somewhat of the Sight is acquired, but not always full-blown, and only temporarily.' After a pause, she said, 'Personally, I think Pod does not have the Sight. I suspect he possesses an extraordinary sense of smell, like animals, or some wights.'

Rohain sipped the drink but could barely swallow one mouthful. A tightness knotted the pit of her stomach. Her heart raced. What she had seen last night—was it true? Could she believe her eyes and ears, or had she been overcome with distress and fallen into a strange hallucination? And what had become of her companions on the road?

'Tell me,' she said to Caitri. 'Featherstone and Pennyrigg, Ustorix and the rest who were with me when I rode out—have they returned?'

'The servant of Master Zimmuth's, he never returned. My lord Callidus was badly wounded. The others are all home and hale, m'lady, which is more than can be said for the many folk of all ranks who were slain or wounded within the Tower's very walls.

Truly, doom came among us, and had not the King-Emperor come to succor us we had all perished. 'Twill be long ere we forget.'

By the Powers, let my meeting with Thorn not be a mere delusion. If I ask the child and her words prove it an invention of my mind, I shall lose hope. Therefore I shall not ask her.

Rohain bathed. Her assistant helped her dress in Stormrider finery. The black armazine gown, equipped with long, tight sleeves that would have been considered screamingly out of mode at Court, was bordered at the collar, cuffs, and hem with wide bands of black ducape stitched with winged crescents in silver. Caitri pinned a scrollwork brooch at the throat. The folds of the sable cloak displayed richly patterned sarcenet linings, and it was fastened at the front by fine chains laced through small silver bosses at either side. A girdle stitched with silver thread in a diamond pattern on a black ground passed around Rohain's waist at the back, but angled down to a V-shape at the front. The shoes were painstakingly embroidered with a pattern of tiny horses.

Dark tresses flowed rampant down Rohain's back, still damp. Caitri raked them with a broken-toothed ivory-and-tortoiseshell comb, then fastened silver stars in the midnight cloud of them, and placed a spangled gauze veil over all, bound with a fillet encrusted with milk-crystals and tiny beads of jet.

'They gave me this to put on you,' she said, fastening a golden chain around Rohain's neck. It was a new tilhal—three bunched hypericum leaves made of jade, clasped in gold.

'Your Ladyship is indeed comely beyond the ordinary, as all have been saying,' she continued gravely, naively unaware of her boldness. 'His Majesty is certain to be pleased when my lady goes before him.'

'Thank you. I am ready now. But I am frightened. I may have dreamed last night, but which is the more terrifying, to be awake or asleep, I know not.'

Sir Flint of the Third Thriesniun, with a clutch of footmen, escorted Rohain to where the King-Emperor presided in the Highest Solar. The fortieth floor was heavily guarded by men-at-arms, but all was calm and serene. It seemed that the evildoers had passed this level by, leaving it intact. Ensconced torches shed a warm light on drab wall-hangings. Their brilliance startling against the black and silver of the Seventh House, yeomen in scarlet-and-gold uniforms stood at every door and window, at every corner. The Royal Standard leaned from wall-brackets, the crowned lion flaunting its splendid colours.

At the door, the visitor's heart galloped as the sentries uncrossed their halberds with due ceremony and allowed her to pass. A wave of dizziness passed over her and she was forced to pause for an instant. Caitri clutched at her elbow.

'Is my lady hale?' Sir Flint voiced his concern. Rohain nodded.

Across an outer room, through another door. Diagonals of sunlight, mellow and pure as honey-mead, lanced in at the windows. Rohain looked up. And there he stood, the King-Emperor.

Through the slashed sleeves of his velvet doublet—gold lions worked on a ground of deepest royal purple—black cambric shirt-sleeves showed in soft, full gathers, tied at three points. A wide belt of goldwork clasped the calf-length doublet, which was slit at each side in the manner of the Dainnan tunic and worn open at the front to show the shirt. Its wide lapels, lined with black and gold samite, jutted at the shoulders to form a *V* with its point finishing at the waist, just above the belt. Black hose fitted closely to his thighs, tucking into knee-boots turned back at the tops. His cloak, thrown back, flared in many folds from his shoulders. Made from purple velvet, it was worked in crowns and heraldic designs both black and gold, and lined with inky satin. His mane of dark hair spilled from beneath a simple low-crowned cap bearing three soft shadowy plumes.

All this finery could not in any way make him foppish; rather, he was magnificent, clad in splendor as rich and somber as a Summer's evening. His vitality filled the hall as though all light, all darkness radiated from him.

At Rohain's entrance, he regarded her without speaking. Viviana had schooled her in how to meet royalty. Like the servant girl, like the warriors flanking her, she dropped to her knees, bowing her head, noticing with intense clarity the detail of the skyriding design on the slightly worn rugs. This was one of the fringed, hooked rugs she had once been accustomed to punishing, in order to free the dust from it. In a detached way, she wondered who was privileged to undertake that job these days and whether they did it as well as she had.

A weight seemed to be pressing upon her eyelids. Soon she would have to look at him, but it would seem an impossible task.

She waited for him to speak.

Two hands lifted her gently to her feet. Their touch was lightning.

'I'll warrant thou wouldst be more comfortable sitting by me.' The voice—rich, tempered, and flawlessly enunciated—a lion's growl. She breathed the cinnamon incense of his presence.

He conducted her to one of two chairs at the head of a table, and seated himself beside her. The table was furnished with a pile of parchments like dessicated leaves, paper-knives with ebony handles, seal containers, red candles, a horn-handled knife, a twist of thin cord, pheasant-quill pens in a silver tray, and inkwells of cold, translucent onyx.

A timid page took a small key and unreeled the taper of a wax-jack on a little silver stand. He trimmed the wick with a pair of pointed snuffers and tremulously lit it, fumbling with the tinderbox.

Thorn's existence was like a terrible furnace flaming at Rohain's side. She was dimly aware that others were present in the hall—great lords, Roxburgh among them, all standing, facing Thorn. Caitri folded her hands neatly to hide her nervousness at being in the presence of the King-Emperor, and arranged herself against the wall where several pages and wigged footmen made bas-reliefs of themselves in scarlet duretty and gold frogging. High on a pelmet, the goshawk Errantry sat dozing, sometimes nervously flicking his tail from side to side. A whitewash of his mutes streaked and splattered the curtains below, as well as any footmen who happened to be standing in the vicinity. One or two hawk-casts decorated the floor with indigestible bits of bone and feather. Errantry opened one fierce eye and closed it again.

'Fear not,' Thorn whispered to Rohain. She found courage to return his smile. 'Gentlemen,' he said loudly, 'here is the Lady Rohain for whom we have all sought high and low.'

Still standing, the lords bowed their heads: Richard of Esgair

Garthen, Lord High Sea Admiral; Octarus Ogier, Lord High Chieftain of Stormriders; Durand Rivenhall, Lord High Chancellor; Istoren Giltornyr, Lord High Sky Admiral; John Drumdunach, Lord High Commander of the Royal Guard. Thorn introduced the chiefest among them by name to the lady at his side, then dismissed them, along with his Private Secretary, his pages and stewards, the guards, and all the other lords and servants, excepting Caitri. He bade the little girl wait in the anteroom.

Rohain sat utterly still, except that a slight tremor ran through her.

'And now thou shalt want to ask some questions,' Thorn said. 'Dost thou wish to use handspeak? Hast thou lost thy tongue again? I confess, I was enjoying the novelty of hearing thy voice.'

She laughed then, joyously.

<<No, I have not lost my speaking,>> she signed, now at ease.

<<Speak, then!>> his hands signaled.

'Thorn,' she said, savoring the name. 'Thorn. Your Dainnan name. That is, Your Majesty's Dainnan name.'

'Gold-Hair,' he said, 'it is hardly necessary to address me like that. Or,' he added, 'to collapse upon the floor when approaching me. Didst thou not pledge thyself to me last night?'

'I did, sir, and most readily.'

'Now thou must learn to be our betrothed, rather than a commoner who brazenly declares herself a lady. It is meet that thou shouldst become accustomed to bearing thyself like the future Queen.'

Her courage returned. 'You know all? But how? Did you know I was residing at Court? Why did I not see you? How may a Dainnan be King?'

'Here come the questions, all of a tumble,' he said, amused. 'But I shall start the tale at the beginning.'

'Oh, but before you do,' she said quickly, basking in his proximity as if it were Summer sunshine, 'I wish to ask you to spare the life of a man imprisoned in your dungeons, condemned to death. His name—'

'He is pardoned, from this moment, whatever his name might be. Now hearken, while I tell the tale. Art thou paying heed?'

'No. I am looking at thee . . .'

Boldly, as though parched and drinking, her eyes travelled over the wiredrawn, flowing lines of his silhouette, the honed planes of his face, stern and laughing at the same time, full of strength, the jawline faintly shadowed with a dark tint, the arch of his throat interrupted by the subtle shadow of the round tumescence midway, and the hollow at the confluence of the collarbone.

His every movement was as graceful and confident as a lion in its prime, his demeanor relaxed yet poised, with the assurance that at need he, as a skilled fighter, could react with speed and power, and there would be only conquest. This time she tried to memorize his flawless beauty. The moment would be ephemeral, as was the wont of moments, and he would vanish soon. *Rare beauty, by nature, must be ephemeral. Without that sting it is no longer rare. But I wish, oh I wish it were not so. I wish that he might endure forever.*

'And I am studying thee,' he replied, 'and I hope to do so more often and more thoroughly at my leisure. But if thou regard'st men in that manner, thou shalt drive them mad.'

'Well, you deserve to be driven mad, sir, for you have already done so to me.'

'Now thou must needs hold conversation with me from the other side of the room,' he said, flame-eyed. 'Else thou might provoke me to encompass and invade thee, here, at this instant.'

'In that case,' she answered breathlessly, 'I remain.'

He regarded her with a strange softness, almost sadness.

'Half child, half woman as thou art. For thee, virtuous maiden,' he said, 'there would be no rightness in that. Not yet.'

She forced herself to look away, suddenly understanding; there were rules that *could not* be abrogated, at this place, at this time, in this century, in Erith.

'You must turn your back on me,' Rohain commanded the King-Emperor of Erith, knowing him well enough to dare light banter, exulting in the play of words between them and the fragile power she wielded, while still unable to believe it was all true. 'Turn your back, whilst you tell me the tale. But look not askance!

Ever since I saw you for the first time I have longed to comb my fingers through your hair.'

He complied, laughing, sprawling back in the chair and stretching out his long legs. She let the dark veils of his locks flow over her fingertips and was amazed, that the very stuff of midnight could lie soft within her own hands, that what she touched was actually of him; he for whom she had ached throughout eternities.

He spoke.

'Through the glades of Tiriendor I roved in Dainnan fashion, which is my wont when it pleases me, and when needs must. For, Gold-Hair, a good sovereign must gauge the state of his realm, and what better way than to explore it unmarked? Several of my chief lords and advisors are persistently alarmed at this habit, and I must forever persuade them it is safer in the greenwood than in the wilderness of Court where poisonous vipers await the turning of every back.

'I had long studied thee and thy companion, Captain Bruadair, ere thou didst meet with me. I was drawn to thee,' he said. 'In thee there burned a passion, right from the first moment—a passion of such intensity as I have never encountered. Thou dost possess a capacity for joyousness and for deep sorrow that bedims the torpid ardencies of others. The crests and troughs of their fervour are but the fickle waves of the ocean, whereas thine are like an island mountain, whose head lifts among the clouds, whose foundations are buried far below on the ocean floor. Thou wouldst try to withhold thy fire, but such duplicity was beyond thy means. When it came time for us to part, I was already lost. Thou wouldst not accompany me then, but I was eager to bring thee to my side if not sooner, then later.'

'Did it hurt you that I would not go with you?' Rohain asked, surprised. Her heart leapt like a deer.

'Hurt? To a degree. Only as a sword piercing the heart. Thou art kissing my hair.'

'Even so.' The strands were silk, lying across her mouth.

'When thou didst hasten to the carlin's house,' he said, 'I ordered guards to be stationed around it, to protect thee, to bring thee to me when your errand was completed. They were to be discreet.'

'The watchers—they were men of yours?'

'They were. I ought to have used Dainnan, but I did not suppose that thou wouldst try to slip through my net.'

She said hesitantly, 'I was a servant here, once.' *Will he now reject me?* He merely nodded, as if it did not matter. Her spirits immeasurably encouraged, she went on: 'I escaped and found the wealth of Waterstair. For the sake of it, others wanted me to keep silence. They hounded me. And in Gilvaris Tarv I sought a cure for paradox ivy from the wizard Korguth. It failed and I thought he pursued me to take revenge for his own ill deed. I believed your men watching Maeve's cottage to be those who hunted me for evil purpose.'

'Why didst thou not enlighten me concerning your pursuers before we went our separate ways?' he asked, his modulated, laughing tones threaded with a hint of gentle exasperation.

'Why did you not declare your heart's truth?' she parried.

'I asked thee to come with me—is that not enough?'

'It was not plain to me. But you tell me plainly now.'

'Because thou hold'st back thine own truth no longer. Thou speakest with thine eyes at last. And thy tongue. And because I would not lose thee a second time.'

Her heart seemed to melt like glass in the fire of his intent. 'Now I do not fear to have you look upon my face. You read now in my eyes that which has long been written in my heart.'

'Thou with thy secret commission to Caermelor—had you but confided to me this tale of treasure-troves, thou hadst saved thyself a deal of toil,' he mocked gently.

'I was to impart the tale only to the King-Emperor!'

'And thus 'tis proven that thou hast that rare quality—thou canst guard a secret well. Wilt thou guard thine affairs so readily now that thou hast found thy tongue?'

He laughed. A sudden wave of concern swept through Rohain. There *was* another secret . . . Should he become aware of her strange history as an amnesiac foundling would he recoil from her? Yet he asked nothing of the past. For him, the present seemed sufficient. Indeed, what could that history matter?

'But tell me,' she said, 'why did your guards not simply knock at Maeve's door and announce that the King-Emperor summoned me?'

'Thou mightst well have refused, as thou didst once before!'

'I could hardly refuse my sovereign . . .'

'So thou sayest, but how could I have known? Then thou didst disappear. Only once before in my life have I been thwarted so thoroughly. There arose a violent anger in my heart that this should have come to pass, that I should lose thee. All those around me suffered from my rage, which was caused by thee!'

'Say no more!' She tugged playfully at his hair.

'No, thou canst not injure me now,' he lightly mocked.

'It was not my fault!'

'Dost thou gainsay me?' he said, feigning to chide her. 'When thou didst alter everything about thy appearance and demeanor, thy mode of communication, calling thyself by another name and coming right into my house, which is the last place I would look for thee, while the town criers were bellowing at every gate in the city, morning, noon, and night, to proclaim the King-Emperor's command that anyone who sees a yellow-haired wench called Imrhien should bring her to him instantly, on pain of imprisonment?'

'I heard them shouting, but I never heeded the words.'

'They cannot be heard distinctly from the palace, unless the wind is in the right quarter. Which I had always counted pleasant, since their rantings are tiresome.'

'Did you have them looking for a yellow-haired wench of exquisite ugliness?'

'No. Thou hadst told me that thou didst want to alter that condition, therefore thou wert bound for the carlin at White Down Rory.'

'Yet in the beginning, how could you warm to someone so ill-made?'

He turned his beautiful head and gave her a measuring look.

'Gold-Hair,' he said, 'I have already told thee.'

'Did you *see* my ugliness?'

'I saw it. I saw thee.'

'How did you recognise me last night?'

'I say again, I saw *thee*. Thine inner worth.'

It was said the D'Armancourt line was set apart from ordinary mortalkind by some puissance of the blood. Likely, that included the Sight; the ability to perceive what lay beneath masks. Thorn looked away, and Rohain resumed her combing. A wonderful silence linked them, filled with unspoken words. *May the Powers of all realms grant that time shall now stand still.*

'I want for nothing now,' she said presently.

'Thou shalt change thy mind, in time, as is the wont of women.'

'I shall not!' She smiled at his light teasing.

'Dost thou not wish to hear the rest of the story?'

'I do!'

'Behold! Thou hast changed it already.'

The goshawk shifted on his perch, shook out his wings, and glided down in a lazy spiral to land upon the back of Rohain's chair. She reached up. Decorously, he nibbled at her hand. Thorn raised his arm and Errantry flew to alight on the leather bracer encircling his wrist. Absently, Thorn stroked the bird's barred plumage.

'We could not find thee,' he said. 'Your red cockerel of a friend at Isenhammer knew nothing. When there was no sign of thee by Imbroltide, we began in earnest to seek the carlin of White Down Rory.'

'I dined in the same hall as you at Imbrol!'

'Alas, that I was unaware of it! My eyes searched beyond the palace walls on that night, my sweet thief of quietude.'

'And my eyes did not search at all! What of Maeve?'

'Her cottage was discovered empty.'

'Empty! Where had she gone?'

'Curiously, she was nowhere to be found, even though the Dainnan and the most proficient of trackers sought her, and messengers were sent to every land. Then we had to depart for the fields of battle. We had tarried too long because of my quest for thee, but the need grew pressing. During my absence the search continued.

'One evening, afar off in northern Eldaraigne, I was riding out with Roxburgh under the early stars, not far from where our troops were bivouacked. In conversation we chanced to look sky-wards, which turned us to the topic of beauty. My Lord High Field-Marshal of the Dainnan let slip the fact that a certain beau-teous young damsel who had brought tidings of treasure to Caermelor had arrived masked. She had been unaware of partic-ular aristocratic protocols and furthermore had recounted a strange story of traveling in the wilderness with a wild Ert by the kenning of 'The Bear'. That sobriquet had once before come to my ears.'

Rohain recalled a conversation by a campfire, Diarmid saying to Thorn: *'When I was a lad, I used to trade words with my—with my uncle.'*

To augment his statement, she had signed, <<*Once I heard Sianadh word-fighting, against some wicked men. He won.*>>

'He always won. Ertishmen are famous for their skill with words; Finvarna is the birthplace of most of the greatest bards. But the Bear could outspar even his own countrymen.'

High in Isse Tower, Thorn again turned the implicit barrage of his gaze upon her.

'I knew then that this "Rohain Tarrenys of the Sorrows" was thee—changed, healed, as thou hadst desired. "Rohain" was a name recently brought to my attention at Court. Ercildoune had once or twice bothered me with it. They had described the lady as *dark-haired*. That thou didst go disguised was proof enough that thou didst fear some imminent peril.'

'Swee-swit,' said the goshawk, dulcet, picking up strands of Thorn's hair in his curved beak.

'Within the hour we departed from the battlefields. The best of our troops rode the skies beside us in haste to Caermelor, with more speed than any Relayer. We were too late—already the Lady of the Sorrows had reached Isse Tower. Pausing only to take fresh eotaurs, we left Caermelor at noon two days since, and rode non-stop, by day and night, arriving here as the festivities of the Antlered One were in full swing.'

'Oh, happy chance! Had you not done so, there must have been massacre on an appalling scale.'

'In that battle, I went through every blood-splashed hall and stair in this worm-bitten pillar, and my sword Arcturus sang metal's song of death as I wielded him, smiting unseelie heads. Yet, thou hadst once again glided away like sand through my fingers, confounding me. Never to me has woman proved so elusive. No sense could be got out of the incoherent servitors and lords of Isse until at last one of them gathered his wits for long enough to inform me that thou wert away to Huntingtowers and might be lying slain upon the road. Roxburgh, who was already mounted, rode out forthwith. I, about to depart, was compelled to turn back. Someone said they had seen thee in the kitchens. When he was sent to bring thee, thou wert not to be found. Many folk confirmed his report that thou wert here, safe, somewhere. The Tower seethed with folk, but it was secure and I knew I should find thee again, sooner or later. I knew it at last.'

He was silent for a while. Then he said, 'Who, at Court, guessed thee as Talith?'

'Only the Lady Dianella.'

'Say further.'

'I told her I was looking for a Dainnan called Thorn. Is your Dainnan name commonly known among the courtiers?'

'As well-known as Roxburgh's "Oak" and Ercildoune's "Ash". That lady connives to be Queen, and brooks no rivals. Constantly she flaunts her charms, like the rest, but she is assisted by her plotting uncle who wishes to lever her on the throne and puppet her on his strings. I would hazard she heard the town criers' proclamations. Her kind hang on their every word in the hope of scandal. Hearing that thou didst search for me and I for thee, that jealous deceiver would have found it necessary to ask no further questions. I'll warrant she and the wizard swiftly planned your downfall, before I could discover thee.'

'Dianella told me to leave Caermelor.'

'I suspect she did so in order that thy demise might occur at a less inconvenient location, and the blame would be looked for elsewhere!' His face darkened. 'Those who cross me are punished.'

A cloud passed across the sun. Shadows rushed in and dammed the room like thin, dark waters.

Thorn seized a curl of paper and a quill-pen from the table, trimming its point with a porcelain-handled penknife. Dipping the point in ink, he dashed off a missive, blotted it dry, rolled the parchment and tied it with cord, dripped wax from a candle and impressed it with the seal-ring he had not been wearing in the wilderness. Calling to Caitri, he directed her to deliver it to one of the messengers waiting outside the door. When she had departed, he resumed his nonchalant position in the chair, reclining on one elbow.

'But surely,' said Rohain earnestly, 'Dianella could not guess that the Tower was to be assailed by the Hunt!'

'One would suppose not,' said Thorn thoughtfully. 'She and her uncle must have prepared some other method of ridding themselves of you, had not Huon intervened.'

Rohain thought: *What a curious coincidence, that the Hunt should choose to assail this fortress precisely at the time of my visit here* . . . And then a hand of ice was laid upon her vitals, bestowing a suspicion so terrible she hardly dared to speak it aloud. *Could the wizard Sargoth possibly wield enough power to summon the Wild Hunt? Worse: if he had not summoned it, then who had? And what had the Antlered One hunted for, besides destruction?*

Thorn said, 'Didst thou tell the Lady Dianella aught of the carlin?'

'I did!' replied Rohain in consternation. 'Cry mercy! Have I endangered the old woman's life? Dianella and her uncle, guessing that Maeve was party to knowledge of Rohain Tarrenys's true identity, might have tried to silence her! Yet surely, mortal men—even the Lord High Wizard's men—could never trace Maeve One-Eye unless she wished it.'

'In truth, Gold-Hair. Yet they were not mortal men who went after her.'

'Then she must be rescued!'

'She shall be, you may believe it.'

'Yet I cannot believe that Sargoth has anything of gramarye at his fingertips, to force unseelie wights to obey him. All his vaunted tricks are only hocus-pocus.'

Thorn plucked a loop of light out of the air and waved it over his shoulder.

'Is that hocus-pocus?'

She laughed. 'A trick, yes—I'll vouch that it was concealed in your sleeve! I am no country lass from Rosedale, to be gulled by sleight-of-hand!'

The shining thing was a small circle of golden leaves spangled with white gems that glittered, having somehow imprisoned the brilliance of stars within their depths. Thorn pulled down her narrow wrist, printed a kiss on it, and slid the leaf-ring upon her finger. Each axonal fiber along her arm turned to hot wire.

'Thou distract'st me, ever, from the tale,' he said, without relinquishing her hand. 'My imagination strays. Thou couldst never understand how difficult it is to remain thus, seemingly unmoved.'

'Whither do thy thoughts wander?'

He leaned back and whispered in her ear. She murmured a reply. The goshawk, screaming, jumped into the air and flapped around the room, scattering a few loose, downy feathers.

'Out, scapegrace!' said his master, and the bird flew through the window. Thorn rose from the chair. Drawing Rohain to her feet, he followed the hawk to the embrasure. They stood close together, she intensely aware of the light pressure of his arm against her shoulder as they looked out through the archway across a wide land and the curve of a dazzling sea.

Thorn leaned his left hand upon the window-frame. It was long-fingered and strong. Around the ring-finger glinted a thin band—three golden hairs, twisted together.

He has kept the token he seized from me! Ah, what would it be like to wake in the night and see him lying against me, hair rayed out upon the pillow, dark lashes fanned upon his cheek, as soft as a sleeping child's?

Below, high in the abyss, the hawk floated.

'Let us speak no more of the past,' murmured Thorn. 'Few yellow leaves, or none, cling upon the boughs; stark, dismantled choirs where erst the birds of Summer sang,' he said, possibly quoting. 'But the dark days of Winter are not unremitting, and clouds have drawn apart on this day to let the sun shine on our contentment.'

'As welcome as sunshine is, storm and wind and rain have

their beauty also,' said Rohain, recalling the rain in the Forest of Tiriendor. 'Each season has a virtue to recommend it; not least Winter.'

'I' faith, I concur! Fain would I be without these walls, and soon we shall be, for we ride this day to Caermelor.'

'By land or sky?'

'By sky. On the wing. Fear'st thou that?' The glance he bestowed on her seemed to fill her bones with water. Her legs would scarcely hold her up.

'On the contrary, I look to it with eagerness! But stay—before I depart from this place, I must first render them aid. Destruction and death have been brought down on innocents. My own apartments were wrecked, although the raiders left this level untouched.'

'Not much was destroyed elsewhere, save flesh and bone. Thy lodgings were the worst ravaged. Other inorganic damage was incidental to their more vile pursuits. Among my men there are dyn-cynnils, an apothecary, and other flesh-tailors. As we speak they tend the wounded of Isse, regardless of rank or birth. I myself have recently walked among the injured and to me it seems there is none so badly hurt as will not recover fully. My physicians shall bide here until their work is done. To Caermelor we shall ride without further ado, I insist. There shall our betrothal be announced, and thou shalt meet Prince Edward.'

A pure, resonant strum went through and through Rohain. She managed to say, 'I approach that meeting with delight.'

'A ball shall be held in thine honour, if that should please thee. Should it?'

'If we should dance the gavotte, as before.'

'To synchronize with thee is joyousness, no matter the choreography, *caileagh faoileag*,' he said lightly.

'Once before you called me that name. What is its meaning?'

'"Beloved bird of the sea". The white bird of freedom is an ocean wanderer. It touches no land for seven years in its voyages around the world, flying over vast tracts of open ocean without landmarks. This fairest, most elusive of winged navigators travels far before it finds its rest.'

At the back of her mind, a thread snapped, but only a thread.

Rohain glanced at her left wrist. Moon-pearls and jet-like chips of black ice embraceleted it, in their setting of white metal; a borrowed trinket of Heligea's. They were not what she had looked for.

'Now I have been called a butterfly and a bird,' she said. 'And Rohain.'

'Which means "beautiful". Each of us has many names. I have the privilege of possessing such a string of them as might arguably stretch from here to Namarre.'

'And one,' she said, 'is James.'

He took her hand. The jolt shook her arm to the shoulder socket.

'Oh!' she said, shivering. 'You take my breath away. Your touch has some alchemy in it.'

'Think'st thou, indeed? Dost thou tolerate it?'

'It is like a shock, but sweeter than anything I have ever endured.'

'How canst thou be certain it is *I* and not *thee* who generates it?'

A silver trumpet sang loudly, somewhere in the machicolations close above. A distant fleck in the southeast shaped itself into a Stormrider.

'A Relayer from Caermelor,' said Thorn. 'And we must tarry no longer. The day matures. Art thou able to be ready to depart before noon, Distraction? The hour is not far away.'

'Easily.'

Rohain called for Caitri. A rattle as of small hard objects scattering upon the floor came from the outer room where she waited—the resourceful child had been playing at knucklebones and at the summons had dropped them.

'At your service, my lady.'

Caitri, kneeling, had not yet overcome awe sufficiently to glance at her sovereign.

'Tell Viviana to be ready to leave at noon.'

'At once, my lady.'

'And send a messenger to Roxburgh. I would confer with the Attriod,' said Thorn.

'Your Majesty,' whispered the maid. Rising, she backed out of the chamber without lifting her eyes.

'I am fond of that child,' said Rohain. 'May I ask her if she would like to accompany us?'

'There is *nothing* thou needs must ask for. All is thine—take it.'

Still clasping her hand, he led her back to the table.

'Is there nought else thou wouldst take from this chimney stack that once housed thee, besides a half-fledged chick?'

His hair held the subtle fragrance of cedar or perhaps wild thyme. Submerged by the barely leashed potency of him, Rohain wrenched her attention away. She recalled a dressing-table in the suite where she had slept on the previous night—one of the many apartments on the fortieth story that had escaped the depredations of the unseelie vandals. The fringed aulmoniere containing Maeve's swan's feather lay there. Beside it lay the crimson vial of Dragon's Blood—Thorn's gift, unchained from around her neck when she had bathed. It had been neglected in the amazement of the morning.

'Yes, there is something. I shall fetch it myself, and return in a trice.'

He raised her hand to his lips. Over it, he studied her with speculative tenderness.

'Your kiss is fire,' she murmured, blushing.

'Burn, then.'

'I do not want to leave your side, even for a trice.'

'Remain, then.'

'Soon, forever. Now I must go.'

He relinquished her hand. Someone's knuckles rapped hesitantly at the outer door. Thorn bade the door-knocker enter, and Rohain fled. Outside in the passageway, a convocation of tall lords stood aside, bowing respectfully, to let her pass. She inclined her head in acknowledgment of their salutes.

In the dressing-chamber a slight figure jerked its head up when she entered in a flurry of silver and black. The dressing-table was bereft of all accoutrements save a bowl and ewer.

'Pod! What are you doing here? Where are my purse and vial?'

'I don't know,' he rapped out, rather implausibly.

'You have them. Give them to me, please.'

He backed away, his hands concealed behind him.

'Prithee, Pod.'

The lad's eyes slid from side to side, like loosely strung beads.

'Such as you,' he said in a stilted voice, 'such as you and such as he shall never find happiness together.'

'Say not that!' shouted Rohain vehemently. 'Take it back! Wish me well instead. Say it is not so!'

'It is so.'

'A king may marry a commoner—why not? He may marry whomsoever he chooses! Why do you hate me?'

'I hate all of you.'

'Do you not wish to find friendship?'

'No.'

She lunged at him, hoping to catch him off guard and retrieve her belongings. He dodged past, skipping lopsidedly to the door and out.

'Take your pessimistic prophecies hence, base villain!' she cried after him. 'They are false, in any event. Never speak to me again!'

She sat before the looking-glass and wiped away a few glassy tears that trembled in her eyes. Pod's prediction had disturbed her deeply. He had stolen the swan's feather and the Dragon's Blood, but it no longer seemed to matter.

A reek of siedo-pods preceded Viviana into the chamber.

'My lady! I am ready to return. I cannot wait to leave this miserable place.'

'Stay back, please!' Rohain held a lace kerchief to her nose.

'There is no ridding oneself of it,' mourned the lady's maid.

Her mistress waved her away. 'Ask Caitri and Pennyrigg and Featherstone and Brand Brinkworth the Storyteller whether they would like to accompany the King-Emperor to Court and abide there. All who wish to do so must assemble at Royal Squadron Level by noon.'

Viviana fluttered from the room. Rohain returned to the Highest Solar, before whose door a second crowd milled. Saluting, murmuring, the concourse parted to allow her through. Silver-and-black hat-hedges lined her path. A daunting assembly of lords and attendants now filled the hall, with the King-Emperor at its focus. All fell silent at Rohain's entrance. Boldly she walked to the window embrasure where once again he stood, framed against the sky, with Errantry positioned on his shoulder. Yes, let them witness how it was.

Smiling that brilliant smile which left her weak, he kissed her hand.

'Our business here is concluded. And so to horse,' he added to the assembly at large.

They led a procession from the hall. Due to his stature, Thorn's cloak was full-yarded enough to billow from his shoulders like a great banner; as he walked its edges flicked the denizens of the Tower in the passageway, who had shrunk to pilose dwarf borders, having removed their hats and fallen to their knees.

There was a stirring in the stones. The procession halted abruptly when Thorn sidestepped, reached into the bruised shadows of a gouge in the wall, and pulled out a small, yelping figure that stank like a goat-pen. Pod quailed, weakly flapping against Thorn's grip like a half-dead fish on a hook.

'Knave!' said Thorn sternly. 'Think you that you can spy on us, hidden, as you erroneously believed?'

Pod hung limply, sullenly.

'Speak!'

The lad pointed an accusing finger.

'She told me not to speak.'

'What?' roared Thorn. 'Have you been troubling the Lady Rohain? I might have your shape shifted to that of a viper's liver and feed you to my hawk.'

'No, no!' squealed Pod pathetically. To Rohain, he looked such a miserable, scrawny thing that compassion and deflection seemed the only possible reaction.

'He has not—' she began then broke off. *He has been troubling me. I would not accuse him, but neither would I lie, especially to Thorn. There have been too many lies, since my tongue was loosened.*

'Any past wrongs are forgiven,' said she. 'He is able, conceivably, to be an amiable lad.'

'He does not look so,' said Thorn. 'Get yourself some clean clouts, lurker, and a courteous tongue in your head.'

He released the boy, who unclotted to a nerveless blob and subsided against the wall.

They moved on.

A phalanx of footmen in mustard livery edged with silver braid stood to attention in straight lines, their gloved hands knotted behind their backs. Saddled and ready, eotaurs cluttered the upper gatehalls with the jangle of their flying-gear and the ring of sildron against stone. Their warm breath scented the air like a harvest.

Lord Ustorix, with Lady Heligea at his elbow, took leave of the King-Emperor and his entourage. The Son of the House croaked his farewells, hoarse with some kind of pent-up emotion.

'Your Majesty has honoured our humble abode by this visit and by the succor Your Majesty has bestowed on Your Majesty's undeserving subjects. May Your Majesty and the Lady Rohain ride with the wind at your backs.' In his pompous efforts at civility he seemed to be tying clove-hitches with his tongue

Thorn nodded and leapt astride his steed, thrusting his boots down between the rustling wings and the smooth flanks.

'Lord Ustorix, are you quite recovered from your ordeal?' inquired Rohain.

'No complaint shall escape my lips, most exalted lady,' he answered with studied fortitude.

'Until you are, I recommend that Heligea take over your Relayer duties. She is adept at riding sky. In fact, I suggest that she should Relay as often as she wishes.'

A murmur of surprise ran through the gathered Household of the Isse Tower. Heligea's grin of triumph eclipsed the scowl of dismay her brother tried to conceal with a low bow.

The sun, at the keypoint of its arch, hung at the centre of the sky's dome. The Imperial Flight, a fleet of some three score mighty Skyhorses, burst from an upper gatehall. Banking to the south-west, they formed an arrowhead and passed away to the distance like charcoaled galleons slowly sinking beneath an azure ocean.

5
CAERMELOR, PART III
Fire and Fleet

If you are the lantern, I am the flame;
If you are the lake, then I am the rain;
If you are the desert, I am the sea;
If you are the blossom, I am the bee;
If you are the fruit, then I am the core;
If you are the rock, then I am the ore;
If you are the ballad, I am the word;
If you are the sheath, then I am the sword.

LOVE SONG OF SEVERNESSE

Viviana and Caitri rode pillion. They had no experience in riding sky, and onhebbing the eotaur flying-gear was too delicate an art for beginners to master. The sliding of andalum chain-plate along the inner courses of the sildron girth-strap to gain or lose altitude took skill born of practice. For the duration of the illicit skyride that had so disjointed the nose of her brother, Heligea—who had secretly practiced for years—had onhebbed like a professional. Rohain, however, had experienced the clumsiness of the novice. Yet this was not the reason Rohain now rode sideways behind Thorn, her arms encircling the wood-hardness of his waist, watching the world dissolve into the flying thunderwrack of his hair.

She leaned against him, almost paralyzed by the exquisite sensation. Later, she could not recall much of that ride save an impression of a storm-whipped shore and a seashell tossed on a dark tide.

Three miles out from Caermelor, the riders heard the trumpets blare. Watchmen on the palace heights had recognised their approach. A mile from the city, the cloud of hugely beating wings began to lose altitude on its long, low final descent. The eotaurs came in over the palace walls, their feathered fetlocks barely clearing the crenellations. They hovered like giant dragonflies over the baileys, churning the air with a backwash as thunderous as a hurricane. From the courtyards below, hats and straw and dust swirled in a chaotic porridge. The cavalcade landed with flawless precision.

Equerries ran to slip off the sildron hoof-crescents and lead away the Skyhorses, to unsaddle them and scrape the sweat from their gleaming flanks, to preen and water and treat the steeds like pampered lords and ladies. Servants hurried to meet the riders, to bear away the jewel-backed riding-gloves they stripped from their hands, to offer fluted cups of wines and cordials. The splendid foot-guards of the Household Division formed two ceremonial columns, creating a human arcade leading to the palace doors. Flowers had been strewn along the cobblestones. Along this arcade walked their sovereign and the dark-haired lady.

As the couple entered the doors of the palace, a slender young man stood upon the flagstones, barring their way. He seemed, in fact, no more than a youth—not much older than Caitri; fourteen or fifteen Summers, a sprout-chinned adolescent. His black hair was impeccably bound into a long horsetail, framing a face that was pale, serious, comely. He bowed briefly to Thorn—a look of understanding flashed between them—and regarded Rohain quizzically from behind soot-coloured eyelashes.

There was no need for introductions.

Rohain performed a deep, gracious curtsey. The youth pronounced her current name in the crack-pitched tones of his years and she replied with his royal title. Then they regarded one another. Rohain glimpsed a flicker of what lay behind the starched facade and smiled.

'I am joyed to greet you.'

'And I you,' he said guardedly, but he smiled too and added, 'well come.'

The Heir Apparent stood aside, that the King-Emperor and Rohain might enter first.

The rooms of Rohain's suite burned with frost and flame. Snowy plaster moldings of milky grapes and vine-leaves twined across the ceilings. Brilliant garlands of flowers had been woven into pure white carpets, upon which stood carmine couches and ottomans. A pale marble chimneypiece was drizzled with sparkling ornaments of ruby red glass. Between the casement windows stretched tall mirrors, polished to perfection.

In one of the three bedchambers—vermilion-carpeted—there stood a bed whose canopy was supported on massive pillars of mahogany. It was hung with curtains of crimson damask embroidered with a twining pattern of clover, over and over. The table at the foot of the bed was muffled in a blood-red cloth. The walls had been painted a soft cream colour with a blush of rose in it, and around them were arranged several clothes-chests, lace-draped tables upholding jewel-caskets and chairs of dark, polished mahogany. A tall cushioned chair had been placed near the head of the bed, with a footstool before it.

The main dressing-room was sumptuously overfurnished with looking-glasses. Boxes on the dressing-table contained numbers of miniature compartments and drawers to hold trinkets and jewellery, with further mirrors fitted to the undersides of the lids, which could be propped open, in case one didn't see enough of oneself elsewhere. In the writing-room, an impressive ink-stand with a double lid and a central handle dominated the polished jarrah escritoire.

Long fingers of windows, half-disguised by festoons and falls of wine-coloured velvet, looked out upon the Winter Garden where crystal wind-chimes had been tied to the boughs, ringing soft and pure, in random melody. Between the green cones of the cypress pines, cornelian fires sprang from high stone dishes, admiring their own fervent lucidity in tarnished ponds.

This, Viviana informed Rohain, was the Luindorn Suite—a

vast and exquisitely furnished apartment usually reserved for state visitors.

After breakfast, two height-matched footmen skilled in the art of unobtrusiveness wheeled out the dining trolley and melted quietly away. Caitri, who had rung for them, leaned wide-eyed from a sitting-room window as though she might presently shift to a linnet's shape and fly out into the sky. She appeared oblivious of Rohain and Viviana, who sat head to head, deep in conversation.

'My lady,' said Viviana, 'that you have found favour in the King-Emperor's eyes is advantageous for us both. As long as his favour lasts, we can *never* be Cut. As for your secret history of service in Isse Tower, why, you can depend on me never to divulge it to anyone. See, you have become a lady after all! I have but one concern—this dresser who has been assigned to you, and this footman also. What next? There is talk that you are to have a noblewoman as your own bodyservant! Are my services to be dispensed with?'

'Of course not. You are to remain as my maid, if you wish it, as I do. And there are to be no ladies-in-waiting—not yet.'

'Ladies-in-waiting?'

As the implications of the term sank in, Viviana's eyes widened. Only a queen would have ladies-in-waiting.

'Six there shall eventually be, chiefed by the Duchess of Roxburgh whenever she is at Court,' whispered Rohain.

Simultaneously, maid and mistress burst out laughing. Seizing each other by the hands, they danced the circumference of the floor like children around a beribboned pole on Whiteflower's Day, finally falling breathlessly on two couches of plum-red velvet.

'So 'tis true!' panted Viviana. 'His Majesty has asked—'

'Yes! We are troth-plighted, he and I. But it is not generally known—the announcement has yet to be officially made.'

'In sooth, rumour has been rife! I did not like to pry, but everyone guesses it. I cannot believe this! My mistress to be Queen-Empress!'

Caitri turned her head, emerging from the haze of her musing. She had been scandalizing at the amount of world that had heretofore been denied her, imprisoned as she had been in Isse Tower.

'Is my lady to be Queen?' She was thunderstruck.

Viviana pranced to the window, grasped the little girl, and whirled her in another polka.

'Yes! Love is the season of the year! What is more, Caitri, when Dain Pennyrigg lifted me from his eotaur just now, he called me his little canary and kissed me. *Kiel varletto!* And he only a stable-hand! Oh, but it was *taraiz* delicious. His kiss thrilled me like lightning!'

Rohain nodded. 'Passion's current. In both senses of the phrase.'

'Skyhorse travel is eminently more pleasurable than Windship travel,' pronounced Viviana. 'Oh, and Master Pennyrigg found this in his saddlebags.' Rummaging in her pocket, she produced the crimson vial of Dragon's Blood.

Rohain clapped her hands. 'Happy day! It is returned to me! Was it companioned by anything else? An aulmoniere perhaps?'

'Why yes, m'lady. Here it is, but it is now putrid with a stink of goats, and I thought to cast it away. I shall have it cleansed for you.'

Her mistress took the dirty purse and felt around inside it. 'Curses! 'Tis empty! Was there naught else?'

'No, m'lady, there was nothing else which Master Pennyrigg himself did not pack. Only an *ensofell* of smelly hair, tied with string—it comes from a dog or a goat methinks—and the bedrag-gled feather of some fowl. Shall I throw them away?'

'No, give the feather to me. It is a powerful talisman.'

Rohain tucked the feather inside a tapestry aulmoniere, fas-tened with buttons of jet. It seemed that Pod was at least capable of thanks for his rescue from Thorn's wrath. However, his return of the vial did not hint at a reversal of his dismal prediction. After all, he was supposed to be a prophet, not a maker of curses.

'Come now, my two birds,' said Rohain, absently retying a seditious lace on Caitri's gown of forget-me-not blue. 'I have been from *his* side for too long. It is fully an hour since we arrived from the Stormrider Tower. That is more than enough time to wash away the stains of travel and recostume ourselves.'

'Look at us!' prattled Viviana, ever conscious of appearances.

'My lady dark-haired in crimson, I fair in daffodil, and cinnamon Caitri in a sky-coloured gown. What a motley bouquet!'

'Yet some among us do not *smell* as a bouquet should,' said her mistress, holding a perfumed pomander to her nose to block out the last odorous traces of siedo-pod oil wafting from Viviana's hair. 'Hasten!'

A rapping at the door announced the Master of the King's Household, a gray-haired gentleman of middle age. 'His Majesty sends greetings, my lady,' he said, bending forward from the waist, 'and regrets to inform you that he has been called away on a matter of uncommon import.'

'So precipitously?' murmured Rohain. 'We have only just arrived!'

'These are fickle times,' said the gentleman. 'Even the best-laid plans may go astray.'

'I thank you, sir, for your advice.'

The palace seemed suddenly devoid of substance and character during Thorn's unexpected absence. Rohain took the opportunity to visit Sianadh in the dungeons.

'You are to be set free,' she told him.

He would not believe her. "Tis kind of you to try to cheer me,' he said in a morose mood, 'but these hard-hearted *skeerdas* would not free their own grandmother if she was in leg-irons.'

'I tell you, I have heard the King-Emperor say so!'

'Ye must have been dreaming,' he said mournfully. 'Ach! I'd give me right arm for a drop o' the pure stuff.'

Thorn returned two days later. He sent a message to Rohain asking her to join him in the Throne Room. Swiftly she made her way through the long galleries and passageways, eager for the reunion.

The columns of the Throne Room aspired to a forty-foot ceiling. This huge space was lit by metallic lusters pendant on thirty-foot chains, and flambeaux on brass pedestals. Twin thrones beneath their dagged and gilded canopy stood atop the grand dais. They were reached by twelve broad stairs.

Around the walls, the history of the world reenacted itself

perpetually on adjoining tapestries that reached to a height of twenty feet and represented years of painstaking stitchery. Above them, every inch of the plasterwork crawled with painted murals—not scenes, but geometric designs, stylized flowers, vegetables, flora and fauna, and fantastic gold-leaf scrollwork that did not stop at the ceiling merely because that was too high to be easily viewed, but surged across it in a prolific efflorescence with the vigor of weeds.

By comparison to this busy overabundance the polished floor seemed austere, parquetried as it was with wood every shade of brown between palest blond and burnt umber. These coloured woods formed the heraldic device of the House of D'Armancourt in repeated tiles six feet square. The hall was so vast that to enter the doors was to dwindle immediately to the proportions of a mouse among cornstalks.

Rohain entered with her small entourage and a froth of footmen and alert courtiers who had entangled themselves in her wake as she sailed through the corridors. Like every cave in the palace, currently the Throne Room was arrayed with a flotsam of courtiers and servants. One of the former—a familiar, foppish figure—bowed low before her.

'My Lady Rohain, His Majesty yet walks in the gardens with the Attriod but will shortly join us here in the Throne Room.'

'Please show me the way to the gardens, Lord Jasper.' He bowed again, but before he could fulfil her request, a footman, whose wig resembled a white rabbit, dropped to his knee. He elevated a silver salver from which Lord Jasper plucked a parchment. The nobleman's brow furrowed as he squinted at the writing of some palace scribe.

'Er—a gentleman begs audience with Your Ladyship. It appears His Majesty sent for him. An Ertishman with an unpronounceable name.'

'Send him in,' said Rohain.

Uproar and a torrent of Ertish curses emanated from outside the Throne Room, reaffirming Sianadh's contempt for formalities. The doors crashed apart and he burst through like a boulder from a mangonel. Catching sight of Rohain, he stood blinking as though dazed. Two footmen who had been shed from his brawny arms stood helplessly by.

'There ye are, *chehrna*,' said the Ertishman meekly, the bear now a lamb. 'The *skeerdas* would not let me through.'

'*Mo gaidair*,' said Rohain warmly. She proffered a hand. He took it with the utmost delicacy and a bewildered look. Nothing else being offered in the way of courtesy, she drew it back with an appreciative sigh. '*Mo gaidair*, your lack of etiquette is a refreshing draught.'

'*Chehrna*, in one breath I am thinking it might be me last, the next they're turning the key in me cell-door and I am a free man. How is this? What have ye done?'

'Lord Jasper, is there some minor chamber where I can converse with my friend? Somewhere less cavernous and popular?'

Lord Jasper's eyebrows shot up to meet his hairline. 'But of course, m'lady,' he said, trying to conceal his disapproval by dabbing his brow with a kerchief of embroidered lawn. 'Methinks the Hall of Audience is unoccupied for the nonce. Allow me to conduct you there.' Calling for footmen to bring lighted tapers, he indicated the Hall's direction with a courtly flourish and a neatly pointed toe.

In a corner of the Hall of Audience, Viviana and Caitri played Cloth-Scissors-Rock. One hundred and sixty candles blazed in gold candlesticks, like banks of radiant flowers. Rohain and Sianadh conversed, she imparting an outline of all that had occurred at Isse Tower. As she spoke, he grew progressively more restive, jubilant at what he was hearing.

'So you see, I did not find what I sought,' she concluded, 'but I found instead something far dearer to my heart.'

'Dear to anyone's heart, the riches of royalty!' he crowed.

'You mistake my meaning. I have no ambition, *mo gaidair*. I did not seek this. I have never desired anything that is theirs— wealth or pomp. Perhaps I have desired respect and ease, who has not? Yet I had hope for an ease that does not live by battening on the toil of others, and a respect that grows from genuine friendship, not social status. I do not need so many jewels, so many costly possessions. All this obsequiousness and etiquette is foreign to me. I suppose I shall get used to it for *his* sake and I doubt not that in time I shall have forgotten that it could be otherwise, and it shall all be enjoyable—for, mistake me not, I am not ungrateful. I entered the world beyond the Tower looking for three things: a face, a voice, a past. In the searching I found the first two, discovered a fourth desire, and lost the third. Now my past matters no longer. The present is all I could desire.'

She fell silent. It occurred to her that now, at last, she was at rest, if not at peace—not seeking anymore. Yet even as she surveyed the luxury surrounding her in the Hall of Audience with its one hundred and sixty lighted candles and three times as many waiting to be lit, a musty wind came funneling out of a past she had forgotten that she had forgotten. Troubled by Pod's words, by a couple of abandoned loam-worms, the lingering breath of forest mold, and withered foliage sprinkled like scraps of torn manuscript in the ruined bedchamber, she shuddered and shrank from remembering. History was too dark; far too dark.

'As my first edict,' she said briskly, 'I shall outlaw the beating of servants throughout Erith.'

'Very right-minded of ye, *chehrna*,' replied Sianadh, 'but ye shall start a rebellion with that kind of thinking.'

'My strength shall be used to shield the vulnerable. All *I* need,' she concluded, 'all I need is air to sustain me, and the one I love.'

'And drink,' rejoined Sianadh prosaically, jumping up, 'and vittles. And him to be good enough for ye.'

Unable to restrain his glee, he jumped in the air and danced, as energetically as Rohain had danced with Viviana not long before. To the disgust of the stone-faced footmen and the door-sentries who for years had practiced outfreezing statues, the wild red-haired man performed an Ertish jig.

'Free!' he trumpeted. 'Free, and pardoned, and in favour with the Queen Apparent! I could kiss ye, *chehrna*, I could kiss ye!'

A wintry gust, clean and sharp, howled through the chamber. It billowed the wall-hangings and blew out seventy-five candles.

Several Dainnan knights in chain mail had entered the chamber and positioned themselves on either side of the door. Sianadh seized up in midpose. Rohain's maids jumped up and snapped to attention and even the guards ossified further.

Thorn stood in the open doorway, a score of lords at his back.

In Dainnan attire, straight as a sword he stood, and as bright. His hair and *dusken* cloak lifted, like shadowy vanes, in the breath of Winter that had entered with him. That cool current blew across the carpets a scatter of leaves from the gardens, leaves that chased each other and skipped like pagan dancers across the floor's rich patterning. Rohain's heart leapt painfully against her ribs, a bird battering itself against its cage. *His beauty is perilous. I could die merely from beholding it.*

Roxburgh, taciturn, stood behind his sovereign's shoulder with two or three others of the Attriod. Like the tail of a comet, a glittering train forever attended the King-Emperor.

This tableau shattered when Thorn stepped forward, crunching dry leaves beneath his boots. Sianadh remained standing. A courtier hissed, 'On your knees, fellow!'

'I grovel before no man,' said Sianadh, 'save the King-Emperor himself.'

'Behold the King-Emperor, block-brain,' muttered Rohain.

'What?' Sianadh jibbed, thrown off balance. Stiffly he sank to his knees, bowing the bushy red head.

'Rise, Kavanagh,' said Thorn, calm as a subterranean lake, as cold.

'Ye have pardoned me,' said Sianadh, stumbling to his feet and moving to Rohain's side with a mixture of gratefulness and wariness, 'and for that I thank ye, Your Majesty. I've a *strong* right arm that has defended Imrhien here and would willingly wield a sword for the Empire, and it has not withered at all despite languishing in your dungeons without so much as a drop of ale to give me fortitude.'

The courtiers murmured against his questionable attitude and his unconscionable manner of addressing the King-Emperor using the second-person pronoun. Their sovereign appeared to ignore these mistakes.

'Indeed?' he said, raising one eyebrow. *A captivating trick,* thought Rohain.

'Aye,' said Sianadh. Lifting an elbow from beneath which emanated an odour of stale body fluids, he rolled up a sleeve. 'Strong, my arm.' Blatantly devoid of finer feeling, he flexed a great pudding of a bicep. Several guards made as if to throw him out for his effrontery. Thorn waved them away.

'Leave us,' he commanded his retinue. 'Stay you, Roxburgh, and my page.' Bowing, the attendants reluctantly began to trickle out of the Hall of Audience.

'You say that arm has defended the Lady Rohain?' Thorn inquired mildly.

'Aye, and no man has ever beaten me in an arm-wrestle,' replied the Ertishman, whose eyes were boldly fixed on Thorn's. Being a few inches shorter, he had to look up to achieve this; an irksome necessity for him.

'Sianadh,' admonished Rohain. 'Do not be *scothy*. Nothing can rescue you this time.'

'Do you make a challenge?' asked Thorn.

'A challenge, by—' Sianadh bit off his words. 'Aye, some might call it that, sir. Now I have said it. There it be.' His face was a mask of defiance.

The last two departing lords fingered their sword-hilts. 'For this insolence his tongue shall be torn out by the roots,' muttered one.

'He's for the scaffold,' murmured another. Roxburgh folded his arms and looked interested. The heavy doors closed.

The corners of Thorn's mouth twitched slightly. He rolled up his right sleeve and took a seat at a small table. His arm, a tawny mellifluity of waterworn driftwood's smoothly contoured undulations, was vastly different from his opponent's. Sianadh's arm was similarly thewed, but adorned by tattoos, freckles, red bristles, and scars.

Suddenly in his element, Sianadh took the opposite stool. They planted their elbows on the tabletop. Their hands came together. Cords bulged, sinews knotted. Elegantly, in the blink of an eye, it was over. Sianadh's hand lay on its back; his shoulders skewed to follow the outward twist of his elbow.

'Two outta three!' he demanded hotly, as though he sat at a

tavern table with a drunken caravaner. Shivering beads stood out on his brow. Thorn nodded. The act was repeated, with identical outcome. Sianadh sat stunned as Thorn rolled down his sleeve.

'Well sir, ye've beaten me fair and square,' the Ertishman admitted with admiration. 'I cannot say as I wasn't ready. I was. But ye might have dignified a man by breaking a sweat. That there is a right arm I'd be proud to fight in the shadow of.'

'My sword arm might cast a darker shadow.'

The Ertishman threw back his head and shouted with laughter, displaying a crescent of broken teeth like stubs of moldy cheese.

'Call me a blind man,' he blurted between guffaws. 'Your skian's buckled on the south side. I've made a right *sgorrama* of meself.'

'True, but not relevant since you have already proven your worth thrice over,' said Thorn. 'What boon would you ask of me?'

'Boon? Sir, ye have already extended the numbering of my days, which I am never sure of. I could not ask for better. However . . .' The Ertishman was struck by a sudden awareness of opportunity. He scratched his beard. 'D'ye need more men-at-arms?'

'Not at this time.'

'Then there's something I have always thought might suit me—to sail on a Windship and trade me way about. Travel, adventure, and wealth. That's my style.'

'A clipper lies idle in Finvarna as we speak. I gift her to you. What more? Ask, while I am generous.'

'I give ye gramercie, sire. As for more, I may not legally set foot in Finvarna. The High Chieftain, Mabhoneen of Finvarna, has banished me. Yet I have a craving to return.'

'You told me he lifted that ban,' interjected Rohain.

'I forgot to tell ye,' said Sianadh. 'He put it back.'

'Why?'

''Tis a long and unjust story, *chebrna*. These days, I yearn for me home something vicious. 'Tis hard to explain—'tis like a sore plague that eats at ye. Aye, I have the homesickness, that which in Finvarna we call the *longarieth*. I would fain set foot on me native sod again.'

'You shall be no longer exiled,' Thorn said.

Sianadh digested this. When he looked at Rohain she beheld in his face a light of joy such as she had never seen there.

'Finvarna,' crooned Sianadh, as if murmuring a love-name. 'Finvarna. I can go back. And a Windship! I shall become a merchant, that I shall. A respectable man. I shall see them, me children, me Granny . . . Ach! The chariot races and the good Ertish cookery—Your Majesty, I cannot find words to show me gratefulness!' He jumped up. 'A Windship! It shall be my beast of burden, my donkey. Therefore I shall call it the *Bear's Ass*, or mayhap the *Bear-Ass*.'

'Unfortunately for the rejuvenation of the Register of Ships' Names, she is already titled,' said Thorn drily. 'Red of canvas, she is called *Rua*.'

'*Rua*—the Red-Haired!' Sianadh chortled.

'You will not return to Finvarna yet?' beseeched Rohain. 'You will stay for the Ball and the Tournament of Jousting, *mo gaidair*? There are to be fireworks!'

'I wouldna miss the festivities for gold angels!'

'We shall be happy and remember happy times past.'

'Aye, times past.' Sianadh quieted abruptly, abashed. 'But it cannot be like those times, not now, not never again, with ye looking like that and all.' His eyes met hers, open but shielded. In them was written the knowledge that he looked upon a friend now contained within a different vessel, a vessel to which he would have responded differently had he known her in it first. He struggled to come to terms with this, having lived all his life in a world whose mores dictated that friendship should not exist between such a man as he and such a woman as she. The awareness discomfited him and made him feel, somehow, a traitor.

Comeliness is a blade with two edges, mused Rohain.

'*Inna shai tithen elion,*' she said, with a sad smile, recalling their first parting—long ago, it seemed in Gilvaris Tarv.

'Kavanagh,' Thorn said, rising to his feet. 'Until you depart you have the freedom of my cellars and my leave to sample their contents in quantities to your liking. This is to indemnify you for the shortages you have ostensibly experienced while living idle at the expense of my Treasury.'

'I shall seek them out at once!' said the Ertishman energetically, clapping the King's Page heartily on the shoulder. 'I have
some drinking to catch up on and I be in need of good fellowship
to do it with. Ye look like a good fellow.'

The courtier stepped back hastily. Sianadh shrugged.

'Have it your way, jack. I'll warrant the kitchen-hands know
how to make merry, if ye do not.'

Bowing with more enthusiasm than style, Sianadh took it upon
himself to walk backward from the Hall of Audience, to demonstrate his knowledge of etiquette. No sooner had he reached the
doors, however, than he was back again. In a sudden, unexpected
gesture, he knelt at Thorn's feet a second time, unbidden, wordless.

Briefly, Thorn laid his hand on the Ertishman's head. '*Sain*
thee,' he said gravely.

This time as Sianadh disappeared around the corner, a high-
pitched whoop drifted back.

'Barbarian.' The whisper rippled knowingly among the
courtiers clustered outside.

'Now,' said Thorn to Rohain, turning the twin shafts of his
gaze on her to penetrate her eyes and plumb the wellspring of her
thought. 'Having dispensed with business, my intent, troth-
plighted, is to walk with thee beneath the trees.'

He took her hand.

Later, as they sauntered together through the gardens, Thorn
said, 'One man leaves the dungeons, another arrives. The Lord
High Wizard is now imprisoned. As for the niece, she is under
durance, confined to rooms, with only poor Georgiana Griffin to
attend her.'

'Good sooth! Are they guilty of conspiring to destroy me, as
you suspected?' asked Rohain.

'As sure as drowners fill their lovers' lungs with water. The one
has demonstrated it, the other has confessed it,' replied Thorn.

'How so?'

'Thou dost recollect I sent a letter from Isse Tower?'

'I do.'

'I bade Tom Ercildoune set a watch on the conjuror. When tidings of our success at Isse reached the Court, the swindler and his

minions instantly fled. The fool thus betrayed himself, for why should he take flight on hearing the Hunt had been defeated and Dianella's supposed rival found safe, unless he feared reprisal for his part in the fiasco?'

'How did you find him?'

'The Dainnan of the Ninth Thriesniun tracked them to the Well in the Wood's Heart. Hast thou heard of it? No? 'Tis a dry and mossy shaft of ancient stone, forever secure from wickedness, and which the carlin further sealed with the powers of her Wand. But she could not leave. She and the lad, her apprentice, were imprisoned there, under eldritch siege. The conjuror, however, walked unharmed among wicked wights winged, tailed, and fanged. Indeed, he was imploring them for aid!'

'Does he wield power over them?' cried Rohain.

'Nay. He is naught but an ill-uttering entertainer, a sly and hollow-hearted man of wax. He had made some pact with them, which ensured his temporary immunity from their wanton wickedness. That is all. When I joined the Ninth Thriesniun we drove back the creatures of unseelie, releasing the two good folk trapped within the Well, and taking the conjuror prisoner. The Dainnan zealously drove the unseelie things far off, whereupon Maeve One-Eye and Tom Coppins went their way on the forest paths again, unafraid.'

'I am glad!'

'The conjurer and his henchmen were brought here to the palace. They were charged with trafficking with wielders of maleficent forces. As for the niece, when confronted with the truth she denied it at first, then, perceiving denial to be sleeveless, she told all. Their murderous conspiracy was revealed.'

'Murderous conspiracy? Is it a fact that Sargoth sent the Hunt against me? That the infamous Huon should bend to a wizard's will seems incredible, but I fear that the attack on Isse Tower at the time of my visit was more than coincidence. Nay,' she said, answering her own question, 'it cannot be so. Sargoth might have achieved his purpose to equal degree with a well-placed ambush of lesser wights.'

'True, *eudail*, no wizard has the power to command Huon. He may have inveigled a hold over some common spriggan or duer-gar, but no mortal man can govern the Wild Hunt. The conjuror has unwittingly plunged himself into deeper trouble than he knows. His meddling has triggered more than he bargained for. He admitted, when questioned, that he sent some minor unseelie destroyer to slay thee, describing thee as a Talith daughter, a gold-haired damsel with her tresses dyed black. I surmise his words were passed on by eldritch tongues, to reach the ears of a might-ier authority.'

Looking directly at Rohain he said gravely, 'My bird, some-thing mighty, unseelie, and malevolent came for thee—the Antlered One himself. *Why should Huon wish to hunt at thy heels?'*

His words accorded with her own suspicions. 'I know not!' she said, and this was true. *Somehow I have incurred the wrath of the Antlered One. It might be that in my travels I inadvertently spied upon him, or took something that belonged to him or his minions. The Lords of Unseelie require only slight motive to persecute mortalkind.*

In her heart she guessed the reason must lie in her forgotten past, but to herself she denied it, blindly hoping that banning such knowledge would negate that past. There was no place here, now, for sorrow and pain. Here was safety and happiness. Why dig up old miseries?

'What is to become of the prisoners?' she asked.

'Time enough to ponder that later. I have turned my mind to other thoughts. Let those who cross me stew awhile, or rot.'

'I would like to visit Dianella.'

'As it please thee, *ionmhuinn.* She cannot harm thee now.'

Rohain made her way to the rooms of durance.

What did she expect? A brooding, bitter courtier, enthroned in shadow and candlelight, who would not turn her head to look at Rohain?

'Come to gloat, have we?' the prisoner would say. 'Come to sneer, now that I am helpless? You have done your work well, have you not? Oh, so successfully!'

'Dianella,' the visitor would reply, 'I have not come to gloat, to miscall you, or to be miscalled. I do not hate you. I never planned that all this should come to pass, I swear it. Dianella, that you loved him, love him still, I now know. If passion drove you to rash deeds I can at least empathize with that passion. I cannot comprehend how any woman who has looked upon him could be anything but lovestruck.'

Then, the courtier might say, 'You understand!' and weep, and beg forgiveness.

Rohain's expectations of the meeting, however, were not to be fulfilled.

The only warning may have been a curious expression that flitted across Dianella's face as Rohain entered with her maidservants—that was all. It might have been a look of surprise.

'Rohain! Dear Heart!' The dark-haired beauty glided forward to bestow an embrace on her visitor and kisses on the air. 'La! You cannot imagine how glad I am to see you. The boredom has been beyond utterance. Griffin sulks, nobody else says a word, and I scarcely have any callers. The dullness defies description!'

'I am sorry for you . . .' Rohain stammered. Somehow, Dianella in the flesh always disarmed her.

'Of course, you look perfectly lovely!' Dianella purred. 'Come—sit by me awhile. Can you spare the time, sweetness? Griffin, we would take a sip. Make arrangements.'

Puzzled and wary, Rohain sat at a table of carved walnut inlaid with copper and nacre. The rooms of durance were far from uncomfortable. They were well-furnished and provided with fireplaces in which flames now leaped cheerfully. Seldom used, the rooms were not dungeon cells but apartments set aside for aristocrats who had fallen under suspicion of crimes such as plotting, treason, or spying.

Dianella chattered on as though she entertained at a garden party; as if nothing had ever existed between them besides close friendship.

'You are simply delicious in seed-pearls and point lace. And your hair—still dark-stained! 'Tis *so fine et gloriana!* Wise of you not to have the dye stripped out, Heart. Doubtless the entire country would believe your goldie-yellow to be fake in any case, the

sillies, or else you would have had half the Talith population begging at your doorstep, claiming you as cousin.' Cocking her head
to one side she added pleasantly, 'Although in sooth, the yellow
would match your skin tones so much more adequately.'

She laughed daintily, with her rose of a mouth closed tight as
a bud. The colour in her cheeks was high. Rohain mumbled a
reply as Georgiana Griffin finished pouring the wine, and
Dianella's flow ran on with barely a pause.

'How do you like my embroidered surcoat and kirtle? See, the
one is worked in motifs of dragonflies and reeds with a border of
butterflies, while on the other, worms are stitched in sundry-
coloured silks, with silver cobwebs and small snails in stumpwork.
Different motifs, yet they match so cleverly in design and colouring, don't you think? La! There it is again.' Dianella broke off,
going to the window. 'Did you hear it, sweetness? Oh look—there
it is!' She pointed with a tapered fingernail. Joining her, Rohain
peered out. She could see nothing but a courtyard below, framed
by walls beyond which the ground fell precipitously away to a distant longbow of shoreline melding with a dragon's spine of
mountains.

'I suppose it was a spriggan or another of those ghastly little
unseelie things,' said Dianella from behind Rohain's back. She was
already seated at the walnut table again, smiling, her red lips
peeled back from her small white teeth. Holding out a chased silver goblet filled with dark liquid she appended, 'They have been
about so very frequently of late.'

As Rohain took the cup, Thorn's leaf-ring on her hand clashed
against the metal. The sound reverberated with extraordinary volume. It resonated and hummed sickeningly inside her head, like
a tocsin, or perhaps a *toxin*.

'To your health!' cried Dianella, lifting her goblet on high. 'No
hard feelings, Heart, let's drink to that!'

Rohain raised the vessel.

'No,' Georgiana Griffin blurted, 'don't drink!'

'Actually, I had no intention of doing so,' said Rohain, watching the thin black tongue of liquid drizzle over the rim of her
tipped goblet. Spilled on the carpet, it gave off a wisp of steam.

She let the vessel fall. Her footman and two guards, who had been standing scarcely noticed beside the door—one was never truly alone in the palace—moved swiftly toward Dianella. At the guard-captain's command they stripped her fingers of the empty compartment-ring, and all other rings for good measure. Rohain's maids clustered at her side, both talking at once. Their eyes, round with shock, were turned in accusation on Dianella. That lady returned their stares sadly.

'Alack! I have failed,' she drawled. 'Yet do not judge me harshly. The decoction would not have harmed you, Dear Heart—it would only have brought upon you a semblance of death. Then, as you lay pale and unmoving in the crypt, my servants would have taken you away. On board a Seaship you would have woken to find yourself banished forever from these domains.'

'Did you not mean to slay me?'

'I swear I did not.'

Rohain met her adversary's eyes. Deep down in their troubled depths smoldered a faint ember of truth. Dianella tossed her head and looked away as if angry to have been deciphered.

'The House of D'Armancourt is a pure bloodline,' she said. 'Royal blood—that is the seat of its power. All its brides have been chosen from royal houses or else from aristocrats of great and ancient families such as mine. Your thin serf's blood shall taint it. Worse—you shall be its downfall.'

'Hold your tongue!' cried Rohain.

At this, the courtier flushed with fury. Her voice became hard and harsh.

'You think yourself so noble, *selevader uncouthant*. No doubt you thought to come here to these rooms to bring me comfort and show your goodness. Yet when they drag me through the streets next week, you will be watching from the window. You will laugh with the rest.'

'What do you mean?'

'Oh, haven't you heard? 'Tis to be the spectacle of a decade! The Lord High Chancellor asked my dear friends Calprisia and Elmaretta to devise a suitable punishment for my so-called crimes. The sweetings suggested that humiliation would be my most dreaded nightmare. My hair is to be shorn off. I am to be dressed in rags and rattled through the streets in a donkey cart. After which, I expect they shall introduce me to the ax. I would prefer it.'

'I shall intercede on your behalf.'

'How gracious of you! You, whom I have wronged so *dreadfully*, sending you from Caermelor so that my uncle could tell the spriggans to carry you away and play with you. Take your pity elsewhere, *malck-drasp*.' Glowering with sheer hatred at Rohain, the wizard's niece spat words from her mouth like poison. 'I will not waste my malison on you. I believe *that* has been done before, and done better.'

Rohain departed.

How foolish to have hoped for better.

Later, she said to Thorn, 'Dianella's sentence must be commuted. Were I she, to be deprived of proximity to you would be far worse than any infliction of hurt or humiliation.'

'Thou art *not* she. Yet if pity moves thee, she shall be merely banished.'

'The Sorrow Isles are remote enough, from all accounts. And her uncle?'

'Thou mayst not pity malice.'

'Welcome back to Court, Rohain,' said Thomas Rhymer. His voice was solemn, but his eyes twinkled. 'We have been the worse without you. Dianella is currently indisposed, but, fed on scandal, the Set thrives more hardily than ever. Were I not incapable of even the slightest exaggeration I would swear they add a new word to the dratted courtingle each instant.'

'Hail, Sir Thomas,' Rohain replied awkwardly.

'Tut. There's no need to be diffident with me, my dear. Of course I guessed as soon as I met you that you had not come from the bleak shores of Sorrow Isles. So did Roxburgh. It mattered little to us—methinks a gentle damsel like you posed no threat to Imperial security! At first your beauty was an intrigue to us both, besides which your manner provided a contrast to the monotonous ways of Court life and the petty obsessions of the so-called Set. It was no time before we found we liked you better, the better we knew you. That you once served in a House of Stormriders does not demean you in our eyes—there is no shame in honest work. Never fear, your secret remains safe. No one else knows.'

'Forgive me, sir, for that deception.'

'Consider it forgiven. Yet your path, and that of His Majesty, might have proved smoother had you entrusted us with a few meager scraps of knowledge.'

'In truth, sir. And I am anguished to think of how much trouble might have been avoided, had I spoken out.' *Blood was shed at Isse because of my presence there.*

'Fiddlesticks!' said the Bard, guessing her thoughts. 'That was not your doing. It was the work of Huon the Hunter! Come now,' he added jovially, 'do not be anguished! Is it not consolation that your Dainnan of the wilderness has found you, whom he sought, and you have found him?' He shook his head regretfully. 'Had I known,' he said, 'had I but known to whom your heart belonged . . .'

'You might have helped me straightway, if I had mentioned the name of Thorn!'

'Indeed, my dear. Howbeit, all that is in the past now. It is time for rejoicing. Come, let me lead you to the Blue Drawing Room. The ladies Rosamonde and Maiwenna would fain keep company with you there, and Alys, with the children of Roxburgh.'

The Winter sun shone cold, a pale doubloon. Lacquered against the sky, evergreens layered with fringes of pungent bristles reached out to offer upright cones like rows of squat candles.

It was the twenty-fourth of Fuarmis, just six days until Primrose Amble with its candles, brides, white lace, horseshoes, and procession of ewes garlanded with the first tentative flowers of Spring. This year the period of the traditional festival was to be extended. It was to culminate in the celebrations for the royal betrothal, beginning on the fifteenth of Sovrachmis, the Primrosemonth. The lacuna between these dates was wadded with a flurry of activity, a cramming of the palace baileys with carters and their conveyances bringing supplies. Every merchant and pedlar in Caermelor had seized the opportunity of a Royal Ball to hawk his wares, whether or not they had been requisitioned for the occasion. In spite of the continuing belligerence simmering in Namarre, which constantly threatened to spill out across the Nenian Landbridge into northern Eldaraigne, the populace applied themselves to the preparations for this year's festivities with an extra abundance of zeal.

Viewed from a more exalted angle, Court seemed an entirely different place. To Rohain it was as though a screen had dropped from her eyes. She was introduced to aristocrats she had never before encountered, she found herself guided to regions of the palace she had not yet seen, she was treated with a respectfulness so novel she could not accustom herself to it. This new state of dignity was almost unnerving.

Courtiers acknowledged Rohain deferentially wherever she went. Crowds thicker than ever jostled at the gates from early morn until late evening. They were hoping for a glimpse of the chosen bride of the King-Emperor, James XVI of the House of D'Armancourt and Trethe, also titled High King and Emperor of Greater Eldaraigne, Finvarna, Severnesse, Luindorn, Rimany, and Namarre; King of his other Realms and Territories. Those who ran the Court machinery had assiduously put it about that his bride-to-be came of a noble line that, impoverished by ill fortune, had sunk into obscurity. If any disapproval evolved, or any questions were whispered about her birth, they were suppressed and popularly passed over. The King-Emperor might follow any whim he chose, and it would be accepted. As the highest of the high, his actions were beyond the context of convention. Besides, the people were glad their sovereign was to wed again at last.

Dianella's dark dye remained fast in Rohain's hair. It proved difficult to wash out. Rohain considered this fortunate, since to be publicly revealed as Talith would inevitably invite further questions as to her origins, and would surely destroy the careful constructions of the senior members of the King's Household, who so ardently desired that His Majesty's troth-plighted should be accepted by the populace as a gentlewoman.

'Thou dost call me Gold-Hair,' she said to Thorn, 'though my locks are now as dark as thine.'

He shrugged. 'Use what paints and colours thou wilt. Thou'rt Gold-Hair, beneath it all.'

To the far reaches of the Empire of Erith the tidings of royal betrothal travelled. Throughout Caermelor, all was noise and traffic, but within the walls of the Palace remained a wonderful, undisturbed tranquillity, an amazing sense of peace. The city whirled, and Rohain was its vortex, the stillness at the storm's eye. To see the evidence of her new authority, her influence as an emblem, took her breath away. Thorn's casual use of power awed her. She wondered how it would be to wield it with such careless assurance.

All this, she would whisper often to herself, *by the Greayte Star—for me?*

And sometimes the prediction of the twisted lad in the Tower would return to tease her.

For her, sheltered, there was no haste, no bustle—only days that slipped by like rain through a colander; days spent sometimes in conversation with Prince Edward, or with Sianadh (when he was not making merry with the butlers, ewerers, and panters in the servants' quarters), or perhaps spent with Thomas Rhymer, or both (the two Ertishmen having formed a drinking and storytelling fellowship), or with the steadfast and ebullient Alys-Jannetta and her lively progeny. Gladly, Rohain was now able to eschew the tiresome company of the Set. Affairs of state took Thorn from her side at times. Then, with her attendants and Maiwenna the Talith gentlewoman and young Rosamonde of Roxburgh, she would ride out in a coach from the Royal Mews, through countryside green-hazed with the buds of an early Spring.

Maiwenna had become a friend. Rohain trusted her almost to the point of revealing her own Talith heritage, but not quite. She asked whether the gentlewoman knew anything of a lost Talith damsel. Maiwenna, however, was nonplussed. She knew of no clues that might lead to discovering Rohain's past. Subsequently, the two spent many hours together, deep in conversation about Avlantia's history.

But most often Rohain's time was spent at the side of he whom she loved beyond others—loved with a passion so intense that it was a wound to the heart.

'Let us go out,' he would say. 'These four walls are like to suffocate me.'

Laughing, chaffing one another, they would saunter in the gardens, or go riding and hawking through the Royal Game Reserves in the ancient Forest of Glincuith. He gave her a sparrowhawk and lessons in archery. He gave her a crimson rose so very dark that it was almost black, whose scent was a dream of Midsummer's Night. And his long hair flowed blacker than Midwinter's Night, glinting with a red sheen like the dark rose. He gave her a palfrey the hue of marshmallow frosting, and a diadem of gems like Sugar crystals. His landhorse, a splendid, swift, and spirited creature that he esteemed as much as he cherished Errantry, was named Altair. Hers was called Firinn.

These hours together, secluded, afforded Rohain rare glimpses of a shy tenderness in her beloved, a hesitancy quite unlike the self-assurance he possessed at other times. It was like the diffidence of wild creatures, such as birds and deer. Most often, he would be as a carefree and wanton youth—zestful, capricious, as merry as a jester, indulging in whimsy and play and foolish nonsense, in which she participated with a footloose joyousness and reckless abandon that surprised her inner self by springing from it. Gentle, witty badinage volleyed between them, taking unexpected turnings. Seldom could he be precognised.

He could be as temperate as the soft winds caressing the northern valleys, or stern as stone and as grim. And when this cold mood was on him it did not affect his manner with Imrhien-Rohain; toward her he was warm always, even though the unmelting snow of all Winters to others.

She knew full well that in these times of unrest he was needed at the helm of the Royal Attriod, but as often as possible he delegated his duties to his commanders and stewards in order to spend time in the company of his betrothed. Fortunately, there had come another unexpected lull in the activities of men and wights in Namarre and northern Eldaraigne. The build-up of minor assaults and skirmishes had again subsided. It seemed they were now gathering their strength, perhaps in readiness for some greater onslaught.

Nonetheless, Thorn could not always be spared from governance. On a day when his duties took him elsewhere, Rohain walked through the palace picture galleries and statue galleries on the arm of the young Prince. They halted beside a window to look out at the dormant Spring Garden with its arches of lichened crab-apples most ancient.

'I should like to see those leafless trees in bloom,' she said. 'Crab-apples bear exquisite blossoms. I think they are my favourites.'

'You shall see them,' said Edward, 'this and every Spring.'

Thorn's silver-clasped hunting-horn was hooked to Edward's belt. As he turned away from the window it chimed against a marble pedestal. Noting the direction of Rohain's gaze, the Prince said, 'Traditionally, the Coirnéad is worn by the reigning monarch—however, he has requested that I bear it now and in the future, saying it may stand me in good stead.'

'The Coirnéad?'

'A horn of Faêran workmanship. For centuries, an heirloom of the Royal Family.'

'A fair ornament.'

A frown crumpled the Prince's brow. They walked on. Edward made as if to speak again, but hesitated.

'You are beauteous, lady,' he stammered suddenly. 'Do not think I flatter you, pray, when I tell you your beauty outshines all other beauties. He has chosen his consort well. His recommendation is law to me. My faith in his wisdom and judgment is implicit. I shall be glad to accept you as my—'

'I can never stand in your mother's place. Pray, allow me to be your friend.'

'Indeed,' he said earnestly, 'and I shall be *your* friend and most devoted admirer. Nothing could make me happier than to welcome you into this family, dear Rohain.' Raising her hand to his lips, he kissed it. His youthful smile was open, ingenuous.

'So saying, you make my own happiness complete,' she said, returning the smile.

The castle hawk-mews was extensive, housing not only hawks but also falcons, and one majestic wedge-tailed eagle named

Audax. The Hawkmaster sported eight taut silver scars on his bald dome where the talons of an eagle owl had once gored him when he was stealing her clutch of eggs. In the mornings, he could be seen in the yards with his falconers and austringers, swinging lures to bring half-trained birds back to the fist. The lures were a pair of moorhens' or magpies' wings dried in an open position and fastened back to back, with a fresh piece of tough beef tied onto the end of a line.

Often, the clear ringing of the tail-bell on a returning gyrfalcon tantalized the early light. The bird would scream a welcome as it flew down, jesses trailing, thrusting its feet forward to lock onto the falconer's tasseled glove, the savage joy of flight still purling in its black, gold-rimmed eye.

The Hawkmaster took Rohain among the sounds of the mews—the tiny tintinnabulation of bells, the bird-screams and whistles and chatter, the rasping whirr of rousing wings, the talk among the austringers and falconers. He proudly showed her the clean gravel-floored pens where roosted goshawks or sparrowhawks, merlins, hobbies, ospreys, peregrines, or the great and noble gyrfalcons, tethered to blocks and perches. Boys were assiduously sweeping up casts and scrubbing mutes off the walls. An austringer coped a tiercel goshawk's beak using a small, bone-handled knife and an abrasive stone. Another imped the damaged tail-feather of a hooded gray hawk, carefully attaching a replacement pinion to the base of the broken one. An apprentice weighed a peregrine on a small set of scales.

'Have to cut him down,' he said. 'He's put on too much.'

'Cut him down?' repeated Rohain, astonished.

'Cut down his feed, m'lady,' explained the apprentice, with a respectful salute.

'The merry merlins fly at larks,' the Hawkmaster said informatively, moving among the birds with Rohain, 'but the gay goshawks be the cooks' birds, so we say, for they will tackle fur or feather. A hunting engine they be, the goshawks, swift as arrows—but 'tis their wont to be peevish and contrary betimes. They must be handled with patience.'

The eagle sat alone in a magnificent pen, fierce-eyed, his irises silver. He was beautiful; black with a pale nape, wing-coverts and under-tail coverts. His legs were long, strong and full-feathered.

'We keeps the hawks and falcons well away from Audax the Great, else he might make a quick meal on 'em,' said the Hawkmaster. 'He will only come to two men—meself, who trained him, and His Imperial Majesty. Only royalty may fly eagles, but no milk-and-water king could do it. Audax's wing-span be more than seven feet, tip to tip. His weight be nigh on seven pound and his hind claw be as thick as a man's little finger. He can bring down small hounds, ye ken, and deer.'

A falconer went past carrying a bucket of day-old chicks and another of frogs and lizards. The eagle roused and shook himself.

'Coo-ee-el,' he whistled. 'Pseet-you, pseet-you.'

'Soothee, soothee,' said the Hawkmaster.

Winter faded. Gone were the moon-spun webs of night, the tinsels of rime lining each edge with glitter, like the shang, and drawing frost feathers on leaf and pane with an exquisite silver pencil. It seemed that every day the sun flew up like a yellow rose and fell down like a red one, and at the end of Winter the stirring of Spring could already be felt as a stirring of the blood; every bare and lichened bough carried the promise of blossom and verdure. The breezes sighed with perfumed breath and sunlight coloured them with pale gold. In the Forest of Glincuith, the only sounds were bright gems of birdsong, and baubles of laughter threaded on strange sweet music drifting from the trees; the piping of eldritch things, like the plaint of weird birds. These sounds Thorn made into a necklace and tossed it over the head of his betrothed. It hung about her shoulders, where it mingled with the abundant spirals and falls of heavy gold from which the dye had at last been stripped after many rinsings, along with the natural sheen, so that most folk believed she had bleached her tresses.

Sometimes Rohain and Thorn rode in open country with their entourage and the Hawkmaster and the falconers and the austringers. Then Thorn would fly Audax at ducks and geese and ptarmigan. The eagle was an expert hunter, with many strategies. He soared on thermals, so high that he vanished from human sight. Up there he could easily see everything that moved over a huge area. Once he had chosen his prey, he would appear abruptly from behind a hill where he had deliberately lost height without being noticed, then fly close to the ground until suddenly appearing only a few yards from his quarry, swooping down over the tops of nearby trees. Or he would start his attack with a long, slow descent up to four miles from his victim, or, most spectacular of all, from hundreds of feet above the ground he would stoop, diving with folded wings like a plummeting stone, flattening out at the last moment, spreading out his wings and tail to decelerate efficiently, pulling his head back and throwing his feet forward with talons outstretched to strike and grasp. The remaining shock of impact would be transferred to the prey.

He never missed his target.

Rohain made a discovery.

It was akin to the memory-dreams of the Three Faces, the Rats, the White Horse. Since her return from Isse and the prematurely terminated journey to Huntingtowers, a verity had been clarifying by degrees in her awareness.

It was Erith, remembered.

Erith's bones had been dredged up out of the waters of forgetfulness, but not much else. None of the history, none of the character—only the formations of the land and the labels of the countries, cities, villages on the map. The bones, and the names of the bones.

Somehow, the knowledge of three dimensions of the world had seeped through to Rohain. The fourth, which was *time*, was still lacking. Yet it strode on toward her betrothal day.

In the glades of Glincuith, the black fretwork of leafless branches formed, by day, a ceiling of sapphire panes; by night, a roof of smoky glass shattered by a gravel of stars. There, Rohain spent pleasant hours learning the courtly dance steps with a partner who moved so lightly and easily over the springy turf that she could swear their feet trod upon nothingness. Here was a lover who was ready, with extraordinary anticipation, to catch her after every pirouette, to whirl her as if she were a child, her skirts billowing like a full-blown camellia; to sustain and guide her, to hold her pressed so close that she thought his heart was beating within her own breast. The scent of pines was snagged like myrrh in his hair. Beneath her left hand, his shoulder was steel, sliding beneath layers of costly fabric. The dim, crimson light of dying suns gleamed through his hair, and his eyes, fixed upon her, were dark-smoldering coals.

At these times, love's anguish and precipitancy threatened to overwhelm her. It was a torment with a terrible sweetness to it—addictive, unconsumed, consuming. From him raged an answering force, a torrent dammed, a ferocity chained, a storm scarcely suppressed, eager, impatient.

The festival of Primrose Amble having passed by, the betrothal was officially announced and celebrated even while more legions of the Empire were making ready to depart for the north to relieve those that had been stationed there for lengthy periods, or to swell the numbers of the King-Emperor's army. The Royal Ball took place in jeweled splendor, attended by royalty, nobility, and dignitaries from all over Erith; more than a thousand guests. The bride-to-be shone like a piece torn out from the very core of the sun. He who moved beside her seemed by contrast the glorious incarnation of night.

The feast was sumptuous. Rohain sat at the high table beneath the canopy, at Thorn's right hand, sharing with him a cup and plate. At their backs, bright heraldic flags adorned the walls. Before them gleamed a swan-shaped cake covered with three thousand hand-molded Sugarpaste feathers. Below, the Banqueting Hall seethed and glistered.

As he conversed with Rohain, Thorn glanced down the table at Roxburgh, who looked splendid in a dress uniform of royal scarlet and gold. The Dainnan Commander had just cleared his trencher of a mighty helping of meats, and with a purposeful air he was contemplating the other dishes.

'The Commander is a renowned trencherman,' said Rohain, noting the object of his gaze.

'Indeed he is!'

Roxburgh having turned aside to speak to his wife, Thorn casually tossed a couple of roasted capons onto his trencher. Roxburgh, helping himself to pie, looked startled at the sight of his erstwhile empty platter. The King's Page made a bursting noise and collapsed behind a gonfalon.

The swan-ship sailed from Waterstair for the occasion, the side of the hill having been knocked out to allow its egress. It was moored over the inner bailey, to the acclamation of the citizens, who could see it from every corner of Caermelor; a giant bird gently lifting in the draughts, bound by iron chains.

In the lists, the jousting knights gave a brave display, sunlight splintering to shards on their harness as their lances shattered on each others' breastplates. The thunderous charge of the armoured war-horses and the impact of their meeting shook the ground. The tournament concluded with a night of fireworks.

Fireworks: traditionally a wizard's stock-in-trade. A city wizard, Feuleth, was handling the preparations. Rohain, dressing for the evening feast, her head swimming with the intoxication of these giddy days and nights, became conscious, at last, of overlooking a new wave of apprehension arising in the city.

'Viviana,' she said, 'what news?'

'A wizard in Gilvaris Tarv, Korguth the Unfeasible or some such, has been Dismantled and struck from the List. And a pirate named Scallywag has been captured.'

'Scalzo?'

'Yes, that was it, m'lady.'

Can it be that at last my enemies are all undone?

But the lady's maid was still speaking. 'And strange things have been happening lately—malign creatures have been creeping into Caermelor. They have been seen in the streets after dark. And in the north, things have gone from bad to worse. They say the barbarian wizard-chieftains and warlords are on the move again. There will be full-scale war, for certain. The times of peace are over.'

'As usual you outstrip me with the latest goings-on. How is it that you are aware of these things, Viviana, and I am not?'

The lady's maid blushed delicately. 'Of late, you have been

occupying yourself with pursuits other than listening to gossip, m'lady,' she replied demurely. 'We have scarcely seen you. You dismiss us when you go out. You are rarely between walls.'

'True enough. What other tidings have been prominent?'

'Only much talk of the forthcoming fireworks!'

After sunset, flaming cressets splashed carnelian light over the city.

Upon the lightless and stony heights of the palace the more privileged crowd waited for the fireworks to begin. The less privileged lingered expectantly beyond the walls, in the streets, on the roofs of houses. Feuleth the Torch-Fingered, a youngish wizard, excitedly prowled the inner bailey. He was setting fuses to last-minute rights in tubes packed with white, prismatic saltpeter, yellow spores of sulfur, and other pyrotechnic generators. For added effect, and to indicate his indispensability, he shouted orders and incantations and waved a staff purportedly imbued with gramarye. Up on the parapets, like a palisade of men, the Royal Attriod surrounded two who stood looking out across the starlit city. She leaned back against him, her head resting next to the base of his throat. He folded his arms around her. Their hands clasped. In the torchlight their profiles formed a double cameo on the somber sky.

With a howl of igniting combustibles, the display commenced. A hundred and eleven coloured fountains leaped: rufescent, iridescent, viridescent. Out of them, fast things shot high into the dome of night, where they destroyed themselves spectacularly, bursting into glittering rain, scintillating arrows, brilliant hail, confetti, baubles, sequins, petals, jewels. On the castle wall, vivid pinwheels began to rotate, spurting sparks and making whizzing noises that could barely be heard over the bangs, hisses, whistles, and roars, and the keening of air split by rapid flight. Comets sizzled past.

The assembly cheered wildly.

'Zounds,' breathed Thomas of Ercildoune on the parapets. 'Old Feu has really outdone himself this time.'

That night, another vision came to Rohain. Later, she named it the Dream of the Feast.

A hall, filled with long tables. An assembly of guests, most stunningly beauteous, some offensively grotesque—paragons and parodies, all at one extreme or the other. As Rohain walked the length of the hall, alone, they turned, one by one, to stare, and the pressure of those stares was a threat. Their power was as strong as desire, as indiscriminating and as ruthless. Fear drowned Rohain in its troubled waters. Did they not mock and sneer? Did they not feint and leer, patently, gleamingly observing her walking through their midst, their very presence plucking at her every nerve? Was not their very maintenance of distance a menace, like a steel bar that held them from her but which they could crumple at will, laughing?

At the end of the hall, someone stood waiting, someone whose back was turned. The face could not be discerned. Dreading the sight of it, Rohain yet fastened her gaze upon that one with fascination. At any moment she would see and recognise the face.

The one turned. And turned, and turned again, repeatedly beginning but never completing the rotation. Always, at the moment the first pale curve of the face came into view, the image would flicker and retreat to its opening, like a shang tableau, and there would be the back of the head again, starting to turn.

Rohain knew that in the last instance this someone would be revealed, but even as the face finally swung into view, there was only a great bird with beating wings, black as oblivion.

She woke with a mad yammering in her ears, white pain splitting her skull.

Fell creatures were being seen in the city at nights. Not before in this long-hundred of years had they dared to penetrate the walls of Caermelor. A curfew was imposed. The citizens made certain their doors were locked at nights, and their abodes well-decked with wight-deterring objects. Wizards and shysters did a brisker trade in charms than usual. Reports came in from outlying areas: The Wild Hunt was active.

The day after the Royal Ball, Thorn came to Rohain and said gravely, 'If the city has become unsafe, it will not be long before the palace itself is challenged by the reeking forces of unseelie. The restlessness of the Wild Hunt concerns me. Theirs is an eternal malignity, a deep-rooted ill-will. A dangerous adversary endeavoured to get to thee, Gold-Hair, and will likely hunt thee again, for these are immortals and able to pursue forever.

'I must leave Caermelor,' he continued. 'The north stirs again. This time there is a difference—after many a feint and false rumour, we are certain that the war-chiefs of Namarre are about to push forward at last, and that after all the skirmishes and raids, battle will soon be joined in earnest. More platoons have departed to take up their positions. A group of two hundred and seventy soldiers from the First Cavalry Division is headed from the Ilian army base to Corvath on a merchant Windship. Two more flights are to take out seven hundred troops early tomorrow, with deployment completed in two or three days. To the killing ground I will not take thee, but here thou must not remain. I will take thee and Edward to the one place thou mightst dwell in safety while I am gone.'

'So we are to be parted . . .' Rohain's blood fused to lead in her veins.

Thorn drew her closer. The effect was not unexpected, the alchemy turning the lead to molten gold. A clear un-scent carried on his breath, like the ether before a storm.

'Dost think I want to leave thee? I want thee by me all ways, day and night, my Pleasure. Yet I will not take thee into danger. A battlefield is no place for thee.'

'I care nothing for danger. Take me with you!'

He placed a finger on her mouth and shook his head.

'No. Until I can be by your side again, Gold-Hair, thou shalt bide in another place.'

6
THE ISLAND
Green Hair, Dark Sea

On rocky shores there used to stand, windblown,
A lonely tower built of graying stone.
O'er dark and restless seas it shone a light,
And beamed a message through the ageless night,
As if to reach the land where roses bloom,
Whose floral kiss abates despair and gloom.

A VERSE FROM 'THE ROSE'S KISS'

Three hundred nautical miles separated Caermelor from that uncertain stretch of water halfway between the Gulf of Mara and the boiling fury of Domjaggar Strait, south of the Cape of Tides and north of the Cape of Winds. Here was a region avoided by Seaship routes, a domain where, no matter how vapid the sky, no matter how placid the sea, mist and cloud gathered their skirts and muffled themselves in their mantles.

The bosun blew his whistle. Blocks squealed overhead as the main yards were braced round. HIMS *King James XVI* hove to at the frayed edges of this foggy obscurity. It was as if a smoky twilight hovered beyond the bowsprit and the starboard taffrail, while elsewhere the day gleamed as lustrous as polished crystals. A mellow sea-breeze came cantering out of the west to lift among the sails the Royal Heraldry of the pennoncels and the long ribbons of streamers, the gay banners and the swallow-tailed gittons, laying them straight along its flowing mane.

Chunks of charcoal imprisoned crimson heat in a brazier suspended on chains from a tripod on the fo'c'sle. Passengers and crew with their taltries thrown back stood watching as a pitch-smeared arrowhead was touched to the coals. Fiery hair sprang forth from that head. In one swift, sudden movement, Thorn fitted the shaft to the string, bent back his longbow—the shaft sliding through his fingers until his right hand almost met the red blossom—and sent it soaring with a twang and a hissing whine, straight into the twilight's heart.

Standing with feet braced apart at right angles to the target, in the classic archer's stance, he watched it fly, high and far.

It vanished.

And then there came a thinning of the fog, and deep within the murk a form manifested as if seen through frosted glass. Across the waters, past a wild spume that was the white blood of waves suiciding in the jaws of reefs, a mountain loomed, indistinct, crowned with a pale cloud. An island, floating in the sea.

'Release the bird,' said Thorn, handing the longbow to his squire. A snowball or a wad of paper scraps was tossed into the air, shaking itself out into the shape of a pigeon. It took wing toward the island. They watched the white chevron disappear, following the red flower. Waves spanked the port side. Ropes creaked, wood complained, and now the faint cries of gulls scratched the wind.

Presently a spark appeared, a brass button against the dark hem of the land.

'There she be!' exclaimed several voices. 'The Beacon!'

At this signal, the crew swung into action again, hauling on the braces to swing the main yards back into position. The helmsman spun the wheel and brought the ship about. Sails filled, and with the wind directly behind her the vessel began to pick up speed, skimming the crests, scooting toward the isle.

The mountain towered ever higher.

Along a narrow channel between the reefs sped HIMS *King James XVI*, guided by the Light. She ran between two headlands that held between them a span of vituperative currents called the Rip, until, skating free of those arms, with the Light in the Tower alone on its rocky promontory to the port side, she fell, like a gull to its haven into a beautiful harbour, tranquil and still.

Above the harbour, basalt terraces snaked up the cliffs to the cloud-bearded summit dominating all with its formidable presence. This peak let down its shadow to ink the water, dwarfing the tall ship with the lily sails now furled and lashed into long buds. The vessel became a mote of light on a dark pond. By the shore, red birds of fishing boats clustered at their moorings, all facing west. Some of these fishers, and other vessels shaped like seedpods, came out toward the *King James XVI*. Crates of snowflake pigeons and a lumpy bag of letters were uploaded. Few other goods were exchanged—this was not a merchant ship, not a trade visit. Most of the islanders had come to look at the King-Emperor's renowned ship and to try to catch a glimpse of him in person—it had been long since he was last on the island—as well as to welcome Prince Edward and the Lady Rohain, tidings of whom had preceded them.

Thorn's hair swung down to brush Rohain's cheek as he leaned to her. While the clipper's longboats were being lowered into the water, the pair took leave of each other, speaking softly, standing on the fo'c'sle while all others kept a respectful distance. But when for the last time their hands unclasped, Rohain felt it was an agony, as though her flesh had grown to his and was now torn.

'Guard her, Thomas,' Thorn had commanded his Bard. 'Guard her well.' But she had thought it was Thorn who needed vigilance and protection, since he was going to war.

Auspiciously, the wind swung around. A sildron floater took Rohain down the ship's side. In a swathe of rose brocade encrusted with carnelians, she sat in the bow, facing astern like the rowers. At the tiller, the coxswain called out a command. Hemmed in by red birds and seed-husks, the line of boats crawled to shore like oar-legged insects on the sun's glittering path.

The fisher families greeted the Crown Prince, the Lady Betrothed, the Duke of Ercildoune, and the Duchess of Roxburgh and her brood with songs, jonquils, and strings of coloured lanterns. They presented them with trinkets and buckles inlaid with mother-of-pearl, all fashioned from carved coral, tusks of walrus, skulls of seals, or teeth of whales. They gave also shell-work bouquets (each shell carefully chosen for its colour and shape to replicate a petal of a particular variety of flower), shell-work trinket boxes and glove boxes. The handful of wealthier islanders presented gifts of pearl necklaces, bracelets, and girdles studded with garnets, peridots, and zeolite crystals and containers covered in shagreen. To these they added amber and agate snuff-boxes, nautilus shell cups with pewter rims and feet, porphyry bowls, and a pristine prismatic bowl imprisoning three live leafy sea-dragons; delicate, innocent creatures that Rohain would later discreetly return to their habitat.

The village mayor made a speech.

The rumbling strains of a shanty drifted from the royal ship, out over the water. On the foredeck the men toiled around the capstan, straining against the bars. The anchor broke the water like some queer fish, flukes streaming. With a rattle and a clang it locked into place. Lengths of canvas dropped from the yardarms and fattened like the bells and scoops of pale pink shells. A phosphorescent wake awoke. Cream curled at the prow.

For as long as possible, Rohain held on to the memory of Thorn in *dusken*, handsome beyond reckoning, resting his elbows on the taffrail, not waving, merely watching her steadily, until distance thinned the bond of that mutual gaze and eventually severed it. Like the tide, terrible grief and longing then rose in her, and she could not speak, made mute again by loss. All the light and laughter in the world was draining out through the Rip, sailing away, far away.

This, then, was the secret island, Tamhania, sometimes called Tavaal. For hundreds of years it had been the private retreat of the kings of the House of D'Armancourt. Some sea-enchantment rendered it safe from all things unseelie. Furthermore, it was hidden from view by mists engendered, it was said, by virtue of a herb that grew extensively over its slopes: *duilleag neoil*, the cloud-leaf, whose effects were complemented by steam from numerous hot springs. If the isle was struck by a red-hot arrow fired from beyond its shores it would become visible for a short time, but no vessel could find the channel through the reefs without the guidance of the Beacon, and the Light would only be kindled in that gray Tower after the reception of a sealed order from the King-Emperor, or a secret rune, carried in by messenger birds.

Rohain had taken leave of Sianadh at Caermelor, where he had boarded a merchant Seaship bound for Finvarna. It had been a parting both sorrowful and joyous.

'No tears, *chehrna!*' he had said, tears standing in his own blue eyes. "Tis not good-bye, in any event! We shall meet again! When the war is over the Queen-Empress must tour the countries of her Empire. Start with the best—the land of the giant elk, and the long rugged shores, and the taverns filled with music and good cheer. Don't ye forget, now!'

He saluted her and swaggered up the gangplank with a jaunty air, waving his cap. That had been the last she had seen of him.

A procession of coaches and riders wound upward along the rutted cliff road from the fishing village on the harbour. Over many an arched bridge of basalt they went, crossing the rills that tumbled down the hillsides, past trees twisted into poetic shapes by salt winds, to the Royal Estate, Tana. High on the mountainside, Tana's castle overlooked the slate roofs of the village, and the cove where flying fish leapt in clear green water.

There the Seneschal of Tana, Roland Avenel, greeted them.

This entire island belonged to the Crown. Of those few Feohrkind folk who had been granted the right to dwell there, some were ancient families, the descendants of generations of islanders: fisher-folk, farmers, and orchardists who for centuries had paid their tithes in services and goods or in gems pried from the gravels and crannies of fissures in the mountain walls. Some had been born on the isle and lived out their span of years on it; others left its cloudy shores when they were full-grown, and never returned. Sometimes, folk came to live on Tamhania who had never set foot there before—men and wives who had sought permission from the official authorities representing the Crown, and been deemed worthy; probably they had some skill or talent to offer the community. Perhaps they themselves longed for peace and seclusion.

The Hall of Tana, the royal residence, was more ethereal by far than the buttressed blocks of Caermelor Palace—a *chastel* out of legend. Its tapering turrets and great ranks of windows rose tier after tier from an ivy-clad plinth that was itself as high as a house—the remains of an old fortress upon which the Hall was founded. Extraordinary masonry adorned the outer walls; pilasters imprisoned in banded stonework, their capitals scrolled or sprouting stone acanthus leaves. Arched niches, ceiled by carvings of giant scallop shells, sheltered statues of mermaids, mermen, porpoises, dolphins, and whales. Over the massive front door loomed the royal coat of arms. Above every ground-floor window, in petrified splendor, the devices of old and noble families were displayed. Swallows darted among the crenellations.

Built upon one of the few level areas on the island, the grounds were parklike. Lawns swept around leafy walks and plantations of ancient, wind-contorted trees that cast their reflections into still ponds, the whole scene overlooking the ocean on the one hand, overlooked by the mountain on the other.

Within, apartments abounded. Huge vaulted cellars with tiled cisterns built into living rock occupied the founding platform. A wide stair led up to the grand salon with its painted wallpaper, heavy-framed portraits, and gilt furniture upholstered in velvet, figured silk, and embroidery. The library was located on this level, as was the dining room, dominated by the marble minstrel's gallery. Higher up, one could find the smaller salons and studies, the bedchambers each with their own sea-theme, and the Hall of the Guards, a gallery one hundred feet long and so wide that ten men could ride abreast through it. Its walls were ornamented with motifs and arabesques in light blues and reds and earthy browns. Throughout the *chastel,* the open-beam ceilings were set with hundreds of paintings of mythic scenes all finished with the highest precision.

In this sumptuous island retreat, the days fled by.

Rohain began to accustom herself to her new environs. It was not like living—it was more like waiting. So she waited, with Prince Edward—as vigorous as Thorn and yet as different from him as father from son—with red-haired Thomas of Ercildoune, and the Duchess Alys, and with Viviana, Caitri, and Georgiana Griffin, who had been dismissed by her invidious mistress and joined Rohain's ever-increasing collection of attendants. Jolly Dain Pennyrigg was with them also, the lad from Isse Tower. He seemed to have become Rohain's equerry by default, even though gray Firinn had not been transported to Tamhania, the steep slopes being unsuitable for thoroughbred riding-horses.

The climate was mild beneath the cloud-blanket, snugged in tepid seas. Turtles the hue of malachite flew under clear waves of jade. Ladybirds crawled or flew everywhere, like tiny buttons, in livery checkered cadmium and black, spotted charcoal and madder.

White vapours trailed from warm springs on the lower slopes. The Hall Of Tana had been built over such pools which now, tamed and shaped by azure-glazed ceramic tiles, were used for bathing. Cloud-leaf grew sharp like dark green fox's ears in basalt clefts, almost the only living things to cling to the sheer rock-faces of the northern slopes. The clouds captured by the eldritch herb seemed to possess the property of allowing one-way vision, so that from the island, the ocean and sky could be seen as far as the horizon—only their edges were softened a little as through a single layer of muslin.

Fisher-folk plied their nets mainly in the calm band of water betwixt shore and reef, for, once past the reef there was no return, not without the kindling of the Light. Without the Light, all vessels foundered, victims of the rocks. That was part of the island's sea-enchantment. When a fleet was to venture out beyond that barrier, the leader would memorize the day's Pass-Sign and cage a pigeon from the lofts in the Light-Tower. When it came time to return, the rune was daubed minutely on a smidgin of papyrus and fastened to the leg of the patient bird. So that the avian aviator could see its way home, a fiery arrow was shot, to make the island visible. Whosoever forgot the sign, or lost the pigeon or the arrows or the fire, could not return; a boat must be sent out to give them aid. It seemed a troublesome affair, but the islanders had grown accustomed to it, and besides, some arcane property of the Light always ensured calm waters in the channel. Once it was lit, safety was assured, even in the most mettlesome storm.

Time passed, but the hours never hung heavily for the bride-in-waiting. Thomas the Bard taught her how to string a lute and make it sing a little, and how to recognise the runes of writing, beginning with the Thorn Rune, **þ**, and how to name the stars. She did not know if she had been able to read and write before she lost her memory, but penmanship and deciphering came easily to her. When personal messages arrived from Thorn at the battle-fields she allowed no one else to read them, and painstakingly composed replies.

From the fisher-folk she learned how to sail the little boats they called *geolas*—'What language is this you islanders speak in snatches?' she asked. 'A version of the Olden Speech. His Majesty is fluent at it,' they told her.

But as well as voyaging and making music, it was time to learn to do harm.

Rohain summoned the Seneschal of Tana, Roland Avenel, a silver-maned, doughty ex-legionary of some fifty Winters. She said, 'It has come to me that knowledge and the wit to use it are the most powerful weapons. The greatest warrior would fail in the wilderness, did he not understand the seasons and the secret ways to find sustenance and the lore of fire-making. Yet a swift and certain sword-arm would stand anyone in good stead. Will you teach me to fight with weapons?'

So the Seneschal tutored her in wielding a light blade and a skian.

When not fencing, strumming, sailing, or shooting arrows at straw bull's-eyes, Rohain would ride with Edward and their companions. They cantered along dark beaches fringed with black pebbles and rocks twisted like slag. Splendid taltries flapped at their backs. The horses' hooves kicked up black sand flecked with glitter, like dominite. Ferny weeds and strings of succulent beads filled rockpools so clear one would not have guessed there was water in them, save for a shimmer and a blur. The sun cast a golden fretwork on the waves—a limpid mesh over living glass, the wave-rims like the veil-flowers of clematis. On the dunes silvery saltbush clung, and kitten-tail grass, and scented tea-tree with its waxy flowers. After sunset, white wings of spray blew back off the rolling breakers, gleaming phosphorescent in the afterglow.

The sea-wind murmured like Thorn's voice in Rohain's ears.

'While thou dost remain here,' he had said, 'I will never be far from thee.'

Could it be that intense, unremitting longing was powerful enough to bridge distance? Rohain imagined he touched her with every caress of the breeze that occasionally tore the mist into strips, and ruffled her skirts, and played with her tresses. She fancied the soft, warm raindrops on her upturned face might be his kisses. At nights, half waking, she heard the susurration of waves breaking on the boulders below the *chastel*, as the breathing of one who lay in slumber beside her, and she would reach out her hand, but there was only the substance of moonlight where he might have been, and shadow for his hair.

Still, she was embraced by a sense of his nearness. She tried to believe it was not all pretense and, convincing herself, found a kind of contentment.

As for the Antlered One and his Hunt, they were far away, on the other side of the island's enchanted barriers, where they could pose no threat. With each day that elapsed they shrank further back in time, until eventually Rohain abandoned all thought of them.

A secret island, Tamhania-Tavaal was an island of secrets, some of which Rohain came to imperfectly recognise, as days linked together in chains of weeks. Riding or walking along the strand, she and her ladies would often find the fishermen's children playing among the seaweed-fringed rockpools—catching crabs, making coronets of sea-grasses, splashing and laughing. There was one little girl among them who always wore a necklace of perfect pearls that shimmered palest pastel green. Luminous were they, worthy of a princess. Rohain thought it curious that the child of one of the poor fisher-folk should wear such a valuable treasure about her neck as carelessly as if it were no more than a string of common shells.

It was the first of several curious matters, she discovered.

Once, rising early after another restless night, she rode out with her retainers before sunrise. Walking their horses along the shore, they spied a woman sitting on a rock at high-tide mark. She did not notice them, for she was staring out across the sea. As the first glimmer of dawn grayed the waters, a big seal came swimming toward the rock. When he came within a pebble's throw, he raised his head and spoke to the woman.

She replied.

Then he walked up out of the sea with the water sliding off him like moon-drops. He cast off his sealskin as he approached, and met her in the form of a man.

The riders turned their horses and hastened away, leaving the couple alone together on the shore bathed by the glance and glimmer of morning light on the waves.

When Rohain told Roland Avenel about this encounter he nodded and said, 'Ah, yes. I too have seen Ursilla once or twice, at early morning, waiting on the rocks. But prithee, bid your attendants to refrain from speaking to anyone about what you and they have witnessed.'

'That I shall, if you say discretion is desirable. But who is she, this Ursilla?'

'She is the wife of a farmer here on the isle, a proud, well-favoured woman who manages her household, her farm, and her husband well. To all outward appearances she possesses all she could desire. Yet beneath the surface, I fear, she is not happy.'

'So I have guessed for myself,' acknowledged Rohain.

Avenel paused and scratched his chin thoughtfully, as though searching for words. 'All three of Ursilla's children,' he went on, 'have webbed hands and webbed feet. The membranes of skin between their fingers and toes are so delicate and thin that the light shows through. A horny epidermis grows on the backs of their hands. Every one of them has soft silken hair, the colour of the water in the first light of dawn.'

'And her lover is one of the island's secrets,' concluded Rohain softly. She recalled, then, the little girl with the pearl necklace. 'Pray tell me, Master Avenel, why the fishermen's children wear such wonderful jewels when they play. I had imagined them to be poor folk.'

'I'll warrant you have seen young Sally,' said Avenel with a laugh. 'Only one other among the fishers owns such wealth. But nobody envies her, or would try to take the thing from her. Oh, no.'

'Why not?'

'Well, because of the way she came by it. 'Tis said that last Summer, Sally was playing with her doll down by the rockpools and when she turned away a mermaid's child stole the toy. Young Sally fled, weeping. On the following day when she returned to look for the doll, the mermaid's child rose from the sea at the edge of the rocks where the spume flies highest.'

'A mermaid's child!' interjected Rohain, fascinated. 'Have you seen the merfolk, sir? What are they like?'

Avenel smiled and drew breath. The Seneschal of Tana was a fair wordsmith; Rohain loved hearing him speak. Now, as he held forth, he led her to imagine entities resembling young women, with waves of hair like sea-leaves, and half their bodies a graceful, sweeping mosaic of verdigrised copper coins. Their skin was the cream of sea-foam and they had long eyes of cucumber green. Avenel related how the merchild came, and in her shell-white hand she held out the pearl necklace, which she gave to Sally in atonement for the theft. In words of alien accent, she told the mortal child that her mother had bade her do so. Then she looked at Sally with her green eyes before flipping away with a flicker of iridescent scales, to plunge beneath the breakers.

'That has been the most recent sighting of the merfolk,' said the Seneschal, 'but that one was only a stripling, not yet a harbinger and bringer of storms—at least, not of disastrous ones.'

'Are they often glimpsed?'

'Not at all, m'lady. To see a mermaid is rare. In all my years on Tavaal, I have never once set eyes on one, nor, in truth, do I wish to do so. Other sea-wights are seen from time to time, but these sightings too are rarities. None easily let themselves be spied by our kind.'

'Who else among the fishers owns a jewel given by sea-folk?'

'The mayor of our village below! In his youth, some thirty years ago, his father was out fishing when one of his comrades caught a wave-maiden on a hook. She promised, if the men let her go, to give them good fortune. The skipper thereupon dropped her over the gunwale and as she swam to her home she sang:

"Muckle gude I wid you gie and mair I wid you wish;
There's muckle evil in the sea, scoom weel your fish."

'Then the six fishermen thought they had been cheated. Only the lad who was later to be our mayor's father took any notice of the sea-maiden's injunction. He scoomed his fish very well indeed, and found a splendid pearl among the scooming, which was kept in the family from that day forth!'

'Oh, fair fortune!' declared Rohain, pleased with his stories. She added, 'I thank you for sharing your knowledge with me, Master Avenel, and while you are doing so, I beg you to solve just one more mystery that has us all intrigued. Last week we rode out to Benvarrey's Bay. There we saw an ancient apple tree on the cliff, leaning right out over the water. Ripe fruit aplenty hung on its boughs but no one gathered them. When the wind shook the tree, several apples dropped into the sea. It seemed a waste. Why do the poor fisher-folk not harvest the fruit of this tree?'

'There is a story attached to that tree,' replied Avenel. 'Years ago, the Sayles were a large fishing family on Tavaal, with a well-tended croft to supplement their living. They prospered. Old Sayle had a great liking for apples, and when they were in season he always took a pile of them in the boat. But when he became too old to go fishing, the family's fortunes began to decline. One by one the sons left the island until only the youngest remained to look after his parents and the farm. His name was Evan.

'One day after Evan had set the *cleibh-giomach*, the lobster creels, he went climbing on the cliff to look for seabirds' eggs. He heard a sweet voice calling to him and when he went down he saw, sitting on a rocky shoal, a maiden of the benvarrey. Comely she was, so it is told, with nacreous skin, and eyes like sea anemones, and a slender waist tapering to a long fluked curve of overlapping scales. Evan was torn between fear and delight but he greeted her courteously. She asked after his father, and the youth told her about all the family's troubles. When he came home Evan told his parents what had happened and his father was well-pleased with him.

'"Next time you go fishing," he said, "take a pile of apples with you."

'The white sea-daughter was delighted to get the "sweet land eggs" once more, and good fortune returned to the Sayles. But Evan was smitten, and he spent so much time out in his boat speaking with her when she appeared, and hoping that she might appear when she was absent, that people began to whisper that he had turned idle. When the youth heard these rumours he was so bothered by them that he decided to leave the island, but before he went he planted the apple tree on the cliff and told the sea-daughter that when the tree matured the sweet land eggs would ripen and drop down for her. Although he went, the good luck stayed, but the lovely wight grew weary of waiting for the apples to form and she went off looking for Evan Sayle. In the end the apples ripened, but neither Evan nor the benvarrey ever came back to look for them. Because the tree was planted there for a sea-wight, no mortal will touch the fruit.'

When she had listened to this tale, Rohain said, 'It seems I have much to learn. You say this sea-girl was a benvarrey, a seelie wight, and yet she had a fish's tail just like a mermaid. How did Evan Sayle recognise she was a benvarrey? And how many kinds of merfolk exist?'

'As to your first question,' answered Avenel, 'it takes an islander, or one who dwells all his life at the margins of the sea, to be able to discern between the different kinds of fishtailed wights, the half piscean and half mortal-seeming. As for your second question, there are five. There are mermaids with their mermen, there are the benvarreys, the sea-morgans, the merrows, and the *maighdeanna na tuinne*, the wave-maidens. The benvarreys do not fail to look kindly on the races of men but the others may be seelie or unseelie or both. Fear not—around the Royal Isle malignity cannot dwell. Unseelie merfolk are repelled from its shores. Indeed, the mermaids of Tavaal *aid* us.'

'In what manner?'

'When the men are fishing off the island a mermaid will warn them of forthcoming storms, calling out *"shiaull er thalloo"*—"sail to land". If they hear this cry, the boats run for shelter at once, or else lose their tackle or their lives. The fishermen fervently hope to never behold a mermaid, for they only show themselves, rising suddenly among the boats, if the forthcoming storm is to be truly terrible, such as the Great Storm of 1079, in which many perished. As you know m'lady, sea-wights of all kinds dislike being viewed by mortals, and few folk have ever set eyes on any of them, excepting the silkies, who are less wary. Tales of actual sightings are part of island history.'

As he finished speaking, Rohain detected a sudden evasiveness, as if he had just then recollected a fact that contradicted his last statement. *I wonder,* she thought, *whether there might be seelie ocean-wights dwelling among us . . .*

'Well,' said Rohain, 'I have not seen a mermaid, but I have glimpsed a silkie, I think. I hope to see more of the eldritch sea-dwellers.'

'Now,' said the Seneschal with a change of tone, 'I have a question for *you*, m'lady. Would it please you to come down to the shore towards evening? There is to be a party and a music-making. The seals will come near—the true seals, the animals that live on the skerries around the island. You shall see *them*, if not the merfolk.'

'Why will they come?'

'They are attracted by any kind of music, even whistling.'

'I should be greatly amused by such a spectacle!'

As the day waned, the islanders gathered great piles of drift-wood and lit fires along the shoreside, then played their pipes and sang their songs. Out where the breakers arched their toss-maned horses' necks, the seals assembled to listen, their soft fur glistening. Burly, wintry-haired Roland Avenel took his bagpipes and walked along the shore playing traditional airs, splashing his bare feet among bubbled crystal garlands of foam strewn like pear-blossom on the ribbed sand.

This delighted the seals. Their heads stuck up out of the water, and they sat up, perpendicular. An enchanting sight it was for Rohain—eighteen to twenty-five seals gathered, all listening, facing different directions, and Avenel playing the pipes to them.

Annie, a serving-girl from Tana, was among the congregated islanders. She touched Rohain lightly on the elbow, saying, 'Most of those creatures out there are *lorraly*, my lady. Others are not.'

Rohain 'Not *lorraly?*' She glanced eagerly toward the seals. 'Are silkies among them?'

'Even so!'

The silkies were the seal-folk, the gentlest of sea-wights. In their seal-form they swam, but in humanlike form they were able to walk on land before returning to the sea. Despite that men were wont to do them great wrong, the silkies had always shown benevolence to mortalkind. They never did harm.

On another day Roland Avenel, knowledgeable in the ways of silkies, took Rohain, Prince Edward, Thomas of Ercildoune, and Caitri down to the strand they called Ronmara. It was a long-light afternoon. The last rays were roseate, the wind temperate, and the tide at its nadir. Not far offshore, out of the sea rose numerous rocky islets formed from tall stacks of hexagonal stones jammed together like honeycomb, a remnant of some past volcanic action. The water was deep on their seaward side and crystalline in shallow bead-fringed pools on the shoreward side.

There, the seal-folk played.

The silkies appeared like a troupe of lithe humans: women and men, youths and maidens and children. All were naked, ivory-skinned. Some lay sunning themselves, while others frolicked and gamboled. Beside them were strewn their downy pelts. Eventually, catching sight of the spies, they seized their sealskins and jumped into the sea in mad haste. Then they swam a little distance before turning, popping up their heads, and, as seals now, gazing at the invaders.

'They are beauteous indeed,' exclaimed the young Prince.

'Indeed!' Caitri echoed, boldly.

"'Tis little wonder mortals sometimes fall in love with them,' said the Bard.

'Do they?' said the little girl, turning to him in surprise.

'But surely,' said Rohain, 'such love must be doomed from the outset! One dwells in the sea, the other on the land. When lovers belong to two different worlds, how shall they be happy together?'

'They shall not,' said Edward, rather sharply. Avenel nodded, his mien somber.

Rohain was about to ask, *How can you know?* when she thought of Rona Wade. She fell silent. Shallow, flat waves played about her feet, rippling with gold scales of sunlight, each delineated by the kohl-line of its own shadow, as she watched the seal-people swim away.

Three times a week, a fisherman's wife would come to the Hall of Tana with her eldest daughter, delivering fish for the tables. Her husband had a knack for catching the best. The woman's name was Rona Wade, and there was a strangeness about her, like the sea, and as profound.

Rohain liked to try broaching the reticence of this gentle wife by speaking with her on the occasions they met, but on subjects pithier than island gossip, she would not be drawn. Rohain could not help noticing the webbed fingers of the children of Hugh and Rona Wade. They bore an affinity with those of Ursilla's progeny, however people wisely refrained from commenting on the likeness. The other island children, if they thought anything of these aberrations, envied them. Webbed fingers made for fine swimmers.

It was obvious that Hugh's love for his bonny wife Rona was unbounded, but she returned it only with cool cordiality. Like Ursilla, she had been seen stealing alone to a deserted shore where she would toss a shell or some other object into the water. Upon this signal a large seal would appear, and she spoke to it in an unknown tongue.

But Rona was not really like Ursilla.

After the conversation, the creature would slip back under the waves, its shape unchanged. Rohain guessed that Rona did not love Hugh, but she was fond of her husband and never betrayed him.

There appeared to be much unreturned love on Tamhania, which the arrival of the visitors had served to increase. Within a few days of her arrival, Georgiana Griffin, Dianella's erstwhile servant, had attracted the attention of one of the island's most eligible young men.

Sevran Shaw was a shipmaster and farmer. Island born, he had travelled far over the seas of Erith on his own sloop, trading profitably, before coming home to settle. Shrewd was he, sensible, good-humored, and comfortably well-off. Now in his thirtieth year, he had never married. Several of the island girls had hoped to snare him, but he had not fallen in love until he set eyes on Georgiana Griffin. This refined lady, bred in the rarefied atmosphere of the Court of Caermelor, refused to hear his suit or to accept him as a friend. Weeks passed and his attachment grew only the stronger, although she avoided him and they hardly ever met. It looked as if his love was ill-fated.

Thus proceeded the secrets and the passions of the isle.

Yet there were other mysteries on Tamhania-Tavaal, not of the affective kind, and these seemed to be more easily solved.

Through the island's only village ran crumbling granite walls, and rows of tall wooden piles driven into the ground for no apparent reason. Some stood or leaned like branchless trees, others supported decrepit piers and condemned jetties that stalked toward the water but finished abruptly far short of it, in the middle of the air. Far above the high-tide line, the dried remains of mussels and barnacles encrusted these thick stems.

When Rohain asked about the useless and ruined structures, Avenel told her the village had risen sixteen feet over the last ten years, and the harbour had had to be rebuilt lower down. Local legend asserted that the island had floated at times during the past centuries, traveling on the ocean currents before catching on some submarine reef or snag and taking root again in a new position.

Market day in the uplifted village was a pleasant diversion for Rohain. At the time of full moon, makeshift stalls would be set up in the Old Village Square, and folk would arrive from all over the island to peddle their wares. Riding through the township one market day, with her nineteen ladies and her equerry, Rohain spied a woman dressed in the geranium-coloured houppelande commonly adopted by the middle classes. Her head was sheathed in a shawl. Walking among the stalls, she was bartering jars of honey, bunches of hyacinths and watercress, apple cider and apple cider vinegar in ceramic bottles.

Her face drew Rohain's attention. There was a look about this woman that stirred some vague memory. Hope sprang in her heart. Could it be she had at last found someone from her past? Dismounting, she gave the reins to her equerry and approached the woman, who curtsied.

'Do you know me?' asked Rohain.

The woman's eyes were two cups filled with reflections. Weather, years, and sorrow had engraved her face with their etchings, but she was not uncomely. 'All on Tamhania know the Lady Rohain Tarrenys, who is to be Queen-Empress.'

'But do you *know* me?'

'No, my lady.'

'Your face, to me, appears familiar. What is your name?'

'Elasaid. Elasaid of the Groves.'

'Are you certain you do not recognise me?'

'Yes.'

'What will you take in return for a bag of apples?'

'Cloth. Good cloth for a new cloak.'

'Mustardevlys? Rylet? Thick woollen frieze?'

'Ratteen, if it please my lady.'

'Give the apples to my equerry. The ratteen shall be sent to you tomorrow.'

A bargain was struck. It was a way of being linked to this woman.

At Tana, Rohain again drew Roland Avenel aside. She said, 'Today I spoke with a woman in the marketplace. She is called Elasaid of the Groves.'

Avenel frowned. 'With respect, does my lady deem it seemly for the future Queen-Empress to associate with commoners in marketplaces?'

Rohain arched her brows in surprise.

'Why, sir, I shall speak with whomsoever pleases me!' she responded. 'There is nothing indecorous about conversing with an honest person in any place, be it public or private. You forget, sir, I am *not* as the courtiers of Caermelor, so rigid in their hierarchies that they cannot recognise a fellow human creature.'

Avenel bowed, murmuring an apology.

'I wish to know,' said Rohain, 'where she dwells, this Elasaid. I shall visit her.'

'She abides low on the eastern slopes above Topaz Bay,' answered the Seneschal. 'To it, there is a path only fit for donkeys or foot traffic. 'Tis very narrow, and an old stone wall runs all along one side. Those who pass that way must beware of Vinegar Tom. He is not unseelie as wights go—haters of mankind cannot abide here. He is a kind of guardian of the path, that's all. There is a rhyme that you must recite if you want to get by him. If it is not said, Vinegar Tom takes you away and leaves you somewhere on the other side of the island where 'tis remote and prickly, and it can take a fistful of days to get back. When I first came here, they taught me the chant:

"Vinegar Tom, Vinegar Tom,
Where by the Powers do you come from?"

'I learned this ditty and went, cocksure, along that path. Vinegar Tom came out and he was like a long-legged greyhound with the head of an ox, with a long tail and huge eyes. When I saw him, I was so flummoxed that I said:

"Vinegar Tom, Vinegar Tom,
Where in the world do you come from?"

'I said it wrong, but the words rhymed, so Vinegar Tom only tossed me over the wall!'

Rohain took a bolt of ratteen and her retinue and went to visit the lady of the apple groves. The narrow track climbed away from the main road and wound over wooded slopes. To the right, the hillsides dropped sharply to the plane of the sea. To the left they escalated to pathless gullies. There, fern sprays prinked the cracks that ran through spills of ropy, wrinkled rock like the sagging hide of some enormous beast, and mist hovered in ravines walled with strange formations in stone, like frozen waterfalls. Ascending, the party passed spindly towers and pinnacles and needles. They went by a rift in a hillside, which emitted occasional plumes of white steam to augment the ambient brume. In deep gullies, water tumbled noisily over pebbles. A light mist rose from the still surfaces of gray rainpools, and from the puddles lying like shattered pieces of the sky clasped between tree-roots.

They passed Vinegar Tom with no difficulty. When they had repeated the rhyme he turned into the likeness of a four-year-old child without a head, and vanished.

The path led them to a level apron where they beheld a vegetable plot, beehives, and a little freshwater runnel skirted by white-flowered cresses. Here nestled a slate-roofed cot, lapped in gnarled-knuckled trees. Purple hyacinths bloomed among their roots. Small birds twittered, and bees gathered in the foaming pink-and-white confectionery of blossom. From behind fissured, sprouting boles, a waif of a child with green-gold hair spied upon the newcomers, then ran away.

Elasaid welcomed her visitors into her cottage.

'There is more cloth here than the worth of the apples,' she said, unfolding a length of ratteen the colour of stormwrack.

'Then pay me the balance in histories,' said Rohain.

'What would my lady wish to know?'

'The roads you have trod. If it pleases you to tell of them.'

'Well, I have trod high roads and low and I don't mind telling at all.'

'Tell me first about yon child with the green-gold hair.'

'Willingly,' said Elasaid of the Groves, 'for I love her well. On an evening seven years ago, when the last afterglow of sunset was still reflecting in the sky and the owls were abroad, I heard beautiful singing coming from among the shadows gathering in Topaz Bay. I thought it might be the sea-morgans, and I was eager to see if I could catch a glimpse, so I made my way down to the bay as quietly as I could. However, I was not careful enough—my foot dislodged a pebble, and all I caught was a flash and a glimmer as the sea-morgans dived off the rocks into the tide.

'In their haste and fright, they inadvertently left one of their babies wriggling and laughing beneath the waterfall that splashes from the cliffs above the bay. When I saw the baby I could not do otherwise than love her. I still grieved deeply for my own daughter, so, rightly or wrongly, I took this child created from foam and seaweed and pearls.

'I took her, and I raised her as my own. I called her Liban. She is like any mortal child in most ways, but I can never get her hair completely dry, not even in the sunshine and the breeze, and the tang of the ocean is always in it. She loves to wade and play in my spring-fed pond, and among the wavelets down at the shore. She is a loving daughter, but there are those among the island-dwellers who, recalling their lives outside Tamhania where unseelie mermaids cause shipwrecks, deem it terribly unlucky even to speak of her kind.

'I have tried to make them forget her origin. I have endeavoured to put it in their minds that she was born of me, but some do not forget and they wish her ill. Minna Scales is the worst. She had never forgiven me since the colt-pixie chased her son when he tried to steal my Gilgandrias, those apples which are said to be seeded from the land of Faêrie. The wight gave him *"cramp and crooking and fault in his footing"*—it made him the laughingstock of the village. But I'm not to blame for the colt-pixie chasing him. The colt-pixie is a guardian of apple trees. 'Tis a wight. I have no command over such.

'Minna Scales will not let up her niggling,' Elasaid continued. '"Odds fish!" she says to Liban. "Look how your hair drips water. Go and dry it like a *lorraly* lass!" Liban just laughs at her. We keep to ourselves mostly, on this side of the island. The child is happy. I have learned to treasure every moment of her happiness. I think of the other daughter I had . . .'

Elasaid's hands trembled.

'I have not always lived this simple life,' she said. 'I voyaged here, to Tavaal, several years ago. Long before I came here, my childhood was spent in a tall and stately house with many servants. I married—perhaps unwisely, but for love. Eight is the number of the children I bore.' Her blanks of eyes sank into weary hollows. She rested her still-handsome head on her hand.

'Evil forces took the first seven from me. I took myself away from the last one. To my eternal regret. For, when I tried to return, I could not. My child, my husband, had gone away in their turn, leaving no trace. I was alone. I searched up and down the Known Lands, to no avail. Finally, sick of the world and its heartbreak, I applied to come here, to live out the rest of my days in seclusion. I found Liban. Abiding with her and my freshet of water, and the apples, I open the doors from one day into the next and close them one by one behind me.'

It was easy to strike up friendships with the good-natured islanders. Elasaid of the rain-eyes was one of many with whom Rohain liked to pass the time in conversation. Another was Rona Wade, the wife of Hugh, whose children had webbed fingers. Rona could never be persuaded to reveal her thoughts and desires, but she knew all that went on around the island, and was happy to share her knowledge.

On a hazy afternoon, Rona Wade and her web-fingered eldest daughter tarried with Rohain by the kitchen door at the Hall of Tana. Outside waited the surly donkey with the empty fish-baskets, while its mistress discussed island lore.

'Why do the children so often dive near the crescent beach beneath the eastern cliffs?' Rohain wanted to know.

'That is where Urchen Conch threw the chest full of money into the water,' said Rona. 'They are looking for gold coins. Ah, but I suspect you have not heard that tale, my lady!'

'I have not, and I burn to understand why anyone would throw treasure into the brine! Who is this Conch?'

'Urchen Conch was a somewhat simpleminded fellow,' said Rona. 'He lived and died a long time ago. Eighty years ago he saved a stranded benvarrey, carrying her back to the sea. He was entitled to three wishes, but did not know to ask, so she rewarded him with information about how to find a treasure. Doing as she bid, he found a chest of antique gold in a great sea-cavern, but he did not know how to dispose of the ancient cash, and at last he threw the coins back into the sea. It is said he threw them from the eastern cliffs.'

'What a strange tale!' said Rohain.

She was about to ask further questions when Rona's two younger children came scrambling up the path, apple-cheeked and breathless.

'Mama!' they cried. 'Luik what we hae fand under a corn-stack! Ain't it pretty!' Delighted with their prize, they held it high. It shimmered with a downy silverescence—a banner long and wide, rippling in the wind off the slopes. A meadow of moon-grass.

A sealskin.

Gazing at the hide, Rona's dark eyes glistened with rapture. She grasped it, shouting aloud in an ecstasy of joy. The children stood gape-mouthed to see their mother put on such an uncharacteristic display, but she turned to them, her happiness suddenly dimming.

'I love you, my darlings,' she said, embracing each one hastily, 'I will always love you.'

The words hung in memory, long after they had been spoken, as if nailed on emptiness. As soon as she had uttered them, Rona fled down the road toward the sea. The children began to sob. The eldest daughter jumped on the donkey's back.

'I'm gaun tae find Da'!'

She whipped the petulant beast into a headlong run, and the younger ones went wailing after. But they never saw their mama again.

Rohain wept for the family, and brought them food and gifts.

Next morning, in the breakfast room at Tana, the residents sat down to dine.

The table-setting was a lavish seascape, dominated by a nef centrepiece filled with rock-salt. This nef had been crafted from a nautilus-shell, which rested beneath the superstructure of a full-rigged sailing galleon, modelled in gold and studded with precious gems. Shell-shapes decorated the gold and mother-of-pearl serviette rings. Over their hands, the ewerer poured phlox-scented water from a dolphin-shaped aquamanile. Meanwhile, a page cranked a serinette in a shellwork case; the miniature barrel-organ tinkled prettily, not with a tune but with the song-notes of the sea-curlew.

The sideboard, whose panels were framed by a graceful relief of crayfish and conger eels carved in apple-wood, had been arranged with figurines of water-serpents and merfolk carved from narwhal tusks. The ornaments were inlaid with nacre and the mottled shell of the sea-turtle. Dome-covered chafing-dishes sat atop charcoal braziers. A silver egg-boiler rested over its small spirit lamp. A sand timer was mounted on the lid, showing that the minutes had almost run out.

The Bard sprinkled allspice from a set of lighthouse-shaped porcelain muffineers. The Prince drank from a nautilus-shell beaker mounted in gold. Someone had left a snuff-box lying on the table alongside a miniature ship carved from bone—the box had been made, not unexpectedly, from a deep-bowled, voluted shell, with an engraved silver lid and silver mounts.

Tana's decor tended to be thematic.

'You have heard the news, my lady?' Master Avenel sipped from a polished driftwood mazer reinforced with a silver foot-rim incised with a pattern of scales.

Rohain nodded assent. 'Rona Wade has gone.'

'Aye, gone back,' said the Seneschal, 'to her first husband. As Hugh returned from the day's fishing, he saw her greet him in the waves. She called a farewell to him. Hugh is a broken man.'

'Well, he was a thief,' said Rohain, stirring medlure in a cup whose bowl was embraced by the claws of two coralline crabs.

'Do not judge too harshly, my lady,' Avenel reproached gently. 'It was love that drove him to the taking of the sealskin.'

'I beg to differ, sir. Love never steals. It does not subjugate.'

In the pause that ensued, a housemaid limped past the doorway carrying a dustpan and broom, on her way upstairs to sweep and clean the bedchambers. At first, Rohain had taken pains to avoid this young woman, because her uneven gait reminded her of Pod and his unpleasantries. On further acquaintance, she discovered Molly Chove to be an amiable and cheerful lass, who took it in good part when the other servants teasingly called her 'Limpet'.

'Master Avenel,' she now said to the Seneschal, 'is there no help for that lame servant?'

'Molly got her lameness through her own fault,' he replied, dabbing at his mouth with a linen serviette. 'A couple of lesser wights inhabit the Hall of Tana—whether they benefit it or not there's no telling, but they've become a habit of a few centuries.'

'Do they help with household duties?'

'Maybe,' said the Seneschal, 'but I think not. They are pixies or bruneys, I believe. So I am told; I have not seen them. Howsoever, our housemaids Mollusc and Ann Chove tell me they were kind to these imps, showing them hospitality and so forth, and in return the wights used to drop a silver coin into a pail of clear water that the wenches would place for them in the chimney-corner of the kitchen every night.'

'Surely there is water enough for wights in the streams and wells?'

'Domestic wights are loath to budge from their chosen dwelling. They like to have clean water put out for their drinking and washing. Once, several years ago, the maids forgot to fill the pail, so the pixies, or whatever they are, went upstairs to their room and shrilly protested about the omission. Annie woke up. She nudged Molly's elbow and recommended that they should both go down to the kitchen to set things aright, but Molly, who likes her sleep, said, "Leave me be! Would it indulge all the wights on Tavaal, I will not get up." Annie went down to the yard and pumped clean water into the pail. Incidentally, next morning she found seven silver threepences in it. Meanwhile, as she was going back to bed that night she overheard the wights discussing ways of penalizing lazy Molly. They decided to cripple her in one leg. At the end of seven years, she heard them say, the lameness might be cured by a certain herb that grew on Windy Spur.'

'Did they mention the name of this wonderful herb?'

'They did, but 'twas such a lengthy and complicated name, Annie could not grasp it. When Molly got up in the morning she was limping, and she has been perpetually lame to this day.'

Prince Edward said, 'The island's wizard, Master Lutey, has a reputation as an excellent healer.'

'He has not been able to help Molly, sir,' replied the Seneschal.

'Then perhaps his reputation is ill-deserved!'

'Do not, I pray you sir, despise the talent of old Robin Lutey,' said Avenel, 'for he is skilled—I can vouch for it. Do you know how Lutey came by his powers?'

'Prithee, remind me.'

'As a young man he was a fisherman near Lizard Point, farming a little, combing along the beaches after the storms. One evening when the tide was far out he went wandering along the shore seeking for some wreckage-find among the seaweed and rocks. As he turned, empty-handed, to go home, he heard a low moan from among some boulders, and there he discovered a stranded mermaid.'

'For a shy race, they are seen surprisingly often,' Rohain interjected.

'Only on Tamhania, my lady,' said Avenel. 'This is a special place.'

'I was given to understand that they only showed themselves before storms.'

'They only *allow* themselves to be seen when they warn of foul weather. This one was stranded. She could not get back to the sea and had no choice but to be seen, despite the fact that no storm was on the way.'

'Next her strange beauty allured him, no doubt?' Rohain was learning the ways of sea-wights.

'Yes, my lady, and he spoke to her, for the sea-folk understand all tongues. She told him that while she combed her long green hair and gazed at herself in the rockpools the tide had gone out without her seeing it. She begged Lutey to carry her over the strip of dry sand, and, giving him her gold-and-pearl Comb as a token, promised him three wishes. She told him that if he was in any trouble, to pass the Comb three times through the sea and call her name, Morvena, and she would come.'

'Now you have me puzzled,' said Rohain. 'How is it that she could not walk, and yet I have heard that some of the sea-damsels when on land have limbs and walk about as well as you or I?'

'That is one of the differences between mermaids and sea-morgans, m'lady.'

'So.' She nodded. 'I continue to learn. And what were Lutey's wishes?'

'The power to break the spells of malign gramarye, to discover thefts, and to cure illness. These she granted, but only to the degree of her own power.'

'He was fortunate.'

'Indeed, but that was not the end of this fish's tale,' said the Seneschal, permitting himself a faint smile at his pun. 'As he walked with her over the sands, she clinging to his neck, she told him of all the wonders of her home under the sea and implored him to go with her and share them all. Robin Lutey was fascinated and would undoubtedly have yielded had not a sharp bark of terror from his dog, which had followed him unnoticed, roused him to look back. At the sight of the faithful hound his wits returned to him. Already the clasp of the mermaid was becoming stronger as she touched the waves, and she might have dragged him under into the deep realms of the great kelp-forests, except that this is Tamhania, the isle of kings, and wickedness thrives not here. She relented. But as she swam away she sang to Lutey—and that, he never forgot. It is said that the song of the mermaid sounds forever in his heart, and that one day she will come for him and he will follow her.'

'A future not unkind awaits him, then,' said the Bard, who had been silent while eating.

'But nay, sir!' said Avenel. 'Master Lutey possesses a terrible gift. He has somewhat of prescience, which allows him to garner an inkling of his own doom. I have gathered, although he has never said as much, that although he shall indeed go with the mermaid he shall not live long thereafter, for the dreaded Marool shall come upon him in its domain, the sea, and shall put an end to his life.'

Rohain pondered on this. Her eyes were wet. Presently she said, 'A mighty wizard is he.'

'Officially he may not carry the title of wizard since he never studied at the College of the Nine Arts, but meanwhile the island benefits from his powers, which are far greater than those of any ordinary wizard.'

'Small praise, in sooth,' said the Bard drily. 'What became of the mermaid's Comb?'

The Seneschal replied, 'It is said that whenever he stroked the sea with it she came to him and taught him many things. The old sea-mage still has the Comb.'

'But he could not cure Molly's lameness?' Rohain persisted.

'It takes wondrous power to cure anyone who has been wight-struck.'

Rohain's hand strayed to her throat. *How true*, she thought. In sudden fear she glanced at her reflection in the mirror-backed sideboard. The face that met her gaze reassured her. *The past is gone. It need not trouble me anymore.*

Days and nights brightened and darkened the shores of Tamhania. They brought a few alterations in life at Tana. On the strand below, the waves washed back and forth, giving and taking. Translucent to the point of transparency were they, only betraying their existence by shadows on the ribbed sand—shadows of floating foam-flecks, the long undulating shadows of ripples, little darknesses made by the water bending the sunlight, robbing the sand of it, throwing it joyously up in brilliant flashes.

One evening Rohain and Viviana entered the kitchens of the Hall of Tana to find Annie and Molly Chove dancing with the cook, while the spit-boy played the fiddle.

'O strange!' cried Rohain, steadying herself against a corner of the well-scrubbed table. 'Molly, how do you caper so well? For I see that you dance better than most, and you limping like a henkie only yesterday! It is beyond all belief!'

'I went mushrooming,' said Molly, panting and red-cheeked.

Uncertainly, Rohain said, 'So you went mushrooming, and that cured you?'

'Nay, mistress! As I were picking a mushroom for me basket an odd-looking boy sprang up out o' the grass, and would not be prevented from smiting me upon the thigh with a sprig of leaves. After that, the pain went right out of me leg and I could walk straight. Now I does the gallopede!'

'Her seven years is over, you see, mistress,' explained Annie,

as Molly and the cook hoofed it around the kitchen in another
mad frenzy. 'Wights always keeps their promises.'

A new month came in, bringing the Beldane Festival, symbolised by flowers and baskets of eggs and butterchurns. At the
Whiteflower's Day Dance, Molly Chove outfooted them all.

After breakfast one morning, Rohain walked beneath the
castle walls amid a crowd of attendants. The sea was apple-juice
green. White feathers ran down the spine of the sky and a peculiar
greenish tinge stained the northwest horizon. Something intangible
about the island began to disturb her. She could not identify it,
could not quite label it a *wrongness*, but there was something.

'Jewel-toads are on the move, my lady,' said young Caitri, 'and
the goats on the hillsides seek the caves. Master Avenel says these
are signs that a bad storm is on the way.'

'Storms frighten me,' stated Viviana. Nervously she toyed with
a silver thimble attached to the well-furnished chatelaine at her
waist.

'I had a dream last night,' said Georgiana Griffin, 'a strange
dream. About that islander.'

'What islander?' asked Rohain, feigning ignorance.

'Master Shaw.'

'I thought you said he was nothing to you.'

'He is. But this dream. I thought I was gathering the primroses
and sea-pinks that grow among the saltbushes on the slope to the
west of the Hanging Cave, when I heard a singing on the rocks
below. I looked down and saw Sevran Shaw lying asleep on the
beach and a fair lady watching beside him. Then he was standing
beside me and when he shook the saltbushes, showers of drops
fell with a tinkling sound and turned as they fell into pure gold,
and I caught sight of the lady floating on the water, far out at sea.
I woke then, but just now as we passed that same flowery slope
I could swear I heard the strange singing coming up from the
rocks, as in the dream.'

'I have more than heard it,' said a male voice. Sevran Shaw
himself was advancing up the path. 'I have seen and conversed
with the singer, the eldritch lady of your dream.' A ripple of

amazement ran through the assembly of courtiers. 'Greetings and hail, Lady Rohain, Lady Georgiana, ladies!' Shaw addressed them with a gallant bow, his plumed hat in his hand.

'Greetings, Master Shaw. You say you have seen a mermaid,' Rohain said.

'Aye, my lady, and it has been long between such sightings. The last time a mermaid appeared near the Hanging Cave was just before the terrible storm in which my father was lost.'

'La!' exclaimed Georgiana. 'Take care not to repeat the mermaid's words, sir, for I have heard that they thrive ill who carry tales from their world to ours.'

Shaw returned, 'There is no need for fear on my account, for I am the master of this sea-girl.' He recounted how he had risen before dawn on the previous day—having not closed his eyes all night, for reasons he would not divulge—and walked to the beach to watch the sun rise across the skerries beyond Seacliffe Head. He had gone down to the Hanging Cave, a place renowned for its strange occurrences. As he stood, he heard a low song coming from a stack of rocks nearby. Moving toward the sound, he saw the singer, a damsel with long green-gold hair falling over her white shoulders, her face turned toward the cave. He knew without a doubt that although for years he had travelled far on the high seas, he was seeing a mermaid for the first time in his life.

Shaw crept toward the rock shelf on which sat this thrilling incarnation, taking cover all the way, but just as he reached it she turned around. Her song changed to a shriek of terror and she attempted to fling herself into the water, but he seized her in his arms. She strove with amazing strength to drag him into the waves with her, but he held her fast and at last bore her down by brute force. She still struggled but at last lay passive on the rock, and as he looked at her he knew he had never seen anything so wild and lovely in all his life.

'Man, what with me?' she had said in a voice sweet and yet so strange that his blood ran cold at the sound.

'Wishes three,' he had replied, aware of the traditional formula.

'What did you wish?' breathed Georgiana.

'I wished that neither myself nor any of my friends should

perish by the sea, like my father did. Next, I wished that I should be fortunate in all my undertakings. As for the third wish, that is my own business, and I shall never tell anyone but the mermaid.'

No one present failed to guess it.

'And she said?' Georgiana murmured.

'"Quit and have," was her reply. I slackened my hold then. Raising her hands, palms together, she dived into the sea.'

Georgiana scarcely spoke after the tale was done. As they climbed the hillside, returning to the *chastel*, Shaw offered his arm and she leaned on it.

But a mermaid had been seen, for the first time in twelve years. Every islander knew what that meant.

Soon, the elements would rise. A terrible storm was on the way.

That afternoon, Rohain went down to the village. Over the village marketplace the greenish stain in the northern sky had darkened to heavy bruising, spreading across the sky, ominous and threatening. Gusts swatted the stalls in fits and starts, like a vexed housewife with a broom. Folk hurried to finish their market chores so that they could get home and begin battening down. The word was out: Master Shaw had seen a mermaid.

Spying Elasaid of the Groves and her child among the last of the market crowd, Rohain approached them. Liban had plucked a posy of sea-pinks from crevices in the stone walls, and was making them into a chain.

'Why do you not hurry home?' Rohain asked. 'Everyone says a storm is on the way.'

Elasaid glanced skyward. 'On the way, but not yet here,' she said. 'Liban has told me it will not arrive before nightfall.'

As they stood in conversation, a weird song came down the wind. It seemed to approach, keening, from far out at sea.

'Whatever is that?' exclaimed Rohain.

Elasaid fell silent, but the melody was heard again, from close by, and this time it was Liban who sang. 'That song is mine,' said the green-eyed scrap of a child with sea-pinks in her hair. 'Someone is calling me. The storm will come tonight.'

'Wisht Liban!' said Elasaid urgently. 'Hush now!' But a rope-faced old woman who had been loitering nearby turned and hurried away. 'Alas, that was Minna Scales, and she heard what Liban said,' said Elasaid sorrowfully. 'She'll be telling the men, those who fear the sea-morgans. What will happen now, I do not know.'

Since Rohain had arrived on Tamhania, shang storms had come with their jinking music like tiny disks of thinly beaten silver shaken in a breeze, and they had gone. But this was the first time a 'natural' storm had menaced. And, by all the signs, what a storm it promised to be. It would bring the world's winds teeming, screaming forth in long, lean, scavenging fronts bearing tons of airborne water. Its brew of pressures would build up tension in powerful charges for sudden, white-hot release. And with all the ruthlessness of something mindless.

This storm was fast approaching, over the sea. And Rohain felt—she was certain . . .

. . . something *wicked* was coming with it.

As darkness crept across the island, objects rattled in the Hall of Tana. Gorgeously decorated pomanders, pounce boxes, and vinaigrettes were clustered on a small marquetry table. All exuded conflicting scents. To add to the sensory confusion, a porcelain pastille-burner discharged aromatic fumes through its pierced lid. Someone had absentmindedly placed this jumble of fragrant ornaments on the table—Molly perhaps, hastening about her business, distracted by the storm's approach. There they sat, abandoned, and clattered—enamel clunking against metal, wood on ceramic, ivory on bone.

Late in the evening the gale's first outriders hooted eerily in the chimneys and chivvied at the tiles of the chastel's pointed rooves. Thomas of Ercildoune, Roland Avenel, and the Bard's apprentice Toby played loudly for Rohain and the young Prince and Duchess Alys of Roxburgh, but although their music increased in volume so did the storm's music, until nature obtained precedence. Then they put away trumpet and bagpipes and drums and sat in the main salon hearkening to the rising howl.

In a sudden burst of thunder, the castle shuddered. A gauntlet fell off a suit of armour, startling the company. It was like a challenge from the elements: *Behold, I throw down the glove. Brave me if you dare.*

They knew, then, that the storm had reached the island.

'If I retired to bed I would not sleep, with this cacophony ringing in my ears,' said the Bard, his tone over-jolly. 'I shall bide here until the tempest abates. Wine, Toby! Have them bring more wine!'

'For my part, presently I shall say good night to all and wend upstairs,' said the Duchess, yawning behind her hand. 'There is no profit in losing sleep.' When next Rohain looked toward her, the Duchess had settled back against the cushions of a brocade couch and fallen into a twitchy doze.

Avenel sat brooding.

Rohain and Prince Edward remained at Ercildoune's side. The Prince toyed with an empty cup, while Rohain stared out at the raging weather. The Bard compensated for the sobriety of his companions by quaffing deeply of his own cup, and calling for his squire to refill it. He was the only loquacious member of the party, loudly regaling them with an assortment of boisterous stories.

The main salon, where they kept company, was beautiful. A multitude of candles illuminated its glory. On the ceiling above the window reveal, stenciled swallows dashed across a painted sky. Bullion-fringed swags of heavy blue velvet in stiff folds festooned the pelmet. The tall windows were divided into smaller panes, each with its own shutter daubed with little pictures of rural idyll.

Through the panes of the embrasure, opalescent and salt-glazed, Rohain and Edward looked out across the village, now in darkness. Its lamplit windows were a scatter of square-cut zircons. Beyond it, the harbour now appeared insubstantial, bathed by the raw murk of night and thunderwrack. The gloom hid any sign of the Light-Tower standing lonely on the ocean's rim. There, the Lightkeeper would be holding vigil, with only the pigeons for company—their cries as soft as dollops of cream—and the great mirrored Light floating at the top of the Tower in its bath of quicksilver.

The storm threw an apoplectic fit. Lightning erratically cast blue-white plaster reliefs of the Light-Tower. For the duration of a thought, it blanched the entire landscape with dazzles so intense they printed specters on the vision of the watchers, against the blackness that smacked down afterward.

The night was at its thickest and the storm had reached an apogee of violence when a brilliant strobe described something *new* out beyond the narrow gap between the headlands. Rohain seized a spyglass, its bronze casing etched with whorls. She trained its round lens on the pale thing that seemed to dance there. After a moment, the cylinder dropped from her nerveless fingers. At her side, Edward deftly retrieved the instrument.

'What is toward?' he asked.

'Oh, I cannot bear it. Something must be done. *The Light must be kindled.*'

The Prince applied the spyglass to his eye.

'A ship!' he muttered wonderingly. 'And in trouble, it seems— too close to the reefs. But what ship? The glass will not let me descry their ensigns.'

By now the Bard had relinquished his winecup and was squinting through a second spyglass. 'Why does the Beacon not shine?' he cried, his voice somewhat slurred. 'Surely by now the ship's master must have sent the message-birds.' Grim-faced, he flung down the instrument. 'But in sooth, what birds could fly in this gale? They would be blown away. And with no Light, that ship shall soon be dashed to pieces.'

Roused from his reverie, Roland Avenel leapt up and strode to the window. 'This is madness,' he said, frowning and peering through the metal tube. 'No vessels are due to put in. Where is this ship from? And who is she?'

'It matters little! Lives are about to be lost!' expostulated the Bard. 'Surely the Lightkeeper knows that. No doubt he'll have seen this ship. It is unavoidable, for the Tower looks out upon the open sea. He is right close to them there—yet inexplicably he remains idle!'

'Has he a heart of ice?' demanded Rohain, pacing the floor, clasping and unclasping her hands.

'He obeys orders,' said Avenel.

'A message must be borne swiftly to him, sir,' the Bard said, leaning unsteadily toward the Prince. 'Your orders to light the flame.'

The Prince replied, 'When an off-island vessel comes in, a foreigner, the command to kindle the Light must bear the Royal Seal. The signet ring bearing that seal is now far from here.'

'Of course—it is upon your father's hand,' said Rohain. 'But do you not wear a similar ring, Edward?'

'No. There is no other.'

'Then,' said the Bard, 'the Lightkeeper must accept the royal command by word of mouth instead! Zounds, methinks the cries of the drowning sailors are already clamoring in my ears. Is that the sound of men calling from the dim and heinous troughs of ocean swell? We must needs hasten!'

'This is madness!' shouted Avenel.

The Duchess Alys woke in fright. 'What's amiss?' she said, hastening to join them at the window.

'Ercildoune would have us kindle the Light, despite that the proper procedure is lacking,' said the Seneschal angrily.

In a low voice the Prince said, 'Good sir, good Thomas, I say to you the Light must not shine on this fell night. Not without the proper directives.'

The Bard stared at him in disbelief. 'Do I hear aright?' he said indistinctly. 'Is Your Highness willing to let those poor folk perish?'

'It may be some trick.'

'Edward, how can you say so?' Rohain trembled, hot with indignation. 'It might *not* be a trick. Would you lay that on your conscience? On ours?'

The Prince's face was troubled. 'Lady, when the Light shines it opens a gate through a shield of gramarye which covers Tamhania like a dome. While that shield is breached, anything unseelie might penetrate.'

The Bard said urgently, 'For one brief instant only shall it be opened! As soon as the vessel slips through, the Light shall be quenched. Where is your heart, lad? I entreat you—ride with me to the Light-Tower and give your command. The Lightkeeper shall not gainsay the Empire's heir.'

'I will ride beside you!' said Rohain.

'May the Powers preserve me from bee-stings and headstrong wenches,' muttered the Bard. He tottered slightly, steadying himself against a marquetry table.

The face of the young Prince was ripped to shreds of anguish and bewilderment. 'Mistress Tarrenys, the weather is too wild for thee,' he said, taking Rohain by the hand. 'Do you not see? Thomas is deep in his cups tonight. The wine leads his thoughts astray. Like many bards he is a passionate man, ruled by his heart; the drink amplifies that tendency. Were he sober, he would not argue against me, for he understands the rules of the island very well. Prithee, do not even contemplate going out in the storm.'

At fourteen, Edward already matched her height. Level with his, her eyes beseeched him. 'Won't you come with me to the Light?' she said.

His visage, pale, dark-eyed against the black brushstroke of his hair, softened. With a shuddering sigh, as though torn in twain, he turned out his hands, palms upward as if in surrender. 'I will ride with thee.'

'Madness!' fumed Avenel.

'Pray think twice!' Alys urged the young man.

'I have made my decision,' replied he, and the Duchess could not gainsay the Crown Prince.

A stony road emerged from the northern end of the village. Hugging the line of the shore, it curved around the sweep of the harbour and along the promontory's spine, ending at Light-Tower Point. Along this road seven riders flew through the fangs of the gale, and slanting spears of rain. The darkness was intense, alleviated only by whips of lightning.

They covered the last lap at a gallop. Pounded by the fists of the ocean, the very ground shook beneath the horses' hooves, and salt spray erupted from the base of the cliff to smite them like a beaded curtain. Only the wall on the seaward side of the road saved them from being flung over the edge. Intermittent flickers of light revealed the ill-timed ship, closer now, foundering on the rocks. Its hull was cracking like a monstrous eggshell. Between blasts of thunder and wind, the riders' ears were assailed by cries of fear and misery as thin as the piping of crickets. The ship, hanged on cruel spurs, slumped sideways, dangling.

'We are too late,' Ercildoune roared, but the words were snatched from his mouth even as he shouted them. The foundering vessel gave a great lurch. With a last macabre wave of its ragged sails it began to crumple slowly into the corrugated sea. A wave crashed against the rocks and jetted up in a pillar of spray.

The Light-Tower seemed to hover at the end of the causeway. Over the archway giving onto its courtyard, runes, weather-stained and eroded, spelled out:

Here, the Tower of Power.
Ye Who Wander Yonder
Keep the Light in Sight.

Tossing their reins to the two squires, the riders burst through the Tower's door in a swirl of drenched cloaks and a clatter of squelching boots. The stairs spiraled up and up. At the top, in a round room, an icicle stood.

The Lightkeeper.

Age had plowed severe furrows into the waxen face. Over heavy robes of overcast gray, a gossamer beard hung to his waist. Moonlight hair flowed halfway down his back, from beneath a broad-brimmed, low-crowned hat. Hollowed out of a face as bleached as parian, the eyes were two glass orbs, limpid, almost colourless. The Lightkeeper was an albino of the kindred calling themselves the Arysk; the Icemen.

He unlidded his eyes, like two silver snuff-boxes.

'Welcome, Your Highness,' this unlit candle declared above the tumult, his phonetics clicking in the Rimanian accent, 'welcome Lords and Ladies.' But it sounded like 'Veltcome, Yourk Hightness, veltcome, Lorcds ant ladties.'

'The ship,' shouted the Prince, pushing past the closed eye of the Light on its pedestal in the room's centre. He looked down from the latticed windows, barred with chill iron against the ocean's siege.

'Vun ist vrecket alreatty,' said the Keeper. 'Aknothert comest.'

'You have doomed one ship and now you say a second follows the same path, Master Grullsbodnr?' the Bard bellowed angrily.

It was true. The second vessel was smaller than her sister. Lanterns swung from the rigging. Their glow spilled sporadically on flowing-haired figures wearing long gowns. Their mouths were open. They were screaming.

The Bard swore vehemently.

'There are women aboard!'

'And yet . . .' Edward murmured. His voice trailed away.

'No kmessagte. No copmandt,' intoned the Lightkeeper glacially.

'Be wary,' cried Alys, 'I mislike the look of this. What ensigns does the captain hoist? I see none.'

'See how the wind has torn the sails! How might ensigns remain untouched?' Ercildoune returned. 'They should be ripped to rags!' He and the Duchess disputed, then, like quarreling rooks, in this high nest on its granite tree, until the Bard bawled, 'While we stand in discussion, the second ship is driven upon the rocks. Master Grullsbodnr, kindle the Light at once!'

The aged Iceman shook his head. 'Ta Light not sheint vidout ta kmessagte.'

'Rohain, I appeal to you!' The Bard drove his fist against the Light's pedestal.

'I am of one mind with you, Thomas. Sir?' Rohain turned to Edward.

'I do not know,' the Prince shouted against the din, desperately grappling with indecision. 'Grullsbodnr is right, and yet if these mariners are indeed mortal and should perish, the shadow of this grievous misdeed will lie heavy on us forever. They might well have been blown off course . . .'

The Duchess Alys plucked at his coat. 'Sir,' she said, 'our own course must not deviate. The mandate is unambiguous. For generations it has obtained security for the royal island. I rode here to prevent folly if I could. The Light must not be kindled this night.'

'And I concur,' Avenel declared.

As they spoke, another blistering flare displayed a ghastly

scene on the rocks below. The second ship had fetched up on their points at last. She tottered. Amid the churning flood, human forms clung to broken spars. Some were overtaken by long valleys, emerging at the summits of crests, sliding down again through dark walls of hyacinth glass, to reappear no more.

'It is too much to be borne,' Rohain exclaimed, 'two ships destroyed. We might have saved the last. We must send boats without delay, to aid any that survive in the water.'

'No boat would live long out there,' Avenel said.

On the second ship, the firefly lanterns had all winked out. Only the nautilus curve of her side now lifted and dropped on the storm's pulse, sinking lower in the water, a mere evanescence of bent wood and ruined canvas, in its death throes no longer a ship, merely a broken thing.

Edward touched Rohain's sleeve. His eyes clouded. 'Forgive me.'

She nodded acknowledgment, unable to speak.

The fenestrations fretted in the gale, the panes rattling in their metal grooves like prisoners shaking the bars of their cells.

'I am sick,' the Bard said. 'I am sick to my very marrow that we should stand thusly by and let this happen on the chance that it is some ruse of unseelie. If this vision is a forgery, what of it? Do we not have Lutey the mage who breaks spells, do we not have strong men and hounds to hunt down any mischief that should infiltrate?'

'Your heart governs your head, Ercildoune,' warned Alys.

'And were that a more prevalent condition, mortalkind must find itself in better state!' he returned warmly. 'Drowned, all drowned, those brave folk, and their corpses to wash up, bloated and staring, along the shores of Tamhania this many a day, a mute reproach, the more terrible in its silence.'

The windows clattered. Between the leading and the wands of iron, the diamond panes wept salt tears. The Tower room was cold and drear. Its freeze seeped through Rohain's sodden clothing and into her sinews. The wind's ululation dropped away somewhat, enabling softer speech, but there was nothing to say.

It was after midnight.

'We should depart,' said Avenel bleakly.

Rohain stole one last glance through the salt-misted lattices, out across the wild sea.

Then, with an altered mien, she turned away from the view. Seizing a candle out of a branch encrusted with dribbles of congealed wax, she stepped up to the Light in its glass cage atop the pedestal.

'Lightkeeper, open the Light's door,' she commanded in a clear voice, 'I shall kindle it myself, if you shall not.'

Edward, filling her place at the window glanced out. Sharply, he said, 'Obey, Master Grullsbodnr.'

'The future king has spoken,' subjoined the Bard, scowling at the Iceman.

The Lightkeeper unfastened the little door. Rohain reached her hand inside. The buttercup candle entered, met the wick, and inflamed it.

The wick was surrounded by polished mirrors. Stark white radiance stood out from them like a solid bar of frost-quartz. Somewhere, clockwork machinery started up. Spring-and-sildron engines whirred and the Light began to rotate. It sent its steely beam through the lattices, far out into the dread of night, over frothing, coughing reefs and farther until, over the trackless ocean, the bounding main, it stretched itself too thin, becoming nothing.

Rohain had espied a third vessel down there—a lifeboat. Its sail seemed as small as a pocket handkerchief.

It was in the channel now. By the Light of the Tower, in protected waters, it steered true—straight for the gap between the headlands. On board were three shipwreck survivors. The young mother stayed at the tiller while two tiny children clung to each other beside the streak of a mast.

The Bard and the Seneschal ran down the stairs, calling to the squires in the stables to launch the Lightkeeper's *geola*, that they might meet the fragile craft as it entered the harbour.

Past the Tower on its northern headland sailed the boat with its three passengers, beneath the single spoke of the wheel of light. The watchers in the upper room could see them clearly, could see their faces now—the courageous, tragic mother, the darling children

standing up and spreading their arms wide for balance. But why
had they done so? Why let go of the mast? And their arms had a
strange look now—they seemed to be stretching . . . the children
were growing.

And she was growing too, and changing, the one who no
longer held the tiller, who could not hold anything anymore
because it had no hands, only terrible wings like two charred fans
of night. The two creatures by the mast extended their black pin-
ions. The darkness was pierced by three pairs of incandescent
coals—red fires burning holes in beaked skulls. One by one they
rose, retracting spurred tridents of talons. The beaks opened.

'Baav!' cawed the first. 'Macha!'

'Neman!' croaked the second.

Effortlessly on those outsized kites of wings, slashing the air
with slow, powerful downstrokes, the three abominations, crow-
things out of nightmare, flapped away over the lightless harbour.
Out of the Light's reach they fled—shadows winging toward
Tamhania's highest point, the mountain's summit.

'Morrigu,' quoth the final corvus in a creaking voice, like the
closing of a coffin-lid.

Then the moon came flying in terror from behind the clouds.
Her light gleamed down. And there on the opposite headland,
on Southern Point just across the Rip from the Light-Tower, was
a child. It was Liban, the adopted daughter of Elasaid. She ran,
spirited and free, like the ocean. The fear that the Crows had
brought was not on her; she was not of mortalkind. Her own
pale tresses flew in the storm wind as she ran along the path to
the sea, laughing. A handful of men chased after her but they
couldn't overtake her, and the last man ran with a crooked gait.
That strange sea-song came again, and the waves thundered
against the rocks. The men halted in fear, staying where they
were up on the cart-track.

The watchers in the Light-Tower heard Liban singing as she
ran out along the reef, and then a mighty wave smashed against
the reef and reared up. It washed over her, and she was gone.

In fitted bursts of moonlight the tempest subsided, rolling away to the southeast. The wind eased. Utter stillness commenced. Fog snakes came coiling out of the sea-harbour and all along the weed-dashed beaches. Although the hour was well before cock-crow, the villagers were astir in the streets. Lanterns passed to and fro in the dark. Much was amiss. The rough weather had wrought severe damage.

Furthermore, it had been discovered in the village that under cover of the storm, John Scales and his wife had incited some of the more superstitious islanders to form a lynch mob and go after the fey girl sheltered by Elasaid of the Groves. Hearing that trouble was afoot, the mayor had taken charge. He mustered certain law-abiding men who were now riding with him to the road from Southern Point, in order to confront Scales's mob as they returned.

A few islanders—mainly those who were known to have a tendency to be fanciful—claimed to have seen three dark shapes flying from the headlands. They said they were like great birds, traveling in a barbed formation like an arrowhead, and they had ascended toward the mountain peak hanging in the sky. But with more pressing matters to attend to, of the alleged Crows little note was taken.

Seven riders hastened back along the crescent road to the village. They drew rein in the marketplace. Overhead, cloud-tendrils unraveled before the face of the bald moon. Frigid radiance bathed the Old Village Square.

'I must find Elasaid,' said Rohain dully. 'She will be here, in the village.'

Her horse was restless, as if sensing her unease. The cold that weighed her limbs like iron chains was generated more by horror than by her soaked raiment. It was a clammy dread that drained her vitality and painted with a lavender hue her nails and lips. She could think of nothing but the appalling Crows, and the child taken by the wave, Elasaid's loss.

''Tis folly to remain here,' remonstrated the Duchess Alys, quietening her own steed with an expert hand. 'I urge you to return with me to hall and hearth.'

'I will not be dissuaded.'

A man ran up to the party of riders.

'My lords, my ladies,' he said, 'the mayor's wife bids ye come to his house, if ye will, and be warmed at his fire, and take a sup.' He bowed.

Suddenly Elasaid was standing at Rohain's stirrup. Her eyes were dark.

'Have you seen Liban, my lady?' she asked. Her tone was flat, without hope.

'Elasaid,' said Rohain, dismounting, 'the child is gone back to the sea. Come with us to the house of the mayor. There we will talk.'

At the home of the village's chieftain, servants brought wine for the guests. A cherry fire burgeoned amid a heap of driftwood, but Rohain was unable to thaw. She had become as one of the Arysk—a glazed and brittle shard, numb to feeling. When she closed her eyes, three ghastly birds flapped across the linings of her lids.

Edward described to Elasaid the entire story as it had been seen from the Light-Tower.

'We heard Liban singing as she ran out along the rocks,' he ended, 'and then a great wave came surging up and swept her away. We saw her no more.'

After a time, Elasaid murmured, 'Another child of mine is gone.' She seemed like one who has been struck blind. 'But I thank you for bearing these tidings,' she went on doggedly. 'I do not grieve for her sake—perhaps somewhat for myself, but self-pity bears no merit. She has returned to her own kind as I always knew she would. She was never my child. Liban has been reclaimed, as is fitting, just as Rona Wade returned to her people not long ago. Those two were not born for the land. Yet I never kept Liban here against her will—she was always free to leave. When it was time, they called her, and it was the song, not any act of credulous, craven mortals; it was the song that brought her to the waves.'

'Those who harried her shall pay the price,' vowed Thomas of Ercildoune, striking his hand against his thigh.

'What of the black birds, the outsized hoodie crows?' asked the Prince. 'Had the child aught to do with them?'

'No sir,' replied Elasaid. 'Of this I am certain. Such creatures are not associated with the sea-morgans—not with any of the merfolk.'

'Do you know their portent?'

'I saw them, the strange birds flying toward the mountain, but I know not from whence these fell things came, or what is their purpose. I know not what they fortoken, but I fear no good will come of this night.'

The cherry fire glowed. Somewhere, a cock crowed. *Uhta* waned—the sun's edge ran a line of tinsel along a diaphanous horizon.

In pain, Rohain said, 'Elasaid Trenowyn, I understand now why I thought your face was familiar to me. On a glass mountain in Rimany a girl with your face opens a lock with her finger, to free seven enchanted rooks. And in the valley they call Rosedale in Eldaraigne, a fine man waits for you and grieves, as he has waited and grieved this many a year. Do not let him wait much longer.'

Elasaid Trenowyn trembled. A spark jumped in her eyes. She picked up her shawl and gave Rohain a wide-eyed look, as though she had never before set eyes on her.

'I hear you.'

Saying nothing more, she left the house and went down to the harbour.

No wreckage from drowned ships, no barrels, planks, spars, or corpses washed up on Tavaal's shores. This proved it—eldritch vessels they had indeed been, all three. What mortal understood the workings of such simulacra? Perhaps they had repaired themselves as they sank. Perhaps they were sailing now, deep down among the benthos, phosphorescent lanterns swinging on the rigging to light up the abysmal darkness.

Today the swell rolled long and slow and blank, as if it had grown as heavy as lead, whose sad colour it reflected. On the beach, the skeleton of a whale lay as it had lain for years—a behemoth beached a decade earlier. The ribs curved skyward, sand-blasted, wind-scoured. Now the skeleton was a framework of great upturned vaults, a vacant hull, a giant cage of ribs that once housed a heart the size of a horse.

It could be seen from the house of the sea-wizard. Lutey's abode perched like a rickety gull's nest on a low cliff overlooking the village and the harbour. Gulls, in fact, went in and out at the windows like accustomed visitors. They spoke with harsh voices at odds with their lines of loveliness, and when the party of riders arrived, loud was their announcement.

Silhouetted against a souring sky, the company of noble visitors and their retainers waited on horseback. Presently the head of Lutey the Gifted appeared between cliff and sea. He came clambering up over the edge, his robes and hair and plaited beard-ends streaming up over his head, blown by vertical drafts. From a pocket in his clothing peeped a fantastically fashioned Comb of pearls and gold.

The riders dismounted and the mage led them to his house. Bowing, he held open the door. As they entered, the structure trembled like a bird's nest in the wind. From somewhere not far off resounded a deep sound as of drums rolling.

The interior smelled of stale seaweed, yet for all its clutter and avian traffic it was surprisingly clean and orderly. Dried seaweeds—pink, rust, cream, and copper—hung from the rafters. A delicate clepsydra dripped by the window. Beside it lay a brass sextant and a folding pocket-spyglass decorated with lacquer, inscribed with the maker's name: *Stodgebeck of Porthery.*

Shelves held nekton memorabilia. The only two chairs had been carved out of coral broken from the reefs by storms. The bed was a giant clam shell, the table a salvaged captain's table inlaid with nacre and scored by daggers. It was set with sea-urchin candleholders, scallop-shell plates, mussel-shell spoons and dark amber-green dishes formed from lacquered bull-kelp—a material light and strong, malleable when fresh yet when dry as hard and impermeable as vitreous. Here in Lutey's house were many things of salt-water origin that, like the sea-wind forced by the cliff to alter direction, had suffered a land-change.

Like some barnacled, weed-grown sea-creature he seemed,

this wizard. His skin was as translucent as a jellyfish, his eyes the windows of an ancient coelacanth. Strung about his throat, a necklace of shark's teeth; scimitars of dentine.

'A force unseelie, a force powerful, has broached our defenses,' said the coelacanth, putting a brass astrolabe aside to make a space on the table. 'I saw them last night. My strength is not great enough to challenge such foes. I know not where they have gone now, the three dark birds, or what will happen. But ye, Princess, should not bear the guilt of it.' He mixed a blue-green potion that he gave to Rohain in a chipped porcelain caudle-cup shaped like an octopus. It burned away the cold dread that had filled her veins with ice since the moment the unseelie entities from the sea had shifted back to their true bird-shapes, and she had at last understood what she had wrought.

'I have Combed the sea,' said the sea-mage, 'but for the first time in my experience there is no reply.' His face was grim. 'What became of the masted lifeboat—the vessel that bore the invaders?'

'It spun around three times,' the Prince replied, 'and then sank, straight down, like a stone.'

An echoing boom rolled up all around, and the shelves racketed.

'Be not unduly alarmed,' said Lutey, observing the discomfiture of his guests. 'It is only the voice of the sea. Alack, that I do not possess its power.'

'It sounds from near,' said the Prince.

'It is near, sir,' said the mage, pulling up a trapdoor set into the floor. Beneath their feet, a great cavern opened out and fell away. Far below, perhaps a hundred feet down in the half-light, a dark swell travelled rapidly toward the inner wall of rock on the last few yards of its journey from the outer ocean.

'The sea-cave undercuts this cliff,' explained Lutey as the wave smashed into the wall and another hollow roar shook his house. 'It is the same sea-cave where Urchen Conch found a chest of antique gold so many years ago, according to local legend—which I doubt not. Here is a ladder. Sometimes I climb down. I have found no gold there,' he added.

He closed the hatch. A gull alighted on his shoulder and wheeled its fierce yellow eye.

'Again I shall Comb the sea this day,' said Lutey. 'Leave a messenger with me, and I will send word of any tidings.'

'What else is to be done?' Avenel asked

'There is naught to be done but watch and wait. Watch and wait, warily and wisely.'

Since the night of the storm, those who dwelt in the Hall of Tana, and some who dwelt in the village, would frequently turn their eyes up toward the roof of the island, hidden in white cloud—that remote peak whence the winged creatures of unseelie had vanished. But there was no sign of anything untoward. The peak seemed to float and dream as always; serene, untroubled. No flocks of ravening hoodie crows came swooping like a black rain, talons extended and toothed beaks gaping, to rip the rooftiles off the village houses and devour the inhabitants. As days passed and all appeared unchanged, the people ceased to raise their heads as often. But always the crown of the mountain overhung them, lost in its steamy wreath.

The Seneschal led a band of riders on eotaurs up to the summit. But the roiling vapors were as obdurate as a wall and the sildron-lifted Skyhorses would not, could not enter that blindfold haze. In such a murk, all orientation could easily be lost. Not knowing up from down, horse and rider might fall out of the sky.

One night as she dozed, it seemed to Rohain that she was still in the sea-mage's house, with the waves booming in the sea-cave underneath, slamming against the foundations.

She awoke.

A kind of fine trembling seemed to pass through the canopied bed. The lamps hanging on chains from the ceiling shivered slightly.

A ship came from the mainland. When it sailed away, Elasaid was aboard. The vessel had brought letters, including a hastily written one for Rohain, in Thorn's beautiful, embellished script that was more like an intertwining of leafy vines than characters. This she deciphered by herself. There were tidings of the business of war, and a brief but forceful line, *I think of thee,* the more earnest in its austerity.

News from the war zone was grim—unseelie forces assailed the Royal Legions and the Dainnan by night while Namarran bands harried them by day. The central stronghold of the subversives, hidden somewhere in the Namarran wastelands, could not be found. It was from there that orders were being issued. It was believed that if this fortress could be discovered and scourged of its wizardly leaders, the uprising might be quelled.

'A letter from my mother,' said Caitri, waving a leaf of paper. 'It seems Isse Tower now harbours a bruney, or a bauchan. It pinches the careless servants and also the masters who beat them. It works hard but Trenchwhistle, now black and blue, is trying to get rid of it, laying out gifts of clothing and so on. It ignores the gifts and won't leave. My mother says the Tower is a better place for it.'

Perusing her missives from Court, Viviana let out a scandalized scream.

'*Kiel varletto!* One of the palace footmen has run away with the sixth granddaughter of the Marquess of Early!'

For days, she would not cease talking about the elopement.

Late on an evening, as she lay abed waiting for sleep, Rohain again thought that a vibration came through the floor. It was as if a heavy wagon had passed the Hall of Tana, loaded with boulders—but when she looked from the window, the road beyond the wall was empty.

The apples of Elasaid's abandoned orchards flourished and ripened. The island's gold-hazed humidity seemed lately to be tinged with a slight smell of rotting—imparted perhaps by the cloud-vapors, or by the seaweed cast up by the waves to wither on the shores, or maybe by the *duilleag neoil* itself. As time passed, one became accustomed to the odour and did not notice it at all.

The weather was unusually warm for early Spring, the sea as temperate as bathwater. Rejoicing at this, the village children dived and swam, especially the children of Ursilla and of Rona Wade. Lutey's warning, 'wait and watch', had lost its urgency. The people of Tamhania had waited and watched, but nothing had happened. A little, their vigilance relaxed. But if their masters were carefree, the tamed beasts of the island were not. They had grown restless, uneasy. To human eyes all seemed peaceful, all seemed well. Yet beneath this veneer, expectancy thrummed like an over-stretched harp-string, drawn taut across land and sea.

On an overcast day, Rohain stood in Tana's library with Roland Avenel. As they conversed, there began a shaking as if an army of armoured war-horses charged around the hill, pulling mangonels and other engines of destruction on iron wheels. Ornaments and girandoles rattled. The walls creaked. An ormulu perfume burner toppled from its stand and one book fell out of the shelves. From the coach-house came the noise of the carriages rocking on their springs.

'Mayhap the island floats again!' exclaimed the Seneschal, shaking his gray head in astonishment. 'Or it is making ready to do so! Mayhap it has grown weary of this location and has pulled up its ancient sea-anchors or cut them adrift, in order to seek another home.'

Tamhania was moving again—at least, that is what they were saying in the village, where the doors and windows of the houses jammed tight in warped frames. And the rainy month of Uiskamis rolled on. On the high spit jutting into the Rip, the grizzled gran-ite Light-Tower seemed to lean into the webs of salt spray, its eye looking far over the silken plain as if it could see past the horizon. At its feet, jagged hunks of rock gripped the uncertain border between land and sea like the Tower's roots, seeming to draw sus-tenance from both. Perhaps the roots did not go down far enough to fix the island in place.

A minor unstorm went over without much ado. The Scales family and their cohorts stood trial in the village hall. They were fined heavily for their cruel and lawless behaviour, after which they became close companions of the stocks in the village square for a couple of days, where, not to waste them, any apples that had rotted in the high humidity were utilized by some of the vil-lage lads for target practice. The general opinion was that the sentence had been too lenient.

Meanwhile, Georgiana Griffin began trysting with Master Sevran Shaw.

Rohain went on with her lessons—the study of music and writing, and the warrior's skills. All the while she probed the thin shell enveloping her lost memories. There was that about this place which disquieted her—had disquieted her from the first, even before the coming of the unseelie hoodie crows. Was the island indeed uprooting itself, to float away? If so, where would it go?

Listlessness overlaid all. Along the shores, layers of water came up with a long *swish* as if some sea-lord in metallic robes rushed past in the shallows. Apart from the cry of the wind, that was the only sound. The terns, the sandpipers, gulls, shearwaters, egrets, and curlews seemed to have vanished.

About a week after Whiteflower's Day, Rohain and her companions sat at dinner in the Hall of Tana. Not one diner spoke or lifted a knife. The hounds stood with hackles raised into ridges all along their spines, their lips peeled back off their curved teeth—but it was no intruder they snarled at, only the doors. These moved gently as if guided by an invisible hand. Presently, they began to open and close by themselves. From out in the stables came the hammering of hooves kicking at stalls. On the dinner-table, wine slopped out of the goblets. Salt cellars shuddered, jumped about, and fell over. Above the heads of the diners, high in the belltower, the bells shivered, unseen, as if their cold metal sides had caught some ague. The clappers rocked but failed to kiss the inner petals of the bronze tulips. They did not ring. Not yet.

The maid Annie rushed in, incoherent, shouting something about Vinegar Tom. Starting up from his seat and drawing his sword, the Seneschal ran outside in case she was in danger from pursuit. He saw no creature, eldritch or otherwise. When they had soothed the girl she told them *not* what they had thought to hear, that Vinegar Tom had chased or harmed someone. Instead she said that Vinegar Tom was gone.

That which had guarded the path for centuries had deserted its post. And now it came out that the colt-pixie had not been seen for some time either, or the domestic wights of Tana, or the silkies, or any others of seelie ilk.

'Is it possible the wights have left Tamhania?' Alys of Roxburgh asked.

No one could answer her.

Over the ocean, thunder rumbled. Horses screamed and goblets toppled, spilling their blood-red wine across the linen battle-plain of Tana's dinner-table.

'These quakes . . .' said the Duchess. She did not finish her sentence.

'Should we not leave here?' Rohain said. 'I fear danger walks the isle.'

'I, too, am troubled,' nodded the Bard.

'Yet it is his Imperial Majesty's command that we remain,' murmured Alys. 'A good soldier never disobeys orders. Neither should we.'

'"Tis the sea,' said the Seneschal overheartily. '"Tis choppy these days. If indeed it floats, the island moves roughly over the waves. We're in for another storm, by the sound of it.'

The words fell from his lips like empty husks, and he knew it.

They sat silent again. Still, no one raised a knife. The salt cellar rolled lazily across the table, leaving a silver trail; an arc, a slice of moon, a fragmented sickle.

No mermaid's cry gave warning of what happened next.

Thunder's iron barrel rolled across the firmament, *but there were no thunderclouds.* The seas lurched. Even the warm waters of the sheltered harbour rose in a brisk, pointy dance, but there was no storm—not in the way storms are usually known. For days this went on, and then the ground picked itself up and shook out its mantle. Many villagers rushed outdoors in fright. It became impossible to walk steadily. Windows and dishes broke. At the Hall of Tana, paintings fell from the walls, and in the stables the small bells rang on the bridles hanging from their hooks.

They jingled, those little bells, and then fell silent as the ground stood still again. Next morning, dawn did not come. Beyond its normal bounds, night stretched out like a long black animal.

'Look at the cloud!' cried Viviana, pointing.

The white wreath that continually lurked upon the mountaintop had now darkened to a wrathful gray. It had grown taller, becoming a column. From the top it forked, like the spreading branches of a gigantic, malevolent tree; billowing, blocking sunlight. Beneath its shadow, the mountainsides sloped as green and lush as always, but particles of sand and dirt moved in the tenebrous air, and flecks like black rain or feathers floated—tiny pieces of ash. This dirty wind irritated the eyes, made breathing difficult. The smell of rottenness had increased a hundredfold, and a stink of putrid cabbage invaded everything. To keep out the dust and stench, the islanders wedged shut their doors and windows. They masked their faces.

'Make ready the sea-vessels,' said the Bard. 'Tell the villagers to prepare to leave.'

But Avenel said, 'This is the Royal Isle! Naught can harm us here. Besides, most of the villagers refuse to even consider abandoning their homes.'

The peculiar storm amplified. Lightning flickered, phosphorescent green, but only within the massive pillar that stood up from the mountain, supporting the sky's congestion. On the island, wells dried up. New ones opened. Streams altered their courses as tremors shook the island to its most profound footings. In the village, the mayor called a meeting.

Thorn had told Rohain: *Do not leave the island. Wait for me.*

She must do as he had bidden. Yet no longer was Tamhania the safe haven it had been when he had spoken those words. Rohain's own hand had lit the candle in the Light-Tower, opening the island to the bringers of doom—just as, somehow, she had also led death and destruction to Isse Tower.

And once he had asked, *'Why should Huon hunt at thy heels?'*

The question confounded her, haunted her. Recent events once again brought it to the forefront.

The real facts must be confronted. No matter how she tried to deny it, *something* sought her. Now that she was willing to face the truth, it blazed like words written in fire. It seemed incredible she could have overlooked anything so obvious. *Never* had Scalzo's scoundrels sought her, *never* had Korguth's mercenaries plagued her. All the time there had been one enemy—one *other* enemy with unseelie forces under its sway—an enemy far more terrible than any small-time brigand or charlatan of a wizard.

In Gilvaris Tarv, on the day she had saved the seelie water-horse from enslavement in the marketplace, she had seen a face. Memory now recalled that face in detail. *Curious, it had been. In fact, 'eldritch' was the word that most described it, and 'malevolent'.* Some unseelie thing in the marketplace had spied her at the very instant her taltry fell back, revealing her extraordinary sun-coloured hair. By her hair, perhaps, the creature had recognised her. Perhaps it had known who she had been in her shadowed past. Perhaps, in that past, she had been hunted—but the hunters were thrown off her trail when she lost her face and her voice. Likely, the creature had gone from the marketplace and told of her whereabouts to her true enemy, the Antlered One. It had been after the market-day that suspicious-looking creatures had begun to watch Ethlinn's house. In a stroke of what turned out to be fortune, Rohain had been mistakenly abducted with Muirne. For a time, while they were incarcerated in the *gilf*-house, her whereabouts had passed out of Huon's knowledge.

Rohain pondered on subsequent events. Had the Antlered One got wind of her as she rode with the wagons along the Road to Caermelor? Had he sent the Dando Dogs after the caravan, resulting in the loss of so many lives?

She had eluded him, only to end up at Court where her Talith ancestry was unmasked by Dianella and Sargoth. The wizard had betrayed her to some unseelie minion of the Antlered One, himself not knowing the full extent of what he did, merely wanting her out of the way so that Dianella's path to the throne would be clear. Doubtless, Sargoth had long been allied with the powers of wickedness. He might have known Huon sought for a Talith damsel, and waited until she was out of Caermelor to betray her.

When Sargoth's tidings reached the Hunter, Isse Tower was attacked. Once again Rohain escaped, but now that she had regained both face and voice, Huon knew her. For whatever reason, he had traced her to the haven of Tamhania and knocked on the door. She, in her folly, had opened it and let his foul creatures enter. Why he hunted at her heels, she had forgotten. *He* had not.

'Let us speak no more of the past.' Close at her side, Thorn had

said these words, while he leaned against a narrow embrasure of Isse Tower and talked with Rohain about Winter, and a hawk had hung suspended in the chalice of the sky.

Those effervescent days had been filled with joyousness. Consequently she, not to spoil it, had not spoken to Thorn of the past, nor told him that it could not be recalled. She had not let him know that in her history there might lie some important, hidden truth.

If he was struck down upon the northern battlefields, he would never know. Swiftly she brushed the thought aside; merely the thought of such loss was like a death-wound to her spirit. But if he triumphed in war, how could she ever return to his side, bringing, as she did, this bane, this curse that shadowed her and touched all those among whom she moved? Thorn was a warrior of extraordinary prowess who had proven his efficacy even against the Wild Hunt, but how long could any mortal man stave off such mighty foes? He and his forces could drive them off once or twice, maybe, but ultimately the immortals, with their unseelie gramarye, must win. This was a peril she would not allow herself to bring upon him.

Thorn—will I ever see thee again? Before I do, I must find out what lies hidden in my past. I must discover why Huon pursues me, so that I, and you my love, will know how to deal with this peril.

Iron bells clanged inside Rohain's skull.

For three days the sun had not been seen. Under darkness, the air was smothering—a blanket stinking of brimstone. The island held still, or perhaps it gathered itself together one last time. And those who dwelled upon its flanks were still blind to its nature, deaf to its peril. Or perhaps they did not want to see or hear, for the probabilities were too mighty, too awful to comprehend. It is a human trait, to dwell in danger zones and be astonished when catastrophe strikes.

Then the land stirred again.

In Tana's oak-paneled west drawing room, Rohain sat playing at card games with Edward, Alys, and Thomas of Ercildoune, to escape the grit and stench of the outdoors. On the window-seat beneath wine-hued velvet hangings, Toby plucked a small ivory lute. His fingernails clicked against the frets. Occasionally, distant laughter and squeals drifted in from the nursery, where the children of the Duchess played hide-and-seek.

A butler glided in carrying a tray in his white-gloved hands. He was followed by a replica bearing a similar tray. Placing their burdens on two of a scattering of small, unstable tables, they proceeded to decant hot spike into small porcelain cups. They poured milk from the mouth of a painted jug fashioned as a cow (which had somehow escaped the eye of Tana's majordomo in his thematic pursuit), and offered cherry tarts and cubes of golden Sugar frosted with tiny pictures of sea-pinks.

Candles blazed in lusters and branches—yellow-white shells of light in the gloom. They lit up gilded chairs and tables, couches, silk-upholstered footrests, ottomans with their embroidered bolsters, polished cherrywood cabinets and toy clockwork confections. Roses gushed from porphyry vases.

'Annie saw those flowers today,' commented Alys, taking note of the roses, 'and was horrified. She said that the blossoming of the burnet rose out of its proper season is an omen of shipwreck and disaster. These small islands breed such superstition.'

'Speaking of local vegetation,' said the Bard, 'I was talking to some coral-fishers the other day. There are some on this island who hold that the surrounding mists are not accumulated, attracted, or given off by cloud-leaf. They hold that *duilleag neoil* has nothing to do with them. The waters around Tamhania are always warm. They say the vapors rise because of'—he picked up a card—'a tremendous heat that burns forever beneath the deeps.'

Toby dropped his ox-horn plectrum, then stooped to retrieve it. In the silence, the clockworkings on the mantels clucked like slow insects. Toby resumed playing.

'Did anyone hear anything last night?' asked the Duchess of Roxburgh, leaning forward to put down the Ten of Wands.

'No. I slept well,' replied Edward.

'I heard nothing,' said the Bard, considering his fan of cards thoughtfully. 'But the servants seemed uneasy.'

Rohain upturned the Queen of Swords on the tablecloth of turquoise baize.

'I thought,' she said, 'I dreamed the sound of uncontrollable sobbing.'

The Duchess's cards slipped through her fingers to the floor. A footman ran to pick them up.

'Shall we abandon the game at this point,' suggested Edward, folding his rising sun of painted cardboard leaves and tapping them on the table, 'and take a cup of best Severnesse spike?'

'An eminently practical idea,' replied the Bard diplomatically, stroking his *pique-devant* beard and auburn mustaches. 'Who can think of playing cards on a day like this?'

"Tis a pretty pack.' Rohain examined the interlocking swan design on the back of each rectangular wafer. It called to her mind the tale of a swanmaiden stolen by a mortal man, and she was about to remark on this when a tremendous vibration went through the floor and walls, and a deep groan of agony emanated from all around. Almost simultaneously, a further commotion arose from the floors below.

'What is it? What's amiss?' The Prince started from his chair. A tremendous clamor and clatter rushed up the stairway.

Footmen hurried to the door, but as they opened it a horseman rode through in a sudden gale, ducking his head under the high lintel. He wheeled to a halt before them. The stallion reared and curvetted, shrilling, its hooves slicing the carpets. The iron-shod fore-hooves struck a glancing blow off an ebony table, which flew across the room, its setting of porcelainware and sweetmeats dashing to pieces. Foam flicked from the beast's snorting mouth, showering the crystal vases. In the dark, gusting wind, the curtains of magenta velvet bellied out. The playing cards, all six suits—Wands, Swords, Cups, Coins, Anchors, and Crowns—flew up like frightened seagulls.

'Master Avenel!' cried Edward. He and his companions stared in disbelief.

'Haste, make haste,' cried the Seneschal of Tana, controlling his mount with difficulty. 'I have just come from the house of Lutey. The island is about to be destroyed.'

When the denouement came, it came rapidly. At the Hall of Tana, furniture collapsed. Plaster cracked, loose bricks fell. The belltower shook, from its foundations upward. At last, up in the murky vapors of their eyrie, all by themselves, their ropes dangling untended by any hand, the great bells of Tana's *chastel* began to toll.

Hot and jarred, the sea chopped and changed without rhythm. Up and down the hillsides the fences undulated like serpents. Cracks unseamed their mouths; sand and mud bubbled out. It was almost impossible for anyone to remain on their feet. People stumbled and rolled, clawing at previously fixed objects that proved treacherous. Apple boughs crashed to the ground. Animals ran to and fro in confusion. Amid the black snow, tiny porous stones hailed down, too hot to touch.

Fishing-boats—the entire fleet—made ready to launch.

The false night was so dense now that it was impossible to discern even an outline of the mountain. Where its top should have loomed, there burned a red glare. Over this spurious sunrise strange lightnings snapped continually in an endless display. It looked like a wicker cage of eerie lightworks forming the death-blue, pumping veins of the smoke-tree whose black leaves continued to pour over the nightscape.

The islanders pushed open their doors with difficulty because of the detritus piled up outside. Down from the village to the harbour they fled with their goats, their hounds and horses, their cattle and sheep. Some folk wept; not many—this was a hardy people. Their strings of lamps, like blobs of grazed yellow resin, could hardly be made out in the gloom. Deep drifts of ash and pumice blocked the streets. Larger stones rattled down, causing hurt; a rain of pain. The darkness was so profound, so unnatural, that it was not like night at all. It was a windowless, doorless chamber. Only the tower of coldly flickering lightnings over the mountain could be clearly seen. Generated by tiny fragments of lava in the ash cloud rubbing against each other to build up enormous charges that tore in thundering bolts through the column, it rose to an unguessed ceiling.

The refugees boarded the boats, stepping from the land they knew in their hearts they would never see again. Great waves leapt up as tall as houses and smacked into one another. Through the chaos, the boats bravely put out into the ashen harbour. They sailed across to the Rip and through it, while smoke roiled on the water and fire boiled in the sky. Now blackened by poisonous effluvium, the brass bells of Tana rang out a lonely farewell from the swaying belfry. As the fleet passed the point, a mild glow as of candlelight exuded from the upper room of the Light-Tower.

'The Lightkeeper!' exclaimed Rohain, in the leading ship. 'He is still within!'

'He refused to leave,' said Avenel, at her side.

Already, while the fleet yet rode out of the harbour, the land woke again and shuddered. As if in answer, the Light beamed forth for the last time, pure and white like a Faêran sword cleaving the murk. Then the mountain roared violently, the scarlet glow flared brightly, and a huge wave opened from the shore, almost swamping the ships, bearing them forward. Bombs of burning rock fell hissing into the sea on all sides. Some went through the rigging and landed, red-hot, on the decks, threatening to set the ships alight before the wary crews scooped them in shovels and tossed them overboard. As the last ship passed through the Rip the island writhed. The Light-Tower itself leaned a little, then, very slowly, as if resisting, it collapsed into the sea. All the way down, the Beacon lanced out courageously, a descending white blade, extinguished only when the waves closed over it.

In a shower of darkness and cinders, the vessels plowed across the deep.

Whether they would escape with their lives or not, none could say.

Behind them, the sea-volcano that was Tamhania had become wildly unstable. Some delicate inner balance had been meddled with. Once it had slept. Now it awakened. A heat so great it was almost inconceivable, hotter than the hottest furnace; a heat that had been lying in wait for more than a millennium at the base of a fracture beneath the island, miles under the sea, now was mobilized. Raising a mindless head, it set its huge shoulders—sinewed with magma, veined with fire—against the scabbed-over crust of soil, to split the lid that held it barely in check. The sea-bed struggled. Deep within the mountain, under tremendous pressure, molten rock welled up through fissures. At temperatures of thousands of degrees, it began to form a dangerous mixture with the volatiles in seawater: venomous fumes to rise like serpents out of vents, stinking sulfurs to belch from fumaroles, asphyxiating exhalations to flow invisibly downhill and gather in hollows, acid vapors to slowly eat through whatever they touched, and strong enough to etch glass, fiery ethers to glow in great veils against the sky, explosive gases to burst open the heart of the volcano with a thunderclap.

Like a chimney catching fire, the central vent began to roar. With each new explosion, blocks the size of palaces hurtled up to the surface, ripped from the throat of the vomiting cone. The air filled with flying rocks. Long streaks of flame arched into the air every few moments. Above the vent a cloud boiled out, convoluted like a brain, its cortex twenty thousand feet above sea level.

A downpour of rain mixed with ash fell on the fishing boats. Some substance in this mud glowed in the dark, and soon the masts and decks looked as if they were covered with a myriad tiny embers. Behind the fleet, the steady roar of the dying mountain-island continued, as the boats sailed on through the night—or was it the day? Missiles screamed like unseelie avengers and howled like frights. A subsonic pounding was going on, as though giants worked at their subterranean forges, their hammer blows *thud-thudding* relentlessly on huge anvils, echoing in caverns where nightmarish bellows pulsed, blaring gouts of smoke up through the chimney. Against the blackness of night, roseate fire-curtains gleamed, speckled with gold. Far away on the slopes of tormented Tamhania, jeweled rocks went spitting, spinning over ash wastes where tall fumes leaned now instead of trees. In the harbour, seawater vaporized like immense billows of smoke. Heavy, deadly gases hugged the contours of the mountainsides, streaming down in rivers. Water floated like smoke, gas flowed as if it were liquid.

But the pressure from miles below did not decrease. Tamhania fought, opening new smoking fissures in its flanks, letting the crimson paste ooze out in languid rivers to incinerate and slowly crush the houses of the village. The island bellowed as it threw its guts into the air.

Hours passed. The fleet now sailed under true night, although all celestial lights were extinguished by the tons of ash and fine debris spreading across the upper skies of Erith. The luminous mud scintillated along the boats' rigging. Tamhania was the light of the plenum: a fire-fountain, its noise circling the rim of the world like an iron wheel rolling around a bowl. Floating rocks—porous, gas-filled chunks of pumice like hard, black sponge—made the water hazardous. Infinitesimal specks of ash mixed with spray plastered the faces, clothes, beards, and hair of the refugees. The mixture stung their eyes and curdled to slippery scum on the decks.

As ring-shaped waves rush away from a stone dropped into a pond of still water, so the ocean reacted to the dreadful murmur of the island. The escaping fleet was rocked by ever-larger swells; long copings dividing extreme abysms. As morning was finally reborn, the sun rose dripping out of the sea like a corrupt gem fastened to the sky's filthy cloak. Those who stood on deck looking back, clutching the railings, saw a brilliant burst of light. Soon, over the continual roaring, the sound of a truly enormous explosion came bounding and crashing across the wavetops. It hit the boats with force and passed away to the horizon. The vessels dipped and lurched, but they held together. The passengers did not rejoice. They knew what would follow. Sound travels faster than ripples in water. Heedless of modesty, all the passengers doffed their footwear and outer clothes in case they should be thrown into the water. Many could not swim.

Viviana pinned her locket-brooch to her chemise, and belted on her chatelaine. 'When I come ashore,' she declared bravely, 'I want to have useful articles about me.'

The sun climbed higher. In the middle of the morning, a second massive explosion shook the entire region as the side of the volcano's central vent was blown off, engendering spectacular outbursts of tephra and huge clouds of steam. Its reverberation smote the vessels with an open hand.

'Make ready,' the word passed from vessel to vessel. 'The first wave comes.'

The crew raced to douse most of the sails, leaving a staysail for steering. As they did so, two helmsmen struggled at the wheel to turn the ship until her bowsprit pointed in the direction of the island, far-off and invisible in a smoky haze wandering ghostlike across the sea. The sailors held the rudder steady, keeping the ship's bow pointed into the volcanic storm.

They saw it, before they heard it—a darkness partitioning the sky.

A wall.

A long, long wall with no end and no beginning that seemed to suck up every drop of water before it. It grew in a beautiful glossy curve, like a shell. Inexorable, stupefying, it approached.

'Hold on!' someone screamed pointlessly against the roaring din of this menace. The helmsmen fought to control the wheel. A swift wind drove against the boats—tons of air displaced by tons of water. The wall rushed across the sea to the fleet, gathered itself up and hung over like a shelf. Timbers shifted and squeaked under the onslaught of elemental forces. Besmirched with mud, Rohain clung to the mizzenmast. She had been lashed to it, because she was unable to keep her feet against the wind's muscle. The wind screeched in her ears, vacuuming out all other sound. Looking up, she saw tons of coiling water suspended over her head. Bellowing, the wave came on, up and over. Rohain felt the deck drop away as she was lifted into the air. She held her breath.

Down she fell. The boat fell with her. Blood rushed to her feet, and an explosion of water assaulted the decks.

Somehow the valiant little vessel had ridden up to the crest and down the other side of the wave, gathering so much speed that she buried her bow in the bottom of the trough. Behind the mother wave came her daughters, rank on rank, rearing to a height of ninety feet. Time and again the boat was wrenched high only to race down and bury herself in the deadly darkness of the troughs, with only the stern jutting from the water. There, half-drowned, she would shudder as though contemplating surrender, eventually raising her bowsprit to lift again. As she came up, tons of water would come sluicing down the bows onto the deck.

No human cry could be heard against the roar of wind and sea. Visibility was almost canceled. At a hundred and thirty-five knots, so strong was the wind that passengers and crew must close their eyes lest it snatch out their inner orbits. Closed or open, there was little difference in what could be seen. Night rode down in the wave-troughs, while their ridges bubbled with a crust of scorched foam so thick that it blocked out everything except the tiny rocks that struck like hammers, and the horizontal daggers of rain or spray.

When the waves of the aftershock had passed, Rohain was able to see that the fleet had broken up, dispersed. No evidence remained of the boat carrying the Duchess of Roxburgh and her children. It was impossible to know which vessels had survived. On the far horizon stood a column of gas, smoke, and vapor, thirty miles high. And the second major wave was on its way.

Too soon, it came roaring after its leader. Not a wall, this was a mountain—a moon-tide altered from the horizontal to the vertical. Tied securely to various pieces of equipment on deck, the ladies-in-waiting screamed. Again Rohain's boat lifted over the crest, borne, incredibly, a hundred and ten feet high to glide down the mountain's spine. Yet this time she did not glide—momentum launched her off the top and thrust her down through the centre of the following wave. She emerged on the other side, her passengers and crew struggling for breath, and immediately fell into the next trough, to be submerged again up to the wheel. The battering of noise and water weakened her seams. The boat began to break up, taking in water. Those who were able manned the hand-pumps.

What was it Thomas had said as they boarded? *'Lutey is aboard with us, Rohain. He can never drown.'* Did merfolk swim beneath this leaking nut-shell hull, bearing it up, protecting it, keeping the promise they had made? What of the rest of the fleet? There was no sign, now, of any of them—not even a broken plank.

Ahead, Rohain glimpsed, between leaning hills of liquid, a striated coagulation that might have been land. Under ragged

remnants of sails like street-beggars' laundry the voyagers travelled on, trying to hold a course for this hopeful sign, largely at
the mercy of wind and water. The waves had subsided to sixty
feet. On the sloshing decks, Rohain waited anxiously with
Edward, Ercildoune, Lutey, the village mayor, Viviana, and Caitri,
hoping that it was all over.

Oh, but it is not over, said her heart. *Three crows, there were.
That is the eldritch number. Yan, tan, tethera. Third time pays for
all, they say.*

Robin Lutey held up the mermaid's Comb. On the ivory, the
mesh-patterns of pearls and gold glinted like sunlight through
waves, even through the dimness. Bracing himself against the
boat's canting, he thrust the Comb into Caitri's hair.

'You are but young,' he shouted, his voice barely audible
against the wind and sea. 'Too young to die.'

'Are you suggesting there will be another wave?' yelled Prince
Edward. He was standing beside Rohain, among their bodyguards.

Lutey nodded, held up his index finger.

'One more.'

'In that event, we must all once again be secured to the boat,'
called Rohain.

'Nay!' Lutey replied. 'Remain free, in case the vessel breaks up.'

'If aught should happen, my lady,' bellowed the Bard, close
to Rohain's ear, 'not that aught shall, but should it, thou shalt be
safe. Thou'rt protected. It is necessary thou shouldst know this.
And the Prince also shall be safe, and now thy little maid also.
Rohain, I may never see thee again. There are so many things I
cannot say. My heart is full, howbeit by my honour I may not
unburden it.'

'But no!' she shouted. 'How should I be safe and not you? And
Viviana, and my ladies!'

'Mayhap Viviana too shall live.' His voice sounded hoarse, as if
he had swallowed gravel. 'She told me she was born with a caul
on her head, which is why her mother named her after a sea-witch.
If she carries it with her then verily, she shall not die by drowning.'

'Thomas . . .'

Rohain's eyes were oceans, overflowing.

Far away, on Tamhania, seawater poured into the volcano's ruined vent and hit the hot magma.

Then the world tore asunder with shocking force.

Such a tumult could only have one source. The whole of the island had been blown upward into the air. Once, long ago, born out of the sea, this strato-volcano had arisen. Now, by the same process, it was being destroyed. After its death, the regulation of the markless sea would disguise its latitude, marching over its former position as though it had never existed.

But for now, the blast travelled out in all directions at more than seven hundred miles per hour. At three hundred and fifty miles per hour, the wave hunted it.

Not so much a wave—the third was an entire ocean standing on end, more than a hundred and fifty feet high. It swamped the entire sky. It was the ocean folding in on itself; the ocean turning inside out. It came, and it picked up Rohain's boat, and the boat travelled on its curling crest in a screaming wind while underneath the sea-bed rose and the water shallowed and the wave gathered until it was a hundred and seventy feet tall and beneath the keel, so dizzyingly far below, there was land.

'Stay close to me!' cried Edward, taking Rohain by the waist. She clutched him tightly.

'Farewell, one and all!' called the Bard through gritted teeth.

Time slowed, or seemed to. In a flash, Rohain realised—a wave like this had happened before. This was not the first time a sea-volcano had erupted in Erith.

. . . to the east, two miles from the sea, lies a thing most curious; the ancient remains of a Watership caught in a cleft between two hills.

Was this to be the fortune of her fishing-boat? To be carried in its entirety, along a river valley for two miles and be deposited, a shattered hulk filled with shattered corpses, far above the level of the distant ocean?

Instead, with a sound curiously reminiscent of the plucking of violin-strings, copper nails began to pull free and pop out of the hull's stressed planking. Timbers burst apart. Caitri clung to Lutey.

Viviana's mouth opened like a tunnel of fear. Rohain reached for her, but she and the Prince were flung forth, out into the maelstrom. His hold was wrenched from her waist. Thomas slid away down the vertical deck. Crumbling, capsizing, shattering to fragments, the boat fell down the back of the ocean.

Ash rained down. It rained on and on.

Fine particles infused the air.

The sun, no longer yellow, had metamorphosed to sea-turquoise. A sunset ranged across one third of the sky—such a sunset as had never been seen by the mortal eyes that now beheld it. Flamboyant it was, brilliant, gorgeous. Burning roses formed from rubies were strewn among flaming orange silks, castles of topaz on fire, and great drifts of melting glass nasturtiums. The horizon itself was ablaze.

Long after the sun had disappeared, the dusty air shimmered with rainbows. An emerald nimbus ringed the bitten moon. This then, was Tamhania's epitaph; that its substance would be dispersed all over Erith, bringing night after night of strange beauty, and that wheresoever its fragments touched, the soil would be nourished with the aftermath of its existence, giving rise to new life. And perhaps in that new life would spring an echo of what had once been.

7
THE CAULDRON
Thyme and Tide

Fires in the core of cores lie quiescent;
Once they jetted from its maws, incandescent.
Lava from the magma bath, effervescent,
Nullified all in its path, heat rubescent.
Once upon a cinder cone light flew sparkling—
Now a crater-lake unknown, deep and darkling.

'Dormancy', a song from Taptharatharath

All the time—through the drag and suck, the lift and toss, through the seethe and sudden swell battering ears to deafness, eyes to blindness, skin to numbness, through the forced drafts of brine gulping and gurning in her stomach, the salt stinging her mouth, the dread inbreathing of water provoking a panic of suffocation, her heart racing for air, splashes of red agony on a black ground like an eruption of the lungs; through it all, the object remained beneath Rohain's hand and bore her up: the Hope, the wooden Hope that floated on the top of the ocean.

Another surge, and the buoyant piece of timber scraped on something. Rohain found solidity beneath her feet. She tiptoed on it and it was snatched away, relinquished, abducted, returned. She walked, emerging from the flood. The wood weighed her hand down now—why so faithful? Why could it not leave her? Wiping blur from her eyes with her free hand she looked down. The leaf-ring on her finger was caught in a bent copper nail, partly dislodged and jutting from the fishing boat's figurehead. Thorn's gift had saved her.

Now she leaned over, unhooked the bright metal band, waded to land, and lay down on a muddy knoll above the tide. Her body spasmed as she gave back to the sea the water that had invaded her lungs. Clad only in a pale shift, she sprawled there like a hank of pallid seaweed, long and lank. Somewhere on the sea or under it, her discarded gown floated; a headless, handless specter among specters more truly terrible.

Drying in the mild night within a thin casing of salt and ash, the girl lifted her aching head. She was conscious now of the care-less clatter and tinkle of water chuckling down a stony sluice. A brackish freshet bounced down a rock wall, like a handful of silk ribbons. Rohain drank a long and delicious draft. As she leaned, two articles fell forward and swung on front of her face: her jade-leaved tilhal and the vial of *nathrach deirge*, both strung on strong, short chains about her neck. At her waist the tapestry aul-moniere remained firmly attached, though bedraggled. For the retaining of these precious accessories she was grateful.

She sat by the laughing trickle and looked about in wonder-ment. This was no rocky shore or strand. Farther uphill, trees were growing, with green turf mantling their feet. Perhaps, after all, the ocean had carried her inland. Under the starless sky, its vestigial moon a haloed sliver of bluish green, the savage waters that had spat her out were now receding, as though the tide were ebbing. They seemed to clutch at the land as they dragged backward, scor-ing the turf with their talons. Through the ash haze Rohain saw the mermaid figurehead, wedged between two tree boles. The monstrous wave was shrinking back into itself, leaving behind a swathe of wrenched-up trees, dragged boulders, plowed ground, doomed seaweed, wreckage, flotsam, and a ragged, half-uprooted wattle-bush that shook itself and sprouted a muddy foot whose ankle was encircled with a gold band and whose toenails were painted with rose enamel.

Staggering and slipping through the blowing ash haze, her own feet squelching in sodden turf where alabaster shells lay among bone-white flowers, Rohain seized the foot.

'Via!' she gasped. Relief surged—one other, at least, had survived. Further than that she could not bear to surmise.

Viviana moaned. Rohain helped her from the network of wattle twigs and boughs that had caught her like some flamboyant fish. Scratched and bleeding in her silken shift, the lady's maid could not speak. The only sounds from her were made by the ringing and clashing of the metal chatelettes of the chatelaine fastened to her belt, which had somehow, through the dunking, been spared.

Her mistress supported the court-servant, leading her to the freshet.

'Drink now.'

She drank, and together they stumbled forward. As the salt water receded, it became clear that the wave had deposited both of them midway up a wall of gentle cliffs sloping down to the original sea level, currently lost beneath the retreating flood.

The brownish mist wafted in streamers that occasionally parted. Rohain strained to look ahead through the haze, trying to glimpse humanlike shapes she had earlier seen or imagined. Staunchly the shapes remained—solidifying, growing larger with every step.

Two embodiments coalesced, dark against umber.

Thorn guaranteed that the leaf-ring would allow its wearer to see the truth and not be tricked by glamour.

The cry that issued from Rohain's throat threatened to tear her flesh in its passing, as lava tears at the walls of its vent. The two incarnations paused in ash night and turned around. One of them, Caitri, ran sobbing and flung herself into Rohain's arms.

'Sweet child,' Rohain said over and over, gripping her in a fierce embrace. Presently she asked, 'Who is with you?'

Viviana sank to her knees, coughing. The figure accompanying Caitri took on the ragged form of the sea-mage, Lutey, who knelt at Viviana's side.

'Courage,' he said. 'Courage.'

'Have you seen others?' asked Rohain.

'No,' Caitri responded.

Lutey said, 'A cottage stands yonder, halfway up the cliff. Go there.'

'Will they help us?' Viviana choked piteously.

'That steading is long abandoned,' said Lutey, 'but of those who once dwelled there, one possessed something of the Sight. When she departed, she left behind provisions to succor the needy, for she prophesied that such a dread night as this might come to pass. I know where we have come to land. This entire region, for miles around, is uninhabited by mankind.'

'How do you know this, Master Lutey?' asked Rohain quietly, guessing, even before she saw.

The choppy waters had sunk a short distance down the cliff face. There at the border, between the domain of death-cold fishes that lived without breath and the realm of beings who stalked on legs and died without breath, *she* sat. She was shining wet, with the seawater still coursing down her limbs. No ash-dust troubled the luminous splendor of those peacock-feather disks traced in helixes, the shot silk of the great translucent double fin, the marble whiteness of the slender arms, the spun-glass tresses that shone green-gold like new willow leaves and flowed over the full length of her graceful lines.

'She lifted me up,' said Caitri, suddenly calm and wondering. 'She carried me.'

'You must give me the Comb now, little one,' said Lutey, holding out his hand for the sparkling thing. 'It is time for me to return it.'

For the first time, Rohain noticed how aged the sea-mage looked, how wizened and weighed down with years—far more so than when she had first seen him, only days ago.

'You tried to stop it happening, did you not?' she said, understanding. 'You tried to work against the birds of unseelie. And it took away your strength.'

'Aye, my lady.' His face crinkled in a grin. 'But sooner or later I'd have been reduced to this, in any event. In some ways'—he glanced at the shining scroll of the sea-girl—'in some ways I'm glad 'tis sooner. She has waited long. So have I.'

'But no!' A sob caught in Caitri's throat. 'You must not go, sir. Perilous things of the Deep lurk out there. The Marool—'

The old man smiled, and kissed her. Beneath the erosion of years, the face that he turned back toward the vision from the sea was young, brave, and gentle. The little girl fell silent.

Taking the Comb, Lutey clambered down the slope, straight-backed, dignified, moving slowly but with surprising surefootedness. It seemed that time sloughed from him with every tread, until he sprang forward like a lithe young man. He reached her. A sparkle passed between them. She flipped the sinuous tail and was gone without a splash. He turned, raised his hand in a gesture of farewell, and followed, walking.

Caitri wept. The sea lapped at Lutey's ankles, his knees, his hips. A swell rolled in and disintegrated against the land. Finally the water closed over his head, and he was never again seen by mortal eyes.

Whitewashed and slate-roofed, the cottage on the cliff over-looked a little drowned harbour. Bordered by guardian rowans, the abandoned garden, once tamed, had burgeoned into wild dishevelment. Mostly one plant ramped over it: a sharp-scented thyme that smothered most of the other vegetation, save for some parsnips and carrots gone to seed.

The latch lifted easily. The door had not been locked. Weatherproof, to keep out the strong sea-winds, the dwelling had resisted much of the ash-sifted air. Only a fine layer of dust greeted the visitors.

Inside, they found munificence.

A chest that stood in one corner was filled with peasant garb, plain and ill-fitting but clean and serviceable. Another ark held fishermen's oilskins, gloves and taltries, stout boots. A drawer contained two or three knives and bent spoons, candles, a ball of twine, salt, and a tinderbox. There was a hatchet and trowel, a bucket to fetch water from the well—even a sack of musty oats that, boiled up in an old iron cauldron over the fire, made a supper of edible porridge. Beds of desiccated straw lay piled against the walls. Here, by the light of the fire and a single candle, the three companions lay down to rest after bolting the door to keep out the eerie night.

Out in the yard, silence seemed to press so strongly upon the cottage's walls that they bowed inward. No sound came, not even the bark of a fox, the sob of an owl, the moan of a hunting wind. Leaves hung stifled under laminae of ash.

The three companions were deeply affected by all that had happened. To see an entire island destroy itself, to survive a storm beyond their most bizarre invention, to be battered and almost drowned, to be suddenly and utterly wrenched from friends and companions, to find themselves in helpless isolation—all these experiences were too intense to bear close scrutiny. When the madness of the world exceeds its usual bounds there comes a time when the captives of that madness must either slam shut the gates of their minds or else be invaded, transformed, and broken by absurdity, horror, and grief. By some unspoken agreement the three castaways endeavoured to avoid the topic of the tragedy in which they had been unwilling participants, with all its disturbing ramifications. They had remained alive; they must persist.

'I suppose the previous occupants must have been wealthy as well as generous, to leave so much behind,' mused Caitri, lying back against the straw bedding. 'I wonder why they chose such poor lodgings.'

'Unless they departed in a hurry. I wonder why they left at all,' said Viviana. She glanced quickly toward a window, as though expecting some sudden, malevolent shape to flit secretively past, or dash itself against the panes.

'Somehow I must send word of our survival to His Majesty,' said Rohain. 'How, I cannot fathom.' She swept salty, tousled hair from her forehead. 'I am weary beyond belief.'

They listened, for a while, to the oppressive silence, wrapped like a muffler about the cottage's walls. The candle flickered.

'Peril walks near this place, I fancy,' said Viviana after a while. 'All is too quiet and still. It is uncanny. And the fog in the air makes it seem more so.' She sniffed. 'The stench of brimstone and burning clings about us. Phew! Only the smell of the garden thyme overpowers it.'

Rohain said, 'Yes, there is an uncanny feeling about this place. This night will prove long, I fear. Make the dark hours fly past, Caitri,' she went on, forcing a smile. 'Tell us a story, prithee.'

The little girl settled back against the wall, drawing her cloak around her shoulders. Her vision turned inward as she told of a man who danced with the Faêran for one night only, as he thought, only to discover when day dawned that he had in fact been absent from the world of men for sixty years. As he stepped once more upon the greensward of the mortal realm his footsteps grew lighter and lighter, until he crumbled and fell to the ground as a meagre heap of ashes.

Caitri stopped speaking. Outside the cottage, along the sea-cliff, no living thing stirred.

She sighed. 'You see,' she said, 'he did not return from the Fair Realm until long after his mortal span had elapsed. Time there had a pace different from time here, yet mortal time and Faêran time seemed to somehow interlock at moments.'

'Entrancing tales,' said Viviana, 'but only dreams, in truth; as are all tales of the Fair and Perilous Realm.' She yawned.

Forgetting the story, drifting into sleep, Rohain thought of all the other questions she ought to have asked the sea-mage. Where was this coast on which they had been cast ashore? What fate had met the other boats? Why was this region empty of mortal men? Where was Prince Edward? Had any others survived—Alys-Jannetta? Thomas? *Ah, Thomas—am I doomed always to grieve for kind-hearted Ertishmen torn from me? If they have perished, it is in large part because I insisted on the kindling at the Light. The guilt weighs heavily on me . . .*

Caitri's smothered sobs came softly to her ears. So much had been lost to them all.

And then Rohain allowed herself to think of Thorn and a piercing, sweet sorrow flooded through her.

Oh, my dark fire! My knight of chivalrous grace whose joyous temper overlays depths unfathomable, as light leaves float on a forest pool . . . Severely I miss your amazing touch, your regard of stern tenderness . . . How shall I send word to thee? Shall I ever again find myself at thy side?

Over all these questions hung another, unanswerable, like a somber mantle. This place, this cottage on the cliff, seemed familiar. *Have I been here before?*

During the night, Rohain woke to silence. Or so it seemed. She fancied she had been roused by the sound of snuffling around the house, as if a dog prowled out there. For a time she lay awake—it made no difference whether she kept her eyes open or not, the darkness was impenetrable.

Abruptly, it gave way to dawn. The colour of the air paled to gray and then to the washed-out blue of diluted ink.

'Last night I dreamed that a bird was beating its wings against the cottage door,' said Caitri, waking. Instinctively, Rohain looked up at the ceiling, as though she might stare beyond, to the sky. Fear tightened its noose around her neck.

'We must away as soon as possible,' she whispered. 'Already we have stayed too long.'

Below the cliffs, the sea had receded noticeably. Still the air looked burned, like toast, yet it had cleared a little. The sun remained blue-green, like an opal, hanging in a yellowish sky. Southwest of the little harbour, not far from shore, a tall, cone-shaped island lifted its head. Farther west another reared up, and beyond it several more in a great sweeping curve dwindling around to the northwest.

'The Chain of Chimneys,' Viviana said, as she stood on the cliff top with Rohain and Caitri. 'My governess told me about them when I was a child, in Wytham. I have never seen them before. I think we are on the desolate western coast of Eldaraigne, not far east of—not far from . . .'

'What?' asked Rohain.

'That place. The place we never reached; Huntingtowers.'

They searched along the shore, calling, but no other survivors could be found. In the trees farther down, they discovered a few fish that had been caught among the branches and left by the receding wave, to suffocate in the air. These victims they fried for breakfast, since the bag of oats was small and would not feed them for long.

'The oats are our only provisions,' said Rohain, 'and they will run out after a few days. Time is not limitless either. For now we must rest and regain our strength, but when we leave here on the morrow, you two must take the oat-bag and follow the coastline to the southeast. Make for the Stormriders' Hold at Isse Tower, keeping well away from the Ringroad and its dangers. Tell the Relayers to take word to His Majesty that I am secure.'

'Ugh! That Tower is *traiz olc*,' muttered Viviana.

'My mother is there, at Isse,' said Caitri, fingering the miniature she wore on a chain around her neck. 'I would that she and I had been placed in service elsewhere. It is a dreadful pile, that Tower. What has it do with you, my lady? Why did you visit there?'

Rohain told the little girl how she had once served alongside her in the Seventh House of the Stormriders. After the tale ended, Caitri waxed pensive.

'So, you were he,' she said at last. Strange events had ceased to astound her.

'Yes.'

'There were some marks on your flesh when they brought you in.'

'I know. My face was disfigured by paradox ivy. My throat— by something else.'

'And your arm also. It looked as though a band or bracelet had dug into your wrist. I could not help noticing. I felt sorry for you. After a time, the weals faded.'

'I do not remember any marks on my wrist.'

All fell silent.

Eventually, Rohain said, 'I have here a vial of Dragon's Blood, see?' She produced the tapestry aulmoniere, which still enclosed the swan's feather and Thorn's gift. '*Nathrach deirge* it is called, yet 'tis not the blood of dragons but an elixir of herbs. It gives warmth and sustenance. You shall take it with you. Our ways must part here. Viviana, you say Huntingtowers lies close by. I shall go and seek it. No, prithee, do not protest! It would be far more perilous for you to accompany me than to do anything else. I am Huon's quarry. This I have come at last to understand, and I know that he will never give up until he finds me. But I do not know *why*.

'As a vulture in human form once pompously stated, "knowledge is power", and if I can find out why I am Huon's target, perhaps I shall have a better chance of eluding him. After all's said and done, there is only one way for me to discover the reason he hunts me. I must retrace my footsteps in earnest. Once, I tried it, and failed. This time, either I will succeed or Huon will win. But until I meet or defeat my doom there will be no safety for those I love. Those who accompany me anywhere shall become his quarry as much as I.'

'But Your Ladyship must come to the Stormriders' Tower yourself, to send the message to Caermelor that you are safe,' Viviana said earnestly. 'Otherwise, how shall we be believed?'

'I wish that none should know my whereabouts. Not even His Majesty. Tell them that I live, send word to His Majesty, but never reveal my purpose or destination. I do not want others to come seeking after me; they would be seeking their doom.' Turning her face away she murmured softly, 'Anyway, I am as good as dead already.'

'In Caermelor they would never let it rest at that,' argued Caitri. 'They would extract the truth from us by fair means or foul. And then they will come after you, for your own good.'

Rohain was forced to concede the truth of this assertion.

'In that case, do not admit that you have seen me at all. Then they shall have no reason to ask further—' She broke off. 'Ah, but to leave His Majesty uninformed cuts me to the quick. Yet if there is no other way to keep them from me . . .'

'We shall not go off without you,' burst out Viviana. 'We shall not leave you in the wastelands.'

'I am able to survive on my own. I have been taught how to find food in the wilderness. This ring I wear, engraved with leaves, has some charm on it, although whether it is strong enough to ward off the Wild Hunt I do not know. I tell you, I must go, and it must be alone and speedily. I am sure that Tamhania's ruin was brought about for the purpose of destroying me or flushing me out of my refuge. My guess is, if such strong forces have been sent against me, wielding the powers of both sea and fire, they will wish to know whether they have succeeded in their mission. Immortal, they will not rest until they are certain of it. Perhaps even now they have learned that I live, and that I walk in this forgotten place. It is possible that as we speak they are drawing nigh. I dare not stay in one place for too long. Haste is imperative.'

'But Your Ladyship is to be Queen-Empress!' Viviana burst out in amazement. 'What is this talk of pursuit and danger? The Dainnan shall guard you. *His Imperial Majesty* shall be your protector. There can be no greater security than that.'

'There is no security against that which threatens me. Do you think mortal arms and wizards' charms can stand against the most malign and feared of eldritch princes? Can the Dainnan blow an island apart?'

'I beg to differ, ma'am. Tamhania was a sleeping volcano. It might have awoken at any time. It destroyed itself with its own life-spirit. I'll warrant the three hoodie crows, great and malevolent though they doubtless are, would not be mighty enough to marshal the elements of heat and pressure.'

'Perhaps not, but Huon's birds set the machinery in motion.'

'Huon's birds?' repeated Caitri. 'My lady is mistaken. Huon commands no birds—at any rate, not in any tale I have heard. His terrible riders and horses and hounds are what he hunts with. Sometimes he enlists spriggans to ride crouching on the cruppers of the fire-eyed shadow-steeds, but no birds. The Crows did not fly at the behest of the Antlered One.'

'You are very learned!' exclaimed Rohain between astonishment and doubt.

'My mother taught me much. She is wise in eldritch lore. Besides, in all of Master Brinkworth's tales there was never a mention of hoodie crows flying with the Wild Hunt.'

'Tarry!' said Rohain quickly. 'Say no more. Your words discomfit me. I thought I knew my enemy but once again I am thrown into chaos and confusion. If Huon did not send the birds, then what did?'

'I know not, but I do know they might sniff you out,' said Caitri. 'Spriggans will, at any rate. They have crafty noses and can trace trails in the same way hounds course after scent, only better. I think they might know the scent of you. They ravaged your chamber at the Tower. And by now, they must know your looks.'

'Indeed they must,' agreed Rohain. 'I fear I betrayed myself in the marketplace of Gilvaris Tarv. These are two problems I do not know how to resolve.'

'That stytchel-thyme all over the garden has a perfume strong enough to cover any odour,' Caitri pointed out. 'You might journey incognito, if masked with the fragrance of it.'

'Caitri, do not *encourage* Her Ladyship to pursue her wild goose chase!' said Viviana.

'Nothing can sway me,' said Rohain. 'I will go to Huntingtowers.'

'But the Wild Hunt issues from that place!'

'Usually at the full of the moon, they say. By my reckoning, we are very early in the month of Duileagmis. The old moon has almost faded. The new moon is yet unborn.'

Viviana sighed deeply. 'Well then, if you must, m'lady. And if there is anything I can do to keep you safe, I shall do it. So, if 'tis disguise you're after, I can help.'

''Tis not more than six or seven leagues due west of here, by my reckoning,' said Viviana, trying to recall the maps her governess had pinned upon the walls of the nursery, 'that horrible place, I mean. A swift all-day's walk.'

In the lonely cottage above the ocean, the courtier had finished dyeing her mistress's golden hair brown, using a crudely made concoction of boiled tree-bark. Now she set about stitching a half-mask for Rohain's eyes and forehead. Viviana was never one to be unprepared. The versatile chatelaine had come through the shipwreck, still tied to her waist-girdle. From its chains dangled various chatelettes made from rustproof materials: brass scissors, a golden etui with a manicure set inside, a bodkin, a spoon, a vinaigrette, a needle-case, a small looking-glass, a cup-sized strainer for spike-leaves, a timepiece that had stopped, and whose case was inlaid with ivory and bronze, a workbox containing small reels of thread, an enameled porcelain thimble and a silver one, silver-handled buttonhooks and a few spare buttons—glass-topped, enclosing tiny pictures—a miniature portrait of her mother worked in enamels, several rowan-wood tilhals, a highly ornamented anlace, a penknife, an empty silver-gilt snuffbox, and a pencil. Only the notecase had been ruined by the salt water.

''Tis a wonder all that motley didn't pull you down like a millstone,' remarked Caitri.

'I carry my caul,' Viviana said demurely, returning a needle to its horn case, which was set about with cabuchons. 'M'lady, with this half-mask over your eyes, and the lower part of your face well-kohled with chimney-soot, you will look like some filthy country itinerant, begging your pardon. Whether you are lad or wench none will discern, if we bundle you in enough rags. And with a little stytchel-thyme rubbed on, any creature that sees you or catches your scent won't be any the wiser.' She cocked her head to one side and gazed critically at Rohain. 'I must admit, it seems a shame, ma'am, to spoil a beauty of the rarest sort—for upon my word, never was such a fair face seen at Court or anywhere else for that matter. 'Tis no wonder His Imperial Majesty was smitten.'

'Mistress Wellesley!' remonstrated Caitri, now schooled in etiquette. 'How boldly you speak before Her Ladyship!'

'Speak plainly before me always, please,' said Rohain absently, her mind on other matters. 'You should both know I always require frankness and do not consider it an impropriety.' She tweaked a lock of her tangled hair over her face to examine its new colour.

'Well, if 'tis frankness you are after, my lady,' said Viviana, 'let me speak my mind now that those other ladies are no longer fluttering about you—*sain* them, I hope they may be safe on land. I do believe you are a lost princess who's slept for a hundred years and been awoken.'

Rohain laughed. 'Thank you for your kind words. I would it were so, but I fear it is not. I would augur that I am by birth greatly inferior to royalty.'

'What exactly do you hope to find at Huntingtowers, m'lady?' asked Caitri.

'I do not know.'

'And if you find nothing?'

'I will keep searching. I have no choice. I am driven.'

Caitri seemed about to say something else, but thought better of it.

That night the snuffling and sniffing sounds came again around the cottage, and a tapping at the window, soft and insistent. A wordless, muttering drone started up. The three sleepers woke and sat still, not moving so much as a toe. They held their breath until they could hold it no longer, and then expelled it in long, silent sighs, fearful that even the slightest noise would betray them.

Toward dawn, the sounds ceased.

In the morning Rohain bade farewell to her companions. Her sense of loss and desolation was magnified by this parting. Always, the burden of guilt associated with the destruction of the island oppressed her; inwardly she lamented for Edward and Thomas, for Alys and Master Avenel and all the other friends she had lost to the violence of fire and water.

She trudged alone to the top of the cliffs and halted, turning to look back at the brooding expanse of the sea. Beneath a leering sky, it was striped with many shades of gray from ashen to lead. The symmetrical cones of the presumably dormant Chimneys stood sentinel, waves outlining their shores with froth. Two petrels winged across the sky. Far below, the cottage looked tiny, like a mantelshelf ornament. After a few more steps it was lost to view altogether. Stunted tea-tree scrub grew on the cliff top, spiking the air with the tang of eucalyptus. In the far distance a disused Mooring Mast stood, a dark web sketched against smudged skies.

This is not the first time I have trodden this path, thought Rohain, without knowing why.

The sharp smell of thyme permeated her disguise—her clothes and knapsack, the brown and lusterless hair combed close about her face to obfuscate her features, the half-mask across her eyes and brow, her roughly kohled jaw. In a mustard-coloured kirtle and snuff-coloured surcoat, a plain leather girdle and an oilskin cloak and taltry, she bore no resemblance to an elegant Court lady. Her slenderness was lost beneath bulky folds.

Is it my fate to go always disguised?

Under the oddly-hued sun, whose face had been transformed by the death of Tamhania, it seemed to Rohain that she no longer moved in the world she had known. Duileagmis, the Leafmonth of Spring, put forth a bounty of darling buds whose colours appeared altered by the stained atmosphere. Greenish flowers bestarred bilious marram grasses, their perfumes dust-clogged. Rohain stooped swiftly. With a knife obtained from the cottage on the cliff, she sliced at some vegetation, hacking off scurvy grass and the fleshy leaves of samphire. She had recognised this wild food from Thorn's teachings. Chewing some, she tucked the rest into her belt.

Once again, she looked back toward the ash-fogged sea. From this angle it gave the illusion of rising up in a broad band, higher than the land on which she stood. As she hesitated, she spied a movement in the scrub. It issued from behind a dune and made off in the direction of the cottage. The thing had a wightish look, no doubt of it. At the same time, dark dots in the southern sky swelled, proving themselves not to be the sea-eagles she had at first taken them for.

Stormriders!

A desire for concealment gripped her. She dashed for cover in a tea-tree thicket. The company of riders swept over, following the shoreline at a low altitude. Thrice they circled the vicinity of the cottage, swooping in close over the roof.

There was little doubt that the Relayers were scouring the coast for survivors of Tamhania's disaster. Rohain hoped fervently that Viviana and Caitri, wherever they were, would wave down the Stormriders and be taken to safety at the Tower on eotaur-back. But wights were abroad too, it was plain. Even in daylight they were on the move. The creature from behind the dune had headed away with a purposeful air that boded ill. She and her companions had not left the bountiful cottage a moment too soon. As soon as the Stormriders had flown away, Rohain hurried onward.

Farther inland, coastal vegetation gave way to lightly wooded hills. Here grew hypericum with its yellow cymes. Hurriedly she gathered it by the armful for its wight-repellent properties, binding the bunches with twine to hang them about her person alongside the stytchel-thyme. Looking up from her work, she made out the distant trapezium of an apparently flat-topped mountain dominating the murky horizon.

On she went. Under her feet, little tracks were born, ran dipping and climbing through the trees and faded among the turf. Among the bushes, leaves stirred. There came a faint, metallic *ching*. Rohain halted.

'Come forth,' she ordered loudly.

More rustlings and a brittle snap were followed by the appearance of Viviana and Caitri from a clump of callistemons.

'You stepped on a twig,' Caitri accused Viviana.

'And I did not!'

Rohain said, 'Ever since I left the cottage I have been hearing you two following me. A herd of oxen might have progressed more quietly. You have no woodcraft whatsoever, and Viviana's chatelaine rings like all the bells of Caermelor. I hoped you might give up. I wished you might attract the attention of those Stormriders and go with them. Turn back now, while you are yet far from Huntingtowers.'

'No.'

'This is to be no picnic in the King's Greenwood.'

Sulkily, the two damsels glared at their mistress. They did not reply.

'Those who walk at my side do so at their peril!' fumed Rohain. She then fervently besought them to leave her, in an exchange that lasted a goodly while—time they could ill afford—but they were adamant in their refusals.

It occurred to Rohain that she might easily abandon them and slip away on her own, drawing off the Hunt. She did not entertain the thought for long. Two untutored maidens, roaming out here without even the benefit of her limited knowledge of survival in the wilderness, must surely perish. Either way, there seemed scant hope of saving the lives of these faithful companions. There was no choice—she must accede at last to their wishes.

'Well,' she said briskly, 'if you are prepared to meet your dooms at such an early age, who am I to stop you? Be it on your own heads. But move discreetly. We are looked for.'

'We spied the Stormriders,' said Viviana. 'Here is your elixir, m'lady.'

'Worse things than Stormriders are abroad,' replied her mistress, accepting the vial and rehanging it around her neck. 'Come. The wind is in the west. We only have to keep our backs to it.'

Chains pulled down Rohain's heart. She foresaw the spilling of the blood of her loyal friends, and guilt flooded her conscience. When she faced the direction of Huntingtowers, an undefined fear also began to take root.

As they hastened along the way, to thrust aside dread she pointed out useful wildflowers, and in a low voice imparted knowledge gleaned from Thorn in the wilderness.

'In tales, adventurers merely stroll along through wood and weald, pulling wild berries and nuts off the hedges,' said Caitri.

'Yes, I have noticed that,' said Rohain. 'Obviously, they only go adventuring in Autumn, the season of ripe fruits.'

'And they do not die of cold,' added Viviana. 'In tales they merely lie down to sleep wrapped in their cloaks, even on bitter nights, with no fire or Dragon's Blood to warm them.'

'Sheer fiction,' said Rohain firmly. White umbels of wild carrot nodded in the breeze, alongside the pinkish-green bells of bilberry. The travellers passed banks of pimpinella, sporting its flat-topped flower heads like lacy plates. 'Common centaury,' instructed Rohain, indicating a herb. 'A bitter tonic can be made from an infusion of the dried plants. Dock leaves for nettle stings. Loosestrife for henna dyes, pretty hemlock, all lace and poison. Poppies for torpid illusions.' She astonished herself with her own erudition. 'Here's chicory. The leaves can be eaten, the roots roasted.'

''Tis a veritable pantry out here,' marvelled Viviana. 'A pharmacopeia.'

'In sooth,' affirmed Rohain, 'but most of it does not taste very nice.'

Everywhere in this pathless land, Spring wildflowers nodded, but there was no time to stop and examine them closely. Instead, Rohain was compelled to rush across the face of the land under unfriendly skies, toward the very bastion of all things unseelie.

'I feel a certain nostalgia for life on the road,' she said, brushing with her fingertips the leaves of an overhanging elder-bough.

'You are bold and brave, my lady,' said Caitri.

'Mayhap. I am bold but I can be craven, I'm free but I'm caged, I'm joyful but I grieve, Caitri, like everyone else. But do not call me by my title now, or even by my name—we might be overheard.'

'What name will you be called instead, my la— my friend?' stuttered Viviana.

'I wish to be called Tahquil. 'Tis a name I heard once, at Court, and did not mislike. It will suffice.'

'A strange-sounding, foreign name. It has the ring of Luindorn.'

'Indeed, I believe it originates from that country. I heard tell it means "Warrior", in feminine form. And warrior I must become. I intend to fight on, despite that fate throws turmoil at me again and again. Whether I will be defeated, I cannot guess.'

After a brief halt for an unappealing meal of cold porridge and samphire leaves, the three companions followed a flowery ridge up wooded slopes and over a shoulder of the hills into wild meadows that once had been well-tended farmlands. Abandonment had made wild the overgrown hedges, the deep brakes of flowering briars. Choked drainage-dikes provided a haven for marsh pennywort, bog asphodel, sedges, and rushes. Under the hedges grew foxgloves and tall spikes of woundwort—'A styptic, used to staunch the bleeding of injuries,' observed Rohain—and white deadnettles, whose dry hollow stems she collected in a bunch.

'Used in concoctions?' inquired Viviana.

'Used to make whistles.'

As she scanned the landscape for provender, words of Thorn's came back to Rohain-Tahquil. He had said, *there is no need to hunger or thirst in the lands of Erith . . . When all else fails, there is always Fairbread.*

The thought brought reassurance.

Later in the afternoon, tattered clouds began to move across the sun's face. A wind gusted, blowing up leaves and dust in sudden spurts. A few spots of dirty rain spattered down. Worse than bad weather, uneasiness crept over the travellers—a cooling of the blood. Rohain-Tahquil shivered, the nape of her neck prickled. Time and time again she would whirl rapidly, knife in hand, only to face emptiness. Yet she could swear she had sensed something following behind. She kept the knife ready in her hand. By unspoken agreement, the companions kept under shelter as much as possible, creeping cautiously from tree to tree or scuttling quickly across open glades. Always their heads turned this way and that as if they expected to see dark shapes of an antlered horseman and other fell manifestations watching them from the shadows, ready to spur forward and ride them down.

Ever ahead loomed the low, flat-topped trapezium of the cauldron-mountain, dark through the haze. The closer they approached it, the heavier was the hush that fell on the landscape. Back along the coast, magpies and larks had warbled their pure bell-tones. From every bush and tree had issued shrill twitterings and pipings. As they pushed farther inland, the birdsong had diminished without the travellers noticing. Now they became aware of a quietude eased only by the murmur of the wind in the leaves.

Acid rain came sluicing down in drowning sheets, hissing in the dust until it made mud of it, before settling down to a steady patter and trickle. Made corrosive by the oxidation of atmospheric nitrogen and brimstone gases from the eruption, water dripped down the collars of the walkers' oilskins, off the edges of their fishermen's taltries, and into their eyes.

'I'd rather an unstorm than this,' grumbled Viviana, shouting to be heard above the downpour. 'This rain bites. It stings.'

'Hush,' warned Rohain-Tahquil. 'Something might hear us.'

As the sun dipped behind their backs, the shower eased. The land had begun to rise steeply. Emerging from a belt of oaks they saw the great sheared-off cone rising ahead of them; the caldera of Huntingtowers, its lower versants leprous with stunted vegetation, pimpled with the low mounds of old, forsaken diggings.

It seemed desolate. Nothing stirred. The ancient caldera lay silent and still. In its mouth where once deadly fires had raged, the waters of the lake were deep, dark and cold.

Now that they stood on its slopes, breathless apprehension laid hold of the damsels. It was so strong it was almost intolerable.

The light was fading. In the east, long clouds shredded to black ribbons. No moon came up behind the summit of the blunted cone.

'I shouldn't like to be any closer to that place at night,' said Rohain-Tahquil.

They found shelter in a mossy stone ruin that had once, in ages long past, conceivably been a byre. Honeysuckle and traveller's joy formed a roof over the few remaining, slug-haunted walls. Against these they piled dry bracken to serve as a bed. Not daring to light a fire, they unwrapped the last slabs of cold porridge from their dock leaves and dined in silence. Rohain-Tahquil offered a sip of *nathrach deirge* all around. Warmed, but wet and cheerless, they huddled together.

'I did not know it would be like this,' complained Viviana. 'I hate slugs.'

'They like you,' said Caitri, subtracting one from Viviana's sleeve. 'Anyway, you said you wanted to come,' she added primly.

'I said I wanted to come but I never said I would not grumble.'

The malachite oval of the sun strayed into a magnificent posteruption sunset, a drifting flowerscape in a profusion of marigold, carnation, primrose, gentian, and lilac—colours that would bleed softly into the air and hang there in frayed, cymophanous striations like shang-reflections for hours after the sun had wasted away.

'We have been fortunate to discover this niche,' said Rohain-Tahquil with a new sense of authority born of her limited knowledge of survival. 'Sometimes farmers inscribed runes into the walls of these animal pens—charms to ward off unseelie wights. See here—' With a loose rock she scraped away a thick nap of moss. 'Some symbols are cut into the stones. They are worn shallow now and hard to see. Still, they may yet hold some efficacy.'

'Of course, all the lesser wights have spied us already,' said Caitri. 'It is to be hoped that they will be deterred by our iron blades and tilhals and salt, and by these great bunches of hypericum.'

'And it is to be hoped they will not go telling their greaters,' said Viviana, using a silver needle from her chatelaine to punch holes in a stalk of deadnettle.

'I have been told that eldritch beings do not cooperate like that, not in the way of our kind,' said Rohain-Tahquil, crushing yet more thyme leaves to release their penetrating aroma. 'Not unless they're forced, by threat or bribe.'

'Some have their own leaders,' said Caitri. 'The siofra bow to their Queen Mab, for example; their little queen no bigger than a man's thumb.'

'Even so,' replied Rohain-Tahquil, 'but fortunately the siofra are given more to glamourish trickery than to war. Their tiny spears would prick no more than a thistle would. Once I travelled with a road-caravan which was dispersed and ravaged by unseelie wights, but I surmise it was not the result of a planned and concerted effort on their part. Many of them happened to be crossing the Road at that time and by ill chance we moved in their way.'

It came to her again that perhaps Huon had planned the devastation of the caravan. But no—hindsight and reason told her there were significant differences in the method of attack. The Wild Hunt had mounted a full-scale, coordinated assault directly on the Tower, while the wights of the Road had appeared at random, following their own hostile instincts rather than obeying a leader.

'Long before that time,' she went on, 'I learned something of the ways of wights from a fellow traveller. Like all creatures of eldritch, the fell things of unseelie are amoral. Left to their own devices they are arbitrary in their choice of victims, neither punishing the bad nor letting alone the good. Spriggans are trooping wights, to be sure, and they have a chieftain—nominally, at any rate—but most unseelie wights are solitary by nature. They do not hold meetings or discussions, they simply act in accordance with the antipathy that drives them. As such, they are the more terrible, being an ungoverned—I will not say lawless, for they are subject to the rigorous laws of their kind—an ungoverned battalion of man-slayers, a division without a major-general, a corps without a head. Yes, a headless horseman would be an apt symbol. But I have said enough, enough to give you nightmares. Sleep now. I shall take the first watch. Caitri, did you want to tell me something?'

Caitri drew breath and looked at her mistress. Then she shook her head and turned away with a sigh.

There being no moon, and the stars being hidden by the last aerial memories of Tamhania, the night waxed as thick as pitch. The wind had dropped. Strangely hushed was the landscape, and devoid of movement. Time dragged on, with no way to mark the hours. A dark melancholia seeped up from the ground. The thoughts of Rohain-Tahquil strayed to Thorn, encamped in the north with his men. This night he would speak and laugh, but not with her.

Not with her.

Tears welled at the inner corners of her eyes. They were tears for Thorn, and for the young Prince and the others who had been subjected to the wrath of Tamhania because of her inexcusable stubbornness. Could her culpability ever be absolved? She thought not.

Slugs meandered across her skin. She flicked at them. Toward what she guessed to be midnight, a sound came through the gloom. Something was coming, *brush, brush, brush.*

It stopped.

She ceased to breathe.

It came again, *brush, brush, brush,* and this time she thought it was accompanied by a dull clanking as of several links of a heavy chain striking together. She strained into the darkness until she fancied her eyes must be bulging from their sockets. Nothing was visible. Groping for the sharp knives she had brought from the cottage, she held them ready in both hands. *Brush, brush, brush,* something came, until it stopped right at the doorstep of the ruined shelter.

A sudden wind blasted Rohain's face. In the sky, clouds of vapor and ash parted momentarily. Dimly the stars shone out. Standing silently in front of the hideaway of crumbling stone was a black dog, huge and shaggy, the size of a calf. It stared with great saucer-eyes as bright as coals of fire.

Tahquil-Rohain's hand groped for the tilhal of jade-carved hypericum leaves that hung beside the vial at her neck. She gripped it tightly. Her thoughts flew to Viviana and Caitri, asleep and innocent at her back.

Let them not wake now, or they will cry out.

There must be no sound, nor sign of fear. This Black Dog might be benign or malign. With luck, it might be a Guardian Black Dog, one of those that had been known to protect travellers. Yet again, it might be one of the unseelie morthadu. In that case, one must not speak or try to strike it, for the morthadu had the power to blast mortals.

She stared at the apparition and it stared back at her. Her body ached with the tension of keeping perfectly still.

It was said that the sight of the morthadu was a presage of death. Whether the thing now before Tahquil-Rohain represented succor or calamity, there was no way of finding out. She sat, rigid as steel, avoiding the burning scarlet gaze, using every ounce of her strength to prevent herself from betraying her fear by the slightest twitch and thus yielding power to the creature.

Toward midnight, the Black Dog was not there anymore.

She kept watch until dawn.

At first light, Tahquil-Rohain roused Viviana to take her turn at the watch. She did not mention their night visitor. No paw marks remained in the sifting ash layer to betray what had come and gone in the night. Tahquil-Rohain surmised there were two possibilities—that the Black Dog was seelie, and had guarded them against some unimaginable menace, or that it was one of the morthadu and had, hopefully, been warded off by one or more of the charms they carried. Either way, she and her friends were safe, for now. She warmed her stiff sinews with a sip of *nathrach deirge*, rolled herself in her cloak, and slept.

When she awoke a third possibility came to her—that the Dog had been unseelie, and had made sure they stayed put all night before going off to spread the news of their whereabouts to others who might be interested. Quickly they departed from the ruin.

Daylight dribbled through clouds and fog. Breakfastless, the travellers climbed among the overgrown mullock heaps of the redundant mines that pocked the foot and heath-covered skirts of the mountain. All the while, the desire to hide pressed on them until it became almost overpowering. Eldritch gramarye seemed to crackle in the air, although nothing untoward could be seen or heard. Nothing was audible at all, in fact, save the wind soughing in their ears. Continually they glanced at the skies and to right and left, every nerve stretched, poised to dive for cover or run for their lives at the first sign of any living thing.

Over their heads, the rim of the caldera hung halfway up the sky. It blocked from view everything within its black walls, including the mysterious architecture of complex towers that, as legend had it, was the stronghold of Huon and his ghastly following. From here the Wild Hunt would put forth on the three nights of every full moon, to sweep out across the countryside and fall upon the unwary, doing to them what harm they chose.

Or not.

Messages received during the sojourn on Tamhania indicated that since the attack on Isse Tower, the Hunt had not been seen to ride . . .

Viviana said, 'My la— Tahquil, there are too many of these slag-heaps—so many pitfalls and potholes. We must be wary. One false step might see one of us toppling down some hidden shaft. The very ground is treacherous. Many places have subsided, while others look to be in danger of collapsing.'

'Wisely spoken, Via. You and Caitri must sit here in the shelter of this scrubby brake. I will wander alone awhile.'

'It is so perilous, ma'am! What do you seek, exactly?'

'I cannot say.'

'Every bush and twig hides something that is ardent to harm us, I am certain. Can we not now go back?'

'I have no choice. I am driven to wander here until I find some clue or key, or perish. There is no life for me in the world if I do not find an answer.'

'And maybe if you do,' said Viviana.

'My—' Caitri twisted her fingers together.

'What is it, Caitri? If you have something of importance to impart to me, say it now.'

'No. No, it is nothing.'

'Stay here.'

'Where are you going?'

'To the very gates of Huntingtowers. I *forbid* you to follow. Wait for me. If I am not back by nightfall, leave with all speed.'

Tahquil left them sitting with their arms about each other; a pathetic picture, like a charcoal sketch of two orphaned waifs. She walked on, stumbling on clods, rocks, and freshly turned dirt, making sure she walked sunwise—for luck and protection— around the eroded mullock heaps. She recalled from descriptions given to her at Isse Tower that somewhere to the right lay a loop of the Ringroad; a section that was dreaded by road-caravans. But this did not concern her. It did not lie in her path. A low cliff did— she changed direction to walk parallel to it, under its briar-tangled overhang.

A creeper trailed across the ground. Its five-pointed leaves were glossy and dark green. Between them sprouted tiny inflo- rescences, pale green like the phosphorescence on rotting corpses. The plant attracted her attention. When her ankle brushed against it, fire ripped through her flesh. She jerked away.

Paradox ivy! You cursed leaf!

She avoided it. In doing so, she missed seeing a mineshaft far- ther along, teetered on the edge of inviolate darkness, and overbalanced, but in the last instant she was able to throw herself backward. To break her fall she flung out her arms, but stones met her as she landed. She lay winded, her hands scrabbling at rubble and weeds.

Rising to her feet painfully, awkwardly, she noticed a scintilla of gold that winked, once, in the corner of her left eye. Where her hands had clutched the ground, something lay uncovered. She picked it up, brushing away the caked dirt.

And something like a memory spun before her eyes.

The ground emptied from beneath its feet. It hurtled downward, to be brought up on a spear-point of agony. A band around its arm had snagged on a projection. The scrawny thing dangled against the cliff face, slowly swinging like bait on a hook.

Then slowly, with great effort, it lifted its other arm. Bird-boned fingers found the catch and released it. The band sprang open and the creature fell.

The band. A bracelet, gold, with a white bird enameled on it. This she held in her hand.

And knew it belonged to her.

The world faded.

Another took its place.

8
AVLANTIA
Quest and Questions

'Tis rumored that the Piper will come soon
And lead us all to Reason with his tune.
New day shall dawn for those who wait, no doubt—
And through the forests, laughter will ring out.

TRADITIONAL FOLK SONG

I n ancient times, when the Ways between the Fair Realm
and Erith were still open, of all the races of Men the Talith
were most favoured by the Faêran—or so it was said. The
people of that northern race were tall and golden-haired, elo-
quent, ardent in scholarship, delighting in poetry, music, and
theater, skilled in the sports of field and track, valorous in war.
Avlantia was their country, and this sun-beloved land was split
into two regions—in the west, Auralonde of the Red Leaves; in the
east, Ysteris of the Flowers.

The eringl trees of Auralonde grew nowhere else in Erith.
Unlike the thorn bushes shipped from the cooler south to be
planted in rows for hedges, their boughs were never bare, for they
could not know the touch of snow in these warm climes. Their
newly budded leaves glowed briefly green-gold. Unfurling, they

swiftly deepened to red-gold, bronze, amber, and scarlet. The roofs of the eringl forests burned deep wine-crimson, and the glossy brown pillars supporting them were wound about with trails of a yellow-leaved vine. Fallen leaves mingled in a bright embroidery on the forest floors, buttoned with fire-bright hemispheres of mushrooms, forming a richly patterned carpet fit for royalty.

Branwyddan, King of the Talith, kept court in Auralonde at Hythe Mellyn, a mighty city built of the golden stone called mellil, which gleamed in the sunlight like pale honey. Tier upon tier, the city's shining roofs, spires, and belfries rose upon the hillside, crowned by the King's palace. Neat shops and taverns bordered the side-streets. Tall and imposing houses flanked the city square, which was overlooked also by the domed Law Courts and the gracious columns of the Council Chambers. In stone horse-troughs, white doves flurried on the water like fallen blossoms.

Below the city sprawled a green and fertile river valley, well-tilled, festooned with orchards, and on the other side of this valley the land climbed suddenly to the steep hills of the Dardenon Ranges, well-clad with the flame-coloured eringls of Auralonde. Hythe Mellyn prospered, as did all of Avlantia.

A plague of rats came to Hythe Mellyn, but though they poured into the city like liquid shadow in a nightmare, it was not their predations that emptied it. The rats were merely the heralds of its doom; many other matters were to come into play before the fate of Hythe Mellyn would be sealed.

At first, when they were few, the needle-eyed, yellow-fanged visitors seemed to be no more than a nuisance. After all, Hythe Mellyn until then had endured no plagues and few vermin. A squeaking and rustling in the night, a chewing of the corners of flour sacks and a depositing of filth in the pantries—these offenses were annoying but could be borne. Traps and baits were laid. It was thought these would eradicate the pests, but the rats' numbers grew steadily despite the efforts of the citizens to destroy them, and they grew bolder. In the hours of darkness they ran across the bedcovers of the citizens. With their septic teeth, they bit people's faces as they lay sleeping, the pain waking them to stare into a mask of horror.

Soon, not only at night were the rats abroad, but also during the hours of daylight. They were to be seen in the street-gutters and on the roofs of houses, scuttling across courtyards, poisoning the carved fountains with their waste. From every cleft and shadow stabbed the knife-point glint of their eyes, and the cold, thin whistling of their squeaks shrilled like spiteful giggling. Never was a pantry door opened without a rain of wriggling black bodies falling from the shelves and scurrying into the corners. Never was the once-sweet air free of the stench of decay and foulness. With sudden bustles of teeth, tails, and spines, the rodents clustered in the cellars like bunches of fat pears. They killed the songbirds in their cages and gnawed unwatched babes in their cradles.

Every countermeasure was tried. More traps and baits were laid, cats were brought in—but for every rodent that was destroyed, two more took its place. In desperation the Lord Mayor posted a reward to whomsoever should rid the city of this scourge—five bags of gold. As the news travelled, it brought in many adventurers from other countries eager to win their fortunes in such an easy way. But it was not easy—in fact, it proved impossible, and the reward grew from five bags to ten, and then to fifteen, as the plague intensified. Rogues and ruffians, itinerants, wizards and conjurers; all came with their bags of tricks, each more bizarre than the last, which they claimed would dispel this curse. None succeeded. The citizens now lived in a state of siege, with every cranny in every house sealed. Many people were too frightened to venture abroad at all, and the city was seized by paralysis, juddering to a standstill.

On the day the Lord Mayor officially increased the reward to twenty bags of gold, a stranger arrived in Hythe Mellyn. Foreigners in outlandish garb being by now a common sight, this one caused no more than the raising of an eyebrow among the few who caught sight of him as he passed through the rat-infested streets toward the Chambers of the City Council in his gaily striped doublet, parti-coloured hose, and versicolour cloak, and his cap like a rainbow with three horns.

But as he entered into the stately oak-paneled halls of the

Council Chambers and bowed before the Lord Mayor and councilors of Hythe Mellyn, his remarkable comeliness suddenly became apparent. Dark eyes, upswept at the outer corners, glittered beneath long lashes. Wavy hair rippled down his back; it was the colour of a blackbird's plumage, with a gleam of chestnut. The clinging fabric of his doublet showed his person to be muscular and lithe, slight but well-proportioned. A faint smile played along his lips, revealing flawless white teeth. His raiment glowed like the Southern Lights—a phenomenon never witnessed in Avlantia but spoken of with awe by travellers who had journeyed to the low, freezing latitudes of the deep south. They said they had seen these lights spread across the skies in luminous mantles of living, shifting colour—fire red, dawn amber, daffodil yellow, leaf green, ocean blue, twilight indigo, and violet. Such was the appearance of the stranger's exotic garb.

Stern-faced, the statesmen of Hythe Mellyn regarded him as he stood before them. Boldly he returned their gaze as if noting their blue eyes and noble features. The ice-white hair of the elders and the corn-yellow locks of the younger men fell across broad Talith shoulders richly cloaked in velvet.

'I shall rid you of the plague, my lords,' the entrancing stranger said cheerfully, 'for the price of twenty-one bags of gold.'

Among themselves the Lord Mayor and the aldermen saw no reason why this 'colourful fellow', as they called him in murmured asides, should succeed where others had failed; and if by some miracle he did, why then they would be glad to shower him with twenty-one bags of gold, the freedom of the city, and more! Thus it was that they readily agreed to his price.

After he heard this, instead of departing to set up traps or wizardly devices, the handsome youth reached into his pocket, took out a set of pipes, and began to play a queer, wild tune. Immediately, the flesh of the listeners crepitated. Astonished and insulted by this odd behaviour, the councilors were about to order the sentries to cast out this offender when they were stayed by an even odder sight.

Down from the wall-hangings and across the floor of the Council Chambers came a thin dark tide, its edges reaching out like crawling tentacles or threads, directed toward the Piper where he stood. Silently, as one organism, rats gathered at his feet. He turned and skipped away, still playing, and they followed him. In sudden fear, the sentries flung wide the brass-bound, oaken doors.

Outdoors and down the street danced the musician, trailed by his invidious entourage. Behind them, the officers of the Council burst out through the doorway. Their shouts and exclamations mingled with the eerie sound of the piping, which, it seemed, could be heard over the entire city. Above the city square, shutters banged open and faces peered out. Rats were gathering—thousands upon thousands of them. From every storehouse and granary, from every wainscot and pantry, attic, cellar, and gutter, from drain, cesspit, cistern, and crevice they came scurrying soundlessly, climbing on one another's backs, crushing their fellows in their haste to join the living spate that grew and overflowed the streets in pursuit of the Piper down King's Avenue, through the East Gate, and out of town.

Never before had such a bizarre and loathsome turmoil been seen in Hythe Mellyn. Frozen in wonder, the citizens stared. Children covered their ears against the shrill keening of the pipes. The tune seemed to remain loud and piercing in the heads of the people even as the Piper danced away down the winding road into the valley, across the bridge, and on toward the hills, for it seemed to tell of queer things waiting on the other side of the valley—the dank holds of Seaships filled with sacks of grain, and stinking scrapheaps, and walled darknesses filled with limitless living flesh to feed on. Yet the melody also described dangers that hunted swiftly from behind: steel-jawed engines, swift monsters with rending teeth and claws, and treacherous, irresistible sweetmeats that tasted delicious but burned caustic through the stomach and brought agonizing death. The rats hearkened and followed. The people hearkened, but did not understand.

As the last of the rodents, the maimed, lame, and slow, struggled to catch up with the horde, the Talith slowly emerged from their dwellings and followed, to see where they would go. Through the wrought-iron gates of the city went the people, until they assembled in a great concourse outside the high walls and looked out across Glisswater Vale, while the more venturesome youths gave chase.

The sun was setting in citrine splendor behind the city. Long light lay across the land, sparkling on the distant ribbon of the River Gliss where golden willows leaned. The thin trilling of the pipes interwove with their leaves and echoed down the valley. The black tide followed the road, with the Piper at its head, and more tributaries ran to join it from the valley farms, until at last it turned off toward Hob's Hill.

The rats never returned.

Those brave youths who had continued the chase reported that a portal had yawned suddenly in the green flank of the hill. There the Piper had entered. The rats followed him faithfully, every one, and were swallowed up inside. Instantly, a pair of double Doors swung shut, meeting in the middle. The sound of the pipes ceased abruptly. There remained no crack or disturbance to show where any Doors had existed. A chill dark wind then blew across the land, and a solemn watchfulness closed in upon Hob's Hill.

But Hythe Mellyn rejoiced. The spires and belfries gave voice with their great brass tongues. After throwing open every gate, door and fenestration, the people danced in the streets. Not a hale rat remained, only a few crushed and crippled ones, soon to be swept away. King Branwyddan, who had removed his court to his palace in Ysteris until such time as the pestilence would be contained, returned soon after. He commanded the refurbishing of the city, so that all should be cleansed and repaired. The Lord Mayor ordered that the coffers be opened and the city's gold be used to buy in what was needed. Only the Piper's promised payment was held in reserve, in expectation of his imminent return, and a hero's welcome was prepared. So began a time of great industry in Hythe Mellyn, but in their happiness the workload seemed light to the populace, and in their business they did not stop to ask, or perhaps did not want to ask, where the Piper had gone and why he had not immediately returned for his reward.

A week slipped by, and another, and another. Still the Piper did not appear, but if he was mentioned at all, it was in whispers.

He was no mortal creature, that was certain. Some thought him one of the Faêran; others said he was naught but an eldritch wight. There was talk of his being unseelie, malicious, and in league with the rats, for one of the councilors vowed he had spied a small black creature in the Piper's pocket when he took out his instrument. Iron horseshoes were placed above every archway, and in the gardens the rowan-trees were hung with bells. But the Piper did not return and the people began to conjecture that he had been trapped under Hob's Hill, or had perished, and that by a stroke of fortune they were rid of this creditor as well as the rats. Many congratulated themselves on their luck, but others shook their heads.

'He will return,' they said quietly among themselves. 'Immortal beings do not forget, nor do they perish so easily. He will return for his payment.'

And they were right.

Seasons changed. Little by little, the gold set aside for the Piper was borrowed for other purposes. Hythe Mellyn returned to its former glory and the stranger who had saved it from the rat-plague was almost forgotten. If ever he was mentioned, it was now postulated that perhaps he had not drawn off the rats after all—every plague eventually comes to an end. Besides, there had not been so very many of the rodents. The baits and traps and cats had wiped most of them out before the ruffian ever showed his face. But a year to the day after he had first appeared, the 'colourful fellow' turned up.

Under the judicious rule of William the Wise, Third King-Emperor of the House of D'Armancourt, no war existed in Erith, and most walled cities did not bother to close their gates at all. During the rat-plague, Hythe Mellyn's gates had been sealed at night in an effort to reduce the numbers of invading vermin. Now they stood open again by night and day. Well-equipped sentries, stationed at the entrances, possessed enough force to turn away the few undesirable outlanders who tried to come in.

They never saw the Piper enter.

In the city's heart, the doors of the Council Chambers also stood open, although sentries were always posted for ceremony's sake. These yeomen jumped and thrust forward their pikes as a shadow crossed the steps, but already the Piper walked within the solemn halls, past the statue of King Branwyddan on its pedestal, to stand before the assembled aldermen. In his gorgeous raiment he appeared like a ray of light piercing a stained-glass window. Amid the throes of their discussion, the councilors paused. Heads were raised. Surrounded by the echoing silence of the high-ceilinged hall, the stranger did not bow. He tilted his head cockily. That same faint smile tweaked the corners of his mouth.

'Gentlemen,' he said, 'I am come to claim my payment. Thrice seven bags of gold.'

His words fell into a hollow space of incredulity and were bounced back from the walls and columns.

A mutter of indignation rippled across the chamber. The Lord Mayor rose from his seat.

'Piper, you are come late.'

'Late or early, I am come,' was the blithe reply.

The Lord Mayor cleared his throat awkwardly.

'But at the time of our bargain, our coffers were full. Now they are depleted, due to the refurbishment of the city. We can ill afford to make such a large payment.'

The Piper offered no response.

'For playing a tune,' continued the Lord Mayor, 'a skilled musician should expect no more than a penny or two. However, we are grateful and not ungenerous, and shall give you a bag of gold. This should be more than enough to keep a thrifty fellow like you in comfort to the end of his days.'

'City of Hythe Mellyn,' came the cool reply, 'you must abide by your promise.'

Mutters of outrage and anger rose from the assembly. The Lord Mayor called for silence. Trouble creased his brow.

'Gentlemen,' he said to his colleagues, 'the Piper speaks truth—a bargain was made.'

'Offer half,' someone shouted, and argument broke out on all sides. Never in the city's history had the orderly proceedings of the council degenerated into such chaos. Ill feeling toward the jaunty fellow ran strangely high. For the Talith were a wise and just people, but perhaps over time, in the comfort of their prosperity, they had become somewhat arrogant, and their wisdom had become clouded by their love of their city. And perhaps there was some alien quality about the beauty of the Piper that, in some, provoked unreasonable fear and hatred.

Said the Piper, 'I do not haggle.'

The Secretary sprang to his feet. 'Then,' he shouted, his face congested with rage, 'you are heartless and no true man. You shall receive nought.'

A storm of approval greeted his words, against which the Lord Mayor remained silent. The Piper smiled, turned swiftly around, and was gone out through the doors. The aldermen heard a burst of clear laughter fading as he passed quickly through the precincts, and they were seized by a unexplained terror.

'We have done amiss,' cried the Lord Mayor in much alarm. 'Send the sheriffs and constables after him. He plots some dangerous mischief and must be caught.'

Hardly had the messengers sped forth than an uncanny sound was heard throughout Hythe Mellyn.

The Piper was playing a different air.

This time, it promised honey-cakes and ponies, swings and sandcastles, hoops and whistles, rainbows, puppies, and Summer picnics—all lying ahead, on the other side of the valley. No man or woman hearkened to it but they wept, for they were taken as in a nostalgic dream back to the lost days of childhood. No child heard it but they must cease what they had been doing and go in quest of these enchanting delights. Thus, as the Piper danced through the streets, he gathered behind him another entourage. Among the bright-eyed, rose-cheeked faces, not one was above the age of sixteen years. From the houses of merchants and lords, aldermen and tradesmen, they came by the scores and by the hundreds—the sun-haired children of the city, the older ones leading the younger by the hand or carrying the babes. The small tots toddled as fast as they could, but the Piper went slowly. For him there was no need for haste, because all the grown-up citizens stood rooted to the spot. Weeping, they stretched out their arms and called the names of their children, who heeded them not. The children had ears only for the Piper's tune, eager eyes only for some distant place. Their little feet moved as if independent of their owners' control.

The tune, dangerous and irresistible, now told also of nightmares and loss, sickness and pain following hard behind, so that the children lagging at the tail end of the crowd wailed and hurried forward. The Piper danced down the valley road, through orchards bubbling with blushing fruit and fields lush with corn. Slowly the city was emptied of its youth. Along the rutted road between the hawthorn hedges they went, across the ivied stone bridge to the other side of the river where hazel bushes burgeoned and blackbirds sang; and on past the turnip-fields and the cow-meadows.

Unable to move, the parents could only shake their fists and scream and call down every curse on the Piper and beg help from the Faêran, or fate, or any source. For half the day the procession crossed Glisswater Vale, swelled by the children from the farms. The farmers could only reach out their empty hands and watch through brimming eyes. They could not see what happened when the children reached Hob's Hill, but they guessed. The great black Doors gaped, this time to admit the cherished flowering of the Talith. Then they snapped shut, as before, leaving no trace save the footprints of the little ones—a trail that ended halfway up the hillside.

With the closing of the Doors in the hill, the citizens found themselves released. They ran, the third living tide to surge down the valley road and across the bridge. They beat on the hillside. They brought shovels and excavated. They dug with their hands and scratched with their fingernails. Night drew in, and they worked on and on until the sun rose, all the while calling and crying until they were hoarse, but nought did they find save cold stones and soil, roots and worms.

In the weeks and months that followed, they brought every piece of gold and every treasure of Hythe Mellyn and laid it before

Hob's Hill, until what was piled there was worth many times twenty-one bags of gold. Still the digging continued, deep into the hill's bowels, but no pick broke through to any secret hole or cavern. Many of the people lay down before the hill among the gold and refused to eat or drink, calling out that they themselves must be taken in exchange for their children. The Secretary of the Council was discovered to have hanged himself from his rafters. King Branwyddan of Avlantia came, bringing chests of treasure as an offering. His own sons had been too old to be taken, yet sorely he grieved for his people.

But no royal gold and no wizard's gramarye or wisdom, and no sacrifice of life or labor could open the Doors of Hob's Hill or even reveal the thinnest hairline crack of an outline.

Hythe Mellyn and all of Avlantia fell into despair.

In later days, travellers who came to the gates of Hythe Mellyn found the city deserted, and went away again. Several explanations were offered. It was reported that a pestilence had arisen and wiped out the population. Some folk said that the children never returned, and the townspeople in their grief hanged themselves on the red trees in the forest, or else travelled to the coast and cast themselves into the sea. Yet others said that the citizens had gone looking for their kin and become trapped under the mountains, and there they wandered still, lost in some strange country. The great Leaving of Hythe Mellyn was a fact, although the manner of the Leaving and the reason behind it were hidden from the knowledge of all, save for a select few.

But the truth of it was this:

When the last child had passed in under Hob's Hill, the Piper, who had stood playing his tune by the Doors as his followers entered, looked back along the road. Far away, just outside the city gates, a small shape crawled in the dust. He played more loudly and the shape moved a little more swiftly, but the sun was setting by this time. The wind bore a faint cry of ineffable sadness and longing over the treetops of the valley. The Piper looked to the sky and laughed, slipping inside the Doors just as they closed.

When the Lord Mayor ran out of the gates he found his little daughter lying in the dust of the road. Gathering her in his arms he brought her home.

Leodogran na Pendran, Lord Mayor of Hythe Mellyn, had given his daughter a pony on her seventh birthday.

'Now, do not let him loose,' he had admonished tenderly, 'as you did with the songbird.'

'Father, he is beautiful!' the child had cried, thanking him with kisses. 'And I shall not set him free, for he cannot fly, and might be eaten by wicked wights. But I shall love him and care for him as best I can.'

'And ride him, for he is already broken to the saddle.'

'Oh no. I shall not ride him unless he wishes it.' She stroked the pony's snowy neck. 'I do not wish to burden him and make him sad, for he has done no harm. But if he comes to love me as I already love him, then one day he will tell me he enjoys my company. And then, since I cannot run as fast as he, he may let me ride.'

Her father shook his head.

'You are too sweet-natured, *elindor*. Be the beast's mistress!'

'Father, pardon me, for I do not wish to be discourteous, but he shall be my friend, and the friend of Rhys too. His name shall be Pero-Hiblinn: Little White Horse in the "Old Speech".'

'I see you have studied your lessons, my little bird,' stated Leodogran kindly. 'But "Pero-Hiblinn" is a tall name for a short horse.'

'Then he shall be "Peri".'

'Come, let us take Peri to stable. But do not leave it too long before you ride him!'

And so it was that some weeks later in the last days of Autumn, Ashalind na Pendran rode on Peri's back across the daisy-speckled sward surrounding her father's house, which stood just outside the city walls. By Leodogran's side, young Rhys, Ashalind's brother, clapped his hands, crowing with delight. His sister had crowned him with Autumn daisies and he looked like a merry woodland sprite. As Peri cantered around the field with his tail flying like a white banner, a bird swooped out of the skies like a bolt, close to the pony's head. Startled, the beast reared up, flailing his front legs. The child was thrown to the ground and the bird flew away. Ashalind lay still, as if in a swoon, but when her father rushed to her side, his heart wrung with concern, he saw her eyelids flutter and knew that she lived.

A servant rode for the apothecary, who, after he had performed his ministrations, said: 'Sir, such a fall might have proved more serious. Fortune has favoured your daughter. She is hale in body save for her left leg, which is broken. I have set it. Let her now rest for three days, but when she rises she will not be able to bear her weight on the limb until it is healed.'

A suitable pair of wooden crutches had been commissioned, but before they were ready the Piper had beckoned, and Ashalind had not been able to follow.

Now all the laughter was gone. It had fled from Hythe Mellyn and Auralonde and out of Avlantia altogether. The amber city was all silence and stillness.

From that execrable day when despair had come to Hythe Mellyn, Ashalind was the only child under the age of sixteen dwelling in all the great city, save for the babes who were born thereafter. No jealousy stained the bereaved hearts of the Talith, only love for this child who was the child of them all. A strange and lonely life it was for her, with no playmates of her age and no small brother with whom to frolic—only older youths and maidens, men and wives, graybeards and dowagers with hearts as heavy and eaten-out as old cast-iron cauldrons. Much of her time was spent with the carlin Meganwy, a woman of wisdom who understood the healing arts and taught her many things. Under Meganwy's guidance, the child grew to be a damsel skilled in herb lore and songs.

For Ashalind there was something more than the heartache of missing all those loved ones and watching the world turn grayhaired. For she had been touched by the Piper's call as none of the adults had, and been drawn by it just like the other children. She had been privy, for a moment, to a world beyond the fences of the world. Never could she forget it. In her inner being a long-ing had awoken, and it smoldered.

Never again, save once, did Ashalind ride upon Peri—and that was at a time of great need. Her father did not care. He cared little for anything now—except his daughter. Nothing she did could displease him. He took off his Lord Mayor's chain of office, for he had not the spirit for it anymore, and his young steward Pryderi Penrhyn, who had been seventeen years old when the children were taken, took over the running of his affairs in the city.

'I have failed in my duty,' said Leodogran. 'I ought to have spoken for the city and paid the Piper. My silence itself proved to be betrayal.'

The delving of Hob's Hill continued at whiles over the years. Graves were raised up there also, for those who had pined away and wished to rest at last near their children. The grass grew over the pits and scars and over the graves, but every year on the first day of Autumn, the Talith of Hythe Mellyn laid on the hillside wreaths of late daisies, leaves, and rowan-berries tied with red ribbons.

The grass grew long on Hob's Hill and the slate-gray hair of Ashalind's father became laced with threads of silver. He withdrew from public life, spending much time in his library—studying, he said, books of lore. But often his daughter would see him there, sitting at the window, staring out into the distance, his eyes clouded like milky opals. His apple orchards, untended, fell into ruin—but his affairs in the city remained well-managed by his trusty steward Pryderi Penrhyn, who did not fail in his duties.

As soon as her leg had healed, Ashalind took to rambling at every chance with her hound Rufus through the wooded hills sur-rounding Glisswater Vale. Endlessly she sought Rhys and the children or looked for another way into the Piper's realm. Love for her father and brother drove her, no more nor less than that fierce white star of Longing kindled by the pipes, now burning within her.

Rarely were unseelie wights encountered in the eringl forests and Ashalind was not troubled by them in her wanderings, for Avlantia was a domain where evil things seldom strayed. This land was said to be beloved by the Faêran, of whom she had once or twice caught a flicker of a glimpse. Folk who had been visited by them told tales of their strange ways and their beauty.

Seven years Ashalind spent searching, never relinquishing hope when it should, reasonably, have long given way to despair.

On her fourteenth birthday, her father gave her a bracelet of gold. Upon it was enameled a white seabird with outstretched wings—the elindor, the bird of freedom, which, after it left the nest, did not touch land for seven years but instead hunted and slept while gliding on the wing or floating on the ocean.

And one evening in late Autumn, just after her birthday, she met a stranger in the woods.

Pale moths were fluttering. A white owl flew into the gathering gloom. There was a glimmer in a clearing. She thought she spied an old gentleman standing there, leaning on a staff and watching her. Approaching without fear, she greeted him courteously.

'Hail to thee, lord.'

'Well met, Ashalind, daughter of Leodogran.'

His voice was as deep and mellow as dawn.

At this the damsel hesitated, for she was startled not only by his use of her name but by the piercing eyes that bent their gaze to her from under the shadow of his hood, eyes like those of a wild creature, but in what way, she could not say. The whiteness of his robes was as pure and perfect as a snowscape. The hoarfrost of his long hair and beard was like the silver of bedewed cobwebs, a fantasy in crystal lace, a symmetry in ice and diamonds hung with long prisms. His glance was a frozen sword catching the sunlight and stabbing it with brilliant sparks. Yet beneath the snow lay warmth. Now that she viewed him closely, she could not say why she had thought him very old, other than the reason of his pastel colouring, for very few lines were graven upon his face.

His strangeness now engendered in Ashalind an uncertainty bordering on fear. Her fingers touched the tilhal at her throat but the whitebeard said:

'I am no unseelie wight, daughter. You have naught to fear. How should I not know who you are, since you are seen wandering our forests day after day, year by year? Such loyalty as yours should not go unrewarded.'

'Sir, I do not know your name but I guess that you are a mighty wizard, such as Razmath the Learned, who fashioned my tilhal.'

'I am called Easgathair.'

Ashalind seized her opportunity.

'I beg leave to ask of you the same questions I ask of all folk I meet, especially the wise and learned.'

'Ask.'

Ashalind hesitated again, for there was something thrilling yet almost perilous about this sage, and his presence disquieted her. It came to her, then, that she stood before one of the Faêran. Nonetheless she gathered up her courage, for never yet had she been daunted in her quest, despite that it had forever been fruitless.

'Do the children of Hythe Mellyn still live, and if so, can they be regained?'

The sun had now set and the white moths were clustered more thickly in the air. All around, eringl leaves spread rumours among themselves. A night-hunting bird hooted. The old gentleman shifted his staff.

'Yes,' he said, 'and yes.'

At this reply, Ashalind caught her breath. Many times she had received this same answer from the learned or the optimistic, but this time the words were declared with more than hope or conviction. They were uttered with knowledge.

'If they have taken any food or drink then the children cannot return to you,' he continued, 'but they may not have done so yet, for seven years of Erith seem shorter than one night to them in the Fair Realm, and they are under the enchantment of their games.'

'What is to be done?'

'One alone may go after them and fetch them back. One who has the courage.'

'I have it. But I do not know the road.'

'Hearken. In view of your faithfulness, and because the treachery of your city was no fault of yours, Ashalind na Pendran, I shall tell you how to find the road. Tomorrow night you must couch yourself beneath the ymp-tree in your father's orchard. Stay awake, and you will find the way. But truly, you are exceeding beauteous and they would keep you, so you must go in disguise. Perhaps they will not expect deception from one so young as you, and may look no deeper. Twine about you sprigs of mint and lavender, so that long-nosed wights may not encounter the fragrance of your skin. Neither speak first, nor give thanks, but show due appreciation. Beware of Yallery Brown and do not reveal your true name.'

Ashalind fell to her knees, trembling.

'I will do it all. Pray tell me, good sir, when I go there, how should I make them hearken to me?'

'The moon waxes to the full, and these are feast nights in the halls of the Crown Prince, Morragan, the Fithiach of Carnconnor. At such times he looks mercifully upon petitioners, and may grant favours. He will never vouchsafe the unconditional return of those you seek, but he may vouchsafe the chance to win them.'

The staff in the sage's hand was a shaft of moonlight. Moths settled along it like snowflakes. An owl sideslipped low overhead with a whoosh and a whirr of predators' wings. It blurred into the night. The Faêran regarded the damsel with a thoughtful stare.

'Think thrice before you take this chance,' he said. 'So far, your path has wended across the ordinary hills and dales of humanity. But if you dare to enter the Realm it will change your life forever. Be careful, be very certain before you choose to step across the boundary.'

'There is no choice to be made. I must bring them back.'

'You are untutored. Beware of the power of gramarye. If on second thought you should decide to continue your normal life, one day perhaps this dream of redemption shall cease to trouble you and you might live in contentment as the years pass by. If you gain entry to the Realm you must pay for it—and the price can be high. No matter which choice you make, you may regret it.'

'Sir, no words shall sway me.'

'Now thrice have you averred this. Go then. I have warned you.'

With that he turned away and went into the shadows under the trees.

'Lord Easgathair, please wait!' she called, following. But he moved swiftly for one so old.

'If you get in, neither eat nor drink until you are out,' were the last words he called over his shoulder, and all she saw was the snow-glimmer of his robes vanishing among the eringls ahead and a few white owl-feathers strewn on the ground among the ferns and mosses.

On the following day, Ashalind made the housekeeper, Oswyn, repeat a vow of secrecy. Delighted by the thought of adventure, the woman bustled about following her mistress's instructions, bringing men's rough garb of tunic and breeches, packing the pockets with fragrant herbs as instructed, dyeing Ashalind's hair with black ink and rubbing pig's grease into it until every filament was snarled and tangled. Between them, they pulled the matted locks forward to conceal most of Ashalind's face and bound the rest in a club at the back. The damsel regarded herself critically in the looking-glass. She practised pulling faces and speaking from the side of her mouth, all the while wondering whether she would have the effrontery to carry this through, and whether she ought to walk with an uneven gait, like a farmer's lad accustomed to clod-hopping among furrows.

That night, Leodogran's daughter stole down to the garden and delved her white hands into the soil, tearing her nails on the stones and smearing her face with cinders and clay. Then she went into her father's orchard and lay down beneath the ymp-tree, the most ancient tree of all, the grafted apple. The leaves fell down around her, lightly covering her as she lay wrapped in a blanket. Under the light of the moon and the stars she tried to stay awake but at last slept, dreaming strange dreams of laughter and the ringing of bells, and songs of joy and grief that wounded like swords. But she saw no road. She awoke damp and cold in the blue light of dawn, her thoughts first straying to her own featherbed in its warm chamber, with her hound lying on the rug, and then to young Rhys, lost and crying in the darkness.

None of her friends in the city had ever beheld the sage Easgathair, and when she sought him in the woods she found no sign. The next night she dressed in disguise and kept vigil as before, but again, sleep took her and she discovered nothing. On the third night as she lay, she twined briars and thorns about her wrist to keep herself awake with their pricking: a wild, lacerating bracelet in place of the smooth gold band she usually wore. Late after middle-night she was still awake when she heard at last a heart-stopping sound; the crystal chime of a bridle-bell.

Then it seemed to her that the wind lifted her suddenly and swung her against the night sky.

The jingling approached like the spangle of sequins, like a woodland of silver bell-flowers rustled by a Summer-silk breeze.

Seen indistinctly in the star-watered gloaming between the apple orchard's fretted boughs, a procession of seven score riders was slowly passing by.

A Faêran Rade.

Breathtakingly fair were they, with a shining beauty that was not of Erith. All were arrayed in splendid raiment of green and gold, and mounted on magnificently caparisoned steeds whose bridles glittered with tiny bells, like chains of stars. The knights among them wore golden helmets. Clasped about their limbs were finely chased greaves. Some bore in their hands golden spears like shafts of pale sunlight. To see these riders was startling, like a first glimpse of new blossom in Spring—a sudden enchantment glimmering against boughs that lately stretched stark and black.

To see them was to truly awaken, for the first time.

A knocking started up under Ashalind's ribs, for the yearning within her, born of the Piper's call, had found an answer at last.

The horses were of a splendid breed, surpassing any she had ever seen in the world—noble, milk-white steeds, moving with the grace of the wind. Each possessed the arched neck, the broad chest, the quivering nostril, and the large eyes of a superb hunter. They seemed made of fire and flame, not of mortal flesh. Each was shod with silver, striking silver sparks with each step, and each bore a jewel on his forehead like a star.

The fair riders made the orchard ring with their clear laughter and song, but other horsemen surrounded them—mounted bodyguards or companions. In contrast, these outriders were of hideous form and face, and mostly smaller in stature.

When the last of the procession had passed, Ashalind sprang

to her feet and followed. Keeping well back so that they would not spy her, she ran after the riders, out through the orchard gate and down Hedgerow Lane and on across the valley. Although the revelers seemed to ride slowly, Ashalind was hard-pressed to keep up. She dropped farther and farther behind. Not once did any face turn back toward her—neither the achingly fair knights and ladies nor the misshapen riders seemed to notice her at all—and thus she grew bolder and more desperate, until after they crossed the bridge there was no more attempt at concealment and she ran openly, gasping for breath, her left leg throbbing deep in the bone.

Ahead loomed Hob's Hill, but now there was a broad road leading to it that had never been there before, and the side of the hill was open. A great light streamed out of the arched Doors. Without pausing, the procession rode inside. Their pursuer was so far behind that she saw the last of them pass within before she could come near. In great fear lest the entrance should close before she could reach it, she sprinted forward, sobbing with agony and longing. Her heart banged so loudly in her chest that she thought it would burst. As the monumental Doors finally began to swing to, Ashalind had almost reached the threshold. With a last effort she flung herself through the portal and heard, at her back, the sonorous clang of stone clapping against stone.

All seemed dark at first, but ahead, as if from beyond a corridor or tunnel, shone a pale pink light like the glow of dawn. Recovering her breath, Ashalind hurried toward it. A breeze blew from there, rose-scented, poignant. An extraordinary excitement surged through her, swelled by a sense of yearning and urgency.

The long hallway ended in a second archway. Its single Door stood open.

Beyond, she beheld a staggering view. Under a sapphire sky, a fair land of wooded hills stretched away to mountains of terrible height and majesty, their keen peaks piercing rings of cloud. She had heard tales and songs of the Fair Realm, and the Piper's tune had described it, but the splendor, the seduction, and the fascination of that realm had never yet come home to her. Her heart was possessed, stabbed by enchantment and desire, and she gazed, almost forgetting her mission, at the land beyond dream or invention. She wept, for it was the land of the Piper's tune, and she had only to walk a few steps to reach it. But those steps were forestalled.

Out of a side opening she had not noticed before sprang two small black figures dressed in mail, crossing their pikes to bar her way. Their ears were long, upstanding and pointed, their mouths wide and their noses broad. They stood about three feet tall and exuded a strong odour of leaf-mold.

In accents unfamiliar, these small and evidently dangerous adversaries demanded, 'Halt stranger. Who trespasses here and on what business?' A gleam darted from their slits of eyes. Their barbed and whiplike tails switched aggressively from side to side.

Ashalind drew herself up to her full height and tried to gain a moment to ponder, for she had not remembered to make a new name for herself. She shrank from giving them the name of any-one she knew in case it brought the owner into danger. Thoughts quarreled in her head—the kenning her father called her, and her golden bracelet, now lying on the dressing-table at home. She spoke in a gruff voice, mumbling.

'I am called Elindor. I am come to ask a boon of the Lord Morragan of Carnconnor.'

Distastefully, the spriggans eyed the filthy peasant lad.

'Steenks,' they agreed, exchanging nods. They spoke to one another in their own creaking tongue.

'Follow,' they said at last, and one entered into the opening from which they had appeared, where a stair led upward. With one last longing glance at the land *beyond* the hill, Ashalind started to climb, and the second spriggan came after.

The stair soared up and up, and opened into a corridor from which led many branches and portals leading to rooms and other stairways, one of which the leading guard climbed. At the top of this second flight was a third. By now Ashalind had been rendered once again breathless, for it was difficult to ascend so far and fast. Fortunately she was not hampered by skirts or a feigned limp, although in the leg that had been broken the bone ached. Already weary from the race across the valley, she was also troubled by thirst.

The wights led her finally to a high room in a tower. The door stood open and a resplendently furnished room lay within. The walls were clad with bright tapestries and leafy vines; the chairs and tables were wrought of gold, embellished with jewels and living flowers. One of the tables was set with goblets and jugs, and dishes piled high with fruits and sweetmeats. Warm air blew softly in at the open windows. What had at first seemed to be a blaze in the hearth was no fire, but a heap of roses so red they seemed aflame. Ashalind had never seen such a splendid room and hardly dared venture in.

'Enter,' said the creaking voice of the leading spriggan sentry.

She went in, but the speaker was no longer to be seen, nor was the other who had been following behind. After examining the room in amazement, she moved to the windows and looked out. There below she saw the spreading of a great garden ringed by a greenwood. Birds and fountains made music, a sea of roses surged and broke like waves against the garden walls, and on the long lawns children played.

The children of Hythe Mellyn.

Unchanged, not a day older than when they had departed seven years before, they frolicked there, lit by brilliant sunlight that seemed peculiarly clear and pink, as if viewed through a pane of roseate quartz. Ashalind dared not call to them, disguised as she was, but tears of joy and pain stung her eyes when she spied Rhys among them. Leaning from the window, she stretched out her arms, but a sound at her back made her start and turn around.

The spriggans had returned. They led her through the thundering halls and extravagant galleries of a fantastic palace, until they came at last to the most amazing hall of all.

Therein, the air was charged.

Lofty trees grew along the walls—indeed they constituted the walls, intersticed by greenery. Their boughs made a serpentine roof of leaves, forming arches laced together by the mellow breeze, tiled by glimmers of azure sky. Flamboyant birds winged across this ceiling and owls perched as if carved.

Merriment resounded, and music of harps and flutes. Long, narrow tables stretched the length of the hall, set with gold-wrought bowls of flowers and platters of food. Seated along them was a splendid company.

At the sight, Ashalind's head spun. For a long instant she thought she fell upward from on a rocky height into a dizziness of open sky where points of light glistered, thick as salt. The song of the stars seemed to choir in her head.

She was among the Faêran.

A faint shimmer of radiance surrounded them. Their voices fell like flower petals on water, as musical as birdsong in the morning. They spoke in a language Ashalind did not understand: a tongue as smooth as polished silver, as rich as the jewel-hoards of dragons. Some wore scarlet and gold and amber like leaping flames, some were clad in green and silver like moonlight on leaves, some in soft gray like curling smoke. Others among them appeared to be as naked as needles, graced only with the beauty of their comely forms and their flowing hair, which was threaded with jewels and flowers.

Courageously, Ashalind stepped forward. Instantaneously, silence fell and all eyes turned to her.

Justly were they called the Fair Folk. Indeed, they were the fairest of all, possessing a beauty that was intoxicating, almost paralyzing. Ashalind had barely caught sight of them through the half-leafless boughs of the apple trees, but now that she was so close, it seemed to her as if her heart and brain had stopped functioning and she could think of nothing to say.

They seemed at first if formed of air and light, yet as strong and living as trees, as lively as wind and fire and swift-flowing waters. Clean and finely drawn were their features, with high cheekbones and sculpted chins. At the outer corners, their eyebrows and their eyes swept up, slanting ever so slightly, as if everything about them was suspended from above and only whimsy anchored them to the ground. Tall and straight as spears were they, the lines of their forms clean and hard. Taut was their peach-blossom skin. Always they smiled and laughed. Indeed, it seemed that gravity and other weighty matters never touched these flower-ladies—fragile and slender, almost waiflike—or these virile lords possessed of the strength and grace of warrior heroes, who were beautiful in another way entirely—not as flowers, but as lions and eagles of immense power. Ashalind thought some among the assembly were older, some younger, but how they gave this impression was hard to say. No heavy jowl, no sagging chin gave evidence of accumulated years. Perhaps the effect of age was lent by an air of greater wisdom and tempered gaiety, in addition to some indefinable aspect of appearance.

Appearing stiff and awkward by comparison with the easy grace of the Faêran, eldritch wights sat among them. These seemed to be mortal men and women, but were not. Some were lovely to look upon, others ordinary—but all were betrayed by some deformity, no matter how minor. Others not so beauteous also mingled with this astonishing company: dangerous fuaths and murderous duergars, unseelie wights of assorted hideousness whose spindly shanks and outsized extremities made a screamingly grotesque contrast to the beauty of their companions. To Ashalind they appeared like fungoid growths and molds sprouting amid wildflowers.

Woodland beasts she saw also—the mask of a narrow-eyed fox, the curve of a deer's neck, lop-eared hares pale as curd flitting over the roots of the wall-trees, a raven on a high branch.

A voice announced, 'Elindor of Erith comes to beg audience of His Royal Highness, Morragan, Crown Prince of the Realm, Fithiach of Carnconnor.'

Bright, melodious laughter rippled around the hall as Ashalind approached the high table and knelt, hardly daring to raise her eyes.

'His Royal Highness bids me welcome you, stranger,' said a corrosive voice. 'Come, drink the guest-cup with us.'

The fellow who had spoken gave a rictus of a smile. He was small and thin, with bloodless lips, a savage, wrinkled face of a yellowish-brown hue, a greasy beard sprouting from his chin. His hair hung lank and stringy, like tangled rats' tails, but it was striped with the colours of dandelions and mud. Clothed in shades of tan and yellow, he stood behind the shoulder of a tall Faêran lord who was seated at the centre of the high table.

As Ashalind dared to lift her gaze for a moment to this lord, a cool, keen wind gusted through the hall.

Or so it seemed.

With eyes as grey as the cold southern seas, *he* was the most grave and comely of all the company. Hair tumbled down in waves to his elbows, and it was the blue-black shade of a raven's wing. The heartbreakingly handsome face betrayed no sign of any passion. Leaning his elbow on the table with the relaxed poise of the omnipotent, he regarded his petitioner, but said nothing.

Bending forward, the wrinkled fellow at the lord's shoulder poured a draught into a jeweled horn and offered it to the new-comer, along with a knowing leer.

'Drink, *erithbunden.*'

'Sir, I respectfully decline your hospitality, but let it be no cause for ill will, I beg of you. I am come but for one task, and I have vowed not to eat or drink until I have accomplished it.'

It was a sore trial to Ashalind to say this, for the wine was sweet-scented, clear and pale green like the new leaves of Spring in Ysteris, and thirst shriveled her palate.

'You are as discourteous as you are decorated with the dirt of your country,' reprimanded the rat-haired fellow, handing the horn to a gargoyle-like creature, which gulped the drink. 'And what may be that task?'

Undaunted she bowed, replying, 'I have come to win back the children of Hythe Mellyn.'

The crowd of Faêran murmured among themselves, and the sound was a brook in Spring, or wind through the cornfields.

'And why do you wish to take them away from this happy place?' barked Rat-Hair. 'For mark you, they dwell in bliss.'

Ashalind found no words for reply but bowed her head in silence, afraid of causing insult and losing her chance to redeem the lost ones.

'His Royal Highness's Piper should have been paid,' continued the puckered fellow. 'A bargain is a bargain. The brats are our playthings now, to toy with as we please. Mayhap we will keep them forever. Mayhap on a whim we will send them back'—with a sudden grin he cocked his head to one side—'in a hundred Erith years'—his head jerked, birdlike, to the other side—'and watch them wither with accumulated age, crumbling to dust as soon as they set foot on Erith's soil!'

This drollery was greeted with joy by several of the more insanely hideous unseelie wights.

Then for the first time the raven-haired prince spoke. His voice was deep and beautiful, like a storm's song.

'What shalt thou give, to earn these children?'

Ashalind, still kneeling, heard her blood thump behind her ears. She chose her words carefully before she made reply.

'Your Royal Highness, ask of me what you will and I will endeavour to provide it—if such is within my power, and causes no evil.'

'Think you, that you can make conditions, *cochal*-eater?' snapped the ocher-faced fellow. As he spoke a large rat ran across his shoulders and disappeared, and the warm wind from the window-arches turned chill, lifting the gray-eyed lord's fall of hair as if he were undersea in a current, spreading the strands like dark wings.

But the prince-lord smiled.

'Elindor of Erith thinks to consider his words wisely,' he said. 'Consider this. If thou canst solve three questions of me, then thou shalt take away thy noisy brats. If not, then they shall stay for ever, and thou also.'

Ashalind bowed low.

'Sir, your offer is accepted as graciously as it is given, and I am ready for the three questions.'

'First, tell me how many stars shine in the skies of Erith. Next, tell me what I am thinking. Last, thou must consider two of the Doors which lead from the chamber below this hall, and tell me which one leads to Erith.'

At these words the ratty fellow laughed hideously, but his master's face still revealed nothing.

Despair threatened to overwhelm Ashalind. She tried to play for time.

'Those questions are . . .' she fumbled for words, 'not easy, sir. I beg leave of you to take time to ponder them anon.'

'Beg, snivel, grovel,' said the servant. 'Now or never.'

'Hold thy tongue, Yallery Brown,' said his master. 'Or I shall have thee again imprisoned beneath the stone. Go then, mortal, I grant thee the time. But speak no word, scribe no symbol, and make no sign until thy return, for the answers must be of thine own inspiration and not of others'. Return when the moon of thy land waxes full again. Give me the answers then or my servant Yallery Brown shall have thee too.' He turned away, to drink from a goblet he held in his hand.

Then the spriggans seized her and rushed her down from that place, and when she came out from Hob's Hill she found herself alone in the night and the falling rain. But the moon was crescent and three weeks had already passed.

When Leodogran's daughter was discovered to have vanished, the city had roused to uproar. She was sought high and low, until Oswyn in fear and shame confessed a garbled version of all that had passed—that Ashalind had met a wizard named Easgathair who had told her how to find a way to the Perilous Realm.

'Alas,' mourned Leodogran, 'for now she too is lost.'

He fell into a fit and would not allow a morsel of food to pass his lips. Oswyn had expected dismissal, but Leodogran told her she was blameless, whereupon she fell to her knees and thanked him for his mercy and justice.

The learned wizard Razmath was consulted.

'Easgathair is not a wizard but the Gatekeeper of the Faêran,' said he. 'Mayhap Ashalind has been ensnared because, after all, she is the One Who Would Not Follow when the Piper played his dire tune. The laws of the Faêran, so it is said, are absolute. It may be that she was marked as their own from the very moment the Piper blew the first note.'

In the house of na Pendran, one rainy eve, Pryderi the loyal young steward sat by the fireside with Leodogran. All the servants were abed, for the hour was late, when the hound Rufus began joyously to bark and there came a knocking on the door. There on the threshold stood Ashalind—wet, dark, dirty, dazed, unspeaking. From her black hair, ink ran in rivulets down her face and her ill-fitting men's garb. Leodogran clasped her in his arms.

'Never shall I let you from my sight again, Elindor mine,' said he. 'My bird, my precious bird is come home.'

But she spoke no reply.

A cool wind was blowing from the south. Leodogran's daughter left her father's lore-books where she had been studying them in the library. Throwing her cloak about her shoulders, she unlatched and opened the front door, but her father, appearing at her elbow, closed it again and took her hand.

'Ashalind, you must not go out.'

He studied her face. He could see that a great conflict was happening within her, and knowing this hurt him grievously.

'How can I help you? Why do you not speak?'

But his daughter was afraid to make any sign, even to shake her head, for the power of the Faêran was everywhere. Somehow they would know, and the chance would be lost forever. She turned again to the door.

'Wait. I shall walk beside you.' Concerned only for her welfare, Leodogran took up his own cloak and his walking-stick. If, in her sickness, she needed to wander, so be it—only he would never let her from his sight.

Thus, every day at dusk in the wooded hills about the city, Ashalind walked with Leodogran and Pryderi, while the dog Rufus followed close in her footsteps. Tears ran unstaunched down the damsel's face, for she sought there Easgathair, believing he might help her in some way, and she feared he would not appear before her unless she walked alone. Yet her father would not leave her nor could she ask it of him. Her hope was that Easgathair would tell her the answers to the three questions without even being asked, for it was certain he would know of the bargain she had struck in the hall under the hill. But all that passed through the eringl woods were the white moths and owls. Without the help of Easgathair, she and the children must be doomed.

The third problem set by the Faêran prince at first appeared not to be difficult. She had seen two Doors leading out from a chamber below the Hall of Feasts, one made of polished silver and the other made of oak. It would seem simple enough to recognise

the portal leading to Erith—but perhaps over-simple. Faêran
things were often not as they seemed, and that task might prove
the most treacherous of all. For the Erith Door to be fashioned of
wood was too obvious. It was a trick—yet what if it were a double trick? Believing she would choose the silver Door, they would
make sure the wooden one barred the way to Erith. Or perhaps
not . . . Alas, that question might be more formidable than she had
supposed, after all. For the second question she had prepared an
answer—whether it would prove acceptable or not was another
matter. But for the first there seemed no solution.

Every night, returning to the house, Ashalind gazed up at the
sky. To look up and suddenly see the majesty of the far-flung net
of stars burning blue-white in their trillions, that was an awesome
experience. Always that moment of first seeing them was like the
moment when, after silence in an echoing hall, a choir of hundreds burst into song, high and deep, accompanied by the
rumbling growl of a pipe organ. The stars, indeed, seemed a heavenly choir if only she could hear their music. The Longing for the
Fair Realm ached in her more gnawingly than before, ever since
she had scented the rosy breeze at the end of the tunnel in the hill
and walked the halls of Carnconnor. The sight of the stars in their
quietude and utterness eased that pain yet exacerbated anxiety.
How could they possibly be counted?

The swiftly waxing moon rode high in the heavens, pooling
shadows in Leodogran's eyes. The glory of the stars blazed like
diamonds thickly sprinkled on velvet. As soon as Ashalind began
to count them, some faded and others twinkled forth, and they
moved as on a great slow wheel, dying and being born.

On the night of the full moon, Ashalind stole secretly from the
house and crept to the stables. There she had hidden a cloak that
laced down the front. With this she covered her gown, adding a
close-fitting wimple to hide her golden hair and a hood to over-
shadow her features. She smeared her face and hands with filth as
before, and embraced the white pony standing in his stall. Silently,
in thought only, she bade him farewell, not daring to even whisper his name. Win or lose, she must now honour her promise to

return to the place beyond the hill. And lose she must, for should she solve the last two problems to the satisfaction of the Faêran, the first she could not answer.

'First, tell me how many stars shine in the skies of Erith. Next, tell me what I am thinking. Last, thou must consider two of the Doors which lead from the chamber below this hall, and tell me which one leads to Erith.'

The final hour was come. She would be separated forever from her father, Pryderi, Meganwy, Oswyn, and her home. She would fall prey to the unseelie, unspeakable thing called Yallery Brown. Imagining what sport he might have with her, she quailed, hesitating. Should she go back, knowing she would fail? What if she never returned to those legendary halls—would they pursue her? Would they hunt her to the fences of Erith, or would they merely laugh at her impotency and faint-heartedness, turning their backs on her forever? She had promised to return. *Honor your word,* her father always said. *Honor your word.* She must keep her promise to return to the Faêran hall. And, though it should be pointless, she must also honour the condition not to speak, scribe, or show sign. No farewell could be spoken, no letter could be left for her father.

She might vanish without clue and spend eternity in the rose garden with Rhys, or in the clutches of Yallery Brown, but in her perverse and willful heart, despite her misgivings, sorrow was mingled with excitement. Since her first glimpse of the Realm the white-hot Longing had begun to excoriate her mind more stringently than ever. That land was the vision of her waking hours and filled all her dreaming, and the pull of it was like the moon to the ocean. The Piper's tune had told all. It was indeed the world wherein lay all the hidden forests of fable, the soaring peaks of dreams, sudden chasms of weird adventure; a land at once dangerous and wild, yet filled with joy and wonders unguessed.

She muffled Peri's hooves, tying on rags. When she ran her fingers through his mane, one or two coarse hairs slid free to cling to her sleeve. One or two more would grow to replace them. The pony swung his head around to look at her. His brown eyes seemed full of wisdom, and as she gazed into them the answer came to her and she knew what to do. From the nearby tack room she fetched a sharp knife and hacked clumps of hair from the mane in several places, letting them fall into the straw. Haltering the now unlovely pony, she led him from the stall.

Beneath the silver penny of the moon went the cloaked damsel and the white horse, among the outbuildings to the overgrown apple orchard. For there was only one way Ashalind could be certain of finding the doors under Hob's Hill once again. She lay down under the ymp-tree.

Middle-night approached. Gnarled lichen-covered trunks leaned, their leafless boughs reaching out to cast shadow-nets on weedy aisles. Feeling the spell of drowsiness coming over her, Ashalind clutched a clump of thistles. Needles of pain shot up her arm, awakening her to the sound of sweetly tinkling bells. The Faêrie Rade passed through the trees like shimmering ghosts. Peri whickered softly and pricked up his ears. Climbing on his back, Ashalind followed.

As before, the Doors of Hob's Hill opened and the light from within revealed a paved way. Lagging several paces behind the end of the procession, Ashalind rode in. The Doors rumbled to, and she slid down to stand beside her steed, who strained toward the far archway. Beyond it now lay a landscape of purple night bejeweled with giant stars of every hue. The everdawn day of Faêrie had altered to soft silver-blue, a sonata in moonlight.

Would Rhys now be sleeping in a bower of blossom somewhere in the Fair Realm? Or would he and the other children still be playing their enchanted games in the rose garden under the canopy of stars? With a rush of tenderness a picture of his face came to mind; his skin soft as a ripe peach, his eyes wide and trusting. Always he had looked to Ashalind as a mother, since their own mother, Niamh, had died giving him birth.

The two spriggan sentries appeared and, complaining, commenced to escort the visitor away.

'Garfarbelserk, Scrimscratcherer,' remarked one, hefting his pike in a knobble-jointed hand.

'Untervoderfort, Spiderstalkenhen,' agreed the other with a nod and a scowl.

Peri snorted and tried to kick the wights, at which they struck at him with the butts of their pikes, screeching. Ashalind-as-Peasant-Lad shouldered her way between the weapons and the pony.

'Stay away from my steed! Hush, hush, Peri. You must come with me.'

His mistress took the tilhal from around her neck and tied it to his halter for protection. This time the sentries led her by a divergent route with no stairs up or down.

Gathering force as she approached, the presence of the Faêran broke over her like a wave.

On this occasion she was brought to a different hall, whose walls were lined with silver trees. The ceiling was high, or else there was no ceiling. Overhead gleamed the shadows and strange fires of the night sky, a fever of stars. To a wild song of fiddles the Faêran danced, clad in rustling silk or living flowers, their hair spangled with miniature lights. Many wights, both seelie and unseelie, danced among them garbed in robes of zaffre and celadon. Repulsive beings, scaled, mailed, leathered, feathered, beastlike or bizarre, mingled with the beauteous. Lace-moths drifted everywhere like bits of torn-up gauze tossed into the air. In the shadows, a pair of agates opened, watched, closed—the eyes of a great black wolf.

When the music ceased the dancers seated themselves around the hall, laughing, conversing in their marvelous language or in the common tongue. The contemptuous sentries beckoned and Ashalind stepped forward, keeping her cloak close-wrapped around her. Instantly a hush fell on the gathering. She felt herself to be truly alien here, a gauche, awkward thing, bound to the soil, bound to ordinariness and eventual mortality. How they must despise her. From under the shadow of her hood, her eyes scanned the gathering. A frisson of excitement surprised her when she saw him. It might have been fear or it might not.

Brighter than the rest was the soft radiance surrounding the gray-eyed lord. He stood on a dais at the far end of the hall, in the midst of a bevy of lords and ladies. Nearby, Yallery Brown sat with some ill-favoured companions of assorted shapes and sizes, some resembling cruel-faced men and others so truly goblinesque as to approximate no living creature Ashalind had ever seen.

From somewhere to the right, a mellow voice announced her presence: 'Elindor of Erith returns to beg audience of His Royal Highness, Morragan of Carnconnor, Crown Prince among the Faêran.'

Whereupon Yallery Brown and his cohorts howled and hooted, prancing with glee. Ashalind waited on bended knee, her head bowed, firmly gripping Peri's halter. Thistledown, like thousands of tiny, pale dancers on tiptoe, floated through the air.

Morragan turned upon her cool, mocking eyes, eyes the colour of smoke. 'Elindor!' he said in his beautiful storm's voice. 'Are they in truth naming young churls after birds in Erith?'

Her blood halted in icy veins. Could it be he saw through her disguise? Was a reply expected?

After a moment he laughed and said:

'No matter. Speak.'

'Sir, I have returned with the answers to Your Royal Highness's three questions. The first was, "How many stars are in the skies of Erith?" And I answer, that there are as many stars as there are living hairs growing on the body of my horse. See here, if it please my lord—it was necessary for me to cut some off to ensure that the total was exact. If anyone doubts this, they may count the hairs themselves and they will find that I do not lie.'

A burst of laughter and applause greeted her words. Yallery Brown gave a shriek and his comrades yowled like cats. The Faêran lord did not smile, but Ashalind's hopes leapt, for he said,

'A clever reply, *erithbunden*, and amusing. So the first question is answered. What of the second? Canst thou tell me what I am thinking?'

'Yes sir,' said Ashalind bravely, using her own clear voice for the first time. 'Your Royal Highness is thinking his humble petitioner is a peasant lad, Elindor of Erith. But your Royal Highness is misled. I am Ashalind na Pendran.'

At this, in a desperate and daring gambit, she threw off her disguise. Bright locks spilled down her back. Using the discarded wimple she wiped her face clean, then stood proud and straight before the astonished assembly, clad in her linen gown. The prince regarded her consideringly. Applause rang louder this time, and praises were shouted from all sides of the hall.

'E'en so!' some of the courtiers cried. ''Tis none other.' For they knew of her, they had seen her wandering on the borders of the Realm, searching, and but for her hound Rufus, she might have been stolen years since.

All eyes turned to the prince, but he offered not a word. Then stepped forth a lady of the Faêran, and her loveliness was a poem. Her dark hair, bound in a silver net laced with glints, reached to her ankles. Her gown was cloth-of-silver overlaid with a kirtle of green lace wrought in a pattern of leaves. Laughing, she said, 'Ashalind, we love clever riddles and tricks—you bring us much merriment this night. We would welcome thee to dwell among us.'

'The golden hair of the Talith is much to our taste,' added another Faêran lady, smiling.

Great wisdom was written in their beautiful faces. Ashalind wondered how such as they could traffic with unseelie things, but she recalled a passage from the lore-books;

The laws, ethics, customs, and manners of the Realm are in many ways unlike those of Erith and are strange to us.'

'That,' said Yallery Brown suddenly, pointing straight toward Ashalind, 'is ours anyway. It was intended to be part of the city's payment.' With unnerving swiftness he crossed to her side, reached up, and spitefully tugged her hair. The pony's eyes rolled and he shied nervously. Icy fire flowed down the damsel's spine. She noted a dandelion flower, yellow as cowardice, peeping from the wight's hideously knotted hair. It might have been growing there, rooted in his skull.

From among the gathering, a Faêran lord spoke. Like the others of his kind, he was comelier than the comeliest of men. A gold-mounted emerald brooch clasped his mantle at the shoulder, and on his head was a velvet cap with a swathe of long spinach-green feathers trailing down to one side.

'In order to find this way in to our country, thou hast spied upon our Rade from under the boughs of the ymp-tree. We of the Realm do not love spies. Other meddlers such as thee have paid the price.'

'My fingers itch to tear out the eyes of this false-tongue mortal, my liege,' said Yallery Brown, turning beseechingly to the prince.

'Yet this smacks of Faêran help and advice,' interjected another Faêran lord. He was garbed in a gaily striped doublet, particoloured hose, and versicolour cloak, his cap a rainbow of three horns. Ashalind thought she recognised him.

'Even this clever deceiver,' Three-Horn-Cap continued, 'could not have come here without the aid of one of our own people—so there can be no forfeit to pay. The Erithan brats were taken because of the perfidy of her kind, those same Men who delved the green slopes of the sithean with iron, and scarred it. But she did not follow me, and thus she is not part of the fee.'

He smiled, showing dazzling white teeth.

'Yes, gentle maid,' he added, 'I am the Piper.'

Of course Ashalind hated the Piper, and yet looking upon him she was forced to admit she loved him, as one must love all the Faêran, even while abhorring them at the same time.

Said Prince Morragan, breaking his silence at last, 'I desire no truck with mortals save for sport, and even that becometh tedious eventually.'

'Never for me, my liege,' whispered the rat-faced Yallery Brown. 'Oh, never for me.'

'She is not thine yet,' replied his master. 'Thus we come to the last question. If this *erithbunden* chooses aright, she and the others shall go free, and it shall be *their* loss. But if she chooses the wrong door, she and they will take the road to doom, Yallery Brown, and perhaps thou shalt be the architect of that doom or perhaps it shall be myself. Behold the Hall of Three Doors!'

As he spoke, the dancers parted, and behold! they stood already in that chamber Ashalind had seen previously. A pathway opened among the crowd revealing not only the Door by which she had entered, but also two closed portals. The Doors of silver and oak faced each other from opposite sides of the hall, and beside each one waited a doughty, grim-faced young man, in ragged plaid and heavy leather, feet planted firmly apart, each holding a pike twined with the dripping red filaments of spirogyra.

These door-wardens stared into the distance, looking neither to right nor left. Their raiment too was wet—indeed water streamed from it in droplets and rivulets to pool around their feet. Seaweed was tangled in their lank hair.

'One of these Doors,' said Yallery Brown, 'leads to Erith. The other leads to your downfall.' He played a little tune on a fiddle and added, 'Think you that you and the brats be the only mortals in the Realm? Not so. For these pikemen of the Doors be Iainh and Caelinh Maghrain, twin sons of the Chieftain of the Western Isles, believed drowned with their comrades in the waters of Corrievreckan. Foolish and arrogant were they, to think they could ride the back of the finest steed in Aia. Now they have learned their lesson well, for they have served in the domain of the Each Uisge this many a long year. Lucky men are these, for their five comrades were torn apart and only their livers washed to shore. And although they look as alike as two peas in a pod they are as different as day from night, for one is forced to be an honest man, while the other never spoke a true word since my lord the Each Uisge became his master. Speak ye the truth, man?'

The guard of the silver Door said, 'Yea.'

'And speak ye also the truth?'

'Yea,' said the guard of the oaken Door.

'You see, it is as I have said,' Yallery Brown continued. 'And this is quite curious to us, for lying is a skill possessed only by mortals. False wench, do not think that we shall tell you which man is which!'

A very pale, exceedingly charming fellow now came forward. He wore close-fitting green armour like the shell of a sea-creature, with a fillet of pearls on his brow and a dagged mantle of brown-green like the leaves of bull-kelp, but he moved like a horse, and despite his finery an unspeakable malevolence hung about him like a ragged shadow.

For a brief moment the mortal damsel looked into his terrible eyes. Cold and expressionless they stared at her, as devoid of emotion or pity as fathomless water, as a drowning pool, as cold rocks and waves that relentlessly smash ships to splinters. Whatever his true shape, here was a thing of horror. She thought:

I am beholding the Each Uisge himself, the Prince of Waterhorses. May all that is benevolent preserve me.

He said, 'My servants only speak two words—yea and nay. They may never say more.' His voice, booming like waves surging in subterranean caverns, ended in the hint of a whicker.

Then said Prince Morragan, 'The mortal may ask one question of one pikeman only.'

Ashalind turned as pale as the Each Uisge and clutched at her pony for support. She had hoped for more clues than this. The wights surrounding Yallery Brown screamed with laughter and leaped about, cutting the most fantastic capers, but the Faêran lady with ankle-length hair said softly:

'Ashalind, fairest, there exists a question which would reveal all to you, if only you could deduce it. We may not aid you in this, but do not despair.'

'When the music stops,' said the raven-haired Fithiach, 'thou must needs choose.'

The dulcet melodies began again, and a whirlpool of dancers flew around Ashalind and the pony, their feet in truth scarcely touching the floor. Time passed, but how much time she could not tell—whether it was a few moments or hours or days. There must be some question she could ask one of the guards, the answer to which would tell her with certainty which was the right Door. If she could not find it out she must choose at random and take a chance, as recklessly as tossing a coin: a chance of losing all, forever—not only for herself but for Hythe Mellyn and the children, for Rhys and their father and for Pryderi. Had she come this far only to fail?

The music and movement distracted her cogitations. She buried her face in the pony's ruined mane and covered her ears. In the darkness her mind raced with a thousand questions, and permutations of what their answers would reveal.

It is like pondering a move in a chess game, she thought. *If I ask this, then if he is the truth-teller he will say that, but if he is the liar he will say the other, and how should that help me in the end?*

With a flash of inspiration she lifted her head. She saw that amid all the motion one tall figure stood and looked down at her and knew the triumph in her eyes.

'Thou hast another choice, Ashalind Elindor,' said Prince Morragan softly. 'To go out by neither Door. I have no love for mortals and would not be grieved if thy race all should perish, but thou'rt passing fair among mortals, and faithful, and acute. Bide here now, and I swear no harm shall come to thee under my protection.'

Beneath straight eyebrows, the smoke-gray eyes were keen and searching. Strands of black-blue hair wafted across his arresting features. This Faêran was indeed comely beyond the dreams of mortals, and he possessed terrible power. The Longing for the Realm pained Ashalind like a wound. He spoke again, more softly than ever:

'I can take thee through fire as through castles of glass. I can take thee through water as through air, and into the sky as through water, untrammeled by saddle or steed or sildron. Flight thou shalt have, and more. Thou hast never known the true wonder of the favour of the Faêran.'

For moments the damsel struggled, pinned by the piercing blade of his gaze, and then her pony blew on her neck and nuzzled her shoulder. At the sudden warmth of his hay-scented breath, she sighed and lowered her eyes.

'Sir, I must take the children home.'

Instantly the gray eyes blazed with a bleak and cold flame. The prince turned away, his cloak flaring, sweeping a shadowy swathe through the air.

The music stopped. The dancers stood still.

'Now choose!' cried the Piper.

Ashalind went to the guard at the oaken Door and asked her question. He replied,

'Nay.'

And she said, 'Then I choose your Door.'

Immediately the Door opened to reveal a long green tunnel of overarching trees beyond which shone the hills of Avlantia in the saffron morning, and the larks were singing, and a merlin hovered in the sky, and the hedges were bare and black along the fallow fields, and blue smoke stenciled the distant skies. And from the city came the sound of bells: 'Awake! Awake!'

But Prince Morragan grasped Ashalind by the hair, pulling her head back so that she must look up at him.

'Thou hast won this game,' he said evenly. 'Thou canst walk the green way and return to thy home. The children will come behind you, but only those who have not tasted of our food and drink. To them it will seem as though they have passed but one hour in the Realm. Go now, but if thou turnest back, even once, thou shalt return here and never leave.' Abruptly he released her.

Tears pricked her eyes as she took the pony by the halter and stepped through the Door. The rumour of a multitude of footsteps came from behind, and childish voices.

Slowly she paced along the vaulted avenue, and soon the first of the children passed her, running down the road, calling to one another in joyful voices. She glanced to the side and saw many whose names she knew, but Rhys was not among them. Had her brother, then, been one of those who had eaten the food of Faêrie?

'Ashalind!' called the compelling voice of the gray-eyed prince. She stumbled, but plodded on. He called her name a second time and she halted and stood, but only for an instant. Onward she went, and now she was halfway along the arched way. More and more children ran past, like leaves blown by an Autumn gale, and there were hundreds of them, but still she could not find her brother, and she thought of Yallery Brown and his flesh-devouring rats, and her courage almost failed her.

'Ashalind.'

This time she fell to her knees and could not arise. The children hurried by. To look over her shoulder, to see one who governed gramarye standing there with the whole of the Fair Realm at his back and that world promised to her—it would be so easy. So sweet it would be, to watch him pivot on his heel and walk away, and to follow. Slowly she clambered to her feet. Despite her desire, she neither looked back nor turned around. She pressed on, her feet and legs heavy, as though she waded through honey. Now the end of the avenue was near, and crowds of children streamed down into the valley, and rushing to meet them down the road from Hythe Mellyn to the bridge flew another crowd—the men and wives of Hythe Mellyn come to bring their children home. Forward into the sunlight went Ashalind.

Then, farther back, she heard the piping tones of her own brother:

'Sister, turn and help me, for I am afraid.'

At that, with a rush of relief, she almost spun about, but she said, 'Do not be afraid, Rhys.' And still she faced toward Erith.

'Sister, turn and help me, for I cannot walk.' Her heart was wrenched, but she hardened it.

'Then, Rhys, you must crawl, for I may not turn back.'

His sobs turned to screams—'Sister, a monster is upon me!'

For the third time, Ashalind stopped, right under the eaves of the last tree, and her neck ached from the effort of not turning her head, and she cried out:

'No, you are not my brother, for he never addressed me as "Sister"!'

Then she heard a crash of thunder and the angry scream of Yallery Brown, and wild laughter. A freezing gust of wind tore leaves from the trees. But her brother came up beside her and she recognised that this time it was he in truth. She set him on the pony's back and they followed the last of the children down the valley.

Sitting on a mullock heap beneath a briar-hung cliff, the young woman blinked. It had been a long time since she had done so and her eyes were filmed with mist, gritty. She looked at the bracelet in her hand, her father's gift. She slipped it on her wrist. Closing, the catch went *click*.

And the memories kept flooding back.

9
THE LANGOTHE
The Longing for Leaving;
the Leaving of Longing

What is Longing that it never lets go? Would that joy could grip us so!
Even the strong oak falls at last, having withstood the south wind's blast.
What is Longing that it never runs out? Even a well may fail in drought.
What is Longing that it never ages, like leaves to dust and youths to
sages?
What is Longing that it will not depart and let peace descend on mortal
heart?

MADE BY LLEWELL, SONGMAKER OF AURALONDE

The tale of the Return of the Children was recounted far and wide in Avlantia. The entire country feted and praised Ashalind na Pendran. A wealth of gifts and the highest honours in the land were bestowed upon her. Bards made songs about the brave maiden who had ventured into the Secret Country, facing not only the Faêran but also the most dangerous of wights, and, against all odds, outwitting them all. The King of Avlantia himself bestowed upon her the title 'Lady of the Circle', with the rank of baroness. Glory and honour paved her way, and happiness ought to have followed—but it was not to be. There remained something the people of Hythe Mellyn had not reckoned with.

'Langothe,' said the wizard Razmath, reading from a lore-book before an Extraordinary Assembly of the citizens of Hythe Mellyn.

'The Green Book of Flandrys describes it as the Longing, or Yearning, for the Fair Realm. All who have visited Tirnan Alainn—as some of the ancients called it—all who have so much as *glimpsed* that country, wish to return. They do no good in the mortal world thereafter. They cannot forget it, even for a little while, and continually search for a Way to return. In severe cases they pine away to their deaths, having no interest in meat or drink and no desire for life in Erith.'

Gravely he raised his eyes to survey the men and women seated before him.

'There is no known cure.' He closed the book.

Stiffly, Leodogran rose to speak. He stood with shoulders bowed.

'Never has there been such joy in this city as on the day our children returned after seven years in the Perilous Realm. On that morn I rose from my couch to find my daughter's bed empty and forsaken. But there came to my door a messenger from Easgathair, Gatekeeper of the Faêran, saying, "Ring the bells and rouse the city, for your daughter is bringing the children home."'

He paused, fighting some inward battle, momentarily unable to speak.

'And on that day we believed all our dreams had come true. The children had indeed been restored to us, but alas, what was lost has never been entirely regained. The Langothe is upon them despite all we have tried. Not love nor gold nor wizardry can bring our children's hearts back to their native land. Though they love us and were overjoyed to be reunited with us, their thoughts constantly stray far away. Ever they wander, ever they search. We have consulted the histories and books of wisdom to no avail. In truth, there is no cure.

'Some lads and lasses never returned from the Perilous Realm because they had partaken of its food or drink. To add to the city's grief, their families have mourned long. My ladies, my lords and gentlemen, we lived in sorrow for seven years, and now for seven long weeks we have watched our neighbours grieve afresh while our children languish and fade. What say ye?'

Then Meganwy, the Carlin of the Herbs, rose to her feet saying,

'I speak for most of us when I declare, we must put an end to sorrow. We cannot let the children's wellbeing continue to decline, nor can we bear to be separated from our darlings. Only one path lies open to us. Together we must seek a way to leave Hythe Mellyn, yea, to leave Erith's dear lands, and journey to dwell in the Realm. How we shall find that place, and whether those that dwell there will admit us, I know not.'

This proposition was greeted with a great outcry, and fiery debate ensued, which continued throughout the many assemblies that followed.

Like the other mortal visitors to the Fair Realm, Ashalind had been brushed by the strange pull of the land beyond the stars. As with them, her interest in the meats of Erith had declined, and her flesh waned, losing the soft curve of youth and conforming closer to the angles of her bones. She did not speak of her own anguish, of the severity with which the Langothe seared her spirit. However, they guessed, her father and Pryderi. Rhys knew only too well; at whiles she and the ailing child would hold one another in a tight embrace.

'What is to be done, Ashli?' he would sigh. 'What is to be done?'

At a loss, she could only shake her head.

The snowy lace of blossom was on the hawthorn when overnight, it seemed, there came a sudden increase in eldritch and Faêran activity throughout all the lands of Erith. Wights of all kinds were abroad in unprecedented numbers, and the Fair Folk were glimpsed much more frequently than ever before, in woodlands and meadows, in high places and by water. Rumors seethed. It was said that some great catastrophe loomed, such as war or the end of the world. People whispered that the King-Emperor in Caermelor knew all about it, for he was in the confidence of the Faêran sovereign, and that they both struggled to avert the mysterious calamity. Many stories circulated, but none knew for certain what the truth might be.

A delegation of wizards, aldermen, and elders of Hythe Mellyn met on many occasions with Branwyddan, King of Avlantia, and his privy council in the palace that crowned the golden city. The fourteen-year-old Lady Ashalind and Pryderi Penrhyn, ten years her senior, were included among them. Hours toiled past in discussion.

'Your Majesty,' said Meganwy of the Herbs, 'in Hythe Mellyn there have been many gatherings of the people, and much ado. The Langothe sorely afflicts our children, and some have died of it. Families yearn vainly for their lost youngsters. Life burdened with this curse is unbearable for many—they wish to leave the city and find a Way into the Fair Realm, there to dwell in peace with their loved ones.'

'How many wish to go?' the king asked, somber of countenance.

Razmath the Learned, wizard of Hythe Mellyn, replied, 'About one third part of the city's population, Your Majesty—those whose children are most severely affected or who never returned.'

'That is many,' sighed the king, 'yet we have looked long upon these silent children and their wan faces. Even the sternest heart could not remain unmoved. I have pondered much on this matter and spoken of it at length with my advisors. Gravely it concerns me, that I cannot furnish contentment for my subjects. Grievously it troubles me that the goodly flower of my people would leave Hythe Mellyn. Yet their sovereign shall not stand in the way of their happiness. So it shall be. If they wish to go, I, Branwyddan, will not gainsay my people, though to lose them will surely be a devastating blow to this land. For many years now the numbers of our race have been dwindling. Sorrow waxes heavy within me— I fear that a Leaving such as this will herald the final days of the Talith.' He added, 'Perhaps only a hastening of the inevitable.'

Leodogran said, 'Your Majesty is gracious and just, and we thank you for your favour. But sire, we need your help, for we do not know how to discover a way to return. My daughter has lain awake beneath the ymp-tree night after night, yet no Faêran procession rides by, no Doors appear in the hillside. Methinks the Hob's Hill traverse is now permanently closed to mortalkind. I have scant knowledge of the Ways between the worlds. What say ye, Orlith?'

The king's wizard spoke. 'Oak coppices, rings of mushrooms, the turf-covered sitheans, circles of standing stones, high places, green roads of leaf and fern, certain wells and tarns, stands of thorn or ash or holly—all these and more are sites where a Way may be found. It is said that these Ways into the Secret Realm, all so different, are each guarded by a Gateway configured like a short passage with a Door at either end, one leading to Erith, the other to the Fair Realm. They are not always doors as we recognise them, with posts and hinges, but Faêran portals that may bear many guises. These Gateways cannot be traversed without the aid or permission of the Faêran.'

Then spoke Gwyneth, Queen of Avlantia.

'William the Wise, King-Emperor in Caermelor, has commerce with the Fair Folk, I believe. It is said that a great friendship exists between them.'

'A messenger shall be dispatched forthwith, asking his help in this matter,' said Branwyddan, 'although I vigorously emphasize that it sorely grieves me to think of losing any of our people.' Sorrow clouded his brow. 'But hearken also to this—of late, unusual occurrences have disturbed all of Erith, as you are well aware, and they have shaken the very foundations of the Royal City in Eldaraigne. An answer from there may come late or not at all, for we hear that William, King-Emperor, is greatly occupied and hardly sleeps. Caermelor has issued orders to open new dominite mines, so that as much of this stone as possible may be dug out of the ground for two purposes: to line the walls of buildings, and to extract the base metal talium for the making of chain mesh. Furthermore, news has been received that heavily guarded shipments of a new kind of metal are being received at the King-Emperor's treasure-houses. What this all means, I may not yet say. But I tell you—time is not unlimited and you must not delay in making your move. Now is the hour to act. Speedily find a Way to the Perilous Realm if that is your desire, citizens of Hythe Mellyn, and end the suffering before it is too late.'

In the soft Spring twilight the air was heavy with honey fragrance. Leodogran remained at the palace in discussion with the wizards Orlith and Razmath, while his daughter walked in the company of Meganwy and Pryderi down the winding streets, through Hythe Mellyn toward the city walls. Ashalind was thinking of her little brother; at the house of na Pendran, the stolen and regained Rhys lay in his bed under Oswyn's care, dreaming of an enchanted rose garden.

'Pray tell us, Mistress Ashalind,' said Pryderi, forgetting, as always, her new title of Lady of the Circle. 'What is the question you asked to find out the Door leading to Erith? For we have all pondered upon it until we are ready to tear out our hair and 'tis most unfair of you to make us suffer so.'

Meganwy said to him, 'But Pryderi, if you had studied the lore-books you would have found it! For although Ashalind reckoned out the answer herself, the riddle is an ancient one, and has been asked and solved before.'

'Do not chide me with ignorance!' returned Pryderi good-naturedly. 'I do not spend my days with my nose buried in books, that is all. There are better things to do. Now, Ashlet, you must relieve me of my misery.'

'Not until you promise not to tease my Meganwy so.'

'Oh, balderdash!' laughed the carlin, her eyes crinkling with merriment. ''Tis merely banter among friends. He only teases those he loves. Besides, I am used to it—after all, I have put up with it since the lad's knees were scabby as two tortoises. And that was a full day ago, at the least.'

Pryderi snorted.

'The question,' interrupted Ashalind, before he could respond with a clever retort, 'which was in fact the *answer*, was, "Would the other guard tell me that this is the door to freedom?"'

They walked awhile in silence, then Pryderi spoke again.

'I see. Well said. Acute, if I may say so. 'Tis fortunate you had perused the same moldy tomes as Meganwy.'

'I had not! It is news to me that this is an old riddle. As Meganwy said, I fathomed it myself!'

'The more credit to you, child,' said Meganwy gently.

'How strange it is,' mused Pryderi, 'that not so long ago we would have given everything we owned if only the children could escape from the Fair Realm. Now we are desperately seeking a Way for them to return. Truly it is said, "misguided are mortals".'

A pale, hollow-eyed child leaning from a casement called out to them. There was an ache in her voice.

'My lady, have you found a Way?'

'Nay,' Ashalind returned, 'not yet.'

A gaunt, lethargic youth lounged beneath the wall by the city gates, looking out across the valley. A reed pipe hung from his belt. As though begging for his life he asked Ashalind, 'Are you bound for Faêrie, my lady? Shall we return now?'

His name was Llewell, and he was one of the returned youths, a brilliant musician and songmaker. He was being driven mad by the Langothe. In his delusion he often believed he was truly one of the Faêran.

'Nay, Llewell,' Ashalind said again, turning away lest the sight of his forlorn and desolate aspect should crush her heart. 'Soon, maybe. Meanwhile, make us a song so that we might forget, for a time.'

So it was, always, with the children. They turned to Ashalind in their blind and urgent need. They clung to hope in the form of her native wit, by which, once, she had achieved the impossible. They wanted to believe she could do it again. And like them, she had been *There*. She understood how they suffered with the Longing.

Outside the gates there was a stirring among the trees, a susurration in the leaves. The rumour of things unseen was every-where; muffled laughter, scamperings, squeakings, shrill whistles, low mutterings and far-off singing. The lands of Erith were alive with the denizens of Faêrie as never before—the Fair Folk them-selves, often heard or sighted but rarely seen clearly, eldritch wights trooping and solitary, wights of water and wood, hill and house, cave and field; incarnations both seelie and unseelie.

'Eldritch creatures lurk all about us,' said Meganwy. 'Surely there must be one who can take a message to Easgathair. From your account, Ashalind, the Faêran sage seemed to hold you in high regard.'

'Then the misguided are not only mortals,' said Pryderi, strid-ing ahead.

Ashalind smiled, as she still sometimes did, despite the dull, sustained pain of unfulfilled yearning. 'Pryderi loves me!' she cried after him chaffingly.

'I do!' he called back over his shoulder.

Ashalind took Meganwy's arm.

'What you say is true, Wise Mother,' she said. 'Let us go direct to the orchard. It is said that apple blossom delights all creatures of gramarye, particularly the Faêran.'

Soft wind, as warm as love, whispered sweet nothings to budding leaves. From far away scraped the raucous hubbub of jackdaws coming home to roost. A skein of swans stitched its way slowly across the mellow west. Passing under the trees and half-hidden by blossom, the urisk was unnoticeable at first, but a flicker of movement caught Meganwy's eye. Silently the carlin took Ashalind by the sleeve, indicating with her forefinger. A small, seelie man-thing moved between the trees on hairy, goatlike legs.

'In the name of Easgathair,' Ashalind called out urgently, 'I bid you tarry.'

With a rustle, the wight jumped away into the trees and was seen no more.

That evening after supper, Ashalind personally set out the pail of clean water and the dish of cream for the household bruney, a task usually carried out by Oswyn. The dark hours came creeping. She sat in the kitchen's inglenook, waiting, waking, and at midnight the bruney came stealing. Its face was ugly and rough, with a stubbly gray beard and wide mouth; its hands were outsized. A conical cap of soft brown deer's hide covered its head; its other clothing consisted of a threadbare coat, patched knee breeches, coarse woollen hose, and large boots. The damsel watched the wight begin its chores, sweeping and scrubbing, scouring the pans to mirror-brightness with preternatural speed and efficiency.

'Bruney,' she said softly into the shadows, never taking her eyes from it, never meeting its gaze. The little manlike thing ceased its industry.

'What are ye doin' sae late awake, Mistress Ashalind?'

'I seek your help, hearth-wight of my home.'

'I seen ye grow up from a bairn no bigger 'n meself, and yer father before ye and his father before that. Have I ever failed this house?'

'No, you've never failed this house. You've been good to us—never a dollop of sour cream, never a drop of unclean water. In return, we've looked after you. Bruney, I seek audience with the Lord Easgathair of the Faêran. Can you bring me before him?'

'I have ways to send messages to the Faêran, Mistress Ashalind, but I wist the Lord Easgathair will nae heed me at this time, if ever, for ill deeds and evil tidings have come upon us all.'

'Of what do you speak?'

'Fell doings and ill fortune,' said the bruney obscurely, 'but there be nocht that such as I can do to change things. Alack that I should see such times as these. Alack for the folly of the great and noble. The world shall be mightily changed and what's tae come of it I know not.'

'But you will try this for me?'

'Aye, that I will, hearth-daughter. Now get ye abed as is proper and leave me to my doings. They's my hours now, not yourn.' He shook his little besom broom at her.

'Good night,' she said, lifting the hems of her skirts as she flitted upstairs.

Toward morning, just before cock-crow, Rufus woke up and began to bark frantically at the bedroom door. Leaping half-awake from her bed, in her linen nightgown, Ashalind collared him.

'Hush, sir. Stay.'

The bruney's head appeared around the door's edge and spoke. ''Tis only me, Rufus. What are ye groazling and bloostering about, ye great lummox?' Lowering his ears sheepishly, the dog wagged his tail. 'Mistress Ashalind,' the bruney went on, 'I hae a message for ye.'

'Yes?'

'Next middle-night ye mun gae to Cragh Tor.'

The head disappeared.

Steep, thickly wooded hills rose close on every side, dark against the star-salted dome of night. Streamlets splashed like threads of spun moonlight down their shoulders. A path wound its way up Cragh Tor, overhung by a cliff on one hand, dropping away precipitously on the other. As the party of three walkers climbed higher, they saw, looking back through a gap in the hills, a scattering of yellow lights shining like fireflies in a dusky dell: the lamplit windows of the city.

Finding the hilltop deserted, they sat down on mossy stones to wait, uneasily. Cragh Tor's summit was flat. No trees grew there; instead it was crowned by a half-circle of granite monoliths, thirty feet high, a ruined cromlech whose other half had collapsed in centuries past. Of the stones that stood, three were still connected by lintels while the others leaned lazily, painted with lichens in rouge, celadon, and fawn. Grass grew over the fallen monoliths, which lay partially buried. Usually this place was dismal and unwelcoming, and this night was no exception. An unquiet breathing of the night soughed and grieved its way in eddies around the angles and edges of the rocks. From somewhere below the ground came the gushing hum of running water. Glowing eyes peered out from shadows near ground level, but no voice answered the inquiries of the incongruous mortals. No Faêran lord or lady appeared.

Ashalind and her companions felt the presence of wights massing thickly all around. The night was full of their mutterings, their lascivious snickerings, sudden wild laughter and unnerving yells. A sneering bogle jumped out, then leapt, spry as a toad, over the rim of the hill. Gray-faced trow-wives peered from shadows and tall tussocks, whispering and pointing, their eyes protruding like onion-bulbs, their oversized heads bound in dun shawls. One of them was clutching a ragged baby. The slight weight of the tilhals at the throats of the mortals felt reassuring, yet inadequate. The trows melted away as slowly the hours of darkness stretched on. The mortals huddled drowsily into their cloaks for warmth.

It was about an hour before dawn when soft music came stealing out of the darkness, subtle but permeating, like jasmine's fragrance. Simultaneously, a rose-petal glow bathed Cragh Tor Circle, like the dawn but untimely. A fox ran across the grass. The monoliths were shining with an inner radiance, like crystal with a heart of fire, and now strange flowers sprang in the turf. Two people of the Faêran were seated upon a fallen monolith while a third stood, one foot braced upon a stone, strumming a small golden harp.

He was like a sudden bird of the night, this harpist; an orchid of many colours, a tonal melody. Twined about his neck was a live snake, slender as grass, yellow-green as unripe lemons. Blinking away the blur of weariness, Ashalind started up, biting off a low cry before it had left her lips.

The harpist was also the Piper.

She turned away, wisely concealing her anger and indignation.

The musician laid down the instrument and spoke softly to his companions. Then the whitebeard with the staff spoke.

'Hail and well met, fair company,' said Easgathair, greeting by name each of the three who now stood before him. He looked indefinably older and more careworn than before, and at this, Ashalind wondered, for the Faêran were said to be immortal, and unaffected by the passage of time.

The three petitioners bowed.

'At your service, Lord Easgathair,' Ashalind said.

'We know your names.' She who uttered these words was seated at Easgathair's right hand—the Faêran lady with the calm and lovely face Ashalind had seen in the halls of the Fithiach of Carnconnor, she whose dark hair reached to her ankles. Green gems now winked like cats' eyes on her hair and girdle. The fox that had run across the grass sat elegantly beside her, looking out from narrow slits of amber. 'But you do not know ours,' she went on. 'I am called Rithindel of Brimairgen.'

'My lady, you gave me courage when I needed it most,' said Ashalind with a curtsey.

'That which is already possessed need not be given.'

'I Cierndanel, the Royal Bard, greet you, mortals,' said the slender young harpist-Piper, bowing with a white smile that seemed, to Ashalind, mocking.

'The musicianship of Cierndanel is renowned amongst our people,' Easgathair said.

While Meganwy and Pryderi saluted the musician, Ashalind faltered, filled with conflicting desires for vengeance and courtesy.

Here before her stood the one who had originated all her troubles, with his irresistible pipe-tunes.

The Faêran bard turned an inquiring eye upon the young woman. Like a nail, it transfixed her.

'Have I offended thee, comeliest of mortals?' (A voice like rain on leaves.) 'Say how, that I might ask forgiveness. A frown blights thy loveliness like late frost upon the early sprouts of Spring.'

'Can you not guess, sir? Yet, offended, I have no wish to offend. I will say no more.'

'Tell on. Our discourse cannot progress until I am satisfied.'

'Well, then.' Ashalind took a deep breath and blurted out, 'You, sir, are the perpetrator of the most heinous thievery of all. You are the Piper. You stole the children. That's your offense.'

'I am all astonishment,' said Cierndanel.

At Ashalind's tidings, Pryderi took an impetuous step forward, raising his fists. Meganwy's eyes snapped fire.

Before they could take issue, Easgathair held up his hand. 'Wait,' he said. 'Cierndanel, thou know'st not the ways of mortals as I do. In their eyes, your accomplishment was not a meting out of justice but a misdeed. Understand, mortals, that Cierndanel was acting on behalf of the justice of the Realm when he led away the children with the music of the Pipes Leantainn. 'Twas not done for revenge or spite, 'twas a lessoning and an upholding of what is just; a fair treatment and due punishment in accordance with equity.'

'Faêran equity,' said Pryderi tightly.

Meganwy said, 'We can hardly applaud the Piper's actions, but let us not quarrel. I have studied somewhat of Faêran customs and mores, and while I cannot approve, I acknowledge. Our moral code is not yours.'

'You all seem to forget,' pursued Cierndanel, the bardic snake sliding around his neck like a pouring of liquid jade and topaz, 'that I piped away your plague of rodents also.'

'But did not Yallery Brown send the rats to begin with?' cried Ashalind.

'The wight Yallery Brown has nought to do with me, sweet daughter. He, like many of his kind, mingles freely with those of our people who tolerate such types, but what mischief they may choose to make outside the Fair Realm is no concern of ours. The crime, the betrayal of promise, was the city's,' he added, stroking the seashell curve of his harp with a long and elegant hand. 'Why hold a grudge against me for being the instrument, so to speak, of retribution?'

The corners of his mouth quirked. A smile tugged at them, as ever.

Said Easgathair, 'Condemned mortals ever rail against the executioner, though 'tis only his given task, and had there been no transgression, there would be no punishment.'

'It seems immortals shall never understand why,' said Pryderi bitterly.

'Immortals we be, yes,' returned Easgathair, 'but filled with passion; swift to laugh and love, swift to anger, slow to weep. We can, like you, be bowed by grief.'

'No, never like us,' replied Pryderi. There was a harsh edge to his tone. 'Never like us, since you cannot know death.'

'An immeasurable gulf,' acknowledged the Lady Rithindel, after a pause, 'sunders our races, one from the other.'

'Nonetheless,' said Meganwy, 'we must let grudges shrivel and be blown away like the leaves of past seasons, for now we are come to ask for your help. Knowing the Fair Ones to be an equitable and just people, we are certain you will not deny us.'

'Indeed, we will not deny that we are equitable and just!' said Easgathair. 'Seat yourselves before us now. We wait to hear what you shall say, although perhaps we have guessed already.'

'We wish to speak of the Langothe,' said Ashalind, guardedly taking a seat beside Pryderi on a mossy stone.

Easgathair nodded.

'We cannot abide with it,' she continued, 'and we beg you to let the children return to the Fair Realm with their families, there to remain. We ask that they may receive protection against unseelie wights such as mingle with the retinue of the Fithiach of Carnconnor, and that they should dwell far from his halls.'

'Far and near do not mean the same in the Realm as they do here,' said Cierndanel lightly. 'Thou mightst cross from one end of

Faêrie to the other and still be close to the place from whence thou proceeded. Indeed, there are no ends or beginnings as thou know'st them.'

The Lady Rithindel said, 'Angavar our High King has always welcomed the gold-haired Talith whenever they have entered our country. You people of the gold have often been a source of delight, aye, and help to us, and this occasion, I wot, would be no exception—despite that he is grievously burdened at this time.'

Ashalind saw Easgathair's fist clench as he gripped his staff. Raising his silver-white head, he directed a calm gaze at the mortals.

'Ashalind,' he said, 'for seven years thou didst wander in the hills and those eringl woodlands where the Faêran take delight in riding and hunting. Thy kindness and loyalty of spirit were marked by those who saw thee pass and that is why I helped thee when thou first asked. For that same reason I will help thee a second time, for it is the way of my people to reward goodness. Also, there are some among us who would perhaps opine that at this time we need, more than ever, a quota of humankind to abide among us. As Gatekeeper to the Realm, I will grant your request. You and your friends and families shall have your admittance, as well as protection against wights. Against Prince Morragan I cannot shield you, but I think he will not harm you.'

The mortal folk jumped up and embraced each other, smiling, bowing deeply to the three Faêran. 'Lord Easgathair, Lady Rithindel, Lord Cierndanel—we greet your generous words with joy!' they cried, mindful, even in the midst of their exultation, to refrain from thanking them, as custom decreed.

A meteor arced down the glistering sky, scoring a trail as fine as diamond-dust. Chaste breezes raced across open spaces, lifting the white silk strands of the Gatekeeper's hair. His proud face, with the erudition of eternity engraved into it, hardened to an uncharacteristic severity.

'It delights us to behold your happiness,' he said, 'but many things you must now learn—for a dire event has come to pass in Aia, and a more disastrous one shall yet befall. Sit yourselves down once more. I must relate to you now a history of Three Contests.'

Perplexed and intrigued, Ashalind and her friends did as he had bid. When they were comfortably settled, the sage began. 'Know first that I, Easgathair White Owl, am the Gatekeeper, the overseer of all the Ways between the Realm and Erith. Some while ago—time runs out of kilter in your country, but it was about the season when Angavar High King traded places with one of your kings for a year and a day, and the two of them became friends— some while ago, I was challenged to a game of Kings-and-Queens, or Battle Royal, as it is sometimes known. The Talith entitle the game "chess". My challenger was the younger brother of the High King—Prince Morragan, the Raven Prince, who is called the Fithiach. Morragan has long been my friend, and such a challenge was not unprecedented. We often vied with one another in amiable gaming.'

'Indeed,' interjected Cierndanel as the whitebeard paused, 'and the prince's bard Ergaiorn follows his lead, for it was then that he won from me in a wager the Pipes Leantainn, the Follow Pipes as mortals might name them, and the very instruments with which thou wouldst have quarrel, sweet maid.'

'Then sir, I would venture to say that you are well rid of them,' rejoined Ashalind with feeling. 'But prithee, Lord Easgathair, do not halt the tale.'

'Alas,' continued the Gatekeeper grimly, 'I did not see then the dark current that ran deep, far below the surface of the charm and wit and mirthfulness of Prince Morragan. I did not suspect the iron acrimony that had become lodged in his once-blithe heart, hardening it over the years, feeding the fires of his pride and arrogance.

'He gifted me with a beautiful Kings-and-Queens set made of gold and jewels, beautifully wrought by Liriel, jewelsmith of Faêrie, and challenged me to find anywhere in the Realm a fairer or cleverer assemblage of pieces for the board. We played the game and, as was our wont, we bet on the outcome.

'Lately the Fithiach had been lamenting the fact that always I must abide near to my post in the Watchtower, from which I can oversee all the rights-of-way, and if I step into Erith I must not stray too far lest I am needed. Until he spoke of this, I had not resented my duties, but when he conjured these ideas I was persuaded perhaps they were at whiles a trifle irksome, and I might enjoy a brief respite, if only for a change.

'"If thou shouldst win the contest," said Morragan, "I shall take thy place in the Watchtower for a space of a year and a day, while thou sojourn'st as thou wishest."

'"But sir," said I, "what stake may I offer thee? Thou dost already possess all thou couldst desire."

'"Wilt thou grant me a boon?" said he, and I made answer—"Provided it is within my scope."

'Eventually we settled that if I should lose I would grant him a boon as yet unasked; that I would pay him whatever he should desire, were it within my power. We played and I defeated him. He assumed my role at the Watchtower for a year and a day.

'Some time later, I in my turn gifted the prince with an equipage of Kings-and-Queens, the pieces being the size of siofra, those diminutive wights who love to mimic our forms and customs.

'"Skilfully is this wrought, I'll allow, my friend," said he, "and 'tis larger than the Golden Set I bestowed on thee, yet 'tis no prettier or more artful."

'Then I showed him how at the touch of a golden wand the pieces moved by themselves, by internal clockworks, and walked to their positions as bid.

'Thus, with the Mechanical Set a second game was played. On this occasion we both wagered the same stake: "The loser shall pay what the winner shall desire," and Prince Morragan ended up the victor.

'"One victory to each of us! This time I have defeated thee, Easgathair," he said, laughing, "but I must beg for time to consider before I ask for what I desire."

'"Sir, thou mightst enjoy as much time as thou wishest," I boasted. "And whilst thou art at it, thou mayst take time also to search high and low for a cleverer or more beautiful set than this, which I'll warrant thou shalt never find in the Realm." At that the brother of the High King smiled and agreed, but added, "Yet, I will bring thee a more marvelous collection and there shall be a third trial. This shall decide the champion."

'Fool that I was to play for unspecified boons,' said Easgathair bitterly. 'And yet how could I suspect? I believed him free of jealous thought. One day, not long—in our reckoning—after thou, Ashalind, hadst taken away the children, he brought me to a glade where a platform was raised. It was inlaid with squares of ivory and ebony and upon it stood sixteen dwarrows in mail, armed, and twelve lords and ladies of Erith including four mounted knights, also a quartet of stone-trolls, all enchanted, all alive. At the player's spoken command they obeyed!'

'But how cruel,' protested Meganwy, 'to enslave living creatures in that way!'

'They were trespassers in the Realm,' explained Cierndanel the Faêran bard with a shrug. 'Those who trespass may, by rights, be taken.'

The mortals looked askance, but held their tongues.

'With this Living Set we played a game,' said the Gatekeeper, 'and once more the Fithiach defeated me. He is an adept player and I began to wonder whether he had allowed me to win the first time. As before, we agreed that the loser must pay what the winner should desire—but this time, having won, he immediately asked for what he wanted. He asked, did the Raven Prince, and I was bound to honour my word. I did not guess it had already become a bitterbynde.'

Easgathair rose and paced around the circle. His feet crushed no blade nor pressed any flower.

'It was then that I discovered the thoughts he harboured. For he made a terrible demand, which was truly anathema to my expectation. I alone am in charge of the Keys to each Gate. If the Ways and the Gates are invisible to you it is because they are merely closed. Rarely are they locked. Once locked, they remain shut forever, according to our Law, as happened to one Gateway after the theft from Lake Coumluch on Whiteflower's Day.' The Gatekeeper shook his silver-maned head. 'I recall precisely the words the Fithiach used when he described the boon he would ask of me. He proclaimed:

'"*Upon thy word, Easgathair White Owl, thou shalt grant me this deed. Thou shalt lock the Gates to the Ways between the Realm and Erith, barring the passage of Faêran, eldritch wights both seelie and unseelie, unspeaking creatures, and all mortal Men. No more shall traffic pass to and from the Realm, which shall remain properly for the Faêran and not be sullied by humankind. At the instant when the Gates finally close, those who bide within the Realm shall remain within and those who bide without shall remain without. After the locking, all the Keys shall be placed in the Green Casket, whose lid shall be sealed by my Password."'*

Pryderi jumped up in a panic.

'Are the Ways to be closed forever? Then we must hasten!'

'I asked him,' said Easgathair, 'for grace of a year and a day. For friendship's sake he granted it.'

'*"Thou might'st enjoy grace of a year and a day,"* he said, *"but do not conjecture that the passage of time shall change my heart. Never shall I retract this demand."'*

'Why should the prince wish to cut Aia in twain, to sunder Erith from the Fair Realm?' asked Meganwy. 'Why does he so despise mingling with mortals?'

'Prince Morragan has no love for your race. There are deeds done by mortals which have aroused his ire, and also stirred the anger of others of our kind—deeds such as spying and stealing, the breaking of promises, slovenly habits, lying, greed, captiousness, the snaring of a Faêran bride by a mortal man. Morragan loves only the Faêran, but traffics also with eldritch wights. His hatred of mortals is not like the bloodthirsty savagery of unseelie wights but rather a desire to shun your kind, to shut them away from his sight.'

'So,' Pryderi summarized, 'it is purely out of contempt for mortal folk that he would lock the Gates to Faêrie.'

'That, and more,' said Easgathair. 'Know that Morragan is the younger brother of Angavar, called Iolaire, High King of the Realm, who is friend to mortals. Your own King-Emperor William once helped Angavar to bring about the fall of the Waelghast, the Chieftain of the Unseelie Hosts, who was a supporter of Prince Morragan. The Waelghast used to plague Angavar in days of yore. Methinks, perhaps Morragan, in his jealousy, encouraged this. Without the Waelghast the unseelie wights are leaderless, but more and more nowadays they are foraying into Erith to harass mortals and mayhap Morragan is behind this also.

'Angavar is powerful. Morragan is the younger and so he must be Crown Prince, instead of King. 'Twould be unwise for me to reveal more, here in this place—even stones may have ears. Suffice to say that rivalry between siblings causes strife in many races, and jealousy is not a trait monopolized by mortals. It hurts Angavar to Close the Ways.'

Clouds of moths gathered around the luminous stones, spattering their tiny X-shaped shadows in evanescent patterns on the lichen. The fox gave a grating, silvery yap like the beat of a wire brush against metal. Down in the mosses, a small stone bobbed up and down as though something were pushing up from underneath it.

'Get thee hence!' said Easgathair, pushing the stone with his foot. It wailed thinly and dropped with a clunk.

An eggshell of silence closed around the Circle, brittle and fragile. Ashalind and her friends were dumbfounded at what they had heard.

'We begged the Fithiach to reconsider,' said Rithindel in low tones, 'but he would not listen. Many of our folk applaud his plan, especially those who have ever given him loyalty and love. Now ill will sunders the Faêran and many go forth to visit Erith, knowing it shall be for the last time. For there are a multitude of things in Erith that please many of us—not least, its mortalkind.'

'Angavar High King,' Cierndanel the Piper said, 'has ordered Giovhnu the Faêran Mastersmith to forge a special metal with which to make gifts of farewell for William of Erith—a metal such as has not before been seen in Aia, a metal with which gramarye is alloyed. *Sildron*, it is called. Your people shall deem it precious.'

'Why then are we mining the yellow metal, the native talium?' asked Pryderi.

'Never have all the Gates been locked,' said Cierndanel. 'It is feared that when the Day of Closing comes, a weaving might be torn; a balance might be shifted. The imbalance may well let loose wild winds of gramarye. Strong forces surround the places where our two countries intersect, and they will be thrown into confusion, striving one against the other. It is possible they will go howling around Erith forever, without guide or purpose. Untamed winds of gramarye can create shape and image out of the thoughts of Men. Only talium can block them out.'

'On the Day of Closing,' said Easgathair with a sigh, 'Midwinter's Day in Erith, three warning calls will be sounded throughout both worlds. On the last call, the Gates shall swing shut, and remain so, seamlessly and forever.'

'Unless Prince Morragan should later reconsider and open the Green Casket of Keys using the Password,' said Meganwy, 'and return the Keys to you, sir.'

'He has vowed never to change his decision once he is sealed within the Realm. What's more, he would have no reason to do so. He is a denizen of the Realm and believes all his happiness can be found therein, throughout eternity. Indeed, he is not mistaken. The delights and adventures of Faêrie are limitless. I can assure you, never shall Morragan change his mind.'

'But might you not divine or guess the Password?'

'There are words and words, in a multitude of tongues. In the Realm, time is infinite. But should the wrong Password be spoken to the Casket three times, its Lock will melt and fuse so that nothing may ever open it, alas.'

'And alas for the Langothe,' said Ashalind resentfully, 'for dearly do I love the good soil of Erith. Had I not heard your tune, Piper, and glimpsed that place, I had rather eat of a fresh-baked brown cob than all the sweet fruits of the Fair Realm. I had rather walk in the briar-tangled woods than the ever-blooming rose gardens, and wear the good linen and coarse wool than dress in Faêran gossamer and moonlight. But now I have no choice, for my blood is changed.'

'Hush, Ashalind,' warned Meganwy; but the Piper laughed.

'We take no insult that a damsel should declare her love for her native land.'

The Lady Rithindel reached down and caressed the ears of the restless fox. She looked out across the land below, its valleys now drowned in mist. The skies were bleaching in the east. A frigid blue light waxed all around.

'The cock crows soon,' she said, 'and we must away.'

'In the morning of Midwinter's Day,' said Easgathair to Ashalind, 'gather together all those who wish to dwell forever in the Realm. Take the way leading west from the city. When you come to the crossroads, take the Green Road.'

'I know of no Green Road,' said Pryderi.

'On that day, those who seek it shall find it. Follow that path to the land of your desire. For now, return to your homes. Farewell.'

Ashalind and her friends took their leave. As they passed beyond the ring of stones they turned back for one last glance, but the Circle was empty. A sense of desolation and abandonment overtook them, as if the last light had faded from the world. They shivered; something more penetrating than chill puncturing their bones. A cock crowed in the distance and the sun peeped over the rim of the world, lighting the dew on the mossy stones and the grass, making jewellery of it.

Thus began the Leaving of Hythe Mellyn, the exodus that no war, plague, or pestilence had brought about. Instead, this migration was initiated by the Langothe; that yearning for a place which all mortals strive to find, in their own way, whether consciously or not, an estate sought either within the known world or beyond.

Throughout Erith in the weeks that remained before the closing of the Gates there was unprecedented mingling of Faêran, mortal, and wight. The Talith families who had resolved to depart set their arrangements in order, and packed the belongings they wished to take with them. As the day drew nearer, more and more of their friends and relations, unable to bear the thought of parting forever, decided to join them.

Thus it happened that early in the morning of Midwinter's Day an immense procession left the golden city by the Western Gate and proceeded down the road, their shadows lying long before them. Of the entire population, only a handful remained behind.

Piled high with boxes and chests, the horses and carriages and wains trundled along. Hounds ran alongside, or rode in the wains with the children. Some folk were mounted, others went on foot.

All were singing. Every voice lifted in the clear morning air, and the song they sang was the love for the green hills, the sun-warmed stone, and the red trees of the homeland they were leaving behind. 'Farewell to Erith,' they sang, 'land of our birth. No more shall we tread your wandering paths or look out across the fields to the sea.'

They smiled as they wept, and hardly knew whether it was gladness or sorrow that they felt; indeed pain and joy seemed, on that journey, to be one and the same.

Behind the procession the city stood almost empty on the hill. Blank windows stared out over deserted courtyards and the streets lay silent, but the amber mellil stone glowed as ever in the sunlight.

At the crossroads where usually roads radiated in four directions, there was now a fifth. A winding Green Road, smooth and unmarked by wheel ruts, stretched out, disappearing over the hills. Bordered with ferns, it was paved not with stone but with pliant turf. Down this path the convoy turned. Those folk who remained standing at the city gates with the Avlantian royal family and their retainers saw them dwindle into the distance, their singing still carried faintly on the breeze. The watchers strained their eyes until they could see their kinsmen no more, but some said later that they had seen a bright light burning white on the horizon and that the procession had passed right into the centre of it.

The King moved his Court from Hythe Mellyn to Filori, in the land called Ysteris of the Flowers. The abandoned city rang hollow, like a great bell. With the Leaving of Hythe Mellyn, the spirit had gone out of the people. As the years passed, fewer children were born to the Talith. Their race dwindled, the last of the royal family died without heirs and the Talith civilization passed into legend. No Feohrkind or Erts or Icemen came from the southern lands to Avlantia, to settle in the abandoned Talith Kingdom—or if they came, they did not remain. Therefore the cities lay dreaming in their crumbling splendor, visited only by the tawny lions and the dragon-lizards that basked in the sun. In later days it was said that a plague or pestilence or unseelie gramarye had emptied the cities of Avlantia. The real reason was forgotten.

Ashalind, riding side-saddle on the black mare Satin—a gift from the city—lagged behind even the most reluctant travellers on the Green Road, despite the urgings of her friends. Only Rufus trotted beside her, alert, reveling in the myriad scents only a hound's nose could trace. Ahead, Rhys rode with their father on the big roan gelding with Peri following on a rope, bearing light packs. Leodogran was gladdened to see how vitality was returning to his young son as they traversed farther along the Road, and colour bloomed in the boy's cheeks.

Pryderi's spirited horse pranced forward eagerly, fighting restraint.

'Don't dally, Ashalind,' the young man called merrily over his shoulder. 'You have made your choice like the rest of us. Lingering only protracts regret. Look forward—we shall be happy when we arrive!'

Leodogran's daughter would not listen, heeding no one. Tugging gently on Satin's reins, she looked up and thought she spied, out toward the coast, a white bird flying.

'I am torn,' she said to herself, 'between the land of my heart and the realm that's infiltrated my blood.'

And she glanced back at the lonely city on the hill.

But her family and friends were advancing down the Road, and so she flicked the reins and rode on. Her hood fell back from her fair head and the edges of her traveling cloak opened like flower petals to reveal her riding-habit, a long-sleeved gown of blond and turquoise saye, worn beneath a short, fitted jacket of ratteen. About her throat was wound a white cambric neckcloth. Nostalgically, she had garlanded her wrists with eringl leaves in place of briars. Beneath the leaves her bracelet glowed on her left arm, like a flame reflected in the rim of a goblet of golden glass.

As they travelled, the road began, imperceptibly, to alter. It became a sunken lane of deep banks, and thick, overhanging hedges. Bright flowers flecked its grassy borders, yet they were not the blooms of Erith.

To either side of the Road, stands of eringls gave way to thick forests, simultaneously bearing fruit and blossom. Rufus ran ahead to join the other hounds frisking and tumbling on the green verge.

When Ashalind looked back at the city again, it was gone. Hythe Mellyn, the trees with their leaves of somber crimson and bronze, the hills—all had vanished. Landscapes, fair and foreign unrolled behind the travellers on all sides, and they were not the hills of home.

The terrible heartache of the Langothe fell away like a discarded mantle, whereupon a form of delirium overswept the mortals. They ran and rode on as though nothing could touch them. Their mood was euphoric, as if they had become invulnerable giants who strode at the top of the world and perceived, through vast gulfs of air, the immensity of a mountain range suspending its ancient blocks from horizon to horizon, each peak stamped on the sky so clearly that they could step out and tread them all.

Now that she had entered the Fair Realm with all of her loved ones and the Langothe was assuaged, it almost seemed to Ashalind that there was naught she could ever lack again. Happiness surrounded her, within her reach, only waiting until she took a sip or sup of Faêran food, when she would possess that happiness and be possessed by it completely. Only the *memory* of the Langothe remained, a fading knowledge that it had once existed. But there was also, still, the memory of Erith, which must be relinquished, wiped out by the act of consuming a part of this new land, in order to be consumed, to gain the utter peace that stems from utter lack of yearning.

A memory too precious?

Afterward, she could never clearly recall those hours in Faêrie when, for a brief efflux, time ran synchronously with time in Erith.

She and her people had come into a marvelous countryside. Here the trees were taller, their foliage denser; the valleys were sharper, the mountains steeper, the shadows more mysterious, thrilling, and menacing. All colours were of greater intensity and brilliance, yet at the same time softer and more various. Through everything ran a promise of excitement that profoundly stirred the psyche.

Avenues of towering trees like rows of pencils led to glimpsed castles of marble and adamant, flecked rose-gold by an *alien* sun. Exuberant brooks flowed through meadows, and on the lower slopes of the hills deer grazed beneath great bowery trees in pastures of flowery sward. Orchards, where fruit hung like lanterns, were yet snowed with full blossom. In the boughs, songbirds trilled melodies to shatter the heart with their poignancy.

Even as the Talith pushed deeper into the Realm, the rosember light paled to the glimmering blue of evening.

The newcomers perceived that a feast was laid out on the starlit lawns, beneath spreading boughs heavy with scalloped leaves. There were pies and puddings, flans and flummeries, saffron seedcakes, cloudy white bread and soft yellow butter, raspberries, pears, strawberries and honeyed figs, creamy curd, truffles, and crystal goblets encircling dark wine. The children who had eaten Faêran food and remained in the Fair Realm now came running forth. Ecstatic families were reunited. Beasts of burden, unhitched from rein and shaft, ran free. Bundles, chests, and boxes were left beside still-laden wains, all abandoned, all *unnecessary* now.

Entranced by the music of fiddle and harp, the yellow-haired people of Hythe Mellyn danced and feasted in the mellow evening. Their cares had been discarded with their belongings on the flower-starred lawns. Caught in the ecstasy of the moment, Ashalind cast off her traveling cloak and prepared to join in. Yet at the last, she did not.

The mortals were being watched. Faêran forms moved among the trees.

When she glimpsed them, something within Ashalind lurched and turned over.

At her elbow, handsome Cierndanel said, 'Thou art honoured, Lady of Erith. The most noble and exalted Lady of the Realm has sent for thee. Come.' He flashed his mercurial grin.

It seemed then to Ashalind that she followed him, or else was transported by some unfathomed means, to another location. In this new place there reclined a Faêran lady; surely a queen among her race. And as Ashalind beheld her she was given to know her name also: Nimriel of the Lake.

Nimriel's tranquillity was that of the calmness of a vast loch at dawn. Her mystery was that of a solitary black tarn in the forest, where, like a breath of steam, a creature of legend comes to drink, its single diamond spire dipping to send swift rings expanding out across the surface. Her beauty bewitched like moonlit reflections of swans moving on water. She was mistress of all the wisdom hidden in deep places; in drowned valleys and starlit lagoons; beneath mountain meres where salmon cruised in the dim, peaty fathoms.

Ashalind looked into a pair of wells, dark and clear.

It was said among mortals that if you stand at the bottom of a deep shaft and look up, then even on a sunny noon you will see the stars shining against pure shadow. That is what it was like to meet the gaze of the Lady of the Lake.

As Ashalind made her duty on bended knee, a dark-haired maiden, lissom as a stemmed orchid, stepped forward: the Lady Rithindel. She offered a two-handled cup.

'Thou art welcome among us, Ashalind na Pendran! My lady Nimriel invites thee to drink.'

Ashalind's hands reached out to take the cup. The red eringl leaves encircling her wrists brushed against it, rustling. Releasing the cup, she drew back with a sigh.

'The Lady Nimriel is generous, but I have promised myself that I shall neither eat nor drink until the last Gate is closed and all links between our two worlds are severed forever.'

On an inland sea the weather might change suddenly. Blinding fogs might form without warning, a wind might come gusting from nowhere to whip up white-capped waves.

The Lady Nimriel spoke, soft and low.

'Many fear me, Ashalind na Pendran.'

'Ought I to be among them, my lady?'

'Thou hast refused my cup. I do not lightly brook refusal of my hospitality. Nevertheless, because thou speakest from thine heart, thou hast no cause to be afraid.'

Ashalind bowed in acknowledgment.

'My custom is to gift newcomers. If thou wilt not accept food or drink, perhaps thou wilt accept other gifts. On thy journeyings, thou may'st need to cheat the moon.' Briefly the lake-queen leaned forward and brushed her fingertips across Ashalind's dagger-slender waist.

'My lady speaks of journeys,' exclaimed the damsel. 'I believed mine to be over.'

'Thy voyage is only just beginning, daughter of Erith. This I see, although as yet I know not the reason. Thou need'st not much in the way of gifts. Thou dost possess many of thine own. Yet mine is bestowed now.'

Confused, at a loss for words, Ashalind stammered a reply. She could not understand what it was the lady had given her.

The two reservoirs of lucency regarded her gravely, as though from a distance.

'Know this, daughter of Erith. The Faêran are in great strife and turmoil at this very hour. Our eyes, from all over the Realm, are turned now toward your country. The time of Closing draweth near, but *all is not as it should be*. Part of the plan goes awry. Go now to Easgathair and thou shalt view, from the Windows of the Watchtower, what the eyes of all who dwell here can see without aid. Farewell.'

Cierndanel escorted Ashalind to the Watchtower. Again, they travelled by some esoteric, indescribable method.

Light as if filtered through geranium-tinted glass washed over a stone building. It was a tower, intricately carved all over, whose slender flying buttresses soared to pointed arches and singing spires. Glossy-leaved ivy climbed there among the rosettes and gargoyles and pinnacles.

Inside the tower, stairs led upward to a chamber where the Gatekeeper stood amid a gathering of the Faêran. Leodogran and Rhys were among them. Eight tall windows reached from floor to ceiling, each facing a different direction. Their crystal panes did not hinder the birds flying in and out. At times these windows would cloud over like breath-misted mirrors. When they cleared, different landscapes would lie beyond them.

Between these fenestrations soared slender golden pillars twined with living ivy leaves and carved ones of peridot, jade, and emerald. The golden ceiling too was festooned with these leaves, and with clusters of jeweled fruit and flowers. In the centre of the room stood a raised plinth draped with mossy velvet, gilt-embroidered. Thereon rested a large gold-clasped green casket with a high-arched lid. The lid was closed.

Easgathair greeted Ashalind, saying grimly, 'I would that I could welcome you here in a happier hour.' His glacial hair and the voluminous folds of his white robes fanned out as he swung around to glance at the Northwest Window, then settled around him again.

'I too, my lord,' replied Ashalind, but her father said gladly:

'Sir, there could be no happier hour.'

Rhys, laughing, chased birds around the hall.

'The Windows may look onto any right-of-way according to my command,' said the Gatekeeper. 'See, the South Window shows the Gate at Carnconnor, that thou call'st the Hob's Hill.'

A curious thought struck Ashalind.

'Does it show the passage which divides the outer Door in the side of Hob's Hill from the inner Door to the Fair Realm? Does that passage lie in Erith or in Faêrie?'

Distracted, Easgathair glanced over his shoulder. 'I must return to the Northwest Window.'

'Allow me to explain.' The fetching Cierndanel, who seemed to be everywhere at once, took the Gatekeeper's place. 'Every Gateway comprises two Doors, an inner and an outer, with a short passageway between. Time flows at different speeds in Erith and the Realm. A Gate-passage is needed to adjust the flow when something passes from one stream to the other. It operates like a lock in a canal.'

'Suppose someone was trapped in there!' said the damsel, thinking of the Gatehouse at the palace in High Mellyn, with its fortified barbican and its ceiling pierced by murder-holes for the destruction of invaders.

'There exists a safeguard to prevent such an accident. When they are locked, the Gates at each end will still open outwards only, permitting traffic to flow *out* of the Gate-passage in either direction.'

'Like eel traps backwards,' put in Rhys, intrigued. Recognizing the Piper, drawn by him, he had ceased his vain attempts to capture a bird in his hands.

'Just so, perspicacious lad. But from this hour, such engines are of use no longer. Already has each Key been turned in each Lock. All Keys, great and small, have been remitted to Easgathair White Owl—from the emerald Key of Geata Duilach, the Leaf Gate, with its intricate wards, to the silver-barreled crystal Key of the Moon Gate; the shell and jade of Geata Cuan's Key and the great basalt Key of Geata Ard. They lie, indestructible but untouchable, in the Green Casket, which is even now sealed by the Password of the Fithiach.' He gestured toward the casket on the plinth. 'Every bond on every Door has been set to lock and link, and now it only remains to join them at the appointed and immutable hour of the Closing. Listen! Do you not hear? The winds of gramarye are awakening at this outrage, the winds of Ang. They flare from the Ringstorm at Erith's rim. Soon they might prowl the lands of thy world, dyed by the imprints of men's designs.'

The smile that usually played about his lips had left him. A shadow crossed his attractive face.

'But something's amiss. Thou seest how the crowds cluster about the Northwest Window, with White Owl at their fore. They look upon a Gate we call the *Geata Poeg na Déanainn*, awaiting Angavar High King and Prince Morragan, who still ride within Erith's boundaries. The royal brothers dare to ride late, as the Closing draws nigh. The first Call is about to sound!'

'Why do they tarry?' asked Ashalind, craning her neck for a better view of the Northwest Window.

'The Fithiach and his followers were returning from a last Rade in Erith, hawking I was informed—but the King and his knights have ridden out to detain them, blocking their path.'

In the Northwest Window a scene revealed itself with startling detail and clarity. A hush fell on the assembly in the Watchtower. Beyond the Window the skies of Erith sheeted storm gray and a strong wind drove the clouds at a cracking pace. Thunderheads boiled over darkly.

Two companies of riders faced each other, one led by Prince Morragan, whose sculpted face could clearly be seen framed by the long dark hair and cloak billowing out behind him. His followers, about a hundred tall Faêran knights, sat motionless upon their horses. Harsh-faced, they gazed upon the King's retinue, which was massed between them and the traverse called the Geata Poeg na Déanainn. The Faêran King's voice could clearly be heard, by the enchantment of the Watchtower Window.

'Brother, renounce thy boon of the Gatekeeper. Shall I drive thee forth before the Gates close and shalt thou be exiled forever from the Realm?'

The watchers cried out in shock and dismay, but the Crown Prince betrayed no sign of disquiet. Calmly, he replied,

'Dost think me a fool? 'Tis a game of bluff.'

'Nay,' replied the King, 'there is no more time for games.'

For an instant, anger flashed from the Crown Prince's eyes, then he smiled and lifted a hand in a signal to his knights. They split into two groups and sprang away, one to the right, the other to the left. Immediately the King's knights spread out to block them, but some broke through and were harried and pursued, and wrestled from their steeds. Faêran-wrought metal flashed up silver against the purple stormwrack of the furious skies. Desperately, the followers of the Fithiach raced to elude their hunters, to reach the portal between the worlds, the Geata Poeg na Déanainn. Among all these knights, two stood out—the High King and his brother. These two, so noble of bearing, strove hardest each against the other. The wind was howling, running before the storm.

Suddenly, cutting across the milling confusion, the sound of a horn rang out, dulcet and virginal, piercing both worlds. Faêran, mortal, and wight alike paused and lifted their eyes.

'The First Call to Faêrie,' cried Easgathair White Owl. 'The appointed hour approaches. Hasten home!'

Some among the assembled Faêran exclaimed to one another in consternation, 'They must hurry! 'Tis too odious a fate they are hazarding!'

Cierndanel said to Ashalind, 'The Sundering of Aia will wreak great changes in Erith, many of which cannot be foretold. The very Gates themselves might become distorted or dislocated beyond recognition. As the instant of Closing draws upon us, Time, habitually unsynchronized, begins to run awry. *The King and the Prince risk misjudging the moment of their return.*'

'Ah,' murmured Ashalind, whose thoughts were far away. 'How I crave to return to *my* home. I cannot bear that this should be my final view of it. Yet, should I return, I would pine away swiftly. The Langothe, incurable, would destroy me.'

'Not necessarily,' said Cierndanel in surprise, wresting his gaze from the Window, 'for there is a cure for the Langothe.' At his throat the eyes of the slender serpent glared, twin peridots, coldly insulted by humanity.

'A cure!' Ashalind whirled to confront him. 'Lord Easgathair never told us!'

'You did not ask for the cure, my lady, but instead for entry into the Realm, which was granted.'

'A cure!' Oppression unchained Ashalind's spirit and she laughed weakly, too stunned at this revelation to be vexed at Faêran literalness. 'Where is this cure? How can I obtain it?'

'Perhaps it is not commonly known among mortals, but the High King of the Realm has the power to take away the Langothe. He is the only one who can do so. Simply by saying the words, *"Forget desire and delight in the Land Beyond the Stars,"* he can annul the Longing.'

'Then I must go now to him before it is too late! Alas, would that I had known before! Would that this fact had been noted in the books of lore, for pity's sake!' she exclaimed passionately.

'It is already too late. There is no time. The Closing is imminent. Besides,' said Cierndanel, 'he does not lightly grant the cure.'

Beyond the Northwest Window, a red-haired rider called to the High King.

'Turn back, sir! Turn back now for home.'

The King's company drew together and swerved, but as they rode toward the Geata Poeg na Déanainn, the riders of Morragan the Fithiach galloped close at their heels. At a shout from the High King, his company wheeled and urged their horses against those who followed, driving them back. Directly over their heads now, lightning struck repeatedly. Hundreds of bolts flashed within the space of a few heartbeats, scalding the sky to white brilliance. A distant pine tree exploded into a living torch.

'Renounce thy boon!' the High King roared to his brother, his voice strong above battle and thunder. His demand was answered by Morragan's mocking laugh.

'The Fithiach knows that the King in desperation tries to trick him,' whispered Cierndanel on breath of lavender. 'I too believe our sovereign is bluffing. He never would banish his brother from the Realm—he is not as ruthless as that—and if his words be examined closely, it will be found that he has not in fact said that he would do so. But what is this madness that overtakes them? They must all make greater haste now!'

From beyond the Window echoed deep-throated yells of anger, the clash of battle, the shrill neighing of Faêran horses. The two sides were evenly matched. They fought magnificently, not to wound or kill, but to prevent progress, and in so doing each impeded the other. Their fighting was a dance of strength and skill, like the clashing of stags in a forest glade, or two thunderstorms meeting to tear open the sky. Conceivably, it was their Faêran rage that now disturbed Erith's elements.

Presently the Call came for the second time, its haunting echoes lifting high overhead—the long, pure notes of the horn, a two-note hook on which to suspend the moment.

'Turn back—the hour is upon us!' cried the High King's captains.

As one, the Faêran lords swung around and began a race, but as before they would not leave off harrying and hunting one another until, nearing the right-of-way, the High King's entourage turned in fury again to assail and drive off their rivals.

'Leave well alone!' shouted Easgathair. About him, the gathering parted as he strode closer to the Window, his white hair flying like shredded gossamer. He seemed taller, and fierce as a hunting owl.

'Can those beyond the traverse see and hear us?' wondered Rhys, at his sister's side.

'They could do so if they wished,' answered Cierndanel, hovering nearby, 'for there is little beyond the power of such mighty ones. But in the heat of this moment it seems they have eyes only for the conflict at hand.'

'We must make the choice now!' said many of the Faêran who watched. 'If Angavar High King does not return in time, we choose exile with him.' In the next blink they were gone.

Others protested that it was unthinkable that the royal brothers and their knights would not return in time. Nevertheless many fled the Watchtower; soon a flood of Faêran, wights, birds, and animals poured through the Geata Poeg na Déanainn to aid the King's return. There was scant chance that they would reach him before the Closing—the combatants fought, in fact, more than a mile from the Gate.

Silently, Ashalind battled an agony of indecision. She lifted her gaze once more toward the knights beyond the Window, staring at the melee. And all at once she forgot to breathe. In that instant her spirit fled out of her eyes and into Erith.

'Father, forgive me,' she cried suddenly, 'I must try to return . . .'

Aghast, Leodogran cried, 'But why?'

'Only that—' His daughter struggled to find words. 'My future lies in Erith, I think. If the High King does not return in time, I will beg him to cure my Langothe, for he has the power to do so.'

'My Elindor, my dearling—would you be parted from us forever?'

'Oh, I do not want that, but it must happen, for just now I have learned where my heart lies, or else my heart has been torn from my body, for I feel a rupture there, as if it were no longer here with me.'

His face was stricken. 'Why do you decide now, at the terminal stroke, to leave forever all the people you love, all you have worked for, in the hour of your triumph? What strange perversity has overtaken you?'

'Father—' She struggled for words, her feet of their own accord stepping away from him as she spoke. 'I do not want to hurt you. This bird must fly the nest, dear Father, or else it will never fly at all. Forgive me. You shall be happy, you and the others I love. Mayhap you shall forget me, here in this land of bliss. My duty is over now. My path is my own. Furthermore, and more importantly—'

'I forbid it!'

Father and daughter opposed one another, the only motionless figures among the swirling multitude.

'Have I not done enough?' Ashalind begged. *My ears strain to hear that last Call. Let it not be now!*

Slowly, Leodogran bowed his head. After a pause he took a pouch, a horn-handled knife, and a dagger from his belt and handed them to his daughter. His movements were stiff, his voice was roughened with grief. 'These heirlooms and this gold, which I bethought in my naivety we would need in this place, I give to you with my benison. They are of no use here. They may do you some good, if you go. But I hope you will not. There must be more to this, more than you have told. I do not understand you.'

He kissed her and quickly turned away.

'Father, when Rhys came back from Faêrie I vowed that I should never weep again, unless it were for happiness. I shed no tears now, but I will carry your loving words with me.'

She leaned to embrace Rhys, whispering comfort in his ear. Rufus had somehow eagerly pushed his way in and she bent down to pet him. Excitement and sadness flooded through her. Her words rose strongly, eagerly.

'Tell Pryderi, Meganwy, and Oswyn I hold them always dear in my heart. And Satin, who is free here—whisper the same in her ear. Cierndanel! If the High King does not turn back in time, I would return to Erith through the Geata Poeg na Déanainn.'

The Faêran Piper looked at her wonderingly, yet knowingly.

Woe the while! thought Ashalind, in an agony of impatience. *The Faêran Herald puts the clarion to his lips.*

'In truth?' said the Piper. 'But the King shall return, he *must* return. The Iolaire is the very quintessence of the Fair Realm. Without him its virtue would be greatly diminished. And those that accompany him right now are the flower of Faêran knighthood, who, if they do not reach the Gateway soon, would be banished until the end of time. But thou, fair damsel, thou mayst not leave, for hast thou not eaten our food and drunk our wine?'

'I have not.'

His comely face sharpened. She caught a spark of anger in his eyes.

'Stay here,' he said.

'As you love me, Cierndanel, benefactor and malefactor of my people, aid me now!'

He paused, as if considering. Then he smiled.

'Very well. Follow me to the right-of-way if you wish, but I think you will never pass through it.'

As the Piper grasped Ashalind's hand, she saw, through the milling crowd, Pryderi. Flailing desperately like a drowning swimmer, he was pushing his way toward her. His jaw knotted, his eyes aghast and fixed, he gasped and lunged forward, but then was gone in what seemed the blink of an eye, and the Watchtower, the assembly vanished with him.

Cierndanel led her to an avenue of trees in blossom, whose boughs arched to intertwine overhead. At the far end of this tunnel, two stone columns capped with a sarsen lintel, framed a scene. Thunderstorms raged in the skies of Erith and the maelstrom of Faêran knights did battle. Behind them, distant peaks reared their heads to the racing clouds. Ice-crystals clung to the grainy surface of the Erith Door, but the perfumed trees of the Realm Door swayed gently. Ashalind and Cierndanel found themselves surrounded by a crowd of Faêran and wights, who paid them no heed, being engrossed in staring through the Gateway toward Erith.

'Thou seest, every traverse has two Doors,' said Cierndanel, speaking quickly, 'and a passage which lies between. Before thee lies the Geata Poeg na Déanainn. In the common speech of Erith, that means the "Gate of Oblivion's Kiss".

'Mark thee, it bears this name for a reason,' he added. 'Over the centuries, several mortal visitors have departed the Realm through this right-of-way and all have been given the same warning. The Gate of Oblivion's Kiss imposes one condition on all those who use it. After passing through into Erith, if thou shouldst ever be kissed by one who is Erith-born, thou shalt lose all memory of what has gone before. The kiss of the *erithbunden* would bring oblivion upon thee, so beware, for then there is no saying whether the bitterbyndings of such a covenant may ever crumble, whether memory ever would return. I think it would not.'

She nodded, trembling. 'I heed.'

'Furthermore,' he insisted, 'the Geata Poeg na Déanainn is a Wandering Gate with no fixed threshold in Erith. When open, it behaves like any other traverse and remains fixed in its location.

But when the Gate is shut it shifts at random, as a butterfly flits erratically from blossom to blossom. Therefore, one is never able to predict its next position. Chiefly it is wont to give onto the country of Eldaraigne, in the north, somewhere in that region known as Arcdur. Always, that was a land uninhabited by your people, but perhaps no longer. Knowing these truths, dost thou still desire to pass through this perilous portal?'

'I do.'

Unexpectedly, the Faêran Piper folded around Ashalind's shoulders a long, hooded cloak the colour of new leaves. He whispered closely in her ear, his words carried on a fragrance of musk roses:

'Fear not, brave daughter of Erith. The Gates are perilous only in the rules by which they exist. If you abide by these, not so much as a hair of your head shall be harmed.'

Ashalind closed her eyes to the strange beauties and perils of the Fair Realm, reaching for the scent of wet soil, the tang of pine, the chill of a storm wind, the cry of elindors on the wing. Her head spun and her mouth was parched taut with a terrible thirst. Easgathair's voice roared from nowhere in the mortal world:

'Return instantly, ye knights, for the time is nigh! The Gates are Closing!'

Ashalind looked through the Gate-passage. At the Erith Gate, one or two of the knights from both sides broke away and rode hard, sparks zapping from their horses' hooves.

'Forget this quarrel!' Easgathair's caveat boomed from somewhere indeterminate. 'Set aside your pride and ride for the Realm!' But the High King and the Crown Prince, intent on their purpose, continued to ignore his warning.

Then red lightning smote from the High King's upraised hand, splitting the sky, and all who looked on heard him shout, 'By the Powers, I will not again petition thee, Crow-Lord. Now thou hast truly stirred my wrath. Consequently, I swear I *shall* exile thee.'

'No!' Hoarse and harsh came Morragan's vehement denial, and for the first time there was a note of alarm in his tone. He flung a zigzag bolt of blue energy from his palm. Confronted with his brother's fury, he gave ground, but even as they battled, the long, clear warning sounded for the third time, rising like a ribbon of bronze over the treetops.

''Tis too late!' thundered the Gatekeeper.

Now at last the High King and the Raven Prince were riding together, flying for the Gateway at breakneck speed with their knights flanking them, and nothing stood in the path of their headlong rush; they spoke not, nor looked to left or right, and all quarrels were abandoned as the threat of permanent expatriation became imminent. Dread fell on the hearts of the assembled audience. A crash like the world's end shook the floor of the Watchtower, the horizon shuddered, and a shadowy veil drew across the vault above. There arose a loud keening and clamor of voices fair and harsh from near and far, and as the beautiful riders almost gained the Gate, a cataclysmic tumult filled the sky and seemed to burst it asunder. The voices of the Faêran joined in a lament like a freezing wind that blights the Spring, for the Gates were swinging shut, and those they loved most would be exiled for eternity.

A sudden terrible gust slammed through the Gate of Oblivion's Kiss with a mighty concussion, snatching mortal breath. It was all over. The Faêran royalty and their companions were forever excluded from the Realm. The Watchtower Windows shattered and fell out in shards, leaving shadowy apertures that stared sorrowfully across the long lawns where the Talith dancers stood poised as if in a frozen tableau.

But with a pang of regret for the land of desire and delight, which spoke of the Langothe already reawakening to haul on its chains, Ashalind had slipped into the Gate of Oblivion's Kiss.

10
DOWNFALL

There's a place that I can tell of, for I've glimpsed it once or twice,
As I've wandered by a misty woodland dell.
I believe I almost saw it on the green and ferny road,
Or beside the trees that shadow the old well.
And I've never dared to whisper, and I've never dared to shout,
Even though it always comes as a surprise,
For I fear that by my movement or the sounding of my voice
I might make it disappear before my eyes.

'Tis a place of great enchantment and wild gramarye; a fair,
Everlasting haunt of timeless mystery,
You'll find danger there, and beauty; strange adventure curs'd and bless'd,
That will seem to wake a longing memory.
But I've heard that if you go there you might stay for far too long,
And you may forget the road by which you came.
Some folk never learn the way. If you should find it then beware,
For if you return, you'll never be the same.

FOLK SONG OF ERITH

For immeasurable moments, all was confusion. Something fluttered and battered softly about her head in the colourless half-light. Ashalind could not comprehend her status. Had she fallen off Peri's back, or perhaps Satin's? Her leg ached. Should it not heal, she would not be able to follow the Piper—oh, the anguish of hearing that call and not being able to respond! She would drag herself through the dust . . . Such a hard bed to lie on, this, and why was everything so hushed and still?

Stung by sudden recollection she sat bolt upright. She looked around for the stony land she had seen at the end of the Gate-passage, and the Faêran knights embattled there. But there was no open sky above her head, no Erith, no tall riders, only a dim, distorted passageway, an arched and twisted tunnel sealed by a Door at either end. The vaulted ceiling was cracked. In places it sagged down like a bag of water. The Gate-passage had been biased, damaged by the unprecedented sundering of the worlds between which it lay. Yet its structure remained viable.

For how long?

In each half of the chamber the walls were different. As they approached one Door they resembled living trees growing closely together, their boughs meeting to interweave as a ceiling. Toward the other portal they merged into rough-hewn rock.

This, then, was the Gate-passage between the Other Country and Erith.

The distraction beat her around the head again, with soft wings. It was a hummingbird. She recalled it rushing by her as she had leapt through the Realm Gate. Now in agitation the tiny creature darted about, seeking escape.

'Which Door shall I open for you?'

But the bird flew up to the wracked ceiling and perched in a niche there.

'Little bird, which Door shall I open for myself? I still have a choice—how odd. I may go out from here to either place, but once out, I may never come back.' She empathized with mailed crustaceans entering a wicker trap; a one-way entrance with no return.

The Lords of Faêrie had been trapped in Erith after all. In her native land, they lingered. Gently, Ashalind pushed the stone Erith Door with one finger. It floated open easily under the slight pressure. Beyond stretched a land of towering rocks: Arcdur, empty of all signs of life. Night reigned.

The hummingbird dashed past. Once outside, it rebelled against the darkness and tried to return, but some invisible barrier prevented this. It flew away, leaving Ashalind bereft.

She let her hand follow it, gingerly, through the Erith Door, out into the airs of home. Her fingertips tingled and she snatched them back. How interesting—it seemed that one could be partway out and still get back in, but if, like the bird, one made a complete exit, a barrier was thrown up. Withdrawing, she allowed the Door to close itself and sat leaning against the wall to ponder, touching the dying eringl leaves that covered the bracelet on her wrist.

The Door would not harm a thing of flesh by closing on it.

Now that this truth was apparent, a plan began to evolve.

She fancied she could hear, at the other end of the Gate-passage, beyond the silver Realm Door with its golden hinges, the sound of sweet, sad singing. If she could somehow prop open the Erith Door then even if she ventured into Erith she could return through the Gate-passage and thus into the Realm whenever she wished. The Gate of Oblivion's Kiss would let no one else pass through it, now that its Key had been turned in its Lock. Prince Morragan's edict had ensured that: '. . . barring the passage of Faêran, eldritch wights both seelie and unseelie, unspeaking creatures and all mortal men . . .' Yet she fitted none of those descriptions! Ashalind laughed, as it came to her that the Raven Prince had overlooked mortal women—over-looked and underestimated. Doubtless Meganwy would have said, *A common trait among males.*

Enchantments must always be carefully worded. The Raven Prince had not been careful enough. The thought of this made the smile linger on Ashalind's lips, and she recalled the remnant of some old tale she had heard in childhood, the story of a man who had outwitted a Lord of Unseelie by hiding in the walls of his home. She thought: *Here in the walls where I now dwell, I am nei-ther within the Realm nor without it . . . Indeed, borders are mysterious, indeterminate places.*

Furthermore, if the Doors could be propped open and the Gate could be duped to allow the unhindered passage to and fro of the only living creature (bar the hummingbird) who had been locked neither in Faêrie nor in Erith, then she might be able to carry a message from one place to the other. What if, in Erith, she could discover the Password to the Green Casket; the Password that would release the Keys to open all the Gates again? Then the High King might be reunited with his Realm!

The preternaturally attractive Prince Morragan, whose dark male beauty cloaked acid and steel, had asked his boon and it had been fulfilled exactly. Once fulfilled, all boons lost their power over whosoever had promised them.

There remained only the danger of the second pledge, the unasked boon that Morragan had cleverly won from the Gatekeeper. But if she, Ashalind, could only find the High King, surely he would be able to put all things to rights, to force his brother to reveal the Password and renounce his second boon in exchange for his own return to the Realm. Surely the Crown Prince would do anything to be reunited with his beloved homeland.

Was it possible? Could she return the generosity of the Faêran by reuniting them with their High King? She would search in Erith for him—surely it was not possible for him to have gone too far away in such a short time—and when she found him, she would beg him to cure the Langothe, which had begun again, of course, to eat at her. Then she would tell him of her secret way back into the Fair Realm and all would be well! The only peril would lie in preventing Prince Morragan from discovering the secret first.

But the Fithiach did not know she was in Erith. No one in Erith knew.

Her fingertip pushed open the stone Erith Door for the second time.

The landscape had changed dramatically. Weather had eroded some monoliths, while others looked sharp and new, as if they had but lately been thrust up from subterranean workshops in some violent upheaval of the ground. It was no longer nighttime. Sunset tinged the air with the delicate pink of blood diluted in water. Puzzled, it took her a moment to work out what was happening, and when she did her insides crawled like cold worms, her stomach flopped like a fish.

Time in Erith was racing past while she remained in the Gate-passage. She must delay no longer—how many years might have passed already? In a panic, she tried to think quickly. Cierndanel, or someone else, had said that time was running all awry because of the Closing. There was no telling how many years might have elapsed by the time she finally slipped through the Door into

Erith—perhaps seven years, perhaps a hundred. All the mortals she had known, who had remained behind, might be long dead. Her world might be altered in many other undreamed-of ways. It might have evolved into a place unknown.

'I shall be a stranger in my own land,' croaked Ashalind, with difficulty forcing words from dehydrated lips.

The Faêran, however, could not be slain; they were immortal. They could choose or be forced by serious injury to pass away into a lesser form, but unchallenged, the exiled knights, the royal lords of the Realm and the lords and ladies who had fled to join them would live on, whatever else.

With a sense of overwhelming urgency she propped her father's knife in the open Erith Door. As soon as she let go, the Door snapped shut, breaking it.

A living hand could keep the Door open, but not an object of metal. If only she could delude this enchanted valve, make it believe that she was partway through it, perpetually half in, half out, it would stay open for her, and her alone. Some part of her must remain in the doorway, to prop it open. A finger? No, that was too gruesome to contemplate. Other measures must be taken. She worked quickly.

For the third and last time she opened the Erith Gate. Arcdur's stony bones leaned up, even more skewed and corroded, shouting against the low-slung sky. A storm was raging, but Ashalind could not wait for it to abate—already too much time had passed. Her preparations were made. Pulling Cierndanel's gift-cloak closer around her shoulders, she stepped out of the quiet passage.

Chaos assailed her. Reflexively she flung herself back against an upright stone pillar, one of the Gateposts. Torrents of rain lashed all around and wind screamed through darkness. Crouching in the lee of the rock, she let the waters of Erith run down her face into her parched mouth, drinking greedily of the chill deluge, feeling it irrigate her body and send silver channels running along her veins, until she had her fill.

Already her riding-habit was sodden. It was strange to recall this was the very costume in which she had made the journey from Hythe Mellyn to the Perilous Realm. That journey now seemed so long ago and far away. The words of Nimriel came back: '*Thy voyage is only just beginning, daughter of Erith.*' Ashalind wrapped herself more tightly in the Faêran cloak. Lightning ripped open the belly of the sky and its dazzle revealed in a black-and-white instant a world of tumbled rocks and oblique crags utterly different from the realm she had departed from moments earlier. Looking back, she noted that on this side the Geata Poeg na Déanainn looked to be no more than a tall crevice between leaning boulders, perilously inviting, its secret recesses wrapped in deep shadow. Intermittent flashes illuminated slanting water-curtains pleated suddenly by gusts of wind. Her thirst slaked, Ashalind felt a great weariness coming over her. She crawled under an overhang, out of the storm's fury. Desiccated leaves flaked from her wrists and turned to dust. The Faêran cloak was warm. Briefly she wondered how this Erithan storm compared to the one in which Morragan had battled against his brother, maybe a hundred years ago.

Then she slept.

Pale dawn revealed a nacreous veil over the sun. Rivulets chattered swiftly over pebbles, droplets fell tinkling from ledges. Boulders had piled themselves high everywhere in fantastic, towering shapes. Water and granite surrounded Ashalind. The only signs of life were mosses and pink lichens.

She drank again, from a rocky cascade, wishing that she had a flask in which to carry water. She was alone in an uncertain place, probably far from human habitation, and she knew nothing of wilderness survival, but good sense told her that thirst and exposure were her two most immediate enemies, and against them she must be prepared. First—survive. Next—fulfil her quest. She decided not to proceed until she had memorized the surroundings in the vicinity of the Geata Poeg na Déanainn, to ensure future recognition.

The furor of the Closing had distorted and dislodged the entire Gate, including both of its Doors. The portal had been blasted out of alignment. Fallen rocks partially covered the Erith Door.

I think the Faêran would no longer know this Gate. Only I am here, to record it in memory.

She began to take careful note of her surroundings, preparing to imprint every detail of the Gate's identity and location on her consciousness. Something nagged, diverting her attention, like a fly buzzing about her ears. She lost concentration . . .

'—*hain?*'

Crackling voices, someone calling out a name.

She took no notice. It was not her name. Or was it?

What was her name?

The interruption faded. A fancy.

She shook her head to rid her ears of the buzzing. The voices faded, giving way to memories.

The Faêran cloak now appeared to be mottled gray in colour, exactly like granite. Its fabric, soft and strong, was unidentifiable and had remained dry, although rain and wind had bedraggled her riding-gown and other garments. Leodogran's dagger and pouch of gold swung from her belt. Ashalind emptied the water out of her riding-boots, braided her long hair, and bound it around her head for convenience, then took a deep breath of the pure, silver-tinged air. It set her blood ringing. The soft luminescence that indicated the sun's position was still low in the sky, behind dully gleaming crags that stood up like pointed teeth.

Northeast of Arcdur, she knew, lay the strait that separated Eldaraigne from Avlantia. Besides having no means of crossing it she was reluctant to return to her homeland lest devastating changes had been wrought on it by the winds of Closing, or by Time. Never had she travelled out of Avlantia, but her thorough education had included studying the maps of the Known Lands of Erith. These she now recalled.

South, a long way south, lay the Royal City, Caermelor, and the Court of the King-Emperor of Erith. It might be the best place to glean news of the whereabouts of Faêran royalty. Besides, the Geata Poeg na Déanainn had spilled her out toward the south, so it seemed somehow meet to continue in the same direction.

Now that excitement, fatigue, and thirst were behind her, Ashalind was aware that hunger, like a rat, gnawed her belly.

Worse than that, the Langothe, which had coiled up like a snake temporarily dormant, now hit her with full force, redoubled now that she had not only breathed the air of the Fair Realm but also left her loved ones there. Retching, she staggered and clutched at an outcrop, half turning toward the Gate.

Now was the time to leave, and leave quickly, before the Langothe's cruel pull drew her back to the Fair Realm at the very outset of her quest. With an effort, as though walking through water rather than air, she forced herself to set out, step by step, aching to turn back, at least to take one extra glance over her shoulder at the Geata Poeg na Déanainn. Instead, as she rounded a granite shoulder she quickened her pace. To deflect her thoughts from hunger and longing she determined to focus her mind on her final glimpse of the Gate, to recall every detail so as to engrave its image deeply into memory. She must never forget.

The Door she left behind, seemingly just another rocky crevice among many, stood still and unnoticeable in the deep shadows of morning, as it had stood for many years. Yet not quite as it had previously stood—a crack was penciled down one side, where it remained slightly ajar. Only a thin crack; a hairline, one might say, as wide as the thickness of three strands of gold, three thin braids of hairs torn out, one by one, from the roots and weighed down at one end by a rock and at the other by a broken knife. A girl's fingernail might have slid into that gap, as it had indeed slid not long before, to test it.

A girl's fingernail could open that Door, as long as the girl was the owner of the hair.

'—hain! Rohain!'

The girl on the mullock heap opened her eyes to darkness. Spicy, intoxicating night enclosed her in its embrace. Someone was calling. Fear drilled her brain, lacerating it with cold skewers.

'Rohain . . .'

How can one move, with wooden limbs?

Closer now: 'Where are you?'

Where indeed? On the slopes of Huntingtowers.

She stood up too late—they were upon her, two white masks of terror in the gloom.

'She's here!'

'My lady, hasten!'

The young woman stared at the masks, unseeing.

''Tis us, Viviana and Caitri—we have been searching for you all day! Quickly—night is come and danger is upon us! Wights are everywhere and not a seelie one among them!'

The urgent tones shattered meditation. An insubstantiality floated away from the dreamer's grasp. Her reverie had been interrupted just as she was about to recreate a visualization of the portal to Faêrie.

Now I shall never recall it.

As her lady's maids grabbed her by the elbows, the damsel had enough presence of mind left to ensure that the bracelet securely encircled her wrist. Then they were off, stumbling through the mountainside's witchy darkness.

Wicked and eldritch indeed was the night. The three mortals were tripped and tricked at every turn, taunted and haunted, jeered at, leered at by the hideous, the horrible, the hateful. Unseelie energies hummed electric in the air like charged wires, for the wind or eldritch fingers to pluck or to slide down with fiendish screams; like cords to snake across their path, to catch in webs at their ankles, transmitting the throbbing menace of the darkness in thin metal slices of pain. On ran the three mortal maidens, expecting at any time to be cut down from behind, or beside, or in front, but there was a globe of soft luminosity illuminating their path.

This light travelled with them. It radiated from the ring worn on the finger of one of them. Things that lunged at the escapers were brushed by the edge of this orb. They yelped and ricocheted away. The boots of the three damsels hammered on the surface of a road as they crossed. On the other side a bank ascended steeply into a wood. Panting, they climbed up into the tangle of undergrowth, pushing in under muffling trees until one of them, the smallest, fell.

'Caitri!'

'I can run no further. Go on without me.'

Green eyes, long and narrow, popped up like sudden lamps. A skinny, pale hand reached for Caitri. Her mistress slashed at it with a knife. Black blood spurted. The screech was like a white-hot arrow through the eardrums. Encouraged, she slashed right and left, back and forth. On her hand, Thorn's leaf-ring flared. Shadows leaped up and away from it, and so did the mad things of the night. Some of the screaming was pouring from the knife-wielder's own mouth, a wordless battle cry of which she had not known she was capable, a song of frenzy. Her knife was every-where, flashing in a kind of whirling cocoon of steel within which her two charges huddled.

When she stopped, arms hanging by her sides, the blade no longer gleamed. Inky blood covered it, splashed her arms and dripped from her clothing. Silence on silver chains hung sus-pended from somewhere far above. The damsel wiped the knife, ineffectually, on her sleeve.

'Trouble us no more!' she shouted into the quiescent shad-ows—or tried to shout. The words emerged in a strangled whisper. She sank to her knees on a whispering carpet of leaves.

'You saved us,' said Viviana, awed. 'Are you hurt?'

'Is there any water?'

In the woods, the night was long. She whose memories had been reborn did not sleep. She sat with her back to her dozing friends, holding a knife in each hand. The ring shone. Strangely, wights' blood had never smeared it.

I must recall the image of the Gate.

Somehow, as she sat through the night, she happened to glance again at the golden bracelet that symbolised her kenning-name. Her eyes began to cloud over. More memories returned . . .

Arcdur. She had travelled through it.

Avlantian riding-habits had not been designed for hard walking. The skirts of blond and turquoise saye tangled about Ashalind's legs and caused her to stumble. On her feet, the soft leather boots yielded to sharp angles of adamant. Only the amazing Faêran cloak flowed with her movements, never snagging on projections, conforming to her body with a gentle caress.

Jumbled stones and scree slopes made progress even slower and more difficult. Constant water and wind kept the rocks swept clean of silt in this region—only in the deepest cracks it found refuge, and there the mosses grew, or the tenacious roots of the blue-green arkenfir.

The cadence of the wind amplified as Ashalind approached the summit of a hill, and it was as if she was at the edge of the world, for there was only the deep sky beyond. In a few steps, a majestic vista of far-flung hills and stacks stalking into the distance unfolded unexpectedly at her feet, and the wind came up over the hill to meet her, soughing in her ears. She paused, looking out over lonely Arcdur, devoid of human habitation. Choughs on the wing caught updrafts. Clothing the opposite ridge was a dark patch of conifers. To her right, a glint on the horizon suggested the sea. She picked her way down the hill and lay flat to drink at a clear beck, then went on, hoping to reach the shelter of the trees before nightfall. The Faêran cloak provided extraordinary warmth and protection, and without it she must surely have perished by now, but fallen pine-needles would be a softer cushion than rock.

She stepped from stone to stone, conscious always of keeping her footing, aware that her next enemy in this remote region was injury. She kept going on a course due south, memorizing landmarks along the way; a stack of flat rocks like giant pancakes, another like loaves of bread . . . most of the constructions reminded her of food, and she wondered how long it was since she had eaten. Searching her memory, she recalled honeyed pears poached in a cardamom and anise sauce, followed by buttered griddle-cakes, eaten for breakfast on the morning of the Leaving. The memory tied knots in her belly, and she turned her musing elsewhere.

She pondered all the strange events that had brought her here, and the foolishness of Men and Faêran that had caused them. Images of her loved ones in the Fair Realm made her choke with longing and she suddenly stopped and hurled herself down among the boulders, digging her fingers into gravel.

'I cannot go on. I must go back.'

There she lay, rigid, while the sun moved a little farther across the pearly sky and the choughs wheeled, inquisitive, above. Eventually, out of her confusion arose a conclusion: she had decided to attempt this venture in order to be rid of the Langothe and to bring the High King back to his Realm. Yet even as she reached this disposition she knew the answer was not really that simple; there was more, if only she had the courage to admit it. For now, however, the important point was that she had freely chosen her own path. No one had coerced her. She had elected to pursue this quest, and all pain, all longing, must be contained and controlled if it were to be achieved.

Hence, with a new strength born of despair, she climbed to her feet again and resumed her journey.

There was no food. It was very beautiful, this land of stone and pine so close to the sky; clear and clean, embroidered with joyous, glimmering waters. But day followed day and Ashalind could find nothing to eat, not even mushrooms down among the gnarled roots of the arkenfirs. Chitinous beetles sometimes crawled in crevices, but she had no mind to consume them. When they opened their wingcases and became airborne, the choughs swooped to snatch them instead.

The light-headedness and aching she had experienced in the first two days vanished, leaving her with a sense of remarkable calm and vigor. She held her course, but on the sixth day of her journey the land to the east started to climb in ragged notches, more precipitous and sheer, while to the west it gentled, and groves of pine and fir marched over undulating hills.

Using a castle-shaped crag as a landmark for her turning-point, she was now forced to veer westward. Somewhere ahead, she knew, lay the northwest coast of Eldaraigne that looked out over a vast sea whose end was in the storm-ring that encircled the rim of the world. A deep ocean current, the Calder Flow, journeyed from the icy southern latitudes past the island country of Finvarna to touch that coast with its chill fingers and keep Arcdur cooler, year-round, than the rest of the country.

On the seventh day she gathered a few handfuls of watercress and wild sage, the first edible plants she had seen. But she noticed that her hands and feet were always cold, and her limbs quaked. Her strength was failing. At night, proper sleep would not come, only a trancelike state, similar to floating on water, buoyed up and unable to sink. She wondered how long anyone could continue to travel without proper sustenance. Perhaps if she could reach the seashore she would find food. If she did not, then she must lie down there and die, within sight of elindors flying over the waves.

Would elindors still navigate the airs of Erith? How many years had passed? Would Men still walk the world, or would their cities lie in ruin? She stumbled, then shook her head to clear it, but could not focus, and recalled vaguely that she had fallen many times that day and her hands were bleeding.

The sky turned from pearl to grape. Another storm blew out of the west that night, bringing strong winds and lashing rain. It lasted all night and through the next day. The Faêran clothes were waterproof, but moisture insinuated itself past the edges to dampen her neck and wrists.

By nightfall on the ninth day the rain had dissipated to the southeast. The falling sun had at last broken through the clouds, and as the traveller plodded up the side of a grassy dune she saw it, low on the horizon, scattering a fish-scale path across the sea. Lulled by the susurration of the waves, she sat among saltbushes and watched the evening's glory fade. Stars appeared. A gibbous moon looked down at the long pale beach, but Ashalind, wrapped in her cloak, her head pillowed on her arms, was already dozing.

It was a fitful sleep, disturbed by dreams of Faêran feasts. The first gleam of dawn wakened her suddenly, and, raising her head, she looked out to sea. A stifled cry escaped her lips, and in the next instant she had sprung to her feet, and, drawing on her last reserves, was running down to the water's edge, waving and calling.

Triangular sails floated, saffron, in the dawnlight. A boat, not far from shore, was silently heading south toward a headland. Onward it tacked without deviation, seeming unaffected by her cries, and she thought it would pass from sight forever and leave her stranded to become, washed by time and tide, sunbleached bones in the sand. But the angle of the hull changed. It had turned, and now cut through water toward her; she could see the curl of white foam beneath the prow. When the vessel was within earshot, she hove to. Her keel prevented her from venturing into the shallows. A man on board dropped anchor and shouted, honouring the time-worn cliché of mariners:

'Ahoy there!'

'Help me,' Ashalind answered. 'I have no food. I am alone.'

The man hesitated.

'Please help me.' The damsel's voice cracked and she sank to the sand, heedless of the lace-edged waves swirling around her knees. Perhaps he did not believe her, or thought she was a decoy for some brigand's ambush, which indicated that *whenever* she was, danger lurked still.

There was a splash. He had stripped to his breeches and was swimming to the beach, towing something buoyant on a rope. A strong swimmer, he soon rose out of the water, dripping, and waded out. He was thickset and bearded, with hair as brown as his body. Bright eyes peered from a weathered face.

'Gramercie. I am grateful,' was all she could think of to say. She tried to stand but collapsed again. He gave her a measuring stare, then asked, in unfamiliar but clear accents,

'Can you swim?'

She nodded, unclasping the cloak and throwing off the ragged gown and jacket.

'Come on now,' the man said to the gaunt, hollow-eyed damsel shivering in hose and gipon. Securing her to the cluster of inflated bladders, he towed her out to the boat and dragged her aboard, then tossed a dry blanket over her while he returned to retrieve her riding-habit and mantle.

There was a small cabin on board, and wicker baskets filled with luminous shells like pale rainbows. An older, grizzle-bearded sailor in the boat handed her a bottle of water and some food: stale bread, cheese, and pickles in a stoneware jar.

'Eat slowly,' he advised.

On his return the younger man dressed himself. Then without

another word he dragged in the anchor. The old man hauled on the jibsheet and took the tiller. The favourable breeze bellied out the lateens against an azure sky. Ashalind lay back on a pile of stinking nets and watched the horizon rise and fall.

'Where are you from? Where are you going?'

'My name is Ashalind na Pendran. I am a traveller, seeking the High King of the Fair Folk. I lost my way.'

This was the truth, as far as it went. She trusted them, these brown sailors—their faces were open and honest. Nonetheless, the secret of the Gate was too precious to be revealed to any save the High King of the Faêran.

'My name is William Javert,' said the younger man, 'and this is my father, Tom. Never have I known a young lass like you to travel alone, but such practices may be common in outlandish regions, I suppose. I doubt not that you seek whom you say you seek, but we have never seen any such people as those you call the Fair Folk. It is not our habit to pay heed to tales and legends of the Strangers. If such folk do exist, maybe 'tis better they remain hidden. To my mind, the less trouble that is stirred up, the better. Some old tales what folks make up when they got nothin' useful to do, tell of a King of the Strangers—the Gentry, as some calls 'em—who sleeps with his warriors under a hill, but I don't put much faith in that. I believe in what I see. In wights I believe, for mickle trouble they do give us. Thought you was one, at first.'

'Old folk used to tell tales of a Perilous Kingdom,' Tom said, squinting at the damsel, 'but I do not know where it was supposed to be. Under the sea perhaps, or under the ground. The Strangers dwelled there, it was said, and their King too. But nowt has been seen of that country since ages long gone, when folks was more ignorant and believed in such fancies. Then again, the world's a queer place.'

The son, William, took his turn at the helm. The boat changed tack and they rounded another headland, still keeping the coast-line in view to the left. The hull rocked on a gentle swell. As they sailed southward, the distant landscape changed from the barren rocks of Arcdur to wooded hills.

'Caermelor . . . who is King there?' asked the passenger.

William regarded her with a quizzical stare.

'Where have you come from, that you don't know our sovereign's name? Your manner of speaking sounds foreign . . .'

'I come from far away. North.'

'Ach, I wouldna have believed any folk did not know of our good King-Emperor, the Sixteenth James D'Armancourt!'

Ashalind fell silent. In her time the sovereign had been William the Wise, who was grandson of the great Unitor, son of James the Second. Had thirteen generations passed? Two or three centuries? It was difficult to credit that such a vast span of time had elapsed.

'How old is the dynasty of D'Armancourt?' she asked.

'Why,' said old Tom, 'it is traced back, they say, a thousand years, that was the first King James. But not all were called James. Some of the D'Armancourt kings bore other names.'

Shocked at this crushing of her hopes, Ashalind clenched her hands. In a spasm of frustration she hammered her fist on a wooden water-barrel. A millennium! It was too much to contemplate. What far-reaching changes had taken place in Erith during such a long period? Why were the exiled Faêran lost or forgotten?

A flock of shearwaters flew overhead. In the water several yards from the keel, something splashed. Instantly the attention of the men was fixed on the spot.

''Tain't *she*, is it?' William asked in a low voice.

'Nay, 'tis one of the *maighdeans*,' said his father. 'But which kind I cannot tell.'

Through the aquamarine depths Ashalind caught a fleeting glimpse of a long, glittering curve, a drifting skein of pale hair, an eldritch face. Then the subaquatic visitor was gone.

'A *maighdean na tuinne*,' explained Tom to the ignorant northerner, 'a damsel of the waves. 'Twould be a good thing to befriend one of them, a seelie one, for they can give warning of storms. The last few days, we were diving for coral and nacrisshell on the northern reefs—that storm blew us off course and away from the fleet. The anchor dragged and we were caught out. Had to run for hours before the wind.'

An eerie crooning of music came blowing to their ears along

the wind. Ashalind saw, on the distant beach, half a dozen figures swaying in dance. The men shaded their eyes with their hands.

William became oddly quiet and appeared to pay a lot of attention to his steering. The distant dancers must have caught sight of the boat. With cries and shouts, they pulled on garments that had lain beside them on the rocks, and slid into the water. The dark shapes of them arrowed toward the small vessel. The young sailor loosened the jib and the sails hung flapping. When the swimmers came cavorting close, the heads that broke the surface were those of seals. William leaned over and spoke to them in a tongue Ashalind could not recognise. He spoke lovingly, gently, and the seals replied in the same language.

'One of the Roane was once wife to Will,' Tom murmured to Ashalind. 'He stole her sealskin while she was dancing, and hid it. 'Tis unlike him to do such a thing, but she were very comely and he were fair taken with her. She begged him to return it, for without it she couldna return to the skerries out in the ocean. But he would not give in and at last persuaded her to marry him. She made a good and dutiful wife to him for three years, although she always had a wistful eye on the sea. One day she chanced to find the skin and then she was off in haste, down to the sea never to return. Will allus asks for news of her. But you see, unions between mortals and immortals allus end in breach and bereavement. Everyone knows that. Will should ha' known.'

'Please, Will, ask the Roane if they know aught of the High King of the Fair Folk.'

William spoke again in the seal language.

'They say they never speak to mortals about the Fair Folk,' he translated, when the seals had given their answer, 'but the eldritch wights of Huntingtowers may be able to tell.'

The Roane went undulating away through the waves, and Tom turned the sail so that the wind filled it. The patched canvas snapped taut as the air crammed into it. Foam creamed at the prow.

Ashalind asked, 'Huntingtowers—what is that?'

'A dreadful unseelie place it is, a caldera infested with powerful wights of gramarye,' said Tom. 'It lies on the other side of the old magmite mines, not more than seven leagues west of a cottage belonging to a good family of fisher-folk known to us—the Caidens. That family lives in fear of the wicked things that issue from the place from time to time.'

'Have you seen any of the creatures that dwell therein?'

'No. But Tavron Caiden has told us of them. And they're not pretty, most of 'em. There's nasty little spriggans and trows as creeps about, and white pigs and hares, but the Caidens wear wizard-*sained* tilhals and the lesser wights don't bother them much—they keep away from the rowan and the iron. The worst things . . .' Here the shell-diver paused and scanned the horizon with a troubled air. 'The worst things is them that goes hunting. Fuaths and duergars and such. Some of them are worse than any nightmare. Others of them look like Men, even right noble and kingly Men, but there's something wrong about them . . .'

'Kingly Men, you say? Then Faêran may be amongst them!' cried Ashalind, dropping the bread on which she had been biting. Her face was flushed.

'That may be so, but there is no mercy in the creatures that infest Huntingtowers, and that place is not where you should seek your King. It is a hub of evil and death. I do not even like to speak of it on a fair day such as this. Leave that sinkhole to the wicked wights, lass. Caermelor's the place for you. News always flows toward big cities.'

'This cottage of your friends—is it far from here?' Ashalind asked.

''Tis near Isse Harbor. It stands alone on the northern coast of the Cape of Tides—twelve to fourteen days away depending on the wind, and if we do not call in at our village on the Isle of Birds. But we have a good haul of nacris-shell already on board, as you can see, and we are heading home to unload it. Besides, we'll not put a slip of a thing like you ashore at the Cape of Tides, not in the shadow of Huntingtowers.'

'If you do, I shall give you gold.' Their passenger rattled the pouch her father had given her, then took some coins from it. The antique disks in her palm glinted, flashing in the sunlight. 'I beg of you—take me there.'

Astonishment registered on the ingenuous faces of the shell-divers, quickly replaced by suspicion.

'How did you come by such wealth? Is it honest gold?'

'It is honest gold, not stolen, nor gold of gramarye to change into leaves and blow away. But it has lain hidden this past millennium and now it is uncovered.'

'Ye'd be better off coming with us to the Isle of Birds. From there you might take the ferry to Finvarna, and thence find passage south to Caermelor on one of the regular shipping runs.'

'Sir, I am grateful for your advice but I will not be dissuaded.'

Putting their heads together, the two boatmen murmured earnestly to one another. From time to time they glanced at their passenger, who lowered her eyes and endeavoured to look as if she took no heed of their discussion.

'Be you steadfastly set on this course, lass?' said Tom at last. 'Is there naught that will change your mind?'

'I am steadfast. If you will not take me to the Cape of Tides, I shall seek another ferryman, in any case.'

A troubled expression clouded the brow of the shell-diver. 'This goes against my better judgment. If you be set on going near Huntingtowers, we will transport you, but not for payment. 'Twould not be right, to bring a starving waif like you into danger and take her gold as well. If you change your mind when you get to Tavron Caiden's place, you might make your way to the Royal City from there.'

'Gramercie!'

Privately, Ashalind decided she would leave payment with them despite their protestations. They had given her food and passage, and it was evident they were not rich folk.

They made landfall thrice during the next fourteen days, entering profound inlets where steps were crudely hewn into the cliffs. William replenished their water supplies from thin waterfalls that trailed like the frayed ends of silk down these walls of adamant, but they met no man there.

'These lands of the northwest coast are deserted,' William said. 'Here dwell only the birds and beasts, and wicked things, and the wind.'

Rugged and rocky was the coastline. The sheer cliffs that lined it were pierced by deep channels and wild, wave-churned sounds cutting far back into the land. For some miles, huge trees crowded down to the very cliff tops. Dense shadows were netted beneath their boughs.

On sighting these ancient woodlands, William remarked in a grim undertone, 'There ends the westernmost arm of the terrible forest.'

At length, the voyagers sailed between islands and arrived on the coast of the mainland at an area where cliffs sloped gently to a tiny harbour. There they tied up the boat and came ashore. The salt breeze stung their faces with a hint of chill. 'Winter's here,' said Tom.

The cottage of the Caidens, whitewashed and slate-roofed, overlooked the neat harbour. Behind it was a large, well-tended vegetable patch, the inevitable bee-skeps, and racks for drying fish. Stunted rowans and plum trees grew all around. A few sea-pinks straggled in the window-boxes facing east. Tavron's wife, Madelinn, kept chickens, goats, and a sheep whose wool she spun.

There were children—a boy, Darvon, and a girl, Tansy. This family welcomed the boatmen and the yellow-haired stranger into their midst, sharing their home and provender, begrudging nothing. Tom and William returned their greetings and hospitality with amiability, but it was evident that the two men were uneasy.

'The lass here had some notion about Huntingtowers,' explained William, 'but instead she may go on to Caermelor, with the next road-caravan that comes this way, or take ship.'

Tom advised, 'Do not be too hasty, lass. Wait until you hear more about that place.'

The next morning the shell-divers sailed away to the Isle of Birds, carrying the gold coins Ashalind had slipped into their pockets while they were not looking.

'Stay awhile, lass,' Tavron Caiden said, 'before you travel on. 'Tis few enough folk who pass this way and we would be glad of the company. Besides, by the look of you, if you don't mind me saying so, a rest would do you good.'

Indeed, the turmoil of the Leaving and the Closing, the shock of finding she had been gone from Erith for a thousand years, and the toilsomeness of hard travel across Arcdur without nourishment had taken their toll. For the first two days the newcomer slept a great deal, woke to eat, and slept again. Good health began to return. The Langothe was on her, nevertheless, pulling toward the north where lay the Gate to the Fair Realm, but she felt driven to quest on, to be rid of the terrible longing at its root. The Caidens bade her tarry longer with them, until strength fully returned. When they saw that she was bent on departing with all haste, they would not tell her the way to Huntingtowers.

'Stay awhile,' they begged. 'Bide just a few days more, then we will tell you the way and set you rightly on it.'

Indeed, their guest was in no state to argue and must submit. They set the best of their simple provender before her. Although she hungered, she had seen Faêran food and breathed its fragrance. No Erithan victuals gave off much flavour in her mouth now, and, above all, the eating of flesh had come to seem abhorrent.

The fisher-folk had never before seen golden hair, and by this she learned for the first time—to her secret sorrow—that the Talith Kingdom was no more. The race had ebbed. Its few remaining representatives were scattered throughout Erith, and in Avlantia red- and bronze-leaved vines grew over the ruins of the cities. Throughout the Known Lands the stockier brown-haired Feorhkind predominated now, far outnumbering even the red Erts of Finvarna. One or two small Feorhkind villages had been established on the fringes of Avlantia, but generally that kindred preferred the cooler southern lands.

Without revealing her origins, Ashalind gleaned much more information from the conversation of her hosts. She learned about the fine talium chain mesh that lined the taltry hoods, used to protect against that wind of gramarye they called the shang, which burned Men's emotions into the ether. She found out about sildron, which (it could only be she who remembered) had been the gift of the High King of the Fair Realm to the D'Armancourt Dynasty. In this new era, sildron lifted Windships and the Skyhorses whose routes never passed over the remote region where the cottage stood. She discovered much concerning the Stormriders and the King's warriors, the Dainnan, and the strifes of past history, and the current unrest in the northeast lands that was wont to erupt into skirmishes.

She was fascinated, numbed by the changes that had happened over a millennium. There seemed so many—yet so few, when such an incredible span of time was considered. Conceivably, the enchantment of the Gate allowed those who passed through it to adapt to alterations in language over the years. As for the evolution of technology, the centuries of ignorance and strife known as the Dark Era had checked the progress of civilization in Erith, or even dragged it backward. Apart from sildron, taltries, and the shang, there seemed little difference between the world as she had known it and the world as she saw it now. Perhaps she would not feel like so much of a misfit in this new age after all.

Yet she marveled and she grieved. A thousand years; it might as well have been forever.

The Caiden children, who had been restraining their curiosity with difficulty, begged their visitor to tell them stories of her travels in the north. After the tale of her hardships in Arcdur was related, they wanted another, and another. Ashalind was happy to oblige as best she could without revealing her secret, so she delved into her hoard of tales learned from Meganwy, and from wandering Storytellers, until Madelinn bade the children cease their pestering and leave the guest some peace.

At nights by the fireside, with the pet whippet lying before the hearth and the sea-sound booming beyond the walls, Ashalind regaled her hosts with all the gestes and songs she could recall. In return they told her about the hollow hill where, it was said, Faêran knights and ladies lay in enchanted sleep with their horses, hounds, and hawks and their treasures of untold wealth, and of how it was supposed to be possible to wake them by certain means if one could find the entrance to their underground halls. But none knew which hills they were, or if the stories were true.

Only one event marred the harmony of these times.

The child Tansy had a tuneful singing voice. Ashalind taught her many songs, including one named 'The Exile,' which had been made by Llewell, the young songmaker who had been among those brought out of Faerie by Ashalind. Well did she remember that youth calling to her at the gates of Hythe Mellyn. He had been driven mad by the Langothe and sometimes believed he was one of the Faêran. But he had never returned to the Fair Realm, for he pined and died before the Leaving. His songs remained.

Full many leagues of foreign soil I've trod.
At last, I would reclaim my native sod.
Alas, it seems I cannot find the way.
Exiled, my heart grows heavy, day by day.
And wondrous as these hills and vales may be,
They're not the mystic realms I crave to see—
The dream'd-of world in childhood's state of bliss—
My land of birth; that is the place I miss.
So am I doomed to seek, forever banned?
A stranger wandering in this strange land?
The strongest measures cannot ease the pain.
Oh, will I ever see my home again?

When she first heard it, Tansy was so taken with this song that she stood on tiptoe to offer Ashalind a kiss. In fright, Ashalind jumped back, covering her face with her hands.

'Oh no! You must not do that!'

The family stared at her, astonished at this peculiar behaviour.

The guest stammered her apologies.

'I must not be kissed. It is a bitterbynde, a geas. It must not be broken.'

The awkward moment passed. A geas must be respected, no matter how strange, and so must the wishes of a guest.

It was a pleasure to help with the many tasks demanded by this solitary life: bread-baking, cheesemaking, drying and salting barrels of fish, gardening, washing, tending the hives and the animals. Immersion in the work of this family temporarily ameliorated the nostalgia Ashalind felt for her own, but always the Langothe corroded the core of her.

One night she was woken with crackling hair, feeling for the first time the prickling exhilaration of the unstorm.

Opening the shutters she saw, below the cliff, every wavecrest foaming with stars. Near at hand, the vegetable patch was powdered with emerald-dust, and even the tethered goat watched with blazing topaz eyes, its horns sculpted of polished agate. It was just as Cierndanel had said— *The winds of gramarye are awakening at this outrage, the winds of Ang. They flare from the Ringstorm at Erith's rim. Soon they shall prowl the lands of thy world, dyed by the imprints of men's designs.'*

On other days the shang came, dimming sunlight, frosting the land and sea with strange lights, but there were no tableaux here in this far-flung outpost.

'Why do you live alone?' Ashalind asked her benefactress as they mended nets down by the harbour. 'Is it not perilous?'

'We have no choice,' replied Madelinn. 'No other folk will live so close to the place of dread. Unseelie things roam near here. Men who venture to the caldera never return, or if they do, they come back raving mad and perish soon after. Sometimes when the moon is full, dark skyriders come to Huntingtowers from the northeast and after that a ghastly Hunt issues from that place. Its leader is Huon, the unseelie prince from whose skull grows a set of antlers like those of a stag, and he is called the Hunter.'

'I have heard the name,' murmured Ashalind. 'Who has not?'

'When the Hunt is abroad, we lock ourselves inside the house, barring all the doors and windows, but the bars do not keep out the horrible baying of black hounds with fiery eyes, and the beating of hooves. It's enough to make your blood curdle.'

'Why then do you live here?'

'Because it is our own.' Madelinn spoke with quiet dignity. 'Eight years ago, when the children were small, we sailed here, from Gilvaris Tarv on the east coast. Tavron and I were raised among fisher-folk, but poverty had forced us to seek employment in that city. It was a terrible life.' She shook her head, frowning.

'Bad conditions; cruelty. Never enough pay to feed the family properly. The children were forever hungry. My uncle lived in this cottage on the cliffs. He died and I inherited it. Here we came, and here we rule ourselves and seldom go hungry, even if it is sometimes fish day after day. We have learned to live in the shadow of Huntingtowers.'

'Will you tell me of that place?'

Madelinn stretched her arm out in a wide gesture to the sea. A tall cone-shaped island reared its peak not far from the shore, southwest of the little harbour. Farther west another thrust up, and beyond it several more in a great sweeping curve dwindling around to the northwest.

'That's what we call the Chain of Chimneys,' she said, 'a line of fire-mountains, ages old, that once lifted themselves out of the sea.'

'I have heard of them by repute,' said Ashalind. 'Called by the old Feorhkind name of Eotenfor, the Giant's Stepping-Stones.'

'Aye,' said Madelinn. 'One of these fire-heads pushed up under the land instead of the sea, and became Huntingtowers Hill. In its top is a vast cauldron more than a mile wide, and inside that are a dozen or so small hills. Ash cones they were. Now they are islands in a lake, for the crater has filled with water. The biggest island is right smack in the middle of it all, but spans and causeways have been built everywhere, it is said, so that the eldritch creatures may cross over. On this central hill is a keep of stone, surrounded by eight other towers all linked by flying bridges.'

Madelinn paused thoughtfully and pushed a stray strand of hair back from her face.

'Well,' she continued, 'I suppose some folk must have gone there to see it all and returned with some wit left, else we wouldn't know what the place looked like, would we? Don't say as how I'd recommend a sightseeing tour, though. The lesser unseelie wights there can be put off with charms, but them things that go a-hunting—they are full wicked.'

But Ashalind was only half listening. Her mind was on Huntingtowers Hill.

If some of the exiled Faêran dwelt there, they must surely

know the whereabouts of King Angavar. But by what Madelinn had said it seemed that they shunned mortals, and would be hardly likely to welcome her in, answer her questions, and wave good-bye. She must approach with caution and try to glean information using stealth. What if they were not Faêran? Wights such as the Each Uisge were able to take on a form resembling Men or Faêran, duping those who did not look too closely. Nonetheless, they could never make the transformation complete and always bore some inconspicuous but betraying sign such as webbed fingers or animal's feet, and when in man-shape they moved like Men, not with Faêran grace.

Prince Morragan had mingled with unseelie wights at Carnconnor. Perhaps it was he who was master at Huntingtowers. At this notion a surge of something akin to shock or exhilaration coursed through Ashalind.

Beside her, the fisherwoman sighed. 'One day we might leave this place. We grow no richer here. The merchants of the road-caravans are miserly in their bartering for dried fish and only come by once a year. And it is not right for the children to be raised in the shadow of fear. One day . . . I don't know where we'd go.'

There came an evening when the moon was almost full. The wind screamed at the gray-green sea and whipped the white-horse crests out beyond the harbour. Inside the cottage, ruby light flickered from the fire, casting deceptive shadows on rough walls.

Ashalind placed the purse of gold sovereigns on the table and loosened the drawstring of its mouth. Coins spilled out, gleaming softly across scored wood. The fisher-folk stared, struck dumb by the sight of so much wealth.

'This is for you,' their guest explained, 'save only for seven pieces, which I may need on my journey. If I do not return within three days take all of it and leave this place, for my efforts might inadvertently arouse the wrath of unseelie wights, and you might find yourselves in peril. If my quest is successful I may not return. If unsuccessful I will ask you to take me in your boat to Caermelor. I go now to Huntingtowers to seek the High King of the Fair Folk.'

The silence was broken by Tavron clearing his throat.

'We shall not take your gold,' he said gruffly. 'Return it to the pouch. Our hospitality asks no fee.'

'I do not mean to insult you,' stammered Ashalind. 'Only, if I do not return I shall not need it. With this you might buy land elsewhere and start a new life.'

Sensing her distress, the white whippet jumped into her lap. Fondly, she caressed it, thinking of her faithful Rufus.

'If you must go, I shall accompany you as your guard,' said Tavron. 'Charms are not enough to ward off such wickedness as lurks there.'

'Would you leave your family unprotected?' asked Ashalind.

'There will be no going to the place of dread, especially now,' interrupted Madelinn. 'Have you not heeded our warnings? The moon will be full tomorrow night, and it is then the Wild Hunt goes forth to scour the surrounding lands. All mortals who love life ought to stay safe behind rowan and iron.'

'I have heeded your words,' replied Ashalind, 'but I am driven. A certain longing burns in me and daily eats me away—longing that can only be appeased when I have found the one I seek. It is the Langothe, and those who have never felt it cannot understand. Nothing you can say will alter my course. I have no choice.'

'You must fight it,' pleaded Tansy. 'Stay with us. Teach us more songs.'

'I must go.'

The next morning, covered by the Faêran mantle, which had subtly altered its hues to match the surroundings, Ashalind left the cottage. She took her father's iron dagger, a wallet of food, some charms, and a leather water-bottle that was a gift from Tavron. The ragged riding-habit lay folded in a wooden chest inside the cottage; in place of it she wore worsted galligaskins, a pair of boys' buskins, and a tunic of brown bergamot, all gifts from the Caidens.

'These garments are old, but fit for traveling,' Tavron Caiden said. 'Unfortunately we have no taltry for you. If an unstorm should come, you must become still, eschew passion—otherwise your image will be painted on the airs for all passersby to see.'

'It may be that the curious cloak you wear has the power to protect from the shang,' suggested Madelinn. 'Cover your head with the hood. It might work.'

At the cottage door the fisher wife made one last appeal.

'Do not go, Ashalind,' she said, looking the damsel squarely in the eyes. 'My mother was a carlin and I possess some of her foresight. I tell you that if you go to Huntingtowers you go to your doom. I tell you that you will be defeated there, and that it will be the end of you as we know you now. You will die or, at best, you will be altered in some terrible, inexplicable way.'

Her entreaties were in vain.

With embraces but no kisses, the family bade farewell. They turned their harrowed faces aside to hide their horror at this obvious suicide.

The damsel set out in a westerly direction toward the tip of the Cape of Tides. She climbed the slope behind the cottage, breathing hard from the exertion. Shreds of morning mist were dissolving in tatters. At the top of the cliff she halted, surveying the satin expanse of the sea. The waters were striped with shades of blue from milky to intense, under a cornflower sky. The perfect cones of the Chimneys stood like guardians, waves creaming on their beaches. A shag perched on a rock, transfixed and cruciform, drying its wings. As yet, Ashalind had seen no elindors in this new era. This morning only shearwaters and petrels rode the sky.

The whippet had followed her. Stoically, she sent it back with a harsh word. The cottage looked tiny, far below. In a few steps it was lost to view.

Low tea-tree scrub grew on the cliff top, spiking the air with the tang of eucalyptus. In the distance, a disused Mooring Mast stood dark against the skyline. Rain had fallen the night before, and puddles made mirrors on the ground.

Despite a growing feeling of trepidation, the traveller made swift progress along the cliffs and past the overgrown mullock heaps of the abandoned mines. Toward nightfall she reached the foot of the long-dead volcano. Its heath-covered flanks rose in a long slow sweep to a brooding summit that appeared flat from her vantage point. Hairs prickled on her arms and neck. The pre-science of danger pressed down like the weight of a mountain. Dark clouds clustered over the sun's face and the air stilled. No birds sang here. Stopping in the shelter of a scrubby brake, Ashalind took a draft of water. Her stomach roiled with trepidation; she could not eat a bite. After tugging the Faêran hood more firmly around her face, she began to ascend as noiselessly and unobtrusively as possible.

As she climbed the hillside, she sensed she was being watched. Bushes rustled furtively, and twin points of viridescent light gleamed out from many an enigmatic shadow. Close by, a shout of loud laughter made her jump. Sweating with more than effort, she labored on, eyes darting from side to side, trying to make sense out of the odd shapes in the gathering darkness. What a fool she had been, she realised too late, to challenge a domain of wights at night. Most of these creatures were nocturnal, and she had placed herself at a grave disadvantage. She ought to have found a sheltered place to sleep and await the dawn. Had she lost her wits already, in her eagerness to be rid of the wearisome Langothe? But there would be no turning back now that she had come so far, and she toiled on until she reached the lip of the caldera.

The waxing moon, risen early, extruded ghostlike shafts through a gash in the cumulus. Its crepuscular light reflected back from the expansive lake that lay stretched out far below Ashalind's feet, strewn with the dark humps of islets like solemn tortoises. The top of the central island rose up level with the caldera's rim, and from it soared, attenuated, the fantastic structure Madelinn Caiden had described, with its towers and flying bridges. From within these towers bluish light pierced the slit windows at many levels. The slits glowed eerily, like blue gas; weird optics watching the night. To the right, a road came through a cutting in the rim and crossed several bridges to reach the towers.

From somewhere to the left a crow harshly said 'cark-cark'. Surely it was unusual for diurnal birds to be calling out at this time of night. The intruder took a deep breath and started to move quietly down the inside wall toward the first bridge.

Her fall was caused by the white hare that ran under her feet. In the next instant, something small but with the strength of a coiled spring landed heavily on her, gouging, beating, pummeling, until her hand found the iron dagger's hilt and she wrenched it from its sheath.

The thing sprang away, shrieking falsetto alarm as it fled into the night. Blood dripped into the damsel's eyes and she wiped it away with her sleeve.

'Cold iron will not serve you far, 'ere,' said a voice like two dry branches rubbing together.

'It serves me well enough,' she said to the spriggan who stood six paces away.

'Only foolish mortals trespass in the domain of 'uon, the Prince of 'unters,' the spriggan said, answering her first question before she had asked it. 'Especially when *he* is on his way. For this, you must die.'

It flinched, blinking as she flicked the dagger to reflect moonlight from the blade into its squinty eyes. This was partly to disguise the fact that her hands were shaking.

'Ah, but if I die, you will not benefit,' Ashalind said steadily. 'In return for certain information, I am prepared to pay gold. True gold.'

She rattled the purse.

'Pah,' sneered the spriggan. 'What use is that yellow metal to me, eh? I 'ave no need of gold, true or otherwise. It cannot buy me juicy caterpillars or sweet cocoons and spiders' eggs.' The wight pranced around, switching its tail restlessly. 'What else does the *erithbunden* offer?'

'Do you like maggots?'

'Love 'em.'

'I passed a dead bird not long ago . . .'

She broke off—the wight had already disappeared in the direction she indicated. Something bit her knee. Reflexively, she kicked it away. With a sigh of relief and disappointment, she decided to retrace her steps after all, and wait on the lower slopes until morning.

As she turned away a nuggety, grotesque shape detached itself from obscurity. Here was a wight even more sinister and repulsive than a spriggan. Ashalind backed away, clutching the charms at her belt, for she recognised this small, manlike being as a black dwarf—a duergar. Battling a sinking feeling, the damsel hoped the rowan and iron charms had some potency against such a dangerous entity.

'What else *do* you offer?' the duergar asked casually.

'I am come to buy information. I offer nothing until I can be sure that you are a trusted henchman of Huon the Hunter, who would have knowledge such as I seek,' she countered. Her hand shivered, gripping the charms. This thing was not to be trifled with—duergars were quick to anger and quicker to strike. She wondered why it had not already torn her head off. Maybe the immutable laws of eldritch forbade it until she showed fear, or else some protective spell of the Lady Nimriel's lingered.

'For instance,' she continued, trying to trick the wight into revealing the information she was after, 'do you know the whereabouts of Angavar High King?'

Out of its puddle of inky shadow, the duergar took a step closer.

'If you want information, I can smuggle you secretly into the Keep of Huon the Horned,' it offered, flexing grimy fingernails and baring long, pointed teeth, 'on the wains that come tonight. First, give us a little suck of your blood.'

Ashalind recalled stories of benighted travellers found by roadsides in the morning, desiccated husks.

'No!' Wildly she cast her mind about, desperate for something with which to buy off this manifestation of iniquity. Fumbling at her wrist, she said, 'A golden bracelet inlaid with a white bird . . . gold coins . . . poppyseed biscuits and blackberry cakes . . .'

'Ignorant flax-wench! How dare you offer trash!'

'If you dislike my offerings, then we cannot do business.' She grew still, but she was too wise to turn her back and walk away.

Noise ceased while the night condensed under a grinning moon.

'Cut off your hair and I will get you into the Keep,' said the duergar eventually.

'The Central Keep? Unharmed and in secret? Yes!'

A whip snaked from the wight's powerful hand. Before the damsel could recoil, it lashed her throat like a tongue of white-hot steel. The duergar emitted a strange mewling noise, which may have been laughter, and muttered, 'Yea indeed.'

Ignoring the searing pang at her throat, Ashalind unbound the long heavy braid from her head and cut it off close to the scalp. She tossed the rope of hair into the wight's hands just as the sound of horses' hooves and wooden wheels came clopping and rattling out of the darkness.

'The bird may enter the cage but it will never sing the songs it learns, and when it pops out its head—pigeon pie!' were the black dwarf's last words. The wicked thing rushed away and Ashalind followed as fast as possible, knowing it was bound to keep its promise to her. Around the caldera's upjutting rim the duergar led her, to the cutting where the road came through from the gentler slopes. Along that road, a convoy of wagons was entering the volcanic basin. The vile creature leaped up beside the driver of the lead wain. What it did to him, Ashalind could not be certain, but the wain and those in procession behind it stopped long enough for her to climb swiftly aboard. As the train moved off again, she found a deep, wooden chest half full of some pungent dried pods and concealed herself inside.

She could tell by the numbness now in her throat that the treacherous duergar had stolen her voice, and she knew by the jolting and swaying and the hollow ring and thud of hooves that the wagons were passing over bridges from island to island. When the wain stopped, the chest was unloaded and propelled upward with nauseating speed before being transferred a second time and left alone in utter silence.

Bleakly the smuggled girl pondered over the loss of her voice, the latest setback of so many in her life. If she could only learn the whereabouts of the King and find him, he might provide some Faêran cure.

After a long while she dared to lift the lid. The chest had been abandoned among others in a dim storeroom, but the door of the room was ajar, admitting a streak of cyanic light. Having ventured out of the redolent container, she nervously peeped around the door. There was only an empty stone-flagged hallway with other recessed doors leading off to either side. A faint smell of charred meat permeated the air.

Waves of weariness washed over Ashalind. She had walked far that day. Fear had kept her senses sharp, but now, in this tomb-like quiet, she was overwhelmed by the need for sleep. After withdrawing into the half-empty storeroom she curled herself in the farthest corner, among a stack of boxes, then pulled the Faêran cloak around her and closed her eyes.

Severing themselves from nightmare, faint echoes woke her. They had sprung from the mutter of distant voices. Feeling in need of sustenance, she took a swig from the water-bottle hanging at her belt and ate the blackberry cakes she had, in desperation, offered the duergar. Refreshed, she emerged from her niche and followed the undercurrent of sound. It led her along the deserted passageways, up spiral stairs, and onto another floor more sump-tuously decorated. Tapestries hung along the walls of the galleries, and rushes strewed the floors. Blue lamps glowed. Hearing the *pad-pad* of multiple footsteps approaching, Ashalind pressed her-self into a recessed doorway. Her Faêran cloak adopted the dusky hues of bluestone and old oak, and without noticing her, half a dozen assorted creatures went past in the wake of a manlike fig-ure with billowing cloak.

'Stinks of siedo-pods up 'ere,' a creaking voice commented as the bevy disappeared around a corner.

Fine droplets beaded the damsel's brow. It dawned on her that siedo-pods' strong odour might well mask the scent of mortal flesh. Following quietly behind the group, she peered around the corner. The mutterings she had been hearing emanated from a doorway farther along, and were accompanied by a clinking of pottery and metal. Beyond that doorway, a grating voice deeper than the tones of spriggans was giving orders to select certain wines and convey them in haste: '. . . and hoof it, you spigot-nosed kerns,' it rasped. 'His Royal Highness will soon be here.'

At these words tempests of blood beat about the temples of

the spy. She could have screamed for sheer delight and terror. Such good fortune, such evil luck! By 'His Royal Highness', the speaker could mean only Prince Morragan. It seemed the Crown Prince was not, after all, comatose beneath a hill, surrounded by Faêran knights. Doubtless he would know the whereabouts of his brother. Had he remained unsleeping throughout the years? Or had he woken not long since? How dreary, how weary, how slow-dragging and tedious would be a millennium of banishment!

But tragedy must follow, if this royal exile should discover and identify her. Instantly he would guess she had come recently from the Fair Realm. How else might a mortal have survived for a thousand years?

That the Prince must recognise her the moment he set eyes on her she had no doubt. He would not forget the mortal maid who had entered his dominions, answered his challenges, reclaimed his captives, refused his invitations and thwarted his desires. He would be fully aware she had accompanied the Talith in their migration to the Realm before the Closing. All these years, he had supposed her locked away in Faêrie with her family. If she had appeared in Erith, there could be only one explanation. Against all possibility, *somewhere*, a Door had been opened.

Assuredly the unseelie wights of Huntingtowers would torment her until she revealed the secret of the Gateway, and then all would be lost. Morragan would send her back to Faêrie with the Password, and when Easgathair opened the Gates, the Prince would be there waiting to enter the Realm in place of his brother, his rival. Then would Morragan use the remaining unasked boon to exile the High King from the Fair Realm, this time truly forever. He would rule in his brother's place. And it would be her fault.

But no, she would not permit discovery. She would be careful. She would listen, and learn what she could.

'Get rid of those miserable slaves below,' a voice bellowed. 'If he finds any cursed mortals here, your heads will roll on the flagstones, then I shall kick 'em out the windows. And while he visits, utter only the common speech, on pain of disembowelment. I will not have the Fithiach disturbed by your squawkings and squeakings. I will cut out the tongue of the first dung-gobbler that disobeys.'

Bowed figures hurried out of the doorway bearing laden trays, and ascended yet another stair.

Soon after, Ashalind's cloaked form glided after them. She had no idea how long the mantle's special qualities might let her remain undetected, but a relatively quick death was preferable to years spent slowly perishing from the agony of the Langothe, and she must persist in her quest.

Thick rugs carpeted the floors of this upper level. More brightly lit, the walls were hung with arras of richer textiles, and shields emblazoned with wonderful devices. The last of the wightish menials entered a chamber by way of richly carved doors inlaid with bronze. The bellowing voice had spoken of mortal slaves in the lower regions of the Keep. Ashalind wondered whether she might possibly pose as a servitor, and thus move freely with less chance of discovery. But no—it was clear that when the Fithiach visited, all mortals were banished from his sight. Nonetheless, he must endure mortal speech, for according to what she had over-heard, he despised the guttural wightish languages but would not permit them to sully the Faêran tongue by employing it. So far, within these walls she had heard only common-speak.

Meanwhile, judging by the sounds in the carved-door cham-ber, further preparations were being made for the arrival of the Raven Prince.

A small insignificant portal was sunk into a niche almost oppo-site the carved doors, across the passageway from them. When Ashalind pushed, its hinges obeyed with a groan. Inside nestled another dark storage cubicle—a good enough vantage point for surveillance when the door was left ajar. Dust arose like phantom brides, and a spider dropped on her face. She might have yelped in surprise, had the duergar not stolen her power of speech.

Her narrow field of vision through the carved doors across the corridor showed lofty arched windows looking out from the larger chamber, which was bustling with activity. A tall, manlike figure moved past one window. Its head was crowned by the branching antlers of a stag. A graceful lady was standing with her back to Ashalind, dressed in a lace-edged green velvet gown sewn thickly all over with peridots. Dark hair cascaded down her back. Gold ornaments glittered on her svelte arms. She might have been a damsel of the Faêran, since several ladies of the Fair Realm had been riding among the ill-fated hawking party exiled on the Day of Closing, and others had fled into Erith as the last Call sounded, when the exile of the royal brethren was in no doubt. But when this green-clad belle turned around, the hem of her dress swished aside. The spy flinched. The 'woman' was neither Faêran nor mortal, but an eldritch wight. How doubly hideous it seemed, that such a fair form should walk upon woolly sheep's hooves.

A glow of firelight to the right illuminated polished furniture and tableware. Nothing else in that room could be observed.

A familiar voice came pummeling like a blow to the stomach:

'Set those goblets aright, nasty little hoglin, or I shall have you flayed like your sniveling cousin whose hide hangs above the Gate of Horn.'

Never had Ashalind erased from memory the coarse tones of Yallery Brown.

Commotion arose to the left. She could not see what caused it.

'Get out,' commanded the unseelie rat-wight. 'His Highness arrives.'

A motley collection of wights hastened from the chamber, disappearing down the corridor. A chill draught followed them, and the clatter of hooves on stone.

'My liege . . .' Yallery Brown's tone was fawning. He had broken off as if in fear or awe.

Several tall figures crossed quickly past the doorway. The carved doors were slammed shut—in the instant before they met, Ashalind discerned a stunning profile that could only be Morragan's. He and his retainers must have entered at the arched windows, which were as vast and high as the front gates of a castle.

Through a gap at the threshold drifted the conversation of those sequestered within. Listening with intense concentration, Ashalind could glean most of what they were saying, but it made little sense. Either they discussed matters far removed from her knowledge, or else she was too tired to comprehend. Eventually she succumbed again to sleep.

By the fluctuations in the window-light when the carved doors were open, Ashalind could tell night from day. She remained concealed hungrily in the spider-haunted cell, sipping her water, and the next night Morragan met again with his followers in the chamber.

There was scant liquid remaining in her leather bottle, and the siedo-pod odour was fading. The Faêran hated spies, and the Raven Prince in particular detested mortals. She began to think that if she were caught there, the manner of her demise at the mercy of unseelie wights might prove more horrible than the Langothe. But she stayed, and she listened, wishing heartily that there were some way of prompting the gathering to speak of the High King.

On the third night, by strange fortune, they did—but it was not as she had hoped. The heavy doors stood ajar. A low buzz of conversation had been proceeding for a good while, when Morragan's Faêran voice carried clearly across the corridor, rich, deep, and melodious in contrast to the harsh, throaty tones and raucous squeaks of the wights.

Gooseflesh raked the listener's spine.

'There has been a restlessness of late,' he said musingly, 'a breath of finer air, as from the Realm. This dusk, I rode down by the fisherman's cot and heard a maid within, warbling a song I have never heard before. In faith, it moved me not a little, although poorly versed.'

Ashalind held her breath. From the unseen fireplace on the right sparks flew into her field of vision and hung dying in midair.

'A song of exile,' said Morragan.

'If it displeased my lord,' murmured Yallery Brown, 'the cottage shall be razed, and those who have dwelt there for far too long shall be punished.'

The eavesdropper stiffened. She must return as soon as possible to warn the Caidens!

'A song of exile,' repeated Morragan, 'reminding me of my own.'

A thicker spray of sparks exploded, as if someone had kicked a burning log.

'Cursed be Angavar, may his reign end!' said the marvelous Faêran voice. 'May his knights rot in their hill grave. Cursed be the White Owl and his Keys. Cursed be the moment the Casket snapped shut with the Word. Might I but live those times over again . . .'

Ashalind, eyes tightly shut, clasped her hands together. Her lips moved soundlessly.

The King, speak again of the High King! Where is this hill beneath which he sleeps amid his noble companions?

'Behold, Your Highness, they bring up the steeds,' said the Winter-wind voice of Huon, Prince of Hunters and steward of the stronghold. 'Tonight we hunt.'

A rush of biting air swung the carved doors open on their hinges. Morragan stood at a window, looking out at the night. The full moon was rising, outlining the statuesque shape of him, the wide shoulders from which his cloak eddied like a piece of darkness.

'The Realm,' he said.

Then softly he spoke, but the night airs carried his voice back to the ears of the eavesdropper. It was a rhyme. The words were Faêran and she did not know what they meant, but their implication was haunting, lyrical, and strummed her Langothed heart with pain.

A half-shang gust lifted Morragan's cloak and hair like a wave. The inked-in outline of a horse appeared at the window. Then the Prince was gone, and several motley figures followed. Bridles jingled, boots scraped on bluestone, and commands were shouted. Far below, hounds began to yelp. A horn sounded. With a dissonance of shrill whoops and strident shouts the Hunt was away, borne aloft on invisible airstreams through the silver-sprayed vaults of darkness.

Abruptly, the fire went out.

Soon afterward, the spy heard two wightish servants come shuffling out of the chamber. As they came through the carved doors, one hoarsely muttered something.

'Shut your snout, clotpoll,' the other wheezed, 'or I'll roll your head in the fire. I'll teach you to speak the low tongue when the Crown Prince is honouring your dunghill with a visit!'

'So high and mighty are you not?' returned the hoarse one sarcastically. 'You may have been chosen for his royal household, scumbag, but you do not deserve it and as soon as they see through you, you'll be thrown out on your muleish ear.'

The wights had by now come to a halt in the corridor.

'You cap of all fools alive!' berated the wheezer. 'And do you plot to take my place? I was chosen for wit and wisdom far beyond the grasp of your greasy claws, boiled-brains.'

'Ha!' retorted Hoarse-Throat. 'The jumped-up feathergoose is even more contemptible when it struts!'

His antagonist could scarcely contain his ire. 'You know not to whom you speak,' he hissed between gritted teeth. 'Be wary, parasite, for your folly outweighs your fat head. I'll warrant you do not even have a notion of the Faêran words spoken this night by his Royal Highness!'

The other spluttered incoherently.

'Anyone with a jot of wit knows the meaning,' said Wheezer triumphantly. 'Even the merfolk sing it in the Gulf of Namarre. It is a riddle, an easy one, but too hard for the likes of *you*, you foul, undigested hodge-pudding.'

'You're full of air!'

'Nay, noisome stench, and I'll prove it!'

The wheezer cleared its throat noisily and began to translate, slowly, as if every word was an effort.

'*Nor bound to dust, ye ocean's bird, the word's thy name, the Key's the word.* So? What's the answer, goat-face?'

But before goat-face could reply a voice thundered out from down the corridor: 'Get along there, you rump-fed idlers, chattering like parrots outside the door! If you utter another word I'll have your lungs!'

With a rattling of spilled trays, the servants fled.

After that there was no more sound, except the wind whining around the Keep and the loud drumming of Ashalind's heart. The riddle was indeed easy. The answer was the elindor, or white bird of freedom, which spent seven years on the wing or water without touching land—her kenning-name. And there was another answer. 'Elindor' was the Password that opened the Green Casket of the Keys, in the Fair Realm.

Like syrup, silence poured forth from the recently vacated chamber. Surely the room was empty. Pulling the hood of the Faêran cloak over her head and tying it securely, Ashalind crossed the corridor, crept inside, and looked around. Indeed, they were all gone. There was no sign of Morragan's erstwhile presence. She was, again, bereft. Perversely, she had hoped for some evidence of him—what, she could not say. But fingering the enameled bracelet on her wrist, she exulted. She had discovered a fact of tremendous significance! She now knew the Password! The elindor, the white bird of freedom—how ironic that Morragan should have chosen it as the master-key. The jest was manifold—the bird that lived free of the bonds of Erith's soil, the kenning of she who had freed the children, the Password to free the Keys from the Green Casket. But she must make haste and escape from Huntingtowers Keep—the danger was too great.

Her ears, strained to the limits of hearing, caught scuffling noises approaching along the corridor. It was too late to leave the chamber through the heavy carved doors. What measure of camouflage the cloak offered, she could not guess. Wildly she looked for a place of concealment among the furnishings, but none offered itself. Nor were there any other exits, save the wide, high openings of the windows, which led to a ledge over sheer nothingness, looking out on lands far below and dark horsemen riding the sky, fell shapes etched against crystal. A huge raven that had been watching her from the sill flapped slowly away. At that moment, enraged screaming broke out in the corridor, just beyond the doors. Terrified, Ashalind ran out to the ledge and dropped down over the side.

For a mere instant she hung by her sliding fingers over a void, knowing full well she would inevitably lose her grip. The chamber above was filled with a cacophony of raucous braying, piercing screeches, and the crashes of laden tables being overturned. Her kicking feet found a toehold just as her left hand lost its grip. Leaves brushed her face; thick tendrils of common ivy. It grew thickly, latticed all over the outer wall, great ancient, arthritic stems of it. Grabbing hold, she began to climb down.

Silent sobs of fear shook her body. Terror melted her sinews like wax and drained them of power, so that her fingers, nerveless, could scarcely grip. The half-shang wind buffeted erratically, alternately flattening her against the wall and wrenching her away, outlining each ivy leaf with green-and-gold rime. Claws of dead stems hooked themselves in her garments. There was no time to disengage them, so they tore great rents in the fabric.

Down she scrambled, seeking blindly for footholds and not knowing when her toes might scrabble against naked bluestone. Farther and farther down she maneuvered, sliding one quivering foot after another, one sweat-slicked hand after another, her heart pounding like a pestle in her chest. How far she must descend she did not know for certain, but the central Keep had looked to be hundreds of feet high. From the corners of her eyes, she could see other towers with their watchful blue-gas windows, and glimpse a couple of soaring spans over an abyss. It was like being a beetle clinging to an open wall, so vulnerable, for all eyes to see, for any predator to pick off with ease.

A chair came hurtling down from above, passed her within a hairsbreadth, and went spinning down to shatter far below. Doggedly she continued to descend. They had discovered her presence. It was only a matter of time before they hunted her down. The water-bottle hampered her. She dropped it.

When her fingers would obey her no longer, she let go of the ivy. After falling a surprisingly short distance, she lay in a crumpled heap, dazedly trying to comprehend that she still lived and had reached the ground safely after all. She tried to stand, but her legs gave way, so she began to crawl, passing by the smashed shards of the fallen chair. Common ivy sprawled all over the ground, covering small bushes and shrubs. Something became hooked on it—her bracelet. Carefully she freed it. The white bird shone in the moonlight, and somehow the sight of this icon gave her strength and courage. Standing up, she broke into a run.

In the rising unstorm, scarlet and silver sparks flew from her iron-shod boots as she fled from island to islet, from bridge to bridge. Shang afterimages pulsed here and there, and the edge of every leaf on every bush was spangled. Up and over the caldera rim she ran, and down the other side, using the iron dagger to slash wildly at small things that sprang, yellow-eyed and malevolent, from the darkness. Away back, the hue and cry gathered momentum. Onward she sped, until she reached the mining grounds, and as she darted in among the heaps she heard the Wild Hunt catching up at her heels. The fire-eyed hounds were baying weirdly now, but there was a jarring note too, a sound that didn't belong. It sounded like a small dog yapping, and its source was up ahead. Rounding a mullock heap, she beheld the white whippet from the cottage of the Caidens. It barked frantically, ran a little distance, then turned to see if she was following. Placing all her faith in the brave little dog, she hastened after it.

The ululation of the pack crescendoed, soon augmented by the deafening blare of horns. She dared not look back, but it seemed as if the Hunt must be almost on her shoulders, when without warning the whippet disappeared into a hole in a hillock. Ashalind followed suit, not a moment too soon, and the horde thundered past overhead.

Gasping for life, the damsel lay with outflung arms in the umbra of a deep cavern whose floor sloped gradually downward. Her throat and chest burned. Somewhere nearby, the little dog whimpered uneasily, and she sensed that it was trying to communicate. Still panting, she crawled in the direction of the sound.

The quietude outside was split by a roar and a concussion that made the ground shake. Handfuls of clay nodules and damp soil showered onto her hair and ragged clothes. After springing up in blind panic, the refugee ran farther into the cave, only to feel the floor drop away beneath her feet. She started to slide. The dagger was still in her hands—swiveling her body like an acrobat, she jammed the blade into the soil to halt her progress. Loose pebbles slipped past and down—she must have stumbled, in her mad rush, over the edge of a shaft. The dagger stayed firmly embedded and she realised she had not fallen far. Her feet dangled over some unguessable depth. She hung from the weapon's hilt. Just above her head the whippet stood, whining. When she looked up she saw its anxious form backlit by gray light from the cave's entrance.

The bellowing roar blared again, and heavy steps caused the ground to vibrate. Something monstrous and massive was approaching, and everything trembled before it. Its weight might cause a cave-in, burying her and the whippet. Doubtless the giant, or whatever it was, intended to do just that. In an agony of effort Ashalind heaved herself up, slid down, tried again, and finally inched herself up over the edge of the shaft. As she crawled up and over, on her elbows, her face level with the dog's muzzle, she saw it wag its tail with delight to see her safe.

'No!' she mouthed in helpless exhaustion. The animal trotted toward her.

'No, no!' she tried to scream; but no words came from her wight-whipped throat, and, unchastized, the white whippet licked her face in innocent and loving greeting—the kiss of the Erith-born.

Some Ertish Words and Phrases

alainn capall dubh: beautiful black horse
Amharcaim!: Look there!
andalum: a dull, blue metal which has the power to neutralise
  sildron's repulsion of the ground
chehrna: dear damsel
clahmor: terrible, tragic
cova donni: blind shotman
culicidae: (plural) deadly, mosquito-like creatures—they are not
  eldritch
daruhshie: self-destructive fool
doch: damned
dominite: black stone, laced with points of talium trihexide—
  used for building, as it blocks out the effects of shang storms
eldritch: supernatural
eotaurs: winged, horned skyhorses bred for the ability to 'ride
  sky' when accoutred with sildron
eringl: a red-leafed tree growing only in Avlantia
gilf: a person who deliberately goes bareheaded in a shang
  storm, or is forced to do so, in order to imprint an image
glissanding: gliding through forests in a sildron harness, using
  branches and/or ropes as a means of propulsion
gramarye: magic
hattocking: the progress of an eotaur over uneven ground

breorig: ruinous
inna shai tithen elion: we have lived the days
lorraly: in the natural order
manscatha: wicked ravager
mo: my
mo gaidair: my friend
mo reigh: my pretty
mor scathach: an unseelie rider that sticks to the shoulders of its prey, becoming as heavy as stone, and rides the life out of it
obban tesh: an expletive
oghi ban Callanan: Callanan's eyes
onhebbing: raising and lowering anything sildron-borne by means of sliding andalum by varying degrees between the sildron and the ground
pishogue: glamour; a spell of illusion
smarin: milksop
Sciobtha!: Hasten!
scothy: mad, crazy
seelie: benevolent towards humankind
sgorrama: stupid (noun or adjective)
shang: a random wind of gramarye which leaves imprints of human passions
shera sethge: poor, unfortunate
sildron: a lustrous, silver metal with the intrinsic property of repelling the ground at a constant distance
skeerda: bad/devious person
Ta ocras orm! Tu faighim moran bia!: I am hungry! I need a lot of food!
taltry: a hood lined with talium metal mesh to protect the wearer from the influence of the shang
tambalai: beloved
tien eun: little one
tilhal: an amulet which may protect against unseelie wights of the lower orders
uhta: the hour before sunrise
unket: supernatural
unseelie: malevolent towards humankind
unstorm: a nickname for shang winds
uraguhne: despicable scum

A Short Pronunciation Guide

Baobansith: *baavan shee*
Buggane: *bug airn*
Cuachag: *cooachack*
Each Uisge: *ech-ooshkya*
Fuath: *foo-a*
Gwragedd Annwn: *gwrageth anoon*

The Elder Tongue

briagha: beautiful
caileagh faoileag: sea-gull damsel
cirean mi coileach: literally, 'cockscomb, my rooster'. It means
     'cocksure boy'
eudail: darling (fem.)
fallaise: a beautiful falling torrent
ionmhuinn: beloved (noun)
nathrach deirge: literally, 'Dragon's blood', a draught to warm and
     nourish the traveller
sabhailte: safe
seirm ceangail: bind-ring

With grateful thanks to the people of Eirinn for their beautiful language, with which the author has taken so many liberties. The usage here is not intended to be accurate.

General Jargon

The Arysk (Icemen) language has thirty-seven words for 'white'
     but for 'green' they have none, and must call it 'blue'
Gold: candlebutter
Sildron: King's Biscuit, Rusty Jack's friend, sinker, cloudpaver,
     moonrafter, frostbite, The Gentry's Farewell, Moonbeam etc
A shang wind: Uncomber, Unstorm

The Monetary System of Erith

Two farthings make a ha'penny—only sometimes a farthing is called a 'zac'—and four make a penny. There is no single coin for tuppence, but there is one for threepence, and it is called a trey bit. Fourpence is called a groat. Six pennies make a tanner, a sixpence. There are two sixpences to a shilling, two shillings to a florin and five shillings to a crown.

Six shillings and eightpence is the value of a noble, but a rose-noble is worth ten shillings. A sovereign is worth twenty shillings—so is a doubloon, but doubloons are used mostly by mariners. Eagles are also equal to sovereigns—the coinage of Stormriders and Windship merchants. A guinea is equal to twenty-one shillings. Twenty-five sovereigns make an angel, which is a hundred crowns, or a pony.

In the west of Earth a penny is equivalent to an early twenty-first century Australian dollar. Thus $240 = a sovereign, $6,000 = a pony/angel. Coins of a penny or less are made of copper; between a penny and a noble all are silver. The rest are gold.

And a shilling is called a 'bob' in the slang of some folk. A 'century' is slang for a hundred shillings. Some call it a 'ton', though there is no coin for it. You can see why Erithans mostly like to barter.

Calendar and Major Festivals of Erith

Winter: Nethilmis the Cloudmonth, Dorchamis the Darkmonth, Fuarmis the Coldmonth. Littlesun Day is on the 1st of Dorchamis, the Winter Solstice. It is the day of the Imbrol Festival, with its puddings and holly.

Spring: Sovrachmis the Primrosemonth, Uiskamis the Rainmonth, Duileagmis the Leafmonth. The Beldane Festival is celebrated at the Spring Equinox on Whiteflowers' Day, with flowers, eggs and dancing around maypoles.

Summer: Uainemis, the Greenmonth, Grianmis the Sunmonth, Teinemis the Firemonth. The Summer Solstice is celebrated at the fiery Lugnais Festival.

Autumn: Arvarmis the Cornmonth, Uvailmis the Applemonth, Gaothmis the Windmonth. The Samdain Harvest Festival celebrates the Autumn Equinox.

Runes

A: *atka*, the thorn, the spindle, the arrowhead
B: *brod*, the loaf
C: *ciedré*, the moon
D: *déanor*, the bow
E: *enen*, the fork
F: *faêrwyrd*, the key
G: *speal*, the scythe or sickle
H: *droichead*, the bridge
I: *idrel*, the sword
J: *crúca*, the hook
K: *kinoré*, the dancer
L: *clúid*, the corner (the turning point)
M: *margran*, the mountain
N: *nenté*, the stitch
O: *orinel*, the ring
P: *meirge*, the flag, the pennant, banner
Q: *sciath*, the shield
R: *sirrig*, the sail
S: *slégorn*, the dragon
T: *tiendir*, the tree
U: *uldris*, the cup
V: *vahlé*, the valley or the furrow
W: *wirroril*, the wave or the water
X: *glas*, the crossroads or the lock
Y: *draíochta*, the dowsing rod
Z: *geata*, the gate

Wight Lore

The high-tide mark is the boundary between the territories of land wights and sea wights.

Although they can prevaricate and trick, wights cannot lie. By the same token, if you make a promise or give your word to a wight you are bound by gramarye to keep it.

Household wights, best exemplified by bruneys (brownies), do not necessarily react adversely to the touch of cold iron. All others do.

Trooping wights wear green coats and red caps, while Solitaries wear red coats.

To steal a swanmaiden, take her cloak of feathers so that she cannot fly. To abduct a mermaid or merrow, take her comb. To kidnap a silkie (selkie), take his or her seal-skin, without which these wights cannot travel underwater. Be aware, it is unkind to do any of these things!

Silkies will not harm you unless you harm them. If you do them a good turn they will return it to you.

Most unseelie and seelie land wights cannot cross running water, especially if it flows south.

An 'awe band' can be put on mortals to stop them telling what they have seen of wights.

Giving wights a gift or verbal thanks means 'goodbye' to them ie, they have been paid therefore their services are no longer required. Some wights take offence at being thanked in any form, and permanently withdraw their services out of sheer indignation. Therefore, thanking wights or the Faêran is taboo.

Warding off Unseelie Wights

Holding Fast, a Steady Look and Silence are three powerful charms against wights.

Conversely (and confusingly), acknowledging their presence by looking at them can be detrimental to them. (Perhaps this is only true outdoors, as The Steady Look has been recorded as being used indoors.)

Having The Last Word is effective in certain cases; also, Rhyme has power over wights.

Many wights are powerless after cock-crow.

To show fear is to give them power over you, to allow them to strike. The ringing of bells is anathema to them. Charms against unseelie wights include ash keys, ground-ivy (*'athair luss'*) and daisies.

A Chant to Repel Wights

Hypericum, salt and bread,
Iron cold and berries red,
Self-bored stone and daisy bright,
Save me from unseelie wight.

Red verbena, amber, bell,
Turned-out raiment, ash as well,
Whistle-tunes and rowan-tree,
Running water, succour me.

Rooster with your cock-a-doo,
Banish wights and darkness too.

Shapeshifting

Even shapeshifters must abide by the laws of their own nature. Not all wights are shapeshifters. For example, urisks are not. Spriggans can alter their size but not their shape. Some wights command two forms. Swanmaidens may become damsels or swans. The Each Uisge and all other waterhorses can take the shape of a man or a horse.

Other wights have the power to metamorphose into three different guises. Two of the waterhorse types, brags and phoukas, have a third native shape; brags, that of a calf with a white handkerchief tied around its neck and phoukas, a bat.

Bogey-beasts and their ilk are true shapeshifters; their possible forms are countless. Some examples include the wight which changes into a bundle of sticks, the Trathley Kow (based on the 'Hedley Kow') which can imitate the form of a man's sweetheart, or any other form it chooses, purely for the purpose of mischief-making and a thing called 'It', which can turn itself into a variety of strange objects.

Note: shapeshifting should not be confused with *glamour*. Glamour is an illusion, a spell cast over the senses of mortals so that they see what is not there. True shapeshifting is more powerful.

Acknowledgments

Yallery Brown: The tale of Yallery Brown is inspired by an article in 'Legends of the Cars', by Mrs Balfour. *Folk-Lore* 11, 1891.

McKeightley and the Antlered One: Inspired by 'The Devil at Ightfield', collected in *English Legends* by Henry Bett, Batsford, London, 1952. This traditional tale has many variants.

Perdret Olvath: Inspired by 'The Fairy Widower', from *Popular Romances of the West of England*, by Robert Hunt. London, 1865.

Eilian: Inspired by a traditional tale collected in *Celtic Folklore, Welsh and Manx, Vol. 1*, by John Rhys. Oxford University Press, 1901. Also inspired by an account of a Faêrie Rade in *Remains of Nithsdale and Galloway Song*, collected by R. H. Cromek. Cadell & Davies, London, 1810.

The Midwife and the Faêran: Inspired by a tale in *Celtic Folklore, Welsh and Manx* (vol. 1) collected by John Rhys. Oxford University Press, 1901.

The Stolen Child: Inspired by the old folktale 'The Stanhope Fairies', collected in *Folk-Tales of the North Country*, by F. Grice. Nelson, London and Edinburgh, 1944.

Lake Coumluch: Inspired by the traditional tale 'The World Below the Water', collected in *Legendary Stories of Wales*, by E. M.

Wilkie. George G. Harrap & Co. Ltd., London, Bombay, Sydney, 1934.

Meroudys and Orfeo: Inspired by MS. Ashmole 61, reproduced in *Illustrations of the Fairy Mythology of Shakespeare*, by Halliwell, reprinted by W. C. Hazlitt in *Fairy Tales, Legends and Romances Illustrating Shakespeare*, 1875.

The Enchanted Knight: Inspired by a traditional ballad recorded in No. 39a, *The English & Scottish Popular Ballads*, edited by F. J. Child. The Folklore Press in Association with the Pagent Book Co., New York, 1957.

Bevan Shaw and the Mermaid: Inspired by 'The Mermaid of Gob-Ny-Ooyl', a folktale collected by Sophia Morrison for *Manx Fairy Tales*. Nutt, London, 1911.

Vinegar Tom: Inspired by a folktale collected by the late Ruth Tongue and reproduced in *County Folklore VIII, Somerset Folklore*. Folklore Society, 1965. The rhyme is a traditional quotation.

Liban: Inspired by the folktale 'The Sea-Morgan's Baby', collected by the late Ruth Tongue for her book *Forgotten Folk-Tales*, 1970.

Evan Sayle and the Mermaid: Inspired by the folktale 'John Reid and the Mermaid', in *Scenes and Legends of the North of Scotland*. Hugh Miller, Edinburgh, 1872.

Scoom Weel Your Fish: Inspired by and partially quoted from the folktale 'The Mermaid Released', *County Folklore III, Orkney and Shetland Islands*. Edited by G. K. Black. Folklore Society, 1903.

The Piper and the Rats: Inspired by 'The Pied Piper', Joseph Jacobs 'More English Fairytales', 1894.

Lutey and the Mermaid: Inspired by a folktale collected in *Traditional and Hearthside Stories of West Cornwall*, 1st series. William Bottrell, Penzance, 1870.

Lazy Molly: Inspired by a folktale collected in *A Book of Folklore*, by Sabine Baring-Gould. Collins, London, n.d.

The Swanmaiden: Inspired by 'The Fairy Maiden', a traditional tale collected in *Legendary Stories of Wales*, by E. M. Wilkie. George Harrap & Co., 1934.

The Guardian Black Dog: Inspired by a passage in *My Solitary Life*, p. 188, by Augustus Hare, n.d., n.p.

The Unseelie Black Dog: Inspired by the traditional tale 'The Mauthe Doog of Peel Castle', collected in *Minstrelsy of the Scottish Border*, with notes and introduction by Sir Walter Scott. Edited by T. F. Henderson. Oliver & Boyd, Edinburgh, 1932.